GREAT
SHORT
NOVELS

R. LARRABURE

R. LARRABURE

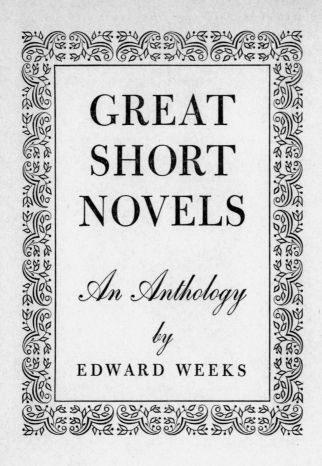

GREAT
SHORT
NOVELS

An Anthology

by

EDWARD WEEKS

The Literary Guild of America, Inc.

NEW YORK

PRINTED AT THE *Country Life Press*, GARDEN CITY, N. Y., U. S. A.

CL

COPYRIGHT, 1941
BY DOUBLEDAY, DORAN & COMPANY, INC.
ALL RIGHTS RESERVED

CONTENTS

FOREWORD

SMALL BOOKS have been a hobby of mine ever since I was a student at Trinity College, Cambridge, when I used to pick them up for a few shillings apiece at the bookstall which Old Man David trundled into the market place. The English have mastered the art of writing and making a small book: their wit is crisp, their paper light, and their bindings supple. They like a small book which can be slid into a pocket or a rucksack and whose contents is worth more than its weight in shillings. In the days I am recalling I was traveling light, going off on my push bike with my good friend Morley Dobson on literary pilgrimages to York or Dover, to the Vales and Dales or the Lake Country, as much as three hundred miles a trip; this led to that most delightful of pastimes, the reading of English authors on their native heath— Hardy in Dorset, Dickens in Kent, Malory in Cornwall. Small books of fiction and poetry were my traveling companions, and I have them yet.

My hobby built up a collection of books small in size and deft in workmanship, and as it persisted I came to have an increasing respect for the skill with which the author had compressed a story within so brief a compass. In particular I was attracted to the short novel: I recognized that in its brevity it was no less distinguished than the more spacious narratives to which we Americans have so often been attracted. Personally I think we put too much emphasis on bigness. We take pride in having "the biggest in the world," and this pride colors to some extent the appreciation of our books. Perhaps in part it explains the enormous popularity we accorded to novels like *Anthony Adverse, Gone with the Wind, The Last Puritan* and *Oliver Wiswell*— to mention four of our recent giants. Now I am not trying to disparage size when it is accompanied by magnificence. *Tom Jones* is a big book, so is *Vanity Fair*, so is *War and Peace* and *The Brothers Karamazov*.

vii

But I am afraid that in our affection for bigness we quite overlook the originality and the delicate art which make for compression in a short novel like *Thaïs, Death in Venice,* or *The Sea of Grass.* In America there has been so much concentration upon the short story in our magazines and the long novel in our bookstores that we have almost lost our appreciation of the short novel, and of the power of suggestion, the swiftness of episode, the terse revelation of character which can make it so appealing.

"What dictates the size of the bottle into which we pour our wine—or vinegar? Certainly not deliberate resolution," writes John Galsworthy, "for then one would have written nothing but stories of from ten to thirty thousand words, instead of only ten tales between those lengths, in five-and-twenty years. . . . The whole thing is a puzzle. Why should one have to write a novel when a certain figure, incident or idea takes possession of the imagination; a short story about a second incident or figure; and a tale of medium length around a third? I cannot answer; but I am convinced that he is in luck to whom the unseen hander-out of bottles offers the pint."

To me that reflection is illuminating. It tells me that the short novel is something of a rarity in the author's trade; that it comes to mind with a recurring challenge and that the author entrusts himself to it only when he is very sure of his ground. After twenty years of editing I do not like to think how many hundred autobiographic novels I have plodded through, which begin with the hero in his cradle, follow him closely through school and college, through marriage and his unhappiness, and at last push him downhill and into his grave. That is the most elementary form of novel-writing, and its loose-gaited, rather self-conscious egotism becomes a weariness of the flesh. Such writing is in painful contrast to the more mature and more exacting art of the short novel.

In the short novel, time must be relative to space: the author cannot afford to pile year upon year. He takes instead a short-cut across time to that crucial year in the life of the man or woman he is writing about. And then, by alternating introspection with the forward movement of the story, by balancing what *has* happened with what *is,* he succeeds in developing his characters to the point where you are caught up heart and mind in the mystery of what will happen to them. You will better understand the problem which the short novelist has to contend with if you will think for a moment of the short story. In the short story the people are invariably subordinate to the situation, and it is the trick of the author to work out that situation as swiftly and dramatically as possible. Whereas in the short novel, as Joseph Conrad puts it, "I insist

not on events, but on their effect on persons." In other words, the people take command. It is the art of the novelist to devise not a single situation, but a succession of "events" which will develop, as in a crescendo, the characters he has in mind.

This short cut across time can be approached in a variety of ways. For instance, in *The Sea of Grass,* the best short novel that has yet been written about our Southwest, Conrad Richter encompasses the whole magnificent struggle between the cattle barons with their ranches "as big as Massachusetts with Connecticut thrown in," and the nesters who would invade them from the East. This struggle consumed roughly twenty-five years. Richter has not the space in which to build up the story year by year. Instead he tells it to you in the person of young Hal, a nephew of the great ranch owner. Hal sees what is happening in his recurring visits to the Cross B. His trips home happen to coincide with the high spots in the conflict. But why not? That's what a novelist is for.

Each author takes the short cut which is most natural to him. Conrad, who is a master of the short novel, takes you straight to the heart of his problem and then holds you in suspense as he weaves his story, now backward, now forward, until you understand perfectly why his people are approaching the climax in view.

Edith Wharton, in her classic *Ethan Frome,* makes a somewhat different approach and her explanation of the method is well worth quoting: "I had known something of New England village life long before I made my home in the same county as my imaginary Starkfield. Even before that final initiation, however, I had had an uneasy sense that the New England of fiction bore little—except a vague botanical and dialectical—resemblance to the harsh and beautiful land as I had seen it. Even the conscientious reproduction of the vernacular left me with the feeling that the outcropping granite had been overlooked. The problem before me, as I saw in the first flash, was this: I had to deal with a subject of which the dramatic climax, or rather the anticlimax, occurs a generation later than the first acts of the tragedy. The theme of my tale was not one on which many variations could be played. It must be treated as starkly and summarily as life had always presented itself to my protagonists. They were, in truth, these figures, my granite outcroppings, but half-emerged from the soil, and scarcely more articulate. This was my task, if I were to tell the story of Ethan Frome; and my scheme of construction—which met with the immediate and unqualified disapproval of the few friends to whom I tentatively outlined it—I still think justified in the given case. It appears to me, indeed, that, while an air of artificiality is lent to a tale of complex and sophisticated people which the novelist causes to be guessed at and interpreted by any mere looker-on, there need be no such drawback if

the looker-on is sophisticated and the people he interprets are simple."
In that revealing statement of Mrs Wharton's you see clearly the sub-
ject which challenged the novelist's imagination, you see the limitations
which made her story necessarily a short one ("the theme of my tale
was not one on which many variations could be played"), and you
see her sophisticated method of unlocking the secret of a taciturn com-
munity. *Ethan Frome* is, in a sense, the standard bearer of those short
novels which suggest the end of the story in their opening pages and
then, by making a short cut back to the beginning of things, intensify
and drive home the poignancy of what is to happen.

The limitations of space impose still other obligations. In a short
novel there can be no elaborate comings and goings. The transitions
are as brief as they are emphatic. The author has to be able to skip his
story as a boy skips a flat stone across a pond. Nor is there space for the
gentle, cantering descriptions which keep Scott and Cooper in the sad-
dle for five pages at a time. The short novel depends upon the power
of selection; it depends upon the author's ability to compress within a
few telling details much more than what he has actually said. When
my daughter was much younger than she is now she had a hearty dis-
taste for the big family reunions of which my clan were so fond. Once,
as she clung to the banisters on her downward path, I heard her say to
her mother, "Just one peek, but no how-d'you-do's!" That's all the
short novelist has time for—just one peek, but no how-do-y'do.

Finally, the short novel does away with vagueness and unintelligi-
bility. To cover a lifetime in 30,000 words means that an author must
be, above all things, definite. He must know his ground; he must know
his people; and, so that you may have no misgivings about either, it is
up to him to devise little signposts, little clues, which will point your
mind in the direction he means to take you. In *The End of the Tether*,
Conrad is concealing something from you. You know that something
is wrong, but you can't put your finger on it at first. Yet if you retrace
your steps when the story is finished, you will find that he has been
warning you of what is to come from the very first sentence.

When you add up these various attributes, I think you will under-
stand why the short novel at its best is so sensitive and challenging to
a writer. In its short cut through time and space, in avoiding the ver-
bose, in its clarity and power of selection, it seems to me a vehicle
streamlined and beautifully in keeping with the temper of our time.

It was in the spring of 1936 that my friend Malcolm Johnson first
suggested the possibility of my bringing together within a single volume
my favorite short novels. He thought we could publish as many as

twelve without straining the wrists of our readers, and it was our original plan that the collection be international. But when I explored this prospect I soon came to the conclusion that the novels in translation ought to be treated in a volume of their own. The French novelists have done some of their most brilliant work in the short form—Guy de Maupassant, Pierre Loti, Anatole France, André Gide and Prosper Mérimée are only a few of a large company we should have to reckon with. From Russia came *A Lear of the Steppes* and *Smoke* by Turgenev, *A Sky-Blue Life* by Gorky and a shelfful of Chekov to choose from. In Germany, Thomas Mann, Arthur Schnitzler and Stefan Zweig were at the moment doing some of their best work in the short form, and back of them were the writers of the *Erzählungen* of the nineteenth century—Storm, Auerback, Keller, Heiser. And I have said nothing of Italy, Spain, or Scandinavia. You can see for yourself that if I was to do justice to the continental novelists in one volume, I simply could not do justice to those English and American authors who were naturally closer to my heart. This led to my first limitation—the necessity of confining my collection to those who wrote in English.

A second caution seemed equally sensible: that for the sake of variety we should take no more than one book from any author. When my arrangements were complete, I found that I had actually selected seven American and five English authors.

Much more involved was the question of length. Where should I draw the dividing lines between the short story, the short novel and the long novel? Admittedly, most short stories disqualify themselves by their structure, yet there were some borderline cases—*Rain* by Somerset Maugham, *Prelude* by Katherine Mansfield and Washington Irving's *Rip Van Winkle*—which made me hesitate. It is my personal belief that, despite their remarkable characterization, each of these is essentially a short story, and so had to be ruled out. In the end I decided arbitrarily to admit to my collection no narrative of less than 20,000 words and none in excess of 60,000. The line had to be drawn somewhere, and I think these are fair boundaries. I must ask you to accept my word for it that a subtle change is discernible in a novel when it moves beyond 60,000 words. The pace slows down and what I have described as the delicate art of condensation is replaced by the more leisurely treatment which one expects from a full-length novel. *Under the Greenwood Tree* is the shortest of Hardy's novels, yet in its structure it simply abbreviates the form of Hardy's longer work. So 60,000 words became my maximum boundary of the short novel, and as a matter of fact there is no book in my collection which runs as long as that. Yet even as I built this necessary fence, I had my regrets, for it shut out *Men Against the Sea* by Charles Nordhoff and James Nor-

man Hall, *The Great Gatsby* which some good critics hold to be the best book ever written by F. Scott Fitzgerald, and *Rogue Male,* the novel about the man who tried to kill Hitler, by that brilliant newcomer, Geoffrey Household.

The word count is a matter of importance to authors and publishers. A full-length novel runs between 90,000 and 120,000 words and a giant will be upwards of twice that length. What I have actually done, therefore, is to qualify as short novels those which were from one third to one half the average size.

Once I had determined to confine myself to novelists who were writing in English and whose books measured between 20,000 and 60,000 words, I was ready to begin my selection. I began by discarding what I did not want. I emphatically did not want the antiques—Samuel Johnson's *Rasselas* or *The Castle of Otranto* by Horace Walpole, both of which have lost their flavor for modern readers. I was not interested in carving out the Book of Ruth nor an excerpt from Malory's *Morte d'Arthur.* Nor was I keen for those stories which have been reprinted so constantly or thumbworn by so much "required reading" that little of their original zest survives. I am thinking specifically of *Dr Jekyll and Mr Hyde* and *Silas Marner.* I had no intention of overlooking the famous or of cottoning to the new simply because it is new. What I wanted was to choose from two centuries books which were full of life today and to which one could honestly apply that diffident word "great." It was my hope that I could so present them, with introductions of my own, that the classics would be read or reread with fresh appetite and the more recent performances accepted with the recognition that they belonged.

The smallest and most tattered darling which I brought back from England was Sterne's *A Sentimental Journey.* For me it is a hardy perennial. I have lost count of how many times I have reread it—not always from cover to cover, but rather for the relish of savoring again twenty or thirty pages of Sterne's teasing and affectionate wit. I think the book is a fascinator, and if at the outset you will make allowance for the style which seems to be jerky but isn't, if you will say to yourself here is a novelist working on the theory of associated ideas one hundred and fifty years before Proust and James Joyce proclaimed the stream of consciousness, if, finally, you will picture to yourself the woman for whom Sterne wrote *A Sentimental Journey,* I believe this book will give you something better than mere refreshment.

I wanted an American novel to compare with *A Sentimental Journey,* and I found it in *Billy Budd,* the last novel written by Herman Melville and certainly one of the best things ever written by this great

American seafarer. There is a rather pathetic story connected with *Billy Budd,* for Melville's prestige with his contemporaries dwindled until at the close of his career no publisher would touch him. This did not deter him from writing, but it did mean that there was no editor curious enough to inquire after his death whether Melville had left behind him a posthumous novel. Thus the manuscript of *Billy Budd* remained among the family papers until the rediscovery of Melville which came in the 1920's. The novel was then published in new editions and now I am glad to have the opportunity of bringing it to a still larger audience. Any modern jury would certainly place it among Melville's three or four best works.

At the time I was studying in England the fraternity between Joseph Conrad and John Galsworthy was still a living thing, not a chapter in a biography. But I had heard enough to realize what Kent meant to Conrad and the Devon moors to the author of the *Forsyte Saga.* Conrad, to my way of thinking, was more at home in the short novel than in the longer novel, as *The Heart of Darkness, Typhoon, The End of the Tether, The Shadow Line* and *The Nigger of the Narcissus* all bear witness. For particular and pressing reasons I put my money on *The End of the Tether.* If you have never read this superb story I envy you the pleasure. If you have read it, I urge you to go back to it for the pathos and prophecy which make it so applicable to English seamen today.

With Galsworthy the choice lay between *The Indian Summer of a Forsyte,* probably the most beautiful single passage of his prose but now an almost inextricable part of *The Forsyte Saga; A Stoic,* the penetrating study of an old bachelor; and *The Apple-Tree* that matchless novel of spring in England—which I chose. Next, for its lovely picture of Edwardian England and for the electricity with which it lights up Cambridge and London in the golden days before the war I turned to *Jacob's Room* by Virginia Woolf. Her eager, sensitive mind, so feminine in its power of observation and so sure in its selection of the telling detail, must have a place in my twelve.

There was a favorite of mine describing a time and place which I myself had known as a volunteer in the French army. I mean *The Spanish Farm* by R. H. Mottram, the story of a Frenchwoman at bay in 1918. "If you are going to have only one war book," said my conscience, "go back and reread *The Red Badge of Courage.*" I did. To a generation which has seen two world wars I submit that the psychology and the imagery of battle which Stephen Crane displayed in his *Red Badge of Courage* is no longer as impressive as it seemed in 1895. That novel, which was rather a stirring innovation then, seems quaint today. So I came back to *The Spanish Farm,* a story written with an artist's

eye for the Flemish terrain and an unerring knowledge of the B.E.F. and of how the Englishmen did their best to get on with the French temperament. I agree emphatically with John Galsworthy when he says that the portrait of Madeleine is the one full, solid, intimate piece of French characterization which resulted from the First World War.

Crossing over to our side of the Atlantic, I soon found that I had more American candidates than I had room for. Two of them, I am sorry to say, were disqualified for reasons over which I had no control. I should certainly have reprinted *Ethan Frome*, had the permission been given me. And I think I should not have been able to resist *A Portrait of Jennie* by Robert Nathan, one of the exquisite miniatures of our time, had it not been for the fact that Mr Nathan's short novels are eventually published in collected form under his own signature.

But to offset these two I had all and more than I could ask for. First in point of time came Henry James. Like Conrad, he was completely at his ease in the short form, and my only question was which of his many to choose. Jacobins with whom I talked were strong for *The Turn of the Screw*. One of them, whose style has never quite recovered from long association with James, reminded me of the interchange between the author and William Lyon Phelps. Said Dr Phelps, "*The Turn of the Screw* made my blood chill, my spine curl, and every individual hair to stand on end." To which James replied that he was very happy to learn of this because, said he, "I meant to scare the whole world with that story; and you had precisely the emotion that I hoped to arouse in everybody. When I wrote it, I was too ill to hold the pen; I therefore dictated the whole thing to a Scot stenographer. I was glad to try this experiment, for I believed that I should be able to judge of its effect on the whole world by its effect on the man who should hear it first. Judge of my dismay when, from first to last page, this iron Scot betrayed not the slightest shade of feeling! I dictated to him sentences that I thought would make him leap from his chair; he short-handed them as though they had been geometry, and whenever I paused to see him collapse, he would inquire in a dry voice, 'What next?'" Well, personally, I have a fellow feeling for that Scot. To make my hair curl a ghost has to be a good, abnormal proposition. At least as good as those in the stories of Montague James (who is, incidentally, no relation). No, the Henry James I wanted was the Henry James of *The Aspern Papers*, a novel which, I think, is just as fresh now as when he wrote it. I like it because of its affiliation with Shelley and that beauty of the past, Jane Clairmont. I like it because it holds the spirit which was—and let us hope still is—Venice.

Of my modern novels, two, I hope, will be read with a sense of discovery: *The Sea of Grass* by Conrad Richter, which I rank as the best

novel, long or short, that has yet come out of the Texas prairies, and *The Trader's Wife* by Jean Kenyon MacKenzie, that terse and vivid story of Newport, West Africa, and an American slaver one hundred years ago. These books are much more than collectors' items. They are the unrewarded classics of our time.

Of the American Negro, what novel has ever spoken with more eloquence, happiness and authenticity than *Porgy*, by DuBose Heyward? Porgy, the lame Negro beggar as he sits silent and rapt in the Charleston sunlight, is a figure to remember. His was a golden age and his story, told with such sympathy by Mr Heyward, reaches straight to the heart.

Our most able and representative novelist of the 1930's—and his craftsmanship rises far above the mere fact of the depression—is John Steinbeck. His short novel, *Of Mice and Men*, I had to have for its humor, for its unerring characterization of our migratory labor, and for its dramatic quality which, as in the case of *Porgy*, made the novel equally effective as a play.

Last but certainly not least I chose *The Bridge of San Luis Rey* by Thornton Wilder, a novel which, as a cub editor, I had tried so hard to have serialized in the *Atlantic* (only in the end to have it turned down by my superiors), and which I regard now, as I did then, as one of the well-tempered and classic novels of our day.

As I went over my line-up to see how well the books would span two centuries I thought, Sterne will stand for the best of the early English novelists, Melville, the best of the mid-nineteenth-century Americans, Henry James for the late Victorians, Joseph Conrad, Galsworthy, Virginia Woolf for the Edwardians, Mottram's *The Spanish Farm* for the best of the First World War; and then, swinging back into our own boundaries, *The Trader's Wife* will stand as a memorable picture of what the slave trader did to the white man here and in Africa; *Porgy*, as a trail-blazer, the best novel that has yet been written by a white man about the Negro in America; *The Sea of Grass*, as the first and best of the short novels to speak for that territory which should be as rich in literature as it is in oil; *The Bridge of San Luis Rey*, which speaks for the golden days of Latin America, and *Of Mice and Men* for the new stirring of conscience and curiosity about migratory labor that came with the depression. A great short novel which has stood the test takes possession of you just as surely as a great play, and for about the same length of time. It is the perfect entertainment for an evening's reading.

Edward Weeks

ACKNOWLEDGMENT

The editor and publishers wish to express their thanks to the following authors, agents and publishers for permission to reprint the novels indicated:

Albert & Charles Boni, Inc., for *The Bridge of San Luis Rey,* by Thornton Wilder.

Coward-McCann, Inc., for *The Trader's Wife,* by Jean Kenyon MacKenzie. Copyright, 1930, by Coward-McCann, Inc., and reprinted by special permission.

J. M. Dent & Sons (Canada), Limited, for *The End of the Tether,* by Joseph Conrad.

The Dial Press, Inc., for *The Spanish Farm,* by R. H. Mottram.

Harcourt, Brace and Company, Inc., for *Jacob's Room,* by Virginia Woolf. Copyright, 1923, by Harcourt, Brace and Company, Inc.

Mrs DuBose Heyward and J. H. McGee, Trust Officer, for *Porgy,* by DuBose Heyward. Copyright, 1925, by Doubleday, Doran & Company, Inc.

Alfred A. Knopf, Inc., for *The Sea of Grass,* by Conrad Richter.

Paul R. Reynolds & Son and Henry James, for *The Aspern Papers,* by Henry James.

Charles Scribner's Sons, for "The Apple-Tree," from *Five Tales,* by John Galsworthy.

The Viking Press, for *Of Mice and Men,* by John Steinbeck.

The Editor wishes to give special thanks to Hervey Allen, for his advice about DuBose Heyward; to Mrs Eleanor Melville Metcalf for advice about her grandfather Herman Melville; to Mrs Emily Flint of the Walker Memorial Library for supplying books and correcting proofs, and to Mrs Jeannette Cloud for the good temper and good judgment with which she kept the work in progress.

xvii

The Sea of Grass

CONRAD RICHTER

CONRAD RICHTER *was born in a small town in Pennsylvania on October 13, 1890. His formal education came to an end when he was fifteen, and thereafter he was on his own, now driving a light wagon over the hills of Schuylkill County, now working in a machine shop, now as a coal breaker, on a farm and for a time in the timber business. He first began to write as the country correspondent for Philadelphia dailies. Once he found his footing in journalism he knew that he would not be satisfied until he was writing on his own. The Sea of Grass, which is a first novel, measures 33,000 words.*

INTRODUCTION

The Sea of Grass is a story of the American Southwest, written with the sweep and native beauty of that limitless country. In time, it covers a period of twenty-five years; in space, a ranch larger than Massachusetts with Connecticut thrown in, the fabulous herds of Texas cattle sprinkled "like grains of cinnamon across the horizons." Such was the domain lorded over by Colonel Jim Brewton before the coming of law and the emigrant.

The story is told to us by the colonel's nephew, Hal, an orphan who was brought up at the big ranch house, who fiercely resented the coming of the colonel's young wife from St Louis and who equally resented the compulsion which sent him East to school. As a young medico Hal comes mack to Salt Fork to take over the practice of old Dr Reid, and it is through his shrewd, young, partisan gaze that we see the struggle which was to deprive the colonel of his empire but never of his pride and his ruthless will. Hal is a good narrator. His uncle's bringing-up and his medical training have made him a realist. Of the nesters—those people who waited till the West was safe and pioneering done—he has been contemptuous since he was old enough to shoot. He had seen them run off the *vega* by his uncle's cow hands and he had heard his uncle's voice ring out in the small, hushed courtroom: "I have sympathy for the pioneer settler who came out here and risked his life and family among the Indians. And I hope I have a little charity for the nester who waited until the country was safe and peaceable before he filed a homestead on someone else's range who fought for it. But when that nester picks country like my big *vega*, that's more than seven thousand feet above the sea, when he wants to plow it up to support his family where there isn't enough rain for crops to grow, where he only kills the grass that will grow, where he starves for

2

water and feeds his family by killing my beef and becomes a man without respect to himself and a miserable menace to the territory, then I have neither sympathy nor charity!"

But no single man could divert the stream of settlers' wagons, taut and white, with their crowded canvas; more and more insistent became the emigrants, tenant farmers from Kansas, artisans and tradesmen whose living had been unsatisfactory in half a dozen states. "Good night, gentlemen," says Colonel Brewton to the cavalry officers who have been ordered in to keep the peace. "You can keep the nesters from being blown away—but God himself can't the prairie. . . ." "And that night as I lay in my sleepless bunk," says Hal, "I fancied that in the milky mist I could see the prairie as I had seen it all my life, with the grass in summer sweeping my stirruped thighs and prairie chicken scuttling ahead of my pony, with the ponds in fall black and noisy with waterfowl, and my uncle's seventy thousand head of cattle rolling in fat, with the tracks of endless game in the winter snow and thousands of tons of wild hay cured and stored on the stem and, when the sloughs of the home range greened up in the spring, with the scent of warming wet earth and swag after swag catching the emerald fire, with horses shedding and snorting and grunting as they rolled and everywhere the friendly, indescribable solitude of that lost sea of grass."

Jim Brewton fought, as every great cattleman did, against the encroachment of the nesters. Arrayed against him he had Brice Chamberlain, the smooth lawyer from the East sent out by Washington to defend the settlers; against him he had his young wife Lutie, who, with her gaiety and willfulness, wanted to tame and prettify the ranch and who could not abide the loneliness, and against him in his old age he had his young, reckless son Brock, the gambler. The story of such opposition takes time, and I must salute the author for the almost effortless skill with which he has compressed his drama within so brief a space and for the almost perfect direction with which, as his climax approaches, he keeps Hal in the background, leaving the center of the stage free for the stirring scenes between the colonel, Lutie and Brock. It is probably asking too much that every character should have his due in a novel of this length. Yet I cannot help remarking that young Jim has been deliberately slighted in favor of his more romantic brother. We are never given to understand why he might not have been a chip of the old block. Nor do we ever see him in his full stature. Perhaps it is enough to say that, had Jimmy entered into the fight, had he stood up to Brock as a true son of the colonel's might, we should not have had a short novel.

I value this story for its spaciousness, for the feeling that the years

have passed and that the changes have taken place which Hal so well observes on his return trips to Salt Fork. I value it for its objectivity. Even at the end it is hard to say if Hal has taken sides and who is the greatest outlaw—the colonel, Judge Chamberlain, Lutie or Brock. I value it for the beauty of its description, a beauty re-enforced by the repetitive phrases which form a refrain toward the close. And finally, I value it for the idiom which no one but an American could have written. When Hal, homesick at boarding school, remembers the Canadian geese he remembers them "rising from the ponds and cutting the sky like Apache lances." In the midst of the quarrel between the colonel and Lutie, Hal feels a strain in the air "like those unseen currents that are said to lift the hair of a wolf before an August thunderclap." When Hal spends the night with his uncle in the cavernous bridal chamber of the Exchange House he sees the elder with his shirt off and "black curls on his chest like hair from a buggy cushion." When news comes that Judge Chamberlain has let Brock off scot free, Hal sees, deep in the colonel's eyes, "red coals like the implacable Indian pueblo fires that are never allowed to go out." And in that last court scene when the old man faces the nester jury—"I realized that those golden wild horses of other days had slipped more deftly out of my uncle's rope than he knew." These similes and others as vivid come straight from the prairie where this story grew.

THE CHARACTERS *and situations in this work are wholly fictional and imaginary, and do not portray and are not intended to portray any actual persons or parties.*

THE SEA OF GRASS

PART I

Lutie

THAT lusty pioneer blood is tamed now, broken and gelded like the wild horse and the frontier settlement. And I think that I shall never see it flowing through human veins again as it did in my Uncle Jim Brewton riding a lathered horse across his shaggy range or standing in his massive ranch house, bare of furniture as a garret, and holding together his empire of grass and cattle by the fire in his eyes.

His rude empire is dead and quartered today like a steer on the meat-block, but I still lie in bed at night and see it tossing, pitching, leaping in the golden sunlight of more than fifty years ago, sweeping up to his very door, stretching a hundred and twenty miles north and south along the river, and rolling as far into the sunset as stock could roam—a ranch larger than Massachusetts with Connecticut thrown in, his fabulous herds of Texas cattle sprinkled like grains of cinnamon across the horizons, his name a legend even then, his brand familiar as the A B C's in every packing-house, and his word the law, not dead sentences in a book, but a moving finger writing on a cottonwood tree where all who rode could very plainly read.

I can see his bedroom, just a bunk in the corner, with a fancy horse-hair bridle and ropes on the wall, and a brown buckskin partly cut away in strips for whang leather. And I can see his huge parlor, without rugs or furniture, piled to the pine rafters with white sacks of flour and burlapped hills of sugar and green coffee, and wooden buttes of boxed tobacco, dried fruits, and canned tomatoes, just the provisions for his hundred hands and everyone else who passed that way, rancher or cowboy, settler or prospector, Mexican, Indian, or outlaw, all welcome at his table.

But what moves across my eye unforgettably is his spring roundup when six or seven wagons working back from the Arizona line reached the headquarters range with a vast, almost mythical herd the like of which will never be seen in this country again. Farther than the eye could strain through the dust, the grass was colored with

5

milling cattle, while bulls rode and fought, and cows and calves bawled, and countless horns clacked, and sixty or seventy of us kept saddling fresh mounts and galloping here and there in a stirring, day-long excitement.

The free wild life we lived on that shaggy prairie was to me the life of the gods. And that there should be anyone who would not love it as we did, who should even hate it passionately and secretly, and yet the memory of whose delicate presence in that violent land still stirs me with emotion after fifty years, had not occurred to me then. But I was only a boy whose face had never known a razor, in a pair of California britches turned up to let my boots into the stirrups, that early fall day I rode with rebellious young back to Salt Fork to be shipped off to Missouri to school before my uncle would fetch back to the ranch the scarcest article in the territory, a woman, the one we had never seen, who was coming all the way from St. Louis to marry him.

At the edge of town I scowled at an encampment of settlers' tents and wagons, the largest I remembered. They seemed to be waiting for something. Then I rode up to the hotel and heard someone say that the telegraph line was open after having been cut again by Indians in the Raton.

"I'm going to let it to you, Hal, to see the Colonel gets this," the red-faced station agent told me mysteriously.

He handed me a sheet of unfolded gray paper, the writing in pencil and dated at St. Louis nearly a week before. It was, I think, the first telegram I had ever seen and for a moment I had the impression that the paper itself had come in some up-to-date manner over the telegraph wire and that the execrable writing was that of this woman who had signed it Lutie and who said with love that she was not stopping off in Denver as she had planned but would arrive in Salt Fork on a morning I knew was tomorrow.

I had not seen my uncle for more than two weeks, and with the telegram unpleasant as a perfumed handkerchief in my pocket, I rode down to the shipping corrals, half expecting to see his herd of fall beef steers come sweeping down off the sand hills into town like the Rio Grande running bankful after the summer rains, washing across the tracks, flooding the stock-pens and overflowing along the river-bank from where, until shipped, they would fill the town night and day with their bawling.

But no Cross B steers were there and neither was my uncle, and I went to the dim adobe courtroom where they were outrageously trying two of our hands for shooting at and running off a nester. I couldn't get any nearer than the door. But from there I could hear the ora-

torical voice of the young district attorney, lately from the East and close to the President, bitterly assailing the high-handed methods on my uncle's vast range and promising new justice for emigrants in all his district from the Rio Grande to the Arizona line.

When the trial adjourned until morning, I pushed myself between groups of soberly talking men to Henry McCurtin, my uncle's lawyer, a ponderous man, who read the telegram over his great drooping dun mustaches.

"I haven't seen the Colonel since the trial opened," he rumbled. "I reckon, son, you better meet this woman tomorrow yourself."

For a long time I lay awake that night in the cavernous Bridal Chamber of the Exchange House, the corner room always reserved for my uncle when he came to town, feeling my hate for this woman who was banishing me to Missouri, and thinking that I had never known the town quite so swarming with men, the livery stable and wagon yards so choked with horses, or the night so deafening with the clatter of pianos and scream of fiddles pouring from open dance-hall windows; with the steady undertone of clinking glasses from half a score of saloons; and men and sporting women talking, laughing, and yelling boisterous songs that paused only for the sudden rap of the six-shooter.

But through it all I could hear, like the wild, unceasing heartbeat of this frontier town, the sound of marching boots on the wooden sidewalk, pounding the planks from bar to bar. And I knew that not all these men, drawn from a hundred and two hundred remote miles, had come to ship beef. It was the trial, this new young district attorney from the East, challenging the power of my uncle and other big cattlemen, that had drawn them. And sitting up in that enormous bed I could see through the long window the distant white tents and sheeted wagons of the emigrants' camp glinting like the wet and treacherous quicksands of the Puerco.

When I awoke in the morning, I found to my regret that I had slept through another shooting. On the way to the depot I saw the dead man's oxen still hitched to his wagon, ten or twelve of them lying down patiently in the yoke, chewing their cud, while the stranger who had done it swung a slow pendulum on the railroad's wooden water-tower, his boots already pulled off by some low wretch and the water dripping over him, his head to one side and one leg curiously longer than the other as if he were trying to reach the ground.

He was cut down by the sheriff under the indignant direction of the new district attorney and laid temporarily under a wagon sheet in the freight house. But as soon as the officers had disappeared into the courthouse, some of the dead teamster's friends dragged him out again just as I faintly heard a bell ringing and hand-brakes screeching from

every open platform. I stayed to watch them take a rope from some-
body's saddle and pull him up again. And when I turned, the train
from St. Louis was long in, with its short coaches coated with the
dust of the Great Plains.

Up until now I expected that at the last moment my uncle would
surely appear. But he wasn't there, and I cast about harshly in my
mind what I should say to this woman and how I might recognize
her. In the territory my uncle attended strictly to business, riding the
range as hard as any of his hands. But in Kansas City, where he went
regularly to sell his cattle, people said that he swung a wide loop and
once when a prominent commission man he much disliked had solic-
ited him too far for his business, even inviting him to a very elite
party, my uncle had forever silenced him by coming in great style with
a notorious and lavishly dressed sporting woman on his arm.

And now I looked for a woman bold and painted like Ready Money
Kate from St. Louis, whom I had often seen sailing up and down
the wooden sidewalks of Salt Fork in vivid silks with parasol to match
and, when she crossed the dusty street, with plenty of red and white
striped stocking showing.

All I saw was a lady standing by the car steps and behind her a
respectful, bearded brakeman holding a pair of valises. Her face was
hidden behind a heavy brown veil, but there was something unfor-
gettable in the slender way she stood there, in a suit of unmistakable
quality and tailoring, gloves and a plumed hat, a fragile feminine
figure, alone and unmet, stared at by blanketed Indians, Mongol-like
Mexicans, and shaggy white men with cartridge belts and with spur
rowels coarse as cart-wheels, and over their heads on the water-tank
the dead man still swinging.

A loafer in a buckskin shirt with all the beading long since lost said
something and pointed to me, and I saw her move toward me. She
did not speak until she was so close I could smell the fragrance of
violets about her and could see the liquid of her eyes through the
veil. Then she lifted it from her face, and although I was only a boy,
I felt that quickening emotion she was always to arouse in me until
the last time I should see her.

"So this is Hal?" she said softly, and kissed me, and I stood there
young and rigid with my face burning in front of everyone. But if
she saw it, she gave no sign. With the dead man slowly turning in
front of her, she went on chatting to me in slightly incoherent but
charming fashion, saying the gayest of things, that required little or
none of my tongue-tied answers, all the while her delicate forehead
shutting out the water-tank and that ring of staring loafers as com-
pletely as if she stood alone with me in my uncle's ranch house. And

I realized that here was a finer-fibered creature than any my long black hair and rope-calloused hands had known.

When I stammered that her telegram had come only last evening and that I hadn't been able to deliver it to my uncle as yet, she took my arm with alive intimacy.

"We'll find him together, Hal," she said confidently.

"He'll come to the hotel, if you'll wait there," I told her.

"The bags can go to the hotel, but not I, Hal," she answered. "I've been shut up in a train for days and days. I want to walk. Miles and miles, until we find him."

Very stiffly and thinking these St. Louis ladies a little mad, I guided her through the deep dust strewn with horns and bones and the forelegs of sheep, between wagon hubs and saddle-pony heels, until we were up on the wooden sidewalk, where I took care to steer her away from the direction of the courthouse. But I couldn't avoid the wagon of the dead freighter, with boys climbing a wheel to stare at what we both could plainly see, a long figure lying on his back, with his red beard still sticking up defiantly from under the blue bandanna across his face. But Lutie Cameron's chatting never stopped. Only her soft live arm tightened in mine like a doeskin band.

I had the pride common in the territory that going about on foot was the mark of a hoeman and close to disgrace. And I was glad when the boardwalk came to an end. But Lutie Cameron had pinned her veil back now; her delicate face was thrown up and there was no stopping her. On and on we went past a few scattered Mexican houses and up the sloping sand hills, where she exclaimed over the common yerba de vibora still in blossom and pinned a yellow spray of it gayly across her coat.

But when we reached the top of the escarpment and, suddenly like coming on the ocean unaware, there in front of us stretched the vast, brown, empty plain, dipping and pitching endlessly like a parched sea, she stopped as if she had run into barbed wire. I tried to point out a remote, nearly indistinguishable cloud shadow that marked the general location of the distant ranch house, but she didn't seem to hear me, chatting almost breathlessly about a traveling acquaintance on the Pullman palace car on her way to join her husband at Fort Ewing, all the while striking out for the white village of tents and covered wagons of the emigrants' camp near by, where life was busily going on.

She waved brightly to a score or more of children tumbling, rolling, and shouting over the ground, and bowed charmingly to tired-looking women in sunbonnets who had been sewing and knitting on a circle of wagon seats and rockers set on the grass and who stood up now

to receive her as some great lady who had deigned to visit their humble abode.

When they told her they had come all the way from her own Missouri and hoped to settle far out on this very plain, something came into her eyes that I hadn't seen there before. She sparkled to grandmothers in knitted caps and wrinkled as Indians, swung a gurgling baby high in the air, and ran and shouted with the children who had clustered around her. And she climbed up into one of the wagons fitted up as a cabin with stove-pipe pushing out of the canvas, where, as I stood stiff and disapproving, I could hear her complimenting the delighted owners on what she found.

"If you see Colonel Brewton," she said gayly before she left, "tell him we've been looking for him everywhere."

I was conscious of a shadow instantly falling over the camp. Even the children seemed to freeze at the sound of my uncle's name.

"I reckon you'll find him at court today, ma'am," a gaunt Missourian answered after a moment.

Lutie Cameron said nothing until we were a quarter-mile away.

"Why did they look at us so queerly, Hal? And why didn't you tell me we might find him at court?"

"We couldn't get in anyhow," I answered sullenly.

And when we reached the square, I could see at the courthouse a little crowd of men packed half-way across the boardwalk to the hitching-rack. I would have gone on to the Exchange House, but she stopped and lifted her head in that gesture I already knew so well, a slight feminine figure against the rude backs of a score of men.

"May we pass, please?" She spoke clearly, and to my surprise that gentle lady's voice of hers turned rough men about and tumbled off their hats as if a bullet had whipped them. A narrow but unmistakable aisle opened in front of us, and presently I found myself inside, with Blackjack Kerns, a rustler and outlaw, rising like a jack-in-the-box to give the lady his seat, and others on the bench moving over to make a few inches of room for me.

§ 2

The Salt Fork County court was stuffed and smelly as a stock corral at shipping time, a dingy adobe room with earthen floor and small Mexican windows darkened by men sitting on the deep ledges so that it seemed as if we had entered a kind of rude twilight.

"Is he here, Hal?" Lutie Cameron whispered to me through her veil.

But even before my eyes grew accustomed to the dimness, I knew by the atmosphere that my uncle wasn't there.

"The jury's comin' in," a cowhand from the Three V's muttered behind me.

I saw now that the jury box of worn and whittled pine benches was empty. Then I heard a stir at the doorway behind us and presently I thought I could feel a wave of restrained excitement rising in the rear of the room and passing from bench to bench until beyond the railing I saw our two accused cowhands twist in their seats and Henry McCurtin turn like a mountain suddenly come to life.

I felt my arm brushed by Lutie Cameron's gloved fingers.

"What is it, Hal?" she whispered.

Then I saw by her veiled eyes that she glimpsed something and, turning my head, I saw it, too, moving erect and towering down the crowded aisle along the wall, a familiar, proud, almost insolent figure in a long gray broadcloth coat with tails and bulging on the side toward us with what I knew was a holster capped with ivory handles, his coal-black eyebrows and mustache white with alkali dust, and in the abrupt quiet of the room the fall of his boot-heels like the shots of a pistol.

Since that day I have been in many a courtroom, but never any so quickly transformed from a dingy room to one kindled and illuminated by the lightning-flash of one man's vitality and power, so that today I can still see it as in the strongest sunshine, the dusty colors of the American flag on the whitewashed wall over the judge's pine bench, and beneath his parted black robe the gold links of his watch-chain, heavy enough for carriage traces, on the court rail a pair of buckled spurs swinging, and that fearless, moving figure of my uncle like some rude territorial czar.

Then I saw that those pitchfork eyes which missed nothing had found us. Deliberately, with scarcely a change in him, he was crossing to our aisle, the men on the bench he chose to pass by scattering for the moment like sheep in front of him. And presently he stood there beside us with bared head and a kind of mellowed dignity, pressing Lutie Cameron's hand, asking her health and welfare in quiet solicitude, his great lusty face gently warmed like the sunlight on a weathered cliff.

Saying he would join us later, he straightened, his black glance swept those close by who had been listening, and he moved majestically on, passing inside the privileged railing where Henry McCurtin stood up in massive welcome and the two accused cowhands grinned and the sheriff hastily brought him the bailiff's chair, while

the district clerk with a pen riding one ear stared respectfully and Judge White, peering as always with a glum and imperturbable face over his pine bench, broke into a friendly smile and his head bobbed in ceremonious greeting.

Only one man inside of the railing showed him no deference, and I watched Brice Chamberlain, the young district attorney appointed by the President, standing there tall and impressive, his plain sack coat buttoned close to his white collar, his brows frowning formidably, and his thick blond hair sweeping back in a kind of masterful and handsome disapproval.

"What's the case about, Hal?" Lutie Cameron whispered. "And who is the scowling gentleman?"

I didn't answer. The faded blue door beyond the railing had opened and men were starting to drift through, in single file, slouching Americans in sagging unbuttoned vests and slightly pompous Mexicans in leather chalecos, one after the other pulling off his hat as he entered, boots shuffling on the adobe floor.

Behind me a voice whispered loudly that for any other man except Jim Brewton the jury would have stayed out with their verdict until they had had their dinner on the county. Then I heard leathery Eli Jones, the jury foreman, answering Judge White's questions.

"We find," he drawled, "that Andy Boggs was shot at and run off the place he wanted to file on, by unknown parties."

I saw the strict face of the judge redden as if over some impropriety. "That's no verdict!" he reminded sharply. "The two defendants—"

"Oh, hell, they're not guilty," Eli waved.

I wanted to give the Apache war-whoop while behind me a row of cowhands stamped their boots and jingled their spurs until Judge White pounded his pine bench in anger. Then he demanded the formal written verdict of the grinning jury foreman and adjourned court.

"Is that the verdict you wanted, Hal?" Lutie Cameron asked eagerly, but I saw that her eyes were not on me or our freed cowhands; rather on the tall young district attorney, who had winced as if thrown by a horse.

Another moment and she had urged me up from our bench. With her arm in mine, she swept up the aisle, chatting with animation at every step, and through the railing, where she stopped beside my uncle, slipping her free arm delicately through his, just as I saw Brice Chamberlain get himself in hand and stiffly congratulate Henry McCurtin.

Then the defeated young district attorney turned to my uncle.

"May I ask you a few questions that I had no opportunity for during the trial, Colonel Brewton?"

His manner was courteous, but there was a faintly challenging ring in his voice and a blue fire in his eyes that kindled the silent attention of those of us standing inside of the railing. He went on without waiting for assent:

"Is it true, Colonel Brewton, that your range runs a hundred miles or more north and south, and west nearly to the Arizona line?"

My uncle merely inclined his head.

"Is it true," Chamberlain went on, his voice suddenly rising, "that of this vast country you control, you actually own only a few scattered water-holes that have been filed on either in your name or those of your men? And that by far the greater part still belongs to the government?"

"Legally, yes," my uncle conceded.

"Is it true, then," Chamberlain concluded, his voice gathering force and indignation, "that this million or more of acres still belonging to the government is the same land that Andrew Boggs, who only wanted a mere hundred and sixty acres for a homestead, was run off from and severely wounded by unknown parties?"

"No," my uncle said quietly but with great firmness and power. "He was not run off because he wanted to settle those hundred and sixty acres but because of what he wanted to do with the land."

So intent had I been on the sparks beginning to fly between the flint and steel of these two men that I had almost forgotten where we were. Now I heard a strong murmur of approval and, looking around, I saw a press of cowhands and cattlemen against the railing.

Brice Chamberlain did not glance around. But something seemed to pass behind his brightly burning blue eyes. His manner changed. An appeal came into his face and voice, and standing there bent persuasively toward my uncle, even I for a moment thought him modest and almost likable.

"Let's forget about this case, Colonel Brewton. Andrew Boggs was only a single man and the court has disposed of him. Waiting at the edge of Salt Fork to see how this trial comes out are other settlers. Not single men, but with families, from babes at the breast to grandmothers. They have given up their homes in the East, driven their wagons more than a thousand miles across the plains, and left their dead from the Mississippi to the Rio Grande—all with the one purpose of finding homes for themselves in this great territory." His voice grew eloquent with pleading. "Now that you have won your case, Colonel Brewton, and can afford to show your sympathy and charity, I want to ask in the names of these families if you won't let them settle

undisturbed on a few acres out of the million or more of government land on your range?"

I saw Lutie Cameron's eyes, soft under her veil, glance expectantly at my uncle. But he didn't see her. He had thrown up his head like an unruly lead steer smelling wolves or water.

"Chamberlain," he said, "I have sympathy for the pioneer settler who came out here and risked his life and family among the Indians. And I hope I have a little charity for the nester who waited until the country was safe and peaceable before he filed a homestead on some-one else's range who fought for it. But—" and his voice began to ring in the small hushed courtroom, "when that nester picks country like my big vega, that's more than seven thousand feet above the sea, when he wants to plow it up to support his family where there isn't enough rain for crops to grow, where he only kills the grass that will grow, where he starves for water and feeds his family by killing my beef and becomes a man without respect to himself and a miserable menace to the territory, then I have neither sympathy nor charity!"

His eyes now were pitch-black, proud, insolent, his great face written with power and almost dissolute ruthlessness. "And I want to say," he finished, "that if I know the temper of the citizens who ran off that worthless nester, Boggs, they'll keep running off every granger who tries to destroy their range!"

For nearly a minute more the two men faced each other, one older, rugged, utterly fearless; the other young and white with emotion.

"They warned me," Brice Chamberlain said in a low burning voice, "not to bring action against you or your men. They told me there was no justice here, that you dominated the country and would never share your land with your less fortunate fellow men."

He turned on his heel and left, but all of us knew this was not the end. I looked at Lutie Cameron. She still hung on my uncle's arm, delicate, silent, rigid, her eyes on the stunned little group of listening Missourians in the patched blue and striped jumpers of farmers huddled there in the courtroom. And when she and my uncle went out to the hotel for dinner, I saw her take the spray of bright yellow blossoms she had pinned so gayly across her coat and throw it away.

With my hat hot and uncomfortable in my hand, I waited as long as I dared that afternoon outside the ladies' parlor of the Exchange House. When I pushed in the door, I saw my uncle standing with dignity in front of the tall window. Beside him stood Lutie Cameron, her head thrown firmly up, her brown veil raised, her plumes at a high and gallant angle, making an unforgettable picture in that dark, cavernous room with a single shaft of sunshine pouring over her, while Judge White in a long black coat with broad silken lapels kept sternly

clearing his throat and compressing his lips as he read the unfamiliar marriage service.

Her cheeks were dusted as if with flour when she turned, but nothing else betrayed her as Dr. Reid, who, I think, must have denied himself liquor all afternoon for the occasion, bowed like the Virginian he was, over her hand, and wished her happiness. And Henry McCurtin, in fresh linen unsullied by a single tobacco stain, asked her jovially through his dun mustaches how she had managed to rope such a shy war-horse.

She and my uncle took me to the depot, and the last thing I saw of Lutie Brewton, she was standing with one arm outstretched waving her handkerchief gayly after me, a gesture I coldly declined to answer. But late that night when the train was puffing through the dark New Mexican hills, I kept thinking about her in that walled island of ranch house on my lost sea of grass.

§ 3

I have hated places in my life, but never any like that academy in Lexington where the woman who had waved me good-by so gayly had imprisoned me, with its brick walls and stone banisters still patched where grape-shot and Minie balls had torn through, with a winter of cold such as I had never known in the territory, with the sun not coming out for weeks at a time and a road of dirt and ashes across the mile-wide Missouri frozen into curious yellow ice.

And when spring came and the eaves dripped a steady tattoo and strange birds cheeped in the wet trees around the school, the ice went out of the Missouri with a roar. And I went, too, between two suns, as my uncle used to say of any man who disappeared. And late that afternoon I was in Kansas City, trying to keep my chin up and my back stiff and not to betray how bewildered I was in this cold young city with wagons and carriages clattering in every direction on the stone paving and no one paying me more attention than if I were a burro dozing in the dusty streets of Old Town in Salt Fork. The thought of those quiet, dusty streets sleeping in the yellow sun made me more homesick for the territory than I have ever been in my life except for a half-hour later when I reached the stockyards and smelled cattle again and saw the familiar colors of longhorns and listened to Nicholas Masters of the Masters Packing Company, the heavy flesh of his face quivering like a kind of purple jelly as he coughed and shook a fat finger at me and sputtered that if he helped me run home, my uncle would never sell him another trainload of steers.

But when I told him it had been the woman my uncle had married and whom I hated that had clapped me into this prison of a school, he stared at me thoughtfully as a companion in distress. And when I left, I had a pass and some money and had given a sacred promise never to let this woman know who it was had befriended me.

All the way out to the ranch on a Salt Fork horse from Dagget's livery stable, with the range already greening up in the sloughs, with Canada geese rising from the ponds and cutting the sky like joined Apache lances, with calves kicking and bucking in the spring sunshine and horses rubbing off winter hair, I felt the bitterness grow in me for the woman who would have kept me from all this. And I planned coldly how I would treat her and what curtness of speech she should hear from me.

Riding up Nester Draw so she should not see me coming, I cut across the rise and up to the rear of the ranch house, where a strange Chinaman cook eyed me suspiciously from the kitchen as I entered by the back door. I scowled to see that there were strange pine settees covered with Navajo blankets in the wide hall. And glancing into the open door of the huge storeroom, I saw with dull anger that the familiar mountains of flour and coffee had vanished and the buttes of dried fruits gone, so that I hardly knew the room with a Brussels carpet on the floor and heavy dark red hangings at the windows and tufted horsehair chairs and sofa around the walls and a square piano with legs curved and lid polished as elegantly and offensively as the piano at school.

It all had an inexpressibly depressing effect on me, as if the old ranch house I had known and loved was gone. And I stood there lonely, bitter, and stiffening as a slender form appeared from the big front bedroom in the dim hall. Oh, she looked a bit thinner and paler, but her dark hair even here on these remote plains was done up in the latest St. Louis fashion; a spray of pink loco weed had been pinned freshly across her basque and she still moved with undiminished sparkle and aliveness.

Then she recognized me.

"Hal!" she almost screamed.

Her intense young arms hugged me as if she had seen no one for weeks. And with her delicate fragrance of violets about me like some sweet drug, I felt the hate go out of me as the ice had gone out of the Missouri at Lexington only a week or two before.

Another moment and she was holding me at arm's length, delightedly looking me over from head to foot, squeezing my hand and laughingly exclaiming what a manly boy I was on the way to becoming, and chattering that she had not had a visitor since day before yesterday

and what a wonderful winter she had spent here on the ranch in this Western climate with blue sky and almost eternal sunshine, and that my uncle was looking more distinguished than ever, and had I seen the trees she had coaxed the hands to plant for summer shade; degrading work, my uncle had called it, that men who rode a horse would never do.

But with nearly every word I observed in her dark eyes the feverish brilliance of the first day I had seen her. And the following year when I came home a little older and taller, it still haunted her eyes although the parlor hummed with company. And I soon found out that scarcely a day was intended to pass without midday dinner guests or overnight guests or guests to stay the week. And most of them crocheted or embroidered, laughed or sang, played charades or whist, and were agreeable to almost anything except to ride out and visit the roundup, which Lutie Brewton kept finding charming excuses to miss.

There were, I remember, the sporting English owners of the Bar 44 and the dancing officers from Fort Ewing, the lively Falconers and important Netherwoods, whose name Lutie Brewton loved to trill over her tongue, the guests from Santa Fe and Albuquerque, and Judge White and Brice Chamberlain on their respective rounds of the district court.

But if I expected my uncle to resent any of their coming, I was mistaken. He rode his range no less hard than before, and it must have seemed to him as it did to me a kind of miracle to step from dark night into a lighted house, from a hard saddle to a cushioned chair, to come from the cold, shaggy plain into warm curtained rooms with Lutie Brewton bare-armed in a silken gown and white candles burning around her as in a cathedral, with silver sparkling and stainless cloth shining and a mellow atmosphere of company talking and laughing around his table.

My uncle would bow with proud courtesy to everyone. But I heard him talk very little, preferring to sit there with a faint desert glow warming his weathered face, his insolent eyes softening a little as he watched or listened to his wife. No matter who came or how large the dinner, Lutie Brewton was the tireless pure flame burning in the center of it, her face flatteringly raised to listen, her talk a highly seasoned language of its own, her headlong treble laughter leading into general bursts of merriment, and her ringed fingers skimming over the white keys of the piano, with the soft light from the tall marble, brass, and china lamp golden on her dark hair.

She never stopped, not even for a moment. And when I watched her so alive on the black horsehair sofa, making ecstatic gestures with her white hands to the gentleman on either side of her, I had the

curious feeling that she never slept, but, stimulated by congenial friends, could go on bubbling night and day.

Certainly she never stopped when she went to town with her fast team of bays to spend the night at the Netherwoods' or the Holdernesses', who were kin of Brice Chamberlain. Once or twice I drove her, and the moment we passed out through the dense wall of cottonwoods and tamarisks, she chatted incessantly, her sensitive face turned away from the wide sea of grass as if it were the plague, so that I swore she never saw the road runner racing with the carriage wheel or the antelope moving among the cattle. And I thought that at last I had begun to understand the reason for her wall of cottonwoods and tamarisks, which had not been planted for summer shade at all.

"She'll settle down once she has babies," I heard Mrs. Netherwood say fondly to Judge White the day of the Holman wedding, when she wore diamond dust in her hair.

§ 4

The babies came soon afterwards. One after the other I found them in the big front bedroom of the ranch house when I came home from school; the first, a fat gurgling girl with dark eyes and scarcely any hair to start with; the second, an unsmiling boy with the blackest of hair and eyes; and the third, a boy whose eyes were an unexpected bright blue, with hair so white and soft it turned and ruffled like a feather in my breath.

Yet neither I nor anyone else could see a change in Lutie Brewton. With her first baby in the cradle, I felt that out of respect I should call her Aunt Lutie, but she turned on me quickly.

"Don't you dare call me that, Hal!" she said and her eyes were black and flashing. "I shall never be old enough to be Auntie to anyone."

Black Hetty, who took care of the babies, showed the broad white of her teeth. But after the second child Lutie Brewton was still the same slender figure, alive, intense, her delicate white skin without a wrinkle. And with the third baby scarcely in his cradle, she danced eight out of ten square dances and waltzes with Brice Chamberlain as her partner in the huge English hall of the Bar 44.

He was at my uncle's ranch house now all too often to suit me, driving out as a rule with his dashing cousin, the young blond Mrs. Holderness, whether my uncle was home or not. The administration at Washington had long since changed and with it his and Judge White's appointments. And Brice Chamberlain had opened a law

office on the dusty Salt Fork plaza next door to Gidding's dance hall, where he specialized in the settling of titles to the huge land grants for profit and filing of homestead entries as a passion.

My uncle paid him little attention, while he treated my uncle with unfailing politeness. But more than once when the latter wasn't looking, I caught Brice Chamberlain's blue eyes measuring him and seeming to say: "You're of the past generation now. Your time is soon over. We will run the world from now on, not you." And to Lutie he openly and eloquently boasted: "Civilization is moving west fast. It will be here soon. And when it comes, the fertile plains around this ranch house will be dotted with farms and schoolhouses."

I paid him no more attention than my uncle. But once when I coldly carried him an invitation to dinner, I saw his desk piled high with semitransparent blueprint maps of township and correction lines and with stacks of letters from scores of land-hungry Easterners he had circularized, a sight that gave me an angry, disturbed feeling.

I was in college at St. Louis when the Washington administration changed again. Almost as I was leaving for home I read with satisfaction in the Salt Fork paper, printed in both English and Spanish, that Brice Chamberlain was closing up his office, turning all his legal matters over to Lawyer Archie Meade and going to establish residence in Denver, where he had been promised the appointment of United States district attorney. And two weeks later when I found him still in Salt Fork, I scowled at his figure crossing the dusty plaza with that impressive long-legged stride, immaculately dressed as always with high-buttoned Eastern suit under an imposing silver-gray Western hat.

I turned to see Henry McCurtin, a little heavier and slower, his drooping dun mustaches a little grayer, standing there ponderously watching him from his inscrutable, deeply buried eyes.

"You glad as I am he's going?" I asked when we had shaken hands.

"I'm not so sure, Hal, not so sure. The town is full of rumors," he rumbled. Then, as if he had said too much, he turned massively away.

For the first time I became sensitive to things unsaid, that the waves of sand hills rolling toward the town held a stormy and faintly ominous look. And when I glanced back, I saw that the landlocked harbor of the square was taut and white with the crowded canvas of settlers' wagons from a dozen Eastern ports. And now I remembered all the small emigrant trains I had glimpsed from my train window across Kansas and through the Raton wherever the wagon trail lay in sight of the tracks.

And when I reached the ranch next day, I thought that I had never seen Lutie Brewton more brilliantly alive and restless, her cheeks flushed, her eyes feverish, almost dazzling. All afternoon her tongue

poured out a stream of gay excitement, one minute warm and frank
and intimate as a sister, the next coaxing and teasing, while my small
cousins burrowed under my chair and climbed on my shoulders and
wore my new silver watch and chain.

As a rule Lutie Brewton treated her children like some gracious
lady who had consented to be their godmother. But tonight to my
mild surprise she told Black Hetty she would put them to bed herself.
And with me standing in the doorway silent at the picture they made,
she poked grave, tender fun at little Jimmy's skinny freckled legs and
arms, and called Sarah Beth's panty waist a corset, which embarrassed
her, and frowned with mock seriousness at the transparent white skin
of Brock, whom, she declared, God had intended to be a girl. And
all the while her facile white hands helped them to slip off their gar-
ments and into their long muslin nightgowns which covered their
toes as they knelt on the brown sheepskin.

But when we were back again in the parlor, I saw her shudder,
and I stared at her until she turned on me like a white tigress.

"Why must you look at me like that, Hal? Am I older? Am I sallow?
What do you see? Have I pouches under my eyes?"

I lied to her that I had seen nothing, telling her the truth that she
looked scarcely older than the day I had met her at the South Fork
depot, and in a moment she had changed back to the sparkling person
I knew. But during the night I thought I heard someone moving about
the great front bedroom, and when I awoke as the sun heaved up red
above the plain, the one who hadn't slept was still walking.

Except for a few minutes at breakfast and noonday dinner, I did
not see her all day. I had planned to ride out to the roundup as was
my custom, but something in her eyes withheld me. All afternoon
I could hear her moving about mysteriously in her room. About six
o'clock I was lying on my back on the slippery horsehair sofa, staring
up at the heavy pine ceiling, when I heard the swish of skirts through
the hall. And when I turned my head, she was standing there.

"You are almost a man now, Hal," she told me. "You've been to
St. Louis and Kansas City, and you know the way of the world. And
I think you'll understand when I tell you I'm going away."

Looking up from where I lay, the light in her eyes seemed almost
blinding. She went on a little breathlessly:

"Run away, perhaps, is what you'd call it, Hal. What people will
call it. I'm running off. Leaving your uncle for always. I'm going
tomorrow morning, and I shan't be back."

I sat up stupefied. I had heard of occasional women deserting their
husbands, but for Lutie Brewton to leave my uncle and her position
in this luxurious ranch house seemed unthinkable. I remembered he

was still out at the roundup, which on our range lasted from spring to summer, and she must have read my thoughts in my eyes.

"Oh, I'm not running off behind his back, Hal," she said to me. "I told him nearly a month ago. When the first emigrant wagons came to Salt Fork. I told him I couldn't stand it another year. Not running them off again and perhaps killing them as they did that poor nester from Louisiana who shot at them last year. He was white trash, but he had a wife and six or seven children. Now, as far as I am concerned, it's all settled—all but the tearing out of a few roots and tendrils."

"But Jimmy and Brock and Sarah Beth?" I stammered.

The first white hardness came into her face.

"I went over it and over it with him, Hal! A thousand times, I think. You know your uncle. He thought he could hold me by holding the children. But nothing can stop me. My lawyer says I can't take them along. But I can fight for them after I'm away. Once we're settled. No jury, Hal, not even Mexicans, can keep three children from their mother."

Something between the lines of what she said troubled me.

"You're going away with somebody?" I heard myself saying coldly.

Unexpected warm color crept up into her faintly wilted cheeks, freshening them like petals, and almost at once she was like a flower rooted again in rich wet earth with that unaccountable power we call life flowing through her.

"If I never knew it before, Hal, I'd know now you had the same blood as your uncle. You ask the same questions. But I shan't tell you any more than I shall him. He's coming now. Don't go, Hal!" she begged quickly as I stiffened and rose. Her slender fingers gripped my arm. "You'll break the ice between us. And don't look so frightened for me, you poor boy!" Something shining and irrevocable came into her face. "I'm not dying and being stuffed into a coffin. I'm going where there's life, Hal. I'm going to balls and theaters and shaded streets and up-to-date stores and where every day people drive in the parks!"

I could hear hoofbeats now. Turning, I saw through the deep windows my uncle riding toward the ranch house, sitting erect as always in his saddle, his right arm held stiffly down against his side with his thumb at the cantle edge as was his custom, unchanged from army days. Presently there was the sound of his boots and spurs through the hall, and he was in the room. But, contrary to what I feared, I had never seen him more quiet.

Lutie Brewton held up her face to be kissed as always and chatted brightly to him of some of the incidents I had told her of college, while

my uncle shook my hand and inquired if I had seen Nicholas Masters as he had written me. There was a curious absence of time and hurry, as if utterly nothing had happened or was expected to happen. Only when I glanced closely to see if Lutie had really told me the truth did I feel the fine filaments of strain in the air like those unseen currents that are said to lift the hair of a wolf before an August thunderclap.

"Supper's on the table, Miz Brewton," stoically called Jeff Calder, the old chuck-wagon cook who had long since followed the Chinaman in the ranch-house kitchen.

I would have given a great deal that night to have avoided the dining-room and the massive silver. My uncle ate gravely while Lutie Brewton single-handed with almost desperate gayety kept conversation alive. But every moment I saw that she curbed her eyes from the windows.

The children had had their supper early tonight as was their custom, and now, with Black Hetty standing by, they were all astride the bare back of Old Cherry, scarcely taller than a pony. Jimmy sat in front; Sarah Beth, who was six or seven, behind him; and Brock to the rear, each holding to a share of the bridle reins. A strip of gunnysack as a blinder had been tied over the gentle old barefoot mare's eyes, and she stood motionless until Jimmy yelled and pulled it off, when she came to life and bobbed up and down until one happily shrieking youngster after the other was deposited on the grass.

I could not look at them myself tonight, and under my breath I muttered that as soon as it was dark I should saddle one of the night horses and ride to the camp at Cottonwood Springs, where I would stay till it was over. Then just before Lutie Brewton rose, she gave me one of her indecipherable glances.

"If I don't see you any more tonight, Hal," she asked, "could you drive me to Salt Fork in the morning?"

My uncle had been sitting quietly on his chair, waiting for her signal to rise, the deferent courtesy he always had for her mellowing his face. Now his head was flung up in the gesture of a challenged wild stallion while his dark eyes flamed with sudden will and power.

"Hal will take your trunk in the buckboard," he told her proudly. "I'll drive you to the train myself."

"Thank you, Colonel Brewton," she said.

But I saw in an instant as she rose that an unusual pallor had swept her face. And when a few moments later I passed the length of the hall to the gallery, I saw her standing rigid in the huge front bedroom with her back toward a pair of ivory handles holstered in a

heavy belt darkened by years of sweat and hanging on a high, brass harness hook out of reach of the children.

<p style="text-align:center">§ 5</p>

For a long time I lay awake that night in the bunk that had once been my uncle's, listening at intervals to the faint bawling of a calf for its mother in some dim, starlit cañada. And when I fell asleep I dreamed that something vaguely beautiful had gone out of this massive ranch house like the kernel of life out of a prairie seed, and all that remained was the brown shell of adobe walls staring from its empty sockets. And everywhere about the house in my dream, the sand was endlessly blowing, burying the print of the coyote and lizard, rattling in the vibora weed, drifting close to the ground like barren snow so that the whole earth seemed to be moving, a restless gray ghost of itself trying to find those full, lusty prairie breasts, fertile as a woman and flowing with milk and wild honey, that used to be.

At the first sound of morning I was up pulling on my clothes in the darkness and drinking coffee in the kitchen to escape the break-fast-table, and lending a hand in the starlight to the hitching of the teams. And when I came back to the long dark hall, I glimpsed in a candle-lighted room, framed like a picture by the heavy doorway, Lutie Brewton, suited, hatted, and one hand gloved, sitting with three sleepy youngsters in their nightgowns about her. And I heard her promising in that clear, delightful, fun-loving voice she always used to children, that she would see them all sooner than soon and would have a double present for each one that Black Hetty should say had been a little lady or gentleman.

Old Jeff helped me carry out her trunk to the sagging buckboard. And soon Lutie Brewton came, a slender, almost jaunty figure in the dim, blue-black light, answering the children's good-by before my uncle helped her up into the top buggy. Before the horses started, she answered again. And from somewhere down beyond the spring I heard her voice a last time, high and clear above the thud of hoofs and rattle of spokes, like some incredibly sweet and lingering bell.

Old Jeff had waited by one of the buckboard wheels, never saying a word, but I could hear him draw hard and furiously on his pipe until the sounds of the buggy grew faint on the night air. Still saying nothing, he moved grimly into the house while I climbed into the rig and my horses without urging followed those that had gone before.

To the newcomer in our Southwestern land it seems that the days

are very much alike, the same blue sky and unchanging sunshine and endless heat waves rising from the plain. But after he is here a year he learns to distinguish nuances in the weather he would never have noticed under a more violent sky; that one day may be clear enough, and yet some time during the night, without benefit of rain or cloud, a mysterious desert influence sweeps the heavens. And the following morning there is air clearer by half than yesterday, as if freshly rinsed by storm and rain.

It was such a morning that I hauled Lutie Brewton's trunk through the crystal air to Salt Fork, with horses and buckboard moving at first under the swinging lamp of the morning planet, and then through a green, velvet twilight that was half-way between stars and sun, and finally in the early purple light that poured over the plain like wine, until it seemed that with every breath I could taste it, and even the stolid cattle feeding beside the trail seemed to lift their heads to stare at it. And when the sun shook the earth finally clear, I saw a wave of antelope flowing inquisitively toward the buggy far ahead, a wave rusty as with kelp, rising and falling over the grassy swells and eventually turning in alarm, so that a thousand white rumps, whirled suddenly into view, were the breaking of that wide prairie wave on some unseen reef of this tossing upland sea.

Most of the way across the vegas I could have reached out my hand and touched the fragrant rows of bee balm starting to bloom on either side of the trail. But all I could smell was the perfume of violets rising from Lutie Brewton's trunk. And all I could see now was a faint, distant column of black smoke hanging in the sky, little more than a smudge in that illimitable air, yet already it threw a shadow over buckboard and trail.

The sun was a branding iron on the back of my neck when we came at last to the edge of the sand hills and I saw the cottonwoods standing already cool in shadow in the river valley below. My spent horses plowed the floury dust of the long street. And the red-faced station agent himself came bustling out to oversee the careful lifting of Lutie Brewton's trunk to the steel-protected baggage truck slatted like a buckboard and trundled like a barrow.

Not until then did I look up and see with relief that everything about the station was normal and everyday, the groups of passengers through the open door of the waiting-room, the loafers playing mumbletypeg on the plank platform, and out near the tracks a circle of friends surrounding Lutie Brewton, laughing and chattering as always, wishing her a pleasant visit to St. Louis and promising gay times when she returned. I could smell the calm unhurried redolence of ties lately simmering in the sun, could hear down in their whitewashed shipping

pens the monotonous baas of a flock of lambs. And nearer, the white dust floated from a car of flour being unloaded in sacks to a dusty wagon.

Then I glimpsed Lawyers Henry McCurtin and Archie Meade talking together in low, grave tones beyond the baggage barrow, and was slowly conscious that all was not quite what it seemed. And when I glanced around again, I was aware that the loafers kept peering up stealthily from under their brows, and a group of passengers whispered from the waiting-room doorway.

And now I was sure that all those happy friends were frantically playing a part and that they really had no more belief that Lutie Brewton was going to St. Louis than I had. And when I stumbled by as if I noticed nothing, I saw that for all her gay animation, her high lace collar was a pale branch whipsawing in the pounding stream of blood at her throat and that the veins on one of my uncle's hands stood out like long-suppressed whipcords of blue lightning.

I couldn't have gone now if I had wished. I could see the grim bulge in my uncle's coat of gray broadcloth and an untamed violence, like a prairie fire rimmed with black smoke, flaring in his dark eyes. Several loafers had risen to their feet licking their lips. Following their eyes, I glimpsed up the street the unmistakable tall figure of Brice Chamberlain in a new brown suit coming out of the Exchange House and pausing for a moment on the high stone steps, a Mexican behind him with a pair of gripsacks. Then both approaching figures were blotted out by the gray clot of rounded emigrant canvas.

PART II

The Colonel

§ 6

There are pictures nearly dead in my memory now that I never thought I should forget: the curl of a yellow sand wave in the black malpais; the bend of grama grass in the June wind; and the glitter of mocking desert snow on the burning alkali flat. But that scene at Salt Fork in the shadow of the sand hills of nearly fifty years ago is still alive and moving in front of my eyes, and I can't wipe it away.

I can see the small red depot and the round gibbet of the railroad water-tower rimmed with the stubs of old posse ropes. Somewhere along the Rio Grande I can hear the whistle of the eastbound train

that was to take Lutie Brewton forever away with the voice of lambs from the shipping pens in her ears, almost human voices that might have been those of little Jimmy and Brock and Sarah Beth calling to her over nearly fifty miles of plain. And I can feel the long-controlled but now violently overflowing passion of my uncle standing there with his gun belt buckled under his long-tailed, gray broadcloth coat, while the man Lutie Brewton had refused to name, but whom we all knew, was coming toward us only a few hundred yards away, somewhere just behind that cloud of emigrant canvas.

I noticed that men were standing on the flat roof of the Baca hide and wool warehouse and that the teamster had finished loading his flat delivery wagon with a high pyramid of flour, but made no effort to drive it away. Above the bullet-punctured fence around the Kingman Mercantile Company store I could see a row of heads belonging to commission-house clerks all turned toward the square. And presently I became aware that young Lawyer Archie Meade had left the side of the troubled Henry McCurtin as if he couldn't bear to see what might happen to his approaching friend.

The train was whistling now by the small river ranchos and finally through the cottonwood bosque where of a summer afternoon the town boys played Jesse James. Some of the silent crowd, I saw, tried not to look up the street, but it was plain that everyone was standing there in a kind of strained expectancy, waiting for Chamberlain's creamy Western hat and brown-checked Eastern suit to appear.

Only Lutie Brewton refused to be still, throwing herself into saying good-by to her friends with an animated gayety that was almost incoherence, laughing to this one and chattering to that, hugging Myra Netherwood and dabbing quick kisses on Cora Holderness's cheeks, while her hands fluttered and flew and drew back like a pair of white falcons on the leash.

Some of the ladies were crying, although when Lutie Brewton turned to say good-by to me, I stood deaf and stony to hide everything I felt.

"Thank you for bringing my trunk," she said brightly, but when I was kissed, with the scent of violets swimming about me, she whispered in my long hair: "Say nice things about me to my babies till I send for them, Hal!"

And now without a sign as yet of Brice Chamberlain, the train was in, with black smoke drifting from the bulging smoke-stack, and with women passengers staring curiously at Lutie Brewton as their full skirts rustled to the train. My uncle himself carried her valises into the palace car, where I could see him standing by her seat as she gracefully chatted and laughed at her open window to her friends outside

on the raised plank platform, her modulated voice clear and charming as if nothing had happened or could happen and she might be only taking a flying trip to Santa Fe.

Even after the conductor, who had waited respectfully for my uncle to alight, gave the signal for the train to start, and when she and everybody else knew that the man who was to be United States district attorney in Colorado had not appeared from that tangle of emigrant canvas to join her, Lutie Brewton sat there alone and gallant as I had ever seen her, leaning from the window to wave gayly and throw kisses to us all.

"Good-by! Good-by!" For a moment the air was filled with eager cries. Then she was gone. And suddenly the platform was silent and most curiously empty, and everyone stood there looking after the train that was already just a retreating door with a narrow window on either side and a streak of dark smoke drifting above it.

Only my uncle refused to look at it. With his head up and his dark eyes a warning to all he met, he walked toward the hotel, a lone, powerful figure to whom no one at the moment dared to speak.

§ 7

As soon as he was gone, the crowd stirred and moved about like a pack of small dogs that had been cowed by the presence of a mastiff. Several men I knew edged to the side of my uncle's lawyer.

"They say Brice Chamberlain's up with Archie Meade in his office now, Mr. McCurtin," one of them said. "What do you reckon Chamberlain'll do now—take the train tomorrow?"

Henry McCurtin's eyes were pits of gray granite in the mountainous bulk of his cheeks.

"Whatever Brice Chamberlain intends to do, he certainly would not inform us, gentlemen." He bowed, and moved stolidly up the street.

And so did I, as well as I was able, knowing no more than Henry McCurtin. Contrary to my expectations, we stayed in town all next day and my uncle drew a thousand dollars in cash from John Kingman, who did a general banking business in his store. And when the time came for the next eastbound train, my uncle was on the plank platform again, with a tensely eager collection of human beings scattered for two hundred yards about the depot, trying to be casual and inconspicuous, clustered about wagons and leaning on saddle horses and board fences tacked with signs of sheep dip, liniment, and tobacco. One and all, friends or enemies, my uncle ignored them,

pacing implacably up and down, a bulge still under one of the tails
of his coat, his great head thrown up like the breech of a twenty-
pounder, his pitch-black eyes from time to time throwing a fearless
look up the street.

Henry McCurtin told me afterwards he believed my uncle had
merely planned to take the train with Brice Chamberlain and stay
with him until he made sure of his man. But Chamberlain did not
appear that day or the next. No one saw either him or his gripsacks
pass on the street, yet common knowledge had it he was staying with
his kin, the John Holdernesses, from whose house a veritable stream
of telegrams, it was said, had begun to pour to Washington.

For Lutie Brewton's sake I felt a kind of shame for him, holing
up like a fox or coyote here in Salt Fork where everybody knew it.
Even Archie Meade seemed embarrassed by his part in the affair,
crossing the square as if in a hurry to shut himself out of sight in
Brice Chamberlain's old office across the alley from the Courthouse
Saloon. And my uncle bore a look of perpetual contempt on his rude
face.

The fourth day he disdained to go to the depot, and several
evenings later he broke his silence to me as we sat at supper in the
hotel eating-room under the mounted heads of antelope and the
long twisted horns of steers that supported rifles belonging to the
diners.

"You can drive your buckboard back to the ranch in the morning,
Hal," he said, I thought, a little wearily.

All week I had slept on the red sofa in the cavernous Bridal
Chamber, still my uncle's room when he came to town. I remember
that when I went to bed that night it was still dusk and so warm I
threw the covers over the pointed back of the sofa, carved with
scrolls and curlicues. And when I awoke I thought a bunch of cow-
hands from some remote ranch had arrived in town for a rowdy
night at the dance halls.

Then I was conscious of an unaccustomed light in the darkened
room and, slipping over to the long window, I saw a procession from
the emigrant camps winding around the plaza, all men, some on
horseback, some on foot, in patched hickory shirts and linsey-woolsey
shirts and faded blue and striped and gray denim jumpers.

A few carried long cap and ball rifles, but most of them held up
hoes and pitchforks and American flags and two or three crude
flares that threw waves of sultry light over their unshaven faces, the
faces of tenant farmers from Kansas, of hunters from Arkansas, of
Missouri backwoodsmen and Louisiana steamboaters and cotton
choppers from East Texas and artisans and tradesmen whose living

had been unsatisfactory in half a dozen Mississippi and Ohio River states.

I watched them pass, then pulled on my boots and clothes and ran down under the swinging red oil lamp on the hotel stairs. When I reached the street, it was empty, but I could see the nesters massed in front of the Holderness house, that stood with proud head and shoulders above all the squat adobe buildings of Salt Fork, the leaping flares lighting up the impressively mortared bricks, the yellow woodwork and round-eyed cupola on the roof.

As I stood in the shadows of the livery stable, a hoarse roar of enthusiasm rose from the emigrants, and I saw the familiar tall figure of Brice Chamberlain on the Holderness front porch, showing himself at last. A bit pale even at this distance in the flares, but resolved and still masterful in a long coat, his blond hair brushed vigorously back from his forehead, he advanced to the ornately runged railing.

What he said at first I do not know, for he spoke in a low tone. Then his voice rang down the street, and I think it could have been heard in the square.

"This much I dare tell you," he challenged, and I imagined I could see the blue fire in his eyes, "that the President is my friend. And he won't stand by in Washington while ruthless forces in this backwood territory oppose and oppress you. That I can promise you as surely as I can that the President of the United States today appointed me judge of your district court. And I have no fear but that he will see to it that the Senate confirms my appointment."

A thunder of approval with shouts of "Judge Chamberlain!" swelled and echoed in the dusty street. But I scarcely heard it, standing there stiff and incredulous, aware that something unexpected and tragic had happened, something that Lutie Brewton with all her quick mind, that saw into everything like a slender golden sword, had not foreseen.

And neither had I until now when everything stepped into its proper place like Dagget's livery horses into their own stalls. And I could see that Brice Chamberlain, lawyer that he was, had moved to clear himself from my uncle's silent threat against the unnamed man going away with Lutie Brewton, and by the same stroke was vindicating himself in the eyes of certain Salt Fork people who would say now that the new judge had never intended to take the train to Denver at all.

All the way back to the hotel, I felt my anger rising against Chamberlain and wondered what Lutie Brewton would do now. And when I entered the room I was uncomfortable to find my uncle

there, his shirt already off, the black growth curling on his chest like hair from a buggy cushion. He paid me no attention until he had worked off his boots and made himself ready for bed. Then he pinned me to the floor with his eyes that still mirrored a reflection of the emigrants' wild flares, and lifted a long leather wallet from the inside pocket of his removed gray coat with tails.

"Put this under your pillow," he said. "You're going to Denver to-morrow. I want you to find Lutie and give it to her. She'll need it."

"Yes, sir," I stammered, aware now that he knew of Chamberlain's change of appointment and thinking I would give almost anything rather than find Lutie Brewton in her humiliation. And yet somewhere in my blood I felt an inexpressible eagerness that I was to see her again.

I wanted to tell him what Brice Chamberlain had promised the nesters, but I didn't dare. Towering there in his long white night-shirt, his untamed black eyes and fierce dark hair and mustache, he re-minded me of one of the uncontrollable Bedouin chiefs of whom I had read at school. Then he laid himself down on the huge Bridal Chamber bed, and even after I had undressed and blown out the light I could feel him there, powerful and motionless on his back, his eyes open, staring at the ceiling.

But some time during the night I heard him tossing and muttering. And once his voice came out thick and strong, like one of his roundup orders bawled above the din of cattle and men, although what he said tonight was sinister and utterly incomprehensible.

"Drink your saddle galls, nesters!" it sounded like. "You've got to plow deeper than that to find him."

§ 8

The brilliant sunshine lay like a golden shawl over the rich mountain city that morning my train set me down for the first time in my life in young Denver. The names of strange railroads incited me from the sides of locomotives at the depot. As I passed up Seventeenth Street, a babel of voices from the doors of clothing stores, auction houses, and pawnbroker shops coaxed and flattered me with "sir" and "young gentleman." There was something in the streets I walked that morning, in the costly dress of the ladies in passing carriages, in the very air that swept down from the mountains, something lavish, dashing and sparkling like Lutie Brewton herself, and I thought I began to under-stand a little of her fever for this prodigal place that was growing by leaps and bounds.

Even in the business house of my uncle's friend, George Twitchell, the lavish touch was there. I felt I was walking on a silver floor as you did in the Silver Dollar Saloon, although the Twitchell establishment was only a hardware house, the largest west of St. Louis, with men from half a dozen states and territories joking and telling stories as they bought everything from six-shooters to mining machinery. And when George Twitchell took me home to noon-day dinner in a fabulous brick mansion behind a tall ornamental fence where a wild Canada goose with one clipped wing swam endlessly around in a fountain, I knew that my uncle, who had said nothing of Lutie Brewton coming back, was aware that a thousand dollars would not let her stay in Denver forever.

That afternoon with the wallet in my pocket, with my hair freshly cut by a Denver barber, my boots shined, and an impressive card supplied and inscribed: "Mr. Harry Brewton" in George Twitchell's blue Spencerian flourishes, I stiffened my young back and pushed myself toward the new Brown Palace Hotel.

A lively bevy of ladies rustled out as I came in. They were hatted and gloved, in silks and satins, with bows and puffs, and laces and flounces, chatting gayly to each other like a group of brilliantly plumaged birds at one of my uncle's ponds on the Cross B. They left the scent of violets and other flowers floating behind them, and if I had doubted it before, I was sure I should find Lutie Brewton here now.

An elegant clerk with a small, trimmed beard, a long tailed coat and immaculate stand-up collar took my card in his fingers.

"Mrs. Colonel Brewton?" he repeated. "Oh, yes, Mrs. Lutie Cameron Brewton." His face lighted and at once he was treating me with respect. I knew now that he had surely seen her and talked to her, and for the moment it was almost as if she were already there in front of me, stepping lightly down the red-carpeted stairs, a lady no one need be ashamed of here, crying: "Hal!" in her clear, modulated voice and throwing her sensitive arms about me.

Then I became aware that his face had clouded and he was speaking to me with genuine regret.

"We all wished Mrs. Brewton might have stayed with us longer."

I stood there stiffly, aware that something beautiful was slipping out of my grasp. The clerk's hands, white as a lady's, were turning the leaves of a leather-bound ledger.

"Mrs. Brewton was here until day before yesterday," he said. "I think she received a letter or telegram. I remember she was very gay, but I had the distinct impression she had been disturbed. She paid her bill and left the hotel and gave us no address. I am very sorry."

When I stepped out into the street, the sun had vanished behind a

cloud and the golden air of the city had fled. And all week while I called at the other hotels and boarding-houses, and while I watched from the mule cars for a delicate face and slender figure, and hung for whole afternoons along Broadway scanning the smart procession of ladies in carriages and fancy carts and rubber-tired runabouts, I never saw it again, although George Twitchell took me by night to the better restaurants, to the Tabor Grand Theater and to a quiet brick house that upstairs turned into a great room of which I remember Soapy Smith in his black ministerial garb and ladies and gentlemen gambling at a score of tables, scarcely noticing huge paintings on the wall that made me blush to my ears.

And when the week was done, all I had for my pains was an endless picture gallery of faces that kept passing me in my sleep, peering and staring at me, ladies' faces, homely and beautiful, soft and hard, sad and glittering. But none of them had that rare something that was Lutie Brewton.

Monday morning I took my uncle's wallet from one of the tall iron safes in the hardware house.

"She's probably gone home," George Twitchell cheered me. "Where else could she go? You'll find her sitting on the ranch-house porch when you ride up."

He was a hearty man, tall and raw-boned, with an air that begat confidence. But when I reached Salt Fork and saw the old town with its dusty streets and plank sidewalks asleep in the yellow sun, I knew they had not been trod the last few days by the slender, alive foot of Lutie Brewton.

On the sugary counter of his mercantile company John Kingman counted the money, his lips moving through his heavy beard in time with his fingers. Once his eyes strayed to the store porch behind me. And when I had passed through the wide-open front doors of the Dagget livery stable, Frank Dagget's did the same. Then I understood.

"Hullo, Hal," he greeted. "See the elephant and hear the owl hoot up in Denver?" And when I nodded briefly, "Shorty Bowen took your buckboard. He said you could hire a buggy if you needed one."

"I don't need any," I said stiffly, knowing what he meant.

The liveryman looked indefinably disappointed.

"Shorty had to pack a couple cases of cartridges out to the ranch," he mentioned.

I felt my ears sharpen, but Frank Dagget's face held no more expression than one of his buggy curtains, neither then nor when he cinched up a horse for me while I forced open its mouth for the bit, a hard unwilling mouth that still dripped with the yellowish green of livery oats.

As I rode out the straggling street Lutie Brewton had walked with me that day now so long ago, Brice Chamberlain drove by me in a hired buggy and an impressive black frock coat like Judge White used to wear. He had always gone out of his way to cultivate my friendship, but today he greeted me with cool and scant ceremony, while I scowled at him in turn and wondered where he had been out here in a direction that led almost nowhere except to the remote ranches.

Then as my pony reached the top of the sand hills, I saw it, a cloud of emigrant canvas rolling where the escarpment fell away to the river, one united tent and covered-wagon city with horses and mules, oxen and milk cows grazing for miles on the mesa.

As the trail took me gradually closer, I grew aware of the unmistakable activity and excitement in the encampment; the sound of hammers on camp anvils and wagon wheels; the movement of nesters in and out of the canvas like ants; the men and women repacking scores of wagons, and voices calling exultantly to each other, while out on the mesa men and boys on horseback were herding the animals toward camp.

It was clear to me now where Brice Chamberlain had been. And if I hadn't guessed it then, I would have known it when I reached the ranch house that evening and found the bunkhouse almost an arsenal of six-shooters and Winchesters while out on the ground around the supper fire sprawled more Cross B hands than I had ever seen together at one time, tin plates of steak and biscuits in their laps, tin cups of black coffee in their hands, and a look in their eyes I well knew.

§ 9

I was glad for all the dark war clouds as an excuse to put off reporting to my uncle about Lutie. But in the end I knew that all the time he stood there in the dim hall listening to what I had to say about the nesters and questioning me about their camp and numbers, there was only one person who walked in his mind.

"You didn't see her?" he demanded at last.

I stammered what had happened in Denver. He made no comment. But when Black Hetty came in from the children's room to light a lamp, I saw that his great arrogant face was lined and his eyes held orange flames that I know now were hatred for the man who had failed Lutie Brewton. And the following day when one of our riders brought word that the nesters had left their camp near the river and already, as if it were a fiesta, were swarming in wagons and on horseback over the eastern part of our fertile big prairie, the violence poured

into his face like a living flood that would tear out any dam in the country, and from the dark clouds of his eyes I could see that torrents of anger were still falling.

"Is Judge Chamberlain with the nesters?" he growled deep in his throat.

"I think it was him in a livery buggy," the cowhand stammered.

"Go out and tell the boys to saddle up," my uncle ordered.

I knew what that meant. And when the hand had gone, my uncle must have seen it in my face, for he fixed his fearful gaze on me.

"Remember, boy," he said, "there are times in your life you've got to be hard. No man respects you for being soft to him today and letting him ruin you and himself tomorrow. You're going to see things before sundown that aren't nice to look at and you better not come along if a college education's made a woman out of you."

"I can be plenty hard to a nester," I told him.

Adamant in his gray broadcloth coat with its tightly fitting shoulders and tails long spread by the saddle; his long, wrinkled boots, far different from the showy footgear of the modern West and unblacked since Lutie Brewton had gone away, he started for the corrals and the big buckskin I knew he would ride today.

Then we passed through the green wall of cottonwoods and misty spraying tamarisks that Lutie Brewton had had planted, I saw the hands at the corrals and bunkhouse watching three horsemen riding over the rise, the sun sparkling like quicksilver on them and their saddle rigging. And when they rode closer, I could make out blue uniforms and polished saber hilts, slouch hats with gold insignia, and the straight-laced backs of officers from Fort Ewing.

My uncle had thrown up his head with that lordly challenge of a wild stallion, and now he waited there in a kind of rude and insolent magnificence until the rider of the bald-faced horse in the lead turned into Major Wilberforce, a soldier of dignity and fierce red mustaches.

He drew off a gauntlet glove and reached down from the saddle to shake hands.

"We're camping by the spring on your big vega, Colonel," he greeted. "We've got a troop of sixty-five men, and the Captain and I couldn't resist riding over to have dinner with you."

What he said was perfectly smooth and friendly, but I could see that our hands had stiffened and were watching my uncle, who stood there now with utter dignity, although his mustache seemed to bristle and his eyes were pitchforks. After what seemed to me an extremely long time, he inclined his head.

"Won't you gentlemen come in? Have your orderly feed your

horses." With powerfully controlled steps and speech, he led the way back to the gallery of the ranch house.

All afternoon I watched the Major and the Captain perspire in their efforts to bring back the friendship of old times as they sat there facing their waiting host, drinking whisky on the tufted horsehair parlor chairs, telling stories of the service, with the children thumping and shouting at play somewhere in the big house, and dinner and supper in the familiar dining-room. No one mentioned Lutie Brewton's name, and yet it was plainly a mockery with her away and the nesters swarming like sheep over our big vega.

At the sound of their horses led to the gallery that evening, the officers rose with relief to ride back to camp. My uncle stood up.

"May I inquire, Major, who ordered the troops to my big prairie?" The officer looked grave under his red mustaches.

"By order of the President, Colonel," he said in a low voice.

"The President," my uncle went on with pitiless irony, "wants you and your troops to stay for some time?"

"Until further orders, Colonel." The Major cleared his throat and looked up. "I hope we shall still be friends."

My uncle did not reply. He stood there with lips tight and eyes pitch-black with contempt for the man who had pulled strings for others to fight his battles for him. I could feel the bitterness working in him like the hot desert winds sweeping the cedars of the rocky canyons of Ladron. In the end the blue veins in his neck and hands gradually relaxed, and I knew the fury of the storm had for the time abated, that he would never send his men to fight against his country's troops, but would relentlessly put himself through the humiliation of sending them back to their respective camps in the morning.

"Good night, gentlemen," he said harshly when they left. "You can keep the nesters from being blown away, but God Himself can't the prairie!"

Long after they had gone, I watched him in the bright June moonlight that was almost like day, standing motionless on the gallery facing the big vega. And that night as I lay in my sleepless bunk staring into the white haze that entered my deep window, I fancied that in the milky mist I could see the prairie as I had seen it all my life and would never see it again, with the grass in summer sweeping my stirruped thighs and prairie chicken scuttling ahead of my pony; with the ponds in fall black and noisy with waterfowl, and my uncle's seventy thousand head of cattle rolling in fat; with the tracks of endless game in the winter snow and thousands of tons of wild hay cured and stored on the stem; and when the sloughs of the home range greened

up in the spring, with the scent of warming wet earth and swag after swag catching the emerald fire, with horses shedding and snorting and grunting as they rolled, and everywhere the friendly indescribable solitude of that lost sea of grass.

§ 10

It struck me as strange to see the sun come up as usual over the eastern plain next morning. And at breakfast I asked my uncle if I could ride west with the Red Lake hands to look for my missing B B mare. He raked me with his coal-black eyes, and I think he knew why I didn't want to stay, but he said nothing, and by the time we reached our Red Lake camp the summer rains were sweeping down from La Ceja.

All night the water dripped from the camp-house roof with a steady clop until my ears seemed to fill with the sound, and suddenly I knew that I hadn't got away from it at all, and what I heard in my brain was the clop, clop, clop of the cloven hoofs of oxen, of wheels slopping in the sloughs, of the gutturals of men and shrill voices of women, of crying babies and crates of cackling barnyard fowl, of the baas of sheep and goats and all the rest of the despised chattels of nesters scattering like a victorious army over our range.

When at last I rode reluctantly back to headquarters, I could see them squatting in likely places on our big vega, digging holes for their dugouts like prairie dogs in the ground, or plastering with mud a frame of cedar poles from Ladron, stringing barbed wire where our cattle and horses and the antelope had always grazed free, or yelling at their teams of mules and steers as they tore up the virgin sod with a breaking plow.

Hot and almost trembling with anger, I came through the wide hall of the ranch house at late dusk and halted, a little ashamed of myself in the sitting-room doorway. Still the same rude, unconquerable figure, my uncle sat with his great proud face over his tan leather account books as if there wasn't a nester within fifty miles, although I knew that from the near-by window he could have seen through the cotton-woods a half-dozen lights beginning to quiver across the dark prairie.

Sitting there that evening and other evenings between the heavy walls of the old ranch house, with my uncle's steel pen scratching arrogantly or his two-weeks-old Kansas paper rattling in lusty gusts in his hands, with my young cousins stretched on the floor cutting out paper horses and cattle from old magazines, and all around us the familiar curtains, furniture, and carpet by lamplight, the feeling kept creeping

over me that Lutie Brewton was somehow still here. And once when a
faint scent of violets seemed to rise in the room from one of her de-
spoiled magazines, I could almost swear that her slender figure was
there in the shadows behind me, alive, delicate, and sparkling, waiting
before calling out in that high clear fun-loving voice she always used
to children.

A few days later Black Hetty whispered to me portentously:

"Heah dem wagons a-rollin' by, Mistah Hal? Miz Brewton come
back mighty soon now. It ain't lonesome round heah no mo'. No, sah.
You wait and see if Hetty doan know."

It was true, I told myself half bitterly, that we weren't a peacefully
remote ranch house any more, forty or fifty miles from the nearest
neighbor. From the bunkhouse doorway you could see fences and
plowed furrows, and smoke rising from mud chimneys. Nearly every
day nesters in spring wagons or road wagons rattled by to town or to
visit other nesters. And nester children began to ride up on the backs
of old horses to borrow matches or sour-dough leaven for biscuits or
baking soda for a cow with the colic.

They avoided the ranch house as they would a pestilence, going
straight to the bunkhouse. I saw little Jimmy and Sarah Beth stand
stiffly under the cottonwoods watching them, but the tow-haired Brock
ran right up and tried to get them to stay and play. It made me think
of the time Lutie Brewton had run and shouted with the emigrant
children, although these nester youngsters today were like another race,
mute, staring, defiant, and yet scared. As soon as they climbed back
on their horse from a wagon wheel, they rode hurriedly away. But I
knew that Lutie Brewton would have coaxed them to stay and talk and
smile with a glass of lemonade and a piece of democrat cake.

Once they were there as my uncle happened to come riding in, and
they huddled together as if they had seen an ogre who would forbid
what Will Lubbock, the bunkhouse cook, had just given them. But if
my uncle saw them, there was no sign of it. In his eyes lately when he
came riding up to the ranch house was a look as if he faintly expected
someone. Tomorrow, always tomorrow, I told myself, we would glance
up and there she would be in one of Frank Dagget's livery buggies as
if she had just been to town. Dagget himself would be looking pleased
and proud for the Colonel. My uncle's face would be grave, and he
would inquire with unfailing courtesy of her health and not a word
about where she had been or the skunk who had failed her. And every
day the headquarters hands would listen to her high clear voice when
she called the children.

But July passed and August passed, and the night before I went back
east to college, my uncle called me into the big front bedroom. I hoped

that he would order me to see the nun, Mercedes, at the convent in St. Louis to ask if she knew where Lutie Brewton was. But he did not mention Lutie's name. Once he glanced at her glove still lying untouched like a delicate part of her, feminine, sensitive, and crushed, on a shelf. And deep in his eyes I saw red coals like the implacable Indian pueblo fires that are never allowed to go out. And the rest of the evening I could feel him far back in his mind stirring the charred embers and laying fresh logs on the blaze.

And when I lay down that night in my bunk I knew my uncle's inner convictions that wherever she was, the sensitive white hand of Lutie Brewton felt humiliated, dishonored, and crushed like its glove on the shelf, and that she would never come back and show herself to the ranch house and town that had idolized her—not even for her children.

§ 11

For three long years, part of them in medical school, I didn't see the massive ranch house, not a grain of sand or blade of grass from the Cross B. I remember the weather as unseasonably dry those years at St. Louis, with the Mississippi gaunt as a trail-driven steer. But the Salt Fork weekly told in glowing italics of the heavy snows that fell west of Kansas and the unusual spring rains that soaked the ranges of the territory until they spouted like the rock of Moses with springs. And every issue there began to be more news of the nesters—emigrants, settlers, homesteaders, and agriculturists, it called them—and less of the cattlemen, until a thousand miles away my thumbs would bite through the paper in anger.

More settlers were landing in Salt Fork by steam and wagon train. The settlers were crowding the Las Cruces land office. The settlers were plowing up the rich brown prairie loam. The settlers were harrowing and planting corn. From the sand hills above Salt Fork the townspeople could see the velvety green patches of the settlers' winter wheat and rye. Judge Chamberlain said as the rains continued that God was clearly on the side of the settlers. The settlers' wheat stood golden in the sun. The heavy heads of the settlers' rye knocked off men's hats. And the settlers' corn could swallow up a horse and rider.

Not that anyone would have known the existence of a settler on the Cross B range from my uncle's letters. Brief as always, the handwriting was still spirited, erect and unquenchable as I had ever seen it, with the final letter of every word sweeping up like a lusty whiplash, and every proper name underlined, not for emphasis, but from an overflow of will and power.

But all those months he wrote me firmly that grass was good and beef high, that my B B mare had a pinto colt, that the hands and children sent me their best and he remained my uncle, Jas. B., I knew from other sources that his favorite saddle horse, Pompey, had thrown and tangled himself in nester barbed wire until he had to be shot; that in sheltered cañadas his cowhands were digging up the telltale buried horns and Cross B hides of butchered beeves; and that a score of nesters were suing him in Judge Chamberlain's court for the destruction by his cattle of their crops and gardens.

I expected the trial to be over before I came home. But in July when I stepped from the train, Salt Fork was like a nesters' holiday with grain wagons choking the square, and the sidewalks crowded with men often thick through the body as their gunnysacks of freshly thrashed wheat and rye, and most of them distinct from cowmen as a draft horse from a saddle pony. And everywhere in the stores the merchants were truckling to the nester women with the smiles and jokes I had thought they reserved for their cattleman friends.

Standing on the steps of the old Exchange House, I could scarcely believe that this was the square for which only a few years ago I would grow desperately homesick. And when I looked for my uncle in Judge Chamberlain's new brick courthouse where Clancy's dance hall used to stand, it did not seem like the Salt Fork county court at all, with no buckled spurs swinging on the railing, with a floor of sawed pine, with pews for seats and all these stolid spectators standing up as in church while the tall figure of Brice Chamberlain swept up to the bar with his bright blond hair waving against the impressive black of his gown. Even the Henry McCurtin I knew had vanished. With sagging cheeks and sunken eyes, he defended my uncle's case like a man who had had his first stroke of paralysis and was calmly resigned to the second.

But it was when my uncle came in and the only notice these sluggish-faced men showed for that proud figure as he towered down the aisle were a few sullen looks and a derisive muttering among themselves that I felt the end had nearly come.

I tried not to listen to the court routine that followed, except when Judge Chamberlain, as if he were rebuking a Mexican cow-thief, reviewed the nester evidence against my uncle to the nester jurors and charged them, as it sounded to me, that they must find my uncle liable and fix the damages. I was remembering a day twelve or fourteen years before when only the whisper that the owner of the Cross B was at the courthouse door had been enough to stir the crowd's emotion. And when he had moved majestically down the aisle and through the railing with as much right as Judge White himself, the whole courtroom had been charged with his presence. And I realized that those

golden wild horses of other days had slipped more deftly out of my
uncle's rope than he knew, and would never be caught again.

First to go had been Lutie Brewton, then the sea of grass. And now
these people who had waited till the West was safe and the pioneering
done, were barking and snapping around my uncle's legs like a pack of
dogs. They had him fairly surrounded, were raising their paws on him
here and tearing out a piece of him there. But after I had watched
him seat himself again in the old, fearless, unconquerable way, with-
out so much as a glance at the nesters beside him, I knew that although
he had lost his case they didn't have him down.

From where I sat I could see only the back of his head like some
dark, shaggy Jove. And yet I was sure that the red coals of his eyes
had fastened themselves on Brice Chamberlain, who might not realize
it, but still had a debt to pay. Times might have changed, but my
uncle never would change, never would forget till he died.

I remember that when I stepped out on the street I found that the
two boys had come along to town with their father. When Brock saw
me, he pulled off Jimmy's hat, waved it, ran up the plank sidewalk
until he was about to be caught, and sailed the hat toward a nester
wagon loaded with towsacks of wheat. For a moment the hat hung
against the sky. Then it missed the wagon and fell into the deep mud.

Little did I think this night that the placid blue sky I saw was
already returning to its old mysterious cycle, that this was the last deep
mud and one of the last wagonloads of wheat that would be seen in
Salt Fork for what the Navajos north of Red Lake called a land of
snows.

§ 12

At the time I thought it only the way the cards happened to fall.
But when I look back on it now, it seems immutable and fixed as a
chapter out of Genesis or Exodus, with the nesters safe on their
Promised Land; with my uncle pushed back with his cattle on a thou-
sand hills; with Brice Chamberlain in the seats of the mighty; and all
the time the red eye of God watching from the burning bush, not to
see that what was to come would be humane and sweet and according
to progress, but that it should be cruel and just and true according to
the book of destiny which blinds a man from properly reading it until
those who would dictate it are dead and fifty or a thousand years have
passed.

When the news reached me that the weather west of Kansas and
Indian Territory had changed, it was as if the God few of us medical
students believed in was in His heaven after all, and my eyes must

have burned with a deep exultation in the dark halls of my school and hospital. The nester women were praying for rain. The nester men were hauling water from my uncle's ponds and windmills. The more responsible nesters were packing up to journey farther west and north, some to join the Mormons. And Judge Chamberlain had made a Fourth of July oration that it was the greatest drouth in the history of the territory. But a letter signed "Cattleman" to the paper said it was no drouth at all, just normal old-fashioned New Mexican weather, and pointed to the native wild grasses that had not been plowed under. With a desperate skill born of long experience in this dry land, they had caught the diminished rains and rushed into growth and seed while the nesters' corn and wheat scarcely sprouted in the ground.

On my way home through Missouri and eastern Kansas the following spring, a veil of gray mist hugged the car windows. But once the train had climbed the high plateaus, the windows were clear, the skies a dull blue, and the plains toasted brown with sod. And when we came close to Salt Fork I had a glimpse from the train of puffs of dust moving over the prairie that were nesters plowing and harrowing a dry land.

I hadn't seen my uncle since I left, and I felt he would be almost insolent with triumph to be vindicated at last. Then I stepped off the train at the familiar red depot and he was there with his buggy to meet me himself, and I wasn't sure of his feelings at all. With his great face plowed and harrowed, his mustache turning gray, but his eyes still pitch-black as I had ever seen them, he drove me home over what had once been his fertile range and was now a waste of barbed wire and bare ground and squalid gates to open and close, with a few of the dugouts empty and already falling in, and the song of an occasional mocking bird or meadow lark a mockery in the dead and dying young fruit trees. And I can still see him sitting in his buggy, silent and deaf, while a nester in an unwashed undershirt tried to sell him his barren, proven-up fields.

It was long after dark when we reached home. The earthen ranch house stood deep in the shadows of its cottonwoods and tamarisks like a forgotten fortress decaying in its ancient bosque. Sarah Beth was east at convent school, the boys asleep in bed, and I saw where, during my uncle's absence in town, the spring winds had deposited miniature dunes of sand and nester field dust along the wall boards as if no walls were there.

And that evening as we sat at the great hulking supper-table, bare of cloth and candles, with only the smoky light from a brass lamp trickling over us; and afterwards as I wandered through the rude hall and silent parlor with boys' quirts and ropes, spurs, bridles, and saddles

scattered over the floor, and boys' rough fingerprints and boot-marks on the dusty lid of the piano; and again next morning when I heard the two boys fighting and tumbling like young savages over the parlor floor and then riding off hard on their ponies, it seemed strange to think that there had ever been a gentle lady in the house.

"She's gone and nobody but my uncle remembers her any more," I told myself, getting up from the bunk where she had once nursed me with the whitest and lightest of hands.

But when I rode out to the remote Cross B camps in the cedar-dotted hills where the nesters had not yet penetrated, and when I talked to some of her old friends in town, I found that they were still talking of the beautiful wife of Colonel Brewton.

Several thought they knew where she was. Young Mrs. Bob Kingman said she had seen Lutie Brewton's face, as young and beautiful as ever, in a nun's wimple on the streets of New Orleans. The gentlemanly wagon boss of the Bar 44, who had won a prize with her as his partner at whist, had seen someone he believed was Mrs. Brewton in a stunning black lace gown and diamonds gambling for high stakes in Tombstone. She was painted and powdered like a dance-hall woman, but he had absolutely remembered the feverish gestures with which she played. And John McCandless, agent for the Mescalero Apaches, had gone to Washington on Indian bureau business and seen a lady he knew but couldn't place, in an open carriage on Pennsylvania Avenue, by the side of a foreign ambassador or someone with ribbons on his coat. She had flushed when stared at and turned her head, and not until they were by did he realize it had been Mrs. Brewton.

Myra Netherwood thought Lutie must be dead. But the story I clung to was told by Superintendent Bedford of the railroad, who had been at the famous Silver Ball given with full orchestra and waxed floor under a waterproof canopy at the bottom of a Colorado silver mine. During the evening a fall of rock in a near-by stope had frightened the dancers off the floor, all but a guest with another name, who was the image of Mrs. Brewton. For several minutes while the rocks continued to fall, she had kept on gayly dancing with her partner, encouraging the orchestra and laughing to her partner as if nothing had happened, until most of the guests were over their scare and back on the floor. Somehow I felt that had been the real Lutie Brewton, and the peculiar emotion I had always felt at the sight of her had welled up in me indescribably at the story.

But later I found that there was something else they were saying about her, although they did not say it to me. And I was to learn that nothing was too romantic and fantastic to speculate about Lutie Brewton.

All I noticed at first was that they took a great interest in young Brock when he came with me to town, laughing at his quick replies and provoking him to others. And all the while the ladies admired his feathery blond hair and treated him to slices of layer cake, and while the men bribed him to strut up and down the Kingman store porch like certain well-known characters of town, I could see them exchange veiled glances and knowing nods. And yet for a medical student I was thick in the skull as a nester and thought nothing of it until in August when we had all driven to town to meet Sarah Beth, who was coming home alone by train from convent school in the morning.

The square swarmed as usual with nester wagons and all their nondescript conveyances, as if having a poor crop year meant nothing to them. My uncle's old friend Dr. Reid, as one professional man to another, invited me into the White Elephant Saloon, and I found several nesters drinking next year's wheat, appropriating the front of the long walnut bar. A little group of cattlemen and cowhands kept themselves distinct at the other end, and while I shook hands with several of them, the doctor gravely waited for me. His face and manner were courteous and serene, but I knew his hand was twitching to wrap itself around a dark bottle, a long white hand marked with veins that as a small boy I was sure must flow with purple wine.

The screen had been moved back from the open door, and across the street I could see young Brock and Jimmy facing each other on the Holderness porch steps as if they had had one of their usual differences and the men around them were tactfully stirring them up to fight. The two boys made a picture I can see now against the rough splintery background of the store, with colored tin signs tacked on the step rises and against the red wall—Jimmy, slim and dark, like a small, stiff image of his father, fists tightly clenched—and Brock leaning forward recklessly to hit him on the nose, his hat pushed back where it hung by its throat latch, his hair a kind of white gold in the afternoon sun.

Then it happened. A bushy, round-headed nubbin of a nester in a hickory shirt ridged like corduroy moved to the doorway.

"I'm a-bettin' on the Chamberlain young 'un," he called.

For a split fraction of a second as his meaning broke over me, I saw Lutie Brewton clear and beautiful as I had ever seen her in the life. And when the nester turned and grinned toward a sand-box, it was almost as if he had spat in her face. I was aware of the grave silence of the cowmen and of a curious wild hate sweeping over me like prairie fire. I had thought myself a medical student soon to go out in the world and save human lives. Now I found that the thin veneer of Eastern schools had cracked and I was only a savage young Brewton from an untamed sea of grass, moving through the little gate where

customers' rifles and pistols stood or lay in their accustomed places on the back bar. I was aware of the cowmen backing out of range and of the bar-keeper ducking. And then I almost wanted to kill Dr. Reid, too, one of whose white hands had with surprising force suddenly thrown up my barrel so that oil from a brass hanging lamp started to pour on the walnut bar.

At the sound of the shot, men from the square began to wedge their heads into the saloon doorway until they were brushed aside like flies and my uncle stood there, sniffing the smell of black powder like an old war-horse, his black eyes sweeping the room until they halted on me standing at the end of the bar with my unsuccessful six-shooter in my hand.

"What's going on, Hal?" he demanded.

I did not dare look at him now, only stood there rigid with my lips closed tight. He waited what seemed a half-hour.

"What was said in here, Walt?" he asked a huge uncomfortable cattleman with open vest and silver watch-chain tangled across it.

The sweat poured from the cattleman's forehead, but he only shook his head. Something came into my uncle's great face. For some little time more he stood there unruly and aroused, dominating the long dim room like old times. Then, following the direction of a half-dozen glances, he turned his head and I saw that Jimmy and Brock had squirmed through the jammed doorway and were now standing there in the barroom with their black and white contrasting heads.

Just whom my uncle looked at the long minute he kept his head turned, I do not know, but I found it was Brock's eager young face and bright blue eyes I was staring at. In that short time I think there passed through my mind everything I had ever seen him do and heard him say, one minute mean and irrepressible, and the next charming and winning as Lutie Brewton herself so that you forgave everything. I remembered his taking to the nesters like his mother and how painstakingly impartial my uncle treated both boys, one like the other, always buying two when he bought one, and dividing equally the lash of his quirt although I felt that Brock usually deserved the most of it. And I wondered of this unnamable thing could have been the source of the deep-seated enmity between the two brothers ever since they had been old enough to walk, or what in God's name it was.

When my uncle finally turned, I saw that something unutterable and terrible had come into his face.

"If any dog has something more to say, now is the time to say it!" he challenged them all, a wild violence fairly leaping from his dark eyes.

There was no sound in the long saloon but a chip someone dropped at a poker-table, the jingle of a horse shaking his harness at a hitching-

rack, and the slow drip of oil on the bar like a clock ticking off the last minutes of the one who would speak. Then with almost a grimace of pain, my uncle nodded at me, and with the boys ahead of me, and my uncle to the rear, we pushed out into the square.

PART III

Brock

§ 13

It was the boy Brock I couldn't get off my mind the next few winters as a student assistant of a high-tempered French surgeon who operated at St. Mary's and the Alexian Brothers' hospitals. And I can't smell chloroform today without some of those old doubts and questionings rising up in front of me like ghosts. All the baffling memories I had of the boy kept turning over in my mind. Young Brock playing he was a priest and singing mass in his high soprano to a herd of grazing longhorns. And young Brock playing posse with the nester children and hanging the outlaw, which was a stray dog, to a nester gate-post. Young Brock leading the half-starved nester youngsters over to the ranch house for sour-dough biscuits and vinegar pies. And young Brock sharpening the rowels of his spur with a blacksmith's file. Young Brock's white hands galloping gracefully through *Black Jack Davey* and *The Gypsy Maid* on the keys of Lutie Brewton's square piano. And the same white hands keeping a tomato-can rolling at fifty feet with the thirty-caliber, rim-fire five-shooter my uncle let him carry because it was hard to get the odd-sized cartridges.

It was Brock loving to talk. And Brock loving to ride. And Brock trading forty-five cartridges from his father's stores two to one for thirty rim-fire. It was Brock shrewd as a judge and reckless as a Brewton and charming and magnificent as his vanished mother as he swindled his and Jimmy's tutor out of their lessons for the afternoon. And all the time his feathery blond hair kept blowing this way and that in my mind.

Peaceably as if he had been a bishop going to his reward, old Dr. Reid back in Salt Fork made ready to depart his life and his well-thumbed books of Robert Ingersoll in his room at the Exchange House, where the older guests would no longer hear his bedside glass and whisky bottle striking the hours of the night. And my uncle telegraphed for me to come home and take the practice.

When I walked up the sandy boardwalk from the train to the hotel, I found the old doctor in a coma. I tried to make him as comfortable as I could, but there was little I could do for him. Even the bottle had been drained of its comfort, and he knew neither me nor my uncle, who, when I came in, had been sitting there for several hours quietly smoking, as the two old friends had often sat in health with only an occasional word between them.

"The thoughts of the señor doctor viejo are not any more on this world," the Mexican woman who had been taking care of him told me.

Once Brock burst eagerly into the room, startling me as some blond Lutie Brewton in boots and spurs, shaking my hand now like a grown man, showing the gold piece he had won at monte, and paying no attention to the bed and its burned-out ember of a man who had brought him into the world. But while the boy stood there laughing and talking, fetching into the sick-room an air like a fresh wind blowing from out of the past, I saw a vestige of life and consciousness struggle into one of the old physician's eyes as if deep down in a well a man with a candle was trying to see and recognize the man at the windlass.

And after Brock had gone whistling down the hall, his boot-heels softened by the red carpet, his spurs jingling a purposefully manipulated tune, the old doctor tried slowly to sit up in bed.

"When did Mrs. Brewton come back?" he asked, staring at me, and I did not dare to look at my uncle, whose puffs on his cigar, I was aware, had suddenly ceased.

"I haven't seen her, doctor," I said in a low voice.

The light went out of his eye like the flame of a candle blown upon and he sank back, his long white hand with its veins of purple wine relaxing on the coverlet. But long after he was silent, the emotion I had always felt at a meeting with Lutie Brewton kept flooding and stirring me at the unexpected sound of her name.

We buried him a week or two later in one of those inexpressibly lonely and barren Southwestern graveyards, so different from the green graves he had known as a boy in his native Virginia. But the mourners, standing there with their hats off as men did forty years ago, did not see that. They were covertly watching the picture of Brock, taller than I, his blond feathery hair faintly yellow, standing only a few feet away from Judge Chamberlain, now a bit portly and distinguished-looking in a long black coat, a shiny high hat in his hand, his yellow hair faintly touched at the temples with silver, but still sweeping back over his head in a kind of masterful distinction.

And from then on, everything I remember of my uncle and Brock is tinctured with iodoform and carbolic acid of the old doctor's office

that became my own, with its green student lamp shining on the white shelves of drug jars and bottles, on the old leather operating-couch strewn with surgical instruments, and on the skeleton that ever since I could remember had stood in a corner.

Before I was back in Salt Fork a year, I found that Brock was already becoming almost as well known a figure in Salt Fork as Ingram Carter, the gambler, whose full-length portrait in oil hung in the White Elephant Saloon. It was blond, gentlemanly Brock Brewton, a favorite with all the dark-haired dance-hall women in Madame Nana's Sala de Baile, and the same Brock Brewton never losing caste but sedately dealing whist and euchre from the best horsehair furniture in town. It was Brock Brewton playing the *Blue Danube* waltz on Myra Netherwood's grand piano, and Brock Brewton driving up and down the town streets with his Choctaw-blooded nester girl beside him on the seat of his red-wheeled open buggy.

And it was Brock Brewton buying out a showcase of candy for the nester children standing around like orphans in the Kingman Mercantile Company store, and the same Brock Brewton shooting Mrs. Olson's three white ducks almost out of her hand while she fed them as he galloped by.

I can still see him in a long-legged brown suit that reminded me of the one Brice Chamberlain had once worn, taking his mother's friend Myra Netherwood devoutly to mass. And I can see him in the same suit, his hat pushed back recklessly and his yellow hair curling, calling for a hundred or two hundred dollars' worth of chips at the White Elephant or Dutch Charley's.

He didn't pay for his chips like ordinary people. He was a Brewton, and if he called for a thousand dollars in gold, they would have tried to give it to him, the bartender marking it down as usual in his jawbone book. And when the Colonel came to town, he would have asked for his bill and there on the wet bar written out a check drawn on the Kingman Mercantile Company.

Brock and all his conflicting ways, together with my uncle's affection for and indulgence toward him, were one of the most puzzling things I had ever tried to solve. Perhaps it was that I refused to see Lutie Brewton as the others did, that to me she was still a young boy's beautiful lady. And it was summer with the bee balm in blossom again along the trail in the cañadas when fate tried to make me see it their way.

I had been called to a prairie dugout where a nester woman had tried to kill herself. She was very low and I couldn't leave her with her small baby fifty miles from a doctor. And several afternoons later when it was all over, I felt that I was no physician at all, only a tired

and defeated ranch boy, and that I wanted nothing so much as to spend a night again among the old familiar things under my uncle's roof.

I was glad I had come. It was dusk when I approached the old ranch house and found light gleaming from a dozen windows, as I had often seen it in the past. And when I stepped into the bare old hall, I had the strange feeling that a lady was there. For a moment the incredible notion came to me that Lutie Brewton had returned. Then Sarah Beth in a girlish white dress with red sash and cuffs sprang out of the massive dining-room doorway and cried a welcome to me and said that she had finished school forever and come through Salt Fork the very morning I left.

They laid a place for me at the table. The white dinner candles and their shades which I had not seen since Lutie Brewton left, the great mass of pink bee balm in the center of the huge old table, and all around me the familiar heavy silver on snowy damask affected me strongly. And all through the meal I observed that my uncle sat very quietly on his chair, the faint desert glow warming his weather-beaten face as I had not seen it for many a year, his pitch-black eyes softening a little as they rested on Sarah Beth. But far back in his eyes I had the impression that it was someone else with dark hair and slender bare arms he saw sitting here with other guests around a gayer and younger table.

We were in the parlor, Sarah Beth had opened the old piano and played some of her convent pieces, and my uncle said he wished Brock were home from town to hear them, when Jimmy was called outside. With the room very still, Sarah Beth's hands strayed into a waltz the name of which I do not know but which her mother's white hands had often played on the same black and yellow keyboard when the room was filled with guests from Fort Ewing to Santa Fe. I saw my uncle hold his cigar motionless in his hand, and for a minute or two with that old melody in the room it was almost as if the plague of nesters had never swarmed and that any minute Black Hetty might appear at the doorway with the three small children to give their mother good-night.

The feeling was so strong that I glanced up at the doorway, and found Jimmy standing there. I thought for the moment he was listening, then I was conscious of the tautening tendons in his tanned young face. And before Sarah Beth had finished, he moved rigidly to where his father sat quiet and proud on the big horsehair armchair.

"I just heard," he said in a low voice, "that Brock shot Dutch Charley in town."

Sarah Beth went on playing without hearing and my uncle, who

still seemed to be in Lutie Brewton's waltz, sat staring at the boy as if the latter had told him that several Cross B cows were bogged down in Red Lake and his loose and bitter lower lip was considering whether or not to send hands at this hour to pull them out.

"Brock shot who?" he repeated, lowering his great head like a powerful bull trying to protect himself from a deep wound already administered.

Guessing that something was wrong, Sarah Beth stopped playing. Somewhere on the trail we could hear a galloping horse. Then Jimmy's low answer came clear enough in the huge room.

"Dutch Charley. He claimed that black-haired woman that deals monte for him was in with Brock and favoring him. He said every time Brock came to the table, the house lost money. They had an argument. Charley went for his gun, but Brock got him before he could shoot."

Sarah Beth gave a little cry, but my uncle had hold of nimself now and was sitting up slowly with his old iron will and power. Only the faint gray showed through his deeply lined face.

"Is Charley dead?" he asked after a little.

"I don't know," Jimmy said. "They locked Brock up."

I knew that must have hit my uncle, but he was sitting there like some rude czar in gray broadcloth and linen, his great unruly face written with the ruthless, almost dissolute pride I remembered, and there was no change in it as Jimmy gave him, bit after bit, what the hands had told him. Only when the boy mentioned the name of Judge Chamberlain did my uncle show emotion, throwing up his head with the old untamed lustiness while his shaggy gray hair bristled.

"What did Chamberlain have to do with it?" he demanded.

By the whiteness of the boy's knuckles I knew that he guessed more than I had supposed. He tried to evade it, but his father's violent eyes were pinning him to the floor and he struggled against them uselessly.

"Judge Chamberlain is the one who got Brock out," he said in a barely audible tone. "He said it was because Brock was so young and he wanted to make a private investigation in the circumstances. If Brock behaves himself, he said the case might not come up at the next term of court. But Brock's got to report to Judge Chamberlain as often as he says."

For a headlong, incredible moment it was as if I had seen the long arm and white hand of Brice Chamberlain, like that of a groomed and masterful colossus, reaching across all Salt Fork county in front of the nesters and the livery-stable loafers, in front of the town ladies, the ranchers' wives and the dance-hall women, to pin a final ugly red brand on the gay, slender figure of Lutie Brewton.

I had seen my uncle angry many times, but never when his blood ran black in his veins as it did now. His face was like a dark storm from which the lightning was constantly hurling. Even across the room I could feel, as physically as I can waves of heat, the rising torrent of flame that, once aroused in him, burned like a prairie conflagration that no man could put out or stand up in front of, but must be let to run its own wild and volcanic course.

Then I saw that he had risen to his feet and was moving toward the door, and I don't think he knew any longer that we were in the room, but all of us knew where he was going. We watched him stop and pick up his old sweated gun belt where it hung from the post of a pine settee in the hall. And at the sight of it, Sarah Beth rose quickly from her stool and moved as far across the room as the painted china parlor lamp on its tall ornamental brass and marble stand.

"Don't go tonight, papa!" she begged him. "Let Hal and Jimmy go in tomorrow."

He stood there bleak and unhearing, strapping the double buckles of the belt before he turned and swept the three of us with his violently smoldering eyes that told us how far we could go and no farther, and that he was still lord of his family, including Brock.

But he did not go. He stood there for a little in the wide hall as if listening. Presently we heard a familiar footstep on the gallery and Brock, his yellow hair curling like a child's, came swinging past him and into the room as fresh and gallant and unscathed as I had ever seen him.

He must have guessed from all our faces that we knew, and it only made him more charming and desperately gayer, throwing himself into lively banter at Sarah Beth as if she wasn't standing there with white cheeks in front of him, ready to burst into tears on his shoulder; chiding her for not waking him up where he slept in the hotel most of the day when she passed through town; laughing and chattering and grimacing; teasing her about Tom Milledeaux's love letters which the nuns rigorously read; and penitently coaxing her to play a duet with him at the piano, where he pulled up a horsehair chair and sat with one arm around her waist while the other ran a brilliant accompaniment on the lower part of the keyboard.

And I thought that no one in the territory, and perhaps no one anywhere but Lutie Brewton herself, could have come in at a moment like this and so disarmed us and held off my uncle until I saw him take again his horsehair armchair, where he sat waiting for the festivities to be over, the eyes in his great intractable face watching Brock with painful and unutterable affection.

At last Sarah Beth went to bed, and my uncle sat looking at the boy.

"I was just starting to town to talk to you, Brock," he began. "Is it true you shot Dutch Charley?"

The boy's face intangibly changed, and he stood there watching my uncle through narrowed eyes.

"I had to shoot him or he'd have shot me."

"Is it true," the older man went on with dogged patience, "that the woman who deals monte for Dutch Charley was favoring you and you knew it?"

"All women like me," Brock said. "Like everybody liked—" His lips closed, but he kept his cool, veiled, almost derisive eyes on my uncle.

The slow color rose in the latter's rude leathery cheeks.

"I don't mind the shooting so much," he said with difficulty. "Boys will fight, and I wouldn't think much of you if you couldn't defend yourself. I told you I'd pay your gambling debts so long as you played fair and square. But I've always told you that cheating was the lowest form of animal life. Now you've cheated, and no matter what anybody else says, I want you to go through trial on your own feet until you clear yourself or take your punishment."

The boy was staring at him with a sudden curious, impersonal hatred.

"No father," he said defiantly, "would send his boy to prison when the judge got him out of it. Besides, I have a job. That's why I'm out here tonight. I'm going to be a counter jumper for George Holderness and Company."

At the sound of the name of Brice Chamberlain's uncle and all it implied, my uncle sat up and the veins swelled in his throat and hands until even the boy was afraid of him and backed across the room. But his eyes were burning in his white face with a restless and brilliant fever, and when he saw he wasn't going to be touched, he began to pace up and down the room.

"You can't keep me out on a ranch!" he was crying. "I'm eighteen. I wasn't cut out for ranching. I've got to be where there's excitement and people. I've got to be where there's stores and lights and music and things going on. Sooner than stay out here in this God-forsaken place, I'd rather be stuffed in a coffin—"

I did not hear any more. There was something fatalistic in the scene and words, as if I had been here before. My uncle and Jimmy seemed to be gone and I was on the same horsehair sofa seeing Lutie Brewton pacing up and down this very Brussels carpet, her eyes burning with a brilliant fever, her lips speaking almost the identical words.

When I looked at my uncle, his face was white and he was breathing heavily as if he had seen a ghost.

"All right, Brock," he brought out thickly. How much it cost him, I could only guess. "I stood in the way of somebody else years ago and I've always been sorry. I won't stand in yours."

Flashing a look of triumph at the dark silent face of his brother standing there, Brock went quickly out of the room. Long after he had gone my uncle sat in his chair staring out of the window. The window was dark and he could see nothing outside, I knew, but I could see him in the pane and I never realized before how utterly furrowed his face was, like a worn-out field, the face of an old man at last. And the rest of him there on the tufted horsehair chair was the once powerful frame of a man in whom some inward drouth had dried up the last few water-holes of life and power.

Only his eyes were the same, burning black and unspeakably bitter in their charred sockets. After a while he rose unsteadily, paying no attention to Jimmy and me standing helplessly by. Then brushing aside Jimmy's proffered help and planting his boots slowly but relentlessly in front of him, he went on without speaking to his lonely and barren bedroom.

§ 14

There was a huge cottonwood that used to stand off the plaza in one of Salt Fork's crooked Mexican streets. Its bark was rougher than any tree I knew and its branches gnarled. It had seen Navajo and Apache raids and the long ox trains crawling on the Chihuahua trail. But it still stood there green and cool, sheltering a lowly adobe house beneath it and all who passed under its branches or pulled chairs into its broad shade.

Of late the nesters had been tying their bony horses to it, and the horses had chewed off half its bark. The lightning had struck it, and the woman of the house and her young son had tried to cut it down. And when of a morning I crossed the plaza to my office, I found myself glancing to see if the old tree had weathered last night's storm.

Back in my mind, I think, it was really not the tree I looked to see if it were still standing there with its roots in the territory and its head in the sky, but an old man who wasn't there at all, who had also known the Navajo and Apache raids and the long ox trains crawling on the Chihuahua trail and now knew the winds that in my profession usually blow in the night.

One evening just before the fall term of court came around, Dutch Charley died of his gunshot wounds in his rooms over the saloon, and

some time during the night, Brock left the dim lights of Salt Fork and an empty money-box of Holderness and Company behind him. I had not seen my uncle since the evening after the shooting. It had not been pleasant to think of him coming to town where everyone would see for himself how deeply he had been stricken. And now it was my conviction that he would not be in Salt Fork, if at all, for a long time to come.

But only a day or two later I met him walking across the plaza, slower, grayer, not much more than a shadow of his old powerful self, yet still painfully erect and implacable in his gray broadcloth tails as I had ever seen him. And the men looked sober when they saw him coming, and said with respect: "Gettin' dry, Colonel," and "Yessirree, Colonel," and looked after him thoughtfully when he had passed.

And when the news came that Brock had been seen in El Paso and called himself Brock Chamberlain now, everybody said it was all over and that you could take one look at Jim Brewton and know himself admitted it. Certainly I seldom heard him mention Brock's name again. But it wasn't over. Once at Sarah Beth's wedding I thought I saw those burned-out eyes deep in their sockets keep staring dully at the guests as if there were someone missing in that familiar ranchhouse parlor, although exactly who was missing I could never be quite sure.

I believe now that every piece of news about Brock my uncle read in the Albuquerque and Denver papers was a secret Apache lance in his heart. His forehead was incommunicable as an old rawhide and branded like one with the mark of the band of his hat. And of what went on behind it he never spoke. All I know was that as months passed and the stories kept coming in about Brock raking eight thousand dollars from a Cripple Creek gambling table and Brock holding up a Mexican sheep herder with three pesos on his person; of Brock a deputy in White Oaks for a day and Brock that night hitching a peddler's cart behind his saddle and shooting up the town; of Brock riding south into Old Mexico ahead of the sheriff, Brock riding west with Cochran's Wild Bunch to hide in the Chiricahuas and Brock riding east alone to bring a jeweled necklace to his Choctaw-blooded nester girl in our next county, he wasn't real to me any more.

He was just a glittering idea, someone I had never seen or known, only a name whose exploits were printed in the Western papers from Omaha to Oregon, talked about over wet bars and dry trails, from horseback to horseback, in the harness-rooms of livery stables and around lonely cow-camp fires.

And when they came to me in my office to drive forty miles into the

next county to dress the wounds of a deputy who could not be moved, I sent word to Jimmy to keep it from my uncle, although it was all fantastic and unreal to me. This Brock Chamberlain, wanted for a dozen things over Arizona Territory, now making fools of a county posse nearer home, holding off twenty or thirty men from an abandoned nester's shack until the sheriff had sent for Judge Chamberlain to come and talk the boy into giving up, could not be the Brock whose feathery white hair had blown with my breath in his cradle.

Then suddenly I knew I was mistaken. The morning train had come and gone, and I was refilling the small bottles of my medicine valise and picking up my surgical instruments when a step sounded in the outer office, and when I looked up, Lutie Brewton was standing there. Oh, her veil hung heavy and dark and I could not distinguish a feature beneath it, and she wore clothes I had never seen before, but there was something in the straining high angle of the plumes of her hat that rang in my ears like calomel.

"Hal!" she said to me in the voice I hadn't heard for fifteen years.

Even without eyes or ears I would have known her. She hugged me in that silent integral part of speech of several generations ago which told things the lips neither would nor could. The familiar scent of violets closed around me again like some delicate, faintly purple cloud. And I was back in a world ten thousand times larger than the brain that contained it, still a long-haired ranch boy, Lutie Brewton had never gone away, and my uncle still rode the range in his lusty prime.

She pinned back her veil, not with the eager gesture of youth I remembered, but almost defensively, and I saw that with all her struggled erectness, her face, dead white against the lifted black plumes, had begun to show the first branding marks of her hated arch-enemy, age. As if she knew I had seen, she threw herself into holding me at arm's length, inspecting me with that critical yet flattering air, telling me almost feverishly how proud she was of me as a doctor, that any woman just to see me must throw herself in my care, and that as a physician's ears must be filled with the woes of his patients, she knew I should never ask her the weary question where she had been all these years.

And I found myself gazing at that brilliant, animated face and asking under my breath if it were true that a few minutes ago I had seen any signs of age. But all the time she plied me with questions about Jimmy and Sarah Beth and Sarah Beth's husband, whom she had never seen, I knew it was Brock that had brought her. And it was strange how I could feel him now for the first time in years, one of those three sleepy youngsters around her in their nightgowns in that

early, candle-lit room so long ago, peering at their mother sitting there, almost jaunty; suited, hatted, and gloved; hearing that she was going on a journey but would see them all sooner than soon, with a double present for each one who had been a little lady or gentleman.

Out of the window I could see across the street men watching from the gallery of Gaylord's saddlery, and I knew that someone had recognized Lutie Brewton. Then there were quick steps in my outer office, and Myra Netherwood, tall and gray-haired, an excited look on her dignified face, was there.

"Doctor, they tell me——" she began. "Lutie!" And they were in each other's arms.

Out in the plaza I heard the rattle of my phaeton's wheels from the livery stable.

"You comin', doc?" called the messenger from the next county.

I moved to finish packing my doctor bag.

"I've got to make a little call—on a sick man," I told Lutie with my back turned. "I know you'll want to be with Mrs. Netherwood. I'll come over as soon as I get in."

I tried to put it as if it were only a near-by nester patient, but I knew when I turned, by the same pale branch whipsawing again in the stream of blood at her throat, that her sensitive mind had guessed where I was going. And all the long trail down into the South Prairie country, while the rancher who had ridden all night dozed beside me, I could see in the endless heat waves two unforgettable looks in Lutie Brewton's brilliant dark eyes. One of them was when she had seen on the wall the framed photograph of my uncle, an old man, a great frame without flesh, sitting in his buggy, holding the reins of his pair of sorrels. The other look she had given me when I left. It concerned nothing of this world, only a small boy in a long nightgown and tousled hair white in the candle-light of a world that had vanished like last year's snows.

§ 15

It was Sunday morning when my horses' shoes splashed silently back again in the floury brown dust of Salt Fork streets. The wooden shutters were up on mercantile houses, the doors of business places closed, and that strange Sabbath stillness hung over everything as if these whitewashed galleries and brown adobe walls had not heard only yesterday the untamed roar of dance hall and six-shooter or seen of an early morning the dregs of the wild night before swinging silently from tree and water-tower.

Even when I turned in my team at Dagget's livery stable, it was

Sunday there among the peacefully munching horses in their stalls. But all the while I drew my straight razor above the wooden wash-stand in my room and while I made my way across the plaza with the Spanish bells from the thick-walled adobe church clanging in my ears, I dreaded meeting Lutie Brewton.

Then I knocked on the Netherwood door, paneled and grained, with a kind of knob I seldom see any more, and Lutie Brewton opened it herself, slender and rigidly erect as I had ever remembered her. Only the plumed hat looked as if it were bearing down too hard on that fragile head and throat, and the eyes in the white face burned with a high fever.

"Don't tell me anything—yet, Hal!" she said. "Just take me to mass. Myra can't go. And I don't want to be stared at alone."

My uncle and I seldom went to church. And I would have given a great deal to escape it this morning. I had never been out with Lutie Brewton before when the nearness of other people had not been the stimulus for the most animated conversation to her companion. But today the only emotion at their approach was the tightening of her arm in mine as it had that day so long ago when together we had passed the murdered teamster lying in the straw of his wagon with a bandanna over his face.

Once we were sitting in the dim church, with the candles mystically winking and the dull red of the sanctuary light glowing in the dark cave of the altar, it was as if she no longer knew I was there. The click of her beads was strangely like the click of six-shooters, and the sibilants of her lips like those of the wind drawing through rusty barbed wire and yerba de vibora. The whitewashed walls of the church kept passing away like mist, and instead of the altar, there in front of me was the barren South Prairie as I had driven through it the last several days, naked in the pitiless Southwestern sunlight, with discouraged nester families watching my phaeton from the doors of occupied dugouts and the doors of the empty houses half-fallen from their hinges. I saw plows rusting and gaunt horses standing motionless where there had once been grass. And the sand still drifted along the crazy pattern of abandoned fence-posts.

And at the end of the journey wounded men stupefied with whisky lay half-undressed under a leafless, sapless apple tree. A fresh mound of earth dried and cracked in the sun like a giant adobe brick. And I knew that around a rough circle of sand hills, hidden men with rifles watched the cañada where a deserted nester's shack stared sullenly from its empty windows.

Chamberlain had not yet arrived, and we had no idea then that he never expected to come, that even at this hour he was boarding

a train for Santa Fe on some unnamed judicial business. And after the sun went down and a horse's hoofs sounded on the trail, we thought it was the judge or news of the judge at last, even when the sound told us there was no buggy. Then as it drew closer through the Western twilight that tonight hung almost red over the land, there was something familiar about the rider hunched on the saddle of a weary, raw-boned roan with lathered shoulders.

"It's the old Colonel," someone muttered after a little.

The men stared at each other and back at the apparition. And now I could make out clearly enough the unmistakable figure of my uncle on his favorite, silver-horned saddle, a weary old man in a gray broadcloth coat too large for his shrunken girth and shoulders, un-armed, his coat-tails spreading behind the cantle, his trousers tucked into boots brown with dust. Who had told him about Brock I had no idea, but he had ridden a direct line across the country from the Cross B, over malpais and timbered ridges where no buggy trail ran. His roan was caked with mud far above the knees where he had plainly forded the treacherous Puerco, and the Navajo blanket protruding from the saddle was dark with sweat.

He halted beside us presently, his great head with its long gray mustaches forward on the soiled linen of his chest. His burned-out eyes seemed to peer at us from far back in his head where life had taken a final stand. And if there was a sign of recognition for any of us, I didn't see it, and for all the attention he showed me, I might have been a stranger instead of Brewton flesh and blood.

"Where's Brock?" was all he asked.

The men stirred uncomfortably. One of them indicated the cañada. For several moments the old eyes peered at the deserted squalid shack, a symbol of all that he hated and that had brought him tragedy and pain. Then the gray wrinkled knees nudged his mount; his old fingers, no more than bone, veins, and skin, twitched the reins, and the tired roan started.

The sheriff caught the bridle.

"You can't go down there," he said. "Not till Judge Chamberlain comes."

For a little it seemed that my uncle didn't understand him, as if it took a long time for that name to penetrate some inner room of his being where the embers of life still glowed. Then he raised his shaggy head in a semblance of that old untamed gesture of a mossy-horned lead steer smelling wolves or water. I had never seen him lift it so slowly, but when the face came up, I saw with a feeling for which there are no words that somewhere in that old Indian-fighter frame still re-mained the breeding-place of the whirlwind and thunderbolt. Already

the hate had begun to pour from his pitch-black eyes, and his face was written again with all those unforgettable black lines of insolent, almost dissolute, will and ruthlessness.

A dozen sheriffs could not have held him now, and none of us tried it, or said anything as we watched him, rigidly erect in the saddle, his right arm held stiffly down against his side with his thumb at the cantle edge as was his custom from army days, ride down alone into the cañada where a low deadly voice we could barely hear hailed him from the nester's shack, warning him he would never give himself up alive for trial, that the old man wasn't his father anyway, and that if he came any closer, he would drop both horse and rider in the trail.

No answer came from my uncle, and the only change in that lone, riding figure was that he seemed to tower in his stirrups so that two hundred yards away, with his back turned, I felt that time had leaped back twenty years, that the clumps of rattlesnake weed melting into each other on the horizon were solid green range, and I might almost see a wave of antelope, rusty as with kelp, rising and falling over my uncle's sea of grass.

He had been in the shack only a few minutes when he was outside ordering me in his old-time thunder to come. When I got there, an unshaven man sat propped up against the wall with rifle and pistol on the floor beside him, mocking and grimacing at me, his yellow hair curling like a child's. And all the time my hand wanted to shake as I tried in the dim light from the doorway to stop the bleeding from a wound in his lung, and while my uncle stood there with tortured stolidity, Brock lay on the dirty floor, paying no attention to my command to be quiet, jibing and mimicking me, calling me a horse doctor, begging tobacco and smoking cigarettes, bantering about Jimmy and Tom Milledeaux and coaxing me to say nice things about him to Sarah Beth, so that no one, not even the sheriff, standing silent and listening some feet beyond the door, could help being won over to him now.

And in the firelight that evening, when he couldn't talk any more and there was no sound but the yapping of the coyotes, I thought I saw his sardonic blue eyes pointing to something behind me. The shack had been systematically riddled with lead by the posse until it was almost a sieve. Only one conspicuous place on the four walls remained untouched by bullets, and I found now that he was derisively drawing my attention to what hung pasted by unknown hands to the center of this spot, a faded, Christmas newspaper print of Christ in the manger, with the well known words: "Peace on Earth, Good Will toward Men."

The ringing of a bell somewhere and the rising and dipping of the

congregation brought the whitewashed walls of the church back again with Lutie Brewton beside me. And when I looked about I was aware now that most of the people around us must have already heard of what had happened on the South Prairie. Their stares at Lutie Brewton carried a questioning as if they were not so sure but that yesterday they had wronged her. Her sensitive mind seemed to feel and respond to their new respect, and when the services were over, I thought she seemed to be again that clear pure flame burning from something far more precious than tallow.

When she went out she lifted her veil and smiled gently to the little Mexican girls admiring her as they kept dipping their knees at aisle and door, and spoke, as she had in the old days, to a sightless, black-shawled Mexican, now an old woman known as La Ciega. The latter, I am sure, had never understood one of Lutie Brewton's sparkling English sentences, although a look had always come into her blind, wrinkled face as if she had talked to someone who had seen the Blessed Virgin.

But today at the sound of that charming, unmistakable voice she had not heard for fifteen years, La Ciega let go of her rebozo and reached out to the speaker, and her hands were tight lumps of brown copper against Lutie Brewton's white slender ones.

"Ay de mi, señora!" she began, and poured out a stream of Spanish from one woman to another.

Lutie stood there delicately responsive and sympathetic, glancing questioningly to me. But when, without translating any of it, I tried to urge her quietly on, she turned attentively to a Mexican youth who rolled barrels and pulled square nails in John Kingman's warehouse.

"What does the blind woman say?"

"She say," the boy said, arching his back with pride to be speaking to Mrs. Brewton in front of everybody, "She say she have a boy too who is kill by a bullet. She said thank to God her boy and your boy don't suffer any more."

"Yes," Lutie Brewton said, drawing in her breath. "Yes, thank her for me."

She was erect again and very white as she took my arm and went on, steadily clearing the multicolored stream of churchgoers still flowing and eddying out of the ancient thick-walled church.

"Now I am ready to go to the ranch, Hal," she said. "Will you have someone from Dagget's livery drive me?"

"I wouldn't go until the funeral, Lutie?" I begged her in a low voice.

The plumes of her hat were suddenly and rigidly higher.

"May I go right away this morning, Hal, please!" she asked, and

I found that her clearly modulated voice impelled me toward the livery stable as effectively as twenty years ago it had turned rough men about and whipped off their hats until the aisle had opened for us into the crowded Salt Fork county courthouse.

A hundred times since she had gone away I had pictured Lutie Brewton coming back to the Cross B. And in my thoughts I was always there, feeling that extraordinary, quickening emotion just the sight of her had always called up in me. But today the old ranch house was the last place on earth I wanted to go with Lutie Brewton. And all the way to the livery stable I could see my uncle's eyes; flaming, terrible eyes as I had seen them in the South Prairie country only yesterday.

Frank Dagget gave me a queer look when I asked him for a pair of fresh horses in my phaeton to drive to the Cross B. And I knew he had guessed who was going with me, for he lifted his best black harness from the long pins, laid it on the back of his fastest team, and said that the boxing of one of the wheels of my old dusty phaeton was loose and he would give me today the fine green-seated buggy he had only last week unloaded from the railroad. And before he let me go, he combed again the manes and tails of his team and flecked the fine particles of dust from shiny black spokes, leather dash and whipstock.

"Is she well?" he asked, not looking at me.

"I think so," I said.

"It takes spunk to go to the old Colonel now," he said as I climbed into the buggy. "But then she always had it."

There are days in our Southwestern country that people call brassy but should be called steel. The sun beats down with a merciless white fire until the cloudless sky is scarcely blue but rather like the blade of a knife that for days has been ground to the stone. And all day it cuts open the breathing body of the prairie and lays its bones dead and bare in the pitiless glare before you.

It was such a morning I drove out of the wide front doors of the livery, and I felt for Lutie Brewton and how she would flinch. But I had no need to. Although Myra Netherwood in a silk wrapper gave me an anguished glance, Lutie Brewton came out of her room delicate and fragile but up and never to be turned back now, showing me the valises to carry to the buggy as if she had been away from the ranch no more than to come to town and would find everything on her return as she had left it a few days before. She gave little sign that the townspeople watched her as we drove away, and once we had reached the prairie, she kept her face turned from all the nester sores and scars, talking in a low incessant voice, as if she could not halt if she wished. But although I listened for any touch here or there that

would reveal the pattern of her hidden years, I knew no more afterwards than before which of the stories of those who said they had seen her was the true one.

Only at dusk when, after pushing the team, we saw the ranch buildings and trees swimming ahead of us like an oasis in a purple desert, was she silent. And she didn't speak again until we had driven through the wall of cottonwoods and tamarisks she herself had had planted and had stopped by the dark familiar walls of the ranch house, dimly lighted by a lantern slung from a hook on the wide front gallery.

I learned that my uncle had not yet returned from the South Prairie, from where he was expected an hour or two ahead of the wagon. But under the candles that Lutie Brewton went about lighting, the whole house was grimly eloquent with his presence; his implacable, sweated gun belt hanging from its accustomed corner of the pine settee in the hall; his wrinkled, unyielding boots standing along the wall in the big front bedroom where Lutie directed me to set down her valises; the inflexible shape of his pipes lying about; and the fierce spartan barrenness of everything.

I wished to God that Jimmy might come in from somewhere in the cedar country, where, they told me, they had sent a rider with the news. As the evening went on, there was no sign of him. But after an hour the older headquarters hands who had known Mrs. Brewton moved in a body from the bunkhouse to greet her and pay their respects, lining up on the front gallery and pushing the foreman first, all grave and embarrassed, ceremoniously shaven and in clean shirts, holding their hats in their hands, scraping the high heels of their boots, feeling tremendously sorry for her about Brock and all that had happened before and all that might happen when the old Colonel came home, but the farthermost notion from their minds that of expressing a word of it.

Soberly each one spoke as he shook hands.

"Nice day, Miz Brewton."

"You have a nice trip from town, Miz Brewton?"

"Find the road pretty fair, Miz Brewton?"

And after that they said little enough, just stood around respectfully until such a time should elapse that it would be fitting for them to go. What few remarks they managed to make they chose with extreme care, avoiding anything that might assume that Brock had ever lived or died or that she had gone away. And all the while Lutie Brewton, her face very pale against her dark hair, tried to make them less uncomfortable, cross-stitching and embroidering their simplest subjects, picking up in her white fingers the most ordinary sentiment spoken with sawdust and awkwardness, and breathing upon it till it

grew golden and exciting and important so that the others looked with surprise at the original speaker for having uttered it.

And when the time they waited for had elapsed, it was as hard for them to go as it had been to come. Once or twice I thought a cow-hand near the door lifted his head to listen. Then even without ears I would have known by the way they stiffened and their features flattened into leather that a step had sounded on the front gallery. And when I looked up, my uncle was towering in the doorway, a picture struck violently on my brain so that today he still seems to be standing there, an untamed shape in the shadows, charged with turbulent will and power, his deep eyes burning with orange flames at what they glimpsed in the wide hallway.

When I glanced back, the cowhands were solemnly taking their leave, mumbling: "Good night, Miz Brewton," going as they came, in single shuffling file, until at last Lutie Brewton stood there alone, a slight, almost frail, feminine figure, rooted against the approaching storm.

My uncle came forward slowly, still a kind of rude king in his tailed gray broadcloth, and when he was under the lights I could see that the forked veins stood out in his neck as he bowed over her hand, asking with unfailing courtesy about her health. But his furrowed face was a mask and his voice granite, and I knew that while all the others in Salt Fork county might tactfully shy from the subject where she had been all these years and what she had been doing, my uncle now would not for a moment avoid it.

And I think Lutie Brewton knew it, too, and resolved in her mind that she would never be cross-examined and compelled to explain as if she were a child, and it only made her eyes more brilliant and tilted back her fragile head piled with its black hair at a gallant, almost defiant angle, while she threw herself not into her old gayety but a grave and desperate incoherence, asking about his welfare, and where was Jimmy, and telling him that Myra had shown her Jimmy's and Sarah Beth's photographs, and mustn't he be terribly tired from his long ride, and couldn't she get something for him to eat and drink? And when my uncle's eyes grew darker with dammed-back questions, she spoke the faster, and her face became very thin and intense ivory, faintly streaked and stained as if by the blood of the creature that had borne it.

Until at last I couldn't bear it any longer and, while my uncle's eyes flared at me, I leaped to my feet and begged her to make us some coffee or rouse the cook to build a fire. Certainly I expected her to seize the chance to leave the room, but she only stood there with her face higher and cut finer, and an indecipherable look in her feverish

eyes, till I was the one who escaped, bolting to the bunkhouse, where I found the hands up far beyond their bedtime, smoking, talking in low tones, waiting for the wagon.

When an hour or two later I went stiffly back across the front gallery, some chemical change had taken place in those ancient walls. The air of the massive old ranch house hung with the elusive scent of violets high on the peaceful fumes of cigar smoke. In the wide hall the brightly colored Navajo rugs had been laid again over the pine settees. A great white cloth hung low from the heavy dining-table set with four places for tomorrow's breakfast. And the parlor I could see was swept and dusted in readiness for the coming visitor who had not been home for many a day. There were fresh doilies on the marble-top tables and clean tidies on the chair backs. The piano still stood closed, but the tall ornamental brass floor-lamp had been lighted, and the blue, entwined flowers bloomed again on the hand-painted china shade.

Then my uncle, who had been sitting quietly on a horsehair armchair, raised his head in that undying gesture of a wild stallion, his half-smoked cigar held suddenly motionless in his hand. Through the door to the front bedroom I saw Lutie Brewton stand perfectly still while she clutched folded clean sheets in her bare white arms. After a moment, far away on the lonely trail under the Southwestern stars I could hear the tolling rumble of the approaching wagon.

There is little more to tell except that the last time I was back the stone my uncle raised was still standing near the broken walls of the old ranch house.

"Brock Brewton, son of James B. and Lutie C. Brewton," it is carved in unequivocal letters that all who ride may read.

I remember very well the first time I saw it. In Salt Fork, people were still divided about Brock and where Mrs. Brewton had been. I was aware that Lutie Brewton herself would never reveal the truth to any of them, perhaps never to me. This particular day she and Sarah Beth, who was home for a month, had driven in the Colonel's pole buggy to the Bar 44. My uncle was sitting on the ranch-house gallery from where he could see the stone. And from what he said to me while his eyes rested on it, his motives were clear to me at last as a + B brand.

"Have you noticed how young she still looks, Hal?" he asked, filling his chair again with that iron dignity and pride I remembered as a boy. "It was a hard thing for a lady to go through. But she's one in a thousand, Hal. No one else will ever be like her." And his deeply lined face warmed like the late afternoon sun touching and mellowing the rugged western slope of a shaggy old mountain.

The Apple-Tree

JOHN GALSWORTHY

JOHN GALSWORTHY *was born in Coombe, a suburb of London, in 1867. He studied law at Oxford and in 1890 was admitted to the bar but, he tells us, he "disliked the profession thoroughly." He began to write when he was twenty-eight, and his first novel,* Jocelyn, *was published in 1899 under the pseudonym John Sinjohn. But it was* The Man of Property *published under his own signature in 1906 which really established him. In 1916, while he was living at his little farmhouse of Wingstone, Galsworthy wrote* The Apple-Tree—*"one of my best stories." It was first published as one of the "Five Tales" (1918) and measures 23,000 words.*

INTRODUCTION

The Apple-Tree is the epitome of Galsworthy. He has informed
the story with his deep sense of chivalry, in this case the chivalry of a
young man caught up in the struggle between chastity and passion; he
has underscored it with that feeling of pity which has made so appeal-
ing the great characters in his novels; last but not least, he has given to
the narrative that singing prose which, as in *The Indian Summer of a
Forsyte,* rises to a poetic beauty unmatched by any English novelist
since his time.

Galsworthy tells us that the narrative "owed its genesis to the chance
sight of a little Welsh maid on the hills of Abergwessin in 1904." I
would give ten-to-one odds that he saw her in the spring of that year—
in April, to be specific. For more than any other novel in my collection,
this is a story of spring and of that peculiar spell which seizes us all
when at last the sun has softened the earth. The alchemy of spring
stirs in all men a new longing, a longing for a responsiveness and a
beauty not to be found among familiar things. The seizure may be as
momentary as the glimpse of "a little Welsh maid on the hills" or it
may linger on as a fever in the blood, as a might-have-been which
plagues a man's thought until the dog days bring him back to normal.

From 1904 until 1916 this story was in the back of Galsworthy's
mind. In April of 1916 he made a determined effort to rise above the
distraction and depression of the war. With his wife he had spent much
of that spring at Wingstone, the farmhouse on the edge of Dartmoor
which had long been their sanctuary, with its meadows, its orchard and
its trout stream. He was reading Hardy—"*The Dynasts* straight through,
as it ought to be read"; he saw a good deal of W. H. Hudson and,
from his talks with the latter, he went straight to the writing of *The
Apple-Tree.* In that spring, when the war was going so badly for

66

the British and when help from America still seemed so far away, Galsworthy found in the short novel the very outlet he was looking for. He worked on *A Stoic* early in the year, finishing its first draft on March twenty-third, "about 30,000 words in forty working days." Then exactly a month later he began "The Apple-Tree," and the story wrote itself with incredible swiftness.

This story is told within the framework of retrospect. At the beginning, so to speak, you are given just a glimpse of the third act. Then the clock turns back; you see things as they were and as the current sweeps you forward you begin to fit the clues together and to guess, with some apprehension, the climax to come. When we first catch sight of him Frank Ashurst is in mid-career, a barrister of means whose marriage has been a complacent, if not a fervid, success. The story begins on his silver-wedding anniversary. The couple are picnicking on the Devon moors, with a car and a chauffeur within reach. And before lunch his wife goes off to do some sketching while Frank stretches out on the hillside, and his gaze wanders over a landscape which seems curiously familiar. As his fancy roams down the valley from the crossroads to the distant apple trees and the farmhouse Frank goes back to the young man he was when twenty-six years before, and fresh from Oxford, he came on a walking tour to this very countryside. So the story begins.

At twenty-two Frank is a lean, athletic figure with that kind of golden glow which is so often characteristic of young Englishmen and with literary aspirations somewhat in conflict with his resolution to be a lawyer. (I do not think it is illegal of me to see in young Frank young J. G.) In the manner of undergraduates, Frank has been jawing with his friend and walking companion, Garton, on the subject of pity, and Garton, who is full of Oxford superiority, remarks that "Pity's only an effect of self-consciousness; it's a disease of the last five thousand years. The world was happier without." This is the first clue, but it might pass unobserved, so natural is the undergraduate patter. Close on its heels comes the second, the reference to the "gypsy bogle," that strange premonition of death which you will find again and again in Galsworthy's writing. And then, breaking into the clear, comes the first theme, Frank's love story, as with swift alchemy it begins to possess his mind. We see how he is led on by his imagination, how his mind grasps at little straws which lovers must always catch— his discovery that Megan has been including "Mr. Ashes" in her prayers, the provocation he feels at her remark, "You laugh at me— you laugh at us," the picture of Megan, her loose dark hair caught in the apple blossoms. And so begins the ceaseless working of his imagination as it projects what may be when next they meet. Skill-

fully and yet discernibly bound up with this is the second theme, the singing, contagious beauty of the spring. "A farm in spring is all birth," writes Galsworthy, and the paragraphs in which he goes on to describe this wonder have in them the lyrical truth of "The Pastoral Symphony." Small wonder that Thomas Hardy "liked best 'The Apple-Tree' because of its poetry."

"If I single out 'The Apple-Tree' to dwell on for a moment," wrote Galsworthy, "it is because the mood behind that story is perennial. In Spring . . . who does not feel himself haunted, looking upon sky and fields, rocks, trees and moorlands—haunted by the Spirit of Nature, though he knows there is no such thing, and that what he is haunted by is, in truth, some emanation of his own longings? It was this 'haunt' I tried to render in 'The Apple-Tree,' the golden wistfulness one feels in Botticelli's Primavera and his Birth of Venus or concreted in the phrase, 'The apple tree, the singing, and the gold,' or even in the single word 'glamour.' The attempt was foolhardy, perhaps blasphemous, but there is no limit to the Instinct of Expression when it sets out of an early morning. Only in the evening, after the work is done, by the fireside, with slippered feet up, does it rub its hands a little, then sigh, thinking of the uncapturable."

THE APPLE-TREE

"The Apple-tree, the singing, and the gold."
——Murray's *Hippolytus of Euripides*.

On their silver-wedding day Ashurst and his wife were motoring along the outskirts of the moor, intending to crown the festival by stopping the night at Torquay, where they had first met. This was the idea of Stella Ashurst, whose character contained a streak of sentiment. If she had long lost the blue-eyed, flower-like charm, the cool slim purity of face and form, the apple-blossom colouring, which had so swiftly and so oddly affected Ashurst twenty-six years ago, she was still at forty-three a comely and faithful companion, whose cheeks were faintly mottled, and whose grey-blue eyes had acquired a certain fullness.

It was she who had stopped the car where the common rose steeply to the left, and a narrow strip of larch and beech, with here and there a pine, stretched out towards the valley between the road and the first long high hill of the full moor. She was looking for a place where they might lunch, for Ashurst never looked for anything; and this, between the golden furze and the feathery green larches smelling of lemons in the last sun of April—this, with a view into the deep valley and up to the long moor heights, seemed fitting to the decisive nature of one who sketched in water-colours, and loved romantic spots. Grasping her paint box, she got out.

"Won't this do, Frank?"

Ashurst, rather like a bearded Schiller, grey in the wings, tall, long-legged, with large remote grey eyes which sometimes filled with meaning and became almost beautiful, with nose a little to one side, and bearded lips just open—Ashurst, forty-eight, and silent, grasped the luncheon basket, and got out too.

"Oh! Look, Frank! A grave!"

By the side of the road, where the track from the top of the common crossed it at right angles and ran through a gate past the narrow wood, was a thin mound of turf, six feet by one, with a moorstone to the west, and on it someone had thrown a blackthorn spray and a

handful of bluebells. Ashurst looked, and the poet in him moved. At
cross-roads—a suicide's grave! Poor mortals with their superstitions!
Whoever lay there, though, had the best of it, no clammy sepulchre
among other hideous graves carved with futilities—just a rough stone,
the wide sky, and wayside blessings! And, without comment, for he
had learned not to be a philosopher in the bosom of his family, he
strode away up on to the common, dropped the luncheon basket under
a wall, spread a rug for his wife to sit on—she would turn up from
her sketching when she was hungry—and took from his pocket Mur-
ray's translation of the "Hippolytus." He had soon finished reading
of "The Cyprian" and her revenge, and looked at the sky instead. And
watching the white clouds so bright against the intense blue, Ashurst,
on his silver-wedding day, longed for—he knew not what. Maladjusted
to life—man's organism! One's mode of life might be high and scrupu-
lous, but there was always an undercurrent of greediness, a hankering,
and sense of waste. Did women have it too? Who could tell? And yet,
men who gave vent to their appetites for novelty, their riotous longings
for new adventures, new risks, new pleasures, these suffered, no doubt,
from the reverse side of starvation, from surfeit. No getting out of it—
a maladjusted animal, civilised man! There could be no garden of
his choosing, of "the Apple-tree, the singing, and the gold," in the
words of that lovely Greek chorus, no achievable elysium in life, or
lasting haven of happiness for any man with a sense of beauty—noth-
ing which could compare with the captured loveliness in a work of
art, set down for ever, so that to look on it or read was always to have
the same precious sense of exaltation and restful inebriety. Life no
doubt had moments with that quality of beauty, of unbidden flying
rapture, but the trouble was, they lasted no longer than the span of a
cloud's flight over the sun; impossible to keep them with you, as Art
caught beauty and held it fast. They were fleeting as one of the glim-
mering or golden visions one had of the soul in nature, glimpses of its
remote and brooding spirit. Here, with the sun hot on his face, a
cuckoo calling from a thorn tree, and in the air the honey savour of
gorse—here among the little fronds of the young fern, the starry
blackthorn, while the bright clouds drifted by high above the hills and
dreamy valleys—here and now was such a glimpse. But in a moment
it would pass—as the face of Pan, which looks round the corner of a
rock, vanishes at your stare. And suddenly he sat up. Surely there was
something familiar about this view, this bit of common, that ribbon of
road, the old wall behind him. While they were driving he had not
been taking notice—never did; thinking of far things or of nothing—
but now he saw! Twenty-six years ago, just at this time of year, from
the farmhouse within half a mile of this very spot he had started for

that day in Torquay whence it might be said he had never returned. And a sudden ache beset his heart; he had stumbled on just one of those past moments in his life, whose beauty and rapture he had failed to arrest, whose wings had fluttered away into the unknown; he had stumbled on a buried memory, a wild sweet time, swiftly choked and ended. And, turning on his face, he rested his chin on his hands, and stared at the short grass where the little blue milkwort was growing. . . .

And this is what he remembered.

§ 1

On the first of May, after their last year together at college, Frank Ashurst and his friend Robert Garton were on a tramp. They had walked that day from Brent, intending to make Chagford, but Ashurst's football knee had given out, and according to their map they had still some seven miles to go. They were sitting on a bank beside the road, where a track crossed alongside a wood, resting the knee and talking of the universe, as young men will. Both were over six feet, and thin as rails; Ashurst pale, idealistic, full of absence; Garton queer, round-the-corner, knotted, curly, like some primeval beast. Both had a literary bent; neither wore a hat. Ashurst's hair was smooth, pale, wavy, and had a way of rising on either side of his brow, as if always being flung back; Garton's was a kind of dark unfathomed mop. They had not met a soul for miles.

"My dear fellow," Garton was saying, "pity's only an effect of self-consciousness; it's a disease of the last five thousand years. The world was happier without."

Ashurst, following the clouds with his eyes, answered:

"It's the pearl in the oyster, anyway."

"My dear chap, all our modern unhappiness comes from pity. Look at animals, and Red Indians, limited to felling their own occasional misfortunes; then look at ourselves—never free from feeling the tooth-aches of others. Let's get back to feeling for nobody, and have a better time."

"You'll never practise that."

Garton pensively stirred the hotch-potch of his hair.

"To attain full growth, one mustn't be squeamish. To starve oneself emotionally's a mistake. All emotion is to the good—enriches life."

"Yes, and when it runs up against chivalry?"

"Ah! That's so English! If you speak of emotion the English always think you want something physical, and are shocked. They're afraid

of passion, but not of lust—oh, no!—so long as they can keep it secret."

Ashurst did not answer; he had plucked a blue floweret, and was twiddling it against the sky. A cuckoo began calling from a thorn tree. The sky, the flowers, the songs of birds! Robert was talking through his hat! And he said:

"Well, let's go on, and find some farm where we can put up." In uttering those words, he was conscious of a girl coming down from the common just above them. She was outlined against the sky, carrying a basket, and you could see that sky through the crook of her arm. And Ashurst, who saw beauty without wondering how it could advantage him, thought: 'How pretty!' The wind, blowing her dark frieze skirt against her legs, lifted her battered peacock tam-o'-shanter; her greyish blouse was worn and old, her shoes were split, her little hands rough and red, her neck browned. Her dark hair waved untidy across her broad forehead, her face was short, her upper lip short, showing a glint of teeth, her brows were straight and dark, her lashes long and dark, her nose straight; but her grey eyes were the wonder—dewy as if opened for the first time that day. She looked at Ashurst—perhaps he struck her as strange, limping along without a hat, with his large eyes on her, and his hair flung back. He could not take off what was not on his head, but put up his hand in a salute, and said:

"Can you tell us if there's a farm here where we could stay the night? I've gone lame."

"There's only our farm near, sir." She spoke without shyness, in a pretty, soft, crisp voice.

"And where is that?"

"Down here, sir."

"Would you put us up?"

"Oh! I think we would."

"Will you show us the way?"

"Yes, sir."

He limped on, silent, and Garton took up the catechism.

"Are you a Devonshire girl?"

"No, sir."

"What then?"

"From Wales."

"Ah! I *thought* you were a Celt; so it's not your farm?"

"My aunt's, sir."

"And your uncle's?"

"He is dead."

"Who farms it, then?"

"My aunt, and my three cousins."

"But your uncle was a Devonshire man?"

"Yes, sir."

"Have you lived here long?"

"Seven years."

"And how d'you like it after Wales?"

"I don't know, sir."

"I suppose you don't remember?"

"Oh, yes! But it is different."

"I believe you!"

Ashurst broke in suddenly:

"How old are you?"

"Seventeen, sir."

"And what's your name?"

"Megan David."

"This is Robert Garton, and I am Frank Ashurst. We wanted to get on to Chagford."

"It is a pity your leg is hurting you."

Ashurst smiled, and when he smiled his face was rather beautiful.

Descending past the narrow wood, they came on the farm suddenly —a long, low, stone-built dwelling with casement windows, in a farm-yard where pigs and fowls and an old mare were straying. A short steep-up grass hill behind was crowned with a few Scotch firs, and in front, an old orchard of apple-trees, just breaking into flower, stretched down to a stream and a long wild meadow. A little boy with oblique dark eyes was shepherding a pig, and by the house door stood a woman, who came towards them. The girl said:

"It is Mrs. Narracombe, my aunt."

"Mrs. Narracombe, my aunt," had a quick, dark eye, like a mother wild-duck's, and something of the same snaky turn about her neck.

"We met your niece on the road," said Ashurst; "she thought you might perhaps put us up for the night."

Mrs. Narracombe, taking them in from head to heel, answered:

"Well, I can, if you don't mind one room. Megan, get the spare room ready, and a bowl of cream. You'll be wanting tea, I suppose."

Passing through a sort of porch made by two yew trees and some flowering-currant bushes, the girl disappeared into the house, her pea-cock tam-o'-shanter bright athwart that rosy-pink and the dark green of the yews.

"Will you come into the parlour and rest your leg? You'll be from college, perhaps?"

"We were, but we've gone down now."

Mrs. Narracombe nodded sagely.

The parlour, brick-floored, with bare table and shiny chairs and sofa stuffed with horsehair, seemed never to have been used, it was so ter-

ribly clean. Ashurst sat down at once on the sofa, holding his lame knee between his hands, and Mrs. Narracombe gazed at him. He was the only son of a late professor of chemistry, but people found a certain lordliness in one who was often so sublimely unconscious of them.

"Is there a stream where we could bathe?"

"There's the strame at the bottom of the orchard, but sittin' down you'll not be covered!"

"How deep?"

"Well, 'tis about a foot and a half, maybe."

"Oh! That'll do fine. Which way?"

"Down the lane, through the second gate on the right, an' the pool's by the big apple-tree that stands by itself. There's trout there, if you can tickle them."

"They're more likely to tickle us!"

Mrs. Narracombe smiled. "There'll be the tea ready when you come back."

The pool, formed by the damming of a rock, had a sandy bottom; and the big apple-tree, lowest in the orchard, grew so close that its boughs almost overhung the water; it was in leaf, and all but in flower —its crimson buds just bursting. There was not room for more than one at a time in that narrow bath, and Ashurst waited his turn, rubbing his knee and gazing at the wild meadow, all rocks and thorn trees and field flowers, with a grove of beeches beyond, raised up on a flat mound. Every bough was swinging in the wind, every spring bird calling, and a slanting sunlight dappled the grass. He thought of Theocritus, and the river Cherwell, of the moon, and the maiden with the dewy eyes; of so many things that he seemed to think of nothing; and he felt absurdly happy.

§ 2

During a late and sumptuous tea with eggs to it, cream and jam, and thin, fresh cakes touched with saffron, Garton descanted on the Celts. It was about the period of the Celtic awakening, and the discovery that there was Celtic blood about this family had excited one who believed that he was a Celt himself. Sprawling on a horsehair chair, with a hand-made cigarette dribbling from the corner of his curly lips, he had been plunging his cold pin-points of eyes into Ashurst's and praising the refinement of the Welsh. To come out of Wales into England was like the change from china to earthenware! Frank, as a d——d Englishman, had not of course perceived the exquisite refinement and emotional capacity of that Welsh girl! And, delicately stirring in the

dark mat of his still wet hair, he explained how exactly she illustrated the writings of the Welsh bard Morgan-ap-Something in the twelfth century.

Ashurst, full length on the horsehair sofa, and jutting far beyond its end, smoked a deeply-coloured pipe, and did not listen, thinking of the girl's face when she brought in a relay of cakes. It had been exactly like looking at a flower, or some other pretty sight in Nature—till, with a funny little shiver, she had lowered her glance and gone out, quiet as a mouse.

"Let's go to the kitchen," said Garton, "and see some more of her."

The kitchen was a white-washed room with rafters, to which were attached smoked hams; there were flower-pots on the window-sill, and guns hanging on nails, queer mugs, china and pewter, and portraits of Queen Victoria. A long, narrow table of plain wood was set with bowls and spoons, under a string of high-hung onions; two sheep-dogs and three cats lay here and there. On one side of the recessed fireplace sat two small boys, idle, and good as gold; on the other sat a stout, light-eyed, red-faced youth with hair and lashes the colour of the tow he was running through the barrel of a gun; between them Mrs. Narra-combe dreamily stirred some savoury-scented stew in a large pot. Two other youths, oblique-eyed, dark-haired, rather sly-faced, like the two little boys, were talking together and lolling against the wall; and a short, elderly, clean-shaven man in corduroys, seated in the window, was conning a battered journal. The girl Megan seemed the only active creature—drawing cider and passing with the jugs from cask to table. Seeing them thus about to eat, Garton said:

"Ah! If you'll let us, we'll come back when supper's over," and without waiting for an answer they withdrew again to the parlour. But the colour in the kitchen, the warmth, the scents, and all those faces, heightened the bleakness of their shiny room, and they resumed their seats moodily.

"Regular gipsy type, those boys. There was only one Saxon—the fellow cleaning the gun. That girl is a very subtle study psycho-logically."

Ashurst's lips twitched. Garton seemed to him an ass just then. Subtle study! She was a wild flower. A creature it did you good to look at. Study!

Garton went on:

"Emotionally she would be wonderful. She wants awakening."

"Are you going to awaken her?"

Garton looked at him and smiled. 'How coarse and English you are!' that curly smile seemed saying.

And Ashurst puffed his pipe. Awaken her! This fool had the best

opinion of himself! He threw up the window and leaned out. Dusk had gathered thick. The farm buildings and the wheel-house were all dim and bluish, the apple-trees but a blurred wilderness; the air smelled of wood smoke from the kitchen fire. One bird going to bed later than the others was uttering a half-hearted twitter, as though surprised at the darkness. From the stable came the snuffle and stamp of a feeding horse. And away over there was the loom of the moor, and away and away the shy stars which had not as yet full light, pricking white through the deep blue heavens. A quavering owl hooted. Ashurst drew a deep breath. What a night to wander out in! A padding of unshod hoofs came up the lane, and three dim, dark shapes passed—ponies on an evening march. Their heads, black and fuzzy, showed above the gate. At the tap of his pipe, and a shower of little sparks, they shied round and scampered. A bat went fluttering past, uttering its almost inaudible "chip, chip." Ashurst held out his hand; on the upturned palm he could feel the dew. Suddenly from overhead he heard little burring boys' voices, little thumps of boots thrown down, and another voice, crisp and soft—the girl's putting them to bed, no doubt; and nine clear words: "No, Rick, you can't have the cat in bed"; then came a skirmish of giggles and gurgles, a soft slap, a laugh so low and pretty that it made him shiver a little. A blowing sound, and the glim of the candle which was fingering the dusk above, went out; silence reigned. Ashurst withdrew into the room and sat down; his knee pained him, and his soul felt gloomy.

"You go to the kitchen," he said; "I'm going to bed."

§ 3

For Ashurst the wheel of slumber was wont to turn noiseless and slick and swift, but though he seemed sunk in sleep when his companion came up, he was really wide awake; and long after Garton, smothered in the other bed of that low-roofed room, was worshipping darkness with his upturned nose, he heard the owls. Barring the discomfort of his knee, it was not unpleasant—the cares of life did not loom large in night watches for this young man. In fact he had none; just enrolled a barrister, with literary aspirations, the world before him, no father or mother, and four hundred a year of his own. Did it matter where he went, what he did, or when he did it? His bed, too, was hard, and this preserved him from fever. He lay, sniffing the scent of the night which drifted into the low room through the open casement close to his head. Except for a definite irritation with his friend, natural when you have tramped with a man for three days, Ashurst's memories

and visions that sleepless night were kindly and wistful and exciting. One vision, specially clear and unreasonable, for he had not even been conscious of noting it, was the face of the youth cleaning the gun; its intent, stolid, yet startled uplook at the kitchen doorway, quickly shifted to the girl carrying the cider jug. This red, blue-eyed, light-lashed, tow-haired face stuck as firmly in his memory as the girl's own face, so dewy and simple. But at last, in the square of darkness through the uncurtained casement, he saw day coming, and heard one hoarse and sleepy caw. Then followed silence, dead as ever, till the song of a blackbird, not properly awake, adventured into the hush. And, from staring at the framed brightening light, Ashurst fell asleep.

Next day his knee was badly swollen; the walking tour was obviously over. Garton, due back in London on the morrow, departed at midday with an ironical smile which left a scar of irritation—healed the moment his loping figure vanished round the corner of the steep lane. All day Ashurst rested his knee, in a green-painted wooden chair on the patch of grass by the yew-tree porch, where the sunlight distilled the scent of stocks and gillyflowers, and a ghost of scent from the flowering-currant bushes. Beatifically he smoked, dreamed, watched.

A farm in spring is all birth—young things coming out of bud and shell, and human beings watching over the process with faint excitement feeding and tending what has been born. So still the young man sat, that a mother-goose, with a stately cross-footed waddle, brought her six yellow-necked grey-backed goslings to strop their little beaks against the grass blades at his feet. Now and again Mrs. Narracombe or the girl Megan would come and ask if he wanted anything, and he would smile and say: "Nothing, thanks. It's splendid here." Towards tea-time they came out together, bearing a long poultice of some dark stuff in a bowl, and after a long and solemn scrutiny of his swollen knee, bound it on. When they were gone, he thought of the girl's soft "Oh!"—of her pitying eyes, and the little wrinkle in her brow. And again he felt that unreasoning irritation against his departed friend, who had talked such rot about her. When she brought out his tea, he said:

"How did you like my friend, Megan?"

She forced down her upper lip, as if afraid that to smile was not polite. "He was a funny gentleman; he made us laugh. I think he is very clever."

"What did he say to make you laugh?"

"He said I was a daughter of the bards. What are they?"

"Welsh poets, who lived hundreds of years ago."

"Why am I their daughter, please?"

"He meant that you were the sort of girl they sang about."

She wrinkled her brows. "I think he likes to joke. Am I?"

"Would you believe me, if I told you?"

"Oh, yes."

"Well, I think he was right."

She smiled.

And Ashurst thought: 'You *are* a pretty thing!'

"He said, too, that Joe was a Saxon type. What would that be?"

"Which is Joe? With the blue eyes and red face?"

"Yes. My uncle's nephew."

"Not your cousin, then?"

"No."

"Well, he meant that Joe was like the men who came over to England about fourteen hundred years ago, and conquered it."

"Oh! I know about them; but is he?"

"Garton's crazy about that sort of thing; but I must say Joe does look a bit Early Saxon."

"Yes."

That "Yes" tickled Ashurst. It was so crisp and graceful, so conclusive, and politely acquiescent in what was evidently Greek to her.

"He said that all the other boys were regular gipsies. He should not have said that. My aunt laughed, but she didn't like it, of course, and my cousins were angry. Uncle was a farmer—farmers are not gipsies. It is wrong to hurt people."

Ashurst wanted to take her hand and give it a squeeze, but he only answered:

"Quite right, Megan. By the way, I heard you putting the little ones to bed last night."

She flushed a little. "Please to drink your tea—it is getting cold. Shall I get you some fresh?"

"Do you ever have time to do anything for yourself?"

"Oh, yes."

"I've been watching, but I haven't seen it yet."

She wrinkled her brows in a puzzled frown, and her colour deepened.

When she was gone, Ashurst thought: 'Did she think I was chaffing her? I wouldn't for the world!' He was at that age when to some men "Beauty's a flower," as the poet says, and inspires in them the thoughts of chivalry. Never very conscious of his surroundings, it was some time before he was aware that the youth whom Garton had called "a Saxon type" was standing outside the stable door; and a fine bit of colour he made in his soiled brown velvetcords, muddy gaiters, and blue shirt; red-armed, red-faced, the sun turning his hair from tow to flax; immovably stolid, persistent, unsmiling he stood. Then, seeing Ashurst looking at him, he crossed the yard at that gait of the young country-

man always ashamed not to be slow and heavy-dwelling on each leg, and disappeared round the end of the house towards the kitchen entrance. A chill came over Ashurst's mood. Clods! With all the good will in the world, how impossible to get on terms with them! And yet—see that girl! Her shoes were split, her hands rough; but—what was it? Was it really her Celtic blood, as Garton had said?—she was a lady born, a jewel, though probably she could do no more than just read and write!

The elderly, clean-shaven man he had seen last night in the kitchen had come into the yard with a dog, driving the cows to their milking. Ashurst saw that he was lame.

"You've got some good ones there!"

The lame man's face brightened. He had the upward look in his eyes which prolonged suffering often brings.

"Yeas; they'm praaper buties; gude milkers tu."

"I bet they are."

"'Ope as yure leg's better, zurr."

"Thank you, it's getting on."

The lame man touched his own: "I know what 'tes, meself; 'tes a main worritin' thing, the knee. I've a 'ad mine bad this ten year."

Ashurst made the sound of sympathy which comes so readily from those who have an independent income, and the lame man smiled again.

"Mustn't complain, though—they mighty near 'ad it off."

"Ho!"

"Yeas; an' compared with what twas, 'tes almost so gude as nu."

"They've put a bandage of splendid stuff on mine."

"The maid she picks et. She'm a gude maid wi' the flowers. There's folks zeem to know the healin' in things. My mother was a rare one for that. 'Ope as yu'll zune be better, zurr. Goo ahn, therr!"

Ashurst smiled. "Wi' the flowers!" A flower herself.

That evening, after his supper of cold duck, junket, and cider, the girl came in.

"Please, auntie says—will you try a piece of our Mayday cake?"

"If I may come to the kitchen for it."

"Oh, yes! You'll be missing your friend."

"Not I. But are you sure no one minds?"

"Who would mind? We shall be very pleased."

Ashurst rose too suddenly for his stiff knee, staggered, and subsided. The girl gave a little gasp, and held out her hands. Ashurst took them, small, rough, brown; checked his impulse to put them to his lips, and let her pull him up. She came close beside him, offering her shoulder. And leaning on her he walked across the room. That shoulder seemed quite the pleasantest thing he had ever touched. But he had presence

of mind enough to catch his stick out of the rack, and withdraw his hand before arriving at the kitchen.

That night he slept like a top, and woke with his knee of almost normal size. He again spent the morning in his chair on the grass patch, scribbling down verses; but in the afternoon he wandered about with the two little boys Nick and Rick. It was Saturday, so they were early home from school; quick, shy, dark little rascals of seven and six, soon talkative, for Ashurst had a way with children. By four o'clock they had shown him all their methods of destroying life, except the tickling of trout; and with breeches tucked up, lay on their stomachs over the trout stream, pretending they had this accomplishment also. They tickled nothing, of course, for their giggling and shouting scared every spotted thing away. Ashurst, on a rock at the edge of the beech clump, watched them, and listened to the cuckoos, till Nick, the elder and less persevering, came up and stood beside him.

"The gipsy bogle zets on that stone," he said.

"What gipsy bogle?"

"Dunno; never zeen 'e. Megan zays 'e zets there; an' old Jim zeed 'e once. 'E was zettin' there naight afore our pony kicked-in father's 'ead. 'E plays the viddle."

"What tune does he play?"

"Dunno."

"What's he like?"

"'E's black. Old Jim zays 'e's all over 'air. 'E's a praaper bogle. 'E don' come only at naight." The little boy's oblique dark eyes slid round. "D'yu think 'e might want to take me away? Megan's feared of 'e."

"Has she seen him?"

"No. She's not afeared o' yu."

"I should think not. Why should she be?"

"She zays a prayer for yu."

"How do you know that, you little rascal?"

"When I was asleep, she said: 'God bless us all, an' Mr. Ashes.' I yeard 'er whisperin'."

"You're a little ruffian to tell what you hear when you're not meant to hear it!"

The little boy was silent. Then he said aggressively:

"I can skin rabbets. Megan, she can't bear skinnin' 'em. I like blood."

"Oh! you do; you little monster!"

"What's that?"

"A creature that likes hurting others."

The little boy scowled. "They'm only dead rabbets, what us eats."

"Quite right, Nick. I beg your pardon."

"I can skin frogs, tu."

But Ashurst had become absent. "God bless us all, and Mr. Ashes!" And puzzled by that sudden inaccessibility, Nick ran back to the stream where the giggling and shouts again uprose at once.

When Megan brought his tea, he said:

"What's the gipsy bogle, Megan?"

She looked up, startled.

"He brings bad things."

"Surely you don't believe in ghosts?"

"I hope I will never see him."

"Of course you won't. There aren't such things. What old Jim saw was a pony."

"No! There are bogles in the rocks; they are the men who lived long ago."

"They aren't gipsies, anyway; those old men were dead long before gipsies came."

She said simply: "They are all bad."

"Why? If there are any, they're only wild, like the rabbits. The flowers aren't bad for being wild; the thorn trees were never planted—and you don't mind them. I shall go down at night and look for your bogle, and have a talk with him."

"Oh, no! Oh, no!"

"Oh, yes! I shall go and sit on his rock."

She clasped her hands together: "Oh, please!"

"Why! What does it matter if anything happens to me?"

She did not answer; and in a sort of pet he added:

"Well, I daresay I shan't see him, because I suppose I must be off soon."

"Soon?"

"Your aunt won't want to keep me here."

"Oh, yes! We always let lodgings in summer."

Fixing his eyes on her face, he asked:

"Would you like me to stay?"

"Yes."

"I'm going to say a prayer for *you* to-night!"

She flushed crimson, frowned, and went out of the room. He sat cursing himself, till his tea was stewed. It was as if he had hacked with his thick boots at a clump of bluebells. Why had he said such a silly thing? Was he just a towny college ass like Robert Garton, as far from understanding this girl?

§ 4

Ashurst spent the next week confirming the restoration of his leg, by exploration of the country within easy reach. Spring was a revelation to him this year. In a kind of intoxication he would watch the pink-white buds of some backward beech tree sprayed up in the sunlight against the deep blue sky, or the trunks and limbs of the few Scotch firs, tawny in violent light, or again on the moor, the gale-bent larches which had such a look of life when the wind streamed in their young green, above the rusty black underboughs. Or he would lie on the banks, gazing at the clusters of dog-violets, or up in the dead bracken, fingering the pink, transparent buds of the dewberry, while the cuckoos called and yaffles laughed, or a lark, from very high, dripped its beads of song. It was certainly different from any spring he had ever known, for spring was within him, not without. In the daytime he hardly saw the family; and when Megan brought in his meals she always seemed too busy in the house or among the young things in the yard to stay talking long. But in the evenings he installed himself in the window seat in the kitchen, smoking and chatting with the lame man Jim, or Mrs. Narracombe, while the girl sewed, or moved about, clearing the supper things away. And sometimes with the sensation a cat must feel when it purrs, he would become conscious that Megan's eyes—those dew-grey eyes—were fixed on him with a sort of lingering soft look which was strangely flattering.

It was on Sunday week in the evening, when he was lying in the orchard listening to a blackbird and composing a love poem, that he heard the gate swing to, and saw the girl come running among the trees, with the red-cheeked, stolid Joe in swift pursuit. About twenty yards away the chase ended, and the two stood fronting each other, not noticing the stranger in the grass—the boy pressing on, the girl fending him off. Ashurst could see her face, angry, disturbed; and the youth's —who would have thought that red-faced yokel could look so dis-traught! And painfully affected by that sight, he jumped up. They saw him then. Megan dropped her hands, and shrank behind a tree-trunk; the boy gave an angry grunt, rushed at the bank, scrambled over and vanished. Ashurst went slowly up to her. She was standing quite still, biting her lip—very pretty, with her fine, dark hair blown loose about her face, and her eyes cast down.

"I beg your pardon," he said.

She gave him one upward look, from eyes much dilated; then, catching her breath, turned away. Ashurst followed.

"Megan!"

But she went on; and taking hold of her arm, he turned her gently round to him.

"Stop and speak to me."

"Why do you beg my pardon? It is not to me you should do that."

"Well, then, to Joe."

"How dare he come after me?"

"In love with you, I suppose."

She stamped her foot.

Ashurst uttered a short laugh. "Would you like me to punch his head?"

She cried with sudden passion:

"You laugh at me—you laugh at us!"

He caught hold of her hands, but she shrank back, till her passionate little face and loose dark hair were caught among the pink clusters of the apple blossom. Ashurst raised one of her imprisoned hands and put his lips to it. He felt how chivalrous he was, and superior to that clod Joe—just brushing that small, rough hand with his mouth! Her shrinking ceased suddenly; she seemed to tremble towards him. A sweet warmth overtook Ashurst from top to toe. This slim maiden, so simple and fine and pretty, was pleased, then, at the touch of his lips. And, yielding to a swift impulse, he put his arms round her, pressed her to him, and kissed her forehead. Then he was frightened—she went so pale, closing her eyes, so that the long, dark lashes lay on her pale cheeks; her hands, too, lay inert at her sides. The touch of her breast sent a shiver through him. "Megan!" he sighed out, and let her go. In the utter silence a blackbird shouted. Then the girl seized his hand, put it to her cheek, her heart, her lips, kissed it passionately, and fled away among the mossy trunks of the apple-trees, till they hid her from him.

Ashurst sat down on a twisted old tree growing almost along the ground, and, all throbbing and bewildered, gazed vacantly at the blossom which had crowned her hair—those pink buds with one white open apple star. What had he done? How had he let himself be thus stampeded by beauty—or—just the spring! He felt curiously happy, all the same; happy and triumphant, with shivers running through his limbs, and a vague alarm. This was the beginning of—what? The midges bit him, the dancing gnats tried to fly into his mouth, and all the spring around him seemed to grow more lovely and alive; the songs of the cuckoos and the blackbirds, the laughter of the yaffles, the level-slanting sunlight, the apple blossom which had crowned her head——! He got up from the old trunk and strode out of the orchard, wanting space, an open sky, to get on terms with these new sensations. He made

for the moor, and from an ash tree in the hedge a magpie flew out to herald him.

Of man—at any age from five years on—who can say he has never been in love? Ashurst had loved his partners at his dancing class; loved his nursery governess; girls in school-holidays; perhaps never been quite out of love, cherishing always some more or less remote admiration. But this was different, not remote at all. Quite a new sensation; terribly delightful, bringing a sense of completed manhood. To be holding in his fingers such a wild flower, to be able to put it to his lips, and feel it tremble with delight against them! What intoxication, and—embarrassment! What to do with it—how meet her next time? His first caress had been cool, pitiful; but the next could not be, now that, by her burning little kiss on his hand, by her pressure of it to her heart, he knew that she loved him. Some natures are coarsened by love bestowed on them; others, like Ashurst's, are swayed and drawn, warmed and softened, almost exalted, by what they feel to be a sort of miracle.

And up there among the tors he was racked between the passionate desire to revel in this new sensation of spring fulfilled within him, and a vague but very real uneasiness. At one moment he gave himself up completely to his pride at having captured this pretty, trustful, dewy-eyed thing! At the next he thought with factitious solemnity: 'Yes, my boy! But look out what you're doing! You know what comes of it!'

Dusk dropped down without his noticing—dusk on the carved, Assyrian-looking masses of the rocks. And the voice of Nature said: "This is a new world for you!" As when a man gets up at four o'clock and goes out into a summer morning, and beasts, birds, trees stare at him and he feels as if all had been made new.

He stayed up there for hours, till it grew cold, then groped his way down the stones and heather roots to the road, back into the lane, and came again past the wild meadow to the orchard. There he struck a match and looked at his watch. Nearly twelve! It was black and unstirring in there now, very different from the lingering, bird-befriended brightness of six hours ago! And suddenly he saw this idyll of his with the eyes of the outer world—had mental vision of Mrs. Narracombe's snake-like neck turned, her quick dark glance taking it all in, her shrewd face hardening; saw the gipsy-like cousins coarsely mocking and distrustful; Joe stolid and furious; only the lame man, Jim, with the suffering eyes, seemed tolerable to his mind. And the village pub!—the gossiping matrons he passed on his walks; and then—his own friends—Robert Garton's smile when he went off that morning ten days ago; so ironical and knowing! Disgusting! For a minute he literally hated this earthly, cynical world to which one belonged, willy-nilly. The gate where he was leaning grew grey, a sort of shimmer passed before him

and spread into the bluish darkness. The moon! He could just see it
over the bank behind; red, nearly round—a strange moon! And turn-
ing away, he went up the lane which smelled of the night and cow-
dung and young leaves. In the straw-yard he could see the dark shapes
of cattle, broken by the pale sickles of their horns, like so many thin
moons, fallen ends-up. He unlatched the farm gate stealthily. All was
dark in the house. Muffling his footsteps, he gained the porch, and,
blotted against one of the yew trees, looked up at Megan's window. It
was open. Was she sleeping, or lying awake perhaps disturbed—un-
happy at his absence? An owl hooted while he stood there peering up,
and the sound seemed to fill the whole night, so quiet was all else, save
for the never-ending murmur of the stream running below the orchard.
The cuckoos by day, and now the owls—how wonderfully they voiced
this troubled ecstasy within him! And suddenly he saw her at her win-
dow, looking out. He moved a little from the yew tree, and whispered:
"Megan!" She drew back, vanished, reappeared, leaning far down. He
stole forward on the grass patch, hit his shin against the green-painted
chair, and held his breath at the sound. The pale blur of her stretched-
down arm and face did not stir; he moved the chair, and noiselessly
mounted it. By stretching up his arm he could just reach. Her hand
held the huge key of the front door, and he clasped that burning hand
with the cold key in it. He could just see her face, the glint of teeth be-
tween her lips, her tumbled hair. She was still dressed—poor child, sit-
ting up for him, no doubt! "Pretty Megan!" Her hot, roughened
fingers clung to his; her face had a strange, lost look. To have been
able to reach it—even with his hand! The owl hooted, a scent of sweet-
briar crept into his nostrils. Then one of the farm dogs' barked; her
grasp relaxed, she shrank back.

"Good-night, Megan!"

"Good-night, sir!" She was gone! With a sigh he dropped back to
earth, and, sitting on that chair, took off his boots. Nothing for it but to
creep in and go to bed; yet for a long while he sat unmoving, his feet
chilly in the dew, drunk on the memory of her lost, half-smiling face,
and the clinging grip of her burning fingers, pressing the cold key into
his hand.

§ 5

He awoke feeling as if he had eaten heavily overnight, instead of
having eaten nothing. And far off, unreal, seemed yesterday's romance!
Yet it was a golden morning. Full spring had burst at last—in one
night the "goldiecups," as the little boys called them, seemed to have

made the field their own, and from his window he could see apple blossoms covering the orchard as with a rose and white quilt. He went down almost dreading to see Megan; and yet, when not she but Mrs. Narracombe brought in his breakfast, he felt vexed and disappointed. The woman's quick eye and snaky neck seemed to have a new alacrity this morning. Had she noticed?

"So you an' the moon went walkin' last night, Mr. Ashurst! Did ye have your supper anywheres?"

Ashurst shook his head.

"We kept it for you, but I suppose you was too busy in your brain to think o' such a thing as that?"

Was she mocking him, in that voice of hers, which still kept some Welsh crispness against the invading burr of the West Country? If she knew! And at that moment he thought: 'No, no; I'll clear out. I won't put myself in such a beastly false position.'

But, after breakfast, the longing to see Megan began and increased with every minute, together with fear lest something should have been said to her which had spoiled everything. Sinister that she had not appeared, not given him even a glimpse of her! And the love poem, whose manufacture had been so important and absorbing yesterday afternoon under the apple trees, now seemed so paltry that he tore it up and rolled it into pipe spills. What had he known of love, till she seized his hand and kissed it! And now—what did he not know? But to write of it seemed mere insipidity! He went up to his bedroom to get a book, and his heart began to beat violently, for she was in there making the bed. He stood in the doorway watching; and suddenly, with turbulent joy, he saw her stoop and kiss his pillow, just at the hollow made by his head last night. How let her know he had seen that pretty act of devotion? And yet if she heard him stealing away, it would be even worse. She took the pillow up, holding it as if reluctant to shake out the impress of his cheek, dropped it, and turned round.

"Megan!"

She put her hands up to her cheeks, but her eyes seemed to look right into him. He had never before realized the depth and purity and touching faithfulness in those dew-bright eyes, and he stammered:

"It was sweet of you to wait up for me last night."

She still said nothing, and he stammered on:

"I was wandering about on the moor; it was such a jolly night. I—I've just come up for a book."

Then, the kiss he had seen her give the pillow afflicted him with sudden headiness, and he went up to her. Touching her eyes with his lips, he thought with queer excitement: 'I've done it! Yesterday all was sudden—anyhow; but now—I've done it!' The girl let her forehead

rest against his lips, which moved downwards till they reached hers.
That first real lover's kiss—strange, wonderful, still almost innocent—
in which heart did it make the most disturbance?

"Come to the big apple-tree to-night, after they've gone to bed.
Megan—promise!"

She whispered back: "I promise!"

Then, scared at her white face, scared at everything, he let her go,
and went downstairs again. Yes! he had done it now! Accepted her
love, declared his own! He went out to the green chair as devoid of a
book as ever; and there he sat staring vacantly before him, triumphant
and remorseful, while under his nose and behind his back the work of
the farm went on. How long he had been sitting in that curious state
of vacancy he had no notion when he saw Joe standing a little behind
him to the right. The youth had evidently come from hard work in the
fields, and stood shifting his feet, breathing loudly, his face coloured
like a setting sun, and his arms, below the rolled-up sleeves of his blue
shirt, showing the hue and furry sheen of ripe peaches. His red lips
were open, his blue eyes with their flaxen lashes stared fixedly at
Ashurst, who said ironically:

"Well, Joe, anything I can do for you?"

"Yeas."

"What, then?"

"Yu can goo away from yere. Us don' want yu."

Ashurst's face, never too humble, assumed its most lordly look.

"Very good of you, but, do you know, I prefer the others should
speak for themselves.

The youth moved a pace or two nearer, and the scent of his honest
heat afflicted Ashurst's nostrils.

"What d'you stay yere for?"

"Because it pleases me."

" 'Twon't please yu when I've bashed yure head in!"

"Indeed! When would you like to begin that?"

Joe answered only with the loudness of his breathing, but his eyes
looked like those of a young and angry bull. Then a sort of spasm
seemed to convulse his face.

"Megan don' want yu."

A rush of jealousy, of contempt, and anger with this thick, loud-
breathing rustic got the better of Ashurst's self-possession; he jumped
up and pushed back his chair.

"You can go to the devil!"

And as he said those simple words, he saw Megan in the doorway
with a tiny brown spaniel puppy in her arms. She came up to him
quickly:

"Its eyes are blue!" she said.

Joe turned away; the back of his neck was literally crimson.

Ashurst put his finger to the mouth of the little brown bullfrog of a creature in her arms. How cosy it looked against her!

"It's fond of you already. Ah! Megan, everything is fond of *you.*"

"What was Joe saying to you, please?"

"Telling me to go away, because you didn't want me here."

She stamped her foot; then looked up at Ashurst. At that adoring look he felt his nerves quiver, just as if he had seen a moth scorching its wings.

"To-night!" he said. "Don't forget!"

"No." And smothering her face against the puppy's little fat, brown body, she slipped back into the house.

Ashurst wandered down the lane. At the gate of the wild meadow he came on the lame man and his cows.

"Beautiful day, Jim!"

"Ah! 'Tes brave weather for the grass. The ashes be later than th' oaks this year. 'When th' oak before th' ash——' "

Ashurst said idly: "Where were you standing when you saw the gipsy bogle, Jim?"

"It might be under that big apple-tree, as you might say."

"And you really do think it was there?"

The lame man answered cautiously:

"I shouldn't like to say rightly that 't *was* there. 'Twas in my mind as 'twas there."

"What do you make of it?"

The lame man lowered his voice.

"They du zay old master, Mist' Narracombe, come o' gipsy stock. But that's tellin'. They'm a wonderful people, yu know, for claimin' their own. Maybe they knu 'e was goin', and sent this feller along for company. That's what I've a-thought about it."

"What was he like?"

" 'E 'ad 'air all over 'is face, an' goin' like this, he was, zame as if 'e 'ad a viddle. They zay there's no such thing as bogles, but I've a-zeen the 'air on this dog standin' up of a dark naight, when I couldn' zee nothin', meself."

"Was there a moon?"

"Yeas, very near full, but 'twas on'y just risen, gold-like be'ind them trees."

"And you think a ghost means trouble, do you?"

The lame man pushed his hat up; his aspiring eyes looked at Ashurst more earnestly than ever.

" 'Tes not for me to zay that—but 'tes they bein' so unrestin'-like.

There's things us don' understand, that's zartin, for zure. There's
people that zee things, tu, an' others that don't never zee nothin'. Now,
our Joe—yu might putt anything under 'is eyes an' 'e'd never see it;
and them other boys, tu, they'm rattlin' fellers. But yu take an' putt our
Megan where there's suthin', she'll zee it, an' more tu, or I'm
mistaken."

"She's sensitive, that's why."

"What's that?"

"I mean, she feels everything."

"Ah! She'm very lovin'-'earted."

Ashurst, who felt colour coming into his cheeks, held out his tobacco
pouch.

"Have a fill, Jim?"

"Thank 'ee, sir. She'm one in an 'underd, I think."

"I expect so," said Ashurst shortly, and folding up his pouch, walked
on.

"Lovin'-'earted!" Yes! And what was he doing? What were his in-
tentions—as they say—towards this loving-hearted girl? The thought
dogged him, wandering through fields bright with buttercups, where
the little red calves were feeding, and the swallows flying high. Yes,
the oaks were before the ashes, brown-gold already; every tree in dif-
ferent stage and hue. The cuckoos and a thousand birds were singing;
the little streams were very bright. The ancients believed in a golden
age, in the garden of the Hesperides! . . . A queen wasp settled on his
sleeve. Each queen wasp killed meant two thousand fewer wasps to
thieve the apples which would grow from that blossom in the orchard;
but who, with love in his heart, could kill anything on a day like this?
He entered a field where a young red bull was feeding. It seemed to
Ashurst that he looked like Joe. But the young bull took no notice of
this visitor, a little drunk himself, perhaps, on the singing and the
glamour of the golden pasture, under his short legs. Ashurst crossed
out unchallenged to the hillside above the stream. From that slope a
tor mounted to its crown of rocks. The ground there was covered with
a mist of bluebells, and nearly a score of crab-apple trees were in full
bloom. He threw himself down on the grass. The change from the
buttercup glory and oak-goldened glamour of the fields to this ethereal
beauty under the grey tor filled him with a sort of wonder; nothing
the same, save the sound of running water and the songs of the
cuckoos. He lay there a long time, watching the sunlight wheel till
the crab-trees threw shadows over the bluebells, his only companions
a few wild bees. He was not quite sane, thinking of that morning's kiss,
and of to-night under the apple-tree. In such a spot as this, fauns and
dryads surely lived; nymphs, white as the crab-apple blossom, retired

within those trees; fauns, brown as the dead bracken, with pointed
ears, lay in wait for them. The cuckoos were still calling when he woke,
there was the sound of running water; but the sun had couched behind
the tor, the hillside was cool, and some rabbits had come out. 'To-
night!' he thought. Just as from the earth everything was pushing up,
unfolding under the soft insistent fingers of an unseen hand, so were
his heart and senses being pushed, unfolded. He got up and broke off
a spray from a crab-apple tree. The buds were like Megan—shell-
like, rose-pink, wild, and fresh; and so, too, the opening flowers, white,
and wild, and touching. He put the spray into his coat. And all the
rush of the spring within him escaped in a triumphant sigh. But the
rabbits scurried away.

§ 6

It was nearly eleven that night when Ashurst put down the pocket
"Odyssey" which for half an hour he had held in his hands without
reading, and slipped through the yard down to the orchard. The moon
had just risen, very golden, over the hill, and like a bright, powerful,
watching spirit peered through the bars of an ash tree's half-naked
boughs. In among the apple-trees it was still dark, and he stood making
sure of his direction, feeling the rough grass with his feet. A black
mass close behind him stirred with a heavy grunting sound, and three
large pigs settled down again close to each other, under the wall. He
listened. There was no wind, but the stream's burbling whispering
chuckle had gained twice its daytime strength. One bird, he could
not tell what, cried "Pip—pip," "Pip—pip," with perfect monotony;
he could hear a night-jar spinning very far off; an owl hooting. Ashurst
moved a step or two, and again halted, aware of a dim living whiteness
all round his head. On the dark unstirring trees innumerable flowers
and buds all soft and blurred were being bewitched to life by the
creeping moonlight. He had the oddest feeling of actual companion-
ship, as if a million white moths or spirits had floated in and settled
between dark sky and darker ground, and were opening and shutting
their wings on a level with his eyes. In the bewildering, still, scentless
beauty of that moment he almost lost memory of why he had come
to the orchard. The flying glamour which had clothed the earth all
day had not gone now that night had fallen, but only changed into this
new form. He moved on through the thicket of stems and boughs cov-
ered with that live powdering whiteness, till he reached the big apple-
tree. No mistaking that, even in the dark, nearly twice the height and
size of any other, and leaning out towards the open meadows and

the stream. Under the thick branches he stood still again, to listen. The
same sounds exactly, and a faint grunting from the sleepy pigs. He put
his hands on the dry, almost warm tree trunk, whose rough mossy
surface gave forth a peaty scent at his touch. Would she come—would
she? And among these quivering, haunted, moon-witched trees he
was seized with doubts of everything! All was unearthly here, fit for
no earthly lovers; fit only for god and goddess, faun and nymph—
not for him and this little country girl. Would it not be almost a relief
if she did not come? But all the time he was listening. And still that
unknown bird went "Pip—pip," "Pip—pip," and there rose the busy
chatter of the little trout stream, whereon the moon was flinging
glances through the bars of her tree-prison. The blossom on a level
with his eyes seemed to grow more living every moment, seemed with
its mysterious white beauty more and more a part of his suspense. He
plucked a fragment and held it close—three blossoms. Sacrilege to
pluck fruit-tree blossom—soft, sacred, young blossom—and throw it
away! Then suddenly he heard the gate close, the pigs stirring again
and grunting; and leaning against the trunk, he pressed his hands to
its mossy sides behind him, and held his breath. She might have been
a spirit threading the trees, for all the noise she made! Then he saw
her quite close—her dark form part of a little tree, her white face part
of its blossom; so still, and peering towards him. He whispered:
"Megan!" and held out his hands. She ran forward, straight to his
breast. When he felt her heart beating against him, Ashurst knew to
the full the sensations of chivalry and passion. Because she was not of
his world, because she was so simple and young and headlong, adoring
and defenceless, how could he be other than her protector, in the dark!
Because she was all simple Nature and beauty, as much a part of this
spring night as was the living blossom, how should he not take all that
she would give him—how not fulfil the spring in her heart and his!
And torn between these two emotions he clasped her close, and kissed
her hair. How long they stood there without speaking he knew not.
The stream went on chattering, the owls hooting, the moon kept
stealing up and growing whiter; the blossom all round them and above
brightened in suspense of living beauty. Their lips had sought each
other's, and they did not speak. The moment speech began all
would be unreal! Spring has no speech, nothing but rustling and
whispering. Spring has so much more than speech in its unfolding
flowers and leaves, and the coursing of its streams, and in its sweet
restless seeking! And sometimes spring will come alive, and, like a
mysterious Presence, stand, encircling lovers with its arms, laying on
them the fingers of enchantment, so that, standing lips to lips, they
forget everything but just a kiss. While her heart beat against him, and

her lips quivered on his, Ashurst felt nothing but simple rapture—
Destiny meant her for his arms, Love could not be flouted! But when
their lips parted for breath, division began again at once. Only, passion
now was so much the stronger, and he sighed:

"Oh! Megan! Why did you come?"

She looked up, hurt, amazed.

"Sir, you asked me to."

"Don't call me 'sir,' my pretty sweet."

"What should I be callin' you?"

"Frank."

"I could not. Oh, no!"

"But you love me—don't you?"

"I could not help lovin' you. I want to be with you—that's all."

"All!"

So faint that he hardly heard, she whispered:

"I shall die if I can't be with you."

Ashurst took a mighty breath.

"Come and be with me, then!"

"Oh!"

Intoxicated by the awe and rapture in that "Oh!" he went on,
whispering:

"We'll go to London. I'll show you the world. And I *will* take care of
you, I promise, Megan. I'll never be a brute to you!"

"If I can be with you—that is all."

He stroked her hair, and whispered on:

"To-morrow I'll go to Torquay and get some money, and get you
some clothes that won't be noticed, and then we'll steal away. And
when we get to London, soon perhaps, if you love me well enough,
we'll be married."

He could feel her hair shiver with the shake of her head.

"Oh, no! I could not. I only want to be with you!"

Drunk on his own chivalry, Ashurst went on murmuring:

"It's I who am not good enough for you. Oh! Megan, when did you
begin to love me?"

"When I saw you in the road, and you looked at me. The first night
I loved you; but I never thought you would want me."

She slipped down suddenly to her knees, trying to kiss his feet.

A shiver of horror went through Ashurst; he lifted her up bodily
and held her fast—too upset to speak.

She whispered: "Why won't you let me?"

"It's I who will kiss your feet!"

Her smile brought tears into his eyes. The whiteness of her moonlit

face so close to his, the faint pink of her opened lips, had the living, unearthly beauty of the apple blossom.

And then, suddenly, her eyes widened and stared past him painfully; she writhed out of his arms, and whispered: "Look!"

Ashurst saw nothing but the brightened stream, the furze faintly gilded, the beech trees glistening, and behind them all the wide loom of the moonlit hill. Behind him came her frozen whisper: "The gipsy bogle!"

"Where?"

"There—by the stone—under the trees!"

Exasperated, he leapt the stream, and strode towards the beech clump. Prank of the moonlight! Nothing! In and out of the boulders and thorn trees, muttering and cursing, yet with a kind of terror, he rushed and stumbled. Absurd! Silly! Then he went back to the apple-tree. But she was gone; he could hear a rustle, the grunting of the pigs, the sound of a gate closing. Instead of her, only this old apple-tree! He flung his arms round the trunk. What a substitute for her soft body; the rough moss against his face—what a substitute for her soft cheek; only the scent, as of the woods, a little the same! And above him, and around, the blossoms, more living, more moonlit than ever, seemed to glow and breathe.

§ 7

Descending from the train at Torquay station, Ashurst wandered uncertainly along the front, for he did not know this particular queen of English watering-places. Having little sense of what he had on, he was quite unconscious of being remarkable among its inhabitants, and strode along in his rough Norfolk jacket, dusty boots, and battered hat, without observing that people gazed at him rather blankly. He was seeking a branch of his London bank, and having found one, found also the first obstacle to his mood. Did he know anyone in Torquay? No. In that case, if he would wire to his bank in London, they would be happy to oblige him on receipt of the reply. That suspicious breath from the matter-of-fact world somewhat tarnished the brightness of his visions. But he sent the telegram.

Nearly opposite to the post office he saw a shop full of ladies' garments, and examined the window with strange sensations. To have to undertake the clothing of his rustic love was more than a little disturbing. He went in. A young woman came forward; she had blue eyes and a faintly puzzled forehead. Ashurst stared at her in silence.

"Yes, sir?"

"I want a dress for a young lady."

The young woman smiled. Ashurst frowned—the peculiarity of his request struck him with sudden force.

The young woman added hastily:

"What style would you like—something modish?"

"No. Simple."

"What figure would the young lady be?"

"I don't know; about two inches shorter than you, I should say."

"Could you give me her waist measurement?"

Megan's waist!

"Oh! anything usual!"

"Quite!"

While she was gone he stood disconsolately eyeing the models in the window, and suddenly it seemed to him incredible that Megan— his Megan—could ever be dressed save in the rough tweed skirt, coarse blouse, and tam-o'-shanter cap he was wont to see her in. The young woman had come back with several dresses in her arms, and Ashurst eyed her laying them against her own modish figure. There was one whose colour he liked, a dove-grey, but to imagine Megan clothed in it was beyond him. The young woman went away, and brought some more. But on Ashurst there had now come a feeling of paralysis. How choose? She would want a hat too, and shoes, and gloves; and, sup-pose, when he had got them all, they commonised her, as Sunday clothes always commonised village folk! Why should she not travel as she was? Ah? But conspicuousness would matter; this was a serious elopement. And, staring at the young woman, he thought: 'I wonder if she guesses, and thinks me a blackguard?'

"Do you mind putting aside that grey one for me?" he said des-perately at last. "I can't decide now; I'll come in again this after-noon."

The young woman sighed.

"Oh! certainly. It's a very tasteful costume. I don't think you'll get anything that will suit your purpose better."

"I expect not," Ashurst murmured, and went out.

Freed again from the suspicious matter-of-factness of the world, he took a long breath, and went back to visions. In fancy he saw the trustful, pretty creature who was going to join her life to his; saw himself and her stealing forth at night, walking over the moor under the moon, he with his arm round her, and carrying her new garments, till, in some far-off wood, when dawn was coming, she would slip off her old things and put on these, and an early train at a distant station would bear them away on their honeymoon journey, till London swallowed them up, and the dreams of love came true.

"Frank Ashurst! Haven't seen you since Rugby, old chap!"

Ashurst's frown dissolved; the face, close to his own, was blue-eyed, suffused with sun—one of those faces where sun from within and without join in a sort of lustre. And he answered:

"Phil Halliday, by Jove!"

"What are you doing here?"

"Oh! nothing. Just looking round, and getting some money. I'm staying on the moor."

"Are you lunching anywhere? Come and lunch with us; I'm here with my young sisters. They've had measles."

Hooked in by that friendly arm Ashurst went along, up a hill, down a hill, away out of the town, while the voice of Halliday, redolent of optimism as his face was of sun, explained how "in this mouldy place the only decent things were the bathing and boating," and so on, till presently they came to a crescent of houses a little above and back from the sea, and into the centre one—an hotel—made their way.

"Come up to my room and have a wash. Lunch'll be ready in a jiffy."

Ashurst contemplated his visage in a looking-glass. After his farm-house bedroom, the comb and one spare shirt *régime* of the last fortnight, this room littered with clothes and brushes was a sort of Capua; and he thought: 'Queer—one doesn't realise——' But what—he did not quite know.

When he followed Halliday into the sitting-room for lunch, three faces, very fair and blue-eyed, were turned suddenly at the words: "This is Frank Ashurst—my young sisters."

Two were indeed young, about eleven and ten. The third was perhaps seventeen, tall and fair-haired too, with pink-and-white cheeks just touched by the sun, and eyebrows, rather darker than the hair, running a little upwards from her nose to their outer points. The voices of all three were like Halliday's, high and cheerful; they stood up straight, shook hands with a quick movement, looked at Ashurst critically, away again at once, and began to talk of what they were going to do in the afternoon. A regular Diana and attendant nymphs! After the farm this crisp, slangy, eager talk, this cool, clean, off-hand refinement, was queer at first, and then so natural that what he had come from became suddenly remote. The names of the two little ones seemed to be Sabina and Freda; of the eldest, Stella.

Presently the one called Sabina turned to him and said:

"I say, will you come shrimping with us?—it's awful fun!"

Surprised by this unexpected friendliness, Ashurst murmured:

"I'm afraid I've got to get back this afternoon."

"Oh!"

"Can't you put it off?"

Ashurst turned to the new speaker, Stella, shook his head, and smiled. She was very pretty! Sabina said regretfully: "You might!" Then the talk switched off to caves and swimming.

"Can you swim far?"

"About two miles."

"Oh!"

"I say!"

"How jolly!"

The three pairs of blue eyes, fixed on him, made him conscious of his new importance. The sensation was agreeable. Halliday said:

"I say, you simply must stop and have a bathe. You'd better stay the night."

"Yes, do!"

But again Ashurst smiled and shook his head. Then suddenly he found himself being catechised about his physical achievements. He had rowed—it seemed—in his college boat, played in his college football team, won his college mile, and he rose from table a sort of hero. The two little girls insisted that he must see "their" cave, and they set forth chattering like magpies, Ashurst between them, Stella and her brother a little behind. In the cave, damp and darkish like any other cave, the great feature was a pool with possibility of creatures which might be caught and put into bottles. Sabina and Freda, who wore no stockings on their shapely brown legs, exhorted Ashurst to join them in the middle of it, and help sieve the water. He too was soon bootless and sockless. Time goes fast for one who has a sense of beauty, when there are pretty children in a pool and a young Diana on the edge, to receive with wonder anything you can catch! Ashurst never had much sense of time. It was a shock when, pulling out his watch, he saw it was well past three. No cashing his cheque to-day—the bank would be closed before he could get there. Watching his expression, the little girls cried out at once:

"Hurrah! Now you'll have to stay!"

Ashurst did not answer. He was seeing again Megan's face, when at breakfast he had whispered: "I'm going to Torquay, darling, to get everything; I shall be back this evening. If it's fine we can go to-night. Be ready." He was seeing again how she quivered and hung on his words. What would she think? Then he pulled himself together, conscious suddenly of the calm scrutiny of this other young girl, so tall and fair and Diana-like, at the edge of the pool, of her wondering blue eyes under those brows which slanted up a little. If they knew what was in his mind—if they knew that this very night he had meant

----! Well, there would be a little sound of disgust, and he would be alone in the cave. And with a curious mixture of anger, chagrin, and shame, he put his watch back into his pocket and said abruptly:

"Yes; I'm dished for to-day."

"Hurrah! Now you can bathe with us."

It was impossible not to succumb a little to the contentment of these pretty children, to the smile on Stella's lips, to Halliday's "Ripping, old chap! I can lend you things for the night!" But again a spasm of longing and remorse throbbed through Ashurst, and he said moodily:

"I must send a wire!"

The attractions of the pool palling, they went back to the hotel. Ashurst sent his wire, addressing it to Mrs. Narracombe: "Sorry, detained for the night, back to-morrow." Surely Megan would understand that he had too much to do; and his heart grew lighter. It was a lovely afternoon, warm, the sea calm and blue, and swimming his great passion; the favour of these pretty children flattered him, the pleasure of looking at them, at Stella, at Halliday's sunny face; the slight unreality, yet extreme naturalness of it all—as of a last peep at normality before he took this plunge with Megan! He got his borrowed bathing dress, and they all set forth. Halliday and he undressed behind one rock, the three girls behind another. He was first into the sea, and at once swam out with the bravado of justifying his self-given reputation. When he turned he could see Halliday swimming along shore, and the girls flopping and dipping, and riding the little waves, in the way he was accustomed to despise, but now thought pretty and sensible, since it gave him the distinction of the only deep-water fish. But drawing near, he wondered if they would like him, a stranger, to come into their splashing group; he felt shy, approaching that slim nymph. Then Sabina summoned him to teach her to float, and between them the little girls kept him so busy that he had no time even to notice whether Stella was accustomed to his presence, till suddenly he heard a startled sound from her. She was standing submerged to the waist, leaning a little forward, her slim white arms stretched out and pointing, her wet face puckered by the sun and an expression of fear.

"Look at Phil! Is he all right? Oh, look!"

Ashurst saw at once that Phil was not all right. He was splashing and struggling out of his depth, perhaps a hundred yards away; suddenly he gave a cry, threw up his arms, and went down. Ashurst saw the girl launch herself towards him, and crying out: "Go back, Stella! Go back!" he dashed out. He had never swum so fast, and reached Halliday just as he was coming up a second time. It was a case of cramp, but to get him in was not difficult, for he did not struggle. The girl, who had stopped where Ashurst told her to, helped as soon

as he was in his depth, and once on the beach they sat down one on each side of him to rub his limbs, while the little ones stood by with scared faces. Halliday was soon smiling. It was—he said—rotten of him, absolutely rotten! If Frank would give him an arm, he could get to his clothes all right now. Ashurst gave him the arm, and as he did so caught sight of Stella's face, wet and flushed and tearful, all broken up out of its calm; and he thought: 'I called her Stella! Wonder if she minded?'

While they were dressing, Halliday said quietly:

"You saved my life, old chap!"

"Rot!"

Clothed, but not quite in their right minds, they went up all together to the hotel and sat down to tea, except Halliday, who was lying down in his room. After some slices of bread and jam, Sabina said:

"I say, you know, you *are* a brick!" And Freda chimed in:

"Rather!"

Ashurst saw Stella looking down; he got up in confusion, and went to the window. From there he heard Sabina mutter: "I say, let's swear blood bond. Where's your knife, Freda?" and out of the corner of his eye could see each of them solemnly prick herself, squeeze out a drop of blood and dabble on a bit of paper. He turned and made for the door.

"Don't be a stoat! Come back!" His arms were seized; imprisoned between the little girls he was brought back to the table. On it lay a piece of paper with an effigy drawn in blood, and the three names Stella Halliday, Sabina Halliday, Freda Halliday—also in blood, running towards it like the rays of a star. Sabina said:

"That's you. We shall have to kiss you, you know."

And Freda echoed:

"Oh! Blow—Yes!"

Before Ashurst could escape, some wettish hair dangled against his face, something like a bite descended on his nose, he felt his left arm pinched, and other teeth softly searching his cheek. Then he was released, and Freda said:

"Now, Stella."

Ashurst, red and rigid, looked across the table at a red and rigid Stella, Sabina giggled; Freda cried:

"Buck up—it spoils everything!"

A queer, ashamed eagerness shot through Ashurst; then he said quietly:

"Shut up, you little demons!"

Again Sabina giggled.

"Well, then, she can kiss her hand, and you can put it against your nose. It *is* on one side!"

To his amazement the girl did kiss her hand and stretch it out. Solemnly he took that cool, slim hand and laid it to his cheek. The two little girls broke into clapping, and Freda said:

"Now, then, we shall have to save your life at any time; that's settled. Can I have another cup, Stella, not so beastly weak?"

Tea was resumed, and Ashurst, folding up the paper, put it in his pocket. The talk turned on the advantages of measles, tangerine oranges, honey in a spoon, no lessons, and so forth. Ashurst listened, silent, exchanging friendly looks with Stella, whose face was again of its normal sun-touched pink and white. It was soothing to be so taken to the heart of this jolly family, fascinating to watch their faces. And after tea, while the two little girls pressed seaweed, he talked to Stella in the window seat and looked at her water-colour sketches. The whole thing was like a pleasurable dream; time and incident hung up, importance and reality suspended. To-morrow he would go back to Megan, with nothing of all this left save the paper with the blood of these children, in his pocket. Children! Stella was not quite that—as old as Megan! Her talk—quick, rather hard and shy, yet friendly—seemed to flourish on his silences, and about her there was something cool and virginal—a maiden in a bower. At dinner, to which Halliday, who had swallowed too much sea-water, did not come, Sabina said:

"I'm going to call you Frank."

Freda echoed:

"Frank, Frank, Franky."

Ashurst grinned and bowed.

"Every time Stella calls you Mr. Ashurst, she's got to pay a forfeit. It's ridiculous."

Ashurst looked at Stella, who grew slowly red. Sabina giggled; Freda cried:

"She's 'smoking'—'smoking!'—Yah!"

Ashurst reached out to right and left, and grasped some fair hair in each hand.

"Look here," he said, "you two! Leave Stella alone, or I'll tie you together!"

Freda gurgled:

"Ouch! You *are* a beast!"

Sabina murmured cautiously:

"*You* call *her* Stella, you see!"

"Why shouldn't I? It's a jolly name!"

"All right; we give you leave to!"

Ashurst released the hair. Stella! What would she call him—after this? But she called him nothing; till at bedtime he said, deliberately:

"Good-night, Stella!"

"Good-night, Mr.—— Good night, Frank! It *was* jolly of you, you know!"

"Oh—that! Bosh!"

Her quick, straight handshake tightened suddenly, and as suddenly, became slack.

Ashurst stood motionless in the empty sitting-room. Only last night, under the apple-tree and the living blossom, he had held Megan to him, kissing her eyes and lips. And he gasped, swept by that rush of remembrance. To-night it should have begun—his life with her who only wanted to be with him! And now, twenty-four hours and more must pass, because—of not looking at his watch! Why had he made friends with this family of innocents just when he was saying good-bye to innocence, and all the rest of it? 'But I mean to marry her,' he thought; 'I told her so!'

He took a candle, lighted it, and went to his bedroom, which was next to Halliday's. His friend's voice called as he was passing:

"Is that you, old chap? I say, come in."

He was sitting up in bed, smoking a pipe and reading.

"Sit down a bit."

Ashurst sat down by the open window.

"I've been thinking about this afternoon, you know," said Halliday rather suddenly. "They say you go through all your past. I didn't. I suppose I wasn't far enough gone."

"What did you think of?"

Halliday was silent for a little, then said quietly:

"Well, I did think of one thing—rather odd—of a girl at Cambridge that I might have—you know; I was glad I hadn't got her on my mind. Anyhow, old chap, I owe it to you that I'm here; I should have been in the big dark by now. No more bed, or baccy; no more anything. I say, what d'you suppose happens to us?"

Ashurst murmured:

"Go out like flames, I expect."

"Phew!"

"We may flicker, and cling about a bit, perhaps."

"H'm! I think that's rather gloomy. I say, I hope my young sisters have been decent to you?"

"Awfully decent."

Halliday put his pipe down, crossed his hands behind his neck, and turned his face towards the window.

"They're not bad kids!" he said.

Watching his friend, lying there, with that smile, and the candle-light on his face, Ashurst shuddered. Quite true! He might have been lying there with no smile, with all that sunny look gone out for ever! He might not have been lying there at all, but "sanded" at the bottom of the sea, waiting for resurrection on the—ninth day, was it? And that smile of Halliday's seemed to him suddenly something wonderful, as if in it were all the difference between life and death—the little flame—the all! He got up, and said softly:

"Well, you ought to sleep, I expect. Shall I blow out?"

Halliday caught his hand.

"I can't say it, you know; but it must be rotten to be dead. Good-night, old boy!"

Stirred and moved, Ashurst squeezed the hand, and went down-stairs. The hall door was still open, and he passed out on to the lawn before the Crescent. The stars were bright in a very dark blue sky, and by their light some lilacs had that mysterious colour of flowers by night which no one can describe. Ashurst pressed his face against a spray; and before his closed eyes Megan started up, with the tiny brown spaniel pup against her breast. "I thought of a girl that I might have—you know. I was glad I hadn't got her on my mind!" He jerked his head away from the lilac, and began pacing up and down over the grass, a grey phantom coming to substance for a moment in the light from the lamp at either end. He was with her again under the living, breathing whiteness of the blossom, the stream chattering by, the moon glinting steel-blue on the bathing-pool; back in the rapture of his kisses on her upturned face of innocence and humble passion, back in the suspense and beauty of that pagan night. He stood still once more in the shadow of the lilacs. Here the sea, not the stream, was Night's voice; the sea with its sigh and rustle; no little bird, no owl, no nightjar called or spun; but a piano tinkled, and the white houses cut the sky with solid curve, and the scent from the lilacs filled the air. A window of the hotel, high up, was lighted; he saw a shadow move across the blind. And most queer sensations stirred within him, a sort of churning, and twining, and turning of a single emotion on itself, as though spring and love, bewildered and confused, seeking the way, were baffled. This girl, who had called him Frank, whose hand had given his that sudden little clutch, this girl so cool and pure—what would *she* think of such wild, unlawful loving? He sank down on the grass, sitting there cross-legged, with his back to the house, motion-less as some carved Buddha. Was he really going to break through in-nocence, and steal? Sniff the scent out of a wild flower, and—perhaps—throw it away? "Of a girl at Cambridge that I might have—you know!" He put his hands to the grass, one on each side, palms down-

wards, and pressed; it was just warm still—the grass, barely moist, soft and firm and friendly. 'What am I going to do?' he thought. Perhaps Megan was at her window, looking out at the blossom, thinking of him! Poor little Megan! 'Why not?' he thought. 'I love her! But do I —really love her? or do I only want her because she is so pretty, and loves me? What am I going to do?' The piano tinkled on, the stars winked; and Ashurst gazed out before him at the dark sea, as if spell-bound. He got up at last, cramped and rather chilly. There was no longer light in any window. And he went in to bed.

§ 8

Out of a deep and dreamless sleep he was awakened by the sound of thumping on the door. A shrill voice called:

"Hi! Breakfast's ready."

He jumped up. Where was he——? Ah!

He found them already eating marmalade, and sat down in the empty place between Stella and Sabina, who, after watching him a little, said:

"I say, do buck up; we're going to start at half-past nine."

"We're going to Berry Head, old chap; you *must* come!"

Ashurst thought: 'Come! Impossible. I shall be getting things and going back.' He looked at Stella. She said quickly:

"Do come!"

Sabina chimed in:

"It'll be no fun without you."

Freda got up and stood behind his chair.

"You've got to come, or else I'll pull your hair!"

Ashurst thought: 'Well—one day more—to think it over! One day more!' And he said:

"All right! You needn't tweak my mane!"

"Hurrah!"

At the station he wrote a second telegram to the farm, and then—tore it up; he could not have explained why. From Brixham they drove in a very little wagonette. There, squeezed between Sabina and Freda, with his knees touching Stella's, they played "Up Jenkins"; and the gloom he was feeling gave way to frolic. In this one day more to think it over, he did not want to think! They ran races, wrestled, paddled—for to-day nobody wanted to bathe—they sang catches, played games, and ate all they had brought. The little girls fell asleep against him on the way back, and his knees still touched Stella's in the wagonette. It seemed incredible that thirty hours ago he had never set

eyes on any of those three flaxen heads. In the train he talked to Stella of poetry, discovering her favourites, and telling her his own with a pleasing sense of superiority; till suddenly she said, rather low:

"Phil says you don't believe in a future life, Frank. I think that's dreadful."

Disconcerted, Ashurst muttered:

"I don't either believe or not believe—I simply don't know."

She said quickly:

"I couldn't bear that. What would be the use of living?"

Watching the frown of those pretty oblique brows, Ashurst answered:

"I don't believe in believing things because one wants to."

"But why should one *wish* to live again, if one isn't going to?"

And she looked full at him.

He did not want to hurt her, but an itch to dominate pushed him on to say:

"While one's alive one naturally wants to go on living for ever; that's part of being alive. But it probably isn't anything more."

"Don't you believe in the Bible at all, then?"

Ashurst thought: 'Now I shall really hurt her!'

"I believe in the Sermon on the Mount, because it's beautiful and good for all time."

"But don't you believe Christ was divine?"

He shook his head.

She turned her face quickly to the window, and there sprang into his mind Megan's prayer, repeated by little Nick: "God bless us all, and Mr. Ashes!" Who else would ever say a prayer for him, like her who at this moment must be waiting—waiting to see him come down the lane? And he thought suddenly: 'What a scoundrel I am!'

All that evening this thought kept coming back; but, as is not unusual, each time with less poignancy, till it seemed almost a matter of course to be a scoundrel. And—strange!—he did not know whether he was a scoundrel if he meant to go back to Megan, or if he did not mean to go back to her.

They played cards till the children were sent off to bed; then Stella went to the piano. From over on the window seat, where it was nearly dark, Ashurst watched her between the candles—that fair head on the long, white neck bending to the movement of her hands. She played fluently, without much expression; but what a picture she made, the faint golden radiance, a sort of angelic atmosphere—hovering about her! Who could have passionate thoughts or wild desires in the presence of that swaying, white-clothed girl with the seraphic head? She played a thing of Schumann's called *"Warum?"* Then Halliday

brought out a flute, and the spell was broken. After this they made
Ashurst sing, Stella playing him accompaniments from a book of
Schumann songs, till, in the middle of *"Ich grolle nicht,"* two small
figures clad in blue dressing-gowns crept in and tried to conceal them-
selves beneath the piano. The evening broke up in confusion, and
what Sabina salled "a splendid rag."

That night Ashurst hardly slept at all. He was thinking, tossing
and turning. The intense domestic intimacy of these last two days, the
strength of this Halliday atmosphere, seemed to ring him round, and
make the farm and Megan—even Megan—seem unreal. Had he really
made love to her—really promised to take her away to live with him?
He must have been bewitched by the spring, the night, the apple
blossom! The notion that he was going to make her his mistress—
that simple child not yet eighteen—now filled him with a sort of
horror, even while it still stung and whipped his blood. He muttered
to himself: "It's awful, what I've done—awful!" And the sound of
Schumann's music throbbed and mingled with his fevered thoughts,
and he saw again Stella's cool, white, fair-haired figure and bending
neck, the queer, angelic radiance about her. 'I must have been—I
must be—mad!' he thought. 'What came into me? Poor little Megan!'
"God bless us all, and Mr. Ashes!" "I want to be with you—only to be
with you!" And burying his face in his pillow, he smothered down a
fit of sobbing. Not to go back was awful! To go back—more awful
still!

Emotion, when you are young, and give real vent to it, loses its
power of torture. And he fell asleep, thinking: 'What was it—a few
kisses—all forgotten in a month!'

Next morning he got his cheque cashed, but avoided the shop of
the dove-grey dress like the plague; and, instead, bought himself
some necessaries. He spent the whole day in a queer mood, cherishing
a kind of sullenness against himself. Instead of the hankering of the
last two days, he felt nothing but a blank—all passionate longing gone,
as if quenched in that outburst of tears. After tea Stella put a book
down beside him, and said shyly:

"Have you read that, Frank?"

It was Farrar's "Life of Christ." Ashurst smiled. Her anxiety about
his beliefs seemed to him comic, but touching. Infectious, too, perhaps,
for he began to have an itch to justify himself, if not to convert her.
And in the evening, when the children and Halliday were mending
their shrimping nets, he said:

"At the back of orthodox religion, so far as I can see, there's always
the idea of reward—what you can get for being good; a kind of beg-
ging for favours. I think it all starts in fear."

She was sitting on the sofa making reefer knots with a bit of string. She looked up quickly:

"I think it's much deeper than that."

Ashurst felt again that wish to dominate.

"You think so," he said; "but wanting the *'quid pro quo'* is about the deepest thing in all of us! It's jolly hard to get to the bottom of it!"

She wrinkled her brows in a puzzled frown.

"I don't think I understand."

He went on obstinately:

"Well, think, and see if the most religious people aren't those who feel that this life doesn't give them all they want. I believe in being good because to be good is good in itself."

"Then you do believe in being good?"

How pretty she looked now—it was easy to be good with her! And he nodded and said:

"I say, show me how to make that knot!"

With her fingers touching his, in manœuvring the bit of string he felt soothed and happy. And when he went to bed he wilfully kept his thoughts on her, wrapping himself in her fair, cool sisterly radiance, as in some garment of protection.

Next day he found they had arranged to go by train to Totnes, and picnic at Berry Pomeroy Castle. Still in that resolute oblivion of the past, he took his place with them in the landau beside Halliday, back to the horses. And, then, along the sea front, nearly at the turning to the railway station, his heart almost leaped into his mouth. Megan— Megan herself!—was walking on the far pathway, in her old skirt and jacket and her tam-o'-shanter, looking up into the faces of the passers-by. Instinctively he threw his hand up for cover, then made a feint of clearing dust out of his eyes; but between his fingers he could see her still, moving, not with her free country step, but wavering, lost-looking, pitiful—like some little dog which has missed its master and does not know whether to run on, to run back—where to run. How had she come like this?—what excuse had she found to get away? —what did she hope for? But with every turn of the wheels bearing him away from her, his heart revolted and cried to him to stop them, to get out, and go to her! When the landau turned the corner to the station he could stand it no more, and opening the carriage door, muttered: "I've forgotten something! Go on—don't wait for me! I'll join you at the castle by the next train!" He jumped, stumbled, spun round, recovered his balance, and walked forward, while the carriage with the astonished Hallidays rolled on.

From the corner he could only just see Megan, a long way ahead now. He ran a few steps, checked himself, and dropped into a walk. With

each step nearer to her, further from the Hallidays, he walked more and more slowly. How did it alter anything—this sight of her? How make the going to her, and that which must come of it, less ugly? For there was no hiding it—since he had met the Hallidays he had become gradually sure that he would not marry Megan. It would only be a wild love-time, a troubled, remorseful, difficult time—and then—well, then he would get tired, just because she gave him everything, was so simple, and so trustful, so dewy. And dew—wears off! The little spot of faded colour, her tam-o'-shanter cap, wavered on far in front of him; she was looking up into every face, and at the house windows. Had any man ever such a cruel moment to go through? Whatever he did, he felt he would be a beast. And he uttered a groan which made a nursemaid turn and stare. He saw Megan stop and lean against the sea-wall, looking at the sea; and he too stopped. Quite likely she had never seen the sea before, and even in her distress could not resist that sight. 'Yes—she's seen nothing,' he thought; 'everything's before her. And just for a few weeks' passion, I shall be cutting her life to ribbons. I'd better go and hang myself rather than do it!' And suddenly he seemed to see Stella's calm eyes looking into his, the wave of fluffy hair on her forehead stirred by the wind. Ah! it would be madness, would mean giving up all that he respected, and his own self-respect. He turned and walked quickly back towards the station. But memory of that poor, bewildered little figure, those anxious eyes searching the passers-by, smote him too hard again, and once more he turned towards the sea. The cap was no longer visible; that little spot of colour had vanished in the stream of the noon promenaders. And impelled by the passion of longing, the dearth which comes on one when life seems to be whiling something out of reach, he hurried forward. She was nowhere to be seen; for half an hour he looked for her; then on the beach flung himself face downward in the sand. To find her again he knew he had only to go to the station and wait till she returned from her fruitless quest, to take her train home; or to take train himself and go back to the farm, so that she found him there when she returned. But he lay inert in the sand, among the indifferent groups of children with their spades and buckets. Pity at her little figure wandering, seeking, was well-nigh merged in the spring-running of his blood; for it was all wild feeling now—the chivalrous part, what there had been of it, was gone. He wanted her again, wanted her kisses, her soft, little body, her abandonment, all her quick, warm, pagan emotion; wanted the wonderful feeling of that night under the moon-lit apple boughs; wanted it all with a horrible intensity, as the faun wants the nymph. The quick chatter of the little bright trout-stream, the dazzle of the buttercups, the rocks of the old

"wild men"; the calling of the cuckoos and yaffles, the hooting of the owls; and the red moon peeping out of the velvet dark at the living whiteness of the blossom; and her face just out of reach at the window, lost in its love-look; and her heart against his, her lips answering his, under the apple-tree—all this besieged him. Yet he lay inert. What was it which struggled against pity and this feverish longing, and kept him there paralysed in the warm sand? Three flaxen heads—a fair face with friendly blue-grey eyes, a slim hand pressing his, a quick voice speaking his name—"So you do believe in being good?" Yes, and a sort of atmosphere as of some old walled-in English garden, with pinks, and cornflowers, and roses, and scents of lavender and lilac— cool and fair, untouched, almost holy—all that he had been brought up to feel was clean and good. And suddenly he thought: 'She might come along the front again and see me!' and he got up and made his way to the rock at the far end of the beach. There, with the spray biting into his face, he could think more coolly. To go back to the farm and love Megan out in the woods, among the rocks, with everything around wild and fitting—that, he knew, was impossible, utterly. To transplant her to a great town, to keep, in some little flat or rooms, one who belonged so wholly to Nature—the poet in him shrank from it. His passion would be a mere sensuous revel, soon gone; in London, her very simplicity, her lack of all intellectual quality, would make her his secret plaything—nothing else. The longer he sat on the rock, with his feet dangling over a greenish pool from which the sea was ebbing, the more clearly he saw this; but it was as if her arms and all of her were slipping slowly, slowly down from him, into the pool, to be carried away out to sea; and her face looking up, her lost face with beseeching eyes, and dark, wet hair—possessed, haunted, tortured him! He got up at last, scaled the low rock-cliff, and made his way down into a sheltered cove. Perhaps in the sea he could get back his control—lose this fever! And stripping off his clothes, he swam out. He wanted to tire himself so that nothing mattered, and swam recklessly, fast and far; then suddenly, for no reason, felt afraid. Suppose he could not reach shore again—suppose the current set him out—or he got cramp, like Halliday! He turned to swim in. The red cliffs looked a long way off. If he were drowned they would find his clothes. The Hallidays would know; but Megan perhaps never—they took no newspaper at the farm. And Phil Halliday's words came back to him again: "A girl at Cambridge I might have—— Glad I haven't got her on my mind!" And in that moment of unreasoning fear he vowed he would not have her on his mind. Then his fear left him; he swam in easily enough, dried himself in the sun, and put on his clothes. His heart felt sore, but no longer ached; his body cool and refreshed.

When one is as young as Ashurst, pity is not a violent emotion. And, back in the Hallidays' sitting-room, eating a ravenous tea, he felt much like a man recovered from fever. Everything seemed new and clear; the tea, the buttered toast, and jam tasted absurdly good; tobacco had never smelt so nice. And walking up and down the empty room, he stopped here and there to touch or look. He took up Stella's work-basket, fingered the cotton reels and a gaily-coloured plait of sewing silks, smelt at the little bag filled with wood-roffe she kept among them. He sat down at the piano, playing tunes with one finger, thinking: 'To-night she'll play; I shall watch her while she's playing; it does me good to watch her.' He took up the book, which still lay where she had placed it beside him, and tried to read. But Megan's little, sad figure began to come back at once, and he got up and leaned in the window, listening to the thrushes in the Crescent gardens, gazing at the sea, dreamy and blue below the trees. A servant came in and cleared the tea away, and he still stood, inhaling the evening air, trying not to think. Then he saw the Hallidays coming through the gate of the Crescent, Stella a little in front of Phil and the children, with their baskets, and instinctively he drew back. His heart, too sore and discomfited, shrank from this encounter, yet wanted its friendly solace—bore a grudge against this influence, yet craved its cool inno-cence, and the pleasure of watching Stella's face. From against the wall behind the piano he saw her come in and stand looking a little blank as though disappointed; then she saw him and smiled, a swift, brilliant smile which warmed yet irritated Ashurst.

"You never came after us, Frank."

"No; I found I couldn't."

"Look! We picked such lovely late violets!" She held out a bunch. Ashurst put his nose to them, and there stirred within him vague longings, chilled instantly by a vision of Megan's anxious face lifted to the faces of the passers-by.

He said shortly: "How jolly!" and turned away. He went up to his room, and, avoiding the children, who were coming up the stairs, threw himself on his bed, and lay there with his arms crossed over his face. Now that he felt the die really cast, and Megan given up, he hated himself, and almost hated the Hallidays and their atmosphere of healthy, happy English homes. Why should they have chanced here, to drive away first love—to show him that he was going to be no better than a common seducer? What right had Stella, with her fair, shy beauty, to make him know for certain that he would never marry Megan; and, tarnishing it all, bring him such bitterness of regretful longing and such pity? Megan would be back by now, worn out by her miserable seeking—poor little thing!—expecting, perhaps, to find

him there when she reached home. Ashurst bit at his sleeve, to stifle
a groan of remorseful longing. He went to dinner glum and silent,
and his mood threw a dinge even over the children. It was a melan-
choly, rather ill-tempered evening, for they were all tired; several
times he caught Stella looking at him with a hurt, puzzled expression,
and this pleased his evil mood. He slept miserably; got up quite early,
and wandered out. He went down to the beach. Alone there with the
serene, the blue, the sunlit sea, his heart relaxed a little. Conceited fool
—to think that Megan would take it so hard! In a week or two she
would almost have forgotten! And he—well, he would have the reward
of virtue! A good young man! If Stella knew, she would give him her
blessing for resisting that devil she believed in; and he uttered a hard
laugh. But slowly the peace and beauty of sea and sky, the flight of the
lonely seagulls, made him feel ashamed. He bathed, and turned home-
wards.

In the Crescent gardens Stella herself was sitting on a camp stool,
sketching. He stole up close behind. How fair and pretty she was, bent
diligently, holding up her brush, measuring, wrinkling her brows.

He said gently:

"Sorry I was such a beast last night, Stella."

She turned round, startled, flushed very pink, and said in her quick
way:

"It's all right. I knew there was something. Between friends it
doesn't matter, does it?"

Ashurst answered:

"Between friends—and we are, aren't we?"

She looked up at him, nodded vehemently, and her upper teeth
gleamed again in that swift, brilliant smile.

Three days later he went back to London, travelling with the Halli-
days. He had not written to the farm. What was there he could say?

On the last day of April in the following year he and Stella were
married. . . .

Such were Ashurst's memories, sitting against the wall among the
gorse, on his silver-wedding day. At this very spot, where he had laid
out the lunch, Megan must have stood outlined against the sky when
he had first caught sight of her. Of all queer coincidences! And there
moved in him a longing to go down and see again the farm and the
orchard, and the meadow of the gipsy bogle. It would not take long;
Stella would be an hour yet, perhaps.

How well he remembered it all—the little crowning group of pine
trees, the steep-up grass hill behind! He paused at the farm gate. The
low stone house, the yew-tree porch, the flowering currants—not

changed a bit; even the old green chair was out there on the grass
under the window, where he had reached up to her that night to take
the key. Then he turned down the lane, and stood leaning on the or-
chard gate—grey skeleton of a gate, as then. A black pig even was
wandering in there among the trees. Was it true that twenty-six years
had passed, or had he dreamed and awakened to find Megan waiting
for him by the big apple-tree? Unconsciously he put up his hand to
his grizzled beard and brought himself back to reality. Opening the
gate, he made his way down through the docks and nettles till he
came to the edge, and the old apple-tree itself. Unchanged! A little
more of the grey-green lichen, a dead branch or two, and for the
rest it might have been only last night that he had embraced that
mossy trunk after Megan's flight and inhaled its woody savour, while
above his head the moonlit blossom had seemed to breathe and live.
In that early spring a few buds were showing already; the blackbirds
shouting their songs, a cuckoo calling, the sunlight bright and warm.
Incredibly the same—the chattering trout-stream, the narrow pool he
had lain in every morning, splashing the water over his flanks and
chest; and out there in the wild meadow the beech clump and the
stone where the gipsy bogle was supposed to sit. And an ache for lost
youth, a hankering, a sense of wasted love and sweetness, gripped
Ashurst by the throat. Surely, on this earth of such wild beauty, one
was meant to hold rapture to one's heart, as this earth and sky held
it! And yet, one could not!

He went to the edge of the stream, and, looking down at the little
pool, thought: 'Youth and spring! What has become of them all, I
wonder?' And then, in sudden fear of having this memory jarred by
human encounter, he went back to the lane, and pensively retraced his
steps to the cross-roads.

Beside the car an old, grey-bearded labourer was leaning on a stick,
talking to the chauffeur. He broke off at once, as though guilty of
disrespect, and, touching his hat, prepared to limp on down the lane.

Ashurst pointed to the narrow green mound. "Can you tell me what
this is?"

The old fellow stopped; on his face had come a look as though he
were thinking: 'You've come to the right shop, mister!'

" 'Tes a grave," he said.

"But why out here?"

The old man smiled. "That's a tale, as yu may say. An' not the first
time as I've a-told et—there's plenty folks asks 'bout that bit o' turf.
'Maid's Grave' us calls et, 'ereabouts."

Ashurst held out his pouch. "Have a fill?"

The old man touched his hat again, and slowly filled an old clay

pipe. His eyes, looking upward out of a mass of wrinkles and hair, were still quite bright.

"If yu don' mind, zurr, I'll zet down—my leg's 'urtin' a bit to-day." And he sat down on the mound of turf.

"There's always a vlower on this grave. An' 'tain't so very lonesome, neither; brave lot o' folks goes by now, in they new motor cars an' things—not as 'twas in th' old days. She've a-got company up 'ere. 'Twas a poor soul killed 'erself."

"I see!" said Ashurst. "Cross-roads burial. I didn't know that custom was kept up."

"Ah! but 'twas a main long time ago. Us 'ad a parson as was very God-fearin' then. Let me see, I've 'ad my pension six year come Michaelmas, an' I were just on fifty when 't 'appened. There's none livin' knows more about et than what I du. She belonged close 'ere; same farm as where I used to work along o' Mrs. Narracombe—'tes Nick Narracombe's now; I dus a bit for 'im still, odd times."

Ashurst, who was leaning against the gate, lighting his pipe, left his curved hands before his face for long after the flame of the match had gone out.

"Yes?" he said, and to himself his voice sounded hoarse and queer.

"She was one in an 'underd, poor maid! I putts a vlower 'ere every time I passes. Pretty maid an' gude maid she was, though they wouldn't burry 'er up tu th' church, nor where she wanted to be burried neither." The old labourer paused, and put his hairy, twisted hand flat down on the turf beside the bluebells.

"Yes?" said Ashurst.

"In a manner of speakin'," the old man went on, "I think as 'twas a love-story—though there's no one never knu for zartin. Yu can't tell what's in a maid's 'ead—but that's wot I think about it." He drew his hand along the turf. "I was fond o' that maid—don' know as there was anyone as wasn' fond of 'er. But she was tu lovin'-'earted—that's where 'twas, I think." He looked up. And Ashurst, whose lips were trembling in the cover of his beard, murmured again: "Yes?"

"'Twas in the spring, 'bout now as 't might be, or a little later—blossom time—an' we 'ad one o' they young college gentlemen stayin' at the farm—nice feller tu, with 'is 'ead in the air. I liked 'e very well, an' I never see nothin' between 'em, but to my thinkin' 'e turned the maid's fancy." The old man took the pipe out of his mouth, spat, and went on:

"Yu see, 'e went away sudden one day, an' never come back. They got 'is knapsack and bits o' things down there still. That's what stuck in my mind—'is never sendin' for 'em. 'Is name was Ashes, or somethin' like that."

"Yes?" said Ashurst once more.

The old man licked his lips.

" 'Er never said nothin', but from that day 'er went kind of dazed lukin'; didn' seem rightly therr at all. I never knu a 'uman creature so changed in me life—never. There was another young feller at the farm—Joe Biddaford 'is name wer', that was praaperly sweet on 'er, tu; I guess 'e used to plague 'er wi' 'is attentions. She got to luke quite wild. I'd zee her sometimes of an avenin' when I was bringin' up the calves; ther' she'd stand in th' orchard, under the big apple-tree, lukin' straight before 'er. 'Well,' I used t' think, 'I dunno what 'tes that's the matter wi' yu, but yu'm lukin' pittiful, that yu be!' "

The old man relit his pipe, and sucked at it reflectively.

"Yes?" said Ashurst.

"I remembers one day I said to 'er: 'What's the matter, Megan?'— 'er name was Megan David, she come from Wales same as 'er aunt, ol' Missis Narracombe. 'Yu'm frettin' about something,' I says. 'No, Jim,' she says, 'I'm not frettin'.' 'Yes, yu be!' I says. 'No,' she says, and tu tears cam' rollin' out. 'Yu'm cryin'—what's that, then?' I says. She putts 'er 'and over 'er 'eart: 'It 'urts me,' she says; 'but 'twill sune be better,' she says. 'But if anything shude 'appen to me, Jim, I wants to be burried under this 'ere apple-tree.' I laughed. 'What's goin' to 'appen to yu?' I says: 'don't 'ee be fulish.' 'No,' she says, 'I won't be fulish.' Well, I know what maids are, an' I never thought no more about et, till tu days arter that, 'bout six in the avenin' I was comin' up wi' the calves, when I see somethin' dark lyin' in the strame, close to that big apple-tree. I says to meself: 'Is that a pig—funny place for a pig to get to!' an' I goes up to et, an' I see what 'twas."

The old man stopped: his eyes, turned upward, had a bright, suffering look.

" 'Twas the maid, in a little narrer pool ther' that's made by the stoppin' of a rock—where I see the young gentleman bathin' once or twice. 'Er was lyin' on 'er face in the watter. There was a plant o' goldie-cups growin' out o' the stone just above 'er 'ead. An' when I come to luke at 'er face, 'twas luvly, butiful, so calm's a baby's— wonderful butiful et was. When the doctor saw 'er, 'e said: ' 'Er culdn' never a-done it in that little bit o' watter ef 'er 'adn't a-been in an extarsy.' Ah! an' judgin' from 'er face, that was just 'ow she was. Et made me cry praaper—butiful et was! 'Twas June then, but she'd a-found a little bit of apple blossom left over somewheres, and stuck et in 'er 'air. That's why I thinks 'er must a-been in an extarsy, to go to et gay, like that. Why! there wasn't more than a fute and 'arf o' watter. But I tell 'ee one thing—that meadder's 'arnted; I knu et, an' she knu et; an' no one'll persuade me as 'tesn't. I told 'em what

she said to me 'bout bein' burried under th' apple-tree. But I think that turned 'em—made et luke tu much 's ef she'd 'ad it in 'er mind deliberate; an' so they burried 'er up 'ere. Parson we 'ad then was very particular, 'e was."

Again the old man drew his hand over the turf.

" 'Tes wonderful, et seems," he added slowly, "what maids 'll du for love. She 'ad a lovin' 'eart; I guess 'twas broken. But us never *knu* nothin'!"

He looked up as if for approval of his story, but Ashurst had walked past him as if he were not there.

Up on the top of the hill, beyond where he had spread the lunch, over, out of sight, he lay down on his face. So had his virtue been rewarded, and "the Cyprian," goddess of love, taken her revenge! And before his eyes, dim with tears, came Megan's face with the sprig of apple blossoms in her dark, wet hair. 'What did I do that was wrong?' he thought. 'What did I do?' But he could not answer. Spring, with its rush of passion, its flowers and song—the spring in his heart and Megan's! Was it just Love seeking a victim! The Greek was right, then—the words of the "Hippolytus" as true to-day!

> *"For mad is the heart of Love,*
> *And gold the gleam of his wing;*
> *And all to the spell thereof*
> *Bend when he makes his spring.*
> *All life that is wild and young*
> *In mountain and wave and stream,*
> *All that of earth is sprung,*
> *Or breathes in the red sunbeam;*
> *Yea, and Mankind. O'er all a royal throne*
> *Cyprian, Cyprian, is thine alone!"*

The Greek was right! Megan! Poor little Megan—coming over the hill! Megan under the old apple-tree waiting and looking! Megan dead, with beauty printed on her! . . .

A voice said:

"Oh, there you are! Look."

Ashurst rose, took his wife's sketch, and stared at it in silence.

"Is the foreground right, Frank?"

"Yes."

"But there's something wanting, isn't there?"

Ashurst nodded. Wanting? The apple-tree, the singing, and the gold!

The Trader's Wife

JEAN KENYON MACKENZIE

She that dwells
Ten leagues beyond man's life; she
that from Naples
Can have no note, unless the sun were post.
THE TEMPEST

JEAN KENYON MACKENZIE *was born in Elgin, Ill., on January 6, 1874. She studied at the University of California and then in Paris. Thereafter she was sent by the Presbyterian Church as a missionary to the German colony of Kamerun on the west coast of Africa. The author of six books about Africa and the life there, Miss MacKenzie's last book and her only novel is* The Trader's Wife, *published in 1930. It measures 21,500 words.*

INTRODUCTION

The Trader's Wife, which I hope will come as a surprise to many readers, is first and foremost a narrative of vivid action in few words. The story begins in Newport, R. I., at a time shortly before the Civil War, when the air is apprehensive with the threat of abolition. The author, Miss Jean Kenyon MacKenzie, is swift to concentrate our attention upon Mr Harford, a brusque, powerful figure, tanned from years at sea and in the tropics. He was once an officer in the United States navy, then a slave trader; now in his forty-seventh year he has earned himself a small fortune and a better reputation by importing ivory and ebony from the African coast. Certainly he seemed a fair catch to Lucy Williams, an eager, pretty woman with some local reputation for her poetry and her stories, whose poverty touched Mr Harford before he knew he was in love. They have been married ten days when the novel begins, and we see them first as they are dressing for dinner and arguing—arguing over Harford's warning that his wife must not accompany him on his trip to Africa. But nothing he can say will dissuade Lucy from her romantic determination to share his exile. Then by one of those swift transitions in which the author is so expert, you watch the couple at the dinner party itself, where the sight of the negro maid reawakens in Harford his African experience. His urbanity is lost, and when he responds to a toast the most he can do is to disclaim the romance of the west coast and to express the hope that his wife will "have the courage and good sense to bear her lot in a dull and monotonous round."

So the story begins, swiftly and with a brief foreboding which captures our attention within a thousand words. I have said that in a short novel the author must be explicit in the use of his clues. In *The Trader's Wife* the clues are evident from the start and very skillfully

they excite your imagination. Africa has a hold upon Harford far stronger than he suspects. You wonder whether Lucy will be able to cope with it. You wonder how much of Harford's desire to keep his wife from Africa proceeds from jealousy and how much of it proceeds from the natural wish to keep her away from the contamination of the slave trade. You know that once Lucy has gone aboard ship in her kid boots and her hoops (the natives were to call them her "cage of reeds") she is destined for an experience which will be the crucial test of her marriage.

Had Lucy been a sea captain's daughter, she might have had less eagerness for Africa. To Harford, who had known it for fifteen years, the coast held a fascination and a repulsion which he could hardly put into words. As the *Arrow* bears them closer to the equator you, the stay-at-home, begin to feel the change that awaits anyone of white blood in Africa. You feel it in the talk at the captain's table. You feel it as Atemba, the castaway slave, is rescued from the sea—and presented to Lucy. You feel it when they anchor at Glass and the Mpongwe girls come aboard and, to the captain's consternation, cluster about Lucy. You feel it in the words which Taylor, the slave trader, whispers to his old friend, Harford—"You damn fool, to bring a lady to this hole!"

The author of *The Trader's Wife* lived for years in Africa as a missionary. She has the woman's gift of seizing upon the most telling details. Her sentences make you see the ooze which gives off the odor of Africa, feel "the great heat which would press upon the canoers," hear the "furious contention of the parrots" in the trees. Not only do her descriptions ring true—what is more, they have in them a narrative movement which keeps the story ever advancing. Watch Lucy's approach to Mr Taylor's house in which she is to spend her first night ashore. "She accepted the poverty of that poor shelter as exceptional—she did not know that there was no better shelter within a month's journey. She did not see a woman's dress hanging on the rude plank wall of Taylor's bedroom and she did not miss that dress when it was whisked away by a stricken Taylor. She sat at table on Taylor's veranda without thought of its fine red-and-white-checked cloth; spreading her wide white skirts, she leaned on her hand and looked out to sea where three vessels hung their lights against the dusk—and she had no knowledge of the ageless intervals when there was no ship there to prick the evening with her lights." There, in that single paragraph, is packed half the story of Taylor's life, his desperation, his loneliness. The tragedy is that Lucy is so unaware.

Lucy's whole life in Africa was a matter of less than a year. You must determine for yourself whether the outcome of that year was

inevitable. If there were mistakes, who made them? Lucy, in her eagerness to see the brave, new world? Harford, who might easily have moved his "factory" beyond reach of the barracoon? You must be the judge. *The Trader's Wife* does what all fine stories should do. It projects your thoughts far beyond the printed word; it makes you participate with Harford and Lucy, a fellow traveler in one of their ten canoes as the Fang rowers drove them far up the river, through the heat, the mist and the moonlight, with the song rising. . . .

BOOK I

The Bride

§ 1

HARFORD WATCHED his wife pack her clothes. It was a strange thing, he thought, that he could not modify her industry. All her savings, the fruit of that life of drudgery from which their marriage had withdrawn her, were transmuted into furbelows that were tossed about the room. An open box received her bodice of green velvet, a lemon-colored dolman with fringe, a padded jacket—he fidgeted and gazed moodily at the padded jacket, remembering the West Coast. He sighed with a memory too heavy of its heavy air. He wished he could prepare his wife for Africa; he roused himself to try again, but she walked away from him into the dimmer end of the long room, to tauten the square end of her Paisley shawl, one end of which he found himself, incredibly, to be holding. Her white arms were busy with the many-colored fabric, folding it with large gestures, intent on bringing it into small compass. She had no inner ear for his warning.

"I understand, Mr. Harford, it will be warm. But a lady must maintain her common state; those about her must be done the honor of an effort to please."

"Those about her!" said Harford. "Who and where are they? I tell you, Lucy, there are not to be five white men in ten days' journey— no, nor in a month of journeying." But he checked himself; he was not a man to persist in futile effort, and his wife's eyes, wide at gaze, were empty of apprehension. She would dress, she said, for the five.

He suddenly wished that she were a sea captain's daughter—there were many of these in the town of Newport. Surely a captain's daughter would entertain some faint misgiving as to the isolations and miseries of the wilderness. And might—the idea visited him—be induced to stay at home. And would be, perhaps, likely enough, less romantic. He sighed. His animosities toward her passionate vanities died down, and in the ebb of these there emerged a fundamental misgiving of the circumstance. How came he to have married her? Not for her beauty —though she was good-looking, he thought, dwelling on her now in

her vivid animations, white-armed among the velvets and silks of her novel and cherished wardrobe. A fine figure of a woman, pressing out into her future like a ship's head, the figure-head on the *Abundance,* that ship on which he had last served his country—like that, with her skirts surging behind her activities like the garments of that eternally wind-blown eager image. Eager, that was the word—how came he to have married an eager woman? And the vast lassitudes of his African experience flowed in upon him. He drowned in that tide.

An hour from then he must dress in the room that was his and Lucy's. He was forty-six years old and had not, until his marriage, occupied a common room. He would not, he thought, in Africa; there, he thought, he would take this matter in hand. "Before we settle down we will settle that"—and he found himself remembering the bark cabin he had built himself on his last tour, silent in its forest clearing halfway round the world, empty of any civilized convenience; and a good thing, too, he told himself, looking about at the clutter of their quarters. His wife at the dressing table drew out the long sweep of her hair—white arms and black hair, the daffodil blossoms of the candles, and a golden light on her breast. He saw that her gesture was noble. Their eyes meeting in the mirror, hers fastened upon this appreciation, and, turning about, she offered her lips with a smiling assurance. Her innocent abandonment moved him; he proceeded in a lighter mood.

The weather was cold; he felt the comfort of the buffalo robe that covered them in the sleigh, and, with his faculties of perception sharpened by his African exile, he appreciated the glowing lights of the house into which they came, shedding their snow at the door. Warmth and warm lights gushed out upon them; they saw the stir of women with sleek hair, their dresses full about them like flowers. His misgiving that he was to suffer the untellable miseries of ennui fell away from his heart; he would be, he promised himself, the ten-day bridegroom that he was, and more truly his wife's husband, taking thought of her pride and the value she put upon her conquest, which she had no art to cover. He swore he would not dwell on this to-night, and forced his attention from her frank display and her dovelike preenings.

He answered with the necessary civility the habitual questions about the West Coast, its climate, its comforts and provender, its peoples; and he watched with his habitual bitterness the uncomprehending laughter at things not humorous and the tentative returns to the aspect of the Negro and his nudity. A black maid was in waiting; she wore a gown of linsey over hoops; she paused in midstream to dwell upon his sayings, something haunted in her eyes. He thought, "There is a fine girl," and he saw her packed in the middle tray of a slaver,

brought out to the air at sunrise and at sunset, sluiced down with water daily, and shivering in the advancing cold of the voyage. He felt the irony of her skirt and hoop; his civilized and determined urbanity was on the ebb, and when he had to answer the toast to his marriage, with its larded phrases of romantic anticipation, its allusions to his wife's reputation as a poetess,—a tenth Muse, and now to be the Muse of travel,—he rose to his feet a rebel, disclaiming the romantic aspects of their future and hoping tersely that his wife would have the courage and the good sense to bear her lot in a dull and monotonous round.

Poetry would never help her to do that, and if she felt herself irrevocably dedicated to the romantic she had best, he said, stay at home among her admirers, while he went abroad about his business. And he sat down, pleased neither with himself—knowing well the degree of his self-indulgence—nor with the company, who were past rallying. Lucy, who was pale, fixed him with a stricken eye, and he looked away from her to meet the gaze of the Negress, wide and fascinated. The glance he gave her was a blow and the very movement of his irritation. She vanished; and so, if he could have had his will, would have vanished the dinner company. But no, they were reviving, and soon he must agree with them that the antislavery activities of Mr. Garrison were unseemly and that the institution of slavery was holy, forecast in the Bible. To his own mind Mr. Garrison had been negligible, an idealist. He had neither read his speeches nor leaned to his reputed opinions, but he felt a present unsuspected repulsion and a bitter negation of these people, so remote from blood and stench. They were telling, without imagination, of the ladies of Boston who had been but recently stoned for their antislavery pretensions.

§ 2

Later he begged Lucy to stay at home. "You haven't an idea of what it is like," he told her; "it is dreary—unspeakably; the surf is a wall, and the forest is another, about an empty room." And while he spoke to her of this, African solitudes possessed his heart like an enchantment. But they were not for her, he was sure. As for slavery and slaving —he could not think either she or her friends would survive the scent of a slave ship, let alone the sight of one or the sound. Lucy, looking at him, was startled out of her mood of self-pity. "It is no more than my duty," she told him.

Lucy's duty, which he had married with Lucy, was to be, he began to feel, a governing factor in his life. He wondered how much of his panic and rebellion was due to bile—the West Coast life, as he well

knew, was a thing of bile and spleen; but Lucy was not to be told when he had a chill, else her duty to nurse him would be more than he could bear.

To church on Sunday, as Lucy's duty, the two of them went, admirable in aspect, as was much observed. A stranger in the pulpit was preaching an abolition sermon—a zealous soul all tortured with his zeal. "This very day," he told them, "while you sit at ease in Zion, a free people in a free country, there are wretched blacks at sea, packed in trays like dried fish, stinking like fish, some of them to die before the sun has set and to be cast into the sea. Who are the murderers of these?"

"The abolitionists do so much exaggerate," Lucy told him on the way home. "They could not exaggerate," he said; and at that she wondered, not knowing how he could speak so, whose business had once been, in his youth, the Trade. She would have questioned him, but his grim look checked her.

"My husband is a stern man," she told her friends, "but not with me"; and she contrived for their benefit a melting Harford, tender and yielding. She had really at first supposed this to be true—else why had he married her? She had only to remember the speed of their courtship to be reassured, even now, that he was tender and yielding. They were not three weeks met when they were married. Lucy and her friends thought this romantic. They had met in Captain Shaw's house at a dinner. Lucy, in white with blue ribbons, had been that gay creature whose sorrows are hidden—all her friends knew this of her, and presently one of them told Harford:—

"There is the pluckiest, the most brilliant girl in the city of Newport. To see her, you would never know that it is her fate to be a drudge. She is a drudge, sir—an orphan; nothing but her own courage and industry lies between her and want." It was told him further that she was much desired as a reader, and that her poetry, written in her rare leisure, was impassioned, noble, and uplifting.

That she was a pretty woman Harford had observed; but her local fame did not hang, it seemed, upon that. Indeed, her local fame was kept bright by her female friends; her schoolmates, grown up and married, assiduously told their husbands how superior a person Lucy Williams was, and the reports passed on to Harford were verbatim. Harford, meeting her, had them by heart, and in a conversation prematurely intimate he had from herself the sad story of her life. All her gayety omitted, she discovered to him her long struggle, her hours of labor late and early, and her present favorable reputation. Harford had, it seemed, read a long tale of hers in verse; he had thought it fine, and told her so. Tears filled her gray eyes; they brimmed

on her curled lashes, and Harford was moved. The evoked image was clear, and it was quite true of him, as Lucy supposed, that he was vulnerable.

But the chink in the armor, if indeed it was over the heart, was not to be pierced by passion. Harford was compassionate to poverty; he knew her to be poor. Newly come from the isolations of Africa, he was more susceptible than was his habit to the appeal of a pretty woman. He was pursued, and he did not shy away. As for Lucy, she knew herself to be incapable of the indelicacies of a pursuit. She was not, she hoped, a woman to love a man unasked—there was that in him, she told her friends, that broke down her reserve. It cannot truly be said that Harford married her from an impulse of pity and in cold blood; it was one of those unions that are fortuitous—the fruit of a favorable season. It is quite certain that if Harford had been married before he would not have married again.

They sailed upon the *Arrow*. Captain Rogers was in measure a partner in Harford's trading venture, had known him for years, and had shipped more than one cargo for him before the slave trade had ceased to be, for Harford, a legitimate business. The captain had brought the trader to Newport, from which a line of goods was to be had of the sort that was replacing, for a growing demand, the slaver's cargo. Rogers had Harford's little fortune in the hold of the *Arrow;* the beads and calicoes and ironware—above all, the rum—were there. Harford would be trading for ivory, ebony, and palm oil. He had a theoretical passion for his venture; it was the fruit of a slow-grown conviction that the commercial future of Africa was dawning with the decline of the slave trade. He brought to his business a perfected technique of contact with the primitive African, and he felt himself to touch upon the time when his many projects, not realizable in the slave trade, would justify themselves. His designs pressed the more upon his attention because there was none with whom he might share them—not the captain, and certainly not his wife.

Captain Rogers had known Lucy Williams all her life, and for him her presence on his ship was a madness. He could not reconcile it with anything he knew either of the West Coast, which in itself he despised, or of Harford, whom he admired. He gave it up once at least every day. Lucy came aboard drowned in tears—and well, he thought, she did to cry. He gave her the best of his cabins, save his own. Vaguely he hoped, and he strangely expected, that she would be seasick the better part of the voyage. He had been sixty days at sea on his last return. He was unprepared for her appearance on deck the third day out and on the next day for her appearance at mess with her assembled airs and graces.

Lucy, pale but affable, put him ill at ease in his own saloon. It annoyed him to put his pipe aside when she entered there. It annoyed him to see his chief mate's head sleeked with pomade and to smell it. It fretted him to find her at his elbow when at midday he took his reckonings, and he dreaded her questioning about the ship's run and the morrow's weather and about his personal adventures—in particular, about the slave trade. It was not in his experience to discuss the slave trade except as a business. He was not ashamed of it; he considered that his equipment was of the best and that his methods were as good as might be. He had never thrown a cargo into the sea—he recounted this to his credit, and he told Lucy of the time when he had with his own hands, after the death of his surgeon, dressed the more deadly sores of his poor wretches. But he found a strange complacency in this young lady who was reconciled to the noted miseries of the middle passage. He supposed that she could hardly know the truth of them, and, musing further, he sniffed the air of his cabin, suffering from an odor which it seemed to him had not quite gone off his ship.

"I hate like hell the smell of those niggers," he told Harford. "The last lot had been a month in barracoon, and for that, or for some other cause, they smelled the worst of any cargo I ever carried. I had the ship painted in Baltimore, but I smell it even in my sleep." Harford, looking at the old man's grimace, said he didn't smell it; but he did, the whiff of it bringing back his own contacts with such cargoes in his time. It was curious that Lucy never spoke of this, the more as they were coming into tropical latitudes, when a ship gives up her essential odor of whatever kind.

§ 3

Lucy, who had at first cried out all day upon the novelty of her circumstance, was now crying out upon its monotony, for with an unbroken easy monotony the ship slid into the tropics. It was a voyage without port of call, and without incident but one. Of this incident the captain loved to tell until the day he died; there was no mate to it in his experience. On the fortieth day out from Newport, the ship then being Lat. 9°, Long. 17°, and off the Ivory Coast, the morning being fair and the sea calm, the ship overhauled a man adrift on the flat of a squared log, very large. The log was such as is shipped from the West Coast, of African mahogany. It was the strangeness of that lonely craft, so dark on the wrinkled brilliance of the morning sea, that struck the captain's imagination. The man was black; he lay upon

the log asprawl—dead to the eye, or dying. But he did not die; the sailors tended him, and with evening he began to revive. Within a day or two he stood upon his legs that were shackled. Naked in his tattoo and chains, he stood before the captain. He had no word to say; he looked at the sea and the ship with a vacant eye. A rag was put about him, and he sat with his back against a capstan.

In the week after this adventure Lucy had a birthday, and said so; the captain then made her a present of the man.

"He is lost from a slaver, ma'am, either by way of escape or because he was thrown away with others when the ship was overhauled by a cruiser—though that would not be likely; those that are put over the side in such a time are weighted. Well, we'll never know from him. He has a look of the people of the Niger—he will be a handsome nigger when his sores are healed and he has put a stone or two on his bones. I trust he will do you many years' service. Bring him aft," he told the steward, "and see that he comes decent to the lady."

Lucy thought this a most romantic present. She waited, smiling, in the pool of the cabin light until the Negro was thrust in and stood by the door. He was now recovered from the blight of his privations; the steward had put a red cloth about his loins. His age would be near to thirty; he was of a good black, tall, and elegant with an animal elegance. In the face that was a tragic mask his eyes were shocking in their vitality—they looked about the world in vain. Coming to light upon Lucy, they rested, they were stayed with wonder; wonder then possessed them, and the poor wretch who had long not known ease from rage and fear was eased by a preoccupation.

Lucy was intimidated by the strangeness of that creature breathing presently so close to her, for the captain had the steward bring him forward, and himself with his hand on the nape of the Negro's neck made him kneel. The dark body bent beside her white skirt.

"This be your Big Massa," the captain told him, and by that word "Massa," or by some intimation that hung in the air, the Negro was informed—Harford knew it; he knew too that he was struck with wonder, asking himself if this were a boy or a girl or a woman, looking with an immediate hunger of curiosity into Lucy's face, pale between bands of dark hair.

Harford saw his wife fluttered. She had thought of a slave as she had known slaves—civilized and broken, dressed in linsey-woolsey, and saying, "Yes, ma'am"; but this man—so striding and so wild, looking at her with such wild eyes—she did not feel to be a slave.

She looked at her husband, and he drew the Negro's eyes. "Get up!" he told him, and the man rose. Smart fellow, Harford thought, and had him led away.

Thereafter Lucy's slave was pupil to the steward and began to learn the difference between a towel and a pillow case. Harford, who had taught many a black boy to lay the cloth, thought well of this one. He gave him the name Atemba. The possession of Atemba was a burning pride in the heart of his mistress, and she became habituated to it. In the letters she wrote home she exploited this event, and a kind of epic account of it appeared a year from then, in the *Newport News*. Old sea captains read it and grinned at Lucy Williams's account of her nigger.

But Harford saw it as a reconciling element in his wife's introduction to the Coast. His imagination began to be busy with this difficulty; he had no illusions as to the bleakness of the prospect, and the captain, with the best will in the world, did nothing to help him. The customary West Coast gossip recurred; the deaths by fever, the misadventures and extremes of nostalgia, the fatalities by poison, by snake bite, the lonely madnesses—all these familiar makings of African biography were, as ever, common talk at the table. Only there were none of the crew so hardy as to talk of women—for all Lucy heard, the white man in West Africa was a celibate.

The ship's course was set to Gaboon, where the captain would take on his Kru boys, discharge his cargo, and turn his vessel over to the Spaniards, with whom his agreement was made and who would assume command and ship the slaves that were gathered and waiting in barracoons. Under Spanish colors the *Arrow*, as the *Esperanza*, would make for a South American port. "But never fear," the captain told Lucy; "the *Arrow* will come to anchor off Newport as clean as she left it, for I'll have her painted once she is discharged at Bahia. Any little thing you will be sending your friends for a present I'll put into their hands myself. An ivory tusk, now; or a grass mat made by the Galway people—though my wife complained when I brought her a mat; she said it smelled of mold. And so it did, ma'am—you'll see for yourself there is a smell of mold that hangs about the equator."

On the forty-seventh day out, the *Arrow* passed within landfall of the lovely small island of Elobi, ringed in its white surf. Every creature on the ship rejoiced to see it shining in an afternoon light on a pale sea. Lucy, holding the captain's glass to an inexpert eye, saw it swing into the empty air, perfectly brilliant. Vines hung down its white cliffs, and on the white sands below dark groups of people gathered and scattered and hailed the ship, their voices lost at sea. The captain told Lucy of a trader who had been killed there, the Benga people claiming that he had robbed them. The captain had rescued the trader's wife, calling a month after the murder; he had found her in a little hut on the west side of the island, where she had kept herself without

harm. The women of the island had fed her, but she had come aboard ship all but dead, and she had died at sea. "It's a hard country for a lady, ma'am," the captain told Lucy, who said that any country was hard for a dishonest man or woman of a poor spirit. And she watched the embowered island set in its ring of surf. She had no question to ask of that woman whose body, as the captain sometimes unhappily remembered, had been let down into the sea. "Your lady has a brave spirit," he told Harford, "but not an idea of this country."

With the next morning Lucy woke to the odor of land; past her porthole green trees drifted, and she heard the quartermaster chanting the mark on the lead line. She had slept while the ship came about into the Gaboon estuary. But Harford had hardly slept the night; he saw the daylight come above the low dark land; presently the morning sky was pricked by the crests of the great trees that stood at the water's edge where the eyes of mariners looked to take their bearings. The surf running up the beach broke enormously, and, when the ship made the bar, broke there. With the sight of that surf, so familiar to him in his wandering, he accepted Africa afresh; the feeling of it came to him across the waters; what had seemed so strange to him in his chosen life as he had thought of it in civilized countries returned to inhabit his very soul, not stranger now than his own breath. Only his absence from these circumscribed and familiar things began already to seem strange; and, already almost forgotten, the sights and the sounds of the North began to sink down over the slope of the sea as the ship came about into the still waters of the estuary.

Atemba leaned on the rail; he looked landward with an empty face. Harford judged that he was not a beach man and that he had no hope of a home beside the sea—of an inland tribe, doubtless, and certainly without the tribal marks of these parts. Harford was familiar with the tribes about the Gaboon; he had gone over this country with a fair degree of interest when he was planning his present venture. And his mind, fresh from his absence, sprang to meet his prospects; he told himself that he had the finest stock of trade goods that had ever been put ashore on these beaches, and the only stock of trade that was not for slaving. He could watch the slave trade perish, as he knew it must, without regret. The day for a legitimate trade had dawned, and he was ready for it.

§ 4

Two schooners lay at anchor off the settlement of Glass. They carried the Spanish flag, Harford knew them for slavers, and he won-

dered whether old mates of his were aboard them. Neither had taken
cargo as yet; their captains would wait for the dark to load, and
would load, when they did, in one night; their trade was now pre-
carious, and their cargo would be brought down in canoes from some
hidden point upriver. A third steamer, a four-master, he made out to
be the *Straw;* she was taking lumber over the side. He rejoiced to see
her, as he must come to agreements with her master. The sound of her
winches, faint across the water, was sweet to him; he would be giving
her cargo on her next voyage—pray God it would not be long. From
the villages that lay along the north shore, and where the small huts
were now visible, he heard the rhythm of drums—or did not hear
them, so well he knew that sound. He marked the long wall of Tay-
lor's barracoon and that no smoke of fires rose above the wattled walls
—it must be that Taylor no longer kept his slaves there and that it
was in disuse since the Patrol had become stricter.

When Lucy brushed in between him and the motionless Atemba,
Harford was shocked to see her, so utterly had she perished from his
mind. Now she leaned on the rail, her sleek hair unruffled in the slight
way of the ship, her cheek brown and red from the long voyage, not
yet heated, her white dress spreading over the hoops she had resumed.
Atemba looked at her without focus; for him she was not there, while
for Harford she was there—strangely present. She began to ask ques-
tions; why had he not prepared himself for these?

He answered her with a half-attention. The Kru boys, laughing and
shouting, were coming alongside in canoes, climbing the rope with
their bundles in their teeth. His two or three friends were coming
in their gigs; they would be looking for their rare letters. Taylor was
first on deck, pulling at the collar of his shirt when he saw a woman,
and, when he saw her to be a lady, entirely confounded. His poor face,
so pallid under the eye of Harford, fresh from home, was unshorn; his
white cotton suit, entirely clean, was threadbare. He bowed as he had
not done these five years, and he told Mrs. Harford, "I am proud to
meet you, ma'am." He woke with a start when Harford told him they
must beg his hospitality for the day or two before they should go up
the river. Taylor was then painfully preoccupied, casting about in his
mind, as Harford well knew, to remember the state of his quarters.
And presently he rushed away.

"I'll not bring her ashore until evening," Harford told him.

"You damn fool, to bring a lady to this hole!" Taylor hissed as he
passed him.

Harford sighed; neither he nor Taylor would have thought it a hole
if it had not been for Lucy, and the two of them had a day's business
pressing them that would not wait. The captain himself must turn his

eyes from his proper concerns because the Mpongwe girls, until to-day so welcome, had begun to clutter the deck. He began to bully them—what were the little sluts doing aboard a decent ship like his? "You take them beach girls for slop side," he told a tall grave Mpongwe youth, who was Taylor's headman, and who had serious business aboard ship.

"Them beach girls be fine too much," said the youth, and he was indignant; "what for they no be fit for live for deck?"

"You no see white woman? You take them beach girls for slop side —white woman no be fit for like them beach girls!"

But the captain was wrong. Between the Mpongwe girls and Lucy there was a strong magnetism and a passionate curiosity. Lucy was looking upon the flower of a notable tribe; those heads so smoothly dressed and set with fretted combs of ivory were all turned her way. Those dark faces, emptied by wonder of any lesser feeling, all fed upon her strangeness. They drifted to her softly, they softly knelt beside her, and when she smiled they laughed, clapping their hands. The odor of the dye of their bright cloths and of trade scent was all about her—a strange odor; their healthy bodies, their dark smooth skins, their dark bright eyes, their white teeth between their laughing brown lips, were strangely near her, in a great perfection of vigor and freedom. Her own image shone in their every eye. Only a mulattress, slim, with tawny hair and a golden skin, leaning against the cabin wall, was withdrawn from Lucy's successes. A small boy, very black, approached Lucy with a gift of pawpaws; the fruit, like yellow melons in a basket, he laid at her feet. And presently all the bright fruits that had come aboard for the crew were heaped before Lucy.

Harford, passing by, was struck by the opulent aspect of that group of girls and fruit. Beauty moved him freshly, and he was released from a burden of care. The evening stole over the estuary of Gaboon—how infinitely sweet it was, with a remembered sweetness. With the failure of the sunlight the shore drew near; he saw the settlement beside the water,—that would be Glass,—and behind the plateau he saw the great trees by which mariners had laid their course for generations, as they would do for years to come. Like acorns fallen from great oaks were the little cabins of the settlements of Gaboon. His business with the captain must wait until the morning. He and Atemba gathered up the weary Lucy and her spoils, intimidating with their busy ways the Mpongwe girls. The captain came to wish her farewell (Harford knew his thought—that she would not live the year out: "And a fine woman too, but hasn't an idea of the country"), and Lucy went over the side, laughing at the difficulties of the ladder, little knowing how she was observed through the captain's glass from the

French ship that lay to leeward of the *Straw*. She would like it if she knew, thought Harford, when he was at leisure in the canoe.

The canoe was his own, and a fine one. It had been made for him in the year of his absence. The young captain of the crew of six was his headman—a Fang. Harford had a liking for the forest tribes; his business, he hoped, would come more and more to be with them, and he had himself trained a group of Fang traders. No other trader had done so, and no other had set himself against the custom of trust that was so smooth a beginning and so inevitable a destruction of friendship. He told the Fang that the canoe was a good one and that he would be paid for it in the morning. They spoke together of the things of trade.

Lucy listened to that strange tongue; the canoers sang and paddled; the shadow of evening was in the water; her attention, weary with strain, drowsed, and they came to shore. Harford gave her a hand as she left the canoe. He thought to himself suddenly, "Never again to be the same!" He thought of the change that waits the white man in Africa—Lucy did not know of this change. She left herself there in the canoe and did not know that it must be so. She gave herself to Africa without thought. She passed the little houses by the sea and did not know that these were now her town; she went up the steps to the door of Taylor's house and did not mark that it was a house with a verandah—a deck house. She was met by a desperate Taylor and did not guess that he was sick with excitement, or that he had never thought to see a formidable white woman there.

She accepted the poverty of that poor shelter as exceptional—she did not know that there was no better shelter within a month's journey. She did not see a woman's dress hanging on the rude plank wall of Taylor's bedroom, and she did not miss that dress when it was whisked away by a stricken Taylor. She sat at table on Taylor's verandah without thought of its fine red and white checked cloth; spreading her wide white skirts, she leaned on her hand and looked out to sea, where three vessels hung their lights against the dusk—and she had no knowledge of the ageless intervals when there was no ship there to prick the evening with her lights.

The nostalgias of Taylor, pushed back into brief surcease, did not weigh upon the air. All went well, thought Taylor, and so it did. What an escape! What a day of escape, and a night! How long, he wondered vaguely, with his eyes upon Lucy. But he did not envy Harford—no, it would be too difficult. He thought of his Iwengosono, with her tawny hair and yellow eyes. She was going to have a baby, and perhaps it would be a black baby—he hoped she would keep well out of the way. Iveki, as good a steward as he could put his hand on, was serving at

the table, Mpongwe hauteur giving dignity to his crude fashion. There was palm oil and other country chop on the table; wine, too, and fine fruit. Behind Lucy stood Atemba, sunk in his own despair—as lost among the Mpongwe as he had been in the sea. Harford supposed that he must have seen the landfall with some hope of his own tribe and country.

With the hour the land breeze fell, and there was a stillness before the sea breeze should rise at eight o'clock; the hurricane lamp brimmed its circle of light, laving the faces that were half in shadow; the sea sighed; the plumes of the bamboo whispered; and in the dark about them— where there was a murmur of comment and laughter—were the curious who gathered to see the white people fresh from the sea. Harford heard the legato of the Mpongwe and the staccato of the Fang tongues. He wished to be seeing his own Fang, who had come down the river in three canoes—they would be bedded near by in Taylor's compound, where they would be without doubt the butt of the fine Mpongwe. He rose, excusing himself. Taylor, in a panic, rose with him, and Lucy was left to look about that bamboo shelter where the white sand drifted on the gray plank of the floor.

Within a little room a bed was spread for her with a bright country cloth. A mirror, gray in a tarnished frame, gave back her image dimmed. Atemba held the lantern for her self-scrutiny, and he looked at himself without a smile. There was a great earthen basin and a jug of water; these were brightly flowered and bore the name of King Toko. The night came in at the windows, where there was no glass, only a shutter that Lucy barred and then threw open again, leaning out to feel against her cheek the stir of the sea breeze. And then, from the dark, dark voices spoke to her softly; Iwengosono and her girl friends were watching her from the ground below the window. They admired her, speaking to her in Mpongwe, which certainly she did not understand; but they saw her smiling in the lamplight. They laughed, and would have come in to her, but the voice of an old woman spoke sharply, and they went away.

Lucy sighed with pleasure. She felt herself deliciously free of the ship; she could not be still in that empty room, and she passionately desired to be abroad. Atemba followed her, the lantern swinging at his knee. She smelt the frangipani that blossoms in beach settlements, and the odor of wood fires. Taylor's little house stood in a trodden clearing surrounded by a brush fence. Beyond this there was a camp ground; the sound of laughter and of drumming came from this compound.

Through a breach in the stockade Lucy saw Africa at play—dark bodies leaping to incredibly accurate rhythms, dark voices joining in an unintelligible phrase and recurrent sudden shout. There were a hun-

dred people there, and on the ground the blaze of twenty fires; there was such a freedom as Lucy had not known. A long time she watched those free people eddying in a dance without logic, struck with firelight and with moonlight. Harford, coming back with Taylor, found her there, Atemba beside her; he drew her with him to the house; he was struck by a lack of focus in her dazzled eyes. She had not complained of the heat—Harford was to find her uncomplaining.

Three days later, in the canoe that pointed upriver, he heard her join the Fang paddlers in their boat song. The Fang shouted with laughter; singing the songs of free men, they shot past the old barracoon. The estuary was clean silver over its whole expanse, and without a sail, the slaves having been loaded in the night and the ships having cleared before dawn. Harford's ten canoes of barter trailed the canoe of the "Big Massa," who was richer now, the Fang told each other, by a woman. A fine woman, bought with a great price, surely. And much goods besides, in his many canoes.

Book II

The Factory

§ 1

Harford settled into the canvas chair that so neatly fitted the sides of his canoe; he savored the morning air of the journey with intense appreciation. He had such a passion for the forests of Africa as he could never have acknowledged, and when his little fleet left the open water for the glassy surface of the Nkomo River he was struck to the heart with a pang of delight. Here the mangrove trees were a hedge about the great park of the forest; the tide was near the full. On a full tide the canoes came to be amid high ground, the mangroves were great trees; in that narrower way the first lustre of the day was lost; the singing ceased, and Harford recognized the familiar rhythm of the journey.

He returned from his solitary excursions to the thought of Lucy's probable miseries during the furies of the day, when the sunlight would flow like a river above the brown water, when with the turn of the tide the obscene roots of the mangrove trees would stand above the slime gnarled with oysters, when the débris of the flood delayed in the ooze would give off the odor of Africa, and the great heat would press upon the canoers in their hollowed tree.

Lucy sat in a canvas chair before him; he saw the back of her wide straw bonnet and her skirts crushed into the narrow compass of the canoe. She bit a pencil and wrote on a pad upon her knee. Every crocodile sprawling on a stone amid-stream and slipping like spilled water back into the flood was a wonder to her. The sinister green lip turned by the brown water against the paddle delighted her. Now and again, when a monkey spread himself like an arabesque, small against the wall of the forest, the paddlers pointed to it, responsive to her zest. She immortalized the monkey then and there with a fine phrase; she wrote about the great and awful forest, the majestic river, the noble savages that bent to the oar. And suddenly she drooped under the sunlight that thrust a wedge between the dark shadows of the river banks. Harford called a halt at the village of Zamaliga. The canoes turned into a bywater that led to the invisible village.

Through a green tunnel of forest they came to a muddy ooze left by the tide below the bank of Zamaliga. Seven men came out of the village stockade; leaning on their spears, they observed the canoes. Those paddlers who were of the clan of the inhabitants of Zamaliga shouted to them, and the villagers, with a marked and lofty deliberation, stepped out into the ooze. They drew up the canoes; one of them lifted Lucy from her chair and set her carefully on the high ground. He left a yellow stain of palm oil on her dress. The forest shed a green stain on her. Her skirts, spread over her hoops, were too wide to pass the narrow way that entered the village; those who watched the strangers through the gun holes in the walls of the headman's house saw her remove her cage of reeds—her laughter woke the village of Zamaliga. Lucy passed into the rectangular clearing, so mediæval in its aspect, of the long narrow village, where she burst upon the vision of the old headman who had come out to greet the white man. From each of the little huts, so low under their cover of palm thatch, a leg was thrust, a head, and a body followed; the clearing, full of sunlight between the walls of the forest, was suddenly stirring with brown bodies. There was a shout from end to end of the village, and a question—was it a lad or a woman?

Lucy, weak with laughter, stooped to the entrance and drew her skirts after her into the headman's house. The headman observed her gravely; he saw the Big Massa spread a grass mat upon a bamboo bed. The woman—for he was assured by the rowers, some of whom were his own people, that this was a woman—lay laughing in the cool gloom of his house. "She is strong for talk," he told himself. He went out under the eaves where he kept his call drum and beat a message summoning his women from their outlying gardens—these people must be fed, he knew. "There are strangers in the village," cried out the beaten

drum. The headman would have liked to inform his neighboring head-men of the wonder of his guests, but there was no phrase in the old drum code that was adequate for this novelty of a white woman, lying in the palaver house of the village, laughing and chattering.

Lucy looked at the rafters; they were studded with little plaintive skulls of animals, brown and varnished with smoke—reminders of the hunt. She saw the fetish images, like dolls, seated on high standing drums in the corner; she averted her eyes from their obscene gestures and their curiously vital and significant faces. The shock of their vitality was without meaning to her. The clutter in the hut, of spears and guns and dogs and hunting nets, did not arrest her. The sound of drums, the heavy air in that brown interior, the warm thick peanut porridge that Atemba brought her and that Harford bade her eat with the bread from her basket, presently made her drowsy, and she slept, lulled by the crowd and the chatter.

The square of golden light that opened on the street was darkened by grave and curious faces; one and then another body entered, the men breeched with bark cloth, the women with bustles of dried grasses. They held their bustles against their thighs as they put their legs over the high threshold. Their heads were dressed with feathers and with disks of brass. They were entirely preoccupied with their scrutiny of Lucy pale in sleep; they understood that this was the white man's woman; they would have rejoiced to see her without the many complications of her coverings, which yet were much to be coveted. Their murmurs in Fang were anatomical in trend; Harford heard them. He wondered to find himself standing guard over a wife in a Fang palaver house, and he greatly wondered to see her sleep there like a veteran.

That night Lucy slept in the bottom of the canoe. The river ran among hills; there was a mist above the river, and a moon gilded the mist. Harford dozed in his chair; the rowers in shifts made against the current; passing canoes hailed them and were hailed again—the word of Hallifodi's white woman went up and down the river and women in villages Lucy was never to see spoke of her daily for many days. The articulate curiosity of the women of the tribes of that river did much to stimulate Harford's trade in those first months of his trading. Through his sleep Harford heard his rowers sing a ballard of the white man and his white woman:—

> "*Hé-yé-é!* Her eyes are like the eyes of the wood dove!
> *Hé-yé-é!*
> Her hair is soft like the hair of the monkey!
> *Hé-yé-é!*

Her husband crossed in a canoe to get her!
Hé-yé-é!
And to her father her husband gave an ivory!
Hé-yé-é!
An ivory as big as your thigh, O Hallifodi!
Hé-yé-é!"

§ 2

On the third day Lucy woke very early in the gray dawn. In the pallor of the morning, and dark against the pale stream of the sky, the trees were full of the furious contention of parrots. That matinal domestic disorder startled her; she could not think where she was that there should be a river of sky above her and her face wet with dew. There was Harford, and his face was not set toward her. The canoe floated toward a landing, a little jetty of logs thrown out against the stream. Trees hung about the water; the river might have been a little lake. A great rectangular clearing was a breach in the forest—the walls of the forest stood sheer about four or five acres of cleared ground that sloped to the river. Along the bank and not more than fifty feet from the water's edge there was a square high stockade. Above this, and on the upper stretch of the clearing where the slope of ground was easy, there was a cabin in a compound with a withy fence about it—this was Harford's house and factory.

Lucy saw that her husband stared at the lower stockade; he stood in the canoe still staring; he wavered and sat down. He asked a question of his headman, who told him that this was De Sopo's barracoon, built in the last dry season; that De Sopo had sent his slaves away by canoes that made one of the Spanish ships.

The barracoon was empty, but the scent of it still hung on the air. Harford was surprised and disheartened; all his plotted future darkened and lost its zest; his distaste for the Trade turned then and there to loathing, and his pleasure in clean barter—which had attracted him as an experiment and a venture—seemed to him now a childish dream, doomed to fail. He could have overturned the canoe in his spleen, but there was Lucy ready to stir herself, to ask her million questions, and to laugh in the face of Africa.

He did not tell her that the barracoon had been built in his absence; he looked at her harshly, begging her to remember that she was in a canoe, and not be throwing herself about. Lucy laughed. She hung on her husband's arm, climbing the slope of the hill on the little footpath that skirted the clearing and that was too narrow. It was still dark in

the forest, and a smell of mold as old as time seeped through that enormous wall.

"Is it not strange, Mr. Harford," Lucy asked him, "that I, who was born in a city and lived in Newport all my life, should have my own first home in such a wild and lonely place? Is it not romantic?" Her husband did not answer her—he was looking grimly at his "factory."

The little cabin, built on stilts and made of wide plates of the bark of trees, stood with its eyes shut in the clearing. Yellow ground was beaten hard about it. At the foot of the stairs that led to the verandah an old Fang caretaker with a broom of twigs was sweeping away what was not there—his Big Massa must see for himself that Ntu Ela swept always and forever the ground that was his care. From one of the lesser cabins behind the factory Harford's carpenter came out to greet him; he was a mulatto from the Gold Coast. He told his wife later that his breath had gone straight away from his body at the sight of the white woman.

The door of the cabin was painted green—a green door! And not another in a thousand miles. Nor any other stairs in that forest. The carpenter who had made the stairs could make anything; he began at first glimpse of Lucy to devise a dress for his wife—wide like Lucy's. He opened the door of the house; in the trade room there were shelves, empty now, and a long counter. He threw back the wooden shutters; he had made these too, and admired them greatly. Off the trade room a door opened to a smaller room. Lucy saw there a slatted wooden bed, and against the wall three wooden boxes laid one above the other; she knew them for shelves, and her mind, weary with wandering among the strange things of the forest, came to rest in that room. Harford could not have guessed how much it was for her a nest. She would not see the house for the poor bleak thing it was—she curtained it and carpeted it and furnished it, and all in the moment the carpenter took to show Harford the bar he had put across the door that opened to the storehouse behind the counter. By a crazy mirror on the trade-room wall she smoothed her hair—laughing at the broken face it gave her.

Harford, standing under the eaves of the house he had thought to live in by himself and where he had thought to be the only trader, looked down the hill and into the barracoon—he could see it plainly. The high stockade of trimmed and sharpened staves was empty now, the ashes of its many little fires cold on the ground. He communed with himself; his wife, calling him, woke him to a forgotten presence. He saw her freshly against the background of the place to which he had brought her: her hardihood and vigor struck him, and it came into his mind that she was a singularly fearless woman. He remembered her lying asleep under the mists and the moonlight in the bottom of the

canoe—impressing upon his inattentive memory an indestructible image, more beautiful than she had seemed to be.

They sat at a table on the verandah. Atemba, having mysteriously achieved a checkered cloth of red and white, served them, as he had learned to do, with what food was to be had, and the acquired arts of Taylor's steward. Behind the constant fabric of Lucy's chatter Harford heard the drums of the neighboring villages. Up and down and across the river, in villages under the cover of the forest, the Fang were drumming out the news that Hallifodi had come back with much goods for barter. Noon, he knew, would find his yard full of his neighbors. Up the path from the river, as his men brought his canoes alongside, others of them carried his bales of cotton, his bales of dried fish, his cases of rum. The great busyness of trade began to furnish his clearing with clamor, with odor, with humanity. Fortified by food and entirely engrossed in the disposal of his goods and the greetings of the headmen who pressed upon him, he was suddenly happy after his own fashion.

Harford was a born trader. He spoke the language of those with whom he traded; he had observed and he practised their customs in trading; he knew their tempo and was neither too swift nor too slow in his greetings and his bargains; he was habitually grave, but he had a reserve of sardonic humor which came into service at a moment accurately timed and effective. He was severe. For these traits he was well liked, and he was not disliked for his moody humors.

The old tattooed shrewd Fang headmen came to greet him now in their patriarchal groups, accompanied by young men beating drums, and young men carrying spears, and keepers of dogs in leashes of three, and women with painted headdresses whose bustles were painted, too. All these people welcomed him, not alone because he was the purveyor of extraordinary novelties, but because they liked him. Was he not their father, returned from paths upon the sea? And had he not passed over the tribe of the arrogant Mpongwe, defying the old Mpongwe taboo that none should trade with the Fang but a son of a beach tribe?

They were consumed with a passion of curiosity about Lucy. Looking at her, they sighed with wonder, snapped their fingers, and slapped their thighs; she saw herself in all those brilliant eyes, adequately mirrored and approved. Chickens were brought to Hallifodi, tied by their feet and hanging head down; fish in green leaf packets were diverted from the cooking pot; eggs—because white men like eggs—were taken from under outraged hens; corn, peanuts, hands of bananas, honey in gourds, wild fruits of the forest—all these were brought, and not without a mingling of reluctance and calculation, to please their white man.

The trade goods were under cover before night; a Fang youth taught by Harford to keep tally had this tally ready, and it was correct. The key was turned on the heaped disorder of the storeroom; the canoe men, who would come for their pay in the morning, wandered off to the villages where they would eat and sleep; the guests, still sighing with acclamation, went away in their tribal groups.

It was cool in the empty clearing. Harford sat on the steps of his house, which looked west, smoking his pipe, dressed once again in no more than a shirt and trousers. Atemba brought good Fang chop to the red and white tablecloth. Lucy, pale with a long day of effort and minus her hoops, was too bewildered and weary to speak, and peace fell upon that little group—so small, so dominant, and so lost in the forest. The dark settled in, and Atemba lit a lantern. Lucy leaned her head on her hand—she was devising a dress that would fit the circumstance. Harford was half asleep when his wife told him that their bed was ready; he had not thought to find a hammock for himself among the loads, and he lay down beside Lucy in the small dark room where he had bunked in times past, and which was already furnished by his wife's undisciplined presence. He felt a movement of tenderness for her fatigue, her innocent trust and courage, her facile abandonment and passion. But when she slept and moonlight fell upon her white arms and her bundles of dark hair, and her clothing hung in billows against the wall, he was oppressed; he rose and went out.

The shadow of his house was black under a blazing moon; silver struck the plumes of the banana trees that stood about his clearing; to the west and down the hill the river wore its veil of mist, and white in the moonlight was the empty yard of the barracoon. He stretched himself in his old canvas chair. The river was audible, and from the villages came the incessant trouble of the dance drums. His circumstance was perfectly familiar to him; nothing of it claimed his attention; every element in it released the man in him that Africa had made in fifteen years.

He thought of De Sopo as he had known him five years before; the two of them were then in the Trade, Harford with a firm of New Yorkers—the last of slave trading for him. De Sopo had been with a group of Portuguese, dealing directly with Bahia. These operations had been off the Muni River, which was then little visited by the British Patrol. De Sopo should be in his early thirties now—grown perhaps, Harford thought to himself, a tricky and a dirty fellow. He would be upriver now, dealing with his slaving chiefs; doubtless he would expect to be lodged when he should come down to his barracoon and while he was holding his kaffle for shipment. Taylor had spoken of De Sopo as shipping with him, but Harford had not thought to ask

where the Portuguese held his slaves. None of the Fang had spoken of the barracoon; it might be, as Harford knew, that they supposed De Sopo to be a partner with himself. He had spent a year in making his clearing and in building his houses, in establishing his trade among the Fang, and in that time he had not bought a slave, though many had been offered him. But the Fang would not so easily disassociate a white man from the Trade, and he must take his measures before De Sopo returned with his new cargo. He considered abandoning this clearing for another, turning over in his mind the locality as he knew it. But he came to the conclusion that he must dispose of his stock before coming to a decision. And he slept under the shadow of his eaves.

§ 3

The Southern Cross leaned to its setting. It was the month of March; the rainy season was near. In the villages the people were making a charm for the felling of trees. Soon Tolo, the constellation of the Hare, would incline to the roofs of the houses in the early dark —then the sons of the Fang would burn the trees they had felled to make their new gardens. Their women would plant the seed, and all the things of man known from the birth of men would go forward. Yet there were these new things in the forest—a trader who did not barter for slaves, and a white woman. Strange things, not to be explained.

On a day soon after Efa Ngoto, with a small company of his young men, came to Harford with a slave. The fame of Harford's goods was irresistible. Efa had no ivory, but he had a girl who had been left in pawn with him by a friend who was now an enemy. She was not a tractable girl—she was given, rather, to audible rehearsals of her irregular position and her grievances. Harford, leaning on the rail of his verandah, heard the account of her virtues as a fine working woman, obedient, sure to breed, for she had done so. He listened to Efa's offer of exchange for the customary tale of goods. He waited with his acquired and admirable patience until Efa had come to an end of oratory and flourishing of his staff. The girl, drawn forward by a bamboo noose about her neck, leaned back against it. Lucy arrived to exclaim and question—and little did she guess how her husband cursed in his heart these rifts in an established contact, based on understood intonations and intervals.

"When the sun is in the middle," Harford told Efa, "I shall call upon the drum all real men of the forest. And when they shall have gathered in answer to my drumming I shall tell them the way and the

kind of my trade—what I shall buy of the tribe of the Fang. Return then with your brothers."

At five o'clock of that afternoon Harford's clearing was filled with headmen and lesser men; with dogs and dog bells; with spears, staves, and guns; with headdresses painted green, yellow, white, strung with beads, studded with shells, buttons, and brass; with bodies painted with clay, with ochre, and with the crimson powder of the camwood tree; with bodies breeched in bark cloth, naked bodies, and bodies striding in leopard skins.

Lucy on the verandah was perfectly silent because Harford had begged her to be so; she put a little parasol between her face and the setting sun and was the more observed for this. She admired her husband deeply, approving the silence with which the noisy crowd attended him when he rose to speak. She could not know what he was saying, but she saw him call for the slave girl who had returned with Efa, and who was drawn by the leash into the center of the group. The girl hung back, intimidated for the moment by the public eye. Harford untied the cord about her neck, telling Efa Ngoto that there— so far as he was concerned—stood every slave girl that was brought him for purchase.

"I will give you for your ivories," he told them, "the right count of goods for an ivory, and all the goods fine. But do not wake me in the night to sell me a slave, thinking, 'He is a man who will not buy a slave in the daytime, but when night comes he will buy a slave.' Do not call me in the morning to sell me a woman who has run away at night and whom with the dawn you have overtaken saying to her, 'Aha, you who run away! I shall take you to the white man, and try running away from him!' Do not hasten back from your quarrels with your enemy tribes bringing young men with you, thinking that I will buy them. Never on any day, rainy season or dry, will I buy a slave from you; and any slave that you bring to my factory in bonds I shall unloose with my own hand and you may deal as you can with the one that stands free. As for your own slaves that you have in your own towns, deal with them after your own fashion—what have I to do with them? Have you heard?"

"We have heard!" The automatic response in its unison and volume startled Lucy, unused to these conventions. A chief rose to ask—what of the barracoon that the white man had built at the foot of the hill and that he had already filled with two fillings of slaves? How were they to understand a tribe of men that both did and did not deal in slaves?

Of white men, as of black men, Harford told them, there are tribes and tribes, customs and customs. De Sopo was of a slaving tribe. For

himself, whose name was Hallifodi and who had been a slaver in his youth, there was now a strong, unbreakable, and permanent taboo without end—he would not slave.

"It is for him taboo!"

Harford knew suddenly that he had said the inevitable, convincing, and last word; he was for the Fang disestablished as a slaver, and that by the logic of a word. His humanity was, moreover, established, for was he not a man with a taboo? A small square bottle of rum went by the hand of Atemba to the hand of every headman, and the palaver was done. In clannish groups and with many words of farewell and of begging, the Fang went away from the clearing. Harford was well-pleased and happily complacent; he rehearsed his speech in part to Lucy, but he did not tell her what he had said when he loosed the rope on the neck of the Fang girl, and Lucy did not know then, or ever, that her husband was a man with a taboo. But Atemba heard, and understood, and he saw the girl released.

§ 4

Lucy had not worn out her first pair of kid shoes when the first rains fell. Harford had put her in a little cabin of one room, built for herself and removed from the smell of salt fish and the constant coming and going of the Fang. Curtains hung at the windows, native mats woven of grass were laid on the floor, and this was made of planks that Harford had had brought upriver. The rough little house, with its thatch of palm mats, its rude shutters, and its green door, delighted Lucy beyond reason; it preoccupied her; she saw it as exiles see their shelters that are achieved at strange expense. She felt for it a mystic attachment that was the beginning in her of the inevitable action of African exile. At night on her slatted bamboo bed in the dark she saw in her mind her little house flooded with light and she rejoiced in all its least arrangement.

Her delight in it was shared by the Fang women who hung about the steps and who saw it after their own fashion and with an excessive admiration. They appropriated to themselves Lucy, on the score of their common sex, and her house as the house of a woman; their innate hardihood overcame their timidity; with a growing boldness they flocked to the spectacle of the white woman with her long hair, her slim waist, her mincing airs that amused them, her excess of clothes that became a legend. Groups of them standing on the ground before her house would summon her in their loud laughing voices; they would question her in the modified tender idiom that the Fang people

reserve for children, and her answers in their own tongue, imperfect and halting, pleased them, increasing in them the conviction that she was a child and the legitimate object of their facile maternal solicitude.

Harford, busy with his own affairs, would be roused by their shouts of laughter, and would look out to wonder at the sight of his wife, in a white dress without hoops, leaning over the rail of her little verandah into a group of the dark bodies of women—tattooed, oiled, painted, turning up to her their faces all smiling and lit with a tender amusement. Their certain uncouthness, their obvious diseases, the known suspicion of cannibalism that hung about the tribe, seemed then to be overlaid by an affinity between women, powerful and touching.

The first rains had not fallen before Lucy ventured into the nearer villages, following Atemba along the tunneled paths of the forest that debouched from a green gloom into the intolerable light of the clearings. A wooden stool would be set for her in one and another of the huts of the village; the clay floor would be swept in her honor; warm curiosities would play about her. Daintily she would taste from a folded leaf the mushroom soup or the fish stew that was the best of the village fare. The headman, getting word of this, would saunter down the clearing to put his head in under the eaves of the favored house, to wonder and laugh at the sight of her; and her personal importance, somehow slipping away, would re-establish itself and would embellish her.

She would come back from these excursions with extravagant talk of the charms of Fang babies, and smelling of the fires that burn on the floors of Fang cabins. And she began to write romantically about her life in the forest. Harford, going about the clearing, would see her sitting at a table she had made of boxes; he knew, he thought, the sort of thing she would be writing—remembering the book of hers that he had read before he met her. He had admired it, liking an authoress to be romantic and sentimental. He remembered that he had read it in a lonely deserted fort on the Gold Coast, sitting in a large, dusty, and empty room, reading Lucy's impossible tale in a small pool of light from a lantern. He had got it from the captain of a ship out of Boston. Life had been at the slack with him then, between two adventures. It was small time he had to be reading now, for his trade was going well, ivory was coming in, was being weighed and sent down the river to Taylor. The Fang of the river valley—the headmen and their favorite wives—were decked in the colored calicoes of his trading; they were drinking his rum and eating his salt fish in all the villages; matches were struck in huts where the fire stick had been the only use; fishhooks were betraying the fish in the river, and gunpowder from Hallifodi furnished the horns of the hunters. Gifted cheats were busy de-

vising ways to overreach him, and he was divining their villainy; all was as it should be in the factory of Hallifodi on the Nkomo River.

A leopard stole a goat that Lucy had meant to milk; Harford had a fever and resented his wife's care; a thief was found to be digging through the ground below the level of the storehouse where Harford kept his reserves; and Atemba was snake-bitten. But. Atemba recovered, Harford recovered, the thief was apprehended and put over the log—Harford calling upon the headman of the recreant's own town to beat him. Only Lucy did not entirely recover from the wound of her husband's ill-humored and morose convalescence, when he had shut his door against her, begging her to send Atemba to serve him. She had then wept bitterly and had written a letter home—speaking of the great loneliness of her life and the unlikeness between men and women in their characters and habits. And indeed it would seem that she was right, for when she sickened with the fever, as she presently did, she accepted her husband's ministrations gratefully, and wrote about them at length in another letter and. another vein. It is not strange, therefore, that Lucy's friends were later divided in their understanding of Harford's character and conduct.

With the passing of time and the falling of the rain, Lucy's letters ceased. Atemba, who was fascinated by the travels of her hand upon the page and by the marks she made, felt aggrieved; her ink, he told her, was drying. He begged her to teach him to write, and so for a little time she did; Harford would see Atemba's face happy and intent above his slow-traveling hand. But Lucy wearied of the teaching; a languor grew upon her in that small house which was shut in by the dark walls of the rain. Atemba thought, "She should visit her father's town." She complained to Harford of the roaches, of the rats that rustled in the leaf thatch of her cabin. There were a hundred roaches on her wall of an evening, she said, and the rats carried away her stockings. She sickened of the daily fare and lost her zest for invention. At the height of the rainy season, when the great rains swept daily through the clearing and fell enormously on the roof, she had black-water fever, and for two nights Harford tended her without hope. On the third night he slept; there was no lantern lit in the white man's clearing, and Lucy, convalescent, lay in the sinister trough of a gray weakness, watching the moonlight on her bark wall.

It was a grievance with her, after this illness, that she had lost track of the days of the week and could not be sure again if it were Sunday or another day. Incessantly she struggled with this problem, calling on Harford to solve it for her—endlessly tracing her way back to a known day and baffled always by her weakness. But with the dry season she forgot this and other obsessions; the falling of the sunlight

among the last light veils of rain flooded her with joy, and she came
back to her housewifery and her visits in the villages.

It began to appear to Harford that her recurrent fevers were antici-
pated by an increase in her vitality—she would then be restless and
her initiative would revive; she would go nutting with the Fang
women in the forest or swimming in the river to the sound of their
joyous cries. He grew to dread these adventures and her returns from
them. Lucy dragging her skirts in from a native village, her hair
smelling of wood smoke and her eyes already shadowed with illness,
was a provocation to Harford; he felt a strangeness in her and his face
was set against her. But Lucy pale and listless, recovering from her
fever, following after him for company and in gratitude for his care
of her, touched him; he softened. He could then suffer it that she
loved him devotedly. He was grateful to her that she spoke less often;
he would find it in his heart to talk with her, recounting the day's
business and the gossip of the neighborhood, and Lucy would listen
in a happy languor.

§ 5

Harford was a careful master and his clearing was well ordered—
a white man might come upon it unannounced and there would be no
scurry there to shame the factor. But no white man came until, on a
day in January, De Sopo arrived in a canoe and was at the door of
the factory before he was observed.

It was noon. Lucy and Harford sat at table under the eaves of the
factory. Lucy, when she saw a white face, felt such a surprise as was
painful; she put her hand to her hair and smoothed her dress; she
remembered the holes in her shoes and that her skirt was short after a
fashion she had devised for her isolated circumstance. She was pale
and intimidated, letting her husband do the honors, and these Har-
ford extended without zeal. With the lapse of time he had ceased to
take account of De Sopo; Mpongwe traders in passing had told him
that the Spaniard was in his own town beyond the sea; and latterly
Harford had heard that he was operating in the Muni River, as the
dangers of the Trade were now excessive in the Gaboon estuary.
The barracoon, so long idle, had ceased to spoil Harford's every
prospect; grass had grown on the floor of it, and the roofs of the
thatch shelter that ran along the inner wall were falling under the
weight of sweet-potato vine. It was a deserted clearing, soon to revert
to forest.

And here at the door was De Sopo.

He was thinner than Harford remembered him to be, of a bad color, and nearly bald. His manner, Harford was bound to agree, was correct. He had heard from his paddlers that Harford had a woman, and he had supposed this to be a Mpongwe woman, such as he himself had. She was with him now; coming in on his heels, she spread out for him a deerskin stool she carried, and then stood against the wall. She was a dark creature, slight and round, without a trace of tattoo, her hair without beads and pinned with a gold ornament; her square of cloth, violet-coloured and bordered with red, was tautened under her arms. Harford wondered where De Sopo had got a girl of her quality. Atemba, who was bringing food to De Sopo, observed her and was by her observed. Only Lucy, looking at her with great pleasure, did not know that she was De Sopo's woman; she did not understand why De Sopo, presently, and when he had found himself in a family, sent her away. She went away down the steps into the violent light of the clearing and down the path to the canoe; but Harford sent Atemba after her to bring her back into the hut of the headman's wife, where she would be fed—if indeed she would eat the food of a Fang woman. Lucy watched the two black people, single file, stride away with an African elegance.

De Sopo, who spoke to Harford in Spanish, spoke to Lucy in beach English, and the corruption of this speech offended her. She made little out of his assurances that he "catch plenty nigger, fine too much, never die for canoe, never kill him for gun, make fine journey two-three moons, keep him now ship live for come. Catch him ship plenty quick." She did not understand when he offered her a fine girl pickaninny, half grown. And later when he went away, and when she would have asked Harford her thousand questions,—the tides of her vitality having risen under excitement,—he was moody and taciturn. He followed De Sopo down to the river, and told him that he could not have him in the house. The Spaniard must sleep in the villages until he should have a shelter of his own.

De Sopo was not of an ill humor—he did not resent his expulsion from a domesticity so remote from his own experience and so unexpected; he gave small attention to Harford's schemes for an unnatural and emasculated trade; he congratulated him elaborately on his marriage with a lady so evidently illustrious, so beautiful, so gracious, and he trusted that his presence in the neighborhood, and the presence of his slaves, would not be offensive. He had got his girl from a partner who had died in the interior, with whom he had been making his way from the upper reaches of the Muni River to the Nkomo. A hard country to travel until they struck the navigable river, by which time his partner had died. De Sopo had missed the aid of a

partner, but his slaves—who were a half day behind him—were a poor-spirited lot and amenable to his Benga overseers. Harford was disarmed more than he had thought to be; they parted on a civil note.

§ 6

"I could not have him here," he told Lucy that night, "as he had hoped to be—both on your account and on my own, because of the reputation I am earning for another sort of trade. But I should like him sometimes to come to see us, unless that would displease you."

Lucy had not dealt with the matter of De Sopo so definitely; she would have been led in any case by Harford. The girl, Harford told her, was doubtless lonely. She had belonged to another man; De Sopo hardly could be attractive to a beautiful girl like that—though it was strange, he said, how now and again you found a·girl who seemed to form such an attachment.

Lucy lay upon her bed, watching Harford move about the room. A silence followed this comment; he saw Lucy perfectly still, her breath suspended, looking at him with a child's amazement. The girl—what was she to De Sopo?

"She is his woman," Harford told her reasonably, but a flood of sympathy filled him when he saw her struggle with this. "It is natural," he told her; "he is a man alone, living in dreary places, and she is a woman, clean, clever—she looks clever—she gives him pleasure— it is customary." Harford felt his way along, and Lucy turned to stone.

"Customary," Lucy murmured; and then she breathed her question into the silence where Harford had felt, curiously enough, so safe:—

"Did you?"

"Yes," said Harford, looking at her without dissimulation; and he had more to say, but she turned to the wall. He waited until his words had sunk back into his heart, and he went away.

Atemba was sitting under the eaves of one of the cabins, and Harford sent him down in the moonlight to invite De Sopo for a drink. The moments dragged until he came. Harford felt a need of masculine conversation; it was almost with relief that he heard the account of the capture of the slaves, who were all war captives, the Fang having raided the villages of the Makae. De Sopo had been gathering food for them on his way down the river; he was expecting old Otolo and his people to bring in several canoe loads of plantain and cassava before the noonday; he had ten hunters out for game, and what rice he had was already under cover—"though the niggers of these parts

will not eat rice unless they are starving." But with all he could do by way of provision either out of his own stock or by purchase from the Fang, he felt a shortage. He had been a long time coming overland, and the Fang by the way had been grudging of their food, seeing that the slaves were Makae. He hoped that Harford had rice and salt to spare, else he would have to go down the river to Taylor, as he had rice for no more than a week, and while he expected news of the *Arrow* within that time, there was no certainty, as Harford knew. And he wondered whether Harford would be able, when the time of shipment came, to lend him five or six canoes.

Harford sighed with irritation; he assured De Sopo that he must not look to him for any help, as his equipment was no more than adequate for his own needs, and he was concerned that the Fang should not have occasion to associate him with any other trade than his own. De Sopo amiably agreed; the idiosyncrasies of his companion were curious, and might perhaps be explained as the Fang were explaining them. Old Otolo had told De Sopo that Hallifodi had a strong taboo and must not trade in slaves. De Sopo had acquired some taboos himself; he could only be grateful that these were minor and not of a nature to interfere with business. He was glad of Harford's presence in the neighborhood, for the barracoon was not of the best, having been hastily made, without proper stronghold; he knew that the presence of a white man's factory would intimidate the slaves, and this, in default of his dead partner, was an end much to be desired. They were in poor shape, he told Harford, having suffered from the journey.

The two men remembered old times—days of youth, captains of ships, old and fantastic headmen; traders and their adventures, their girls, their deaths, the fates of their half-breed children, were remembered until the moon was low and De Sopo must go back to his cabin in the village that was nearest the barracoon. The slaves, he said, should be coming along in the morning. He had a crew of Benga men with them, an armed man to a canoe, and that was not enough.

He went down to the clearing, his shadow, with its broad hat, black behind him. Harford marked how thin the Spaniard was—as he had already marked his pallor. De Sopo walked like a man without a care in the world. As for himself—he looked about his clearing where his goods were stored and his crew of Fang were sleeping, to the cabin where his wife lay and where a light still shone at the window, and he felt a kind of envy of homeless, reckless, disreputable vagabonds.

With the dawn there came a wailing on the river; Harford wakened to the sound and wondered that De Sopo would put up with it—he should be able, Harford thought, to control the wailing of his slaves. The wailing grew as the canoes multiplied at the landing—the high

desolate wailing that is the voice of the sorrows of Africa. That rhythmic crying presently filled the river valley. The devil must have a million of them, Harford thought. And he heard a sobbing at the door of the factory—thinking it a strange thing, until he knew it to be Lucy. She fell against him sobbing; she could not get her breath to ask him what it was she heard, and her terror released in him a fresh sense of the authentic anguish of the wailing. He took her to his bed and warmed her, soothing her; he gave her brandy that she took with a child's obedience, sobbing as she put her lip against the cup. He lay beside her, telling her that she must be reassured, that it was the slaves come down the river into the barracoon. And when he was done, the sound of wailing filled the room; his wife wept against him. Neither of them ever spoke again of the union of black girls and white men.

Book III

The Barracoon

§ 1

With the morning there was silence in the river valley. The clearing between the walls of the barracoon was alive with human activities; above the thatch which roofed the lean-to that ran along the inner walls smoke rose; fires burned here and there in the compound, and pots were on the fires. Harford could see, with his eye to his spy-glass, all that remembered routine of the encampment waiting shipment; he noted that the slaves were ill-fed, and he thought, in view of the disrepair of the stockade, that this was a good thing. The lot was mixed in age and sex, though women were in the majority, as is customary among captives of tribal wars. The men were chained in pairs, but the women were not shackled.

When he put his glass down Lucy picked it up. She was not expert in its use, and into the frame of its single round there swung the green wall of the forest across the river, where, among the branches of a tree in flower, a golden snake imperceptibly drew its length. She lowered the glass; there was a canoe, brown on the brown flood of the river. Bracing the barrel of the glass against a stanchion of the verandah, she found the range of the barracoon and she caught her breath. On that day, and on the days that followed, for hour after hour she inspected the barracoon.

Harford's attention was eventually caught; he watched her, wonder-

ing at her concentration. He saw the glass, shifted delicately, rake the
sunny open and the shadows under the thatch of the long roof. He saw
that Lucy was pale and that she leaned against the stanchion, but she
would not be dissuaded. "I see them living," she told her husband
when he asked her what was there. And was again absorbed.

The slaves were ten days in the barracoon before Harford forbade
Lucy the use of the spyglass. He had been away overnight, little as he
liked to leave his wife alone at the factory; but he trusted Atemba,
and he took advantage of the presence of De Sopo, knowing that the
Spaniard was within hail. He returned light-hearted, with three
ivories bought from under the bamboo bed of a difficult old headman.
His carriers sang as they came out of the forest path into the factory
clearing; Harford thought that Lucy would be hearing them, and glad
of his return. But Lucy, in the blaze of the afternoon sun, was on
the verandah, looking through the glass. Harford was on the steps
before she took account of him. The degree of her preoccupation re-
pelled him; her dress was disordered and her hair unkempt; their
greetings were brief. She returned to her post at the stanchion, and
pointed her glass again with a practised hand.

Atemba brought him his food, and Lucy did not join him. Harford
observed her from where he sat at table behind the bamboo screen
that shaded the north end of the little verandah—it came into his
mind that she might be ill. He bade her go to the shade of her room,
and this she did, but with reluctance. Later in the afternoon she
came to him where he was alone in the musty gloom of the storehouse;
she was then hysterical—telling him that she could not bear her life
and must get away. He turned from the shelves where he was going
over his bales of calico. "This," he thought, "is nostalgia"—and he
thought himself to be overtaken by the difficulties he had foreseen
from the first day of his marriage. She said again that she must get
away, and she wrung her hands. He considered her seriously; he told
her that when he had finished with an ivory deal now pending with
Efa Ngoto they would take a holiday down the river—though he
sighed when he said this, and did not see his way clear. "It will be a
long time, perhaps," he told her, and said that she must not count
on it.

Lucy turned her back and leaned her forehead on the door jamb;
he felt her struggle to control her voice. "It is the slaves," she said.
"I can't—I can't—Mr. Harford, the children—" But she could not
bring herself to tell him more.

He drew her out of the storeroom; with his habit of caution he
paused to lock the door. Going to the verandah, he trained the glass
on the barracoon. He must see for himself what it was that so pos-

sessed his wife—though it was a fever in the making, he told himself.
He swept his eye about that clearing, full of late afternoon sunlight
and of slaves. The accommodations were certainly not of the best—
De Sopo had been doing a makeshift sort of business, and there was
obviously a shortage of food. He especially observed the women and
children, as Lucy had done; he tried to see them with her eyes, and he
agreed that it was a sorry sight. When he lowered the glass he put
it away in a chest of his own belongings, telling her that she must
oblige him by not using it again so long as the slaves were there—"and
that will not be long," he told her; De Sopo was hoping to send them
down the river any day and any hour. He begged her to contain her-
self. His own business was urgent for the time, and he could not go
away.

"Let me go with Atemba," she urged. "I could go down the river
with Atemba—we should be safe."

"Yes," he said. "and find yourself in a fleet of slave canoes—or sleep-
ing in Taylor's house when the cargo is landing! You must content
yourself," he told her, "for you are a trader's wife. It will not be long."

§ 2

But it was long. Two long days from then, when Lucy sat before
a dressing table she had made of packing boxes and muslin, De Sopo
came to confer with Harford, and his Mpongwe girl—breaking bounds
—came with him. Lucy saw her shadow in the mirror, dark against the
orange daylight at the door. She turned and looked at her; the girl
moved into the room as though Lucy's glance were a summons; she
came near, looking gravely about at the white woman's possessions.

"How you health, Mamee?" she said in her soft insinuating voice.
And the aura of her femininity, fostered as it was and cultured in its
kind, startled Lucy, so long used to men and to the hardy alien Fang
women.

"What for you come here, Mamee?" asked the girl. "This never
be proper town for beach woman."

"What for *you* come here?" asked Lucy.

"My white man come; he speak for you man. He ask you man:
'What for you no fit for give proper food for them slaves? They live
for die they no catch food. Plenty pickaninny die; night come we
throw him for bush!' My massa ask you man: 'What for you no give
proper chop? You like all my slaves die, we throw him for river?' "

Lucy sat staring at the girl, not knowing all that she had said. And
the soft voice went on: "Hallifodi say he never be fit for feed all

them slaves. My massa say, 'You please feed all them sick slaves, all them pickaninny—those women holler all night you never feed them!' Hallifodi say, 'No, goddam, I never feed them slaves—I got big taboo, I never feed slaves!' "

Lucy's hand fell from her head, letting her hair fall, and the Mpongwe, grown bolder, touched it softly as she had often wished to do. She sang a little chant of admiration in her own tongue. Lucy did not draw away; she was grown used to the pleasure of black women in her hair and skin. She answered Esala perfunctorily when the girl asked, "What tribe be your slave Atemba? Where you get that boy?" She was sunk in dark thoughts. She did not know when Esala went away.

At table that night she asked Harford if De Sopo came to see him, and when he answered "Yes" and no more, she asked him, "Why?"

"He cannot let me alone about food for his slaves—he says they will starve if Taylor doesn't send for them soon. He has cleaned out the Fang—they had little to spare. And he cannot agree that I am not here to sell him food."

"Cannot you?" questioned Lucy heavily.

"I cannot. I have vowed that I am not a slaver, nor a partner of slavers. Either I do a legitimate trade in Africa or I get out!" Harford flung himself sidewise to the table—he had hoped to put away this palaver long enough to eat his palm-oil chop and baked plantain. He felt himself to be harried to death. De Sopo would go down the river that night, he told her, to see what could be done, though fearing to leave the barracoon in charge of the crew of Benga. A gang of slaves should be under the surveillance of not less than three white men.

"He says he cannot trust the Benga not to sleep at night. He had the hardihood to ask me if I would not serve him in his absence. He isn't such a bad fellow, either; I'd do him a service if I could, and I pity him."

Harford presently went down to the landing to see De Sopo off; he asked Lucy if she could spare half a dozen of her soda biscuits for De Sopo, and a pot of the preserve she had made of an edible forest fruit. She made a little pack of these; she saw her husband go away with his hurricane lamp, and she went to his chest, from which she took his spyglass.

Atemba lighted her way to her cabin, as was his habit at night. The soft dark of the tropics was vibrant with the ineluctable unbroken singing of insects in the grass at the edge of the forest wall. The rains were near again and the insects and the frogs spread an immense fabric beneath the stars. There was no moon; the drumming in the villages was desultory. Suddenly the slaves wailed—faintly,

and stronger, and fully, the voice of wailing filled the river valley. Lucy trembled; she sank upon the lower step of her cabin.

"Oh, why, Atemba," she shuddered, "do they wail?" And he told her they wailed because their father was going away. De Sopo was going down the river, so they wailed.

But how was he their father, she asked. Had he not bought them, and would he not sell them? How was he their father? "He is certainly that," Atemba told her, "their father. Without him they would starve, and they fear to see him go. They say, 'O our Father, O! We die of hunger, O! Pity your children, O! Do not leave us, lest we starve!' And perhaps they will starve," Atemba added dispassionately.

The wailing flowed like a river through the dark. Atemba listened to his mistress's anguished command that he go to the slaves and beg them not to wail. He thought this a silly invention, but he did not cross his white woman. He would go, he said, if they did not stop— but it would not be a long wailing, for it was no more than a farewell.

It ceased. Atemba went away, and an hour later Harford found Lucy seated on the step of her cabin, the light from her hurricane lamp shining sweetly on her white dress and up into her face. Her mournful dark eyes met his that answered them sternly. "This woman," he thought, "is out of place."

§ 3

At noon the next day, Harford, who was surrounded by a rustic group and was weighing ivory, did not see Lucy return his glass to his chest. At their midday meal she questioned him closely as to De Sopo's plans and whether he would be home the next day or the day after that. Not for three days, he told her, and added that the cargo canoes would be longer in coming than that. It was De Sopo's plan to make a place for the slaves on the beach, although that was against his interest and judgment; but the loss if they were to remain in the barracoon, with food so scarce, would be heavy. He must risk the move to the beach.

Harford hoped—and he wished, in his present preoccupation, to believe—that Lucy did not know the death rate among the slaves. He was glad to forget that he could not see his way to help, and he was elated at the spread of his trade. A company from Ayos had traveled a week by canoe to sell him their ivories; they came, trailing their leopard skins and speaking a modified dialect, from a remote people whose trade he had labored to develop. When night came, and the last man

and dog on leash had gone down the hill and off up the river, Harford sank into his chair with a tot of rum, and he could have wished to be alone in his clearing. He wished he need not see his wife at table lest she trouble him with questions. But she was as silent as himself. Had he looked at her he would not have known her for the laughing girl who had hung on his arm when they had first climbed the hill to the factory not a year ago. He would have been struck, had he looked at her, by her thinness, her look of strain, her pallor, her rough and broken hair. But, after the custom of companions who live together without lapse, neither of these two was attentive to the aspect of the other, and Lucy sank away into the shadow of her obsession unobserved.

When Atemba lit the lamp in her cabin that night, Lucy spoke with him. She asked him if he had been born a slave. Atemba was a headman's son, he told her. "It is a strange thing," he thought, "how long the white people are in framing the first of questions." She asked him if the big gate to the barracoon was locked with a key. Atemba said it was, barred and locked with a key, and that there were other precautions about the outer wall—there was an outer wall and an inner door. A passage, very short, led from the gate to the inner door. All the building, Atemba told her, was rough. The barracoon in which he himself had been imprisoned once was strong; none could have looked into that barracoon. And with that memory a terrible excitement began to flow into his heart, threatening his control. He felt a current of intention, obscure as yet, lift him from his accepted groove. He gave his attention, suddenly creative, subtly perceptive, to Lucy— trying to penetrate her secret thought, conscious of an intense dynamic at work beneath her fixed composure.

She asked him who had the key to the gate—if De Sopo had it; and he said he did not know. He was silent. And then he said there was one who knew who had the key, and if his Mamee commanded him to ask that one he would do so. When Lucy pressed him for the name of that one, he said it was Esala, De Sopo's woman. She would know who had the key. If his Mamee commanded him to do so, he would return, when night was in the middle, with that knowledge.

While Lucy pondered upon this, he looked in her mirror, taking counsel with his dark and secret image that spoke to him there, eye to eye. Behind him in the dim reflection stood the white woman listening to a strong inner voice. She would tell him to go. And if she did not tell him, still he would go—for he felt an irresistible quickening toward a course that was clearing, like a path when dawn reveals it. When Lucy told him that he must do as he had said, his going was a passion of acquiescence. The swift withdrawal of his energy from her cabin

and from the clearing left Lucy like a castaway, with the tide on the ebb—she felt a vast fatigue and the hurry of her heart beating.

Harford's window shed an orange light and then was dark; there was now no light in the forest. Upon the dark the Southern Cross was erected and leaned again to its decline; occasionally a bird called or a band of monkeys clamored briefly; a late moon rose behind the cabins, and their black shadows bit into the flooding light.

At something like two o'clock Atemba stood in the shadow of Lucy's west window; he had the key and gave it to her. Esala, he said, had given him the key to hold until the dark before the dawn. "What shall I tell the white woman," he thought, "if she asks me why Esala gave me the key?" But Lucy did not ask that or any other question— she seemed to dream.

Atemba came to the door and opened it; beyond the shadow where he stood there was a wash of moonlight in the clearing. "Mamee," he asked her with an utmost urgency, "when you let the slaves go—am I then free?"

He saw Lucy startle as if she woke. She asked him if he saw the Benga guards and if they were sleeping. He had found them sleeping—and that was because their master was away and because the slaves, they knew, were weak from sickness and from hunger. Atemba had wakened the guards as he passed, telling them there was a leopard abroad in the clearing on moonlight nights. Only strangers and white men, he told them, were ignorant of this—all others seeking a shelter to sleep in. The Benga men, he said, had given him thanks and had said that they must lie outside to watch the slaves. There was a house, he had told them, near the gate; they had better lie there. If the leopard caught them, who would watch the slaves? Would their master not then blame them that they had not listened to the warning of Hallifodi's man? After which reasoning, Atemba told Lucy, they had risen from their bed of leaves upon the ground and had gone away into the house. The house, Atemba told her, looked away from the barracoon. It was a strange thing, he told her, but they went into that house. "Ah, Mamee," he said in a voice of profoundest passion, "when you let the slaves go—"

She did not answer him—she moved past him down the steps into the moonlight. She took no account of him. But later, when they were in the shadow of the trail to the river, he pressed his fate again: "Ah, Mamee, am I, too, free? When it is taboo for you to have a slave, and it is taboo for Hallifodi to have a slave, am I free?" He was behind her in the trail; he heard her say yes. He took the key from her hand; her hand was hot, and, with his faculty of perception at its highest level, he was aware, among a multitude of impressions, that she had a fever. He wished that her dress were dark; it glimmered, and her

skirt was noisy among the grasses. He wished that she were sure to do as he might find occasion to tell her; he wished that he were in control, as a man should be—and his will leaped before him in the path. When she came to the end of the shadowed trail and to the verge of the clearing about the barracoon, he bade her wait, and they stood still.

In the mild clear light of the moon the stockade of the barracoon rose to the height of about twelve feet; they were standing a hundred feet from its southeast corner. Midway of the eastern wall there was, curiously, a great tree; it was incorporated in the stockade, and it made, of a morning, shade upon the glare on the floor of the barracoon. It is to be supposed that De Sopo had left it there because it presented difficulties in felling, and its crest of branches, high upon the pillar of its bole, was not hospitable to escape. The river ran fifty yards from the west wall; the space between was cleared and was now in shadow. The gate was in the south wall; it was barred, and the lock was a padlock. The guards were not in sight; the fire by which they had slept was sunk to embers, and their leafy beds were dark on the ground. There was no sound of life, only the river's running.

Suddenly from behind the wall of the barracoon there rose a woman's faint and plaintive wailing—like a thread of smoke from a small fire on a windless air. Atemba knew it for a cry of remembrance. Without warning Lucy floated out into the moonlight; she was at the gate before he was; her hand was at her lip while he unlocked the gate. They stepped swiftly into the passage; Atemba drew the gate to; the key was in his hand. The passage was eight feet long—the depth of the lean-to that ran about the inner wall; the door at the end of this short passage was barred but not locked. The delicate cry rose again. Lucy threw up the iron bar, and they were in the yard of the barracoon.

§ 4

The moon was above the eastern wall; the shadow of the great tree was upon the trodden ground of the western half of the enclosure. Under the thatch of the lean-to the slaves slept in the shadow. Lucy —who had brooded so many days upon the comings and goings of the many dark bodies, now cooking, now eating, now lamenting—was alone with the moonlight in the clearing. She was arrested in a still enchantment. Atemba saw that she did not see a woman gray with dust who lay upon the earth, and swifter than her perception he sprang to where the woman lay. Catching her about the middle, he brought her to her feet, one hand over her mouth. Her eyes stared at Lucy while he dragged her to the passageway. Atemba summoned Lucy with a

movement of his head; they were in the passage before she had caught her breath, and Atemba was speaking in the woman's ear. He instructed her; Lucy saw her eyes focus on his words. He released her—she was a young woman ravaged with hunger; she was gone back into the compound like the flowing of water.

Atemba drew Lucy through the outer gate; he closed it, and they slid by the south wall in the moonlight to the shadow under the west wall. In that shadow Lucy fell to trembling, her teeth chattered, and she leaned against the wall. Presently she vomited. Atemba, seeing that she could not stand, supported her. She moaned, and he was appalled, but his decision was as swift as breath. He carried her to the water's edge; the jetty was in moonlight, and he was too much a forest creature to move that way; he laid Lucy among the leaves at the foot of the forest wall, first stirring them with his foot; he covered her white dress with his own dark cloth. He let himself down into the water that ran deep by this bank, and returned with a small canoe —it was the ferryman's canoe and its anchorage well known. Lucy was past speech. He laid her in the seepage in the bottom of the canoe; drawing her dress along her sides, he spread his cloth over her and pushed off into the stream. He could see a flowing of dark bodies along the bright south wall of the barracoon; they disappeared into the shadow of the west wall. He dipped his paddle, making upstream.

A river silence fell on the canoe; Lucy's sigh was light. Coming to a little beach landing, the canoe wavered. Atemba gave a bird call; there was no answer. Under the deep shade of a wooded bank he whistled again and waited, but not long; Lucy moaned and stirred; he cleared the bank and paddled upstream. He dipped his paddle three or four times before he heard an answer to his call—a bird whistled among the branches that swung from the near margin. Atemba held the canoe and scanned the forest wall. He drew in to a log and found a backwater in the thicket; the river glittered in midstream, but here was a moon dusk. Esala crept out on the log, and Atemba held out to her the key. She took it, thrusting it into the basket under her arm; drawing the canoe alongside, she boarded, startling when she felt Lucy's body under the cloth. The paddle sank into the water, the canoe shot out into the stream, and there was silence on the river.

In the moonlight Atemba saw that Esala had whitened her face with clay, after the manner of the Fang who mourn, and that she was as naked as a Fang woman, that she had painted dark designs on her body, which was smooth and without the inevitable Fang tattoo. He understood that she was joining her fate with his, and he felt a rush of pride and passion. It was true of Atemba that he was a chief's son and of no mean tribe. How far his home was, or where it might be, he

could not know; he could look up at the stars and take counsel of them; soon, too, he must counsel with Esala. It did not appear to him what he must do with the white woman; his swift planning had not foreseen the present difficulty—he had thought that Lucy would steal away to her cabin when they had left the barracoon. But there was no hope of that now; he knew the course of her fevers, and that she would be helpless for not less than a day. Nothing in his heart swerved from his intention of escape; he was as single as an arrow that has been released from the bow; all his wisdom was fused to an instinct, and he knew that he must go upriver swiftly all the night—and without words.

Neither he nor Esala could pass in prolonged intercourse as Fang. A canoe from upriver hailed them, surveyed them in the moonlight, and, seeing the ashen face of Esala, the paddler asked them who had died. "A child," said Atemba. Esala wailed faintly, and the canoe went its way. But Lucy, when Esala wailed, stirred again, moaned, and would have sat up. Atemba steered into a backwater; the canoe stole up this dark shallow until he knew by the evil smell that he was at the end of the inlet, and in a pool where the women of a village were used to soak their manioc. He shipped his paddle and crept along the length of the canoe to Esala in the bow. He began to speak to her softly in their only common tongue, which was Fang. Under the intense dark Lucy sighed and slept.

Presently from the forest the guinea fowl called the near approach of morning, and in the dark the two dark heads drew apart, the murmur of voices ceased, the canoe slid back to the river. Time was pressing, but they knew what they must do. Before the pallor of dawn Esala had guided Atemba to a trodden beach; it was the landing of the headman Efa Ngoto, who had a village near by in the forest. She knew that place well, having camped there with De Sopo more than once. A shelter with three walls under thatch was in common use at the landing. It stood clear of the forest, which was here of great trees, and open. They must work quickly before day. Coming ashore, they drew up the canoe, and Atemba lifted Lucy, who was now in a stupor. Esala was before him in the shelter; she found the embers of a fire that was always there upon the ground of the hut, and that would be renewed many times in the day by the villagers as they came and went upon the river. With a burning log for a light, she looked about the hut; there was no snake, no filth, no menace. Atemba, standing with Lucy across his shoulder, watched her; he was ready at the signal to lay his mistress down. She sighed, relaxing on the bed and turning her head away upon the wooden pillow. Esala adjusted her dress. Atemba would have thrown his cloth about her, but Esala caught it up; she

drew the logs together, and a thread of smoke rose. Swift as shadows the two were gone, and the canoe, dark a moment on the glitter of the river, disappeared.

§ 5

The smoke among the logs became a flame; the mists of morning rose in the moonlight; the river spoke and spoke against the little beach; a monkey looked into the open shelter with surprise, and was intimidated; with the gray light a million parrots woke to their domestic disagreements and were articulate. The clamor of day woke in the forest. And the first fisherman coming down the village trail looked in at the hut. As if he were winged, he stood again in the street of the village. "There is a magic by the river!" he told his friends. "A strange one is there!"

But the headman, when he saw the strange one, knew it for the wife of Hallifodi, having seen that woman many times. He was appalled.

Behind him and pressing upon him and upon one another, the people of his village crowded, struck with wonder. Their voices, discreet at first, grew in volume and in stress, but Lucy did not move until an old woman broke into a high crying wail. Other women wailed, and the white woman, moaning faintly, moved her head, moved her hand, and was still again.

"She lives! She breathes!" cried out the agitated people of the village of Efa Ngoto.

Efa himself, though much against his will,—for who knew how the matter stood either with the white woman's husband or in the more supernatural implications?—got himself ready to go to Hallifodi. He was deliberate in his preparations, wishing that his experience had fitted him for the present adventure and for the part he had to play. He put on the best he had—and that was a military coat and a red fez cap, both bought of Hallifodi himself. He chose swift rowers. He gave instructions that no one of his village was to approach the white woman, none was to go under the thatch, but that his head wife herself, with those women whom she should choose, was to watch from without the hut. Only Evina was not to watch. She was his present favorite wife and was with child; she must beware dark powers. He went away in the sunlight.

It was presently warm in the shadow of the thatch, and with the passage of the day the sun shone there. The women, four and five at a time, pitied the white woman with their eyes. They sang plaintive songs—spontaneous little ballads about the white woman who had

come to lie upon the bed of their village. She had come by the river, O! She had no child, O! Alone she had come, O! She said no word, O! Her beautiful hair, O! Her fine white cloth, O! They struck their hands softly for an accompaniment to their songs.

The white woman whimpered and sighed, and the black women more than ever sang their plaintive songs. These songs, they thought, were good for that magic, for with the afternoon Lucy was still. Harford heard them singing at the bend of the river, and his heart turned over.

The Fang women fell away when the white man came to look at his woman. They had not gone near her all day; they could in no way be to blame for her death—if indeed she was dead.

She was dead. The women saw her hand fall from Harford's. They saw him look into her eyes. They burst into a wail, and the entire village of Efa Ngoto wailed.

Harford sat down on a piece of firewood; he could no longer stand on his feet. Nothing of all this was clear to him. The face of his wife was a secret silence in a great clamor. He had not eaten that day; news of the empty barracoon had shattered his morning, and with noon Efa Ngoto had stood at the door with news of a wife he had hardly missed. No, he had not missed her; he had been all morning with the Benga guards and with the straggling slaves who had returned to beg from him a handful of rice.

How had she come here, and why? Was this really his wife? A laughing girl, a chatterer—now to be lying so pale and sunken in this rude shelter—lost here in a strange forest. Lying here without a word. No answer. How had she come here? Had she been poisoned? Her dress was draggled. Her hair was disordered. He stooped to put her poor hands beside her, and on the dust of the ground he saw a key. Abstractedly with his foot he pushed it aside—the headman should have a care of his keys.

The Spanish Farm

R. H. MOTTRAM

RALPH HALE MOTTRAM *was born in Norwich, England,
October 30, 1883. He was educated first at a private school
in Norwich and then in Lausanne, Switzerland. Despite his
Quaker antecedents, he enlisted at the outbreak of the First
World War, and here his command of French proved an
invaluable pass key in his duties as a battalion commander,
interpreter and general peacemaker with the Flemish peas-
ants. His first novel,* The Spanish Farm, *was published in
1924 and shortly thereafter was awarded the Hawthornden
Prize. The novel measures 59,000 words.*

TO ·

MY WIFE

INTRODUCTION

Please understand that the Spanish Farm—which gives the title to this novel—has no connection whatever with the Spain of Alfonso or Franco. To that extent the title is misleading. In reality the Spanish Farm was a single-storied building of immensely thick walls of red brick which had been built three hundred years ago in the Flemish borderlands; it was surrounded by a wide and deep moat and guarded by a shot tower whose loopholed bulk now served as a tool shed. In its time the Spanish Farm had sheltered Neapolitan mercenaries fighting the French, Spanish colonists fighting the Flemish and Frenchmen fighting the English or the Dutch. In between wars it had been occupied with the more placid business of tilling the best soil in Europe. And now as the story opens in the autumn of 1915 it is once more packed tight with humanity, two companies of Kitchener's Mob sent here to lick their wounds and reorganize after the disastrous offensive at Loos. The farm took its name from the Spanish colonists who had built it at the time of Alva and down through the three centuries it had acquired a personality of its own. It symbolized the implacable spirit of that borderland so often fought over but never really conquered.

Madeleine Vanderlynden, who is in her twentieth year at the beginning of the novel, was born on the Spanish Farm, and in her blood is that tenacity, that masterful spirit with which her peasant forebears clung to the old blockhouse farm through war and peace. Madeleine herself, as we see her in these pages, might have been painted by one of the old Flemish masters. She is square and strong but so close knit that she does not look disproportionately broad. ("That great Flanders mare ought to have two seats allowed her!" said a Parisian cocotte—but the girl was jealous!) Madeleine's figure, kept in check by hard

work and frugal feeding, would have held the eye of any man; her gray eyes with their level and serene brows, her dark hair and her skin with its pallor of health would have prompted the exclamation, "What a handsome woman!"—not "What a pretty girl!" The girl in her had been subdued some time ago.

Why she is so self-contained, why she resists the usual temptations of the flesh is a question which at the outset neither her English visitors nor her French neighbors can answer. What we do know is that she manages men adroitly and that for some reason she is herself remote. Her father alone suspects the reason for her preoccupation. All that Madeleine shows to those billeted at the farm (and practically the whole English army must have passed through or near it at one time or another) was her slow-burning resentment against the war—this *bêtise,* this great "stupidity," which was cutting so irrevocably into her life. The front was only twenty miles away, and the passing of troops, the sound of the guns and the threat of the German attack give tension to the scene. To live day by day in such a surrounding calls for sturdy individuality, and Madeleine's spirit came straight from the farm itself. "She was that spirit that forgets nothing and forgives nothing but maintains itself, amid all disasters, and necessarily." But with all this she was highly desirable—as the French interpreter makes only too clear before he is bowled over by the crockery.

Madeleine had been educated at a convent in St Omer, and, whether it was her education or her inspiration, the fact remains that she started with the English cavalry officers a sort of understanding that she would never have attempted with French troops. The English paid her liberally and treated her respectfully, probably confusing her in their minds with English farmers' wives to whom they were in the habit of paying for hunt damage. They had money; Madeleine had eggs, coffee, soft bread, *pommes frites* and beer. She could launder shirts and collars and she realized that every English officer required so many gallons of water to wash in at least once a day. All this, as Mr Mottram says with a quiet smile, she attended to at a small charge.

"Careful, even grudging in everything, when she gave she gave generously—no half measures." To three men she reveals herself. Between her father and herself there was an almost wordless understanding; to reach Skene she had to pass through the barriers of language and association, and one is never sure for how long their intimacy can survive; whereas beneath the cool, efficient concealment of her affair with Georges there runs a maternal feeling and a passion as natural as anything in the world.

"For four years and three months," said John Galsworthy, speaking of the First World War, "the British army was in France, and, so far

as I know, Madeleine is the only full, solid, intimate piece of French characterization which has resulted from that long and varied contact." It is Mr Mottram's forte to have made us understand, as it were, a French woman at bay and, incidentally, to have illuminated by contrasts so true that they constantly make us smile those small differences in temperament and behavior which separate the English and the French. The author accomplishes this, not by long interjections of French, but by the deftest suggestions in English to indicate the differences in speech and in character. He himself served in Flanders from 1914 to 1919—"partly as a troop commander, partly as a sort of military diplomat." Not otherwise could he have gained such an artist's feeling for the Flemish landscape, such unerring knowledge of Englishmen without women, of Madeleine and the Spanish Farm.

THE SPANISH FARM

PART I

La Patrie est en danger

A FARMER stood watching a battalion of infantry filing into his pasture. A queerer mixture of humanity could not have been imagined. The farmer wore a Dutch cap, spoke Flemish by preference, but could only write French. His farm was called Ferme l'Éspagnole—The Spanish Farm—and stood on French soil. The soldiers were the usual English mixture—semi-skilled townsmen, a number of agricultural and other laborers, fewer still of seafaring and waterside folk, and a sprinkling of miners and shepherds, with one or two regulars.

The farmer, Mr. Vanderlynden, Jerome, described in the Communal records as a Cultivator, sixty-five years of age, watching his rich grass being tramped to liquid mud under the heavy boots of the incoming files, and the shifting of foot-weary men as they halted in close column, platoon by platoon, made no protest. This was not merely because under the French law he was bound to submit to the needs of the troops, but also because, after twelve months' experience, he had discovered that there were compensations attached to the billeting and encampment of English. They paid—so much per officer or man—not always accurately, but promptly always, and what would you more in war-time? The Spanish Farm was less than twenty kilometers from the "Front," the actual trenches, whose ground-shaking gun-rumble was always to be heard, whose scouting aeroplanes were visible and audible all day, whose endless flicker of star shells made green the eastern horizon all night. The realities of the situation were ever present to Mr. Jerome Vanderlynden, who besides could remember a far worse war, that of 1870. Moreover, the first troops passing that way in the far-off days of 1914 had been French, and had wanted twice as much attention, and had never paid, had even threatened him when he suggested it.

.

Standing with his great knotted earthy fists hanging by his side, as the khaki stream poured and poured through the wide-set gate, he passed in review the innumerable units or detachments that had billeted in the Spanish Farm or encamped in its pastures. Uncritical, almost unreasoning, the old peasant was far from being able to define the difference he had felt when the first English arrived. He had heard tell of them, read of them in the paper, but was far from imagining what they might have been like, having no data to go on and no power of imagination. He had been coming in from getting up the last of the potato crop of 1914 when he had found flat-capped, mud-coloured horsemen at his gate. Sure that they were Germans (the Uhlans had been as near as Hazebrouck only a few weeks before), he hastily tied the old white horse in the tombereau, and had gone forward cap in hand. But his daughter Madeleine had already met the soldiers at the gate. A widower for many years, Jerome Vanderlynden's house was kept by his youngest child, this Madeleine, now in her twentieth year. To say that he believed in her does not do justice to his feelings. She had been the baby of the family, had had a better education than he or his sons, at a convent in St. Omer; added to all this, plus her woman's prestige, was the fact that she inherited (from heaven knows where!) a masterful strain. What she said (and she was not lavish of words) was attended to. Whether it were education, inspiration, or more probably an appreciation beyond the powers of her father, that told her that English cavalry officers would agree with her, it is certain that she started with those first squadrons of the Cavalry Division a sort of understanding that she would never have attempted with French troops. They paid her liberally and treated her respectfully, probably confusing her in their minds with English farmers' wives to whom they were in the habit of paying for hunt damage. They had money—officers and men wanted to supplement their rations and the horses' forage. Madeleine had eggs, coffee, soft bread, beer, fried potatoes, beans, oats. She could and did wash collars and shirts better than the average soldier servant. It took her some time to understand that every English officer required many gallons of water to wash in, at least once a day. But once she had grasped that too, she attended to it, at a small charge.

And now it was October, 1915; more troops than ever, especially infantry, were in the commune, and an interpreter had warned Jerome Vanderlynden that he would have a whole battalion in the farm. He made no remark, but Madeleine had asked several questions. More awake mentally than her father, it had not escaped her close reading of

the paper that a new sort of English troops were coming to France. They were described indifferently as "Territorials" and as "New Army" or "Kitchener's Army," and neither Madeleine nor indeed the newspapers of the Department du Nord knew of any difference between them and the Territoriaux of the French system. Madeleine put them down as second-line troops and stored the fact in her vigilant mind.

She came and stood beside her father, as the 10th Battalion Easthamptonshire Regiment broke up and moved off to its billets. Two of the sadly depleted companies went to adjacent farms, two remained on the premises. The officers—of whom only twelve survived the battle of Loos—were busy with non-coms., going through nominal rolls, lists of missing men or damaged equipment, trying to disentangle some sort of parade state and indent for replacements.

Madeleine did not bother about them. She said to her father: "I am going to find the Quarta-mastere!"

She found him, standing amid his stores in the hop-press, and knew him by his gray hair and white-red-white ribbon. She had long ago inquired and found out that this rank in the English Army were chosen from among the old soldiers, and were quickest at getting to business. It had been explained to her that the white-red-white ribbon was for length of good conduct, and secretly tolerant of men's foibles as of a child's, she stored this fact also, for identification purposes.

In this instance the Mess President having been killed, the old ranker, Lieutenant and Quartermaster John Adams, was acting Mess President, and doing nearly every other duty in the disorganization and readjustment that followed the tragic bungle of the New Army's first offensive.

He greeted her with his professional aplomb: "Good day, Maddam, dinner for twelve officers; compris, douze!" He held up the fingers of both hands and then two fingers separately.

"All right!" returned Madeleine in English. "Where are their rations?"

He replied, "Ah, you're sharp!" and called to his storekeeper, "Jermyn, officers' rations to Maddam and tell the mess cook!" He went on to bargain for other things—beds for the Colonel, the Adjutant and himself—and in the course of the argument Madeleine informed him that according to General Routine Orders there was to be no smoking in the barns and no insanitary practices, that all gates must be kept closed, and no movables removed. Handing him her price list, she withdrew to her long coffin-shaped stove in the brick-floored kitchen.

Dusk settled down on the Spanish Farm—autumn dusk—with swathed mists on the small flat chocolate-coloured fields, richest and best tilled in the world—not bare of crops. The brilliant colours of the last hop-leaves and of the regular rows of elms that bordered each pasture were hidden, but the tops of the trees towered above the mist-line into that wide blue vault that the old painters loved, nowhere wider than in the Flemish plain. The Spanish Farm stood on the almost imperceptible southern slope of the sandy ridge that divides in some degree the valley of the Yser from that of the Lys, whose flat meadows lay spread out, almost from Aire to the factory smoke of Armentières, at a slightly lower level to the south. Northward, behind the house, the ground rose very gradually in fertile field and elm-encircled pasture. Westward, black against the last glow of the sunset, two little 'planes droned their way from the aerodromes round St. Omer toward the eastern horizon where the evening "hate" was toned down by the distance to the low boom of "heavies," the sharper note of the field-guns, the whip-lash crack of rifles and machine-guns, and the flatter squashed-out reports of mortars and grenades.

The house itself was a single-storied building of immensely thick walls of red brick—much as the settlers under Alva had left it three hundred years before—except for enlargement of windows and re-thatching—though the existing thatch was so old that wall-flowers tasselled its ridge from one octagonal spoke-tiled chimney-stack to the other. Originally a simple block with door in the middle, outbuildings had been added at each end, giving it the form of an unfinished quad-rangle, the gap toward the south, enclosing the great steaming midden of golden dung. Completely surrounded by a deep wide moat, access to it was only possible by a brick bridge on the southern side, guarded by a twenty-foot extinguisher-roofed "shot" tower, whose loopholed bulk now served for tool shed below and pigeonloft above.

Further outbuildings stood outside the moat, a few to the north in the smaller pasture behind the house, but a long broad range of cowshed, stable, and hop-press stretched into the ten-acre "home" or "manor" pasture.

Never, since Alva last marched that way, had the old semi-fortress been so packed with humanity. Two companies, which even at their present weakness must have numbered over three hundred men, were getting rid of their arms and equipment and filing round to the north pasture where the cookers flared and smoked, the cooks, demoniac in their blackened faces and clothes, ladled out that standard compost that, at any time before nine in the morning was denominated "coffee," at any hour before or after noon "soup," until the end of the day, when, as a last effort, it became "tea." Derisive shouts of "Gyp-oh!"

intended to convey that it was accepted for what it was—yesterday's bacon grease, hot water and dust from the floor of a lorry—greeted it, as it splashed into the tendered mess-tins of the jostling crowd.

Within the house, in the westward of the two principal rooms, Madeleine, with Berthe, most useful of the Belgian refugees about the place, had got her stove nearly red hot, and was silently, deftly handling her pots and dishes, while the mess cooks unpacked the enamelled plates and cups and carried them through to the other room where the table was being set by the simple process of spreading sheets of newspapers upon it and arranging the drinking-cups, knives and forks thereon. Bread being cut, there only remained for "Maddam," as they called Madeleine, to say that all was ready, so that the brass shell-case in the passage could be used as a gong. The Colonel appeared, and the Adjutant, both regular soldiers, masking whatever they felt under professional passivity. There were no other senior officers; the only surviving Major was with a captainless outlying company. The two companies in the farm were commanded by lieutenants. The junior officers were all Kitchener enlistments. Some of them had hoped to spend that night in Lille.

The conversation was not so brilliant as the meal. In many a worse billet, the Easthamptons looked back to their night at Spanish Farm. Every one was dog tired and bitterly depressed. The Colonel only sat the length of one cigarette. Adams took his food in his "bunk." The junior officers clattered up the narrow candle-lit stair into the loft where two of them had a bedstead and two others the floor. The Adjutant was left collating facts and figures, with the Doctor, who was going through his stores. To them came the runner from the guard-room (improvised in a tent at the brick-pillared gate of the pasture).

"Reinforcement officers, sir!"

There entered two rather bewildered young men who had passed during the previous forty-eight hours through every emotion from a desperate fear that the "victory" of Loos would end the war without their firing a shot, to sheer annoyance at being dumped at a railhead and told to find a battalion in the dark. They had lost everything they had except what they carried on them, and were desperately hungry.

The Adjutant surprised even himself at the cordial greeting he gave the two strangers—untried officers from a reserve battalion he had never seen. He knew nothing of their history or capabilities, but the sense of more people behind, coming to fill the gaps, warmed even the professional soldier's trained indifference. He got up, and went to

the door of the kitchen, calling for "Maddam" and repeating "Man-gay" in a loud voice to indicate that further refreshment was required.

Madeleine had just finished, with Berthe, the washing and cleaning up of her cooking utensils, and was about to go to bed in her little single bedroom that looked out over the northern pasture. She was just as inclined to cook another meal as a person may be, who has already worked eighteen hours and expects to rise at half-past five in the morning. Nor was there anything in the stare of the shorter, fair-haired new arrival, with his stolid silence, to encourage her. But the taller and darker of the two asked her in fair French if she could manage an omelet and some coffee. They regretted deranging her, but had the hunger of a wolf and had not eaten since the morning. Whether it was being addressed in her own tongue, or the fact that the young officer had hit on the things that lay next her hand and would not take five minutes, or whether it was something in the voice, Madeleine acquiesced politely, and set about providing what was asked.

The Adjutant stared. He was not accustomed to interpolations in foreign tongues in his orders. But this young officer was so obviously unconscious of offense, and the interference so opportune, that there was nothing to be said. He talked to the new-comers as they supped, and, apologizing for having to put them in the little ground-floor room with the orderly officer, retired to his own.

Silence and darkness fell upon the Spanish Farm, only broken by the steps of the sentries, the change of guard, and the dull mutter and star-shell flicker from the line, and for some hours all those human beings that lay in and around the old house, lost consciousness of their hopes, fears, and wants.

.

English officers and men who billeted in the Spanish Farm (and practically the whole English Army must have passed through or near it at one time or another) to this day speak of it as one of the few places they can still distinguish in the blur of receding memories, one of the few spots of which they have nothing but good to tell. In part this may be easily explained. The old house was comparatively roomy, well kept, water-tight. There was less overcrowding, no leaking roof to drip on one's only dry shirt—and besides, though the regu-lations were more strictly observed here than anywhere, that fact gave almost an impression of home—order, cleanliness, respect ruled here yet a little—but perhaps there is another reason—perhaps houses, so old and so continually handled by human beings, have almost a personality of their own: perhaps the Spanish Farm that had sheltered

Neapolitan mercenaries fighting the French, Spanish Colonists fighting the Flemish, French fighting English or Dutch—and now English and Colonials fighting Germans—perhaps the old building bent and brooded over these last of its many occupants—perhaps knew a little better than other houses what men expected of it.

.

Madeleine thought no more of the War, and the population it had brought to the Spanish Farm, until half-past seven, when the mess-orderlies began to prepare breakfast. Obstinately refusing to allow any-one to touch her stove, she cooked that incomprehensible meal of oat-soup ("porridge" they called it!), and bacon and eggs, after which she knew, they ate orange confiture. She, her father, and the farm hands, had long taken their lump of bread and bowl of coffee, stand-ing. Her attention was divided between the hum of the separator in the dairy and her washing drying on the line, when she heard her father's voice calling: "Madeleine, leinsche!" ("Little Madeleine!"). She called out that she was in the kitchen.

The old man came, moving more quickly than usual, voluble in Flemish, excited. The soldiers had moved out all the flax-straw lying in the long wooden drying-shed behind the house, on the pasture, and all the machines, reapers and binders, drills and rakes. Moreover, they had taken for firewood hop-poles that had been expressly forbidden.

Madeleine washed her hands at the sink, saying she would see about it. But she was saved the trouble. Her father went out into the yard, unable to keep still in his impatience, and she heard him in altercation with old Adams. They drifted into the mess-room. As she was drying her hands, there was a knock on the kitchen door, and she saw her father ushering in the dark young officer of the evening before. Her brow cleared. She had not the least doubt she could "manage" the young man.

The young man surpassed expectations. Madeleine found it un-necessary to keep to her rather limited English. His French, while not correct, was expansive. He admitted her version of the farmer's rights under Billeting Law, but would not accept the sum, running into hundreds of francs, which Jerome Vanderlynden, typical peasant at a bargain, asked for compensation. It appeared that the quiet-looking young man knew something of flax culture and more of agricultural machinery. He quoted within a very little the cost of re-stacking the flax, oiling the machinery, with the price of two burnt hop-poles. He offered forty francs.

Old Vanderlynden made his usual counter: "What if I go to Brigade Head-quarters about it!"

"Then you will get nothing at all. They are too busy, and we move on to-day!"

The old man laughed and slapped his leg.

Madeleine, knowing by experience that the officer had been authorized to spend fifty francs (a sum which appealed to the English, being recognizable as a couple of sovereigns), began to respect him, took the money, and signed the receipt.

Left alone, old Jerome remarked that the young man was very well brought up. Madeleine was looking carefully through her pots and pans to see that nothing had disappeared into the big mess-box.

From the window she saw the battalion paraded, and watched them move off, as she passed hastily from room to room, counting things. Her father was round the outbuildings. The last to go was old Adams with the wagons. A great stillness fell on the old farm, the litter of papers, tins and ashes, and all the unmistakable atmosphere of a crowded place suddenly deserted.

.

The day following the departure of the battalion was fine and still. Even the Front was quieting down. After the early midday meal of soup and bread, Madeleine put on her second-best frock, washed, did her hair, spent a little time over her hands, and putting on her fur but no hat, picked her way over the cobbles and left the farm by the main gate.

She walked with the ease of a person of perfect health, who knew what she wanted and where she was going, and who had habitually no time to stroll, no need to think. The clumsiness of a life of hard physical labor had been corrected by a good education, and she might well have passed in her dress that had so evidently been best, and was going to be everyday, for an English girl. Only the boots and the hatless head marked her for a follower of the continental tradition, though her strong ankles and round neck would have well supported the low shoes and simple felt or straw of an outdoor English-woman.

She said nothing to her father or to the farmhands as to her errand. No one inquired. For a long while, ever since she had left the convent school, she had been mistress of her own actions and of other people's. Old Vanderlynden, if he ever spoke of her to others, used not the peasant's usual "Ma fille"—"my little girl," but "Ma demoiselle"—"my young lady." Her dress indicated nothing, for etiquette forbade her going beyond the farm in her old worn "every-day" and apron, clogs and upturned sleeves. Old men and women and children were plowing, manuring and weed-burning in the fields bordering the hedgeless road. She spoke to no one, and no one spoke to her. She

met them all once a week, at Mass, and that was sufficient. One or
two of them, glancing at her straight figure and level, unswerving gait,
glanced at each other and grinned. The usual surmises were probably
made, for it was known that she was keeping company with none of
the young men of her generation before they were all hurried off to the
War—and it was plainly unnatural that a good-looking young woman
with a dowry should not be sought in marriage. These surmises were
all the more interesting because nothing definite was known.

Some hundreds of yards before reaching the Lille-Calais road,
Madeleine passed under the shadow of one of those little woods of
oak, crowning a small conical hill, that constitute the only untilled
plots of the hard-worked Flemish border. Like its counterpart in all
the neighboring parishes, this wood also was called the "Kruysabel"
or Poplar-cross, on account of the crucifix that hid in its highest and
thickest part, where its five "rides" met in a tiny clearing. To the
south of this clearing was a little hunting shelter, brick, with mock-
Gothic windows and leaded lights, encircled by a timber-pillared
verandah, on which the thatch of the eaves descended, in the worst
style of Lille garden-furnishing ("rustic work" in England). After
entering the wood by a wicket, it was to this erection that Madeleine
mounted by a soft squashy "ride" between impenetrable walls of oak
sapling, planted as close as it would grow, and cut regularly, section
by section, according to age, so that little could be seen but slim
straight gray-green stems on all sides.

Arrived at the little clearing on the summit, the girl took out a key
and entered the hunting shelter. The ornamental porch led straight
into a dining-place almost filled by the long table surrounded by
benches. The porch and windows filled the north wall, a great open
birch-hearth with fire-dogs, the western. Opposite was a long rack of
antlers, false or real, for greatcoats, guns and bags. On the remaining
side was a partition pierced by two doors. The apartment was clean
and well kept—nor was this wonderful to anyone who could have seen
Madeleine produce feather brush and duster, and go carefully along
the pine-boarded wainscot, round mouldings and window-ledges, and
along the frames of the photographs of many a jolly party—photo-
graphs in which a man, appearing variously from middle age to past
it, mustached and whiskered in the fashion of his youth—which must
have been the fall of the Second Empire—and a youth who passed
to manhood in the newest group—were surrounded by male com-
panions who tended to be less and less hairy the newer the picture—
and women in every fashion from crinolines to gaiters and deerstalkers
—live horses and dogs and dead birds and beasts, on a background of
hunting shelter and trees. Madeleine hardly paused to gaze at one,

but passed on, chasing spiders, fly marks, dust, and looking for damp or wormholes. She was far from being a person to stand in front of a photograph while there was work to do.

Next she opened the left-hand door and peered into the little kitchen almost filled by the vase-and-coffin-style stove, at which she and others had cooked many a hot-pot and lapin-chasseur. All was in order here, and she only glanced to see that no invading hand had touched the stacked fuel, and that the iron-ringed flagstone that opened on a diminutive cellar had not been moved. She left the kitchen. Before the other door some little animation gleamed through the naturally passive, almost defensive expression—behind which she habitually concealed her thoughts. Entering this third apartment, a little upholstered lounge, twelve feet square, she closed the door softly and stood a moment without moving. It had been originally a gun-room, but the present Baron, her father's proprietor, owner of two thousand hectares of shooting of which this shelter was the center, had turned it into a withdrawing-room for ladies, as their presence at the shooting parties became more and more usual. A divan ran under the curtained windows, west and south, a tiny fireplace was beside the door, while a corner had been carved off the kitchen for toilet purposes. Otherwise it was pine boarded and upholstered in plaited straw like the rest of the building. But the straw surfaces were covered with cushions, mats and covers, chiefly Oriental, and all collected, like the Flemish china on the walls, and the fancy photographs "Kruysabel by Moonlight," "Morning in the Woods," etc., etc., by Georges, the present Baron's son.

.

It was this very Georges—spoiled, lovable, perverse, self-indulgent, whose taste and personality penetrated and overcame the rococo-rustic architecture and upholstery—that Madeleine had met in this very room, every time she could and he would, all that summer that led up to the declaration of war. How many times they had spent the Catholic five to seven o'clock—she protected by endless subterfuges and evasions—he coming easily of right—she was far from counting. Nor did she cast back in her mind to the commencement of the thing. Indeed, there had been nothing remarkable about it. It happened like this:

Her father was the old Baron's chief tenant and head gamekeeper (as that office is understood in France). She had known Georges as a thin, dark-eyed, imperious, tyrannical boy. As a girl she had helped carry the materials of the midday feast, that, cooked and served at the Kruysabel, was the converging-point of the morning drives of the

Baron's shooting parties. The last shoot of the spring of 1914 had finished in darkness, and she had been left, as usual, to clear up. Her basket packed, the place all squared-up and tidy, she had stood by candle-light, munching a strip of buttered spiced-bread and finishing, careless of the dregs, the last of a bottle of Burgundy that her Flemish soul loved as only a Flemish soul can. She had caught Georges' prominent brown eyes on her, more than once during the day, as she moved about, waiting at table. Conscious of looking her best, this had pleased her, beneath her preoccupation with her duties of cooking and serving. Moreover, she had a good day's work behind her (the Baron paid well if he was satisfied), and the Burgundy warmed her heart.

She heard footsteps behind her, and a tune hummed, and knew instinctively who it was. She kept quite still. Instinct told her that this was the most effective thing to do. Two arms, under hers, bent her backwards, and Georges fastened his lips to hers. Self-controlled, she neither called out nor resisted. Careful, even grudging in everything, when she gave, she gave generously, no half measures. That was how it had started. The most natural thing in the world. It had gone on in spasms of passion, and interludes, as far as she was concerned, of cool efficient concealment. Georges was a little younger, far less healthy in mind or body, probably less strong, physically, than she. There may have been an undercurrent of almost maternal feeling on her part, and certainly not the least illusion as to the consequences of being found out. And no one had found out.

.

But now, as she stood in the empty room, on this October afternoon of 1915, she was as far from ruminating on the beginnings of the affair as she was from the neo-classic tower of Merville Church, visible fifteen kilometers away, in the pale sunshine, through a gap in the branches. She had to stop for a moment to get used to the atmosphere, as a diver adjusts himself to the pressure of a lower level, but it was an unconscious pause; then, pressing her lips together, she dusted and swept, opened the windows, banged mats and covers. Not that she hoped by the elaborate preparation of a room unused these fifteen months, and destined to be empty many another, to charm back the man through whom alone that room interested her. Madeleine's point of view was much simpler. Her father had charge of the shooting. She had automatically undertaken the care of the shelter. Having done so, unasked and unpaid, as part of the general unwritten arrangement between her father and the Baron, she could be trusted to go through with it, whatever happened.

Her task finished, she straightened her back and stood, hands on her hips, looking at nothing. From somewhere beyond Estaires, Civenchy or Festubert perhaps, came the sound of guns; some petty incident of the four-hundred-mile year-long battle was dragging out its squalid tragedy. Her lips moved, formed the words "Bêtes—sales bêtes!" which mean so much more than "dirty beasts" and something more immediate than "foul brutes" in English. No sound came. All that feeling of hers was too deep down to struggle into active expression through her habitual reserve and acquiescence with current manners. Not hers to criticize or revolt, hers only to feel, to feel with all the depth of a narrow, obstinate nature. Anyone might have supposed that she was thinking of the Germans who had killed one brother, and held another prisoner since Charleroi. Could she have been induced to express herself, she might have said, from mere habit of convention, that she meant the Germans. But it was deeper than that, so deep as to be almost impersonal.

Years before, when she was but a little girl, she had stood by the bedside of her mother, dying for want of proper medical attention, the fees for which had been grudged until it was too late. Her mother had said: "Pray to the Virgin, now that you are alone!" She had answered, sobbing: "I will pray, and I will take care of father and brothers, and they of me!" "Pray to the Virgin!" the mother repeated. "She is the only one that will take care of you!" That unique effort of expression of a life worn down with toil, and given up to save expense, had sunk into Madeleine's mind, been confirmed by the teaching of the convent school, where the nuns seemed to be perpetually clearing up the mess men made of things. When the war came Madeleine dumbly recognized it for a thing that men did. She had none of the definite sex-antagonism of an English suffragist, was affectionately tolerant of her father and brothers, and constructively tender to Georges, would have loved to have surrounded him with perpetual comfort and indulgence. But in the bulk, men were always doing things like this war. Her smouldering, almost sulky resentment had not decreased one particle during the fifteen months that had passed. For her, the day of mobilization had been catastrophic. Georges, grandson of an ennobled "industrialist" and of bourgeois blood of the official classes, surprised everybody, surprised Madeleine, surprised perhaps himself. The manifesto "La Patrie est en danger" had just been issued. He seemed to have swallowed its sentiments whole. His papers arrived, and found him in uniform—he was (of course) in the cuirassiers. He mounted and rode off. Like so many others, the indolent, expensive young man lost all thought of anything except what he deemed "duty."

Madeleine, who knew as well as anyone that his depot would be at Lille, had taken her stand, that August morning, just inside the gate of the Kruysabel. She had chosen that place for easy concealment, and she knew he must pass that way; she was prepared to give him anything he might want. He passed her at the trot, looking rather fine in his regimentals, and well mounted. He raised his hand to the salute, but did not draw rein. She had gone home and taken up her work where she had laid it down.

Going about the endless jobs of a farmer's daughter, her slow-moving temper had risen and risen. She knew Georges, his impulses, his absorption in the matter that held him for the moment, his spoiled thriftlessness. He would rush into military life, engulf himself in it, never thinking for a moment to take his fill of happiness first. He would not write. She hoped he would not. There would be no means of keeping the arrival of letters secret from the whole village. Nor would she write to him. She made no bones over social distinctions, upheld them rather. He was the young master. It was not for her to write. This left a great ache in her, for which she presently found a partial cure. It came to her as she was packing up parcels of small luxuries for her brothers. She packed a third one, more carefully than the first two. As the billeting of English troops on the farm became increasingly regular, she managed to vary and improve that third parcel, obtaining from the—to her—sumptuously overstocked canteens and private presents of the men in khaki—tinned stuff, toilet wares, and the beautiful English cigarettes Georges loved. She posted this third packet from Hazebrouck each weekly market day, for however well known she was to the farming community, she was a stranger to the small postal and other officials of the railway town. She comforted herself that if anything (it was always called "anything" by the women of the War, whatever their nationality) had happened to Georges the parcel would be returned. She was far from picturing the trenches to herself. So, with steady, profitable work at the farm, now a camp and barrack as well, with a weekly parcel to send, and a weekly visit to the shelter at Kruysabel, the interminable months had passed. People—her father with one son dead and one a prisoner—her sister, down in Laventie, within bullet-range of the trenches—got accustomed to the war.

But not Madeleine.

So, as she stood in the fading light of the October sunset, resting a moment before she returned to the farm, there was nothing petty or personal in the grim set of her features, the slow-burning anger of

her eyes. She might have posed there for a symbolic figure of Woman contemplating Fate. She stood straight in her neat, almost careful dress, bought with one eye on looks and one on usefulness, solid well-kept boots and stockings, thick but without hole or wrinkle. Large boned, but so close-knit that she did not look disproportionately broad, her figure, kept in check by hard work and frugal feeding, promised to grow thick only with middle age. Anyone looking at her face would have said, "What a handsome woman," not "What a pretty girl." There was something below the surface that kept the red lips closed in their firm line, the round chin lifted, the gray eyes and level brows serene. Her dark hair, which she kept, while at work, tied in a duster, was neat and smooth. Her skin had the pallor of health.

That internal quality that made her simple shapeliness so much more arresting than any trick of dimple, glance, or elaborate preparation and high color, was, like anything else worth having, the gradual distillation of the hard-lived generations gone before. How much of it came from the cultivators who had hung on to that low ridge between the marshes and the sea, as French and Norman, English, Burgundian and Spaniard swept over it, and how much from the Spanish blood of Alva's colonists who had held the old block-house-farm amid all the unfriendliness of climate, native inhabitants, and chance, none can now say.

Jerome Vanderlynden had a hook nose and beady brown eyes. Madeleine rather took after her mother, a Delplice of Bailleul, in her straight nose and fair complexion. But there it was, outwardly, obstinacy; inwardly—something more. It was that "something more" that clouded her smooth forehead and flashed in her stabbing, side-to-side stare. She never even dreamed of envying the properly married women who had received official and private recognition of the trouble the War had brought them. Nor did she stop to pity the hundreds of thousands of women of irregular position, who had been abandoned on the outbreak of hostilities, without resources. Her feeling, if almost impersonal, was simple, direct. This War, this "Bêtise," this great Stupidity had taken Georges from her. She would be even with it. She put away her duster and brush, wrapped herself in her fur, and locking up, descended the ride to the wicket without glancing at the scuttling rabbits, crossed two arable fields by their narrow grass borders, and so through the north pasture entered the house by the plank bridge and the scullery door. Hanging her fur in her room, she slipped on her long blue apron, went to the kitchen, and began doing the next thing.

.

Nearly a week passed before the advance-party of a new battalion, consisting of an interpreter in the blue uniform of the French Mission and an English officer, rode into the courtyard. They were received by Madeleine, who gave them coffee and began to explain herself in English as usual, as to what she was disposed to do, and charge, and the rules she expected to be observed. The Englishman was the usual square, blond, sheepishly-grinning grown-up boy, who nodded and said "All right" whenever there was a pause. The interpreter was a middle-aged commercial traveler for a colonial house, who talked glibly and respectfully, while under the table his foot pursued Madeleine's. The arrangements completed, Madeleine left the two, who had obviously lunched well in Hazebrouck or Cassel, to measure up and ticket the various rooms, barns, and stables, according to their requirements.

It was again her day for the Kruysabel, and she went to her room, slipping off her apron and her stained and mended dress, to tidy herself. Her room was a small cell-like apartment looking out across the moat to the north pasture. The distempered walls were marked with damp, but the tiled floor was clean and the places round the window where the plaster had come away were hidden by short curtains. Before this window, which was in a corner, stood a chest of drawers, bearing the cheap deal looking-glass and an old inlaid box containing the girl's few treasures. The remaining wallspace of the outside wall was filled by the great wooden bedstead, above the head of which was a little china bracket carrying the inevitable sprig of box-tree. The bed came so far down the little room that there was only place for a wooden chair between its foot and the door, on the other side of which stood a tall press, reaching to the ceiling, and a wooden washstand, surmounted by a shelf that held the relics of Madeleine's first communion under a glass bell, such as used to be seen in England encasing Dresden clocks. The washstand just allowed for the drawers to open.

Thus, as she did her hair before the glass in the window, Madeleine could see her door softly opened, to admit the interpreter, who had drawn off his boots and tiptoed in, his brown eyes gleaming greasily at the sight of her bare arms and neck, muttering: "What luck!" The words died on shaking lips and the creased eyelids fluttered over downcast eyes, as she turned in cold fury: "Get out of my bedroom!"

He hesitated, and catching the ewer of common white china she slung it forward with the force of muscles accustomed to tossing swedes to feed the mashing-machine. It broke on his forehead, cutting his eyebrow and deluging him with water. With a gasp he was gone.

She called to Berthe to bring a swab and broom. When the mess was cleared: "That imbecile of an interpreter!" she said.

"It is a dirty type," grunted the philosophic Berthe. Madeleine forgot the incident.

She recalled it, however, before the new battalion had been under the roof of the Spanish Farm many hours. They broke every rule, stole, destroyed, trespassed, and worst of all, left open the gate from the pasture to the "plain" (the level range of arable), so that the cattle got out and had to be chased back. Madeleine, having expostulated with N.C.O.'s and men, finally appealed to the Major, who sent for the Adjutant. The latter, not allowing for Madeleine's English, said bluntly that the interpreter had informed him that the people were Germans in disguise, and would be better for a lesson.

Madeleine interposed with such energy and point that the officers promised, in order to get rid of her, to issue orders. Not believing in stones left unturned, Madeleine also wrote to the Chief of the French Mission at Cassel. Then an idea struck her. She looked in her account book, where under the heading "Easthamptonshire Regiment" she noted the name of the dark young officer who spoke French so well, Lieutenant Geoffrey Skene. She wrote to him as well, asking if he would come over and intercede with the troops.

.

The day after, the battalion left, the Major giving her twenty francs for wood burnt, fowls and eggs. As there had been over twenty officers in the mess and nearly nine hundred men in the battalion, Madeleine added up the billeting and mess money and was content. She received an acknowledgment of her letter from the French Mission, but nothing else. Again peace and emptiness fell on the Spanish Farm.

Again, nearly a week elapsed, when Madeleine, stirring the midday soup, saw an officer ride into the courtyard. She called to her father, who was sorting haricots. He went out and returned with Lieutenant Skene.

Madeleine did not understand the English and it did not worry her. She had indeed required this young man to deal with a difficulty, but the need had passed. Still, he might be useful, and she invited him to stay to lunch, calling to Berthe to kill a fowl, while her father got up a bottle of Burgundy. She heard politely a long explanation as to the receipt of her letter, and the impossibility of replying sooner, owing to conditions prevailing in the trenches. She understood what was said, but paid little heed, not being interested. She had found this young man so far "well brought up" and "malin," "sharp at money" in contest with her father. She now began to see that he was

"serviable," "willing." This thought, striking against her eternal preoccupation with Georges, kindled a spark.

It was when the young officer mentioned that he lay in the trenches next some French troops that the spark caught, flamed, became an idea. She showed nothing, of course, presiding with her usual competence at the long Flemish midday meal, which she felt to be his due, after having got him to come so far on his useless errand. But as the four courses followed one another, and a carafe of beer gave place to more Burgundy, she was thinking. Her father went back to work, leaving the Lieutenant smoking over his coffee and glass of Lille gin.

She began to question him with infinite caution, trying to find out what his strange view of life might be. She made up her mind, after rallying him (as was rather the fashion) on his conquests of her sex in France, that he was very innocent, well brought up, sharp at money, willing, and now she added in her mind, "rather a child," "un peu enfant." It did not displease her. On the contrary, it was all to the good. She rather expected the English to be like that. He did not take the subject up and feign interest in her, as a Frenchman would have done, but remained serious. She was therefore obliged to say right out what was in her mind. It was to ask him, next time he went up to the trenches, next to the French troops, to try and obtain news of Georges for her. She had heard that his regiment was in the northern sector. She formed no idea of the trenches, of the camps and resting places next to them. She simply said what she wanted. Once the words were out she had to use all her self-control. The sound of her request, the speaking aloud of what had been going round and round in her mind for so long, brought a rush of feeling such as she had not experienced since the first day of mobilization. She bit her lips to keep back tears and sobs. Then she was glad to hear the Lieutenant promising to do what he could. There was some difficulty about it, apparently, she was not curious to understand. She was glad she had asked an Englishman, realizing now how the thing sounded, and what a tale a Frenchman would have made of it. All she cared about now was for this young man to go—she was aching with the effort of restraint—and get her the news she wanted. She had no clear idea what. She pictured in a dim way Georges sending a message that he was all right, and making an appointment to meet her, in St. Omer—Calais—where he liked. Further than that her imagination could not take her.

She thanked the young man cordially, and offered him more gin. He refused, and went away, assuring her that he was at her service in this as in other matters. She forgot him before he was out of the yard, and fearing that she would cry—a thing she had not done since

she was a tiny girl—she went to her room. But she did not cry. She
sat on the wooden chair at the foot of the bed, her hands on the
wooden rail, her face upon her hands. Nothing happened. She soon
went back to her work, for her feelings were even worse in that little
room of hers than in the big kitchen where she had so much to do.
Gradually her heart ceased to thump, her eyes to smart. But she had
taken the first active step towards getting Georges back—towards that
recovery of anything taken away from her, that was her deepest
instinct. And she knew that she would not stop at any first step—
not she!

.

It took more than a mere European war twenty miles off to in-
terrupt the regular life of the Spanish Farm. Troops came and troops
went, and Madeleine watched them, watched the payments made
by the messes for extra accommodation and cooking, and the weekly
payments through the Mairie for billeting and stabling, watched the
storing of the crops, the thrashing, the milking, the feeding of the
fowls. Every week she went to market, sold what she could, bought
as little as possible, and sent her parcel, surreptitiously, from the
post office. She neither heard nor saw anything of Georges. She
neither heard nor saw anything of Lieutenant Skene. But, sure enough,
on the first opportunity, she was obliged to try to get news of Georges.

It happened, as winter came on, that "the château" had need of
some things, eggs, and hare pâté—nowhere so good as at the Spanish
Farm—and Madame la Baronne wanted some sewing done, rather
special, better than any of her women could do. A message came
via the Baron, who shouted from horseback, as he rode by, to Vander-
lynden, at work in the plain. Old Vanderlynden handed it on to
Madeleine, as he bent in an attitude half of prayer, half a crouching
ape's, over the midday soup.

Madeleine nodded and told him to put in the horse—not that she
could not have done it, but she must clean herself. Accordingly,
half an hour later, there might have been seen issuing from the yard
of the Spanish Farm, over the brick bridge, along the earth road that
divided the manor pasture, out by the brick-pillared gate on to the
road, surely the oldest, most repaired of high black gigs, drawn by an
old white horse whose sonorous walk took it along at perhaps two miles
an hour. Framed in the dark aperture of the hood, upright, expression-
less, sat Madeleine, bareheaded, but in her best dress, holding the reins
in a gloved hand, basket between her feet. Silent, expressionless, she
may have been, but when she turned into the Lille-Calais road and met
a string of English transports, limbers and wagons, it was noticeable

that the Quartermaster-Sergeant, after glancing at her face, instead of shouting to her to get out of the way, turned in his saddle and shouted to the drivers, "Right o' the road!"

She came to the village and crossed the empty Grand' Place, where the old houses stared unchanged over the notice-boards of the offices of the Head-quarters of an English Division, and the church, newly faced with red brick, showed the zeal of the pious Flemings. Turning sharply out of this, she mounted, at the snail pace of the old white horse, a steep street between little houses of people who had retired to live on about the equivalent of forty pounds English per annum (as people do in France). It ended in a great eighteenth-century iron grille, the entry to the château. The central gates stood open and she drove straight along a road deep between high banks covered with shrubs, which followed for some fifty yards the old line of the moat, until she came under the back part of the château where a broad terrace of gravel separated the basement offices from the kitchen garden. Leaving the old horse, with perfect confidence, looking down his nose into a laurel bush, Madeleine took her basket on her arm, and entered the great square kitchen.

One of the things that renders life so easy in France is the absence of change. Anywhere outside Paris, and often in it, change seems to have worn itself out, and to have ceased. In that remote corner of Flanders, Madeleine had no shyness, hesitation, or doubt, in entering the house of her father's landlord and her lover's mother. She would not have dreamed of entering by the front. No less would she have thought of leaving the house without seeing Madame la Baronne in person. She was not alone in this. The establishment was ruled by a lean, gaunt, gray-mustached person, discernible to be of the female sex only by her clothes, named Placide. Just as for Madeleine, so for Placide, life was an easy riddle. She knew her place to a hair's breadth, between God, and her master and her mistress, on the one hand, and the servants, tenants, tradespeople on the other. The great square block of a house, the main building of the older castle, whose wings had been thrown into its moat, whose forecourt had become flower gardens in the revolution of 1790, went on its even way under her iron rule, undisturbed by wars. The presence of a mess of English officers in the Baron's quarters, east of the main staircase, the absence of young Master Georges, of all the men-servants, and of some of the women who had gone to work on farms, did not throw Placide out of her stride. When Madeleine entered, she was standing with her back to the dresser with its shining pots and pans, telling a maid-servant her duties. The following conversation ensued:

"Good morning, Madeleine, how goes it?"

"Good morning, Placide, not too badly!"

"You have brought the things!"

"Here they are."

"What will you have to take?"

"Nothing, thank you!"

"Come, a glass of beer, a cup of coffee!"

"Nothing, thank you all the same!"

"But you will say 'Good day' to Madame!"

"Why yes, if Madame wishes it."

This little formality, for both speakers had said just those words hundreds of times and knew them by heart, being over, Placide went to see if Madame were free to see Madeleine, and Madeleine sipped coffee as though she had not refused it, and gossiped with the girls.

She was then ushered through the paved and plastered back passage, smelling of all the game that had been carried through it, and of all the corks that had been drawn in it, to the front hall floored with black and white stone, on which stood heavy old furniture, a little of each period and a good deal of 1860 to 1870, between walls that were painted in landscape as a background to the plaster statues of classical deities and symbolic figures of the virtues, holding lamps. From this, the high double doors opened into the drawing-room or salon, where Madame sat since the use of Monsieur's apartments by English troops had forced her to relinquish her boudoir to serve as his bedroom.

Madame la Baronne d'Archeville had been married when the Empress Eugénie was the first lady of Europe, and taking marriage very seriously, had never tried to change since. Although she had neither the height nor carriage of her imperial example, she continued in 1915 doing her hair and wearing her clothes as she had begun, and the effect was all her own. Herself of high bourgeois blood, she had married when told to, without demur, the Baron, who, son of an army contractor and, so he said, great-grandson of an emigré of 1792, had re-purchased with money made out of républiques and empires, what those empires and républiques had taken from his ancestors, real or imaginary.

The room in which Madame sat looked like it. Originally the banqueting hall of the small feudal castle from which the château had grown, it ran from back to front of the modernized building, with two tall windows looking on to the kitchen garden behind, and two others, opposite, looking on to the flower garden in front, and over trees and village roofs into the rich undulations of the plain. The great beams that held the roof were visible, but below them the walls that had been panelled were papered cream and gold. Against this

background hung two rows of pictures, the upper row smallish and very dark, displaying, as far as could be seen, grim old men in more or less armor, and stolid ladies in stuffs, laces and jewels hardly less resisting. The lower row was composed of portraits of whiskered men in uniforms of recent eras, and women, all in evening dresses of the nineteenth century, varied by landscapes, some good, some too good to be true, in pairs. Below the pictures were marble slabs on gilt brackets, tables shining with brass inlay. The floor space was occupied with curly armed, heavily stuffed chairs and settees. It was a room into which the Second Empire seemed to have burst in flood, washing up the drift of earlier ages, and to have ebbed, leaving a carpet shiny from use.

But to Madame la Baronne, and Madeleine, no such thoughts occurred. To Madame it was her salon. To Madeleine it was Madame's salon. To Madeleine, Madame said:

"Good day, Madeleine. All goes well at the farm?"

"Yes, Madame la Baronne. I hope that the health of Monsieur and Madame is good, and that there is good news of Monsieur Georges."

She stood, square planted and upright, not quite so near the door as a servant, not quite so near Madame's chair as a visitor. She was perfectly conscious that on her left, in the curve of the grand piano, was a red, blue and white draped easel on which was a picture in oils of Georges, as a boy, in a white sailor suit, lips parted, eyes staring a little, evidently just going to say, "I want so-and-so," in his spoiled way. But she spoke his name without tremor, and heard the reply:

"Thank you, we are well; we have no news of my son, but that is good news, is it not?"

"Yes, Madame. I have brought the things."

"Very well. Placide will pay you. Good day."

"Good day, Madame la Baronne, and thank you."

Backing with a curtsy to the door, she let herself out, took her money from Placide, received her basket with her cloths and terrine, jerked up the head of the old white horse, and drove back to the farm. She had got what she wanted—the assurance of no ill news of Georges.

.

That evening in the lamp-lit salon, after Madame had said, "There is nothing more; good night, Placide," there was silence only broken by the Baron puffing his cigar. He supported the war very badly. He was too old to serve and was prevented from fishing or shooting by English water-supply officers, who dammed up and filtered his waters, and by French Gendarmerie Commandants, who stopped his supplies of cartridges. At last he exploded:

"Nothing ever happens in this cursed war. You, what have you done to-day?"

Madame la Baronne replied, after a moment's silence that was partly protest at his manners and partly some tiny instinctive defensiveness, "I have seen Madeleine Vanderlynden!"

"Ah, she brought the ham and the hare pâté!"

"Yes." Madame was struggling with that tiny instinct—could not quite catch what it prompted—her feeling only materialized into the words:

"She has bold eyes!"

"It is a fine girl. Probably she knows it!" qualified the Baron, and mused.

Madame mused too. But the necessity, forced upon her early in married life with the Baron, of shutting one's eyes and ears to what men did and said about women, prevented her connecting Madeleine's composure with her own family. She could only fall back on her stock complaint.

"She will never be like her mother, that poor Sylvie!"

But irritation had supervened with the Baron: "You're not obliged to receive the girl!"

"One has to do what one can for one's people. They wouldn't like it if one didn't say a word to them when they come with things."

"Do what you like so long as I have hare pâté," yawned the Baron. "Ugh, this war, I do nothing but yawn and sleep!"

"I pray!" said Madame to herself, and rose to go to the little "chapel" in the turn of the stairs to do so.

.

Madeleine had no theory of the Irony of Fate. She had a merely hard experience of it, gained from watching crops and prices. Reassured as to Georges' safety by what she had heard at the château, she took what comfort she could.

Three days after her visit, she was sewing and mending by the kitchen stove, using the light of the dying sunset to the last glimmer. There were no English troops in the farm on that day, and outside were the sounds of her father putting up the horses, on a background of damp late-autumn silence, and behind that, the muffled vibration of the eternal battle, that made the window-panes tremble ever so little.

Suddenly there came the sound of whistling—the last bars of the well-worn tune:

> *"Madelon—lon—lon*
> *Madelon donne-moi ton cœur!"*

and shouted greetings. Then her father's slouching tread and a brisk military stride. Then her father's voice:

"Mad'leine, here is Victor Dequidt, home on leave!"

She got up, pushed the ever-ready coffee-pot over the heat of the fire, and greeted the guest. He was the son of a neighboring farmer, and if she ever bothered her head about such things, Madeleine was perhaps conscious deep down in herself that he liked her more than a little. They had played together as children, grown to adolescence together, had experiences in common, wandering in the Kruysabel. But ever since her mother's death had forced her to early maturity, Madeleine had been very busy, then, with Georges, very busy and very happy, and since the War, very busy and preoccupied. Any memories of Victor hardly disturbed the surface of her mind. If he liked to follow her about with his blue eyes, and pay her small compliments, why, let him. Most men looked at her, so might he. She poured him out coffee, and some of the rum she had got from the quartermasters of various English units, and listened politely, but without interest, to his talk.

It was the usual talk of men on leave. All that he said was being said in English, French, German, Italian, during years, whenever men got home for a few brief days. It was about food, railways, jokes, old acquaintances—never about the cosmic murder in which they were engaged, or their daily decreasing belief that they might escape alive. In the middle of the commonplaces that she had heard from different lips a hundred times in that kitchen, Madeleine heard the words:

"It was a good job, that stretcher-bearing business at the hospital, miles from the line—good food—a bunk to sleep in at night, and who do you think was the last stretcher-case I carried?"

Silence. Old Vanderlynden was not good at guessing. Madeleine was bored. Victor went on:

"Why, the young Baron Georges!"

Silence again. Old Vanderlynden, who could hardly see to fill his pipe, said:

"It's as dark as a nigger's back in here!" and held a paper spill to the candle on the mantelshelf.

Madeleine cried with a stamp of her foot:

"Don't light up! don't light up!"

Her father obediently lit his pipe, knocked out the half-burnt spill against the fireplace and put it back.

Victor, disappointed at the way his anecdote was received, said gallantly:

"One sees you are a good housekeeper, and not one to burn good money!"

But Madeleine was just succeeding, by sheer will-power in swallowing—swallowing down It—the maniacal desire that had come rushing up from her heart into her head—the strong frenzy of a strong nature —bidding her catch up the great steel harl from the hearth and smash in the heads—not so much of her father and Victor, but of these two men—prototypes of all the other careless, mischievous, hopeless men, that had let Georges be hurt in their insane war. She swallowed, and the fury of that instant was gone, battened down, under control. She replied to Victor in a steady off-hand voice:

"Oh no, we have plenty of candles from the English. After all, you might as well light up, Father!"

As he did so, the old man asked:

"What had he the matter with him, the poor young Baron?"

"He had become consumptive, owing to the life."

As the candle took heart and shone, Madeleine's courage rose to meet the necessity for showing nothing and finding out everything which she deliberately courted. Sure of herself, she said gently:

"To which base hospital did you say he was going?" She saw her mistake in a moment. She was not so completely mistress of herself as she had thought. No hospital had been mentioned. But there was nothing subtle about Victor. He was only too pleased to have interested her. He replied:

"The English hospital in tents at Naes' farm, there beside the St. Omer line. Ours are full."

His gossiping talk flickered on like the candle flame—dim and alone. Madeleine and her father said scarcely a word, the former deliberately, wanting to be alone, the latter lacking the habit of speech. As no interest was shown and no further refreshment offered, Victor eventually rose to go. They bade him good night at the door, locked up, and turned to their rooms, with their usual brief word of nightly affection. The old man was snoring directly. Madeleine lay for hours on her back, her eyes burning at the dim ceiling of her little room, her legs and feet straight and rigid, hands clasped on her thumping heart. Surely he was a lucky man for whom she planned and schemed and longed so in her short, hard-earned time of rest!

.

The next day Jerome Vanderlynden and Madeleine set out in the dark early morning and reached Hazebrouck before most of the market had foregathered. This the old man understood and agreed to. One got one's own price by this means from people who were in

a hurry. What he did not understand was why Madeleine had on her very best instead of her second best that she usually wore to market, without a hat. Incurious and incapable of challenging her decisions, he said nothing. The stuff sold well. By eight o'clock the basket and receptacles were almost empty. Then Madeleine said:

"We must go and see the young baron."

"What do we want to go tra'passin' over there for?"

"Because Victor may be wrong. The Baron and Madame had not heard the other day."

"That's their affair."

"If it's true, they'll be glad enough to know."

"It will cost something."

"Leave the money to me."

She had made up her mind and she was going. Independent as were few girls of her sort, she was too conventional to risk the journey alone. That would be to court scandal. So her father must come with her.

At the station they got into some difficulty about tickets. The line was almost entirely military. The gray-haired Commissioner was an acquaintance.

"What are you going to do there, you two?"

Madeleine pushed before her father.

"We are going to see a wounded relative in hospital!"

"Well, you can have privilege tickets. All you want is the certificate of the Mairie."

Madeleine knew better than to argue on such a point. She drew the old man outside.

"Get down to the 'Golden Key' and come back with the cart. Look sharp!"

"Why not drive all the way?"

"Twenty kilometers there and twenty back; we should not be home all night, and supposing an English regiment comes to the farm when I'm not there?"

One of the great advantages Madeleine possessed over her father was that she could think so much quicker. The old man had fetched the cart, Madeleine had done her shopping, and they were two kilometers on the road home before he had thought of the next objection:

"What are you going to say to Blanquart?"

Blanquart was the schoolmaster and secretary of the Mairie.

"That I want a certificate that we have relatives at the war."

"But that won't get you a cheap ticket to visit the young baron in hospital."

"You leave it to me."

Obedient, the old man left it.

Blanquart was not at the Mairie, he was measuring fields for an "expertise," a professional assessment.

Leaving the cart on the road, Madeleine lifted her best skirt and stepped over the clods to him. He was busy and interested in his job, and didn't want to be dragged home to the Mairie. At her suggestion he wrote the certificate on the next fair page of the big square pocket-book he was covering with figures. He was not very curious about the matter. The Vanderlyndens were the best-known family in the parish. The loss of the two boys was no secret. He was asked every day for the endless certificates, questionnaires, lists and returns by which France is governed: "You are going to join the Society of the Friends of the Prisoners of War, I suppose?"

Madeleine let him suppose, only murmuring that one did what one could in such times.

He wrote: "I, Anastasius Amadeus Blanquart, Secretary of the Mairie of the Commune of Hondebecq, certify that Vanderlynden, Jerome, cultivator, has male relatives mobilized for military service," and signed.

"Now you'll want the official stamp. Ask my little Cécile. She knows where it is."

"Perfectly. And we thank you many times."

"There is nothing. Always at your service."

"Good day, Monsieur Blanquart."

Sure enough, at the schoolhouse, also in all Flemish villages the office of the Mairie, little Cécile Blanquart was proud to affix the official stamp, with its "République Française, Commune de Honde-becq" inscription in violet ink.

So back went the old gig, down the same road it had just come. In the distance rumbled the battle. Each side of the hedgeless road with its grassy stone pavé and "dirt" paths, the rich heavy lands gleamed with moisture in their nakedness, in the pastures the last leaves of the elms fluttered down upon thick grass that soaked and soaked. Flanders, the real Flanders, the strip of black alluvial soil between the chalky downs of France and the gravelly or stony waste border where the Germanic peoples begin, was preparing herself for another fruitful year, as she had, time out of mind, in war and in peace, paying as little attention to this war as to any other of the long series she had seen. And across her breast, on that Route Nationale that a French Emperor had built with stone from Picardy, went old Vander-lynden, child of her soil, inheritor of her endless struggle, and Made-leine, the newer, more self-conscious, better-educated generation, per-

haps even more typical of her country than her father, showing the endless adaptability of her mixed border race, absorbing the small steps of human progress, and emerging even more Flemish than before.

The old man, in his black suit and high-crowned peaked Dutch cap, sat almost crouching on the seat of the gig, knees nearly as high as his chin, wrists on knees, dark eyes fixed on the road ahead, speaking from time to time to the old white horse, who paid no attention nor varied its wooden shamble. Madeleine, whose clothes were almost those of a modern girl of the towns, sat upright, hands folded in her lap, head erect, in face and figure just another of those strongly built, tranquil, slightly "managing" Madonnas of the pictures of the old Flemish painters, if ever Madonna had so grim an immobility, such a slow-burning, unquenchable spark in the gray eye.

They reached the "Golden Key," put up the horse and gig, and walked to the station. There was a train in ten minutes. They each took a bowl of coffee and slice of bread, not at the station buffet where the tariff was aimed at the hurried traveler, but at the little café outside, where the small ill-paid world employed at a French station gets itself served for twenty centimes a time less than other people. Then Madeleine went with her certificate, her own and her father's identity cards, and her hand full of small notes, to the booking-office.

"Two third-class privilege tickets to Schaexen Halte, and return, to see a wounded relative!"

The booking-clerk took the papers and looked at them.

"This is no good," he muttered through his decayed teeth.

Madeleine, with all the contempt of the comparatively free and wealthy farmer's daughter for the small railway official, and all the cunning of one who deals with beasts and the law, held her peace.

The booking-office clerk was in that category of age and infirmity which alone in those days could exempt a man from mobilization. He worked fifteen hours a day in a pigsty of an office, whose glazed wicket made a perpetual draught. He was easily flustered.

"You asked for two privilege tickets to go and see a wounded relative in hospital."

"That is what I said!"

"This certificate is incomplete!"

Madeleine said never a word, but leaned calmly on the ledge of the wicket, making herself look as stupid as she could, by letting her lower lip droop. Behind her a queue was forming. Already there were cries of: "Come on!" "The train goes in five minutes," and a wag, "They are making a film for the cinema!"

Tears of exasperation came into the little man's eyes and his hand began to tremble. He stamped his foot.

"Write the name of the relative you are going to visit."

"I have no pen."

Men were hammering on the partition and women were saying, "Are we going to miss the train in addition to all our other miseries?"

The booking-office clerk flung his hairy crossed-nibbed pen at Madeleine. She took it, and wrote in the margin of Blanquart's certificate the name of her dead brother, carefully using the Flemish script, which the railway people, mainly pure French, could not read. The paper was seized; the cards of identity, the privilege tickets, the change were thrust into her hands. She moved away, counting her change and smiling a very little to herself, and giving just a glance each to the English military policeman and the French gendarme at the platform entrance, both amused spectators of the scene. Behind her, the booking-office clerk kept chewing over the words "sacred peasants," "swine's luck," and other expressions of feeling, as he jabbed the date on tickets and served them in frenzied haste to the crowd that besieged his wicket.

On the wooden benches of the third-class compartment old Vanderlynden and Madeleine found many an acquaintance. There were cries of: "How goes it, Madeleine?" "Jerome, what are you jolly-well doing here, since when did you live St. Omer way?"

.

Madeleine, who had foreseen this contingency, nudged her father, and replied for both:

"We have a little business to attend to," having made up her mind that no one would guess what it was. She was right. Thus she set running the right stream of vague gossip. For weeks after, the news ran through all the surrounding communes, and flowed back to Hondebecq, that she and her father had been to St. Omer by train. It circulated from the inn of "Lion of Flanders" to the restaurant "The Three Crown-pieces," even descended to mere estaminets like the "Return from the Congo" and the "Brave Sapeur-Pompier." No one could make it out. Victor Dequidt soon rejoined his regiment, and if he mentioned the young baron, no one except Madeleine was curious enough to ask which hospital he had gone to. Nor did anyone know of Madeleine's particular interest in him. At last, when the tale got to the café-restaurant "de la Gare et de Commerce," one of the gaziers or bullock merchants who used that more business quarter of the village was able to propound a theory. There was an English Forage Officer at St. Omer, and he had his depôt just exactly at Naes'

farm, by the new sidings the English had had to make at Schaexen
Halte for their hospital, so as to be out of the way of the bombing.
No doubt old Vanderlynden had worked the trick all right with that
officer (who was buying large quantities), and done well out of it.
The certificate of having mobilized relatives that Blanquart had
given in such a hurry (and which, of course, was known through
Cécile and the other school-children), might be on account of Marcel
Vanderlynden, or might be merely a blind. The original paper on
which Madeleine had written her brother's name remained in the
archives of the station until all were burnt in the bombardment of
December, 1917.

.

Descending at Schaexen Halte, Madeleine and her father made
their way to the block of white marquees and tents that almost filled the
manor pasture of Naes' farm. In spite of the fresh air, the smell of
anæsthetics and disinfectants hung over the duck-board paths and
cindered drives, and mingled with the odor of cooking maconochie
and the smoke of a giant incinerator that, never quenched, burned
the daily load of discarded clothing and bandages, filthy with human
refuse and trench mud. Near by, in the corner where Naes used to
grow his maize, was a small neat cemetery of little mounds with in-
scribed wooden crosses, destined to grow with the years into a bigger
area than the hospital and the sidings together, until lawyers had to
argue out the compensation due to Naes for the expropriation. At
this point luck deserted Madeleine, for no sooner had she and her
father got into conversation with an orderly, than up rolled a convoy
of a dozen ambulances, out ran all the available orderlies, and the
whole place hummed like a railway station. There was no getting an
answer to a question, and the pair were obliged to step into the
nearest tent to avoid being run over. They found themselves, in the
peculiar half light of such places, before a wooden table at which a
sergeant was writing hurriedly. At Madeleine's question he called over
his shoulder:

"What about these civilians, sir, are they allowed?"

A young doctor came in from somewhere behind, buckling on a
belt. He spoke kindly in French, but was obviously preoccupied. There
had been some French casualties in the hospital, he thought, but it
had not been his tour of duty, and they had been passed on at once.

"Besides," he added, "all next-of-kin are informed if it is a serious
case, and you will soon hear for certain."

Aware of the truth of this, and of her false position, Madeleine did
not press the matter. She knew the English were queer about such

things. So were the French, but she understood their sort of queerness and sympathized with it, not the English sort.

The officer and sergeant went outside, and began examining, questioning, listing, sorting the long line of stretchers, each with its pale, patient face above dirty blankets, a line that grew faster than it could be dealt with. Madeleine drew her father outside and sent him off to the halte on the railway, to drink a glass of beer. She herself pried about among tent-pegs and ropes, canvas flaps and damp twilight. She managed to get into one big tent with iron beds in rows, and was going from one to the other when she was stopped by a girl of her own age, in the ugly gray and red uniform and beautiful white coif of English nurses. The girl said:

"Défendu!" She spoke with a queer accent.

Madeleine had a flash of inspiration:

"I am looking for my fiancé, a French soldier," she said in English. The girl's eyes melted.

"I'm so sorry, there are no French here, all gone!" She called an orderly to "show the lady out!"

Madeleine tried to question him, but all she got was: "Straight down the cinder track you'll find the road!" and "Now then, mum, get on, 'ow the 'ell am I to evacuate these bloody blessays with you in the gangway. 'Tisn't decent, besides!"

She made a détour and tried once more, but only once. She pushed her way into a tent behind some screens, and peeping over, saw a sergeant-major, followed by bearers with a stretcher covered by a Union Jack. They put it on the iron table, lifted the flag and began fetching water, unbinding and washing the helpless thing. She slipped away behind the screens unnoticed. She tried no more. She did not connect the dead body with Georges. She could not imagine him dead. But it was unlucky. Deep down some superstition was touched.

.

She rejoined her father, and they caught a train that got back to Hazebrouck at four. Suddenly she wished to be alone, felt a necessity for a moment to gather herself for the next stroke, as it were. Her father had not said a word since the hospital, but she wanted him to go away. She sat in the salle d'attente and sent him for the horse and gig. She stared in front of her at the gathering shadows, between the sand-bagged windows. She heard the feet of the old horse, the rattle of the gig-wheels. Then suddenly her father appeared with Lieutenant Skene. She had not thought of him, but she thought fast enough now. Quickly, using the word "fiancé" for Georges, she explained her plight. He was the same well-brought-up, handy, decorous

young officer. In a moment he had broken into the Railway Trans-
port Office, pushed aside the corporal, possessed himself of the tele-
phone and was trying to get something definite from the hospital
as to Georges' destination after leaving the place. He came back dis-
appointed; they could not trace the name.

Meantime, the fighting half of her spirit had got its breath, and
cutting short his apologies, she went rapidly on to the next thing.
Could he get her a lift in a car or lorry to the English base to which
alone, so he said, casualties passing through English clearing-stations
would go? In a moment she saw her mistake, she had asked too much,
had run across some inexplicable—to her, unreasonable, prejudice
in the young officer's mind. She knew well enough that it was for-
bidden for civilians to travel in British vehicles, but had counted
hastily on his position as an officer and her powers of persuasion.
He began to use commonplaces, to inquire how she was getting on
with the troops at the farm. Briefly, tartly, she replied she must be
getting home, and rose to go. She did not bother about the look of
concern on his face, but turning to say good-bye from the gig, as it
got slowly in motion, she reflected that it was foolish to throw away
possible friends and their help, and called to him, "Come and see
us soon." He made a gesture and she accepted the fact that he was
rather taken with her. He would be.

Driving home in the twilight, however, she had only one thought—
rather one feeling. This war had dealt her a blow. She admitted that,
on the day's doings, she was worsted. Was she going to give in? Not
she! Silent beside her father, up the road between the silent fields,
one process only was going on in her. A hardening, a storing-up of
strength. Done? She was only just beginning!

.

She had plenty of time for reflection as the winter wore on. Madame
la Baronne did not send down to the farm for anything special enough
to be made a pretext for a visit to the château. Moreover, though she
longed to go and ask boldly what had happened to Georges, and was
only prevented by a sure knowledge of his resentment if she exposed
herself and him in that way, yet she was able to tell herself with con-
fidence that if the very worst had happened, it would have got known
—would have filtered out through the servants, through Masses an-
nounced in church, through mourning worn by the Baron and
Madame. But there were no rumors, no horror-stricken whispers, no
sign of black in Madame's dress or in what the Baron called his
"sports" (indicating cloths of material that meant to be Scotch tweed,
color meant to be khaki, cut meant to be that of an English gentle-

man out shooting—but which failed at all points, as Frenchmen's clothes so often do). So far, so good.

There existed in Madeleine, as in so many women of those days, the queerest contradiction. Fearing daily and desperately the very worst—death to their loved man—they never could believe in it happening, often even when it did actually happen, as was usual in those years. Relieved, respited at least from the major anxiety —for Georges must be in hospital or depôt somewhere, and out of the fighting, Madeleine began to be a prey to a lesser—to know what had happened to him? which led her curiosity to explore the unknown at least once a day.

.

Meanwhile, the war that had dealt her that private blow was gentle with her. The English kept on increasing. Seldom was the farm without its happy-go-lucky khaki crowd, whose slang, mixed with Indian words learned from old regular soldiers, and cheerful attempts at anglicized French phrases, Madeleine learned and used, as she learned the decorous politeness of the older officers, the shy good humor of the younger ones. Many a good sum did Blanquart pay her for billeting, many a neat bill did she receipt for anxious Mess Presidents. It was a queer education for a girl of her sort. At the convent school she had committed to memory certain facts about England and its people, not because they interested her, but because she soon discovered that it was easier to do lessons than to be punished for not doing them, and because her scheming mind knew by practice, if not by theory, that knowledge is power. And now she was having an object-lesson in very deed.

All the communes lying close to the line, whose population had been decimated by general mobilization, were being re-peopled by English-speaking men and women, in billets and horselines, rest-camps and hospitals, aerodromes and manœuver grounds. Night after night she heard the winter darkness atremble with traffic on the road, and learned to know it as the sound of "caterpillars" (which she took to be the name of some new kind of road engine, and was not wrong) bringing up guns and yet more guns. This was interesting, comforting, profitable, there were no dull hours, no sense of danger, and plenty of money to be made. But it had an indirect effect which Madeleine saw clearly enough, if she did not trace the connection very closely. The more ships were torpedoed by German submarines, the fewer ships there were. The more English there were, the more ships were wanted. Therefore the still fewer ships to import foodstuffs. Therefore appeals from deputies, maires, publicists, parliamentarians of all

sorts, praising, cajoling, inciting the "honest peasants" to grow more and more food. The greater waxed the importance of the question, the more the endless bargaining and speculating to which she and her father, instinctively prone, needed little encouragement.

Jerome Vanderlynden and all his sort—all backed up by wives and daughters more or less like Madeleine—hung on to their produce for better and better prices. Subsidies had to be granted, taxes eased, bounties promised, facilities given. Then they would go on and grow some more—and then hang out again for greater and greater benefits. Beet, haricots, potatoes, wheat, barley, oats, all served their turn. Flax doubled in price, and doubled again. Hops were worth their weight in gold. Chicory had to be the object of special legislation. The farmers learned slowly, but surely. There was no brisk, open "business as usual" propaganda—and no need for it. The dour old men, and quiet, careful women and girls, were not likely to miss the opportunity. The atmosphere was right. If death and disaster come to-morrow—"gather ye rosebuds while ye may." Gathering rosy thousand-franc notes is even better. And who would blame an old man with one son dead and one a prisoner, with his barn full of English soldiers who smoked pipes and set lighted candles among the straw as they wrote home, not to mention the ever-present possibility of shells—like all the farms Armentières way—or bombs— like all those toward St. Omer.

.

As a side issue, the social position of the peasant farmer began to improve. He had been accustomed to brief spells of flattery at election times—not to the wave of adulation that now engulfed him. He began to look the whole world in the face, and fear not any man. But many a man began, if not to fear him, at least to seek his good offices. Besides all the politicians, the contractors, the endless train of semi-public opportunists the War had created, the easy-going world of retired middle-aged people that are to be found in every French Department, suddenly discovered that the only way to remain easy-going was to get the farmer to befriend them. Everything from coals to chicken meal, from bread to cotton was being rationed. That facile plenty which is the basis of the French provincial middle class was threatened. Thus, as 1916 advanced, and the long sordid epic of Verdun began to string out its desperate incidents, the Baron Louis d'Archeville, walking round his shooting with the air of a child gazing at a birthday cake it has been forbidden to touch, bowler hat, "sports," camp-stool, all complete, stumped over the pavement of the

yard, and found Madeleine putting her week's washing through the portable wringer.

Having it in his mind to ask for wooden logs, eggs, ham, and anthracite, he naturally began:

"Ah, good day, Madeleine, pretty as ever!"

"Good day, Monsieur le Baron."

"And this brave Jerome, he goes well? A glass of beer? I shall not say no!" He sat down on a wheelbarrow and waited for her to call her father.

Old Jerome came at Madeleine's cry of "Papa, kom ben t'haus!" from picking over his seed potatoes.

Madeleine, who wanted the men out of the way, let it pass for politeness that she took the carafe of beer and two hastily washed glasses into the kitchen, swabbed the table and invited the Baron to place himself. She went back to her wringer, leaving the door into the scullery open. One never knew. She had kept her secret in her heart ever since her visit to the English hospital. She had no news, and had been able to think of no new way of getting even with the War, but she had forgotten nothing, forgiven nothing, renounced nothing.

Old Jerome, who, even a year before, would have stood in the Baron's presence until told to be seated, now sat down beside his landlord without apology.

The Baron did not remark on this, but said: "Then, you have your farm all full of English?"

"They do damage enormously."

"Very likely, but you have the right to be paid!"

"They pay, but they do damage all the same."

Old Jerome was not going to let go a possible advantage.

The Baron, whose feelings against the English had been cool from 1870 until Fashoda, then violent until the idea of the Entente and its meaning had filtered into his unreceptive mind, had just been reading propagandist literature, "The English Effort," and so forth, designed for just such as he. Expanding with the new ideas he had received, he reviewed the situation at some length, dwelling on England's immense resources of material, untouched reserves of men, all that cheerful unknown which was so comforting in face of unpleasant known facts of the growing wastage of France.

Jerome added one remark born of the unaccustomed way money was now handed about. "Besides, they are rich!" which led the Baron on again, along the path pointed out by yet another pamphlet he had been reading, on the subject of the new war loan.

Much of the verbiage and all the argument was lost on old Jerome.

He was thinking of his sons and poured out another glass for himself and the Baron. "It's a grievous business, this war," he sighed. "You must feel that as much as I."

The Baron did not miss the allusion, blinked a moment, for what is one to say to a man who has two sons, one of whom is dead and forever gone, and the other a prisoner, with uncertain prospects. He concluded that the most comforting thing was to talk of his own son. Besides, he preferred to.

"At last we have news of Georges. He has written to us, you will never divine from whence!"

He waited a moment, but old Jerome was not good at guessing. In the scullery the wringer was no longer creaking as it turned, and the splashing of water and the soft flop of the clothes into the tin pail had ceased.

"He has written from Monte Carlo. It seems that the army surgeons found he was making himself a bad chest, and sent him to the south for convalescence. He is being marked inapt for service, but he still wishes to do his part, and they will put him in this French Mission with the English Army as Officer-Interpreter. One day or another, we may see him here, if he is attached to a division that passes this way."

In the scullery Madeleine was standing over the wringer, allowing herself to smile ever so little. Within her breast her blood was dancing to the tune "I knew it, I knew it!" Now, that terribly serious Georges of the day of mobilization that she did not understand and for whom she could do nothing would be changed back to the gay Georges (Monte Carlo, she had heard him speak of it, could see and hear him doing so now) that she did understand, and who would want her. The Baron was talking of other things now, of how the French would take it easy, and how the English would come in and finish the War. It was quite their turn. One had made sufficient sacrifices. Could Jerome let him have—this, that, and the other? She paid little heed. Her father bargained a bit, then acquiesced. She thought it fitting, when the Baron rose to go, to come to the door of the kitchen and say:

"Au revoir, Monsieur le Baron."

"Au revoir, Madeleine, remain young and pretty, is all one asks of you!"

.

She on her side asked little. She would get Georges back. She was sure now. The days might pass, nothing happen, no news come, but she was sure, sure as though he had written giving the date of his arrival.

Spring came—never more beautiful than in Flanders, where beauty can only exist on a basis of utility. It came shyly, a northern spring. The sodden grayness of the marshland winter on flat hedgeless fields gave way to cold and fitful sunshine that shone on rich young green everywhere, while the black dripping leaves of the elms in the dank pastures seemed blurred in vapor, that, upon examination, proved to be but a profusion of tiny light-colored buds. And then something happened. It began happening so far away and so high up among the principalities and powers of this world that it was weeks before Madeleine felt its effects.

As the horrors of Verdun dragged on, the wastage that was obvious to so mediocre an observer as the Baron began to be acutely felt at the more sensitive Great Head-quarters. So much so that Great Head-quarters of France insisted to British Great Head-quarters that something must be done. British Great Head-quarters, well groomed, well mannered, had a long way then still to go before it should shake off its slightly patronizing attitude towards its ally. It merely said that something should be done when it was ready. Great Head-quarters of France, doubting when that time would come to a people who had to be so well groomed and well mannered, insisted still harder. British Great Head-quarters replied good-humoredly, "Oh, very well then!" It became known that there was to be a British offensive in the Somme. Gigantic rearrangements were necessary, and among the million schemes, orders and moves, was the establishment of Corps Head-quarters at Hondebecq. This necessitated a lot of room, and the mere fighting troops had to be pushed farther out. Thus Madeleine, one fine morning early in March, only just saved herself from dropping a saucepan of boiling soup. An officer-interpreter, in the uniform of the French Mission, had ridden into the yard. She knew the uniform well, had seen many such a one, but since the Baron's last visit it meant to her only one person. Her emotion, kept well under, was gone in a flash. She saw directly, as the officer dismounted, it was not Georges. He came from the new Corps Head-quarters to say that no more infantry would be billeted at the farm. Instead, she would be expected to house the Corps Salvage Officer.

Madeleine knew little and cared less as to what this might mean, except as it affected the work of the farm. She waited, and in a few days an elderly gentleman appeared who had the tall angular figure, whiskers, and prominent teeth of French caricatures of English people of the nineteenth century. With him came a gig, a motor-car, three riding horses, servant, groom, chauffeur and sundry dogs. He surveyed the room offered him coolly enough, had some alterations made in the position of bed and washstand, but warmed in his manner at once

when he discovered, in the course of a few hours, that Madeleine could speak really resourceful if slangy English, and understood about his cold bath. He had had such difficulty, he told her, and the French were so dirty. Madeleine smiled (for he had passed her estimate for accommodation and cooking without a murmur) and took him under her wing. There was something about him that she dimly associated with what her father might have been, in totally different circumstances—a mixture of helplessness and partiality to herself. She mended his bed-socks and filled his india-rubber hot-water bottle almost with affection. He on his side would often say words which she took for endearment, in what he conceived to be French—was less trouble than the ever-changing battalion messes, and paid, in the long run, nearly as much. She was glad to have the barns freed from everlasting fear of fire, and to get them empty before the summer. The space which the Salvage required she had Blanquart measure up, and charged at the rate laid down in the billeting regulations. It came to nearly as much as housing infantry.

.

This old gentleman, by name Sir Montague Fryern, and his "salvage dump" were merely concrete evidence which slowly revealed to Madeleine what was going on. The idea of "salvage" had been imposed upon English fighting formations unwillingly, from somewhere high up and far off, some semi-political Olympus near Whitehall. Divisional and Corps Staffs knew better than to resist. They thought it silly and superfluous—the war was trouble enough, and already much too long and dangerous for the average regular soldier, without having to economize material as well. But, wise with eighteen months of such a war as they had never dreamed of, and hoped never to see again, they had found out that the way to deal with these mad ideas invented by people at home, was to acquiesce, and then to side-track them. So when pressed for the third time for reasons why they had not appointed a Salvage officer, the Corps Staff now functioning at Hondebecq looked at one another, and some one said jokingly, "Let's make old Fryern do the job!"

The baronet had been almost a national joke. In 1914 dapper old gentlemen in London clubs had said:

"Heard about old Fryern?"

"No!"

"He's joined up as a private in the R.A.M.C."

Some one said it was to avoid commanding a battalion, some that it was to escape scandal or a writ, others that it was merely "just

like old Fryern!" In the course of a year he had become notorious for prolonging officers' convalescence with illicit drink, and the King, it was said, had insisted on his taking a commission. Too eccentric to be put in a responsible position, and insisting on not remaining in England, he had drifted about Divisional, and then Corps Head-quarters until this heaven-sent opportunity housed him in a suitable nook. A man of unexpected resource, no sooner had he understood what was required of him than he began to gather at the Spanish Farm the most miscellaneous collection of objects ever seen together since Rabelais compiled his immortal lists of omnium gatherum. A field-gun, a motor-car, other people's servants, several animals, French school books, Bosch pamphlets, sewing machines, plows and tinned food; nothing came amiss to him. What good he did, no one could say. Little of the stuff was re-issued and served the purpose of economy, but when Dignitaries from British Great Head-quarters came down to see Corps Head-quarters and said to its old friends: "I say, Charles, you were awfully slack about the Salvage Order, you know!" the old friends were able to answer:

"Well, we aren't now; you come and see old Fryern's dump after lunch—say about three!"

"What, old 'Chops' Fryern?"

"No other, I assure you!" and so on.

.

It happened, only a week or so after Sir Montague's arrival at the farm, that a lorry stopped in the yard. There was nothing un-usual in that. They did so at all hours of the day and most of the night. The English, so wits said, fought on rubber tyres. Old Jerome, leaning on his hoe, type of primitive man drudging with his primitive implement to wring a subsistence from inscrutable Nature, often stood to watch these powerful, docile servants of a younger age, that could do the work of ten men and four horses in half an hour. He was doing so now, and Madeleine, if she thought about it at all, thought like this: "Poor old father, he's making old bones; it's the boys he misses," when she saw Jerome drop his hoe and run to the lorry to help out a woman with a shawl over her head.

In another moment Madeleine had no doubt. It was her sister Marie from Laventie. In a moment she was out. The men on the lorry, with the queer, dumb, unexpected kindliness of the poorer Englishman, were handing down Emilienne, Marie's little girl, in a sort of frozen stupor of cold and fright. Madeleine ran to take the child, while her father helped Marie, who seemed dazed, into the house. Round the kitchen stove, quickly stoked until the top shone

red, Madeleine plied them with the inevitable coffee, and presently with slabs of staunch farm bread.

Jerome stood by, the mere helpless male in the face of calamity. It was he who said first:

"What is it, my girl?"

At first Marie could only say, "O, my God!" and rock herself. But presently, reviving under the influence of food and drink, and the still more potent surroundings of safety in that familiar, warm old kitchen, where she had grown up, began to tell of the daily increase in shelling and bombing. In her half-empty farm-house, with the glass long gone from its shuttered windows, and the machine-gun bullets in its walls, relics of the first engagement with the Germans in 1914, she had billeted some English Engineers. The sector had been quiet ever since Neuve Chapelle, a year before. Suddenly, as the English sat with her around the fire, the shell had come. It had fallen in the doorway of the farm and had flung half the house upon the soldiers. Marie, protected by the solid brick chimney-piece, as soon as she got her breath, had scrambled under the débris to the room where Emilienne was crying to her. The door was jammed by a fallen beam. Some soldiers had run from a neighboring billet, had broken in the door and got the child out. How they had all tramped up the road, shells ahead, shells behind, shells falling each side, with the sky red and the air rocking with the English artillery retaliation, she could not tell. At last, at a dump of some sort the Engineers had put her on a lorry that had taken her to Strazeele. Farther than that they could not go; it was the limit of their Corps area. Marie and Madeleine had been educated by the past eighteen months, and knew better than to expect a lorry to go outside its Corps area. So Marie had had to walk, with the child in her arms, to Caestre, where she had found, thank God! plenty of lorries running back from railhead. On hearing her tale, an officer had allowed her to get into one that was going to Hondebecq, and she had easily persuaded the driver to go as far as Spanish Farm.

At this point there was a tap on the door, which was opened by a khaki-clad figure, with a sheepish face and unmistakable Cockney accent.

"Beg parding, mum, but 'ow's yer little gal?"

"Give them something to take, they had been so——" she used the untranslatable word "gentil," for which "decent" is perhaps the nearest equivalent. But Marie meant what the word perhaps originally meant—human as against inhuman, civilized as against barbarous.

Madeleine took out mugs of coffee and rum, and was rewarded by a cheerful, "Thank ye, kindly, miss, and here's the very best!"

Madeleine came back, stepping softly. Emilienne had sunk into a deep, heavy sleep, interrupted by twitching and muttering, in the chimney corner. Giving her a glance, Madeleine clasped her hands.

"O Marie, all your things! The brass bedstead, the beer glasses, the clock!"

Marie shook her head, tears ran down her face.

Above her, old Jerome, caring little for woman's fallals, muttered: "Thank God, the little one was spared!"

Like all other incidents of the War, there it was. Shells fell, something was destroyed. One went on as well as one could. That was the history of the past eighteen months, was to be the history of another two years and a half—just a perpetual narrow margin of human survival over all the disasters humanity could bring upon itself. Not that the Vanderlyndens took the large impersonal view. Marie and Emilienne slept most of that day. The next, they started in to work, their varying capacities. The first thing Marie did was to spend a day, bribing lorry drivers and cajoling officers, to get back to Laventie and see what was left. The beetroot had been sold, the potatoes had gone with the horse and cart to Aunt Delobeau's near Bailleul, because for some time Marie had been unable to keep a man on the farm, and had worked it with such village women as had been stranded like herself by general mobilization, the Government being only too glad to leave them there, to cultivate almost under machine-gun fire, as long as they would. But since the fatal night, the gendarmerie had become nervous of the place, though the actual shelling had ceased. They would not allow her to sow the ground, and were moving the powers that watch over France to obtain an order of general evacuation of the commune, which they no longer desired to patrol. With difficulty she obtained permission to fetch away the seed and one or two agricultural implements. The dwelling-house had burnt out, for the split stove had flung its flaming coals on thatch and beams. She was spared the spectacle of inevitable looting by Allies, and on returning to the Spanish Farm, settled down into the position she had left, in 1910, to be married.

Outwardly, Madeleine acquiesced. Marie was the elder sister—eldest child, in fact—and had all the prestige of a married woman. She was also more purely peasant than Madeleine and easily jealous of her rights. Madeleine, since she had had Georges, had ceased to envy her sister. Now, losing Georges, she lost her secret comfort, and any satisfaction she may have drawn from being mistress of the house, brains of the farm. But Madeleine by long brooding on her secret fixed idea—Georges—had come to that point at which she accepted these outward superficial happenings, estimating their im-

portance solely by the standard of that Fixed Idea. At first she was unable to see how the advent of Marie and Emilienne affected her reconquest of Georges.

.

She was soon to learn.

Marie, for a few days preoccupied with herself, startled by what had happened, and rather grateful for home and shelter, soon emerged from that numbed state which, medically the result of concussion, is one of the first universal symptoms of shell-shock. She began to be masterful and critical of Madeleine's former management. She had run two messes for the Engineers in her small Lys valley house, with far less scope than the Spanish Farm afforded. Madeleine pointed out that she had done all that, and would have continued but for movements of troops over which she had no control. Marie agreed, sighing for the busy days when she had cooked and done for three officers, and scores of hungry men, just out or just going into the trenches, to whom Emilienne had sold chocolate, cigarettes, writing paper and candles to great advantage. Perhaps also she was jealous of Madeleine, of the younger girl's smarter looks, less peasant-like and matronly than her own, of her untouched good luck during the long anxiety of the war, for, like all the world, Marie knew nothing of the secret about Georges. But things kept happening. Presently the right thing happened.

Podevin, who kept the "Lion of Flanders" inn, on the Grand' Place of Hondebecq, gave up. He had made money, of course, especially latterly since the Corps Head-quarters had been in the village, and had enabled him to open a dining-room for officers. But, like so many, he had lost his only son at Verdun, and, heartbroken, cared no longer even to amass wealth. The long, biscuit-colored house, with its two storeys and old steep-tiled roof was for sale. Marie saw the notice and told Madeleine at once:

"There's your chance!"

Madeleine took her habitual half-minute of reflection, trying this new idea against her Fixed Idea. They suited marvellously. Why had she not thought of it before? (The true answer was that she was not sufficiently imaginative.) She saw now that in taking the "Lion of Flanders" she would be placing herself exactly where Georges must come if his division were moved this way, which was sure to happen sooner or later. And the whole thing was so natural that he would never be able to make her the one reproach she feared so much— of running after him and making their liaison obvious.

The two women went to see Podevin together, before they told

old Jerome. Podevin could only say, "I've lost my son—let me alone!"

They fetched in Blanquart, as was usual in such cases. The grizzled schoolmaster arranged it. Madeleine pretended to be shocked at the price, standing in Blanquart's little parlor, with the sound of the school classes grinding out the morning lesson like some gigantic gramophone gone mad, just through the wall. But secretly she nudged Marie. The worst was over. The price named was well within what she kept about her in the house in notes. She would not have to draw on the savings bank at Hazebrouck. That made all the difference in tackling her father. But when the two daughters broached the subject that evening, he acquiesced. It would be a good business, he said. Madeleine, who had never forgotten how he had, all unasked, fetched Lieutenant Skene to help her on the day of the visit to the hospital, wondered how much her father guessed of her secret. Something, surely. But it was just the sort of subject on which neither of them could speak to each other. So all she said was, "You know, you're a good father!"

.

The War, that had wounded her so deeply where she was most vulnerable, was kind to her in little things. No sooner was she installed in the "Lion of Flanders," and had got together some three or four village women who had young families or other domestic ties that had made them anxious to get any work they could within a hundred yards of their doors, while forbidding them to go out for the day to the farms that needed them, than Corps Head-quarters arranged a Horse Show, a form of amusement that became very fashionable in the B.E.F. as the years went on. Officially, it was inaugurated to keep drivers and orderlies up to their work. Subconsciously it indulged that national failing, love or horses and open air, so curious in a town-bred nation. Madeleine, of course, paid no more heed to this than she did to any other of the curious foibles of those incomprehensible English, until she found that most of the officers of three divisions would be in the village nearly all day for this function, many of them ten miles from their own messes, and glad enough to find a decent meal. She laid her plans and purchased wisely and well. Then, only two days before the festival, Sir Montague offered to take her to the show. She thought for half a minute, and accepted, almost jubilantly.

.

She was feeling the long strain, however much she concealed it with silent composure. And, as with all women in her particular "ir-

regular" position, she had begun to hug the golden illusion that goes with it, and makes it for some so possible to bear. She had lost Georges; he was gone from her side, in spite of her, pulled away by something he held dearer. He had not come back, not written. She could not, dare not if she could, go or write to him. But she still believed, as all such women do, "Oh, if I could only see him!" She still nourished that pathetic faith, still believed that if only she could stand face to face with him, things would be again as they had been. There was, however, that terrible danger haunting the attempt to get face to face with him. He might think or feel she was following him. That, she knew, would be fatal. In Sir Montague, therefore, she saw a heaven-sent angel. Too old, too cranky, too well known (as she had soon discovered) to be the object of scandal regarding her, he would take her under his wing and she would be at the Horse Show, to be seen. Georges, if he were there, would see her. That was the safest. Once he saw her she had perfect confidence in herself. She would know instinctively, would not look, not she. But she would will it, and he would have to come. She recognized clearly enough now, how simply, passively, unconsciously she had made their first hour alone together, when she had given herself, in the shelter at the Kruysabel. She had only to do it again. This also comforted her, for she was not original. She accepted Sir Montague's invitation graciously, and took care to look her best on the day.

.

The day came, and she was ready. Radiant with health, wishing to be dressed in her own way, in a mixture of country primness and the English style she secretly admired (coat and skirt and all-weather hat), she had compromised at the skirt of her pigeon-gray saxony costume, a cream-colored blouse that left her elbows and neck bare, with nothing on her head but her own crisp dark hair. Thus adorned, she esteemed herself as nearly a lady (i.e. a person who does no work) as she had any need to be, while not too far removed from the mistress of the "Lion of Flanders."

Before Sir Montague came to fetch her, as she was perfecting her arrangements at her restaurant, Lieutenant Skene appeared with a gunner officer she did not like, who was obviously joking about her. She greeted her friend kindly, in English, and ignored the other. She was flattered to see that the lieutenant was evidently taking her part, trying to make the other behave, looking very sheepish and funny as he clumsily concealed his obvious feeling for her. They reserved a table and went away. Sir Montague was punctual and she stepped up into the gig with the ease of one who has always had to use her

limbs. She was elated. Men looked after her. The sun shone. In the queer gauche Flemish springtime, buds and shoots hung stiffly in the still air like heraldic emblems. A band was playing, people were moving about. Everything whipped her excitement. They drove on to Verbaere's big pasture, behind the mill, and put the gig with the other vehicles, all parked and stewarded as on an English race-course. Sir Montague had a way of arching his elbow, twirling his whip, and fetching a great circle before he brought his conveyance to a stand-still that caused, she noticed, much laughter, and the beginnings of a cheer.

He handed her into a rough enclosure, where English nurses in gray and red and white coifs, Canadian nurses in blue and scarlet, Australian sisters in gray-brown, fine big girls in their mannish hats, mixed with a sprinkling of the wives of local maires and notaries, small French officialdom and business circles. Some of these ignored Madeleine, perhaps did not know her, but the brewer's wife from the next village, invited by the A.S.C. colonel billeted on her, gave a cheery "Good day, Madeleine," that would have put anyone at ease. But Madeleine was already at her ease. She saw she was getting more attention than any other woman on the ground. She had dressed just right, awakened none of the submerged sensibilities of those queer English. That and a glance at the lovely horses, shining, prancing, bobbing head and floating tail—for she loved fine animals—was all she cared to notice before she settled herself, eyes straight to the front, and put out all her feelers for the one purpose for which she had come. Poor Madeleine, no one had bothered to tell her that there were already over fifty English divisions in France, and among the men before her she stood one chance in seventeen of finding Georges. They passed about her, Easthamptons, Lincolns, Norfolks, A.S.C., R.A.M.C., R.A.F., gunners, Engineers, French Mission in blue and strawberry, wonderful staff people, in khaki and leather so perfect that it outshone all the bright colors of the French. She took it all in, tried to sort it out, mused over it, especially the name "Lincoln," which, like all French people, she was incapable of pro-nouncing. She could form no idea of which group was the likeliest to be Georges', glanced over the face and figures of the French Mission officers. More than any close examination, her instinct told her, Georges was not there. A sort of numbness came over her, she felt it almost like a physical sensation. It seemed to be in her legs. She fought against it, would not give in to it. Then, all of a sudden, too suddenly for her strong, resolute, unimaginative nature, she did give in.

The corps officials had hardly begun judging the riding-horses when

she slipped from her place, round behind the stand, out between the wagon-teams, waiting their turn, with cunning drivers of all arms surreptitiously dabbing metal and leather with handkerchiefs, looking stolidly over the exhibits they belong to, speaking gently to them in low voices. She found a well-known gap in the hedge and got through into the back lane that ran towards Verbaere's mill. Up this, picking her way in the mud to save her best boots, she came into the village by the yard of the "Lion of Flanders." The numbness was gone from her legs. Instead, her pulse beat in her temples so loud that she hardly heard the band playing "Watch your Step," and the cheering as the riding-horses, classed by the judges, filed round the ring, and out.

.

She let herself into the "Lion of Flanders" by the back door, which she shut with a clang. She looked magnificent and just a bit desperate, so that, of her waiting-women, one said to another, "She's in fine fettle this morning, our young patronne!" But she was not the woman to do the more ordinary desperate things. No—yes. A stitch of her close-sewn self-control had parted. She was not going to stand it. Her mental attitude contained nothing of an English suffragette's logical, theoretical stand upon "rights." Her pride was hurt. Georges was Georges, dearer than life, but there now glimmered behind him something dearer than that—her dignity, what was due to her— Herself, of course, in reality.

She swept a glance round the neat, well-laid tables, sniffed the redolent preparation of the kitchen. She—dragged about behind a man's shadow that ever eluded her! Of course, her feeling was incoherent, ill-defined, just a sense of resentment against something she did not trouble to identify, but it was there. Reckless, she went down the stone steps into the cellar. Among the casks of weak beer and carefully "lengthened" wine she had taken over from Podevin, was a bottle marked "Chambertin," which she recognized as an oversight. It was good stuff. She had hidden it with the English Expeditionary Force canteen whisky and the rum she had got out of Sir Montague. Now her thought was, "They shan't have it, those English!" She took it up, glanced at the coating of the bottle neck, and mounted the stairs with it.

"Berthe," she cried—she had borrowed the girl from the farm for the day—"four glasses and some bread!"

Putting on her black alpaca apron, she pulled the cork, holding the bottle steady with a firm wrist, and poured out. Raising her glass, she said to them: "I give you that!" and drank amid a

murmur of "Thank you, Madeleine." Outside the services of the Church, the only ceremonial she had ever been taught to observe was connected with good wine. The Chambertin lived up to her gesture, with its broad, almost coarse flavor, a legend among the frugal Flemish at their rare feasts. Outwardly, what she did was just a bit of unexpected generosity toward four employees who could do with a heartening for the twelve hours' hard work that lay ahead of them, from which she intended to draw handsome profit. Within her heart it was, unconsciously, perhaps, almost a sacramental act, the opening of a new life. The blood in her was beating out the time, "I won't stand it any longer!"

.

The square-footed beakers, of the sort which would be called "rummers" in England, were empty, the substantial finger-pieces munched and swallowed, before there came the sound of spurred boots on the cobbles and the clients began to arrive. First two Canadian majors with the Maire came to claim the table they had reserved, and found it kept for them, the coarse napkins starched, the heavy cutlery and glass in place, and Madeleine with her best smile and hardly a trace of accent asking: "What would you like for lunch?" at which the Maire stared. Behind them trooped others. The room was soon full, the glass windows clouded with steam, the noise of conversation and table-ware deafening.

Imperturbable, Madeleine moved among it. The waiting may have been amateur. The cooking was thorough in the solid Flemish fashion. At least, no one was left staring at an empty plate or glass. Madeleine, a smile for every one, and a glib English explanation for every difficulty, used the mental arithmetic she had learnt at the market, in calculating bills. Her clients went off with heightened color and laughing voices, amid trails of tobacco smoke. Manfully, Madeleine and her staff cleared the place, fed themselves and washed up. They had only got the tables reset before that extraordinary meal "afternoon tea" was demanded of them. Madeleine was equal to the occasion. It might be a foolish custom, but it paid. And this merged into dinner, long and heavy as is the Flemish custom. Younger officers, and especially those down from the line, were getting boisterous, rude. She had to put up with many a clumsy joke, many a suggestion. She was too busy and too utterly unafraid to care. One thing did rather amuse her. At the table he had reserved for his party, the Lieutenant Skene was following her with his eyes and ears, and getting so cross at the treatment she was receiving. At length, just as it was all becoming too boisterous, and the younger officers were

getting out of hand, suddenly, from the little private room that had been reserved for Brigadier-General Devlin and his friends, came the sound of a piano—the good piano she had got from the château. Not musical, and unwilling to spend time over such trifles, she was forced to stop and listen. It was Chopin, some one said. It had the most extraordinary effect. General Devlin and the officer who had been playing went away. The rest of the crowd in the big room went also, the rowdiness gone from them, subdued, seduced from their daily selves by the music. On Madeleine the effect was strongest. Wrought up by the events of the day and by sheer fatigue (she had been on her feet twelve hours), the lovely stuff, that could not act on her unreceptive spirit, antipathetic to it, merely saddened her. After another laborious wash up, she dismissed her helpers, locked the house and started for home. It was past midnight, and the day that had been so fine left a dark windy night, promising rain before morning. As she trod the pavé of the grand'route and the earth of the farm road, she felt miserable and beaten. It was easy enough to say, "I won't stand it!" Like so many other people, she found it so difficult to do. How not to stand and what not to stand? Forget Georges? Could she? Would she if she could? Go and find him, and thus make him forget her? Which?

.

The corps did not have a horse show every day, but the one just passed had been a good advertisement for the "Lion of Flanders," and Madeleine began to do a quiet, regular business in luncheons and teas for the officers that incessantly circled round and about Corps Head-quarters. To be busy soothed her feeling of helplessness, and the necessity for this soothing kept her polite, skilful, attentive. Some weeks passed, and then again, far away, and high up, undreamed of by her, things began to happen.

The English offensive in the Somme, heralded as a great victory, had in reality made infinitesimal gains at the cost of enormous loss. The British Great Head-quarters, then still functioning in complete disunity with Great Head-quarters of France, and often in good-humored disregard of the advice given it, went on butting, like an obstinate ram, at the same place. This, though it surprised the Germans more than the most subtle strategy would have done, cost the lives of many a thousand English soldiers. It was necessary to economize and economize again. The reserve corps would have to disappear, the line northward be more sparsely held. Here the long chain of action and reaction touched Madeleine.

For two days she was feverishly busy, officers wanting meals at

all hours in great numbers. On the third morning, as she came down in the blaze of July seven-o'clock weather, she found a long string of lorries, grinding and jolting, behind them officers' servants with led horses, mess-carts, police. They went. A silence as of peace-time settled on the remote Flemish village, lost in the undulating fertile plateau between Dunkirk and Lille. Twenty kilometers eastward was the line, full of troops. Twenty kilometers west were the great manœuver areas where men learned to kill and not be killed more and more scientifically. At Hondebecq, nothing. It took nearly a week to convince Madeleine, who was interested in the more general aspects of the War. She was not really convinced until the Baron walked into her empty dining-room.

"Good day, Madeleine, you have lost all your clients."

Looking up from her knitting, she said gravely:

"It seems so!" But secretly she now believed it. If it were not true he would not have come. He disliked the crowd of junior officers who joked about his beard.

What was to be done? Not retain an empty restaurant where no one ever came. She saw enough at home in the evenings to know that Marie was firmly settled in, and didn't want her. The situation was beyond her. Her practical mind focussed on the immediate was baffled. But things went on happening and once again the long arm of chance touched her.

It was about a fortnight after Hondebecq had been plunged in its unnatural silence. She was going home in the long July twilight. She no longer waited to serve late dinners, her only customers being occasional passing troops during the day. No local people used the "Lion of Flanders," it was essentially an English restaurant. She was stopped at the level-crossing by the evening train from Calais going southward. As the smoke and noise faded away, she ran into Blanquart, the schoolmaster and communal secretary, stumbling over the platform-edging, wiping his eyes. The sight of that familiar figure in tears gave her pause.

"Why, Monsieur Blanquart, what is it?"

"It is my little Cécile!"

"What has she got, Cécile?"

Monsieur Blanquart blew his nose and said: "I ought not to complain. She was a good girl. Naturally she has got a good job."

"What job has she got? Where has she gone, then?"

"But to Amiens! You haven't seen the discourse of M. Paul Deschanel on the Recruitment of Women? It is hanging in the Mairie if that gives you any pleasure."

Madeleine, gray-eyed, her mouth a straight line, her hands crossed

over the little bag that contained the day's takings, stared at him between the eyes a full half-minute. Then she said:

"Ah, I sympathize with you. Good evening, Monsieur Blanquart." She went away thinking, and thought to some effect.

.

First, a refugee Belgian family was installed in the derelict "Lion of Flanders," where they all lived in the dining-room round the stove, boarded up the big windows, and got jobs in the village. Then Madeleine was seen in earnest consultation with Blanquart. Finally it was known that she had got a job in a Government office at Amiens, from which the men had just been combed out.

"Tiens!" said the gossips. "Cécile Blanquart first, now Madeleine Vanderlynden. Who next?"

The formalities took a week. Then Madeleine emerged with the papers of her appointment in her hands. She went first to the "Lion of Flanders" and told the refugee family in no equivocal terms, how, when and where to pay their rent to Marie. Leaving them in a state of guttural exclamation, half gratefulness, half apprehension, she turned for a moment into the church, and stood by the high-backed prie-Dieu that bore the initials V.D.—Vanderlynden-Delplace—staring at the gimcrack ornaments of the altar, the eternal childish innocence of the Catholic Church decoration. Old Justine Schact was fidgeting about her verger's duties. Birds scuffled in the belfry as the chimes played their verse and a half of hymn tune that marked the quarter hour.

Madeleine's lips, set by habit to utter a prayer in those surroundings, formed something like this: "Saint Madeleine, out of your divine pity, grant me that I may see him, then it will be all right!" Her lips ceased to move. In her unbowed head, her steady eyes took on the gleam of frosted marsh-pools. She squared her fine shoulders and clasped her large, capable hands on the chair-back. She might have been an allegory of indomitable Flanders. There was no mistaking the glance she bent on the altar. It said, "Saint Madeleine, if you don't . . ." But the threat was never articulated. She turned and walked out, erect and sure-footed. At the farm she told her father what time to put the horse in, and when it came, appeared from her room, her canvas-covered wooden box locked and corded. She made her adieu thus shortly:

"Good-bye, Marie, what luck you came. I can go with a tranquil heart. Berthe will help you well. Good-by, Berthe. Good-by, Emilienne, I will send you a pretty postcard!" To the old house, in which she and her father, and no one knows how many ancestors, had been

born, in which her mother had died, not a look. Either it was too familiar, or simply did not appeal to her. To the Kruysabel where she had known her brief hours of bliss—not a look. She was going to something better. Or perhaps, in her narrow personal way, she felt that these things were part of her, and that, so far as they existed, they went with her.

At the station, standing beside her box as the train came in, she turned with real affection to her father, probably the one being in the world she thoroughly understood and sympathized with. But she only said, "Au revoir, Father," and he only replied, "Au revoir, my girl." Then with a hoist of strong arms and legs, she was into the train, after which the old man stood a moment, staring. But she was already settling herself in her place, taking stock of her neighbors, girding herself for her new campaign.

PART II

"On les aura"

Madeleine went to Amiens, but it hardly describes what happened to say that she went by herself without other companions than chance fellow-travelers, for, in her, there entered the capital of Northern France more than a single Flemish girl. She took up with her, all about her, an atmosphere of the frontier, of staunch Flanders, of the Spanish Farm. Countrified she might be, certainly a stranger, but there was nothing callow or helpless about her. She showed that maturity that connoisseurs of wine mean when they speak of "body." Generations, a whole race, living in one way, confronted century after century with much the same environments, had prepared that quality in her, which led no one to wonder at or pity her. Had there been any Society for the Protection of Young Girls at the station at Amiens, it would not have considered her a "case," as she swung down on to the platform, produced her ticket and papers, and bargained with an old man with a barrow to take her box—a bargain she struck much to her advantage by shouldering the said box and starting to carry it herself.

The Amiens to which Madeleine went was the Amiens of mid-war —that is to say, a general manufacturing town of eighty thousand people, provincial, antiquated as such towns can be only in France —which town, plunged into European war, had seen the Germans march through its streets. It was now reserve railhead, camping-

ground, last-civilized-spot for the avalanches of reinforcements the English were pouring into the line. Most of the French who fought beside them in that northern sector had to pass through it. Madeleine had not been able to calculate with any nicety how her move had increased her chances of meeting Georges, but she got as far as beginning to understand what the Baron had meant by the "English effort," the immensity of that Volunteer Army, the constant watching and waiting that would be necessary to find Georges among the hundreds of French Mission officers that went with it. But like all vague steps, the one that she had taken was comforting because of its novelty, its unplumbed depths of possibility. Once cut adrift from home, and having suppressed a tiny shyness, rising in the throat, she flung herself into the new life with gusto. She was not wholly ignorant of towns, had been to Hazebrouck and St. Omer, to Dunkirk even, once, and was ready as any country-grown girl to fall under the spell of town life and strive desperately to look as if she had always lived it.

.

Her job was in one of those Government Departments, whose staff, depleted by general mobilization, and further by repeated "combing-out," hardly sufficed to keep going that multiplicity of printed forms by which France is governed. She wrote a good hand, having acquired that art at a convent school where it, at least, was not reckoned among the subversive sciences. Perhaps she dimly saw in the power to write and read one of the advantages that such as she possessed over the less lucky. Handwriting, at any rate, was no difficulty. Figures she handled with respect, almost with appetite. As the first newness of the life thawed and broke before her, she began to prepare herself to take the lead in the office, as she had taken it at the farm. By the time August was turning into September, she almost smiled as she took her week's money. She would not have paid Berthe so much for doing such a job. Eight to twelve and two to six seemed to her a ridiculously light day. The heat of the town was sometimes oppressive, but the office, about the ill-kept state of which she grimaced to herself, was on the north side of one of those rococo barrack-like buildings that link the architecture of the chef-lieux of Northern France to that of Mediterranean civilization. That is, it had the dank chill of a tomb. She survived. As for the life in general, her iron health stood it well. She missed the air and exercise, but her diet was not full enough to allow her to fatten. She had been welcomed, of course, by Cécile Blanquart, and taken, not without a shade of kindly patronage, to lodge with the

aunt who sheltered Cécile. The aunt was one of those widows of
the small official class who seemed to have disappeared from England
since Dickens. She was poorer, prouder, more impossibly ugly and
mean than anything surviving to us. She would have housed Madeleine,
had not each of her tiny rooms already contained two people at
least. Clinging to any ha'pence that were to be had, she arranged
that the new-comer should dine at the frugal common table she
kept, and sleep a few streets away in the third-floor attic over the
pork butcher's. Madeleine appeared to her what is called in France
"sérieuse." To Madeleine, the arrangement appeared nothing short
of heaven sent.

She had applied herself to her job. She had put out all her most
feminine sensibilities to catch the right note in dress and looks, for
she was nothing if not conventional. But in her heart she was simply
passing the days and waiting her chance to find Georges. As she did
her work, altered and supplemented her clothes, took little evening
walks or visited the cinema with the other girls, to all appearance
just a strapping country cousin fitting herself into new surroundings,
she was, all the time, vigilant, relentless. She drew the others down
to the station on the pretext of buying a paper at the hour the troop
trains passed or stopped. She preferred for her small needs the shops
that fronted the well-known officers' restaurant, for Georges, she
knew, would do himself well if he had the chance. As to what exactly
she would say or do if she saw him she was not the girl to wonder.
She had perfect faith in her illusion—just to see him face to face,
anyhow, anywhere.

.

Her companions with whom she worked, ate, and spent her eve-
nings did not annoy her. That is as much as she felt about them.
Although only a year or so her juniors, there was nothing about
them to excite her jealousy or even her respect. As she listened to
them, making little muddles over their jobs, giving way to small
passions and routine indispositions, chattering with affected solemnity
or secrecy of their opinions, hopes, fears—above all of their love
affairs—she almost smiled. She put more of herself into even the
purchase of hairpins than they did into their liaisons. Not that she
was more generous or less acquisitive than they, but simply because
there was more of her. She had known real work, hard bargains,
the utter depth of passion—things undreamed of in their little world
of petty officialdom and shop-assistantship. Even the country girls
like Cécile stood mentally where she, Madeleine, had not done
since her mother died. Probably her principal minor preoccupation (as

distinct from her one great secret preoccupation) was the size of her body. She was half a head taller and much more substantial than most of them. She knew she was dressing herself right, somber colors, good material and cut, little or no ornament—but her hands and feet gave her some anxious moments, they seemed so big. She gave considerable attention to her hands, using every means she could hear of to whiten them, and manicuring them elaborately, bringing to the work much patience and sense and no imagination. For her feet, she simply bought the best she could afford, not attempting to pinch them, relying on her strong ankles, straight back, and developed hips to keep her extremities in proportion. She was right. Men turned to look at her often enough and never with the superior, amused eye that she saw bent on her companions. She did not consciously care whether men looked or not, but there was just that comfort in it that she could tell that she was interpreting this strange new world rightly. Had she but known, she possessed two of the greatest advantages over most of the women in those surroundings —radiant health, that brightened her glance, polished her skin, burnished her hair—and, in spite of her quiet clothes and steady eyes, an air of independence of which she was probably unconscious, but which was far more attractive than the air of facile complicity with male patronage that many girls wore. Like all advantages, these carried with them their own inconvenience, as she soon discovered.

.

Among Aunt Blanquart's lodgers were men, too weedy or too well protected to have been mobilized. They functioned on the railway, or some other public service, she did not care what, with colored brassards on their arms. She had paid no heed to them, secure in the fatal confidence of a strong nature, merely getting out of them anything they knew about the movements of troops, feigning the fatuous gossiping curiosity that was common enough. She was so immersed in her Fixed Idea that she was astonished when the more pimply of them slipped past Aunt Blanquart's semi-official vigilance, as she was going home to her room, and following her, proposed, "Suppose we take a little walk, as the English say!"

Madeleine turned on him a freezing stare:

"What for?" she demanded, standing her ground.

The pimply-faced one faded back into the house, muttering excuses, only to confide in his friends later that Madeleine was a "rosse," "an awkward beast," as one should say.

Then again, when the skull-capped old gentleman who controlled

her room went sick, the worried head of the department came across to Madeleine naturally with: "Give out the work to the room, while this old Do-nothing is away, will you?"

She did the distribution of the endless schedules, minutes and circulars deftly enough, and corrected the errors with a firm hand. It took far less thought than most of her days at the farm. When the "old Do-nothing" returned, skull-capped, pallid, smelling of lozenges, she met him with, "I have done" so and so, and "you will find this" there and that "under the paper weight!" etc., going quietly back to her desk. At night he lingered, and was left alone with her, because she was never in such a hurry as the others to crowd downstairs, squabble in the lobby over the inadequate space allowed for dressing oneself for the walk home. She turned and stared as he asked her to dine with him.

An idea—one of her rare, slowly born ideas—had come to being in her head. In her seriousness she hardly noticed that he had taken it for granted that she would go with him. But she almost smiled when he began to detail his little plan. She, who had known not merely trials of cunning with Belgian horse dealers and hop merchants, but desperate evasion and deceit to meet Georges in the Kruysabel, agreed to pretend to Aunt Blanquart that she had a headache, and to meet this old man at the corner of the street. Fortunately it was dark at the hour named—dark with that war-time darkness of a town within the bombing area. She had a difficulty to recognize him in the crowd—and a great temptation to help his shuffling steps. She felt a sort of charity towards him, an inclination to take his arm and help him—a feeling which increased as she saw what careful plans he had laid. He did not take her to a restaurant, where the unequal couple they made would certainly have been the object of more or less concealed amusement, but to the back sitting-room of an old servant of his, who was now caretaker at a big shop. It was discreet, cozy. The cooking was good, the dinner ample, chosen from the more easily digested dishes. She was so touched by his evident enjoyment—though she had her own quiet confidence in her desirability—and by his desire to give her a good time—and things had been rather thin since mobilization—that the only tyranny she practised on him was to make him send out for a bottle of Burgundy; the pale sweet wines he offered seemed to her below the occasion.

There was no awkwardness during the meal, for she asked prudent, calculated questions—who really moved, housed and regulated the flow of troops—did he know the numbers or composition of the English divisions—all the small details most Frenchwomen—utterly innocent of spying—asked eternally out of sheer curiosity and interferingness.

And when they had done eating she had to put up with the demonstrations that men make, who have either not had their fill in middle life, or who have come to regard it as a necessity not to be foregone. She had found that he did possess information and perhaps connections that might be useful to her Fixed Idea, and tolerated his attempts to solace his waning instincts, until, hearing the hour chime, she shook herself free, put herself tidy, and left him to find his way home—only, because he might be useful and sounded disappointed, she murmured, "Another time," at the door. Once in the street, she stepped briskly home, arrived at the door of her lodging about the usual hour of her return from Aunt Blanquart's, and went up to bed. She was plotting and scheming busily and had already forgotten her entertainer as though he had never existed.

.

Indeed, he might have saved himself that trouble. In that last week of September, just as she was beginning to feel no more strange as a government clerk in Amiens that she had felt as a farmer's daughter in Hondebecq, there spread through the minor French circles the news of a further English offensive. From what source it came and how it took shape no one will ever know, but the perpetual hungry curiosity of the sort of people among whom Madeleine now lived, was suddenly glutted with the news that there was to be an offensive, and that the Prince of Wales was taking part. This set flame to the French imagination, among whose republican embers a royalist spark has ever glowed.

To Madeleine, whose restricted imagination conjured up some long defile of troops through the cobbled streets, led by a fair-haired English boy, the news seemed of great promise. Georges was certain to be there. She saw him, accurately enough, in the blue and strawberry of the French Mission, riding in the cavalcade. She got a day off—her old man was "complaisant," as the French say, and she found herself with a whole day on her hands, an equinoctial day of chill drafts and paling sunshine, of fluttering leaves and a stir in the blood.

She had tried to get some idea as to when and where the troops would pass, but all that she could gather was that the English police had been doubled. This only endorsed her preconceived notion of a parade through the town. She rose in good time and dressed herself carefully—in somber colors, in coat and skirt, inclining rather to the English model, implacably neat, well-buttoned, without a spot of bright color or a trace of expression on her face. She went out and down to the station, bought a paper, lingered about, tried to feel what was going on. The streets were crowded, and as she was seldom about at

this hour she drew comfort from the fact. It was of course the usual crowd of the nearest town behind the line of an offensive, men of all ranks going and coming on leave, base and line-of-communication people, young officers with a day off, grizzled officers' servants sent in from the innumerable camps for shopping. There were English, of north country and south country, London and Liverpool, Welsh, Scotch, Irish, Channel Isles. There were Canadians talking Yankee, Anglo-Indians, in wonderful blouses with mailed shoulder-straps, tall gaunt Australians, fresh-faced New Zealanders, swarthy or tanned English South Americans, South Africans and Naval details. More than once she was stared at, twice spoken to, once followed. If the Prince of Wales did pass down that street, it was in one of those fleet Vauxhall cars, with red-capped staff officers. There was no cheering, no procession, nothing of the crude, out-of-date spectacle that would have delighted and encouraged her. By one o'clock she was desperately hungry and tired, and burning with a sort of spiritual fever.

She did not give up, however. Partly faithful, partly merely obstinate, she stuck to her furtive prowling, keeping ever closer to the well-known Restaurant "à la Paysanne Flamande." She knew her Georges. A thousand accidents might take him into this or that street, by rail or car, on horseback or on foot, but, between noon and two o'clock, there was no possible error, Georges would be sitting before the best-laid table he could find, napkin tucked into his buttonhole, saying he had the hunger of a wolf, making caustic fun of the bill of fare, and standing no nonsense with the waiter. The celebrated restaurant, entirely a creation of the War, before which it had led a struggling existence dependent on a billiard-table and a mixed clientèle, presented a glass swing-door between two large plate-glass windows, protected by round iron tables and chairs set among desolate shrubs in boxes. The door opened into a little-used café-lounge; the eating-room had replaced the billiard-table on the raised portion of the floor up four steps at the back. Thus the public in the street could see the legs and half the bodies of the diners, but not their faces. Outside, a great sign-board, swung English-fashion on a bracket, depicted an alleged Flemish peasant-woman, in national costume, with international features, and the immemorial vulgarity of such efforts. Madeleine never even guessed that the square of brilliant paint was an allegorical representation of herself, and would have been much astonished to have been told so.

Two o'clock struck, and half-past, and suddenly she had a physical qualm. What was it? She realized she was faint with hunger. Together with the bodily emptiness and dizziness, there rose in her a bitter wave of disgust and disillusionment. For the second time she set

her teeth. She would not stand it. Careless of the fact that she was
doing what was only done by women of a sort she despised, because
she considered they were driving a dangerous, badly paid trade, she
pushed open the door, walked steadily into the café, and sat down
just as the tables were beginning to go round. It was partly want of
food, as she told herself, but partly, if she had admitted it, the moisture
of desperate vexation in her eyes. She ordered a café crême of an un-
willing waiter, who did not want French people there, in such a way
that he brought it, at once, and properly done. The scalding sips
soon revived her. She began to think, if thinking it can be called.
Rather she just sat and felt. She felt the French equivalents of "I'm
fed up with this"—"I'm going to put an end to it"—whatever It ex-
actly was. Then less articulately she just felt sore. It was not in her to
feel passively sore, but how to express her feeling by activity she could
not see, at the moment.

.

The souls of women come, perhaps rather more often than those of
men, to steep places down which the least touch will cause them to
hurl themselves. Madeleine had been hanging on some such edge
ever since the day of the Horse Show. It needed by the stroke of a
feather to send her over.

Her trance was broken by the sound of field-boots on the steps that
led down from the dining-room. Two officers were passing to the door,
middle-aged junior officers of infantry or artillery, with cleaned-up,
discolored uniforms, and faces and voices of those who had been
"through it," and had a good deal more to go through before they
would have done with "it"—"it" being the War. Madeleine had seen
hundreds such, going up to the line, coming down from the line, sitting
round her father's table, taking charge of parties of men, with shy
resolution. Little given to guessing, she could have told almost of what
they were talking—of what they had done on leave, what sort of
"show" they were going to be involved in, possibly of the very inn of
the "Lion of Flanders" where they might have snatched a comfortable
meal in the intervals of sleeping in their clothes and eating out of their
hands. They passed beside her and she smiled involuntarily. Her long
vigil had not been in vain. All the English divisions were bound to pass
into the Somme offensive sooner or later, and there was nothing
wonderful in her meeting two officers whom she had seen before. Nor
was it because she was feeling the homesickness or the loneliness of the
acutely sensitive. But just because the starvation of her Fixed Idea had
wrought her up to a point culminating at that moment, she smiled.

The shorter, fairer of the two, whose mere name she remembered

(for she had that sort of memory, very useful for checking billeting returns), recognized her and spoke to his companion. The other turned. It was Lieutenant Skene, whom she had not seen, or indeed thought of, since the Horse Show. He turned, and their glances met. She saw in a moment that it mattered intensely to both of them what she did, how or why she could not see, but she knew that it mattered. She kept perfectly still, her face molded in a smile. The door clicked. They were alone. Skene sat before her. What had she done? Nothing. By doing nothing she had placed him there.

He began questioning her: what was she doing in Amiens? and she replied briefly, not thinking of the words. She pushed aside her cup and rested one elbow on the table, her chin in her hand. She stared into his eyes, gray-brown, dilated by shell-fire, and reddened at the rims by gas, but full of feeling which she recognized at a glance as genuine. That feeling was concern for her welfare. She did not admit to herself, still less to him, that there was anything to be concerned about. But it warmed her in the depths of her heart, just as the liqueur he had ordered for her (with sweet cakes, and the way in which he did it showed his solicitude) warmed her stomach. It was true he was talking about himself. She knew in a moment that this was not egotism but English shyness. She answered him in a dream, rocking her body ever so slightly on her chair, as if she were nursing something. Indeed, she was—nursing some part of her spirit, bruised just as violently as her knees had been when the old horse fell down and threw her on to the pavé of the Lille road—for she had just been thrown out of her closed self-control, that hid unwelcome Truth even from herself, on to the bare realization of the long fast of two years, the sharp starvation of two months.

Now he was talking about *her,* with the polite candor which had made her say, the first time she saw him, that he was "well brought up" and "willing." More, he was inquiring about Georges. She was not surprised; that was all part of it. She heard herself, as another person, replying coolly: "He is dead!" and when pressed further: "He is dead for me." She could have laughed aloud at the same time, not for joy, but from the steady mounting beat of her own heart. His concern was trebled. Her heart beat faster, not feverishly, steadily. She had thought of her trouble: "I'll put an end to this!" She was putting an end to it!

Then he actually touched her, and made sympathetic remarks. He was advising her not to frequent officers' restaurants, and she replied she did not care. It was true. She cared for nothing at the moment, had never felt more lighthearted. He asked what she was going to do next. She wanted to laugh more than ever as she said, "Nothing!" He pro-

posed a cinema. She assented delightedly, feeling as though she would
have proposed it herself in a moment, it was so inevitable. She made
a quick calculation. Cécile Blanquart and the other girls were at the
office. Aunt Blanquart and the pork butcher's wife, at whose house she
lodged, would not be shopping in the main streets, rendered expensive
by English custom. It was safe enough.

Out in the street she stepped beside him with a pride which, she sud-
denly realized, she had never known. There are inconveniences about
clandestine liaisons. She almost enjoyed the publicity. Fortified by
coffee, cakes and brandy, as tall as he was to an inch or so, she seemed
to float along on the wings of new-found comfort, effortless, smiling.

The cinema was full. He was nonplussed, she could see, did not
know what to do next—knew what he wanted (as she did, and hugged
herself), but, being English, had a difficulty in saying it. He wanted
her. That was natural enough. She knew herself to be desirable. It
amused her to hear him proposing to see her home to her "Aunt's"—
for thus she had described her lodging. She let him. It seemed now she
had only to go on letting him, and the riddle of life was solved. She
had not known an hour before that there was a riddle. Now she only
knew she was approaching a solution.

They arrived in the narrow by-street near the cathedral as the clocks
chimed four. At that hour the place was deserted. Their footsteps
echoed, they might have been treading a world of their own. Made-
leine felt it, but noticed that he was feeling something stronger. He
had almost shed his English reserve—was talking volubly, about him-
self—how he had been twice in hospital, and must now go back to the
fighting—how men like himself wanted a little comfort before they
died. He spoke in English, but she understood most of the words and
all the drift. His feelings coincided with hers and saved her the
trouble of expressing them, to which she was unused and averse. At
the door of her lodging they both stopped, she with her key in the lock,
he looking at her with eyes that he immediately averted, and which
pivoted round, in spite of him, to her. As she turned the key and
opened the door, she said, with the feeling of turning something in
her heart and opening it: "Here we are!" Inevitably, as if she had
taught him the words, he was saying: "Don't send me away, let me
stay!" and with a great sigh of happiness such as she had felt once
before in her life—another life, surely—she retreated into the dark
entry before him with: "Well then, my poor friend!"

．　　　．　　　．　　　．　　　．　　　．　　　．

When Madeleine next had attention to spare for such matters, the
chimes were telling six o'clock, and through the glass of the skylight-

window a little star twinkled. She became conscious that he was slowly awakening from the stupor in which they had plunged each other, and was lying, open-eyed, waiting for her to move (just like him). Her mind sprang at once to the practical:

"What time is your train?"

"Gone this half-hour!"

She sat up in alarm: "You will have trouble!"

"They can't tell to a few hours when I left camp!"

Reassured, she passed on to the next thing.

"You are hungry!"

"Yes!"

She was fully alive to the situation. The pork butcher's wife down-stairs had opened, like every one in Amiens who could manage it, an eating-room. The particular public for which it catered were English and French N.C.O.'s of garrison formations, not a field for high profit, but respectable and regular. There was a back room. It was better than courting trouble by going outside. She explained this to Skene as she sat up, shivered slightly at the contact of the air, lit the candle, and tidied herself. She was not ill at ease before him. Thorough in every-thing, when she gave she knew no stint. She did not boggle over the irregularity of their situation, any more than over her semi-nudity. Why should she? She had perfect confidence in what she had done, just as in her things, which were clean and good in quality, and in her body, which was firm and fresh with health. Of course, out in the street the conventions constrained one to dissemble, to conceal what one did, and only to show as much of one's skin as fashion allowed for the mo-ment. But with Skene she was as frank as she had been with herself, poured him out clean water, and explained that with a small gratuity and a generous order, Madame would make no scruple of their having the best time they could. There were the French police to bribe, pos-sibly, and worse still, the English, but it could be managed.

She was proud of Skene when they interviewed Madame. He spoke French with some fluency, and knew just how to flatter the old lady's sensibility and appeal to her greed. When they sat opposite each other in the little back room, he turned on her eyes still bemused, and looked at his watch with frank pleasure: "No train till six-thirty. Still nearly twelve hours!" he said. Under the table she rubbed his ankle with her slippered foot. Their little dinner ended, as, alas! all dinners must. The pork butcher's wife, overpaid and adroitly flattered, rallied them, almost blessed them, as, his arm around her waist, her arm round his neck, they mounted slowly the dark, narrow stairs.

Hardly a breath of disillusionment spoiled their few hours together. He took what life could give him—life that was likely to end for him

so soon and so abruptly. She, woman-like, put into it something almost sacramental, as though she were devoting to flames some cherished possession, and devoting it willingly. There was nothing Skene could not have asked her for that she would not have given him, from money to her heart's blood. He asked simply to be loved—comforted, more exactly, in his starved, war-worn body. That was easy. She gloried in it, even went so far outside her usual self as to point out the bare cleanliness and order of her little room. That was just about the length of her knowledge of English character. A clean room would appeal to him. She never even stopped to wonder that she should be so anxious to please this chance acquaintance—this man of different race, religion, and language. She had never read a novel and was innocent of the romantic theories of love at first sight. She acted as she did from one of her slow-moving, undemonstrative impulses—just then so strong that it amounted to a feeling of almost physical well-being in her limbs—traceable, possibly, if she had been the sort to theorize about origins of feeling, to starved maternal instinct. She missed something—petulance, perversity—the whims of a spoiled child that she would have loved to gratify, as she had, long before, in the secrecy of the hut in the Kruysabel. But she did not miss her spoiled child much, for she had instead this good child—this man of quiet good manners, whose behavior she had noted the first time she saw him, and who now accepted her suggestions without a murmur. So she invited him gently to see how she had moved the few articles of furniture, scrubbed the floor, cleaned the sky-light, pasted paper on the damp-stained walls, hung her few dresses on hooks beneath a curtain, and put a rose-colored paper shade round her candle. She was gratified to see how pleased he was, little suspected that she had laid her finger on the very deepest desire in him. He had told her that he was no soldier, but a member of a profession that he had practised for twenty years before volunteering in August, 1914. Yet she was very far from forming any conception of the decent orderliness of the life he had left, the life of an assistant diocesan architect in a provincial English town, with its rooted habit of cleanly comfort and moderate happiness, that the war had hurt so horribly; and she never guessed what dim echoes her own Flemish domestic virtues aroused, of all he had ever felt to be the necessities of existence.

She was even farther away from him when his self-consciousness, awakening with the small hours, drew him to think of the future—of his and of hers. Like many another man in those years, his courage ebbed at the false dawn, and he questioned Fate aloud as to whether he would see another—whether he would ever again know the comfort of her. The simple cunning of her kind led her to propose ar-

rangements to meet him again. This in turn led to the question of where she was to be found. This drew from him anxious questions, that flattered her immensely by the importance he attached to her welfare, but brought back unpleasantly into prominence that other whom she was trying so hard, so unconsciously, to forget. She burst out with a few fierce words, stamping and stamping on that dead image of love to make it disappear from view. It was when she did this, brutally dismissing from memory that spoiled child of her affections, that her new, good, well-behaved child gave her the first taste of his imperfections. He was solicitous, punctilious to a degree, questioned if he ought to take what was Georges'. She would have been angry with him in another moment had not a stronger, surer, more positive instinct prevailed. They had such a little time, might never have another. She wound her bare arms round his head and stifled his questions and doubts against the present reality of her tangible self. And surely she was right. In all those years of loss and waste it occurred to her naturally to build and replace what she could, and all the love and care she could not give to the children she might not bear, she gave to this grown-up child, who needed it, and took it willingly enough, once he ceased to think.

.

In the gray dawn she was up and about, making coffee, heating water for him to shave, helping clean his endless buckles and straps. She let him out in good time for his train, and sweetened her kiss with the eternal hopefulness of that "à bientôt," "until soon," that is the happiest thing in French farewells. Then slowly, carefully, she made herself ready for the day at the office, proud of the dark touches under her eyes, of the mat-pallor of her skin, of the little smiles that curled the corners of her mouth. And many a man, seeing her, wished he had been the source of the deep secret satisfaction she seemed to give herself that day.

All that week she retained the feeling of having done a good action—or, as she would have expressed it, had she expressed it at all—driven a good bargain with Fate. At the end of the week "Papa," as the girls in the office called the head of the room, waited for her and asked her to spend the Sunday afternoon with him. It was his birthday, and he. and she would celebrate it with a little Festivity. She did not look at him for fear she should laugh, for, taller than he by inches, she caught the sparkle of the electric light reflected on the top of his bald head. She asked, with averted face, "Will there be many invitations?"

"But no—you and I alone, naturally!"

She shook her head slowly from side to side as she hooked her

fur under her chin and surveyed herself in the little glass that hung on the door of the girls' lobby.

"But you promised last time that there should be other times——" His voice had risen, his eyes darkened. It was wonderful what malignity could still reside in a little old man. Something stronger still inhabited Madeleine, since those few hours she had spent with Skene. Once again the blood in her veins had run like molten honey, and she, no spendthrift of herself, had felt in every limb as she gave herself up utterly: "This is right—right—right!"

She was in no mood for senile trifling, and turned on him with the arrogance of youth, blazing, magnificent: "And now I promise you there will not!" and left him, breathless and a little afraid.

.

Another week passed. Madeleine became uneasy. The strongest emotional impression will not last. The time she had had with Skene began to fade into the background. It had been such a minute. It had no result. Instead of feeling perversely resentful against Georges, she now felt so against both of them. Skene neither wrote nor made any sign. He did not even give her the dubious satisfaction of obliterating the shame she felt at Georges' neglect. All this lay, a dumb ache, in her uncritical soul. But she had more immediate cause for annoyance. She became conscious that she was being looked at, whispered about. It did nothing more than ruffle the surface of her self-confidence, but when she and Cécile Blanquart went to the cinema together—she hardly noticed a half-unwillingness on Cécile's part, and that the other girls who often accompanied them had made excuses—she was brought face to face with the matter. Cécile said shyly, in the melodious darkness of the one-franc seats, where one had to keep one's hands in one's lap, because so many soldiers were lonely:

"You know what they are saying about you at the office?"

"No—what?"

"Oh—I daren't tell you!"

Madeleine did not press her. There is only one thing said by girls who cannot mind their own business—having, indeed, no business to mind. Madeleine had never spread nor listened with interest to rumors about other girls, simply because she minded her own business, having always had business to mind. But she knew well enough what the village gossip of Hondebecq was, and had found out that an office in a provincial town is only a village without elbow-room. She pondered a little over the matter, which grew increasingly serious as she did so. She did not bother greatly as to the source of any rumor about her. Spite on the part of "Papa," love of scandal in the heart of the

pork butcher's wife of her lodging—mere empty interest on the part of some person or persons who had seen her with Skene or with "Papa," it might be! The point that disturbed her was the possible effect on her freedom of action. It might make it more difficult for her to profit by the next opportunity of seeing Skene-Georges—for the two were slowly merging into one at the back of her mind. This roused her. She began to think seriously, but in her slow way.

.

Then came a letter from home—from Marie.

She read it several times, by candle-light, lying on her back in her narrow iron bed, one hand holding the pages of British Expeditionary Force canteen block note-paper, which Marie used because it cost nothing, covered with Marie's sloping convent-school writing—the other hand below her head, on which a handkerchief protected the long plaits of her hair, that she had never bobbed at the command of fashion. Gradually she mastered it. Marie was no correspondent; none of the sort that she belonged to, cultivated letter-writing or exceeded what was strictly necessary. The motive of her letter was badly stated: "Father demands to know how goes his daughter." There followed a brief résumé of village news. Victor Dequidt was reported missing. Other persons had been married. There had been more bombing near St. Omer. There was no news of brother Marcel; they feared the worst. Then followed the words: "Father has seen Monsieur le Baron lately. He was furious. It seems that his son Georges has left the French Mission, where he was in safety, and has gone to make his training for an aviator in Paris. Madame is deso-lated"; and then commonplaces to the end. "His son Georges" was a way of speaking Marie had picked up from living in the Lys valley, in the influence of Lille. It was not how they spoke in Hondebecq. This displeased Madeleine an instant. Then the real meaning of the letter dawned on her. Her father had shown by his conduct on the day of their visit to the hospital how thoroughly he understood what was be-tween Georges and herself. He had made Marie write—Marie who knew and suspected nothing. Madeleine—the youngest, the one who had lived longest with him, who had replaced her mother in the house —responded to the old man's partiality for her. Unspoken, never visible, there was a stronger link between them than existed with the others of the family. She thought of him with affection. Her mind moved on. She could see the Baron, stumping up and down the earth roads, with "Merde!" and "Name of a name!" at every step; and the dining-room at the château, into which she had been allowed to peep, when running errands from the farm. She could hear Placide's nasal

chant announcing dinner: "Madame la Baronne is served!" and the Baron, still "Merde"-ing and "Name of a name"-ing, and the Baronne's tearful but dignified "Voyons, Charles!" Paris, Georges was in Paris! Although affectionate in her way, she hardly paused to think of her brother Marcel, giving no sign from his German prison.

.

Then she had one of her intuitions. The very thing. She would teach the gossips of Amiens to tell tales about her—and give them something to tell of, all in one blow. The very economy of the idea appealed to her. There were always vacancies in the big Ministries in Paris, she had heard "Papa" say. "Papa!" she almost laughed. He would have his Festivity, after all. He should be made to work it. The idea was so new and beautiful that it actually kept her awake for half an hour after she had blown out her candle—a rare thing for a girl of her habits and physique.

The first person who was astonished at the turn of affairs was "Papa." He became aware, as he snuffed with rage and ill-health at his desk behind the screen by the stove, of kind looks and lingerings. His resentment and small suspicions soon melted. He ventured half-apologetic remarks, was not rebuffed. Nor did she hurry away with the other girls, as she had done all the week since his last propositions. Eventually he timidly complained that he had not had his little Festivity, that his birthday had passed unhonored.

Madeleine felt something, almost compunction, but her Fixed Idea soon resumed its empire over her mind. She listened to him.

On the following Sunday, having drunk her coffee and eaten her roll, she replied to Marie's letter. She expressed her sympathy with all those in the village who had suffered bereavement, sent her congratulations to all those who had bettered their state of life. She asked to hear further of Marcel. She mentioned the Baron and the Baronne in the former category, also the Dequidts. She sent her father much affection and promised to come and see him soon. This was a mere convention. He would have been astonished had she carried it into effect, but it was testimony of her gratitude to him for having guessed her Fixed Idea, and having so astutely helped her. The letter, evidence of an orderly, unimaginative mind, wound up with sisterly affection for Marie—also a convention—for the two girls, realists to the core, knew well enough that they were friendly so long as they remained apart—and kisses for Emilienne. Having completed this, and posted it, she went to second mass at the cathedral. There, when it was over, she sat in the dimness of the sand-bagged windows and the ancient stones. She had never read Mr. Ruskin, never glanced at the moral

carvings of the west front, the historical carvings of the ambulatory—sand-bagged as were the first, and removed as were the second now—and would probably have made very little of them, save that they were the sort of carvings one saw in churches. Of all the long romance of that storied pile, from Robert de Luzarches to the German occupation of 1870, she knew and cared nothing—neither for its tons of masonry, glass and wood, nor for the million prayers that drifted on its stagnant air. Nor did she sit there alone from any religious motive. She was not truly religious—too sure of herself, too incurious, she kept of the faith of her fathers nothing but some habits, and some rags of superstition. She left, at one o'clock, when all the English officers were in their messes, and all the French homes had that air of preoccupation which accompanies the most important meal of the week. The streets were empty. She passed rapidly to the big shop at which "Papa's" servant was caretaker, and found the side door unlocked. In the back sitting-room Papa was waiting for her, skull-cap, clean collar, eyes watering with pleasure. There, amid solid furniture, marble-topped chiffoniers and chests of drawers, hermetically sealed, chairs and settees upholstered as if for ever, they held "Papa's Festivity." Once again Madeleine was touched when she saw he had ordered red wine to please her. But after the table had been cleared and his senile familiarities began, she hardened her heart. She questioned him straightly and searchingly, making him buy, with information, every liberty she allowed him. She knew well enough how quickly men changed, once they were satisfied, and chose the very moment before he lay back on the plush settee, exhausted by the violence of his emotions, to extract a promise that he would get her transferred to Paris, and a second promise of secrecy—because, she told him, there were so many spiteful tongues. She looked him full in the eyes as she said this, but he was at the stage at which he could only say, "Yes, yes!" intent on gratifying his momentary needs. After this she poured him out some wine, and kissing him on his bald head—for his skull-cap had slipped off—she left him to reflect. She went to an appointment with Cécile Blanquart, whose father was visiting her for the day and chatted to him of village affairs. Her crude psychology was not at fault. For a day or two "Papa" left her alone, but before a week was out he was pestering her again. She took it as a right, believing that men who had once desired her must do so again. In fact, it was this point at which Georges' neglect had so hurt her. But she had made her terms and stuck to them. She reminded "Papa" of his promises, and he demurred, temporized. She cut him severely for two days and brought him to heel. He was not likely to find many women who would have patience with him, feeble and mean about money as he was, in

face of the chances of a good time with some English officer. He did as he was told. She had to interview the Controller of the Service, but fortunately Paris was always calling for more and more help to fill the places of men combed out, and she got her transfer, and all the accompanying papers, complete. She was to go the following Sunday. She knew enough of the working of things now to see that she was already out of the power of "Papa." With this, all compunction left her. She promised gaily to dine with him, and he little suspected the real source of her pleasure: the feeling that at last she would be near Georges, easily able to meet him face to face as she desired, and that, once met, she would work on him her charm, in which she had such implicit trust.

She arranged to meet "Papa" at the station, because, she said, she wanted information about her train on the morrow. The information she really required was about that evening's train, the 18.05 for Paris. He drew her into the buffet, anxious to prime himself for his evening's enjoyment, and she went willingly, careless of appearances now. He ordered two of those compounds known as Quinine Tonics. She gulped hers down as the Boulogne-Paris train thundered in, bent forward to kiss him, and crying, "Au revoir, mind you are decent to the girls!" swung out of the door, across the waiting-hall, and through the wicket, where he could not follow, as he had no permit. In fact, he did not try. He was first so astonished, then so enraged, that he choked over his drink, and dropped his glass, for the breakage of which a callous waitress charged him forty centimes. Alas, that a long career of getting the most out of women, and giving the least, should descend to this!

.

Although so short a time had elapsed, the Madeleine who traveled from Amiens to Paris was a very different girl from the Madeleine who had left Hondebecq three months earlier. The very manner of her shaking off "Papa" showed it. The habit of the village in which she had grown up, regarding railways, consisted in going to the station, hearing when the next train went to the required destination, and waiting for it. To possess and understand a time-table—more, to have mastered the complicated regulations of a military station in war-time, was the measure of how far Madeleine had advanced.

She found herself in a Paris that had an air of forced cheerfulness and dumb expectancy. True, the panic of the day of mobilization, growing right up to the Aisne battle, was over; the alarums of 1918 were not yet in sight. But it was a Paris bereft of men, many a shutter closed; a Paris as yet unhaunted by Americans, but beginning to be desperate in its pleasures. What its best historians, its great lovers,

Murger or Victor Hugo, would have thought of it, cannot be con-
jectured. Its fabled gaiety was gone for good. Its heroism had that
poisoned quality that makes women cover broken hearts with cheap
finery.

Madeleine, who had never imagined a town of the size before,
spent the first two months quietly taking it all in. She had the sense to
see that she must start all over again. She did her work with zest—it
suited her. That suited her Controller, who put her to lodge with rela-
tives—retired people of official class, who lived in an "apartment,"' a
tiny flat in a huge block of buildings situated just where the scholarly
Pantheon district trails off into the poverty of St. Étienne du Mont.
No one could be more self-effacing than Madeleine when she wished
to. During her first weeks in Paris she attended to her work, lived
quietly with Monsieur and Madame Petit, dressed soberly, glanced
at no one in the street, or in the great office where her duties lay. She
made herself amiable and useful in the small precise household, left it
in time to catch her 'bus, that landed her opposite the bridge, across
which towered the world-famous gallery in which the Ministry to
which she was attached was housed. She made herself agreeable to the
girls with whom she worked. Some were country girls, shy or inefficient,
but there was not a Fleming amongst them, and she concealed her
opinion that she knew better than they about most things. As for
the native Parisiennes, of whom all sorts and conditions were gathered
into that great harbor of steady work and sure pay, she admired their
ferocious femininity and put up with their moods—even when they
called her "Boche du Nord"—the equivalent of calling a Worcester-
shire girl a Welshwoman—which they did at times, out of sheer dislike
of her demure capacity. To have seen her, no one would have sus-
pected that she was gleaning every scrap of information she could with
regard to the Flying Corps units that formed the Air defence of Paris.
And she had better opportunity now. Paris was by no means the town-
just-behind-the-line that Madeleine was used to. Information was to
be had, people got to know things and talked of them. Her Ministry,
engaged in rationing one of the necessities of life, rationed Flying
Corps troops among other people. She missed nothing. At last she
found what she was looking for.

.

In one of those innumerable lists of men that were being produced
by Government Departments all over the world, as well as in her
particular Ministry, she saw the name Georges d'Archeville. It was a
list of those young men designated, with the picturesque appropriate-
ness of the French language, as "aspiring aviators" who were "di-

rected towards the Front," that is, being sent into the line of battle. Madeleine and another girl were crossing them off the lists of the garrison of Paris. She stared so long and heavily that her companion bent over her: "What! You can't find it—but there it is!"

Madeleine ticked the beloved name and went on, as in a stupor. This was really a blow. To come to Paris had seemed to her, somehow, the satisfactory culmination of her long vigil. She felt sure she would be successful in finding him. She had found him indeed. What now! The Paris garrison was not concerned with the fate of "aspiring aviators" once they were struck off its rolls. Their fate was not indeed in much doubt, but there remained the horrible uncertainty as to which of the graveyards behind the four hundred miles of Front would hold his grave. At this point her common-sense and practical knowledge of affairs deserted her. She just wanted him, that was all. Feigning a headache, she excused herself and got leave to go home; but instead of going, she lingered about the quays and bridges, never lovelier than in winter twilight, with golden wraiths of leaves spinning in the bitter wind along the severe, well-proportioned gray lines of masonry. The fresh air calmed her; hunger at length drove her back to the Petits' apartment. She did not notice at first anything in the manner of her hosts. The only thing that she noticed was that M. Petit, as he handed her a letter, used the phrase:

"It came about four o'clock!"

That was the hour at which her eye had caught the name in the fatal list. All the threads and tatters of superstition that clung to her Flemish soul took life and substance at this. She muttered the words, "Ah, yes! I expected it. It is a word from home!" She passed, quiet and self-possessed, to her little bedroom, one of those little rooms which lead one to ask if they were intended by the architect for anything, or whether they might not be an inadvertence. Lighting her candle, she sat on the thin coverlet of her bed, that reached from the tall window to the door, and resting her feet on the lower shelf of the washstand, thrust her thumb into the envelope and burst it open. It was from Skene. It was what is called in those English romances Madeleine had never read or imagined, a "love letter." It asked her to spend his week's leave with him. That much she saw, and then put it down and buried her face in her hands. She had expected it to contain news of the death of Georges. Why or how she thought anyone should write to her on such a subject is one of those mysteries that hang about the most clear-minded, least bemused of people. She had felt rather than thought it, and the revulsion was for the moment too much for her. She was roused by the clatter of plates, and the acrid voice of Madame Petit, keeping the supper within the smallest possible bounds. She

changed her blouse, washed and did her hair, and hurried out to help
Madame.

During a meal whose frugality would have driven a monk from his
vows, she heard M. Petit say, "Well, have you good news from home!"
and herself replying: "Yes. My brother writes to say he has leave, and
asks me to go home to see him!"

She afterwards reflected that she could not have invented a better
answer. The envelope was stamped with the British military postmark.
The old man was inquisitive, and there was no knowing what use
he might not make of any conclusion he drew. To have a brother in
the English area was the one feasible explanation.

.

These considerations did not weigh heavily with her, however. She
slipped away as soon as she could, and read her letter through again
and then again. There was much in it that she did not come within a
long way of understanding—descriptions of the life of decent civilized
men in camp and billet, not to mention trench and dugout. These
simply conveyed nothing and did not interest her. Then there was an
involved scrupulousness that she had no means of sharing. But the
main motive that had caused the writing of those four sheets was
clear enough—Skene really wanted her. And if she did not admit it to
herself, she wanted to be wanted. She did not reply to the letter, but
put it away in a safe place, a little lock-up box in which she kept her
immediate savings and a trinket or two, and went to her work in the
morning, a changed woman. She had regained in a breath her old
sureness. She now saw herself again the woman she desired to be. "If
I can only see him face to face" still ran in her mind, but this time it
was Skene whom she hoped to see. Insensibly the symbol had changed,
the emotions remained. She thought the matter over in her cautious
way. He had supposed her still to be in Amiens and had written there.
By good luck she had sent a card (one of those war postcards, all khaki
and azure and sentiment) to Cécile Blanquart, having it in her mind
that Cécile would describe to the full, in her next letter home (for
Cécile was the sort that wrote once a week), anything that she, Made-
leine did. It had been an act of petty pride. It now seemed like the
work of Providence—Cécile had redirected the letter, and here it was.
Madeleine did not mistake what it meant. He wanted a week, like the
few hours he had had, in Amiens. That was natural enough; she saw
nothing in it. In her experience men were like that, and she secretly
approved. For a week, at least, she would have some one belonging to
her; beyond that she did not look.

After twenty-four hours' consideration she took the letter from its

hiding-place, replied to it in most measured terms—judging to a nicety, by some instinct, what would make him say a little more and say it a little plainer, without committing her in any way. A week passed, and back came a further letter. It filled her with a sort of steady glow. There was no mistaking it. He had written for a room in an hotel he knew of at the other end of the city, on the steep hill that leads from behind the big stations to Montmartre. She did not reply until old M. Petit, looking at her over his spectacles, asked her: "Well, and your brother?"

She gathered herself together mentally. Of course, she had to fend off all that sort of thing. She replied briefly: "I am going home for a week!"

That evening she sent Skene a card on which Union Jack and Tricolor were entwined. She wrote with a sort of exultation: "I wish to be all yours." Such an outburst must have been caused by something deeper than the paltry bickering of a little old man, or the prospect of meeting a young one with whom she had once passed a few hours of intimacy under the stress of strong emotion.

.

The day came. She got her week's leave. It is one of the victories of women's entry into ordinary commercial activities of business houses and Government offices, that they have forced some humanity and reason into the mechanical discipline of such places. Having made no plans, she had put her few belongings into one of those black hold-alls that make all French travelers seem countrified, and stood on the platform of the Gare du Nord, waiting. She had dressed herself carefully—more carefully than usual, with hardly a spot of color, and was conscious that every inch of her that was covered showed the finest possible value for the money. Her hands, neck and face had lost nothing in their firmness and pallor. The figure she cut seemed to culminate in the little leather satchel clasped against her fur—as if she were holding her heart in reserve, and defending it at the same time. The train roared into the station, and after a moment's confusion, she saw Skene coming towards her. She had been wondering fearfully for a moment if he would come, if she would recognize him, if any unforeseen obstacle would arise. When he reached her, she turned up her face and gave him her rare smile. When he slid his hand under her arm and hurried her down the platform to catch one of the few taxis, she pressed ever so little against him. Never in her life had she been happier than in hearing those heavy boots clanking beside her. Now that he had come she knew she was right. Skene was neither exceptionally handsome, brave nor rich—and she would have thought nothing the more of him if he had been. She neither knew nor cared

for heroes of fiction, but admired the clean, athletic type of young man just then beginning to be popularized by the cinema. Skene had the looks and bearing of what he was—an average Englishman of the professional classes, who had passed through the successive stages of discomfort, danger, all but death. He had the sure movements, straight glance, and agreeable carelessness begotten of this, grafted on to middle-class standards of manners. Superficially, at any rate, he was more considerate than his nearest French equivalent would have been.

All this, which would have disappointed or amused many a French-woman, captivated Madeleine, and in the taxi she gave up her lips to him with rich joy at the unmistakable warmth of his feelings. The moment, however, the taxi stopped at the restaurant she had indicated, she made herself prim and aloof. She had not wasted her time since she had been in Paris, and knew her way about. The restaurant dated from the period of those great Exhibitions that had served to rehabili-tate Paris after 1870. Originally the home of the sort of people who gave some shadowy substance to Murger's bohemian Paris, it had long become the classic rendezvous of English and American visitors and of Frenchmen who wanted to sacrifice style to price. It still had the red-plush benches and gaily frescoed walls of romance, but the service and cooking were what Frenchmen call "serious." The place had just been worth preserving on a commercial basis in the commercial era, and consequently had been preserved.

Madeleine had lost nothing of her idea of celebrating an occasion. She ate heartily and did not refuse to drink with Skene. He was, of course, ravenous, and in the state in which drink had no effect on him. She smiled demurely across the table at him, more at home every moment. He was also amused at something. He had only known Paris fifteen years earlier, as a young architect half-way through his A.R.I.B.A., and was marveling at the change—at the figure she cut in those surroundings that had for him such different associations: she almost bourgeois—he in the fancy dress of his uniform. Her manner with the waiter was perfect, and perfect her assumption of respect-ability. He loved it, felt almost at home, too. For in their secret hearts both of them were domesticated, conventional to the core. Both of them loathed the War and all it had brought. It was the queerest of contradictions that forced them to comfort their ultra-respectable as-pirations in such a place and such a manner, both spoken of even in war-time by many people, as "irregular."

.

The meal at an end, they went, as a matter of course, to a cinema. One did, in war-time. Skene, who at home would hardly have walked

to the end of the street with such an object—Madeleine, who had hardly heard of such a thing before she went to Amiens—went to the nearest cinema because it was war-time and no one wanted to think. Walking in the brisk air of a Parisian winter evening, good meat and drink within them, they enjoyed themselves prodigiously, Skene because he had existed in dubious snatches of comfort for a long time, and was likely to so exist for an indefinite period—Madeleine because of the reality of a man at her side. He was making jokes about the Place Clichy being the Place Cliché! She did not understand in the least, but laughed because he was happy beside her. And so to the gaping portico of one of those establishments which advertise what is known in France as "spectacle de famille." This last was being loudly cried by a person, paid to do so, at the door—who added in stentorian tones that soldiers went in free, and nursemaids half-price. It was typical of Skene that he paid for two of the most expensive seats, and placed Madeleine in the one that gave him the best view of her profile. The film, unfortunately, was a French one, not an American. That is to say, instead of being confronted with the improbable adventures of a man looking somewhat like Skene, Madeleine realized with a start that she was watching a love story in which the principal character was a tolerable travesty of Georges d'Archeville, and behaved with just his perverse petulance. She turned her head, smiled at Skene, played with her program, smoothed her gloves, and arranged herself with minute care for her costume and the possible effect of the seat on it. It was no good. Cinema screens are insistent. It is difficult to avoid that great glare of white, with its intriguing figures in motion. It revealed to her what she would never have invented for herself—the idea that, like the hero of the film, Georges neglected her because he was engrossed by some other woman. She could not dismiss the idea; did not try, perhaps. She felt suddenly more wounded than she had ever felt since August, 1914. That Georges might be hurt at her sharing an English officer's week of Leave never occurred to her. To her practical soul, with its incapacity for flights of imagination, things seemed all too readily what they appeared to the eye. Suddenly she rose.

"This representation is rasant," she said to Skene, and marveled a moment, as they threaded their way out, at his docile good temper. Not a grumble, not a protest. He just followed her and snapped up a taxi. In it he was more solicitous than ever, gentle, kind, with a Mid-Victorian kindness she had never known—the manners of one whose boyhood has been unspoiled by bitter thoughts about money.

They reached the little hotel at which they had dropped their baggage, and he handed her in. By this time his way with her was having

the queerest effect. Had he been thoughtless, brutal, she would easily have braced herself to meet it. As it was, she felt something slowly dissolving in her. She held herself in yet a little, approving the place he had chosen, clean and reasonable in price. But when the door of their little room was bolted, and she stood in front of the mirror by the rose-colored curtains, unpinning her hat, he came gently behind her and slipped his hands under her arms. It was just Georges' way. She burst into tears. The moment the first sob had shaken itself free—for she did nothing by halves, and when, rarely, she cried, she cried bitterly —she knew she would feel better. Skene let her droop on to the bed and sat beside her, one arm round her, making very small comforting remarks in French and English alternately, but no inquiries. She kept her handkerchief tight pressed upon her eyes with both hands, but her sobs were lessening, and with every moment the agonizing vision of Georges with some one else grew smaller and fainter. She leaned ever so gently against Skene, who tended her as a woman might a child, did every little service for her, amazing her, who had never been so treated since she was four years old. Gradually she slipped down into the comfort of those hard hands, whose fingers kept something of the skill and discrimination of such as have been used for wise, gentle occupations. But only when she was at ease, with dry bright eyes and braided hair, did he seem to think of himself, and then only to ask so humbly for what he wanted. She gave him all herself, fiercely, as if for ever to prevent any of her from escaping again into those other hands that had neglected her so. More, when they two swam slowly back to the surface of normal existence again, in the quiet of the night only broken by the discreet bubbling of the calorifère in the corner, she told him the stark truth of herself and Georges, with a bareness of exposure of her very soul she had never before permitted, of which, perhaps, she had never before been capable. And when at last they slept, in each other's arms, it was the deep sleep of emotional reaction, for no less than she, Skene had looked for years past on utter shipwreck—obliteration of his individuality in the dark mud of Flemish trenches—and knew from a different point of view all she suffered, and what comfort she clutched at.

The next day passed in that atmosphere known to English honeymooners. Not a trace remained of the emotions of the evening before —nothing but two healthy young people out for a holiday, both in the most incurious state of mind, and easily amused. The things they missed seeing far out-numbered those they noticed, as is the case with honeymooners.

Madeleine was so used to the English that she hardly smiled when he turned the little hotel upside down in order to have a hot bath and an egg for breakfast. The establishment, at length conceding these recondite advantages, ceased to interest them. They went out into the busy streets, in the frosty air, Skene's hands in the pockets of his "British warm," Madeleine with one hand tucked into his arm, the other holding her fur tippet close across her throat, as she saw other girls doing. To Skene, a free morning in Paris could only, by habit and association, mean one thing:—pictures. To Madeleine it could only mean another:—shops. As they descended into the roaring heart of the city, never busier than in mid-war, they found some of the galleries were still open, and Skene took her from room to room, pointing out old favorites, lamenting new gaps left by careful storage of some of the more valuable masterpieces. She moved beside him, confused, uncertain whether to blush or look away in front of many a splendid nudity, but drawn by the spirit that was on both, to squeeze his arm a little. In the mood of the moment she unconsciously identified herself with all feminine beauty, and he acquiesced. But he was not less in holiday mind than she, stood patiently for half an hour at a time in big shops, watching her wringing out to the uttermost centime the best value from scowling shop-girls. Skene begged to give her what she wanted—he had managed to visit three field cashiers and get francs from each—he had a pocket full of money. She accepted, loyally keeping herself within limits and wasting nothing. Both of them had their shocks. In one of the turnings off the rue de Rivoli they met a tall fresh-cheeked young man, scented and glittering, in a gray-green uniform Skene identified as Russian. Skene fell into a growling condemnation of all "Base Pups," "Head-quarter people," etc., etc., incomprehensible to her, save its long-stored ill-humor. But she was after all only saying the same thing in French, when a frail, fair, over-arranged lady kept her waiting in the glove department of the Bon Marché, when Skene heard her grind her white teeth, with: "That sort of animal doesn't know what time's worth!"

.

The next day was still queerer. Skene wanted what he called "a day in the country." Madeleine had no idea what he might mean, her notions of a holiday being confined to Church Festivals. She went with him, however, down the Seine Valley, as far as the regulations permitted. She gathered he once had regular haunts here, had gone by steamer with companions. She taunted him laughingly with having been one to "rigoler" in his youth. She began to suspect that he was much richer than his worn khaki and careful trench habits made ap-

parent. He took her to a well-known beauty spot, all shuttered and sad with war and winter, roused the proprietor and persuaded him to give them food and drink in the mournfulness of the dismantled salle à manger. The proprietor, like so many others, had lost an only son. It took a lot of gentleness and some of Skene's Expeditionary Force canteen cigarettes to thaw him. But gradually he expanded into the graveyard interest of his kind. What were the trenches like? Were the dead buried properly? Would one find their graves? Skene told all he could, painted a true picture as far as he could, exaggerating no horror, slurring over none of the stark facts. The old man was appeased. He liked to know. So his son was lying like that, was he, amid the Meuse hillocks!

Madeleine took no part in the conversation, but sat looking at Skene, totally uninterested in what he was saying, enjoying the masculinity of his movements and gestures. She was beginning to be curious about the one thing that ever aroused her speculation. What was this man's position in life? The men talked on into the winter dusk, the "patron" offering liqueurs and cigars. She and Skene missed their train back and had to walk to a neighboring depôt, and get seats on an army lorry. Skene tipped the driver and Madeleine saw the man's face. That night, as they lay side by side in the sober companionship that both of them felt so right and justifiable, she asked him of his home. She was somewhat astonished at the result. He talked for twenty minutes, and was all the time incomprehensible to her. The old house in the Cathedral Close, the hereditary sinecure descending in the one family—the semi-public school, wholly leisured-class prejudices and scruples—the circle of maiden aunts living on railway dividends—the pet animals—the social functions—made her pucker her smooth, regular forehead with complete mystification. She could make nothing of it except that every one in England was rolling in money.

.

Another day followed, and another. The end of the week was at hand. As it approached, they both regarded the impending separation calmly. The emotions that had brought them together were of the sort that will not keep. Neither of them were bohemians of the true water. The life of the little hotel where they slept and the restaurants where they fed was soon drained of its attractiveness. If Skene really wanted anything, it was to be back at his job in England. If Madeleine ever asked herself what she found lacking in those brief days, the answer would have been a farm of her own, a settled place in some village community, and, perhaps, children. But she did not ask herself such questions, nor did Skene admit for a moment that there

was anything to desire other than what they shared. But there fell long silences between them. The tittle-tattle about topical events interested neither of them. The little news they could tell each other was told. They could not talk of Georges. Their only common memories were of the farm and the Easter Horse Show of the division. Both subjects were stale. The small attempt Madeleine made to understand Skene had led her into perplexity. Skene had let her more intimate self alone, having neat provincial notions of chivalry. The excursions of peace-time Paris no longer existed. The cinema and most theaters bored Skene. Madeleine could not sit out concerts. The day before the last, they went at Skene's suggestion to the Sorbonne. He wanted to feast his eyes, that must so soon look at decauville railways and trench-mortar ammunition, on the Fresco, by Puvis de Chavannes, which decorates the lecture hall of that institution.

He had first seen it as a young man, and the impression it had made was undimmed. He loved that blue-green twilight in which statuesque people stood in attitudes among Greek pillars and poplar trees. He loved it with an English love of things as they are not. Madeleine gazed at the great lecture hall. At last she said, "It is not then a church!" No fool, she had grasped the speculative, investigating atmosphere.

"No," Skene replied, "it is a higher grade school!"

"As school decoration, it is not ver' useful!"

Skene had nothing to say.

Later, as Skene wished to dawdle over some architectural drawings in the Cluny Museum, she said frankly she would look at the shops. Their time was drawing to a close. The next day was the last. Skene did not know how to say that he hoped to meet her again. Did he?

.

For Madeleine it was easier. She simply went on behaving beautifully. The week had not been spoiled by one cross word. To the end, she found no fault with Skene, herself, or Fate. Such tenderness as life had not already rubbed out of her, showed itself in her solicitude as to his sandwiches and half-bottle of wine. It would be cold, she warned him, as they paced the platform of the Gare du Nord. If he passed by the farm he would say a word to her father and Marie. He promised, stoical as she, and habituated to War-time farewells. He did not allude to the future. She kept herself wrapped in uncritical passivity. The train was made up. She saw his out-of-shape cap, khaki back, and tightly clothed legs disappear successively in the doorway of the carriage. He came out again, having secured his corner, and they paced the asphalt of the station for yet a few minutes, in silence. Then

at shoutings and whistlings and blowings of tin trumpets, without which no French train can start, he disappeared again, but, the door closed, hung out of the window. The train was full of French leave-men, many drunk. One in particular, who was wearing a bowler hat on his uniform, noticed Skene and Madeleine just as the train began to move, and shouted, "I know what you've been doing, English officer and little lady!" Skene waved and was gone. Madeleine turned and went. "Know what you've been doing" rang in her ears. A smile curled the corners of her mouth. Men looked after her again now that she was alone. She walked, taking pleasure in exercise and the keen air, to the little hotel in the stony street, paid the bill, with the money Skene had given her, reclaimed her hold-all, strained to bursting with the things he had bought for her. Then she demanded a taxi, which she dismissed in front of the Pantheon, and walked on foot to Monsieur and Madame Petit's. She ascended the stone stairs, cold and bare as penury, and knocked.

Monsieur opened to her with a short piece of candle, carefully screened in his hand. He closed the door and led her into the fireless dining-room, from which her room opened. He peered at her.

"Well, this war, how goes it?"

"But gently!" she replied, not guessing what he was driving at.

"Come, your brother told you nothing?"

In a moment it came back to her, that she had been spending a week's "leave" with her "brother." She faced the peering old eyes.

"You know that the men in the trenches never say anything!"

He was rebuffed, but tried again.

"The Boulogne train must have been very late!"

But she was on her guard now, and replied readily enough:

"Very late. The Bosche were bombing Amiens!"

The old man grunted and left her. In her own room she smiled at her reflection in the glass. She was looking magnificent, feeling magnificent. To come from at least some degree of luxury, if not from home and love, at least from entertainment and admiration, to the bleak realities of her daily life, did not daunt her Flemish heart. She unpacked and undressed methodically, passed her hands over that flesh that had been so generously caressed, and seemed rounded and fortified by it, and wrapped herself in the hard-worn bed-clothes, warming them with her vitality. Could Skene, buttoned up in his "British warm," miles away on the northern railway, have seen her, he might have been attracted, he would not have been harrowed or flattered. She had rubbed off the contact with him by the passage of her hands over herself. She rubbed him off her soul no less easily. She was at her

place in the Ministry on the morrow, and save that her appearance of well-being excited desire or envy, created no sensation.

Then as the days passed, very slowly, and all the more surely, reaction began to set in. She did not analyze it or express it, but it was there. The old feeling of having been done, cheated! There was the old void—and Skene, against whom she bore no malice, was partial, rather—had tried to fill it and failed. It was not in him. Too well behaved, too incomprehensible, too English, he had, in fact, not asked enough of her. She would have felt more at home with him had he been subject to those moods of feverish desire and cold disgust that she associated with all that was most admirable in men. For that male perversity which, when it existed in her father and the Baron, in "Papa," and Monsieur Blanquart, in fact in all men, was the very thing by which war had been brought about, and caused her separation from Georges—when it appeared in that Georges himself, became simply one of his attributes. Her "good child" bored her. Her spoiled, imperious one was what she needed.

The evenings lengthened. February came, and the Bosche retreat. Marie wrote that she was trying to get back to Laventie, where things were in a pitiable state, but good land must not be allowed to lie waste. They despaired of Marcel. Madeleine did not reply to this letter. The farm and all it had contained seemed very remote. Yet the letter was a comfort; it brought no bad news, and no news was good news. Already, she thought again of nothing but Georges. As for any practical plan to find him, she had long come to the end of the expedients that her not very strong imagination could devise. She just wanted, and waited.

The chief of her department in the Ministry was one of those politicians who found the War dull. Its concentration upon the one great effort to beat the Bosche, and preserve the French nation alive, robbed such a politician of his living. There was little scope for anything but messing with contracts, trying and necessarily unspectacular. This one among the party-bosses of the French Chamber hit upon a plan which would advertise him, and at the same time give a sort of rallying-cry and style for the next political stunt. He saw shrewdly enough that Peace would one day burst upon an astonished world, and that those who were unprepared for it would be badly left. And what would be the best starting-place in the new Peace atmosphere? Why, obviously, to be hailed in a million farms, a million small shops, as "That brave Monsieur Dantrigues—he was good to our poor boys in the hospitals during the War!" It could be used as common ground

for Action Française on the one hand, and the extreme socialists on the other. And no one dared raise hand or word against it. The quickest, cheapest and best way to set it afoot was, of course, to make use of the organizing power of his immense department, the ocean of needy vanity in which the hundreds of temporary typists and girl war-clerks swam; the comic papers could be got to blaze it about—they were invariably hard up.

So it was that Madeleine, in common with all her companions, found herself invited to take part in a gigantic Charitable Fête. They were given little cards with the particulars—certain elements of costume were to be uniform, also an electric lamp in the hair, and a basket of gifts. They were to meet in the Tuileries, at certain spots indicated by numbers, from which decorated lorries would take them to the various hospitals of the metropolitan area, to distribute an Easter gift to every sick or wounded soldier. Monsieur Dantrigues was smart enough to see that this was much more effective than the same thing carried out near the Front. For if a man has incurred a gumboil guarding a railway in the Seine Valley, he likes just as well to be treated as a "brave wounded," and is just as likely to vote subsequently for the man who organized people to think him so. On the other hand, the real fighting soldiers, nearer the Front, would mostly be killed and never vote at all.

The idea caught on. Generals, clerics, ladies old and young, blessed it and gave funds for costumes and presents.

.

Never did government department function so ill as that which contained Madeleine, as the ten thousand charitable maidens prepared themselves for the fray. Madeleine entered into the affair rather than make herself conspicuous. She had no sentiment about other people's soldiers, no anxiety to please men who did not interest her. But she went, took her number, arranged herself with sense and taste, and found a little comfort from looking nice. She managed to get a double supply of gifts and send one lot to her brother Marcel, hoping that it might bring a sign from him in his German prison.

The day came. Released at an early hour, the girls dispersed to costume themselves. The short-sleeved tunic of thin white material, with its girdle of artificial ivy leaves, suited Madeleine. Even Monsieur and Madame Petit, never prodigal of praise, admitted that she looked well. When she arrived at the rendezvous, she created some sensation. The uniform dress brought out precisely her better proportions and carriage, all her good looks that depended on health and hard work. As the lorries that were to take them to their places swung alongside

the pavement, one of the girls said to her, "That great Flanders mare ought to have two seats allowed her!" but the very spite of the speech was a compliment to Madeleine. They were set down on the steps of one of those great palaces of stone, common in Paris, that had been aroused from centuries of slumber by the War, and now sheltered hundreds of narrow white beds. Among these, up and down great vistas of ward and corridor, the girls processed, music in front, bearers of lighted candles behind. The fête, designed by a lady of cosmopolitan education, just then very intimate with Dantrigues, had elements of English carol-singing and German Christmas-tree effect, mixed with French delight in spectacle and uniform. Then the girls were divided into pairs, and given so many beds each for the distribution of gifts.

Madeleine was frankly bored with the whole thing. She hardly bothered to make herself agreeable to the men in her section of beds —passing them with a word or two of conventional good wishes, holding her clean, fair-skinned, smiling, slightly obtuse profile high above them, stepping easily, unencumbered by the basket on her hip. At the end of her bit were several empty beds, the nursing sister on duty explaining that the occupants were more or less convalescent, and had leave. She did not trouble to hurry off elsewhere, nor to obtain a fresh supply of gifts. The more or less innocent flirtations, which the other girls saw as one of the chief attractions of the business, did not excite her. The electric globe in her hair, which annoyed her, went out, and seeing a glass door leading on to a verandah, all dark and quiet, she slipped through unseen. She had hardly drawn the door to behind her than she had a peculiar sensation. She had stepped into a mild, humid spring night, the stars of which shone above the garden plantation of the place, beyond the stone pillars of the balcony on which she stood. But in her own mind she had stepped through the separation of over two years, as one puts one's foot through a paper screen. Georges was near her, she knew. The back of the balcony, against the glazed windows of the ward, was lined with a kind of fixed garden seat used by the convalescent. One of these convalescents was seated, lying there rather, his attitude expressive more of exasperation than of physical weakness. Before she could analyze or act upon her queer feeling of nearness of Georges, his voice arose from the recumbent figure, in the quakerish simplicity of French intimacy: "It is thou!" was all he said.

She flung down her basket and sunk on the seat beside him. Galvanized into sudden life, he heaved himself up, clutched her in his arms, bent down her face to his. For some time, who can tell how long, neither of them thought of anything, content just to feel the emotions of the moment. Amid these arose the jangle of a bell. It brought

Madeleine to her senses at once. It was the arranged signal—five minutes' warning before the charitable maidens rejoined their lorries. M. Dantrigues' lady friend had thoughtfully suggested that some of the young women might want to put themselves tidy. Madeleine stood up, telling Georges briefly what was intended. He replied with an army word, intimating how much he cared. She was tender, docile, careful with him, spoiling him every minute.

"Yes, yes, my little one. I know. But it is worth more to arrange where we can meet. Your Mado will wait for you wherever you say!"

It was the pet name he had for her those ages ago in the Kruysabel. At the sound of it, spoken as she spoke, all that lost Peace-time ease arose ghostly before them. He vented his indignation against Fate by picking up her basket and flinging it into the night, where it crashed softly among earth and leaves. The gesture delighted her. It was the old Georges, the real "young master" of first love. She had been terribly frightened by his first greeting, that meek "It is thou!" so unlike him, that he had uttered. He pleased her still more when he went on:

"If that's your bell, you'd better go. Don't get caught in this sacred box, whatever you do!"

"Tell me where," she whispered.

"I'll find a place and let you know. I must get out of here. If not, I'll burst myself as I have bursted so many Bosches. Where do you live?"

She told him, pressed a kiss on his lips, and was gone in a flash, quiet, confident, alert. She was herself again.

The journey back to the rendezvous in the lorry was noisy and amusing. A score or two of young women, mainly at the minx stage of unattachment, chattered and squabbled, mimicked and raved. Madeleine sat in a corner unheeding. From the rendezvous home she took no account of time, nor place, could not have said by which street she passed, or at what hour she sat down to the Petits' supper. They were rather nicer than usual to her that night, feeling perhaps that she was a credit to them—for the charitable fête had been discussed from every possible point of view in that quarter of shabby gentility, and every one in the block of flats knew that the Petits' lodger had taken part. Madame Petit had seen to that. But Madeleine was not responsive—wrapped herself in a brown study—or was it a golden dream? —and retired early to her room.

.

The next day she was the same—quiet, polite, but detached, went to the office as usual, returned at the same hour, replied to questions in monosyllables, went to bed early. Monsieur Petit began to have his

suspicions—could it be that the young woman had fallen in love ("made a friend" was the expression he used to his wife) at the fête?

The next morning, as they sipped coffee in their several déshabillés, there came a knock on the door. A message! Monsieur Petit, who took it in, handed it to Madeleine through the two inches that she opened her door. He dressed hurriedly, agog with excitement. The hour at which she usually left for the office passed, and she did not appear. Finally, she did leave her room, at nearly ten o'clock, dressed in her best, carrying her hold-all and a hat-box.

"Good-bye," she said. "I have left everything in order and the week's money on the dressing-table."

Monsieur Petit stammered, "But why?"

Madeleine's eyes gleamed in such a way that he stood aside to let her pass. "Because I am leaving," she said. "Make my adieux to Madame. She is occupied, I know!"

And the old man stamped with rage as he heard her firm footfall descending the stone stairs. She was going, taking away a secret with her. Almost as well have taken one of the bronze figures of saints or knights on horseback from the dining-room—that would have been no more robbery than to take away a secret from that little home where bronze statuettes and curiosity about other people's affairs were the only luxuries.

At the foot of the stairs Madeleine hailed a taxi and gave an address in the northwestern quarter of the city, from the paper in her hand. Then she folded the paper carefully, and replaced it in her hand-bag with her money and little mirror, as the vehicle bounded down the Boulevard St. Michel. Poor Monsieur Petit was not to be allowed to forget her departure. Three days later the postman brought a letter for Madeleine. Monsieur Petit turned it over and over, his fingers itched. Then something in his memory of superannuated government service stirred. He knew what it was, and told his wife, nodding and glaring malignantly.

"I have sent hundreds in my time. It is the dismissal!"

It appeased him somewhat, for naturally he could imagine nothing more fatal than to be dismissed from the service of the government he had served for fifty years, and which paid him his pension in consequence. Retribution indeed had fallen on Madeleine, in Monsieur Petit's eyes.

.

Could Monsieur Petit have divined whither Madeleine had flown, could he have followed her, confronted her as he longed to, crying, "See, abandoned girl, cheater of my curiosity, how Fate has overtaken

you!" it is doubtful if Madeleine would have bothered even to laugh at him. She sat perfectly upright, swaying with the rocking vehicle, staring at the chauffeur's back, as she was carried down steep crowded streets, across wide vistas of bridge and quay, square and avenue, up into quiet, almost sinister-quiet, respectable streets. Dismissing and paying her taxi, and watching him out of sight, she shouldered her baggage and found her way along by sign and number to a tall block of small flats, like a hundred other such. She waited a moment, hesitating between dislike of the concierge and equal dislike of becoming conspicuous by standing in the road. Finally, she walked boldly in, disregarding the gaping eyes and mouth that followed her from the basement, mounted to the floor she required, and knocked. She had to repeat her knock more than once before it was answered and the door was left unlocked for her to push open. There was no one in the little vestibule. She dropped her things, and, guided by Georges' voice, found the bedroom, where Georges, who had pulled the clothes over him again, was cursing the cold floor he had had to tread. That was the real Georges, the man who wanted her without bothering to get up to open the door for her, the man for whom she would have died. She put her arms around his neck, and bent down to him, so that he could have her.

.

He was very much real Georges that day. He lay in bed until hunger forced him to rise, and then would neither dress nor shave. He was not of that type that lives on the interest of the past, nor hurriedly discounts the future. Nor can it be said that the thought of Lieutenant Skene crossed Madeleine's mind. Had it done so, she might have reflected how much more she loved this, her spoiled child, than that, her good one. But she, too, was absorbed in the present. She did not even remember the Ministry, whose service she had so peremptorily abandoned.

When the first gladness of reunion was slowing down into the assurance that she really had got him back, and had now only to devise how to keep him—a task she did not feel very difficult—she began to question him, very gently and indirectly, as to his plans. She remonstrated with him on the folly of their being there together, an object of interest to the concierge, still more on his insistence that she should stay there. But he only shouted that he would "burst up" all the concierges, and she had to humor him and promise to stay for the present at least. Not that he threatened to leave her, but that she would not and could not threaten to leave him. At length, in the evening, as he sat in gown

and slippers before the fire she had made, at the supper she had fetched and set, while she tidied the room strewn with his things, he began to think of her, asked for her father. He only asked one or two brief questions not being the man to take deep interest in anything outside his own comfort. When she had answered, he just said: "This sacred war!" Nothing else. But Madeleine knew what he meant. There it was, all round and over them, enveloping, threatening, thwarting. No less than he, she rebelled against it, in her decorous woman's way. But for him she rebelled against it twice over, hated it, made it responsible for his loss of health that was new, and his violence that was habitual—forgave him, on account of it, his carelessness of her—this way in which he wanted to live—the obvious fact that he had had other women in this room. She did not reflect upon her own record, then. But she coaxed him to take supper—she had bought the war-products that were nearest to the hare pâté and spicebread and confiture of old times—gave him a bowl of hot wine and water, as she had many a time that he had found her, he, glowing and triumphant, with a dog at his heels. And sure enough, under the spell of her magic, in that firelit bed-sitting room of the little flat in Paris, there came back, gradually but surely, the Georges of old days. His worn cheeks filled out, his eyes were less sunken, his hand less thin and shaky. He began to hold up his head and hum a tune. She hung near him, watching him, foreseeing not only every need, but every whim. He became almost liberal, expansive. He had fourteen days' "convalo"—a visit every day to the hospital, which institution would not otherwise bother about him. At the end of that time he would either go back to hospital, or up to the front. He did not care which, he said, smiling. For the first time since she had rediscovered him, he did not call anything sacred, wish to "burst" anyone, or use the expressive, untranslatable verb "foutre." She cleared away and tidied up and prepared herself for the night, as he sat glancing through the newspapers humming to himself, content, asking nothing. When he felt tired, he just turned out the light, and rolled into the place she had made warm for him.

.

Days so spent soon pass, nor is there anything more tragic than physical satiety, with its wiping out of what has gone before. Madeleine, not naturally apprehensive, would have gone on had not hard facts pulled her up. Georges had spent his pocket-money on paying the quarter's rent of their retreat. She had spent hers on food for him and herself. No bohemian, she began to take counsel with herself as to how

to obtain fresh supplies. One source of funds she dismissed at once. She would not ask Georges for a penny. That would have seemed outrageous to her. She did not attempt it. She had a handsome sum in the Savings Bank at Hazebrouck. But how get it? She did not want to write to Monsieur Blanquart or to Marie. Even if they could have withdrawn it for her (and the difficulties of such a step she did not clearly foresee), they would both of them have found out sooner or later something about Georges. And that she would not have for all the world. Her father she could trust, but she also knew his ingrained habits regarding money, his incapacity for reading and writing. A letter would simply stupefy him. If he got some one to read it to him, he would simply be stupefied the more. His Madeleine spending her savings? Never! He would do nothing. Should she, then, go by train and get the money? There would be endless difficulties in getting authority to journey into the British Military Zone—but the great difficulty to her mind, the insurmountable one, was to leave Georges for two days. She was nonplussed.

Just then it happened that Georges, turning towards her in one of his more expansive moments, said, in his spoiled way: "My God, how I want you!"

Occupied fully with him at the moment, her mind retained the words, her memory searching for the last occasion on which she had heard them. Georges went out to his club that morning, leaving her sewing, washing, doing a hundred and one jobs in her thorough housekeeper's way. She sat brooding, almost waiting for some stroke of luck to help her with her difficulty. Suddenly she remembered who it was that last used that phrase—Lieutenant Skene. She sat down at once and wrote to him. She had no scruples. All the English were rich. This one had no outlet for his money. She had been worth it. The reply came in three days, to the post-office address she had given. It brought a hundred francs. They lasted a week, and few people could have made them last more, save that Georges only came in to supper now. He was getting restless, smelled of drink. She wrote again to Skene. No reply came. Instead there came the end of the fortnight of Georges' "convalo." That day she sat alone waiting for two things, a letter bringing money, or Georges bringing fatal news. Either he was not well enough to go back to the front, so that his state must indeed be serious, or he was well enough, which was even worse. She dared not ask him; he vouchsafed nothing, seemed well enough, but restless. She, meanwhile, for the first time in her life was feeling really ill. She had never met before with this particular cruelty of Fate, resented it, but only felt worse. Perhaps the town life had sapped her vitality. Perhaps Georges had brought home from his hospital, on his clothes, in his

breath, the germ of some war fever. The following day Georges was excited, and talked loud and long when he came back from the club. Her head felt so strange she did not understand.

.

Perhaps it was as well she did not. Georges had been granted another fortnight "convalo," but it was not that. It was the news of the battle of Vimy that excited him. The English, of whom he was good-humoredly jealous, had taken that battered ridge, disputed for years. There was talk of eleven thousand prisoners and a quantity of guns. He had missed being "in it." But with the news came rumor more important still. The French were preparing a great offensive in Champagne. He would not miss that one, sacred name, not he! The spirit of that period of the war, the spirit of "On Les Aura" burned in his veins like fire. As he strode and shouted about the room, cursing his "convalo," that a week ago was all he desired, because now it prevented his being in the show.

Madeleine had the queerest feeling of all her life up to that day, for she was not a girl to faint—a sinking feeling, not painful, rather comforting. Then nothing. Then a reawakening, not so comfortable, dismay, weakness. Georges, who did nothing by halves, became, for the nonce, generous to the utmost limit of the nature of a man born with a silver spoon in his mouth and a cheque-book in the pocket of his first suit. Probably it never crossed his mind that she had taken infection from some carelessness of his. But he did better. He promptly called a young doctor of his set, who, having been badly wounded, was now permanently attached to the Paris garrison. Between affection for Georges and a handsome bribe—for the proceeding was thoroughly irregular—flat contrary to every by-law of the town and every order of the Medical Service—this young man took Madeleine in hand, visited her daily, did what was necessary in the way of prescribing, got a discreet sister of charity to nurse her. Being a man of the world, he further suggested to her, as soon as she was well enough to make inquiries, that she would not care for Georges to see her in her present state. That kept her quiet during the weeks of recovery. But there came a fine June day when she was well enough to walk out a little in a Paris ever more feverish and deserted. Then the young doctor, as thorough as Georges or herself, told her the truth. Georges' thoroughness had taken the form of borrowing the identity disc and paybook of a hospital casualty whom he resembled in height and complexion. The young doctor had connived at the fraud, with the cynicism of Georges himself and all his set. Thus furnished, Georges had gone straight into the heart of that ghastly failure of the French in Cham-

pagne, during May, 1917. The hurried scrutiny of his credentials had not found him out, he was in the line and fighting when his half-recovered health broke down once more, and fatally. He was buried in a huge, ever-growing cemetery, near the Aerodrome, at Avenant-le-Petit.

.

When Madeleine realized it, she sat still, looking at nothing, gathering within her all her physical vitality to meet this blow to the spirit. On her face, refined by illness, was something· of the look that horses have under heavy shell-fire, bewildered resistance to the unknown. The young doctor let her alone for twenty-four hours, and then very gently led her mind back to practical considerations. The period for which Georges had hired the flat was expiring shortly. Had she money, or the means of getting some? It did not take her long to run over the alternatives—an attempt to get back into some sort of office—or a begging letter to Skene? She avoided both, not from any sense of shame, but simply because now Paris and its life had no meaning for her. She had wanted Georges. She had said, "If I could only see him!" She had seen him. Now she would never see him again. Why bother?

The young doctor then suggested that he could obtain her a permission to travel by train to Hazebrouck. This brought to her mind the almost certain death of her brother, Marcel, in his German prison camp, and of Marie's return to Laventie. The mere name of the market town called up at once associations so potent, so much more real than all that had happened since. The farm understaffed, the old father being swindled out of billeting money! Those were realities. Those things appealed to her more than this tragic dream-life. She accepted gladly the young doctor's offer, and left him looking after her and muttering: "What a type, all the same!" But she had no special contempt or dislike for him.

She left Paris in the same way as she left him. The old sacred towers, the new garish restaurants, the keen bitter energy, the feminine grace, of that metropolis of the world, that had once again had the enemy at its gates, and was yet to be bombarded by such engines as had never before been turned upon city of man—she turned her back upon it all, and, for her, it was not. On a gray July day she entered the train. As she traveled homewards, the day grew grayer and wetter. She passed, unheeding, through an immense bustle between Abbeville and Calais, and down to St. Omer. Her train stopped frequently, and she glanced, uninterested, at the trains and trucks, materials and men, that choked rail and road. About her, people talked of the great offensive the English had begun, from Ypres to the sea. She looked at the crops

and houses, thought of her father, whose very double, tall, old, dark-clothed, and bent, she saw in almost every teeming field of flax or hops, grain or roots, of that rich valley. Perhaps she had occasional bitter spasms of anger against this war, that had enslaved, and then destroyed Georges. But to her, facts were facts, and she did not deny them.

.

Outside Hazebrouck the train stopped interminably. The guns had been audible, loud and angry for some time, but the long roll of them was punctuated now by a sharper nearer sound, that clubbed one about the ears at regular intervals—artillery practising, no doubt, she thought. After waiting in the motionless train as long as she considered reasonable, she got out, finding a perverse satisfaction in the use of her limbs, swinging down the steep side of the second-class carriage of the Nord Railway, and asking for her box and "cardboard" (containing hats) to be handed down to her. Shouldering these, she marched along the asphalt with which the prodigal English had re-enforced the embankment, showing no concern at the cries of "They bombard!" shouted to her by her fellow-passengers. She passed the engine, from which the driver and firemen were peering ahead. The fields were very deserted, but she was hardly the sort to be frightened in daylight, or dark either. She passed the points where the Dunkirk line joined that from St. Omer. Near by, stood a row of cottages, known as the "Seven Chimneys," the first houses of Hazebrouck, on the station side. Her idea was to leave her trunk at the estaminet, for her father to fetch in the morning. To her astonishment, the whole row appeared deserted, empty, doors open, fires burning, food cooking. Somewhat nonplussed, she stopped a moment to get her breath, pushed her box behind the counter of the estaminet, where she was known, and then passed on, with her "cardboard," keeping the path that separates the St. Omer road from the railway. Where this reached its highest point, just at the entry to the town, she happened to glance across the rich, lonely, hedgeless fields towards the Aire road, and saw, on that side, every wall and alley black with people. She had no time to reflect on this peculiarity before she was deafened by such a roaring upheaval of earth as she had certainly never imagined. It took away her breath, wrenched her "cardboard" out of her hands. For some seconds she could hear nothing, see nothing, but when her senses returned, the first thing she noticed was the patter of falling débris. The shell had fallen in the ditch of the railway embankment, and made a hole the size of the midden at home, and three times as deep. She picked herself up from her knees, dusted herself, re-captured her "cardboard," and passed on, greeted by a long "Ah—

a—ah!" from scores of throats of the spectators, a quarter of a mile away. The incident annoyed her. They were bombarding, and no mistake. But it would take worse than that to prevent her from crossing the railway under the arch, and taking the Calais road. The rue de St. Omer was empty, but undamaged. They were a jumpy lot, she thought; it revolted her to see all those good houses, left unlocked and open to all the ills that attack abandoned property. There was not even another shell-hole nearer than the station, so far as she could see. She would have liked a cup of coffee and a slice of bread, but the town was empty as an eggshell. She heard another explosion behind her as she reached the Calais pavé. The persistence of those Bosches! But she was persistent too, and gathered her damp clothes and battered "cardboard" to her, as she strode vigorously home. She was not sentimental—no one less so, but it may well have been that her blood quickened, and her rooted strength returned, as she found herself, once more, facing that salt wind, under those low gray skies, among which she had been bred and born.

At length she came to the earth road, the signpost, and the turning, and saw the farm, the fringe of dead wallflower stalks on the ridge of the thatch, the old "shot" tower by the bridge over the moat. It was between six and seven when she passed the brick-pillared gate, noted a new bomb-hole, and signs of military occupation. Entering by the door, she found her father in the passage.

"It's our Madeleine," he said quietly.

Madeleine kissed him and told him to fetch her box in the morning, from "Seven Chimneys."

He said, "Thy room is empty," and went into the kitchen, while she said a word to Berthe. It was true, her little room was just as she had left it a year before. She noted the fact with quiet satisfaction, but did not bother over the significance of it—over the fact that her father, who usually paid so little heed to anything that went on in the house, had kept her room untouched and empty for her. She quietly accepted the fact, conscious that he felt that neither the God to whom he muttered prayers on Sunday, nor the various temporal powers whom he obeyed, when he had to, on weekdays, really understood him or cared for him as his younger daughter did. She sat down with him, in the dim kitchen, to the evening meal, by the light of the day that was dying in thin drizzle and incessant mutter of guns. Once some fearful counter-barrage made the old panes of the oriel window rattle, and the old man said:

"It's a swine of a war, all the same!"

Madeleine replied: "It's something new for them to be bombarded in Hazebrouck!"

"I'm going to take the money out of the Savings Bank," he commented. In his mind, unused to the facilities of bookkeeping, and cradled in the cult of the worsted stocking for savings, he probably thought of his money as being held in notes or coin in the stoutly-barred vault behind the Mairie. After a long pause, during which he surveyed her hands, busy with household mending, somewhat neglected since Marie had relinquished it to Berthe, he spoke again:

"You are quite a fine lady of the town!"

"That will soon pass," she answered, without ceasing to ply her needle.

Later he said: "You know Marie has returned to Laventie?"

Madeleine nodded. The remark was not so stupid as it sounded. He knew she knew the fact. It was his way of appealing to her.

"Now you have come back, you will be just the Madeleine you used to be, and all will go on as before, won't it?"

Her nod was all the answer he asked.

Once again he spoke: "You know Marcel is dead?"

Again she nodded. Again it was only his way of saying, "Come what may, you will see me through, we shall not be worse off for the cruelties of Fate!" She understood and acquiesced. Nothing else passed until with "Good night, father," and "Good night, my girl," they parted.

Of her life during the past twelve months and all it had contained, not a word.

PART III

La Galette

The late summer of 1917, the summer of Haig's offensive from Ypres, was one of the wettest of the war, but the days following Madeleine's return opened fine.

She was up betimes, and soon made herself apparent in the life of the farm. Harvest must begin the moment things were dry enough, and before they became too dry, so that the cut grain would neither sprout as it lay, nor spill itself as it fell. Besides herself and her father, they had Berthe, and the family of Belgian refugees, two boys too young for service, and eight women of all ages. A thoughtful government had added two Territorial soldiers of the very oldest class, who could easily be spared from such military duty as they were fit for; and to this, a still more thoughtful Madeleine mentally added some

amount of help that could be extracted, by one means or another, from English troops resting in the area. At the moment of her return there were no troops, but artillery came on the following day. There also came a platelayer's family from Hazebrouck, whose house was too near the big shells that had fallen. Madeleine drove a hard bargain with them, work in the fields as the price of a loft in the outhouses, until the latter should be required for potatoes. But these matters were not her first concern. She made a long and careful scrutiny of the billeting money that had been paid during her absence. Marie was too accustomed to the rough methods of those who live on the edge of the trenches, and knew little of the fine art of making the English pay.

Madeleine went to see Monsieur Blanquart in the morning recess of the school, and found him perceptibly grayer and more harassed, almost snowed under by the immense weight of paper, by which a government, in sore straits, discharged its expedients upon its humbler representatives. In addition to the correspondence and registration necessitated by general mobilization, and by the occupation of an allied army, there were now circulars and returns concerning food production, waste prevention, aircraft precautions, counter-espionage, and the surveillance of prices. In such circumstances, Blanquart probably wished her back in Paris, but she insisted. After bitter argument, he suddenly surveyed her with a gleam of interest.

"There, you aren't greatly changed; but what induced you to leave a good job in the Ministry?"

Madeleine realized that she was an object of admiring interest, with who-knows-what history invented for her by Cécile. She pushed it all aside. "I had better things to do than to go moldy in an office. Now, Monsieur Blanquart, for the month of March, there is only seventy-five francs marked down. How do you explain it?" and so on.

.

She came back from the village across the fields, scrutinizing the crops, the workers, the new drains and telegraph wires the English were putting in everywhere. Already, in a few hours, her short assumption of town life and habit was dropping from her. She had put it away with the town hats Skene and Georges had bought for her, in the "cardboard," on the half-tester of her bed. She went bareheaded, already stepping longer and holding her skirt, with both hands, up from the wetness of the knee-high root crops, and away from the waist-high grains. Her illness had squared and filled out her figure, deprived it of its virginal severity, and now the refinement that in-door life, suffering, and impaired health had given to her features

and skin, was yielding before fresh air, good food, vigorous action, and the habit of command. Only her straight glance, and erect carriage, that she had taken to town remained as the town was forgotten. The town could not take those from her, the country could only confirm them. Two officers' servants, who had let the charges they were leading graze surreptitiously on the rich second cut of the watermeadows by the little stream that issued from the moat, hastily pulled up the horses' heads, and resumed the road. She had made herself known to the new unit that morning, already.

In the dark passage she ran into a dragoon-like figure, that even her accustomed eyes mistook for the moment for that of a soldier. Then she saw who it was, swallowed a lump in the throat, and said:

"Hold, it is you, Placide, enter then, and be seated!"

"Ah, it is you, Madeleine, returned. How do you go on?"

"But well! and you? You can surely take a cup of coffee!"

"I shall not say no! One wants something to give courage in these times that are passing!"

Madeleine was busy over the coffee-pot, and only said: "Monsieur the Baron and Madame the Baronne have had a sad loss!"

Placide sighed like an eight-day clock running down, and then began. It took ten minutes for her to give her description of the reception of the news of Georges' death at the château—of Monsieur's fit of crying and swearing—of Madame's fainting and prayers. Madeleine stood before her, hands on hips, planted, resisting the sudden, unexpected agony of reviving grief. When Placide remembered what she had come for (eggs and anthracite) and had gone, accompanied by a Belgian with a barrow, Madeleine poured her untasted coffee carefully back into the pot, and slipped out by the back door and away over the fields.

In a few minutes she was mounting the steep sodden path to the Kruysabel. The sun was coming out, and all around the earth steamed. The hunting shelter, intact and not noticeably weathered, had yet an air of neglect. Grass grew where grass should not, the windows were dim with cobweb and fly-smut. The door stuck, and inside the air was warm and moldy. The photos stared at her, the guardian spirit of the place, as she moved from room to room, tried handles, dusted, rubbed, and shook things. The seats invited her, the mirrors showed her active restlessness. At last she stood still, and some spasm of acute realization seemed to gather and descend on her, and she wrung her hands. "What will become of it all?" she cried aloud. It, undefined, being the old happy easy life of pre-war. A great sob broke from her, and at its sound in that lonely place of memories, she pulled herself together, put away her things, and looked up. As

she trod the reeking moss and gluey mud on the way home, she seemed to be treading something down into the earth, as, alas, many another was to do, like her, throwing in vain a little mold of forgetfulness on the face of recollection that, buried, yet refused to die.

.

Day succeeded day, mostly wet, almost always noisy. The interminable offensive dragged to its sodden end. Unit succeeded unit, and then French succeeded English, and even the heroes of Verdun, Champagne, the Argonne had no good word to say of their new sector. Gas they knew, and shells and machine-gun fire, but to be Drowned was the last refinement of a war that had already surpassed all notions of possible evil, all tales of Sedan, all histories of old-time carnage.

All this made little or no impression upon Madeleine. The old life had slipped back upon her like a glove. German bombs dropped in or about the pasture, spoiled her sleep, made her apprehensive of fire and damage. Otherwise she merely learned from the talk around the kitchen stove that the war was just what she had always felt it to be—a crowning imbecility of insupportable grown-up children. All that one wanted was to be left tranquil. There was always plenty to do, and, if one were only left alone, money to be made. Economics, politics, sociology were beyond her, and had they not been so, they would have weighed with her no more than they ever have done with agricultural, self-contained, home-keeping three-quarters of France. That Germany was anxious for her young industries, England for her old ones, France for her language and racial existence, that governments grow naturally corrupt as milk gets sour, by mere effluxion of time, that captains of industry must be ruthless or perish, all this did not sway her mind. All one wanted was to be left tranquil. Tranquillity being denied, she did the best she could.

The officers who hired the front rooms, the men and animals billeted in the farm buildings, the N.C.O.'s, orderlies, what-not, might be dispirited, jumpy, no longer the easy-going confident English of other years, but they still bought what she had to sell, and paid for what they had—more rather than less, as the conscripted civilian, craving the comforts from which he had been torn, replaced the regular soldier or early volunteer, who had never known or had disdained them. She got a good deal of help with the harvest. The English had all sorts of stores, appliances, above all, plenty of willing arms, that she wanted. The troops "in rest" were glad enough for the most part, when off duty, to do any small job to take their minds off the

world-wide calamity that enveloped them, or that gave the momentary illusion of peace-time ease and freedom. Owing to the submarine campaign they were rather encouraged than otherwise. The harvest, though not magnificent, was fair, and the ever-rising scale of officially fixed prices left always a larger margin of profit. Thus "One does what one can!" was Madeleine's appropriate comment, when asked. Very little escaped her, as that murderous sodden autumn closed in.

.

It was about Christmas time that the bombardment of all the back areas, especially Hazebrouck, recommenced in earnest. It was the period at which the Germans regained the initiative. Madeleine noticed a fact like that. She noticed also the extraordinary thinning out of the troops. They either went forward into the line or far back, into rest, beyond St. Omer. But the headlines of the papers, the rumors her father brought home from the estaminet, moved her not one whit. The Russian revolution, the advent of America, the British and French man-power questions, Roumanian or Syrian affairs, all left her cold. She read of them in French and English impartially, with all the distrust of her sort for the printed word. It was not until she heard the Baron descant upon the situation, during a visit he paid her father, that she began to take any serious account of the way the war was trending. The Baron had been severely shaken by the death of his son. A view of life, which seldom went beyond personal comfort, had been vitally disconcerted by the final dispersal of one of its cherished comforts, the idea of a son to succeed to and prolong the enjoyment of life. He had the gloomiest forebodings, blamed Russians, Roumanians, English, Americans, Portuguese, Turks, Germans, in turn for the dark days certainly ahead. Madeleine listened with the tolerant submission proper from a chief tenant's daughter toward the master. When the Baron spoke of "my son," her just appreciation was never misled into thinking that he meant her lover. The two were distinct. She had her own bitter memories, black moods, tears even. That was her affair. The Baron's loss of his son was his, a different matter. She sympathized demurely. As for the news he brought, the probable German offensive in the spring, she made a rapid calculation, and dismissed the matter. Not good at imagining, she could not conceive of anything the Germans might do that she would not outwit. The crops and animals, she reckoned, could be stored in safety, the money and valuables she could trust herself to take care of; the solid old house and furniture she could not picture as suffering much damage. Of any personal fear for herself she felt no qualm. Except

for a few moments during her illness in Paris, she had known no physical terror since, an infant, she had ceased to be afraid of the dark, finding by experience that it did not touch her. She poured out the Baron's drink at her father's request, and let him talk.

Poor Baron, though Madeleine did not realize it, what else could he do? Born so that he was four years too young to take part in the war of 1870, he was now eight years too old to take part in that of 1914. He could only fight with his tongue, and that he did. But he was fundamentally unchanged, rallied Madeleine on the havoc her good looks must have wrought in Amiens and Paris. Madeleine smiled dutifully. To her he represented one of the guarantees of order and stability. Without an elaborate argument, she concluded that so long as there was a baron above her, and her father, there would be, at the other end of the social scale, laborers, refugees, all sorts of humble folk just as far beneath the level at which she and hers swam. It seemed just that those above and those below should be equally exploitable by the adroit farmer's daughter, anchored securely midway.

Spring came, the spring of 1918: surely the most tragically beautiful of all the springs the old world has seen! The frosts and darkness passed. Flowers came out in the Kruysabel. It was a busy time of mucking, plowing, rolling, sowing. Nothing happened. Hazebrouck, too much bombarded, ceased to hold its market. Madeleine went to Cassel instead. The news of the great German break-through on the Somme did not even impress her, she was busy preparing to get the main-crop potatoes in, before Easter. Let them fight on the Somme, so she might sow Flanders.

But three weeks later there did occur at length something to impress her. On the unforgettable 11th of April, 1918, the guns were very loud. On the 12th there were hurried movements of troops. All sorts of odd rumors came floating back from all points between Ypres and La Bassée. The Germans had broken through! The Germans had not broken through, but had been thrown back! Estaires was on fire! Locre was taken, and so on. Madeleine had occasion to go to the Mairie, to argue as to why her old Territorials should have been recalled from the farm, and found Monsieur Blanquart packing all his records into a great wooden case. He stopped and stared at her.

"What are you doing, Monsieur Blanquart?"

He raised his hands with unaccustomed nervousness.

"It is a formal order from the Government!"

He would not listen to her tale of billeting money unpaid, and

government fertilizer not delivered: "There are other things to do at this moment," was all he would say. For once Madeleine did not get her way. That impressed her. The next day the horizon to the south and east was black with pillars of smoke. By night these became pillars of flame, biblical, ominous. The incessant sounds of battle changed in timbre. The heavy bombardment ceased. Nearer and nearer crept the rattle of machine guns. Madeleine had one or two errands, and returning by the village shortly afterwards, was astonished to find all the shops shut. Vanhove, the butcher, was loading his best brass bedstead and mattress on to—what of all conceivable vehicles? Madeleine stared before she took it in. It was the roller, the road roller. None other. The well-known road roller the English had installed. Built by Aveling & Porter at Rochester in the 'eighties, it had ground and panted its unwieldy frame northward through many a township and village of England, passing from hand to ever poorer hand, as it deteriorated, until finally the obscure and almost penniless Rural District Council of Marsham and Little Uttersfield, failing to sell it, had painted their name on its boiler and kept it. Unloaded, like so many other derelicts, into the arms of the British Expeditionary Force in the glad enthusiasm of 1915, it had served the turn of an intelligent English Engineer, who, early in the war, had discovered that roads and railways, food and patience alone could win in such a struggle. He had soon been shipped off to the East, lest he bring shame upon his betters, but his roller had remained for years now, on that section of the Joint Road Control of the Second English Army, with the French Ponts et Chaussées Authority, who divided acrimoniously between them the control of the Hazebrouck sub-area. The machine had become a portent in Hondebecq. The children had swung behind it, horses ceased to shy at it, and Madeleine herself had come, in time, to have something almost like affection for it, as a monument of the queer, wayward genius of the English. No such rollers ever rolled the roads of France, but Madeleine had found it useful for both rolling and traction. She had made friends with the two middle-aged, sooty-khakied Derbyshire men who lived with it and got them to do jobs for her. Now she laid a hand gingerly on the warm shining rail of the "cab" and asked of the driver:

"What are you doing!"

"Got to go, Mamzelle, partee, you know!"

"You like a ride, miss? Get up and we'll take you as far as St. Omer!" his mate added. "Alleman's coming, you know!"

Something fierce prompted Madeleine to say: "I'm not going to run away!" But Vanhove, having hoisted his bedstead into the tender, was persuading the men to drive on.

Madeleine saw the lever put over, and the ponderous machine of another generation roar away upon the cobbles, its single cylinder panting desperately. Then she felt indeed disturbed, as though she had been forced to part with a conviction.

.

As she went back to the farm through the fairy beauty of the evening—(were ever evenings so beautiful as those of the April retreat?)—her step was no less firm, her glance as calm, as usual. Passing over the plank bridge, and entering the house by the back, she was confronted by the spectacle of Berthe in her best hat, with a bundle.

"I'm going!" said the apparition simply.

"What has come over you?"

"After you were gone, an English wagon came, all full of people from Armentières way. The secretary of Nieppe told the patron that the Bosche are in Laventie, and that Marie has left, so the Patron has taken the tumbril and gone after her potatoes!"

Madeleine was at no loss. She even approved the old man's determination. Only she considered that it would have been better for her to go.

"You stay here," she said. "I'm going up to the château to borrow the young Baron's bicycle!" She knew well enough that Georges' machine was stowed away in the coachhouse. On that she could catch her father, and send him back. But she had not reckoned up the situation.

"No," said Berthe, "I'm going!"

"Why, you're not frightened like that silly lot from Armentières?"

But the terror-stricken faces and bandaged heads of those civilians in the lorry, who had so narrowly escaped the battle, had broken Berthe's nerve—which was never the equal of Madeleine's. She shouldered her bundle.

"I'm going!" she said simply.

Madeleine was not accustomed to being disobeyed, and there is no knowing what she might not have done had she not been in a hurry herself.

"Very well, go then! Tell the Picquart family to lock up the sheds. I'm going after the patron!"

"The Picquarts are gone, this half-hour, with their things in the wheelbarrow!"

Just then the breeze that stirs at dusk blew open the door, and there entered into the darkening passage with startling nearness the rat-tat-tat-tat-tat of German machine guns. Madeleine flung away: "Go and

burst yourselves as quick as possible, heap of dirtiness!" she cried, and set off at a run for the château.

The village seemed even more ominous than before, now it was half dark, and not a light in the abandoned houses. Some English transport was crossing the square, however, with the patient sour look of men going "into it" again—"it," the battle. She turned into the steep silent alley that led through the iron grille, to the "drive" of the château, and broke into a run again on the smooth gravel. She had not gone twenty yards before she jumped as if shot. A black figure had risen behind the trunk of a tree with a sharp "Hish!" She fell sideways, clutching an elm sapling that bent with her, staring. The figure made two steps towards her, and she, petrified, could only maintain her balance and stare. Then with infinite relief she heard: "Tiens, it's you, Madeleine! What do you want?"

"Why, Monsieur le Baron, I didn't know you!"

"Be quiet then. There is some one wandering round the château. It may be the Bosche!"

"What, are they here?"

"The village has been formally evacuated. One expects them from one moment to another!"

At that instant steps and voices could be heard on the terrace surrounding the house, which, on account of the winding of the drive by way of the old moat, was just above the level of their eyes. The Baron, quivering all over, not with fear, but with sporting instinct, brought his spiked camp stool to the charge, and tiptoed noiselessly up the bank. Madeleine, clutching her skirt with one hand, swinging herself up by the undergrowth with the other, arrived beside him just in time to see two familiar Australian figures looming leisurely in the darkness. In another instant the Baron would have sprung, with no one knows what results. Madeleine pushed past him, stepped over the flower-bed that bordered the terrace, and walked up to the visitors, addressing them in their own inimitable language, learned from their own lips in the kitchen of the Spanish Farm:

"Hello, Digger, what you want?"

The tall lean men turned without surprise:

"To get in," replied the nearer.

Madeleine hastily translated. The Baron, after staring a moment, led the way to the back.

The château possessed, of course, no bell or knocker, as Leon, the concierge, or his wife, were always to be found near the gate, to steer front-door visitors round to their appropriate entrance, and open for them. Lesser mortals came to the kitchen door, where Placide dealt with them as St. Peter is reported to deal with ambitious souls in

another place. Since the war, and more especially since the concierge and all his family had been evacuated, the whole of the windows and doors were closed, bolted and shuttered.

The first object that met the gaze of the little party, as they rounded the corner of the building, was Leon's garden ladder, reared against the window of the Baron's dressing-room, in the eastern wing, from which protruded the hindquarters and legs of a man, in stout service riding breeches and dirty boots.

"Thunder of God," cried the Baron, seizing the ladder and shaking it violently, "come down, or I'll bring you!"

An Australian added quietly, "You'd best come down, Mercadet, and tell Jim!"

A few hurried calls in Franco-English and laconic Australian replies, and a French interpreter climbed, an Australian soldier slid, down the ladder.

"Well, sir," demanded the Baron of the former, "you have large views of your duties!"

"Sir," replied the interpreter, "the place is officially evacuated. We have a right here. You have not!"

"I have said I will not budge," replied the Baron, folding his arms, "and budge I will not!"

"Monsieur le Baron," interposed Madeleine, "all these will be very useful if the Bosche come!"

The Baron strode to the heavy kitchen door and struck a succession of blows with his stick, shouting at the top of his voice, "Placide, open then, you are as lazy as stupid!"

Very shortly a light glimmered and the bolts shot back. The door turned, and Placide barred the way, as an old-fashioned clothes-horse covers a blazing fire. It took her a moment or two to understand.

"Ah, it is you, Monsieur le Baron!"

"Did you think it was the devil?"

"I was upstairs seeing to the calorifère of Madame, who is in the chapel. I thought you were gone to the village!"

Her master pushed past. "Here are officers come to billet. Are the rooms ready?"

He had, of course, assumed that none but officers would dream of coming to the château of Hondebecq.

Madeleine, by the light of Placide's candle, soon knew better. The Australian who had spoken was a Colonel, the other two and the French interpreter were privates. As they trooped into the passage, the Colonel called over his shoulder, "Come on, boys!"

From the kitchen garden, where they had sat silent and unnoticed spectators of the scene, there emerged a Lewis-gun section and order-

lies. Beyond them transport was dimly visible: mules silent as their drivers, standing as if cut in stone.

"Madeleine," called the Baron, "explain to these gentlemen that all my servants have run off, but that Placide will serve supper as soon as may be!"

The Colonel, however, was busy with his machine gunners. The "cubby hutch," as he called Leon's potting shed, half-way up the drive would do for one position well, but he wished to command the garden and meadow beyond, and the fields skirting the village on that side. Madeleine understood perfectly. "There is the cellar skylight, level with the ground."

The Colonel went to look. "It fits like the tail of Barnes' donkey!" was his only comment.

Before he would sit down to his meal he asked: "Do I get the old man right, that his wife is here still?"

"She is praying for her son in the chapel!"

"Is he wounded?"

"He is dead."

"He'll be just as happy if she keeps alive. I've got a limber going back St. Omer way. She'd better go in that! Tell 'em!"

Madeleine explained the offer to the Baron, who thanked the Colonel profusely, saying that it was worthy of one gentleman to another.

The Colonel not understanding, when his mouth was empty, bowed as one unaccustomed and inquired: "It is his wife, isn't it, all correct?"

Madeleine confirmed that the Baroness was "all correct."

But the Baroness was an obstacle. First Placide, then the Baron himself went up to see her. She would only moan: "No, let them kill me, I shall see him again all the sooner. Besides, it is too late, and I am at least warm with the calorifère!"

Then Madeleine went up. There was nothing dramatic in the meeting between those two, the mother and the mistress of a dead man. Madeleine said steadily: "Madame, Monsieur Georges would prefer you to go!"

"You think so?"

"I am sure, madame!"

"In that case, I will!"

Madeleine helped her. But no one, unless it was the French interpreter, realized the pathos of the moment. The limber had been furnished with cushions, a small trunk, and a wooden box of Placide's. The driver had announced that he was "going by the dirt roads, it's easier for wimmen." Then that faded lady kissed the man whom she

had married because the Second Empire told her to, and replied to his "Courage, Eugènie," simply: "I think I shall not catch cold!" and went away in an army limber, with Placide stalking behind.

.

Madeleine watched them go. Alone of all those present she, perhaps, noticed the change which seemed to settle down on the house, almost at once. It was not yet abandoned, but its women, its natural guardians, had gone from it.

The orderly, ration "fag" in mouth, cleared the table with a clatter, spilling grease on the floor. The marble overmantel, between the vases a former D'Archeville had brought from the sack of Pekin, and the Sèvres clock, became, as though by magic, littered with pipes, ashes, revolver ammunition, maps, indelible pencils—all the flotsam of men campaigning far from the decencies of property and housewifery. She tried to get the Baron on one side, having not for a moment forgotten her business at the château, but he was busy giving the Colonel, and a young officer who had come quietly in, as if by chance, some detail of the district. Before she could make her wants known, the Colonel, who had swept back the cloth, silver salts, plates, flower vases, all at one sweep, planted his 1 in 40,000 army map, and had his finger on the square pasture, and centerless E of building labeled "Ferme l'Éspagnole"—the Spanish Farm.

"That belongs to mademoiselle," the interpreter interposed, prompted by the Baron, indicating her.

"Arthur," said the Colonel to the young officer, "your platoon can make a 'strong point' there, where the roads join, and sleep in the house, while it's worth it!"

In an instant, Madeleine relinquished all thoughts of pursuing her father on the Baron's bicycle. It was not merely that if she had had to choose between loyalty to her father and loyalty to the home, she would have chosen the latter. It was also that, had her father been there to counsel her, he would certainly have said, "Garde la maison, ma fille!" "Stick to the house, my girl."

"I'll go with you," she told the lieutenant, and went out into the darkness with him.

The horizon, from beyond Ypres, to the northeast, right round to near Béthune to the south, was ablaze. Over captured Merville, Estaires, Armentières, hung floating lights. The bombardment had ceased, the Bosche being too fearful of hitting their own advanced parties. The machine gun clamor was subsiding, both sides no longer knowing in the darkness where their bullets went. The farm Madeleine found already occupied. Tall lean figures, magnified in the candle-

light, had stripped lengths of fabric from an aeroplane that had come down in the pasture, and lay half buried, grotesquely mangled, a putrefying mass of charred human flesh, wood and delicate machinery in the middle. They were covering every crevice in the kitchen windows. They made shelters, and gun-pits, and loopholes. By midnight the house was no longer a farm, it was a tactical "strong point." Madeleine had too much sense to protest, and declined firmly to be evacuated. Calling the officer and sergeant together, she pointed to her door:

"This my room. I lock the door. See, diggers?"

"All serene, missy, sleep well," was the reply.

Madeleine did so. Like all those strong enough to stand it, she felt a kind of exaltation rising above any fear. Many a man felt like her that night. The long-distance bombardment, under which a human being was matched against a lump of steel as large and many times harder than himself, was over. To it succeeded the direct struggle of man against man, with machine gun, rifle and grenade. The Bosche were no longer awe-inspiring once they got beyond the range of their big guns. Let them come, the sooner the better. The great offensive had been threatened for months. It was here. Some would survive it. Meantime the chances were even. Madeleine slept.

.

No one knows, to this day, why the Bosche never got to Hondebecq, but they halted a mile short of it. Nothing happened. Anticlimax ruled. War moods of exaltation, begotten of danger, and the vitality that rises to meet it, cannot last. The battle of Bailleul dwindled out in gray, cold spring weather. The trench line stiffened and became as fixed as the old line from the Ypres salient to La Bassée had been, before Messines and Paschendaele. The Bosche tried again and again farther south with no more effect. In the north the reorganized English line held good. The mood which came with this new state of things began to show itself, in civilians and soldiers alike, to be one of steady exasperation. For what did all this endless effort amount to? One lived in a state not comparable to that of Peace, as regards comfort, business, or personal liberty. One side or the other made an offensive. The discomfort increased, the hectic war-time business was dislocated, personal liberty disappeared. But one thing remained—War. Enormously expensive, omnipresent, exasperating. Civilians and soldiers, the latter nearly all unwilling civilians now, felt its exasperation. Madeleine felt it. The Baron felt it. The troops billeted in the château and the farm felt it. The Baron, relieved from his wife's querulous exactions, Madeleine, set free

from dutiful if doubtful belief in her father's methods of business, found the first Australian troops, if not charming visitors, at least good companions for the work in hand.

When it became certain that the enemy could get no farther, they were relieved, first by French troops, then by a Clydeside labor battalion. The Baron found his salle-à-manger filled with officers, who, though not actively ill-behaved, and probably well-meaning, he could see, whether he spoke their language or not, came of no particular family.

Madeleine found herself confronted with a set of cooks and quarter-masters as businesslike as herself, far more akin to her in methods and outlook than had ever been the original volunteer army of England—who had paid what she asked with shy good humor. The neat walks and formal "bosquets" of the château garden, box-hedged, and decorated with plaster figures of nymphs and cupids, situate amid greenish pools, became pitted with latrines, and scarred with dugouts.

The village was beyond bullet range, but a 5.9 shell crashed in the top of the "shot" tower in the yard of the Spanish Farm. But worse than these evils were the continual thefts from the cellar of the château of wine, coal, and mattresses (for half the village had readily obtained leave to store their possessions there). At the farm, Madeleine was amazed to find herself forced to sell beer and butter, at less than cost price, by well-organized "strikes" that threatened to leave her merchandise on her hands.

The Baron, moreover, like so many of his age and nation at that time, had his private sorrow. Sharing his meals with the ever-changing messes of officers that filled his salle-à-manger (for the village being evacuated, there were no shops, and he was glad enough to trade away the accommodation he could provide for food), he would stare round the youthful, unwarlike faces about him, faces of professional or business men, farmers or engineers from all corners of Great Britain or the Colonies, and would mutter, "I have no longer my son!"

Madeleine, more self-controlled, wore black. No funeral service had been said for Jerome Vanderlynden. He had "disappeared" in the trite phrase of the Casualty Lists. The old church in the "place" of Hondebecq had three gaping shell-holes in the roof. The doors were closed, and it was declared in brief official notice "Unsafe." She did not even know if her numerous cousins and relations by marriage, scattered by the evacuation all across France from Evreux to Bordeaux, had heard what had happened to him. Nor did the thought of them greatly trouble her, accustomed to think and act for herself. She was doing what she knew so well her father was expecting of her. She was looking after the farm. The crops were sown. Such beasts as remained

were tended. Jerome Vanderlynden had disappeared! That could not be helped, any more than the thefts of all the fowls from the yard. Madeleine just went on.

.

The days went by, and the two civilians left in Hondebecq hardly noticed a change that came over things in the last week of July, 1918. That war, continuing year in and year out, could not be measured according to its "victories" of one side or the other, by people so intensely intimate with it, because they lived on the edge of the trenches. The most perhaps that they noticed was the gradual cessation of the shelling. It was no longer necessary to run to dugouts from one's bed at dawn, or from one's evening meal. Yet, at last, something really had happened. Madeleine was dimly conscious of a new atmosphere in the shuttered and sand-bagged salle-à-manger, when she went up on one of her usual errands to the château. The old interpreter, Mercadet, attached to the area, was sticking flags in the map of the Western Front, with his melancholy precision. "One has still some force left!" he announced, and Madeleine saw without heeding that he was *moving the flags forward, instead of back*. It was, of course, Mangin's flank attack of July, the turning-point of the war. She paid more attention, however, a week or two later, when the troops in the farm began to move. The Bosche were gone from Kemmel Hill, was all they said. She lost touch with the war at this point, having no one to give her news.

She contrived to secure a couple of mules she found wandering about, and being handy with animals, shut them up and fed them sparingly. Probably nothing in the whole war frightened her so much as those weeks of the month of September, when she was quite alone. Even the dog had been killed by the shell on the "shot" tower. Then, as the troops abandoned the château she found there a couple of aged veterans, left as billet wardens, and induced them, by pointing out truthfully how much better they would fare with her than in the Baron's company in the lonely château, to move to the farm. These two old casual laborers, who had enlisted in 1914 when drunk or workless, and had ever since been living better than before the war, made no difficulties. But it was no object to her to make hardships for the Baron, once she had gained her point, and secured potential guardians and laborers for the farm. She invited him to take his meals with her, and neither laughed nor chided as he stumped off, cigar glowing in the dark, to sleep on the moth-eaten rugs in his gun-room, revolver beside him, lest the château should be robbed—though what indeed there remained to steal in the darkened rooms, save the heavy

furniture, no one could have said—wine, food, bedding, small objects had gone one by one, for use, or as souvenirs. The silver had been buried by Mercadet in the garden. But the Baron slept in the empty château, by instinct.

He was not alone long.

There was an almost dramatic fitness about the Army's choice of his one companion. A red-headed Welshman, answering to the name of Jacobs, was posted there, as District Sanitary Engineer. The glamor and intensity was gone from the war, and the situation was now one for Municipal Health Officers. The appointment was additionally fitting. For though adorned by the title of "doctor," and adorning the rank of Captain, Jacobs was by profession a Borough Sanitary Engineer, one of those species peculiar to Great Britain. In its dying stages, those who ran the war were at last learning to put men to the job they could do best.

.

Such was the situation of what the French staff aptly called the "open town" of Hondebecq in the last weeks of the war. By daylight, the Spanish Farm was at work, Madeleine and her two veterans, with the two mules, getting in all the undamaged crops—for nearly a quarter of the total acreage of the farm was lost in trench and wire, dugout and shell-hole. Hardly a day passed but had its hair-breadth escape from buried "duds" or unexploded shell, or caved-in gun-pit. Madeleine worked because it was natural to her—because she had nothing else to do, possibly with some unconscious idea of dedication to her father's memory. At dusk, Jacobs and the Baron would arrive, on bicycles, the one having toured his area, which stretched from the line of evacuation that ran from the Belgian border, through Hazebrouck down to Aire—away to the maze of desultory trenches from which the English troops were slowly pushing the last German machine gunners. The Baron usually acted as his guide, and in Jacobs' company avoided otherwise certain arrest. Madeleine would just be finishing her evening meal with the veterans. Jacobs would produce a field message book in which he had noted the map reference of any unburied offence, human or otherwise, and at his order the old men would jog off with one of the tireless mules in a salvaged limber, two shovels, a tin of disinfectant, and a lantern clattering in the springless vehicle. Madeleine cleared the table and served dinner to Jacobs and the Baron, who would sit over it, drinking canteen whisky and discussing in English-French and French-English the submarine menace and surface drainage, by means of any daily papers they had gleaned during the day's wandering, and with the help of Made-

leine's translation. By the time both were ready to return to their never-made "beds" in the château, the veterans would come clattering back, the mules going at an unearthly amble in the darkness, and all was ready for the morrow.

.

The War had been full of surprises—had been one great catastrophic surprise, since its declaration, and had kept up its pyrotechnic suddenness of change through all its four years. But the change that extinguished it outdid all else in strangeness. Late in October, the inhabitants of the château and the farm had heard the familiar sound of twelve-inch shells falling in Dunkirk, and never dreamed that they were never to hear that sound again. All day the roads and rail had been busy with French and English troops. They had halted in and around Hondebecq and passed on. The inhabitants of the farm and the château little dreamed that no more were to pass that way. The days and nights became quieter and ever more strangely quiet. There was a continual tension of the ear to catch that familiar rat-tat-tat, swish, boom. No sound came. Then, early in gray November, Jacobs and the Baron returned earlier than usual from their eternal cycling tour. In all the cellars of Hazebrouck, in all the hastily contrived, already-forgotten "strong points" in the area, they had not found one unburied mule, one neglected latrine. Or Jacobs had forgotten to take map references, for both were excited. Instead, they bent over a day-old English paper, that pretended to have the terms of the Armistice.

At first it was mere meaningless words. Nothing happened. The daily life of Hondebecq did not change. But soon a phenomenon was observed. Up the solid gray pavé road that Napoleon built from Lille to Dunkirk, along which the victorious armies of mid-October had advanced, there flowed, in the opposite direction, another human stream. No army this, and nothing victorious about it, though here and there a dirty old hat, or wonderfully made, decrepit wheelbarrow was decorated with the flags of the Allies, bought from Germans who had been selling them during the last weeks in the French industrial area. By one and two, here a family, there an individual with a dog, all those civilians who had been swept within the German lines in the offensives of 1914 or 1918, were walking home. Such a homecoming surely never was since misery began. Doré used to picture such events in his illustrations to the Bible, but no one has even seen the like in reality. For censors had been strict, and the line of trenches where the Allies had fronted the Germans unpassable. Many a man of the Flemish border, or the Somme downs, had hoped to find his

house or his field spared, and had to go to look himself in order to be finally disillusioned. Madeleine, superintending the cleaning of the fields, the weed burning, and autumn plowing, saw them come incuriously, not able to realize that even she, who had seen the whole War through, with the trenches only just beyond the sight of her eyes and never out of her hearing, had only now to begin to learn what it really had been.

She left the veterans and the mules, busy in the fields, and stood, for a few moments, on the edge of the pavé, where the by-road to the farm left it, watching the melancholy procession. True, some were laughing, or greeted her with a cheer, but the general impression of those pinched faces and anxious eyes, above worn and filthy clothes, gave a better idea than any historian will ever do, of the rigors of the blockade. Madeleine gained from the sight just her first inkling of the irreparable loss, that was to weigh upon the lifetime of her generation. War, the Leviathan, was giving up that which it had swallowed, but there was no biblical jubilation in them, none of those sharp terrors that, in scripture, foretell everlasting joy. Madeleine, better than any Bible-reading Protestant, comprehended. These poor souls (as she called them to herself, pityingly, for they had been "caught out," a defect she did not admit) had now got to work to catch up the wastage. A bright chance for most of them!

She returned to the farm, and now, finally convinced of the Armistice, yoked the mules to the strongest tackle she could find amid the abandoned and salvaged engineer stores that Jacobs had gathered, and began to pull away the barbed wire that laced the farm about, fifty yards at a time.

· · · · · · ·

She worked thus with the veterans, beating, shouting at, jerking the mouths of the mules, tugging, cutting, coiling the rusted venomous strands, piling the stout pickets on one side for further use, until it was nearly dark. Hastening home to prepare supper she noticed a dark bent figure standing irresolutely in the courtyard. She was walking over the slippery furrows by aid of a half pick-handle, but, though thus armed, was unafraid, and found something unaccountably familiar in that listless bent-shouldered form. Coming up to it, she gave a cry. It was the ghost of Jerome Vanderlynden. She took him by the hand, called him "Father," told him with a choke in her voice that she was glad to see him back. He just stared at her, but when spoken to with decision, sat in the settle by the stove, and smiled at the warmth and the smell of food. Other sign of animation he would not give, nor could she elicit what he thought, or how he had found

his way home. When her veterans came in from the stable, she introduced him, and they displayed all the kindliness of their sort, seemed to understand at a glance the nature of the case, called him "Poor old gentleman" and offered him a ration cigarette, which he took, and immediately laid aside, as if he did not know its use. He appeared better for the food and rest, and was willing to be led to the bare tiled bedroom in which he had always occupied the crazy old double bed, where his children had been born and his wife had died, and which, with the big old press, two pegs, and two photos of the children, constituted the whole furniture. He allowed Madeleine to help him off with his sodden, shapeless boots, rolled on the bed, and slept. Madeleine covered him and left him. In the morning he appeared, awakened apparently by habit, or the smell of food, but replied only by vacant looks to his daughter's questions—pertinently designed as they were—"What has happened to the horse and tumbril?" "Where have you been?" "Do you remember me?"

To the blandishments of the veterans (well-meant attempts to cheer him up), he paid no regard. It was not Jerome Vanderlynden who had returned. It was his ghost, something that, having lost its human mortal life, could not quite die, but must wander about the scenes to which it was accustomed, handle the objects it had used, but nothing more.

.

The condition of her father might have weighed heavily on Madeleine's mind had it been her only preoccupation, but fortunately it was not. First of all there was work. She was working harder than anybody ever works in England. From before the gray wet winter dawn, until long after the solitary army candle had been lighted in the kitchen, making grotesque shadows in the broken glass of the oriel window, her hands were never still, tugging, smoothing, shifting earth, timber, wire, weeds, produce; housework, cooking, mending, were relaxations. Her mind and voice, thinking for and directing the veterans, the mules, presently the four bullocks and two milch cows, she contrived to obtain from those wandering loose after the break-up of the trench lines, were never still except during the six or so hours that she slept. She regarded the Armistice as a piece of personal good luck. She would get the ground into some sort of order before the spring sowing. There would be manure, too, now that she had beasts, and with manure at hand, no Fleming ever quite loses heart. But besides work, the Peace that had so suddenly descended upon earth (without, alas, bringing that Goodwill supposed for centuries to accompany it) proved itself more inexorable than War.

Things began to move, released from the numbing strangulation of four and a quarter years. Jacobs and the veterans got orders to proceed to Courtrai, and continue the good work of cleansing the ornamental waters of that town from the use to which the German officers had put them. This disturbance of her source of labor gave Madeleine some moments' thought, but the sight of the Dequidt family, trudging back to their farm on foot, having been returned from evacuation in the Cherbourg district, opened up a new means of dealing with the problem. Her farm was nearly in order, her house more or less intact, her larder stocked with the good tinned stuff of the British Expeditionary Force Canteen. Theirs would not be so. She would give of her ample store, in return for work. There was one duty with which, however, she preferred to trust the two veterans, rather than any of her neighbors. Now that they were going, she thought of them in the terms in which she had once thought of a lieutenant called Skene. They were willing and well behaved. Moreover, they were going back to England (indicated by their saying to her, "What Ho, for Blighty," many times a day), so that they were safe. With smiles and encouraging words she led them to the foot of the shot tower. It was badly cracked by the shell that had hit the top, and great lumps of brickwork, a yard cube, had fallen, blocking the door; elm beams a foot square lay jammed across the broken floor. It took three hours' hard work to effect an entrance. Then Madeleine kneeled down, put her arms through the broken boards, and fished up a length of stout iron chain. "Pull," she commanded, handing it over. The veterans, spitting on their hands, and setting their heels against the cobbles, called "Heave-ho!" as the chain emerged link by link. Finally, with a clatter and smash, a great iron box was retrieved. Madeleine unhooked it from the chain and bade them carry it to the house.

Once she had it on the kitchen table, having wiped the worst of the muddy water from it, and assured herself it was intact, she gave a sigh of relief. It was the savings of her father's lifetime, that had been withdrawn from the Savings Bank, when Hazebrouck was first bombarded, and hidden thus by her. Seeing it before her, Madeleine made what the French call a "gesture"—one of those actions prompted by emotions deeper than reason—in this case by the only genuine feeling at the base of the otherwise politician-manufactured Entente Cordiale. She had found the English friends in need, not too exacting, fairly ready to pay for what they wanted. They had been a comfort at the beginning of, through the long length of, and now at the daily growing aftermath of disillusionment with, the War. She took two notes, 20 francs each, from her purse, and distributed them to the

veterans. Those members of England's Last Hope pocketed the money, exclaiming with one voice, "Thank you, Maddam," winking solemnly at each other.

That evening Jacobs took his leave, and she charged him for exactly what he had had. He departed into the darkness, to catch the newly established train service over the hastily repaired line, the veterans wheeling his valise and their own packs on a salved Lewis-gun hand cart.

· · · · · · · ·

With the departure of that party the British Army in Flanders finally left the Spanish Farm, after four years. The longed-for golden reign of Peace was re-established. And anything less golden cannot be imagined. Madeleine lost no time in getting into touch with the evacuated neighbors now returning to their farms. They were nearly all women, and though they were willing enough to work, they had neither the dexterity nor the resources of the British Army. Madeleine wished indeed, before many weeks were over, that the War had lasted longer. There was the big kitchen window, not to mention sundry other panes broken by carelessness, or by concussion of bombing and shelling, to be reglazed. There were leaks in the roof to mend, there was the shot tower to rebuild—unless indeed she built some other stowage room for all the things it used to hold—sacks, "fertilizer," tools, roots, grain, hops, spare cart covers, timber. There were nineteen gates missing, endless lengths of hedge and ditch practically to be made over again. The hurdles were all gone, and worst of all, the great fifteen-feet hop-poles and stout wire. As was usual throughout French Flanders, the British Army had burned every piece of wood upon the farm. Madeleine did not blame them. A French or any other army would have done the same. There was, however, one good job that the War had done: the tall elms round the pasture had been completely barked by the numerous mounted units that had succeeded each other. They would die, and the proprietor (the Baron, to wit) would do well to sell them at once, while the price was so high. The ground would be disencumbered, more grass would grow and the great roots would no longer suck up all the manure one put down. The only loser would be the Baron. It was his affair.

· · · · · · · ·

For already Peace had brought that endless attempt to go one better than one's neighbor, which, for four years, had been hidden under the more immediate necessity to go one better than the Bosche. Thus Madeleine, perceiving that whatever the eventual scheme of

compensation, she must pay, in the first instance, nearly all the loss occasioned, began actually to grudge the English their demobilization. Had they (and their dumps of material) remained in the neighborhood, she would have got them to do plumbing and glazing, ditching and joinery, and to give her good telephone wire, aeroplane canvas, oil, paint and nails. Instead of which, every day that she went as far as the Lille road, she saw trainloads of useful English, singing and cheering on their way to Dunkirk, where they were being demobbed by thousands a day. So she grew bitter, and having no one else to blame (for who could blame old Jerome, wandering helpless like a worn-out horse) she began to blame the English for going away. Madame la Baronne had returned to the château. Placide was once more functioning, and the Baron was only seen at the farm on his walks, as before the offensive of 1918. So that there was absolutely no one but the English to blame for having departed so inopportunely. There was nothing exceptional in Madeleine's case. It was, indeed, the common feeling in all those French and Flemish farms on the border of what had been the trenches (the frontiers of civilization) and was now the Devastated Area (something no one wanted, and everybody was tired of hearing about). This being so, the Government, depending upon votes, saw that something must be done to retain those sources of its power and emoluments, less they be filched by Bolsheviks, Germans, Socialists or other enemies—in fact by persons who might come to wield the power, and enjoy the resulting advantages, which every government looks upon as the permanent reward of the endless corruption by which it has maintained itself in power.

Thus, about this time, Madeleine began to hear of things called "Reparations," that the Germans were going to be made to pay. She was invited to inscribe at the Mairie the list of damage done by the War to the farm. She went to see Monsieur Blanquart, and furnished him with a list that totaled 131,415 francs 41 centimes (the total market value of the farm in 1914 being about 120,000 francs). Monsieur Blanquart inscribed the lot. He did more. Like every one else, he felt that he had had an atrocious time for many years, and that nothing was too good for him. Keeping in close touch with his daughter Cécile, at Amiens, he had been quite sharp enough to see how things were shaping. He had hung in the windows of his little parlor, and all round the mayoral office at the Estaminet de la Mairie, in place of the patriotic appeals by M. Deschanel to fortitude and patience, in place of lists of conscripts, and of ever-mounting food prices, little cards inscribed "Blanquart, financial agent"; "Blanquart, bonds, shares, assurances." He unfolded golden schemes to Madeleine, who listened with her special "stupid peasant" expression that she

kept for the occasions when she was thinking hard. Her list of war
damages was based not so much on facts and figures as on her one
idea of any monetary transaction—namely, to ask twice as much as a
thing is worth, in the certainty that you will be beaten down by at
least a quarter. She was no more deceived by the talk in the papers
than by Blanquart's "financial operations." She knew how difficult it
was for her to part with money or money's worth, and judged the
Germans, and Blanquart's stocks and shares, by her own standards.
Pay! Not likely, Germans or Royal Dutch, not if they could help it.
But standing hatless and vacant-faced before Blanquart, she was
working out in her mind one of her slowly conceived plans, so much
less simple than one would have supposed from her appearance.
She had enough cash in the iron box to buy two horses and get along
until harvest.

"Look here, Monsieur Blanquart, I'll take 50,000 francs' worth of
your bonds, and pay you when I get my 'Reparations.'"

But Blanquart had not lived in the village all those years for
nothing. "You comprehend," he replied, "your reparations are subject
to discussion!"

"No doubt; but I suppose one will pay us something!"

"Undoubtedly, but how much?—That's the point!"

Madeleine got up and moved toward the door. "Oh, well, it's
a pity!" she said.

Blanquart hated to see her go. She was one of the richest "heiresses"
in the village (as heiresses go in France), and there was only Marie
to divide it with her when old Jerome died. Moreover, she had quite
a reputation for the part she had played in the last phases of the
War, and it would be a great help to be able to say to the others:
"Madeleine Vanderlynden has taken 50,000." He offered: "Look here,
I'll buy your reparations for 40,000!"

"No, nothing to be done," was the answer, hand on the latch.

In his heart Monsieur Blanquart pested the sacred peasants. But
something must be arranged. "Very well, I sell you 40,000 worth of
securities, and you can pay me when you get your 'Reparations'!"

Madeleine left the doorway and came back to the table. Looking
through his stocked portfolio she chose only bearer bonds (coupons
appealed to her; the less tangible dividend warrant or inscribed or
registered stock did not), some national, some industrial, some lottery.
Thus armed, she returned to the farm.

.

Thus came what Politicians called "Peace," but mostly French
people, realists in a sense that the English public never is, spoke of

it as the "era of La Galette"—the cake which one could eat and yet have again, the pie in which every one's finger might be—the lucky-bag into which all might dip.

Upon the mentality of France, with its dominant peasant outlook, only one deep impression was made. The Germans were beaten. Therefore their money could be got at. Anyone who did not get at it was a fool, simply. This was not piracy. The Germans had invited a contest, and lost. The loser pays—that is logic as well as human nature. When the first hints were dropped that there might be delays, even a dwindling of the golden stream that was to flow from Berlin—public feeling became so strong that Government had hastily to vote sums "on account of" the Reparations to be exacted. In every village, men, and more often women, asked each other: "What have you estimated your damages at?" "What have you received on account?" In place of the War-time watchwords "La Patrie est en danger" and "On les aura," there might very reasonably have been displayed another: "La Galette"—The Cake that every one might take. "L'assiette au beurre"—The butter-dish to grease every itching palm. "Le pot au vin"—The loving-cup that was ever full.

.

Before she could put the War finally away from her, Madeleine had to go through a process which might be called in English, the laying of ghosts. Without active belief in the supernatural, and prone to laughter at those who dared not pass the Kruysabel, after dusk, without crossing themselves (this superstition was one of the safeguards that had kept her meetings with Georges secure), she preserved to the full the clear feeling of all primitives, that the Living are connected with, influenced by, the Departed. The most immediate case was that of her father. Jerome Vanderlynden had never recovered his reason, but had recaptured a few words, and most of his bodily functions. What had been done, or not done, to him, during his eight months behind the German lines, will never be known. A neighbor, also swallowed up by the swift invasion of April, 1918, had seen him, near Lille, working in a field, under German direction, but had not been recognized. At that date, even, the old man had lost his senses. He bore no particular signs of ill-usage, other than the common starvation caused by blockade, and, after weeks of loving care, Madeleine, nearest to him, most like him of all people on earth, managed to make out what he mumbled to himself, with that scared look, when his food was set before him: "There's nothing left to eat!" he whispered, with a frightened glance around. Then, when coaxed, he would eat, rapidly, defensively.

Madeleine, no theorist, came to the conclusion that the fact that he had been interrupted in the middle of sowing his potatoes, and had then found the stock of food at Marie's farm destroyed or taken, had unhinged his mind. At that she had to leave it, and although the old man's iron health did not vary, she had sorrowfully to admit that, as father and parent, as companion and guide, he was gone from her, just as effectively as though she had buried him in the churchyard, beneath the battered, spireless old church, that filled all one side of the grande place of the village. So strongly did she feel this, that she refused to let the curé worry him about his soul.

Thus was one ghost laid.

．　　　．　　　．　　　．　　　．　　　．　　　．

There was another ghost, one that haunted her with no material presence, did not inhabit the farm, but hovered, a dim gray figure at the back of her mind.

About Christmas, 1919, in the dead slack of the year, when most of the clearing of the land was done, when the autumn sowing was over and it was too early for the spring one, she had leisure to go up to the Kruysabel. She had neglected this ceremony since the invasion of 1918, chiefly because the disappearance of her father had left the whole weight of the farm on her shoulders, partly because, steadfast as she was, she changed as must every living thing, and Georges was receding from her, with the past. She knew that the place had been fortified into a "strong point," and had she not known, she would have guessed from the fact that the wooden-gate was gone, and the alley that led up the hill, beaten into pulp by military traffic. She scrambled up among the undergrowth, untouched save for shell-holes, and a few places where the vegetation had fired, or hung gray and sickly, reeking of gas. This made her frown and put on her expression as of one about to smack a naughty child. At the top, treading some barbed wire, she came out into the little clearing, leapt a half-decayed trench, and stood by the hunting shelter. Outwardly it was not much changed. A woman, looking at it with the eyes of Madeleine, could see that it was no longer the same place, although its greeny-gray woodland color, and shape that blurred into the surrounding undergrowth, had been carefully preserved, so that it was probably imperceptible to the best glasses a few hundred yards away. The door was undone, and she pushed it open, stood and gasped. Nothing in the previous four years and a half had quite prepared her for what she found. The place had been skilfully gutted. Not only the glass from the windows, the whole of the rugs, cushions, seats, and fittings were gone, but the actual partitions had been re-

moved, leaving the brick chimney-piece alone supporting an empty shell. The trap of the cellar had been forced, and in the aperture left was a steel and concrete "pill-box," its machine gun embrasures level with the window-sills. At the opposite end, just where there had stood the divan on which she had held Georges in her arms, the floor had been torn up, the earth dug away, to make room for a similar erection. The only recognizable remains of the furniture were some of the animal heads and photographs of hunting groups, all adorned with mustaches or other attributes, obscene or merely grotesque, in army indelible pencil, or fastened with field telephone wire. It took Madeleine's plodding mind a moment to size it all up, from the gas-gong hanging from a nail, to the painted wooden notice-board, in English: "Any person found using this Strong Point as a latrine will be severely dealt with. C.R.E. Defence lines."

Then she let the door swing to, turned her back on the place, and walked away. It was not in her to philosophize. What had been done, she felt like a personal injury. If the place had merely been dirtied and damaged by billeting or shell-fire, she would have shrugged her shoulders and put it straight. But this systematic conversion struck deep at her sense of personal possession. They had challenged her right to something she felt to be most deeply her own. For once she was at a loss, was done, beaten, did not know how to adjust herself, hit back. Georges seemed smaller, further off, than she had ever felt him. Her love for him now seemed almost ridiculous, temporary, and forever done with. She was aroused from her reverie by the thick undergrowth that barred her steps, and realized that she was walking down the northeastern slope of the wood, with her back to the farm. That recalled her to herself. She retraced her steps, skirted the clearing, dodged the trenches and wire, and descended the hill towards home, head up, face impenetrable, mistress of herself. But in her heart she was banking up the slow burning fires of resentment. The less easy it was to find legitimate fuel for them, the more she fed them with the first thing or person that came to hand, feeling herself wronged and slighted by all the world.

　·　　　·　　　·　　　·　　　·　　　·　　　·

There remained one more ghost to be laid, one thin wraith that Madeleine hardly noticed, hovering at the back of her war-memories. She did not call up this last apparition, it came to her.

As gray January slid into February, she became aware, amid her engrossing preoccupation with the farm, that a Labor Corps battalion was working on the clearance of the neighboring trench-lines. They were composed of German prisoners and Chinese, officered by a few

English. Presently an orderly called, a German orderly, sent to buy
eggs. She sent him about his business, curtly. This brought an officer,
fair, bald, thick-set, speaking little French. He smiled at her with an
irritating cocksureness, and inquired for her father. Then she recog-
nized him. It was the Lieutenant Millgate who had come to the farm
late one night in 1915 with Lieutenant Skene, to join the East-
hamptons. She found him some eggs for old times' sake, charged
him a pre-war price and forgot him again. He was no ghost; he was
an insignificant fact, and did not haunt her.

But there came a gray day when he reappeared, and not alone.
Another officer in khaki, taller but slighter, was riding behind him,
and tried to greet old Jerome, who ignored the greeting. Before she
knew what had happened, Geoffrey Skene stood before her. Almost
mechanically, for she could not say what she felt, she bade him enter
and sit down. Once he was seated, following her with his eyes, all
her vindictiveness found vent in the words:

"Will you have some coffee? The Allies stole all our wine!" Then
she softened again, and gave him good coffee, because, like all women,
she had a tender spot somewhere for a man who had once desired
her. But it was only for a moment. He sat there, unaltered, just
as he had sat when she had sent him to deliver a message to Georges.
And the thought that Georges had gone out of her life, and that this
lesser man of hers was on his way to England, to go out of her
life just as effectually, hurt her possessive and domineering instincts.
She said bitterly, "I lost my fiancé, after all!" and as he murmured
some condolence her spleen overcame her, and she lashed out with
her tongue at all the damage done to the farm and to her father,
the destruction of her brothers and Georges, at all the work there was
to do, and no one to do it.

She saw Millgate fidget, heard him say in English, "Come on!"
Then she saw Skene rise, bid her good-bye, and go. She moved to the
door, but for the life of her she could not say if she wanted him to go
or stay.

Then, as he swung his leg, in its soiled army clothes, over his
horse's back, straightened up, and clattered away, she knew. She did
not want him, had never wanted him, nor any Englishman, nor any-
thing English. He was just one of the things the War, the cursed War,
had brought on her, and now it, and they, were going. Good riddance.
Nor was her feeling unreasonable. The only thing she and Skene
had in common, was the War. The War removed, they had absolutely
no means of contact. Their case was not isolated. It was national.

So Madeleine remained in the Spanish Farm, and saw no more English, for the Labor Corps soon broke up and went, and she did not care. She was engrossed in one thing only: to get back, sou by sou, everything that had been lost or destroyed, plundered or shattered, by friend or foe, and pay herself for everything she had suffered and dared. And as there was a Madeleine more or less, widowed and childless, bereaved and soured, in every farm in northeastern France, she became a portent. Statesmen feared or wondered at her, schemers and the new business men served her and themselves through her, while philosophers shuddered. For she was the Spanish Farm, the implacable spirit of that borderland so often fought over, never really conquered. She was that spirit that forgets nothing and forgives nothing, but maintains itself, amid all disasters, and necessarily. For she was perhaps the most concrete expression of humanity's instinctive survival in spite of its own perversity and ignorance. There must she stand, slow-burning revenge incarnate, until a better, gentler time.

The End of the Tether

JOSEPH CONRAD

JOSEPH CONRAD (*Josef Teodor Konrad Nalecz Korzeni-owski*) *was born on December 3, 1857, at Berdiczew, Poland. When he was seventeen he joined the French Marine Service and four years later (1878) he first landed on English soil. At that time, when he was twenty-one, he began his study of English. For the next sixteen years he sailed the seas of the British Empire as officer and commander in the British Merchant Service. It was while he was on a vacation in London that he wrote his first novel, "Almayer's Folly" in 1892. In 1894, after more than twenty years of sea life, Conrad retired from the service. The End of the Tether was in the author's mind as early as 1899. The actual writing was begun in 1902, but the original manuscript was destroyed by fire—a lamp on Conrad's study table exploded—and in October of that year Conrad pains-takingly rewrote the novel from start to finish. The book measures 59,000 words.*

INTRODUCTION

Sailor that he was, Joseph Conrad liked to have things shipshape; his stories are made to fit effortlessly within the briefest compass, with no loose thread or unresolved character at the end. In his writing he was like an old bosun, intent on stowing a full-rigged ship within the confines of an empty bottle. His intentness was such that he never failed to tell a good story, one you can read with perennial refreshment, and this is because of the exquisite care with which he has packed every sentence. At his desk Conrad drove himself with the hard discipline he had learned at sea. He wrote in longhand and with the most painstaking care: as little as three hundred words—the equivalent of a page and a half of typewriting—was often a day's work (many a contemporary novelist writing directly on the typewriter will average two thousand words over a considerable stretch), and when it was done the words were as taut as a great mariner and a great artist could make them.

Conrad was at his best in the short novel. The form came naturally to him, and he used it frequently. My problem was which one to choose. As I have explained in my foreword, I might have taken any one of the big four—*Heart of Darkness, Typhoon, The End of the Tether* and *The Shadow Line*. I have picked *The End of the Tether* because it has more heart in it and because, as you read it today, the story has a far-reaching application which is little short of prophecy. For me, Captain Whalley is the embodiment of the English command of the sea. In his youth he had been a fearless navigator who had opened up new passages in the East in his famous white clipper, the *Condor*. He had made, and lost, his fortune at sea; his forty years in the East had spanned the building up of the Treaty Ports, and in his time he had seen Singapore grow from a mucky little landing with

mud huts to the great harbor it is; he had built up a reputation known through the China Station and he had seen his authority dwindle as steam dispersed the clipper fleet; he had watched the German tramps snatch up cargoes until the Sailors' Home was full of English officers without a command and, as age closed in, he himself had been forced to sell to the Japanese the *Fair Maid,* the darling barque on which he had hoped to end his days. Fit together these telltale bits of Captain Whalley's background and then ask yourself with how much foreboding Conrad planned this narrative back in 1899. Could he have foreseen so surely the blows which were to fall upon the Empire? Whether you take this novel for its personal or its prophetic tragedy, there is no doubt that it has in it the elements of endurance and heartbreak which must stir the sympathies of any reader in the English-speaking world here and now.

Captain Whalley is sixty-seven when the novel opens, and you notice at once that he is not standing but seated on his bridge. That fact is a half acknowledgment of what age and time have done to him. As Conrad tells us, "The physical traits of the old captain, his powerful frame, his reposeful mien, his intelligent, handsome face, the big limbs, the benign courtesy, the touch of rugged severity in the shaggy eyebrows made up a seductive personality." In no time he has you in his pocket, and it is your chief concern that neither old age nor the mortification of his partner Massey shall bring him low. You know that the captain has invested every penny he possesses in his last command but you do not know the odds against him. Conrad has taken, so to speak, the perfect opening, an opening which allows full play for that shuttling back and forth, that alternation of past and present, which is his favorite device. As he shows us the captain in his prime, admiration is underscored by pity, and both become the more acute as, with the most skillful nudges, the story moves forward under its painful necessity.

We have all known men who for a time appeared to be impervious to age, who for a time were indestructible. The slow-dawning suspicion that the old captain is suffering from a secret wound (when your reading is at an end recall, if you can, what first aroused your suspicion) is a certain cause of pity. But I think what draws us still closer to Captain Whalley is his great capacity for loyalty and the realization of what he means to others. Trace this in the ascending scale. The little Malay Serang, the "captain's pilot fish," has a veneration for him which one suspects he felt for no other white man, a veneration expressed dramatically and almost entirely in monosyllables. The man-to-man affection which passes between the captain and his contemporary, Ned Elliott, the master attendant of the port, is as direct a

current as the more youthful affection of the Dutch recluse, Van Wyk. And the loyalty goes deeper when the women appear. Anyone who has lived on the seacoast will remember days when the scudding clouds open suddenly and sunlight pours down on a ship or an island a mile away. So in a moment of recollection far beyond reach Captain Whalley could live again the days with his wife in the big main cabin, all white and gold, of the *Condor*. The cluster of home flowers with which she decorated every panel, the faint flavor of turpentine which made old Swinburne, the mate, less hearty than usual in tackling his food and the piano which had been shipped from London round the cape—"Mrs Whalley is a regular out-and-out nightingale, sir," the mate would pronounce after listening profoundly over the skylight— these were the sunlit episodes of a time that would never come again.

After his wife's death it was his daughter Ivy to whom his life was dedicated. That is easy enough to understand, for Ivy "resembled her mother in the color of her eyes and in character—and also in this, that she understood him without many words." And as if this were not enough, Ivy has made a completely improvident marriage in far-off Australia, so that her father had double cause for remembering her and her need. So he had every occasion for helping her, which, be it said, he does with a certain proud satisfaction. Indeed, were Ivy's need less insistent, it is doubtful if he would have taken the risks he did.

I have by now borrowed enough of Conrad's pigment to suggest the compelling force and intimacy of this narrative. There remains the pleasure of conning over in my own mind those scenes which make you pause in admiration of any man who can see things so clearly and write them down with such terse perfection. I see the captain as he sits alone in his cabin on the *Fair Maid;* I see the great unclouded glare of the sun on the water, the grief-stricken face of old Swinburne, the mate; I remember the journey up-river where the forests of big trees came down to the brink and where the floods had left "a mass of roots intertwined as if wrestling underground"; I hear the plunge of the lead as the native takes the sounding just before the *Sofala* grazes on the bar and I feel the betrayal of the old man as he gropes so pathetically for that wretched jacket on the bridge. Imagery like this compels us to read on—hoping against hope.

THE END OF THE TETHER

FOR A LONG TIME after the course of the steamer *Sofala* had been altered for the land, the low swampy coast had retained its appearance of a mere smudge of darkness beyond a belt of glitter. The sunrays fell violently upon the calm sea—seemed to shatter themselves upon an adamantine surface into sparkling dust, into a dazzling vapour of light that blinded the eye and wearied the brain with its unsteady brightness.

Captain Whalley did not look at it. When his Serang, approaching the roomy cane arm-chair which he filled capably, had informed him in a low voice that the course was to be altered, he had risen at once and had remained on his feet, face forward, while the head of his ship swung through a quarter of a circle. He had not uttered a single word, not even the word to steady the helm. It was the Serang, an elderly, alert, little Malay, with a very dark skin, who murmured the order to the helmsman. And then slowly Captain Whalley sat down again in the arm-chair on the bridge and fixed his eyes on the deck between his feet.

He could not hope to see anything new upon this lane of the sea. He had been on these coasts for the last three years. From Low Cape to Malantan the distance was fifty miles, six hours' steaming for the old ship with the tide, or seven against. Then you steered straight for the land, and by and by three palms would appear on the sky, tall and slim, and with their dishevelled heads in a bunch, as if in confidential criticism of the dark mangroves. The *Sofala* would be headed towards the sombre strip of the coast, which at a given moment, as the ship closed with it obliquely, would show several clean shining fractures—the brimful estuary of a river. Then on through a brown liquid, three parts water and one part black earth, on and on between the low shores, three parts black earth and one part brackish water, the *Sofala* would plough her way upstream, as she had done once every month for these seven years or more, long before he was aware of her existence, long before he had ever thought of having anything to do with her and her

invariable voyages. The old ship ought to have known the road better than her men, who had not been kept so long at it without a change; better than the faithful Serang, whom he had brought over from his last ship to keep the captain's watch; better than he himself, who had been her captain for the last three years only. She could always be depended upon to make her courses. Her compasses were never out. She was no trouble at all to take about, as if her great age had given her knowledge, wisdom, and steadiness. She made her landfalls to a degree of the bearing, and almost to a minute of her allowed time. At any moment, as he sat on the bridge without looking up, or lay sleepless in his bed, simply by reckoning the days and the hours he could tell where he was—the precise spot of the beat. He knew it well, too, this monotonous huckster's round, up and down the Straits; he knew its order and its sights and its people. Malacca to begin with, in at daylight and out at dusk, to cross over with a rigid phosphorescent wake this highway of the Far East. Darkness and gleams on the water, clear stars on a black sky, perhaps the lights of a home steamer keeping her unswerving course in the middle or maybe the elusive shadow of a native craft with her mat sails flitting by silently—and low land on the other side in sight at daylight. At noon the three palms of the next place of call, up a sluggish river. The only white man residing there was a retired young sailor, with whom he had become friendly in the course of many voyages. Sixty miles farther on there was another place of call, a deep bay with only a couple of houses on the beach. And so on, in and out, picking up coastwise cargo here and there, and finishing with a hundred miles' steady steaming through the maze of an archipelago of small islands up to a large native town at the end of the beat. There was a three days' rest for the old ship before he started her again in inverse order, seeing the same shores from another bearing; hearing the same voices in the same places, back again to the *Sofala's* port of registry on the great highway to the East, where he would take up a birth nearly opposite the big stone pile of the harbour office till it was time to start again on the old round of 1,600 miles and thirty days. Not a very enterprising life, this, for Captain Whalley, Henry Whalley, otherwise Dare-devil Harry Whalley, of the *Condor*, a famous clipper in her day. No. Not a very enterprising life for a man who had served famous firms, who had sailed famous ships (more than one or two of them his own); who had made famous passages, had been the pioneer of new routes and new trades; who had steered across the unsurveyed tracts of the South Seas, and had seen the sun rise on uncharted islands. Fifty years at sea, and forty out in the East ("a pretty thorough apprenticeship," he used to remark smilingly),

had made him honourably known to a generation of shipowners and merchants in all the ports from Bombay clear over to where the East merges into the West upon the coast of the two Americas. His fame remained writ, not very large but plain enough, on the Admiralty charts. Was there not somewhere between Australia and China a Whalley Island and a Condor Reef? On that dangerous coral formation the celebrated clipper had hung stranded for three days, her captain and crew throwing her cargo overboard with one hand and with the other, as it were, keeping off her a flotilla of savage war-canoes. At that time neither the island nor the reef had any official existence. Later the officers of her Majesty's steam-vessel *Fusilier,* despatched to make a survey of the route, recognized in the adoption of these two names the enterprise of the man and the solidity of the ship. Besides, as any one who cares may see, the *General Directory* vol. ii. p. 410, begins the description of the "Malotu or Whalley Passage" with the words "This advantageous route, first discovered in 1850 by Captain Whalley in the ship *Condor,*" etc., and ends by recommending it warmly to sailing vessels leaving the China ports for the south in the months from December to April inclusive.

This was the clearest gain he had out of life. Nothing could rob him of this kind of fame. The piercing of the Isthmus of Suez, like the breaking of a dam, had let in upon the East a flood of new ships, new men, new methods of trade. It had changed the face of the Eastern seas and the very spirit of their life; so that his early experiences meant nothing whatever to the new generation of seamen.

In those bygone days he had handled many thousands of pounds of his employers' money and of his own; he had attended faithfully, as by law a shipmaster is expected to do, to the conflicting interests of owners, charterers, and underwriters. He had never lost a ship or consented to a shady transaction; and he had lasted well, outlasting in the end the conditions that had gone to the making of his name. He had buried his wife (in the Gulf of Petchili), had married off his daughter to the man of her unlucky choice, and had lost more than an ample competence in the crash of the notorious Travancore and Deccan Banking Corporation, whose downfall has shaken the East like an earthquake. And he was sixty-seven years old.

§ 2

His age sat lightly enough on him; and of his ruin he was not ashamed. He had not been alone in believing in the stability of the Banking Corporation. Men whose judgment in matters of finance was

as expert as his seamanship had commended the prudence of his investments, and had themselves lost much money in the great failure. The only difference between him and them was that he had lost his all. And yet not his all. There had remained to him from his lost fortune a very little barque, *Fair Maid,* which he had bought to occupy his leisure of a retired sailor—"to play with," as he expressed it himself.

He had formally declared himself tired of the sea the year preceding his daughter's marriage. But after the young couple had gone to settle in Melbourne he found out that he could not make himself happy on shore. He was too much of a merchant sea-captain for mere yachting to satisfy him. He wanted the illusion of affairs; and his acquisition of the *Fair Maid* preserved the continuity of his life. He introduced her to his acquaintances in various ports as "my last command." When he grew too old to be trusted with a ship, he would lay her up and go ashore to be buried, leaving directions in his will to have the barque towed out and scuttled decently in deep water on the day of the funeral. His daughter would not grudge him the satisfaction of knowing that no stranger would handle his last command after him. With a fortune he was able to leave her, the value of a 500-ton barque was neither here nor there. All this would be said with a jocular twinkle in his eye: the vigorous old man had too much vitality for the sentimentalism of regret; and a little wistfully withal, because he was at home in life, taking a genuine pleasure in its feelings and its possessions; in the dignity of his reputation and his wealth, in his love for his daughter, and in his satisfaction with the ship—the plaything of his lonely leisure.

He had the cabin arranged in accordance with his simple ideal of comfort at sea. A big bookcase (he was a great reader) occupied one side of his stateroom; the portrait of his late wife, a flat bituminous oil-painting representing the profile of one long black ringlet of a young woman, faced his bedplace. Three chronometers ticked him to sleep and greeted him on waking with the tiny competition of their beats. He rose at five every day. The officer of the morning watch, drinking his early cup of coffee aft by the wheel, would hear through the wide orifice of the copper ventilators all the splashings, blowings, and splutterings of his captain's toilet. These noises would be followed by a sustained deep murmur of the Lord's Prayer recited in a loud earnest voice. Five minutes afterwards the head and shoulders of Captain Whalley emerged out of the companion-hatchway. Invariably he paused for a while on the stairs, looking all round at the horizon; upwards at the trim of the sails; inhaling deep draughts of the fresh air. Only then he would step out on the poop, acknowledging the hand

raised to the peak of the cap with a majestic and benign "Good morning to you." He walked the deck till eight scrupulously. Sometimes, not above twice a year, he had to use a thick cudgel-like stick on account of a stiffness in the hip—a slight touch of rheumatism, he supposed. Otherwise he knew nothing of the ills of the flesh. At the ringing of the breakfast bell he went below to feed his canaries, wind up the chronometers, and take the head of the table. From there he had before his eyes the big carbon photographs of his daughter, her husband, and two fat-legged babies—his grandchildren—set in black frames into the maple-wood bulkheads of the cuddy. After breakfast he dusted the glass over these portraits himself with a cloth, and brushed the oil painting of his wife with a plummet kept suspended from a small brass hook by the side of the heavy gold frame. Then with the door of his state-room shut, he would sit down on the couch under the portrait to read a chapter out of a thick pocket Bible—her Bible. But on some days he only sat there for half an hour with his finger between the leaves and the closed book resting on his knees. Perhaps he had remembered suddenly how fond of boat-sailing she used to be.

She had been a real shipmate and a true woman, too. It was like an article of faith with him that there never had been, and never could be, a brighter, cheerier home anywhere afloat or ashore than his home under the poop-deck of the *Condor,* with the big main cabin all white and gold, garlanded as if for a perpetual festival with an unfading wreath. She had decorated the centre of every panel with a cluster of home flowers. It took her a twelvemonth to go round the cuddy with this labour of love. To him it had remained a marvel of painting, the highest achievement of taste and skill; and as to old Swinburne, his mate, every time he came down to his meals he stood transfixed with admiration before the progress of the work. You could almost smell these roses, he declared, sniffing the faint flavour of turpentine which at that time pervaded the saloon, and (as he confessed afterwards) made him somewhat less hearty than usual in tackling his food. But there was nothing of the sort to interfere with his enjoyment of her singing. "Mrs. Whalley is a regular out-and-out nightingale, sir," he would pronounce with a judicial air after listening profoundly over the skylight to the very end of the piece. In fine weather, in the second dog-watch, the two men could hear her trills and roulades going on to the accompaniment of the piano in the cabin. On the very day they got engaged he had written to London for the instrument; but they had been married for over a year before it reached them, coming out round the Cape. The big case made part of the first direct general cargo landed in Hongkong harbour—an event

that to the men who walked the busy quays of to-day seemed as hazily remote as the dark ages of history. But Captain Whalley could in a half-hour of solitude live again all his life, with its romance, its idyl, and its sorrow. He had to close her eyes himself. She went away from under the ensign like a sailor's wife, a sailor herself at heart. He had read the service over her, out of her own prayer-book, without a break in his voice. When he raised his eyes he could see old Swinburne facing him with his cap pressed to his breast, and his rugged, weather-beaten, impassive face streaming with drops of water like a lump of chipped red granite in a shower. It was all very well for that old sea-dog to cry. He had to read on to the end; but after the splash he did not remember much of what happened for the next few days. An elderly sailor of the crew, deft at needlework, put together a mourning frock for the child out of one of her black skirts.

He was not likely to forget; but you cannot dam up life like a sluggish stream. It will break out and flow over a man's troubles, it will close upon a sorrow like the sea upon a dead body, no matter how much love has gone to the bottom. And the world is not bad. People had been very kind to him; especially Mrs. Gardner, the wife of the senior partner in Gardner, Patteson & Co., the owners of the *Condor*. It was she who volunteered to look after the little one, and in due course took her to England (something of a journey in those days, even by the overland mail route) with her own girls to finish her education. It was ten years before he saw her again.

As a little child she had never been frightened of bad weather; she would beg to be taken up on deck in the bosom of his oilskin coat to watch the big seas hurling themselves upon the *Condor*. The swirl and crash of the waves seemed to fill her small soul with a breathless delight. "A good boy spoiled," he used to say of her in joke. He had named her Ivy because of the sound of the word, and obscurely fascinated by a vague association of ideas. She had twined herself tightly round his heart, and he intended her to cling close to her father as to a tower of strength; forgetting while she was little, that in the nature of things she would probably elect to cling to someone else. But he loved life well enough for even that event to give him a certain satisfaction, apart from his more intimate feeling of loss.

After he had purchased the *Fair Maid* to occupy his loneliness, he hastened to accept a rather unprofitable freight to Australia simply for the opportunity of seeing his daughter in her own home. What made him dissatisfied there was not to see that she clung now to somebody else, but that the prop she had selected seemed on closer examination "a rather poor stick"—even in the matter of health. He disliked his son-in-law's studied civility perhaps more than his method of

handling the sum of money he had given Ivy at her marriage. But of his apprehensions he said nothing. Only on the day of his departure, with the hall-door open all ready, holding her hands and looking steadily into her eyes, he had said, "You know, my dear, all I have is for you and the chicks. Mind you write to me openly." She had answered him by an almost imperceptible movement of her head. She resembled her mother in the colour of her eyes, and in character—and also in this, that she understood him without many words.

Sure enough she had to write; and some of these letters made Captain Whalley lift his white eye-brows. For the rest he considered he was reaping the true reward of his life by being thus able to produce on demand whatever was needed. He had not enjoyed himself so much in a way since his wife had died. Characteristically enough his son-in-law's punctuality in failure caused him at a distance to feel a sort of kindness towards the man. The fellow was so perpetually being jammed on a lee shore that to charge it all to his reckless navigation would be manifestly unfair. No, no! He knew well what that meant. It was bad luck. His own had been simply marvellous, but he had seen in his life too many good men—seamen and others—go under with the sheer weight of bad luck not to recognize the fatal signs. For all that, he was cogitating on the best way of tying up very strictly ever penny he had to leave, when with a preliminary rumble of rumours (whose first sound reached him in Shanghai as it happened), the shock of the big failure came; and, after passing through the phases of stupor, of incredulity, of indignation, he had to accept the fact that he had nothing to speak of to leave.

Upon that, as if he had only waited for this catastrophe, the unlucky man, away there in Melbourne, gave up his unprofitable game, and sat down—in an invalid's bath-chair at that, too. "He will never walk again," wrote the wife. For the first time in his life Captain Whalley was a bit staggered.

The *Fair Maid* had to go to work in bitter earnest now. It was no longer a matter of preserving alive the memory of Dare-devil Harry Whalley in the Eastern Seas, or of keeping an old man in pocket-money and clothes, with, perhaps, a bill for a few hundred first-class cigars thrown in at the end of the year. He would have to buckle-to, and keep her going hard on a scant allowance of gilt for the ginger-bread scrolls at her stem and stern.

This necessity opened his eyes to the fundamental changes of the world. Of his past only the familiar names remained, here and there, but the things and the men, as he had known them, were gone. The name of Gardner, Patteson & Co. was still displayed on the walls of warehouses by the waterside, on the brass plates and window-panes

in the business quarters of more than one Eastern port, but there was no longer a Gardner or a Patteson in the firm. There was no longer for Captain Whalley an arm-chair and a welcome in the private office, with a bit of business ready to be put in the way of an old friend, for the sake of bygone services. The husbands of the Gardner girls sat behind the desks in that room where, long after he had left the employ, he had kept his right of entrance in the old man's time. Their ships now had yellow funnels with black tops, and a time-table of appointed routes like a confounded service of tramways. The winds of December and June were all one to them; their captains (excellent young men he doubted not) were, to be sure, familiar with Whalley Island, because of late years the Government had established a white fixed light on the north end (with a red danger sector over the Condor Reef), but most of them would have been extremely surprised to hear that a flesh-and-blood Whalley still existed—an old man going about the world trying to pick up a cargo here and there for his little barque.

And everywhere it was the same. Departed the men who would have nodded appreciatively at the mention of his name, and would have thought themselves bound in honour to do something for Dare-devil Harry Whalley. Departed the opportunities which he would have known how to seize; and gone with them the white-winged flock of clippers that lived in the boisterous uncertain life of the winds, skimming big fortunes out of the foam of the sea. In a world that pared down the profits to an irreducible minimum, in a world that was able to count its disengaged tonnage twice over every day and in which lean charters were snapped up by cable three months in advance, there were no chances of fortune for an individual wandering haphazard with a little barque—hardly indeed any room to exist.

He found it more difficult from year to year. He suffered greatly from the smallness of remittances he was able to send his daughter. Meantime he had given up good cigars, and even in the matter of inferior cheroots limited himself to six a day. He never told her of his difficulties, and she never enlarged upon her struggle to live. Their confidence in each other needed no explanations, and their perfect understanding endured without protestations of gratitude or regret. He would have been shocked if she had taken it into her head to thank him in so many words, but he found it perfectly natural that she should tell him she needed two hundred pounds.

He had come in with the *Fair Maid* in ballast to look for a freight in the *Sofala's* port of registry, and her letter met him there. Its tenor was that it was no use mincing matters. Her only resource was in opening a boarding-house, for which the prospects, she judged, were good.

Good enough, at any rate, to make her tell him frankly that with two hundred pounds she could make a start. He had torn the envelope open, hastily, on deck, where it was handed to him by the ship-chandler's runner, who had brought his mail at the moment of anchoring. For the second time in his life he was appalled, and remained stock-still at the cabin door with the paper trembling between his fingers. Open a boarding-house! Two hundred pounds for a start! The only resource! And he did not know where to lay his hands on two hundred pence.

All that night Captain Whalley walked the poop of his anchored ship, as though he had been about to close with the land in thick weather, and uncertain of his position after a run of many gray days without a sight of sun, moon, or stars. The black night twinkled with the guiding lights of seamen and the steady straight lines of lights on shore; and all around the *Fair Maid* the riding lights of ships cast trembling trails upon the water of the roadstead. Captain Whalley saw not a gleam anywhere till the dawn broke and he found out that his clothing was soaked through with the heavy dew.

His ship was awake. He stopped short, stroked his wet beard, and descended the poop ladder backwards, with tired feet. At the sight of him the chief officer, lounging about sleepily on the quarterdeck, remained open-mouthed in the middle of a great early-morning yawn.

"Good morning to you," pronounced Captain Whalley, solemnly, passing into the cabin. But he checked himself in the doorway, and without looking back "By the bye," he said, "there should be an empty wooden case put away in the lazarette. It has not been broken up—has it?"

The mate shut his mouth, and then asked as if dazed, "What empty case, sir?"

"A big flat packing-case belonging to that painting in my room. Let it be taken upon deck and tell the carpenter to look it over. I may want to use it before long."

The chief officer did not stir a limb till he had heard the door of the captain's stateroom slam within the cuddy. Then he beckoned aft the second mate with his forefinger to tell him that there was something "in the wind."

When the bell rang Captain Whalley's authoritative voice boomed out through a closed door, "Sit down and don't wait for me." And his impressed officers took their places, exchanging looks and whispers across the table. What! No breakfast? And after apparently knocking about all night on deck, too! Clearly, there was something in the wind. In the skylight above their heads, bowed earnestly over the plates, three wire cages rocked and rattled to the restless jumping of the

hungry canaries; and they could detect the sounds of their "old man's" deliberate movements within his stateroom. Captain Whalley was methodically winding up the chronometers, dusting the portrait of his late wife, getting a clean white shirt out of the drawers, making himself ready in his punctilious, unhurried manner to go ashore. He could not have swallowed a single mouthful of food that morning. He had made up his mind to sell the *Fair Maid*.

§ 3

Just at that time the Japanese were casting far and wide for ships of European build, and he had no difficulty in finding a purchaser, a speculator who drove a hard bargain, but paid cash down for the *Fair Maid,* with a view to a profitable resale. Thus it came about that Captain Whalley found himself on a certain afternoon descending the steps of one of the most important post offices of the East with a slip of bluish paper in his hand. This was the receipt of a registered letter enclosing a draft for two hundred pounds, and addressed to Melbourne. Captain Whalley pushed the paper into his waistcoat-pocket, took his stick from under his arm, and walked down the street.

It was a recently opened and untidy thoroughfare with rudimentary side-walks and a soft layer of dust cushioning the whole width of the road. One end touched the slummy street of Chinese shops near the harbour, the other drove straight on, without houses, for a couple of miles, through patches of jungle-like vegetation, to the yard gates of the new Consolidated Docks Company. The crude frontages of the new Government buildings alternated with the blank fencing of vacant plots, and the view of the sky seemed to give an added spaciousness to the broad vista. It was empty and shunned by natives after business hours, as though they had expected to see one of the tigers from the neighbourhood of the New Waterworks on the hill coming at a loping canter down the middle to get a Chinese shopkeeper for supper. Captain Whalley was not dwarfed by the solitude of the grandly planned street. He had too fine a presence for that. He was only a lonely figure walking purposefully, with a great white beard like a pilgrim, and with a thick stick that resembled a weapon. On one side the new Courts of Justice had a low and unadorned portico of squat columns half concealed by a few old trees left in the approach. On the other the pavilion wings of the new Colonial Treasury came out to the line of the street. But Captain Whalley, who had now no ship and no home, remembered in passing that on that very site when he first came out from England there had stood a fishing village, a few mat huts

erected on piles between a muddy tidal creek and a miry pathway that went writhing into a tangled wilderness without any docks or waterworks.

No ship—no home. And his poor Ivy away there had no home either. A boarding-house is no sort of home though it may get you a living. His feelings were horribly rasped by the idea of the boarding-house. In his rank of life he had that truly aristocratic temperament characterized by a scorn of vulgar gentility and by prejudiced views as to the derogatory nature of certain occupations. For his own part he had always preferred sailing merchant ships (which is a straight-forward occupation) to buying and selling merchandise of which the essence is to get the better of somebody in a bargain—an undignified trial of wits at best. His father had been Colonel Whalley (retired) of the H.E.I. Company's service, with very slender means besides his pension, but with distinguished connections. He could remember as a boy how frequently waiters at the inns, country tradesmen and small people of that sort, used to "My lord" the old warrior on the strength of his appearance.

Captain Whalley himself (he would have entered the Navy if his father had not died before he was fourteen) had something of a grand air which would have suited an old and glorious admiral; but he became lost like a straw in the eddy of a brook amongst the swarm of brown and yellow humanity filling a thoroughfare, that by contrast with the vast and empty avenue he had left seemed as narrow as a lane and absolutely riotous with life. The walls of the houses were blue; the shops of the Chinamen yawned like cavernous lairs, heaps of nondescript merchandise overflowed the gloom of the long range of arcades, and the fiery serenity of sunset took the middle of the street from end to end with a glow like the reflection of a fire. It fell on the bright colours and the dark faces of the bare-footed crowd, on the pallid yellow backs of the half-naked jostling coolies, on the accoutrements of a tall Sikh trooper with a parted beard and fierce moustaches on sentry before the gate of the police compound. Looming very big above the heads in a red haze of dust, the tightly packed car of the cable tram-way navigated cautiously up the human stream, with the incessant blare of its horn, in the manner of a steamer groping in a fog.

Captain Whalley emerged like a diver on the other side, and in the desert shade between the walls of closed warehouses removed his hat to cool his brow. A certain disrepute attached to the calling of a land-lady of a boarding-house. These women were said to be rapacious, un-scrupulous, untruthful; and though he condemned no class of his fellow-creatures—God forbid!—these were suspicions to which it was unseemly that a Whalley should lay herself open. He had not expostu-

lated with her, however. He was confident she shared his feelings; he was sorry for her; he trusted her judgment; he considered it a merciful dispensation that he could help her once more—but in his aristocratic heart of hearts he would have found it more easy to reconcile himself to the idea of her turning seamstress. Vaguely he remembered reading years ago a touching piece called the "Song of the Shirt." It was all very well making songs about poor women. The granddaughter of Colonel Whalley, the landlady of a boarding-house! Pooh! He replaced his hat, dived into two pockets, and stopping a moment to apply a flaring match to the end of a cheap cheroot, blew an embittered cloud of smoke at a world that could hold such surprises.

Of one thing he was certain—that she was the own child of a clever mother. Now he had got over the wrench of parting with his ship, he perceived clearly that such a step had been unavoidable. Perhaps he had been growing aware of it all along with an unconfessed knowledge. But she, far away there, must have had an intuitive perception of it, with the pluck to face that truth and the courage to speak out—all the qualities which had made her mother a woman of such excellent counsel.

It would have had to come to that in the end! It was fortunate she had forced his hand. In another year or two it would have been an utterly barren sale. To keep the ship going he had been involving himself deeper every year. He was defenceless before the insidious work of adversity, to whose more open assaults he could present a firm front; like a cliff that stands unmoved the open battering of the sea, with a lofty ignorance of the treacherous backwash undermining its base. As it was, every liability satisfied, her request answered, and owning no man a penny, there remained to him from the proceeds a sum of five hundred pounds put away safely. In addition he had upon his person some forty odd dollars—enough to pay his hotel bill, providing he did not linger too long in the modest bedroom where he had taken refuge.

Scantily furnished, and with a waxed floor, it opened into one of the side-verandahs. The straggling building of bricks, as airy as a birdcage, resounded with the incessant flapping of rattan screens worried by the wind between the whitewashed square pillars of the sea-front. The rooms were lofty, a ripple of sunshine flowed over the ceilings; and the periodical invasions of tourists from some passenger steamer in the harbour flitted through the wind-swept dusk of the apartments with the tumult of their unfamiliar voices and impermanent presences, like relays of migratory shades condemned to speed headlong round the earth without leaving a trace. The babble of their irruptions ebbed out as suddenly as it had arisen: the draughty corridors and the long

chairs of the verandahs knew their sight-seeing hurry or their prostrate repose no more; and Captain Whalley, substantial and dignified, left well nigh alone in the vast hotel by each light-hearted skurry, felt more and more like a stranded tourist with no aim in view, like a forlorn traveller without a home. In the solitude of his room he smoked thoughtfully, gazing at the two sea-chests which held all that he could call his own in this world. A thick roll of charts in a sheath of sailcloth leaned in a corner; the flat packing-case containing the portrait in oils and the three carbon photographs had been pushed under the bed. He was tired of discussing terms, of assisting at surveys, of all the routine of the business. What to the other parties was merely the sale of a ship was to him a momentous event involving a radically new view of existence. He knew that after this ship there would be no other; and the hopes of his youth, the exercise of his abilities, every feeling and achievement of his manhood, had been indissolubly connected with ships. He had served ships; he had owned ships; and even the years of his actual retirement from the sea had been made bearable by the idea that he had only to stretch out his hand full of money to get a ship. He had been at liberty to feel as though he were the owner of all the ships in the world. The selling of this one was weary work; but when she passed from him at last, when he signed the last receipt, it was as though all the ships had gone out of the world together, leaving him on the shore of inaccessible oceans with seven hundred pounds in his hands.

Striding firmly, without haste, along the quay, Captain Whalley averted his glances from the familiar roadstead. Two generations of seamen born since his first day at sea stood between him and all these ships at the anchorage. His own was sold, and he had been asking himself, What next?

From the feeling of loneliness, of inward emptiness—and of loss, too, as if his very soul had been taken out of him forcibly—there had sprung at first a desire to start right off and join his daughter. "Here are the last pence," he would say to her; "take them, my dear. And here's your old father: you must take him, too."

His soul recoiled, as if afraid of what lay hidden at the bottom of this impulse. Give up! Never! When one is thoroughly weary all sorts of nonsense come into one's head. A pretty gift it would have been for a poor woman—this seven hundred pounds with the incumbrance of a hale old fellow more than likely to last for years and years to come. Was he not as fit to die in harness as any of the youngsters in charge of these anchored ships out yonder? He was as solid now as ever he had been. But as to who would give him work to do, that was another matter. Were he, with his appearance and antecedents, to go about

looking for a junior's berth, people, he was afraid, would not take him seriously; or else if he succeeded in impressing them, he would maybe obtain their pity, which would be like stripping yourself naked to be kicked. He was not anxious to give himself away for less than nothing. He had no use for anybody's pity. On the other hand, a command—the only thing he could try for with due regard for common decency—was not likely to be lying in wait for him at the corner of the next street. Commands don't go a-begging nowadays. Ever since he had come ashore to carry out the business of the sale he had kept his ears open, but had heard no hint of one being vacant in the port. And even if there had been one, his successful past itself stood in his way. He had been his own employer too long. The only credential he could produce was the testimony of his whole life. What better recommendation could any one require? But vaguely he felt that the unique document would be looked upon as an archaic curiosity of the Eastern waters, a screed traced in obsolete words—in a half-forgotten language.

§ 4

Revolving these thoughts, he strolled on near the railings of the quay, broad-chested, without a stoop, as though his big shoulders had never felt the burden of the loads that must be carried between the cradle and the grave. No single betraying fold or line of care disfigured the reposeful modelling of his face. It was full and untanned; and the upper part emerged, massively quiet, out of the downward flow of silvery hair, with the striking delicacy of its clear complexion and the powerful width of the forehead. The first cast of his glance fell on you candid and swift, like a boy's; but because of the ragged snowy thatch of the eye-brows the affability of his attention acquired the character of a keen and searching scrutiny. With age he had put on flesh a little, had increased his girth like an old tree presenting no symptoms of decay; and even the opulent, lustrous ripple of white hairs upon his chest seemed an attribute of unquenchable vitality and vigour.

Once rather proud of his great bodily strength, and even of his personal appearance, conscious of his worth, and firm in his rectitude, there had remained to him, like the heritage of departed prosperity, the tranquil bearing of a man who had proved himself fit in every sort of way for the life of his choice. He strode on squarely under the projecting brim of an ancient Panama hat. It had a low crown, a crease through its whole diameter, a narrow black ribbon. Imperishable and a little discoloured, this headgear made it easy to pick him out from

afar on thronged wharves and in the busy streets. He had never adopted the comparatively modern fashion of pipeclayed cork helmets. He disliked the form; and he hoped he could manage to keep a cool head to the end of his life without all these contrivances for hygienic ventilation. His hair was cropped close, his linen always of immaculate whiteness; a suit of thin gray flannel, worn threadbare but scrupulously brushed, floated about his burly limbs, adding to his bulk by the looseness of its cut. The years had mellowed the good-humoured, imperturbable audacity of his prime into a temper carelessly serene; and the leisurely tapping of his iron-shod stick accompanied his footfalls with a self-confident sound on the flag-stones. It was impossible to connect such a fine presence and this unruffled aspect with the belittling troubles of poverty; the man's whole existence appeared to pass before you, facile and large, in the freedom of means as ample as the clothing of his body.

The irrational dread of having to break into his five hundred pounds for personal expenses in the hotel disturbed the steady poise of his mind. There was no time to lose. The bill was running up. He nourished the hope that this five hundred would perhaps be the means, if everything else failed, of obtaining some work which, keeping his body and soul together (not a matter of great outlay), would enable him to be of use to his daughter. To his mind it was her own money which he employed, as it were, in backing her father and solely for her benefit. Once at work, he would help her with the greater part of his earnings; he was good for many years yet, and this boarding-house business, he argued to himself, whatever the prospects, could not be much of a gold-mine from the first start. But what work? He was ready to lay hold of anything in an honest way so that it came quickly to his hand; because the five hundred pounds must be preserved intact for eventual use. That was the great point. With the entire five hundred one felt a substance at one's back; but it seemed to him that should he let it dwindle to four-fifty or even four-eighty, all the efficiency would be gone out of the money, as though there were some magic power in the round figure. But what sort of work?

Confronted by that haunting question as by an uneasy ghost, for whom he had no exorcising formula, Captain Whalley stopped short on the apex of a small bridge spanning steeply the bed of a canalized creek with granite shores. Moored between the square blocks a sea-going Malay prau floated half hidden under the arch of masonry, with her spars lowered down, without a sound of life on board, and covered from stem to stern with a ridge of palm-leaf mats. He had left behind him the overheated pavements bordered by the stone frontages that, like the sheer face of cliffs, followed the sweep of the quays; and

an unconfined spaciousness of orderly and sylvan aspect opened before him its wide plots of rolled grass, like pieces of green carpet smoothly pegged out, its long ranges of trees lined up in colossal porticos of dark shafts roofed with a vault of branches.

Some of these avenues ended at the sea. It was a terraced shore; and beyond, upon the level expanse, profound and glistening like the gaze of a dark-blue eye, an oblique band of stippled purple lengthened itself indefinitely through the gap between a couple of verdant twin islets. The masts and spars of a few ships far away, hull down in the outer roads, sprang straight from the water in a fine maze of rosy lines pencilled on the clear shadow of the eastern board. Captain Whalley gave them a long glance. The ship, once his own, was anchored out there. It was staggering to think that it was open to him no longer to take a boat at the jetty and get himself pulled off to her when the evening came. To no ship. Perhaps never more. Before the sale was concluded, and till the purchase-money had been paid, he had spent daily some time on board the *Fair Maid*. The money had been paid this very morning, and now, all at once, there was positively no ship that he could go on board of when he liked; no ship that would need his presence in order to do her work—to live. It seemed an incredible state of affairs, something too bizarre to last. And the sea was full of craft of all sorts. There was that prau lying so still swathed in her shroud of sewn palm-leaves—she, too, had her indispensable man. They lived through each other, this Malay he had never seen, and this high-sterned thing of no size that seemed to be resting after a long journey. And of all the ships in sight, near and far, each was provided with a man, the man without whom the finest ship is a dead thing, a floating and purposeless log.

After his one glance at the roadstead he went on since there was nothing to turn back for, and the time must be got through somehow. The avenues of big trees ran straight over the Esplanade, cutting each other at diverse angles, columnar below and luxuriant above. The interlaced boughs high up there seemed to slumber; not a leaf stirred overhead: and the reedy cast-iron lamp-posts in the middle of the road, gilt like sceptres diminished in a long perspective, with their globes of white porcelain atop, resembling a barbarous decoration of ostriches' eggs displayed in a row. The flaming sky kindled a tiny crimson spark upon the glistening surface of each glassy shell.

With his chin sunk a little, his hands behind his back, and the end of his stick marking the gravel with a faint wavering line at his heels. Captain Whalley reflected that if a ship without a man was like a body without a soul, a sailor without a ship was of not much more account in this world than an aimless log adrift upon the sea. The

log might be sound enough by itself, tough of fibre, and hard to destroy
—but what of that! And a sudden sense of irremediable idleness
weighted his feet like a great fatigue.

A succession of open carriages came bowling along the newly opened
sea-road. You could see across the wide grass-plots the discs of vibra-
tion made by the spokes. The bright domes of the parasols swayed
lightly outwards like full-blown blossoms on the rim of a vase; and
the quiet sheet of dark-blue water, crossed by a bar of purple, made a
background for the spinning wheels and the high action of the horses,
whilst the turbaned heads of the Indian servants elevated above the
line of the sea horizon glided rapidly on the paler blue of the sky. In
an open space near the little bridge each turn-out trotted smartly in a
wide curve away from the sunset; then pulling up sharp, entered the
main alley in a long slow-moving file with the great red stillness of the
sky at the back. The trunks of mighty trees stood all touched with red
on the same side, the air seemed aflame under the high foliage, the
very ground under the hoofs of the horses was red. The wheels turned
solemnly; one after another the sunshades drooped, folding their
colours like gorgeous flowers shutting their petals at the end of the
day. In the whole half-mile of human beings no voice uttered a dis-
tinct word, only a faint thudding noise went on mingled with slight
jingling sounds, and the motionless heads and shoulders of men and
women sitting in couples emerged stolidly above the lowered hoods—
as if wooden. But one carriage and pair coming late did not join the
line.

It fled along in a noiseless roll; but on entering the avenue one of
the dark bays snorted, arching his neck and shying against the steel-
tipped pole; a flake of foam fell from the bit upon the point of a
satiny shoulder, and the dusky face of the coachman leaned forward
at once over the hands taking a fresh grip of the reins. It was a
long dark-green landau, having a dignified and buoyant motion
between the sharply curved C-springs, and a sort of strictly official
majesty in its supreme elegance. It seemed more roomy than is usual,
its horses seemed slightly bigger, the appointments a shade more
perfect, the servants perched somewhat higher on the box. The dresses
of three women—two young and pretty, and one, handsome, large,
of mature age—seemed to fill completely the shallow body of the
carriage. The fourth face was that of a man, heavy lidded, distin-
guished and sallow, with a sombre, thick, iron-gray imperial and
moustaches, which somehow had the air of solid appendages. His
Excellency——

The rapid motion of that one equipage made all the others appear
utterly inferior, blighted, and reduced to crawl painfully at a snail's

pace. The landau distanced the whole file in a sort of sustained rush; the features of the occupants whirling out of sight left behind an impression of fixed stares and impassive vacancy; and after it had vanished in full flight as it were, notwithstanding the long line of vehicles hugging the curb at a walk, the whole lofty vista of the avenue seemed to lie open and emptied of life in the enlarged impression of an august solitude.

Captain Whalley had lifted his head to look, and his mind, disturbed in its meditation, turned with wonder (as men's minds will do) to matters of no importance. It struck him that it was to this port, where he had just sold his last ship, that he had come with the very first he had ever owned, and with his head full of a plan for opening a new trade with a distant part of the Archipelago. The then governor had given him no end of encouragement. No Excellency he—this Mr. Denham—this governor with his jacket off; a man who tended night and day, so to speak, the growing prosperity of the settlement with the self-forgetful devotion of a nurse for a child she loves; a lone bachelor who lived as in a camp with the few servants and his three dogs in what was called then the Government Bungalow: a low-roofed structure on the half-cleared slope of a hill, with a new flagstaff in front and a police orderly on the verandah. He remembered toiling up that hill under a heavy sun for his audience; the unfurnished aspect of the cool shaded room; the long table covered at one end with piles of papers, and with two guns, a brass telescope, a small bottle of oil with a feather stuck in the neck at the other—and the flattering attention given to him by the man in power. It was an undertaking full of risk he had come to expound, but a twenty minutes' talk in the Government Bungalow on the hill had made it go smoothly from the start. And as he was retiring Mr. Denham, already seated before the papers, called out after him, "Next month the *Dido* starts for a cruise that way, and I shall request her captain officially to give you a look-in and see how you get on." The *Dido* was one of the smart frigates on the China station—and five-and-thirty years make a big slice of time. Five-and-thirty years ago an enterprise like his had for the colony enough importance to be looked after by a Queen's ship. A big slice of time. Individuals were of some account then. Men like himself; men, too, like poor Evans, for instance, with his red face, his coal-black whiskers, and his restless eyes, who had set up the first patent slip for repairing small ships, on the edge of the forest, in a lonely bay three miles up the coast. Mr. Denham had encouraged that enterprise, too, and yet somehow poor Evans had ended by dying at home deucedly hard up. His son, they said, was squeezing oil out of cocoanuts for a living on some God-forsaken islet of the Indian Ocean;

but it was from that patent slip in a lonely wooded bay that had sprung the workshops of the Consolidated Docks Company, with its three graving basins carved out of solid rock, its wharves, its jetties, its electric-light plant, its steam-power houses—with its gigantic sheer-legs, fit to lift the heaviest weight ever carried afloat, and whose head could be seen like the top of a queer white monument peeping over bushy points of land and sandy promontories, as you approached the New Harbour from the west.

There had been a time when men counted: there were not so many carriages in the colony then, though Mr. Denham, he fancied, had a buggy. And Captain Whalley seemed to be swept out of the great avenue by the swirl of a mental backwash. He remembered muddy shores, a harbour without quays, the one solitary wooden pier (but that was a public work) jutting out crookedly, the first coal-sheds erected on Monkey Point, that caught fire mysteriously and smouldered for days, so that amazed ships came into a roadstead full of sulphurous fog, and the sun hung blood-red at midday. He remembered the things, the faces, and something more besides—like the faint flavour of a cup quaffed to the bottom, like a subtle sparkle of the air that was not to be found in the atmosphere of to-day.

In this evocation, swift and full of detail like a flash of magnesium light into the niches of a dark memorial hall, Captain Whalley contemplated things once important, the efforts of small men, the growth of a great place, but now robbed of all consequence by the greatness of accomplished facts, by hopes greater still; and they gave him for a moment such an almost physical grip upon time, such a comprehension of our unchangeable feelings, that he stopped short, struck the ground with his stick, and ejaculated mentally, "What the devil am I doing here!" He seemed lost in a sort of surprise; but he heard his name called out in wheezy tones once, twice—and turned on his heels slowly.

He beheld then, waddling towards him autocratically, a man of an old-fashioned and gouty aspect, with hair as white as his own, but with shaved, florid cheeks, wearing a necktie—almost a neckcloth—whose stiff ends projected far beyond his chin; with round legs, round arms, a round body, a round face—generally producing the effect of his short figure having been distended by means of an air-pump as much as the seams of his clothing would stand. This was the Master-Attendant of the port. A master-attendant is a superior sort of harbour-master; a person, out in the East, of some consequence in his sphere; a Government official, a magistrate for the waters of the port, and possessed of vast but ill-defined disciplinary authority over seamen of all classes. This particular Master-Attendant was reported to consider

it miserably inadequate, on the ground that it did not include the power of life and death. This was a jocular exaggeration. Captain Eliott was fairly satisfied with his position, and nursed no inconsiderable sense of such power as he had. His conceited and tyrannical disposition did not allow him to let it dwindle in his hands for want of use. The uproarious, choleric frankness of his comments on people's character and conduct caused him to be feared at bottom. Though in conversation many pretended not to mind him in the least, others would only smile sourly at the mention of his name, and there were even some who dared to pronounce him "a meddlesome old ruffian." But for almost all of them one of Captain Eliott's outbreaks was nearly as distasteful to face as a chance of annihilation.

§ 5

As soon as he had come up quite close he said, mouthing in a growl—

"What's this I hear, Whalley? Is it true you're selling the *Fair Maid?*"

Captain Whalley, looking away, said the thing was done—money had been paid that morning; and the other expressed at once his approbation of such an extremely sensible proceeding. He had got out of his trap to stretch his legs, he explained, on his way home to dinner. Sir Frederick looked well at the end of his time. Didn't he?

Captain Whalley could not say; had only noticed the carriage going past.

The Master-Attendant, plunging his hands into the pockets of an alpaca jacket inappropriately short and tight for a man of his age and appearance, strutted with a slight limp, and with his head reaching only to the shoulder of Captain Whalley, who walked easily, staring straight before him. They had been good comrades years ago, almost intimates. At the time when Whalley commanded the renowned *Condor,* Eliott had charge of the nearly as famous *Ringdove* for the same owners; and when the appointment of Master-Attendant was created, Whalley would have been the only other serious candidate. But Captain Whalley, then in the prime of life, was resolved to serve no one but his own auspicious Fortune. Far away, tending his hot irons, he was glad to hear the other had been successful. There was a worldly suppleness in bluff Ned Eliott that would serve him well in that sort of official appointment. And they were so dissimilar at bottom that as they came slowly to the end of the avenue before the Cathedral, it had never come into Whalley's head that he

might have been in that man's place—provided for to the end of his days.

The sacred edifice, standing in solemn isolation amongst the converging avenues of enormous trees, as if to put grave thoughts of heaven into the hours of ease, presented a closed Gothic portal to the light and glory of the west. The glass of the rosace above the ogive glowed like fiery coal in the deep carvings of a wheel of stone. The two men faced about.

"I'll tell you what they ought to do next, Whalley," growled Captain Eliott suddenly.

"Well?"

"They ought to send a real live lord out here when Sir Frederick's time is up. Eh?"

Captain Whalley perfunctorily did not see why a lord of the right sort should not do as well as any one else. But this was not the other's point of view.

"No, no. Place runs itself. Nothing can stop it now. Good enough for a lord," he growled in short sentences. "Look at the changes in our own time. We need a lord here now. They have got a lord in Bombay."

He dined once or twice every year at the Government House—a many-windowed, arcaded palace upon a hill laid out in roads and gardens. And lately he had been taking about a duke in his Master-Attendant's steam-launch to visit the harbour improvements. Before that he had "most obligingly" gone out in person to pick out a good berth for the ducal yacht. Afterwards he had an invitation to lunch on board. The duchess herself lunched with them. A big woman with a red face. Complexion quite sunburnt. He should think ruined. Very gracious manners. They were going on to Japan. . . .

He ejaculated these details for Captain Whalley's edification, pausing to blow out his cheeks as if with a pent-up sense of importance, and repeatedly protruding his thick lips till the blunt crimson end of his nose seemed to dip into the milk of his moustache. The place ran itself; it was fit for any lord; it gave no trouble except in its Marine department—in its Marine department, he repeated twice, and after a heavy snort began to relate how the other day her Majesty's Consul-General in French Cochin-China had cabled to him—in his official capacity—asking for a qualified man to be sent over to take charge of a Glasgow ship whose master had died in Saigon.

"I sent word of it to the officers' quarters in the Sailors' Home," he continued, while the limp in his gait seemed to grow more accentuated with the increasing irritation of his voice. "Place's full of them. Twice as many men as there are berths going in the local trade.

All hungry for an easy job. Twice as many—and—What d'you think, Whalley? . . . "

He stopped short; his hands, clenched and thrust deeply downwards, seemed ready to burst the pockets of his jacket. A slight sigh escaped Captain Whalley.

"Hey? You would think they would be falling over each other. Not a bit of it. Frightened to go home. Nice and warm out here to lie about a verandah waiting for a job. I sit and wait in my office. Nobody. What did they suppose? That I was going to sit there like a dummy with the Consul-General's cable before me? Not likely. So I looked up a list of them I keep by me and sent word for Hamilton—the worst loafer of them all—and just made him go. Threatened to instruct the steward of the Sailors' Home to have him turned out neck and crop. He did not think the berth was good enough—if you—please. 'I've your little record by me,' said I. 'You came ashore here eighteen months ago, and you haven't done six months' work since. You are in debt for your board now at the Home, and I suppose you reckon the Marine Office will pay in the end. Eh? So it shall; but if you don't take this chance, away you go to England, assisted passage, by the first homeward steamer that comes along. You are no better than a pauper. We don't want any white paupers here.' I scared him. But look at the trouble all this gave me.'"

"You would not have had any trouble," Captain Whalley said almost involuntarily, "if you had sent for me."

Captain Eliott was immensely amused; he shook with laughter as he walked. But suddenly he stopped laughing. A vague recollection had crossed his mind. Hadn't he heard it said at the time of the Travancore and Deccan smash that poor Whalley had been cleaned out completely? "Fellow's hard up, by heavens!" he thought; and at once he cast a sidelong upwards glance at his companion. But Captain Whalley was smiling austerely straight before him, with a carriage of the head inconceivable in a penniless man—and he became reassured. Impossible. Could not have lost everything. That ship had been only a hobby of his. And the reflection that a man who had confessed to receiving that very morning a presumably large sum of money was not likely to spring upon him a demand for a small loan put him entirely at his ease again. There had come a long pause in their talk, however, and not knowing how to begin again, he growled out soberly, "We old fellows ought to take a rest now."

"The best thing for some of us would be to die at the oar," Captain Whalley said, negligently.

"Come, now. Aren't you a bit tired by this time of the whole show?" muttered the other, sullenly.

"Are you?"

Captain Eliott was. Infernally tired. He only hung on to his berth so long in order to get his pension on the highest scale before he went home. It would be no better than poverty, anyhow; still, it was the only thing between him and the workhouse. And he had a family. Three girls, as Whalley knew. He gave "Harry, old boy," to understand that these three girls were a source of the greatest anxiety and worry to him. Enough to drive a man distracted.

"Why? What have they been doing now?" asked Captain Whalley with a sort of amused absent-mindedness.

"Doing! Doing nothing. That's just it. Lawn-tennis and silly novels from morning to night. . . . "

If one of them at least had been a boy! But all three! And, as ill-luck would have it, there did not seem to be any decent young fellows left in the world. When he looked around in the club he saw only a lot of conceited popinjays too selfish to think of making a good woman happy. Extreme indigence stared him in the face with all that crowd to keep at home. He had cherished the idea of building himself a little house in the country—in Surrey—to end his days in, but he was afraid it was out of the question . . . and his staring eyes rolled upwards with such a pathetic anxiety that Captain Whalley charitably nodded down at him, restraining a sort of sickening desire to laugh.

"You must know what it is yourself, Harry. Girls are the very devil for worry and anxiety."

"Ay! But mine is doing well," Captain Whalley pronounced slowly, staring to the end of the avenue.

The Master-Attendant was glad to hear this. Uncommonly glad. He remembered her well. A pretty girl she was.

Captain Whalley, stepping out carelessly, assented as if in a dream: "She was pretty."

The procession of carriages was breaking up.

One after another they left the file to go off at a trot, animating the vast avenue with their scattered life and movement; but soon the aspect of dignified solitude returned and took possession of the straight wide road. A syce in white stood at the head of a Burmah pony harnessed to a varnished two-wheel cart; and the whole thing waiting by the curb seemed no bigger than a child's toy forgotten under the soaring trees. Captain Eliott waddled up to it and made as if to clamber in, but refrained; and keeping one hand resting easily on the shaft, he changed the conversation from his pension, his daughters, and his poverty back again to the only other topic in the world—the Marine Office, the men and the ships of the port.

He proceeded to give instances of what was expected of him; and

his thick voice drowsed in the still air like the obstinate droning of an enormous bumble-bee. Captain Whalley did not know what was the force or the weakness that prevented him from saying good-night and walking away. It was as though he had been too tired to make the effort. How queer. More queer than any of Ned's instances. Or was it that overpowering sense of idleness alone that made him stand there and listen to these stories? Nothing very real had ever troubled Ned Eliott; and gradually he seemed to detect deep in, as if wrapped up in the gross wheezy rumble, something of the clear hearty voice of the young captain of the *Ringdove*. He wondered if he, too, had changed to the same extent; and it seemed to him that the voice of his old chum had not changed so very much—that the man was the same. Not a bad fellow the pleasant, jolly Ned Eliott, friendly, well up to his business—and always a bit of a humbug. He remembered how he used to amuse his poor wife. She could read him like an open book. When the *Condor* and the *Ringdove* happened to be in port together, she would frequently ask him to bring Captain Eliott to dinner. They had not met often since those old days. Not once in five years, perhaps. He regarded from under his white eyebrows this man he could not bring himself to take into his confidence at this juncture; and the other went on with his intimate outpourings, and as remote from his hearer as though he had been talking on a hill-top a mile away.

He was in a bit of a quandary now as to the steamer *Sofala*. Ultimately every hitch in the port came into his hands to undo. They would miss him when he was gone in another eighteen months, and most likely some retired naval officer had been pitchforked into the appointment—a man that would understand nothing and care less. That steamer was a coasting craft having a steady trade connection as far north as Tenasserim; but the trouble was she could get no captain to take her on her regular trip. Nobody would go in her. He really had no power, of course, to order a man to take a job. It was all very well to stretch a point on the demand of a consul-general, but. . . .

"What's the matter with the ship?" Captain Whalley interrupted in measured tones.

"Nothing's the matter. Sound old steamer. Her owner has been in my office this afternoon tearing his hair."

"Is he a white man?" asked Whalley in an interested voice.

"He calls himself a white man," answered the Master-Attendant scornfully; "but if so, it's just skin-deep and no more. I told him that to his face, too."

"But who is he, then?"

"He's the chief engineer of her. See *that*, Harry?"

"I see," Captain Whalley said, thoughtfully. "The engineer. I see."

How the fellow came to be a shipowner at the same time was quite a tale. He came out third in a home ship nearly fifteen years ago, Captain Eliott remembered, and got paid off after a bad sort of row both with his skipper and his chief. Anyway, they seemed jolly glad to get rid of him at all costs. Clearly a mutinous sort of chap. Well, he remained out here, a perfect nuisance, everlastingly shipped and unshipped, unable to keep a berth very long; pretty nigh went through every engine-room afloat belonging to the colony. Then suddenly, "What do you think happened, Harry?"

Captain Whalley, who seemed lost in a mental effort as of doing a sum in his head, gave a slight start. He really couldn't imagine. The Master-Attendant's voice vibrated dully with hoarse emphasis. The man actually had the luck to win the second great prize in the Manila lottery. All these engineers and officers of ships took tickets in that gamble. It seemed to be a perfect mania with them all.

Everybody expected now that he would take himself off home with his money, and go to the devil in his own way. Not at all. The *Sofala,* judged too small and not quite modern enough for the sort of trade she was in, could be got for a moderate price from her owners, who had ordered a new steamer from Europe. He rushed in and bought her. This man had never given any signs of that sort of mental intoxication the mere fact of getting hold of a large sum of money may produce—not till he got a ship of his own; but then he went off his balance all at once: came bouncing into the Marine Office on some transfer business, with his hat hanging over his left eye and switching a little cane in his hand, and told each one of the clerks separately that "Nobody could put him out now. It was his turn. There was no one over him on earth, and there never would be either." He swaggered and strutted between the desks, talking at the top of his voice, and trembling like a leaf all the while, so that the current business of the office was suspended for the time he was in there, and everybody in the big room stood open-mouthed looking at his antics. Afterwards he could be seen during the hottest hours of the day with his face as red as fire rushing along up and down the quays to look at his ship from different points of view: he seemed inclined to stop every stranger he came across just to let them know "that there would be no longer any one over him; he had bought a ship; nobody on earth could put him out of his engine-room now."

Good bargain as she was, the price of the *Sofala* took up pretty near all the lottery-money. He had left himself no capital to work with. That did not matter so much, for these were the halcyon days of steam

coasting trade, before some of the home shipping firms had thought of establishing local fleets to feed their main lines. These, when once organized, took the biggest slices out of that cake, of course; and by and by a squad of confounded German tramps turned up east of Suez Canal and swept up all the crumbs. They prowled on the cheap to and fro along the coast and between the islands, like a lot of sharks in the water ready to snap up anything you let drop. And then the high old times were over for good; for years the *Sofala* had made no more, he judged, than a fair living. Captain Eliott looked upon it as his duty in every way to assist an English ship to hold her own; and it stood to reason that if for want of a captain the *Sofala* began to miss her trips she would very soon lose her trade. There was the quandary. The man was too impracticable. "Too much of a beggar on horseback from the first," he explained. "Seemed to grow worse as the time went on. In the last three years he's run through eleven skippers; he had tried every single man here, outside of the regular lines. I had warned him before that this would not do. And now, of course, no one will look at the *Sofala*. I had one or two men up at my office and talked to them; but, as they said to me, what was the good of taking the berth to lead a regular dog's life for a month and then get the sack at the end of the first trip? The fellow, of course, told me it was all nonsense; there has been a plot hatching for years against him. And now it had come. All the horrid sailors in the port had conspired to bring him to his knees, because he was an engineer." Captain Eliott emitted a throaty chuckle.

"And the fact is, that if he misses a couple more trips he need never trouble himself to start again. He won't find any cargo in his old trade. There's too much competition nowadays for people to keep their stuff lying about for a ship that does not turn up when she's expected. It's a bad lookout for him. He swears he will shut himself on board and starve to death in his cabin rather than sell her—even if he could find a buyer. And that's not likely in the least. Not even the Japs would give her insured value for her. It isn't like selling sailing-ships. Steamers *do* get out of date, besides getting old."

"He must have laid by a good bit of money though," observed Captain Whalley, quietly.

The Harbour-master puffed out his purple cheeks to an amazing size.

"Not a stiver, Harry. Not—a—single sti-ver."

He waited; but as Captain Whalley, stroking his beard slowly, looked down on the ground without a word, he tapped him on the forearm, tiptoed, and said in a hoarse whisper—

"The Manila lottery has been eating him up."

He frowned a little, nodding in tiny affirmative jerks. They all were going in for it; a third of the wages paid to ships' officers ("in my port," he snorted) went to Manila. It was a mania. That fellow Massy had been bitten by it like the rest of them from the first; but after winning once he seemed to have persuaded himself he had only to try again to get another big prize. He had taken dozens and scores of tickets for every drawing since. What with this vice and his ignorance of affairs, ever since he had improvidently bought that steamer he had been more or less short of money.

This, in Captain Eliott's opinion, gave an opening for a sensible sailor-man with a few pounds to step in and save that fool from the consequences of his folly. It was his craze to quarrel with his captains. He had had some really good men, too, who would have been too glad to stay if he would only let them. But no. He seemed to think he was no owner unless he was kicking somebody out in the morning and having a row with the new man in the evening. What was wanted for him was a master with a couple of hundred or so to take an interest in the ship on proper conditions. You don't discharge a man for no fault, only because of the fun of telling him to pack up his traps and go ashore, when you know that in that case you are bound to buy back his share. On the other hand, a fellow with an interest in the ship is not likely to throw up his job in a huff about a trifle. He had told Massy that. He had said: " 'This won't do, Mr. Massy. We are getting very sick of you here in the Marine Office. What you must do now is to try whether you could get a sailor to join you as partner. That seems to be the only way.' And that was sound advice, Harry."

Captain Whalley, leaning on his stick, was perfectly still all over, and his hand, arrested in the act of stroking, grasped his whole beard. And what did the fellow say to that?

The fellow had the audacity to fly out at the Master-Attendant. He had received the advice in a most impudent manner. "I didn't come here to be laughed at," he had shrieked. "I appeal to you as an Englishman and a shipowner brought to the verge of ruin by an illegal conspiracy of your beggarly sailors, and all you condescend to do for me is to tell me to go and get a partner!" The fellow had presumed to stamp with rage on the floor of the private office. Where was he going to get a partner? Was he being taken for a fool? Not a single one of that contemptible lot ashore at the "Home" had twopence in his pocket to bless himself with. The very native curs in the bazaar knew that much. . . . "And it's true enough, Harry," rumbled Captain Eliott, judicially. "They are much more likely one and all to owe money to the Chinamen in Denham Road for the clothes on their backs. 'Well,' said I, 'you make too much noise over it for my

taste, Mr. Massy. Good morning.' He banged the door after him; he dared to bang my door, confound his cheek!"

The head of the Marine department was out of breath with indignation; then recollecting himself as it were, "I'll end by being late to dinner—yarning with you here . . . wife doesn't like it."

He clambered ponderously into the trap; leaned out side-ways, and only then wondered wheezily what on earth Captain Whalley could have been doing with himself of late. They had had no sight of each other for years and years till the other day when he had seen him unexpectedly in the office.

What on earth. . . .

Captain Whalley seemed to be smiling to himself in his white beard.

"The earth is big," he said, vaguely.

The other, as if to test the statement, stared all round from his driving-seat. The Esplanade was very quiet; only from afar, from very far, a long way from the sea-shore, across the stretches of grass, through the long ranges of trees, came faintly the toot—toot—toot of the cable car beginning to roll before the empty peristyle of the Public Library on its three-mile journey to the New Harbour Docks.

"Doesn't seem to be so much room on it," growled the Master-Attendant, "since these Germans came along shouldering us at every turn. It was not so in our time."

He fell into deep thought, breathing stertorously, as though he had been taking a nap open-eyed. Perhaps he, too, on his side, had detected in the silent pilgrim-like figure, standing there by the wheel, like an arrested wayfarer, the buried lineaments of the features belonging to the young captain of the *Condor*. Good fellow—Harry Whalley —never very talkative. You never knew what he was up to—a bit too off-hand with people of consequence, and apt to take a wrong view of a fellow's actions. Fact was he had a too good opinion of himself. He would have liked to tell him to get in and drive him home to dinner. But one never knew. Wife would not like it.

"And it's funny to think, Harry," he went on in a big subdued drone, "that of all the people on it there seems only you and I left to remember this part of the world as it used to be. . . ."

He was ready to indulge in the sweetness of a sentimental mood had it not struck him suddenly that Captain Whalley, unstirring and without a word, seemed to be awaiting something—perhaps expecting. . . . He gathered the reins at once and burst out in bluff hearty growls—

"Ha! My dear boy. The men we have known—the ships we've sailed—ay! and the things we've done. . . . "

The pony plunged—the syce skipped out of the way, Captain Whalley raised his arm.

"Good-bye."

§ 6

The sun had set. And when, after drilling a deep hole with his stick, he moved from that spot the night had massed its army of shadows under the trees. They filled the eastern ends of the avenue as if only waiting the signal for a general advance upon the open spaces of the world; they were gathering low between the deep stone-faced banks of the canal. The Malay prau, half concealed under the arch of the bridge, had not altered its position a quarter of an inch. For a long time Captain Whalley stared down over the parapet, till at last the floating immobility of that beshrouded thing seemed to grow upon him into something inexplicable and alarming. The twilight abandoned the zenith; its reflected gleams left the world below, and the water of the canal seemed to turn into pitch. Captain Whalley crossed it.

The turning to the right, which was his way to his hotel, was only a very few steps farther. He stopped again (all the houses of the sea-front were shut up, the quayside was deserted, but for one or two figures of natives walking in the distance) and began to reckon the amount of his bill. So many days in the hotel at so many dollars a day. To count the days he used his fingers: plunging one hand into his pocket, he jingled a few silver coins. All right for three days more; and then, unless something turned up, he must break into the five hundred—Ivy's money—invested in her father. It seemed to him that the first meal coming out of that reserve would choke him—for certain. Reason was of no use. It was a matter of feeling. His feelings had never played him false.

He did not turn to the right. He walked on, as if there still had been a ship in the roadstead to which he could get himself pulled off in the evening. Far away, beyond the houses, on the slope of an indigo promontory closing the view of the quays, the slim column of a factory-chimney smoked quietly straight up into the clear air. A Chinaman, curled down in the stern of one of the half-dozen sampans floating off the end of the jetty, caught sight of a beckoning hand. He jumped up, rolled his pigtail round his head swiftly, tucked in two rapid movements his wide dark trousers high up his yellow thighs, and by a single, noiseless, finlike stir of the oars, sheered the sampan alongside the steps with the ease and precision of a swimming fish.

"*Sofala*," articulated Captain Whalley from above; and the China-

man, a new emigrant probably, stared upwards with a tense attention as if waiting to see the queer word fall visibly from the white man's lips. *"Sofala,"* Captain Whalley repeated; and suddenly his heart failed him. He paused. The shores, the islets, the high ground, the low points, were dark: the horizon had grown sombre; and across the eastern sweep of the shore the white obelisk, marking the landing-place of the telegraph-cable, stood like a pale ghost on the beach before the dark spread of uneven roofs, intermingled with palms, of the native town. Captain Whalley began again:

"Sofala. Savee *So-fa-la,* John?"

This time the Chinaman made out that bizarre sound, and grunted his assent uncouthly, low down in his bare throat. With the first yellow twinkle of a star that appeared like the head of a pin stabbed deep into the smooth, pale, shimmering fabric of the sky, the edge of a keen chill seemed to cleave through the warm air of the earth. At the moment of stepping into the sampan to go and try for the command of the *Sofala* Captain Whalley shivered a little.

When on his return he landed on the quay again, Venus, like a choice jewel set low on the hem of the sky, cast a faint gold trail behind him upon the roadstead, as level as a floor made of one dark and polished stone. The lofty vaults of the avenues were black—all black overhead—and the porcelain globes on the lamp-posts re-sembled egg-shaped pearls, gigantic and luminous, displayed in a row whose farther end seemed to sink in the distance, down to the level of his knees. He put his hands behind his back. He would now con-sider calmly the discretion of it before saying the final word to-morrow. His feet scrunched the gravel loudly—the discretion of it. It would have been easier to appraise had there been a workable alternative. The honesty of it was indubitable: he meant well by the fellow; and periodically his shadow leaped up intense by his side on the trunks of the trees, to lengthen itself, oblique and dim, far over the grass— repeating his stride.

The discretion of it. Was there a choice? He seemed already to have lost something of himself; to have given up to a hungry spectre some-thing of his truth and dignity in order to live. But his life was necessary. Let poverty do its worst in exacting its toll of humiliation. It was certain that Ned Eliott had rendered him, without knowing it, a service for which it would have been impossible to ask. He hoped Ned would not think there had been something underhand in his action. He supposed that now when he heard of it he would understand—or perhaps he would only think Whalley an eccentric old fool. What would have been the good of telling him—any more than of blurting the whole tale to that man Massy? Five hundred pounds ready to

invest. Let him make the best of that. Let him wonder. You want a captain—I want a ship. That's enough. B-r-r-r. What a disagreeable impression that empty, dark, echoing steamer had made upon him. . . .

A laid-up steamer was a dead thing and no mistake; a sailing-ship somehow seems always ready to spring into life with the breath of the incorruptible heaven; but a steamer, thought Captain Whalley, with her fires out, without the warm whiffs from below meeting you on her decks, without the hiss of steam, the clangs of iron in her breast —lies there as cold and still and pulseless as a corpse.

In the solitude of the avenue, all black above and lighted below, Captain Whalley, considering the discretion of his course, met, as it were incidentally, the thought of death. He pushed it aside with dislike and contempt. He almost laughed at it; and in the unquenchable vitality of his age only thought with a kind of exultation how little he needed to keep body and soul together. Not a bad investment for the poor woman this solid carcass of her father. And for the rest—in case of anything—the agreement should be clear: the whole five hundred to be paid back to her integrally within three months. Integrally. Every penny. He was not to lose any of her money whatever else had to go—a little dignity—some of his self-respect. He had never before allowed anybody to remain under any sort of false impression as to himself. Well, let that go—for her sake. After all, he had never *said* anything misleading—and Captain Whalley felt himself corrupt to the marrow of his bones. He laughed a little with the intimate scorn of his worldly prudence. Clearly, with a fellow of that sort, and in the peculiar relation they were to stand to each other, it would not have done to blurt out everything. He did not like the fellow. He did not like his spells of fawning loquacity and bursts of resentfulness. In the end—a poor devil. He would not have liked to stand in his shoes. Men were not evil, after all. He did not like his sleek hair, his queer way of standing at right angles, with his nose in the air, and glancing along his shoulder at you. No. On the whole, men were not bad—they were only silly or unhappy.

Captain Whalley had finished considering the discretion of that step—and there was the whole long night before him. In the full light his long beard would glisten like a silver breastplate covering his heart; in the spaces between the lamps his burly figure passed less distinct, loomed very big, wandering, and mysterious. No; there was not much real harm in men: and all the time a shadow marched with him, slanting on his left hand—which in the East is a presage of evil.

"Can you make out the clump of palms yet, Serang?" asked Captain Whalley from his chair on the bridge of the *Sofala* approaching the bar of Batu Beru.

"No, Tuan. By and by see." The old Malay, in a blue dungaree suit, planted on his bony dark feet under the bridge awning, put his hands behind his back and stared ahead out of the innumerable wrinkles at the corners of his eyes.

Captain Whalley sat still, without lifting his head to look for himself. Three years—thirty-six times. He had made these palms thirty-six times from the southward. They would come into view at the proper time. Thank God, the old ship made her courses and distances trip after trip, as correct as clockwork. At last he murmured again—

"In sight yet?"

"The sun makes a very great glare, Tuan."

"Watch well, Serang."

"Ya, Tuan."

A white man had ascended the ladder from the deck noiselessly, and had listened quietly to this short colloquy. Then he stepped out on the bridge and began to walk from end to end, holding up the long cherrywood stem of a pipe. His black hair lay plastered in long lanky wisps across the bald summit of his head; he had a furrowed brow, a yellow complexion, and a thick shapeless nose. A scanty growth of whisker did not conceal the contour of his jaw. His aspect was of brooding care; and sucking at a curved black mouthpiece, he presented such a heavy overhanging profile that even the Serang could not help reflecting sometimes upon the extreme unloveliness of some white men.

Captain Whalley seemed to brace himself up in his chair, but gave no recognition whatever to his presence. The other puffed jets of smoke; then suddenly—

"I could never understand that new mania of yours of having this Malay here for your shadow, partner."

Captain Whalley got up from the chair in all his imposing stature and walked across to the binnacle, holding such an unswerving course that the other had to back away hurriedly, and remained as if intimidated, with the pipe trembling in his hand. "Walk over me now," he muttered in a sort of astounded and discomfited whisper. Then slowly and distinctly he said—

"I—am—not—dirt." And then added defiantly, "As you seem to think."

The Serang jerked out—

"See the palms now, Tuan."

Captain Whalley strode forward to the rail; but his eyes, instead

of going straight to the point, with the assured keen glance of a sailor, wandered irresolutely in space, as though he, the discoverer of new routes, had lost his way upon this narrow sea.

Another white man, the mate, came up on the bridge. He was tall, young, lean, with a moustache like a trooper, and something malicious in the eye. He took up a position beside the engineer. Captain Whalley with his back to them inquired—

"What's on the log?"

"Eighty-five," answered the mate quickly, and nudged the engineer with his elbow.

Captain Whalley's muscular hands squeezed the iron rail with an extraordinary force; his eyes glared with an enormous effort; he knitted his eyebrows, the perspiration fell from under his hat—and in a faint voice he murmured, "Steady her, Serang—when she is on the proper bearing."

The silent Malay stepped back, waited a little, and lifted his arm warningly to the helmsman. The wheel revolved rapidly to meet the swing of the ship. Again the mate nudged the engineer. But Massy turned upon him.

"Mr. Sterne," he said, violently, "let me tell you—as a shipowner—that you are no better than a confounded fool."

§ 7

Sterne went down smirking and apparently not at all disconcerted, but the engineer Massy remained on the bridge, moving about with uneasy self-assertion. Everybody on board was his inferior—everyone without exception. He paid their wages and found them in their food. They ate more of his bread and pocketed more of his money than they were worth; and they had no care in the world, while he alone had to meet all the difficulties of shipowning. When he contemplated his position in all its menacing entirety, it seemed to him that he had been for years the prey of a band of parasites; and for years he had scowled at everybody connected with the *Sofala* except, perhaps, at the Chinese firemen who served to get her along. Their use was manifest: they were an indispensable part of the machinery of which he was the master.

When he passed along his decks he shouldered those he came across brutally; but the Malay deck hands had learned to dodge out of his way. He had to bring himself to tolerate them because of the necessary manual labour of the ship which must be done. He had to struggle and plan and scheme to keep the *Sofala* afloat—and what did

he get for it? Not even enough respect. They could not have given him enough of that if all their thoughts and all their actions had been directed to that end. The vanity of possession, the vainglory of power, had passed away by this time, and there remained only the material embarrassments, the fear of losing that position which had turned out not worth having, and an anxiety of thought which no abject subservience of men could repay.

He walked up and down. The bridge was his own after all. He had paid for it; and with the stem of the pipe in his hand he would stop short at times as if to listen with a profound and concentrated attention to the deadened beat of the engines (his own engines) and the slight grinding of the steering chains upon the continuous low wash of water alongside. But for these sounds, the ship might have been lying as still as if moored to a bank, and as silent as if abandoned by every living soul; only the coast, the low coast of mud and mangroves with the three palms in a bunch at the back, grew slowly more distinct in its long straight line; without a single feature to arrest attention. The native passengers of the *Sofala* lay about on mats under the awnings; the smoke of her funnel seemed the only sign of her life and connected with her gliding motion in a mysterious manner.

Captain Whalley on his feet, with a pair of binoculars in his hand and the little Malay Serang at his elbow, like an old giant attended by a wizened pigmy, was taking her over the shallow water of the bar.

This submarine ridge of mud, scoured by the stream out of the soft bottom of the river and heaped up far out on the hard bottom of the sea, was difficult to get over. The alluvial coast having no distinguishing marks, the bearings of the crossing-place had to be taken from the shape of the mountains inland. The guidance of a form flattened and uneven at the top like a grinder tooth, and of another smooth, saddle-backed summit, had to be searched for within the great unclouded glare that seemed to shift and float like a dry fiery mist, filling the air, ascending from the water, shrouding the distances, scorching to the eye. In this veil of light the near edge of the shore alone stood out almost coal-black with an opaque and motionless solidity. Thirty miles away the serrated range of the interior stretched across the horizon, its outlines and shades of blue, faint and tremulous like a background painted on airy gossamer on the quivering fabric of an impalpable curtain let down to the plain of alluvial soil; and the openings of the estuary appeared, shining white, like bits of silver let into the square pieces snipped clean and sharp out of the body of the land bordered with mangroves.

On the forepart of the bridge the giant and the pigmy muttered to each other frequently in quiet tones. Behind them Massy stood sideways with an expression of disdain and suspense on his face. His globular eyes were perfectly motionless, and he seemed to have forgotten the long pipe he held in his hand.

On the fore-deck below the bridge, steeply roofed with the white slopes of the awnings, a young lascar seaman had clambered outside the rail. He adjusted quickly a broad band of sail canvas under his armpits, and throwing his chest against it, leaned out far over the water. The sleeve of his thin cotton shirt, cut off close to the shoulder, bared his brown arm of full rounded form and with a satiny skin like a woman's. He swung it rigidly with the rotary and menacing action of a slinger: the 14-lb. weight hurtled circling in the air, then suddenly flew ahead as far as the curve of the bow. The wet thin line swished like scratched silk running through the dark fingers of the man, and the plunge of the lead close to the ship's side made a vanishing silvery scar upon the golden glitter; then after an interval the voice of the young Malay uplifted and longdrawn declared the depth of the water in his own language.

"Tiga stengah," he cried after each splash and pause, gathering the line busily for another cast. "Tiga stengah," which means three fathom and a half. For a mile or so from seaward there was a uniform depth of water right up to the bar. "Half-three. Half-three. Half-three,"— and his modulated cry, returned leisurely and monotonous, like the repeated call of a bird, seemed to float away in sunshine and disappear in the spacious silence of the empty sea and of a lifeless shore lying open, north and south, east and west, without the stir of a single cloud-shadow or the whisper of any other voice.

The owner-engineer of the *Sofala* remained very still behind the two seamen of different race, creed, and colour; the European with the time-defying vigour of his old frame, the little Malay, old, too, but slight and shrunken like a withered brown leaf blown by a chance wind under the mighty shadow of the other. Very busy looking forward at the land, they had not a glance to spare; and Massy, glaring at them from behind, seemed to resent their attention to their duty like a personal slight upon himself.

This was unreasonable; but he had lived in his own world of unreasonable resentments for many years. At last, passing his moist palm over the rare lanky wisps of coarse hair on the top of his yellow head, he began to talk slowly.

"A leadsman, you want! I suppose that's your correct mail-boat style. Haven't you enough judgment to tell where you are by looking at the land? Why, before I had been a twelvemonth in the trade *I*

was up to that trick—and I am only an engineer. I can point to you from here where the bar is, and I could tell you besides that you are likely as not to stick her in the mud in about five minutes from now; only you would call it interfering, I suppose. And there's that written agreement of ours, that says I mustn't interfere."

His voice stopped. Captain Whalley, without relaxing the set severity of his features, moved his lips to ask in a quick mumble—

"How near, Serang?"

"Very near now, Tuan," the Malay muttered, rapidly.

"Dead slow," said the Captain aloud in a firm tone.

The Serang snatched at the handle of the telegraph. A gong clanged down below. Massy with a scornful snigger walked off and put his head down the engine-room skylight.

"You may expect some rare fooling with the engines, Jack," he bellowed. The space into which he stared was deep and full of gloom; and the gray gleams of steel down there seemed cool after the intense glare of the sea around the ship. The air, however, came up clammy and hot on his face. A short hoot on which it would have been impossible to put any sort of interpretation came from the bottom cavernously. This was the way in which the second engineer answered his chief.

He was a middle-aged man with an inattentive manner, and apparently wrapped up in such a taciturn concern for his engines that he seemed to have lost the use of speech. When addressed directly his only answer would be a grunt or a hoot, according to the distance. For all the years he had been in the *Sofala* he had never been known to exchange as much as a frank Good-morning with any of his shipmates. He did not seem aware that men came and went in the world; he did not seem to see them at all. Indeed he never recognized his shipmates on shore. At table (the four white men of the *Sofala* messed together) he sat looking into his plate dispassionately, but at the end of the meal would jump up and bolt down below as if a sudden thought had impelled him to rush and see whether somebody had not stolen the engines while he dined. In port at the end of the trip he went ashore regularly, but no one knew where he spent his evenings or in what manner. The local coasting fleet had preserved a wild and incoherent tale of his infatuation for the wife of a sergeant in an Irish infantry regiment. The regiment, however, had done its turn of garrison duty there ages before, and was gone somewhere to the other side of the earth, out of men's knowledge. Twice or perhaps three times in the course of the year he would take too much to drink. On these occasions he would return on board at an earlier hour than usual; run across the deck balancing himself with his spread arms

like a tight-rope walker; and locking the door of his cabin, he would
converse and argue with himself the livelong night in an amazing
variety of tones; storm, sneer, and whine with an inexhaustible per-
sistence. Massy in his berth next door, raising himself on his elbow,
would discover that his second remembered the name of every white
man that had passed through the *Sofala* for years and years back. He
remembered the names of men that had died, that had gone home,
that had gone to America: he remembered in his cups the names of
men whose connection with the ship had been so short that Massy
had almost forgotten its circumstances and could barely recall their
faces. The inebriated voice on the other side of the bulkhead com-
mented upon them all with an extraordinary and ingenious venom of
scandalous inventions. It seems they had all offended him in some
way, and in return he had found them all out. He muttered darkly;
he laughed sardonically; he crushed them one after another; but
of his chief, Massy, he babbled with an envious and naïve admiration.
Clever scoundrel! Don't meet the likes of him every day. Just look at
him. Ha! Great! Ship of his own. Wouldn't catch *him* going wrong.
No fear—the beast! And Massy, after listening with a gratified smile
to these artless tributes to his greatness, would begin to shout, thump-
ing at the bulkhead with both fists—

"Shut up, you lunatic! Won't you let me go to sleep, you fool!"

But a half smile of pride lingered on his lips; outside the solitary
lascar told off for night duty in harbour, perhaps a youth fresh from
a forest village, would stand motionless in the shadows of the deck
listening to the endless drunken gabble. His heart would be thumping
with breathless awe of white men: the arbitrary and obstinate men
who pursue inflexibly their incomprehensible purposes—beings with
weird intonations in the voice, moved by unaccountable feelings,
actuated by inscrutable motives.

§ 8

For a while after his second's answering hoot Massy hung over
the engine-room gloomily. Captain Whalley who, by the power
of five hundred pounds, had kept his command for three years, might
have been suspected of never having seen that coast before. He
seemed unable to put down his glasses, as though they had been glued
under his contracted eyebrows. This settled frown gave to his face an
air of invincible and just severity; but his raised elbow trembled
slightly, and the perspiration poured from under his hat as if a
second sun had suddenly blazed up at the zenith by the side of the

ardent still globe already there, in whose blinding white heart the
earth whirled and shone like a mote of dust.

From time to time, still holding up his glasses, he raised his other
hand to wipe his streaming face. The drops rolled down his cheeks,
fell like rain upon the white hairs of his beard, and brusquely, as if
guided by an uncontrollable and anxious impulse, his arm reached
out to the stand of the engine-room telegraph.

The gong clanged down below. The balanced vibration of the
dead-slow speed ceased together with every sound and tremor in the
ship, as if the great stillness that reigned upon the coast had stolen in
through her sides of iron and taken possession of her innermost
recesses. The illusion of perfect immobility seemed to fall upon her
from the luminous blue dome without a stain arching over a flat
sea without a stir. The faint breeze she had made for herself ex-
pired, as if all at once the air had become too thick to budge; even
the slight hiss of the water on her stem died out. The narrow, long
hull, carrying its way without a ripple, seemed to approach the shoal
water of the bar by stealth. The plunge of the lead with the mournful,
mechanical cry of the lascar came at longer and longer intervals; and
the men on her bridge seemed to hold their breath. The Malay at the
helm looked fixedly at the compass card, the Captain and the Serang
stared at the coast.

Massy had left the skylight, and, walking flat-footed, had returned
softly to the very spot on the bridge he had occupied before. A slow,
lingering grin exposed his set of big white teeth: they gleamed evenly
in the shade of the awning like the keyboard of a piano in a dusky
room.

At last, pretending to talk to himself in excessive astonishment, he
said not very loud—

"Stop the engines now. What next, I wonder?"

He waited, stooping from the shoulders, his head bowed, his glance
oblique. Then raising his voice a shade—

"If I dared make an absurd remark I would say that you haven't
the stomach to. . . . "

But a yelling spirit of excitement, like some frantic soul wandering
unsuspected in the vast stillness of the coast, had seized upon the
body of the lascar at the lead. The languid monotony of his sing-song
changed to a swift, sharp clamour. The weight flew after a single
whirr, the line whistled, splash followed splash in haste. The water had
shoaled, and the man, instead of the drowsy tale of fathoms, was call-
ing out the soundings in feet.

"Fifteen feet. Fifteen, fifteen! Fourteen, fourteen. . . . "

Captain Whalley lowered the arm holding the glasses. It descended

slowly as if by its own weight; no other part of his towering body stirred; and the swift cries with their eager warning note passed him by as though he had been deaf.

Massy, very still, and turning an attentive ear, had fastened his eyes upon the silvery, close-cropped back of the steady old head. The ship herself seemed to be arrested but for the gradual decrease of depth under her keel.

"Thirteen feet . . . Thirteen! Twelve!" cried the leadsman anxiously below the bridge. And suddenly the barefooted Serang stepped away noiselessly to steal a glance over the side.

Narrow of shoulder, in a suit of faded blue cotton, an old gray felt hat rammed down on his head, with a hollow in the nape of his dark neck, and with his slender limbs, he appeared from the back no bigger than a boy of fourteen. There was a childlike impulsiveness in the curiosity with which he watched the spread of the voluminous, yellowish convolutions rolling up from below to the surface of the blue water like massive clouds driving slowly upwards on the un-fathomable sky. He was not startled at the sight in the least. It was not doubt, but the certitude that the keel of the *Sofala* must be stirring the mud now, which made him peep over the side.

His peering eyes, set aslant in a face of the Chinese type, a little old face, immovable, as if carved in old brown oak, had informed him long before that the ship was not headed at the bar properly. Paid off from the *Fair Maid*, together with the rest of the crew, after the completion of the sale, he had hung, in his faded blue suit and floppy gray hat, about the doors of the Harbour Office, till one day, seeing Captain Whalley coming along to get a crew for the *Sofala*, he had put himself quietly in the way, with his bare feet in the dust and an upward mute glance. The eyes of his old commander had fallen on him favourably—it must have been an auspicious day—and in less than half an hour the white men in the "Ofiss" had written his name on a document as Serang of the fire-ship *Sofala*. Since that time he had repeatedly looked at that estuary, upon that coast, from this bridge and from this side of the bar. The record of the visual world fell through his eyes upon his unspeculating mind as on a sensitized plate through the lens of a camera. His knowledge was absolute and precise; nevertheless, had he been asked his opinion, and especially if questioned in the down-right, alarming manner of white men, he would have displayed the hesitation of ignorance. He was certain of his facts—but such a certitude counted for little against the doubt what answer would be pleasing. Fifty years ago, in a jungle village, and before he was a day old, his father (who died without ever seeing a white face) had had his nativity cast by a man of skill

and wisdom in astrology, because in the arrangement of the stars may be read the last word of human destiny. His destiny had been to thrive by the favour of various white men on the sea. He had swept the decks of ships, had tended their helms, had minded their stores, had risen at last to be a Serang; and his placid mind had remained as incapable of penetrating the simplest motives of those he served as they themselves were incapable of detecting through the crust of the earth the secret nature of its heart, which may be fire or may be stone. But he had no doubt whatever that the *Sofala* was out of the proper track for crossing the bar at Batu Beru.

It was a slight error. The ship could not have been more than twice her own length too far to the northward; and a white man at a loss for a cause (since it was impossible to suspect Captain Whalley of blundering ignorance, of want of skill, or of neglect) would have been inclined to doubt the testimony of his senses. It was some such feeling that kept Massy motionless, with his teeth laid bare by an anxious grin. Not so the Serang. He was not troubled by any intellectual mistrust of his senses. If his captain chose to stir the mud it was well. He had known in his life white men indulge in outbreaks equally strange. He was only genuinely interested to see what would come of it. At last, apparently satisfied, he stepped back from the rail.

He had made no sound: Captain Whalley, however, seemed to have observed the movements of his Serang. Holding his head rigidly, he asked with a mere stir of his lips—

"Going ahead still, Serang?"

"Still going a little, Tuan," answered the Malay. Then added casually, "She is over."

The lead confirmed his words; the depth of water increased at every cast, and the soul of excitement departed suddenly from the lascar swung in the canvas belt over the *Sofala's* side. Captain Whalley ordered the lead in, set the engines ahead without haste, and averting his eyes from the coast directed the Serang to keep a course for the middle of the entrance.

Massy brought the palm of his hand with a loud smack against his thigh.

"You grazed on the bar. Just look astern and see if you didn't. Look at the track she left. You can see it plainly. Upon my soul, I thought you would! What made you do that? What on earth made you do that? I believe you are trying to scare me."

He talked slowly, as it were circumspectly, keeping his prominent black eyes on his captain. There was also a slight plaintive note in his rising choler, for, primarily, it was the clear sense of a wrong suffered undeservedly that made him hate the man who, for a beggarly

five hundred pounds, claimed a sixth part of the profits under the
three years' agreement. Whenever his resentment got the better of
the awe the person of Captain Whalley inspired he would positively
whimper with fury.

"You don't know what to invent to plague my life out of me. I
would not have thought that a man of your sort would con-
descend. . . . "

He paused, half hopefully, half timidly, whenever Captain Whalley
made the slightest movement in the deck-chair, as though expecting
to be conciliated by a soft speech or else rushed upon and hunted
off the bridge.

"I am puzzled," he went on again, with the watchful, unsmiling
baring of his big teeth. "I don't know what to think. I do believe you
are trying to frighten me. You very nearly planted her on the bar
for at least twelve hours, besides getting the engines choked with
mud. Ships can't afford to lose twelve hours on a trip nowadays—as
you ought to know very well, and do know very well to be sure,
only. . . . "

His slow volubility, the sideways cranings of his neck, the black
glances out of the very corners of his eyes, left Captain Whalley un-
moved. He looked at the deck with a severe frown. Massy waited for
some little time, then began to threaten plaintively.

"You think you've got me bound hand and foot in that agreement.
You think you can torment me in any way you please. Ah! But
remember it has another six weeks to run yet. There's time for me
to dismiss you before the three years are out. You will do yet some-
thing that will give me the chance to dismiss you, and make you wait
a twelvemonth for your money before you can take yourself off and
pull out your five hundred, and leave me without a penny to get
the new boilers for her. You gloat over that idea—don't you? I do
believe you sit here gloating. It's as if I had sold my soul for five
hundred pounds to be everlastingly damned in the end. . . . "

He paused, without apparent exasperation, then continued evenly—

" . . . With the boilers worn out and the survey hanging over my
head, Captain Whalley—— Captain Whalley, I say, what do you
do with your money? You must have stacks of money somewhere—
a man like you must. It stands to reason. I am not a fool, you know,
Captain Whalley—partner."

Again he paused, as though he had done for good. He passed his
tongue over his lips, gave a backward glance at the Serang conning
the ship with quiet whispers and slight signs of the hand. The wash
of the propeller sent a swift ripple, crested with dark froth, upon a
long flat spit of black slime. The *Sofala* had entered the river; the

trail she had stirred up over the bar was a mile astern of her now, out of sight, had disappeared utterly; and the smooth, empty sea along the coast was left behind in the glittering desolation of sunshine. On each side of her, low down, the growth of sombre twisted mangroves covered the semi-liquid banks; and Massy continued in his old tone, with an abrupt start, as if his speech had been ground out of him, like the tune of a music-box, by turning a handle.

"Though if anybody ever got the best of me, it is you. I don't mind saying this. I've said it—there! What more can you want? Isn't that enough for your pride, Captain Whalley? You got over me from the first. It's all of a piece, when I look back at it. You allowed me to insert that clause about intemperance without saying anything, only looking very sick when I made a point of it going in black on white. How could I tell what was wrong about you? There's generally something wrong somewhere. And, lo and behold! when you come on board it turns out that you've been in the habit of drinking nothing but water for years and years."

His dogmatic, reproachful whine stopped. He brooded profoundly, after the manner of crafty and unintelligent men. It seemed inconceivable that Captain Whalley should not laugh at the expression of disgust that overspread the heavy, yellow countenance. But Captain Whalley never raised his eyes—sitting in his arm-chair, outraged, dignified, and motionless.

"Much good it was to me," Massy remonstrated, monotonously, "to insert a clause of dismissal for intemperance against a man who drinks nothing but water. And you looked so upset, too, when I read my draft in the lawyer's office that morning, Captain Whalley—you looked so crestfallen, that I made sure I had gone home on your weak spot. A shipowner can't be too careful as to the sort of skipper he gets. You must have been laughing at me in your sleeve all the blessed time. . . . Eh? What were you going to say?"

Captain Whalley had only shuffled his feet slightly. A dull animosity became apparent in Massy's sideways stare.

"But recollect that there are other grounds of dismissal. There's habitual carelessness, amounting to incompetence—there's gross and persistent neglect of duty. I am not quite as big a fool as you try to make me out to be. You have been careless of late—leaving everything to that Serang. Why! I've seen you letting that old fool of a Malay take bearings for you, as if you were too big to attend to your work yourself. And what do you call that silly touch-and-go manner in which you took the ship over the bar just now? You expect me to put up with that."

Leaning on his elbow against the ladder abaft the bridge, Sterne,

the mate, tried to hear, blinking the while from the distance at the second engineer, who had come up for a moment, and stood in the engine-room companion. Wiping his hands on a bunch of cotton waste, he looked about with indifference to the right and left at the river banks slipping astern of the *Sofala* steadily.

Massy turned full at the chair. The character of his whine became again threatening.

"Take care. I may yet dismiss you and freeze to your money for a year. I may. . . ."

But before the silent, rigid immobility of the man whose money had come in the nick of time to save him from utter ruin, his voice died out in his throat.

"Not that I want you to go," he resumed after a silence, and in an absurdly insinuating tone. "I want nothing better than to be friends and renew the agreement, if you will consent to find another couple of hundred to help with the new boilers, Captain Whalley. I've told you before. She must have new boilers; you know it as well as I do. Have you thought this over?"

He waited. The slender stem of the pipe with its bulky lump of a bowl at the end hung down from his thick lips. It had gone out. Suddenly he took it from between his teeth and wrung his hands slightly.

"Don't you believe me?" He thrust the pipe bowl into the pocket of his shiny black jacket.

"It's like dealing with the devil," he said. "Why don't you speak? At first you were so high and mighty with me I hardly dared to creep about my own deck. Now I can't get a word from you. You don't seem to see me at all. What does it mean? Upon my soul, you terrify me with this deaf and dumb trick. What's going on in that head of yours? What are you plotting against me there so hard that you can't say a word? You will never make me believe that you—you—don't know where to lay your hands on a couple of hundred. You have made me curse the day I was born. . . ."

"Mr. Massy," said Captain Whalley, suddenly, without stirring.

The engineer started violently.

"If that is so I can only beg you to forgive me."

"Starboard," muttered the Serang to the helmsman; and the *Sofala* began to swing round the bend into the second reach.

"Ough!" Massy shuddered. "You make my blood run cold. What made you come here? What made you come aboard that evening all of a sudden, with your high talk and your money—tempting me? I always wondered what was your motive. You fastened yourself on me to have easy times and grow fat on my life blood, I tell you. Was that

it? I believe you are the greatest miser in the world, or else why. . . . "

"No. I am only poor," interrupted Captain Whalley, stonily.

"Steady," murmured the Serang. Massy turned away with his chin on his shoulder.

"I don't believe it," he said in his dogmatic tone. Captain Whalley made no movement. "There you sit like a gorged vulture—exactly like a vulture."

He embraced the middle of the reach and both the banks in one blank, unseeing, circular glance, and left the bridge slowly.

§ 9

On turning to descend Massy perceived the head of Sterne the mate loitering, with his sly, confident smile, his red moustaches and blinking eyes, at the foot of the ladder.

Sterne had been a junior in one of the larger shipping concerns before joining the *Sofala*. He had thrown up his berth, he said, "on general principles." The promotion in the employ was very slow, he complained, and he thought it was time for him to try and get on a bit in the world. It seemed as though nobody would ever die or leave the firm; they all stuck fast in their berths till they got mildewed; he was tired of waiting; and he feared that when a vacancy did occur the best servants were by no means sure of being treated fairly. Besides, the captain he had to serve under—Captain Provost—was an unaccountable sort of man and had taken a dislike to him for some reason or other. For doing rather more than his bare duty as likely as not. When he had done anything wrong he could take a talking to, like a man; but he expected to be treated like a man, too, and not to be addressed invariably as though he were a dog. He had asked Captain Provost plump and plain to tell him where he was at fault, and Captain Provost, in a most scornful way, had told him that he was a perfect officer, and that if he disliked the way he was being spoken to there was the gangway—he could take himself off ashore at once. But everybody knew what sort of man Captain Provost was. It was no use appealing to the office. Captain Provost had too much influence in the employ. All the same, they had to give him a good character. He made bold to say there was nothing in the world against him, and, as he had happened to hear that the mate of the *Sofala* had been taken to the hospital that morning with a sunstroke, he thought there would be no harm in seeing whether he would not do. . . .

He had come to Captain Whalley freshly shaved, red-faced, thin-

flanked, throwing out his lean chest; and had recited his little tale with an open and manly assurance. Now and then his eyelids quivered slightly, his hand would steal up to the end of the flaming moustache; his eyebrows were straight, furry, of a chestnut colour, and the directness of his gaze seemed to tremble on the verge of impudence. Captain Whalley had engaged him temporarily; then, the other man having been ordered home by the doctors, Sterne had remained for the next trip, and then the next. He had now attained permanency, and the performance of his duties was marked by an air of serious, single-minded application. Directly he was spoken to, he began to smile attentively, with a great deference expressed in his whole attitude; but there was in the rapid winking which went on all the time something quizzical, as though he had possessed the secret of some universal joke cheating all creation and impenetrable to other mortals.

Grave and smiling he watched Massy come down step by step; when the chief engineer had reached the deck he swung about, and they found themselves face to face. Matched as to height and utterly dissimilar, they confronted each other as if there had been something between them—something else than the bright strip of sunlight that, falling through the wide lacing of two awnings, cut crosswise the narrow planking of the deck and separated their feet as it were a stream; something profound and subtle and incalculable, like an unexpressed understanding, a secret mistrust, or some sort of fear.

At last Sterne, blinking his deep-set eyes and sticking forward his scraped, clean-cut chin, as crimson as the rest of his face, murmured—

"You've seen? He grazed! You've seen?"

Massy, contemptuous, and without raising his yellow, fleshy countenance, replied in the same pitch—

"Maybe. But if it had been you we would have been stuck fast in the mud."

"Pardon me, Mr. Massy. I beg to deny it. Of course a shipowner may say what he jolly well pleases on his own deck. That's all right; but I beg to. . . . "

"Get out of my way!"

The other had a slight start, the impulse of suppressed indignation perhaps, but held his ground. Massy's downward glance wandered right and left, as though the deck all round Sterne had been bestrewn with eggs that must not be broken, and he had looked irritably for places where he could set his feet in flight. In the end he, too, did not move, though there was plenty of room to pass on.

"I heard you say up there," went on the mate—"and a very just remark it was, too—that there's always something wrong. . . . "

"Eavesdropping is what's wrong with *you*, Mr. Sterne."

"Now, if you would only listen to me for a moment, Mr. Massy, sir, I could. . . . "

"You are a sneak," interrupted Massy in a great hurry, and even managed to get so far as to repeat, "a common sneak," before the mate had broken in argumentatively—

"Now, sir, what is it you want? You want. . . . "

"I want—I want," stammered Massy, infuriated and astonished— "I want? How do you know that I want anything? How dare you? What do you mean? . . . What are you after—you. . . ."

"Promotion." Sterne silenced him with candid bravado. The engineer's round soft cheeks quivered still, but he said quietly enough—

"You are only worrying my head off," and Sterne met him with a confident little smile.

"A chap in business I know (well up in the world he is now) used to tell me that this was the proper way. 'Always push on to the front,' he would say. 'Keep yourself well before your boss. Interfere whenever you get a chance. Show him what you know. Worry him into seeing you.' That was his advice. Now I know no other boss than you here. You are the owner, and no one else counts for *that* much in my eyes. See, Mr. Massy? I want to get on. I make no secret of it that I am one of the sort that means to get on. These are the men to make use of, sir. You haven't arrived at the top of the tree, sir, without finding that out—I daresay."

"Worry your boss in order to get on," repeated Massy, as if awestruck by the irreverent originality of the idea. "I shouldn't wonder if this was just what the Blue Anchor people kicked you out of their employ for. Is that what you call getting on? You shall get on in the same way here if you aren't careful—I can promise you."

At this Sterne hung his head, thoughtful, perplexed, winking hard at the deck. All his attempts to enter into confidential relations with his owner had led of late to nothing better than these dark threats of dismissal; and a threat of dismissal would check him at once into a hesitating silence as though he were not sure that the proper time for defying it had come. On this occasion he seemed to have lost his tongue for a moment, and Massy, getting in motion, heavily passed him by with an abortive attempt at shouldering. Sterne defeated it by stepping aside. He turned then swiftly, opening his mouth very wide as if to shout something after the engineer, but seemed to think better of it.

Always—as he was ready to confess—on the lookout for an opening to get on, it had become an instinct with him to watch the conduct of his immediate superiors for something "that one could lay hold

of." It was his belief that no skipper in the world would keep his command for a day if only the owners could be "made to know." This romantic and naïve theory had led him into trouble more than once, but he remained incorrigible; and his character was so instinctively disloyal that whenever he joined a ship the intention of ousting his commander out of the berth and taking his place was always present at the back of his head, as a matter of course. It filled the leisure of his waking hours with the reveries of careful plans and compromising discoveries—the dreams of his sleep with images of lucky turns and favourable accidents. Skippers had been known to sicken and die at sea, than which nothing could be better to give a smart mate a chance of showing what he's made of. They also would tumble overboard sometimes: he had heard of one or two such cases. Others again. . . . But, as it were constitutionally, he was faithful to the belief that the conduct of no single one of them would stand the test of careful watching by a man who "knew what's what" and who kept his eyes "skinned pretty well" all the time.

After he had gained a permanent footing on board the *Sofala* he allowed his perennial hope to rise high. To begin with, it was a great advantage to have an old man for captain: the sort of man besides who in the nature of things was likely to give up the job before long from one cause or another. Sterne was greatly chagrined, however, to notice that he did not seem anyway near being past his work yet. Still, these old men go to pieces all at once sometimes. Then there was the owner-engineer close at hand to be impressed by his zeal and steadiness. Sterne never for a moment doubted the obvious nature of his own merits (he was really an excellent officer); only, nowadays, professional merit alone does not take a man along fast enough. A chap must have some push in him, and must keep his wits at work, too, to help him forward. He made up his mind to inherit the charge of this steamer if it was to be done at all; not indeed estimating the command of the *Sofala* as a very great catch, but for the reason that, out East especially, to make a start is everything, and one command leads to another.

He began by promising himself to behave with great circumspection; Massy's sombre and fantastic humours intimidated him as being outside one's usual sea experience; but he was quite intelligent enough to realize almost from the first that he was there in the presence of an exceptional situation. His peculiar prying imagination penetrated it quickly; the feeling that there was in it an element which eluded his grasp exasperated his impatience to get on. And so one trip came to an end, then another, and he had begun his third before he saw an opening by which he could step in with any sort of effect. It had all

been very queer and very obscure; something had been going on near him, as if separated by a chasm from the common life and the working routine of the ship, which was exactly like the life and the routine of any other coasting steamer of that class.

Then one day he made his discovery.

It came to him after all these weeks of watchful observation and puzzled surmises, suddenly, like the long-sought solution of a riddle that suggests itself to the mind in a flash. Not with the same authority, however. Great heavens! Could it be that? And after remaining thunderstruck for a few seconds he tried to shake it off with self-contumely, as though it had been the product of an unhealthy bias toward the Incredible, the Inexplicable, the Unheard-of—the Mad!

This—the illuminating moment—had occurred the trip before, on the return passage. They had just left a place of call on the mainland called Pangu; they were steaming straight out of a bay. To the east a massive headland closed the view, with the tilted edges of the rocky strata showing through its ragged clothing of rank bushes and thorny creepers. The wind had begun to sing in the rigging; the sea along the coast, green and as if swollen a little above the line of the horizon, seemed to pour itself over, time after time, with a slow and thundering fall, into the shadow of the leeward cape; and across the wide opening the nearest of a group of small islands stood enveloped in the hazy yellow light of a breezy sunrise; still farther out the hummocky tops of other islets peeped out motionless above the water of the channels between, scoured tumultuously by the breeze.

The usual track of the *Sofala* both going and returning on every trip led her for a few miles along this reef-infested region. She followed a broad lane of water, dropping astern, one after another, these crumbs of the earth's crust resembling a squadron of dismasted hulks run in disorder upon a foul ground of rocks and shoals. Some of these fragments of land appeared, indeed, no bigger than a stranded ship; others, quite flat, lay awash like anchored rafts, like ponderous, black rafts of stone; several, heavily timbered and round at the base, emerged in squat domes of deep green foliage that shuddered darkly all over to the flying touch of cloud shadows driven by the sudden gusts of the squally season. The thunderstorms of the coast broke frequently over that cluster; it turned then shadowy in its whole extent; it turned more dark, and as if more still in the play of fire; as if more impenetrably silent in the peals of thunder; its blurred shapes vanished—dissolving utterly at times in the thick rain—to reappear clear-cut and black in the stormy light against the gray sheet of the cloud—scattered on the slaty round table of the sea. Unscathed by storms, resisting the work of years, unfretted by the

strife of the world, there it lay unchanged as on that day, four hundred years ago, when first beheld by Western eyes from the deck of a high-pooped caravel.

It was one of those secluded spots that may be found on the busy sea, as on land you come sometimes upon the clustered houses of a hamlet untouched by men's restlessness, untouched by their need, by their thought, and as if forgotten by time itself. The lives of uncounted generations had passed it by, and the multitudes of seafowl, urging their way from all the points of the horizon to sleep on the outer rocks of the group, unrolled the converging evolutions of their flight in long, sombre streamers upon the glow of the sky. The palpitating cloud of their wings soared and stooped over the pinnacles of the rocks, over the rocks slender like spires, squat like martello towers; over the pyramidal heaps like fallen ruins, over the lines of bald boulders showing like a wall of stones battered to pieces and scorched by lightning—with the sleepy, clear glimmer of water in every breach. The noise of their continuous and violent screaming filled the air.

This great noise would meet the *Sofala* coming up from Batu Beru; it would meet her on quiet evenings, a pitiless and savage clamour enfeebled by distance, the clamour of seabirds settling to rest, and struggling for a footing at the end of the day. No one noticed it especially on board; it was the voice of their ship's unerring landfall, ending the steady stretch of a hundred miles. She had made good her course, she had run her distance till the punctual islets began to emerge one by one, the points of rocks, the hummocks of earth . . . and the cloud of birds hovered—the restless cloud emitting a strident and cruel uproar, the sound of the familiar scene, the living part of the broken land beneath, of the outspread sea, and of the high sky without a flaw.

But when the *Sofala* happened to close with the land after sunset she would find everything very still there under the mantle of the night. All would be still, dumb, almost invisible—but for the blotting out of the low constellations occulted in turns behind the vague masses of the islets whose true outlines eluded the eye amongst the dark spaces of the heaven: and the ship's three lights, resembling three stars—the red and the green with the white above—her three lights, like three companion stars wandering on the earth, held their unswerving course for the passage at the southern end of the group. Sometimes there were human eyes open to watch them come nearer, travelling smoothly in the sombre void; the eyes of a naked fisherman in his canoe floating over a reef. He thought drowsily: "Ha! The fire-ship that once in every moon goes in and comes out of Pangu

Bay." More he did not know of her. And just as he had detected the faint rhythm of the propeller beating the calm water a mile and a half away, the time would come for the *Sofala* to alter her course, the lights would swing off him their triple beam—and disappear.

A few miserable, half-naked families, a sort of outcast tribe of long-haired, lean, and wild-eyed people, strove for their living in this lonely wilderness of islets, lying like an abandoned outwork of the land at the gates of the bay. Within the knots and loops of the rocks the water rested more transparent than crystal under their crooked and leaky canoes, scooped out of the trunk of a tree: the forms of the bottom undulated slightly to the dip of a paddle; and the men seemed to hang in the air, they seemed to hang enclosed within the fibres of a dark, sodden log, fishing patiently in a strange, unsteady, pellucid, green air above the shoals.

Their bodies stalked brown and emaciated as if dried up in the sunshine; their lives ran out silently; the homes where they were born, went to rest, and died—flimsy sheds of rushes and coarse grass eked out with a few ragged mats—were hidden out of sight from the open sea. No glow of their household fires ever kindled for a seaman a red spark upon the blind night of the group: and the calms of the coast, the flaming long calms of the equator, the unbreathing, concentrated calms like the deep introspection of a passionate nature, brooded awfully for days and weeks together over the unchangeable inheritance of their children; till at last the stones, hot like live embers, scorched the naked sole, till the water clung warm, and sickly, and as if thickened about the legs of lean men with girded loins, wading thigh-deep in the pale blaze of the shallows. And it would happen now and then that the *Sofala,* through some delay in one of the ports of call, would heave in sight making for Pangu Bay as late as noonday.

Only a blurring cloud at first, the thin mist of her smoke would arise mysteriously from an empty point on the clear line of sea and sky. The taciturn fishermen within the reefs would extend their lean arms toward the offing; and the brown figures stooping on the tiny beaches, the brown figures of men, women, and children grubbing in the sand in search of turtles' eggs, would rise up, crooked elbow aloft and hand over the eyes, to watch this monthly apparition glide straight on, swerve off—and go by. Their ears caught the panting of that ship; their eyes followed her till she passed between the two capes of the mainland going at full speed as though she hoped to make her way unchecked into the very bosom of the earth.

On such days the luminous sea would give no sign of the dangers lurking on both sides of her path. Every thing remained still, crushed

by the overwhelming power of the light; and the whole group, opaque in the sunshine,—the rocks resembling pinnacles, the rocks resembling spires, the rocks resembling ruins; the forms of islets resembling bee-hives, resembling mole-hills; the islets recalling the shapes of hay-stacks, the contours of ivy-clad towers—would stand reflected together upside down in the unwrinkled water, like carved toys of ebony dis-posed on the silvered plate-glass of a mirror.

The first touch of blowing weather would envelop the whole at once in the spume of the windward breakers, as if in a sudden cloud-like burst of steam; and the clear water seemed fairly to boil in all the passages. The provoked sea outlined exactly in a design of angry foam the wide base of the group; the submerged level of broken waste and refuse left over from the building of the coast near by, projecting its dangerous spurs, all awash, far into the channel, and bristling with wicked long spits often a mile long: with deadly spits made of froth and stones.

And even nothing more than a brisk breeze—as on that morning, the voyage before, when the *Sofala* left Pangu Bay early, and Mr. Sterne's discovery was to blossom out like a flower of incredible and evil aspect from the tiny seed of instinctive suspicion—even such a breeze had enough strength to tear the placid mask from the face of the sea. To Sterne, gazing with indifference, it had been like a revelation to behold for the first time the dangers marked by the hissing livid patches on the water as distinctly as on the engraved paper of a chart. It came into his mind that this was the sort of day most favourable for a stranger attempting the passage: a clear day, just windy enough for the sea to break on every ledge, buoying, as it were, the channel plainly to the sight; whereas during a calm you had nothing to depend on but the compass and the practised judgment of your eye. And yet the successive captains of the *Sofala* had had to take her through at night more than once. Nowadays you could not afford to throw away six or seven hours of a steamer's time. That you couldn't. But then use is everything, and with proper care. . . . The channel was broad and safe enough; the main point was to hit upon the entrance correctly in the dark—for if a man got him-self involved in that stretch of broken water over yonder he would never get out with a whole ship—if he ever got out at all.

This was Sterne's last train of thought independent of the great discovery. He had just seen to the securing of the anchor, and had remained forward idling away a moment or two. The captain was in charge on the bridge. With a slight yawn he had turned away from his survey of the sea and had leaned his shoulders against the fish davit.

These, properly speaking, were the very last moments of ease he was to know on board the *Sofala*. All the instants that came after were to be pregnant with purpose and intolerable with perplexity. No more idle, random thoughts; the discovery would put them on the rack, till sometimes he wished to goodness he had been fool enough not to make it at all. And yet, if his chance to get on rested on the discovery of "something wrong," he could not have hoped for a greater stroke of luck.

§ 10

The knowledge was too disturbing, really. There was "something wrong" with a vengeance, and the moral certitude of it was at first simply frightful to contemplate. Sterne had been looking aft in a mood so idle, that for once he was thinking no harm of any one. His captain on the bridge presented himself naturally to his sight. How insignificant, how casual was the thought that had started the train of discovery—like an accidental spark that suffices to ignite the charge of a tremendous mine!

Caught under by the breeze, the awnings of the foredeck bellied upwards and collapsed slowly, and above their heavy flapping the gray stuff of Captain Whalley's roomy coat fluttered incessantly around his arms and trunk. He faced the wind in full light, with his great silvery beard blown forcibly against his chest; the eyebrows overhung heavily the shadows whence his glance appeared to be staring ahead piercingly. Sterne could just detect the twin gleam of the whites shifting under the shaggy arches of the brow. At short range these eyes, for all the man's affable manner, seemed to look you through and through. Sterne never could defend himself from that feeling when he had occasion to speak with his captain. He did not like it. What a big heavy man he appeared up there, with that little shrimp of a Serang in close attendance—as was usual in this extraordinary steamer! Confounded absurd custom that. He resented it. Surely the old fellow could have looked after his ship without that loafing native at his elbow. Sterne wriggled his shoulders with disgust. What was it? Indolence or what?

That old skipper must have been growing lazy for years. They all grew lazy out East here (Sterne was very conscious of his own unimpaired activity); they got slack all over. But he towered very erect on the bridge; and quite low by his side, as you see a small child looking over the edge of a table, the battered soft hat and the brown face of the Serang peeped over the white canvas screen of the rail.

No doubt the Malay was standing back, nearer to the wheel; but the great disparity of size in close association amused Sterne like the observation of a bizarre fact in nature. There were as queer fish out of the sea as any in it.

He saw Captain Whalley turn his head quickly to speak to his Serang; the wind whipped the whole white mass of the beard sideways. He would be directing the chap to look at the compass for him, or what not. Of course. Too much trouble to step over and see for himself. Sterne's scorn for that bodily indolence which overtakes white men in the East increased on reflection. Some of them would be utterly lost if they hadn't all these natives at their beck and call; they grew perfectly shameless about it, too. He was not of that sort, thank God! It wasn't in him to make himself dependent for his work on any shrivelled-up little Malay like that. As if one could ever trust a silly native for anything in the world! But that fine old man thought differently, it seems. There they were together, never far apart; a pair of them, recalling to the mind an old whale attended by a little pilot-fish.

The fancifulness of the comparison made him smile. A whale with an inseparable pilot-fish! That's what the old man looked like; for it could not be said he looked like a shark, though Mr. Massy had called him that very name. But Mr. Massy did not mind what he said in his savage fits. Sterne smiled to himself—and gradually the ideas evoked by the sound, by the imagined shape of the word pilot-fish, the ideas of aid, of guidance needed and received, came uppermost in his mind: the word pilot awakened the idea of trust, of dependence, the idea of the welcome, clear-eyed help brought to the seaman groping for the land in the dark: groping blindly in fogs: feeling his way in the thick weather of the gales that, filling the air with a salt mist blown up from the sea, contract the range of sight on all sides to a shrunken horizon that seems within reach of the hand.

A pilot sees better than a stranger, because his local knowledge, like a sharper vision, completes the shapes of things hurriedly glimpsed; penetrates the veils of mist spread over the land by the storms of the sea; defines with certitude the outlines of a coast lying under the pall of fog, the forms of landmarks half buried in a starless night as in a shallow grave. He recognizes because he already knows. It is not to his far-reaching eye but to his more extensive knowledge that the pilot looks for certitude; for this certitude of the ship's position on which may depend a man's good fame and the peace of his conscience, the justification of the trust deposited in his hands, with his own life, too, which is seldom wholly his to throw away, and the

humble lives of others rooted in distant affections, perhaps, and made as weighty as the lives of kings by the burden of the awaiting mystery. The pilot's knowledge brings relief and certitude to the commander of a ship; the Serang, however, in his fanciful suggestion of a pilot-fish attending a whale, could not in any way be credited with a superior knowledge. Why should he have it? These two men had come on that run together—the white and the brown—on the same day: and of course a white man would learn more in a week than the best native would in a month. He was made to stick to the skipper as though he were of some use—as the pilot-fish, they say, is to the whale. But how—it was very marked—how? A pilot-fish—a pilot—a . . . But if not superior knowledge then. . . .

Sterne's discovery was made. It was repugnant to his imagination, shocking to his ideas of honesty, shocking to his conception of mankind. This enormity affected one's outlook on what was possible in this world: it was as if for instance the sun had turned blue, throwing a new and sinister light on men and nature. Really in the first moment he had felt sickish, as though he had got a blow below the belt: for a second the very colour of the sea seemed changed—appeared queer to his wandering eye; and he had a passing, unsteady sensation in all his limbs as though the earth had started turning the other way.

A very natural incredulity succeeding this sense of upheaval brought a measure of relief. He had gasped; it was over. But afterwards, during all that day, sudden paroxysms of wonder would come over him in the midst of his occupations. He would stop and shake his head. The revolt of his incredulity had passed away almost as quick as the first emotion of discovery, and for the next twenty-four hours he had no sleep. That would never do. At meal-times (he took the foot of the table set up for the white men on the bridge) he could not help losing himself in a fascinated contemplation of Captain Whalley opposite. He watched the deliberate upward movements of the arm; the old man put his food to his lips as though he never expected to find any taste in his daily bread, as though he did not know anything about it. He fed himself like a somnambulist. "It's an awful sight," thought Sterne; and he watched the long period of mournful, silent immobility, with a big brown hand lying loosely closed by the side of the plate, till he noticed the two engineers to the right and left looking at him in astonishment. He would close his mouth in a hurry then, and lowering his eyes, wink rapidly at his plate. It was awful to see the old chap sitting there: it was even awful to think that with three words he could blow him up sky-high. All he had to do was to raise his voice and pronounce a single short

sentence, and yet that simple act seemed as impossible to attempt as moving the sun out of its place in the sky. The old chap could eat in his terrific mechanical way; but Sterne, from mental excitement, could not—not that evening, at any rate.

He had had ample time since to get accustomed to the strain of the meal-hours. He would never have believed it. But then use is everything; only the very potency of his success prevented anything resembling elation. He felt like a man who, in his legitimate search for a loaded gun to help him on his way through the world, chances to come upon a torpedo—upon a live torpedo with a shattering charge in its head and a pressure of many atmospheres in its tail. It is the sort of weapon to make its possessor careworn and nervous. He had no mind to be blown up himself; and he could not get rid of the notion that the explosion was bound to damage him, too, in some way.

This vague apprehension had restrained him at first. He was able now to eat and sleep with that fearful weapon by his side, with the conviction of its power always in his mind. It had not been arrived at by any reflective process; but once the idea had entered his head, the conviction had followed overwhelmingly in a multitude of observed little facts to which before he had given only a languid attention. The abrupt and faltering intonations of the deep voice; the taciturnity put on like an armour; the deliberate, as if guarded, movements; the long immobilities, as if the man he watched had been afraid to disturb the very air: every familiar gesture, every word uttered in his hearing, every sigh overheard, had acquired a special significance, a confirmatory import.

Every day that passed over the *Sofala* appeared to Sterne simply crammed full with proofs—with incontrovertible proofs. At night, when off duty, he would steal out of his cabin in pyjamas (for more proofs) and stand a full hour, perhaps, on his bare feet below the bridge, as absolutely motionless as the awning stanchion in its deck socket near by. On the stretches of easy navigation it is not usual for a coasting captain to remain on deck all the time of his watch. The Serang keeps it for him as a matter of custom; in open water, on a straight course, he is usually trusted to look after the ship by himself. But this old man seemed incapable of remaining quietly down below. No doubt he could not sleep. And no wonder. This was also a proof. Suddenly in the silence of the ship panting upon the still, dark sea, Sterne would hear a low voice above him exclaiming nervously—

"Serang!"

"Tuan!"

"You are watching the compass well?"

"Yes, I am watching, Tuan."

"The ship is making her course?"

"She is, Tuan. Very straight."

"It is well; and remember, Serang, that the order is, that you are to mind the helmsmen and keep a lookout with care, the same as if I were not on deck."

Then, when the Serang had made his answer, the low tones on the bridge would cease, and everything round Sterne seemed to become more still and more profoundly silent. Slightly chilled and with his back aching a little from long immobility, he would steal away to his room on the port side of the deck. He had long since parted with the last vestige of incredulity; of the original emotions, set into a tumult by the discovery, some trace of the first awe alone remained. Not the awe of the man himself—he could blow him up sky-high with six words—rather it was an awestruck indignation at the reckless perversity of avarice (what else could it be?), at the mad and sombre resolution that for the sake of a few dollars more seemed to set at nought the common rule of conscience and pretended to struggle against the very decree of Providence.

You could not find another man like this one in the whole round world—thank God. There was something devilishly dauntless in the character of such a deception which made you pause.

Other considerations occurring to his prudence had kept him tongue-tied from day to day. It seemed to him now that it would yet have been easier to speak out in the first hour of discovery. He almost regretted not having made a row at once. But then the very monstrosity of the disclosure . . . Why! he could hardly face it himself, let alone pointing it out to somebody else. Moreover, with a desperado of that sort one never knew. The object was not to get him out (that was as well as done already), but to step into his place. Bizarre as the thought seemed, he might have shown fight. A fellow up to working such a fraud would have enough cheek for anything; a fellow that, as it were, stood up against God Almighty Himself. He was a horrid marvel—that's what he was: he was perfectly capable of brazening out the affair scandalously till he got him (Sterne) kicked out of the ship and everlastingly damaged his prospects in this part of the East. Yet if you want to get on something must be risked. At times Sterne thought he had been unduly timid of taking action in the past; and what was worse, it had come to this, that in the present he did not seem to know what action to take.

Massy's savage moroseness was too disconcerting. It was an in-

calculable factor of the situation. You could not tell what there was behind that insulting ferocity. How could one trust such a temper? it did not put Sterne in bodily fear for himself, but it frightened him exceedingly as to his prospects.

Though of course inclined to credit himself with exceptional powers of observation, he had by now lived too long with his discovery. He had gone on looking at nothing else, till at last one day it occurred to him that the thing was so obvious that no one could miss seeing it. There were four white men in all on board the *Sofala*. Jack, the second engineer, was too dull to notice anything that took place out of his engine-room. Remained Massy—the owner—the interested person—nearly going mad with worry. Sterne had heard and seen more than enough on board to know what ailed him; but his exasperation seemed to make him deaf to cautious overtures. If he had only known it, there was the very thing he wanted. But how could you bargain with a man of that sort? It was like going into a tiger's den with a piece of raw meat in your hand. He was as likely as not to rend you for your pains. In fact, he was always threatening to do that very thing; and the urgency of the case, combined with the impossibility of handling it with safety, made Sterne in his watches below toss and mutter open-eyed in his bunk, for hours, as though he had been burning with fever.

Occurrences like the crossing of the bar just now were extremely alarming to his prospects. He did not want to be left behind by some swift catastrophe. Massy being on the bridge, the old man had to brace himself up, and make a show, he supposed. But it was getting very bad with him, very bad indeed, now. Even Massy had been emboldened to find fault this time; Sterne, listening at the foot of the ladder, had heard the other's whimpering and artless denunciations. Luckily the beast was very stupid and could not see the why of all this. However, small blame to him; it took a clever man to hit upon the cause. Nevertheless, it was high time to do something. The old man's game could not be kept up for many days more.

"I may yet lose my life at this fooling—let alone my chance," Sterne mumbled angrily to himself, after the stooping back of the chief engineer had disappeared round the corner of the skylight. Yes, no doubt—he thought; but to blurt out his knowledge would not advance his prospects. On the contrary, it would blast them utterly as likely as not. He dreaded another failure. He had a vague consciousness of not being much liked by his fellows in this part of the world; inexplicable enough, for he had done nothing to them. Envy, he supposed. People were always down on a clever chap who made no bones about his determination to get on. To do your duty

and count on the gratitude of that brute Massy would be sheer folly. He was a bad lot. Unmanly! A vicious man! Bad! Bad! A brute! A brute without a spark of anything human about him; without so much as simple curiosity even, or else surely he would have responded in some way to all these hints he had been given. . . . Such insensibility was almost mysterious. Massy's state of exasperation seemed to Sterne to have made him stupid beyond the ordinary silliness of shipowners.

Sterne, meditating on the embarrassments of that stupidity, forgot himself completely. His stony, unwinking stare was fixed on the planks of the deck.

The slight quiver agitating the whole fabric of the ship was more perceptible in the silent river, shaded and still like a forest path. The *Sofala*, gliding with an even motion, had passed beyond the coastbelt of mud and mangroves. The shores rose higher, in firm sloping banks, and the forest of big trees came down to the brink. Where the earth had been crumbled by the floods it showed a steep brown cut, denuding a mass of roots intertwined as if wrestling underground; and in the air, the interlaced boughs, bound and loaded with creepers, carried on the struggle for life, mingled their foliage in one solid wall of leaves, with here and there the shape of an enormous dark pillar soaring, or a ragged opening, as if torn by the flight of a cannonball, disclosing the impenetrable gloom within, the secular inviolable shade of the virgin forest. The thump of the engines reverberated regularly like the strokes of a metronome beating the measure of the vast silence, the shadow of the western wall had fallen across the river, and the smoke pouring backwards from the funnel eddied down behind the ship, spread a thin dusky veil over the sombre water, which, checked by the flood-tide, seemed to lie stagnant in the whole straight length of the reaches.

Sterne's body, as if rooted on the spot, trembled slightly from top to toe with the internal vibration of the ship; from under his feet came sometimes a sudden clang of iron, the noisy burst of a shout below; to the right the leaves of the tree-tops caught the rays of the low sun, and seemed to shine with a golden green light of their own shimmering around the highest boughs which stood out black against a smooth blue sky that seemed to droop over the bed of the river like the roof of a tent. The passengers for Batu Beru, kneeling on the planks, were engaged in rolling their bedding of mats busily; they tied up bundles, they snapped the locks of wooden chests. A pockmarked pedlar of small wares threw his head back to drain into his throat the last drops out of an earthenware bottle before putting it away in a roll of blankets. Knots of travelling traders standing about

the deck conversed in low tones; the followers of a small Rajah from down the coast, broad-faced simple young fellows in white drawers and round white cotton caps with their coloured sarongs twisted across their bronze shoulders, squatted on their hams on the hatch, chewing betel with bright red mouths as if they had been tasting blood. Their spears, lying piled up together within the circle of their bare toes, resembled a casual bundle of dry bamboos; a thin, livid Chinaman, with a bulky package wrapped up in leaves already thrust under his arm, gazed ahead eagerly; a wandering Kling rubbed his teeth with a bit of wood, pouring over the side a bright stream of water out of his lips; the fat Rajah dozed in a shabby deck-chair— and at the turn of every bend the two walls of leaves reappeared running parallel along the banks, with their impenetrable solidity fading at the top to a vaporous mistiness of countless slender twigs growing free, of young delicate branches shooting from the topmost limbs of hoary trunks, of feathery heads of climbers like delicate silver sprays standing up without a quiver. There was not a sign of a clearing anywhere; not a trace of human habitation, except when in one place, on the bare end of a low point under an isolated group of slender tree-ferns, the jagged, tangled remnants of an old hut on piles appeared with that peculiar aspect of ruined bamboo walls that look as if smashed with a club. Farther on, half hidden under the drooping bushes, a canoe containing a man and a woman together with a dozen green cocoanuts in a heap, rocked helplessly after the *Sofala* had passed, like a navigating contrivance of venturesome insects, of travelling ants; while two glassy folds of water streaming away from each bow of the steamer across the whole width of the river ran with her upstream smoothly, fretting their outer ends into a brown whispering tumble of froth against the miry foot of each bank.

"I must," thought Sterne, "bring that brute Massy to his bearings. It's getting too absurd in the end. Here's the old man up there buried in his chair—he may just as well be in his grave for all the use he'll ever be in the world—and the Serang's in charge. Because that's what he is. In charge. In the place that's mine by rights. I must bring that savage brute to his bearings. I'll do it at once, too. . . ."

When the mate made an abrupt start, a little brown, half-naked boy, with large black eyes, and the string of a written charm round his neck, became panic-struck at once. He dropped the banana he had been munching, and ran to the knee of a grave dark Arab in flowing robes, sitting like a Biblical figure, incongruously, on a yellow tin trunk corded with a rope of twisted rattan. The father, unmoved, put out his hand to pat the little shaven poll protectingly.

§ 11

Sterne crossed the deck upon the track of the chief engineer. Jack, the second, retreating backwards down the engine-room ladder, and still wiping his hands, treated him to an incomprehensible grin of white teeth out of his grimy hard face; Massy was nowhere to be seen. Sterne scratched at the door softly, then, putting his lips to the rose of the ventilator, said—

"I must speak to you, Mr. Massy. Just give me a minute or two."

"I am busy. Go away from my door."

"But pray, Mr. Massy. . . ."

"You go away. D'you hear? Take yourself off altogether—to the other end of the ship—quite away. . . ." The voice inside dropped low. "To the devil."

Sterne paused: then very quietly—

"It's rather pressing. When do you think you will be at liberty, sir?"

The answer to this was an exasperated "Never"; and at once Sterne, with a very firm expression of face, turned the handle.

Mr. Massy's stateroom—a narrow, one-berth cabin—smelt strongly of soap, and presented to view a swept, dusted, unadorned neatness, not so much bare as barren, not so much severe as starved and lacking in humanity, like the ward of a public hospital, or rather (owing to the small size) like the clean retreat of a desperately poor but exemplary person. Not a single photograph frame ornamented the bulk-heads; not a single article of clothing, not as much as a spare cap, hung from the brass hooks. All the inside was painted in one plain tint of pale blue; two big sea-chests in sail-cloth covers and with iron padlocks fitted exactly in the space under the bunk. One glance was enough to embrace all the strip of scrubbed planks within the four unconcealed corners. The absence of the usual settee was striking; the teak-wood top of the washing-stand seemed hermetically closed, and so was the lid of the writing-desk, which protruded from the partition at the foot of the bed-place, containing a mattress as thin as a pancake under a threadbare blanket with a faded red stripe, and a folded mosquito-net against the nights spent in harbour. There was not a scrap of paper anywhere in sight, no boots on the floor, no litter of any sort, not a speck of dust anywhere; no traces of pipe-ash even, which, in a heavy smoker, was morally revolting, like a manifestation of extreme hypocrisy; and the bottom of the old wooden arm-chair (the only seat there), polished with much use, shone as if its shabbiness had been waxed. The screen of leaves on

the bank, passing as if unrolled endlessly in the round opening of the port, sent a wavering network of light and shade into the place.

Sterne, holding the door open with one hand, had thrust in his head and shoulders. At this amazing intrusion Massy, who was doing absolutely nothing, jumped up speechless.

"Don't call names," murmured Sterne, hurriedly. "I won't be called names. I think of nothing but your good, Mr. Massy."

A pause as of extreme astonishment followed. They both seemed to have lost their tongues. Then the mate went on with discreet glibness:

"You simply couldn't conceive what's going on on board your ship. It wouldn't enter your head for a moment. You are too good—too —too upright, Mr. Massy, to suspect anybody of such a . . . It's enough to make your hair stand on end."

He watched for the effect: Massy seemed dazed, uncomprehending. He only passed the palm of his hand on the coal-black wisps plastered across the top of his head. In a tone suddenly changed to confidential audacity Sterne hastened on:

"Remember that there's only six weeks left to run. . . ." The other was looking at him stonily. . . "So anyhow you will require a captain for the ship before long."

Then only, as if that suggestion had scarified his flesh in the manner of red-hot iron, Massy gave a start and seemed ready to shriek. He contained himself by a great effort.

"Require—a—captain," he repeated with scathing slowness. "Who requires a captain? You dare tell me that I need any of you humbugging sailors to run my ship. You and your likes have been fattening on me for years. It would have hurt me less to throw my money overboard. Pam—pe—red us—e—less f-f-f-frauds. The old ship knows as much as the best of you." He snapped his teeth audibly and growled through them. "The silly law requires a captain."

Sterne had taken heart of grace meantime.

"And the silly insurance people, too, as well," he said, lightly. "But never mind that. What I want to ask is: Why shouldn't *I* do, sir? I don't say but you could take a steamer about the world as well as any of us sailors. I don't pretend to tell *you* that it is a very great trick. . . ." He emitted a short, hollow guffaw, familiarly. . . . "I didn't make the law—but there it is; and I am an active young fellow; I quite hold with your ideas; I know your ways by this time, Mr. Massy. I wouldn't try to give myself airs like that—that— er—lazy specimen of an old man up there."

He put a marked emphasis on the last sentence, to lead Massy away from the track in case . . . but he did not doubt of now holding

his success. The chief engineer seemed nonplussed, like a slow man invited to catch hold of a whirligig of some sort.

"What you want, sir, is a chap with no nonsense about him, who would be content to be your sailing-master. Quite right, too. Well, I am fit for the work as much as that Serang. Because that's what it amounts to. Do you know, sir, that a dam' Malay like a monkey is in charge of your ship—and no one else? Just listen to his feet pit-patting above us on the bridge—real officer in charge. He's taking her up the river while the great man is wallowing in the chair—perhaps asleep; and if he is, that would not make it much worse either—take my word for it."

He tried to thrust himself farther in. Massy, with lowered forehead, one hand grasping the back of the arm-chair, did not budge.

"You think, sir, that the man has got you tight in his agreement. . . ." Massy raised a heavy snarling face at this. . . . "Well, sir, one can't help hearing of it on board. It's no secret. And it has been the talk on shore for years; fellows have been making bets about it. No, sir! It's *you* who have got him at your mercy. You will say that you can't dismiss him for indolence. Difficult to prove in court, and so on. Why, yes. But if you say the word, sir, I can tell you something about his indolence that will give you the clear right to fire him out on the spot and put me in charge for the rest of this very trip—yes, sir, before we leave Batu Beru—and make him pay a dollar a day for his keep till we get back, if you like. Now, what do you think of that? Come, sir. Say the word. It's really well worth your while, and I am quite ready to take your bare word. A definite statement from you would be as good as a bond."

His eyes began to shine. He insisted. A simple statement—and he thought to himself that he would manage somehow to stick in his berth as long as it suited him. He would make himself indispensable; the ship had a bad name in her port; it would be easy to scare the fellows off. Massy would have to keep him.

"A definite statement from me would be enough," Massy repeated, slowly.

"Yes, sir. It would." Sterne stuck out his chin cheerily and blinked at close quarters with that unconscious impudence which had the power to enrage Massy beyond anything.

The engineer spoke very distinctly:

"Listen well to me, then, Mr. Sterne: I wouldn't—d'ye hear?—I wouldn't promise you the value of two pence for anything *you* can tell me."

He struck Sterne's arm away with a smart blow, and catching hold of the handle pulled the door to. The terrific slam darkened

the cabin instantaneously to his eyes as if after the flash of an explosion. At once he dropped into the chair. "Oh, no! You don't!" he whispered faintly.

The ship had in that place to shave the bank so close that the gigantic wall of leaves came gliding like a shutter against the port; the darkness of the primeval forest seemed to flow into that bare cabin with the odour of rotting leaves, of sodden soil—the strong muddy smell of the living earth steaming uncovered after the passing of a deluge. The bushes swished loudly alongside; above there was a series of crackling sounds, with a sharp rain of small broken branches falling on the bridge; a creeper with a great rustle snapped on the head of a boat davit, and a long, luxuriant green twig actually whipped in and out of the open port, leaving behind a few torn leaves that remained suddenly at rest on Mr. Massy's blanket. Then, the ship sheering out in the stream, the light began to return, but did not augment beyond a subdued clearness: for the sun was very low already, and the river, wending its sinuous course through a multitude of secular trees as if at the bottom of a precipitous gorge, had been already invaded by a deepening gloom—the swift precursor of the night.

"Oh, no, you don't!" murmured the engineer again. His lips trembled almost imperceptibly; his hands, too, a little: and to calm himself he opened the writing-desk, spread out a sheet of thin grayish paper covered with a mass of printed figures and began to scan them attentively for the twentieth time this trip at least.

With his elbows propped, his head between his hands, he seemed to lose himself in the study of an abstruse problem in mathematics. It was the list of the winning numbers from the last drawing of the great lottery which had been the one inspiring fact of so many years of his existence. The conception of a life deprived of that periodical sheet of paper had slipped away from him entirely, as another man, according to his nature, would not have been able to conceive a world without fresh air, without activity, or without affection. A great pile of flimsy sheets had been growing for years in his desk, while the *Sofala,* driven by the faithful Jack, wore out her boilers in tramping up and down the Straits, from cape to cape, from river to river, from bay to bay; accumulating by that hard labour of an overworked, starved ship the blackened mass of these documents. Massy kept them under lock and key like a treasure. There was in them, as in the experience of life, the fascination of hope, the excitement of a half-penetrated mystery, the longing of a half-satisfied desire.

For days together, on a trip, he would shut himself up in his berth with them: the thump of the toiling engines pulsated in his ear; and

he would weary his brain poring over the rows of disconnected figures, bewildering by their senseless sequence, resembling the hazards of destiny itself. He nourished a conviction that there must be some logic lurking somewhere in the results of chance. He thought he had seen its very form. His head swam; his limbs ached; he puffed at his pipe mechanically; a contemplative stupor would soothe the fretfulness of his temper, like the passive bodily quietude procured by a drug, while the intellect remains tensely on the stretch. Nine, nine, nought, four, two. He made a note. The next winning number of the great prize was forty-seven thousand and five. These numbers of course would have to be avoided in the future when writing to Manila for the tickets. He mumbled, pencil in hand . . . "and five. Hm . . . hm." He wetted his finger: the papers rustled. Ha! But what's this? Three years ago, in the September drawing, it was number nine, nought, four, two that took the first prize. Most remarkable. There was a hint there of a definite rule! He was afraid of missing some recondite principle in the overwhelming wealth of his material. What could it be? and for half an hour he would remain dead still, bent low over the desk, without twitching a muscle. At his back the whole berth would be thick with a heavy body of smoke, as if a bomb had burst in there, unnoticed, unheard.

At last he would lock up the desk with the decision of unshaken confidence, jump up and go out. He would walk swiftly back and forth on that part of the foredeck which was kept clear of the lumber and of the bodies of the native passengers. They were a great nuisance, but they were also a source of profit that could not be disdained. He needed every penny of profit the *Sofala* could make. Little enough it was, in all conscience! The incertitude of chance gave him no concern, since he had somehow arrived at the conviction that, in the course of years, every number was bound to have its winning turn. It was simply a matter of time and of taking as many tickets as he could afford for every drawing. He generally took rather more; all the earnings of the ship went that way, and also the wages he allowed himself as chief engineer. It was the wages he paid to others that he begrudged with a reasoned and at the same time a passionate regret. He scowled at the lascars with their deck brooms, at the quartermasters rubbing the brass rails with greasy rags; he was eager to shake his fist and roar abuse in bad Malay at the poor carpenter— a timid, sickly, opium-fuddled Chinaman, in loose blue drawers for all costume, who invariably dropped his tools and fled below, with streaming tail and shaking all over, before the fury of that "devil." But it was when he raised up his eyes to the bridge where one of these sailor frauds was always planted by law in charge of his ship

that he felt almost dizzy with rage. He abominated them all; it was
an old feud, from the time he first went to sea, an unlicked cub with
a great opinion of himself, in the engine-room. The slights that had
been put upon him. The persecutions he had suffered at the hands
of skippers—of absolute nobodies in a steamship after all. And now
that he had risen to be a shipowner they were still a plague to him:
he had absolutely to pay away precious money to the conceited useless
loafers:—As if a fully qualified engineer—who was the owner as
well—were not fit to be trusted with the whole charge of a ship. Well!
he made it pretty warm for them; but it was a poor consolation. He
had come in time to hate the ship, too, for the repairs she required,
for the coal-bills he had to pay, for the poor beggarly freights she
earned. He would clench his hand as he walked and hit the rail
a sudden blow, viciously, as though she could be made to feel pain.
And yet he could not do without her; he needed her; he must hang
on to her tooth and nail to keep his head above water till the ex-
pected flood of fortune came sweeping up and landed him safely on
the high shore of his ambition.

It was now to do nothing, nothing whatever, and have plenty of
money to do it on. He had tasted of power, the highest form of it
his limited experience was aware of—the power of shipowning. What
a deception! Vanity of vanities! He wondered at his folly. He had
thrown away the substance for the shadow. Of the gratification of
wealth he did not know enough to excite his imagination with any
visions of luxury. How could he—the child of a drunken boiler-
maker—going straight from the workshop into the engine-room of
a north-country collier! But the notion of the absolute idleness of
wealth he could very well conceive. He revelled in it, to forget his
present troubles; he imagined himself walking about the streets of
Hull (he knew their gutters well as a boy) with his pockets full of
sovereigns. He would buy himself a house; his married sisters, their
husbands, his old workshop chums, would render him infinite homage.
There would be nothing to think of. His word would be law. He
had been out of work for a long time before he won his prize, and
he remembered how Carlo Mariani (commonly known as Paunchy
Charley), the Maltese hotel-keeper at the slummy end of Denham
Street, had cringed joyfully before him in the evening, when the news
had come. Poor Charley, though he made his living by ministering to
various abject vices, gave credit for the food to many a piece of white
wreckage. He was naïvely overjoyed at the idea of his old bills being
paid, and he reckoned confidently on a spell of festivities in the
cavernous grogshop downstairs. Massy remembered the curious, re-
spectful looks of the "trashy" white men in the place. His heart

had swelled within him. Massy had left Charley's infamous den directly he had realized the possibilities open to him, with his nose in the air. Afterwards the memory of these adulations was a great sadness.

This was the true power of money—and no trouble with it, nor any thinking required either. He thought with difficulty and felt vividly; to his blunt brain the problems offered by any ordered scheme of life seemed in their cruel toughness to have been put in his way by the obvious malevolence of men. As a shipowner everyone had conspired to make him a nobody. How could he have been such a fool as to purchase that accursed ship? He had been abominably swindled; there was no end to this swindling, and as the difficulties of his improvident ambition gathered thicker round him, he really came to hate everybody he had ever come in contact with. A temper naturally irritable and an amazing sensitiveness to the claims of his own personality had ended by making life for him a sort of inferno— a place where his lost soul had been given up to the torment of savage brooding.

But he had never hated any one so much as that old man who turned up one evening to save him from an utter disaster,—from the conspiracy of the wretched sailors. He seemed to have fallen on board from the sky. His footsteps echoed on the empty steamer, and the strange deep-toned voice on deck repeating interrogatively the words, "Mr. Massy, Mr. Massy there?" had been startling like a wonder. And coming up from the depths of the cold engine-room, where he had been pottering dismally with a candle amongst the enormous shadows, thrown on all sides by the skeleton limbs of machinery, Massy had been struck dumb by astonishment in the presence of that imposing old man with a beard like a silver plate, towering in the dusk rendered lurid by the expiring flames of sunset.

"Want to see me on business? What business? I am doing no business. Can't you see that this ship is laid up?" Massy had turned at bay before the pursuing irony of his disaster. Afterwards he could not believe his ears. What was that old fellow getting at? Things don't happen that way. It was a dream. He would presently wake up and find the man vanished like a shape of mist. The gravity, the dignity, the firm and courteous tone of that athletic old stranger impressed Massy. He was almost afraid. But it was no dream. Five hundred pounds are no dream. At once he became suspicious. What did it mean? Of course it was an offer to catch hold of for dear life. But what could there be behind?

Before they had parted, after appointing a meeting in a solicitor's office early on the morrow, Massy was asking himself, What is his

motive? He spent the night in hammering out the clauses of the agreement—a unique instrument of its sort whose tenor got bruited abroad somehow and became the talk and wonder of the port.

Massy's object had been to secure for himself as many ways as possible of getting rid of his partner without being called upon at once to pay back his share. Captain Whalley's efforts were directed to making the money secure. Was it not Ivy's money—a part of her fortune whose only other asset was the time-defying body of her old father? Sure of his forbearance in the strength of his love for her, he accepted, with stately serenity, Massy's stupidly cunning paragraphs against his incompetence, his dishonesty, his drunkenness, for the sake of other stringent stipulations. At the end of three years he was at liberty to withdraw from the partnership, taking his money with him. Provision was made for forming a fund to pay him off. But if he left the *Sofala* before the term, from whatever cause (barring death), Massy was to have a whole year for paying. "Illness?" the lawyer had suggested: a young man fresh from Europe and not overburdened with business, who was rather amused. Massy began to whine unctuously, "How could he be expected? . . ."

"Let that go," Captain Whalley had said with a superb confidence in his body. "Acts of God," he added. In the midst of life we are in death, but he trusted his Maker with a still greater fearlessness—his Maker who knew his thoughts, his human affections, and his motives. His Creator knew what use he was making of his health—how much he wanted it. . . . "I trust my first illness will be my last. I've never been ill that I can remember," he had remarked. "Let it go."

But at this early stage he had already awakened Massy's hostility by refusing to make it six hundred instead of five. "I cannot do that," was all he had said, simply, but with so much decision that Massy desisted at once from pressing the point, but had thought to himself, "Can't! Old curmudgeon. *Won't!* He must have lots of money, but he would like to get hold of a soft berth and the sixth part of my profits for nothing if he only could."

And during these years Massy's dislike grew under the restraint of something resembling fear. The simplicity of that man appeared dangerous. Of late he had changed, however, had appeared less formidable and with a lessened vigour of life, as though he had received a secret wound. But still he remained incomprehensible in his simplicity, fearlessness, and rectitude. And when Massy learned that he meant to leave him at the end of the time, to leave him confronted with the problem of the boilers, his dislike blazed up secretly into hate.

It had made him so clear-eyed that for a long time now Mr. Sterne could have told him nothing he did not know. He had much ado in trying to terrorize that mean sneak into silence; he wanted to deal alone with the situation; and—incredible as it might have appeared to Mr. Sterne—he had not yet given up the desire and the hope of inducing that hated old man to stay. Why! there was nothing else to do, unless he were to abandon his chances of fortune. But now, suddenly, since the crossing of the bar at Batu Beru things seemed to be coming rapidly to a point. It disquieted him so much that the study of the winning numbers failed to soothe his agitation: and the twilight in the cabin deepened, very sombre.

He put the list away, muttering once more, "Oh, no, my boy, you don't. Not if I know it." He did not mean the blinking, eavesdropping humbug to force his action. He took his head again into his hands; his immobility confined in the darkness of this shut-up little place seemed to make him a thing apart infinitely removed from the stir and the sounds of the deck.

He heard them: the passengers were beginning to jabber excitedly; somebody dragged a heavy box past his door. He heard Captain Whalley's voice above—

"Stations, Mr. Sterne." And the answer from somewhere on deck forward—

"Ay, ay, sir."

"We shall moor head upstream this time; the ebb has made."

"Head upstream, sir."

"You will see to it, Mr. Sterne."

The answer was covered by the autocratic clang of the engine-room gong. The propeller went on beating slowly: one, two, three; one, two, three—with pauses as if hesitating on the turn. The gong clanged time after time, and the water churned this way and that by the blades was making a great noisy commotion alongside. Mr. Massy did not move. A shore-light on the other bank, a quarter of a mile across the river, drifted, no bigger than a tiny star, passing slowly athwart the circle of the port. Voices from Mr. Van Wyk's jetty answered the hails from the ship; ropes were thrown and missed and thrown again; the swaying flame of a torch carried in a large sampan coming to fetch away in state the Rajah from down the coast cast a sudden ruddy glare into his cabin, over his very person. Mr. Massy did not move. After a few last ponderous turns the engines stopped, and the prolonged clanging of the gong signified that the captain had done with them. A great number of boats and canoes of all sizes boarded the off-side of the *Sofala*. Then after a time the tumult of splashing, of cries, of shuffling feet, of packages dropped with a

thump, the noise of the native passengers going away, subsided slowly. On the shore, a voice, cultivated, slightly authoritative, spoke very close alongside—

"Brought any mail for me this time?"

"Yes, Mr. Van Wyk." This was from Sterne, answering over the rail in a tone of respectful cordiality. "Shall I bring it up to you?"

But the voice asked again—

"Where's the captain?"

"Still on the bridge, I believe. He hasn't left his chair. Shall I. . . ."

The voice interrupted negligently—

"I will come on board."

"Mr. Van Wyk," Sterne suddenly broke out with an eager effort, "will you do me the favour. . . ."

The mate walked away quickly towards the gangway. A silence fell. Mr. Massy in the dark did not move.

He did not move even when he heard slow shuffling footsteps pass his cabin lazily. He contented himself to bellow out through the closed door—

"You—Jack!"

The footsteps came back without haste; the doorhandle rattled, and the second engineer appeared in the opening, shadowy in the sheen of the skylight at his back, with his face apparently as black as the rest of his figure.

"We have been very long coming up this time," Mr. Massy growled, without changing his attitude.

"What do you expect with half the boiler tubes plugged up for leaks?" the second defended himself loquaciously.

"None of your lip," said Massy.

"None of your rotten boilers—I say," retorted his faithful subordinate without animation, huskily.

"Go down there and carry a head of steam on them yourself—if you dare. I don't."

"You aren't worth your salt then," Massy said. The other made a faint noise which resembled a laugh but might have been a snarl.

"Better go slow than stop the ship altogether," he admonished his admired superior. Mr. Massy moved at last. He turned in his chair, and grinding his teeth—

"Dam' you and the ship! I wish she were at the bottom of the sea. Then you would have to starve."

The trusty second engineer closed the door gently.

Massy listened. Instead of passing on to the bathroom where he should have gone to clean himself, the second entered his cabin, which was next door. Mr. Massy jumped up and waited. Suddenly he heard

the lock snap in there. He rushed out and gave a violent kick to the door.

"I believe you are locking yourself up to get drunk," he shouted.

A muffled answer came after a while.

"My own time."

"If you take to boozing on the trip I'll fire you out," Massy cried.

An obstinate silence followed that threat. Massy moved away, perplexed. On the bank two figures appeared, approaching the gangway. He heard a voice tinged with contempt—

"I would rather doubt your word. But I shall certainly speak to him of this."

The other voice, Sterne's, said with a sort of regretful formality—

"Thanks. That's all I want. I must do my duty."

Mr. Massy was surprised. A short, dapper figure leaped lightly on the deck and nearly bounded into him where he stood beyond the circle of light from the gangway lamp. When it had passed towards the bridge, after exchanging a hurried "Good evening," Massy said surlily to Sterne, who followed with slow steps—

"What is it you're making up to Mr. Van Wyk for, now?"

"Far from it, Mr. Massy. I am not good enough for Mr. Van Wyk. Neither are you, sir, in his opinion, I am afraid. Captain Whalley is, it seems. He's gone to ask him to dine up at the house this evening."

Then he murmured to himself darkly—

"I hope he will like it."

§ 12

Mr. Van Wyk, the white man of Batu Beru, an ex-naval officer who, for reasons best known to himself, had thrown away the promise of a brilliant career to become the pioneer of tobacco-planting on that remote part of the coast, had learned to like Captain Whalley. The appearance of the new skipper had attracted his attention. Nothing more unlike all the diverse types he had seen succeeding each other on the bridge of the *Sofala* could be imagined.

At that time Batu Beru was not what it has become since: the centre of a prosperous tobacco-growing district, a tropically suburban-looking little settlement of bungalows in one long street shaded with two rows of trees, embowered by the flowering and trim luxuriance of the gardens, with a three-mile-long carriage-road for the afternoon drives and a first-class Resident with a fat, cheery wife to lead the society of married estate-managers and unmarried young fellows in the service of the big companies.

All this prosperity was not yet; and Mr. Van Wyk prospered alone

on the left bank of his deep clearing carved out of the forest, which
came down above and below to the water's edge. His lonely bungalow
faced across the river the houses of the Sultan: a restless and melan-
choly old ruler who had done with love and war, for whom life no
longer held any savour (except of evil forebodings) and time never
had any value. He was afraid of death, and hoped he would die
before the white men were ready to take his country from him. He
crossed the river frequently (with never less than ten boats crammed
full of people), in the wistful hope of extracting some information on
the subject from his own white man. There was a certain chair on the
verandah he always took: the dignitaries of the court squatted on the
rugs and skins between the furniture: the inferior people remained
below on the grass-plot between the house and the river in rows three
or four deep all along the front. Not seldom the visit began at day-
break, Mr. Van Wyk tolerated these inroads. He would nod out of
his bedroom window, toothbrush or razor in hand, or pass through the
throng of courtiers in his bathing robe. He appeared and disappeared
humming a tune, polished his nails with attention, rubbed his shaved
face with eau-de-Cologne, drank his early tea, went out to see his
coolies at work; returned, looked through some papers on his desk,
read a page or two in a book or sat before his cottage piano leaning
back on the stool, his arms extended, fingers on the keys, his body
swaying slightly from side to side. When absolutely forced to speak
he gave evasive, vaguely soothing answers out of pure compassion: the
same feeling perhaps made him so lavishly hospitable with the
aerated drinks that more than once he left himself without soda-water
for a whole week. That old man had granted him as much land as he
cared to have cleared: it was neither more nor less than a fortune.

Whether it was fortune or seclusion from his kind that Mr. Van
Wyk sought, he could not have pitched upon a better place. Even
the mail-boats of the subsidized company calling on the veriest clusters
of palm-thatched hovels along the coast steamed past the mouth of
Batu Beru river far away in the offing. The contract was old: perhaps
in a few years' time, when it had expired, Batu Beru would be in-
cluded in the service: meantime all Mr. Van Wyk's mail was addressed
to Malacca, whence his agent sent it across once a month by the
Sofala. It followed that whenever Massy had run short of money
(through taking too many lottery tickets), or got into a difficulty
about a skipper, Mr. Van Wyk was deprived of his letters and news-
papers. In so far he had a personal interest in the fortunes of the
Sofala. Though he considered himself a hermit (and for no passing
whim evidently, since he had stood eight years of it already), he liked
to know what went on in the world.

Handy on the verandah upon a walnut étagère (it had come last year by the *Sofala*—everything came by the *Sofala*) there lay, piled up under bronze weights, a pile of *The Times* weekly edition, the large sheets of the *Rotterdam Courant*, the *Graphic* in its world-wide green wrappers, an illustrated Dutch publication without a cover, the numbers of a German magazine with covers of the "Bismarck malade" colour. There were also parcels of new music—though the piano (it had come years ago by the *Sofala*) in the damp atmosphere of the forests was generally out of tune. It was vexing to be cut off from everything for sixty days at a stretch sometimes, without any means of knowing what was the matter. And when the *Sofala* reappeared Mr. Van Wyk would descend the steps of the verandah and stroll over the grass-plot in front of his house, down to the water-side, with a frown on his white brow.

"You've been laid up after an accident, I presume."

He addressed the bridge, but before anybody could answer Massy was sure to have already scrambled ashore over the rail and pushed in, squeezing the palms of his hands together, bowing his sleek head as if gummed all over the top with black threads and tapes. And he would be so enraged at the necessity of having to offer such an explanation that his moaning would be positively pitiful, while all the time he tried to compose his big lips into a smile.

"No, Mr. Van Wyk. You would not believe it. I couldn't get one of those wretches to take the ship out. Not a single one of the lazy beasts could be induced, and the law, you know, Mr. Van Wyk. . . . "

He moaned at great length apologetically; the words conspiracy, plot, envy, came out prominently, whined with greater energy. Mr. Van Wyk, examining with a faint grimace his polished fingernails, would say, "H'm. Very unfortunate," and turn his back on him.

Fastidious, clever, slightly sceptical, accustomed to the best society (he had held a much-envied shore appointment at the Ministry of Marine for a year preceding his retreat from his profession and from Europe), he possessed a latent warmth of feeling and a capacity for sympathy which were concealed by a sort of haughty, arbitrary indifference of manner arising from his early training; and by a something an enemy might have called foppish, in his aspect—like a distorted echo of past elegancies. He managed to keep an almost military discipline amongst the coolies of the estate he had dragged into the light of day out of the tangle and shadows of the jungle; and the white shirt he put on every evening with its stiff glossy front and high collar looked as if he had meant to preserve the decent ceremony of evening-dress, but had wound a thick crimson sash above his hips as a concession to the wilderness, once his adversary, now his vanquished com-

panion. Moreover, it was a hygienic precaution. Worn wide open in front, a short jacket of some airy silken stuff floated from his shoulders. His fluffy, fair hair, thin at the top, curled slightly at the sides; a carefully arranged moustache, an ungarnished forehead, the gleam of low patent shoes peeping under the wide bottom of trousers cut straight from the same stuff as the gossamer coat, completed a figure recalling, with its sash, a pirate chief of romance, and at the same time the elegance of a slightly bald dandy indulging, in seclusion, a taste for unorthodox costume.

It was his evening get-up. The proper time for the *Sofala* to arrive at Batu Beru was an hour before sunset, and he looked picturesque, and somehow quite correct, too, walking at the water's edge on the background of grass slope crowned with a low, long bungalow with an immensely steep roof of palm thatch, and clad to the eaves in flowering creepers. While the *Sofala* was being made fast he strolled in the shade of the few trees left near the landing-place, waiting till he could go on board. Her white men were not of his kind. The old Sultan (though his wistful invasions were a nuisance) was really much more acceptable to his fastidious taste. But still they were white; the periodical visits of the ship made a break in the well-filled sameness of the days without disturbing his privacy. Moreover, they were necessary from a business point of view; and through a strain of preciseness in his nature he was irritated when she failed to appear at the appointed time.

The cause of the irregularity was too absurd, and Massy, in his opinion, was a contemptible idiot. The first time the *Sofala* reappeared under the new agreement swinging out of the bend below, after he had almost given up all hope of ever seeing her again, he felt so angry that he did not go down at once to the landing-place. His servants had come running to him with the news, and he had dragged a chair close against the front rail of the verandah, spread his elbows out, rested his chin on his hands, and went on glaring at her fixedly while she was being made fast opposite his house. He could make out easily all the white faces on board. Who on earth was that kind of patriarch they had got there on the bridge now?

At last he sprang up and walked down the gravel path. It was a fact that the very gravel for his paths had been imported by the *Sofala*. Exasperated out of his quiet superciliousness, without looking at any one right or left, he accosted Massy straightway in so determined a manner that the engineer, taken aback, began to stammer unintelligibly. Nothing could be heard but the words: "Mr. Van Wyk . . . Indeed, Mr. Van Wyk. . . . For the future, Mr. Van Wyk"—and by the suffusion of blood Massy's vast bilious face acquired an unnatural

orange tint, out of which the disconcerted coal-black eyes shone in an extraordinary manner.

"Nonsense. I am tired of this. I wonder you have the impudence to come alongside my jetty as if I had it made for your convenience alone."

Massy tried to protest earnestly. Mr. Van Wyk was very angry. He had a good mind to ask that German firm—those people in Malacca—what was their name?—boats with green funnels. They would be only too glad of the opening to put one of their small steamers on the run. Yes; Schnitzler, Jacob Schnitzler, would in a moment. Yes. He had decided to write without delay.

In his agitation Massy caught up his falling pipe.

"You don't mean it, sir!" he shrieked.

"You shouldn't mismanage your business in this ridiculous manner."

Mr. Van Wyk turned on his heel. The other three whites on the bridge had not stirred during the scene. Massy walked hastily from side to side, puffed out his cheeks, suffocated.

"Stuck-up Dutchman!"

And he moaned out feverishly a long tale of griefs. The efforts he had made for all these years to please that man. This was the return you got for it, eh? Pretty. Write to Schnitzler—let in the green-funnel boats—get an old Hamburg Jew to ruin him. No, really he could laugh. . . . He laughed sobbingly. . . . Ha! ha! ha! And make him carry the letter in his own ship presumably.

He stumbled across a grating and swore. He would not hesitate to fling the Dutchman's correspondence overboard—the whole confounded bundle. He had never, never made any charge for that accommodation. But Captain Whalley, his new partner, would not let him probably; besides, it would be only putting off the evil day. For his own part he would make a hole in the water rather than look on tamely at the green funnels overrunning his trade.

He raved aloud. The China boys hung back with the dishes at the foot of the ladder. He yelled from the bridge down at the deck, "Aren't we going to have any chow this evening at all?" then turned violently to Captain Whalley, who waited, grave and patient, at the head of the table, smoothing his beard in silence now and then with a forbearing gesture.

"You don't seem to care what happens to me. Don't you see that this affects your interests as much as mine? It's no joking matter."

He took the foot of the table growling between his teeth.

"Unless you have a few thousands put away somewhere. I haven't."

Mr. Van Wyk dined in his thoroughly lit-up bungalow, putting a point of splendour in the night of his clearing above the dark bank of

the river. Afterwards he sat down to his piano, and in a pause he became aware of slow footsteps passing on the path along the front. A plank or two creaked under a heavy tread; he swung half round on the music-stool, listening with his finger-tips at rest on the keyboard. His little terrier barked violently, backing in from the verandah. A deep voice apologized gravely for "this intrusion." He walked out quickly.

At the head of the steps the patriarchal figure, who was the new captain of the *Sofala* apparently (he had seen a round dozen of them, but not one of that sort), towered without advancing. The little dog barked unceasingly, till a flick of Mr. Van Wyk's handkerchief made him spring aside into silence. Captain Whalley, opening the matter, was met by a punctiliously polite but determined opposition.

They carried on their discussion standing where they had come face to face. Mr. Van Wyk observed his visitor with attention. Then at last, as if forced out of his reserve—

"I am surprised that you should intercede for such a confounded fool."

This outbreak was almost complimentary, as if its meaning had been, "That such a man as you should intercede!" Captain Whalley let it pass by without flinching. One would have thought he had heard nothing. He simply went on to state that he was personally interested in putting things straight between them. Personally. . . .

But Mr. Van Wyk, really carried away by his disgust with Massy, became very incisive—

"Indeed—if I am to be frank with you—his whole character does not seem to me particularly estimable or trustworthy. . . ."

Captain Whalley, always straight, seemed to grow an inch taller and broader, as if the girth of his chest had suddenly expanded under his beard.

"My dear sir, you don't think I came here to discuss a man with whom I am—I am—h'm—closely associated."

A sort of solemn silence lasted for a moment. He was not used to asking favours, but the importance he attached to this affair had made him willing to try. . . . Mr. Van Wyk, favourably impressed, and suddenly mollified by a desire to laugh, interrupted—

"That's all right if you make it a personal matter; but you can do no less than sit down and smoke a cigar with me."

A slight pause, then Captain Whalley stepped forward heavily. As to the regularity of the service, for the future he made himself responsible for it; and his name was Whalley—perhaps to a sailor (he was speaking to a sailor, was he not?) not altogether unfamiliar. There was a lighthouse now, on an island. Maybe Mr. Van Wyk himself. . . .

"Oh, yes. Oh, indeed." Mr. Van Wyk caught on at once. He indicated a chair. How very interesting. For his own part he had seen some service in the last Acheen War, but had never been so far East. Whalley Island? Of course. Now that was very interesting. What changes his guest must have seen since.

"I can look further back even—on a whole half-century."

Captain Whalley expanded a bit. The flavour of a good cigar (it was a weakness) had gone straight to his heart, also the civility of that young man. There was something in that accidental contact of which he had been starved in his years of struggle.

The front wall retreating made a square recess furnished like a room. A lamp with a milky glass shade, suspended below the slope of the high roof at the end of a slender brass chain, threw a bright round of light upon a little table bearing an open book and an ivory paper-knife. And, in the translucent shadows beyond, other tables could be seen, a number of easy-chairs of various shapes, with a great profusion of skin rugs strewn on the teakwood planking all over the verandah. The flowering creepers scented the air. Their foliage clipped out between the uprights made as if several frames of thick, unstirring leaves reflecting the lamplight in a green glow. Through the opening at his elbow Captain Whalley could see the gangway lantern of the *Sofala* burning dim by the shore, the shadowy masses of the town beyond the open lustrous darkness of the river, and, as if hung along the straight edge of the projecting eaves, a narrow black strip of the night sky full of stars—resplendent. The famous cigar in hand he had a moment of complacency.

"A trifle. Somebody must lead the way. I just showed that the thing could be done; but you men brought up to the use of steam cannot conceive the vast importance of my bit of venturesomeness to the Eastern trade of the time. Why, that new route reduced the average time of a southern passage by eleven days for more than half the year. Eleven days! It's on record. But the remarkable thing—speaking to a sailor—I should say was. . . ."

He talked well, without egotism, professionally. The powerful voice, produced without effort, filled the bungalow even into the empty rooms with a deep and limpid resonance, seemed to make a stillness outside; and Mr. Van Wyk was surprised by the serene quality of its tone, like the perfection of manly gentleness. Nursing one small foot, in a silk sock and a patent leather shoe, on his knee, he was immensely entertained. It was as if nobody could talk like this now, and the over-shadowed eyes, the flowing white beard, the big frame, the serenity, the whole temper of the man, were an amazing survival from the prehistoric times of the world coming up to him out of the sea.

Captain Whalley had been also the pioneer of the early trade in the Gulf of Petchili. He even found occasion to mention that he had buried his "dear wife" there six-and-twenty years ago. Mr. Van Wyk, impassive, could not help speculating in his mind swiftly as to the sort of woman that would mate with such a man. Did they make an adventurous and well-matched pair? No. Very possibly she had been small, frail, no doubt very feminine—or most likely commonplace with domestic instincts, utterly insignificant. But Captain Whalley was no garrulous bore, and shaking his head as if to dissipate the momentary gloom that had settled on his handsome old face, he alluded conversationally to Mr. Van Wyk's solitude.

Mr. Van Wyk affirmed that sometimes he had more company than he wanted. He mentioned smilingly some of the peculiarities of his intercourse with "My Sultan." He made his visits in force. Those people damaged his grass-plot in front (it was not easy to obtain some approach to a lawn in the tropics), and the other day had broken down some rare bushes he had planted over there. And Captain Whalley remembered immediately that, in 'forty-seven, the then Sultan, "this man's grandfather," had been notorious as a great protector of the piratical fleets of praus from farther East. They had a safe refuge in the river at Batu Beru. He financed more especially a Balinini chief called Haji Daman. Captain Whalley, nodding significantly his bushy white eyebrows, had very good reason to know something of that. The world had progressed since that time.

Mr. Van Wyk demurred with unexpected acrimony. Progressed in what? he wanted to know.

Why, in knowledge of truth, of decency, in justice, in order—in honesty, too, since men harmed each other mostly from ignorance. It was, Captain Whalley concluded quaintly, more pleasant to live in.

Mr. Van Wyk whimsically would not admit that Mr. Massy, for instance, was more pleasant naturally than the Balinini pirates.

The river had not gained much by the change. They were in their way every bit as honest. Massy was less ferocious than Haji Daman no doubt, but. . . .

"And what about you, my good sir?" Captain Whalley laughed a deep soft laugh. "*You* are an improvement, surely."

He continued in a vein of pleasantry. A good cigar was better than a knock on the head—the sort of welcome he would have found on this river forty or fifty years ago. Then leaning forward slightly, he became earnestly serious. It seems as if, outside their own sea-gipsy tribes, these rovers had hated all mankind with an incomprehensible, bloodthirsty hatred. Meantime their depredations had been stopped, and what was the consequence? The new generation was orderly, peaceable, settled

in prosperous villages. He could speak from personal knowledge. And even the few survivors of that time—old men now—had changed so much, that it would have been unkind to remember against them that they had ever slit a throat in their lives. He had one especially in his mind's eye: a dignified, venerable headman of a certain large coast village about sixty miles sou'west of Tampasuk. It did one's heart good to see him—to hear that man speak. He might have been a ferocious savage once. What men wanted was to be checked by superior intelligence, by superior knowledge, by superior force, too—yes, by force held in trust from God and sanctified by its use in accordance with His declared will. Captain Whalley believed a disposition for good existed in every man, even if the world were not a very happy place as a whole. In the wisdom of men he had not so much confidence.

The disposition had to be helped up pretty sharply sometimes, he admitted. They might be silly, wrong-headed, unhappy; but naturally evil—no. There was at bottom a complete harmlessness at least. . . .

"Is there?" Mr. Van Wyk snapped acrimoniously.

Captain Whalley laughed at the interjection, in the good humour of large, tolerating certitude. He could look back at half a century, he pointed out. The smoke oozed placidly through the white hairs hiding his kindly lips.

"At all events," he resumed after a pause, "I am glad that they've had no time to do you much harm as yet."

This allusion to his comparative youthfulness did not offend Mr. Van Wyk, who got up and wriggled his shoulders with an enigmatic half-smile. They walked out together amicably into the starry night towards the river-side. Their footsteps resounded unequally on the dark path. At the shore end of the gangway the lantern, hung low to the handrail, threw a vivid light on the white legs and the black feet of Mr. Massy waiting about anxiously. From the waist upwards he remained shadowy, with a row of buttons gleaming up to the vague outline of his chin.

"You may thank Captain Whalley for this," Mr. Van Wyk said, curtly, to him before turning away.

The lamps on the verandah flung three long squares of light between the uprights far over the grass. A bat flitted before his face like a circling flake of velvety blackness. Along the jasmine hedge the night air seemed heavy with the fall of perfumed dew; flower-beds bordered the path; the clipped bushes uprose in dark, rounded clumps here and there before the house; the dense foliage of creepers filtered the sheen of the lamplight within in a soft glow all along the front; and everything near and far stood still in a great immobility, in a great sweetness.

Mr. Van Wyk (a few years before he had had occasion to imagine himself treated more badly than anybody alive had even been by a woman) felt for Captain Whalley's optimistic views the disdain of a man who had once been credulous himself. His disgust with the world (the woman for a time had filled it for him completely) had taken the form of activity in retirement, because, though capable of great depth of feeling, he was energetic and essentially practical. But there was in that uncommon old sailor, drifting on the outskirts of his busy solitude, something that fascinated his scepticism. His very simplicity (amusing enough) was like a delicate refinement of an upright character. The striking dignity of manner could be nothing else, in a man reduced to such a humble position, but the expression of something essentially noble in the character. With all his trust in mankind he was no fool; the serenity of his temper at the end of so many years, since it could not obviously have been appeased by success, wore an air of profound wisdom. Mr. Van Wyk was amused at it sometimes. Even the very physical traits of the old captain of the *Sofala,* his powerful frame, his reposeful mien, his intelligent, handsome face, the big limbs, the benign courtesy, the touch of rugged severity in the shaggy eyebrows, made up a seductive personality. Mr. Van Wyk disliked littleness of every kind, but there was nothing small about that man, and in the exemplary regularity of many trips an intimacy had grown up between them, a warm feeling at bottom under a kindly stateliness of forms agreeable to his fastidiousness.

They kept their respective opinions on all worldly matters. His other convictions Captain Whalley never intruded. The difference of their ages was like another bond between them. Once, when twitted with the uncharitableness of his youth, Mr. Van Wyk, running his eye over the vast proportions of his interlocutor, retorted in friendly banter—

"Oh. You'll come to my way of thinking yet. You'll have plenty of time. Don't call yourself old: you look good for a round hundred."

But he could not help his stinging incisiveness, and though moderating it by an almost affectionate smile, he added—

"And by then you will probably consent to die from sheer disgust."

Captain Whalley, smiling, too, shook his head. "God forbid!"

He thought that perhaps on the whole he deserved something better than to die in such sentiments. The time of course would have to come, and he trusted to his Maker to provide a manner of going out of which he need not be ashamed. For the rest he hoped he would live to a hundred if need be; other men had been known; it would be no miracle. He expected no miracles.

The pronounced, argumentative tone caused Mr. Van Wyk to raise his head and look at him steadily. Captain Whalley was gazing fixedly

with a rapt expression, as though he had seen his Creator's favourable decree written in mysterious characters on the wall. He kept perfectly motionless for a few seconds, then got his vast bulk on to his feet so impetuously that Mr. Van Wyk was startled.

He struck first a heavy blow on his inflated chest: and, throwing out horizontally a big arm that remained steady, extended in the air like the limb of a tree on a windless day—

"Not a pain or an ache there. Can you see this shake in the least?"

His voice was low, in an awing, confident contrast with the headlong emphasis of his movements. He sat down abruptly.

"This isn't to boast of it, you know. I am nothing," he said in his effortless strong voice, that seemed to come out as naturally as a river flows. He picked up the stump of the cigar he had laid aside, and added peacefully, with a slight nod, "As it happens, my life is necessary; it isn't my own, it isn't—God knows."

He did not say much for the rest of the evening, but several times Mr. Van Wyk detected a faint smile of assurance flitting under the heavy moustache.

Later on Captain Whalley would now and then consent to dine "at the house." He could even be induced to drink a glass of wine. "Don't think I'm afraid of it, my good sir," he explained. "There was a very good reason why I should give it up."

On another occasion, leaning back at ease, he remarked, "You have treated me most—most humanely, my dear Mr. Van Wyk, from the very first."

"You'll admit there was some merit," Mr. Van Wyk hinted, slily. "An associate of that excellent Massy. . . . Well, well, my dear captain, I won't say a word against him."

"It would be no use your saying anything against him," Captain Whalley affirmed a little moodily. "As I've told you before, my life— my work, is necessary, not for myself alone. I can't choose. . . ." He paused, turned the glass before him right round. . . . "I have an only child—a daughter."

The ample downward sweep of his arm over the table seemed to suggest a small girl at a vast distance. "I hope to see her once more before I die. Meantime it's enough to know that she has me sound and solid, thank God. You can't understand how one feels. Bone of my bone, flesh of my flesh; the very image of my poor wife. Well, she . . ."

Again he paused, then pronounced stoically the words, "She has a hard struggle."

And his head fell on his breast, his eyebrows remained knitted, as

by an effort of meditation. But generally his mind seemed steeped in the serenity of boundless trust in a higher power. Mr. Van Wyk wondered sometimes how much of it was due to the splendid vitality of the man, to the bodily vigour which seems to impart something of its force to the soul. But he had learned to like him very much.

§ 13

This was the reason why Mr. Sterne's confidential communication, delivered hurriedly on the shore alongside the dark silent ship, had disturbed his equanimity. It was the most incomprehensible and unexpected thing that could happen; and the perturbation of his spirit was so great that, forgetting all about his letters, he ran rapidly up the bridge ladder.

The portable table was being put together for dinner to the left of the wheel by two pig-tailed "boys," who as usual snarled at each other over the job, while another, a doleful, burly, very yellow Chinaman, resembling Mr. Massy, waited apathetically with the cloth over his arm and a pile of thick dinner-plates against his chest. A common cabin lamp with its globe missing, brought up from below, had been hooked to the wooden framework of the awning; the side-screens had been lowered all round; Captain Whalley, filling the depths of the wicker-chair, seemed to sit benumbed in a canvas tent crudely lighted, and used for the storing of nautical objects; a shabby steering-wheel, a battered brass binnacle on a stout mahogany stand, two dingy life-buoys, an old cork fender lying in a corner, dilapidated deck-lockers with loops of tin rope instead of door-handles.

He shook off the appearance of numbness to return Mr. Van Wyck's unusually brisk greeting, but relapsed directly afterwards. To accept a pressing invitation to dinner "up at the house" cost him another very visible physical effort. Mr. Van Wyk, perplexed, folded his arms, and leaning back against the rail, with his little, black, shiny feet well out, examined him covertly.

"I've noticed of late that you are not quite yourself, old friend."

He put an affectionate gentleness into the last two words. The real intimacy of their intercourse had never been so vividly expressed before.

"Tut, tut, tut!"

The wicker-chair creaked heavily.

"Irritable," commented Mr. Van Wyk to himself; and aloud, "I'll expect to see you in half an hour, then," he said, negligently, moving off.

"In half an hour," Captain Whalley's rigid silvery head repeated behind him as if out of a trance.

Amidships, below, two voices, close against the engine-room, could be heard answering each other—one angry and slow, the other alert.

"I tell you the beast has locked himself in to get drunk."

"Can't help it now, Mr. Massy. After all, a man has a right to shut himself up in his cabin in his own time."

"Not to get drunk."

"I heard him swear that the worry with the boilers was enough to drive any man to drink," Sterne said, maliciously.

Massy hissed out something about bursting the door in. Mr. Van Wyk, to avoid them, crossed in the dark to the other side of the deserted deck. The planking of the little wharf rattled faintly under his hasty feet.

"Mr. Van Wyk! Mr. Van Wyk!"

He walked on: somebody was running on the path. "You've forgotten to get your mail."

Sterne, holding a bundle of papers in his hand, caught up with him. "Oh, thanks."

But, as the other continued at his elbow, Mr. Van Wyk stopped short. The overhanging eaves, descending low upon the lighted front of the bungalow, threw their black straight-edged shadow into the great body of the night on that side. Everything was very still. A tinkle of cutlery and a slight jingle of glasses were heard. Mr. Van Wyk's servants were laying the table for two on the verandah.

"I am afraid you give me no credit whatever for my good intentions in the matter I've spoken to you about," said Sterne.

"I simply don't understand you."

"Captain Whalley is a very audacious man, but he will understand that his game is up. That's all that anybody need ever know of it from me. Believe me, I am very considerate in this, but duty is duty. I don't want to make a fuss. All I ask you, as his friend, is to tell him from me that the game's up. That will be sufficient."

Mr. Van Wyk felt a loathsome dismay at this queer privilege of friendship. He would not demean himself by asking for the slightest explanation; to drive the other away with contumely he did not think prudent—as yet, at any rate. So much assurance staggered him. Who could tell what there could be in it? he thought. His regard for Captain Whalley had the tenacity of a disinterested sentiment, and his practical instinct coming to his aid, he concealed his scorn.

"I gather, then, that this is something grave."

"Very grave," Sterne assented, solemnly, delighted at having produced an effect at last. He was ready to add some effusive protestations

of regret at the "unavoidable necessity," but Mr. Van Wyk cut him short—very civilly, however.

Once on the verandah Mr. Van Wyk put his hands in his pockets, and, straddling his legs, stared down at a black panther skin lying on the floor before a rocking-chair. "It looks as if the fellow had not the pluck to play his own precious game openly," he thought.

This was true enough. In the face of Massy's last rebuff Sterne dared not declare his knowledge. His object was simply to get charge of the steamer and keep it for some time. Massy would never forgive him for forcing himself on; but if Captain Whalley left the ship of his own accord, the command would devolve upon him for the rest of the trip; so he hit upon the brilliant idea of scaring the old man away. A vague menace, a mere hint, would be enough in such a brazen case; and, with a strange admixture of compassion, he thought that Batu Beru was a very good place for throwing up the sponge. The skipper could go ashore quietly, and stay with that Dutchman of his. Weren't these two as thick as thieves together? And on reflection he seemed to see that there was a way to work the whole thing through that great friend of the old man's. This was another brilliant idea. He had an inborn preference for circuitous methods. In this particular case he desired to remain in the background as much as possible, to avoid exasperating Massy needlessly. No fuss! Let it all happen naturally.

Mr. Van Wyk all through the dinner was conscious of a sense of isolation that invades sometimes the closeness of human intercourse. Captain Whalley failed lamentably and obviously in his attempts to eat something. He seemed overcome by a strange absent-mindedness. His hand would hover irresolutely, as if left without guidance by a preoccupied mind. Mr. Van Wyk had heard him coming up from a long way off in the profound stillness of the river-side, and had noticed the irresolute character of the footfalls. The toe of his boot had struck the bottom stair as though he had come along mooning with his head in the air right up to the steps of the verandah. Had the captain of the *Sofala* been another sort of man he would have suspected the work of age there. But one glance at him was enough. Time—after, indeed, marking him for its own—had given him up to his usefulness, in which his simple faith would see a proof of Divine mercy. "How could I contrive to warn him?" Mr. Van Wyk wondered, as if Captain Whalley had been miles and miles away, out of sight and earshot of all evil. He was sickened by an immense disgust of Sterne. Even to mention his threat to a man like Whalley would be positively indecent. There was something more vile and insulting in its hint than in a definite charge of crime—the debasing taint of blackmailing. "What could any one bring against him?" he asked himself. This was a limpid personality.

"And for what object?" The Power that man trusted had thought fit to leave him nothing on earth that envy could lay hold of, except a bare crust of bread.

"Won't you try some of this?" he asked, pushing a dish slightly. Suddenly it occurred to Mr. Van Wyk that Sterne might possibly be coveting the command of the *Sofala*. His cynicism was quite startled by what looked like a proof that no man may count himself safe from his kind unless in the very abyss of misery. An intrigue of that sort was hardly worth troubling about, he judged; but still, with such a fool as Massy to deal with, Whalley ought to and must be warned.

At this moment Captain Whalley, bolt upright, the deep cavities of the eyes overhung by a bushy frown, and one large brown hand resting on each side of his empty plate, spoke across the table-cloth abruptly—

"Mr. Van Wyk, you've always treated me with the most humane consideration."

"My dear captain, you make too much of the simple fact that I am not a savage." Mr. Van Wyk, utterly revolted by the thought of Sterne's obscure attempt, raised his voice incisively, as if the mate had been hiding somewhere within earshot. "Any consideration I have been able to show was no more than the rightful due of a character I've learned to regard by this time with an esteem that nothing can shake."

A slight ring of glass made him lift his eyes from the slice of pine-apple he was cutting into small pieces on his plate. In changing his position Captain Whalley had contrived to upset an empty tumbler.

Without looking that way, leaning sideways on his elbow, his other hand shading his brow, he groped shadily for it, then desisted. Van Wyk stared blankly, as if something momentous had happened all at once. He did not know why he should feel so startled; but he forgot Sterne utterly for the moment.

"Why, what's the matter?"

And Captain Whalley, half-averted, in a deadened, agitated voice, muttered—

"Esteem!"

"And I may add something more," Mr. Van Wyk, very steady-eyed, pronounced slowly.

"Hold! Enough!" Captain Whalley did not change his attitude or raise his voice. "Say no more! I can make you no return. I am too poor even for that now. Your esteem is worth having. You are not a man that would stoop to deceive the poorest sort of devil on earth, or make a ship unseaworthy every time he takes her to sea."

Mr. Van Wyk, leaning forward, his face gone pink all over, with

the starched table-napkin over his knees, was inclined to mistrust his senses, his power of comprehension, the sanity of his guest.

"Where? Why? In the name of God!—what's this? What ship? I don't understand who. . . ."

"Then, in the name of God, it is I! A ship's unseaworthy when her captain can't see. I am going blind."

Mr. Van Wyk made a slight movement, and sat very still afterwards for a few seconds; then, with the thought of Sterne's "The game's up," he ducked under the table to pick up the napkin which had slipped off his knees. This was the game that was up. And at the same time the muffled voice of Captain Whalley passed over him—

"I've deceived them all. Nobody knows."

He emerged flushed to the eyes. Captain Whalley, motionless under the full blaze of the lamp, shaded his face with his hand.

"And you had that courage?"

"Call it by what name you like. But you are a humane man—a—a—gentleman, Mr. Van Wyk. You may have asked me what I had done with my conscience."

He seemed to muse, profoundly silent, very still in his mournful pose.

"I began to tamper with it in my pride. You begin to see a lot of things when you are going blind. I could not be frank with an old chum even. I was not frank with Massy—no, not altogether. I knew he took me for a wealthy sailor fool, and I let him. I wanted to keep up my importance—because there was poor Ivy away there—my daughter. What did I want to trade on his misery for? I did trade on it—for her. And now, what mercy could I expect from him? He would trade on mine if he knew it. He would hunt the old fraud out, and stick to the money for a year. Ivy's money. And I haven't kept a penny for myself. How am I going to live for a year? A year! In a year there will be no sun in the sky for her father."

His deep voice came out, awfully veiled, as though he had been overwhelmed by the earth of a landslide and talking of the thoughts that haunt the dead in their graves. A cold shudder ran down Mr. Van Wyk's back.

"And how long is it since you have. . . ?" he began.

"It was a long time before I could bring myself to believe in this—this—visitation." Captain Whalley spoke with gloomy patience from under his hand.

He had not thought he had deserved it. He had begun by deceiving himself from day to day, from week to week. He had the Serang at hand there—an old servant. It came on gradually, and when he could no longer deceive himself. . . .

His voice died out almost.

"Rather than give her up I set myself to deceive you all."

"It's incredible," whispered Mr. Van Wyk. Captain Whalley's appalling murmur flowed on.

"Not even the sign of God's anger could make me forget her. How could I forsake my child, feeling my vigour all the time—the blood warm within me? Warm as yours. It seems to me that, like the blinded Sampson, I would find the strength to shake down a temple upon my head. She's a struggling woman—my own child that we used to pray over together, my poor wife and I. Do you remember that day I as well as told you that I believed God would let me live to a hundred for her sake? What sin is there in loving your child? Do you see it? I was ready for her sake to live for ever. I half believed I would. I've been praying for death since. Ha! Presumptuous man—you wanted to live. . . ."

A tremendous, shuddering upheaval of that big frame, shaken by a gasping sob, set the glasses jingling all over the table, seemed to make the whole house tremble to the roof-tree. And Mr. Van Wyk, whose feeling of outraged love had been translated into a form of struggle with nature, understood very well that, for that man whose whole life had been conditioned by action, there could exist no other expression for all the emotions; that, to voluntarily cease venturing, doing, enduring, for his child's sake, would have been exactly like plucking his warm love for her out of his living heart. Something too monstrous, too impossible, even to conceive.

Captain Whalley had not changed his attitude, that seemed to express something of shame, sorrow, and defiance.

"I have even deceived you. If it had not been for that word 'esteem.' These are not the words for me. I would have lied to you. Haven't I lied to you? Weren't you going to trust your property on board this very trip?"

"I have a floating yearly policy," Mr. Van Wyk said almost unwittingly, and was amazed at the sudden cooping up of a commercial detail.

"The ship is unseaworthy, I tell you. The policy would be invalid if it were known. . . ."

"We shall share the guilt, then."

"Nothing could make mine less," said Captain Whalley.

He had not dared to consult a doctor; the man would have perhaps asked who he was, what he was doing; Massy might have heard something. He had lived on without any help, human or divine. The very prayers stuck in his throat. What was there to pray for? and death seemed as far as ever. Once he got into his cabin he dared not come out again; when he sat down he dared not get up; he dared not raise

his eyes to anybody's face, he felt reluctant to look upon the sea or up to the sky. The world was fading before his great fear of giving himself away. The old ship was his last friend; he was not afraid of her; he knew every inch of her deck; but at her, too, he hardly dared to look, for fear of finding he could see less than the day before. A great incertitude enveloped him. The horizon was gone; the sky mingled darkly with the sea. Who was this figure standing over yonder? what was this thing lying down there? And a frightful doubt of the reality of what he could see made even the remnant of sight that remained to him an added torment, a pitfall always open for his miserable pretence. He was afraid to stumble inexcusably over something—to say a fatal Yes or No to a question. The hand of God was upon him, but it could not tear him away from his child. And, as if in a nightmare of humiliation, every featureless man seemed an enemy.

He let his hand fall heavily on the table. Mr. Van Wyk, arms down, chin on breast, with a gleam of white teeth pressing on the lower lip, meditated on Sterne's "The game's up."

"The Serang of course does not know."

"Nobody," said Captain Whalley, with assurance.

"Ah, yes. Nobody. Very well. Can you keep it up to the end of the trip? That is the last under the agreement with Massy."

Captain Whalley got up and stood erect, very stately, with the great white beard lying like a silver breastplate over the awful secret of his heart. Yes; that was the only hope there was for him of ever seeing her again, of securing the money, the last he could do for her, before he crept away somewhere—useless, a burden, a reproach to himself. His voice faltered.

"Think of it! Never see her any more: the only human being besides myself now on earth that can remember my wife. She's just like her mother. Lucky the poor woman is where there are no tears shed over those they loved on earth and that remain to pray not to be led into temptation—because, I suppose, the blessed know the secret of grace in God's dealings with His created children."

He swayed a little, said with austere dignity—

"I don't. I know only the child He has given me."

And he began to walk. Mr. Van Wyk, jumping up, saw the full meaning of the rigid head, the hesitating feet, the vaguely extended hand. His heart was beating fast; he moved a chair aside, and instinctively advanced as if to offer his arm. But Captain Whalley passed him by, making for the stairs quite straight.

"He could not see me at all out of his line," Van Wyk thought, with a sort of awe. Then going to the head of the stairs, he asked a little tremulously—

"What is it like—like a mist—like. . . ." Captain Whalley, half-way down, stopped, and turned round undismayed to answer:

"It is as if the light were ebbing out of the world. Have you ever watched the ebbing sea on an open stretch of sands withdrawing farther and farther away from you? It is like this—only there will be no flood to follow. Never. It is as if the sun were growing smaller, the stars going out one by one. There can't be many left that I can see by this. But I haven't had the courage to look of late. . . ." He must have been able to make out Mr. Van Wyk, because he checked him by an authoritative gesture and a stoical—

"I can get about alone yet."

It was as if he had taken his line, and would accept no help from men, after having been cast out, like a presumptuous Titan, from his heaven. Mr. Van Wyk, arrested, seemed to count the footsteps right out of earshot. He walked between the tables, tapping smartly with his heels, took up a paper-knife, dropped it after a vague glance along the blade; then happening upon the piano, struck a few chords, standing up before the keyboard with an attentive poise of the head like a piano-tuner; closing it, he pivoted on his heels brusquely, avoided the little terrier sleeping trustfully on crossed forepaws, came upon the stairs next, and, as though he had lost his balance on the top step, ran down headlong out of the house. His servants, beginning to clear the table, heard him mutter to himself (evil words no doubt) down there, and then after a pause go away with a strolling gait in the direction of the wharf.

The bulwarks of the *Sofala* lying alongside the bank made a low, black wall on the undulating contour of the shore. Two masts and a funnel uprose from behind it with a great rake, as if about to fall: a solid, square elevation in the middle bore the ghostly shapes of white boats, the curves of davits, lines of rail and stanchions, all confused and mingling darkly everywhere; but low down, amidships, a single lighted port stared out on the night, perfectly round, like a small, full moon, whose yellow beam caught a patch of wet mud, the edge of trodden grass, two turns of heavy cable wound round the foot of a thick wooden post in the ground.

Mr. Van Wyk, peering alongside, heard a muzzy boastful voice apparently jeering at a person called Prendergast. It mouthed abuse thickly, choked; then pronounced very distinctly the word "Murphy," and chuckled. Glass tinkled tremulously. All these sounds came from the lighted port. Mr. Van Wyk hesitated, stooped; it was impossible to look through unless he went down into the mud.

"Sterne," he said half aloud.

The drunken voice within said gladly:

"Sterne—of course. Look at him blink. Look at him! Sterne, Whalley, Massy. Massy, Whalley, Sterne. But Massy's the best. You can't come over him. He would just love to see you starve."

Mr. Van Wyk moved away, made out farther forward a shadowy head stuck out from under the awnings as if on the watch, and spoke quietly in Malay, "Is the mate asleep?"

"No. Here, at your service."

In a moment Sterne appeared, walking as noiselessly as a cat on the wharf.

"It's so jolly dark, and I had no idea you would be down to-night."

"What's this horrible raving?" asked Mr. Van Wyk, as if to explain the cause of a shudder that ran over him audibly.

"Jack's broken out on a drunk. That's our second. It's his way. He will be right enough by to-morrow afternoon, only Mr. Massy will keep on worrying up and down the deck. We had better get away."

He muttered suggestively of a talk "up at the house." He had long desired to effect an entrance there, but Mr. Van Wyk nonchalantly demurred: it would not, he feared, be quite prudent, perhaps; and the opaque black shadow under one of the two big trees left at the landing-place swallowed them up, impenetrably dense by the side of the wide river that seemed to spin into threads of glitter the light of a few big stars dropped here and there upon it outspread and flowing stillness.

"The situation is grave beyond doubt," Mr. Van Wyk said. Ghostlike in their white clothes they could not distinguish each other's features, and their feet made no sound on the soft earth. A sort of purring was heard. Mr. Sterne felt gratified by such a beginning.—

"I thought, Mr. Van Wyk, a gentleman of your sort would see at once how awkwardly I was situated."

"Yes, very. Obviously his health is bad. Perhaps he's breaking up. I see, and he himself is well aware—I assume I am speaking to a man of sense—he is well aware that his legs are giving out."

"His legs—ah!" Mr. Sterne was disconcerted, and then turned sulky. "You may call it his legs if you like; what I want to know is whether he intends to clear out quietly. That's a good one, too! His legs! Pooh!"

"Why, yes. Only look at the way he walks," Van Wyk took him up in a perfectly cool and undoubting tone. "The question, however, is whether your sense of duty does not carry you too far from your true interest. After all, I, too, could do something to serve you. You know who I am."

"Everybody along the Straits has heard of you, sir."

Mr. Van Wyk presumed that this meant something favourable. Sterne had a soft laugh at this pleasantry. He should think so! To the

opening statement, that the partnership agreement was to expire at the end of this very trip, he gave an attentive assent. He was aware. One heard of nothing else on board all the blessed day long. As to Massy, it was no secret that he was in a jolly deep hole with these worn-out boilers. He would have to borrow somewhere a couple of hundred first of all to pay off the captain; and then he would have to raise money on mortgage upon the ship for the new boilers—that is, if he could find a lender at all. At best it meant loss of time, a break in the trade, short earnings for the year—and there was always the danger of having his connection filched away from him by the Germans. It was whispered about that he had already tried two firms. Neither would have anything to do with him. Ship too old, and the man too well known in the place. . . . Mr. Sterne's final rapid winking remained buried in the deep darkness sibilating with his whispers.

"Supposing, then, he got the loan," Mr. Van Wyk resumed in a deliberate undertone, "on your own showing he's more than likely to get a mortgagee's man thrust upon him as captain. For my part, I know that I would make that very stipulation myself if I had to find the money. And as a matter of fact I am thinking of doing so. It would be worth my while in many ways. Do you see how this would bear on the case under discussion?"

"Thank you, sir. I am sure you couldn't get anybody that would care more for your interests."

"Well, it suits my interest that Captain Whalley should finish his time. I shall probably take a passage with you down the Straits. If that can be done, I'll be on the spot when all these changes take place, and in a position to look after *your* interests."

"Mr. Van Wyk, I want nothing better. I am sure I am infinitely. . . ."

"I take it, then, that this may be done without any trouble."

"Well, sir, what risk there is can't be helped; but (speaking to you as my employer now) the thing is more safe than it looks. If anybody had told me of it I wouldn't have believed it, but I have been looking on myself. That old Serang has been trained up to the game. There's nothing the matter with his—his—limbs, sir. He's got used to do things on his own in a remarkable way. And let me tell you, sir, that Captain Whalley, poor man, is by no means useless. Fact. Let me explain to you, sir. He stiffens up that old monkey of a Malay, who knows well enough what to do. Why, he must have kept captain's watches in all sorts of country ships off and on for the last five-and-twenty years. These natives, sir, as long as they have a white man close at the back, will go on doing the right thing most surprisingly well—even if left quite to themselves. Only the white man must be of the sort to put

starch into them, and the captain is just the one for that. Why, sir, he has drilled him so well that now he needs hardly speak at all. I have seen that little wrinkled ape made to take the ship out of Pangu Bay on a blowy morning and on all through the islands; take her out first-rate, sir, dodging under the old man's elbow, and in such quiet style that you could not have told for the life of you which of the two was doing the work up there. That's where our poor friend would be still of use to the ship even if—if—he could no longer lift a foot, sir. Providing the Serang does not know that there's anything wrong."

"He doesn't."

"Naturally not. Quite beyond his apprehension. They aren't capable of finding out anything about us, sir."

"You seem to be a shrewd man," said Mr. Van Wyk in a choked mutter, as though he were feeling sick.

"You'll find me a good enough servant, sir."

Mr. Sterne hoped now for a handshake at least, but unexpectedly with a "What's this? Better not to be seen together," Mr. Van Wyk's white shape wavered, and instantly seemed to melt away in the black air under the roof of boughs. The mate was startled. Yes. There was that faint thumping clatter.

He stole out silently from under the shade. The lighted port-hole shone from afar. His head swam with the intoxication of sudden success. What a thing it was to have a gentleman to deal with! He crept aboard, and there was something weird in the shadowy stretch of empty decks, echoing with shouts and blows proceeding from a darker part amidships. Mr. Massy was raging before the door of the berth: the drunken voice within flowed on undisturbed in the violent racket of kicks.

"Shut up! Put your light out and turn in, you confounded swilling pig—you! D'you hear me, you beast?"

The kicking stopped, and in the pause the muzzy oracular voice announced from within—

"Ah! Massy, now—that's another thing. Massy's deep."

"Who's that aft there? You, Sterne? He'll drink himself into a fit of horrors." The chief engineer appeared vague and big at the corner of the engine-room skylight.

"He will be good enough for duty to-morrow. I would let him be, Mr. Massy."

Sterne slipped away into his berth, and at once had to sit down. His head swam with exultation. He got into his bunk as if in a dream. A feeling of profound peace, of pacific joy, came over him. On deck all was quiet.

Mr. Massy, with his ear against the door of Jack's cabin, listened

critically to a deep, stertorous breathing within. This was a dead-drunk sleep. The bout was over: tranquillized on that score, he, too, went in, and with slow wriggles got out of his old tweed jacket. It was a garment with many pockets, which he used to put on at odd times of the day, being subject to sudden chilly fits, and when he felt warmed he would take it off and hang it about anywhere all over the ship. It would be seen swinging on belaying-pins, thrown over the heads of winches, suspended on people's very door-handles for that matter. Was he not the owner? But his favourite place was a hook on a wooden awning stanchion on the bridge, almost against the binnacle. He had even in the early days more than one tussle on that point with Captain Whalley, who desired the bridge to be kept tidy. He had been overawed then. Of late, though, he had been able to defy his partner with impunity. Captain Whalley never seemed to notice anything now. As to the Malays, in their awe of that scowling man not one of the crew would dream of laying a hand on the thing, no matter where or what it swung from.

With an unexpectedness which made Mr. Massy jump and drop the coat at his feet, there came from the next berth the crash and thud of a headlong, jingling, clattering fall. The faithful Jack must have dropped to sleep suddenly as he sat at his revels, and now had gone over chair and all, breaking, as it seemed by the sound, every single glass and bottle in the place. After the terrific smash all was still for a time in there, as though he had killed himself on the spot. Mr. Massy held his breath. At last a sleepy, uneasy groaning sigh was exhaled slowly on the other side of the bulkhead.

"I hope to goodness he's too drunk to wake up now," muttered Mr. Massy.

The sound of a softly knowing laugh nearly drove him to despair. He swore violently under his breath. The fool would keep him awake all night now for certain. He cursed his luck. He wanted to forget his maddening troubles in sleep sometimes. He could detect no movements. Without apparently making the slightest attempt to get up, Jack went on sniggering to himself where he lay; then began to speak, where he had left off as it were—

"Massy! I love the dirty rascal. He would like to see his poor old Jack starve—but just you look where he has climbed to. . . ." He hiccoughed in a superior, leisurely manner. . . . "Shipowning it with the best. A lottery ticket you want. Ha! ha! I will give you lottery tickets, my boy. Let the old ship sink and the old chum starve—that's right. He don't go wrong—Massy don't. Not he. He's a genius—that man is. That's the way to win your money. Ship and chum must go."

"The silly fool has taken it to heart," muttered Massy to himself.

And, listening with a softened expression of face for any slight sign of returning drowsiness, he was discouraged profoundly by a burst of laughter full of joyful irony.

"Would like to see her at the bottom of the sea! Oh, you clever, clever devil! Wish her sunk, eh? I should think you would, my boy; the damned old thing and all your troubles with her. Rake in the insurance money—turn your back on your old chum—all's well—gentleman again."

A grim stillness had come over Massy's face. Only his big black eyes rolled uneasily. The raving fool. And yet it was all true. Yes. Lottery tickets, too. All true. What? Beginning again? He wished he wouldn't. . . .

But it was even so. The imaginative drunkard on the other side of the bulkhead shook off the deathlike stillness that after his last words had fallen on the dark ship moored to a silent shore.

"Don't you dare to say anything against George Massy, Esquire. When he's tired of waiting he will do away with her. Look out! Down she goes—chum and all. He'll know how to. . . ."

The voice hesitated, weary, dreamy, lost, as if dying away in a vast open space.

". . . Find a trick that will work. He's up to it—never fear. . . ."

He must have been very drunk, for at last the heavy sleep gripped him with the suddenness of a magic spell, and the last word lengthened itself into an interminable, noisy, indrawn snore. And then even the snoring stopped, and all was still.

But it seemed as though Mr. Massy had suddenly come to doubt the efficacy of sleep as against a man's troubles; or perhaps he had found the relief he needed in the stillness of a calm contemplation that may contain the vivid thoughts of wealth, of a stroke of luck, of long idleness, and may bring before you the imagined form of every desire; for, turning about and throwing his arms over the edge of his bunk, he stood there with his feet on his favourite old coat, looking out through the round port into the night over the river. Sometimes a breath of wind would enter and touch his face, a cool breath charged with the damp, fresh feel from a vast body of water. A glimmer here and there was all he could see of it; and once he might after all suppose he had dozed off, since there appeared before his vision, unexpectedly and connected with no dream, a row of flaming and gigantic figures—three nought seven one two—making up a number such as you may see on a lottery ticket. And then all at once the port was no longer black: it was pearly gray, framing a shore crowded with houses, thatched roof beyond thatched roof, walls of mats and bamboo, gables of carved teak timber. Rows of dwellings raised on a

forest of piles lined the steely bank of the river, brimful and still, with the tide on the turn. This was Batu Beru—and the day had come.

Mr. Massy shook himself, put on the tweed coat, and, shivering nervously as if from some great shock, made a note of the number. A fortunate, rare hint that. Yes; but to pursue fortune one wanted money —ready cash.

Then he went out and prepared to descend into the engine-room. Several small jobs had to be seen to, and Jack was lying dead drunk on the floor of his cabin, with the door locked at that. His gorge rose at the thought of work. Ay! But if you wanted to do nothing you had to get first a good bit of money. A ship won't save you. True, all true. He was tired of waiting for some chance that would rid him at last of that ship that had turned out a curse on his life.

§ 14

The deep, interminable hoot of the steam-whistle had, in its grave, vibrant note, something intolerable, which sent a slight shudder down Mr. Van Wyk's back. It was the early afternoon; the *Sofala* was leaving Batu Beru for Pangu, the next place of call. She swung in the stream, scantily attended by a few canoes, and, gliding on the broad river, became lost to view from the Van Wyk bungalow.

Its owner had not gone this time to see her off. Generally he came down to the wharf, exchanged a few words with the bridge while she cast off, and waved his hand to Captain Whalley at the last moment. This day he did not even go as far as the balustrade of the verandah. "He couldn't see me if I did," he said to himself. "I wonder whether he can make out the house at all." And this thought somehow made him feel more alone than he had ever felt for all these years. What was it? six or seven? Seven. A long time.

He sat on the verandah with a closed book on his knee, and, as it were, looked out upon his solitude, as if the fact of Captain Whalley's blindness had opened his eyes to his own. There were many sorts of heartaches and troubles, and there was no place where they could not find a man out. And he felt ashamed, as though he had for six years behaved like a peevish boy.

His thought followed the *Sofala* on her way. On the spur of the moment he had acted impulsively, turning to the thing most pressing. And what else could he have done? Later on he should see. It seemed necessary that he should come out into the world, for a time at least. He had money—something could be arranged; he would grudge no time, no trouble, no loss of his solitude. It weighed on him now—and

Captain Whalley appeared to him as he had sat shading his eyes, as if, being deceived in the trust of his faith, he were beyond all the good and evil that can be wrought by the hands of men.

Mr. Van Wyk's thoughts followed the *Sofala* down the river, winding about through the belt of the coast forest, between the buttressed shafts of the big trees, through the mangrove strip, and over the bar. The ship crossed it easily in broad daylight, piloted, as it happened, by Mr. Sterne, who took the watch from four to six, and then went below to hug himself with delight at the prospect of being virtually employed by a rich man—like Mr. Van Wyk. He could not see how any hitch could occur now. He did not seem able to get over the feeling of being "fixed up at last." From six to eight, in the course of duty, the Serang looked alone after the ship. She had a clear road before her now till about three in the morning, when she would close with the Pangu group. At eight Mr. Sterne came out cheerily to take charge again till midnight. At ten he was still chirruping and humming to himself on the bridge, and about that time Mr. Van Wyk's thought abandoned the *Sofala*. Mr. Van Wyk had fallen asleep at last.

Massy, blocking the engine-room companion, jerked himself into his tweed jacket surlily, while the second waited with a scowl.

"Oh. You came out! You sot! Well, what have you got to say for yourself?"

He had been in charge of the engines till then. A sombre fury darkened his mind: a hot anger against the ship, against the facts of life, against the men for their cheating, against himself, too—because of an inward tremor in his heart.

An incomprehensible growl answered him.

"What? Can't you open your mouth now? You yelp out your infernal rot loud enough when you are drunk. What do you mean by abusing people in that way?—you old useless boozer, you!"

"Can't help it. Don't remember anything about it. You shouldn't listen."

"You dare to tell me! What do you mean by going on a drunk like this?"

"Don't ask me. Sick of the dam' boilers—you would be. Sick of Life."

"I wish you were dead, then. You've made me sick of you. Don't you remember the uproar you made last night? You miserable old soaker!"

"No; I don't. Don't want to. Drink is drink."

"I wonder what prevents me from kicking you out. What do you want here?"

"Relieve you. You've been long enough down there, George."

"Don't you George me—you tippling old rascal, you! If I were to die to-morrow you would starve. Remember that. Say Mr. Massy."

"Mr. Massy," repeated the other, stolidly.

Dishevelled, with dull blood-shot eyes, a snuffy, grimy shirt, greasy trousers, naked feet thrust into ragged slippers, he bolted in head down directly Massy had made way for him.

The chief engineer looked around. The deck was empty as far as the taffrail. All the native passengers had left in Batu Beru this time, and no others had joined. The dial of the patent log tinkled periodically in the dark at the end of the ship. It was a dead calm, and, under the clouded sky, through the still air that seemed to cling warm, with a seaweed smell, to her slim hull, on a sea of sombre gray and unwrinkled, the ship moved on an even keel, as if floating detached in empty space. But Mr. Massy slapped his forehead, tottered a little, and caught hold of a belaying-pin at the foot of the mast.

"I shall go mad," he muttered, walking across the deck unsteadily. A shovel was scraping loose coal down below—a fire-door clanged. Sterne on the bridge began whistling a new tune.

Captain Whalley, sitting on the couch, awake and fully dressed, heard the door of his cabin open. He did not move in the least, waiting to recognize the voice, with an appalling strain of prudence.

A bulkhead lamp blazed on the white paint, the crimson plush, the brown varnish of mahogany tops. The white wood packing-case under the bed-place had remained unopened for three years now, as though Captain Whalley had felt that, after the *Fair Maid* was gone, there could be no abiding-place on earth for his affections. His hands rested on his knees; his handsome head with the big eyebrows presented a rigid profile to the doorway. The expected voice spoke out at last.

"Once more, then. What am I to call you?"

Ha! Massy. Again. The weariness of it crushed his heart—and the pain of shame was almost more than he could bear without crying out.

"Well. It is to be 'partner' still?"

"You don't know what you ask."

"I know what I want. . . ."

Massy stepped in and closed the door.

". . . And I am going to have a try for it with you once more."

His whine was half persuasive, half menacing.

"For it's no manner of use to tell me that you are poor. You don't spend anything on yourself, that's true enough; but there's another name for that. You think you are going to have what you want out of me for three years, and then cast me off without hearing what I think of you. You think I would have submitted to your airs if I had

known you had only a beggarly five hundred pounds in the world? You
ought to have told me."

"Perhaps," said Captain Whalley, bowing his head. "And yet it has
saved you. . . ." Massy laughed scornfully. . . . "I have told you
often enough since."

"And I don't believe you now. When I think how I let you lord it
over my ship! Do you remember how you used to bullyrag me about
my coat and *your* bridge? It was in his way. *His* bridge! 'And I won't
be a party to this—and I couldn't think of doing that.' Honest man!
And now it all comes out. 'I am poor, and I can't. I have only this five
hundred in the world.' "

He contemplated the immobility of Captain Whalley, that seemed to
present an inconquerable obstacle in his path. His face took a mourn-
ful cast.

"You are a hard man." .

"Enough," said Captain Whalley, turning upon him. "You shall
get nothing from me, because I have nothing of mine to give away
now."

"Tell that to the marines!"

Mr. Massy, going out, looked back once; then the door closed, and
Captain Whalley, alone, sat as still as before. He had nothing of his
own—even his own past of honour, of truth, of just pride, was gone.
All his spotless life had fallen into the abyss. He had said his last good-
bye to it. But what belonged to *her*, that he meant to save. Only a little
money. He would take it to her in his own hands—this last gift of a
man that had lasted too long. And an immense and fierce impulse, the
very passion of paternity, flamed up with all the unquenched vigour
of his worthless life in a desire to see her face.

Just across the deck Massy had gone straight to his cabin, struck
a light, and hunted up the note of the dreamed number whose figures
had flamed up also with the fierceness of another passion. He must
contrive somehow not to miss a drawing. That number meant some-
thing. But what expedient could he contrive to keep himself going?

"Wretched miser!" he mumbled.

If Mr. Sterne could at no time have told him anything new about
his partner, he could have told Mr. Sterne that another use could
be made of a man's affliction than just to kick him out, and thus defer
the term of a difficult payment for a year. To keep the secret of the
affliction and induce him to stay was a better move. If without means,
he would be anxious to remain; and that settled the question of re-
funding him his share. He did not know exactly how much Captain
Whalley was disabled; but if it so happened that he put the ship

ashore somewhere for good and all, it was not the owner's fault—was it? He was not obliged to know that there was anything wrong. But probably nobody would raise such a point, and the ship was fully insured. He had had enough self-restraint to pay up the premiums. But this was not all. He could not believe Captain Whalley to be so confoundedly destitute as not to have some more money put away somewhere. If he, Massy, could get hold of it, that would pay for the boilers, and everything went on as before. And if she got lost in the end, so much the better. He hated her: he loathed the troubles that took his mind off the chances of fortune. He wished her at the bottom of the sea, and the insurance money in his pocket. And as, baffled, he left Captain Whalley's cabin, he enveloped in the same hatred the ship with the worn-out boilers and the man with the dimmed eyes.

And our conduct after all is so much a matter of outside suggestion, that had it not been for his Jack's drunken gabble he would have there and then had it out with this miserable man, who would neither help, nor stay, nor yet lose the ship. The old fraud! He longed to kick him out. But he restrained himself. Time enough for that—when he liked. There was a fearful new thought put into his head. Wasn't he up to it after all? How that beast Jack had raved! "Find a safe trick to get rid of her." Well, Jack was not so far wrong. A very clever trick had occurred to him. Ay! But what of the risk?

A feeling of pride—the pride of superiority to common prejudices —crept into his breast, made his heart beat fast, his mouth turn dry. Not everybody would dare; but he was Massy, and he was up to it!

Six bells were struck on deck. Eleven! He drank a glass of water, and sat down for ten minutes or so to calm himself. Then he got out of his chest a small bull's-eye lantern of his own and lit it.

Almost opposite his berth, across the narrow passage under the bridge, there was, in the iron deck-structure covering the stokehold fiddle and the boiler-space, a storeroom with iron sides, iron roof, iron-plated floor, too, on account of the heat below. All sorts of rubbish was shot there: it had a mound of scrap-iron in a corner; rows of empty oil-cans; sacks of cotton-waste, with a heap of charcoal, a deck-forge, fragments of an old hen-coop, winch-covers all in rags, remnants of lamps, and a brown felt hat, discarded by a man dead now (of a fever on the Brazil coast), who had been once mate of the *Sofala,* had remained for years jammed forcibly behind a length of burst copper pipe, flung at some time or other out of the engine-room. A complete and impervious blackness pervaded that Capharnaum of forgotten things. A small shaft of light from Mr. Massy's bull's-eye fell slanting right through it.

His coat was unbuttoned; he shot the bolt of the door (there was no

other opening), and, squatting before the scrap-heap, began to pack
his pockets with pieces of iron. He packed them carefully, as if the
rusty nuts, the broken bolts, the links of cargo chain, had been so much
gold he had that one chance to carry away. He packed his side-
pockets till they bulged, the breast-pocket, the pockets inside. He
turned over the pieces. Some he rejected. A small mist of powdered
rust began to rise about his busy hands. Mr. Massy knew something of
the scientific basis of his clever trick. If you want to deflect the mag-
netic needle of a ship's compass, soft iron is the best; likewise many
small pieces in the pockets of a jacket would have more effect than a
few large ones, because in that way you obtain a greater amount of
surface for weight in your iron, and it's surface that tells.

He slipped out swiftly—two strides sufficed—and in his cabin he
perceived that his hands were all red—red with rust. It disconcerted
him, as though he had found them covered with blood: he looked
himself over hastily. Why, his trousers, too! He had been rubbing his
rusty palms on his legs.

He tore off the waistband button in his haste, brushed his coat,
washed his hands. Then the air of guilt left him, and he sat down to
wait.

He sat bolt upright and weighted with iron in his chair. He had a
hard, lumpy bulk against each hip, felt the scrappy iron in his pockets
touch his ribs at every breath, the downward drag of all these pounds
hanging upon his shoulders. He looked very dull, too, sitting idle there,
and his yellow face, with motionless black eyes, had something
passive and sad in its quietness.

When he heard eight bells struck above his head, he rose and made
ready to go out. His movements seemed aimless, his lower lip had
dropped a little, his eyes roamed about the cabin, and the tremendous
tension of his will had robbed them of every vestige of intelligence.

With the last stroke of the bell the Serang appeared noiselessly on
the bridge to relieve the mate. Sterne overflowed with good nature,
since he had nothing more to desire.

"Got your eyes well open yet, Serang? It's middling dark; I'll wait
till you get your sight properly."

The old Malay murmured, looked up with his worn eyes, sidled
away into the light of the binnacle, and, clasping his hands behind his
back, fixed his eyes on the compass-card.

"You'll have to keep a good lookout ahead for land, about half-past
three. It's fairly clear, though. You have looked in on the captain as
you came along—eh? He knows the time? Well, then, I am off."

At the foot of the ladder he stood aside for the captain. He watched
him go up with an even, certain tread, and remained thoughtful for

a moment. "It's funny," he said to himself, "but you can never tell whether that man has seen you or not. He might have heard me breathe this time."

He was a wonderful man when all was said and done. They said he had had a name in his day. Mr. Sterne could well believe it; and he concluded serenely that Captain Whalley must be able to see people more or less—as himself just now, for instance—but not being certain of anybody, had to keep up that unnoticing silence of manner for fear of giving himself away. Mr. Sterne was a shrewd guesser.

This necessity of every moment brought home to Captain Whalley's heart the humiliation of his falsehood. He had drifted into it from paternal love, from incredulity, from boundless trust in divine justice meted out to men's feelings on this earth. He would give his poor Ivy the benefit of another month's work; perhaps the affliction was only temporary. Surely God would not rob his child of his power to help, and cast him naked into a night without end. He had caught at every hope; and when the evidence of his misfortune was stronger than hope, he tried not to believe the manifest thing.

In vain. In the steadily darkening universe a sinister clearness fell upon his ideas. In the illuminating moments of suffering he saw life, men, all things, the whole earth with all her burden of created nature, as he had never seen them before.

Sometimes he was seized with a sudden vertigo and an overwhelming terror; and then the image of his daughter appeared. Her, too, he had never seen so clearly before. Was it possible that he should ever be unable to do anything whatever for her? Nothing. And not see her any more? Never.

Why? The punishment was too great for a little presumption, for a little pride. And at last he came to cling to his deception with a fierce determination to carry it out to the end, to save her money intact, and behold her once more with his own eyes. Afterwards—what? The idea of suicide was revolting to the vigour of his manhood. He had prayed for death till the prayers had stuck in his throat. All the days of his life he had prayed, for daily bread, and not to be led into temptation, in a childlike humility of spirit. Did words mean anything? Whence did the gift of speech come? The violent beating of his heart reverberated in his head—seemed to shake his brain to pieces.

He sat down heavily on the deck-chair to keep the pretence of his watch. The night was dark. All the nights were dark now.

"Serang," he said, half aloud.

"Ada, Tuan. I am here."

"There are clouds on the sky?"

"There are, Tuan."

"Let her be steered straight. North."

"She is going north, Tuan."

The Serang stepped back. Captain Whalley recognized Massy's footfalls on the bridge.

The engineer walked over to port and returned, passing behind the chair several times. Captain Whalley detected an unusual character as of prudent care in his prowling. The near presence of that man brought with it always a recrudescence of moral suffering for Captain Whalley. It was not remorse. After all, he had done nothing but good to the poor devil. There was also a sense of danger—the necessity of greater caution.

Massy stopped and said—

"So you still say you must go?"

"I must indeed."

"And you couldn't at least leave the money for a term of years?"

"Impossible."

"Can't trust it with me without your care, eh?"

Captain Whalley remained silent. Massy sighed deeply over the back of the chair.

"It would just do to save me," he said in a tremulous voice.

"I've saved you once."

The chief engineer took off his coat with careful movements, and proceeded to feel for the brass hook screwed into the wooden stanchion. For this purpose he placed himself right in front of the binnacle, thus hiding completely the compass-card from the quartermaster at the wheel. "Tuan!" the lascar at last murmured softly, meaning to let the white man know that he could not see to steer.

Mr. Massy had accomplished his purpose. The coat was hanging from the nail, within six inches of the binnacle. And directly he had stepped aside the quartermaster, a middle-aged, pock-marked, Sumatra Malay, almost as dark as a negro, perceived with amazement that in that short time, in this smooth water, with no wind at all, the ship had gone swinging far out of her course. He had never known her to get away like this before. With a slight grunt of astonishment he turned the wheel hastily to bring her head back north, which was the course. The grinding of the steering-chains, the chiding murmurs of the Serang, who had come over to the wheel, made a slight stir, which attracted Captain Whalley's anxious attention. He said, "Take better care." Then everything settled to the usual quiet on the bridge. Mr. Massy had disappeared.

But the iron in the pockets of the coat had done its work; and the *Sofala*, heading north by the compass made untrue by this simple device, was no longer making a safe course for Pangu Bay.

The hiss of water parted by her stem, the throb of her engines, all the sounds of her faithful and laborious life, went on uninterrupted in the great calm of the sea joining on all sides the motionless layer of cloud over the sky. A gentle stillness as vast as the world seemed to wait upon her path, enveloping her lovingly in a supreme caress. Mr. Massy thought there could be no better night for an arranged ship-wreck.

Run up high and dry on one of the reefs east of Pangu—wait for daylight—hole in the bottom—out boats—Pangu Bay same evening. That's about it. As soon as she touched he would hasten on the bridge, get hold of the coat (nobody would notice in the dark), and shake it upside down over the side, or even fling it into the sea. A detail. Who could guess? Coat been seen hanging there from that hook hundreds of times. Nevertheless, when he sat down on the lower step of the bridge-ladder his knees knocked together a little. The waiting part was the worst of it. At times he would begin to pant quickly, as though he had been running, and then breathe largely, swelling with the intimate sense of a mastered fate. Now and then he would hear the shuffle of the Serang's bare feet up there: quiet, low voices would exchange a few words, and lapse almost at once into silence. . . .

"Tell me directly you see any land, Serang."

"Yes, Tuan. Not yet."

"No, not yet," Captain Whalley would agree.

The ship had been the best friend of his decline. He had sent all the money he had made by and in the *Sofala* to his daughter. His thought lingered on the name. How often he and his wife had talked over the cot of the child in the big stern-cabin of the *Condor;* she would grow up, she would marry, she would love them, they would live near her and look at her happiness—it would go on without end. Well, his wife was dead, to the child he had given all he had to give; he wished he could come near her, see her, see her face once, live in the sound of her voice, that could make the darkness of the living grave ready for him supportable. He had been starved for love too long. He imagined her tenderness.

The Serang had been peering forward, and now and then glancing at the chair. He fidgeted restlessly, and suddenly burst out close to Captain Whalley—

"Tuan, do you see anything of the land?"

The alarmed voice brought Captain Whalley to his feet at once. He! See! And at the question, the curse of his blindness seemed to fall on him with a hundredfold force.

"What's the time?" he cried.

"Half-past three, Tuan."

"We are close. You *must* see. Look, I say. Look."

Mr. Massy, awakened by the sudden sound of talking from a short doze on the lowest step, wondered why he was there. Ah! A faintness came over him. It is one thing to sow the seed of an accident and another to see the monstrous fruit hanging over your head ready to fall in the sound of agitated voices. "There's no danger," he muttered thickly to himself.

The horror of incertitude had seized upon Captain Whalley, the miserable mistrust of men, of things—of the very earth. He had steered that very course thirty-six times by the same compass—if anything was certain in this world it was its absolute, unerring correctness. Then what had happened? Did the Serang lie? Why lie? Why? Was he going blind, too?

"Is there a mist? Look low on the water. Low down, I say."

"Tuan, there's no mist. See for yourself."

Captain Whalley steadied the trembling of his limbs by an effort. Should he stop the engines at once and give himself away? A gust of irresolution swayed all sorts of bizarre notions in his mind. The unusual had come, and he was not fit to deal with it. In this passage of inexpressible anguish he saw her face—the face of a young girl—with an amazing strength of illusion. No, he must not give himself away after having gone so far for her sake. "You steered the course? You made it? Speak the truth."

"Ya, Tuan. On the course now. Look."

Captain Whalley strode to the binnacle, which to him made such a dim spot of light in an infinity of shapeless shadow. By bending his face right down to the glass he had been able before. . . .

Having to stoop so low, he put out, instinctively, his arm to where he knew there was a stanchion to steady himself against. His hand closed on something that was not wood but cloth. The slight pull adding to the weight, the loop broke, and Mr. Massy's coat falling, struck the deck heavily with a dull thump, accompanied by a lot of clicks.

"What's this?"

Captain Whalley fell on his knees, with groping hands extended in a frank gesture of blindness. They trembled, these hands feeling for the truth. He saw it. Iron near the compass. Wrong course. Wreck her! His ship. Oh, no. Not that.

"Jump and stop her!" he roared out in a voice not his own.

He ran himself—hands forward, a blind man, and while the clanging of the gong echoed still all over the ship, she seemed to butt full tilt into the side of a mountain.

It was low water along the north side of the strait. Mr. Massy had

not reckoned on that. Instead of running aground for half her length, the *Sofala* butted the sheer ridge of a stone reef which would have been awash at high water. This made the shock absolutely terrific. Everybody in the ship that was standing was thrown down headlong: the shaken rigging made a great rattling to the very trucks. All the lights went out; several chain-guys, snapping, clattered against the funnel; there were crashes, pings of parted wire-rope, splintering sounds, loud cracks; the masthead lamp flew over the bows, and all the doors about the deck began to bang heavily. Then, after having hit, she rebounded, hit the second time the very same spot like a battering-ram. This completed the havoc: the funnel, with all the guys gone, fell over with a hollow sound of thunder, smashing the wheel to bits, crushing the frame of the awnings, breaking the lockers, filling the bridge with a mass of broken wood. Captain Whalley picked himself up and stood knee-deep in wreckage, torn, bleeding, knowing the nature of the danger he had escaped mostly by the sound, and holding Mr. Massy's coat in his arms.

By this time Sterne (he had been flung out of his bunk) had set the engines astern. They worked for a few turns, then a voice bawled out, "Get out of the damned engine-room, Jack!"—and they stopped; but the ship had gone clear of the reef and lay still, with a heavy cloud of steam issuing from the broken deck-pipes, and vanishing in wispy shapes into the night. Notwithstanding the suddenness of the disaster there was no shouting, as if the very violence of the shock had half-stunned the shadowy lot of people swaying here and there about her decks. The voice of the Serang pronounced distinctly above the confused murmurs—

"No bottom." He had heaved the lead.

Mr. Sterne cried out next in a strained pitch—

"Where the devil has she got to? Where are we?"

Captain Whalley replied in a calm bass—

"Amongst the reefs to the eastward."

"You know it, sir? Then she will never get out again."

"She will be gone in five minutes. Boats, Sterne. Even one will save you all in this calm."

The Chinaman stokers went in a disorderly rush for the port boats. Nobody tried to check them. The Malays, after a moment of confusion, became quiet, and Mr. Sterne showed a good countenance. Captain Whalley had not moved. His thoughts were darker than this night in which he had lost his first ship.

"He made me lose a ship."

Another tall figure standing before him amongst the litter of the smash on the bridge whispered insanely—

"Say nothing of it."

Massy stumbled closer. Captain Whalley heard the chattering of his teeth.

"I have the coat."

"Throw it down and come along," urged the chattering voice. "B-b-b-b-boat!"

"You will get five years for this."

Mr. Massy had lost his voice. His speech was a mere dry rustling in his throat.

"Have mercy!"

"Had you any when you made me lose my ship? Mr. Massy, you shall get five years for this!"

"I wanted money! Money! My own money! I will give you some money. Take half of it. You love money yourself."

"There's a justice. . . ."

Massy made an awful effort, and in a strange, half-choked utterance—

"You blind devil! It's you that drove me to it."

Captain Whalley, hugging the coat to his breast, made no sound. The light had ebbed for ever from the world—let everything go. But this man should not escape scot-free.

Sterne's voice commanded—

"Lower away!"

The blocks rattled.

"Now then," he cried, "over with you. This way. You, Jack, here. Mr. Massy! Mr. Massy! Captain! Quick, sir! Let's get——"

"I shall go to prison for trying to cheat the insurance, but you'll get exposed; you, honest man, who has been cheating me. You are poor. Aren't you? You've nothing but the five hundred pounds. Well, you have nothing at all now. The ship's lost, and the insurance won't be paid."

Captain Whalley did not move. True! Ivy's money! Gone in this wreck. Again he had a flash of insight. He was indeed at the end of his tether.

Urgent voices cried out together alongside. Massy did not seem able to tear himself away from the bridge. He chattered and hissed despairingly—

"Give it up to me! Give it up!"

"No," said Captain Whalley; "I could not give it up. You had better go. Don't wait, man, if you want to live. She's settling down by the head fast. No; I shall keep it, but I shall stay on board."

Massy did not seem to understand; but the love of life, awakened suddenly, drove him away from the bridge.

Captain Whalley laid the coat down, and stumbled amongst the heaps of wreckage to the side.

"Is Mr. Massy with you?" he called out into the night.

Sterne from the boat shouted—

"Yes; we've got him. Come along, sir. It's madness to stay longer."

Captain Whalley felt along the rail carefully, and without a word, cast off the painter. They were expecting him still down there. They were waiting, till a voice suddenly exclaimed—

"We are adrift! Shove off!"

"Captain Whalley! Leap! . . . pull up a little . . . leap! You can swim."

In that old heart, in that vigorous body, there was, that nothing should be wanting, a horror of death that apparently could not be overcome by the horror of blindness. But after all, for Ivy he had carried his point, walking in his darkness to the very verge of a crime. God had not listened to his prayers. The light had finished ebbing out of the world; not a glimmer. It was a dark waste; but it was unseemly that a Whalley who had gone so far to carry a point should continue to live. He must pay the price.

"Leap as far as you can, sir; we will pick you up."

They did not hear him answer. But their shouting seemed to remind him of something. He groped his way back, and sought for Mr. Massy's coat. He could swim indeed; people sucked down by the whirlpool of a sinking ship do come up sometimes to the surface, and it was unseemly that a Whalley, who had made up his mind to die, should be beguiled by chance into a struggle. He would put all these pieces of iron into his own pockets.

They, looking from the boat, saw the *Sofala,* a black mass upon a black sea, lying still at an appalling cant. No sound came from her. Then, with a great bizarre shuffling noise, as if the boilers had broken through the bulkheads, and with a faint muffled detonation, where the ship had been there appeared for a moment something standing upright and narrow, like a rock out of the sea. Then that, too, disappeared.

When the *Sofala* failed to come back to Batu Beru at the proper time, Mr. Van Wyk understood at once that he would never see her any more. But he did not know what had happened till some weeks afterwards, when, in a native craft lent him by his Sultan, he had made his way to the *Sofala's* port of registry, where already her existence and the official inquiry into her loss were beginning to be forgotten.

It had not been a very remarkable or interesting case, except for the fact that the captain had gone down with his sinking ship. It

was the only life lost; and Mr. Van Wyk would not have been able to learn any details had it not been for Sterne, whom he met one day on the quay near the bridge over the creek, almost on the very spot where Captain Whalley, to preserve his daughter's five hundred pounds intact, had turned to get a sampan which would take him on board the *Sofala*.

From afar Mr. Van Wyk saw Sterne blink straight at him and raise his hand to his hat. They drew into the shade of a building (it was a bank), and the mate related how the boats with the crew got into Pangu Bay about six hours after the accident, and how they had lived for a fortnight in a state of destitution before they found an opportunity to get away from that beastly place. The inquiry had exonerated everybody from all blame. The loss of the ship was put down to an unusual set of the current. Indeed, it could not have been anything else: there was no other way to account for the ship being set seven miles to the eastward of her position during the middle watch.

"A piece of bad luck for me, sir."

Sterne passed his tongue on his lips and glanced aside. "I lost the advantage of being employed by you, sir. I can never be sorry enough. But here it is: one man's poison, another man's meat. This could not have been handier for Mr. Massy if he had arranged that shipwreck himself. The most timely total loss I've ever heard of."

"What became of that Massy?" asked Mr. Van Wyk.

"He, sir? Ha! ha! He would keep on telling me that he meant to buy another ship; but as soon as he had the money in his pocket he cleared out for Manila by mail-boat early in the morning. I gave him chase right aboard, and he told me then he was going to make his fortune dead sure in Manila. I could go to the devil for all he cared. And yet he as good as promised to give me the command if I didn't talk too much."

"You never said anything. . . . " Mr. Van Wyk began.

"Not I, sir. Why should I? I mean to get on but the dead aren't in my way," said Sterne. His eyelids were beating rapidly, then drooped for an instant. "Besides, sir, it would have been an awkward business. You made me hold my tongue just a bit too long."

"Do you know how it was that Captain Whalley remained on board? Did he really refuse to leave? Come now! Or was it perhaps an accidental. . . . ?"

"Nothing!" Sterne interrupted with energy. "I tell you I yelled for him to leap overboard. He simply *must* have cast off the painter of the boat himself. We all yelled to him— hat is, Jack and I. He wouldn't even answer us. The ship was as silent as a grave to the last.

Then the boilers fetched away, and down she went. Accident! Not it! The game was up, sir, I tell you."

This was all that Sterne had to say.

Mr. Van Wyk had been of course made the guest of the club for a fortnight, and it was there that he met the lawyer in whose office had been signed the agreement between Massy and Captain Whalley.

"Extraordinary old man," he said. "He came into my office from nowhere in particular as you may say, with his five hundred pounds to invest, and that engineer fellow following him anxiously. And now he is gone out a little inexplicably, just as he came. I could never understand him quite. There was no mystery at all about that Massy, eh? I wonder whether Whalley refused to leave the ship. It would have been foolish. He was blameless, as the court found."

Mr. Van Wyk had known him well, he said, and he could not believe in suicide. Such an act would not have been in character with what he knew of the man.

"It is my opinion, too," the lawyer agreed. The general theory was that the captain had remained too long on board trying to save something of importance. Perhaps the chart which would clear him, or else something of value in his cabin. The painter of the boat had come adrift of itself, it was supposed. However, strange to say, some little time before that voyage poor Whalley had called in his office and had left with him a sealed envelope addressed to his daughter, to be forwarded to her in case of his death. Still it was nothing very unusual, especially in a man of his age. Mr. Van Wyk shook his head. Captain Whalley looked good for a hundred years.

"Perfectly true," assented the lawyer. "The old fellow looked as though he had come into the world full grown and with that long beard. I could never, somehow, imagine him either younger or older— don't you know. There was a sense of physical power about that man, too. And perhaps that was the secret of that something peculiar in his person which struck everybody who came in contact with him. He looked indestructible by any ordinary means that put an end to the rest of us. His deliberate, stately courtesy of manner was full of significance. It was as though he were certain of having plenty of time for everything. Yes, there was something indestructible about him; and the way he talked sometimes you might have thought he believed it himself. When he called on me last with that letter he wanted me to take charge of, he was not depressed at all. Perhaps a shade more deliberate in his talk and manner. Not depressed in the least. Had he a presentiment, I wonder? Perhaps! Still it seems a miserable end for such a striking figure."

"Oh, yes! It was a miserable end," Mr. Van Wyk said, with so much

fervour that the lawyer looked up at him curiously; and afterwards, after parting with him, he remarked to an acquaintance—

"Queer person that Dutch tobacco-planter from Batu Beru. Know anything of him?"

"Heaps of money," answered the bank manager. "I hear he's going home by the next mail to form a company to take over his estates. Another tobacco district thrown open. He's wise, I think. These good times won't last for ever."

In the southern hemisphere Captain Whalley's daughter had no presentiment of evil when she opened the envelope addressed to her in the lawyer's handwriting. She had received it in the afternoon; all the boarders had gone out, her boys were at school, her husband sat upstairs in his big arm-chair with a book, thin-faced, wrapped up in rugs to the waist. The house was still, and the grayness of a cloudy day lay against the panes of the windows.

In a shabby dining-room, where a faint cold smell of dishes lingered all the year round, sitting at the end of a long table surrounded by many chairs pushed in with their backs close against the edge of the perpetually laid table-cloth, she read the opening sentences: "Most profound regret—painful duty—your father is no more—in accordance with his instructions—fatal casualty—consolation—no blame attached to his memory. . . . "

Her face was thin, her temples a little sunk under the smoother bands of black hair, her lips remained resolutely compressed, while her dark eyes grew larger, till at last, with a low cry, she stood up, and instantly stooped to pick up another envelope which had slipped off her knees on to the floor.

She tore it open, snatched out the enclosure. . . .

"My dearest child," it said, "I am writing this while I am able yet to write legibly. I am trying hard to save for you all the money that is left; I have only kept it to serve you better. It is yours. It shall not be lost; it shall not be touched. There's five hundred pounds. Of what I have earned I have kept nothing back till now. For the future, if I live, I must keep back some—a little—to bring me to you. I must come to you. I must see you once more.

"It is hard to believe that you will ever look on these lines. God seems to have forgotten me. I want to see you—and yet death would be a greater favour. If you ever read these words, I charge you to begin by thanking a God merciful at last, for I shall be dead then, and it will be well. My dear, I am at the end of my tether."

The next paragraph began with the words: "My sight is going. . . . "

She read no more that day. The hand holding up the paper to her eyes fell slowly, and her slender figure in a plain black dress walked rigidly to the window. Her eyes were dry: no cry of sorrow or whisper of thanks went up to heaven from her lips. Life had been too hard, for all the efforts of his love. It had silenced her emotions. But for the first time in all these years its sting had departed, the carking care of poverty, the meanness of a hard struggle for bread. Even the image of her husband and of her children seemed to glide away from her into the gray twilight; it was her father's face alone that she saw, as though he had come to see her, always quiet and big, as she had seen him last, but with something more august and tender in his aspect.

She slipped his folded letter between the two buttons of her plain black bodice, and leaning her forehead against a window-pane remained there till dusk, perfectly motionless, giving him all the time she could spare. Gone! Was it possible? My God, was it possible? The blow had come softened by the spaces of the earth, by the years of absence. There had been whole days when she had not thought of him at all— had no time. But she had loved him, she felt she had loved him after all.

Of Mice And Men

JOHN STEINBECK

BORN *in Salinas, Calif., February 27, 1902, John Steinbeck*
studied at the Salinas High School and then—intermit-
tently—at Stanford University. But the manual half of
his education came to him as he worked on the ranches
along the Salinas River, with the fruit pickers or high up in
the Sierras. Tortilla Flat *and* In Dubious Battle *were*
early novels of his which caught the critics' attention. Of
Mice and Men, *his sixth book, was published in 1937. It*
measures 36,000 words.

INTRODUCTION

I would not know where to find an American novelist more characteristic of the 1930's than John Steinbeck. In his stories about the fruit pickers, the ranch hands and the Okies he exemplifies that openhanded attitude toward labor which was characteristic of so much of the fiction submitted to an editor in the post-Depression years. But Steinbeck's writing has a warmth which sets it apart from the didactic and accusing writing of that period. He is more interested in people than in problems: he must make you believe in the characters he sees in his mind; once that is accomplished he trusts his people to bring home the truth. Finally, he has to a greater degree than any other American of his time that element which has been lost sight of in the intensity of our reform—a sense of humor.

There is nothing of the exhibitionist, nothing of what Robert Frost calls the "tenderer-than-thou" philosopher in John Steinbeck's attitude toward his bindle stiffs and ranch hands. He writes about them because he happens to know them and to like them. In his youth and during his years of intermittent study at Stanford he lived and worked on ranches in the Salinas Valley. He worked with his hands in the heights of the California Sierras, in a sugar refinery and in a fish hatchery; he was at home in a bunkhouse, with the fruit pickers or in a "jungle." In the course of such experience he learned how to roll brown paper cigarettes (which he still smokes) and he learned more than most of us know—at that age—about human nature. He had the heft that commands respect and the quiet understanding which induces other men to talk and, like O. Henry, he did not forsake his habit of fraternization when his stories began to appear. After *Of Mice and Men* had run its course as a best seller, the play went into production. But the author, instead of marking time on Broadway,

was on his way to Oklahoma, there to gather material for *The Grapes of Wrath*. He joined up with the Okies, lived with them in their over-night camps, worked with them in the fields when they had reached California. He bet his publishers a barrel of California muscatel that his play wouldn't run a week in New York and was still unconvinced when the report of the first-night success was telephoned to the ranch house where he was staying. Let me repeat that the experience which Stein-beck picked up the hard way has not turned him into a crusader for the underprivileged; it has simply sharpened his senses and left him with an authentic knowledge of a life which has been too little fre-quented by American novelists. I have yet to see the story that ought to be written about skilled labor in the United States. But, unless I miss my guess, the man to write it will be John Steinbeck.

Of Mice and Men is a story, not of skilled labor, but of men who have no skill, the migratory workers who follow the harvest from county to county, always dreaming of the day when they will "get a little place and live off the fatta the lan' " and always moving from place to place with the same hope and restlessness which took many of our first "settlers" to the frontier. George and Lennie are, if you like, the 1937 model of our American frontiersman—just as shiftless, just as rattletrap and in their own way just as proud as the dissatisfied men who went West a hundred years earlier. In the boom days I lived with some of these bindle stiffs as a harvest hand in Kansas and I know from my limited experience with what fidelity Mr. Steinbeck has set them down. Lewis Gannett has well said that "one reason the world loves Irishmen is that in them, as in John Steinbeck, tough-ness and tenderness walk hand in hand." And with George and Lennie toughness and tenderness do walk hand in hand. Their friendship is the very core of the novel. Lennie, a huge bear of a man, shapeless of face, with large pale eyes and wide, sloping shoulders, Lennie so powerful and blundering that he cannot live without a keeper, and George, who, for all his exasperation (". . . if I was alone I could live so easy") and his courage, is simply not smart enough to avoid trouble. So they blunder on from job to job, cheered up by the dream of the chicken farm which will be theirs someday—a dream which, as George recites it, makes other men like old Candy and Crooks catch fire. " 'Guys like us, that work on ranches, are the loneliest guys in the world. They got no family. They don't belong no place. With us it ain't like that. We got a future. We got somebody to talk to that gives a damn about us. We don't have to sit in no barroom blowin' in our jack jus' because we got no place else to go. Someday—we're gonna get the jack together and we're gonna have a little house and a couple of acres. We'll have a big vegetable patch and a rabbit hutch and

chickens. And when it rains in the win'er we'll just say the hell with goin' to work and we'll build up a fire in the stove and set around it an' listen to the rain comin' down on the roof. Nuts!' He took out his pocketknife. 'I hain't got time for no more.' " I can imagine that there will be some readers who will wince at the dialogue in this book and not accept it because life is like that. For their sake I would point out that the friendship between George and Lennie, that incongruous loyalty of man to man, lifts the story above the plane of raw reality and that the dream which keeps them going and which is repeated by other lonely people like Candy stands out in the end as a yearning common to us all. Actually that dream is an old inheritance in our American blood.

We know today that *Of Mice and Men* was written with an impulse different from that which prompted the other novels in this volume. A friend of the author's, Joseph Henry Jackson, literary editor of the San Francisco *Chronicle,* tells us that Steinbeck wanted to see *how like a play he could write a short novel*. This is the trigger to our understanding of the book's structure. It explains the clear division of the story into six scenes; it explains the dramatic way in which each scene is impressed upon the mind—the details are not many, but every one is made to count; it explains the curious curtain fall which comes at the end of each chapter and the absence of interpretation (by the author) which is expected in a more leisurely narrative. Here the entire emphasis is on dialogue, action and reaction.

The question is, do Steinbeck's people carry home to you the truth that is in them? Are they, as someone has said, down-at-the-heel bums who were better dead? Or are they individuals in whose hopes and disappointments we can recognize our own? For the answer I urge you to keep your eye on Slim. Slim, the foreman, is the umpire in this story. He is the cool, collected observer whose sympathies are so unerring, and his is the authority which the other men respect. When at the end George turns to him for vindication, you have your answer.

OF MICE AND MEN

A FEW MILES south of Soledad, the Salinas River drops in close to the hillside bank and runs deep and green. The water is warm too, for it has slipped twinkling over the yellow sands in the sunlight before reaching the narrow pool. On one side of the river the golden foothill slopes curve up the strong and rocky Gabilan mountains, but on the valley side the water is lined with trees—willows fresh and green with every spring, carrying in their lower leaf junctures the debris of the winter's flooding; and sycamores with mottled, white, recumbent limbs and branches that arch over the pool. On the sandy bank under the trees the leaves lie deep and so crisp that a lizard makes a great skittering if he runs among them. Rabbits come out of the brush to sit on the sand in the evening, and the damp flats are covered with the night tracks of 'coons, and with the spread pads of dogs from the ranches, and with the split-wedge tracks of deer that come to drink in the dark.

There is a path through the willows and among the sycamores, a path beaten hard by boys coming down from the ranches to swim in the deep pool, and beaten hard by tramps who come wearily down from the highway in the evening to jungle-up near water. In front of the low horizontal limb of a giant sycamore there is an ash pile made by many fires; the limb is worn smooth by men who have sat on it.

Evening of a hot day started the little wind to moving among the leaves. The shade climbed up the hills toward the top. On the sand banks the rabbits sat as quietly as little gray, sculptured stones. And then from the direction of the state highway came the sound of footsteps on crisp sycamore leaves. The rabbits hurried noiselessly for cover. A stilted heron labored up into the air and pounded down river. For a moment the place was lifeless, and then two men emerged from the path and came into the opening by the green pool.

They had walked in single file down the path, and even in the open one stayed behind the other. Both were dressed in denim trousers and in denim coats with brass buttons. Both wore black, shapeless hats and both carried tight blanket rolls slung over their shoulders. The first man was small and quick, dark of face, with restless eyes and sharp, strong features. Every part of him was defined: small, strong hands, slender arms, a thin and bony nose. Behind him walked his opposite, a huge man, shapeless of face, with large, pale eyes, with wide, sloping shoulders; and he walked heavily, dragging his feet a little, the way a bear drags his paws. His arms did not swing at his sides, but hung loosely.

The first man stopped short in the clearing, and the follower nearly ran over him. He took off his hat and wiped the sweat-band with his forefinger and snapped the moisture off. His huge companion dropped his blankets and flung himself down and drank from the surface of the green pool; drank with long gulps, snorting into the water like a horse. The small man stepped nervously beside him.

"Lennie!" he said sharply. "Lennie, for God' sakes don't drink so much." Lennie continued to snort into the pool. The small man leaned over and shook him by the shoulder. "Lennie. You gonna be sick like you was last night."

Lennie dipped his whole head under, hat and all, and then he sat up on the bank and his hat dripped down on his blue coat and ran down his back. "Tha's good," he said. "You drink some, George. You take a good big drink." He smiled happily.

George unslung his bindle and dropped it gently on the bank. "I ain't sure it's good water," he said. "Looks kinda scummy."

Lennie dabbled his big paw in the water and wiggled his fingers so the water arose in little splashes; rings widened across the pool to the other side and came back again. Lennie watched them go. "Look, George. Look what I done."

George knelt beside the pool and drank from his hand with quick scoops. "Tastes all right," he admitted. "Don't really seem to be running, though. You never oughta drink water when it ain't running, Lennie," he said hopelessly. "You'd drink out of a gutter if you was thirsty." He threw a scoop of water into his face and rubbed it about with his hand, under his chin and around the back of his neck. Then he replaced his hat, pushed himself back from the river, drew up his knees and embraced them. Lennie, who had been watching, imitated George exactly. He pushed himself back, drew up his knees, embraced them, looked over to George to see whether he had it just right. He pulled his hat down a little more over his eyes, the way George's hat was.

George stared morosely at the water. The rims of his eyes were red with sun glare. He said angrily, "We could just as well of rode clear to the ranch if that bastard bus driver knew what he was talkin' about. 'Jes' a little stretch down the highway,' he says. 'Jes' a little stretch,' God damn near four miles, that's what it was! Didn't wanta stop at the ranch gate, that's what. Too God damn lazy to pull up. Wonder he isn't too damn good to stop in Soledad at all. Kicks us out and says, 'Jes' a little stretch down the road.' I bet it was *more* than four miles. Damn hot day."

Lennie looked timidly over to him. "George?"

"Yeah, what ya want?"

"Where we goin', George?"

The little man jerked down the brim of his hat and scowled over at Lennie. "So you forgot that awready, did you? I gotta tell you again, do I? Jesus Christ, you're a crazy bastard!"

"I forgot," Lennie said softly. "I tried not to forget. Honest to God I did, George."

"O.K.—O.K. I'll tell ya again. I ain't got nothing to do. Might jus' as well spen' all my time tellin' you things and then you forget 'em, and I tell you again."

"Tried and tried," said Lennie, "but it didn't do no good. I remember about the rabbits, George."

"The hell with the rabbits. That's all you ever can remember is them rabbits. O.K.! Now you listen and this time you got to remember so we don't get in no trouble. You remember settin' in that gutter on Howard street and watchin' that blackboard?"

Lennie's face broke into a delighted smile. "Why sure, George. I remember that but what'd we do then? I remember some girls come by and you says you say"

"The hell with what I says. You remember about us goin' into Murray and Ready's, and they give us work cards and bus tickets?"

"Oh, sure, George. I remember that now." His hands went quickly into his side coat pockets. He said gently, "George I ain't got mine. I musta lost it." He looked down at the ground in despair.

"You never had none, you crazy bastard. I got both of 'em here. Think I'd let you carry your own work card?"

Lennie grinned with relief. "I I thought I put it in my side pocket." His hand went into the pocket again.

George looked sharply at him. "What'd you take outa that pocket?"

"Ain't a thing in my pocket," Lennie said cleverly.

"I know there ain't. You got it in your hand. What you got in your hand—hidin' it?"

"I ain't got nothin', George. Honest."

"Come on, give it here."

Lennie held his closed hand away from George's direction. "It's on'y a mouse, George."

"A mouse? A live mouse?"

"Uh-uh. Jus' a dead mouse, George. I didn' kill it. Honest! I found it. I found it dead."

"Give it here!" said George.

"Aw, leave me have it, George."

"Give it here!"

Lennie's closed hand slowly obeyed. George took the mouse and threw it across the pool to the other side, among the brush. "What you want of a dead mouse, anyways?"

"I could pet it with my thumb while we walked along," said Lennie.

"Well, you ain't petting no mice while you walk with me. You remember where we're goin' now?"

Lennie looked startled and then in embarrassment hid his face against his knees. "I forgot again."

"Jesus Christ," George said resignedly. "Well—look, we're gonna work on a ranch like the one we come from up north."

"Up north?"

"In Weed."

"Oh, sure. I remember. In Weed."

"That ranch we're goin' to is right down there about a quarter mile. We're gonna go in an' see the boss. Now, look—I'll give him the work tickets, but you ain't gonna say a word. You jus' stand there and don't say nothing. If he finds out what a crazy bastard you are, we won't get no job, but if he sees ya work before he hears ya talk, we're set. Ya got that?"

"Sure, George. Sure I got it."

"O.K. Now when we go in to see the boss, what you gonna do?"

"I I," Lennie thought. His face grew tight with thought. "I ain't gonna say nothin'. Jus' gonna stan' there."

"Good boy. That's swell. You say that over two, three times so you sure won't forget it."

Lennie droned to himself softly, "I ain't gonna say nothin' I ain't gonna say nothin' I ain't gonna say nothin'."

"O.K.," said George. "An' you ain't gonna do no bad things like you done in Weed, neither."

Lennie looked puzzled. "Like I done in Weed?"

"Oh, so ya forgot that too, did ya? Well, I ain't gonna remind ya, fear ya do it again."

A light of understanding broke on Lennie's face. "They run us outa Weed," he exploded triumphantly.

"Run us out, hell," said George disgustedly. "We run. They was lookin' for us, but they didn't catch us."

Lennie giggled happily. "I didn't forget that, you bet."

George lay back on the sand and crossed his hands under his head, and Lennie imitated him, raising his head to see whether he were doing it right. "God, you're a lot of trouble," said George. "I could get along so easy and so nice if I didn't have you on my tail. I could live so easy and maybe have a girl."

For a moment Lennie lay quiet, and then he said hopefully, "We gonna work on a ranch, George."

"Awright. You got that. But we're gonna sleep here because I got a reason."

The day was going fast now. Only the tops of the Gabilan mountains flamed with the light of the sun that had gone from the valley. A water snake slipped along on the pool, its head held up like a little periscope. The reeds jerked slightly in the current. Far off toward the highway a man shouted something, and another man shouted back. The syca-more limbs rustled under a little wind that died immediately.

"George—why ain't we goin' on to the ranch and get some supper? They got supper at the ranch."

George rolled on his side. "No reason at all for you. I like it here. Tomorra we're gonna go to work. I seen thrashin' machines on the way down. That means we'll be bucking grain bags, bustin' a gut. Tonight I'm gonna lay right here and look up. I like it."

Lennie got up on his knees and looked down at George. "Ain't we gonna have no supper?"

"Sure we are, if you gather up some dead willow sticks. I got three cans of beans in my bindle. You get a fire ready. I'll give you a match when you get the sticks together. Then we'll heat the beans and have supper."

Lennie said, "I like beans with ketchup."

"Well, we ain't got no ketchup. You go get wood. An' don't you fool around. It'll be dark before long."

Lennie lumbered to his feet and disappeared in the brush. George lay where he was and whistled softly to himself. There were sounds of splashings down the river in the direction Lennie had taken. George stopped whistling and listened. "Poor bastard," he said softly, and then went on whistling again.

In a moment Lennie came crashing back through the brush. He carried one small willow stick in his hand. George sat up. "Awright," he said brusquely. "Gi'me that mouse!"

But Lennie made an elaborate pantomime of innocence. "What mouse, George? I ain't got no mouse."

George held out his hand. "Come on. Give it to me. You ain't puttin' nothing over."

Lennie hesitated, backed away, looked wildly at the brush line as though he contemplated running for his freedom. George said coldly, "You gonna give me that mouse or do I have to sock you?"

"Give you what, George?"

"You know God damn well what. I want that mouse."

Lennie reluctantly reached into his pocket. His voice broke a little. "I don't know why I can't keep it. It ain't nobody's mouse. I didn't steal it. I found it lyin' right beside the road."

George's hand remained outstretched imperiously. Slowly, like a terrier who doesn't want to bring a ball to its master, Lennie approached, drew back, approached again. George snapped his fingers sharply, and at the sound Lennie laid the mouse in his hand.

"I wasn't doin' nothing bad with it, George. Jus' strokin' it."

George stood up and threw the mouse as far as he could into the darkening brush, and then he stepped to the pool and washed his hands. "You crazy fool. Don't you think I could see your feet was wet where you went acrost the river to get it?" He heard Lennie's whimpering cry and wheeled about. "Blubberin' like a baby! Jesus Christ! A big guy like you." Lennie's lip quivered and tears started in his eyes. "Aw, Lennie!" George put his hand on Lennie's shoulder. "I ain't takin' it away jus' for meanness. That mouse ain't fresh, Lennie; and besides, you've broke it pettin' it. You get another mouse that's fresh and I'll let you keep it a little while."

Lennie sat down on the ground and hung his head dejectedly. "I don't know where there is no other mouse. I remember a lady used to give 'em to me—ever' one she got. But that lady ain't here."

George scoffed. "Lady, huh? Don't even remember who that lady was. That was your own Aunt Clara. An' she stopped givin' 'em to ya. You always killed 'em."

Lennie looked sadly up at him. "They was so little," he said, apologetically. "I'd pet 'em, and pretty soon they bit my fingers and I pinched their heads a little and then they was dead—because they was so little."

"I wish't we'd get the rabbits pretty soon, George. They ain't so little."

"The hell with the rabbits. An' you ain't to be trusted with no live mice. Your Aunt Clara give you a rubber mouse and you wouldn't have nothing to do with it."

"It wasn't no good to pet," said Lennie.

The flame of the sunset lifted from the mountaintops and dusk came into the valley, and a half darkness came in among the willows and

the sycamores. A big carp rose to the surface of the pool, gulped air and then sank mysteriously into the dark water again, leaving widening rings on the water. Overhead the leaves whisked again and little puffs of willow cotton blew down and landed on the pool's surface.

"You gonna get that wood?" George demanded. "There's plenty right up against the back of that sycamore. Floodwater wood. Now you get it."

Lennie went behind the tree and brought out a litter of dried leaves and twigs. He threw them in a heap on the old ash pile and went back for more and more. It was almost night now. A dove's wings whistled over the water. George walked to the fire pile and lighted the dry leaves. The flame cracked up among the twigs and fell to work. George undid his bindle and brought out three cans of beans. He stood them about the fire, close in against the blaze, but not quite touching the flame.

"There's enough beans for four men," George said.

Lennie watched him from over the fire. He said patiently, "I like 'em with ketchup."

"Well, we ain't got any," George exploded. "Whatever we ain't got, that's what you want. God a'mighty, if I was alone I could live so easy. I could go get a job an' work, an' no trouble. No mess at all, and when the end of the month come I could take my fifty bucks and go into town and get whatever I want. Why, I could stay in a cat house all night. I could eat any place I want, hotel or any place, and order any damn thing I could think of. An' I could do all that every damn month. Get a gallon of whisky, or set in a pool room and play cards or shoot pool." Lennie knelt and looked over the fire at the angry George. And Lennie's face was drawn with terror. "An' whatta I got," George went on furiously. "I got you! You can't keep a job and you lose me ever' job I get. Jus' keep me shovin' all over the country all the time. An' that ain't the worst. You get in trouble. You do bad things and I got to get you out." His voice rose nearly to a shout. "You crazy son-of-a-bitch. You keep me in hot water all the time." He took on the elaborate manner of little girls when they are mimicking one another. "Jus' wanted to feel that girl's dress—jus' wanted to pet it like it was a mouse—— Well, how the hell did she know you jus' wanted to feel her dress? She jerks back and you hold on like it was a mouse. She yells and we got to hide in a irrigation ditch all day with guys lookin' for us, and we got to sneak out in the dark and get outta the country. All the time somethin' like that—all the time. I wisht I could put you in a cage with about a million mice an' let you have fun." His anger left him suddenly. He looked across

the fire at Lennie's anguished face, and then he looked ashamedly at the flames.

It was quite dark now, but the fire lighted the trunks of the trees and the curving branches overhead. Lennie crawled slowly and cautiously around the fire until he was close to George. He sat back on his heels. George turned the bean cans so that another side faced the fire. He pretended to be unaware of Lennie so close beside him.

"George," very softly. No answer. "George!"

"Whatta you want?"

"I was only foolin', George. I don't want no ketchup. I wouldn't eat no ketchup if it was right here beside me."

"If it was here, you could have some."

"But I wouldn't eat none, George. I'd leave it all for you. You could cover your beans with it and I wouldn't touch none of it."

George still stared morosely at the fire. "When I think of the swell time I could have without you, I go nuts. I never get no peace."

Lennie still knelt. He looked off into the darkness across the river. "George, you want I should go away and leave you alone?"

"Where the hell could you go?"

"Well, I could. I could go off in the hills there. Some place I'd find a cave."

"Yeah? How'd you eat. You ain't got sense enough to find nothing to eat."

"I'd find things, George. I don't need no nice food with ketchup. I'd lay out in the sun and nobody'd hurt me. An' if I foun' a mouse, I could keep it. Nobody'd take it away from me."

George looked quickly and searchingly at him. "I been mean, ain't I?"

"If you don' want me I can go off in the hills an' find a cave. I can go away any time."

"No—look! I was jus' foolin', Lennie. 'Cause I want you to stay with me. Trouble with mice is you always kill 'em." He paused. "Tell you what I'll do, Lennie. First chance I get I'll give you a pup. Maybe you wouldn't kill *it*. That'd be better than mice. And you could pet it harder."

Lennie avoided the bait. He had sensed his advantage. "If you don't want me, you only jus' got to say so, and I'll go off in those hills right there—right up in those hills and live by myself. An' I won't get no mice stole from me."

George said, "I want you to stay with me, Lennie. Jesus Christ, somebody'd shoot you for a coyote if you was by yourself. No, you stay with me. Your Aunt Clara wouldn't like you running off by yourself, even if she is dead."

Lennie spoke craftily, "Tell me—like you done before."

"Tell you what?"

"About the rabbits."

George snapped, "You ain't gonna put nothing over on me."

Lennie pleaded, "Come on, George. Tell me. Please, George. Like you done before."

"You get a kick outta that, don't you? Awright, I'll tell you, and then we'll eat our supper. . . ."

George's voice became deeper. He repeated his words rhythmically as though he had said them many times before. "Guys like us, that work on ranches, are the loneliest guys in the world. They got no family. They don't belong no place. They come to a ranch an' work up a stake and then they go inta town and blow their stake, and the first thing you know they're poundin' their tail on some other ranch. They ain't got nothing to look ahead to."

Lennie was delighted. "That's it—that's it. Now tell how it is with us."

George went on. "With us it ain't like that. We got a future. We got somebody to talk to that gives a damn about us. We don't have to sit in no bar room blowin' in our jack jus' because we got no place else to go. If them other guys gets in jail they can rot for all anybody gives a damn. But not us."

Lennie broke in. *"But not us! An' why? Because because I got you to look after me, and you got me to look after you, and that's why."* He laughed delightedly. "Go on now, George!"

"You got it by heart. You can do it yourself."

"No, you. I forget some a' the things. Tell about how it's gonna be."

"O.K. Someday—we're gonna get the jack together and we're gonna have a little house and a couple of acres an' a cow and some pigs and——"

"An' live off the fatta the lan'," Lennie shouted. "An' have *rabbits*. Go on, George! Tell about what we're gonna have in the garden and about the rabbits in the cages and about the rain in the winter and the stove, and how thick the cream is on the milk like you can hardly cut it. Tell about that, George."

"Why'n't you do it yourself? You know all of it."

"No you tell it. It ain't the same if I tell it. Go on George. How I get to tend the rabbits."

"Well," said George, "we'll have a big vegetable patch and a rabbit hutch and chickens. And when it rains in the winter, we'll just say the hell with goin' to work, and we'll build up a fire in the stove and set around it an' listen to the rain comin' down on the roof—Nuts!" He took out his pocket knife. "I ain't got time for no more." He drove

his knife through the top of one of the bean cans, sawed out the top and passed the can to Lennie. Then he opened a second can. From his side pocket he brought out two spoons and passed one of them to Lennie.

They sat by the fire and filled their mouths with beans and chewed mightily. A few beans slipped out of the side of Lennie's mouth. George gestured with his spoon. "What you gonna say tomorrow when the boss asks you questions?"

Lennie stopped chewing and swallowed. His face was concentrated. "I I ain't gonna say a word."

"Good boy! That's fine, Lennie! Maybe you're gettin' better. When we get the coupla acres I can let you tend the rabbits all right. 'Specially if you remember as good as that."

Lennie choked with pride. "I can remember," he said.

George motioned with his spoon again. "Look, Lennie. I want you to look around here. You can remember this place, can't you? The ranch is about a quarter mile up that way. Just follow the river?"

"Sure," said Lennie. "I can remember this. Di'n't I remember about not gonna say a word?"

" 'Course you did. Well, look. Lennie—if you jus' happen to get in trouble like you always done before, I want you to come right here an' hide in the brush."

"Hide in the brush," said Lennie slowly.

"Hide in the brush till I come for you. Can you remember that?"

"Sure I can, George. Hide in the brush till you come."

"But you ain't gonna get in no trouble, because if you do, I won't let you tend the rabbits." He threw his empty bean can off into the brush.

"I won't get in no trouble, George. I ain't gonna say a word."

"O.K. Bring your bindle over here by the fire. It's gonna be nice sleepin' here. Lookin' up, and the leaves. Don't build up no more fire. We'll let her die down."

They made their beds on the sand, and as the blaze dropped from the fire the sphere of light grew smaller; the curling branches disappeared and only a faint glimmer showed where the tree trunks were. From the darkness Lennie called, "George—you asleep?"

"No. Whatta you want?"

"Let's have different color rabbits, George."

"Sure we will," George said sleepily. "Red and blue and green rabbits, Lennie. Millions of 'em."

"Furry ones, George, like I seen in the fair in Sacramento."

"Sure, furry ones."

" 'Cause I can jus' as well go away, George, an' live in a cave."

"You can jus' as well go to hell," said George. "Shut up now."

The red light dimmed on the coals. Up the hill from the river a coyote yammered, and a dog answered from the other side of the stream. The sycamore leaves whispered in a little night breeze.

§ 2

The bunk house was a long, rectangular building. Inside, the walls were whitewashed and the floor unpainted. In three walls there were small, square windows, and in the fourth, a solid door with a wooden latch. Against the walls were eight bunks, five of them made up with blankets and the other three showing their burlap ticking. Over each bunk there was nailed an apple box with the opening forward so that it made two shelves for the personal belongings of the occupant of the bunk. And these shelves were loaded with little articles, soap and talcum powder, razors and those Western magazines ranch men love to read and scoff at and secretly believe. And there were medicines on the shelves, and little vials, combs; and from nails on the box sides, a few neckties. Near one wall there was a black cast-iron stove, its stovepipe going straight up through the ceiling. In the middle of the room stood a big square table littered with playing cards, and around it were grouped boxes for the players to sit on.

At about ten o'clock in the morning the sun threw a bright dust-laden bar through one of the side windows, and in and out of the beam flies shot like rushing stars.

The wooden latch raised. The door opened and a tall, stoop-shouldered old man came in. He was dressed in blue jeans and he carried a big push-broom in his left hand. Behind him came George, and behind George, Lennie.

"The boss was expectin' you last night," the old man said. "He was sore as hell when you wasn't here to go out this morning." He pointed with his right arm, and out of the sleeve came a round stick-like wrist, but no hand. "You can have them too beds there," he said, indicating two bunks near the stove.

George stepped over and threw his blankets down on the burlap sack of straw that was a mattress. He looked into his box shelf and then picked a small yellow can from it. "Say. What the hell's this?"

"I don't know," said the old man.

"Says 'positively kills lice, roaches and other scourges.' What the hell kind of bed you giving us, anyways. We don't want no pants rabbits."

The old swamper shifted his broom and held it between his elbow

and his side while he held out his hand for the can. He studied the label carefully. "Tell you what—" he said finally, "last guy that had this bed was a blacksmith—hell of a nice fella and as clean a guy as you want to meet. Used to wash his hands even *after* he ate."

"Then how come he got graybacks?" George was working up a slow anger. Lennie put his bindle on the neighboring bunk and sat down. He watched George with open mouth.

"Tell you what," said the old swamper. "This here blacksmith— name of Whitey—was the kind of guy that would put that stuff around even if there wasn't no bugs—just to make sure, see? Tell you what he used to do— At meals he'd peel his boil' potatoes, an' he'd take out ever' little spot, no matter what kind, before he'd eat it. And if there was a red splotch on an egg, he'd scrape it off. Finally quit about the food. That's the kinda guy he was—clean. Used ta dress up Sundays even when he wasn't going no place, put on a necktie even, and then set in the bunkhouse."

"I ain't so sure," said George skeptically. "What did you say he quit for?"

The old man put the yellow can in his pocket, and he rubbed his bristly white whiskers with his knuckles. "Why he just quit, the way a guy will. Says it was the food. Just wanted to move. Didn't give no other reason but the food. Just says 'gimme my time' one night, the way any guy would."

George lifted his tick and looked underneath it. He leaned over and inspected the sacking closely. Immediately Lennie got up and did the same with his bed. Finally George seemed satisfied. He unrolled his bindle and put things on the shelf, his razor and bar of soap, his comb and bottle of pills, his liniment and leather wrist-band. Then he made his bed up neatly with blankets. The old man said, "I guess the boss'll be out here in a minute. He was sure burned when you wasn't here this morning. Come right in when we was eatin' breakfast and says, 'Where the hell's them new men?' An' he give the stable buck hell, too."

George patted a wrinkle out of his bed, and sat down. "Give the stable buck hell?" he asked.

"Sure. Ya see the stable buck's a nigger."

"Nigger, huh?"

"Yeah. Nice fella too. Got a crooked back where a horse kicked him. The boss gives him hell when he's mad. But the stable buck don't give a damn about that. He reads a lot. Got books in his room."

"What kind of a guy is the boss?" George asked.

"Well, he's a pretty nice fella. Gets pretty mad sometimes, but he's pretty nice. Tell ya what—know what he done Christmas? Brang a

gallon of whisky right in here and says, 'Drink hearty boys. Christmas comes but once a year.'"

"The hell he did! Whole gallon?"

"Yes sir. Jesus, we had fun. They let the nigger come in that night. Little skinner name of Smitty took after the nigger. Done pretty good, too. The guys wouldn't let him use his feet, so the nigger got him. If he coulda used his feet, Smitty says he woulda killed the nigger. The guys said on account of the nigger's got a crooked back, Smitty can't use his feet." He paused in relish of the memory. "After that the guys went into Soledad and raised hell. I didn't go in there. I ain't got the poop no more."

Lennie was just finishing making his bed. The wooden latch raised again and the door opened. A little stocky man stood in the open doorway. He wore blue jean trousers, a flannel shirt, a black, unbuttoned vest and a black coat. His thumbs were stuck in his belt, on each side of a square steel buckle. On his head was a soiled brown Stetson hat, and he wore high-heeled boots and spurs to prove he was not a laboring man.

The old swamper looked quickly at him, and then shuffled to the door rubbing his whiskers with his knuckles as he went. "Them guys just come," he said, and shuffled past the boss and out the door.

The boss stepped into the room with the short, quick steps of a fat-legged man. "I wrote Murray and Ready I wanted two men this morning. You got your work slips?" George reached into his pocket and produced the slips and handed them to the boss. "It wasn't Murray and Ready's fault. Says right here on the slip that you was to be here for work this morning."

George looked down at his feet. "Bus driver give us a bum steer," he said. "We hadda walk ten miles. Says we was here when we wasn't. We couldn't get no rides in the morning."

The boss squinted his eyes. "Well, I had to send out the grain teams short two buckers. Won't do any good to go out now till after dinner." He pulled his time book out of his pocket and opened it where a pencil was stuck between the leaves. George scowled meaningfully at Lennie, and Lennie nodded to show that he understood. The boss licked his pencil. "What's your name?"

"George Milton."

"And what's yours?"

George said, "His name's Lennie Small."

The names were entered in the book. "Le's see, this is the twentieth, noon the twentieth." He closed the book. "Where you boys been working?"

"Up around Weed," said George.

"You, too?" to Lennie.

"Yeah, him too," said George.

The boss pointed a playful finger at Lennie. "He ain't much of a talker, is he?"

"No, he ain't, but he's sure a hell of a good worker. Strong as a bull."

Lennie smiled to himself. "Strong as a bull," he repeated.

George scowled at him, and Lennie dropped his head in shame at having forgotten.

The boss said suddenly, "Listen, Small!" Lennie raised his head. "What can you do?"

In a panic, Lennie looked at George for help.

"He can do anything you tell him," said George. "He's a good skinner. He can rassel grain bags, drive a cultivator. He can do anything. Just give him a try."

The boss turned on George. "Then why don't you let him answer? What you trying to put over?"

George broke in loudly, "Oh! I ain't saying he's bright. He ain't. But I say he's a God damn good worker. He can put up a four hundred pound bale."

The boss deliberately put the little book in his pocket. He hooked his thumbs in his belt and squinted one eye nearly closed. "Say—what you sellin'?"

"Huh?"

"I said what stake you got in this guy? You takin' his pay away from him?"

"No, 'course I ain't. Why ya think I'm sellin' him out?"

"Well, I never seen one guy take so much trouble for another guy. I just like to know what your interest is."

George said, "He's my cousin. I told his old lady I'd take care of him. He got kicked in the head by a horse when he was a kid. He's awright. Just ain't bright. But he can do anything you tell him."

The boss turned half away. "Well, God knows he don't need any brains to buck barley bags. But don't you try to put nothing over, Milton. I got my eye on you. Why'd you quit in Weed?"

"Job was done," said George promptly.

"What kinda job?"

"We we was diggin' a cesspool."

"All right. But don't try to put nothing over, 'cause you can't get away with nothing. I seen wise guys before. Go on out with the grain teams after dinner. They're pickin' up barley at the threshing machine. Go out with Slim's team."

"Slim?"

"Yeah. Big tall skinner. You'll see him at dinner." He turned

abruptly and went to the door, but before he went out he turned and looked for a long moment at the two men.

When the sound of his footsteps had died away, George turned on Lennie. "So you wasn't gonna say a word. You was gonna leave your big flapper shut and leave me do the talkin'. Damn near lost us the job."

Lennie stared hopelessly at his hands. "I forgot, George."

"Yeah, you forgot. You always forget, an' I got to talk you out of it." He sat down heavily on the bunk. "Now he's got his eye on us. Now we got to be careful and not make no slips. You keep your big flapper shut after this." He fell morosely silent.

"George."

"What you want now?"

"I wasn't kicked in the head with no horse, was I, George?"

"Be a damn good thing if you was," George said viciously. "Save ever'body a hell of a lot of trouble."

"You said I was your cousin, George."

"Well, that was a lie. An' I'm damn glad it was. If I was a relative of yours I'd shoot myself." He stopped suddenly, stepped to the open front door and peered out. "Say, what the hell you doin' listenin'?"

The old man came slowly into the room. He had his broom in his hand. And at his heels there walked a dragfooted sheepdog, gray of muzzle, and with pale, blind old eyes. The dog struggled lamely to the side of the room and lay down, grunting softly to himself and licking his grizzled, moth-eaten coat. The swamper watched him until he was settled. "I wasn't listenin'. I was jus' standin' in the shade a minute scratchin' my dog. I jus' now finished swampin' out the wash house."

"You was pokin' your big ears into our business," George said. "I don't like nobody to get nosey."

The old man looked uneasily from George to Lennie, and then back, "I jus' come there," he said. "I didn't hear nothing you guys was sayin'. I ain't interested in nothing you was sayin'. A guy on a ranch don't never listen nor he don't ast no questions."

"Damn right he don't," said George, slightly mollified, "not if he wants to stay workin' long." But he was reassured by the swamper's defense. "Come on in and set down a minute," he said. "That's a hell of an old dog."

"Yeah. I had 'im ever since he was a pup. God, he was a good sheep dog when he was younger." He stood his broom against the wall and he rubbed his white bristled cheek with his knuckles. "How'd you like the boss?" he asked.

"Pretty good. Seemed awright."

"He's a nice fella," the swamper agreed. "You got to take him right."

At that moment a young man came into the bunk house; a thin young man with a brown face, with brown eyes and a head of tightly curled hair. He wore a work glove on his left hand, and, like the boss, he wore high-heeled boots. "Seen my old man?" he asked.

The swamper said, "He was here jus' a minute ago, Curley. Went over to the cook house, I think."

"I'll try to catch him," said Curley. His eyes passed over the new men and he stopped. He glanced coldly at George and then at Lennie. His arms gradually bent at the elbows and his hands closed into fists. He stiffened and went into a slight crouch. His glance was at once calculating and pugnacious. Lennie squirmed under the look and shifted his feet nervously. Curley stepped gingerly close to him. "You the new guys the old man was waitin' for?"

"We just come in," said George.

"Let the big guy talk."

Lennie twisted with embarrassment.

George said, "S'pose he don't want to talk?"

Curley lashed his body around. "By Christ, he's gotta talk when he's spoke to. What the hell are you gettin' into it for?"

"We travel together," said George coldly.

"Oh, so it's that way."

George was tense, and motionless. "Yeah, it's that way."

Lennie was looking helplessly to George for instruction.

"An' you won't let the big guy talk, is that it?"

"He can talk if he wants to tell you anything." He nodded slightly to Lennie.

"We jus' come in," said Lennie softly.

Curley stared levelly at him. "Well, nex' time you answer when you're spoke to." He turned toward the door and walked out, and his elbows were still bent out a little.

George watched him out, and then he turned back to the swamper. "Say, what the hell's he got on his shoulder? Lennie didn't do nothing to him."

The old man looked cautiously at the door to make sure no one was listening. "That's the boss's son," he said quietly. "Curley's pretty handy. He done quite a bit in the ring. He's a lightweight, and he's handy."

"Well, let him be handy," said George. "He don't have to take after Lennie. Lennie didn't do nothing to him. What's he got against Lennie?"

The swamper considered. "Well tell you what.

Curley's like a lot of little guys. He hates big guys. He's alla time picking scraps with big guys. Kind of like he's mad at 'em because he ain't a big guy. You seen little guys like that, ain't you? Always scrappy?"

"Sure," said George. "I seen plenty tough little guys. But this Curley better not make no mistakes about Lennie. Lennie ain't handy, but this Curley punk is gonna get hurt if he messes around with Lennie."

"Well, Curley's pretty handy," the swamper said skeptically. "Never did seem right to me. S'pose Curley jumps a big guy an' licks him. Ever'body says what a game guy Curley is. And s'pose he does the same thing and gets licked. Then ever'body says the big guy oughtta pick somebody his own size, and maybe they gang up on the big guy. Never did seem right to me. Seems like Curley ain't givin' nobody a chance."

George was watching the door. He said ominously, "Well, he better watch out for Lennie. Lennie ain't no fighter, but Lennie's strong and quick and Lennie don't know no rules." He walked to the square table and sat down on one of the boxes. He gathered some of the cards together and shuffled them.

The old man sat down on another box. "Don't tell Curley I said none of this. He'd slough me. He just don't give a damn. Won't ever get canned 'cause his old man's the boss."

George cut the cards and began turning them over, looking at each one and throwing it down on a pile. He said, "This guy Curley sounds like a son-of-a-bitch to me. I don't like mean little guys."

"Seems to me like he's worse lately," said the swamper. "He got married a couple of weeks ago. Wife lives over in the boss's house. Seems like Curley is cockier'n ever since he got married."

George grunted, "Maybe he's showin' off for his wife."

The swamper warmed to his gossip. "You seen that glove on his left hand?"

"Yeah. I seen it."

"Well, that glove's fulla vaseline."

"Vaseline? What the hell for?"

"Well, I tell ya what—Curley says he's keepin' that hand soft for his wife."

George studied the cards absorbedly. "That's a dirty thing to tell around," he said.

The old man was reassured. He had drawn a derogatory statement from George. He felt safe now, and he spoke more confidently. "Wait'll you see Curley's wife."

George cut the cards again and put out a solitaire lay, slowly and deliberately. "Purty?" he asked casually.

"Yeah. Purty but——"

George studied his cards. "But what?"

"Well—she got the eye."

"Yeah? Married two weeks and got the eye? Maybe that's why Curley's pants is full of ants."

"I seen her give Slim the eye. Slim's a jerkline skinner. Hell of a nice fella. Slim don't need to wear no high-heeled boots on a grain team. I seen her give Slim the eye. Curley never seen it. An' I seen her give Carlson the eye."

George pretended a lack of interest. "Looks like we was gonna have fun."

The swamper stood up from his box. "Know what I think?" George did not answer. "Well, I think Curley's married a tart."

"He ain't the first," said George. "There's plenty done that."

The old man moved toward the door, and his ancient dog lifted his head and peered about, and then got painfully to his feet to follow. "I gotta be settin' out the wash basins for the guys. The teams'll be in before long. You guys gonna buck barley?"

"Yeah."

"You won't tell Curley nothing I said?"

"Hell no."

"Well, you look her over, mister. You see if she ain't a tart." He stepped out the door into the brilliant sunshine.

George laid down his cards thoughtfully, turned his piles of three. He built four clubs on his ace pile. The sun square was on the floor now, and the flies whipped through it like sparks. A sound of jingling harness and the croak of heavy-laden axles sounded from outside. From the distance came a clear call. "Stable Buck—ooh, sta-able Buck!" And then, "Where the hell is that God damn nigger?"

George stared at his solitaire lay, and then he flounced the cards together and turned around to Lennie. Lennie was lying down on the bunk watching him.

"Look, Lennie! This here ain't no set up. I'm scared. You gonna have trouble with that Curley guy. I seen that kind before. He was kinda feelin' you out. He figures he's got you scared and he's gonna take a sock at you the first chance he gets."

Lennie's eyes were frightened. "I don't want no trouble," he said plaintively. "Don't let him sock me, George."

George got up and went over to Lennie's bunk and sat down on it. "I hate that kinda bastard," he said. "I seen plenty of 'em. Like the old guy says, Curley don't take no chances. He always wins." He thought for a moment. "If he tangles with you, Lennie, we're gonna get the can. Don't make no mistake about that. He's the boss's son.

Look, Lennie. You try to keep away from him, will you? Don't never speak to him. If he comes in here you move clear to the other side of the room. Will you do that, Lennie?"

"I don't want no trouble," Lennie mourned. "I never done nothing to him."

"Well, that won't do you no good if Curley wants to plug himself up for a fighter. Just don't have nothing to do with him. Will you remember?"

"Sure, George. I ain't gonna say a word."

The sound of the approaching grain teams was louder, thud of big hooves on hard ground, drag of brakes and the jingle of trace chains. Men were calling back and forth from the teams. George, sitting on the bunk beside Lennie, frowned as he thought. Lennie asked timidly, "You ain't mad, George?"

"I ain't mad at you. I'm mad at this here Curley bastard. I hope we was gonna get a little stake together—maybe a hundred dollars." His tone grew decisive. "You keep away from Curley, Lennie."

"Sure I will, George. I won't say a word."

"Don't let him pull you in—but—if the son-of-a-bitch socks you— let 'im have it."

"Let 'im have what, George?"

"Never mind, never mind. I'll tell you when. I hate that kind of a guy. Look, Lennie, if you get in any kind of trouble, you remember what I told you to do?"

Lennie raised up on his elbow. His face contorted with thought. Then he eyes moved sadly to George's face. "If I get in any trouble, you ain't gonna let me tend the rabbits."

"That's not what I meant. You remember where we slep' last night? Down by the river?"

"Yeah. I remember. Oh, sure I remember! I go there an' hide in the brush."

"Hide till I come for you. Don't let nobody see you. Hide in the brush by the river. Say that over."

"Hide in the brush by the river, down in the brush by the river."

"If you get in trouble."

"If I get in trouble."

A brake screeched outside. A call came, "Stable—Buck. Oh! Sta-able Buck."

George said, "Say it over to yourself, Lennie, so you won't forget it."

Both men glanced up, for the rectangle of sunshine in the doorway was cut off. A girl was standing there looking in. She had full, rouged lips and wide-spaced eyes, heavily made up. Her fingernails were red. Her hair hung in little rolled clusters, like sausages. She wore a cotton

house dress and red mules, on the insteps of which were little bouquets of red ostrich feathers. "I'm lookin' for Curley," she said. Her voice had a nasal, brittle quality.

George looked away from her and then back. "He was in here a minute ago, but he went."

"Oh!" She put her hands behind her back and leaned against the door frame so that her body was thrown forward. "You're the new fellas that just come, ain't ya?"

"Yeah."

Lennie's eyes moved down over her body, and though she did not seem to be looking at Lennie she bridled a little. She looked at her fingernails. "Sometimes Curley's in here," she explained.

George said brusquely, "Well he ain't now."

"If he ain't, I guess I better look some place else," she said playfully.

Lennie watched her, fascinated. George said, "If I see him, I'll pass the word you was looking for him."

She smiled archly and twitched her body. "Nobody can't blame a person for lookin'," she said. There were footsteps behind her, going by. She turned her head. "Hi, Slim," she said.

Slim's voice came through the door. "Hi, Good-lookin'."

"I'm tryin' to find Curley, Slim."

"Well, you ain't tryin' very hard. I seen him goin' in your house."

She was suddenly apprehensive. "'Bye, boys," she called into the bunk house, and she hurried away.

George looked around at Lennie. "Jesus, what a tramp," he said. "So that's what Curley picks for a wife."

"She's purty," said Lennie defensively.

"Yeah, and she's sure hidin' it. Curley got his work ahead of him. Bet she'd clear out for twenty bucks."

Lennie still stared at the doorway where she had been. "Gosh, she was purty." He smiled admiringly. George looked quickly down at him and then he took him by an ear and shook him.

"Listen to me, you crazy bastard," he said fiercely. "Don't you even take a look at that bitch. I don't care what she says and what she does. I seen 'em poison before, but I never seen no piece of jail bait worse than her. You leave her be."

Lennie tried to disengage his ear. "I never done nothing, George."

"No, you never. But when she was standin' in the doorway showin' her legs, you wasn't looking the other way, neither."

"I never meant no harm, George. Honest I never."

"Well, you keep away from her, 'cause she's a rat-trap if I ever seen one. You let Curley take the rap. He let himself in for it. Glove fulla

vaseline," George said disgustedly. "An' I bet he's eatin' raw eggs and writin' to the patent medicine houses."

Lennie cried out suddenly—"I don' like this place, George. This ain't no good place. I wanna get outta here."

"We gotta keep it till we get a stake. We can't help it, Lennie. We'll get out jus' as soon as we can. I don't like it no better than you do." He went back to the table and set out a new solitaire hand. "No, I don't like it," he said. "For two bits I'd shove out of here. If we can get jus' a few dollars in the poke we'll shove off and go up the American River and pan gold. We can make maybe a couple of dollars a day there, and we might hit a pocket."

Lennie leaned eagerly toward him. "Le's go, George. Le's get outta here. It's mean here."

"We gotta stay," George said shortly. "Shut up now. The guys'll be comin' in."

From the washroom nearby came the sound of running water and rattling basins. George studied the cards. "Maybe we oughtta wash up," he said. "But we ain't done nothing to get dirty."

A tall man stood in the doorway. He held a crushed Stetson hat under his arm while he combed his long, black, damp hair straight back. Like the others he wore blue jeans and a short denim jacket. When he had finished combing his hair he moved into the room, and he moved with a majesty only achieved by royalty and master craftsmen. He was a jerkline skinner, the prince of the ranch, capable of driving ten, sixteen, even twenty mules with a single line to the leaders. He was capable of killing a fly on the wheeler's butt with a bull whip without touching the mule. There was a gravity in his manner and a quiet so profound that all talk stopped when he spoke. His authority was so great that his word was taken on any subject, be it politics or love. This was Slim, the jerkline skinner. His hatchet face was ageless. He might have been thirty-five or fifty. His ear heard more than was said to him, and his slow speech had overtones not of thought, but of understanding beyond thought. His hands, large and lean, were as delicate in their action as those of a temple dancer.

He smoothed out his crushed hat, creased it in the middle and put it on. He looked kindly at the two in the bunk house. "It's brighter'n a bitch outside," he said gently. "Can't hardly see nothing in here. You the new guys?"

"Just come," said George.

"Gonna buck barley?"

"That's what the boss says."

Slim sat down on a box across the table from George. He studied the

solitaire hand that was upside down to him. "Hope you get on my team," he said. His voice was very gentle. "I gotta pair of punks on my team that don't know a barley bag from a blue ball. You guys ever buckled any barley?"

"Hell, yes," said George. "I ain't nothing to scream about, but that big bastard there can put up more grain alone than most pairs can."

Lennie, who had been following the conversation back and forth with his eyes, smiled complacently at the compliment. Slim looked approvingly at George for having given the compliment. He leaned over the table and snapped the corner of a loose card. "You guys travel around together?" His tone was friendly. It invited confidence without demanding it.

"Sure," said George. "We kind a look after each other." He indicated Lennie with his thumb. "He ain't bright. Hell of a good worker, though. Hell of a nice fella, but he ain't bright. I've knew him for a long time."

Slim looked through George and beyond him. "Ain't many guys travel around together," he mused. "I don't know why. Maybe ever'body in the whole damn world is scared of each other."

"It's a lot nicer to go around with a guy you know," said George.

A powerful, big-stomached man came into the bunk house. His head still dripped water from the scrubbing and dousing. "Hi, Slim," he said, and then stopped and stared at George and Lennie.

"These guys jus' come," said Slim by way of introduction.

"Glad ta meet ya," the big man said. "My name's Carlson."

"I'm George Milton. This here's Lennie Small."

"Glad ta meet ya," Carlson said again. "He ain't very small." He chuckled softly at his joke. "Ain't small at all," he repeated. "Meant to ask you, Slim—how's your bitch? I seen she wasn't under your wagon this morning."

"She slang her pups last night," said Slim. "Nine of 'em. I drowned four of 'em right off. She couldn't feed that many."

"Got five left, huh?"

"Yeah, five. I kept the biggest."

"What kinda dogs you think they're gonna be?"

"I dunno," said Slim. "Some kinda shepherds, I guess. That's the most kind I seen around here when she was in heat."

Carlson went on, "Got five pups, huh. Gonna keep all of 'em?"

"I dunno. Have to keep 'em a while so they can drink Lulu's milk."

Carlson said thoughtfully, "Well, looka here, Slim. I been thinkin'. That dog of Candy's is so God damn old he can't hardly walk. Stinks like hell, too. Ever' time he comes into the bunk house I can smell him for two, three days. Why'n't you get Candy to shoot his old dog and

give him one of the pups to raise up? I can smell that dog a mile away. Got no teeth, damn near blind, can't eat. Candy feeds him milk. He can't chew nothing else."

George had been staring intently at Slim. Suddenly a triangle began to ring outside, slowly at first, and then faster and faster until the beat of it disappeared into one ringing sound. It stopped as suddenly as it had started.

"There she goes," said Carlson.

Outside, there was a burst of voices as a group of men went by.

Slim stood up slowly and with dignity. "You guys better come on while they's still something to eat. Won't be nothing left in a couple of minutes."

Carlson stepped back to let Slim precede him, and then the two of them went out the door.

Lennie was watching George excitedly. George rumpled his cards into a messy pile. "Yeah!" George said, "I heard him, Lennie. I'll ask him."

"A brown and white one," Lennie cried excitedly.

"Come on. Le's get dinner. I don't know whether he got a brown and white one."

Lennie didn't move from his bunk. "You ask him right away, George, so he won't kill no more of 'em."

"Sure. Come on now, get up on your feet."

Lennie rolled off his bunk and stood up, and the two of them started for the door. Just as they reached it, Curley bounced in.

"You seen a girl around here?" he demanded angrily.

George said coldly, " 'Bout half an hour ago maybe."

"Well what the hell was she doin'?"

George stood still, watching the angry little man. He said insultingly, "She said—she was lookin' for you."

Curley seemed really to see George for the first time. His eyes flashed over George, took in his height, measured his reach, looked at his trim middle. "Well, which way'd she go?" he demanded at last.

"I dunno," said George. "I didn' watch her go."

Curley scowled at him, and turning, hurried out the door.

George said, "Ya know, Lennie, I'm scared I'm gonna tangle with that bastard myself. I hate his guts. Jesus Christ! Come on. They won't be a damn thing left to eat."

They went out the door. The sunshine lay in a thin line under the window. From a distance there could be heard a rattle of dishes.

After a moment the ancient dog walked lamely in through the open door. He gazed about with mild, half-blind eyes. He sniffed, and then lay down and put his head between his paws. Curley popped into the

doorway again and stood looking into the room. The dog raised his head, but when Curley jerked out, the grizzled head sank to the floor again.

§ 3

Although there was evening brightness showing through the windows of the bunk house, inside it was dusk. Through the open door came the thuds and occasional clangs of a horseshoe game, and now and then the sound of voices raised in approval or derision.

Slim and George came into the darkening bunkhouse together. Slim reached up over the card table and turned on the tin-shaded electric light. Instantly the table was brilliant with light, and the cone of the shade threw its brightness straight downward, leaving the corners of the bunk house still in dusk. Slim sat down on a box and George took his place opposite.

"It wasn't nothing," said Slim. "I would of had to drowned most of 'em anyways. No need to thank me about that."

George said, "It wasn't much to you, maybe, but it was a hell of a lot to him. Jesus Christ, I don't know how we're gonna get him to sleep in here. He'll want to sleep right out in the barn with 'em. We'll have trouble keepin' him from getting right in the box with them pups."

"It wasn't nothing," Slim repeated. "Say, you sure was right about him. Maybe he ain't bright, but I never seen such a worker. He damn near killed his partner buckin' barley. There ain't nobody can keep up with him. God awmighty I never seen such a strong guy."

George spoke proudly. "Jus' tell Lennie what to do an' he'll do it if it don't take no figuring. He can't think of nothing to do himself, but he sure can take orders."

There was a clang of horseshoe on iron stake outside and a little cheer of voices.

Slim moved back slightly so the light was not on his face. "Funny how you an' him string along together." It was Slim's calm invitation to confidence.

"What's funny about it?" George demanded defensively.

"Oh, I dunno. Hardly none of the guys ever travel together. I hardly never seen two guys travel together. You know how the hands are, they just come in and get their bunk and work a month, and then they quit and go out alone. Never seem to give a damn about nobody. It jus' seems kinda funny a cuckoo like him and a smart little guy like you travelin' together."

"He ain't no cuckoo," said George. "He's dumb as hell, but he ain't

crazy. An' I ain't so bright neither, or I wouldn't be buckin' barley for my fifty and found. If I was bright, if I was even a little bit smart, I'd have my own little place, an' I'd be bringin' in my own crops, 'stead of doin' all the work and not getting what comes up outa the ground." George fell silent. He wanted to talk. Slim neither encouraged nor discouraged him. He just sat back quiet and receptive.

"It ain't so funny, him an' me goin' aroun' together," George said at last. "Him and me was both born in Auburn. I knowed his Aunt Clara. She took him when he was a baby and raised him up. When his Aunt Clara died, Lennie just come along with me out workin'. Got kinda used to each other after a little while."

"Umm," said Slim.

George looked over at Slim and saw the calm, God-like eyes fastened on him. "Funny," said George. "I used to have a hell of a lot of fun with 'im. Used to play jokes on 'im 'cause he was too dumb to take care of 'imself. But he was too dumb even to know he had a joke played on him. I had fun. Made me seem God damn smart alongside of him. Why he'd do any damn thing I tol' him. If I tol' him to walk over a cliff, over he'd go. That wasn't so damn much fun after a while. He never got mad about it, neither. I've beat the hell outa him, and he coulda bust every bone in my body jus' with his han's, but he never lifted a finger against me." George's voice was taking on the tone of confession. "Tell you what made me stop that. One day a bunch of guys was standin' around up on the Sacramento River. I was feelin' pretty smart. I turns to Lennie and says, 'Jump in.' An' he jumps. Couldn't swim a stroke. He damn near drowned before we could get him. An' he was so damn nice to me for pullin' him out. Clean forgot I told him to jump in. Well, I ain't done nothing like that no more."

"He's a nice fella," said Slim. "Guy don't need no sense to be a nice fella. Seems to me sometimes it jus' works the other way around. Take a real smart guy and he ain't hardly ever a nice fella."

George stacked the scattered cards and began to lay out his solitaire hand. The shoes thudded on the ground outside. At the windows the light of the evening still made the window squares bright.

"I ain't got no people," George said. "I seen the guys that go around on the ranches alone. That ain't no good. They don't have no fun. After a long time they get mean. They get wantin' to fight all the time."

"Yeah, they get mean," Slim agreed. "They get so they don't want to talk to nobody."

" 'Cause Lennie's a God damn nuisance most of the time," said George. "But you get used to goin' around with a guy an' you can't get rid of him."

"He ain't mean," said Slim. "I can see Lennie ain't a bit mean."

" 'Course he ain't mean. But he gets in trouble alla time because he's so God damn dumb. Like what happened in Weed——" He stopped, stopped in the middle of turning over a card. He looked alarmed and peered over at Slim. "You wouldn't tell nobody?"

"What'd he do in Weed?" Slim asked calmly.

"You wouldn't tell? No, 'course you wouldn'."

"What'd he do in Weed?" Slim asked again.

"Well, he seen this girl in a red dress. Dumb bastard like he is, he wants to touch ever'thing he likes. Just wants to feel it. So he reaches out to feel this red dress an' the girl lets out a squawk, and that gets Lennie all mixed up, and he holds on 'cause that's the only thing he can think to do. Well, this girl squawks and squawks. I was jus' a little bit off, and I heard all the yellin', so I comes running, an' by that time Lennie's so scared all he can think to do is jus' hold on. I socked him over the head with a fence picket to make him let go. He was so scairt he couldn't let go of that dress. And he's so God damn strong, you know."

Slim's eyes were level and unwinking. He nodded very slowly. "So what happens?"

George carefully built his line of solitaire cards. "Well, that girl rabbits in an' tells the law she been raped. The guys in Weed start a party out to lynch Lennie. So we sit in a irrigation ditch under water all the rest of that day. Got on'y our heads sticking outa water, an' up under the grass that sticks out from the side of the ditch. An' that night we scrammed outa there."

Slim sat in silence for a moment. "Didn't hurt the girl none, huh?" he asked finally.

"Hell, no. He just scared her. I'd be scared too if he grabbed me. But he never hurt her. He jus' wanted to touch that red dress, like he wants to pet them pups all the time."

"He ain't mean," said Slim. "I can tell a mean guy a mile off."

" 'Course he ain't, and he'll do any damn thing I——"

Lennie came in through the door. He wore his blue denim coat over his shoulders like a cape, and he walked hunched way over.

"Hi, Lennie," said George. "How you like the pup now?"

Lennie said breathlessly, "He's brown an' white jus' like I wanted." He went directly to his bunk and lay down and turned his face to the wall and drew up his knees.

George put down his cards very deliberately. "Lennie," he said sharply.

Lennie twisted his neck and looked over his shoulder. "Huh? What you want, George?"

"I tol' you you couldn't bring that pup in here."

"What pup, George? I ain't got no pup."

George went quickly to him, grabbed him by the shoulder and rolled him over. He reached down and picked the tiny puppy from where Lennie had been concealing it against his stomach.

Lennie sat up quickly. "Give 'um to me, George."

George said, "You get right up an' take this pup back to the nest. He's gotta sleep with his mother. You want to kill him? Just born last night an' you take him out of the nest. You take him back or I'll tell Slim not to let you have him."

Lennie held out his hands pleadingly. "Give 'um to me, George. I'll take 'um back. I didn't mean no harm, George. Honest I didn't. I jus' wanted to pet 'um a little."

George handed the pup to him. "Awright. You get him back there quick, and don't you take him out no more. You'll kill him, the first thing you know." Lennie fairly scuttled out of the room.

Slim had not moved. His calm eyes followed Lennie out the door. "Jesus," he said. "He's jes' like a kid, ain't he."

"Sure he's jes' like a kid. There ain't no more harm in him than a kid neither, except he's so strong. I bet he won't come in here to sleep tonight. He'd sleep right alongside that box in the barn. Well—let 'im. He ain't doin' no harm out there."

It was almost dark outside now. Old Candy, the swamper, came in and went to his bunk, and behind him struggled his old dog. "Hello, Slim. Hello, George. Didn't neither of you play horseshoes?"

"I don't like to play ever' night," said Slim.

Candy went on, "Either you guys got a slug of whisky? I gotta gut ache."

"I ain't," said Slim. "I'd drink it myself if I had, an' I ain't got a gut ache neither."

"Gotta bad gut ache," said Candy. "Them God damn turnips give it to me. I knowed they was going to before I ever eat 'em."

The thick-bodied Carlson came in out of the darkening yard. He walked to the other end of the bunk house and turned on the second shaded light. "Darker'n hell in here," he said. "Jesus, how that nigger can pitch shoes."

"He's plenty good," said Slim.

"Damn right he is," said Carlson. "He don't give nobody else a chance to win——" He stopped and sniffed the air, and still sniffing, looked down at the old dog. "God awmighty, that dog stinks. Get him outa here, Candy! I don't know nothing that stinks as bad as an old dog. You gotta get him out."

Candy rolled to the edge of his bunk. He reached over and patted the ancient dog, and he apologized, "I been around him so much I never notice how he stinks."

"Well, I can't stand him in here," said Carlson. "That stink hangs around even after he's gone." He walked over with his heavy-legged stride and looked down at the dog. "Got no teeth," he said. "He's all stiff with rheumatism. He ain't no good to you, Candy. An' he ain't no good to himself. Why'n't you shoot him, Candy?"

The old man squirmed uncomfortably. "Well—hell! I had him so long. Had him since he was a pup. I herded sheep with him." He said proudly, "You wouldn't think it to look at him now, but he was the best damn sheep dog I ever seen."

George said, "I seen a guy in Weed that had an Airedale could herd sheep. Learned it from the other dogs."

Carlson was not to be put off. "Look, Candy. This ol' dog jus' suffers hisself all the time. If you was to take him out and shoot him right in the back of the head—" he leaned over and pointed, "—right there, why he'd never know what hit him."

Candy looked about unhappily. "No," he said softly. "No, I couldn't do that. I had 'im too long."

"He don't have no fun," Carlson insisted. "And he stinks to beat hell. Tell you what. I'll shoot him for you. Then it won't be you that does it."

Candy threw his legs off his bunk. He scratched the white stubble whiskers on his cheek nervously. "I'm so used to him," he said softly. "I had him from a pup."

"Well, you ain't bein' kind to him keepin' him alive," said Carlson. "Look, Slim's bitch got a litter right now. I bet Slim would give you one of them pups to raise up, wouldn't you, Slim?"

The skinner had been studying the old dog with his calm eyes. "Yeah," he said. "You can have a pup if you want to." He seemed to shake himself free for speech. "Carl's right, Candy. That dog ain't no good to himself. I wisht somebody'd shoot me if I get old an' a cripple."

Candy looked helplessly at him, for Slim's opinions were law. "Maybe it'd hurt him," he suggested. "I don't mind takin' care of him."

Carlson said, "The way I'd shoot him, he wouldn't feel nothing. I'd put the gun right there." He pointed with his toe. "Right back of the head. He wouldn't even quiver."

Candy looked for help from face to face. It was quite dark outside by now. A young laboring man came in. His sloping shoulders were bent forward and he walked heavily on his heels, as though he carried the invisible grain bag. He went to his bunk and put his hat on his

shelf. Then he picked a pulp magazine from his shelf and brought it to the light over the table. "Did I show you this, Slim?" he asked.

"Show me what?"

The young man turned to the back of the magazine, put it down on the table and pointed with his finger. "Right there, read that." Slim bent over it. "Go on," said the young man. "Read it out loud."

" 'Dear Editor' ": Slim read slowly. " 'I read your mag for six years and I think it is the best on the market. I like stories by Peter Rand. I think he is a whing-ding. Give us more like the Dark Rider. I don't write many letters. Just thought I would tell you I think your mag is the best dime's worth I ever spent.' "

Slim looked up questioningly. "What you want me to read that for?"

Whit said, "Go on. Read the name at the bottom."

Slim read, " 'Yours for success, William Tenner.' " He glanced up at Whit again. "What you want me to read that for?"

Whit closed the magazine impressively. "Don't you remember Bill Tenner? Worked here about three months ago?"

Slim thought. . . . "Little guy?" he asked. "Drove a cultivator?"

"That's him," Whit cried. "That's the guy!"

"You think he's the guy wrote this letter?"

"I know it. Bill and me was in here one day. Bill had one of them books that just come. He was lookin' in it and he says, 'I wrote a letter. Wonder if they put it in the book!' But it wasn't there. Bill says, 'Maybe they're savin' it for later.' An' that's just what they done. There it is."

"Guess you're right," said Slim. "Got it right in the book."

George held out his hand for the magazine. "Let's look at it?"

Whit found the place again, but he did not surrender his hold on it. He pointed out the letter with his forefinger. And then he went to his box shelf and laid the magazine carefully in. "I wonder if Bill seen it," he said. "Bill and me worked in that patch of field peas. Run cultivators, both of us. Bill was a hell of a nice fella."

During the conversation Carlson had refused to be drawn in. He continued to look down at the old dog. Candy watched him uneasily. At last Carlson said, "If you want me to, I'll put the old devil out of his misery right now and get it over with. Ain't nothing left for him. Can't eat, can't see, can't even walk without hurtin'."

Candy said hopefully, "You ain't got no gun."

"The hell I ain't. Got a Luger. It won't hurt him none at all."

Candy said, "Maybe tomorra. Le's wait till tomorra."

"I don't see no reason for it," said Carlson. He went to his bunk, pulled his bag from underneath it and took out a Luger pistol. "Le's get it over with," he said. "We can't sleep with him stinkin' around in here." He put the pistol in his hip pocket.

Candy looked a long time at Slim to try to find some reversal. And Slim gave him none. At last Candy said softly and hopelessly, "Awright —take 'im." He did not look down at the dog at all. He lay back on his bunk and crossed his arms behind his head and stared at the ceiling.

From his pocket Carlson took a little leather thong. He stooped over and tied it around the old dog's neck. All the men except Candy watched him. "Come, boy. Come on, boy," he said gently. And he said apologetically to Candy, "He won't even feel it." Candy did not move nor answer him. He twitched the thong. "Come on, boy." The old dog got slowly and stiffly to his feet and followed the gently pulling leash.

Slim said, "Carlson."

"Yeah?"

"You know what to do."

"What ya mean, Slim?"

"Take a shovel," said Slim shortly.

"Oh, sure! I get you." He led the dog out into the darkness.

George followed to the door and shut the door and set the latch gently in its place. Candy lay rigidly on his bed staring at the ceiling.

Slim said loudly, "One of my lead mules got a bad hoof. Got to get some tar on it." His voice trailed off. It was silent outside. Carlson's footsteps died away. The silence came into the room. And the silence lasted.

George chuckled, "I bet Lennie's right out there in the barn with his pup. He won't want to come in here no more now he's got a pup."

Slim said, "Candy, you can have any one of them pups you want."

Candy did not answer. The silence fell on the room again. It came out of the night and invaded the room. George said, "Anybody like to play a little euchre?"

"I'll play out a few with you," said Whit.

They took places opposite each other at the table under the light, but George did not shuffle the cards. He rippled the edge of the deck nervously, and the little snapping noise drew the eyes of all the men in the room, so that he stopped doing it. The silence fell on the room again. A minute passed, and another minute. Candy lay still, staring at the ceiling. Slim gazed at him for a moment and then looked down at his hands; he subdued one hand with the other, and held it down. There came a little gnawing sound from under the floor and all the men looked down toward it gratefully. Only Candy continued to stare at the ceiling.

"Sounds like there was a rat under there," said George. "We ought to get a trap down there."

Whit broke out, "What the hell's takin' him so long? Lay out some

cards, why don't you? We ain't going to get no euchre played this way."

George brought the cards together tightly and studied the backs of them. The silence was in the room again.

A shot sounded in the distance. The men looked quickly at the old man. Every head turned toward him.

For a moment he continued to stare at the ceiling. Then he rolled slowly over and faced the wall and lay silent.

George shuffled the cards noisily and dealt them. Whit drew a scoring board to him and set the pegs to start. Whit said, "I guess you guys really come here to work."

"How do ya mean?" George asked.

Whit laughed. "Well, ya come on a Friday. You got two days to work till Sunday."

"I don't see how you figure," said George.

Whit laughed again. "You do if you been around these big ranches much. Guy that wants to look over a ranch comes in Sat'day afternoon. He gets Sat'day night supper an' three meals on Sunday, and he can quit Monday mornin' after breakfast without turning his hand. But you come to work Friday noon. You got to put in a day an' a half no matter how you figure."

George looked at him levelly. "We're gonna stick aroun' a while," he said. "Me an' Lennie's gonna roll up a stake."

The door opened quietly and the stable buck put in his head; a lean negro head, lined with pain, the eyes patient. "Mr. Slim."

Slim took his eyes from old Candy. "Huh? Oh! Hello, Crooks. What's'a matter?"

"You told me to warm up tar for that mule's foot. I got it warm."

"Oh! Sure, Crooks. I'll come right out an' put it on."

"I can do it if you want, Mr. Slim."

"No. I'll come do it myself." He stood up.

Crooks said, "Mr. Slim."

"Yeah."

"That big new guy's messin' around your pups out in the barn."

"Well, he ain't doin' no harm. I give him one of them pups."

"Just thought I'd tell ya," said Crooks. "He's takin' 'em outa the nest and handlin' them. That won't do them no good."

"He won't hurt 'em," said Slim. "I'll come along with you now."

George looked up. "If that crazy bastard's foolin' around too much, jus' kick him out, Slim."

Slim followed the stable buck out of the room.

George dealt and Whit picked up his cards and examined them. "Seen the new kid yet?" he asked.

"What kid?" George asked.

"Why, Curley's new wife."

"Yeah, I seen her."

"Well, ain't she a looloo?"

"I ain't seen that much of her," said George.

Whit laid down his cards impressively. "Well, stick around an' keep your eyes open. You'll see plenty. She ain't concealin' nothing. I never seen nobody like her. She got the eye goin' all the time on everybody. I bet she even gives the stable buck the eye. I don't know what the hell she wants."

George asked casually, "Been any trouble since she got here?"

It was obvious that Whit was not interested in his cards. He laid his hand down and George scooped it in. George laid out his deliberate solitaire hand—seven cards, and six on top, and five on top of those.

Whit said, "I see what you mean. No, they ain't been nothing yet. Curley's got yella-jackets in his drawers, but that's all so far. Ever' time the guys is around she shows up. She's lookin' for Curley, or she thought she lef' somethin' layin' around and she's lookin' for it. Seems like she can't keep away from guys. An' Curley's pants is just crawlin' with ants, but they ain't nothing come of it yet."

George said, "She's gonna make a mess. They's gonna be a bad mess about her. She's a jail bait all set on the trigger. That Curley got his work cut out for him. Ranch with a bunch of guys on it ain't no place for a girl, specially like her."

Whit said, "If you got idears, you ought ta come in town with us guys tomorra night."

"Why? What's doin'?"

"Jus' the usual thing. We go in to old Susy's place. Hell of a nice place. Old Susy's a laugh—always crackin' jokes. Like she says when we come up on the front porch las' Sat'day night. Susy opens the door and then she yells over her shoulder, 'Get yor coats on, girls, here comes the sheriff.' She never talks dirty, neither. Got five girls there."

"What's it set you back?" George asked.

"Two an' a half. You can get a shot for two bits. Susy got nice chairs to set in, too. If a guy don't want a flop, why he can just set in the chairs and have a couple or three shots and pass the time of day and Susy don't give a damn. She ain't rushin' guys through and kickin' 'em out if they don't want a flop."

"Might go in and look the joint over," said George.

"Sure. Come along. It's a hell of a lot of fun—her crackin' jokes all the time. Like she says one time, she says, 'I've knew people that if they got a rag rug on the floor an' a kewpie doll lamp on the phonograph they think they're running a parlor house.' That's Clara's house

she's talkin' about. An' Susy says, 'I know what you boys want,' she says. 'My girls is clean,' she says, 'an' there ain't no water in my whisky,' she says, 'If any you guys wanta look at a kewpie doll lamp an' take your own chance gettin' burned, why you know where to go.' An' she says, 'There's guys around here walkin' bow-legged 'cause they like to look at a kewpie doll lamp.' "

George asked, "Clara runs the other house, huh?"

"Yeah," said Whit. "We don't never go there. Clara gets three bucks a crack and thirty-five cents a shot, and she don't crack no jokes. But Susy's place is clean and she got nice chairs. Don't let no goo-goos in, neither."

"Me an' Lennie's rollin' up a stake," said George. "I might go in an' set and have a shot, but I ain't puttin' out no two and a half."

"Well, a guy got to have some fun sometime," said Whit.

The door opened and Lennie and Carlson came in together. Lennie crept to his bunk and sat down, trying not to attract attention. Carlson reached under his bunk and brought out his bag. He didn't look at old Candy, who still faced the wall. Carlson found a little cleaning rod in the bag and a can of oil. He laid them on his bed and then brought out the pistol, took out the magazine and snapped the loaded shell from the chamber. Then he fell to cleaning the barrel with the little rod. When the ejector snapped, Candy turned over and looked for a moment at the gun before he turned back to the wall again.

Carlson said casually, "Curley been in yet?"

"No," said Whit. "What's eatin' on Curley?"

Carlson squinted down the barrel of his gun. "Lookin' for his old lady. I seen him going round and round outside."

Whit said sarcastically, "He spends half his time lookin' for her, and the rest of the time she's lookin' for him."

Curley burst into the room excitedly. "Any you guys seen my wife?" he demanded.

"She ain't been here," said Whit.

Curley looked threateningly about the room. "Where the hell's Slim?"

"Went out in the barn," said George. "He was gonna put some tar on a split hoof."

Curley's shoulders dropped and squared. "How long ago'd he go?"

"Five—ten minutes."

Curley jumped out the door and banged it after him.

Whit stood up. "I guess maybe I'd like to see this," he said. "Curley's just spoilin' or he wouldn't start for Slim. An' Curley's handy, God damn handy. Got in the finals for the Golden Gloves. He got

newspaper clippings about it." He considered. "But jus' the same, he better leave Slim alone. Nobody don't know what Slim can do."

"Thinks Slim's with his wife, don't he?" said George.

"Looks like it," Whit said. " 'Course Slim ain't. Least I don't think Slim is. But I like to see the fuss if it comes off. Come on, let's go."

George said, "I'm stayin' right here. I don't want to get mixed up in nothing. Lennie and me got to make a stake."

Carlson finished the cleaning of the gun and put it in the bag and pushed the bag under his bunk. "I guess I'll go out and look her over," he said. Old Candy lay still, and Lennie, from his bunk, watched George cautiously.

When Whit and Carlson were gone and the door closed after them, George turned to Lennie. "What you got on your mind?"

"I ain't done nothing, George. Slim says I better not pet them pups so much for a while. Slim says it ain't good for them; so I come right in. I been good, George."

"I coulda told you that," said George.

"Well, I wasn't hurtin' 'em none. I jus' had mine in my lap pettin' it."

George asked, "Did you see Slim out in the barn?"

"Sure I did. He tol' me I better not pet that pup no more."

"Did you see that girl?"

"You mean Curley's girl?"

"Yeah. Did she come in the barn?"

"No. Anyways I never seen her."

"You never seen Slim talkin' to her?"

"Uh-uh. She ain't been in the barn."

"O.K.," said George. "I guess them guys ain't gonna see no fight. If there's any fightin', Lennie, you keep out of it."

"I don't want no fights," said Lennie. He got up from his bunk and sat down at the table, across from George. Almost automatically George shuffled the cards and laid out his solitaire hand. He used a deliberate, thoughtful, slowness.

Lennie reached for a face card and studied it, then turned it upside down and studied it. "Both ends the same," he said. "George, why is it both end's the same?"

"I don't know," said George. "That's jus' the way they make 'em. What was Slim doin' in the barn when you seen him?"

"Slim?"

"Sure. You seen him in the barn, an' he tol' you not to pet the pups so much."

"Oh, yeah. He had a can a' tar an' a paint brush. I don't know what for."

"You sure that girl didn't come in like she come in here today?"

"No. She never come."

George sighed. "You give me a good whore house every time," he said. "A guy can go in an' get drunk and get ever'thing outa his system all at once, an' no messes. And he knows how much it's gonna set him back. These here jail baits is just set on the trigger of the hoosegow."

Lennie followed his words admiringly, and moved his lips a little to keep up. George continued, "You remember Andy Cushman, Lennie? Went to grammar school?"

"The one that his old lady used to make hot cakes for the kids?" Lennie asked.

"Yeah. That's the one. You can remember anything if there's anything to eat in it." George looked carefully at the solitaire hand. He put an ace up on his scoring rack and piled a two, three and four of diamonds on it. "Andy's in San Quentin right now on account of a tart," said George.

Lennie drummed on the table with his fingers. "George?"

"Huh?"

"George, how long's it gonna be till we get that little place an' live on the fatta the lan—an' rabbits?"

"I don' know," said George. "We gotta get a big stake together. I know a little place we can get cheap, but they ain't givin' it away."

Old Candy turned slowly over. His eyes were wide open. He watched George carefully.

Lennie said, "Tell about that place, George."

"I jus' tol' you, jus' las' night."

"Go on—tell again, George."

"Well, it's ten acres," said George. "Got a little win'mill. Got a little shack on it, an' a chicken run. Got a kitchen, orchard, cherries, apples, peaches, 'cots, nuts, got a few berries. They's a place for alfalfa and plenty water to flood it. They's a pig pen——"

"An' rabbits, George."

"No place for rabbits now, but I could easy build a few hutches and you could feed alfalfa to the rabbits."

"Damn right, I could," said Lennie. "You God damn right I could."

George's hands stopped working with the cards. His voice was growing warmer. "An' we could have a few pigs. I could build a smoke house like the one gran'pa had, an' when we kill a pig we can smoke the bacon and the hams, and make sausage an' all like that. An' when the salmon run up river we could catch a hundred of 'em an' salt 'em down or smoke 'em. We could have them for breakfast. They ain't nothing so nice as smoked salmon. When the fruit come in we could

can it—and tomatoes, they're easy to can. Ever' Sunday we'd kill a chicken or a rabbit. Maybe we'd have a cow or a goat, and the cream is so God damn thick you got to cut it with a knife and take it out with a spoon."

Lennie watched him with wide eyes, and old Candy watched him too. Lennie said softly, "We could live offa the fatta the lan'."

"Sure," said George. "All kin's a vegetables in the garden, and if we want a little whisky we can sell a few eggs or something, or some milk. We'd jus' live there. We'd belong there. There wouldn't be no more runnin' round the country and gettin' fed by a Jap cook. No, sir, we'd have our own place where we belonged and not sleep in no bunk house."

"Tell about the house, George," Lennie begged.

"Sure, we'd have a little house an' a room to ourself. Little fat iron stove, an' in the winter we'd keep a fire goin' in it. It ain't enough land so we'd have to work too hard. Maybe six, seven hours a day. We wouldn't have to buck no barley eleven hours a day. An' when we put in a crop, why, we'd be there to take the crop up. We'd know what come of our planting."

"An' rabbits," Lennie said eagerly. "An' I'd take care of 'em. Tell how I'd do that, George."

"Sure, you'd go out in the alfalfa patch an' you'd have a sack. You'd fill up the sack and bring it in an' put it in the rabbit cages."

"They'd nibble an' they'd nibble," said Lennie, "the way they do. I seen 'em."

"Ever' six weeks or so," George continued, "them does would throw a litter so we'd keep plenty rabbits to eat an' to sell. An' we'd keep a few pigeons to go flyin' around the win'mill like they done when I was a kid." He looked raptly at the wall over Lennie's head. "An' it'd be our own, an' nobody could can us. If we don't like a guy we can say, 'Get the hell out,' and by God he's got to do it. An' if a fren' come along, why we'd have an extra bunk, an' we'd say, 'Why don't you spen' the night?' an' by God he would. We'd have a setter dog and a couple stripe cats, but you gotta watch out them cats don't get the little rabbits."

Lennie breathed hard. "You jus' let 'em try to get the rabbits. I'll break their God damn necks. I'll I'll smash 'em with a stick." He subsided, grumbling to himself, threatening the future cats which might dare to disturb the future rabbits.

George sat entranced with his own picture.

When Candy spoke they both jumped as though they had been caught doing something reprehensible. Candy said, "You know where's a place like that?"

George was on guard immediately. "S'pose I do," he said. "What's that to you?"

"You don't need to tell me where it's at. Might be any place."

"Sure," said George. "That's right. You couldn't find it in a hundred years."

Candy went on excitedly, "How much they want for a place like that?"

George watched him suspiciously. "Well—I could get it for six hundred bucks. The ol' people that owns it is flat bust an' the ol' lady needs an operation. Say—what's it to you? You got nothing to do with us."

Candy said, "I ain't much good with on'y one hand. I lost my hand right here on this ranch. That's why they give me a job swampin'. An' they give me two hunderd an' fifty dollars 'cause I los' my hand. An' I got fifty more saved up right in the bank, right now. Tha's three hunderd, and I got fifty more comin' the end a the month. Tell you what——" He leaned forward eagerly. "S'pose I went in with you guys. Tha's three hunderd an' fifty bucks I'd put in. I ain't much good, but I could cook and tend the chickens and hoe the garden some. How'd that be?"

George half-closed his eyes. "I gotta think about that. We was always gonna do it by ourselves."

Candy interrupted him, "I'd make a will an' leave my share to you guys in case I kick off, 'cause I ain't got no relatives nor nothing. You guys got any money? Maybe we could do her right now?"

George spat on the floor disgustedly. "We got ten bucks between us." Then he said thoughtfully, "Look, if me an' Lennie work a month an' don't spen' nothing, we'll have a hunderd bucks. That'd be four fifty. I bet we could swing her for that. Then you an' Lennie could go get her started an' I'd get a job an' make up the res', an' you could sell eggs an' stuff like that."

They fell into a silence. They looked at one another, amazed. This thing they had never really believed in was coming true. George said reverently, "Jesus Christ! I bet we could swing her." His eyes were full of wonder. "I bet we could swing her," he repeated softly.

Candy sat on the edge of his bunk. He scratched the stump of his wrist nervously. "I got hurt four year ago," he said. "They'll can me purty soon. Jus' as soon as I can't swamp out no bunk houses they'll put me on the county. Maybe if I give you guys my money, you'll let me hoe in the garden even after I ain't no good at it. An' I'll wash dishes an' little chicken stuff like that. But I'll be on our own place, an' I'll be let to work on our own place." He said miserably, "You seen what they done to my dog tonight? They says he wasn't no good

to himself nor nobody else. When they can me here I wisht somebody'd shoot me. But they won't do nothing like that. I won't have no place to go, an' I can't get no more jobs. I'll have thirty dollars more comin', time you guys is ready to quit."

George stood up. "We'll do her," he said. "We'll fix up that little old place an we'll go live there." He sat down again. They all sat still, all bemused by the beauty of the thing, each mind was popped into the future when this lovely thing should come about.

George said wonderingly, "S'pose they was a carnival or a circus come to town, or a ball game, or any damn thing." Old Candy nodded in appreciation of the idea. "We'd just go to her," George said. "We wouldn't ask nobody if we could. Jus' say, 'We'll go to her,' an' we would. Jus' milk the cow and sling some grain to the chickens an' go to her."

"An' put some grass to the rabbits," Lennie broke in. "I wouldn't never forget to feed them. When we gon'ta do it, George?"

"In one month. Right squack in one month. Know what I'm gon'ta do? Im gon'ta write to them old people that owns the place that we'll take it. An' Candy'll send a hunderd dollars to bind her."

"Sure will," said Candy. "They got a good stove there?"

"Sure, got a nice stove, burns coal or wood."

"I'm gonna take my pup," said Lennie. "I bet by Christ he likes it there, by Jesus."

Voices were approaching from outside. George said quickly, "Don't tell nobody about it. Jus' us three an' nobody else. They li'ble to can us so we can't make no stake. Jus' go on like we was gonna buck barley the rest of our lives, then all of a sudden some day we'll go get our pay an' scram outa here."

Lennie and Candy nodded, and they were grinning with delight. "Don't tell nobody," Lennie said to himself.

Candy said, "George."

"Huh?"

"I ought to of shot that dog myself, George. I shouldn't ought to of let no stranger shoot my dog."

The door opened. Slim came in, followed by Curley and Carlson and Whit. Slim's hands were black with tar and he was scowling. Curley hung close to his elbow.

Curley said, "Well, I didn't mean nothing, Slim. I just ast you."

Slim said, "Well, you been askin' me too often. I'm gettin' God damn sick of it. If you can't look after your own God damn wife, what you expect me to do about it? You lay offa me."

"I'm jus' tryin' to tell you I didn't mean nothing," said Curley. "I jus' thought you might of saw her."

"Why'n't you tell her to stay the hell home where she belongs?" said Carlson. "You let her hang around bunk houses and pretty soon you're gonna have som'pin on your hands and you won't be able to do nothing about it."

Curley whirled on Carlson. "You keep outa this les' you wanta step outside."

Carlson laughed. "You God damn punk," he said. "You tried to throw a scare into Slim, an' you couldn't make it stick. Slim throwed a scare inta you. You're yella as a frog belly. I don't care if you're the best welter in the country. You come for me, an' I'll kick your God damn head off."

Candy joined the attack with joy. "Glove fulla vaseline," he said disgustedly. Curley glared at him. His eyes slipped on past and lighted on Lennie; and Lennie was still smiling with delight at the memory of the ranch.

Curley stepped over to Lennie like a terrier. "What the hell you laughin' at?"

Lennie looked blankly at him. "Huh?"

Then Curley's rage exploded. "Come on, ya big bastard. Get up on your feet. No big son-of-a-bitch is gonna laugh at me. I'll show ya who's yella."

Lennie looked helplessly at George, and then he got up and tried to retreat. Curley was balanced and poised. He slashed at Lennie with his left, and then smashed down his nose with a right. Lennie gave a cry of terror. Blood welled from his nose. "George," he cried. "Make 'um let me alone, George." He backed until he was against the wall, and Curley followed, slugging him in the face. Lennie's hands remained at his sides; he was too frightened to defend himself.

George was on his feet yelling, "Get him, Lennie. Don't let him do it."

Lennie covered his face with his huge paws and bleated with terror. He cried, "Make 'um stop, George." Then Curley attacked his stomach and cut off his wind.

Slim jumped up. "The dirty little rat," he cried, "I'll get 'um myself."

George put out his hand and grabbed Slim. "Wait a minute," he shouted. He cupped his hands around his mouth and yelled, "Get 'im, Lennie!"

Lennie took his hands away from his face and looked about for George, and Curley slashed at his eyes. The big face was covered with blood. George yelled again, "I said get him."

Curley's fist was swinging when Lennie reached for it. The next minute Curley was flopping like a fish on a line, and his closed fist was

lost in Lennie's big hand. George ran down the room. "Leggo of him, Lennie. Let go."

But Lennie watched in terror the flopping little man whom he held. Blood ran down Lennie's face, one of his eyes was cut and closed. George slapped him in the face again and again, and still Lennie held on to the closed fist. Curley was white and shrunken by now, and his struggling had become weak. He stood crying, his fist lost in Lennie's paw.

George shouted over and over, "Leggo his hand, Lennie. Leggo. Slim, come help me while the guy got any hand left."

Suddenly Lennie let go his hold. He crouched cowering against the wall. "You tol' me to, George," he said miserably.

Curley sat down on the floor, looking in wonder at his crushed hand. Slim and Carlson bent over him. Then Slim straightened up and regarded Lennie with horror. "We got to get him in to a doctor," he said. "Looks to me like ever' bone in his han' is bust."

"I didn't wanta," Lennie cried. "I didn't wanta hurt him."

Slim said, "Carlson, you get the candy wagon hitched up. We'll take 'um into Soledad an' get 'um fixed up." Carlson hurried out. Slim turned to the whimpering Lennie. "It ain't your fault," he said. "This punk sure had it comin' to him. But—Jesus! He ain't hardly got no han' left." Slim hurried out, and in a moment returned with a tin cup of water. He held it to Curley's lips.

George said, "Slim, will we get canned now? We need the stake. Will Curley's old man can us now?"

Slim smiled wryly. He knelt down beside Curley. "You got your senses in hand enough to listen?" he asked. Curley nodded. "Well, then listen," Slim went on. "I think you got your han' caught in a machine. If you don't tell nobody what happened, we ain't going to. But you jus' tell an' try to get this guy canned and we'll tell ever'body, an' then will you get the laugh."

"I won't tell," said Curley. He avoided looking at Lennie.

Buggy wheels sounded outside. Slim helped Curley up. "Come on now. Carlson's gonna take you to a doctor." He helped Curley out the door. The sound of wheels drew away. In a moment Slim came back into the bunk house. He looked at Lennie, still crouched fearfully against the wall. "Let's see your hands," he asked.

Lennie stuck out his hands.

"Christ awmighty, I hate to have you mad at me," Slim said.

George broke in, "Lennie was jus' scairt," he explained. "He didn't know what to do. I told you nobody ought never to fight him. No, I guess it was Candy I told."

Candy nodded solemnly. "That's jus' what you done," he said.

"Right this morning when Curley first lit intil your fren', you says, 'He better not fool with Lennie if he knows what's good for 'um.' That's jus' what you says to me."

George turned to Lennie. "It ain't your fault," he said. "You don't need to be scairt no more. You done jus' what I tol' you to. Maybe you better go in the wash room an' clean up your face. You look like hell."

Lennie smiled with his bruised mouth. "I didn't want no trouble," he said. He walked toward the door, but just before he came to it, he turned back. "George?"

"What you want?"

"I can still tend the rabbits, George?"

"Sure. You ain't done nothing wrong."

"I di'n't mean no harm, George."

"Well, get the hell out and wash your face."

§ 4

Crooks, the negro stable buck, had his bunk in the harness room; a little shed that leaned off the wall of the barn. On one side of the little room there was a square four-paned window, and on the other, a narrow plank door leading into the barn. Crooks' bunk was a long box filled with straw, on which his blankets were flung. On the wall by the window there were pegs on which hung broken harness in process of being mended; strips of new leather; and under the window itself a little bench for leather-working tools, curved knives and needles and balls of linen thread, and a small hand riveter. On pegs were also pieces of harness, a split collar with the horsehair stuffing sticking out, a broken hame, and a trace chain with its leather covering split. Crooks had his apple box over his bunk, and in it a range of medicine bottles, both for himself and for the horses. There were cans of saddle soap and a drippy can of tar with its paint brush sticking over the edge. And scattered about the floor were a number of personal possessions; for, being alone, Crooks could leave his things about, and being a stable buck and a cripple, he was more permanent than the other men, and he had accumulated more possessions than he could carry on his back.

Crooks possessed several pairs of shoes, a pair of rubber boots, a big alarm clock and a single-barreled shotgun. And he had books, too; a tattered dictionary and a mauled copy of the California civil code for 1905. There were battered magazines and a few dirty books on a special shelf over his bunk. A pair of large gold-rimmed spectacles hung from a nail on the wall above his bed.

This room was swept and fairly neat, for Crooks was a proud, aloof man. He kept his distance and demanded that other people keep theirs. His body was bent over to the left by his crooked spine, and his eyes lay deep in his head, and because of their depth seemed to glitter with intensity. His lean face was lined with deep black wrinkles, and he had thin, pain-tightened lips which were lighter than his face.

It was Saturday night. Through the open door that led into the barn came the sound of moving horses, of feet stirring, of teeth champing on hay, of the rattle of halter chains. In the stable buck's room a small electric globe threw a meager yellow light.

Crooks sat on his bunk. His shirt was out of his jeans in back. In one hand he held a bottle of liniment, and with the other he rubbed his spine. Now and then he poured a few drops of the liniment into his pink-palmed hand and reached up under his shirt to rub again. He flexed his muscles against his back and shivered.

Noiselessly Lennie appeared in the open doorway and stood there looking in, his big shoulders nearly filling the opening. For a moment Crooks did not see him, but on raising his eyes he stiffened and a scowl came on his face. His hand came out from under his shirt.

Lennie smiled helplessly in an attempt to make friends.

Crooks said sharply, "You got no right to come in my room. This here's my room. Nobody got any right in here but me."

Lennie gulped and his smile grew more fawning. "I ain't doing nothing," he said. "Just come to look at my puppy. And I seen your light," he explained.

"Well, I got a right to have a light. You go on get outta my room. I ain't wanted in the bunk house, and you ain't wanted in my room."

"Why ain't you wanted?" Lennie asked.

"'Cause I'm black. They play cards in there, but I can't play because I'm black. They say I stink. Well, I tell you, you all of you stink to me."

Lennie flapped his big hands helplessly. "Ever'body went into town," he said. "Slim an' George an' ever'body. George says I gotta stay here an' not get in no trouble. I seen your light."

"Well, what do you want?"

"Nothing—I seen your light. I thought I could jus' come in an' set."

Crooks stared at Lennie, and he reached behind him and took down the spectacles and adjusted them over his pink ears and stared again. "I don't know what you're doin' in the barn anyway," he complained. "You ain't no skinner. They's no call for a bucker to come into the barn at all. You ain't no skinner. You ain't got nothing to do with the horses."

"The pup," Lennie repeated. "I come to see my pup."

"Well, go see your pup, then. Don't come in a place where you're not wanted."

Lennie lost his smile. He advanced a step into the room, then remembered and backed to the door again. "I looked at 'em a little. Slim says I ain't to pet 'em very much."

Crooks said, "Well, you been takin' 'em out of the nest all the time. I wonder the old lady don't move 'em someplace else."

"Oh, she don't care. She let's me." Lennie had moved into the room again.

Crooks scowled, but Lennie's disarming smile defeated him. "Come on in and set a while," Crooks said. " 'Long as you won't get out and leave me alone, you might as well set down." His tone was a little more friendly. "All the boys gone into town, huh?"

"All but old Candy. He just sets in the bunk house sharpening his pencil and sharpening and figuring."

Crooks adjusted his glasses. "Figuring? What's Candy figuring about?"

Lennie almost shouted, " 'Bout the rabbits."

"You're nuts," said Crooks. "You're crazy as a wedge. What rabbits you talkin' about?"

"The rabbits we're gonna get, and I get to tend 'em, cut grass an' give 'em water, an' like that."

"Jus' nuts," said Crooks. "I don't blame the guy you travel with for keepin' you outa sight."

Lennie said quietly, "It ain't no lie. We're gonna do it. Gonna get a little place an' live on the fatta the lan'."

Crooks settled himself more comfortably on his bunk. "Set down," he invited. "Set down on the nail keg."

Lennie hunched down on the little barrel. "You think it's a lie," Lennie said, "But it ain't no lie. Ever' word's the truth, an' you can ast George."

Crooks put his dark chin into his pink palm. "You travel aroun' with George, don't ya?"

"Sure. Me an' him goes ever' place together."

Crooks continued. "Sometimes he talks, and you don't know what the hell he's talkin' about. Ain't that so?" He leaned forward, boring Lennie with his deep eyes. "Ain't that so?"

"Yeah sometimes."

"Jus' talks on, an' you don't know what the hell it's all about?"

"Yeah sometimes. But not always."

Crooks leaned forward over the edge of the bunk. "I ain't a southern negro," he said. "I was born right here in California. My old man had a chicken ranch, 'bout ten acres. The white kids come to play at our

place, an' sometimes I went to play with them, and some of them was pretty nice. My ol' man didn't like that. I never knew till long later why he didn't like that. But I know now." He hesitated, and when he spoke again his voice was softer. "There wasn't another colored family for miles around. And now there ain't a colored man on this ranch an' there's jus' one family in Soledad." He laughed. "If I say something, why it's just a nigger sayin' it."

Lennie asked, "How long you think it'll be before them pups will be old enough to pet?"

Crooks laughed again. "A guy can talk to you an' be sure you won't go blabbin'. Couple of weeks an' them pups'll be all right. George knows what he's about. Jus' talks, an' you don't understand nothing." He leaned forward excitedly. "This is just a nigger talkin', an' a busted-back nigger. So it don't mean nothing, see? You couldn't remember it anyways. I seen it over an' over—a guy talkin' to another guy and it don't make no difference if he don't hear or understand. The thing is, they're talkin', or they're settin' still not talkin'. It don't make no difference, no difference." His excitement had increased until he pounded his knee with his hand. "George can tell you screwy things, and it don't matter. It's just the talking. It's just bein' with another guy. That's all." He paused.

His voice grew soft and persuasive. "S'pose George don't come back no more. S'pose he took a powder and just ain't coming back. What'll you do then?"

Lennie's attention came gradually to what had been said. "What?" he demanded.

"I said s'pose George went into town tonight and you never heard of him no more." Crooks pressed forward some kind of private victory. "Just s'pose that," he repeated.

"He won't do it," Lennie cried. "George wouldn't do nothing like that. I been with George a long time. He'll come back tonight——" But the doubt was too much for him. "Don't you think he will?"

Crooks' face lighted with pleasure in his torture. "Nobody can't tell what a guy'll do," he observed calmly. "Le's say he wants to come back and can't. S'pose he gets killed or hurt so he can't come back."

Lennie struggled to understand. "George won't do nothing like that," he repeated. "George is careful. He won't get hurt. He ain't never been hurt, 'cause he's careful."

"Well, s'pose, jus' s'pose he don't come back. What'll you do then?"

Lennie's face wrinkled with apprehension. "I don' know. Say, what you doin' anyways?" he cried. "This ain't true. George ain't got hurt."

Crooks bored in on him. "Want me ta tell ya what'll happen?

They'll take ya to the booby hatch. They'll tie ya up with a collar, like a dog."

Suddenly Lennie's eyes centered and grew quiet, and mad. He stood up and walked dangerously toward Crooks. "Who hurt George?" he demanded.

Crooks saw the danger as it approached him. He edged back on his bunk to get out of the way. "I was just supposin'," he said. "George ain't hurt. He's all right. He'll be back all right."

Lennie stood over him. "What you supposin' for? Ain't nobody goin' to suppose no hurt to George."

Crooks removed his glasses and wiped his eyes with his fingers. "Jus' set down," he said. "George ain't hurt."

Lennie growled back to his seat on the nail keg. "Ain't nobody goin' to talk no hurt to George," he grumbled.

Crooks said gently, "Maybe you can see now. You got George. You *know* he's goin' to come back. S'pose you didn't have nobody. S'pose you couldn't go into the bunk house and play rummy 'cause you was black. How'd you like that? S'pose you had to sit out here an' read books. Sure you could play horseshoes till it got dark, but then you got to read books. Books ain't no good. A guy needs somebody—to be near him." He whined, "A guy goes nuts if he ain't got nobody. Don't make no difference who the guy is, long's he's with you. I tell ya," he cried, "I tell ya a guy gets too lonely an' he gets sick."

"George gonna come back," Lennie reassured himself in a frightened voice. "Maybe George come back already. Maybe I better go see."

Crooks said, "I didn't mean to scare you. He'll come back. I was talkin' about myself. A guy sets alone out here at night, maybe readin' books or thinkin' or stuff like that. Sometimes he gets thinkin', an' he got nothing to tell him what's so an' what ain't so. Maybe if he sees somethin', he don't know whether it's right or not. He can't turn to some other guy and ast him if he sees it too. He can't tell. He got nothing to measure by. I seen things out here. I wasn't drunk. I don't know if I was asleep. If some guy was with me, he could tell me I was asleep, an' then it would be all right. But I jus' don't know." Crooks was looking across the room now, looking toward the window.

Lennie said miserably, "George wun't go away and leave me. I know George wun't do that."

The stable buck went on dreamily, "I remember when I was a little kid on my old man's chicken ranch. Had two brothers. They was always near me, always there. Used to sleep right in the same room, right in the same bed—all three. Had a strawberry patch. Had an alfalfa patch. Used to turn the chickens out in the alfalfa on a sunny

morning. My brothers'd set on a fence rail an' watch 'em—white chickens they was."

Gradually Lennie's interest came around to what was being said. "George says we're gonna have alfalfa for the rabbits."

"What rabbits?"

"We're gonna have rabbits an' a berry patch."

"You're nuts."

"We are too. You ast George."

"You're nuts." Crooks was scornful. "I seen hunderds of men come by on the road an' on the ranches, with their bindles on their back an' that same damn thing in their heads. Hunderds of them. They come, an' they quit an' go on; an' every damn one of 'em's got a little piece of land in his head. An' never a God damn one of 'em ever gets it. Just like heaven. Ever'body wants a little piece of lan'. I read plenty of books out here. Nobody never gets to heaven, and nobody gets no land. It's just in their head. They're all the time talkin' about it, but it's jus' in their head." He paused and looked toward the open door, for the horses were moving restlessly and the halter chains clinked. A horse whinnied. "I guess somebody's out there," Crooks said. "Maybe Slim. Slim comes in sometimes two, three times a night. Slim's a real skinner. He looks out for his team." He pulled himself painfully upright and moved toward the door. "That you, Slim?" he called.

Candy's voice answered. "Slim went in town. Say, you seen Lennie?"

"Ya mean the big guy?"

"Yeah. Seen him around any place?"

"He's in here," Crooks said shortly. He went back to his bunk and lay down.

Candy stood in the doorway scratching his bald wrist and looking blindly into the lighted room. He made no attempt to enter. "Tell ya what, Lennie. I been figuring out about them rabbits."

Crooks said irritably, "You can come in if you want."

Candy seemed embarrassed. "I do' know. 'Course, if ya want me to."

"Come on in. If ever'body's comin' in, you might just as well." It was difficult for Crooks to conceal his pleasure with anger.

Candy came in, but he was still embarrassed. "You got a nice cozy little place in here," he said to Crooks. "Must be nice to have a room all to yourself this way."

"Sure," said Crooks. "And a manure pile under the window. Sure, it's swell."

Lennie broke in, "You said about them rabbits."

Candy leaned against the wall beside the broken collar while he scratched the wrist stump. "I been here a long time," he said. "An'

Crooks been here a long time. This's the first time I ever been in his room."

Crooks said darkly, "Guys don't come into a colored man's room very much. Nobody been here but Slim. Slim an' the boss."

Candy quickly changed the subject. "Slim's as good a skinner as I ever seen."

Lennie leaned toward the old swamper. "About them rabbits," he insisted.

Candy smiled. "I got it figured out. We can make some money on them rabbits if we go about it right."

"But I get to tend 'em," Lennie broke in. "George says I get to tend 'em. He promised."

Crooks interrupted brutally. "You guys is just kiddin' yourself. You'll talk about it a hell of a lot, but you won't get no land. You'll be a swamper here till they take you out in a box. Hell, I seen too many guys. Lennie here'll quit an' be on the road in two, three weeks. Seems like ever' guy got land in his head."

Candy rubbed his cheek angrily. "You God damn right we're gonna do it. George says we are. We got the money right now."

"Yeah?" said Crooks. "An' where's George now? In town in a whore house. That's where your money's goin'. Jesus, I seen it happen too many times. I seen too many guys with land in their head. They never get none under their hand."

Candy cried, "Sure they all want it. Everybody wants a little bit of land, not much. Jus' som'thin' that was his. Som'thin' he could live on and there couldn't nobody throw him off of it. I never had none. I planted crops for damn near ever'body in this state, but they wasn't my crops, and when I harvested 'em, it wasn't none of my harvest. But we gonna do it now, and don't you make no mistake about that. George ain't got the money in town. That money's in the bank. Me an' Lennie an' George. We gonna have a room to ourself. We're gonna have a dog an' rabbits an' chickens. We're gonna have green corn an' maybe a cow or a goat." He stopped, overwhelmed with his picture.

Crooks asked, "You say you got the money?"

"Damn right. We got most of it. Just a little bit more to get. Have it all in one month. George got the land all picked out, too."

Crooks reached around and explored his spine with his hand. "I never seen a guy really do it," he said. "I seen guys nearly crazy with loneliness for land, but ever' time a whore house or a blackjack game took what it takes." He hesitated. ". . . . If you guys would want a hand to work for nothing—just his keep, why I'd come an' lend a hand. I ain't so crippled I can't work like a son-of-a-bitch if I want to."

"Any you boys seen Curley?"

They swung their heads toward the door. Looking in was Curley's wife. Her face was heavily made up. Her lips were slightly parted. She breathed strongly, as though she had been running.

"Curley ain't been here," Candy said sourly.

She stood still in the doorway, smiling a little at them, rubbing the nails of one hand with the thumb and forefinger of the other. And her eyes traveled from one face to another. "They left all the weak ones here," she said finally. "Think I don't know where they all went? Even Curley. I know where they all went."

Lennie watched her, fascinated; but Candy and Crooks were scowling down away from her eyes. Candy said, "Then if you know, why you want to ast us where Curley is at?"

She regarded them amusedly. "Funny thing," she said. "If I catch any one man, and he's alone, I get along fine with him. But just let two of the guys get together an' you won't talk. Jus' nothing but mad." She dropped her fingers and put her hands on her hips. "You're all scared of each other, that's what. Ever' one of you's scared the rest is goin' to get something on you."

After a pause Crooks said, "Maybe you better go along to your own house now. We don't want no trouble."

"Well, I ain't giving you no trouble. Think I don't like to talk to somebody ever' once in a while? Think I like to stick in that house alla time?"

Candy laid the stump of his wrist on his knee and rubbed it gently with his hand. He said accusingly, "You gotta husban'. You got no call foolin' aroun' with other guys, causin' trouble."

The girl flared up. "Sure I gotta husban'. You all seen him. Swell guy, ain't he? Spends all his time sayin' what he's gonna do to guys he don't like, and he don't like nobody. Think I'm gonna stay in that two-by-four house and listen how Curley's gonna lead with his left twict, and then bring in the ol' right cross? 'One-two' he says. 'Just the ol' one-two an' he'll go down.'" She paused and her face lost its sullenness and grew interested. "Say—what happened to Curley's han'?"

There was an embarrassed silence. Candy stole a look at Lennie. Then he coughed. "Why Curley he got his han' caught in a machine, ma'am. Bust his han'."

She watched for a moment, and then she laughed. "Baloney! What you think you're sellin' me? Curley started som'pin' he didn' finish. Caught in a machine—baloney! Why, he ain't give nobody the good ol' one-two since he got his han' bust. Who bust him?"

Candy repeated sullenly, "Got it caught in a machine."

"Awright," she said contemptuously. "Awright, cover 'im up if ya wanta. Whatta I care? You bindle bums think you're so damn good. Whatta ya think I am, a kid? I tell ya I could of went with shows. Not jus' one, neither. An' a guy tol' me he could put me in pitchers. . . ." She was breathless with indignation. "—Sat'iday night. Ever'body out doin' som'pin'. Ever'body! An' what am I doin'? Standin' here talkin' to a bunch of bindle stiffs—a nigger an' a dum-dum and a lousy ol' sheep—an' likin' it because they ain't nobody else."

Lennie watched her, his mouth half open. Crooks had retired into the terrible protective dignity of the negro. But a change came over old Candy. He stood up suddenly and knocked his nail keg over backward. "I had enough," he said angrily. "You ain't wanted here. We told you you ain't. An' I tell ya, you got floozy idears about what us guys amounts to. You ain't got sense enough in that chicken head to even see that we ain't stiffs. S'pose you get us canned. S'pose you do. You think we'll hit the highway an' look for another lousy two-bit job like this. You don't know that we got our own ranch to go to, an' our own house. We ain't got to stay here. We gotta house and chickens an' fruit trees an' a place a hunderd time prettier than this. An' we got fren's, that's what we got. Maybe there was a time when we was scared of gettin' canned, but we ain't no more. We got our own lan', and it's ours, an' we c'n go to it."

Curley's wife laughed at him. "Baloney," she said. "I seen too many you guys. If you had two bits in the worl', why you'd be in gettin' two shots of corn with it and suckin' the bottom of the glass. I know you guys."

Candy's face had grown redder and redder, but before she was done speaking, he had control of himself. He was the master of the situation. "I might of knew," he said gently. "Maybe you just better go along an' roll your hoop. We ain't got nothing to say to you at all. We know what we got, and we don't care whether you know it or not. So maybe you better jus' scatter along now, 'cause Curley maybe ain't gonna like his wife out in the barn with us 'bindle stiffs.' "

She looked from one face to another, and they were all closed against her. And she looked longest at Lennie, until he dropped his eyes in embarrassment. Suddenly she said, "Where'd you get them bruises on your face?"

Lennie looked up guiltily. "Who—me?"

"Yeah, you."

Lennie looked to Candy for help, and then he looked at his lap again. "He got his han' caught in a machine," he said.

Curley's wife laughed. "O.K., Machine. I'll talk to you later. I like machines."

Candy broke in. "You let this guy alone. Don't you do no messing aroun' with him. I'm gonna tell George what you says. George won't have you messin' with Lennie."

"Who's George?" she asked. "The little guy you come with?"

Lennie smiled happily. "That's him," he said. "That's the guy, an' he's gonna let me tend the rabbits."

"Well, if that's all you want, I might get a couple rabbits myself."

Crooks stood up from his bunk and faced her. "I had enough," he said coldly. "You got no rights comin' in a colored man's room. You got no rights messing around in here at all. Now you jus' get out, an' get out quick. If you don't, I'm gonna ast the boss not to ever let you come in the barn no more."

She turned on him in scorn. "Listen, Nigger," she said. "You know what I can do to you if you open your trap?"

Crooks stared hopelessly at her, and then he sat down on his bunk and drew into himself.

She closed on him. "You know what I could do?"

Crooks seemed to grow smaller, and he pressed himself against the wall. "Yes, ma'am."

"Well, you keep your place then, Nigger. I could get you strung up on a tree so easy it ain't even funny."

Crooks had reduced himself to nothing. There was no personality, no ego—nothing to arouse either like or dislike. He said, "Yes, ma'am," and his voice was toneless.

For a moment she stood over him as though waiting for him to move so that she could whip at him again; but Crooks sat perfectly still, his eyes averted, everything that might be hurt drawn in. She turned at last to the other two.

Old Candy was watching her, fascinated. "If you was to do that, we'd tell," he said quietly. "We'd tell about you framin' Crooks."

"Tell an' be damned," she cried. "Nobody'd listen to you, an' you know it. Nobody'd listen to you."

Candy subsided. "No" he agreed. "Nobody'd listen to us."

Lennie whined, "I wisht George was here. I wisht George was here."

Candy stepped over to him. "Don't you worry none," he said. "I jus' heard the guys comin' in. George'll be in the bunk house right now, I bet." He turned to Curley's wife. "You better go home now," he said quietly. "If you go right now, we won't tell Curley you was here."

She appraised him coolly. "I ain't sure you heard nothing."

"Better not take no chances," he said. "If you ain't sure, you better take the safe way."

She turned to Lennie. "I'm glad you bust up Curley a little bit. He

got it comin' to him. Sometimes I'd like to bust him myself." She slipped out the door and disappeared into the dark barn. And while she went through the barn, the halter chains rattled, and some horses snorted and some stamped their feet.

Crooks seemed to come slowly out of the layers of protection he had put on. "Was that the truth what you said about the guys come back?" he asked.

"Sure. I heard 'em."

"Well, I didn't hear nothing."

"The gate banged," Candy said, and he went on, "Jesus Christ, Curley's wife can move quiet. I guess she had a lot of practice, though."

Crooks avoided the whole subject now. "Maybe you guys better go," he said. "I ain't sure I want you in here no more. A colored man got to have some rights even if he don't like 'em."

Candy said, "That bitch didn't ought to of said that to you."

"It wasn't nothing," Crooks said dully. "You guys comin' in an' settin' made me forget. What she says is true."

The horses snorted out in the barn and the chains rang and a voice called, "Lennie. Oh, Lennie. You in the barn?"

"It's George," Lennie cried. And he answered, "Here, George. I'm right in here."

In a second George stood framed in the door, and he looked disapprovingly about. "What you doin' in Crooks' room. You hadn't ought to be here."

Crooks nodded. "I tol' 'em, but they come in anyways."

"Well, why'n't you kick 'em out?"

"I di'n't care much," said Crooks. "Lennie's a nice fella."

Now Candy aroused himself. "Oh, George! I been figurin' and figurin'. I got it doped out how we can even make some money on them rabbits."

George scowled. "I thought I tol' you not to tell nobody about that."

Candy was crestfallen. "Didn't tell nobody but Crooks."

George said, "Well you guys get outta here. Jesus, seems like I can't go away for a minute."

Candy and Lennie stood up and went toward the door. Crooks called, "Candy!"

"Huh?"

" 'Member what I said about hoein' and doin' odd jobs?"

"Yeah," said Candy. "I remember."

"Well, jus' forget it," said Crooks. "I didn' mean it. Jus' foolin'. I wouldn' want to go no place like that."

"Well, O.K., if you feel like that. Good-night."

The three men went out of the door. As they went through the barn the horses snorted and the halter chains rattled.

Crooks sat on his bunk and looked at the door for a moment, and then he reached for the liniment bottle. He pulled out his shirt in back, poured a little liniment in his pink palm and, reaching around, he fell slowly to rubbing his back.

§ 5

One end of the barn was piled high with new hay and over the pile hung the four-taloned jackson fork suspended from its pulley. The hay came down like a mountain slope to the other end of the barn, and there was a level place as yet unfilled with the new crop. At the sides the feeding racks were visible, and between the slats the heads of horses could be seen.

It was Sunday afternoon. The resting horses nibbled the remaining wisps of hay, and they stamped their feet and they bit the wood of the mangers and rattled the halter chains. The afternoon sun sliced in through the cracks of the barn walls and lay in bright lines on the hay. There was the buzz of flies in the air, the lazy afternoon humming.

From outside came the clang of horseshoes on the playing peg and the shouts of men, playing, encouraging, jeering. But in the barn it was quiet and humming and lazy and warm.

Only Lennie was in the barn, and Lennie sat in the hay beside a packing case under a manger in the end of the barn that had not been filled with hay. Lennie sat in the hay and looked at a little dead puppy that lay in front of him. Lennie looked at it for a long time, and then he put out his huge hand and stroked it, stroked it clear from one end to the other.

And Lennie said softly to the puppy, "Why do you got to get killed? You ain't so little as mice. I didn't bounce you hard." He bent the pup's head up and looked in its face, and he said to it, "Now maybe George ain't gonna let me tend no rabbits, if he fin's out you got killed."

He scooped a little hollow and laid the puppy in it and covered it over with hay, out of sight; but he continued to stare at the mound he had made. He said, "This ain't no bad thing like I got to hide in the brush. Oh! no. This ain't. I'll tell George I foun' it dead."

He unburied the puppy and inspected it, and he stroked it from ears to tail. He went on sorrowfully, "But he'll know. George always knows. He'll say, 'You done it. Don't try to put nothing over on me.' An' he'll say, 'Now jus' for that you don't get to tend no rabbits!' "

Suddenly his anger arose. "God damn you," he cried. "Why do you got to get killed? You ain't so little as mice." He picked up the pup and hurled it from him. He turned his back on it. He sat bent over his knees and he whispered, "Now I won't get to tend the rabbits. Now he won't let me." He rocked himself back and forth in his sorrow.

From outside came the clang of horseshoes on the iron stake, and then a little chorus of cries. Lennie got up and brought the puppy back and laid it on the hay and sat down. He stroked the pup again. "You wasn't big enough," he said. "They tol' me and tol' me you wasn't. I di'n't know you'd get killed so easy." He worked his fingers on the pup's limp ear. "Maybe George won't care," he said. "This here God damn little son-of-a-bitch wasn't nothing to George."

Curley's wife came around the end of the last stall. She came very quietly, so that Lennie didn't see her. She wore her bright cotton dress and the mules with the red ostrich feathers. Her face was made up and the little sausage curls were all in place. She was quite near to him before Lennie looked up and saw her.

In a panic he shoveled hay over the puppy with his fingers. He looked sullenly up at her.

She said, "What you got there, sonny boy?"

Lennie glared at her. "George says I ain't to have nothing to do with you—talk to you or nothing."

She laughed. "George giving you orders about everything?"

Lennie looked down at the hay. "Says I can't tend no rabbits if I talk to you or anything."

She said quietly, "He's scared Curley'll get mad. Well, Curley got his arm in a sling—an' if Curley gets tough, you can break his other han'. You didn't put nothing over on me about gettin' it caught in no machine."

But Lennie was not to be drawn. "No, sir. I ain't gonna talk to you or nothing."

She knelt in the hay beside him. "Listen," she said. "All the guys got a horseshoe tenement goin' on. It's on'y about four o'clock. None of them guys is goin' to leave that tenement. Why can't I talk to you? I never get to talk to nobody. I get awful lonely."

Lennie said, "Well, I ain't supposed to talk to you or nothing."

"I get lonely," she said. "You can talk to people, but I can't talk to nobody but Curley. Else he gets mad. How'd you like not to talk to anybody?"

Lennie said, "Well, I ain't supposed to. George's scared I'll get in trouble."

She changed the subject. "What you got covered up there?"

Then all of Lennie's woe came back on him. "Jus' my pup," he said

sadly. "Jus' my little pup." And he swept the hay from on top of it.

"Why, he's dead," she cried.

"He was so little," said Lennie. "I was jus' playin' with him
an' he made like he's gonna bite me an' I made like I was gonna
smack him an' an' I done it. An' then he was dead."

She consoled him. "Don't you worry none. He was jus' a mutt. You
can get another one easy. The whole country is fulla mutts."

"It ain't that so much," Lennie explained miserably. "George ain't
gonna let me tend no rabbits now."

"Why don't he?"

"Well, he said if I done any more bad things he ain't gonna let me
tend the rabbits."

She moved closer to him and she spoke soothingly. "Don't you worry
about talkin' to me. Listen to the guys yell out there. They got four
dollars bet in that tenement. None of them, ain't gonna leave till it's
over."

"If George sees me talkin' to you he'll give me hell," Lennie said
cautiously. "He tol' me so."

Her face grew angry. "Wha's the matter with me?" she cried. "Ain't
I got a right to talk to nobody? Whatta they think I am, anyways?
You're a nice guy. I don't know why I can't talk to you. I ain't doin'
no harm to you."

"Well, George says you'll get us in a mess."

"Aw, nuts!" she said. "What kinda harm am I doin' to you? Seems
like they ain't none of them cares how I gotta live. I tell you I ain't
used to livin' like this. I coulda made somethin' of myself." She said
darkly, "Maybe I will yet." And then her words tumbled out in a pas-
sion of communication, as though she hurried before her listener could
be taken away. "I lived right in Salinas," she said. "Come there when
I was a kid. Well, a show come through, an' I met one of the actors.
He says I could go with that show. But my ol' lady wouldn' let me. She
says because I was on'y fifteen. But the guy says I coulda. If I'd went,
I wouldn't be livin' like this, you bet."

Lennie stroked the pup back and forth. "We gonna have a little
place—an' rabbits," he explained.

She went on with her story quickly, before she should be interrupted.
" 'Nother time I met a guy, an' he was in pitchers. Went out to the
Riverside Dance Palace with him. He says he was gonna put me in the
movies. Says I was a natural. Soon's he got back to Hollywood he
was gonna write to me about it." She looked closely at Lennie to see
whether she was impressing him. "I never got that letter," she said.
"I always thought my ol' lady stole it. Well, I wasn't gonna stay no
place where I couldn't get nowhere or make something of myself, an'

where they stole your letters. I ast her if she stole it, too, an' she says no. So I married Curley. Met him out to the Riverside Dance Palace that same night." She demanded, "You listenin'?"

"Me? Sure."

"Well, I ain't told this to nobody before. Maybe I ought'n to. I don' *like* Curley. He ain't a nice fella." And because she had confided in him, she moved closer to Lennie and sat beside him. "Coulda been in the movies, an' had nice clothes—all them nice clothes like they wear. An' I coulda sat in them big hotels, an' had pitchers took of me. When they had them previews I coulda went to them, an' spoke in the radio, an' it wouldn'ta cost me a cent because I was in the pitcher. An' all them nice clothes like they wear. Because this guy says I was a natural." She looked up at Lennie, and she made a small grand gesture with her arm and hand to show that she could act. The fingers trailed after her leading wrist, and her little finger stuck out grandly from the rest.

Lennie sighed deeply. From outside came the clang of a horseshoe on metal, and then a chorus of cheers. "Somebody made a ringer," said Curley's wife.

Now the light was lifting as the sun went down, and the sun streaks climbed up the wall and fell over the feeding racks and over the heads of the horses.

Lennie said, "Maybe if I took this pup out and threw him away George wouldn't never know. An' then I could tend the rabbits without no trouble."

Curley's wife said angrily, "Don't you think of nothing but rabbits?"

"We gonna have a little place," Lennie explained patiently. "We gonna have a house an' a garden and a place for alfalfa, an' that alfalfa is for the rabbits, an' I take a sack and get it all fulla alfalfa and then I take it to the rabbits."

She asked, "What makes you so nuts about rabbits?"

Lennie had to think carefully before he could come to a conclusion. He moved cautiously close to her, until he was right against her. "I like to pet nice things. Once at a fair I seen some of them long-hair rabbits. An' they was nice, you bet. Sometimes I've even pet mice, but not when I could get nothing better."

Curley's wife moved away from him a little. "I think you're nuts," she said.

"No I ain't," Lennie explained earnestly. "George says I ain't. I like to pet nice things with my fingers, sof' things."

She was a little bit reassured. "Well, who don't?" she said. "Ever'-body likes that. I like to feel silk an' velvet. Do you like to feel velvet?"

Lennie chuckled with pleasure. "You bet, by God," he cried happily.

"An' I had some, too. A lady give me some, an' that lady was—my own Aunt Clara. She give it right to me—'bout this big a piece. I wisht I had that velvet right now." A frown came over his face. "I lost it," he said. "I ain't seen it for a long time."

Curley's wife laughed at him. "You're nuts," she said. "But you're a kinda nice fella. Jus' like a big baby. But a person can see kinda what you mean. When I'm doin' my hair sometimes I jus' set an' stroke it 'cause it's so soft." To show how she did it, she ran her fingers over the top of her head. "Some people got kinda coarse hair," she said complacently. "Take Curley. His hair's jus' like wire. But mine is soft and fine. 'Course I brush it a lot. That makes it fine. Here—feel right here." She took Lennie's hand and put it on her head. "Feel right aroun' there an' see how soft it is."

Lennie's big fingers fell to stroking her hair.

"Don't you muss it up," she said.

Lennie said, "Oh! That's nice," and he stroked harder. "Oh, that's nice."

"Look out, now, you'll muss it." And then she cried angrily, "You stop it now, you'll muss it all up." She jerked her head sideways, and Lennie's fingers closed on her hair and hung on. "Let go!" she cried. "You let go!"

Lennie was in a panic. His face was contorted. She screamed then, and Lennie's other hand closed over her mouth and nose. "Please don't," he begged. "Oh! Please don't do that. George'll be mad."

She struggled violently under his hands. Her feet battered on the hay and she writhed to be free; and from under Lennie's hand came a muffled screaming. Lennie began to cry with fright. "Oh! Please don't do none of that," he begged. "George gonna say I done a bad thing. He ain't gonna let me tend no rabbits." He moved his hand a little and her hoarse cry came out. Then Lennie grew angry. "Now don't," he said. "I don't want you to yell. You gonna get me in trouble jus' like George says you will. Now don't you do that." And she continued to struggle, and her eyes were wild with terror. He shook her then, and he was angry with her. "Don't you go yellin'," he said, and he shook her; and her body flopped like a fish. And then she was still, for Lennie had broken her neck.

He looked down at her, and carefully he removed his hand from over her mouth, and she lay still. "I don't want ta hurt you," he said, "but George'll be mad if you yell." When she didn't answer nor move he bent closely over her. He lifted her arm and let it drop. For a moment he seemed bewildered. And then he whispered in fright, "I done a bad thing. I done another bad thing."

He pawed up the hay until it partly covered her.

From outside the barn came a cry of men and the double clang of shoes on metal. For the first time Lennie became conscious of the outside. He crouched down in the hay and listened. "I done a real bad thing," he said. "I shouldn't of did that. George'll be mad. An' he said an' hide in the brush till he come. He's gonna be mad. In the brush till he come. Tha's what he said." Lennie went back and looked at the dead girl. The puppy lay close to her. Lennie picked it up. "I'll throw him away," he said. "It's bad enough like it is." He put the pup under his coat, and he crept to the barn wall and peered out between the cracks, toward the horseshoe game. And then he crept around the end of the last manger and disappeared.

The sun streaks were high on the wall by now, and the light was growing soft in the barn. Curley's wife lay on her back, and she was half covered with hay.

It was very quiet in the barn, and the quiet of the afternoon was on the ranch. Even the clang of the pitched shoes, even the voices of the men in the game seemed to grow more quiet. The air in the barn was dusky in advance of the outside day. A pigeon flew in through the open hay door and circled and flew out again. Around the last stall came a shepherd bitch, lean and long, with heavy, hanging dugs. Half-way to the packing box where the puppies were she caught the dead scent of Curley's wife, and the hair arose along her spine. She whimpered and cringed to the packing box, and jumped in among the puppies.

Curley's wife lay with a half-covering of yellow hay. And the meanness and the plannings and the discontent and the ache for attention were all gone from her face. She was very pretty and simple, and her face was sweet and young. Now her rouged cheeks and her reddened lips made her seem alive and sleeping very lightly. The curls, tiny little sausages, were spread on the hay behind her head, and her lips were parted.

As happens sometimes, a moment settled and hovered and remained for much more than a moment. And sound stopped and movement stopped for much, much more than a moment.

Then gradually time awakened again and moved sluggishly on. The horses stamped on the other side of the feeding racks and the halter chains clinked. Outside, the men's voices became louder and clearer.

From around the end of the last stall old Candy's voice came. "Lennie," he called. "Oh, Lennie! You in here? I been figuring some more. Tell you what we can do, Lennie." Old Candy appeared around the end of the last stall. "Oh, Lennie!" he called again; and then he stopped, and his body stiffened. He rubbed his smooth wrist on his

white stubble whiskers. "I di'n't know you was here," he said to Curley's wife.

When she didn't answer, he stepped nearer. "You oughten to sleep out here," he said disapprovingly; and then he was beside her and— "Oh, Jesus Christ!" He looked about helplessly, and he rubbed his beard. And then he jumped up and went quickly out of the barn.

But the barn was alive now. The horses stamped and snorted, and they chewed the straw of their bedding and they clashed the chains of their halters. In a moment Candy came back, and George was with him.

George said, "What was it you wanted to see me about?"

Candy pointed at Curley's wife. George stared. "What's the matter with her?" he asked. He stepped closer, and then he echoed Candy's words. "Oh, Jesus Christ!" He was down on his knees beside her. He put his hand over her heart. And finally, when he stood up, slowly and stiffly, his face was as hard and tight as wood, and his eyes were hard.

Candy said, "What done it?"

George looked coldly at him. "Ain't you got any idear?" he asked. And Candy was silent. "I should of knew," George said hopelessly. "I guess maybe way back in my head I did."

Candy asked, "What we gonna do now, George? What we gonna do now?"

George was a long time in answering. "Guess we gotta tell the guys. I guess we gotta get 'im an' lock 'im up. We can't let 'im get away. Why, the poor bastard'd starve." And he tried to reassure himself. "Maybe they'll lock 'im up an' be nice to 'im."

But Candy said excitedly, "We oughtta let 'im get away. You don't know that Curley. Curley gon'ta wanta get 'im lynched. Curley'll get 'im killed."

George watched Candy's lips. "Yeah," he said at last, "that's right, Curley will. An' the other guys will." And he looked back at Curley's wife.

Now Candy spoke his greatest fear. "You an' me can get that little place, can't we, George? You an' me can go there an' live nice, can't we, George? Can't we?"

Before George answered, Candy dropped his head and looked down at the hay. He knew.

George said softly, "—I think I knowed from the very first. I think I knowed we'd never do her. He usta like to hear about it so much I got to thinking maybe we would."

"Then—it's all off?" Candy asked sulkily.

George didn't answer his question. George said, "I'll work my month

an' I'll take my fifty bucks an' I'll stay all night in some lousy cat house. Or I'll set in some poolroom till ever'body goes home. An' then I'll come back an' work another month an' I'll have fifty bucks more."

Candy said, "He's such a nice fella. I didn' think he'd do nothing like this."

George still stared at Curley's wife. "Lennie never done it in meanness," he said. "All the time he done bad things, but he never done one of 'em mean." He straightened up and looked back at Candy. "Now listen. We gotta tell the guys. They got to bring him in, I guess. They ain't no way out. Maybe they won't hurt 'im." He said sharply, "I ain't gonna let 'em hurt Lennie. Now you listen. The guys might think I was in on it. I'm gonna go in the bunk house. Then in a minute you come out and tell the guys about her, and I'll come along and make like I never seen her. Will you do that? So the guys won't think I was in on it?"

Candy said, "Sure, George. Sure I'll do that."

"O.K. Give me a couple minutes then, and you come runnin' out an' tell like you jus' found her. I'm going now." George turned and went quickly out of the barn.

Old Candy watched him go. He looked helplessly back at Curley's wife, and gradually his sorrow and his anger grew into words. "You God damned tramp," he said viciously. "You done it, di'n't you? I s'pose you're glad. Ever'body knowed you'd mess things up. You wasn't no good. You ain't no good now, you lousy tart." He sniveled, and his voice shook. "I could of hoed in the garden and washed dishes for them guys." He paused, and then went on in a sing-song. And he repeated the old words: "If they was a circus or a baseball game we would of went to her jus' said 'ta hell with work,' an' went to her. Never ast nobody's say so. An' they'd of been a pig and chickens an' in the winter the little fat stove an' the rain comin' an' us jus' settin' there." His eyes blinded with tears and he turned and went weakly out of the barn, and he rubbed his bristly whiskers with his wrist stump.

Outside the noise of the game stopped. There was a rise of voices in question, a drum of running feet and the men burst into the barn. Slim and Carlson and young Whit and Curley, and Crooks keeping back out of attention range. Candy came after them, and last of all came George. George had put on his blue denim coat and buttoned it, and his black hat was pulled down low over his eyes. The men raced around the last stall. Their eyes found Curley's wife in the gloom, they stopped and stood still and looked.

Then Slim went quietly over to her, and he felt her wrist. One lean finger touched her cheek, and then his hand went under her slightly

twisted neck and his fingers explored her neck. When he stood up the men crowded near and the spell was broken.

Curley came suddenly to life. "I know who done it," he cried. "That big son-of-a-bitch done it. I know he done it. Why—ever'body else was out there playin' horseshoes." He worked himself into a fury. "I'm gonna get him. I'm going for my shot gun. I'll kill the big son-of-a-bitch myself. I'll shoot 'im in the guts. Come on, you guys." He ran furiously out of the barn. Carlson said, "I'll get my Luger," and he ran out too.

Slim turned quietly to George. "I guess Lennie done it, all right," he said. "Her neck's bust. Lennie coulda did that."

George didn't answer, but he nodded slowly. His hat was so far down on his forehead that his eyes were covered.

Slim went on, "Maybe like that time in Weed you was tellin' about." Again George nodded.

Slim sighed. "Well, I guess we got to get him. Where you think he might of went?"

It seemed to take George some time to free his words. "He—would of went south," he said. "We come from north so he would of went south."

"I guess we gotta get 'im," Slim repeated.

George stepped close. "Couldn' we maybe bring him in an' they'll lock him up? He's nuts, Slim. He never done this to be mean."

Slim nodded. "We might," he said. "If we could keep Curley in, we might. But Curley's gonna want to shoot 'im. Curley's still mad about his hand. An' s'pose they lock him up an' strap him down and put him in a cage. That ain't no good, George."

"I know," said George. "I know."

Carlson came running in. "The bastard's stole my Luger," he shouted. "It ain't in my bag." Curley followed him, and Curley carried a shotgun in his good hand. Curley was cold now.

"All right, you guys," he said. "The nigger's got a shotgun. You take it, Carlson. When you see 'um, don't give 'im no chance. Shoot for his guts. That'll double 'im over."

Whit said excitedly, "I ain't got a gun."

Curley said, "You go in Soledad an' get a cop. Get Al Wilts, he's deputy sheriff. Le's go now." He turned suspiciously on George. "You're comin' with us, fella."

"Yeah," said George. "I'll come. But listen, Curley. The poor bastard's nuts. Don't shoot 'im. He di'n't know what he was doin'."

"Don't shoot 'im?" Curley cried. "He got Carlson's Luger. 'Course we'll shoot 'im."

George said weakly, "Maybe Carlson lost his gun."

"I seen it this morning," said Carlson. "No, it's been took."

Slim stood looking down at Curley's wife. He said, "Curley—maybe you better stay here with your wife."

Curley's face reddened. "I'm goin'," he said. "I'm gonna shoot the guts outa that big bastard myself, even if I only got one hand. I'm gonna get 'im."

Slim turned to Candy. "You stay here with her then, Candy. The rest of us better get goin'."

They moved away. George stopped a moment beside Candy and they both looked down at the dead girl until Curley called, "You George! You stick with us so we don't think you had nothin' to do with this."

George moved slowly after them, and his feet dragged heavily.

And when they were gone, Candy squatted down in the hay and watched the face of Curley's wife. "Poor bastard," he said softly.

The sound of the men grew fainter. The barn was darkening gradually and, in their stalls, the horses shifted their feet and rattled the halter chains. Old Candy lay down in the hay and covered his eyes with his arm.

§ 6

The deep green pool of the Salinas River was still in the late afternoon. Already the sun had left the valley to go climbing up the slopes of the Gabilan mountains, and the hilltops were rosy in the sun. But by the pool among the mottled sycamores, a pleasant shade had fallen.

A water snake glided smoothly up the pool, twisting its periscope head from side to side; and it swam the length of the pool and came to the legs of a motionless heron that stood in the shallows. A silent head and beak lanced down and plucked it out by the head, and the beak swallowed the little snake while its tail waved frantically.

A far rush of wind sounded and a gust drove through the tops of the trees like a wave. The sycamore leaves turned up their silver sides, the brown, dry leaves on the ground scudded a few feet. And row on row of tiny wind waves flowed up the pool's green surface.

As quickly as it had come, the wind died, and the clearing was quiet again. The heron stood in the shallows, motionless and waiting. Another little water snake swam up the pool, turning its periscope head from side to side.

Suddenly Lennie appeared out of the brush, and he came as silently as a creeping bear moves. The heron pounded the air with its wings, jacked itself clear of the water and flew off down river. The little snake slid in among the reeds at the pool's side.

Lennie came quietly to the pool's edge. He knelt down and drank, barely touching his lips to the water. When a little bird skittered over the dry leaves behind him, his head jerked up and he strained toward the sound with eyes and ears until he saw the bird, and then he dropped his head and drank again.

When he was finished, he sat down on the bank, with his side to the pool, so that he could watch the trail's entrance. He embraced his knees and laid his chin down on his knees.

The light climbed on out of the valley, and as it went, the tops of the mountains seemed to blaze with increased brightness.

Lennie said softly, "I di'n't forget, you bet, God damn. Hide in the brush an' wait for George." He pulled his hat down low over his eyes. "George gonna give me hell," he said. "George gonna wish he was alone an' not have me botherin' him." He turned his head and looked at the bright mountain tops. "I can go right off there an' find a cave," he said. And he continued sadly, "—an' never have no ketchup—but I won't care. If George don't want me I'll go away. I'll go away."

And then from out of Lennie's head there came a little fat old woman. She wore thick bull's-eye glasses and she wore a huge gingham apron with pockets, and she was starched and clean. She stood in front of Lennie and put her hands on her hips, and she frowned disapprovingly at him.

And when she spoke, it was in Lennie's voice. "I tol' you an' tol' you," she said. "I tol' you, 'Min' George because he's such a nice fella an' good to you.' But you don't never take no care. You do bad things."

And Lennie answered her, "I tried, Aunt Clara, ma'am. I tried and tried. I couldn' help it."

"You never give a thought to George," she went on in Lennie's voice. "He been doin' nice things for you alla time. When he got a piece a pie you always got half or more'n half. An' if they was any ketchup, why he'd give it all to you."

"I know," said Lennie miserably. "I tried, Aunt Clara, ma'am. I tried and tried."

She interrupted him. "All the time he coulda had such a good time if it wasn't for you. He woulda took his pay an' raised hell in a whore house, and he coulda set in a pool room an' played snooker. But he got to take care of you."

Lennie moaned with grief. "I know, Aunt Clara, ma'am. I'll go right off in the hills an' I'll fin' a cave an' I'll live there so I won't be no more trouble to George."

"You jus' say that," she said sharply. "You're always sayin' that,

an' you know sonofabitching well you ain't never gonna do it. You'll jus' stick around an' stew the b'Jesus outa George all the time."

Lennie said, "I might jus' as well go away. George ain't gonna let me tend no rabbits now."

Aunt Clara was gone, and from out of Lennie's head there came a gigantic rabbit. It sat on its haunches in front of him, and it waggled its ears and crinkled its nose at him. And it spoke in Lennie's voice too.

"Tend rabbits," it said scornfully. "You crazy bastard. You ain't fit to lick the boots of no rabbit. You'd forget 'em and let 'em go hungry. That's what you'd do. An' then what would George think?"

"I would *not* forget," Lennie said loudly.

"The hell you wouldn'," said the rabbit. "You ain't worth a greased jack-pin to ram you into hell. Christ knows George done ever'thing he could to jack you outa the sewer, but it don't do no good. If you think George gonna let you tend rabbits, you're even crazier'n usual. He ain't. He's gonna beat hell outa you with a stick, that's what he's gonna do."

Now Lennie retorted belligerently, "He ain't neither. George won't do nothing like that. I've knew George since—I forget when— and he ain't never raised his han' to me with a stick. He's nice to me. He ain't gonna be mean."

"Well, he's sick of you," said the rabbit. "He's gonna beat hell outa you an' then go away an' leave you."

"He won't," Lennie cried frantically. "He won't do nothing like that. I know George. Me an' him travels together."

But the rabbit repeated softly over and over, "He gonna leave you, ya crazy bastard. He gonna leave ya all alone. He gonna leave ya, crazy bastard."

Lennie put his hands over his ears. "He ain't, I tell ya he ain't." And he cried, "Oh! George—George—George!"

George came quietly out of the brush and the rabbit scuttled back into Lennie's brain.

George said quietly, "What the hell you yellin' about?"

Lennie got up on his knees. "You ain't gonna leave me, are ya, George? I know you ain't."

George came stiffly near and sat down beside him. "No."

"I knowed it," Lennie cried. "You ain't that kind."

George was silent.

Lennie said, "George."

"Yeah?"

"I done another bad thing."

"It don't make no difference," George said, and he fell silent again.

Only the topmost ridges were in the sun now. The shadow in the valley was blue and soft. From the distance came the sound of men shouting to one another. George turned his head and listened to the shouts.

Lennie said, "George."

"Yeah?"

"Ain't you gonna give me hell?"

"Give ya hell?"

"Sure, like you always done before. Like, 'If I di'n't have you I'd take my fifty bucks——' "

"Jesus Christ, Lennie! You can't remember nothing that happens, but you remember ever' word I say."

"Well, ain't you gonna say it?"

George shook himself. He said woodenly, "If I was alone I could live so easy." His voice was monotonous, had no emphasis. "I could get a job an' not have no mess." He stopped.

"Go on," said Lennie. "An' when the enda the month come——"

"An' when the end of the month come I could take my fifty bucks an' go to a cat house" He stopped again.

Lennie looked eagerly at him. "Go on, George. Ain't you gonna give me no more hell?"

"No," said George.

"Well, I can go away," said Lennie. "I'll go right off in the hills an' find a cave if you don' want me."

George shook himself again. "No," he said. "I want you to stay with me here."

Lennie said craftily—"Tell me like you done before."

"Tell you what?"

" 'Bout the other guys an' about us."

George said, "Guys like us got no fambly. They make a little stake an' then they blow it in. They ain't got nobody in the worl' that gives a hoot in hell about 'em——"

"*But not us,*" Lennie cried happily. "Tell about us now."

George was quiet for a moment. "But not us," he said.

"Because——"

"Because I got you an'——"

"An' I got you. We got each other, that's what, that gives a hoot in hell about us," Lennie cried in triumph.

The little evening breeze blew over the clearing and the leaves rustled and the wind waves flowed up the green pool. And the shouts of men sounded again, this time much closer than before.

George took off his hat. He said shakily, "Take off your hat, Lennie. The air feels fine."

Lennie removed his hat dutifully and laid it on the ground in front of him. The shadow in the valley was bluer, and the evening came fast. On the wind the sound of crashing in the brush came to them.

Lennie said, "Tell how it's gonna be."

George had been listening to the distant sounds. For a moment he was business-like. "Look acrost the river, Lennie, an' I'll tell you so you can almost see it."

Lennie turned his head and looked off across the pool and up the darkening slopes of the Gabilans. "We gonna get a little place," George began. He reached in his side pocket and brought out Carlson's Luger; he snapped off the safety, and the hand and gun lay on the ground behind Lennie's back. He looked at the back of Lennie's head, at the place where the spine and skull were joined.

A man's voice called from up the river, and another man answered.

"Go on," said Lennie.

George raised the gun and his hand shook, and he dropped his hand to the ground again.

"Go on," said Lennie. "How's it gonna be. We gonna get a little place."

"We'll have a cow," said George. "An' we'll have maybe a pig an' chickens an' down the flat we'll have a little piece alfalfa——"

"For the rabbits," Lennie shouted.

"For the rabbits," George repeated.

"And I get to tend the rabbits."

"An' you get to tend the rabbits."

Lennie giggled with happiness. "An' live on the fatta the lan'."

"Yes."

Lennie turned his head.

"No, Lennie. Look down there acrost the river, like you can almost see the place."

Lennie obeyed him. George looked down at the gun.

There were crashing footsteps in the brush now. George turned and looked toward them.

"Go on, George. When we gonna do it?"

"Gonna do it soon."

"Me an' you."

"You an' me. Ever'body gonna be nice to you. Ain't gonna be no more trouble. Nobody gonna hurt nobody nor steal from 'em."

Lennie said, "I thought you was mad at me, George."

"No," said George. "No, Lennie. I ain't mad. I never been mad, an' I ain't now. That's a thing I want ya to know."

The voices came close now. George raised the gun and listened to the voices.

Lennie begged, "Le's do it now. Le's get that place now."

"Sure, right now. I gotta. We gotta."

And George raised the gun and steadied it, and he brought the muzzle of it close to the back of Lennie's head. The hand shook violently, but his face set and his hand steadied. He pulled the trigger. The crash of the shot rolled up the hills and rolled down again. Lennie jarred, and then settled slowly forward to the sand, and he lay without quivering.

George shivered and looked at the gun, and then he threw it from him, back up on the bank, near the pile of old ashes.

The brush seemed filled with cries and with the sound of running feet. Slim's voice shouted, "George. Where you at, George?"

But George sat stiffly on the bank and looked at his right hand that had thrown the gun away. The group burst into the clearing, and Curley was ahead. He saw Lennie lying on the sand. "Got him, by God." He went over and looked down at Lennie, and then he looked back at George. "Right in the back of the head," he said softly.

Slim came directly to George and sat down beside him, sat very close to him. "Never you mind," said Slim. "A guy got to sometimes."

But Carlson was standing over George. "How'd you do it?" he asked.

"I just done it," George said tiredly.

"Did he have my gun?"

"Yeah. He had your gun."

"An' you got it away from him and you took it an' you killed him?"

"Yeah. Tha's how." George's voice was almost a whisper. He looked steadily at his right hand that had held the gun.

Slim twitched George's elbow. "Come on, George. Me an' you'll go in an' get a drink."

George let himself he helped to his feet. "Yeah, a drink."

Slim said, "You hadda, George. I swear you hadda. Come on with me." He led George into the entrance of the trail and up toward the highway.

Curley and Carlson looked after them. And Carlson said, "Now what the hell ya suppose is eatin' them two guys?"

A Sentimental Journey through France and Italy

LAURENCE STERNE

Laurence Sterne *was born in Clonmel, Ireland, on November 24, 1713. He was educated for the church at Jesus College, Cambridge, where his reading of Locke's "Essay concerning Human Understanding" had much to do with the formation of his own style. He married Elizabeth Lumley in 1741 and up to his forty-sixth year had spent most of his married life in York as a prebendary of York Cathedral and vicar of Sutton. A Sentimental Journey was published in February 1768, a month before the author's death. Sterne himself saw the first edition through the press, to which there were 281 subscribers. The novel measures 46,000 words.*

INTRODUCTION

A Sentimental Journey should be read in the setting it deserves. Unless the reader knows how and why it was written he may miss the essence of what is actually one of the most teasing and affectionate books ever written in English.

In our time there is no telling what profession Laurence Sterne would have embraced. It is my private guess that he would have been a free-lance writer or a university professor—if the university was remarkable for its latitude—but in the eighteenth century, which was more openly tolerant in matters of behavior than we are today, Sterne was a minister. In his graver moments he was a man of God and a preacher of ability, as his volumes of sermons bear witness; in his sunnier moods he was as impulsive and witty a man as ever lived in the British Isles, and it is in this aspect that he comes down to us today.

Thin, with aquiline features, his pallor—for tuberculosis had threatened him ever since he was an undergraduate—set off by his black clothes, his eyes gleaming as he launched on one of his inimitable stories or gazing at you as in the Gainsborough portrait, in that quiet, searching way which unlocked a woman's heart, Laurence Sterne was at once a grace and a torment to the cloth. Family influence had destined him for a place in the Church of England, and in it during his middle years he found a livelihood and a security which he could never have earned as a writer. The problem was to keep him within bounds. "He went to the limit," says Dr Wilbur L. Cross in his magnificent biography, "that is, as far as he could without being unfrocked."

Sterne's marriage was not a happy one, nor were his duties all-absorbing. In his early forties he took sides in a squabble which involved the dignitaries of the cathedral. He wrote a pamphlet lampooning the whole affair, and, while it made people laugh, its ridicule stung the archbishop. To save the author, his friends bought up and burned

every copy of it they could lay their hands on. The humorist was now hot in rebellion and in this mood he settled down to write his much more outrageous novel, *Tristram Shandy*. That manuscript escaped to London where it could not be suppressed, and the fame which it brought Parson Yorick after its publication was his best defense. He was lionized in London and in Bath; he made a triumphant tour to Paris and Rome, and back home in York the church found discretion to be the better part of valor.

But Sterne's constitution, as Dr Cross rightly says, was not strong enough to play the part of a social lion. Everywhere he went the notables flocked to see him, and he was confronted with invitations a fortnight deep. Even when he retired to his Yorkshire parsonage, renamed Shandy Hall, there were distractions. He must, the picture comes from Dr. Cross, chaperon a lady or two over to Scarborough, preach as a celebrity in the cathedral on Sunday . . . sup late at night or race chariots in the morning along the hard sands by the sea. Sterne knew that this was living under the sentence of death: hemorrhages threatened him with an increasing severity, and thus it was inevitable that the hard humor of *Tristram Shandy* should in the next book give way to something closer to the heart.

For years Sterne had been indulging in flirtations—"in love," he said, "with one princess or another almost all my life." Like Dean Swift before him, he found delight and consolation in literary endearments. *A Sentimental Journey* is the direct result of the last flirtation he had time for. In the winter of his fifty-third year Sterne, despite his ill health, was enjoying as much as he could of London society. At the home of his loyal friend Mrs James he met a Mrs Elizabeth Draper, newly arrived from Bombay. Mrs Draper was twenty-six with, as Sterne first thought, "the air and simper of fine ladies bent upon conquest." But when he discovered that she was married to a man twenty years her senior, a man with neither affection nor imagination, Yorick's heart was touched. Sterne and Mrs Draper were soon inseparable, and this time he took the flirtation more seriously. He had Eliza's portrait painted by Cosway, the famous miniaturist, and it went with him everywhere as a token of the woman who might one day be his wife. At last the time had come for a clean break with Mrs Sterne, who had lately been residing in France. When Eliza returned to India it was with the understanding that they would keep intimate journals, "mutual testimonies which would be acknowledged on the happy day of their reunion." Sterne was literally prostrated after Eliza's departure and not for some weeks could he be shipped home to Shandy Hall, "a bale of cadaverous goods consigned to Pluto and Company," as he put it.

Back in his beloved Yorkshire, however, he took a tenuous new lease on life. Fortified by ass's milk, which was his main staple after a hemorrhage, he wrote at his desk or puttered about the place, planning such alterations as he would make for Eliza's coming to Shandy Hall. All of this he wrote down in his journal under the spell of an enchantment which made him believe implicitly in the future, and out of this journal, out of his ceaseless longing for Eliza came the impulse to write *A Sentimental Journey*.

You may ask what license I have to call this book a novel. *A Sentimental Journey through France and Italy* runs the full title, which sounds much more like a travel book. We know that Sterne had earlier been antagonized by a travel book which Smollett had written about those same countries and that ever since then he had had the determination to do a better job himself. Then unforeseen circumstances intervened—his meeting with Mrs Draper and that "hypnotism," as Dr Cross calls it, which arose from his flirtation and which allowed him a few more golden months of life in which to project himself and Eliza into the future. To my way of thinking, *A Sentimental Journey* can be more easily defended as an autobiographic novel than as a work of travel. Laurence Sterne himself is the hero, and Eliza Draper the heroine, whether you see her as the beautiful Fleming, the Grisette or the *fille de chambre*. Instead of a plot, instead of a central situation, you accept that series of dramatic portraits, "ebbing and flowing with the author's emotions"—the Franciscan, the master of the hotel, Monsieur Dessein, the servant La Fleur, the dwarf and, from first to last, that sensitive and capricious first person singular, Yorick himself.

Madame Saurd, watching the effect of *A Sentimental Journey* upon Sterne's contemporaries who read it in France, put her finger unerringly upon the particular beauty of this short volume. "Sterne's merit," she wrote, "lies in his having caught a thousand impressions, a thousand fleeting emotions which pass through the heart or the imagination of a sensitive man, and in having rendered them all in piquant phrase and image. He enlarges the human heart by portraying his own sensations. . . ."

A SENTIMENTAL JOURNEY THROUGH
FRANCE AND ITALY

THEY ORDER, said I, this matter better in France—
You have been in France? said my gentleman, turning quick upon me with the most civil triumph in the world.—Strange! quoth I, debating the matter with myself, That one and twenty miles sailing, for 'tis absolutely no further from Dover to Calais, should give a man these rights—I'll look into them: so giving up the argument—I went straight to my lodgings, put up half a dozen shirts and a black pair of silk breeches—"the coat I have on," said I, looking at the sleeve, "will do"—took a place in the Dover stage; and the packet sailing at nine the next morning—by three I had got sat down to my dinner upon a fricasseed chicken, so incontestably in France, that had I died that night of an indigestion, the whole world could not have suspended the effects of the *Droits d'aubaine**—my shirts, and black pair of silk breeches—portmanteau and all must have gone to the King of France—even the little picture which I have so long worn, and so often have told thee, Eliza, I would carry with me into my grave, would have been torn from my neck.—Ungenerous!—to seize upon the wreck of an unwary passenger, whom your subjects had beckon'd to their coast—by heaven! SIRE, it is not well done; and much does it grieve me, 'tis the monarch of a people so civilized and courteous, and so renowned for sentiment and fine feelings, that I have to reason with—
But I have scarce set foot in your dominions—

Calais

When I had finis'd my dinner, and drank the King of France's health, to satisfy my mind that I bore him no spleen, but, on the

*All the effects of strangers (Swiss and Scotch excepted) dying in France, are seized by virtue of this law, though the heir be upon the spot—the profit of these contingencies being farmed, there is no redress.

contrary, high honour for the humanity of his temper—I rose up an inch taller for the accommodation.

—No—said I—the Bourbon is by no means a cruel race: they may be misled like other people; but there is a mildness in their blood. As I acknowledged this, I felt a suffusion of a finer kind upon my cheek—more warm and friendly to man, than what Burgundy (at least of two livres a bottle, which was such as I had been drinking) could have produced.

—Just God! said I, kicking my portmanteau aside, what is there in this world's goods which should sharpen our spirits, and make so many kind-hearted brethren of us fall out so cruelly as we do by the way?

When a man is at peace with man, how much lighter than a feather is the heaviest of metals in his hand! he pulls out his purse, and holding it airily and uncompress'd, looks round him, as if he sought for an object to share it with.—In doing this, I felt every vessel in my frame dilate—the arteries beat all cheerily together, and every power which sustained life, performed it with so little friction, that 'twould have confounded the most *physical précieuse* in France: with all her materialism, she could scarce have called me a machine—

I'm confident, said I to myself, I should have overset her creed.

The accession of that idea carried nature, at that time, as high as she could go—I was at peace with the world before, and this finish'd the treaty with myself—

Now, was I a King of France, cried I—what a moment for an orphan to have begg'd his father's portmanteau of me!

The Monk—Calais

I had scarce uttered the words, when a poor monk of the order of St. Francis came into the room to beg something for his convent. No man cares to have his virtues the sport of contingencies—or one man may be generous, as another man is puissant—*sed non quo ad hanc*—or be it as it may—for there is no regular reasoning upon the ebbs and flows of our humours; they may depend upon the same causes, for aught I know, which influence the tides themselves—'twould oft be no discredit to us, to suppose it was so: I'm sure at least for myself, that in many a case I should be more highly satisfied, to have it said by the world, "I had had an affair with the moon, in which there was neither sin nor shame," than have it pass altogether as my own act and deed, wherein there was so much of both.

—But be this as it may. The moment I cast my eyes upon him,

I was predetermined not to give him a single sous; and accordingly I put my purse into my pocket—button'd it up—set myself a little more upon my centre, and advanced up gravely to him: there was something, I fear, forbidding in my look: I have his figure this moment before my eyes, and think there was that in it which deserved better.

The monk, as I judged from the break in his tonsure, a few scatter'd white hairs upon his temples being all that remained of it, might be about seventy—but from his eyes, and that sort of fire which was in them, which seemed more temper'd by courtesy than years, could be no more than sixty—Truth might lie between—He was certainly sixty-five; and the general air of his countenance, notwithstanding something seem'd to have been planting wrinkles in it before their time, agreed to the account.

It was one of those heads which Guido has often painted—mild, pale—penetrating, free from all common-place ideas of fat contented ignorance looking downwards upon the earth—it look'd forwards; but look'd at something beyond this world. How one of his order came by it, heaven above, who let it fall upon a monk's shoulders, best knows; but it would have suited a Bramin, and had I met it upon the plains of Indostan, I had reverenced it.

The rest of his outline may be given in a few strokes; one might put it into the hands of any one to design, for 'twas neither elegant or otherwise, but as character and expression made it so: it was a thin, spare form, something above the common size, if it lost not the distinction by a bend forward in the figure—but it was the attitude of Entreaty; and as it now stands presented to my imagination, it gain'd more than it lost by it.

When he had entered the room three paces, he stood still; and laying his left hand upon his breast (a slender white staff with which he journey'd being in his right)—when I had got close up to him, he introduced himself with the little story of the wants of his convent, and the poverty of his order—and did it with so simple a grace—and such an air of deprecation was there in the whole cast of his look and figure —I was bewitch'd not to have been struck with it—

—A better reason was, I had predetermined not to give him a single sous.

The Monk—Calais

'Tis very true, said I, replying to a cast upwards with his eyes, with which he had concluded his address—'tis very true—and heaven be their resource who have no other but the charity of the world, the stock

of which, I fear, is no way sufficient for the many *great claims* which are hourly made upon it.

As I pronounced the words *great claims,* he gave a slight glance with his eye downwards upon the sleeve of his tunic—I felt the full force of the appeal—I acknowledge it, said I—a coarse habit, and that but once in three years, with meagre diet—are no great matters; and the true point of pity is, as they can be earn'd in the world with so little industry, that your orders should wish to procure them by pressing upon a fund which is the property of the lame, the blind, the aged, and the infirm—the captive who lies down counting over and over again the days of his afflictions, languishes also for his share of it; and had you been of the *order of mercy,* instead of the order of St. Francis, poor as I am, continued I, pointing at my portmanteau, full cheerfully should it have been open'd to you, for the ransom of the unfortunate—The monk made me a bow—but of all others resumed I, the unfortunate of our own country, surely, have the first rights; I have left thousands in distress upon our own shore—The monk gave a cordial wave with his head—as much as to say, No doubt, there is misery enough in every corner of the world, as well as within our convent—But we distinguish, said I, laying my hand upon the sleeve of his tunic, in return for his appeal—we distinguish, my good father! betwixt those who wish only to eat the bread of their own labour—and those who eat the bread of other people's, and have no other plan in life, but to get through it in sloth and ignorance, *for the love of God.*

The poor Franciscan made no reply: a hectic of a moment pass'd across his cheek, but could not tarry—Nature seemed to have done with her resentments in him; he shewed none—but letting his staff fall within his arm, he press'd both his hands with resignation upon his breast, and retired.

The Monk—Calais

My heart smote me the moment he shut the door—Psha! said I, with an air of carelessness, three several times—but it would not do: every ungracious syllable I had utter'd, crowded back into my imagination: I reflected, I had no right over the poor Franciscan, but to deny him; and that the punishment of that was enough to the disappointed, without the addition of unkind language—I considered his grey hairs—his courteous figure seem'd to re-enter and gently ask me what injury he had done me?—and why I could use him thus?— I would have given twenty livres for an advocate—I have behaved

very ill, said I within myself; but I have only just set out upon my travels; and shall learn better manners as I get along.

The Desobligeant—Calais

When a man is discontented with himself, it has one advantage however, that it puts him into an excellent frame of mind for making a bargain. Now there being no travelling through France and Italy without a chaise—and nature generally prompting us to the thing we are fittest for, I walk'd out into the coach-yard to buy or hire something of that kind to my purpose: an old Desobligeant* in the furthest corner of the court hit my fancy at first sight, so I instantly got into it, and finding it in tolerable harmony with my feelings, I ordered the waiter to call Monsieur Dessein, the master of the hôtel— but Monsieur Dessein being gone to vespers, and not caring to face the Franciscan, whom I saw on the opposite side of the court, in conference with a lady just arrived at the inn—I drew the taffeta curtain betwixt us, and being determined to write my journey, I took out my pen and ink, and wrote the preface to it in the *Desobligeant.*

Preface—In the Desobligeant

It must have been observed by many a peripatetic philosopher, That nature has set up by her own unquestionable authority certain boundaries and fences to circumscribe the discontent of man: she has effected her purpose in the quietest and easiest manner, by laying him under almost insuperable obligations to work out his ease, and to sustain his suffering at home. It is there only that she has provided him with the most suitable objects to partake of his happiness, and bear a part of that burthen, which, in all countries and ages, has ever been too heavy for one pair of shoulders. 'Tis true, we are endued with an imperfect power of spreading our happiness sometimes beyond *her* limits, but 'tis so ordered, that from the want of languages, connections, and dependencies, and from the difference in educations, customs, and habits, we lie under so many impediments in communicating our sensations out of our own sphere, as often amount to a total impossibility.

It will always follow from hence, that the balance of sentimental commerce is always against the expatriated adventurer: he must buy

*A Chaise, so called in France, from its holding but one person.

what he has little occasion for, at their own price—his conversation will seldom be taken in exchange for theirs without a large discount— and this, by the bye, eternally driving him into the hands of more equitable brokers, for such conversation as he can find, it requires no great spirit of divination to guess at his party—

This brings me to my point; and naturally leads me (if the see-saw of this *Desobligeant* will but let me get on) into the efficient as well as final causes of travelling—

Your idle people that leave their native country, and go abroad for some reason or reasons which may be derived from one of these general causes—

Infirmity of body,
Imbecility of the mind, or
Inevitable necessity.

The two first include all those who travel by land or by water, labouring with pride, curiosity, vanity, or spleen, subdivided and combined *in infinitum.*

The third class includes the whole army of peregrine martyrs; more especially those travellers who set out upon their travels with the benefit of the clergy, either as delinquents travelling under the direction of governors recommended by the magistrate—or young gentlemen transported by the cruelty of parents and guardians, and travelling under the direction of governors recommended by Oxford, Aberdeen, and Glasgow.

There is a fourth class, but their number is so small, that they would not deserve a distinction, was it not necessary in a work of this nature to observe the greatest precision and nicety, to avoid a confusion of character. And these men I speak of, are such as cross the seas and sojourn in a land of strangers, with a view of saving money for various reasons and upon various pretences: but as they might also save themselves and others a great deal of unnecessary trouble by saving their money at home—and as their reasons for travelling are the least complex of any other species of emigrants, I shall distinguish these gentlemen by the name of

Simple Travellers.

Thus the whole circle of travellers may be reduced to the following *heads:*

Idle Travellers,
Inquisitive Travellers,
Lying Travellers,
Proud Travellers,

Vain Travellers,
Splenetic Travellers.

Then follow

The Travellers of Necessity,
The delinquent and felonious Traveller,
The unfortunate and innocent Traveller,
The simple Traveller.

And last of all (if you please) The Sentimental Traveller (meaning thereby myself), who have travell'd, and of which I am now sitting down to give an account—as much out of *Necessity,* and the *besoin de Voyager,* as any one in the class.

I am well aware, at the same time, as both my travels and observations will be altogether of a different cast from any of my fore-runners; that I might have insisted upon a whole nitch entirely to myself —but I should break in upon the confines of the *Vain* Traveller, in wishing to draw attention towards me, till I have some better grounds for it, than the mere *Novelty of my Vehicle.* It is sufficient for my reader, if he has been a Traveller himself, that with study and reflection hereupon he may be able to determine his own place and rank in the catalogue—it will be one step towards knowing himself, as it is great odds but he retains some tincture and resemblance of what he imbibed or carried out, to the present hour.

The man who first transplanted the grape of Burgundy to the Cape of Good Hope (observe he was a Dutchman) never dreamt of drinking the same wine at the Cape, that the same grape produced upon the French mountains—he was too phlegmatic for that—but undoubtedly he expected to drink some sort of vinous liquor; but whether good, bad, or indifferent—he knew enough of this world to know, that it did not depend upon his choice, but that what is generally called *chance* was to decide his success: however, he hoped for the best: and in these hopes, by an intemperate confidence in the fortitude of his head, and the depth of his discretion, *Mynheer* might possibly overset both in his new vineyard; and by discovering his nakedness, become a laughing-stock to his people.

Even so it fares with the poor Traveller, sailing and posting through the politer kingdoms of the globe, in pursuit of knowledge and improvements.

Knowledge and improvements are to be got by sailing and posting for that purpose; but whether useful knowledge and real improvements, is all a lottery—and even where the adventurer is successful, the acquired stock must be used with caution and sobriety, to turn to any profit—but as the chances run prodigiously the other way,

both as to the acquisition and application, I am of opinion, That a man would act as wisely, if he could prevail upon himself to live contented without foreign knowledge or foreign improvements, especially if he lives in a country that has no absolute want of either—and indeed, much grief of heart has it oft and many a time cost me, when I have observed how many a foul step the inquisitive Traveller has measured to see sights and look into discoveries; all which, as Sancho Pança said to Don Quixote, they might have seen dry-shod at home. It is an age so full of light, that there is scarce a country or corner of Europe, whose beams are not crossed and interchanged with others— Knowledge in most of its branches, and in most affairs, is like music in an Italian street, whereof those may partake, who pay nothing— But there is no nation under heaven—and GOD is my record (before whose tribunal I must one day come and give an account of this work) —that I do not speak it vauntingly—But there is no nation under heaven abounding with more variety of learning—where the sciences may be more fitly woo'd, or more surely won, than here—where art is encouraged, and will soon rise high—where Nature (take her altogether) has so little to answer for—and, to close all, where there is more wit and variety of character to feed the mind with—Where then, my dear countrymen, are you going—

—We are only looking at this chaise, said they—Your most obedient servant, said I, skipping out of it, and pulling off my hat—We were wondering, said one of them, who, I found, was an *inquisitive Traveller,*—what could occasion its motion.—'Twas the agitation, said I coolly, of writing a preface.—I never heard, said the other, who was a *simple Traveller,* of a preface wrote in a *Desobligeant.*—It would have been better, said I, in a *Vis à Vis.*

As an Englishman does not travel to see Englishmen, I retired to my room.

Calais

I perceived that something darken'd the passage more than myself, as I stepp'd along it to my room; it was effectually Mons. Dessein, the master of the hôtel, who had just returned from vespers, and, with his hat under his arm, was most complaisantly following me, to put me in mind of my wants. I had wrote myself pretty well out of conceit with the *Desobligeant;* and Mons. Dessein speaking of it, with a shrug, as if it would no way suit me, it immediately struck my fancy that it belong'd to some *innocent Traveller,* who, on his return home, had left it to Mons. Dessein's honour to make the most of. Four months had elapsed since it had finished its career of Europe

in the corner of Mons. Dessein's coach-yard; and having sallied out from thence but a vampt-up business at the first, though it had been twice taken to pieces on Mount Sennis, it had not profited much by its adventures—but by none so little as the standing so many months unpitied in the corner of Mons. Dessein's coach-yard. Much indeed was not to be said for it—but something might—and when a few words will rescue misery out of her distress, I hate the man who can be a churl of them.

—Now was I the master of this hôtel, said I, laying the point of my fore-finger on Mons. Dessein's breast, I would inevitably make a point of getting rid of this unfortunate *Desobligeant*—it stands swinging reproaches at you every time you pass by it—

Mon Dieu! said Mons. Dessein—I have no interest—Except the interest, said I, which men of a certain turn of mind take, Mons. Dessein, in their own sensations—I'm persuaded, to a man who feels for others as well as for himself, every rainy night, disguise it as you will, must cast a damp upon your spirits—You suffer, Mons. Dessein, as much as the machine—

I have always observed, when there is as much *sour* as *sweet* in a compliment, that an Englishman is eternally at a loss within himself, whether to take it or let it alone: a Frenchman never is: Mons. Dessein made me a bow.

C'est bien vrai, said he—But in this case I should only exchange one disquietude for another, and with loss: figure to yourself, my dear Sir, that in giving you a chaise which would fall to pieces before you had got half way to Paris—figure to yourself how much I should suffer, in giving an ill impression of myself to a man of honour, and lying at the mercy, as I must do, *d' un homme d' esprit.*

The dose was made up exactly after my own prescription; so I could not help taking it—and returning Mons. Dessein his bow, without more casuistry we walk'd together towards his Remise, to take a view of his magazine of chaises.

In the Street—Calais

It must needs be a hostile kind of a world, when the buyer (if it be but of a sorry post-chaise) cannot go forth with the seller thereof into the street, to terminate the difference betwixt them, but he instantly falls into the same frame of mind, and views his conventionist with the same sort of eye, as if he was going along with him to Hyde-park-corner to fight a duel. For my own part, being but a poor swordsman, and no way a match for Monsieur *Dessein,* I felt the rotation of all the movements within me, to which the situation is incident—I looked at

Monsieur *Dessein* through and through—eyed him as he walk'd along in profile—then, *en face*—thought he look'd like a Jew—then a Turk —disliked his wig—cursed him by my gods—wished him at the devil—

—And is all this to be lighted up in the heart for a beggarly account of three or four louis d'ors, which is the most I can be over-reach'd in? —Base passion! said I, turning myself about, as a man naturally does upon a sudden reverse of sentiment—base ungentle passion! thy hand is against every man, and every man's hand against thee— Heaven forbid! said she, raising her hand up to her forehead, for I had turned full in front upon the lady whom I had seen in conference with the monk—she had followed us unperceived—Heaven forbid, indeed! said I, offering her my own—she had a black pair of silk gloves, open only at the thumb and two fore-fingers, so accepted it without reserve—and I led her up to the door of the Remise.

Monsieur *Dessein* had *diabled* the key above fifty times, before he found out he had come with a wrong one in his hand: we were as impatient as himself to have it open'd; and so attentive to the obstacle, that I continued holding her hand almost without knowing it: so that Monsieur *Dessein* left us together, with her hand in mine, and with our faces turned towards the door of the Remise, and said he would be back in five minutes.

Now a colloquy of five minutes, in such a situation, is worth one of as many ages with your faces turned towards the street: in the latter case, 'tis drawn from the objects and occurrences without—when your eyes are fixed upon a dead blank—you draw purely from yourselves. A silence of a single moment upon Mons. *Dessein's* leaving us, had been fatal to the situation—she had infallibly turned about—so I began the conversation instantly—

—But what were the temptations (as I write not to apologise for the weaknesses of my heart in this tour,—but to give an account of them)—shall be described with the same simplicity, with which I felt them.

The Remise Door—Calais

When I told the reader that I did not care to get out of the *Desobligeant*, because I saw the monk in close conference with a lady just arrived at the inn—I told him the whole truth; for I was full as much restrained by the appearance and figure of the lady he was talking to. Suspicion crossed my brain, and said, he was telling her what had passed, something jarred upon it within me—I wished him at his convent.

When the heart flies out before the understanding, it saves the

judgment a world of pains—I was certain she was of a better order of beings—however, I thought no more of her, but went on and wrote my preface.

The impression returned upon my encounter with her in the street; a guarded frankness with which she gave me her hand, shewed, I thought, her good education and her good sense; and as I led her on, I felt a pleasurable ductility about her, which spread a calmness over all my spirits—

—Good God! how a man might lead such a creature as this round the world with him!

I had not yet seen her face—'twas not material; for the drawing was instantly set about, and long before we had got to the door of the Remise, *Fancy* had finish'd the whole head, and pleased herself as much with its fitting goddess, as if she had dived into the TIBER for it —but thou art a seduced, and a seducing slut; and albeit thou cheatest us seven times a day with thy pictures and images, yet with so many charms dost thou do it, and thou deckest out thy pictures in the shapes of so many angels of light, 'tis a shame to break with thee.

When we had got to the door of the Remise, she withdrew her hand from across her forehead, and let me see the original—it was a face of about six and twenty—of a clear transparent brown, simply set off without rouge or powder—it was not critically handsome, but there was that in it, which, in the frame of mind I was in, attached me much more to it—it was interesting; I fancied it wore the characters of a widow'd look, and in that state of its declension, which had passed the two first paroxysms of sorrow, and was quietly beginning to recon- cile itself to its loss—but a thousand other distresses might have traced the same lines; I wish'd to know what they had been—and was ready to enquire (had the same *bon ton* of conversation permitted, as in the days of Esdras)—"*What aileth thee? and why art thou disquieted? and why is thy understanding troubled?*"—In a word, I felt benevo- lence for her; and resolv'd some way or other to throw in my mite of courtesy—if not of service.

Such were my temptations—and in this disposition to give way to them, was I left alone with the lady with her hand in mine, and with our faces both turned closer to the door of the Remise than what was absolutely necessary.

The Remise Door—Calais

This certainly, fair lady! said I, raising her hand up a little lightly as I began, must be one of Fortune's whimsical doings: to take two

utter strangers by their hands—of different sexes, and perhaps from different corners of the globe, and in one moment place them together in such a cordial situation as Friendship herself could scarce have achieved for them, had she projected it for a month—

—And your reflection upon it, shews how much, Monsieur, she has embarrassed you by the adventure—

When the situation is what we would wish, nothing is so ill-timed as to hint at the circumstances which make it so: you thank Fortune, continued she—you had reason—the heart knew it, and was satisfied; and who but an English philosopher would have sent notice of it to the brain to reverse the judgment?

In saying this she disengaged her hand with a look which I thought a sufficient commentary upon the text.

It is a miserable picture which I am going to give of the weakness of my heart, by owning that it suffered a pain, which worthier occasions could not have inflicted—I was mortified with the loss of her hand, and the manner in which I had lost it carried neither oil nor wine to the wound: I never felt the pain of a sheepish inferiority so miserable in my life.

The triumphs of a true feminine heart are short upon these discomfitures. In a very few seconds she laid her hand upon the cuff of my coat, in order to finish her reply; so some way or other, God knows how, I regained my situation.

—She had nothing to add.

I forthwith began to model a different conversation for the lady, thinking from the spirit as well as moral of this, that I had been mistaken in her character; but upon turning her face towards me, the spirit which had animated the reply was fled—the muscles relaxed, and I beheld the same unprotected look of distress which first won me to her interest—melancholy! to see such sprightliness the prey of sorrow—I pitied her from my soul; and though it may seem ridiculous enough to a torpid heart—I could have taken her into my arms, and cherished her, though it was in the open street, without blushing.

The pulsations of the arteries along my fingers pressing across hers, told her what was passing within me: she looked down—a silence of some moments followed.

I fear, in this interval, I must have made some slight efforts towards a closer compression of her hand, from a subtle sensation I felt in the palm of my own—not as if she was going to withdraw hers—but as if she thought about it—and I had infallibly lost it a second time, had not instinct more than reason directed me to the last resource in these dangers—to hold it loosely and in a manner as if I was every moment going to release it, of myself; so she let it continue, till

Monsieur *Dessein* returned with the key; and in the mean time I set myself to consider how I should undo the ill impressions which the poor monk's story, in case he had told it her, must have planted in her breast against me.

The Snuff-Box—Calais

The good old monk was within six paces of us, as the idea of him cross'd my mind; and was advancing towards us a little out of the line, as if uncertain whether he should break in upon us or no—He stopp'd, however, as soon as he came up to us, with a world of frankness: and having a horn snuff-box in his hand, he presented it open to me—You shall taste mine—said I, pulling out my box (which was a small tortoise one) and putting it into his hand—'Tis most excellent, said the monk; Then do me the favour, I replied, to accept of the box and all, and when you take a pinch out of it, sometimes recollect it was the peace-offering of a man who once used you unkindly, but not from his heart.

The poor monk blush'd as red as scarlet. *Mon Dieu!* said he, pressing his hands together—you never used me unkindly.—I should think, said the lady, he is not likely. I blush'd in my turn; but from what movements I leave to the few who feel to analyse—Excuse me, Madame, replied I—I treated him most unkindly; and from no provocations. 'Tis impossible, said the lady—My God! cried the monk, with a warmth of asseveration which seem'd not to belong to him—the fault was in me, and in the indiscretion of my zeal—The lady opposed it, and I joined with her in maintaining it was impossible, that a spirit so regulated as his, could give offence to any.

I knew not that contention could be rendered so sweet and pleasurable a thing to the nerves as I then felt it.—We remained silent without any sensation of that foolish pain which takes place, when in such a circle you look for ten minutes in one another's faces without saying a word. Whilst this lasted, the monk rubb'd his horn box upon the sleeve of his tunick; and as soon as it had acquired a little air of brightness by the friction—he made a low bow, and said, 'twas too late to say whether it was the weakness or goodness of our tempers which had involved us in this contest—but be it as it would—he begg'd we might exchange boxes—In saying this, he presented his to me with one hand, as he took mine from me in the other; and having kissed it—with a stream of good-nature in his eyes he put it into his bosom—and took his leave.

I guard this box, as I would the instrumental parts of my religion,

to help my mind on to something better: in truth, I seldom go abroad without it: and oft and many a time have I called up by it the courteous spirit of its owner to regulate my own, in the justlings of the world; they had found full employment for his, as I learnt from his story, till about the forty-fifth year of his age, when upon some military services ill requited, and meeting at the same time with a disappointment in the tenderest of passions, he abandoned the sword and the sex together, and took sanctuary, not so much in his convent as in himself.

I feel a damp upon my spirits, as I am going to add, that in my last return through Calais, upon inquiring after Father Lorenzo, I heard he had been dead near three months, and was buried, not in his convent, but, according to his desire, in a little cemetery belonging to it, about two leagues off: I had a strong desire to see where they had laid him—when upon pulling out his little horn box, as I sat by his grave, and plucking up a nettle or two at the head of it, which had no business to grow there, they all struck together so forcibly upon my affections, that I burst into a flood of tears—but I am as weak as a woman; and I beg the world not to smile, but pity me.

The Remise Door—Calais

I had never quitted the lady's hand all this time; and had held it so long, that it would have been indecent to have let it go, without first pressing it to my lips: the blood and spirits, which had suffered a revulsion from her, crowded back to her, as I did it.

Now the two travellers, who had spoke to me in the coach-yard, happened at that crisis to be passing by, and observing our communications, naturally took it into their heads that we must be *man and wife,* at least; so stopping as soon as they came up to the door of the Remise, the one of them, who was the inquisitive Traveller, ask'd us, if we set out for Paris the next morning?—I could only answer for myself, I said; and the lady added, she was for Amiens—We dined there yesterday, said the simple Traveller—You go directly through the town, added the other, in your road to Paris. I was going to return a thousand thanks for the intelligence, *that Amiens was in the road to Paris;* but upon pulling out my poor monk's little horn box to take a pinch of snuff, I made them a quiet bow, and wished them a good passage to Dover—they left us alone—

—Now where would be the harm, said I to myself, if I was to beg of this distressed lady to accept of half of my chaise?—and what mighty mischief could ensue?

Every dirty passion, and bad propensity in my nature, took the alarm, as I stated the proposition—It will oblige you to have a third horse, said AVARICE, which will put twenty livres out of your pocket— You know not what she is, said CAUTION—or what scrapes the affair may draw you into, whispered COWARDICE—

Depend upon it, Yorick! said DISCRETION, 'twill be said you went off with a mistress, and came by assignation to Calais for that purpose.

—You can never after, cried HYPOCRISY aloud, shew your face in the world—or rise, quoth MEANNESS, in the church—or be any thing in it, said PRIDE, but a lousy prebendary.

But 'tis a civil thing, said I—and as I generally act from the first impulse, and therefore seldom listen to these cabals, which serve no purpose, that I know of, but to encompass the heart with adamant— I turn'd instantly about to the lady—

—But she had glided off unperceived, as the cause was pleading, and had made ten or a dozen paces down the street, by the time I had made the determination; so I set off after her with a long stride, to make her the proposal with the best address I was master of; but observing she walk'd with her cheek half resting upon the palm of her hand—with the slow, short-measur'd step of thoughtfulness, and with her eyes, as she went step by step, fixed upon the ground, it struck me, she was trying the same cause herself. God help her! said I, she has some mother-in-law, or tartufish aunt, or nonsensical old woman, to consult upon the occasion, as well as myself: so not caring to interrupt the processe, and deeming it more gallant to take her at discretion than surprise, I faced about, and took a short turn or two before the door of the Remise, whilst she walk'd musing on one side.

In the Street—Calais

Having, on the first sight of the lady, settled the affair in my fancy, "that she was of the better order of beings"—and then laid it down as a second axiom, as indisputable as the first, that she was a widow, and wore a character of distress—I went no further; I got ground enough for the situation which pleased me—and had she remained close beside my elbow till midnight, I should have held true to my system, and considered her only under that general idea.

She had scarce got twenty paces distant from me, ere something within me called out for a more particular inquiry—it brought on the idea of a further separation—I might possibly never see her more— the heart is for saving what it can; and I wanted the traces through which my wishes might find their way to her, in case I should never

rejoin her myself: in a word, I wish'd to know her name—her family's—her condition; and as I knew the place to which she was going, I wanted to know from whence she came: but there was no coming at all this intelligence: a hundred little delicacies stood in the way. I form'd a score different plans—There was no such thing as a man's asking her directly—the thing was impossible.

A little French *débonnaire* captain, who came dancing down the street, shewed me, it was the easiest thing in the world; for popping in betwixt us, just as the lady was returning back to the door of the Remise, he introduced himself to my acquaintance, and before he had well got announced, begg'd I would do him the honour to present him to the lady—I had not been presented myself—so turning about to her, he did it just as well by asking her, if she had come from Paris? No, she was going that route, she said.—*Vous n'êtes pas de Londres?*—She was not, she replied.—Then Madame must have come through Flanders—*Apparemment vous êtes Flammande?* said the French captain—The lady answered, she was—*Peut-être de Lisle?* added he—She said, she was not of Lisle.—Nor Arras?—nor Cambray?—nor Ghent?—nor Brussels? She answered, she was of Brussels.

He had had the honour, he said, to be at the bombardment of it last war—that it was finely situated, *pour cela*—and full of noblesse when the Imperialists were driven out by the French (the lady made a slight curtsy)—so giving her an account of the affair, and of the share he had had in it—he begg'd the honour to know her name—so made his bow.

Et Madame a son Mari? said he, looking back when he had made two steps—and without staying for an answer—danced down the street.

Had I served seven years' apprenticeship to good breeding, I could not have done as much.

The Remise—Calais

As the little French captain left us, Mons. Dessein came up with the key of the Remise in his hand, and forthwith let us into his magazine of chaises.

The first object which caught my eye, as Mons. Dessein open'd the door of the Remise, was another old tatter'd *Desobligeant:* and notwithstanding it was the exact picture of that which had hit my fancy so much in the coach-yard but an hour before—the very sight of it stirr'd up a disagreeable sensation within me now; and I thought 'twas a churlish beast into whose heart the idea could first enter,

to construct such a machine; nor had I much more charity for the man who could think of using it.

I observed the lady was as little taken with it as myself: so Mons. Dessein led us on to a couple of chaises which stood abreast, telling us, as he recommended them, that they had been purchased by my Lord A. and B. to go the *grand tour,* but had gone no further than Paris, so were in all respects as good—as new—They were too good—so I pass'd on to a third, which stood behind, and forthwith began to chaffer for the price. But 'twill scarce hold two, said I, opening the door and getting in—Have the goodness, Madam, said Mons. Dessein, offering his arm, to step in—The lady hesitated half a second, and stepp'd in; and the waiter that moment beckoning to speak to Mons. Dessein, he shut the door of the chaise upon us, and left us.

The Remise—Calais

C'est bien comique, 'tis very droll, said the lady smiling, from the reflection that this was the second time we had been left together by a parcel of nonsensical contingencies—*c'est bien comique,* said she—

—There wants nothing, said I, to make it so, but the comic use which the gallantry of a Frenchman would put it to—to make love the first moment, and an offer of his person the second.

'Tis their *fort,* replied the lady.

It is supposed so at least—and how it has come to pass, continued I, I know not: but they have certainly got the credit of understanding more of love, and making it better than any other nation upon earth; but for my own part, I think them arrant bunglers, and in truth the worst set of marksmen that ever tried Cupid's patience.

—To think of making love by *sentiments!*

I should as soon think of making a genteel suit of cloaths out of remnants:—and to do it—pop—at first sight by declaration—is submitting the offer and themselves with it, to be sifted with all their *pours* and *contres,* by an unheated mind.

The lady attended as if she expected I should go on.

Consider then, madam, continued I, laying my hand upon hers—

That grave people hate Love for the name's sake—

That selfish people hate it for their own—

Hypocrites for heaven's—

And that all of us, both old and young, being ten times worse frighten'd than hurt by the very *report*—

—What a want of knowledge in this branch of commerce a man

betrays, who ever lets the word come out of his lips, till an hour or two at least after the time, that his silence upon it becomes tormenting. A course of small, quiet attentions, not so pointed as to alarm—nor so vague as to be misunderstood—with now and then a look of kindness, and little or nothing said upon it—leaves nature for your mistress, and she fashions it to her mind—

Then I solemnly declare, said the lady, blushing—you have been making love to me all this while.

The Remise—Calais

Monsieur Dessein came back to let us out of the chaise, and acquaint the lady, Count de L——, her brother, was just arrived at the hôtel. Though I had infinite good-will for the lady, I cannot say, that I rejoiced in my heart at the event—and could not help telling her so— for it is fatal to a proposal, Madam, said I, that I was going to make to you—

You need not tell me what the proposal was, said she, laying her hand upon both mine, as she interrupted me.—A man, my good Sir, has seldom an offer of kindness to make to a woman, but she has a presentiment of it some moments before—

Nature arms her with it, said I, for immediate preservation—But I think, said she, looking in my face, I had no evil to apprehend—and to deal frankly with you, had determined to accept it.—If I had— (she stopped a moment)—I believe your good-will would have drawn a story from me, which would have made pity the only dangerous thing in the journey.

In saying this, she suffered me to kiss her hand twice, and with a look of sensibility mixed with a concern, she got out of the chaise—and bid adieu.

In the Street—Calais

I never finished a twelve-guinea bargain so expeditiously in my life: my time seemed heavy upon the loss of the lady, and knowing every moment of it would be as two, till I put myself into motion—I ordered post-horses directly, and walked towards the hôtel.

Lord! said I, hearing the town-clock strike four, and recollecting that I had been little more than a single hour in Calais—

What a large volume of adventures may be grasped within this little span of life, by him who interests his heart in every thing, and who, having eyes to see what time and chance are perpetually holding

out to him as he journeyeth on his way, misses nothing he can *fairly* lay his hands on.—

—If this won't turn out something—another will—no matter—'tis an assay upon human nature—I get my labour for my pains—'tis enough—the pleasure of the experiment has kept my senses and the best part of my blood awake, and laid the gross to sleep.

I pity the man who can travel from *Dan* to *Beersheba,* and cry, 'Tis all barren—and so it is; and so is all the world to him, who will not cultivate the fruits it offers. I declare, said I, clapping my hands cheerily together, that was I in a desert, I would find out wherewith in it to call forth my affections—If I could not do better, I would fasten them upon some sweet myrtle, or seek some melancholy cypress to connect myself to—I would court their shade, and greet them kindly for their protection—I would cut my name upon them, and swear they were the loveliest trees throughout the desert: if their leaves wither'd, I would teach myself to mourn, and when they rejoiced, I would rejoice along with them.

The learned SMELFUNGUS travelled from Boulogne to Paris—from Paris to Rome—and so on—but he set out with the spleen and jaundice, and every object he pass'd by was discoloured or distorted—He wrote an account of them, but 'twas nothing but the account of his miserable feelings.

I met Smelfungus in the grand portico of the pantheon—he was just coming out of it—*'Tis nothing but a huge cockpit,** said he—I wish you had said nothing worse of the Venus of Medicis, replied I—for in passing through Florence, I had heard he had fallen foul upon the goddess, and used her worse than a common strumpet, without the least provocation in nature.

I popp'd upon Smelfungus again at Turin, in his return home; and a sad tale of sorrowful adventures he had to tell, "wherein he spoke of moving accidents by flood and field, and of the cannibals which each other eat: the Anthropophagi"—he had been flay'd alive, and bedevil'd, and used worse than St. Bartholomew, at every stage he had come at—

—I'll tell it, cried Smelfungus, to the world. You had better tell it, said I, to your physician.

Mundungus, with an immense fortune, made the whole tour; going on from Rome to Naples—from Naples to Venice—from Venice to Vienna—to Dresden, to Berlin, without one generous connection or pleasurable anecdote to tell of; but he had travell'd straight on, looking neither to his right hand or his left lest Love or Pity should seduce him out of his road.

*Vide S[mollett]'s Travels.

Peace be to them! if it is to be found; but heaven itself, was it possible to get there with such tempers, would want objects to give it —every gentle spirit would come flying upon the wings of Love to hail their arrival—Nothing would the souls of Smelfungus and Mundungus hear of, but fresh anthems of joy, fresh raptures of love, and fresh congratulations of their common felicity—I heartily pity them: they have brought up no faculties for this work; and was the happiest mansion in heaven to be allotted to Smelfungus and Mundungus, they would be so far from being happy, that the souls of Smelfungus and Mundungus would do penance there to all eternity.

Montriul

I had once lost my portmanteau from behind my chaise, and twice got out in the rain, and one of the times up to the knees in dirt, to help the postillion to tie it on, without being able to find out what was wanting—Nor was it till I got to Montriul, upon the landlord's asking me if I wanted not a servant, that it occurred to me, that that was the very thing.

A servant! That I do most sadly, quoth I—Because, Monsieur, said the landlord, there is a clever young fellow, who would be very proud of the honour to serve an Englishman.—But why an English one, more than any other?—They are so generous, said the landlord—I'll be shot if this is not a livre out of my pocket, quoth I to myself, this very night—But they have wherewithal to be so, Monsieur, added he— Set down one livre more for that, quoth I—It was but last night, said the landlord, *qu'un my Lord Anglois presentoit un ecu à la fille de chambre—Tant pis, pour Mademoiselle Janatone,* said I.

Now Janatone being the landlord's daughter, and the landlord supposing I was young in French, took the liberty to inform me, I should not have said *tant pis*—but, *tant mieux. Tant mieux, toujours, Monsieur,* said he, when there is any thing to be got—*tant pis,* when there is nothing. It comes to the same thing, said I. *Pardonnez moi,* said the landlord.

I cannot take a fitter opportunity to observe once for all, that *tant pis* and *tant mieux* being two of the great hinges in French conversation, a stranger would do well to set himself right in the use of them, before he gets to Paris.

A prompt French Marquis at our ambassador's table demanded of Mr. H——, if he was H—— the poet? No, said H—— mildly— *Tant pis,* replied the Marquis.

It is H—— the historian, said another—*Tant mieux,* said the

Marquis. And Mr. H——, who is a man of an excellent heart, return'd thanks for both.

When the landlord had set me right in this matter, he called in La Fleur, which was the name of the young man he had spoke of—saying only first, That as for his talents, he would presume to say nothing—Monsieur was the best judge what would suit him; but for the fidelity of La Fleur, he would stand responsible in all he was worth.

The landlord deliver'd this in a manner which instantly set my mind to the business I was upon—and La Fleur, who stood waiting without, in that breathless expectation which every son of nature of us have felt in our turns, came in.

Montriul

I am apt to be taken with all kinds of people at first sight; but never more so, than when a poor devil comes to offer his service to so poor a devil as myself; and as I know this weakness, I always suffer my judgment to draw back something on that very account—and this more or less, according to the mood I am in, and the case—and I may add the gender too of the person I am to govern.

When La Fleur entered the room, after every discount I could make for my soul, the genuine look and air of the fellow determined the matter at once in his favour; so I hired him first—and then began to enquire what he could do: But I shall find out his talents, quoth I, as I want them—besides, a Frenchman can do every thing.

Now poor La Fleur could do nothing in the world but beat a drum, and play a march or two upon the fife. I was determined to make his talents do: and can't say my weakness was ever so insulted by my wisdom, as in the attempt.

La Fleur had set out early in life, as gallantly as most Frenchmen do, with *serving* for a few years: at the end of which, having satisfied the sentiment, and found moreover, That the honour of beating a drum was likely to be its own reward, as it open'd no further track of glory to him—he retired *à ses terres,* and lived *comme il plaisoit à Dieu*—that is to say, upon nothing.

—And so, quoth *Wisdom,* you have hired a drummer to attend you in this tour of yours through France and Italy! Psha! said I, and do not one half of our gentry go with a humdrum *compagnon du voyage* the same round, and have the piper and the devil and all to pay besides? When a man can extricate himself with an *equivoque* in such an unequal match—he is not ill off—But you can do something

else, La Fleur? said I—*O qu'oui!*—he could make spatterdashes, and play a little upon the fiddle—Bravo! said Wisdom—Why I play a bass myself, said I—we shall do very well. You can shave, and dress a wig a little, La Fleur?—He had all the dispositions in the world— It is enough for heaven! said I, interrupting him—and ought to be enough for me—So supper coming in, and having a frisky English spaniel on one side of my chair, and a French valet, with as much hilarity in his countenance as ever nature painted in one, on the other —I was satisfied to my heart's content with my empire; and if monarchs knew what they would be at, they might be satisfied as I was.

Montriul

As La Fleur went the whole tour of France and Italy with me, and will be often upon the stage, I must interest the reader a little further in his behalf, by saying, that I had never less reason to repent of the impulses which generally do determine me, than in regard to this fellow—he was a faithful, affectionate, simple soul as ever trudged after the heels of a philosopher; and notwithstanding his talents of drum-beating and spatterdash-making, which, though very good in themselves, happened to be of no great service to me, yet was I hourly recompensed by the festivity of his temper—it supplied all defects—I had a constant resource in his looks, in all difficulties and distresses of my own—I was going to have added, of his too; but La Fleur was out of the reach of every thing; for whether it was hunger or thirst, or cold or nakedness, or watchings, or whatever stripes of ill luck La Fleur met with in our journeyings, there was no index in his physiognomy to point them out by—he was eternally the same; so that if I am a piece of a philosopher, which Satan now and then puts into my head I am—it always mortifies the pride of the conceit, by reflecting how much I owe to the complexional philosophy of this poor fellow, for shaming me into one of a better kind. With all this, La Fleur had a small cast of the coxcomb—but he seemed at first sight to be more a coxcomb of nature than of art; and before I had been three days in Paris with him—he seemed to be no coxcomb at all.

Montriul

The next morning, La Fleur entering upon his employment, I delivered to him the key of my portmanteau, with an inventory of my

half a dozen shirts and silk pair of breeches; and bid him fasten all upon the chaise—get the horses put to—and desire the landlord to come in with his bill.

C' est un garçon de bonne fortune, said the landlord, pointing through the window to half a dozen wenches who had got round about La Fleur, and were most kindly taking their leave of him, as the postillion was leading out the horses. La Fleur kissed all their hands round and round again, and thrice he wiped his eyes, and thrice he promised he would bring them all pardons from Rome.

The young fellow, said the landlord, is beloved by all the town, and there is scarce a corner in Montriul, where the want of him will not be felt: he has but one misfortune in the world, continued he, "He is always in love."—I am heartily glad of it, said I—'twill save me the trouble every night of putting my breeches under my head. In saying this, I was making not so much La Fleur's eloge, as my own, having been in love, with one princess or other, almost all my life, and I hope I shall go on so till I die, being firmly persuaded, that if ever I do a mean action, it must be in some interval betwixt one passion and another: whilst this interregnum lasts, I always perceive my heart locked up—I can scarce find in it to give Misery a sixpence; and therefore I always get out of it as fast as I can, and the moment I am rekindled, I am all generosity and good-will again; and would do any thing in the world, either for or with any one, if they will but satisfy me there is no sin in it.

—But in saying this—sure I am commending the passion—not myself.

A Fragment

The town of Abdera, notwithstanding Democritus lived there, trying all the powers of irony and laughter to reclaim it, was the vilest and most profligate town in all Thrace. What for poisons, conspiracies, and assassinations—libels, pasquinades, and tumults, there was no going there by day—'twas worse by night.

Now, when things were at the worst, it came to pass, that the Andromeda of Euripides being represented at Abdera, the whole orchestra was delighted with it: but of all the passages which delighted them, nothing operated more upon their imaginations, than the tender strokes of nature, which the poet had wrought up in that pathetic speech of Perseus, *O Cupid, prince of God and men* &c. Every man almost spoke pure iambics the next day, and talk'd of nothing but Perseus his pathetic address—"O Cupid, prince of God and men"— in every street of Abdera, in every house—"O Cupid! Cupid!"—in

every mouth, like the natural notes of some sweet melody which drops from it whether it will or no—nothing but "Cupid! Cupid! prince of God and men"—The fire caught—and the whole city, like the heart of one man, open'd itself to Love.

No pharmacopolist could sell one grain of helebore—not a single armourer had a heart to forge one instrument of death—Friendship and Virtue met together, and kiss'd each other in the street—the golden age returned, and hung over the town of Abdera—every Abderite took his oaten pipe, and every Abderitish woman left her purple web, and chastely sat her down and listened to the song—

'Twas only in the power, says the Fragment, of the God whose empire extendeth from heaven to earth, and even to the depths of the sea, to have done this.

Montriul

When all is ready, and every article is disputed and paid for in the inn, unless you are a little sour'd by the adventure, there is always a matter to compound at the door, before you can get into your chaise, and that is with the sons and daughters of poverty, who surround you. Let no man say, "let them go to the devil"—'tis a cruel journey to send a few miserables, and they have had sufferings enow without it: I always think it better to take a few sous out in my hand; and I would counsel every gentle traveller to do so likewise; he need not be so exact in setting down his motives for giving them—They will be register'd elsewhere.

For my own part, there is no man gives so little as I do; for few, that I know, have so little to give: but as this was the first public act of my charity in France, I took the more notice of it.

A well-a-way! said I, I have but eight sous in the world, shewing them in my hand, and there are eight poor men and eight poor women for 'em.

A poor tatter'd soul, without a shirt on, instantly withdrew his claim, by retiring two steps out of the circle, and making a disqualifying bow on his part. Had the whole parterre cried out, *Place aux dames,* with one voice, it would not have conveyed the sentiment of a deference for the sex with half the effect.

Just Heaven! for what wise reasons hast thou ordered it, that beggary and urbanity, which are at such variance in other countries, should find a way to be at unity in this?

—I insisted upon presenting him with a single sous, merely for his *politesse.*

A poor little dwarfish, brisk fellow, who stood over-against me in

the circle, putting something first under his arm, which had once been a hat, took his snuff-box out of his pocket, and generously offer'd a pinch on both sides of him: it was a gift of consequence, and modestly declined—The poor little fellow press'd it upon them with a nod of welcomeness—*Prenez en—prenez*, said he, looking another way; so they each took a pinch—Pity thy box should ever want one, said I to myself; so I put a couple of sous into it—taking a small pinch out of his box, to enhance their value, as I did it.—He felt the weight of the second obligation more than of the first—'twas doing him an honour—the other was only doing him a charity—and he made me a bow down to the ground for it.

—Here! said I to an old soldier with one hand, who had been campaign'd and worn out to death in the service—here's a couple of sous for thee. *Vive le Roi!* said the old soldier.

I had then but three sous left: so I gave one, simply *pour l'amour de Dieu*, which was the footing on which it was begg'd—The poor woman had a dislocated hip; so it could not be well upon any other motive.

Mon cher et tres charitable Monsieur—There's no opposing this, said I.

My Lord Anglois—the very sound was worth the money—so I gave *my last sous* for it. But in the eagerness of giving, I had overlooked a *pauvre honteux*, who had no one to ask a sous for him, and who, I believed, would have perished ere he could have ask'd one for himself: he stood by the chaise, a little without the circle, and wiped a tear from a face which I thought had seen better days—Good God! said I—and I have not one single sous left to give him—But you have a thousand! cried all the powers of nature, stirring within me—so I gave him—no matter what—I am ashamed to say *how much*, now—and was ashamed to think how little, then; so if the reader can form any conjecture of my disposition, as these two fixed points are given him, he may judge within a livre or two what was the precise sum.

I could afford nothing for the rest, but *Dieu vous benisse—Et le bon Dieu vous benisse encore*—said the old soldier, the dwarf, &c. The *pauvre honteux* could say nothing—he pull'd out a little handkerchief, and wiped his face as he turned away—and I thought he thanked me more than them all.

The Bidet

Having settled all these little matters, I got into my post-chaise with more ease than ever I got into a post-chaise in my life; and La Fleur

having got one large jack-boot on the far side of a little *bidet*,* and
another on this (for I count nothing of his legs)—he canter'd away
before me as happy and as perpendicular as a prince—

—But what is happiness! what is grandeur in this painted scene
of life! A dead ass, before we had got a league, put a sudden stop to
La Fleur's career—his bidet would not pass by it—a contention arose
betwixt them, and the poor fellow was kick'd out of his jack-boots the
very first kick.

La Fleur bore his fall like a French christian, saying neither more
or less upon it, than, Diable! so presently got up and came to the
charge again astride his bidet, beating him up to it as he would have
beat his drum.

The bidet flew from one side of the road to the other, then back
again—then this way—then that way, and in short every way but by
the dead ass—La Fleur insisted upon the thing—and the bidet threw
him.

What's the matter, La Fleur, said I, with this bidet of thine?—
Monsieur, said he, *c'est un cheval le plus opiniatre du monde*—Nay,
if he is a conceited beast, he must go his own way, replied I—so La
Fleur got off him, and giving him a good sound lash, the bidet took
me at my word, and away he scamper'd back to Montriul—*Peste!* said
La Fleur.

It is not *mal-à-propos* to take notice here, that though La Fleur
availed himself but of two different terms of exclamation in this
encounter—namely, *Diable!* and *Peste!* that there are nevertheless
three, in the French language; like the positive, comparative, and
superlative, one or the other of which serve for every unexpected
throw of the dice in life.

Le Diable! which is the first, and positive degree, is generally used
upon ordinary emotions of the mind, where small things only fall out
contrary to your expectations—such as—the throwing once doublets—
La Fleur's being kick'd off his horse, and so forth—Cuckoldom, for
the same reason, is always—*Le Diable!*

But in cases where the cast has something provoking in it, as in
that of the bidet's running away after, and leaving La Fleur aground
in jack-boots—'tis the second degree.

'Tis then *Peste!*

And for the third—

—But here my heart is wrung with pity and fellow-feeling, when
I reflect what miseries must have been their lot, and how bitterly
so refined a people must have smarted, to have forced them upon
the use of it—

*Post horse.

Grant me, O ye powers which touch the tongue with eloquence in distress!—whatever is my *cast,* grant me but decent words to exclaim in, and I will give my nature way.

—But as these were not to be had in France, I resolved to take every evil just as it befel me without any exclamation at all.

La Fleur, who had made no such covenant with himself, followed the bidet with his eyes till it was got out of sight—and then, you may imagine, if you please, with what word he closed the whole affair.

As there was no hunting down a frighten'd horse in jack-boots, there remained no alternative but taking La Fleur either behind the chaise, or into it—

I preferred the latter, and in half an hour we got to the post-house at Nampont.

Nampont—The Dead Ass

And this, said he, putting the remains of a crust into his wallet— and this, should have been thy portion, said he, hadst thou been alive to have shared it with me.—I thought by the accent, it had been an apostrophe to his child; but 'twas to his ass, and to the very ass we had seen dead in the road, which had occasioned La Fleur's misadventure. The man seemed to lament it much; and it instantly brought into my mind Sancho's lamentation for his; but he did it with more true touches of nature.

The mourner was sitting upon a stone-bench at the door, with the ass's pannel and its bridle on one side, which he took up from time to time—then laid them down—look'd at them and shook his head. He then took his crust of bread out of his wallet again, as if to eat it; held it some time in his hand—then laid it upon the bit of his ass's bridle—looked wistfully at the little arrangement he had made—and then gave a sigh.

The simplicity of his grief drew numbers about him, and La Fleur amongst the rest, whilst the horses were getting ready; as I continued sitting in the post-chaise, I could see and hear over their heads.

—He said he had come last from Spain, where he had been from the furthest borders of Franconia; and had got so far on his return home, when his ass died. Every one seemed desirous to know what business could have taken so old and poor a man so far a journey from his own home.

It had pleased Heaven, he said, to bless him with three sons, the finest lads in all Germany; but having in one week lost two of the

eldest of them by the small-pox, and the youngest falling ill of the same distemper, he was afraid of being bereft of them all; and made a vow, if Heaven would not take him from him also, he would go in gratitude to St Iago in Spain.

When the mourner got thus far on his story, he stopp'd to pay nature his tribute—and wept bitterly.

He said, Heaven had accepted the conditions, and that he had set out from his cottage with this poor creature, who had been a patient partner of his journey—that it had eat the same bread with him all the way, and was unto him as a friend.

Every body who stood about, heard the poor fellow with concern— La Fleur offered him money—The mourner said, he did not want it —it was not the value of the ass—but the loss of him—The ass, he said, he was assured loved him—and upon this told them a long story of a mischance upon their passage over the Pyrenean mountains which had separated them from each other three days; during which time the ass had sought him as much as he had sought the ass, and that they had neither scarce eat or drank till they met.

Thou hast one comfort, friend, said I, at least in the loss of thy poor beast; I'm sure thou hast been a merciful master to him.—Alas! said the mourner, I thought so, when he was alive—but now that he is dead I think otherwise.—I fear the weight of myself and my afflictions together have been too much for him—they have shortened the poor creature's days, and I fear I have them to answer for.—Shame on the world! said I to myself—Did we love each other, as this poor soul but loved his ass—'twould be something.—

Nampont—The Postillion

The concern which the poor fellow's story threw me into required some attention: the postillion paid not the least to it, but set off upon the *pavé* in a full gallop.

The thirstiest soul in the most sandy desert of Arabia could not have wished more for a cup of cold water, than mine did for grave and quiet movements; and I should have had an high opinion of the postillion, had he but stolen off with me in something like a pensive pace—On the contrary, as the mourner finished his lamentation, the fellow gave an unfeeling lash to each of his beasts, and set off clattering like a thousand devils.

I called to him as loud as I could, for heaven's sake to go slower— and the louder I called, the more unmercifully he galloped—The duce take him and his galloping too—said I—he'll go on tearing my nerves

to pieces till he has worked me into a foolish passion, and then he'll go slow, that I may enjoy the sweets of it.

The postillion managed the point to a miracle: by the time he had got to the foot of a steep hill about half a league from Nampont, —he had put me out of temper with him—and then with myself, for being so.

My case then required a different treatment; and a good rattling gallop would have been of real service to me—

Then, prithee, get on—get on, my good lad, said I.

The postillion pointed to the hill—I then tried to return back to the story of the poor German and his ass—but I had broke the clue—and could no more get into it again, than the postillion could into a trot.

—The duce go, said I, with it all! Here am I sitting as candidly disposed to make the best of the worst, as ever wight was, and all runs counter.

There is one sweet lenitive at least for evils, which Nature holds out to us: so I took it kindly at her hands, and fell asleep; and the first word which roused me was *Amiens*.

Bless me! said I, rubbing my eyes—this is the very town where my poor lady is to come.

Amiens

The words were scarce out of my mouth, when the count de L——'s post-chaise, with his sister in it, drove hastily by: she had just time to make me a bow of recognition—and of that particular kind of it, which told me she had not yet done with me. She was as good as her look; for, before I had quite finished my supper, her brother's servant came into the room with a billet, in which she said she had taken the liberty to charge me with a letter, which I was to present myself to Madame R—— the first morning I had nothing to do at Paris. There was only added, she was sorry, but from what *penchant* she had not considered, that she had been prevented telling me her story—that she still owed it me; and if my route should ever lay through Brussels, and I had not by then forgot the name of Madame de L—— —that Madame de L—— would be glad to discharge her obligation.

Then I will meet thee, said I, fair spirit! at Brussels—'tis only returning from Italy through Germany to Holland, by the route of Flanders, home—'twill scarce be ten posts out of my way; but were it ten thousand! with what a moral delight will it crown my journey, in sharing in the sickening incidents of a tale of misery told to me by such a sufferer! to see her weep! and though I cannot

dry up the fountain of her tears, what an exquisite sensation is there still left, in wiping them away from off the cheeks of the first and fairest of women, as I'm sitting with my handkerchief in my hand in silence the whole night beside her?

There was nothing wrong in the sentiment; and yet I instantly reproached my heart with it in the bitterest and most reprobate of expressions.

It had ever, as I told the reader, been one of the singular blessings of my life, to be almost every hour of it miserably in love with some one; and my last flame happening to be blown out by a whiff of jealousy on the sudden turn of a corner, I had lighted it up afresh at the pure taper of Eliza but about three months before—swearing as I did it, that it should last me through the whole journey—Why should I dissemble the matter? I had sworn to her eternal fidelity—she had a right to my whole heart—to divide my affections was to lessen them— to expose them, was to risk them: where there is risk, there may be loss:—and what wilt thou have, Yorick! to answer a heart so full of trust and confidence—so good, so gentle and unreproaching!

—I will not go to Brussels, replied I, interrupting myself—but my imagination went on—I recalled her looks at that crisis of our separation, when neither of us had power to say adieu! I look'd at the picture she had tied in a black ribband about my neck—and blush'd as I look'd at it—I would have given the world to have kiss'd it— but was ashamed—and shall this tender flower, said I, pressing it between my hands—shall it be smitten to its very root—and smitten, Yorick! by thee, who hast promised to shelter it in thy breast?

Eternal fountain of happiness! said I, kneeling down upon the ground—be thou my witness—and every pure spirit which tastes it, be my witness also, That I would not travel to Brussels, unless Eliza went along with me, did the road lead me towards heaven.

In transports of this kind, the heart, in spite of the understanding, will always say too much.

The Letter—Amiens

Fortune had not smiled upon La Fleur; for he had been unsuccessful in his feats of chivalry—and not one thing had offered to signalize his zeal for my service from the time he had entered into it, which was almost four-and-twenty hours. The poor soul burn'd with impatience; and the Count de L——'s servant coming with the letter, being the first practicable occasion which offered, La Fleur had laid hold of it; and in order to do honour to his master, had taken him

into a back parlour in the Auberge, and treated him with a cup or two of the best wine in Picardy; and the Count de L——'s servant in return, and not to be behind-hand in politeness with La Fleur, had taken him back with him to the Count's hotel. La Fleur's *prevenancy* (for there was a passport in his very looks) soon set every servant in the kitchen at ease with him; and as a Frenchman, whatever be his talents, has no sort of prudery in showing them, La Fleur, in less than five minutes, had pulled out his fife, and leading off the dance himself with the first note, set the *fille de chambre,* the *maitre d'hotel,* the cook, the scullion, and all the household, dogs and cats, besides an old monkey, a-dancing: I suppose there never was a merrier kitchen since the flood.

Madame de L——, in passing from her brother's apartments to her own, hearing so much jollity below stairs, rung up her *fille de chambre* to ask about it; and hearing it was the English gentleman's servant who had set the whole house merry with his pipe, she ordered him up.

As the poor fellow could not present himself empty, he had loaden'd himself in going up stairs with a thousand compliments to Madame de L——, on the part of his master—added a long apocrypha of enquiries after Madame de L——'s health—told her, that Monsieur his master was *au desespoire* for her re-establishment from the fatigues of her journey—and, to close all, that Monsieur had received the letter which Madame had done him the honour—And he has done me the honour, said Madame de L——, interrupting La Fleur, to send a billet in return.

Madame de L—— had said this with such a tone of reliance upon the fact, that La Fleur had not power to disappoint her expectations —he trembled for my honour—and possibly might not altogether be unconcerned for his own, as a man capable of being attached to a master who could be wanting *en egards vis à vis d' une femme!* so that when Madame de L—— asked La Fleur if he had brought a letter— *O qu'oui,* said La Fleur; so laying down his hat upon the ground, and taking hold of the flap of his right-side pocket with his left-hand, he began to search for the letter with his right—then contrary-wise— *Diable!*—then sought every pocket, pocket by pocket, round, not forgetting his fob—*Peste!*—then La Fleur emptied them upon the floor—pulled out a dirty cravat—a hankerchief—a comb—a whiplash—a night-cap—then gave a peep into his hat—*Quelle etourderie!* He had left the letter upon the table in the Auberge—he would run for it, and be back with it in three minutes.

I had just finished my supper when La Fleur came in to give me an account of his adventure: he told the whole story simply as it was; and only added, that if Monsieur had forgot (*par hazard*) to

answer Madame's letter, the arrangement gave him an opportunity to recover the *faux pas*—and if not, that things were only as they were.

Now I was not altogether sure of my *etiquette,* whether I ought to have wrote or no; but if I had—a devil himself could not have been angry: 'Twas but the officious zeal of a well-meaning creature for my honour; and however he might have mistook the road, or embarrassed me in so doing—his heart was in no fault—I was under no necessity to write—and what weighed more than all—he did not look as if he had done amiss.

—'Tis all very well, La Fleur, said I—'Twas sufficient. La Fleur flew out of the room like lightning, and return'd with pen, ink, and paper, in his hand; and coming up to the table, laid them close before me, with such a delight in his countenance, that I could not help taking up the pen.

I begun and begun again; and though I had nothing to say, and that nothing might have been expressed in half a dozen lines, I made half a dozen different beginnings, and could no way please myself.

In short, I was in no mood to write.

La Fleur stepp'd out and brought a little water in a glass to dilute my ink—then fetched sand and seal-wax—It was all one; I wrote, and blotted, and tore off, and burnt, and wrote again—*Le diable l'emporte,* said I half to myself—I cannot write this self-same letter; throwing the pen down despairingly as I said it.

As soon as I had cast down the pen, La Fleur advanced with the most respectful carriage up to the table, and making a thousand apologies for the liberty he was going to take, told me he had a letter in his pocket wrote by a drummer in his regiment to a corporal's wife, which, he durst say, would suit the occasion.

I had a mind to let the poor fellow have his humour—Then prithee, said I, let me see it.

La Fleur instantly pulled out a little dirty pocket book cramm'd full of small letters and billet-doux in a sad condition, and laying it upon the table, and then untying the string which held them all together, run them over one by one, till he came to the letter in question —*La voila,* said he, clapping his hands: so unfolding it first, he laid it before me, and retired three steps from the table whilst I read it.

The Letter

Madame, Je suis penetré de la douler la plus vive, et reduit en même temps au desespoir par ce retour imprevû du Corporal qui rend notre entrevue de ce soir la chose du monde la plus impossible.

Mais vive la joie! et toute la mienne sera de penser à vous.

L'amour n'est *rien* sans sentiment.

Et le sentiment est encore *moins* sans amour.

On dit qu'on ne doit jamais se desesperer.

On dit aussi que Monsieur le Corporal monte la garde Mercredi: alors ce sera mon tour.

Chacun à son tour.

En attendant—Vive l'amour! et vive la bagatelle!

Je suis, MADAME,
*Avec toutes les sentiments les
plus respectueux et les plus
tendres, tout à vous.*

JAQUES ROQUE,

It was but changing the Corporal into the Count—and saying nothing about mounting guard on Wednesday—and the letter was neither right or wrong—so to gratify the poor fellow, who stood trembling, for my honour, his own, and the honour of his letter— I took the cream gently off it, and whipping it up in my own way— I seal'd it up and sent him with it to Madame de L—— —and the next morning we pursued our journey to Paris.

Paris

When a man can contest the point by dint of equipage, and carry on all floundering before him with half a dozen lackies and a couple of cooks—'tis very well in such a place as Paris—he may drive in at which end of a street he will.

A poor prince who is weak in cavalry, and whose whole infantry does not exceed a single man, had best quit the field; and signalize himself in the cabinet, if he can get up into it—I say *up into it*— for there is no descending perpendicular amongst 'em with a *"Me voici, mes enfans"*—here I am—whatever many may think.

I own my first sensations, as soon as I was left solitary and alone in my own chamber in the hotel, were far from being so flattering as I had prefigured them. I walked up gravely to the window in my dusty black coat, and looking through the glass saw all the world in yellow, blue, and green, running at the ring of pleasure.—The old with broken lances, and in helmets which had lost their vizards— the young in armour bright which shone like gold, beplumed with each gay feather of the east—all—all—tilting at it like fascinated knights in tournaments of yore for fame and love—

Alas, poor Yorick! cried I, what art thou doing here? On the very first onset of all this glittering clatter thou art reduced to an atom—seek—seek some winding alley, with a tourniquet at the end of it, where chariot never rolled or flambeau shot its rays—there thou mayest solace thy soul in converse sweet with some kind *grisset* of a barber's wife, and get into such coteries!—

—May I perish! if I do, said I, pulling out a letter which I had to present to Madame de R——. —I'll wait upon this lady, the very first thing I do. So I called La Fleur to go seek me a barber directly —and come back and brush my coat.

The Wig—Paris

When the barber came, he absolutely refused to have any thing to do with my wig: 'twas either above or below his art: I had nothing to do, but to take one ready made of his own recommendation.

—But I fear, friend! said I, this buckle won't stand.—You may immerge it, replied he, into the ocean, and it will stand—

What a great scale is every thing upon in this city! thought I— The utmost stretch of an English periwigmaker's ideas could have gone no further than to have "dipped it into a pail of water."— What difference! 'tis like time to eternity.

I confess I do hate all cold conceptions, as I do the puny ideas which engender them; and am generally so struck with the great works of nature, that for my own part, if I could help it, I never would make a comparison less than a mountain at least. All that can be said against the French sublime in this instance of it, is this— that the grandeur is *more* in the *word;* and *less* in the *thing.* No doubt the ocean fills the mind with vast ideas; but Paris being so far inland, it was not likely I should run post a hundred miles out of it, to try the experiment—the Parisian barber meant nothing.—

The pail of water standing beside the great deep, makes certainly but a sorry figure in speech—but 'twill be said—it has one advantage —'tis in the next room, and the truth of the buckle may be tried in it without more ado, in a single moment.

In honest truth, and upon a more candid revision of the matter, *The French expression professes more than it performs.*

I think I can see the precise and distinguishing marks of national characters more in these nonsensical *minutiæ,* than in the most important matters of state; where great men of all nations talk and stalk so much alike, that I would not give ninepence to chuse amongst them.

I was so long in getting from under my barber's hands, that it was too late to think of going with my letter to Madame R—— that night: but when a man is once dressed at all points for going out, his reflections turn to little account, so taking down the name of the Hotel de Modene, where I lodged, I walked forth without any determination where to go—I shall consider of that, said I, as I walk along.

The Pulse—Paris

Hail ye small sweet courtesies of life, for smooth do ye make the road of it! like grace and beauty which beget inclinations to love at first sight: 'tis ye who open this door and let the stranger in.

—Pray, Madame, said I, have the goodness to tell me which way I must turn to go to the Opera comique:—Most willingly, Monsieur, said she, laying aside her work—

I had given a cast with my eye into half a dozen shops as I came along in search of a face not likely to be disordered by such an interruption; till at last, this hitting my fancy, I had walked in.

She was working a pair of ruffles as she sat in a low chair on the far side of the shop facing the door—

—*Tres volontiers;* most willingly, said she, laying her work down upon a chair next her, and rising up from the low chair she was sitting in, with so cheerful a movement and so cheerful a look, that had I been laying out fifty louis d'ors with her, I should have said—"This woman is grateful."

You must turn, Monsieur, said she, going with me to the door of the shop, and pointing the way down the street I was to take—you must turn first to your left hand—*mais prenez garde*—there are two turns; and be so good as to take the second—then go down a little way and you'll see a church, and when you are past it, give yourself the trouble to turn directly to the right, and that will lead you to the foot of the *Pont Neuf,* which you must cross—and there any one will do himself the pleasure to shew you—

She repeated her instructions three times over to me, with the same good-natur'd patience the third time as the first;—and if *tones and manners* have a meaning, which certainly they have, unless to hearts which shut them out—she seemed really interested, that I should not lose myself.

I will not suppose it was the woman's beauty, notwithstanding she was the handsomest Grisset, I think, I ever saw, which had much to do with the sense I had of her courtesy; only I remember, when

I told her how much I was obliged to her, that I looked very full in her eyes,—and that I repeated my thanks as often as she had done her instructions.

I had not got ten paces from the door, before I found I had forgot every tittle of what she had said—so looking back, and seeing her still standing in the door of the shop as if to look whether I went right or not—I returned back, to ask her whether the first turn was to my right or left—for that I had absolutely forgot.—Is it possible? said she, half laughing.—'Tis very possible, replied I, when a man is thinking more of a woman, than of her good advice.

As this was the real truth—she took it, as every woman takes a matter of right, with a slight courtesy.

—*Attendez,* said she, laying her hand upon my arm to detain me, whilst she called a lad out of the back-shop to get ready a parcel of gloves. I am just going to send him, said she, with a packet into that quarter, and if you will have the complaisance to step in, it will be ready in a moment, and he shall attend you to the place.— So I walk'd in with her to the far side of the shop, and taking up the ruffle in my hand which she laid upon the chair, as if I had a mind to sit, she sat down herself in her low chair, and I instantly sat myself down beside her.

—He will be ready, Monsieur, said she, in a moment—And in that moment, replied I, most willingly would I say something very civil to you for all these courtesies. Any one may do a casual act of good-nature, but a continuation of them shews it is a part of the temperature; and certainly, added I, if it is the same blood which comes from the heart, which descends to the extremes (touching her wrist), I am sure you must have one of the best pulses of any woman in the world—Feel it, said she, holding out her arm. So laying down my hat, I took hold of her fingers in one hand, and applied the two fore-fingers of my other to the artery—

—Would to heaven! my dear Eugenius, thou hadst passed by, and beheld me sitting in my black coat, and in my lack-a-day-sical manner, counting the throbs of it, one by one, with as much true devotion as if I had been watching the critical ebb or flow of her fever—How wouldst thou have laugh'd and moralized upon my new profession!—and thou shouldst have laugh'd and moralized on— Trust me, my dear Eugenius, I should have said, "there are worse occupations in this world *than feeling a woman's pulse.*"—But a Grisset's! thou wouldst have said—and in an open shop! Yorick—

—So much the better: for when my views are direct, Eugenius, I care not if all the world saw me feel it.

The Husband—Paris

I had counted twenty pulsations, and was going on fast towards the fortieth, when her husband coming unexpected from a back parlour into the shop, put me a little out of my reckoning.—'Twas nobody but her husband, she said—so I began a fresh score—Monsieur is so good, quoth she, as he pass'd by us, as to give himself the trouble of feeling my pulse—The husband took off his hat, and making me a bow, said, I did him too much honour—and having said that, he put on his hat and walk'd out.

Good God! said I to myself, as he went out—and can this man be the husband of this woman!

Let it not torment the few who know what must have been the grounds of this exclamation, if I explain it to those who do not.

In London a shopkeeper and a shopkeeper's wife seem to be one bone and one flesh: in the several endowments of mind and body, sometimes the one, sometimes the other has it, so as in general to be upon a par, and to tally with each other as nearly as a man and wife need to do.

In Paris, there are scarce two orders of beings more different: for the legislative and executive powers of the shop not resting in the husband, he seldom comes there—in some dark and dismal room behind, he sits commerceless in his thrum night-cap, the same rough son of Nature that Nature left him.

The genius of a people where nothing but the monarchy is *salique,* having ceded this department, with sundry others, totally to the women—by a continual higgling with customers of all ranks and sizes from morning to night, like so many rough pebbles shook long together in a bag, by amicable collisions, they have worn down their asperities and sharp angles, and not only become round and smooth, but will receive, some of them, a polish like a brilliant— Monsieur *le Mari* is little better than the stone under your foot—

—Surely—surely, man! it is not good for thee to sit alone—thou wast made for social intercourse and gentle greetings, and this improvement of our natures from it, I appeal to, as my evidence.

—And how does it beat, Monsieur? said she.—With all the benignity, said I, looking quietly in her eyes, that I expected—She was going to say something civil in return—but the lad came into the shop with the gloves—*A propos,* said I, I want a couple of pair myself.

The Gloves—Paris

The beautiful Grisset rose up when I said this, and going behind the counter, reach'd down a parcel and untied it: I advanced to the side over-against her: they were all too large. The beautiful Grisset measured them one by one across my hand—It wou'd not alter the dimensions—She begg'd I would try a single pair, which seemed to be the least—She held it open—my hand slipped into it at once—It will not do, said I, shaking my head a little—No, said she, doing the same thing.

There are certain combined looks of simple subtlety—where whim, and sense, and seriousness, and nonsense, are so blended, that all the languages of Babel set loose together could not express them— they are communicated and caught so instantaneously, that you can scarce say which party is the infector. I leave it to your men of words to swell pages about it—it is enough in the present to say again, the gloves would not do; so folding our hands within our arms, we both loll'd upon the counter—it was narrow, and there was just room for the parcel to lay between us.

The beautiful Grisset look'd sometimes at the gloves, then side-ways to the window, then at the gloves—and then at me. I was not disposed to break silence—I follow'd her example: so I looked at the gloves, then to the window, then at the gloves, and then at her— and so on alternately.

I found I lost considerably in every attack—she had a quick black eye, and shot through two such long and silken eye-lashes with such penetration, that she look'd into my very heart and veins—It may seem strange, but I could actually feel she did—

It is no matter, said I, taking up a couple of the pairs next me, and putting them into my pocket.

I was sensible the beautiful Grisset had not ask'd above a single livre above the price—I wish'd she had ask'd a livre more, and was puzzling my brains how to bring the matter about—Do you think, my dear Sir, said she, mistaking my embarrassment, that I could ask a *sous* too much of a stranger—and of a stranger whose politeness more than his want of gloves, has done me the honour to lay himself at my mercy?—*M'en croyez capable?*—Faith! not I, said I; and if you were, you are welcome—So counting the money into her hand, and with a lower bow than one generally makes to a shop-keeper's wife, I went out, and her lad with his parcel followed me.

The Translation—Paris

There was nobody in the box I was let into but a kindly old French officer. I love the character, not only because I honour the man whose manners are softened by a profession which makes bad men worse; but that I once knew one—for he is no more—and why should I not rescue one page from violation by writing his name in it, and telling the world it was Captain Tobias Shandy, the dearest of my flock and friends, whose philanthropy I never think of at this long distance from his death—but my eyes gush out with tears. For his sake, I have a predilection for the whole corps of veterans; and so I strode over the two back rows of benches, and placed myself beside him.

The old officer was reading attentively a small pamphlet, it might be the book of the opera, with a large pair of spectacles. As soon as I sat down, he took his spectacles off, and putting them into a shagreen case, return'd them and the book into his pocket together. I half rose up, and made him a bow.

Translate this into any civilized language in the world—the sense is this:

"Here's a poor stranger come into the box—he seems as if he knew nobody; and is never likely, was he to be seven years in Paris, if every man he comes near keeps his spectacles upon his nose—'tis shutting the door of conversation absolutely in his face—and using him worse than a German."

The French officer might as well have said it all aloud: and if he had, I should in course have put the bow I made him into French too, and told him, "I was sensible of his attention, and return'd him a thousand thanks for it."

There is not a secret so aiding to the progress of sociality, as to get master of this *short hand,* and be quick in rendering the several turns of looks and limbs, with all their inflections and delineations, into plain words. For my own part, by long habitude, I do it so mechanically, that when I walk the streets of London, I go translating all the way; and have more than once stood behind in the circle, where not three words have been said, and have brought off twenty different dialogues with me, which I could have fairly wrote down and sworn to.

I was going one evening to Martini's concert at Milan, and was just entering the door of the hall, when the Marquisina di F—— was coming out in a sort of a hurry—she was almost upon me before I

saw her; so I gave a spring to one side to let her pass—She had done the same, and on the same side too: so we ran our heads together: she instantly got to the other side to get out: I was just as unfortunate as she had been; for I had sprung to that side, and opposed her passage again—We both flew together to the other side, and then back—and so on—it was ridiculous; we both blush'd intolerably; so I did at last the thing I should have done at first— I stood stock still, and the Marquisina had no more difficulty. I had no power to go into the room, till I had made her so much reparation as to wait and follow her with my eye to the end of the passage— She look'd back twice, and walk'd along it rather sideways, as if she would make room for any one coming up stairs to pass her— No, said I—that's a vile translation: the Marquisina has a right to the best apology I can make her; and that opening is left for me to do it in—so I ran and begg'd pardon for the embarrassment I had given her, saying it was my intention to have made her way. She answered, she was guided by the same intention towards me—so we reciprocally thank'd each other. She was at the top of the stairs; and seeing no *chichesbee* near her, I begg'd to hand her to her coach —so we went down the stairs, stopping at every third step to talk of the concert and the adventure—Upon my word, Madame, said I, when I had handed her in, I made six different efforts to let you go out—And I made six different efforts, replied she, to let you enter—I wish to heaven you would make the seventh, said I—With all my heart, said she, making room—Life is too short to be long about the forms of it—so I instantly stepp'd in, and she carried me home with her—And what became of the concert, St. Cecilia, who, I suppose, was at it, knows more than I.

I will only add, that the connection which arose out of the translation, gave me more pleasure than any one I had the honour to make in Italy.

The Dwarf—Paris

I had never heard the remark made by any one in my life, except by one; and who that was will probably come out in this chapter: so that being pretty much unprepossessed, there must have been grounds for what struck me the moment I cast my eyes over the *parterre*—and that was, the unaccountable sport of nature in forming such numbers of dwarfs—No doubt she sports at certain times in almost every corner of the world; but in Paris, there is no end to her amusements—The goddess seems almost as merry as she is wise.

As I carried my idea out of the *opera comique* with me, I measured every body I saw walking in the streets by it—Melancholy application! especially where the size was extremely little—the face extremely dark—the eyes quick—the nose long—the teeth white—the jaw prominent—to see so many miserables, by force of accidents driven out of their own proper class into the very verge of another, which it gives me pain to write down—every third man a pigmy!—some by ricketty heads and hump backs—others by bandy legs—a third set arrested by the hand of Nature in the sixth and seventh years of their growth—a fourth, in their perfect and natural state, like dwarf apple-trees; from the first rudiments and stamina of their existence, never meant to grow higher.

A medical traveller might say, 'tis owing to undue bandages—a splenetic one, to want of air—and an inquisitive traveller, to fortify the system, may measure the height of their houses—the narrowness of their streets, and in how few feet square in the sixth and seventh stories such numbers of the *Bourgoisie* eat and sleep together; but I remember, Mr. Shandy the elder, who accounted for nothing like any body else, in speaking one evening of these matters, averred, that children, like other animals, might be increased almost to any size, provided they came right into the world; but the misery was, the citizens of Paris were so coop'd up, that they had not actually room enough to get them—I did not call it getting anything, said he—'tis getting nothing—Nay, continued he, rising in his argument, 'tis getting worse than nothing, when all you have got, after twenty or five-and-twenty years of the tenderest care and most nutritious aliment bestowed upon it, shall not at last be as high as my leg. Now, Mr. Shandy being very short, there could be nothing more said of it.

As this is not a work of reasoning, I leave the solution as I found it, and content myself with the truth only of the remark, which is verified in every lane and by-lane of Paris. I was walking down that which leads from the Carousal to the Palais Royal, and observing a little boy in some distress at the side of the gutter, which ran down the middle of it, I took hold of his hand, and help'd him over. Upon turning up his face to look at him after, I perceived he was about forty—Never mind, said I; some good body will do as much for me, when I am ninety.

I feel some little principles within me, which incline me to be merciful towards this poor belighted part of my species, who have neither size or strength to get on in the world.—I cannot bear to see one of them trod upon; and had scarce got seated beside my old French officer, ere the disgust was exercised, by seeing the very thing happen under the box we sat in.

At the end of the orchestra, and betwixt that and the first side-box, there is a small esplanade left, where, when the house is full, numbers of all ranks take sanctuary. Though you stand, as in the parterre, you pay the same price as in the orchestra. A poor defenceless being of this order had got thrust somehow or other into this luckless place —the night was hot, and he was surrounded by beings two feet and a half higher than himself. The dwarf suffered inexpressibly on all sides; but the thing which incommoded him most, was a tall corpulent German, near seven feet high, who stood directly betwixt him and all possibility of his seeing either the stage or the actors. The poor dwarf did all he could to get a peep at what was going forwards by seeking for some little opening betwixt the German's arm and his body, trying first one side, then the other; but the German stood square in the most unaccommodating posture that can be imagined —the dwarf might as well have been placed at the bottom of the deepest draw-well in Paris; so he civilly reach'd up his hand to the German's sleeve, and told him his distress—The German turn'd his head back, look'd down upon him as Goliath did upon David—and unfeelingly resumed his posture.

I was just then taking a pinch of snuff out of my monk's little horn box—And how would thy meek and courteous spirit, my dear monk! so temper'd to *bear and forbear!*—how sweetly would it have lent an ear to this poor soul's complaint!

The old French officer, seeing me lift up my eyes with an emotion, as I made the apostrophe, took the liberty to ask me what was the matter—I told him the story in three words, and added, how inhuman it was.

By this time the dwarf was driven to extremes, and in his first transports, which are generally unreasonable, had told the German he would cut off his long queue with his knife.—The German look'd back coolly, and told him he was welcome, if he could reach it.

An injury sharpen'd by an insult, be it to whom it will, makes every man of sentiment a party: I could have leap'd out of the box to have redressed it—The old French officer did it with much less confusion; for leaning a little over, and nodding to a centinel, and pointing at the same time with his finger at the distress—the centinel made his way to it.—There was no occasion to tell the grievance— the thing told itself; so thrusting back the German instantly with his musket—he took the poor dwarf by the hand, and placed him before him—This is noble! said I, clapping my hands together— And yet you would not permit this, said the old officer, in England.

—In England, dear Sir, said I, *we sit all at our ease.*

The old French officer would have set me at unity with myself,

in case I had been at variance,—by saying it was a *bon mot*—and as a *bon mot* is always worth something at Paris, he offered me a pinch of snuff.

The Rose—Paris

It was now my turn to ask the old French officer, "what was the matter?" for a cry of *"Haussez les mains, Monsieur l'Abbé,"* re-echoed from a dozen different parts of the parterre, was as unintelligible to me, as my apostrophe to the monk had been to him.

He told me, it was some poor Abbé in one of the upper loges, who he supposed had got planted perdu behind a couple of grissets, in order to see the opera, and that the parterre espying him, were insisting upon his holding up both his hands during the representation.—And can it be supposed, said I, that an ecclesiastic would pick the grissets' pockets? The old French officer smiled, and whispering in my ear, opened a door of knowledge which I had no idea of.

Good God! said I, turning pale with astonishment—is it possible, that a people so smit with sentiment should at the same time be so unclean, and so unlike themselves—*Quelle grossiereté!* added I.

The French officer told me it was an illiberal sarcasm at the church, which had begun in the theatre about the time the Tartuffe was given in it, by Moliere—but, like other remains of Gothic manners, was declining—Every nation, continued he, have their refinements and *grossieretés,* in which they take the lead, and lose it of one another by turns—that he had been in most countries, but never in one where he found not some delicacies, which others seemed to want. *Le* POUR *et le* CONTRE *se trouvant en chaque nation;* there is a balance, said he, of good and bad every where; and nothing but the knowing it is so, can emancipate one-half of the world from the prepossession which it holds against the other—that the advantage of travel, as it regarded the *sçavoir vivre,* was by seeing a great deal both of men and manners; it taught us mutual toleration; and mutual toleration, concluded he, making me a bow, taught us mutual love.

The old French officer delivered this with an air of such candour and good sense, as coincided with my first favourable impressions of his character—I thought I loved the man; but I fear I mistook the object—'twas my own way of thinking—the difference was, I could not have expressed it half so well.

It is alike troublesome to both the rider and his beast—if the latter goes pricking up his ears, and starting all the way at every object which he never saw before—I have as little torment of this

kind as any creature alive; and yet I honestly confess, that many a thing gave me pain, and that I blush'd at many a word the first month—which I found inconsequent and perfectly innocent the second.

Madame de Rambouliet, after an acquaintance of about six weeks with her, had done me the honour to take me in her coach about two leagues out of town.—Of all women, Madame de Rambouliet is the most correct; and I never wish to see one of more virtues and purity of heart—In our return back, Madame de Rambouliet desired me to pull the cord—I asked her if she wanted any thing—*Rien que pisser,* said Madame de Rambouliet.

Grieve not, gentle traveller, to let Madame de Rambouliet p—ss on—And, ye fair mystic nymphs! go each one *pluck your rose,* and scatter them in your path—for Madame de Rambouliet did no more —I handed Madame de Rambouliet out of the coach; and had I been the priest of the chaste CASTALIA, I could not have served at her fountain with a more respectful decorum.

The Fille de Chambre—Paris

What the old French officer had delivered upon travelling, bringing Polonius's advice to his son upon the same subject into my head— and that bringing in Hamlet; and Hamlet the rest of Shakespeare's works, I stopp'd at the Quai de Conti in my return home, to purchase the whole set.

The bookseller said he had not a set in the world—*Comment!* said I; taking one up out of a set which lay upon the counter betwixt us— He said, they were sent him only to be got bound, and were to be sent back to Versailles in the morning to the Count de B——.

—And does the Count de B——, said I, read Shakespeare? *C'est un Esprit fort,* replied the bookseller.—He loves English books; and what is more to his honour, Monsieur, he loves the English too. You speak this so civilly, said I, that it is enough to oblige an Englishman to lay out a Louis d'or or two at your shop—The bookseller made a bow, and was going to say something, when a young decent girl about twenty, who by her air and dress seemed to be *fille de chambre* to some devout woman of fashion, come into the shop and asked for *Les Egarements du Cœur & de l'Esprit:* the bookseller gave her the book directly; she pulled out a little green sattin purse run round with ribband of the same colour, and putting her finger and thumb into it, she took out the money and paid for it. As I had nothing more to stay me in the shop, we both walk'd out of the door together.

—And what have you to do, my dear, said I, with *The Wanderings of the Heart,* who scarce know yet you have one; nor, till love has first told you it, or some faithless shepherd has made it ache, canst thou ever be sure it is so.—*Le Dieu m'en garde!* said the girl.— With reason, said I—for if it is a good one, 'tis pity it should be stolen; 'tis a little treasure to thee, and gives a better air to your face, than if it was dress'd out with pearls.

The young girl listened with a submissive attention, holding her sattin purse by its ribband in her hand all the time—'Tis a very small one, said I, taking hold of the bottom of it—she held it towards me—and there is very little in it, my dear, said I; but be as good as thou art handsome, and heaven will fill it: I had a parcel of crowns in my hand to pay for Shakespeare; and as she had let go the purse entirely, I put a single one in; and tying up the ribband in a bow-knot, returned it to her.

The young girl made me more a humble courtesy than a low one— 'twas one of those quiet, thankful sinkings, where the spirit bows itself down—the body does no more than tell it. I never gave a girl a crown in my life which gave me half the pleasure.

My advice, my dear, would not have been worth a pin to you, said I, if I had not given this along with it: but now, when you see the crown, you'll remember it—so don't, my dear, lay it out in ribbands.

Upon my word, Sir, said the girl, earnestly, I am incapable—in saying which, as is usual in little bargains of honour, she gave me her hand—*En veritè, Monsieur, je mettrai cet argent apart,* said she.

When a virtuous convention is made betwixt man and woman, it sanctifies their most private walks: so notwithstanding it was dusky, yet as both our roads lay the same way, we made no scruple of walking along the Quai de Conti together.

She made me a second courtesy in setting off, and before we got twenty yards from the door, as if she had not done enough before, she made a sort of a little stop to tell me again—she thank'd me.

It was a small tribute, I told her, which I could not avoid paying to virtue, and would not be mistaken in the person I had been rendering it to for the world—but I see innocence, my dear, in your face— and foul befal the man who ever lays a snare in its way!

The girl seem'd affected some way or other with what I said—she gave a low sigh—I found I was not impowered to inquire at all after it—so said nothing more till I got to the corner of the Rue de Nevers, where we were to part.

—But is this the way, my dear, said I, to the Hotel de Modene? she told me it was—or, that I might go by the Rue de Gueneguault,

which was the next turn.—Then I'll go, my dear, by the Rue de Gueneguault, said I, for two reasons; first I shall please myself, and next I shall give you the protection of my company as far on your way as I can. The girl was sensible I was civil—and said, she wish'd the Hotel de Modene was in the Rue de St. Pierre—You live there? said I—She told me she was *fille de chambre* to *Madame R——*—Good God! said I, 'tis the very lady for whom I have brought a letter from Amiens—The girl told me that Madame R——, she believed, expected a stranger with a letter, and was impatient to see him—so I desired the girl to present my compliments to Madame R——, and say I would certainly wait upon her in the morning.

We stood still at the corner of the Rue de Nevers whilst this pass'd—We then stopped a moment whilst she disposed of her *Egarements du Cœur,* &c. more commodiously than carrying them in her hand—they were two volumes; so I held the second for her whilst she put the first into her pocket; and then she held her pocket, and I put in the other after it.

'Tis sweet to feel by what fine-spun threads our affections are drawn together.

We set off afresh, and as she took her third step, the girl put her hand within my arm—I was just bidding her—but she did it of herself, with that undeliberating simplicity, which shew'd it was out of her head that she had never seen me before. For my own part, I felt the conviction of consanguinity so strongly, that I could not help turning half round to look in her face, and see if I could trace out any thing in it of a family likeness—Tut! said I, are we not all relations?

When we arrived at the turning up of the Rue de Gueneguault, I stopp'd to bid her adieu for good and all: the girl would thank me again for my company and kindness—She bid me adieu twice—I repeated it as often; and so cordial was the parting between us, that had it happened any where else, I'm sure not but I should have signed it with a kiss of charity, as warm and holy as an apostle.

But in Paris, as none kiss each other but the men—I did, what amounted to the same thing—

—I bid God bless her.

The Passport—Paris

When I got home to my hotel, La Fleur told me I had been enquired after by the Lieutenant de Police—The duce take it! said I—I know the reason. It is time the reader should know it, for in

the order of things in which it happened, it was omitted; not that it was out of my head; but that, had I told it then, it might have been forgot now—and now is the time I want it.

I had left London with so much precipitation, that it never enter'd my mind that we were at war with France; and had reached Dover, and looked through my glass at the hills beyond Boulogne, before the idea presented itself; and with this in its train, that there was no getting there without a passport. Go but to the end of a street, I have a mortal aversion for returning back no wiser than I set out; and as this was one of the greatest efforts I had ever made for knowledge, I could less bear the thoughts of it; so hearing the Count de —— had hired the packet, I begg'd he would take me in his *suite*. The Count had some little knowl-edge of me, so made little or no difficulty—only said, his inclination to serve me could reach no farther than Calais, as he was to return by way of Brussels to Paris; however, when I had once pass'd there, I might get to Paris without interruption; but that in Paris I must make friends and shift for myself—Let me get to Paris, Monsieur le Count, said I—and I shall do very well. So I embark'd, and never thought more of the matter.

When La Fleur told me the Lieutenant de Police had been enquiring after me—the thing instantly recurred—and by the time La Fleur had well told me, the master of the hotel came into my room to tell me the same thing, with this addition to it, that my passport had been particularly asked after: the master of the hotel concluded with saying, He hoped I had one—Not I, faith! said I.

The master of the hotel retired three steps from me, as from an infected person, as I declared this—and poor La Fleur advanced three steps towards me, and with that sort of movement which a good soul makes to succour a distress'd one—the fellow won my heart by it; and from that single *trait,* I knew his character as perfectly, and could rely upon it as firmly, as if he had served me with fidelity for seven years.

Mon seigneur! cried the master of the hotel—but recollecting himself as he made the exclamation, he instantly changed the tone of it—if Monsieur, said he, has not a passport (*apparemment*) in all likelihood he has friends in Paris who can procure him one— Not that I know of, quoth I, with an air of indifference.—Then, *certes,* replied he, you'll be sent to the Bastile or the Chatelet, *au moins.* Poo! said I, the king of France is a good-natur'd soul —he'll hurt nobody.—*Cela n'empeche pas,* said he—you will cer-tainly be sent to the Bastile to-morrow morning.—But I've taken your lodgings for a month, answer'd I, and I'll not quit them a

day before the time for all the kings of France in the world. La
Fleur whispered in my ear, That nobody could oppose the king
of France.

Pardi! said my host, *ces Messieurs Anglois sont des gens tres ex-
traordinaires*—and having both said and sworn it—he went out.

The Passport—The Hotel at Paris

I could not find in my heart to torture La Fleur's with a serious
look upon the subject of my embarrassment, which was the reason
I had treated it so cavalierly; and to shew him how light it lay
upon my mind, I dropt the subject entirely; and whilst he waited
upon me at supper, talk'd to him with more than usual gaiety
about Paris, and of the opera comique.—La Fleur had been there
himself, and had followed me through the streets as far as the
bookseller's shop; but seeing me come out with the young *fille de
chambre* and that we walk'd down the Quai de Conti together,
La Fleur deem'd it unnecessary to follow me a step further—so
making his own reflections upon it, he took a shorter cut—and
got to the hotel in time to be inform'd of the affair of the police
against my arrival.

As soon as the honest creature had taken away, and gone down
to sup himself, I then began to think a little seriously about my
situation.—

—And here, I know, Eugenius, thou wilt smile at the remem-
brance of a short dialogue which pass'd betwixt us the moment I
was going to set out—I must tell it here.

Eugenius, knowing that I was as little subject to be overburthen'd
with money as thought, had drawn me aside to interrogate me how
much I had taken care for; upon telling him the exact sum,
Eugenius shook his head, and said it would not do; so pull'd out
his purse in order to empty it into mine.—I've enough in con-
science, Eugenius, said I.—Indeed, Yorick, you have not, replied
Eugenius—I know France and Italy better than you—But you
don't consider, Eugenius, said I, refusing his offer, that before I
have been three days in Paris, I shall take care to say or do some-
thing or other for which I shall get clapp'd up into the Bastile,
and that I shall live there a couple of months entirely at the king
of France's expence. I beg pardon, said Eugenius, drily: really
I had forgot that resource.

Now the event I treated gaily came seriously to my door.

Is it folly, or nonchalance, or philosophy, or pertinacity—or what

is it in me, that, after all, when La Fleur had gone down stairs, and I was quite alone, I could not bring down my mind to think of it otherwise than I had then spoken of it to Eugenius?

—And as for the Bastile; the terror is in the word—Make the most of it you can, said I to myself, the Bastile is but another word for a tower—and a tower is but another word for a house you can't get out of—Mercy on the gouty! for they are in it twice a year—but with nine livres a day, and pen and ink and paper and patience, albeit a man can't get out, he may do very well within —at least for a month or six weeks; at the end of which, if he is a harmless fellow, his innocence appears, and he comes out a better and wiser man than he went in.

I had some occasion (I forgot what) to step into the courtyard, as I settled this account; and remember I walk'd down stairs in no small triumph with the conceit of my reasoning—Beshrew the *sombre* pencil! said I vauntingly—for I envy not its power, which paints the evils of life with so hard and deadly a colouring. The mind sits terrified at the objects she has magnified herself, and blackened: reduce them to their proper size and hue, she over-looks them—'Tis true, said I, correcting the proposition—the Bastile is not an evil to be despised—But strip it of towers—fill up the fossé—unbarricade the doors—call it simply a confinement, and suppose 'tis some tyrant of a distemper—and not of a man which holds you in it—the evil vanishes, and you bear the other half without complaint.

I was interrupted in the hey-day of this soliloquy, with a voice which I took to be of a child, which complained "it could not get out."—I look'd up and down the passage, and seeing neither man, woman or child, I went out without further attention.

In my return back through the passage, I heard the same words repeated twice over; and looking up, I saw it was a starling hung in a little cage—"I can't get out—I can't get out," said the starling.

I stood looking at the bird: and to every person who came through the passage it ran fluttering to the side towards which they ap-proach'd it, with the same lamentation of its captivity—"I can't get out," said the starling—God help thee! said I—but I'll let thee out, cost what it will; so I turned about the cage to get to the door; it was twisted and double twisted so fast with wire, there was no getting it open without pulling the cage to pieces—I took both hands to it.

The bird flew to the place where I was attempting his deliverance, and thrusting his head through the trellis, pressed his breast against it, as if impatient—I fear, poor creature! said I, I cannot set thee

at liberty—"No," said the starling—"I can't get out—I can't get out," said the starling.

I vow I never had my affections more tenderly awakened; or do I remember an incident in my life, where the dissipated spirits, to which my reason had been a bubble, were so suddenly call'd home. Mechanical as the notes were, yet so true in tune to nature were they chanted, that in one moment they overthrew all my systematic reasonings upon the Bastile; and I heavily walk'd up stairs, unsaying every word I had said in going down them.

Disguise thyself as thou wilt, still, Slavery! said I—still thou art a bitter draught! and though thousands in all ages have been made to drink of thee, thou art no less bitter on that account.—'Tis thou, thrice sweet and gracious goddess, addressing myself to LIBERTY, whom all in public or in private worship, whose taste is grateful, and ever will be so, till NATURE herself shall change—no *tint* of words can spot thy snowy mantle or chymic power turn thy sceptre into iron—with thee to smile upon him as he eats his crust, the swain is happier than his monarch, from whose court thou art exiled—Gracious heaven! cried I, kneeling down upon the last step but one in my ascent, grant me but health, thou great Bestower of it, and give me but this fair goddess as my companion—and shower down thy mitres, if it seems good unto thy divine providence, upon those heads which are aching for them.

The Captive—Paris

The bird in his cage pursued me into my room; I sat down close to my table, and leaning my head upon my hand, I began to figure to myself the miseries of confinement. I was in a right frame for it, and so I gave full scope to my imagination.

I was going to begin with the millions of my fellow-creatures, born to no inheritance but slavery: but finding, however affecting the picture was, that I could not bring it near me, and that the multitude of sad groups in it did but distract me—

—I took a single captive, and having first shut him up in his dungeon, I then look'd through the twilight of his grated door to take his picture.

I beheld his body half wasted away with long expectation and confinement, and felt what kind of sickness of the heart it was which arises from hope deferr'd. Upon looking nearer I saw him pale and feverish: in thirty years the western breeze had not once fann'd his blood—he had seen no sun, no moon, in all that time

—nor had the voice of friend or kinsman breathed through his lattice:—his children—

But here my heart began to bleed—and I was forced to go on with another part of the portrait.

He was sitting upon the ground upon a little straw, in the furthest corner of his dungeon, which was alternately his chair and bed: a little calendar of small sticks were laid at the head, notch'd all over with the dismal days and nights he had passed there—he had one of these little sticks in his hand, and with a rusty nail he was etching another day of misery to add to the heap. As I darkened the little light he had, he lifted up a hopeless eye towards the door, then cast it down—shook his head, and went on with his work of affliction. I heard his chains upon his legs, as he turned his body to lay his little stick upon the bundle.—He gave a deep sigh—I saw the iron enter into his soul—I burst into tears—I could not sustain the picture of confinement which my fancy had drawn—I started up from my chair, and called La Fleur, I bid him bespeak me a *remise,* and have it ready at the door of the hotel by nine in the morning.

—I'll go directly, said I, myself to Monsieur le Duc de Choiseul.

La Fleur would have put me to bed; but not willing he should see any thing upon my cheek which would cost the honest fellow a heart-ache—I told him I would go to bed by myself—and bid him go do the same.

The Starling—Road to Versailles

I got into my *remise* the hour I promised: La Fleur got up behind, and I bid the coachman make the best of his way to Versailles.

As there was nothing in this road, or rather nothing which I look for in travelling, I cannot fill up the blank better than with a short history of this self-same bird, which became the subject of the last chapter.

Whilst the Honourable Mr—— was waiting for a wind at Dover, it had been caught upon the cliffs before it could well fly, by an English lad who was his groom; who not caring to destroy it, had taken it in his breast into the packet—and by course of feeding it, and taking it once under his protection, in a day or two grew fond of it, and got it safe along with him to Paris.

At Paris the lad had laid out a livre in a little cage for the starling, and as he had little to do better the five months his master staid there,

he taught it in his mother's tongue the four simple words—(and no more)—to which I own'd myself so much its debtor.

Upon his master's going on for Italy—the lad had given it to the master of the hotel—But his little song for liberty being in an *unknown* language at Paris, the bird had little or no store set by him—so La Fleur bought both him and his cage for me for a bottle of Burgundy.

In my return from Italy I brought him with me to the country in whose language he had learn'd his notes—and telling the story of him to Lord A——, Lord A begg'd the bird of me—in a week Lord A gave him to Lord B——; Lord B made a present of him to Lord C——; and Lord C's gentleman sold him to Lord D's for a shilling—Lord D gave him to Lord E——, and so on—half round the alphabet—From that rank he pass'd into the lower house, and pass'd the hands of as many commoners—But as all these wanted to *get in*—and my bird wanted to *get out*—he had almost as little store set by him in London as in Paris.

It is impossible but many of my readers must have heard of him; and if any by mere chance have ever seen him,—I beg leave to inform them, that bird was my bird—or some vile copy set up to represent him.

I have nothing farther to add upon him, but that, from that time to this, I have borne this poor starling as the crest to my arms.—Thus

—And let the heralds' officers twist his neck about if they dare.

The Address—Versailles

I should not like to have my enemy take a view of my mind when I am going to ask protection of any man; for which reason I generally endeavour to protect myself; but this going to Monsieur le Duc de C—— was an act of compulsion—had it been an act of choice, I should have done it, I suppose, like other people.

How many mean plans of dirty address, as I went along, did my servile heart form! I deserve the Bastile for every one of them.

Then nothing would serve me, when I got within sight of Versailles, but putting words and sentences together, and conceiving attitudes and tones to wreath myself into Monsieur le Duc de C——'s good graces—This will do, said I—Just as well, retorted I again, as a coat carried up to him by an adventurous taylor, without taking his measure—Fool! continued I,—see Monsieur le Duc's face first—observe what character is written in it—take notice in what posture he stands to hear you—mark the turns and expression of his body and limbs—and for the tone—the first sound which comes from his lips will give it you; and from all these together you'll compound an address at once upon the spot, which cannot disgust the Duke—the ingredients are his own, and most likely to go down.

Well! said I, I wish it well over—Coward again! as if man to man was not equal throughout the whole surface of the globe; and if in the field—why not face to face in the cabinet too? And trust me, Yorick, whenever it is not so, man is false to himself, and betrays his own succours ten times where nature does it once. Go to the Duc de C—— with the Bastile in thy looks—My life for it, thou wilt be sent back to Paris in half an hour with an escort.

I believe so, said I—Then I'll go to the Duke, by Heaven! with all the gaiety and debonairness in the world.——

——And there you are wrong again, replied I—A heart at ease, Yorick, flies into no extremes—'tis ever on its centre—Well! well! cried I, as the coachman turn'd in at the gates, I find I shall do very well: and by the time he had wheel'd round the court, and brought me up to the door, I found myself so much the better for my own lecture, that I neither ascended the steps like a victim to justice, who was to part with life upon the topmost—nor did I mount them with a skip and a couple of strides, as I do when I fly up, Eliza! to thee, to meet it.

As I entered the door of the saloon I was met by a person who possibly might be the maitre d'hotel, but had more the air of one

of the under-secretaries, who told me the Duc de C—— was busy,—
I am utterly ignorant, said I, of the forms of obtaining an audience,
being an absolute stranger, and what is worse in the present conjunc-
ture of affairs, being an Englishman too.—He replied, that did
not increase the difficulty.—I made him a slight bow, and told him, I
had something of importance to say to Monsieur le Duc. The Secretary
look'd towards the stairs, as if he was about to leave me to carry up
this account to some one—But I must not mislead you, said I,—for
what I have to say is of no manner of importance to Monsieur le Duc
de C—— —but of great importance to myself.—*C'est une autre affaire,*
replied he—not at all, said I, to a man of gallantry. But pray, good
Sir, continued I, when can a stranger hope to have *accesse?*—In not
less than two hours, said he, looking at his watch. The number of
equipages in the court-yard seemed to justify the calculation, that I
could have no nearer a prospect—and as walking backwards and
forwards in the saloon, without a soul to commune with, was for the
time as bad as being in the Bastile itself, I instantly went back to my
remise, and bid the coachman to drive me to the *Cordon Bleu,* which
was the nearest hotel.

I think there is a fatality in it—I seldom go to the place I set out
for.

Le Patisser—Versailles

Before I had got half way down the street I changed my mind: as
I am at Versailles, thought I, I might as well take a view of the town;
so I pull'd the cord, and ordered the coachman to drive round some
of the principal streets—I suppose the town is not very large, said I.—
The coachman begg'd pardon for setting me right, and told me it was
very superb, and that numbers of the first dukes and marquisses and
counts had hotels—The count de B——, of whom the bookseller at
the Quai de Conti had spoke so handsomely the night before, came
instantly into my mind—And why should I not go, thought I, to the
Count de B——, who has so high an idea of English books, and
English men—and tell him my story? so I changed my mind a second
time—In truth it was the third; for I had intended that day for
Madame de R—— in the Rue St Pierre, and had devoutly sent
her word by her *fille de chambre* that I would assuredly wait upon
her—but I am governed by circumstances—I cannot govern them; so
seeing a man standing with a basket on the other side of the street, as
if he had something to sell, I bid La Fleur go up to him and enquire
for the Count's hotel.

La Fleur returned a little pale: and told me it was a Chevalier de St Louis selling *patés*—It is impossible, La Fleur, said I.—La Fleur could no more account for the phænomenon than myself; but persisted in his story: he had seen the croix set in gold, with its red ribband, he said, tied to his button-hole—and had looked into the basket and seen the *patés* which the Chevalier was selling; so could not be mistaken in that.

Such a reverse in man's life awakens a better principle than curiosity: I could not help looking for some time at him as I sat in the *remise*—the more I look'd at him, his croix, and his basket, the stronger they wove themselves into my brain—I got out of the *remise,* and went towards him.

He was begirt with a clean linen apron which fell below his knees, and with a sort of a bib that went half way up his breast; upon the top of this, but a little below the hem, hung his croix. His basket of little *patés* was covered over with a white damask napkin; another of the same kind was spread at the bottom; and there was a look of *propreté* and neatness throughout, that one might have bought his *patés* of him, as much from appetite as sentiment.

He made an offer of them to neither; but stood still with them at the corner of a hotel, for those to buy who chose it, without solicitation.

He was about forty-eight—of a sedate look, something approaching to gravity. I did not wonder.—I went up rather to the basket than him, and having lifted up the napkin, and taken one of his *patés* into my hand—I begg'd he would explain the appearance which affected me.

He told me in a few words, that the best part of his life had pass'd in the service, in which, after spending a small patrimony, he had obtain'd a company and the croix with it; but that, at the conclusion of the last peace, his regiment being reformed, and the whole corps, with those of some other regiments, left without any provision, he found himself in a wide world without friends, without a livre—and indeed, said he, without any thing but this—(pointing, as he said it, to his croix)—The poor Chevalier won my pity, and he finished the scene with winning my esteem too.

The king, he said, was the most generous of princes, but his generosity could neither relieve or reward every one, and it was only his misfortune to be amongst the number. He had a little wife, he said, whom he loved, who did the *patisserie;* and added, he felt no dishonour in defending her and himself from want in this way—unless Providence had offer'd him a better way.

It would be wicked to withhold a pleasure from the good, in passing

over what happen'd to this poor Chevalier of St Louis about nine
months after.

It seems he usually took his stand near the iron gates which lead
up to the palace, and as his croix had caught the eye of numbers,
numbers had made the same inquiry which I had done—He had told
the same story, and always with so much modesty and good sense, that
it had reach'd at last the king's ears—who hearing the Chevalier had
been a gallant officer, and respected by the whole regiment as a man
of honour and integrity—he broke up his little trade by a pension of
fifteen hundred livres a year.

As I have told this to please the reader, I beg he will allow me to
relate another, out of its order, to please myself—the two stories
reflect light upon each other—and 'tis a pity they should be parted.

The Sword—Rennes

When states and empires have their periods of declension, and feel
in their turns what distress and poverty is—I stop not to tell the causes
which gradually brought the house d'E—— in Britanny into decay.
The Marquis d'E—— had fought up against his condition with great
firmness; wishing to preserve, and still shew to the world, some little
fragments of what his ancestors had been—their indiscretions had put
it out of his power. There was enough left for the little exigencies of
obscurity—But he had two boys who look'd up to him for *light*—he
thought they deserved it. He had tried his sword—it could not open
the way—the *mounting* was too expensive—and simple œconomy was
not a match for it—there was no resource but commerce.

In any other province in France, save Britanny, this was smiting
the root for ever of the little tree his pride and affection wish'd to see
re-blossom—But in Britanny, there being a provision for this, he avail'd
himself of it; and taking an occasion when the states were assembled
at Rennes, the Marquis, attended with his two boys, entered the court;
and having pleaded the right of an ancient law of the duchy, which,
though seldom claim'd, he said, was no less in force, he took his sword
from his side—Here, said he, take it; and be trusty guardians of it, till
better times put me in condition to reclaim it.

The president accepted the Marquis's sword—he staid a few minutes
to see it deposited in the archives of his house, and departed.

The Marquis and his whole family embarked the next day for Mar-
tinico, and in about nineteen or twenty years of successful application
to business, with some unlook'd-for bequests from distant branches of
his house, return'd home to reclaim his nobility and to support it.

It was an incident of good fortune which will never happen to any traveller, but a sentimental one, that I should be at Rennes at the very time of this solemn requisition: I call it solemn—it was so to me.

The Marquis enter'd the court with his whole family: he supported his lady—his eldest son supported his sister, and his youngest was at the other extreme of the line next his mother—he put his handkerchief to his face twice—

—There was a dead silence. When the Marquis had approach'd within six paces of the tribunal, he gave the Marchioness to his youngest son, and advancing three steps before his family—he reclaim'd his sword. His sword was given him, and the moment he got it into his hand he drew it almost out of the scabbard—'twas the shining face of a friend he had once given up—he look'd attentively along it, beginning at the hilt, as if to see whether it was the same—when observing a little rust which it had contracted near the point, he brought it near his eye, and bending his head down over it—I think I saw a tear fall upon the place: I could not be deceived by what followed.

"I shall find," said he, "some *other way* to get it off."

When the Marquis had said this, he return'd his sword into its scabbard, made a bow to the guardians of it—and with his wife and daughter, and his two sons following him, walk'd out.

O how I envied him his feelings!

The Passport—Versailles

I found no difficulty in getting admittance to Monsieur le Count de B——. The set of Shakespeares was laid upon the table, and he was tumbling them over. I walk'd up close to the table, and giving first such a look at the books as to make him conceive I knew what they were—I told him I had come without any one to present me, knowing I should meet with a friend in his apartment, who, I trusted, would do it for me—it is my countryman the great Shakespeare, said I, pointing to his works—*et ayez la bonté, mon cher ami,* apostrophizing his spirit, added I, *de me faire cet honneur-là.*—

The Count smiled at the singularity of the introduction; and seeing I look'd a little pale and sickly, insisted upon my taking an armchair: so I sat down; and to save him conjectures upon a visit so out of all rule, I told him simply of the incident in the bookseller's shop, and how that had impelled me rather to go to him with the story of a little embarrassment I was under, than to any other man in France—And what is your embarrassment? let me hear it, said the Count. So I told him the story just as I have told it the reader.—

—And the master of my hotel, said I, as I concluded it, will needs have it, Monsieur le Count, that I should be sent to the Bastile—but I have no apprehensions, continued I—for in falling into the hands of the most polish'd people in the world, and being conscious I was a true man, and not come to spy the nakedness of the land, I scarce thought I laid at their mercy.—It does not suit the gallantry of the French, Monsieur le Count, said I, to shew it against invalids.

An animated blush came into the Count de B——'s cheeks as I spoke this—*Ne craignez rien*—Don't fear, said he—Indeed I don't, replied I again—Besides, continued I a little sportingly, I have come laughing all the way from London to Paris, and I do not think Monsieur le Duc de Choiseul is such an enemy to mirth, as to send me back crying for my pains.

—My application to you, Monsieur le Count de B—— (making him a low bow) is to desire he will not.

The Count heard me with great good-nature, or I had not said half as much—and once or twice said—*C'est bien dit*. So I rested my cause there—and determined to say no more about it.

The Count led the discourse: we talk'd of indifferent things—of books, and politics, and men—and then of women—God bless them all! said I, after much discourse about them—there is not a man upon earth who loves them as much as I do: after all the foibles I have seen, and all the satires I have read against them, still I love them; being firmly persuaded that a man, who has not a sort of an affection for the whole sex, is incapable of ever loving a single one as he ought.

Heh bien! Monsieur l'Anglois, said the Count, gaily—You are not come to spy the nakedness of the land—I believe—*ni encore*, I dare say *that* of our women—But permit me to conjecture—if, *par hazard,* they fell into your way, that the prospect would not affect you.

I have something within me which cannot bear the shock of the least indecent insinuation: in the sport-ability of chitchat I have often endeavoured to conquer it, and with infinite pain have hazarded a thousand things to a dozen of the sex together—the least of which I could not venture to a single one to gain heaven.

Excuse me, Monsieur le Count, said I—as for the nakedness of your land, if I saw it, I should cast my eyes over it with tears in them—and for that of your women (blushing at the idea he had excited in me), I am so evangelical in this, and have such a fellow-feeling for whatever is *weak* about them, that I would cover it with a garment, if I knew how to throw it on—But I could wish, continued I, to spy the *nakedness* of their hearts, and through the different disguises of customs, climates, and religion, find out what is good in them to fashion my own by—and therefore am I come.

It is for this reason, Monsieur le Count, continued I, that I have not seen the Palais Royal—nor the Luxembourg—nor the Façade of the Louvre—nor have attempted to swell the catalogues we have of pictures, statues, and churches—I conceive every fair being as a temple, and would rather enter in, and see the original drawings, and loose sketches hung up in it, than the transfiguration of Raphael itself.

The thirst of this, continued I, as impatient as that which inflames the breast of the connoisseur, has led me from my own home into France—and from France will lead me through Italy—'tis a quiet journey of the heart in pursuit of NATURE, and those affections which arise out of her, which make us love each other—and the world, better than we do.

The Count said a great many civil things to me upon the occasion; and added, very politely, how much he stood obliged to Shakespeare for making me known to him—But, *à-propos,* said he,—Shakespeare is full of great things—he forgot a small punctilio of announcing your name—it puts you under a necessity of doing it yourself.

The Passport—Versailles

There is not a more perplexing affair in life to me, than to set about telling any one who I am—for there is scarce anybody I cannot give a better account of than myself; and I have often wish'd I could do it in a single word—and have an end of it. It was the only time and occasion in my life I could accomplish this to any purpose—for Shakespeare lying upon the table, and recollecting I was in his books, I took up Hamlet, and turning immediately to the grave-diggers' scene in the fifth act, I laid my finger upon YORICK, and advancing the book to the Count, with my finger all the way over the name—*Me! voici!* said I.

Now whether the idea of poor Yorick's skull was put out of the Count's mind by the reality of my own, or by what magic he could drop a period of seven or eight hundred years, makes nothing in this account—'tis certain the French conceive better than they combine— I wonder at nothing in this world, and the less at this; inasmuch as one of the first of our own church, for whose candour and paternal sentiments I have the highest veneration, fell into the same mistake in the very same case,—"He could not bear," he said, "to look into the sermons wrote by the king of Denmark's jester."—Good, my lord! said I; but there are two Yoricks. The Yorick your lordship thinks of has been dead and buried eight hundred years ago; he flourish'd in Horwendillus's court—the other Yorick is myself, who have flourish'd, my

lord, in no court—He shook his head—Good God! said I, you might as well confound Alexander the Great with Alexander the Copper-smith, my lord—'Twas all one, he replied.

—If Alexander king of Macedon could have translated your lord-ship, said I, I'm sure your lordship would not have said so.

The poor Count de B—— fell but into the same *error*—

—*Et, Monsieur, est il Yorick?* cried the Count.—*Je le suis,* said I.— *Vous?—Moï—moi qui ai l'honneur de vous parler, Monsieur le Comte—Mon Dieu!* said he, embracing me—*Vous êtes Yorick!*

The Count instantly put the Shakespeare into his pocket, and left me alone in his room.

The Passport—Versailles

I could not conceive why the Count de B—— had gone so abruptly out of the room, any more than I could conceive why he had put the Shakespeare into his pocket—*Mysteries which must explain themselves are not worth the loss of time which a conjecture about them takes up:* 'twas better to read Shakespeare; so taking up *"Much ado about Nothing,"* I transported myself instantly from the chair I sat in to Messina in Sicily, and got so busy with Don Pedro and Benedict and Beatrice, that I thought not of Versailles, the Count, or the Passport.

Sweet pliability of man's spirit, that can at once surrender itself to illusions, which cheat expectation and sorrow of their weary mo-ments!—Long—long since had ye number'd out my days, had I not trod so great a part of them upon this enchanted ground; when my way is too rough for my feet, or too steep for my strength, I get off it, to some smooth velvet path which fancy has scattered over with rose-buds of delights; and having taken a few turns in it, come back strengthen'd and refresh'd—When evils press sore upon me, and there is no retreat from them in this world, then I take a new course—I leave it—and as I have a clearer idea of the elysian fields than I have of heaven, I force myself, like Æneas, into them—I see him meet the pensive shade of his forsaken Dido, and wish to recognize it—I see the injured spirit wave her head, and turn off silent from the author of her miseries and dishonors—I lose the feelings for myself in hers, and in those affections which were wont to make me mourn for her when I was at school.

Surely this is not walking in a vain shadow—nor does man disquiet himself in vain *by it*—he oftener does so in trusting the issue of his com-motions to reason only—I can safely say for myself, I was never able to conquer any one single bad sensation in my heart so decisively, as by

beating up as fast as I could for some kindly and gentle sensation to fight it upon its own ground.

When I had got to the end of the third act, the Count de B—— entered with my passport in his hand. Mons. le Duc de C——, said the Count, is as good a prophet, I dare say, as he is a statesman—*Un homme qui rit,* said the duke, *ne sera jamais dangereux.*—Had it been for any one but the king's jester, added the Count, I could not have got it in these two hours.—*Pardonnez moi,* Mons. le Count, said I—I am not the king's jester. But you are Yorick?—Yes.—*Et vous plaisantez?* —I answered, Indeed I did jest—but was not paid for it—'twas entirely at my own expence.

We have no jester at court, Mons. le Count, said I: the last we had was in the licentious reign of Charles II.—since which time our manners have been so gradually refining, that our court at present is so full of patriots, who wish for *nothing* but the honours of wealth of their country—and our ladies are all so chaste, so spotless, so good, so devout—there is nothing for a jester to make a jest of—

Voila un persiflage! cried the Count.

The Passport—Versailles

As the Passport was directed to all lieutenant-governors, governors, and commandants of cities, generals of armies, justiciaries, and all officers of justice, to let Mr. Yorick the king's jester, and his baggage, travel quietly along—I own the triumph of obtaining the Passport was not a little tarnish'd by the figure I cut in it—But there is nothing unmix'd in this world; and some of the gravest of our divines have carried it so far as to affirm, that enjoyment itself was attended even with a sigh—and that the greatest *they knew of* terminated *in a general way* in little better than a convulsion.

I remember the grave and learned Bevoriskius, in his Commentary upon the Generations from Adam, very naturally breaks off in the middle of a note to give an account to the world of a couple of sparrows upon the out-edge of his window, which had incommoded him all the time he wrote, and at last had entirely taken him off from his genealogy.

—'Tis strange! writes Bevoriskius; but the facts are certain, for I have had the curiosity to mark them down one by one with my pen— but the cock-sparrow, during the little time that I could have finished the other half of this note, has actually interrupted me with the reiteration of his caresses three-and-twenty times and a half.

How merciful, adds Bevoriskius, is heaven to his creatures!

Ill-fated Yorick! that the gravest of thy brethren should be able to write that to the world, which stains thy face with crimson, to copy in even thy study.

But this is nothing to my travels—So I twice—twice beg pardon for it.

Character—Versailles

And how do you find the French? said the Count de B——, after he had given me the Passport.

The reader may suppose, that after so obliging a proof of courtesy, I could not be at a loss to say something handsome to the enquiry.

—*Mais passe, pour cela*—Speak frankly, said he: do you find all the urbanity in the French which the world give us the honour of?—I had found everything, I said, which confirmed it—*Vraiment,* said the Count—*les François sont polis*—To an excess, replied I.

The Count took notice of the word *excesse;* and would have it I meant more than I said. I defended myself a long time as well as I could against it—he insisted I had a reserve, and that I would speak my opinion frankly.

I believe, Mons. le Count, said I, that man has a certain compass, as well as an instrument; and that the social and other calls have occasion by turns for every key in him; so that if you begin a note too high or too low, there must be a want either in the upper or under part, to fill up the system of harmony.—The Count de B—— did not understand music, so desired me to explain it some other way. A polish'd nation, my dear Count, said I, makes every one its debtor; and besides, urbanity itself, like the fair sex, has so many charms, it goes against the heart to say it can do ill; and yet, I believe, there is but a certain line of perfection, that man, take him altogether, is impower'd to arrive at—if he gets beyond, he rather exchanges qualities than gets them. I must not presume to say, how far this has affected the French in the subject we are speaking of—but should it ever be the case of the English, in the progress of their refinements, to arrive at the same polish which distinguishes the French, if we did not lose the *politesse du cœur,* which inclines men more to humane actions, than courteous ones—we should at least lose that distinct variety and originality of character, which distinguishes them, not only from each other, but from all the world besides.

I had a few of King William's shillings as smooth as glass in my pocket; and foreseeing they would be of use in the illustration of my hypothesis, I had got them into my hand, when I had proceeded so far—

See, Mons. le Count, said I, rising up, and laying them before him upon the table—by jingling and rubbing one against another for seventy years together in one body's pocket or another's, they are become so much alike, you can scarce distinguish one shilling from another.

The English, like ancient medals, kept more apart, and passing but few people's hands, preserve the first sharpnesses which the fine hand of Nature has given them—they are not so pleasant to feel—but, in return, the legend is so visible, that at the first look you see whose image and superscription they bear. But the French, Mons. le Count, added I (wishing to soften what I had said), have so many excellencies, they can the better spare this—they are a loyal, a gallant, a generous, an ingenious, and good-temper'd people as is under heaven—if they have a fault, they are too *serious*.

Mon Dieu! cried the Count, rising out of his chair.

Mais vous plaisantez, said he, correcting his exclamation.—I laid my hand upon my breast, and with earnest gravity assured him it was my most settled opinion.

The Count said he was mortified he could not stay to hear my reasons, being engaged to go that moment to dine with the Duc de C——.

But if it is not too far to come to Versailles to eat your soup with me, I beg, before you leave France, I may have the pleasure of knowing you retract your opinion—or, in what manner you support it.—But if you do support it, Mons. Anglois, said he, you must do it with all your powers, because you have the whole world against you—I promised the Count I would do myself the honour of dining with him before I set out for Italy—so took my leave.

The Temptation—Paris

When I alighted at the hotel, the porter told me a young woman with a bandbox had been that moment enquiring for me.—I do not know, said the porter, whether she is gone away or no. I took the key of my chamber of him, and went up stairs; and when I had got within ten steps of the top of the landing before my door, I met her coming easily down.

It was the fair *fille de chambre* I had walked along the Quai de Conti with: Madame de R—— had sent her upon some commission to a *merchante de modes* within a step or two of the hotel de Modene; and as I had fail'd in waiting upon her, had bid her enquire if I had left Paris; and if so, whether I had not left a letter addressed to her.

As the fair *fille de chambre* was so near my door, she return'd back and went into the room with me for a moment or two whilst I wrote a card.

It was a fine still evening in the latter end of the month of May —the crimson window-curtains (which were of the same colour of those of the bed) were drawn close—the sun was setting, and reflected through them so warm a tint into the fair *fille de chambre's* face—I thought she blush'd—the idea of it made me blush myself— we were quite alone; and that superinduced a second blush before the first could get off.

There is a sort of a pleasing half-guilty blush, where the blood is more in fault than the man—'tis sent impetuous from the heart, and virtue flies after it—not to call it back, but to make the sensation of it more delicious to the nerves—'tis associated.—

But I'll not describe it—I felt something at first within me which was not in strict unison with the lesson of virtue I had given her the night before—I sought five minutes for a card—I knew I had not one. I took up a pen—I laid it down again—my hand trembled—the devil was in me.

I know as well as any one he is an adversary, whom if we resist he will fly from us—but I seldom resist him at all; from a terror, that though I may conquer, I may still get a hurt in the combat—so I give up the triumph for security; and instead of thinking to make him fly, I generally fly myself.

The fair *fille de chambre* came close up to the bureau where I was looking for a card—took up first the pen I cast down, then offer'd to hold me the ink; she offer'd it so sweetly, I was going to accept it— but I durst not—I have nothing, my dear, said I, to write upon.— Write it, said she, simply, upon any thing—

I was just going to cry out, Then I will write it, fair girl! upon thy lips.—

If I do, said I, I shall perish—so I took her by the hand, and led her to the door, and begg'd she would not forget the lesson I had given her—She said, indeed she would not—and as she uttered it with some earnestness, she turn'd about, and gave me both her hands, closed together, into mine—it was impossible not to compress them in that situation—I wish'd to let them go; and all the time I held them, I kept arguing within myself against it—and still I held them on.—In two minutes I found I had all the battle to fight over again— and I felt my legs and every limb about me tremble at the idea.

The foot of the bed was within a yard and a half of the place where we were standing—I had still hold of her hands—and how it hap-

pened I can give no account, but I neither ask'd her—nor drew her —nor did I think of the bed—but so it did happen, we both sat down.

I'll just shew you, said the fair *fille de chambre,* the little purse I have been making to-day to hold your crown. So she put her hand into her right pocket, which was next me, and felt for it some time—then into the left—"She had lost it."—I never bore expectation more quietly—it was in her right pocket at last—she pull'd it out; it was of green taffeta, lined with a little bit of white quilted sattin, and just big enough to hold the crown—she put it into my hand;—it was pretty; and I held it ten minutes with the back of my hand resting upon her lap—looking sometimes at the purse, sometimes on one side of it.

A stitch or two had broke out in the gathers of my stock—the fair *fille de chambre,* without saying a word, took out her little housewife, threaded a small needle, and sew'd it up—I foresaw it would hazard the glory of the day; and as she pass'd her hand in silence across and across my neck in the manœuvre, I felt the laurels shake which fancy had wreath'd about my head.

A strap had given way in her walk, and the buckle of her shoe was just falling off—See, said the *fille de chambre,* holding up her foot— I could not from my soul but fasten the buckle in return, and putting in the strap—and lifting up the other foot with it, when I had done, to see both were right—in doing it too suddenly—it unavoidably threw the fair *fille de chambre* off her centre—and then—

The Conquest

Yes—and then—Ye whose clay-cold heads and lukewarm hearts can argue down or mask your passions, tell me, what trespass is it that man should have them? or how his spirit stands answerable to the Father of spirits but for his conduct under them.

If Nature has so wove her web of kindness that some threads of love and desire are entangled with the piece—must the whole web be rent in drawing them out?—Whip me such stoics, great Governor of nature! said I to myself—Wherever thy providence shall place me for the trials of my virtue—whatever is my danger—whatever is my situation—let me feel the movements which rise out of it, and which belong to me as a man—and if I govern them as a good one, I will trust the issues to thy justice: for thou hast made us, and not we ourselves.

As I finish'd my address, I raised the fair *fille de chambre* up by the hand, and led her out of the room—she stood by me till I lock'd the door and put the key in my pocket—*and then*—the victory being quite

decisive—and not till then, I press'd my lips to her cheek, and taking her by the hand again, led her safe to the gate of the hotel.

The Mystery—Paris

If a man knows the heart, he will know it was impossible to go back instantly to my chamber—it was touching a cold key with a flat third to it, upon the close of a piece of music, which had call'd forth my affections—therefore when I let go the hand of the *fille de chambre,* I remain'd at the gate of the hotel for some time, looking at every one who pass'd by, and forming conjectures upon them, till my attention got fix'd upon a single object which confounded all kind of reasoning upon him.

It was a tall figure of a philosophic, serious, adust look, which pass'd and repass'd sedately along the street, making a turn of about sixty paces on each side of the gate of the hotel—the man was about fifty-two—had a small cane under his arm—was dress'd in a dark drab-colour'd coat, waistcoat, and breeches, which seem'd to have seen some years service—they were still clean, and there was a little air of frugal *propreté* throughout him. By his pulling off his hat, and his attitude of accosting a good many in his way, I saw he was asking charity; so I got a sous or two out of my pocket ready to give him, as he took me in his turn—He pass'd by me without asking any thing—and yet did not go five steps farther before he ask'd charity of a little woman —I was much more likely to have given of the two—He had scarce done with the woman, when he pull'd his hat off to another who was coming the same way.—An ancient gentleman came slowly—and, after him, a young smart one—He let them both pass, and ask'd nothing; I stood observing him half an hour, in which time he had made a dozen turns backwards and forwards, and found that he invariably pursued the same plan.

There were two things very singular in this, which set my brain to work, and to no purpose—the first was, why the man should *only* tell his story to the sex—and secondly—what kind of story it was, and what species of eloquence it could be, which soften'd the hearts of the women, which he knew 'twas to no purpose to practise upon the men.

There were two other circumstances which entangled this mystery —the one was, he told every woman what he had to say in her ear, and in a way which had much more the air of a secret than a petition —the other was, it was always successful—he never stopp'd a woman, but she pull'd out her purse, and immediately gave him something.

I could form no system to explain the phænomenon.

I had got a riddle to amuse me for the rest of the evening, so I walk'd up stairs to my chamber.

The Case of Conscience—Paris

I was immediately followed up by the master of the hotel, who came into my room to tell me I must provide lodgings elsewhere.—How so, friend? said I.—He answer'd, I had had a young woman lock'd up with me two hours that evening in my bed-chamber, and 'twas against the rules of his house—Very well, said I, we'll all part friends then—for the girl is no worse—and I am no worse—and you will be just as I found you.—It was enough, he said, to overthrow the credit of his hotel.—*Voyez vous, Monsieur,* said he, pointing to the foot of the bed we had been sitting upon—I own it had something of the appearance of an evidence; but my pride not suffering me to enter into any detail of the case, I exhorted him to let his soul sleep in peace, as I resolved to let mine do that night, and that I would discharge what I owed him at breakfast.

I should not have minded, *Monsieur,* said he, if you had had twenty girls—'Tis a score more, replied I, interrupting him, than I ever reck-on'd upon—Provided, added he, it had been but in a morning.—And does the difference of the time of the day at Paris make a difference in the sin?—It made a difference, he said, in the scandal.—I like a good distinction in my heart; and cannot say I was intolerably out of temper with the man.—I own it is necessary, resumed the master of the hotel, that a stranger at Paris should have the opportunities presented to him of buying lace and silk stockings and ruffles, *et tout cela*—and 'tis nothing if a woman comes with a bandbox.—O' my conscience, said I, she had one; but I never look'd into it.—Then *Monsieur,* said he, has bought nothing.—Not one earthly thing, replied I.—Because, said he, I could recommend one to you who would use you *en conscience.*—But I must see her this night, said I.—He made me a low bow, and walk'd down.

Now shall I triumph over this *maître d'hotel,* cried I—and what then? Then I shall let him see I know he is a dirty fellow.—And what then?—What then! I was too near myself to say it was for the sake of others.—I had no good answer left—there was more of spleen than principle in my project, and I was sick of it before the execution.

In a few minutes the Grisset came in with her box of lace—I'll buy nothing, however, said I, within myself.

The Grisset would shew me every thing—I was hard to please: she would not seem to see it; she open'd her little magazine, and laid all

her laces one after another before me—unfolded and folded them up again one by one with the most patient sweetness—I might buy—or not —she would let me have every thing at my own price—the poor creature seem'd anxious to get a penny; and laid herself out to win me, and not so much in a manner which seem'd artful, as in one I felt simple and caressing.

If there is not a fund of honest cullibility in man, so much the worse —my heart relented, and I gave up my second resolution as quietly as the first—Why should I chastise one for the trespass of another? If thou art tributary to this tyrant of an host, thought I, looking up in her face, so much harder is thy bread.

If I had not had more than four Louis d'ors in my purse, there was no such thing as rising up and shewing her the door, till I had first laid three of them out in a pair of ruffles.

—The master of the hotel will share the profit with her—no matter —then I have only paid as many a poor soul has *paid* before me, for an act he *could* not do, or think of.

The Riddle—Paris

When La Fleur came up to wait upon me at supper, he told me how sorry the master of the hotel was for his affront to me in bidding me change my lodgings.

A man who values a good night's rest will not lie down with enmity in his heart, if he can help it—So I bid La Fleur tell the master of the hotel, that I was sorry on my side for the occasion I had given him— and you may tell him, if you will, La Fleur, added I, that if the young woman should call again, I shall not see her.

This was a sacrifice not to him, but myself, having resolved, after so narrow an escape, to run no more risks, but to leave Paris, if it was possible, with all the virtue I enter'd it.

C'est deroger à noblesse, Monsieur, said La Fleur, making me a bow down to the ground as he said it—*Et encore, Monsieur,* said he, may change his sentiments—and if (*par hazard*) he should like to amuse himself—I find no amusement in it, said I, interrupting him—

Mon Dieu! said La Fleur—and took away.

In an hour's time he came to put me to bed, and was more than commonly officious—something hung upon his lips to say to me, or ask me, which he could not get off: I could not conceive what it was, and indeed gave myself little trouble to find it out, as I had another riddle so much more interesting upon my mind, which was that of the man's asking charity before the door of the hotel—I would have given

anything to have got to the bottom of it; and that, not out of curiosity —'tis so low a principle of enquiry, in general, I would not purchase the gratification of it with a two-sous piece—but a secret, I thought, which so soon and so certainly soften'd the heart of every woman you came near, was a secret at least equal to the philosopher's stone: had I had both the Indies, I would have given up one to have been master of it.

I toss'd and turn'd it almost all night long in my brains to no manner of purpose: and when I awoke in the morning, I found my spirit as much troubled with my *dreams,* as ever the king of Babylon had been with his; and I will not hesitate to affirm, it would have puzzled all the wise men of Paris as much as those of Chaldea, to have given its interpretation.

Le Dimanche—Paris

It was Sunday; and when La Fleur came in, in the morning, with my coffee and roll and butter, he had got himself so gallantly array'd, I scarce knew him.

I had covenanted at Montriul to give him a new hat with a silver button and loop and four Louis d'ors *pour s'adoniser,* when we got to Paris; and the poor fellow, to do him justice, had done wonders with it.

He had bought a bright, clean, good scarlet coat, and a pair of breeches of the same—They were not a crown worse, he said, for the wearing—I wish'd him hang'd for telling me—They look'd so fresh, that tho' I knew the thing could not be done, yet I would rather have imposed upon my fancy with thinking I had bought them new for the fellow, than that they had come out of the Rue de Friperie.

This is a nicety which makes not the heart sore at Paris.

He had purchased moreover a handsome blue sattin waistcoat, fancifully enough embroidered—this was indeed something the worse for the service it had done, but 'twas clean scour'd—the gold had been touch'd up, and upon the whole was rather showy than otherwise— and as the blue was not violent, it suited with the coat and breeches very well: he had squeez'd out of the money, moreover, a new bag and a solitaire; and had insisted with the *fripier* upon a gold pair of garters to his breeches knees—He had purchased muslin ruffles, *bien brodées,* with four livres of his own money—and a pair of white silk stockings for five more—and, to top all, nature had given him a handsome figure, without costing him a sous.

He entered the room thus set off, with his hair drest in the first style, and with a handsome bouquet in his breast—in a word, there was that look of festivity in every thing about him, which at once

put me in mind it was Sunday—and by combining both together, it instantly struck me, that the favour he wish'd to ask of me the night before, was to spend the day as every body in Paris spent it besides. I had scarce made the conjecture, when La Fleur, with infinite humility, but with a look of trust, as if I should not refuse him, begg'd I would grant him the day, *pour faire le galant vis-à-vis de sa maîtresse.*

Now it was the very thing I intended to do myself *vis-à-vis* Madame de R—— —I had retained the Remise on purpose for it, and it would not have mortified my vanity to have had a servant so well dress'd as La Fleur was, to have got up behind it: I never could have worse spared him.

But we must *feel,* not argue in these embarrassments—the sons and daughters of service part with liberty, but not with nature, in their contracts; they are flesh and blood, and have their little vanities and wishes in the midst of the house of bondage, as well as their task-masters—no doubt they have set their self-denials at a price—and their expectations are so unreasonable, that I would often disappoint them, but that their condition puts it so much in my power to do it.

Behold—Behold, I am thy servant—disarms me at once of the powers of a master—

—Thou shalt go, La Fleur! said I.

—And what mistress, La Fleur, said I, canst thou have pick'd up in so little a time at Paris? La Fleur laid his hand upon his breast, and said 'twas a *petite demoiselle,* at Monsieur le Count de B——'s—La Fleur had a heart made for society; and, to speak the truth of him, let as few occasions slip him as his master—so that somehow or other—but how—Heaven knows—he had connected himself with the *demoiselle* upon the landing of the stair-case, during the time I was taken up with my passport; and as there was time enough for me to win the Count to my interest, La Fleur had contrived to make it do to win the maid to his. The family, it seems, was to be at Paris that day, and he had made a party with her, and two or three more the Count's household, upon the *boulevards.*

Happy people! that once a week at least are sure to lay down all your cares together, and dance and sing, and sport away the weights of grievance, which bow down the spirit of other nations of the earth.

The Fragment—Paris

La Fleur had left me something to amuse myself with for the day more than I had bargain'd for, or could have entered either into his head or mine.

He had brought the little print of butter upon a currant-leaf; and as the morning was warm, he had begg'd a sheet of waste paper to put betwixt the currant-leaf and his hand—As that was plate sufficient, I bade him lay it upon the table as it was; and as I resolved to stay within all day, I ordered him to call upon the *traiteur,* to bespeak my dinner, and leave me to breakfast by myself.

When I had finished the butter, I threw the currant-leaf out of the window, and was going to do the same by the waste paper—but stopping to read a line first, and that drawing me on to a second and third—I thought it better worth; so I shut the window, and drawing a chair up to it, I sat down to read it.

It was in the old French of Rabelais's time, and for aught I know might have been wrote by him—it was moreover in a Gothic letter, and that so faded and gone off by damps and length of time, it cost me infinite trouble to make any thing of it—I threw it down; and then wrote a letter to Eugenius—then I took it up again and embroiled my patience with it afresh—and then to cure that, I wrote a letter to Eliza—Still it kept hold of me; and the difficulty of understanding it increased but the desire.

I got my dinner; and after I had enlightened my mind with a bottle of Burgundy, I at it again—and after two or three hours poring upon it, with almost as deep attention as ever Gruter or Jacob Spon did upon a nonsensical inscription, I thought I made sense of it; but to make sure of it, the best way, I imagined, was to turn it into English, and see how it would look then—so I went on leisurely as a trifling man does, sometimes writing a sentence—then taking a turn or two— and then looking how the world went out of the window; so that it was nine o'clock at night before I had done it—I then began and read it as follows.

The Fragment—Paris

Now as the Notary's wife disputed the point with the Notary with too much heat—I wish, said the Notary (throwing down the parchment) that there was another Notary here only to set down and attest all this—

—And what would you do then, Monsieur? said she, rising hasily up—the Notary's wife was a little fume of a woman, and the Notary thought it well to avoid a hurricane by a mild reply—I would go, answered he, to bed—You may go to the devil answer'd the Notary's wife.

Now there happening to be but one bed in the house, the other

two rooms being unfurnished, as is the custom at Paris, and the Notary not caring to lie in the same bed with a woman who had but that moment sent him pell-mell to the devil, went forth with his hat and cane and short cloak, the night being very windy, and walk'd out ill at ease towards the *Pont Neuf*.

Of all the bridges which ever were built, the whole world who have pass'd over the *Pont Neuf* must own, that it is the noblest—the finest—the grandest—the lightest—the longest—the broadest that ever conjoin'd land and land together upon the face of the terraqueous globe—

By this it seems as if the author of the fragment had not been a Frenchman.

The worst fault which divines and the doctors of the Sorbonne can allege against it, is, that if there is but a cap-full of wind in or about Paris, 'tis more blasphemously *sacre Dieu'd* there than in any other aperture of the whole city—and with reason, good and cogent, Messieurs; for it comes against you without crying *garde d'eau*, and with such unpremeditable puffs, that of the few who cross it with their hats on not one in fifty but hazards two livres and a half, which is its full worth.

The poor Notary, just as he was passing by the sentry, instinctively clapp'd his cane to the side of it, but in raising it up, the point of his cane catching hold of the loop of the centinel's hat, hoisted it over the spikes of the ballustrade clear into the Seine—

—*'Tis an ill wind*, said a boat-man, who catch'd it, *which blows nobody any good*.

The sentry, being a Gascon, incontinently twirl'd up his whiskers, and levell'd his harquebuss.

Harquebusses in those days went off with matches; and an old woman's paper lantern at the end of the bridge happening to be blown out she had borrow'd the sentry's match to light it—it gave a moment's time for the Gascon's blood to run cool, and turn the accident better to his advantage—*'Tis an ill wind*, said he, catching off the Notary's castor, and legitimating the capture with the boatman's adage.

The poor Notary cross'd the bridge, and passing along the rue de Dauphine into the fauxbourg of St. Germain, lamented himself as he walked along in this manner:

Luckless man that I am! said the Notary, to be the sport of hurricanes all my days—to be born to have the storm of ill language levell'd against me and my profession wherever I go—to be forced into marriage by the thunder of the church to a tempest of a woman—to be driven forth out of my house by domestic winds, and despoil'd of my

castor by pontific ones—to be here, bare-headed, in a windy night at the mercy of the ebbs and flows of accidents—where am I to lay my head?—miserable man! what wind in the two-and-thirty points of the whole compass can blow unto thee, as it does to the rest of thy fellow-creatures, good!

As the Notary was passing on by a dark passage, complaining in this sort, a voice call'd out to a girl, to bid her run for the next Notary —now the Notary being the next, and availing himself of his situation, walk'd up the passage to the door, and passing through an old sort of a saloon, was usher'd into a large chamber, dismantled of every thing but a long military pike—a breast-plate—a rusty old sword, and bandoleer, hung up equidistant in four different places against the wall.

An old personage, who had heretofore been a gentleman, and unless decay of fortune taints the blood along with it, was a gentleman at that time, lay supporting his head upon his hand, in his bed; a little table with a taper burning was set close beside it, and close by the table was placed a chair—the Notary sat him down in it; and pulling out his inkhorn and a sheet or two of paper which he had in his pocket, he placed them before him, and dipping his pen in his ink, and leaning his breast over the table, he disposed every thing to make the gentleman's last will and testament.

Alas! Monsieur le Notaire, said the gentleman, raising himself up a little, I have nothing to bequeath, which will pay the expence of bequeathing, except the history of myself, which I could not die in peace unless I left it as a legacy to the world; the profits arising out of it I bequeath to you for the pains of taking it from me—it is a story so uncommon, it must be read by all mankind—it will make the fortunes of your house—the Notary dipp'd his pen into his inkhorn— Almighty Director of every event in my life! said the old gentleman, looking up earnestly, and raising his hands towards heaven—Thou, whose hand hast led me on through such a labyrinth of strange passages down into this scene of desolation, assist the decaying memory of an old, infirm, and broken-hearted man—direct my tongue by the spirit of thy eternal truth, that this stranger may set down nought but what is written in that Book, from whose records, said he, clasping his hands together, I am to be condemn'd or acquitted!—The Notary held up the point of his pen betwixt the taper and his eye—

—It is a story, Monsieur le Notaire, said the gentleman, which will rouse up every affection in nature—it will kill the humane, and touch the heart of cruelty herself with pity—

—The Notary was inflamed with a desire to begin, and put his pen a third time into his inkhorn—and the old gentleman turning a little

more towards the Notary, began to dictate his story in these words—
—And where is the rest of it, La Fleur? said I—as he just then entered the room.

The Fragment and the Bouquet*—Paris

When La Fleur came up close to the table, and was made to comprehend what I wanted, he told me there were only two other sheets of it, which he had wrapt round the stalks of a bouquet to keep it together, which he had presented to the *demoiselle* upon the *boulevards*—Then prithee, La Fleur, said I, step back to her to the Count de B——'s hotel, and *see if thou canst get it*—There is no doubt of it, said La Fleur—and away he flew.

In a very little time the poor fellow came back quite out of breath, with deeper marks of disappointment in his looks than could arise from the simple irreparability of the fragment—*Juste ciel!* in less than two minutes that the poor fellow had taken his last tender farewell of her —his faithless mistress had given his *gage d'amour* to one of the Count's footmen—the footman to a young sempstress—and the sempstress to a fidler, with my fragment at the end of it—Our misfortunes were involved together—I gave a sigh—and La Fleur echo'd it back again to my ear.

—How perfidious! cried La Fleur—How unlucky! said I.

—I should not have been mortified, Monsieur, quoth La Fleur, if she had lost it—Nor I, La Fleur, said I, had I found it.

Whether I did or no will be seen hereafter.

The Act of Charity—Paris

The man who either disdains or fears to walk up a dark entry, may be an excellent good man, and fit for a hundred things; but he will not do to make a good sentimental traveller. I count little of the many things I see pass at broad noonday, in large and open streets. —Nature is shy, and hates to act before spectators; but in such an unobserved corner you sometimes see a single short scene of hers, worth all the sentiments of a dozen French plays compounded together—and yet they are *absolutely* fine;—and whenever I have a more brilliant affair upon my hands than common, as they suit a preacher just as well as a hero, I generally make my sermon out of

*Nosegay.

'em—and for the text—"Cappadocia, Pontus and Asia, Phrygia and Pamphylia"—is as good as any one in the Bible.

There is a long dark passage issuing out from the opera comique into a narrow street; 'tis trod by a few who humbly wait for a *fiacre,** or wish to get off quietly o' foot when the opera is done. At the end of it, towards the theatre, 'tis lighted by a small candle, the light of which is almost lost before you get half-way down, but near the door—'tis more for ornament than use: you see it as a fix'd star of the least magnitude; it burns—but does little good to the world, that we know of.

In returning along this passage, I discern'd, as I approach'd within five or six paces of the door, two ladies standing arm in arm with their backs against the wall, waiting, as I imagined, for a *fiacre*—as they were next the door, I thought they had a prior right; so edged myself up within a yard or little more of them, and quietly took my stand— I was in black, and scarce seen.

The lady next me was a tall lean figure of a woman, of about thirty-six; the other of the same size and make, of about forty; there was no mark of wife or widow in any one part of either of them—they seem'd to be two upright vestal sisters, unsapp'd by caresses, unbroke in upon by tender salutations: I could have wish'd to have made them happy —their happiness was destin'd that night, to come from another quarter.

A low voice, with a good turn of expression, and sweet cadence at the end of it, begg'd for a twelve-sous piece betwixt them, for the love of Heaven. I thought it singular that a begger should fix the quota of an alms—and that the sum be twelve times as much as what is usually given in 'the dark. They both seem'd astonish'd at it as much as my-self.—Twelve sous! said one—A twelve-sous piece! said the other— and made no reply.

The poor man said, he knew not how to ask less of ladies of their rank; and bow'd down his head to the ground.

Poo! said they—we have no money.

The beggar remained silent for a moment or two, and renew'd his supplication.

Do not, my fair young ladies, said he, stop your good ears against me—Upon my word, honest man! said the younger, we have no change—Then God bless you, said the poor man, and multiply those joys which you can give to others without change!—I observed the elder sister put her hand into her pocket—I'll see, said she, if I have a sous.—A sous! give twelve, said the supplicant; Nature has been bountiful to you, be bountiful to a poor man.

*Hackney-coach.

I would, friend, with all my heart, said the younger, if I had it.

My fair charitable! said he, addressing himself to the elder—What is it but your goodness and humanity which makes your bright eyes so sweet, that they outshine the morning even in this dark passage? and what was it which made the Marquis de Santerre and his brother say so much of you both as they just pass'd by?

The two ladies seemed much affected; and impulsively at the same time they both put their hands into their pocket, and each took out a twelve-sous piece.

The contest betwixt them and the poor supplicant was no more—it was continued betwixt themselves, which of the two should give the twelve-sous piece in charity—and to end the dispute, they both gave it together, and the man went away.

The Riddle Explained—Paris

I stepped hastily after him: it was the very man whose success in asking charity of the women before the door of the hotel had so puzzled me—and I found at once his secret, or at least the basis of it —'twas flattery.

Delicious essence! how refreshing art thou to nature! how strongly are all its powers and all its weaknesses on thy side! how sweetly dost thou mix with the blood, and help it through the most difficult and tortuous passages to the heart!

The poor man, as he was not straiten'd for time, had given it here in a larger dose: 'tis certain he had a way of bringing it into less form, for the many sudden cases he had to do with in the streets; but how he contrived to correct, sweeten, concentre, and qualify it—I vex not my spirit with the inquiry—it is enough, the beggar gained two twelve-sous pieces—and they can best tell the rest who have gained much greater matters by it.

Paris

We get forwards in the world, not so much by doing services, as receiving them; you take a withering twig, and put it in the ground; and then you water it because you have planted it.

Mons. le Count de B——, merely because he had done me one kindness in the affair of my passport, would go on and do me another, the few days he was at Paris, in making me known to a few people of rank; and they were to present me to others, and so on.

I had got master of my *secret* just in time to turn these honours to some little account; otherwise, as is commonly the case, I should have din'd or supp'd a single time or two round, and then by *translating* French looks and attitudes into plain English, I should presently have seen, that I had gold out of the *couvert** of some more entertaining guest; and in course should have resigned all my places one after another, merely upon the principle that I could not keep them.—As it was, things did not go much amiss.

—I had the honour of being introduced to the old Marquis de B——: in days of yore he had signaliz'd himself by some small feats of chivalry in the *Cour d'amour,* and had dress'd himself out to the idea of tilts and tournaments ever since—the Marquis de B—— wish'd to have it thought the affair was somewhere else than in his brain. "He could like to take a trip to England," and ask'd much of the English ladies. Stay where you are, I beseech you, Mons. le Marquis, said I— Les Messrs. Anglois can scarce get a kind look from them as it is— The Marquis invited me to supper.

Mons. P—— the farmer-general was just as inquisitive about our taxes—They were very considerable, he heard—If we knew but how to collect them, said I, making him a low bow.

I could never have been invited to Mons. P——'s concerts upon any other terms.

I had been misrepresented to Madame de Q—— as an *esprit*— Madame de Q—— was an *esprit* herself: she burnt with impatience to see me, and hear me talk. I had not taken my seat, before I saw she did not care a sous whether I had any wit or no—I was let in, to be convinced she had.—I call Heaven to witness I never once open'd the door of my lips.

Madame de V—— vow'd to every creature she met, "She had never had a more improving conversation with a man in her life."

There are three epochas in the empire of a French woman—She is coquette—then deist—then *dévote:* the empire during these is never lost—she only changes her subjects: when thirty-five years and more have unpeopled her dominions of the slaves of love, she repeoples it with slaves of infidelity—and then with the slaves of the church.

Madame de V—— was vibrating betwixt the first of these epochas: the colour of the rose was fading fast away—she ought to have been a deist five years before the time I had the honour to pay my first visit. She placed me upon the same sopha with her, for the sake of disputing the point of religion more closely—In short, Madame de V—— told me she believed nothing.

I told Madame de V—— it might be her principle; but I was sure

*Plate, napkin, knife, fork, and spoon.

it could not be her interest to level the outworks, without which I could not conceive how such a citadel as hers could be defended—that there was not a more dangerous thing in the world than for a beauty to be a deist—that it was a debt I owed my creed, not to conceal it from her—that I had not been five minutes sat upon the sopha beside her, but I had begun to form designs—and what is it, but the sentiments of religion, and the persuasion they had excited in her breast, which could have check'd them as they rose up?

We are not adamant, said I, taking hold of her hand—and there is need of all restraints, till age in her own time steals in and lays them on us —but, my dear lady, said I, kissing her hand—'tis too—too soon—

I declare I had the credit all over Paris of unperverting Madame de V—— ——She affirmed to Mons. D—— an the Abbe M——, that in one half-hour I had said more for revealed religion, than all their Encyclopedia had said against it—I was lifted directly into Madame de V——'s *Coterie*—and she put off the epocha of deism for two years.

I remember it was in this *Coterie*, in the middle of a discourse, in which I was shewing the necessity of a *first cause*, that the young Count de Faineant took me by the hand to the farthest corner of the room, to tell me my *solitaire* was pinn'd too strait about my neck —It should be *plus badinant,* said the Count, looking down upon his own—but a word, Mons. Yorick, *to the wise*—

—And *from the wise,* Mons. le Count, replied I, making him a bow—*is enough.*

The Count de Faineant embraced me with more ardour than ever I was embraced by mortal man.

For three weeks together, I was of every man's opinion I met.— *Pardi! ce Mons. Yorick a autant d'esprit que nous autres—Il raisonne bien,* said another—*C'est un bon enfant,* said a third.—And at this price I could have eaten and drank and been merry all the days of my life at Paris; but 'twas a dishonest *reckoning*—I grew ashamed of it.— It was the gain of a slave—every sentiment of honour revolted against it—the higher I got, the more was I forced upon my *beggarly system* —the better the *Coterie*—the more children of Art—I languish'd for those of Nature: and one night, after a most vile prostitution of myself to half a dozen different people, I grew sick—went to bed—order'd La Fleur to get me horses in the morning to set out for Italy.

Maria—Moulines

I never felt what the distress of plenty was in any one shape till now —to travel it through the Bourbonnois, the sweetest part of France—in

the heyday of the vintage, when Nature is pouring her abundance into every one's lap and every eye is lifted up—a journey through each step of which Music beats time to *Labour*, and all her children are rejoicing as they carry in their clusters—to pass through this with my affections flying out, and kindling at every group before me—and every one of them was pregnant with adventures.

Just Heaven!—it would fill up twenty volumes—and alas! I have but a few small pages left of this to crowd it into—and half of these must be taken up with the poor Maria my friend Mr. Shandy met with near Moulines.

The story he had told of that disorder'd maid affected me not a little in the reading; but when I got within the neighborhood where she lived, it returned so strong into my mind, that I could not resist an impulse which prompted me to go half a league out of the road, to the village where her parents dwelt, to enquire after her.

'Tis going, I own, like the Knight of the Woeful Countenance, in quest of melancholy adventures—but I know not how it is, but I am never so perfectly conscious of the existence of a soul within me, as when I am entangled in them.

The old mother came to the door, her looks told me the story before she open'd her mouth—She had lost her husband; he had died, she said, of anguish, for the loss of Maria's senses, about a month before. —She had feared at first, she added, that it would have plunder'd her poor girl of what little understanding was left—but, on the contrary, it had brought her more to herself—still she could not rest—her poor daughter, she said, crying, was wandering somewhere about the road—

—Why does my pulse beat languid as I write this? and what made La Fleur, whose heart seem'd only to be tuned to joy, to pass the back of his hand twice across his eyes, as the woman stood and told it? I beckoned to the postillion to turn back into the road.

When we had got within half a league of Moulines, at a little opening in the road leading to a thicket, I discovered poor Maria sitting under a poplar—she was sitting with her elbow in her lap, and her head leaning on one side within her hand—a small brook ran at the foot of the tree.

I bid the postillion go on with the chaise to Moulines—and La Fleur to bespeak my supper—and that I would walk after him.

She was dress'd in white, and much as my friend described her, except that her hair hung loose, which before was twisted within a silk net.—She had, super-added likewise to her jacket, a pale green ribband, which fell across her shoulder to the waist; at the end of which hung her pipe.—Her goat had been as faithless as her lover; and she had got a little dog in lieu of him, which she had kept tied by a string

to her girdle: as I look'd at her dog, she drew him towards her with the string.—"Thou shalt not leave me, Sylvio," said she. I look'd in Maria's eyes, and saw she was thinking more of her father than of her lover or her little goat; for as she utter'd them, the tears trickled down her cheeks.

I sat down close by her; and Maria let me wipe them away as they fell, with my handkerchief.—I then steep'd it in my own—and then in hers—and then in mine—and then I wip'd hers again—and as I did it, I felt such undescribable emotions within me, as I am sure could not be accounted for from any combinations of matter and motion.

I am positive I have a soul; nor can all the books with which materialists have pestered the world ever convince me to the contrary.

Maria

When Maria had come a little to herself, I ask'd her if she remembered a pale thin person of a man, who had sat down betwixt her and her goat about two years before? She said, she was unsettled much at that time, but remember'd it upon two accounts—that ill as she was, she saw the person pitied her; and next, that her goat had stolen his handkerchief, and she had beat him for the theft—she had wash'd it, she said, in the brook, and kept it ever since in her pocket to restore it to him in case she should ever see him again, which, she added, he had half promised her. As she told me this, she took the handkerchief out of her pocket to let me see it; she had folded it up neatly in a couple of vine-leaves, tied round with a tendril—on opening it, I saw an S. marked in one of the corners.

She had since that, she told me, strayed as far as Rome, had walk'd round St. Peter's once—and return'd back—that she found her way alone across the Apennines—had travell'd over all Lombardy without money—and through the flinty roads of Savoy without shoes—how she had borne it, and how she had got supported, she could not tell —but *God tempers the wind*, said Maria, to the shorn lamb.

Shorn indeed! and to the quick, said I; and wast thou in my own land, where I have a cottage, I would take thee to it and shelter thee: thou shouldst eat of my own bread, and drink of my own cup—I would be kind to thy Sylvio—in all thy weaknesses and wanderings I would seek after thee and bring thee back—when the sun went down I would say my prayers; and when I had done thou shouldst play thy evening song upon thy pipe, nor would the incense of my sacrifice be worse accepted for entering heaven along with that of a broken heart.

Nature melted within me, as I utter'd this; and Maria observing, as I took out my handkerchief, that it was steep'd too much already to be of use, would needs go wash it in the stream.—And where will you dry it, Maria? said I.—I'll dry it in my bosom, said she—'twill do me good.

And is your heart still so warm, Maria? said I.

I touched upon the string on which hung all her sorrows—she look'd with wistful disorder for some time in my face; and then, without saying any thing, took her pipe, and play'd her service to the Virgin —The string I had touch'd ceased to vibrate—in a moment or two Maria returned to herself—let her pipe fall—and rose up.

And where are you going, Maria? said I.—She said, to Moulines— Let us go, said I, together.—Maria put her arm within mine, and lengthening the string, to let the dog follow—in that order we enter'd Moulines.

Maria—Moulines

Tho' I hate salutations and greetings in the market-place, yet when we got into the middle of this, I stopp'd to take my last look and last farewel of Maria.

Maria, though not tall, was nevertheless of the first order of fine forms—affliction had touch'd her looks with something that was scarce earthly—still she was feminine—and so much was there about her of all that the heart wishes, or the eye looks for in woman, that could the traces be ever worn out of her brain, and those of Eliza out of mine, she should *not only eat of my bread and drink of my own cup,* but Maria should lie in my bosom, and be unto me as a daughter.

Adieu, poor luckless maiden!—Imbibe the oil and wine which the compassion of a stranger, as he journeyeth on his way, now pours into thy wounds—the Being who has twice bruised thee can only bind them up for ever.

The Bourbonnois

There was nothing from which I had painted out for myself so joyous a riot of the affections, as in this journey in the vintage, through this part of France; but pressing through this gate of sorrow to it, my sufferings have totally unfitted me: in every scene of festivity I saw Maria in the background of the piece, sitting pensive under her poplar; and I had got almost to Lyons before I was able to cast a shade across her.

—Dear sensibility! source inexhausted of all that's precious in our joys, or costly in our sorrows! thou chainest thy martyr down upon his bed of straw—and 'tis thou who lift'st him up to HEAVEN—Eternal fountain of our feelings!—'tis here I trace thee—and this is thy *"divinity which stirs within me"*—not, that in some sad and sickening moments, *"my soul shrinks back upon herself, and startles at destruction"*—mere pomp of words!—but that I feel some generous joys and generous cares beyond myself—all comes from thee, great—great SENSORIUM of the world! which vibrates, if a hair of our heads but falls upon the ground, in the remotest desert of thy creation—Touch'd with thee, Eugenius draws my curtain when I languish—hears my tale of symptoms, and blames the weather for the disorder of his nerves. Thou giv'st a portion of it sometimes to the roughest peasant who traverses the bleakest mountains—he finds the lacerated lamb of another's flock—This moment I beheld him leaning with his head against his crook, with piteous inclination looking down upon it!—Oh! had I come one moment sooner!—it bleeds to death—his gentle heart bleeds with it—

Peace to thee, generous swain!—I see thou walkest off with anguish —but thy joys shall balance it—for happy is thy cottage—and happy is the sharer of it—and happy are the lambs which sport about you.

The Supper

A shoe coming loose from the forefoot of the thill-horse, at the beginning of the ascent of mount Taurira, the postillion dismounted, twisted the shoe off, and put it in his pocket; as the ascent was of five or six miles and that horse our main dependence, I made a point of having the shoe fasten'd on again, as well as we could; but the postillion had thrown away the nails, and the hammer in the chaise-box being of no great use without them, I submitted to go on.

He had not mounted half a mile higher, when coming to a flinty piece of road, the poor devil lost a second shoe, and from off his other fore-foot. I then got out of the chaise in good earnest; and seeing a house about a quarter of a mile to the left-hand, with a great deal to do I prevailed upon the postillion to turn up to it. The look of the house, and of every thing about it, as we drew nearer, soon reconciled me to the disaster.—It was a little farm-house, surrounded with about twenty acres of vineyard, about as much corn—and close to the house, on one side, was a *potagerie* of an acre and a half, full of every thing which could make plenty in a French peasant's house—and on the other side was a little wood, which furnished wherewithal to dress it.

It was about eight in the evening when I got to the house—so I left the postillion to manage his point as he could—and for mine, I walk'd directly into the house.

The family consisted of an old grey-headed man and his wife, with five or six sons and sons-in-law and their several wives, and a joyous genealogy out of them.

They were all sitting down together to their lentil-soup; a large wheaten loaf was in the middle of the table; and a flaggon of wine at each end of it, promised joy through the stages of the repast—'twas a feast of love.

The old man rose up to meet me, and with a respectful cordiality would have me sit down at the table; my heart was set down the moment I enter'd the room; so I sat down at once like a son of the family; and to invest myself in the character as speedily as I could, I instantly borrowed the old man's knife, and taking up the loaf, cut myself a hearty luncheon; and as I did it, I saw a testimony in every eye, not only of an honest welcome but of a welcome mix'd with thanks that I had not seem'd to doubt it.

Was it this; or tell me, Nature, what else it was that made this morsel so sweet—and to what magic I owe it, that the draught I took of their flaggon was so delicious with it, that they remain upon my palate to this hour?

If the supper was to my taste—the grace which followed it was much more so.

The Grace

When supper was over, the old man gave a knock upon the table with the haft of his knife, to bid them prepare for the dance: the moment the signal was given, the women and girls ran all together into a back apartment to tye up their hair—and the young men to the door to wash their faces, and change their sabots; and in three minutes every soul was ready upon a little esplanade before the house to begin —The old man and his wife came out last, and placing me betwixt them, sat down upon a sopha of turf by the door.

The old man had some fifty years ago been no mean performer upon the vielle—and, at the age he was then of, touch'd it well enough for the purpose. His wife sung now-and-then a little to the tune—then intermitted—and join'd her old man again as their children and grandchildren danced before them.

It was not till the middle of the second dance, when for some pauses in the movement wherein they all seem'd to look up, I fancied I

could distinguish an elevation of spirit different from that which is the cause or the effect of simple jollity.—In a word, I thought I beheld *Religion* mixing in the dance—but as I had never seen her so engaged, I should have look'd upon it now as one of the illusions of an imagination which is eternally misleading me, had not the old man, as soon as the dance ended, said, that this was their constant way; and that all his life long he had made it a rule after supper was over, to call out his family to dance and rejoice; believing, he said, that a cheerful and contented mind was the best sort of thanks to Heaven that an illiterate peasant could pay—

—Or a learned prelate either, said I.

The Case of Delicacy

When you have gain'd the top of mount Taurira, you run presently down to Lyons—adieu then to all rapid movements! 'Tis a journey of caution; and it fares better with sentiments, not to be in a hurry with them; so I contracted with a Voiturin to take his time with a couple of mules, and convey me in my own chaise safe to Turin through Savoy.

Poor, patient, quiet, honest people! fear not: your poverty, the treasury of your simple virtues, will not be envied you by the world, nor will your vallies be invaded by it.—Nature! in the midst of thy disorders, thou art still friendly to the scantiness thou hast created —with all thy great works about thee, little hast thou left to give, either to the scythe or to the sickle—but to that little thou grantest safety and protection; and sweet are the dwellings which stand so shelter'd.

Let the way-worn traveller vent his complaints upon the sudden turns and dangers of your roads—your rocks,—your precipices—the difficulties of getting up—the horrors of getting down—mountains impracticable—and cataracts, which roll down great stones from their summits, and block his road up—The peasants had been all day at work in removing a fragment of this kind between St. Michael and Madane; and by the time my Voiturin got to the place, it wanted full two hours of completing before a passage could any how be gain'd: there was nothing but to wait with patience—'twas a wet and tempestuous night: so that by the delay, and that together, the Voiturin found himself obliged to take up five miles short of his stage at a little decent kind of an inn by the road-side.

I forthwith took possession of my bed-chamber—got a good fire— order'd supper; and was thanking Heaven it was no worse—when a voiture arrived with a lady in it and her servant-maid.

As there was no other bed-chamber in the house, the hostess, without much nicety, led them into mine, telling them, as she usher'd them in, that there was nobody in it but an English gentleman—that there were two good beds in it, and a closet within the room which held another.—The accent in which she spoke of this third bed did not say much for it—however, she said there were three beds, and but three people—and she durst say, the gentleman would do any thing to accommodate matters.—I left not the lady a moment to make a conjecture about it—so instantly made a declaration that I would do any thing in my power.

As this did not amount to an absolute surrender of my bed-chamber, I still felt myself so much the proprietor, as to have a right to do the honours of it—so I desired the lady to sit down—pressed her into the warmest seat—call'd for more wood—and desired the hostess to enlarge the plan of the supper, and to favour us with the very best wine.

The lady had scarce warm'd herself five minutes at the fire, before she began to turn her head back, and give a look at the beds; and the oftener she cast her eyes that way, the more they return'd perplex'd—I felt for her—and for myself; for in a few minutes, what by her looks, and the case itself, I found myself as much embarrassed as it was possible the lady could be herself.

That the beds we were to lie in were in one and the same room, was enough simply by itself to have excited all this—but the position of them, for they stood parallel, and so very close to each other, as only to allow space for a small wicker chair betwixt them, rendered the affair still more oppressive to us—they were fixed up moreover near the fire, and the projection of the chimney on one side, and a large beam which cross'd the room on the other, form'd a kind of recess for them that was no way favourable to the nicety of our sensations—if any thing could have added to it, it was that the two beds were both of them so very small, as to cut off from every idea of the lady and the maid lying together; which in either of them, could it have been feasible, my lying beside them, though a thing not to be wish'd, yet there was nothing in it so terrible which the imagination might not have pass'd over without torment.

As for the little room within, it offer'd little or no consolation to us; 'twas a damp cold closet, with a half dismantled window-shutter, and with a window which had neither glass or oil paper in it to keep out the tempest of the night. I did not endeavour to stifle my cough when the lady gave a peep into it; so it reduced the case in course to this alternative—that the lady should sacrifice her health to her feelings, and take up with the closet herself, and abandon the bed next mine to her maid—or that the girl should take the closet, &c. &c.

The lady was a Piedmontese of about thirty, with a glow of health in her cheeks.—The maid was a Lyonoise of twenty, and as brisk and lively a French girl as ever moved.

—There were difficulties every way—and the obstacle of the stone in the road, which brought us into the distress, great as it appeared whilst the peasants were removing it, was but a pebble to what lay in our ways now—I have only to add, that it did not lessen the weight which hung upon our spirits, that we were both too delicate to communicate what we felt to each other upon the occasion.

We sat down to supper; and had we not had more generous wine to it than the little inn in Savoy could have furnish'd, our tongues had been tied, till necessity herself had set them at liberty—but the lady having a few bottles of Burgundy in her voiture, sent down her Fille de Chambre for a couple of them; so that by the time supper was over, and we were left alone, we felt ourselves inspired with a strength of mind sufficient to talk, at least, without reserve upon our situation. We turn'd it every way, and debated and considered it in all kind of lights in the course of a two hours negotiation; at the end of which the articles were settled finally betwixt us, and stipulated for in form and manner of a treaty of peace—and I believe with as much religion and good faith on both sides, as in any treaty which has yet had the honour of being handed down to posterity.

They were as follows:

First, As the right of the bed-chamber is in Monsieur—and he thinking the bed next to the fire to be the warmest, he insists upon the concession on the lady's side of taking up with it.

Granted, on the part of Madame; with a proviso, That as the curtains of that bed are of a flimsey transparent cotton, and appear likewise too scanty to draw close, that the Fille de Chambre shall fasten up the opening, either by corking pins, or needle and thread, in such manner as shall be deem'd a sufficient barrier on the side of Monsieur.

2dly. It is required on the part of Madame, that Monsieur shall lie the whole night through in his robe de chambre.

Rejected: inasmuch as Monsieur is not worth a robe de chambre; he having nothing in his portmanteau but six shirts and a black silk pair of breeches.

The mentioning of the silk pair of breeches made an entire change of the article—for the breeches were accepted as an equivalent for the robe de chambre; and so it was stipulated and agreed upon, that I should lie in my black silk breeches all night.

3dly. It was insisted upon, and stipulated for by the lady, that after Monsieur was got to bed, and the candle and fire extinguished, that Monsieur should not speak one single word the whole night.

Granted; provided Monsieur's saying his prayers might not be deem'd an infraction of the treaty.

There was but one point forgot in this treaty, and that was the manner in which the lady and myself should be obliged to undress and get to bed—there was one way of doing it, and that I leave to the reader to devise; protesting as I do, that if it is not the most delicate in nature, 'tis the fault of his own imagination—against which this is not my first complaint.

Now when we were got to bed, whether it was the novelty of the situation, or what it was, I know not; but so it was, I could not shut my eyes; I tried this side and that and turn'd and turn'd again, till a full hour after midnight; when Nature and patience both were wearing out—O my God! said I.

You have broke the treaty, Monsieur, said the lady, who had no more sleep than myself.—I begg'd a thousand pardons—but insisted it was no more than an ejaculation—she maintained 'twas an entire infraction of the treaty—I maintain'd it was provided for in the clause of the third article.

The lady would by no means give up the point, though she weaken'd her barrier by it; for in the warmth of the dispute, I could hear two or three corking pins fall out of the curtain to the ground.

Upon my word and honour, Madame, said I—stretching my arms out of bed by way of asseveration—

(—I was going to have added, that I would not have trespass'd against the remotest idea of decorum for the world)—

—But the Fille de Chambre hearing there were words between us, and fearing that hostilities would ensue in course, had crept silently out of her closet, and it being totally dark, had stolen so close to our beds, that she had got herself into the narrow passage which separated them, and had advanced so far up as to be in a line betwixt her mistress and me—

So that when I stretch'd out my hand, I caught hold of the Fille de Chambre's—

Porgy

A Novel

DUBOSE HEYWARD

DuBose Heyward *was born in Charleston, S. C., August 31, 1885. His father died when he was two, and from his tenth year on DuBose was doing what he could to support his family. First he sold papers, then at fourteen he left the Charleston public schools and went to work in a hardware store. At the end of two years he came down with a serious illness, and it was in the long convalescence which ensued, when books were his constant companions, that he completed his self-education. Porgy, his first novel, was published in 1925. It measures 39,000 words.*

For

DOROTHY HEYWARD

Porgy, Maria, and Bess,
Robbins, and Peter, and Crown;
Life was a three-stringed harp
Brought from the woods to town.
Marvelous tunes you rang
From passion, and death, and birth,
You who had laughed and wept
On the warm, brown lap of the earth.
Now in your untried hands
An instrument, terrible, new,
Is thrust by a master who frowns,
Demanding strange songs of you.
God of the White and Black,
Grant us great hearts on the way
That we may understand
Until you have learned to play.

INTRODUCTION

Porgy is the first work in prose of an artist who started as a painter, then shifted to poetry and finally found his full stature as a novelist. It is a novel which broke away from what I call the "Colonel Massa" tradition: the story comes from one of the most aristocratic cities of the old South and yet it carries the reader with perfect confidence and beautiful fidelity through those partitions which so often have set apart the white man and the Negro in fiction as in life.

Porgy takes its name and its central character from a Negro beggar who within recent memory was a familiar figure about the streets of Charleston, S. C. Porgy had lost both legs and in order to navigate at will he had built himself a tiny wooden cart, only a few inches above the ground, which he harnessed to a most odoriferous goat. So much comes down to us in fact. Here, as Mr Heyward recognized, was the perfect vehicle for admitting us to old Catfish Row, the huge Negro tenement on the Charleston water front. Catfish Row in a far-off age had entertained governors and ambassadors but now, with its high ceilings, its battered colonial mantels and its Adam designs still showing in the broken plaster, it is the sanctuary for some forty Negroes, its walls and great court boxing the story as perfectly as if they had been made for no other purpose.

It is Porgy who first leads us into Catfish Row, and it is he and his neighbors who keep us there, beguiled by a life so full of light and shadow, of easy laughter and sudden grief—a life at all times so full of sound, the plucking of a guitar, the thunder of wheels as the great cotton drays roll over the cobbles and the singing which makes the dark throb like an old wound. Porgy and his hefty ally, Maria, the great Negress who keeps the cookshop, Crown, the stevedore, with his sinister strength, and Bess, who comes when Crown calls, Jake, the fishermen and Sportin' Life with his Northern clothes and his "happy dust"— these are individuals each one of whom is a story in himself. It is the free play of their affairs which carries the story along. Notice also that, for all of their wrangling and jealousy, they are bound together by a communal spirit which is their only solace in sorrow and their only defense against the detective and the law they do not understand.

The poet in DuBose Heyward comes out strongly in his feeling for the Negro speech. To him it is much more than mere dialect; he knows their happy gift of improvising; he knows the rhythm of their talk, the awkwardness of their grammar and the old Biblical phrases into which they slip so naturally when in trouble. There may be times when you have to read the dialogue aloud in order to get the sense from the sound. If you could have a Carolinian read it to you you would realize in an instant the beauty which flows out with the words. Listen to Porgy as he talks to his dice: " 'Oh, little stars, roll me some light!' he sang softly, made a pass and won. 'Roll me a sun an' moon!' he urged, and again the cubes did his bidding." Again when Porgy and his stinking goat are stationed outside the lawyer's office and they hear the sound of laughter from within Porgy whispers to the goat: "No, no, bubber. Ain't yuh hear de boss laugh? When nigger mek de buckra laugh, den he know he done won. Dis wey we goin' spen' we libe. You watch." When Peter speaks of "shemale sense," when Maria lashes out at Sportin' Life and his "happy dust," when Simon Frasier, the Negro lawyer, protests that his divorce papers "ain't no mo' dan a license tuh 'dulterate" you know that the novelist is laughing as he says it—but that the words ring true.

Mr Heyward came by such source material in the most natural way possible. It was part—perhaps the most valuable part—of his inheritance. He was born in Charleston of a family rich in ancestors (one of them had signed the Declaration) but poor in property. His family, like so many thousand others, had been thoroughly dispossessed by the Civil War, and young Heyward at an early age had to get out and scramble. He sold papers, worked in a hardware store, was checker in a cotton warehouse, then a salesman of life insurance; through all these lean years the city itself was his recreation. He loved the cotton

wharves, the sea islands and the bay, the old houses and the bells. But not until he was almost forty did he have time to raise his head from the grindstone, withdraw to the hills and write down what he knew. Long patience, love of the city he was born in and personal suffering —these endowed the novelist with that power of sympathy which one feels in his narrative from first to last. From his close friend Hervey Allen I have had this intimate account of how *Porgy* took shape:

"The whole story of *Porgy* is pretty much literally true. DuBose shaped it and, of course, applied the background of old Charleston, of the hurricane, which, by the way, he had been through and which he often spoke of. I remember I told him to read the description of the hurricane in Mrs Atherton's *Conqueror*. He did so and said he could do better than that for his purposes, as he had seen a hurricane at firsthand. I might also say, although you will appreciate that it is somewhat a delicate reference, that I think DuBose was attracted to the character of Porgy because Porgy was a cripple, and so was DuBose. When Heyward was a young boy he had a terrible attack of infantile paralysis and only those who knew him well understood how marvelously he handled himself and how well he concealed his twisted body. Undoubtedly into the making of *Porgy* went that personal understanding that enabled DuBose to tell his tale with passionate sympathy. I can remember many long discussions together about the use of the colorful background of Charleston and DuBose's enthusiasm as the story grew. I do not mean to say that it grew only when we talked about it. That would not be at all correct. It seemed to occur to him in a series of scenes, and we did talk about how to string them together. That was for the novel and not for the play."

Because he was first a painter Mr Heyward naturally saw his story as "a series of scenes," each with its own high lights and shadows, each with its action in the foreground and each in itself distinct. Whether your impressions of Porgy come to you through reading the book or from seeing the play, what you will remember long, long after will be the sunlight and shadow, the laughter and heart-piercing sadness of separate scenes. You will remember Porgy as you first saw him, sitting rapt and intense in the tropical sunlight. You will remember the crap game and the goat cart and Maria as she swings her cleaver through the shark steaks. You will remember Bess in prison after the happy dust has done its work. You will remember the cocky little fishing fleet and how the hurricane roared down and how in that once magnificent ballroom of Catfish Row the Negroes crowded together and swayed and poured their griefs and fears into a rhythm which swept the hours into oblivion.

PORGY

PART I

Porgy lived in the Golden Age. Not the Golden Age of a remote and legendary past; nor yet the chimerical era treasured by every man past middle life, that never existed except in the heart of youth; but an age when men, not yet old, were boys in an ancient, beautiful city that time had forgotten before it destroyed.

In this city there persisted the Golden Age of many things, and not the least among them was that of beggary. In those days the profession was one with a tradition. A man begged, presumably, because he was hungry, much as a man of more energetic temperament became a stevedore from the same cause. His plea for help produced the simple reactions of a generous impulse, a movement of the hand, and the gift of a coin, instead of the elaborate and terrifying processes of organized philanthropy. His antecedents and his mental age were his own affair, and, in the majority of cases, he was as happily oblivious of one as of the other.

Had it all been otherwise, had Porgy come a generation, or even a score of years, later, there would have been a repetition of the old tragedy of genius without opportunity. For, as the artist is born with the vision of beauty, and the tradesman with an eye for barter, so was Porgy equipped by a beneficent providence for a career of mendicancy. Instead of the sturdy legs that would have predestined him for the life of a stevedore on one of the great cotton wharves, he had, when he entered the world, totally inadequate nether extremities, quick to catch the eye, and touch the ready sympathy of the passer-by. Either by birth, or through the application of a philosophy of life, he had acquired a personality that could not be ignored, one which at the same time interested and subtly disturbed. There was that about him which differentiated him from the hordes of fellow practitioners who competed with him for the notice of the tender-hearted. Where others bid eagerly for attention, and burst into voluble thanks and blessings, Porgy sat silent, rapt. There was something Eastern and

563

mystic about the intense introspection of his look. He never smiled, and he acknowledged gifts only by a slow lifting of the eyes that had odd shadows in them. He was black with the almost purple blackness of unadulterated Congo blood. His hands were very large and muscular, and, even when flexed idly in his lap, seemed shockingly formidable in contrast with his frail body. Unless one were unusually preoccupied at the moment of dropping a coin in his cup, he carried away in return a very definite, yet somewhat disquieting, impression: a sense of infinite patience, and beneath it the vibration of unrealized, but terrific, energy.

No one knew Porgy's age. No one remembered when he first made his appearance among the ranks of the local beggars. A woman who had married twenty years before remembered him because he had been seated on the church steps, and had given her a turn when she went in.

Once a child saw Porgy, and said suddenly, "What is he waiting for?" That expressed him better than anything else. He was waiting, waiting with the concentrating intensity of a burning-glass.

As consistent in the practice of his profession as any of the business and professional men who were his most valued customers, Porgy was to be found any morning, by the first arrival in the financial district, against the wall of the old apothecary shop that stands at the corner of King Charles Street and The Meeting House Road. Long custom, reinforced by an eye for the beautiful, had endeared that spot to him. He would sit there in the cool of the early hours and look across the narrow thoroughfare into the green freshness of Jasper Square, where the children flew their kites, and played hide-and-seek among the shrubs. Then, when the morning advanced, and the sun poured its semi-tropical heat between the twin rows of brick, to lie impounded there, like a stagnant pool of flame, he would experience a pleasant atavistic calm, and would doze lightly under the terrific heat, as only a full-blooded negro can. Toward afternoon a slender blue shadow would commence to grow about him that would broaden with great rapidity, cool the baking flags, and turn the tide of customers home before his empty cup.

But Porgy best loved the late afternoons, when the street was quiet again, and the sunlight, deep with color, shot level over the low roof of the apothecary shop to paint the cream stucco on the opposite dwelling a ruddy gold and turn the old rain-washed tiles on the roof to burnished copper. Then the slender, white-clad lady who lived in the house would throw open the deep French windows of the second story drawing-room, and sitting at the piano, where Porgy could see

her dimly, she would play on through the dusk until old Peter drove
by with his wagon to carry him home.

§

Porgy had but one vice. With his day reduced to the dead level
of the commonplace, he was by night an inveterate gambler. Each
evening his collections were carefully divided into a minimum for
room and food, and the remainder for the evening's game. Seen in
the light of the smoking kerosene lamp, with the circle of excited faces
about him, he was no longer the beggar in the dust. His stagnant
blood leaped to sudden life. He was the peer of the great, hulking
fellows who swung cotton bales and stank intolerably from labor in
the fertilizer mills. He even knew that he had won their grudging
respect, for he had a way of coaxing and wheedling the little ivory
cubes that forced them to respond. The loud "Oh, my Baby," and ex-
plosive "Come seben," of his fellow-gamesters seldom brought silver
when he experienced that light, keen feeling and thought of the new,
soft-spoken words to say. In those hours he lost his look of living in the
future. While the ivories flew, he existed in an intense and burning
present.

One Saturday night in late April, with the first premonitory breath
of summer in the air, Porgy sat in the gaming circle that had gathered
before his door in Catfish Row, and murmured softly to his gods of
chance. All day he had been conscious of a vague unrest. There had
been no breeze from the bay, and from his seat outside the apothecary
shop the sky showed opaque blue-grey and bore heavily upon the town.
Towards evening, a thunder-head had lifted over the western horizon
and growled ominously; but it had passed, leaving the air hot, vitiated,
and moist. The negroes had come in for the night feeling irritable,
and, instead of the usual Saturday night of song and talk, the rooms
were for the most part dark and silent, and the court deserted.

The game started late, and there were few players. Opposite Porgy,
sitting upon his haunches, and casting his dice in moody silence, was
a negro called Crown. He was a stevedore, had the body of a gladia-
tor, and a bad name. His cotton-hook, hanging from his belt by a
thong, gleamed in the lamplight, and rang a clear note on the flags
when he leant forward to throw. Crown had been drinking with
Robbins, who sat next to him, and the air was rank with the effluvium
of vile corn whisky. Robbins was voluble, and as usual, when in liquor,
talked incessantly of his wife and children, of whom he was inordi-

nately proud. He was a good provider, and, except for his Saturday night drink and game, of steady habits.

"Dat lady ob mine is a born white-folks nigger," he boasted. "She fambly belong tuh Gob'ner Rutledge. Ain't yet see Miss Rutledge sheself come tuh visit she when she sick? An' dem chillen ob mine, dem is raise wid *ways*."

"Yo' bes sabe yo' talk for dem damn dice. Dice ain't gots no patience wid 'oman!" cut in a young negro of the group.

"Da's de trut'," called another. "Dey is all two after de same nigger money. Dat mek um can't git 'long."

"Shet yo' damn mout' an' t'row!" growled Crown.

Robbins, taken aback, rolled the dice hastily. Scarcely had they settled before Crown scooped them fiercely into his great hand, and, swearing foully at them, sent them tumbling out across the faintly illuminated circle, to lose them on the first cast. Then Porgy took them up tenderly, and held them for a moment cupped in his muscular, slim-fingered hand.

"Oh, little stars, roll me some light!" he sang softly; made a pass, and won. "Roll me a sun an' moon!" he urged; and again the cubes did his bidding.

"Porgy witch dem dice," Crown snarled, as he drained his flask and sent it shattering against the pavement.

Under the beetling walls of the tenement the game went swiftly forward. In a remote room several voices were singing drowsily, as though burdened by the oppression of the day. In another part of the building some one was picking a guitar monotonously, chord after chord, until the dark throbbed like an old wound. But the players were oblivious of all except the splash of orange light that fell upon the flags, and the living little cubes that flashed or dawdled upon it, according to the mood of the hand that propelled them. Peter, the old wagoner, sat quietly smoking in Porgy's doorway, and looked on with the indulgent smile of tolerant age. Once when Crown lost heavily, and turned snarling upon Robbins with, "T'row dem damn dice fair, nigger," he cautioned mildly, "Frien' an' licker an' dice ain't meant tuh 'sociate. Yo' mens bes' go slow."

Then, in a flash, it happened.

Robbins rolled again, called the dice, and retrieved them before Crown's slow wits got the count, then swept the heap of coins into his pocket.

With a low snarl, straight from his crouching position, Crown hurled his tremendous weight forward, shattering the lamp, and bowling Robbins over against the wall. Then they were up and facing each other. The oil from the broken lamp settled between two flags and

blazed up ruddily. Crown was crouched for a second spring, with lips drawn from gleaming teeth. The light fell strong upon thrusting jaw, and threw the sloping brow into shadow. One hand touched the ground lightly, balancing the massive torso. The other arm held the cotton-hook forward, ready, like a prehensile claw. In comparison Robbins was pitifully slender and inadequate. There was a single desperate moment of indecision; then he took his only chance. Like a thrown spear, he hurled his lithe body forward under the terrifying hook, and clinched. Down, down, down the centuries they slid. Clothes could not hold them. Miraculously the tawny, ridged bodies tore through the thin coverings. Bronze ropes and bars slid and wove over great shoulders. Bright, ruddy planes leaped out on backs in the fire flare, then were gulped by sliding shadows. A heady, bestial stench absorbed all other odors. A fringe of shadowy watchers crept from cavernous doorways, sensed it, and commenced to wail eerily. Backward and forward, in a space no larger than a small room, the heaving, inseparable mass rocked and swayed. Breath labored like steam. At times the fused single body would thrust out a rigid arm, or the light would point out, for one hideous second, a tortured, mad face. Again the mass would rise as though propelled a short distance from the earth, topple, and crash down upon the pavement with a jarring impact.

Such terrific expenditure of human energy could not last. The end came quickly, and with startling suddenness. Crown broke his adversary's weakening hold, and held him the length of one mighty arm. The other swung the cotton-hook downward. Then he dropped his victim, and swaggered drunkenly toward the street. Even to the most inexperienced the result would have been obvious. Robbins was dead: horribly dead.

A scream rose to a crescendo of unendurable agony, and a woman broke through the circle of spectators and cast herself upon the body. The fire flickered to a faint, blue flame, unearthly, terrifying.

Porgy shivered violently, whimpered in the gloom; then drew himself across his threshold and closed the door.

§

Catfish Row, in which Porgy lived, was not a row at all, but a great brick structure that lifted its three stories about the three sides of a court. The fourth side was partly closed by a high wall, surmounted by jagged edges of broken glass set firmly in old lime plaster, and pierced in its center by a wide entrance-way. Over the entrance there

still remained a massive grill of Italian wrought iron, and a battered capital of marble surmounted each of the lofty gate-posts. The court itself was paved with large flag-stones, which even beneath the accumulated grime of a century, glimmered with faint and varying pastel shades in direct sunlight. The south wall, which was always in shadow, was lichened from pavement to rotting gutter; and opposite, the northern face, unbroken except by rows of small-paned windows, showed every color through its flaking stucco, and, in summer, a steady blaze of scarlet from rows of geraniums that bloomed in old vegetable tins upon every window-sill.

Within the high-ceilinged rooms, with their battered colonial mantels and broken decorations of Adam designs in plaster, governors had come and gone, and ambassadors of kings had schemed and danced. Now before the gaping entrance lay only a narrow, cobbled street, and beyond, a tumbled wharf used by negro fishermen. Only the bay remained unchanged. Beyond the litter of the wharf, it stretched to the horizon, taking its mood from the changing skies; always different —invariably the same.

Directly within the entrance of the Row, and having upon the street a single bleary window, wherein were displayed plates of fried fish, was the "cook-shop" which catered to the residents of the tenement.

Porgy's room was opposite the shop and enjoyed the great advantage of having a front window that commanded the street and harbor, and an inner door where he could sit and enter into the life of the court. To him, the front window signified adventure, the door—home.

§

It was Porgy's custom, when the day's work was done and he had exchanged a part of his collections for his evening meal of fish and bread, to sit at his front window and watch the world pass by. The great cotton wharves lay up the river, beyond the Row; and when the cotton season was on, he loved to sit in the dusk and see the drays go by. They would sweep into view with a loud thunder of wheels on the cobbles; and from his low seat they loomed huge and mysterious in the gathering dark. Sometimes there would be twenty of them in a row, with great swiftly-stepping mules, crouched figures of drivers, and bales piled toweringly above them. Always Porgy experienced a vague and not unpleasant fear when the drays swung past. There was power, vast, awe-inspiring; it could so easily crush him were he in its path. But here, safe within his window, he could watch it with per-

fect safety. At times when the train was unusually long, the sustained, rhythmic thunder and the sweep of form after form past his window produced an odd pleasurable detachment in his mind, and pictures of strange things and places would brighten and fade. But the night following the killing, the window was closed, and through the open door behind him beat the rhythm of a dirge from Robbins' room.

"What de matter, chillen?" came the strophe. And the antistrophe swelled to the answer:

"Pain gots de body, an' I can't stan' still."

Porgy sat upon his floor counting the day's collection: one dollar and twenty cents. It had been a good day. Perhaps the sorrow that had brooded over his spirit had quickened the sympathy of the passers-by.

"What de matter, Sister?"

"Jedus gots our brudder, an' I can't stan' still."

Ever since Porgy had come home the air had swung to the rhythm of the chant. He divided his pile into equal portions, and commenced to pocket one. The burden swayed out again.

"Pain gots de body, an' I can't stan' still."

He hesitated a moment, poured all the coins together again, selected a twenty-five-cent piece which he put into his pocket, and, taking the remainder in his hand, went out and drew himself across the short distance to the room of mourning.

The body lay upon a bed in the corner of the room, sheeted to the eyes, and upon its breast rested a large blue saucer. Standing in a circle about the bed, or seated upon the floor, backs to the wall, were a score of negroes, some singing, and others swaying, patting the floor with their large feet. For not a single moment since the body had been laid out had the rhythm slackened. With each hour it gathered weight until it seemed to swing the massive structure.

Porgy had heard that Robbins had left no burial insurance, the customary Saturday night festivities having consumed the slender margin between daily wage and immediate need. Now, at sight of the saucer, he knew that rumor had not erred. It had been an old custom among penniless negroes to prepare the corpse thus, then to sing dirges until neighborhood sympathy provided the wherewithal for proper interment. Recent years had introduced the insurance agent and the "buryin' lodge," and the old custom had fallen into disuse. It had even become a grievous reproach to have a member of the family a "saucer-buried nigger."

At the foot of the bed, bowed by the double weight of sorrow and disgrace, the widow sat swaying to the rhythm like a beach palm in the ebb and flow of a bleak sea wind.

The sight of her grief, the close room, the awful presence beneath

the sheet, and the unceasing pulse of sound that beat against his ears, all contributed to stir a strange desire into being within Porgy. Suddenly he threw his head back and wailed long and quaveringly. In rushed a vast feeling of relief. He wailed again, emptied his handful of small coins into the saucer, and sank to the floor at the head of the bed. Presently he commenced to croon with the others, and a sense of exaltation flooded his being, compelling him from the despair of the dirge to a more triumphant measure.

"Oh, I gots a little brudder in de new grabe-yahd. What outshine de sun," he sang.

Without missing the beat, the chorus shifted: "An' I'll meet um in the primus lan'."

Then came a rude interruption. A short yellow negro bustled into the room. His voice was low, oily, and penetrating. He was dressed entirely in black, and had an air of great importance. The song fell away to scarcely more than a throbbing silence. The man crossed the room to where the widow sat huddled at the foot of the bed, and touched her on the shoulder. She raised a face like a burned out ember.

"How de saucer stan' now, my sister?" he whispered, at the same time casting an appraising glance toward the subject of his inquiry.

"Dere ain't but fifteen dollar," she replied in a flat, despairing voice.

"An' he gots tuh git buried termorrer," called an awed voice, "or de boahd ob healt' will take um, an' give um tuh de students."

The widow's scream shrilled wildly. She rose to her knees and clutched the man's hand between both of hers. "Oh, fuh Gawd's sake bury um in de grabe-yahd. I goin' tuh work Monday, and I swear tuh Gawd I goin' tuh pay yuh ebery cent."

For a second even the rhythm ceased, leaving an aching suspense in the air. Watchers waited tensely. Wide eyes, riveted on the man's face, pleaded silently. Presently his professional manner slipped from him. "All right, Sister," he said simply. "Wid de box, an' one ca'age it will cost me more dan twenty-five. But I'll see yuh t'rough. Yuh can all be ready at eight tumorruh. It's a long trip tuh de cemetery."

The woman relaxed silently across the foot of the bed, her head between her outflung arms. Then from the narrow confines of the room, the song beat up and out triumphantly:

"Oh, I gots a little brudder in de new grabe-yahd. What outshine de sun!"

The rhythm swelled, and voices in the court and upper rooms took it up, until the deeply-rooted old walls seemed to rock and surge with the sweep of it.

§

In the cool of the early morning, the procession took its departure for the cemetery that lay beyond the city limits to the north. First went the dilapidated hearse, with its rigid wooden plumes, and faded black velvet draperies that nodded and swayed inside the plate glass panels. Then followed the solitary carriage, in which could be seen massed black accentuated by several pairs of white cotton gloves held to lowered eyes. Behind the carriage came the mourners in a motley procession of wagons and buggies that had been borrowed for the occasion.

Porgy drove with Peter, and four women, seated on straight chairs in the wagon behind them, completed their company. From time to time a long-drawn wail would rise from one of the conveyances, to be taken up and passed back from wagon to wagon like a dismal echo.

Moving from the negro district into the wide thoroughfare of Meeting House Road, with its high buildings and its white faces that massed and scattered on the pavements, the cortége appeared almost grotesque, with the odd fusion of comedy and tragedy so inextricably a part of negro life in its deep moments.

The fat German who kept the shop on the corner of King Charles Street and Summer Road, called his clerk from the depths of the building, and their stomachs shook with laughter. But the little, dark Russian Jew in the next shop, who dealt in abominably smelling clothing, gave them a reproving look, and disappeared indoors.

The cemetery lay several miles beyond the city limits. The lot was bare of trees, but among the graves many bright flowering weeds masked the ugliness of the troubled earth. To the eastward a wide marsh stretched away to a far, bright line of sea. Westward, ploughed fields swept out to a distant forest of yellow pine. From the sea to the far tree tops, the sky swung a dizzy arch of thin blue, high in the center of which several buzzards hung motionless, watching.

In the vast emptiness of the morning the little procession crawled out to the edge of the broken wooden fence that marked the enclosure, and stopped.

By the time the last wagon had arrived, the cheap pine casket was resting upon battens over the grave, and the preacher, robed in white, was preparing to commence the service.

The mourners gathered close about the grave.

"Death, ain't yuh gots no shame?" called a clear, high, soprano voice; and immediately the mortal embodiment of infinite sorrow

broke and swayed about the grave in the funeral chant. Three times the line swung its curve of song, shrill, keen, agonizing; then it fell away to a heart-wrenching minor on the burden:

> *"Take dis man an' gone—gone.*
> *Death, ain't yuh gots no shame?"*

When the singing ceased, the burial service commenced, the preacher extemporizing fluently. Taking his rhythm from the hymn, he poured his words along its interminable reiteration until the cumulative effect rocked the entire company.

The final moment of the ritual arrived. The lid was removed from the casket, and the mourners were formed into line to pass and look upon the face of the dead. A very old, bent negress went first. She stooped, then suddenly, with a shriek of anguish, cast herself beside the coffin.

"Tell Peter tuh hold de do' open fuh me. I's comin' soon!" she cried.

"Yes, Gawd, goin' soon," responded a voice in the crowd. Others pressed about the grave, and the air was stabbed by scream on scream. Grief spent itself freely, terrifyingly.

Slowly the clashing sounds merged into the regular measure of a spiritual. Beautiful and poignant it rose, swelling out above the sounds of falling earth as the grave was filled:

> *"What yuh goin' ter do when yuh*
> > *come out de wilderness,*
> *Come out de wilderness,*
> *Come out de wilderness;*
> *What yuh goin' ter do when yuh*
> > *come out de wilderness*
> *Leanin' on my Lord.*

> *"Leanin' on my Lord,*
> *Leanin' on my Lord,*
> *Leanin' on my Lord*
> *Who died on Calvary."*

The music faded away in vague, uncertain minors. The mood of the crowd changed almost tangibly. There was an air of restless apprehension. Nervous glances were directed toward the entrance. Peter, always sagacious, unless taken unawares, had conferred in advance with Porgy about this moment. When he had helped him from the wagon, he had stationed him just inside the fence, where he could be lifted quickly into the road.

"De las' man in de grabe-yahd goin' tuh be de nex' one tuh git buried," he had reminded his friend.

Now, as the final shovelful of earth was thrown upon the grave, he came running to Porgy, and lifted him quickly into the road. Behind them broke a sudden earth-shaking burst of sound, as of the stampeding of many cattle, and past them the mourners swept, stumbling, fighting for room; some assisting weaker friends, others fighting savagely to be free of the enclosure. In the center of the crowd, plunging forward with robes flying, was the preacher. In an incredibly short time the lot was cleared. Then, from a screening bush near the grave, arose the old negress who had been the first to wail out her grief. She had lain there forgotten, overcome by the storm of her emotion. She tottered feebly into the road.

"Nebber you min', Sister," the preacher assured her comfortingly. "Gawd always lub de righteous."

Dazed, and much pleased at the attention that she was receiving, while still happily unmindful of its cause, the old woman smiled a vague smile, and was hoisted into the wagon.

During the funeral the sun had disappeared behind clouds that had blown in swiftly from the sea, and now a scurry of large drops swept over the vehicles, and trailed away across the desolate graves.

"Dat's all right now fer Robbins," commented Porgy. "Gawd done sen' he rain already fuh wash he feet-steps offen dis eart'."

"Oh, yes, Brudder!" contributed a woman's voice; and, "Amen, my Jedus!" added another.

§

In the early afternoon of the day of the funeral, Porgy sat in his doorway communing with Peter. The old man was silent for awhile, his grizzled head bowed, and an expression of brooding tenderness upon his lined face.

"Robbins war a good man," he reflected at length, "an' dat nigger, Crown, war a killer, an' fuhebber gettin' intuh trouble. Yet, dere lie Robbins, wid he wife an' fadderless chillen; an' Crown done gone he ways tuh do de same t'ing ober again somewheres else."

"Gone fuh true. I reckon he done lose now on Kittiwar Islan', in dem palmettuh t'icket; an' de rope ain't nebber make fuh ketch um an' hang um." Porgy stopped suddenly, and motioned with his head toward someone who had just entered the court. The new arrival was a white man of stocky build, wearing a wide-brimmed hat, and a goatee. He was swinging a heavy cane, and he crossed the court

directly and paused before the two. For a moment he stood looking down at them with brows drawn fiercely together. Then he drew back his coat, exhibiting a police badge, and a heavy revolver in a breast holster.

"You killed Robbins," he shot out suddenly at Peter. "And I'm going to hang you for it. Come along now!" and he reached out and laid a firm hand upon the old man's shoulder.

Peter shook violently, and his eyes rolled in his head. He made an ineffectual effort to speak, tried again, and finally said, " 'Fore Gawd, Boss, I ain't nebber done it."

Like a flash, the pistol was out of its holster, and pointing between his eyes. "Who did it, then?" snapped the man.

"Crown, Boss. I done see him do um," Peter cried in utter panic.

The man laughed shortly. "I thought so," he said. Then he turned to Porgy.

"You saw it too, eh?"

There was panic in Porgy's face, and in his lap his hands had clinched upon each other. But his eyes were fixed upon the paving. He drew a deep breath, and waited.

A flare of anger swept the face above him. "Come. Out with it. I don't want to have to put the law on you."

Porgy's only answer was a slight tremor that shook the hands in his lap. The detective's face darkened, and sweat showed under his hatbrim. Suddenly his temper bolted.

"Look at me, you damned nigger!" he shouted.

Slowly the sitting figure before him relaxed, almost it seemed, muscle by muscle. At last the hands fell apart, and lay flexed and idle. Finally Porgy raised eyes that had become hard and impenetrable as onyx. They met the angry glare that beat down upon them without flinching. After a long moment, he spoke slowly, and with great quietness.

"I ain't know nuttin' 'bout um. I been inside, asleep on my bed, wid de do' closed."

"You're a damn liar," the man snapped.

He shrilled a whistle, and two policemen entered.

"He saw the killing," the detective said, indicating Peter. "Take him along, and lock him up as a material witness."

"How about the cripple?" asked one of the officers.

"He could not have helped seeing it," the man said sourly. "That's his room right there. But I can't make him come through. But it don't matter. One's enough to hang Crown, if we ever get him. Come, get the old man in the wagon."

The policeman lifted the shaking old negro to his feet. "Come

along, Uncle. It ain't going to be as bad for you as Crown, anyway,"
encouraged one of them. Then the little party passed out of the en-
trance, leaving Porgy alone.

From the street sounded the shrill gong of the patrol wagon, fol-
lowed by the beat of swiftly receding hoofs upon the cobbles.

§

Ten days had passed since the detective had taken Peter away. For
a week the wagon had waited under the tottering shed, and the de-
jected old horse had subsisted upon a varied diet brought to him by
the friends of his absent master. Then a man had come and taken
the outfit away. In answer to the protests of the negroes, he had ex-
hibited a contract, dated three years previous, by which Peter was
to pay two dollars a week for an indefinite period, on an exorbitant
purchase price. Failure to pay any installment would cause the prop-
erty to revert to the seller. It all looked thoroughly legal. And so the
dilapidated old rig rattled over the cobbles and departed.

Then the man from the installment furniture house came. He was
a vile-mouthed, bearded Teuton, and swore so fiercely that no one
dared to protest when he loaded Peter's furniture on his truck and
drove away.

Now there remained in a corner of Porgy's room, where he had
taken them into custody, only a battered leather trunk, a chromo of
"The Great Emancipator," and a bundle of old clothes; mute re-
minders of their kindly and gentle old owner.

Part II

The languor of a Southern May was in the air. It was a season dear
to the heart of a negro. Work on the wharves was slowing down, and
the men were putting in only two or three days a week. There were
always some of them lying about the court, basking in the sun, laugh-
ing, and telling stories while they waited for their women to come
from the "white folks'" kitchens, with their full dinner pails.

Near the entrance, the stevedores usually lounged, their great size
differentiating them from most of the other men. They had bright
bandanas about their thick necks, and under their blue cotton shirts
moved broad, flat backs that could heft a five hundred pound cotton

bale. Earning more money than the others, and possessing vast physical strength in a world of brute force, they lorded it swaggeringly about the court; taking the women that they wanted, and dressing them gorgeously in the clashing crimsons and purples that they loved.

Grief over the loss of Robbins had stormed itself out at the funeral. Peter's ill fortune still occasioned general comment, but slight concern to the individual. There was an air of gaiety about. The scarlet of the geraniums was commencing to flicker in a run of windy flame on each window sill; and from the bay came the smell of salt air blown across young marsh-grass.

At the wharf, across the narrow street, the fishermen were discharging strings of gleaming whiting and porgy. Vegetable sloops, blowing up from the Sea Islands, with patched and tawny sails, broke the flat cobalt of the inner harbor with the cross-wash of their creamy wakes.

Through the back door of the cook-shop Maria, the huge proprietress, could be seen cutting shark-steaks from a four-foot hammerhead that one of the fishermen had given her. All in all, it was a season for the good things of life, to be had now for scarcely more than the asking.

Only Porgy sat lonely and disconsolate in his doorway and watched the sunlight creep up the eastern wall until it faded to a faint red at the top, then the blue dusk grew under the wharf, and swirled through the street and court. He had not been able to get to his stand since Peter's departure; and the small store of coins, which he kept under a loose brick in his hearth, was nearing exhaustion. Also, he missed his old friend keenly and could not enter into the lighthearted life about him.

Presently two women entered. Porgy saw that they were Robbins' widow, and her sister, who now shared her room. He had been awaiting their coming eagerly, as they had left in the early afternoon to carry bed-clothing and food to the jail for Peter.

"How yuh fin' um, Sister?" he hailed.

The younger woman paused, standing in the shadow, and the widow lowered herself to a seat beside Porgy. She had put her grief aside, and gone resolutely about her task of earning a living for the three children.

"I can't puzzle dis t'ing out," she said after a while. "De old man ain't done nuttin', an' dey done gots um lock up like a chicken t'ief. Dey say dey gots tuh keep um till dat nigger Crown get ketch; an, Gawd knows when dat debble ob a t'ing goin' tuh happen."

"It sho pay nigger tuh go blin' in dis world," contributed the young woman. "Porgy ain't gots much leg, but he sho got sense."

After a moment of reflection, Porgy replied: "Sense do berry well; but he can't lift no weight."

A big stevedore was crossing the court, his body moving easily with the panther-like flow of enormous muscular power under absolute control.

The beggar's eyes became wistful.

"Sense gots power tuh take a t'ing atter yuh gits dere," he said. "But he nebber puts bittle in a belly what can't leabe he restin' place. What I goin' do now sence Peter gone, an' I can't git on de street?"

"Pray, Brudder, pray," said the widow devoutly. "Ain't yuh see Gawd done soffen de haht of dat yalluh buryin' ondehtakuh attuh I done pray tuh him fuh a whole day an' night? Gawd gots leg fuh de cripple."

"Bless de Lord!" ejaculated the young woman.

"An' he gots comfort fuh de widder."

"Oh, my Jedus!" crooned Porgy, beginning to sway.

"An' food fuh de fadderless."

"Yes, Lord!"

"An' he goin' raise dis poor nigger out de dus'."

"Allelujah!"

"An' set um in de seat ob de righteous."

"Amen, my Sister!"

For a little while the three figures, showing now only as denser shadows in a world of shade, swayed slowly from side to side. Then, without saying a word, Porgy drew himself across his threshold, and closed the door very softly.

§

It was not yet day when Porgy awakened suddenly. His eyes were wide, and his face was working with unwonted emotion. In the faint light that penetrated his bleared window from a street lamp, he made his way to the hearth, and removed the brick from his secret depository. With feverish haste he counted his little store, placing the coins in a row before him. Then with the utmost care he recounted them, placing them in little piles, one for the coppers, one for the nickels, and one for the dimes. When he had fully satisfied himself as to the extent of his wealth, his tension relaxed, and, tying the money in a rag which he tore from his bedclothing, he closed his hand firmly upon it, crawled back into bed, and immediately fell asleep.

§

Two days later, Porgy drove his chariot out through the wide entrance into a land of romance and adventure. He was seated with the utmost gravity in an inverted packing-case that proclaimed with unconscious irony the virtues of a well-known toilet soap. Beneath the box two solid lop-sided wheels turned heavily. Before him, between a pair of improvised shafts, a patriarchal goat tugged with the dogged persistence of age which has been placed upon its mettle, and flaunted an intolerable stench in the face of the complaisant and virtuous soap box.

As oblivious of the mirth-provoking quality of his appearance, as he was of a smell to which custom had inured him, Porgy turned his equipage daringly into a new thoroughfare, and drove through a street where high, bright buildings stood between wide gardens, and where many ladies passed and re-passed on the sidewalks, or in glittering carriages.

But the magic that had come to pass, even in the triumph of that first morning, stirred vague doubts and misgivings within him. He noticed that while he occasioned slight comment in the negro quarter, no sooner had he entered the white zone, than people commenced to pass him with averted faces, and expressions that struggled between pity and laughter. When he finally reached his old stand before the apothecary shop, these misgivings crystallized into a definite fear.

Several of his clients happened to be passing the shop together. One of them was clerk to an apothecary further down the street. He seized his nose with one hand, while he pointed at Porgy with the other. Then all seized their noses, shaking with laughter, and waited to see what would happen.

Porgy looked his outfit over carefully. Certainly it was working with the utmost satisfaction. Somewhat mystified, he tied the ancient animal to a post, and, with great gravity, swung himself out of his wagon, across the pavement, and to his old stand.

The boys who had laughed stood nearby, and were joined by others, until soon there was quite a group.

Presently there issued from the shop the loud voice of the proprietor: "Oh, Mary, come quick, and bring the broom. Something has died again." Then followed the sound of boxes being overturned, while dust from a prodigious sweeping bellied in clouds from the door. Then the apothecary, very red in the face, came out for air, and found the goat. The burst of laughter that greeted him increased his irrita-

tion. Brandishing the broom, and in no uncertain language, he drove Porgy from his door.

But the bystanders had so enjoyed the joke at the apothecary's expense, and were feeling in such high good humor, that when Porgy had an opportunity to appraise his collections, he found that they amounted to more than he frequently got from a whole day of patient waiting.

§

It is impossible to conceive of a more radical change than that brought about in Porgy's life by his new emancipation. From his old circumstances which had conspired to anchor him always to one spot, he was now in the grip of new forces that as inevitably resulted in constant change of scene. Soon he became quite a metropolitan, and might have been seen in any part of the city, either sitting in his wagon at the curb, or, if the residents of the locality seemed lenient in their attitude toward goats, disembarking, and trying his luck in the strip of shade along the wall.

In those days, everyone tolerated Porgy—for a while. He had become "a character." The other beggars gnashed their teeth, but were powerless.

On certain days he would turn to the south when he left the court, and soon would emerge into a land of such beauty that he never lost the illusion that it was unreal. No one seemed to work in that country, except the happy, well-clothed negroes who frequently came to back gates when he passed, and gave him tender morsels from the white folks' kitchens. The great, gleaming houses looked out at him with kindly eyes that peered between solid walls of climbing roses. Ladies on the deep piazzas would frequently send a servant running out to give him a coin and speed him on his way.

Before the houses and the rose-trellises stretched a broad drive, and beyond its dazzling belt of crushed shell the harbor lay between its tawny islands, like a sapphire upon a sailor's weathered hand. Sometimes Porgy would steal an hour from the daily rounds, pause there, and watch a great, blunt-nosed steamer heave slowly out of the unknown, to come to rest with a sigh of spent steam, and a dusty thundering of released anchor chains.

"Gawd sho gots a long arm," he would murmur; or, "Porgy, yo' sho is a little somethin' aftuh all."

Then there would be other days when he would repair to the narrow retail street, with its unbelievable windows, and drawing near to the

curb, between the tall carriages of the shoppers would fall heir to the pennies which they got with their change, and which were of no value to such as they.

Always kind hands dropped coins in his cup, and sped him on. They were great days for Porgy. And great were the nights when he would tell of his adventures to the envious circle that gathered in the dusk of the court.

But Porgy was by nature a dreamer, and there were times even in those days, when his mind returned with wistful longing to the old uninterrupted hours when he used to sit, lost in meditation, under the unmarked drift of time. Some day, he would tell himself, there would come one with a compassion so great that he would give both Porgy and the goat place by his doorstep. Then life would be perfect indeed.

§

June, and the cotton season was over. The last tramp steamer had faded into the horizon. Great sheds that linked land and sea lay empty and dark, and through their cavernous depths echoed the thud and suck of waves against the bulkheads. The last of the stevedores had departed, some to the plantations, others to the phosphate mines, and still others to the river barges.

The long, hot days, so conducive to indolence, brought a new phase of life to Catfish Row. The loud talk and noisy comings and goings diminished. Men came in earlier in the evenings, and spent more time with their women.

Porgy sat alone in his doorway. In a room overhead a man and his wife were engaged in a friendly quarrel that ended in laughter. From an open window nearby came the sound of drowsy child voices. In the crowded dark about him, Life, with cruel preoccupation, was engrossed with its eternal business.

A large, matronly woman who lived near him, passed, carrying a pail of water. She stopped, set down her burden, and dropped a hand on Porgy's shoulder.

"What de matter wid dis man, he ain't gots nuttin' tuh say?" she asked him kindly.

Porgy's face contracted with emotion. He caught her hand and hurled it from him. "Lemme be," he rasped, in a tight, husky voice. "Yuh done gots yuh own man. Ain't yuh?"

"Oh, Lawd!" she laughed, as she turned away. "Yuh ain't t'ink I wantin' *yuh*, is yuh? Do listen tuh de man."

§

Through the early night a woman had lain in the dust against the outer wall of Maria's cook-shop. She was extremely drunk and unpleasant to look upon. Exactly when she had dropped, or been dropped there, no one knew. Porgy had not seen her when he had driven in at sunset. But he had heard some talk of her among those who had entered later. One of the men had come in laughing.

"I seen Crown's Bess outside," he said. "Must be she come aroun' tuh look fur um."

"She sho goin' tuh hab one long res', ef she goin' wait dere fur um. Dat nigger gone f'om hyuh fas' and far!" another had averred.

It was ten o'clock; and Maria was closing her shop. The great negress was in the act of fastening the window, when the tall, gaunt form of the woman lurched through the door into the faint illumination of the smoking lamp. The visitor measured the distance to the nearest bench with wandering and vacant eyes, plunged for it, and collapsed, with head and arms thrown across a table.

Maria was exasperated, but equal to the emergency. Catching the woman around the middle, she swung her easily to the door, dropped her into outer darkness, and returned to the window.

A crash caused her to turn suddenly. There was the woman again, sprawled across the table as before.

"I swear tuh Gawd!" exclaimed the provoked negress. "Ef yuh ain't de persistentes' nigger I ebber seen." She went over, lifted the woman's head, and looked into eyes in the far depths of which a human soul was flickering feebly.

"Somethin' tuh eat," the woman whispered. "Lemme hab somethin' tuh eat, an' I'll go."

Growling like an approaching equinoctial gale, Maria brought bread and fish; and emptying the dregs of the coffeepot into a cup, placed it before her.

"Now, eat an' trabble, Sister," she advised laconically.

The woman raised her head. An ugly scar marked her left cheek, and the acid of utter degradation had etched hard lines about her mouth; but eyes into which human consciousness was returning looked fearlessly into the determined face of the big negress. For a moment she ate wolfishly; then asked suddenly:

"Who lib in dat room 'cross de way?"

"Porgy," she was informed, "but such as yuh ain't gots no use fuh he. He a cripple, an' a beggar."

"He de man wid goat?"

"Yes, he gots goat."

The woman's eyes narrowed to dark, unfathomable slits.

"I hyuh say he gits good money fum de w'ite folks," she said slowly.

In silence the meal was finished. Then the woman steadied herself a moment with hands against a table, and, without a word to Maria, walked quickly, with an almost haughty carriage, from the room.

She crossed the narrow drive with a decisive tread, opened the door of Porgy's room, entered, and closed the door behind her.

§

It was late afternoon. Serena Robbins entered the court, paused at Porgy's door, and gave a sharp rap on the weathered panel. The door was opened by a woman. The visitor looked through her, and spoke directly to Porgy, who sat within.

"I gots good news," she announced. "I done been tuh see my w'ite folks 'bout Peter; an' dey say dey gots a frien' who is a lawyer, an' he kin git um out. I tell um tuh sen' um tuh see you 'bout um, 'cause yuh gots so much sense when yuh talks tuh w'ite folks."

Having delivered her message, Serena turned a broad back upon the woman who stood silently in the doorway, and with the bearing of an arbiter of social destinies, strode to her corner of the court.

Across the drive, Maria, vast and moist, hung over her stove in a far corner of her cook-shop. Several negroes sat at the little tables, eating their early suppers, laughing and chaffing.

"Yuh sho got good-lookin' white gals in dis town," drawled a slender young octoroon. He was attired in sky-blue, peg-top trousers, yellow spats, and in the center of a scarlet bow-tie gleamed an immense paste horseshoe.

"Do listen tuh Sportin' Life!" said a black, loutish buck admiringly. "Ef he ain't lookin' at de rollin' bones, he always gots he eye on de women."

Maria's heavy tread shook the room as she crossed and stood, with arms akimbo, scowling down at her iridescent guest. The man looked up, lowered his eyes quickly, and shifted uneasily in his chair.

"Nigger!" she finally shot at him, and the impact almost jarred him from his chair. "I jus' tryin' ter figger out wedder I bettuh kill yuh decent now, wid yuh frien's about yuh; or leabe you fuh de w'ite gentlemens tuh hang attuh a while."

"Come now, old lady, don't talk like dese old-fashioned lamp-oil

niggers what have had no adwantage. Why, up in New York, where I been waitin' in a hotel—"

But he got no further.

"Noo Yo'k," she shouted. "Don't yuh try any Noo Yo'kin' aroun' dis town. Ef I had my way, I'd go down tuh dat Noo Yo'k boat, an' take ebbery Gawd's nigger what come up de gang plank wid er Joseph coat on he back an' a glass headlight on he buzzom and drap um tuh de catfish befo' he foot hit decent groun'! Yas; my belly fair ache wid dis Noo Yo'k talk. De fus t'ing dat dem nigger fuhgit is dat dem is nigger. Den dem comes tuh dese decent country mens, and fills um full ob talk wut put money in de funeral ondehtakuh pocket." Breathless, she closed her arraignment by bringing a fist the size of a ham down upon the table with such force that her victim leapt from his chair and extended an ingratiating hand toward her.

"Dat' all right, Auntie. Le's you an' me be frien'."

"Frien' wid yuh?" and her tone dripped scorn. "One ob dese days I might lie down wid er rattlesnake, and when dat time come, yuh kin come right along an' git intuh de bed. But till den, keep yuh shiny carcase in Noo Yo'k till de debbil ready tuh take chaage ob um!"

Suddenly the anger left her eyes, and her face became grave. She leaned over, and spoke very quietly into his face.

"Fuh Gawd's sake, don't talk dat kind ob talk tuh dese hyuh boys. Dis county ain't nebber yit see a black man git lynch. Dese nigger knows folks, an' dey knows nigger. Fer Gawd' sake keep yuh mout' off w'ite lady. Yuh gots plenty ob yuh own color fuh talk 'bout. Stick tuh dem, an' yuh ain't git inter no trouble."

During Maria's attack upon her guest, the court had been full of the many-colored sounds that accompanied its evening life. Now, gradually the noise shrunk, seeming to withdraw into itself. All knew what it meant. A white man had entered. The protective curtain of silence which the negro draws about his life when the Caucasian intrudes hung almost tangibly in the air. No one appeared to notice the visitor. Each was busily preoccupied with his task. Yet the newcomer made no move that was not noted by fifty pairs of inscrutable eyes.

The man wore a soft hat drawn well down over his face. He was slender and tall, and walked with his body carried slightly forward, like one who is used to meeting and overcoming difficulties.

A young woman passed him. He reached out and touched her on the arm. She stopped, and turned immediately toward him, her eyes lowered, her manner submissive, but utterly negative.

"I am looking for a man by the name of Porgy," he said in a clear pleasant voice. "Can you direct me to his room?"

"Porgy?" she repeated slowly, as though trying to remember. Then

she called aloud: "Anybody hyuh know a man by de name ob Porgy?"

Several of the silent bystanders looked up. "Porgy?" they repeated, one after another, with shakes of the head.

The white man laughed reassuringly, as though quite used to the proceeding. "Come," he urged, "I am his friend, Mr. Alan Archdale; I know that he lives here, and I want to help him."

From behind her tubs, Serena advanced, knocking the ashes from her clay pipe as she came. When she was quite close, she stopped, and peered up into the face above her. Then she turned upon the girl.

"Go 'long an' call Porgy," she commanded. "Can't yuh tell *folks* when yuh see um?"

A light broke over the young woman's face.

"Oh, yuh means *Porgy?*" she cried, as though she had just heard the name for the first time; "I ain't understan' wut name yuh say, Boss," and echoes arose from different parts of the court. "Oh, yes, de gentleman mean *Porgy*. How come we ain't understan'." Then the tension in the air broke, and life resumed its interrupted flow.

The young woman stepped to Porgy's door, and called. Presently the door opened, and a woman helped the beggar out to his seat upon the sill, then seated herself behind him in the deep gloom of the room.

Archdale crossed the short distance, and seated himself on the sill beside the negro.

"Tell me about your friend who got locked up on account of the Robbins murder," he asked, without preamble.

In the dim light, Porgy leaned forward and looked long into the keen, kindly face of his questioner.

Archdale gave a surprised exclamation: "Why, you're the old man who used to beg in front of the apothecary shop on King Charles Street!" he said. Then, after a moment of scrutiny: "But you are not old, after all, are you?" and he studied the face intently. There was a touch of grey in the wool above the ears, and strong character lines flared downward from the nose to corners of a mouth that was, at once, full-lipped and sensuous, yet set in a resolute line most unusual in a negro. With the first indications of age upon it, the face seemed still alive with a youth that had been neither spent nor wasted.

"But, tell me about your friend," said the visitor, breaking a silence that was commencing to become tense.

Porgy's face still wore its mask. "How come yuh tuh care, Boss?" he queried.

"Why, I am the Rutledge's lawyer; and I look after their colored folks for them. I think they must have owned half the slaves in the country. A woman here, Serena Robbins, is the daughter of their old coachman, or something; and she asked them to help her friend out."

"Peter ain't gots no money, yuh know, Boss. An' I jes begs from do' to do'." There was still a shade of suspicion in Porgy's voice.

Archdale laughed reassuringly. "It will not take any money. At least, not much; and I am sure that Mrs. Rutledge will take care of that. So you can go right ahead and tell me all about it."

Fully satisfied at last, Porgy told the tale of the killing and the subsequent arrest of Peter.

When he had finished the recital, Archdale sat silent for a while. "The dirty hounds!" he said under his breath. Finally he turned wearily to Porgy, and explained slowly:

"Of course we can go to law about this; but it will take no end of time. There is an easier way. He must have someone, who is acceptable to the magistrate, to go his bond. Do you know a man by the name of Huysenberg, who keeps a corner-shop down by the West-end wharf?"

Porgy, listening intently, nodded.

Archdale handed him a bill. "Take this ten dollars to him, and tell him that you want him to go Peter's bond. He hasn't any money of his own, and his shop is in his wife's name; but he has an arrangement with the magistrate that makes him entirely satisfactory."

He handed Porgy a card with an address pencilled under a printed name. "You will find me here," he said. "If Peter is not out in two days after you hand over the ten, let me know." Then, with a brisk, but friendly "Good night," he left the court.

§

There was great rejoicing in Catfish Row. Peter had returned. The ten dollar bill which Archdale had given Porgy had worked the miracle. Except for the fact that the old negro's shoulders drooped, and his grip on actualities seemed weakened by his confinement, there was no evidence to show that he had been absent. He had gone to the horse-dealer, and had found his ancient beast still awaiting a purchaser. Another contract had been signed which had started him off again on the eternal weekly payment. The German had driven back with the furniture, which Peter had docilely purchased for the second time. Again "The Great Emancipator" had been hung in his accustomed place above the mantel. Now, each morning, the old wagon rattled out over the cobbles, with the usual number of small, ecstatic, black bodies pendant from its dilapidated superstructure.

"De buckra sho gots nigger figgered out tuh a cent!" said Peter philosophically, and even with a note of admiration in his voice. "Dem

knows how much money wagon make in er week; an' de horse man, de furniture man, an' de lan'lo'd mek dey 'rangement' accordin'. But I done lib long 'nough now tuh beat 'em all, 'cause money ain't no use tuh a man attuh he done pass he prime, nohow."

When the old man had settled firmly back into his nook, and had an opportunity to look about him, he noticed a change in Porgy.

"I tell yuh dat nigger happy," he said to Serena, one evening while they were smoking their pipes together on her washing bench.

"Go 'long wid yuh!" she retorted. "Dat 'oman ain't de kin' tuh mek man happy. It tek a killer like Crown tuh hol' she down."

"Dat may be so," agreed the old man sagely. "But Porgy don' know dat yit. An' 'side, ef a man is de kin' wut needs er 'oman, he goin' be happy regahdless. Him dress she up in he own eye till she look lak de Queen of Sheba tuh um. Porgy t'ink right now dat he gots a she-gawd in he room."

"He sho' gots de kin' wut goin' gib um hell," Serena commented cynically. "Dat 'oman ain't fit tuh 'sociate wid. Much as I like Porgy, I wouldn't swap t'ree wo'd wid she."

"Dat's all so, Sister," conceded Peter. "But yuh keep yo' eye on Porgy. He usen tuh hate all dese chillen. Ain't he? Now watch um. Ebery day w'en he come home he gots candy-ball fuh de crowd. An' wut mo', yistuhday I hyuh he an' she singin' tuhgedduh in dey room."

Serena motioned to him to be quiet. Porgy's woman crossed the court to draw a bucket of water from the common tap near Serena's corner. She was neatly dressed, and passed them as though they did not exist. Filling her pail, she swung it easily to her head, and, steadying it lightly with one hand, returned close to them with an air of cool scorn that produced entirely different effects upon her two observers. Serena watched her departure in silence.

"Dat de t'ing!" said Peter, a note of admiration in his voice. "She sho ain't axin' no visit offen none of she neighbor." And he emitted an indiscreet chuckle, which was too much for his friend.

"Yuh po', ole, wall-eyed, sof'-headed gran'daddy! Ain't yuh 'shame' tuh set dey befo' me, an' talk sweet-mout' 'bout dat murderin' Crown's Bess? Ef I wuz yo' age, an' er man, I'd sabe my sof' wo'd fer de Gawd-farin' ladies."

"Ef yuh wuz my age, an' a man—" commenced Peter. He hesitated, and looked long at her with his dim, kindly eyes; then he shook his head. "No; it ain't no use. Yuh wouldn't onderstan'. Dat somet'ing shemale sense ain't goin' tuh help yuh none wid." And, still shaking his head, he knocked out his pipe, and departed in the direction of the stable, where he was presently greeted by a soft, comprehending whinny.

Bess entered Porgy's room and swung her pail of water to its place beside the new wood stove that had superseded the old, open hearth, and busied herself with preparations for supper.

Porgy was seated in a low chair near the door. He was smoking contentedly, and the odd tension that had characterized him, even in his moments of silent thought, had given place to a laxed attitude of body and an expression of well-being.

An infinitesimal negro passed with a whistle and a double shuffle.

"Look hyuh, sonny!" called Porgy.

The boy paused, hesitated, and advanced slowly. Porgy held out a large round ball, striped red and white. "How 'bout er sweet?" he said a little self-consciously. The boy took the candy, and shuffled uneasily from foot to foot.

"Dat's right," said Porgy, with a burst of sudden, warm laughter, that somehow startled the child. "Now yuh come again an' see Porgy an' Bess."

Part III

Porgy drove slowly down King Charles Street, and appraised the prospects for hitching and settling awhile in the narrow strip of shade against the walls of the buildings. The day was sweltering, and both cripple and goat were drooping beneath the steady pressure of the sun.

A man passed, walking briskly. Porgy at once recognized the long, easy stride, and the soft felt hat drawn rather low over the eyes. He reached out and gave a slight twist to the tail of his somnambulant animal, which resulted in a shambling trot that brought the vehicle abreast of the pedestrian. But at that moment the gentleman stopped, produced a key, and opening the door of an office, passed in without looking around.

Porgy eyed the office and its environs with evident satisfaction. The building stood very near the old apothecary shop; and between it and its neighbor to the east was an entrance way several feet in width, which breathed forth an inviting coolness from its deep shade. No one was passing at the moment. Porgy turned the head of his beast toward the entrance, gave a sudden twist to the tail, and drove audaciously across the pavement, and into the retreat. Then he hitched his wagon a few feet from the street, and seated himself, cup in hand, at the pavement's inner edge.

"Yuh bes' git along out of Mr. Alan' do'way wid dat goat befo' he fin' yuh. Ain't yuh onduhstan' gentlemen ain't likes tuh smell goat?"

Porgy looked up and met the threatening gaze of Simon Frasier.

Frasier was a practising attorney-at-law. He was well past fifty years of age, and his greying wool looked very white in comparison with his uncompromisingly black skin. He had voted the democratic ticket in the dark period of reconstruction, when such action on his part took no little courage, and accordingly enjoyed the almost unlimited toleration of the aristocracy. Without possessing the official sanction of the State for the practice of his profession, he was, by common consent among the lawyers, permitted to represent his own people in the police and magistrates' courts and to turn his hand to other small legal matters into which it was thought inadvisable to enquire too deeply.

Porgy regarded his accuser stonily.

"Ob course gentlemen ain't likes tuh smell goat," he replied.

The door opened, and Archdale looked out. From where Porgy sat he could have touched him with his hand; yet the cripple's gaze never wavered from the face of the negro, and his expression remained unchanged. Forestalling an interruption, he hastened on, in a voice that had become mildly incredulous, as he continued, "But it can't be dat attuh knowing buckra long as yuh been know um, yuh ain't onduhstan' um any better dan tuh t'ink dey would dribe away po' cripple in de heat."

Archdale made a movement that actually crossed Porgy's line of vision; but the beggar's face gave no sign of recognition. His voice rose to a pitch of indignation:

"Yuh might be a lawyuh, an' all dat; but I ain't goin' tuh hab yuh stan' dey an' tell me dat Mistuh Archdale gots dem po' w'ite-trash ways. Ob course he don't likes de smell ob goat; but he gots er haht in he breas' fuh de po' cripple nigger."

A wry smile tugged at the corner of Archdale's mouth.

"All right, Porgy," he said, "I got it all; but, gentleman or no gentleman, I can't have a goat on my doorstep. I would not have one client left in a week."

At the sound of Archdale's voice, Porgy looked around. His entire body seemed to express amazement.

"Why, hyuh's de Boss now!" he cried. Then he turned triumphantly to the negro, and added, "Wut I done tells yuh 'bout de real quality; ain't yuh done see he say I kin stay?"

Archdale became desperate. "I did not say you could," he cried, with the manner of one who puts his foot in the crack of a closing door. "You can wait there today, as I will be in court all morning; but tomorrow you must find somewhere else."

"By tuhmorruh I goin' hab dis goat wash till yuh can't tell um from one of dem rosebush in de pahk!" Porgy assured him with an ingenuous smile. "Yuh is goin' to be mighty lubbin' of dis goat attuh a while, Boss."

"No; goats don't wash, Porgy. Away you go after today." But the power of absolute conviction was not in Archdale's voice. His foot was still in the crack; but he knew that the door was closing.

"All right, Frasier; I'll see you now about your divorce business," he said to the other negro, and showed him into the office.

Presently through an open window behind Porgy came the sound of Archdale's voice:

"All right, Frasier. Out with it. The gentleman who has come down to improve moral conditions among the negroes thinks you are a menace. He is going to have you indicted for granting divorces illegally."

In a voice very different from the one in which he had arraigned Porgy, Frasier began:

"I fin' so much nigger onsattify wid dere marriage, an' I hyuh tell ob a t'ing dey calls divorce."

"Yes?" encouraged his questioner.

"So fuh a long time now I been separate dem wid a divorce wut I mek up fuh de pu'pose. An' he go fine, Boss. I done mek too much nigger happy."

"Have you one of the papers with you?"

Silence; and then Archdale's voice again.

" 'I, Simon Frasier, hereby divorce Rachel Smalls and Columbus Devo for the charge of one dollar; signed, Simon Frasier.' Well, that is simple enough. Where did you get this seal?"

"I done buy um from de junk-shop Jew, Boss."

"Don't you know there is no such thing as divorce in this State?"

"I hyuh tell dere ain't no such t'ing fuh de w'ite folks; but de nigger need um so bad, I ain't see no reason why I can't mek up one wut sati'fy de nigger? He seem tuh work berry well, too, till dat sof' mout' gentleman come 'roun' an' onsettle all my client."

A groan floated through the window to Porgy's ears, causing him to indulge in a slow, malicious smile. Then in a pained voice the negro lawyer proceeded: "He been keepin' me alibe, Boss. An' wut mo', he keep de nigger straight. Dis gentleman say dat dey gots tuh lib tuh-gedduh anyhow till dey done dead. Dat's de law, he say. But nigger ain't mek dataway. I done get um all properly moralize, and dis same gentleman tell um dat my paper ain't no mo' dan a license tuh 'dul-terate. So now dey just leabe each odduh anyhow, and I ain't gets no dollar. An' now he say he goin' jail me, wut mo'!"

There was a moment of silence, then Porgy heard Archdale's voice calling a number; then: "Hello! Is that the Solicitor's office? Mr. Dennis, please.

"Oh—this is Archdale, Dennis. Yes, another negro. This time it is Frasier, you know, the divorce decree case. Yes, I have him here in my office. Look here; you have a terrifically heavy docket this term. There is no use taking the State's money and your valuable time on this case."

There followed a pause; then Archdale said hastily, "Oh, no; I am not trying anything; but he is perfectly innocent of any deliberate wrongdoing. Yes, of course; it would be serious if he were responsible; but you know no one takes old Frasier seriously. A no-bill from the grand jury would save no end of time and trouble.

"Yes; I will guarantee that he will stop."

Porgy listened intently; and after a moment he heard Archdale say, "Thank you," and turn his chair toward his client. Then he heard him address the negro.

"We are not going to lock you up this time, Simon. But you will have to stop divorcing your people. I have given my word. If you do it again, snap! to jail we both go. Do you understand?"

A relieved gasp greeted the announcement followed by "Gawd bless yuh, Boss!" and a moment later Frasier stood blinking in the white glare of the street.

Porgy looked up, and in an exact imitation of Frasier's professional manner, said testily, "Mobe on, please; mobe on. I gots a berry perlite goat hyuh wut objec' tuh de smell ob de jail-bird."

A chuckle sounded from Archdale's office.

Immediately the light of victory, carefully veiled, but bright, shone in Porgy's eyes. He reached behind him and tweaked the goat by the ear. The dejected animal mistook the signal, and started forward.

"No, no, bubber," whispered Porgy. "Ain't yuh hear de Boss laugh? When nigger mek de buckra laugh, den he know he done won. Dis wey we goin' spen' we libe. You watch."

§

The change in Porgy, which Peter had been the first to notice, was now apparent to all who knew him. The defensive barrier of reserve that he had built about his life was down. The long hours when he used to sit fixed and tense, with the look of introspection upon his face, were gone. Even the most skeptical of the women were beginning to admit that Bess was making him a good mate. Not that they mingled

freely with the other residents of the court. On the contrary, they seemed strangely sufficient unto themselves in the midst of the intensely gregarious life that was going on about them. Porgy's earnings were adequate to their modest needs, and Bess was always up and out with the first of the women, and among them all there was none who could bargain more shrewdly with the fishermen and hucksters who sold their wares on the wharf.

Like Porgy, Bess had undergone a subtle change that became more evident from day to day. Her gaunt figure had rounded out, bringing back a look of youthful comeliness, and her face was losing its hunted expression. The air of pride that had always shown in her bearing, which had amounted almost to disdain, that had so infuriated the virtuous during her evil days, was heightened, and, in her bettered condition forced a resentful respect from her feminine traducers.

One morning while she was doing her marketing on the wharf, one of the river men who had known her in the past, hailed her too familiarly. He was at that moment stepping from the top round of a ladder on to the wharf.

"How 'bout ternight?" he asked with a leer.

She was holding a string of whiting in her left hand, and was hanging upon the final penny of a bargain with the fishman. She half turned, and delivered a resounding slap with her right hand. The man staggered backward, hung for a moment, then vanished. There was a tremendous splash from the shallow water.

"Twenty cent fuh dis string, an' not one cent mo'," Bess continued coolly to the fishman.

He accepted the price. Bess gave him eighteen cents, and a hard look. He counted the money, glanced at the hand that now hung innocently against her apron, then laughed.

"Just as yuh say, Sister. I ain't quarrelin' none wid *yuh dis* mornin'."

Bess gave him one of the faint, cryptic smiles that always made men friends and women enemies for her, and departed for Catfish Row, as if nothing had happened to break the dull routine of the morning's chores.

§

Saturday night, and the court had flung off its workaday clothes and mood. In the corner by Serena's washbench a small intimate circle had gathered about a smoking kerosene lamp. Several women sat on the bench with drowsy little negroes in their laps. A man near the light leaned over a guitar, with a vague wistfulness in his face, and plucked

successive chords with a swift, running vibrance of sound. Then a deep
baritone hummed for a second and raised an air:

> *"Ain't it hahd tuh be a nigger;*
> *Ain't it hahd tuh be a nigger;*
> *Ain't it hahd tuh be a nigger;*
> *'Cause yuh can't git yo' rights w'en yuh do.*

> *"I was sleepin' on a pile ob lumber,*
> *Jus' as happy as uh man kin be,*
> *W'en a w'ite man come wake me from my slumber,*
> *An' he say, 'Yuh gots tuh work now, 'cause yuh free!' "*

Then they were all in on the chorus:

> *"Ain't it hahd tuh be a nigger,"*

and the gloom hummed with the low, close harmonies.

In another corner the crap circle had gathered. Porgy's delight in
the game had not waned with his increasing interests, and he sat fon-
dling the small white cubes, and whispering to them in his old confi-
dential manner.

"Little w'ite babies," he crooned, "come sing fuh dis nigger."

He cast—and won.

Gathering the little heap of pennies and nickels, he passed them be-
hind him to Bess, who squatted in the shadows. She took the money
in silence, counted it, dropped it into her apron pocket, and continued
to watch the game intently, smiling her cryptic smile when Porgy won,
but saying scarcely anything at all.

The negro known as Sportin' Life had come in just as the game
was commencing, and had sat in. That he was not altogether above
suspicion was evidenced by the fact that the little circle of men refused
to allow him to use his own dice, and told him so frankly. He scowled
at them, dropped the dice back into his pocket, and started to leave.
Then he seemed to think better of it, and joined the circle.

As the game proceeded it became evident that Porgy's luck was with
him; he was the most consistent winner, and Sportin' Life was bearing
most of the burden. But the mulatto was too good a gambler to evince
any discomfiture. He talked steadily, laughed much, and missed no
opportunity to drop a sly word of suspicion when Porgy drew in a pot.
There was nothing that could be taken up and resented, but Porgy
was mystified, and Bess' face was dark with anger more than once. He
had a way of leaning over just as Porgy cast, and placing his face
almost on the flags so that he could see under the dice when they

struck. Then he would look up, laugh meaningly into Porgy's face, and sometimes clap his hands as though the cripple had managed something very cleverly.

When the game finally broke up it was clear that he had poisoned the minds of the company, and the good nights lacked their usual warmth.

Bess reached into her apron pocket, and drew out the evening's winnings. The coins made quite a little weight in her hand. A late fragment of moon swung over the wall and poured its diminished light into her open palm. She commenced to count the money. Porgy left her, and drew himself into his room. She proceeded to count, absorbed in her task.

§

"Porgy lucky," said a low voice beside her. "Mus' be yer gots two dollar dere fer um." Sportin' Life lifted his elegant trousers, so that the knees would not bag, and squatted on the flags at her side. He removed his stiff straw hat, with its bright band, and spun it between his hands. The moonlight was full upon his face, with its sinister, sensuous smile.

She looked at him squarely a moment, then said in a cold, level voice:

"I can't 'member ebber meetin' a nigger dat I like less dan I does you."

"Thank yer kindly," he replied, not in the least degree daunted. "But jus' de same, I wants ter be frien' wid yer. Me and you ain't usen ter dese small-town slow ways. We ain't been above seein' night-life what is night-life, an' I jus' wants ter talk to you now and den; dat's all."

"I gots no time fuh talk," she told him. "An' wut mo', I t'rough wid de kin' ob nights you is t'inking 'bout."

"No mo' red-eye; none 'tall?" he queried. "Nebber gits t'irsty, eh?"

"Yes, Gawd knows, I does git t'irsty now and den," she said impulsively; then added sharply, "But I done t'rough now, I tells yer; I done t'rough."

She arose to go. "Yo' kin' mek me sick," she told him; "an' I ain't wants tuh hab no mo' talk wid yuh."

He got spryly to his feet, and stood beside her. "Oh, come on, le's let bygone be bygone, an' be frien'." Then his voice became low and ingratiating: "Come; gimme yer han', Sister," he said.

Acquiescent, but mystified, she held out her open palm.

He poured a little pile of white powder into it. There it lay in the

moonlight, very clean and white on her dark skin. "Happy dus'!" she said, and her voice was like a gasp. "Take dat t'ing away, nigger. I t'rough wid um, I tells yuh." But she did not turn her hand over and let it fall upon the ground.

"Jus' a little touch fer ole time sake," he whispered. " 'Tain't 'nough ter hurt er fly. An' it ain't goin' ter cos' yer one cent."

She stood a moment longer, and her hand trembled, spilling a few grains between her fingers. Then suddenly she clapped her palm over her mouth. When she took it away it was quite empty.

Sportin' Life heaved a sigh of relief, turned and leant against the wall—and waited.

In the corner by Serena's bench the party was breaking up. Only a few women were left, and instead of the blur of general talk, remarks leapt clear. They were discussing the crap game that had just closed.

"Dey is somet'ing berry queer 'bout de way de money always go tuh de same place," a voice was saying.

The moonlight ebbed from the corner where Bess and Sportin' Life stood. Five minutes had passed since she had made her sudden decisive gesture. She stood oddly rigid, with her hands clenched at her sides.

Abruptly she spun around. "Yuh gots mo' ob dat?" Her voice was low and taut.

"Sho' I has!" came the answer, with a confident laugh. "But it don't come cheap. Gimme dat money yer got dere."

Silently she held out her hand, and poured the coins into his palm. He gave her a small folded paper.

"I got more ob dat when yer needs it," he said, as he turned away.

But she did not hear him. She snatched the paper, opened it, and threw the contents into her mouth.

The court was sinking to sleep. One by one the lighted windows went blank. The women at the washbench got to their feet. One yawned noisily, and another knocked her clay pipe out on the flags in a shower of sparks. Then a voice came clearly—the one that had complained before about the crap game.

"I ain't sayin' ef it conjer, er jus' plain loaded dice. All I gots tuh say is dat dam nigger, Porgy, steal my Sam' wages off him now t'ree week runnin'."

Out of the shadows and across the moonlit square a figure flashed, gesturing wildly.

The women leapt back. The one who had done the talking screamed once, the shrill note echoing around the walls. The advancing figure closed convulsive hands upon her shoulders and snatched her body forward. Wide, red-lit eyes glared into her face. A voice half sobbed, half screamed, "Yuh say dat 'bout Porgy? Yuh say Porgy is t'ief?"

The victim was young and strong. She tore the hands from her shoulders and raised her arms before her face. One of the other women reached out to seize the intruder, but was met with a glare so insanely malignant that she retreated screaming.

Above them windows were leaping to light. Dark bodies strained from sills. Feet sounded, running down clapping dilapidated stairways. A shrill, long, terrifying shriek cut across the growing noise, and the women clinched and fell. Bystanders rushed to intervene, and became involved. Always in the centre of the storm a maddened woman whirled like a dervish and called horribly upon her God, striking and clawing wildly.

The babel became terrific. The entire population of the court contributed to the general confusion. In the rooms above, children wailed out a nameless terror.

Suddenly over the tumult sounded the gong of the patrol wagon, and through the gateway half-a-dozen policemen advanced with pistols out, and clubs ready.

The uproar stopped suddenly at its peak. Shadows dropped back and were gulped by deeper shadow. Feet made no sound in retreating. Solid bodies became fluid, sliding. Yawning doorways drew them in. Miraculously the court was converted into a vacant, walled square, in which stood six erect figures, looking a little theatrical and foolish with their revolvers and clubs, and a woman who shook menacing hands at nothing at all and swore huskily at phantoms.

"No trouble finding the cause of the disturbance," said an authoritative voice. "Get her, men. Better use bracelets. Can't tell about dope cases."

The squad closed quickly. For a moment a grotesque shadow tumbled and shifted in the centre of the court; then a voice said, "Steady now." The mass broke into individual figures, and, under the ebbing moonlight, moved toward the entrance with a manacled woman in their midst.

Porgy had opened his door at the first outcry and sat on the sill trying to get the import of the disturbance. Now, as the group passed close to him, he looked up. The woman had ceased her outcry, and was looking about with vague, unseeing eyes. As they walked past his doorway, so close that he could have touched the nearest officer with his hand, she looked down, and her gaze focussed upon the sitting figure. Her body stiffened, and her head lifted with the old, incongruous gesture of disdain.

"Bess!" called Porgy once very loudly; and again, in a voice that sagged, "Bess!"

One of the policemen paused and looked down upon the speaker.

But the woman turned deliberately away, and he hastened to rejoin the party. Then the wagon clanged down the darkened street.

§

Under the gas light that supplemented a far, dusty window in the Recorder's Court, stood Bess. She swayed, and her face twitched occasionally; but her glance was level, and her head erect.

Behind a high desk sat a man well past middle age. His florid complexion caused his long grey mustache to appear very white. His eyes were far apart and suggested a kindness that was born of indolence, rather than of wide compassion. His hands were slender and beautifully made, and he sat with elbows on desk, and finger-tips touching. When he spoke it was in a drawl that suggested weariness.

"What is the charge, Officer?" he asked.

"Bein' under the influence of dope, an' creatin' a disturbance in Catfish Row, yer Honor," replied the policeman who stood by the prisoner.

"Anybody hurt?"

"Not as we was able to see, yer Honor."

The judge turned to the prisoner.

"Have you ever been here before?"

"No, suh," came the reply in a low, clear tone.

"The officer of the day thinks she has, yer Honor," put in the policeman, "but he can't swear to it. She looks like a hundred others, he says, scar and all; an' they change names so fast you get nothing from the records."

The judge regarded the prisoner with amiability. The thermometer on the wall beside him registered ninety. It was asking too much of good-nature to require it to subvert itself in such heat.

"I suppose we will have to give you the benefit of the doubt," he said. Then he turned to the officer.

"After all, it's the man who sold her the poison we want. I was kept here three hours yesterday by dope cases. I want it put a stop to."

He contracted his brows in a weak attempt at sternness, and directed a steady gaze at Bess.

"Who sold you that dope?"

She met his eyes squarely.

"I don't t'ink I know um again," she said in a low, even tone. "I buy from um in de dark, las' night, an' he gone off right away."

"It's no use, Your Honor," put in the policeman. "They won't give each other away."

The judge fixed the culprit with a long scrutiny. Then he asked:
"Have you any money to pay a fine?"

"No, suh. Yuh'll jus' hab tuh gib' me my time."

A man entered the room.

"I beg your pardon, Your Honor," he said, "but there is a cripple outside in a goat-cart who says he is prepared to pay the woman's fine."

"Eh; what's that?" exclaimed the judge. "Is it that black scoundrel, Porgy, the beggar?"

"That's him, Yer Honor," replied the man, with a grin.

"Why, the highwayman takes a dime from me every time I venture on King Charles Street. And here he has the audacity to come and offer to pay a fine."

"Don't tek he money, Boss."

The prisoner said the words steadily, then caught her lower lip with her strong, white teeth.

"Address the Court as 'Your Honor,' not 'Boss,' " ordered the judge.

"Yo' Honuh," amended the culprit.

For a long moment the Recorder sat, his brow contracted. Then he drew a large, cool, linen handkerchief from his pocket and mopped his face.

"Go out and take ten dollars from the beggar," he told the policeman. "It's a small fine for the offence." Then turning to the woman, he said:

"I am going to lock you up for ten days; but any time you give the name of that dope peddler to the jailer you can leave. Do you understand?"

Bess had nothing to say in reply, and after a moment the policeman took her by the arm.

"This way to the wagon," he directed, and led her from the court room.

The street was a blaze of early morning sun, and the woman covered her eyes with her hand. The wagon stood, step to curb, and the officer hurried her across the narrow pavement and into the conveyance.

.The bell clanged, and the heavy horse flung its weight against the collar.

Something impelled Bess to remove her hand and to look down.

Below the high side of the patrol, looking rather like a harbor tug beside an ocean liner, stood the goat-cart. For a moment she looked into Porgy's face. It told her nothing, except that he seemed suddenly to have grown older, and that the real Porgy, who had looked out at her from the eyes for a little while, had gone back into his secret places and closed the door.

The wagon lunged forward.

Then Porgy spoke.

"How long?" he called.

The incessant clamor of the gong commenced, and the hoofs beat their noisy tattoo upon the stones.

Bess raised both hands with fingers extended.

The wagon rounded a corner and disappeared.

§

The jail in which Bess was incarcerated was no better, and no worse, than many others of its period, and the score of negro women with whom she found herself could not be said to suffer acutely under their imprisonment. When life reaches a certain level of misery, it envelopes itself in a protective anesthesia which deadens the senses to extremes; and having no tasks to perform, the prisoners awaited the expiration of their brief sentences with sodden patience, or hastened the passage of time with song.

By day they were at liberty to exercise in the jail yard, a square of about half an acre surrounded by a high brick wall, containing not so much as a single blade of grass. Like a great basin, the yard caught and held the heat which poured from the August sun until it seemed to overflow the rim, and quiver, as though the immense vessel had been jarred from without. But the soaring walls gave always a narrow strip of shade to which the prisoners clung, moving around the sides as the day advanced, with the accuracy of the hand of a sundial.

Before nightfall the prisoners were herded into the steaming interior of the building, and Bess and the other women were locked in a steel cage, which resembled a large dog-pound and stood in the centre of a high, square room, with a passageway around it. A peculiarly offensive moisture clung to the ceiling, and streamed in little rivulets down the walls. An almost unbreathable stench clogged the atmosphere.

The jailers were not vindictive. They were not even unkind. Some of them evidenced a mild affection for their charges, and would pause to exchange greetings with them on their rounds. But it would have meant effort to better the living conditions, and effort on the part of a white warden in August was not to be considered. They locked them up, gave them a sufficiency of hominy and white pork to sustain life, allowed them to see their visitors, talk, and sing to their hearts' content. If they were suffering from tuberculosis, or one of a hundred nameless and communicable diseases, when they entered, it was none

of the County's affair. And if they left showing that ash-pallor so unmistakable in a negro, it was as lamentable as it was unavoidable. But when all was said and done, what must one expect if one added to the handicap of a dark skin the indiscretion of swallowing cocaine and indulging in a crap game?

Bess received but one visitor during her imprisonment. When the callers were admitted, on the day following her arrival, Maria loomed in the centre of the small, timid group. She went directly to Bess where she sat by the wall, with her eyes closed against the glare. The big negress wore an expression of solicitude, and her voice was low and surprisingly gentle as she said:

"Porgy ask me tuh bring yer dis blanket fuh lie on, an' dese fish an' bread. How yuh is feelin' now?" Then she bent over and placed a bundle in the prisoner's lap.

Bess opened her eyes in surprise.

"I ain't been expectin' no fabors off none ob you folks," she replied. "How come yuh tuh care ef I lib er die, attuh dat row I mek?"

Maria lowered herself to a seat beside her.

"I lubs dat nigger, Porgy, lak he been my chile," she told her. "An' wut mo', I t'ink I know what done happen tuh yuh."

"Wut yuh know?"

"I been in my do' dat night; an' I seen dat skunk, Sportin' Life, sell yuh dat stuff. Ef I had er known den wut it wuz, I'd a been hyuh long side ob yuh now fuh murder."

After a moment, she asked: "Wut mek yuh don't tell de jailluh who done um, an' come on home?"

Bess remained silent for a moment; then she raised her head and looked into the eyes of the older woman.

"I's a 'oman grown. Ef I tek dope, dat muh own business. Ef I ebber gits muh han' on dat nigger, I goin' fix um so he own mammy ain't know um! But I ain't goin' gib um 'way tuh de w'ite folks."

The hard lines about her mouth softened, and, in scarcely more than a whisper, she added:

"I gots tuh be decent 'bout somet'ing, 'less I couldn't go back an' look in Porgy face."

Maria got heavily to her feet. The other visitors were leaving, and she longed to be free of the high, brick walls. She dropped a hand on Bess's shoulder.

"Yuh do right, Sister. But ef dat yalluh nigger come tuh Catfish Row agin—leabe him fuh me—dat's all!" Then the big negress joined the departing group, and passed out through the small steel doorway that pierced the massive gate.

Bess sat for a long while without moving. The sun lifted over the

high wall, and drove its white-hot tide into her lap, and upon her folded hands.

"Wut mek yuh ain't mobe intuh de shade?" a neighbor asked curiously.

Bess looked up and smiled.

"I jes' settin' hyuh t'inkin' 'bout muh frien'," she said. "Yuh done hear um call me 'Sister,' ain't yuh? Berry well den. Dat mean me and she is frien'."

§

Bess lay upon the bed in Porgy's room and stared at the ceiling with hard, bright eyes. From time to time she would pluck at the sheet that covered her and utter hurried, indistinct sentences that bore not the slightest relation to existing circumstances. A week had passed since her release, and its seven interminable days had been spent in this fashion.

Porgy was out upon the day's rounds. Occasionally the door to the sick-room would open, and an awed, black face peer in. The mystery of delirium frightened and perplexed the negroes, and limited the manifestations of kindness and sympathy that they usually bestowed upon unfortunate friends. Even Maria was not proof against this dread, and the irrelevant observations that greeted her when she went in with the daily lunch sent her hurrying wide-eyed from the room.

Porgy returned early in the evening. His face was deeply marked, but the lines were those of anxiety, and his characteristic firmness of mouth and jaw was gone. He closed the door on the curious glances of his neighbors, and lifted himself to a seat upon the bed.

"How Bess now?" he asked softly.

She shifted her gaze from the ceiling to his face.

"Eighteen miles tuh Kittiwar!" she muttered. "Rattlesnake', palm-ettuh bush, an' such."

Her eyes were suddenly fearful, and she closed her hand tightly upon his.

Porgy cast a hurried glance over his shoulder. Then, reassured, stroked her brow, and comforted her in his deep, gentle voice.

"Yuh hyuh wid Porgy now; an' nuttin' can't hurt yuh. Soon de cool wedder comin' an' chill off dese febers. Ain't yuh 'member how dat cool win' come tuh town wid de smell ob pine tree; an' how de star is all polish up lak w'ite folks' silber? Den ebbery body git well. Ain't yuh know? Yuh jus' keep still, an' watch wut Porgy say."

She was silent after that, and closed her eyes. Presently, to his relief, he saw that she was sleeping. This was the moment for which

he had been waiting. He went out, closing the door very gently, and joined a group of sympathisers in the court.

"Wut we goin' do now?" he asked. "A week gone, an' she ain't none better."

Peter knocked out his clay pipe on a flag-stone, with three staccato little raps, thus gaining the attention of the circle.

"Ef yuh wants tuh listen tuh me," he remarked weightily, "I adwise yer tuh sen' she tuh de w'ite folk' hospital."

His words were received with a surprise amounting to incredulity.

"Fuh Gawd sake, Daddy Peter!" an awed voice said at last. "Ain't yuh knows dey lets nigger die dey, so dey kin gib um tuh de student?"

But the old negro stood his ground.

"De student ain't gits um 'til he done dead. Ain't dat so? Den he can't hurt um none. Ain't dat so, too? An' I gots dis tuh say. One ob my w'ite folks is er nuss tuh de hospital; and dat lady is er pure angel wid de sick nigger. Ef I sick tuhmorruh I goin' tuh she; an' wut she say is good wid me. I wants dis carcase tek care ob w'ile he is alibe. W'en he done dead, I ain't keer."

"Yuh ain't keer whedder yuh is cut up an' scatter, 'stead of bein' bury in Gawd own grabe-yahd?" someone asked the iconoclast.

Under this direct attack, the old man weakened.

"Well, mebbe I ain't sayin' I jus' as lief," he compromised. "But I t'ink Gawd onduhstan' de succumstance, an' mek allowance."

Serena Robbins broke the silence which followed.

"How come yuh ain't ax me fuh pray ober um?" she enquired in a slightly offended voice. "Mus' be yuh is done fergit how Gawd done answer we las' prayeh, and sen' dat goat tuh sabe yu' life, when starbation done stan' dey an' look yuh in de eye."

Porgy brightened at that, and turned eagerly from the dark horror of Peter's suggestion.

"Dat so, my Sister," he commenced; but her eyes were already closed, and her body was swaying from side to side, as she sat cross-legged on the flags. Presently she began to intone:

"Oh, Jedus, who done trouble de wateh in de sea of Gallerie—"

"Amen!" came the chorus, led by Porgy.

"An' likewise who done cas' de Debbil out ob de afflicted, time an' time agin—"

"Oh, Jedus!"

"Wut mek yuh ain't lay yo' han' on dis sister' head?"

"Oh, my fadder!"

"An' sen' de Debbil out ob she, down er steep place intuh de sea, lak yuh use' tuh do, time an' time agin?"

"Time an' time agin!"

"Ain't dis po' cripple done lif' up out de dus' by we prayeh?"

"Da's de trut', Jedus."

"Eben so, lif' up he woman, an' mek she well, time an' time agin!"

"Time an' time ag'in! Allelujah!"

After the prayer the group scattered, each going silently away in the late dusk, until there remained only Porgy, who sat with bowed head, and Maria, massive and inscrutable, beside him.

When the last retreating footstep died away, the great negress bent her turbaned head over until it almost touched Porgy's face.

"Listen tuh me," she whispered. "Yuh wants dat 'oman cure up; ain't yuh?"

"Yuh knows I does." And, already suffering from the reaction from religious enthusiasm, his voice was flat and hopeless.

"Berry well den. De ribber boat leabe fum de wharf at sebben o'clock, tuhmorruh mo'nin'. Yuh knows dat deck-han' by de name Mingo?"

Porgy nodded assent, his eyes intent upon her face.

"Well; git on de wharf early, an' gib um two dollar. Tell um w'en de boat done git tuh Ediwander Islan' at eight tuhmorruh night, tuh go right tuh Lody cabin, an' tell she tuh mek a conjer tuh cas' de debbil out Bess."

"Yuh t'ink dat cure she?" asked Porgy, with a glimmer of new hope in his eyes.

"I ain't t'ink. I knows," came in tones of absolute conviction. "Now, min'; an' do wut I say."

The big negress shuffled away to her room, leaving Porgy alone in the gloom.

The bent, solitary figure raised its eyes to the square of sky, with its bewildering profusion of stars, that fitted like a lid over the high rim of the court. There were no sounds except a weary land breeze that fingered the lichens on the south wall, and a whisper from the bay, as the tide lifted its row of shells and pebbles a notch further up the littered beach.

Now that all human companionship had been withdrawn, the watcher felt strangely alone, and smaller than the farthest star or most diminutive shell. Like a caged squirrel, his tired mind spun the rounds of his three alternatives: First, the white man's science, gaunt, clean, and mysterious, with the complete and awful magistracy which it assumed over the luckless bodies that fell into its possession. He knew that it returned some healed in body. He knew that others had passed into its portals, and had been obliterated utterly. Then his second alternative: the white man's God, vague and abstract as the wind that moved among the lichens, with his Jesus, who could stir him sud-

denly to his most beautiful songs and make his heart expand until, for a moment, it embraced all mankind with compassionate love, but who passed, as the wind passes, leaving him cold and disillusioned. One of these he must choose, or else turn his face back to the old blurred trail that receded, down, down, down to the beginning of things: to the symbols one might hold, tangible and terrifying; to the presciences that shuddered like dawn at the back of the brain and told one what to do without the process of thought.

As though bent beneath a great physical weight, Porgy sat without moving, until the pattern on his glittering ceiling had changed and shifted. Then he lifted his face slowly, drew his sleeve across his moist forehead, and entered his room.

§

Just before sunrise Porgy left his room and hitched up his goat. In the upper air over Catfish Row a single buzzard hung poised. Slowly it careened to a current of air, and its belly and under-wings lit to a ruddy glory from the sun, which was still below the horizon. Porgy saw it and winced. But as he went about his task there was no indecision in his face. He harnessed the goat with steady hands, drove out of the court and to the pier-head.

He experienced no difficulty in finding his man. Mingo accepted the mission and the handful of pennies and nickels; and Porgy, having closed the bargain, returned at once to the court.

Maria was opening her shop as he entered, and paused with a shutter in her hands. She could scarcely believe her eyes. The beggar's face was bright, and he was humming a tune.

"Wut de news?" she asked. "Bess done git well?"

"Not jus' yit," he replied. "But I done had me a dream las' night; an' de dream say tuh sen' tuh de conjer 'oman; an' Bess goin' break she feber tuhnight."

"Da's right, my Brudder," Maria responded heartily. "Dat 'oman good as well now. You watch!"

All day, sitting by Archdale's office, Porgy hummed his tune, and counted off the hours of the steamboat's voyage. Now she would be passing Kittiwar and, in only a few hours more, she would be coming to rest for the night at Ediwander.

The counting off continued after he went to bed, and he was strangely undisturbed by Bess's mutterings. Now the boat had arrived, he finally told himself. Maria had said that the cabin was near the landing. Surely it would not take the woman long to brew the spell.

His excitement increased to a mood of exaltation. He lay with his hand upon Bess's forehead, waiting.

Far away St. Christopher struck the hour. The mellow bells threw the quarter hours out like a handful of small gold coins to ring down upon the drowsy streets. Then, very deliberately, they dropped ten round, heavy notes into the silence.

This should be the moment. Porgy pressed his hand harder, and sweat broke out upon his brow. For a moment it seemed to him that life hung suspended.

"Porgy," said a weak, flat voice beside him. "Porgy, dat you dey, ain't it? Why you ain't talk tuh me?"

The cripple's answer was a sudden high laugh that broke to a sob. "T'ank Gawd!" he said; and again, "T'ank Gawd!"

§

On the evening following the day upon which Bess had taken her turn for the better, Maria was alone in her shop. The supper hour was over, and her patrons had departed. She was busy at her stove, and did not turn immediately when someone entered. When she finally looked over her shoulder, her customer had buried his face in his hands, and she failed to recognize him. Of one fact there could be little doubt: the man was drunk, for the close, little room was already heavy with the exhalations of vile corn whiskey.

She crossed the room, and touched the man on the shoulder. He lowered his hands and attempted to focus his eyes on her face.

"Oh, it's you, Mingo?" she said, and even then she did not grasp the significance of his presence in the city at that time.

"Gimme some supper," he growled; and, with an uncertain movement, drew some change from his pocket and spilled it in a small pile on the table.

Maria looked at the money. There was about half a dollar in all, but there were only two nickels, and the remainder was in pennies. It looked suspiciously like the currency in which Porgy paid his debts. Then, as she stood looking down at the little heap of copper, the full import of the man's presence dawned upon her.

"Wut yuh doin' here now?" she demanded of him in a tense whisper; "when de ribber boat ain't due back fuh annoder day?"

The question stirred her customer's consciousness to a faint gleam of life; but it did not vitalize it sufficiently for adroit prevarication.

"I miss de boat dis trip," he managed to articulate. "I take er drink wid er frien', and when I git tuh de wharf, de boat done gone."

Two powerful hands gripped his shoulders and flung him back against the wall. He opened his eyes wide and looked into a face of such cold ferocity that his loose lips emitted a sudden "Oh, Jedus!" and he became immediately sober, and very much afraid.

Then Maria poured into his ears words that had the heat and dead weight of molten lead.

"Now I goin' lock yuh up in dat closet till de ribber boat is back at de wharf," she concluded. "Den I goin' let yuh loose. But I all de time goin' be where I kin git my hand on yuh again. Ef yuh ebber tells Porgy, or any libbin' soul, dat yuh ain't deliber dat message tuh Lody, I goin' tuh hab nigger blood on my soul w'en I stan' at de jedgement. Now yuh gots dat straight in yuh head?"

Mingo nodded assent. He was beyond the power to speak.

The big negress jerked him suddenly to his feet, propelled him across the room and into the stygian recesses of the closet. Then she slammed the door, and turned the immense iron key in the lock, and dropped it in her pocket.

"Well, dat's dat!" she remarked, as she wiped a moist, mystified face upon a corner of her apron. "Mus' hab been Jedus done um atter all." Then, as though to dismiss the matter, she added: "No, I be damn ef he did. He ain't gots it in um."

Part IV

It was the day set for the grand parade and picnic of "The Sons and Daughters of Repent Ye Saith the Lord," and, with the first light of morning, Catfish Row had burst into a fever of preparation. Across the narrow street, the wharf, from which the party was to leave, bustled and seethed with life. A wagon rattled out to the pier-head and discharged an entire load of watermelons. Under the vigilant eyes of a committee a dozen volunteers lifted the precious freight from the vehicle, and piled it ready for the steamer.

From behind the next pier, with a frenzied threshing of its immense stern paddle, came the excursion boat. Tall open exhaust funnels flanked the walking-beam, and coughed great salmon-colored plumes of steam into the faint young sunlight. A fierce torrent of wood-smoke gushed from the funnel and went tumbling away across the harbor. Painters were hurled, missed, coiled, and hurled again. Then, amid a babblement of advice and encouragement, the craft was finally moored in readiness for the Lodge.

The first horizontal rays of the sun were painting the wall a warm claret, when Porgy opened his door, to find Peter already dressed for the parade, and perched upon the back of his gaily blanketed horse. He wore a sky-blue coat, white pants which were thrust into high black leggings, and a visored cap, from beneath which he scowled fiercely down upon the turmoil around the feet of his mount. Across his breast, from right shoulder to left hip, was a broad scarlet sash, upon which was emblazoned, "Repent Ye Saith the Lord!" and from his left breast fluttered a white ribbon bearing the word "MARSHAL." From time to time, he would issue orders in hoarse, menacing gutturals, which no one heeded; and twice, in the space of half an hour, he rode out to the pier-head, counted the watermelons, and returned to report the number to an important official who had arrived in a carriage to supervise the arrangements.

Momently the confusion increased, until at eight o'clock it culminated in a general exodus toward the rendezvous for the parade.

The drowsy old city had scarcely commenced its day when, down through King Charles Street, the procession took its way. Superbly unselfconscious of the effect that it produced, it crashed through the slow, restrained rhythm of the city's life like a wild, barbaric chord. All of the stately mansions along the way were servantless that day, and the aristocratic matrons broke the ultimate canon of the social code and peered through front windows at the procession as it swept flamboyantly across the town.

First came an infinitesimal negro boy, scarlet-coated, and aglitter with brass buttons. Upon his head was balanced an enormous shako; and while he marched with left hand on hip and shoulders back, his right hand twirled a heavy gold-plated baton. Then the band, two score boys attired in several variations of the band master's costume, strode by. Bare, splay feet padded upon the cobbles; heads were thrown back, with lips to instruments that glittered in the sunshine, launching daring and independent excursions into the realm of sound. Yet these improvisations returned always to the eternal boom, boom, boom of an underlying rhythm, and met with others in the sudden weaving and ravelling of amazing chords. An ecstasy of wild young bodies beat living into the blasts that shook the windows of the solemn houses. Broad, dusty, blue-black feet shuffled and danced on the many-colored cobbles and the grass between them. The sun lifted suddenly over the housetops and flashed like a torrent of warm, white wine between the staid buildings, to break on flashing teeth and laughing eyes.

After the band came the men members of the lodge, stepping it out to the urge of the marshals who rode beside them, reinforcing the marching rhythm with a series of staccato grunts, shot with crisp,

military precision from under their visored caps. Breast cross-slashed with the emblems of their lodge, they passed.

Then came the carriages, and suddenly the narrow street hummed and bloomed like a tropic garden. Six to a carriage sat the sisters. The effect produced by the colors was strangely like that wrought in the music; scarlet, purple, orange, flamingo, emerald; wild, clashing, unbelievable discords; yet, in their steady flow before the eye, possessing a strange, dominant rhythm that reconciled them to each other and made them unalterably right. The senses reached blindly out for a reason. There was none. They intoxicated, they maddened, and finally they passed, seeming to pull every ray of color from the dun buildings, leaving the sunlight sane, flat, dead.

For its one brief moment out of the year the pageant had lasted. Out of its fetters of civilization this people had risen, suddenly, amazingly. Exotic as the Congo, and still able to abandon themselves utterly to the wild joy of fantastic play, they had taken the reticent, old Anglo-Saxon town and stamped their mood swiftly and indelibly into its heart. Then they passed, leaving behind them a wistful envy among those who had watched them go,—those whom the ages had rendered old and wise.

§

When the exodus from the Row was completed, Bess helped Porgy out to the boat and established him in an angle of the main-deck cabin, where he could see and enjoy the excursion to the full. Below them on the wharf, Maria, who had the direction of the refreshment committee in hand, moved about among the baskets and boxes, looking rather like a water-front conflagration, in a voluminous costume of scarlet and orange. Bess left Porgy and descended the ladder.

"I gots a ready hand wid bundle," she announced diffidently.

The immense negress paused, and looked her up and down.

"Well, well, it looks like yer tryin' ter be decent," she commented.

Instantly the woman chilled. "Yuh kin go tuh Hell!" she said deliberately. "I ain't axin' fuh no sermon. I want a job. Does yuh want a han' wid dem package, or not?"

For a moment their eyes met. Then they laughed suddenly, loudly together, with complete understanding.

"All right, den," the older woman said. "Ef yuh is dat independent, yuh kin tek dem basket on board."

After that they worked together, until the procession arrived, without the interchange of further remarks.

§

Down the quiet bay, like a great, frenzied beetle, the stern-wheeler kicked its way. On the main deck the band played without cessation. In a ring before it, a number of negroes danced, for the most part shuffling singly. The sun hurled the full power of an August noon upon the oil-smooth water, and the polished surface cast it upward with added force under the awnings. The decks sagged with color, and repeated explosions of laughter rode the heat waves back to the drowsing, lovely old city long after the boat had turned the first bend in the narrow river and passed from view on its way to the negro picnic grounds on Kittiwar Island.

Thrashing its way between far-sweeping marshes and wooded sea islands, the boat would burst suddenly into lagoon after lagoon, that lay strewn along the coast, that blazed in the noon like great fire-opals held in silver mesh.

Finally a shout went up. Kittiwar lay before them, thrusting a slender wharf from its thickly wooded extremity into the slack tide.

The debarkation over, Maria took possession of a clearing that stood in a dense forest of palmettoes and fronted on the beach, and marshalled her committee to prepare the lunch. From the adjacent beach came the steady, cool thunder of the sea and the unremitting hum of sand, as tireless winds scooped it from the dunes and sent it in low, flat-blown layers across the hard floor of the beach.

The picnickers heard it, and answered with a shout. Soon the streaming whiteness of the inner surf was dotted with small, glistening black bodies; the larger figures, with skirts hoisted high, were wading in the shallows.

Porgy sat with a large myrtle bush in one hand, with which he brushed flies from several sleeping infants. The sun lay heavy and comforting upon him. One of the children stirred and whimpered. He hummed a low, bumbling song to it. There was a new contentment in his face. After a while he commenced to nod.

§

"I go an' git some palmettuh leaf fuh tablecloth," Bess told Maria; and, without waiting for an answer, she took a knife from a basket, and entered the dense tangle of palm and vine that walled the clearing.

Almost immediately she was in another world. The sounds behind

her became faint, and died. A rattler moved its thick body sluggishly out of her way. A flock of wood ibis sprang suddenly up, broke through the thick roof of palm leaves, and streamed away over the treetops toward the marsh with their legs at the trail.

She cut a wide fan-shaped leaf from the nearest palmetto. Behind her some one breathed—a deep interminable breath.

The woman's body stiffened slowly. Her eyes half closed and were suddenly dark and knowing. Some deep ebb or flow of blood touched her face, causing it to darken heavily, leaving the scar livid. Without turning, she said slowly:

"Crown!"

"Yas, yuh know berry well, dis Crown."

The deep sound shook her. She turned like one dazed, and looked him up and down.

His body was naked to the waist, and the blue cotton pants that he had worn on the night of the killing had frayed away to his knees. He bent slightly forward. The great muscles of his torso flickered and ran like the flank of a horse. His small wicked eyes burned, and he moistened his heavy lips.

Earth had cared for him well. The marshes had provided eggs of wild fowl, and many young birds. The creek had given him fish, crabs and oysters in abundance, and the forest had fed him with its many berries, and succulent palmetto cabbage.

"I seen yuh land," he said, "an' I been waitin' fuh yuh. I mos' dead ob lonesome on dis damn island, wid not one Gawd's person to swap a word wid. Yuh gots any happy-dus' wid yuh?"

"No," she said; then with an effort, "Crown, I gots somethin' tuh tell yuh. I done gib up dope; and beside dat, I sort ob change my way."

His jaw shot forward, and the huge shoulder muscles bulged and set. His two great hands went around her throat and closed like the slow fusing of steel on steel. She stopped speaking. He drew her to him until his face touched hers. Under his hands her arteries pounded, sending fierce spurts of flame through her limbs, beating redly behind her eyeballs. His hands slackened. Her face changed, her lips opened, but she said nothing. Crown broke into low, shaken laughter, and threw her from him.

"Now come wid me," he ordered.

Into the depths of the jungle they plunged; the woman walking in front with a trance-like fixity of gaze. They followed one of the narrow hard-packed trails that had been beaten by the wild hogs and goats that roamed the island.

On each side of them, the forest stood like a wall, its tough low trees and thick-bodied palmettos laced and bound together with wire-

strong vines. Overhead the foliage met, making the trail a tunnel as inescapable as though it had been built of masonry.

The man walked with a swinging, effortless stride, but his breath sounded in long, audible inhalations, as though he labored physically.

When they had journeyed for half an hour they crossed a small cypress swamp. The cypress-knees jutted grotesquely from the yellow water, and trailing Spanish moss extended drab stalactites that brushed their faces as they threaded the low, muddy trail.

Finally Bess emerged into a small clearing, in the centre of which stood a low hut with sides of plaited twigs and roof of palmetto leaves laid on top of each other in regular rows like shingles.

Crown was close behind her. At the low door of the hut she paused and turned toward him. He laughed suddenly and hotly at what he saw in her face.

"I know yuh ain't change," he said. "Wid yuh an' me it always goin' tuh be de same. See?"

He snatched her body toward him with such force that her breath was forced from her in a sharp gasp. Then she inhaled deeply, threw back her head, and sent a wild laugh out against the walls of the clearing.

Crown swung her about and threw her face forward into the hut.

§

The sun was so low that its level rays shot through the tunnels of the forest and bronzed its ceiling of woven leaves when Bess returned to the clearing. She paused for a moment. Behind her, screened by the underbrush, stood Crown.

"Now 'member wut I tells yuh," he said. "Yuh kin stay wid de cripple 'til de cotton come. Den I comin'. Davy will hide we on de ribber boat fur as Sawannah. Den soon de cotton will be comin' in fas', an' libbin will be easy. Yuh gits dat?"

For a moment she looked into the narrow, menacing eyes, then nodded.

"Go 'long den, an' tote fair, les yuh wants tuh meet yo' Gawd."

She stepped into the open. Already most of the party were on the boat. She crossed the narrow beach to the wharf.

Maria stood by the gangplank and looked at her with suspicious eyes. "Wuh yuh been all day?" she demanded.

"I git los' in de woods, an' I can't git my bearin's 'til sundown. But dat ain't nobody' business 'cep' me an' Porgy, ef yuh wants tuh know."

She found Porgy on the lower deck near the stern, and seated herself

by him in silence. He was looking into the sunset, and gave no evidence
of having noticed her arrival.

Through the illimitable, mysterious night, the steamer took its way.
Presently it swung out of one of the narrow channels and wallowed
like an antediluvian monster into the stillness of a wide lagoon. Out
of the darkness, low, broad waves moved in upon it, trailing stars
along their swarthy backs to shatter into silver dust against the un-
couth bows.

To Porgy and Bess, still sitting silent in the stern, came only the
echoes of drowsy conversations, sounds of sleeping, and the rhythmic
splash and drip of the single great wheel behind them. The boat forged
out into the centre of the lagoon, and the shore line melted out behind
it. Where it had shown a moment before, could now be seen only the
steady climb of constellations out of the water's rim, and the soft,
humid lamps of low, near stars. The night pressed in about the two
quiet figures.

Porgy had said no word since their departure. His body had assumed
its old, tense attitude. His face wore again its listening look. Now, he
said slowly:

"Yuh nebber lie tuh me, Bess."

"No," came an even, colorless voice, "I nebber lie tuh yuh. Yuh gots
tuh gib me dat."

Another interval, then:

"War it Crown?"

A sharp, indrawn breath beside him, and a whisper:

"How yuh know?"

"Gawd gib cripple many t'ings he ain't gib strong men." Then
again, patiently, "War it Crown?"

"Yes, it war."

"Wut he say?"

"He comin' fuh me when de cotton come tuh town."

"Yuh goin'?"

"I tell um—yes."

After a while the woman reached out a hand and closed it lightly
about the man's arm. Under the sleeve she felt the muscles go rigid.
What power! She tried to circle it with her hand. It was almost as big
as Crown's. It was strange that she had not noticed that before.
She opened her mouth to speak, but no sound came. Presently she
sighed, and withdrew her hand.

Through the immense emptiness of sea and sky the boat forged
slowly toward the distant city's lights.

§

"I gots er feelin' yistuhday," announced Maria to Serena Robbins, as she took a batch of wet clothing from the latter's tub, gave it one twist with her enormous hands, and set it aside to go upon the line.

"Wut yuh gots er feelin' 'bout?"

"I gots er feelin' w'en Porgy 'oman come out de wood on de picnic, she done been wid Crown."

At the mention of the murderer's name Serena stepped back, and her usual expression of sanctimonious complacency slowly changed. Her lower lip shot forward, and her face darkened.

"Yuh t'ink dat nigger on Kittiwar?" she asked.

"I allus figgered he bin dey in dem deep palmetters," Maria replied. "But w'en I look in Bess's eye las' night, I sho ob two t'ing: one, dat he is dey, an' two, dat she been wid um."

"Yuh b'lieb she still run wid dat nigger?"

"Dem sort ob mens ain't need tuh worry 'bout habin' 'omen," Maria told her. "Dey kin lay de lash on um, an' kick um in de street; den dey kin whistle w'en dey ready, an' dere dey is ag'in lickin' dey han'."

"She goin' stay wid Porgy, ef she know wut good fuh she."

"She know all right, an' she lub Porgy. But ef dat nigger come attuh she, dey ain't goin' tuh be noboddy roun' hyuh but Porgy an' de goat."

A sudden dark flame blazed in Serena's face, sweeping the acquired complacency before it, and changing it utterly. She leant forward, and spoke heavily:

"Dat nigger bes' t'ank he Gawd dat I gots My Jedus now fuh hol' back my han'!"

"Yuh ain't means dat yuh is goin' tuh gib um up tuh de w'ite folks ef he come back to town, 'stead ob settle wid um yu'self?" Maria asked incredulously.

"I ain't know wut fuh do," the other replied, the hatred in her face giving way to a look of perplexity. "Ef dat nigger come tuh town he sho tuh git kill' sooner er later. Den de w'ite folks goin' lock me up. Dey gots it on de writin's now dat I been Robbins' wife; an' dey goin' figger I like as not kill um. I knows two people git lock up dat way, an' dey ain't do one Gawd t'ing."

"Nigger sho' gots fuh keep he eye open in dis worl'," the big negress observed. "But we can't turn no nigger ober tuh de police."

A man paused before the entrance of the court, and looked in. To the two women he was only a silhouette standing under the arch

against a dazzling expanse of bay; but the foppish outlines of the indolent, slender figure were unmistakable.

A smile of pleased anticipation grew about Maria's wide mouth. She dried her hands upon her apron.

"Jus' like I been tellin' yuh!" she remarked to Serena. "T'ank Gawd, Jedus ain't gots me yit wuh he gots you; an' I still mens enough tuh straighten out a crooked nigger. See dat yalluh snake wrigglin' in de do'way? He de one wut sell Bess dat happy-dus'."

Drying her hands and bared forearms with ominous thoroughness, she crossed to her shop. The room was empty when she entered. She went at once to the stove which stood in its corner, with its legs set upon four bricks. She bent forward, placed a shoulder against one of its corners, gave a heave, and threw out a brick. Then she straightened up, spat first on one hand, then on the other, and, carrying the brick in her immense right, lightly, and with a certain awful fondness, stepped out of her door.

Sportin' Life was now within the entrance, and presented an unsuspecting profile to the cook-shop.

With frightful deliberation, Maria swung her long arm back; then, like the stroke of a rattler, it shot forward. The brick caught the mulatto full on the side of the head. He crumpled among his gaudy habiliments like a stricken bird.

After a space of time the victim blinked feebly, then opened his eyes upon Maria's face. She was mopping his head with a wet rag, and his first glance discovered an expression of gentleness on her heavy features. Reassured, he opened his eyes wide. But the gentleness was gone. He felt himself gripped by the shoulders, and suddenly snatched upward to be placed upon unsteady legs. Then he was propelled rapidly toward the gate.

At the pavement's edge Maria swung her victim around until his wandering and reluctant gaze met hers.

"De las' time yuh wuz aroun' hyuh, I ain't hab nuttin' on yuh but my eyes. Now I knows yuh—yuh damn, dirty, dope-peddler, wreckin' de homes ob dese happy niggers!"

Her arms shot forward and back like locomotive pistons. The man's head snapped to an acute angle, and righted itself with difficulty.

"Now, w'en I done flingin' yuh out dis gate," she proceeded, "it's de las' time yuh is goin' tuh leabe it erlibe. Eberybody say I is er berry t'orough nigger, an' ef yuh ebber comes roun' hyuh agin, drunk or sobuh, I ain't goin' to be t'rough wid yuh carcase ontil I t'row yuh bones out tuh de buzza'd one by one."

Abruptly she reversed the luckless man and placed a foot in the small of his back. Then with a heave that seemed to bring into play

every muscle of her huge bulk, she catapulted him once and for all out of Catfish Row and the lives of its inhabitants.

Part V

"Fish runnin' well outside de bar, dese days," remarked Jake one evening to several of his seagoing companions.

A large, bronze-colored negro paused in his task of rigging a line, and cast an eye to sea through the driveway.

"An' we mens bes' make de mores ob it," he observed. "Dem Septumbuh storm due soon, an' fish ain't likes eas' win' an' muddy watuh."

Jake laughed reassuringly.

"Go 'long wid yuh. Ain't yuh done know we hab one stiff gale las' summer, an' he nebber come two yeah han' runnin'.''

His wife came toward him with a baby in her arms, and, giving him the child to hold, took up the mess of fish which he was cleaning in a leisurely fashion.

"Ef yuh ain't mans enough tuh clean fish no fastuh dan dat, yuh bes' min' de baby, an' gib um tuh a 'oman fuh clean!" she said scornfully, as she bore away the pan.

The group laughed at that, Jake's somewhat shamefaced merriment rising above the others. He rocked the contented little negro in his strong arms, and followed the retreating figure of the mother with admiring eyes.

"All right, mens," he said, returning to the matter in hand. "I'm all fuh ridin' luck fer as he will tote me. Turn out at fo' tuhmorruh mornin', and we'll push de 'Seagull' clean tuh de blackfish banks befo' we wets de anchor. I gots er feelin' in my bones dat we goin' be gunnels undeh wid de pure fish when we comes in tuhmorruh night."

The news of Jake's prediction spread through the negro quarter. Other crews got their boats hastily in commission and were ready to join the "Mosquito Fleet" when it put to sea.

On the following morning, when the sun rose out of the Atlantic, the thirty or forty small vessels were mere specks teetering upon the water's rim against the red disc that forged swiftly up beyond them.

Afternoon found the wharf crowded with women and children, who laughed and joked each other as to the respective merits of their men and the luck of the boats in which they went to sea.

Clara, Jake's wife, sought the head of the dock long before sundown, and sat upon the bulkhead with her baby asleep in her lap. Occasionally she would exchange a greeting with an acquaintance; but for the

most part she gazed toward the harbor mouth and said no word to any one.

"She always like dat," a neighbor informed a little group. "A conjer 'oman once tell she Jake goin' git drownded; an' she ain't hab no happiness since, 'cept when he feet is hittin' de dirt."

Presently a murmur arose among the watchers. Out at the harbor mouth, against the thin greenish-blue of the horizon, appeared the "Mosquito Fleet." Driven by a steady breeze, the boats swept toward the city with astonishing rapidity.

Warm sunlight flooded out of the west, touched the old city with transient glory, then cascaded over the tossing surface of the bay to paint the taut, cupped sails salmon pink, as the fleet drove forward directly into the eye of the sun.

Almost before the crowd realized it, the boats were jibing and coming about at their feet, each jockeying for a favorable berth.

Under the skillful and daring hand of Jake, the "Seagull" took a chance, missed a stern by a hairbreadth, jibed suddenly with a snap and boom, and ran in, directly under the old rock steps of the wharf.

A cheer went up from the crowd. Never had there been such a catch. The boat seemed floored with silver which rose almost to the thwarts, forcing the crew to sit on gunnels, or aft with the steersman.

Indeed the catch was so heavy that as boat after boat docked, it became evident that the market was glutted, and the fishermen vied with each other in giving away their surplus cargo, so that they would not have to throw it overboard.

§

By the following morning the weather had become unsettled. The wind was still coming out of the west; but a low, solid wall of cloud had replaced the promising sunset of the evening before, and from time to time the wind would wrench off a section of the black mass, and volley it with great speed across the sky, to accumulate in unstable pyramids against the sunrise.

But the success of the day before had so fired the enthusiasm of the fishermen that they were not easily to be deterred from following their luck, and the first grey premonition of the day found the wharf seething with preparation.

Clara, with the baby in her arms, accompanied Jake to the pierhead. She knew the futility of remonstrance; but her eyes were fearful when the heavy, black clouds swept overhead. Once, when a wave slapped a pile, and threw a handful of spray in her face, she moaned

and looked up at the big negro by her side. But Jake was full of the business in hand, and besides, he was growing a little impatient at his wife's incessant plea that he sell his share of the "Seagull" and settle on land. Now he turned from her, and shouted:

"All right, mens!"

He bestowed a short, powerful embrace upon his wife, with his eyes looking over her shoulder into the Atlantic's veiled face, turned from her with a quick, nervous movement, and dropped from the wharf into his boat.

Standing in the bow, he moistened his finger in his mouth, and held it up to the wind.

"You mens bes' git all de fish yuh kin tuhday," he admonished. "Win' be in de eas' by tuhmorruh. It gots dat wet tas' ter um now."

One by one the boats shoved off, and lay in the stream while they adjusted their spritsails and rigged their full jibs abeam, like spin-nakers, for the free run to sea. The vessels were similar in design, the larger ones attaining a length of thirty-five feet. They were very nar-row, and low in the waist, with high, keen bows, and pointed sterns. The hulls were round-bottomed, and had beautiful running lines, the fishermen, who were also the designers and builders, taking great pride in the speed and style of their respective craft. The boats were all open from stem to stern and were equipped with thole-pins for row-ing, an expedient to which the men resorted only in dire emergency.

Custom had reduced adventure to commonplace; yet it was incon-ceivable that men could put out, in the face of unsettled weather, for a point beyond sight of land, and exhibit no uneasiness or fear. Yet bursts of loud, loose laughter, and snatches of song, blew back to the wharf long after the boats were in mid-stream.

The wind continued to come in sudden flaws, and, once the little craft had gotten clear of the wharves, the fleet made swift but erratic progress. There were moments when they would seem to mark time upon the choppy waters of the bay; then suddenly a flaw would bear down on them, whipping the water as it came, and, filling the sails, would fairly lift the slender bows as it drove them forward.

By the time that the leisurely old city was sitting down to its break-fast, the fleet had disappeared into the horizon, and the sun had climbed over its obstructions to flood the harbor with reassuring light.

The mercurial spirits of the negroes rose with the genial warmth. Forebodings were forgotten. Even Clara sang a lighter air as she rocked the baby upon her lap. But the sun had just lifted over the eastern wall, and the heat of noon was beginning to vibrate in the court, when suddenly the air of security was shattered. From the center of town sounded the deep, ominous clang of a bell.

At its first stroke life in Catfish Row was paralyzed. Women stopped their tasks, and, not realizing that they did, clasped each others' hands tightly, and stood motionless, with strained, listening faces.

Twenty times the great hammer fell, sending the deep, full notes out across the city that was holding its breath and counting them as they came.

"Twenty!" said Clara, when it had ceased to shake the air.

She ran to the entrance and looked to the north. Almost at the end of vision, between two buildings, could be seen the flagstaff that surmounted the custom-house. It was bare when she looked—just a thin, bare line against the intense blue, but even as she stood there, a flicker of color soared up its length; then fixed and flattened, showing a red square with a black center.

"My Gawd!" she called over her shoulder. "It's de trut'. Dat's de hurricane signal on top de custom-house."

Bess came from her room, and stood close to the terrified woman.

"Dat can't be so," she said comfortingly. "Ain't yuh 'member de las' hurricane, how it tek two day tuh blow up. Now de sun out bright, an' de cloud all gone."

But Clara gave no sign of having heard her.

"Come on in!" urged Bess. "Ef yuh don't start tuh git yuh dinner, yuh won't hab nuttin' ready fuh de mens w'en dey gits in."

After a moment the idea penetrated, and the half-dazed woman turned toward Bess, her eyes pleading.

"You come wid me, an' talk a lot. I ain't likes tuh be all alone now."

"Sho' I will," replied the other comfortingly, "I min' de baby fuh yuh, an' yuh kin be gittin' de dinner."

Clara's face quivered; but she turned from the sight of the far red flag and opened her door for Bess to pass in.

After the two women had remained together for half an hour, Bess left the room for a moment to fetch some sewing. The sun was gone, and the sky presented a smooth, leaden surface. She closed the door quickly so that Clara might not see the abrupt change, and went out of the entrance for a look to sea.

Like the sky, the bay had undergone a complete metamorphosis. The water was black, and strangely lifeless. Thin, intensely white crests rode the low, pointed waves; and between the opposing planes of sky and sea a thin westerly wind roamed about like a trapped thing and whined in a complaining treble key. A singularly clear half-light pervaded the world, and in it she could see the harbor mouth distinctly, as it lay ten miles away between the north and south jetties that stretched on the horizon like arms with the finger-tips nearly touching.

Her eyes sought the narrow opening. Guiltless of the smallest speck, it let upon utter void.

"It'd take 'em t'ree hour tuh mek harbor from de banks wid good win'," said a woman who was also watching. "But dere ain't no powuh in dis breeze, an' it a head one at dat."

"Dey kin row it in dat time," encouraged Bess. "An' de storm ain't hyuh yit."

But the woman hugged her forebodings, and stood there shivering in the close, warm air.

§

Except for the faint moan of the wind, the town and harbor lay in a silence that was like held breath.

Many negroes came to the wharf, passed out to the pier-head, and sat quietly watching the entrance to the bay.

At one o'clock the tension snapped. As though it had been awaiting St. Christopher's chimes to announce "Zero Hour," the wind swung into the east, and its voice dropped an octave, and changed its quality. Instead of the complaining whine, a grave, sustained note came in from the Atlantic, with an undertone of alarming variations, that sounded oddly out of place as it traversed the inert waters of the bay.

The tide was at the last of the ebb, and racing out of the many rivers and creeks toward the sea. All morning the west wind had driven it smoothly before it. But now, the stiffening eastern gale threw its weight against the water, and the conflict immediately filled the bay with large waves that leapt up to angry points, then dropped back sullenly upon themselves.

"Choppy water," observed a very old negro who squinted through half-closed eyes. "Dem boat nebbuh mek headway in dat sea."

But he was not encouraged to continue by the silent, anxious group.

Slowly the threatening undertone of the wind grew louder. Then, as though a curtain had been lowered across the harbor mouth, everything beyond was blotted by a milky screen.

"Oh, my Jedus!" a voice shrilled. "Here he come, now! Le's we go!"

Many of the watchers broke for the cover of buildings across the street. Some of those whose men were in the fleet crowded into the small wharf-house. Several voices started to pray at once, and were immediately drowned in the rising clamor of the wind.

With the mathematical precision that it had exhibited in starting, the gale now moved its obliterating curtain through the jetties, and thrust it forward in a straight line across the outer bay.

There was something utterly terrifying about the studied manner in which the hurricane proceeded about its business. It clicked off its moves like an automaton. It was Destiny working nakedly for the eyes of men to see. The watchers knew that for at least twenty-four hours it would stay, moving its tides and winds here and there with that invincible precision, crushing the life from those whom its preconceived plan had seemed to mark for death.

With that instant emotional release that is the great solace of the negro, the tightly packed wharf-house burst into a babblement of weeping and prayer.

The curtain advanced to the inner bay and narrowed the world to the city, with its buildings cowering white and fearful, and the remaining semi-circle of the harbor.

And now from the opaque surface of the screen came a persistent roar that was neither of wind or water, but the articulate cry of the storm itself. The curtain shot forward again and became a wall, grey and impenetrable, that sunk its foundations into the tortured sea and bore the leaden sky upon its soaring top.

The noise became deafening. The narrow strip of water that was left before the wharves seemed to shrink away. The buildings huddled closer and waited.

Then it crossed the strip, and smote the city.

From the roofs came the sound as though ton after ton of ore had been dumped from some great eminence. There was a dead weight to the shocks that could not conceivably be delivered by so unsubstantial a substance as air, yet which was the wind itself, lifting abruptly to enormous heights, then hurling its full force downward.

These shocks followed the demoniac plan, occurring at exact intervals, and were succeeded by prying fingers, as fluid as ether, as hard as steel, that felt for cracks in roofs and windows.

One could no longer say with certainty, "This which I breathe is air, and this upon which I stand is earth." The storm had possessed itself of the city and made it its own. Tangibles and intangibles alike were whirled in a mad, inextricable nebula.

The waves that moved upon the bay could be dimly discerned for a little distance. They were turgid, yellow, and naked; for the moment they lifted a crest, the wind snatched it and dispersed it, with the rain, into the warm semi-fluid atmosphere with which it delivered its attack upon the panic-stricken city.

Notch by notch the velocity increased. The concussions upon the roofs became louder, and the prying fingers commenced to gain a purchase, worrying small holes into large ones. Here and there the wind would get beneath the tin, roll it up suddenly, whirl it from a

building like a sheet of paper, and send it thundering and crashing down a deserted street.

Again it would gain entrance to a room through a broken window, and, exerting its explosive force to the full, would blow all of the other windows outward, and commence work upon the walls from within.

It was impossible to walk upon the street. At the first shock of the storm, the little group of negroes who had sought shelter in the wharf-house fled to the Row. Even then, the force of the attack had been so great that only by bending double and clinging together were they able to resist the onslaughts and traverse the narrow street.

Porgy and Bess sat in their room. The slats had been taken from the bed and nailed across the window, and the mattress, bundled into a corner, had been pre-emptied by the goat. Bess sat wrapped in her own thoughts, apparently unmoved by the demoniac din without. Porgy's look was one of wonder, not unmixed with fear, as he peered into the outer world between two of the slats. The goat, blessed with an utter lack of imagination, revelled in the comfort and intimacy of his new environment, expressing his contentment in suffocating waves, after the manner of his kind. A kerosene lamp without a chimney, smoking straight up into the unnatural stillness of the room, cast a faint, yellow light about it, but only accentuated the heavy gloom of the corners.

From where Porgy sat, he could catch glimpses of what lay beyond the window. There would come occasional moments when the floor of the storm would be lifted by a burrowing wind, and he would see the high, naked breakers racing under the sullen pall of spume and rain.

Once he saw a derelict go by. The vessel was a small river sloop, with its rigging blown clear out. A man was clinging to the tiller. One wave, larger than its fellows, submerged the little boat, and when it wallowed to the surface again, the man was gone, and the tiller was kicking wildly.

"Oh, my Jedus, hab a little pity!" the watcher moaned under his breath.

Later, a roof went by.

Porgy heard it coming, even above the sound of the attack upon the Row, and it filled him with awe and dread. He turned and looked at Bess, and was reassured to see that she met his gaze fearlessly. Down the street the roar advanced, growing nearer and louder momentarily. Surely it would be the final instrument of destruction. He held his breath, and waited. Then it thundered past his narrow sphere of vision. Rolled loosely, it loomed to the second story windows, and flapped and tore at the buildings as it swept over the cobbles.

When a voice could be heard again, Porgy turned to his companion.

"You an' me, Bess," he said with conviction. "We *sho'* is a little somet'ing attuh all."

After that, they sat long without exchanging a word. Then Porgy looked out of the window and noticed that the quality of the atmosphere was becoming denser. The spume lifted for a moment, and he could scarcely see the tormented bay.

"I t'ink it mus' be mos' night," he observed. "Dey ain't much light now on de outside ob dis storm."

He looked again before the curtain descended, and what he saw caused his heart to miss a beat.

He knew that the tide should be again at the ebb, for the flood had commenced just after the storm broke. But as he looked, the water, which was already higher than a normal flood, lifted over the far edge of the street, and three tremendous waves broke in rapid succession, sending the deep layers of water across the narrow way to splash against the wall of the building.

This reversal of nature's law struck terror into the dark places of Porgy's soul. He beckoned to Bess, his fascinated eyes upon the advancing waves.

She bent down and peered into the gloom. "Oh, yes," she remarked in a flat tone. "It been dis way in de las' great storm. De win' hol' de watuh in de jetty mout' so he can't go out. Den he pile up annoder tide on him."

Suddenly an enormous breaker loomed over the backs of its shattered and retreating fellows. The two watchers could not see its crest, for it towered into, and was absorbed by, the low-hanging atmosphere. Yellow, smooth, and with a perpendicular, slightly concave front, it flashed across the street, and smote the solid wall of the Row. They heard it roar like a mill-race through the drive, and flatten, hissing in the court. Then they turned, and saw their own door give slightly to the pressure, and a dark flood spurt beneath it, and debouch upon the floor.

Bess took immediate command of the situation. She threw an arm about Porgy, and hurried him to the door. She withdrew the bolt, and the flimsy panels shot inward. The court was almost totally dark. One after another now the waves were hurtling through the drive and impounding in the walled square.

The night was full of moving figures, and cries of fear; while, out of the upper dark, the wind struck savagely downward.

With a powerful swing, Bess got Porgy to a stairway that providentially opened near their room, and, leaving him to make his way up alone, she rushed back, and was soon at his heels with an armful of belongings.

They sought refuge in what had been the great ball-room of the mansion, a square, high-ceilinged room on the second story, which was occupied by a large and prosperous family. There were many refugees there before them. In the faint light cast by several lanterns, the indestructible beauty of the apartment was evident, while the defacing effects of a century were absorbed in shadow. The noble open fireplace, the tall, slender mantel, with its Grecian frieze and intricate scrollwork, the high panelled walls were all there. And then, huddled in little groups on the floor, or seated against the walls, with eyes wide in the lantern-shine, the black, fear-stricken faces.

Like the ultimate disintegration of a civilization—there it was; and upon it, as though to make quick work of the last, tragic chapter, the scourging wrath of the Gods—white, and black.

§

The night that settled down upon Catfish Row was one of nameless horror to the inhabitants, most of whom were huddled on the second floor in order to avoid the sea from beneath, and deafening assaults upon the roof above their heads.

With the obliteration of vision, sound assumed an exaggerated significance, and the voice of the gale, which had seemed by day only a great roar, broke up in the dark into its various parts. Human voices seemed to cry in it; and there were moments when it sniffed and moaned at the windows.

Once, during a silence in the room, a whinny was distinctly heard.

"Dat my ole horse!" wailed Peter. "He done dead in he stall now, an' dat he woice goin' by. Oh, my Gawd!"

They all wailed out at that; and Porgy, remembering his goat, whimpered and turned his face to the wall.

Then someone started to sing:

> *"I gots uh home in de rock, don't yuh see?"*

With a feeling of infinite relief, Porgy turned to his Jesus. It was not a charm that he sought now for the assuaging of some physical ill, but a benign power, vaster perhaps even than the hurricane. He lifted his rich baritone above the others:

> *"Oh, between de eart' an' sky,*
> *I kin see my Sabior die.*
> *I gots uh home in de rock,*
> *Don't yuh see!"*

Then they were all in it, heart and soul. Those who had fallen into a fitful sleep, awoke, rubbed their eyes, and sang.

Hour after hour dragged heavily past. Outside, the storm worked its will upon the defenceless city. But in the great ball-room of Catfish Row, forty souls sat wrapped in an invulnerable garment. They swayed and patted, and poured their griefs and fears into a rhythm that never missed a beat, which swept the hours behind it into oblivion, and that finally sang up the faint grey light that penetrated the storm, and told them that it was again day.

§

At about an hour after daybreak the first lull came. Like the other moves of the hurricane, it arrived without warning. One moment the tumult was at its height. The next, there was utter suspension. Abruptly, like an indrawn breath, the wind sucked back upon itself, leaving an aching vacuum in its place. Then from the inundated water-front arose the sound of the receding flood.

The ebb-tide was again overdue, and with the second tide piled upon it, the whole immeasurable weight of the wind was required to maintain its height. Now, with the pressure removed, it turned and raced beneath the low-lying mist toward the sea, carrying its pitiful loot upon its back.

To the huddled figures in the great room of the Row came the welcome sound, as the court emptied itself into the street. The negroes crowded to the windows, and peered between the barricades at the world without.

The water receded with incredible speed. Submerged wreckage lifted above the surface. The street became the bed of a cataract that foamed and boiled on its rush to the sea. Presently the wharf emerged, and at its end even a substantial remnant of the house could be descried. How it had survived that long was one of the inexplicable mysteries of the storm.

Suddenly Peter, who was at one of the windows, gave a cry, and the other negroes crowded about him to peer out.

The sea was still running high, and as a large wave lifted above the level of the others, it thrust into view the hull of a half submerged boat. Before the watchers could see, the wave dropped its burden into a trough, but the old man showed them where to look, and presently a big roller caught it up, and swung it, bow on, for all to see. There was a flash of scarlet gunnel, and, beneath it, a bright blue bird with open wings.

"De 'Seagull'!" cried a dozen voices together. "My Gawd! dat Jake' boat!"

All night Clara had sat in a corner of the room with the baby in her arms, saying no word to anyone. She was so still that she seemed to be asleep, with her head upon her breast. But once, when Bess had gone and looked into her face, she had seen her eyes, wide and bright with pain.

Now the unfortunate woman heard the voices, and sprang to the window just in time to see the craft swoop into a hollow at the head of the pier.

She did not scream out. For a moment she did not even speak. Then she spun around on Bess with the dawn of a wild hope in her dark face.

"Tek care ob dis baby 'til I gits back," she said, as she thrust the child almost savagely into Bess's arms. Then she rushed from the room.

The watchers at the window saw her cross the street, splashing wildly through the knee-deep water. Then she ran the length of the wharf, and disappeared behind the sheltering wall of the house.

It was so sudden, and tired wits move slowly. Several minutes had passed before it occurred to anyone to go with her. Finally Peter turned from the window.

"Dat 'oman ain't ought tuh be out dey by sheself," he said. "Who goin' out dey wid me, now?"

One of the men volunteered, and they started for the door.

A sound like the detonation of a cannon shook the building to its foundations. The gale had returned, smashing straight downward from some incredible height to which it had lifted during the lull.

The men turned and looked at one another.

Shock followed shock in rapid succession. Those who stood by the windows felt them give inward, and instinctively threw their weight against the frames. The explosions merged into a steady roar of sound that surpassed anything that had yet occurred. The room became so dark that they could no longer see one another. The barricaded windows were vaguely discernible in bars of muddy grey and black. Deeply rooted walls swung from the blows, and then settled slowly back on the recoil.

A confused sound of praying filled the room. And above it shrilled the terror of the women.

For an appreciable space of time the spasm lasted. Then, slowly, as though by the gradual withdrawing of a lever, the vehemence of the attack abated. The muddy grey bars at the windows became lighter, and some of the more courageous of the negroes peered out.

The wharf could be seen dimly extending under the low floor of

spume and mist. The breakers were higher than at any previous time, but instead of smashing in upon the shore, they raced straight up the river and paralleled the city. As each one swung by it went clean over the wharf, obliterating it for the duration of its passage.

Suddenly from the direction of the lower harbor a tremendous mass appeared, showing first only a vast distorted stain against the grey fabric of the mist. Then a gigantic wave took it, and drove it into fuller view.

"Great Gawd A'mighty!" some one whispered. "It's dat big lumbuh schooner bruck loose in de harbor."

The wave hunched its mighty shoulders under the vessel and swung it up—up, for an interminable moment. The soaring bowsprit lifted until it was lost in mist. Tons of water gushed from the steep incline of the deck, and poured over the smooth, black wall of the side, as it reared half out of the sea. Then the wave swept aft, and the bow descended in a swift, deadly plunge.

A crashing of timbers followed that could be heard clearly above the roaring of the storm. The hull had fallen directly across the middle of the wharf. There was one cataclysmic moment when the whole view seemed to disintegrate. The huge timbers of the wharf up-ended, and were washed out like straws. The schooner rolled half over, and her three masts crashed down with their rigging. The shock burst the lashings of the vessel's deck. load, and as the hull heeled, an avalanche of heavy timbers took the water. The ruin was utter.

Heavy and obliterating, the mist closed down again.

Bess turned from the window holding the sleeping infant in her arms, raised her eyes and looked full at Porgy.

With an expression of awe in his face, the cripple reached out a timid hand and touched the baby's cheek.

§

The windows of the great ball-room were open to the sky, and beyond them, a busy breeze was blowing across its washed and polished expanse, gathering cloud-remnants into little heaps, and sweeping them in tumbling haste out over the threshold of the sea.

Most of the refugees had returned to their rooms, where sounds of busy salvaging could be heard. Porgy's voice arose jubilantly announcing that the goat had been discovered, marooned upon the cook-stove; and that Peter's old horse had belied his whinny, and was none the worse for a thorough wetting.

Serena Robbins paused before Bess, who was gathering her things

preparatory to leaving the room, placed her hands upon her hips, and looked down upon her.

"Now, wut we all goin' do wid dis po' mudderless chile?" she said, addressing the room at large.

The other occupants of the room gathered behind Serena, but there was something about Bess's look that held them quiet. They stood there waiting and saying nothing.

Slowly Bess straightened up, her face lowered and pressed against that of the sleeping child. Then she raised her eyes and met the gaze of the complacent older woman.

What Serena saw there was not so much the old defiance that she had expected, as it was an inflexible determination, and, behind it, a new-born element in the woman that rendered the scarred visage incandescent. She stepped back, and lowered her eyes.

Bess strained the child to her breast with an elemental intensity of possession, and spoke in a low, deep voice that vested her words with sombre meaning.

"Is Clara come back a'ready, since she dead, an' say somet'ing 'bout 'we' tuh yuh 'bout dis chile?"

She put the question to the group, her eyes taking in the circle of faces as she spoke.

There was no response; and at the suggestion of a possible return of the dead, the circle drew together instinctively.

"Berry well den," said Bess solemnly. "Ontell she do, I goin' stan' on she las' libbin' word an' keep dis chile fuh she 'til she do come back."

Serena was hopelessly beaten, and she knew it.

"Oh, berry well," she capitulated. "All I been goin' tuh do wuz jus' tuh puhwide um wid er propuh Christian raisin'. But ef she done gib um tuh yuh, dere ain't nuttin mo' I kin do, I guess."

Part VI

October blew down from the north, bracing, and frosty-clear. It sent a breeze racing like mad over the bay and bouncing into the court to toss the clothes-lines like lanyards of signal flags. The torpid city and wide, slumbrous marshes were stung to sudden life and laughed up at the far, crisp blue of the sky.

Out in the harbor mouth, a faint wisp of smoke grew and blackened, and presently beneath it the rusty hull of a tramp lifted from

the Atlantic, and thrust its blunt nose into the waters of the bay.

Summer had gone. Soon the cotton would be coming through.

It was nine o'clock, and still Porgy lingered in the court. His blood leapt swiftly in his veins, and he experienced that sweet upsurge of life that the North knows with the bursting of spring, but that comes most keenly to the sultry lands with the strong breath of autumn. Yet, when he looked up at the sky, a vague prescience of disaster darkened his spirit. He sat beside Bess in the doorway, with his eyes upon the child in her lap. After a while he took the baby into his arms, and then the foreboding suddenly became pain.

He looked up and met the gaze of the woman. It was there in her eyes also, plain for him to see.

Out in the silence of the street a sound commenced to grow. Only a faint, far murmur at first, it gathered weight until it became a steady rumble, with a staccato clip, clip, clip running through it.

There were a few women and children about, and they ran to the entrance to see. But Porgy and Bess sat and looked fixedly at the bay, where it lay beyond the gate.

Then the drays came, and the bay was blotted out by the procession.

The great mules, fat and strong from their summer in pasture, moved swiftly with a sharp click of shoes, and the drivers cracked their whips and laughed down at the crowd. The low platforms of the vehicles seemed almost to brush the ground; and, upon them, clear to the top of the entrance arch, the bales towered, with the fibre showing in dazzling white patches where the bagging was torn. Twenty or more in the train they passed.

Scarcely had the rumble receded in the distance, than a burst of heavy laughter sounded in the street, and two tall figures strode through the entrance and into the group of women and children. There was a bright flash from bandanas, and one of the men swung a child to his shoulder. Loud greetings followed, and another burst of laughter, heavy, deep-chested and glad.

From an upper window a woman's voice called, "Come on, Sister; le's we go down. De stevedore is comin' back."

Porgy turned toward Bess, and moistened his lips with his tongue. Then he spoke in a low husky voice:

"Us ain't talk much sence de picnic, Bess, you an' me. But I gots tuh talk now. I gots tuh know how you an' me stan'."

Bess regarded him dumbly. For a moment the look which Serena had seen when she had tried to take the baby brushed her face, then it passed, leaving it hopeless.

Porgy leaned forward. "Yuh is wantin' tuh go wid Crown w'en he come?"

Then she answered: "W'en I tek dat dope, I know den dat I ain't yo' kin'. An' w'en Crown put he han' on me dat day, I run tuh he like water. Some day dope comin' agin. An' some day Crown goin' put he han' on my t'roat. It goin' be like dyin' den. But I gots tuh talk de trut' tuh yuh. W'en dem time come, I goin' tuh go."

"Ef dey warn't no Crown?" Porgy whispered. Then before she could answer, he hurried on: "Ef dey wuz only jes' de baby an' Porgy, wut den?"

The odd incandescence flared in her face, touching it with something eternal and beautiful beyond the power of human flesh to convey. She took the child from Porgy with a hungry, enfolding gesture. Then her composure broke.

"Oh, fuh Gawd sake, Porgy, don't let dat man come an' handle me! Ef yuh is willin' tuh keep me, den lemme stay. Ef he jus' don't put dem hot han' on me, I kin be good, I kin 'member, I kin be happy."

She broke off abruptly, and hid her face against that of the child.

Porgy patted her arm. "Yuh ain't needs tuh be 'fraid," he assured her. "Ain't yuh gots yo' man? Ain't you gots Porgy? Wut kin' of a nigger yuh t'inks yuh gots anyway, fuh let annuduh nigger carry he 'oman? No, suh! yuh gots yo' man now; yuh gots Porgy."

§

From behind a sea island the full October moon lifted its chill disc and strewed the bay with cold, white fire. The lights were out in Catfish Row, except for a shaft of firelight that fell across the dark from Serena's room, and a faint flicker in the cook-shop where Maria was getting her fire laid in readiness for the early breakfast.

A cry sounded in the court, which was quickly muffled; then followed low, insolent laughter.

Maria was at her door instantly. Across the court, a man could be seen for one moment, seated on Serena's wash-bench; then behind him the door closed with a bang, shutting off the shaft of firelight.

Maria crossed the court, and when she had reached the man's side he looked up. The moonlight fell upon his face. It was Crown.

"What yuh doin' hyuh?" she asked him.

"Jus' droppin' in on a few ole frien'."

"Come tuh de shop," she commanded. "I gots tuh hab talk wid yuh."

He arose obediently, and followed her.

Maria turned up the lamp and faced about as Crown entered the

room. He had to bend his head to pass under the lintel, and his shoulders brushed the sides of the opening.

The big negress stood for a long moment looking at him. Her gaze took in the straight legs with their springing thighs straining the fabric of the cotton pants, the slender waist, and the almost unbelievable outward flare of the chest to the high, straight span of the shoulders.

A look of deep sadness grew in her somber face.

"Wid uh body like dat!" she said at last, "why yuh is goin' aroun' huntin' fuh deat'?"

Crown laughed uneasily, stepped into the room, and sat at a table. He placed his elbows upon it, hunched his shoulders forward with a writhing of muscle beneath the shirt, then dropped his chin in his hands, and regarded the woman.

"I know dese hyuh niggers," he replied. "Dey is a decent lot. Dey wouldn't gib no nigger away tuh de w'ite folks."

"Dat de Gawd' trut'. Only dey is odder way ob settlin' up er debt."

"Serena?" he asked, with a sidelong look, and a laugh. "Dat sister gots de fear ob Gawd in she heart. I ain't 'fraid none ob she."

After a moment of silence he asked abruptly:

"Bess still libbin' wid de cripple?"

"Yes; an' she a happy, decent 'oman. Yuh bes' leabe she alone."

"Fer Gawd' sake! Wut yuh t'ink I come tuh dis damn town fuh? I ain't jus' huntin' fuh deat'! I atter my 'oman."

Maria placed her hands on the table opposite the man and bent over to look into his face.

"'Oman is all berry much de same," she said in a low, persuasive voice. "Dey comes an' dey goes. One sattify a man quick as annuduh. Dey is lots ob bettuh lookin' gal dan Bess. She fix fuh life now wid dat boy. I ax yuh go an' lef she. Gib she uh chance."

"It tek long time tuh learn one 'oman," he said slowly. "Me an' Bess done fight dat all out dese fibe year gone."

"Yuh ain't goin' leabe she den?" There was an unusual note of pleading in the heavy voice.

"Not till Hell freeze."

After a moment he arose and turned to her.

"I gots tuh go out now. I ain't sho' wedder I goin' away tuhnight or wait fuh tuhmorruh night. I goin' look aroun' an' see how de lan' lay; but I'll be seein' yuh agin befo' I goes."

Maria regarded him for a long moment; the look of sadness in her face deepened to a heavy melancholy; but she said nothing.

Crown started for the street with his long, swaggering stride. The big woman watched him until he turned to the north at the entrance

and passed from view. Then she locked the door and, with a deep sigh, walked to her own room.

§

Porgy opened his eyes suddenly. The window, which had been luminous when he went to sleep, was now darkened. He watched it intently. Slowly he realized that parts of the little square still showed the moonlit waters of the bay, and that only the centre was blocked out by an intervening mass. Then the mass moved, and Porgy saw that it was the torso and shoulders of a man. The window was three feet in width, yet the shoulders seemed to brush both sides of it as the form bent forward. The sash was down, and presently there came a sound as though hands were testing it to see whether it could be forced up.

Porgy was lying on his back. He reached his left hand over the covers and let the fingers touch ever so lightly the sleeping faces of first the baby, then the woman. His right hand slid beneath his pillow, and his strong, slender fingers closed about the handle of a knife.

At the window the slight, testing noise continued.

§

It was certainly after midnight when Maria looked from her doorway; for the moon was tottering on the western wall, and while she stood looking, slowly it dropped over and vanished.

The vague forebodings that she had felt when she talked to Crown earlier in the evening had kept sleep from her; with each passing hour her fears increased, and with them a sense of imminence that finally forced her to get up, slip on a wrapper, and prepare to make the rounds of the court.

But on opening her door, she was at once reassured. The square stood before her like a vast cistern brimmed with misty dark and roofed with a lid of sky. A cur grovelled forward on its belly from a near-by nook, and licked one of her bare feet with its moist, warm tongue.

Above her, in the huge honeycomb of the building, someone was snoring in a slow, steady rhythm.

The big negress drew a deep sigh of relief and turned back toward her room.

A sound of cracking wood snapped the silence. Then, like a flurry of small bells, came a shiver of broken glass on the stones.

Maria spun around, and tried to locate the sound; but no noise followed. Silence flowed back over the court and settled palpably into its recesses. The faint, not unpleasant rhythm of the snoring came insistently forward.

Suddenly Maria turned, her face quick with apprehension. She drew her wrapper closely about her, and crossed to Porgy's door. With only half of the distance traversed, she heard a sound from the room. It was more of a muffled thump than anything else, and with it, something very like a. gasp.

When her hand closed over the knob all was silent again, except that she could hear a long, slightly shuddering breath.

Then came a sound that caused her flesh to prickle with primal terror. It was so unexpected, there in the chill, silent night. It was Porgy's laugh, but different. Out of the stillness it swelled suddenly, deep, aboriginal, lustful. Then it stopped short.

Maria heard the baby cry out; then Bess's voice, sleepy and mystified. "Fuh Gawd' sake, Porgy, what yuh laughin' 'bout?"

"Dat all right, honey," came the answer. "Don't yuh be worryin'. Yuh gots Porgy now, an' he look atter he 'oman. Ain't I done tells yuh: Yuh gots er *man* now."

Maria turned the knob, entered the room, and closed the door quickly behind her.

Night trailed westward across the city. In the east, out beyond the ocean's rim, essential light trembled upward and seemed to absorb rather than quench the morning stars. Out of the sliding planes of mist that hung like spent breath above the city, shapes began to emerge and assume their proper values.

Far in the upper air over Catfish Row a speck appeared. It took a long, descending spiral, and became two, then three. Around a wide circle the specks swung, as though hung by wires from a lofty pivot. The light brightened perceptibly. The specks dropped to a lower level, increased in size, and miraculously became a dozen. Then some of them dropped in from the circumference of the circle, cutting lines across like the spokes of a wheel, and from time to time flapping indolent wings. Dark and menacing when they flew to the westward, they would turn easily toward the east, and the sun, still below the horizon, would gild their bodies with ruddy gold, as they sailed, breast on, toward it.

Down, down they dropped, reaching low, and yet lower levels, until at last they seemed to brush the water-front buildings with their sombre wings. Then gradually they narrowed to a small circle that

patrolled the air directly over a shape that lay awash in the rising tide, across the street from Catfish Row.

Suddenly from the swinging circle a single bird planed down and lit with an awkward, hopping step directly before the object. For a moment he regarded it with bleak, predatory eyes; then flew back to his fellows. A moment later the whole flock swooped down, and the shape was hidden by flapping wings and black awkward bodies that hopped about and fought inward to the centre of the group.

A negro who had been sleeping under an overturned bateau awoke and rubbed his eyes; then he sprang up and, seizing an oar, beat the birds away with savage blows.

He bent over the object for a moment, then turned and raced for the street with eyes showing white.

"Fuh Gawd' sake, folks," he cried, "come hyuh quick! Hyuh Crown, an' he done dead."

§

A group of three white men stood over the body. One was the plain-clothes man with the goatee and stick who had investigated the Robbins' murder. Behind him stood a uniformed policeman. The third, a stout, leisurely individual, was stooping over the body, in the act of making an examination.

"What do you make of it, Coroner?" asked the plain-clothes man.

"Knife between fifth and sixth ribs; must have gone straight through the heart."

"Well, he had it comin' to him," the detective observed. "They tell me he is the nigger, Crown, who killed Robbins last April. That gives us the widow to work on fer a starter, by the way; and Hennessy tells me that he used to run with that dope case we had up last August. She's livin' in the Row, too. Let's go over and have a look."

The Coroner cast an apprehensive glance at the forbidding structure across the way.

"Can't be so sure," he cautioned. "Corpse might have been washed up. Tide's on the flood."

"Well, I'm goin' to have a look at those two women, anyway," the plain-clothes man announced. "That place is alive with crooks. I'd like to get something on it that would justify closing it up as a public nuisance, and throwing the whole lot of 'em out in the street. One murder and a happy-dust riot already this summer; and here we are again."

Then turning to the policeman, he gave his orders.

"Get the wagon and take the body in. Then you had better come right back. We might have some arrests. The Coroner and I'll investigate while you're gone."

He turned away toward the Row, assuming that he would be followed.

"All right, Cap; what do you say?" he called.

The Coroner shook his ponderous figure down into his clothes, turned with evident reluctance, and joined him.

"All right," he agreed. "But all I need is a couple of witnesses to identify the body at the inquest."

Across the street a small negro boy detached himself from the base of one of the gateposts and darted through the entrance.

A moment later the white men strode into an absolutely empty square. Their heels made a sharp sound on the flags, and the walls threw a clear echo down upon them. A cur that had been left napping in the sun woke with a start, looked about in a bewildered fashion, gave a frightened yelp, and bolted through a doorway.

It was all clearly not to the taste of the Coroner, and he cast an uneasy glance about him.

"Where do we go?" he asked.

"That's the widow's room over there, if she hasn't moved. We'll give it a look first," said the detective.

The door was off the latch, and, without knocking, he kicked it open and walked in.

The room was small, but immaculately clean. Beneath a patched white quilt could be seen the form of a woman. Two other women were sitting in utter silence beside the bed.

The form under the covers moaned.

"Drop that," the detective commanded. "And answer some questions."

The moaning stopped.

"Where were you yesterday and last night?"

The reply came slowly, as though speaking were great pain.

"I been sick in dis bed now t'ree day an' night."

"We been settin' wid she, nursin' she, all dat time," one of the women said.

And the other supplemented. "Dat de Gawd' trut'."

"You would swear to that?" asked the Coroner.

Three voices answered in chorus:

"Yes, Boss, we swear tuh dat."

"There you are," said the Coroner to the plain-clothes man, "an air-tight alibi."

The detective regarded him for a moment with supreme contempt. Then he stepped forward and jerked the sheet from Serena's face, which lay upon the pillow as immobile as a model done in brown clay.

"You know damn well that you were out yesterday!" he snapped. "I have a good mind to get the wagon and carry you in."

Silence followed.

"What do you say to that?" he demanded.

But Serena had nothing to say, and neither had her handmaidens.

Then he turned a menacing frown upon them, as they sat motionless with lowered eyes.

"Well!"

They jumped slightly, and their eyes showed white around the iris. Suddenly they began to speak, almost in unison.

"We swear tuh Gawd, we done been hyuh wid she t'ree day."

"Oh, Hell!" said the exasperated detective. "What's the use? You might as well argue with a parrot-cage."

"That woman is just as ill at this moment as you are," he said to his unenthusiastic associate when they were again in the sunlight. "Her little burlesque show proves that, if nothing else. But there is her case all prepared. I don't believe she killed Crown; she doesn't look like that kind. She is either just playing safe, or she has something entirely different on her chest. But there's her story; and you'll never break in without witnesses of your own; and you'll never get 'em."

The Coroner was not a highly sensitized individual; but as he moved across the empty court, he found it difficult to control his nerves under the scrutiny which he felt leveled upon him from behind a hundred shuttered windows. Twice he caught himself looking covertly over his shoulders; and, as he went, he bore hopefully away toward the entrance.

But the detective was intent upon his task, and presently called him back.

"This is the cripple's room," he said. "He ain't much of a witness. I tried to break him in the Robbins case; but he wouldn't talk. I want to have a look at the woman, though."

He kicked the door open suddenly. Porgy and Bess were seated by the stove, eating breakfast from tin pans. On the bed in the corner the baby lay.

Porgy paused, with his spoon halfway to his mouth, and looked up. Bess kept her eyes on the pan, and continued to eat.

The Coroner stopped in the doorway, and made a businesslike show of writing in a notebook.

"What's your name?" he asked Porgy.

The cripple studied him for a long moment, taking in the ample

proportions of the figure and the heavy, but not unsympathetic, face. Then he smiled one of his fleeting, ingenuous smiles.

"Jus' Porgy," he said. "Yuh knows me, Boss. Yuh is done gib me plenty ob penny on King Charles Street."

"Of course, you're the goat-man. I didn't know you without your wagon," he said amiably. Then, becoming businesslike, he asked:

"This nigger, Crown. You knew him by sight. Didn't you?"

Porgy debated with himself for a moment, looked again into the Coroner's face, was reassured by what he saw there, and replied:

"Yes, Boss; I 'member um w'en he usen tuh come hyuh, long ago."

"You could identify him, I suppose?"

Porgy looked blank.

"You'd know him if you saw him again?"

"Yes, Boss; I know um."

The Coroner made a note in his book, closed it with an air of finality, and put it in his pocket.

During the brief interview, the detective had been making an examination of the room. The floor had been recently scrubbed, and was still damp in the corners. He gave the clean, pine boards a close scrutiny, then paused before the window. The bottom of the lower sash had been broken, and several of the small, square panes were missing.

"So this is where you killed Crown, eh?" he announced.

The words fell into the silence and were absorbed by it, causing them to seem theatrical and unconvincing. Neither Porgy nor Bess spoke. Their faces were blank and noncommittal.

After a full moment, the woman said:

"I ain't onduhstan', Boss. Nobody hyuh ain't kill Crown. My husban' he fall t'rough dat winduh yisterday when he leg gib 'way. He er cripple."

"Any one see him do it?" enquired the Coroner from the door.

"Oh, yes, Boss," replied Bess, turning to him. "T'ree or four ob de mens was in de street; dey will tell yuh all 'bout um."

"Yes, of course; more witnesses," sneered the detective. Then turning to the Coroner, he asked with a trace of sarcasm in his tone:

"That satisfies you fully, I suppose?"

The Coroner's nerves were becoming edgy.

"For God's sake," he retorted, "do you expect me to believe that a cripple could kill a two-hundred pound buck, then tote him a hundred yards? Well, I've got what I need now anyway. As far as I'm concerned, I'm through."

They were passing the door of Maria's shop when the detective caught sight of something within that held his gaze.

"You can do as you please," he told his unwilling companion. "But

I'm going to have a look in here. I have never been able to get anything on this woman; but she is a bad influence in the neighborhood. I'd trust her just as far as I could throw her."

The Coroner heaved a sigh of resignation, and they stepped back, and entered the shop.

Upon the flooring, directly before the door, and not far from it, was a pool of blood. Standing over the pool was a table, and upon it lay the carcass of a shark. Maria sat on a bench behind the table. As the men entered she swung an immense cleaver downward. A cross-section of the shark detached itself and fell away on a pile of similar slices. A thin stream of blood dribbled from the table, augmenting the pool upon the floor.

Maria did not raise her eyes from her task. Again the cleaver swung up, and whistled downward.

From the street sounded the clatter of the returning patrol.

"I'll wait for you in the wagon," said the Coroner hastily, and stepped back into the sunlight.

But he was not long alone. The uninterrupted swing of the dripping cleaver was depressing, and the enthusiasm of his associate waned.

The bell clanged. Hoofs struck sparks from the cobbles, and the strong but uncertain arm of the law was withdrawn, to attend to other and more congenial business.

§

The sound from the retreating wagon dwindled and ceased.

For a moment Catfish Row held its breath; then its windows and doors flew open, and poured its life out into the incomparable autumn weather. The crisis had passed. There had been no arrests.

Serena stepped forth, her arms filled with the morning's wash.

" 'Ain't it hahd tuh be er nigger!' " someone sang in a loud, clear voice. And everybody laughed.

Down the street, like an approaching freight train, came the drays, jarring the building and rattling the windows, as the heavy tires rang against the cobbles.

Bess and Porgy came out with the others, and seated themselves against the wall in the gracious sunlight. Of the life, yet apart from it, sufficient unto each other, they did not join in the loud talk and badinage that was going on about them. Like people who had come on a long, dark journey, they were content to sit, and breathe deeply of the sun. The baby was sleeping in Bess's arms, and from time to time she would sing a stave to it in a soft, husky voice.

Into the court strode a group of stevedores. Their strong white teeth flashed in the sunshine, and their big, panther-like bodies moved easily among the women and children that crowded about them.

"Wey all de gals?" called one in a loud, resonant voice. "Mus' be dey ain't know dat dis is pay-day."

Two women who were sitting near Porgy and Bess rose and went forward, with their arms twined about each other's waists. In a few minutes they were out of the crowd again, each looking up with admiring eyes into the face of one of the men.

"Mens an' 'omans ain't de same," said Porgy. "One mont' ago dem gals been libbin' wid dey own mens. Den de storm tek um. Now dey is fuhgit um a'ready, an' gibbin' dey lub tuh de nex'."

"No; dey is diff'rent fuh true," replied Bess. "An' yuh won't nebber onduhstan'. All two dem gal gots baby fuh keep alibe." She heaved a deep sigh; and then added, "Dey is jus' 'oman, an' nigger at dat. Dey is doin' de bes' dey kin—dat all."

She was looking down at the baby while she spoke, and when she raised her eyes and looked at Porgy, he saw that they were full of tears.

"But you, Bess; you is diff'rent f'om dat?" he said, with a gently interrogating note in his voice.

"Dat 'cause Gawd ain't mek but one Porgy!" she told him. "Any 'oman gots tuh be decent wid you. But I gots fuh tell yuh de trut', widout Porgy I is jus' like de res'."

A shadow drifted across their laps, and they lifted their faces to the sky.

A solitary buzzard had left the circle that had swung high in the air all morning, and was swinging back and forth over the Row, almost brushing the parapet of the roof as it passed. While Porgy and Bess looked, it suddenly raised the points of its wings, reached tentative legs downward, spread its feet wide, and lit on the edge of the roof directly over their room.

"My Gawd!" exclaimed Maria, who was standing near. "Crown done sen' he buzzud back fuh bring trouble. Knock um off, Porgy. Fer Gawd' sake, knock um off befo' he settle!"

The cripple reached out and picked up a brick-bat. The happiness had left his face, and his eyes were filled with fear. With a swing of his long, powerful arm, he sent the missile on its errand.

It struck a parapet directly beneath the bird.

With a spasmodic flap of wings, the black body lifted itself a few feet from the building, then settled suddenly back. For a moment it hopped awkwardly about, as though the roof were red hot beneath its feet, then folded its wings, drew its nude head in upon its breast, and surveyed the court with its aloof, malevolent eyes.

"T'row agin," Maria called, handing **Porgy** another brick-bat. But he seemed not to hear. His face quivered, and he hid it in his hands.

"Sonny," the big negress called to a small boy who was standing near, looking at the bird with his mouth open. "Git out on de roof wid uh stick, an' run dat bird away."

But Porgy plucked at her skirt, and she looked down.

"Let um be," he said in a hopeless voice. "It too late now. Ain't yuh see he done settle, an' he pick my room fuh light ober? It ain't no use now. Yuh knows dat. It ain't no use."

§

The next morning Porgy sat in his accustomed place by Archdale's door. Autumn had touched the oaks in the park across the way, and they brushed the hard, bright sky with a slow circling motion, and tossed handfuls of yellow leaves down upon the pedestrians who stepped briskly along.

King Charles Street was full of hurrying men on their way to the cotton offices and the big wholesale warehouses that fronted on the wharves. Like the artery of a hale old man who has lain long asleep, but who wakens suddenly and springs into a race, the broad thoroughfare seemed to pound and sing with life.

The town was in a generous mood. Again and again the bottom of Porgy's cup gave forth its sharp, grateful click as a coin struck it and settled. But the cripple had not even his slow glance of thanks for his benefactors on that flashing autumn morning. Always he kept veiled, apprehensive eyes directed either up or down the street, or lifted frightened glances to the sky, as though fearing what he might see there.

At noon a white man stopped before him. But he did not drop a coin and pass on.

After a moment, Porgy brought his gaze back, and looked up.

The white man reached forward, and handed him a paper.

"Dah fuh me?" asked Porgy, in a voice that shook.

"You needn't mind takin' it," the man assured him with a laugh. "It's just a summons as witness to the Coroner's inquest. You knew that nigger, Crown, didn't you?"

He evidently took Porgy's silence for assent, for he went on.

"Well, all you got to do is to view the body in the presence of the Coroner, tell him who it is, and he'll take down all you say."

Porgy essayed speech, failed, tried again, and finally whispered:

"I gots tuh go an' look on Crown' face wid all dem w'ite folks lookin' at me. Dat it?"

His voice was so piteous that the constable reassured him:

"Oh, cheer up; it's not so bad. I reckon you've seen a dead nigger before this. It will all be over in a few minutes."

"Dey ain't goin' be no nigger in dat room 'cept me?" Porgy asked.

"Just you and Crown, if you still call him one."

After a moment, Porgy asked:

"I couldn't jus' bring a 'oman wid me? I couldn't eben carry my—my 'oman?"

"No," said the white man positively. "Now I've got to be gettin' along, I reckon. Just come over to the Court House in half an hour, and I'll meet you and take you in. Only be sure to come. If you don't show up it's jail for you, you know."

For a moment after the man had gone, Porgy sat immovable, with his eyes on the pavement. Then a sudden change swept over him. He cast once glance up and down the hard, clean street, walled by its uncompromising, many-eyed buildings. Then in a panic he clambered into his cart, gave a cruel twist to the tail of his astonished goat, and commenced a spasmodic, shambling race up Meeting House Road in the direction in which he knew that, miles away, the forests lay.

§

To many, the scene which ensued on the upper Meeting House Road stands out as an exquisitely humorous episode, to be told and retold with touching up of high lights and artistic embellishments. To these, in the eyes of whom the negro is wholly humorous, per se, there was not the omission of a single conventional and readily recognizable stage property.

For, after all, what could have been funnier than an entirely serious race between a negro in a dilapidated goat-cart, and the municipality's shining new patrol wagon, fully officered and clanging its bell for the crowds to hear as it came.

The finish took place in the vicinity of the railway yards and factories, and the street was filled with workmen who smoked against the walls, or ate their lunch, sitting at the pavement's edge—grand-stand seats, as they were quite accurately described in the telling.

The street cars ran seldom that far out; and Porgy had the thoroughfare almost entirely to himself. His face wore a demented look, and was working pitifully. In his panic, he wrung the tail of his unfortunate beast without mercy. The lunchers along the pavement saw him com-

ing, and called to friends further along; so that as he came, he was greeted with shouts of laughter and witty sallies from the crowd.

Then the wagon appeared, a mere speck in the distance, but sending the sound of its bell before it as an advertisement of its presence. It grew rapidly until it reached the cheering crowds. Then it seemed that even the sedate officers of the law were not above a sly humor of their own, for the vehicle slackened its pace perceptibly and prolonged the final moment of capture.

The big buildings had been left behind, and there lay before Porgy only the scattered, cheap bungalows of the labor quarters; and beyond, as elusive and desirable as the white man's heaven, glimmered the far line of the woods, misty and beautiful in the pink autumn haze.

The patrol forged ahead and came to a clanging stop. The officers leapt out and, amid shouts of laughter from the crowd, lifted wagon, goat and man into the vehicle. The driver jerked the horse back into its breechings, swung the wagon with a dramatic snap that was not wasted upon his gallery, and sent it clanging and rocking back in the direction from which it had come.

Porgy fell forward, with his arms thrown out upon the back of the goat, and buried his face between them in the shaggy, evil-smelling hair.

The workmen upon the sidewalks cheered and shouted with mirth. Surely it had been a great day. They would not soon have another laugh to match it.

§

When the wagon reached the down-town district, the inquest was over. It had been a simple matter to secure another witness for the identification of the body. The jury had made short work of their task, and had found that Crown had come to his death as the result of a chest wound at the hands of person or persons unknown.

Porgy was taken at once to the station house, where the charge of "Contempt of Court" was formally entered against him on the blotter, and he was locked up to await trial early the following morning.

Under the wheezing gas jet, the Recorder looked Porgy over with his weary glance, brought the tips of his slender fingers together; gave him "five days," in his tired drawl, and raised his eyes to the next negro on the morning's list.

They hoisted the outfit, goat and all, into the patrol for the trip to the jail, thus again brightening a day for a group of light-hearted Nordics upon the pavement.

A large, red-faced policeman took his seat at the rear of the wagon. "You sure beat all!" he confided to Porgy, with a puzzled frown. "Runnin' away like the devil was after you, from bein' a witness; an' now goin' to jail with a face like Sunday mornin'."

§

In the fresh beauty of an early October morning, Porgy returned home. There were few of his friends about, as work was now plentiful, and most of those who could earn a day's wage were up and out. He drove through the entrance, pulled his goat up short, and looked about him.

Serena was seated on her bench with a baby in her arms.

Porgy gave her a long look, and a question commenced to dawn in his eyes. The child turned in her arms, and his suspicions were confirmed. It was his baby—his and Bess's.

Then Serena looked up and saw him. She arose in great confusion, clasped the infant to her ample bosom, and, without a word of greeting, stepped through her doorway. Then, as though struck by an afterthought, she turned, thrust her head back through the opening, and called loudly:

"Oh, Maria! hyuh Porgy come home."

The she disappeared and the door slammed shut.

Mystified and filled with alarm, Porgy turned his vehicle toward the cook-shop and arrived at the door just as Maria stepped over the threshold.

She seated herself on the sill and brought her face level with his. Then she looked into his eyes.

What Porgy saw there caused him to call out sharply:

"Where's Bess? Tell me, quick, where's Bess?"

The big negress did not answer, and after a moment her ponderous face commenced to shake.

Porgy beat the side of his wagon with his fist.

"Where, where—" he began, in a voice that was suddenly shrill.

But Maria placed a steadying hand over his frantic one and held it still.

"Dem dutty dogs got she one day w'en I gone out," she said in a low, shaken voice. "She been missin' yuh an' berry low in she min' 'cause she can't fin' out how long yuh is lock up fuh. Dat damn houn' she knock off de wharf las' summer fin' she like dat an' git she tuh tek er swalluh ob licker. Den half a dozen of de mens gang she, an' mek she drunk."

"But wuh she now?" Porgy cried. "I ain't keer ef she wuz drunk. I want she now."

Maria tried to speak, but her voice refused to do her bidding. She covered her face with her hands, and her throat worked convulsively.

Porgy clutched her wrist. "Tell me," he commanded. "Tell me, now."

"De mens all carry she away on de ribber boat," she sobbed. "Dey leabe word fuh me dat dey goin' tek she all de way tuh Sawannah, an' keep she dey. Den Serena, she tek de chile, an' say she is goin' gib um er Christian raisin'."

Deep sobs stopped Maria's voice. For a while she sat there, her face buried in her hands. But Porgy had nothing to say. When she finally raised her head and looked at him, she was surprised at what she saw.

The keen autumn sun flooded boldly through the entrance and bathed the drooping form of the goat, the ridiculous wagon, and the bent figure of the man in hard, satirical radiance. In its revealing light, Maria saw that Porgy was an old man. The early tension that had characterized him, the mellow mood that he had known for one eventful summer, both had gone; and in their place she saw a face that sagged wearily, and the eyes of age lit only by a faint reminiscent glow from suns and moons that had looked into them, and had already dropped down the west.

She looked until she could bear the sight no longer; then she stumbled into her shop and closed the door, leaving Porgy and the goat alone in an irony of morning sunlight.

Billy Budd, Foretopman

HERMAN MELVILLE

HERMAN MELVILLE, *the third of eight children, was born in New York City on August 1, 1819. His parents were well-born and originally well-to-do. The father went through bankruptcy before his death in 1832, and the boy, who had been educated in a sheltered fashion, had to find his feet as best he could. He was first employed as a bank clerk, tried his hand at farming and at teaching, and then, when he was eighteen, he shipped on a freighter to Liverpool. In 1841 he again went to the sea, and this time served the whaling fleet in the Pacific; later, on an American man-of-war. From these seafaring years came the material for his best writing. Billy Budd, his last novel, was begun in 1888 and finished in 1891. It measures 32,500 words.*

WHAT BEFELL HIM IN THE YEAR OF THE GREAT MUTINY

Begun—Friday, November 16, 1888.
Revision begun—March 2, 1889.
Finished—April 19, 1891.

DEDICATED

TO

JACK CHASE

ENGLISHMAN

WHEREVER THAT GREAT HEART MAY NOW BE
HERE ON EARTH OR HARBOURED IN PARADISE.
CAPTAIN OF THE MAINTOP IN THE YEAR 1843 IN
THE U.S. FRIGATE "UNITED STATES"

INTRODUCTION

Billy Budd, Foretopman—"An inside Narrative" as the author wrote on his title page—was completed five months before Herman Melville's death in 1891. It is his last novel, a novel written in a firm serenity of mind and one which the American critic Grant Overton marked as "his single triumph aside from *Moby Dick*." Any modern jury would place it among the best things Melville ever wrote, and yet, as luck would have it, the manuscript was not published until 1924 and then only as part of his collected works. During his lifetime Melville's writing fell on evil days. No publisher wanted *Clarel*, the publication of which his uncle financed, and after his death no publisher was enough interested to inquire whether there was a posthumous novel. Thus *Billy Budd* had to await the new esteem for Melville which came with the rediscovery of *Moby Dick* in the centennial year 1919.

Billy Budd, as the title tells you, is a story of the sea. Or, to be more specific, of the seamen aboard the seventy-four-gun ship Indomitable, in the days of Nelson. Melville's call to the sea was one of the strongest impulses in his character. He was not bred for it, for his father was at one time a well-to-do merchant in New York City, and the boy's first years were on the side of luxury. When he was seven, we have this thumbnail sketch of him by his uncle Peter Gansevoort: "He is very backward in speech and somewhat slow in comprehension, but you

will find him as far as he understands men and things both solid and profound and of a docile and amiable disposition. . . . Let him avoid green fruit and unseasonable exposure to the sun." Ten years later Herman's father was dead, his family was impoverished and the boy was on his own. After a brief bout in a bank he answered the call to the sea, serving before the mast in what was unquestionably the hardest manual labor America had to offer in his time. In John Freeman's splendid monograph on Herman Melville there is a delightful account of the boy's preparation for his life as a sailor. Having signed his first ship's papers, he bought himself a red shirt, a tarpaulin hat, a belt and a jackknife. Then "after dinner I went into my room, locked the door carefully and hung a towel over the knob, so that no one could peep through the keyhole, and then went to trying on my red woolen shirt before the glass, to see what sort of a looking sailor I was going to make. As soon as I got into the shirt I began to feel a sort of warm and red about the face, which I found was owing to the reflection of the dyed wool upon my skin. After that I took a pair of scissors and went to cutting my hair, which was very long. I thought every little would help in making me a light hand to run aloft."

Melville's first berth was on a freighter bound for Liverpool. The disillusionment of this voyage was as nothing compared with that of 1841 when he served before the mast on a whaler. He deserted the ship at Nukuheva in the Marquesas Islands after fifteen months of hard usage and brutality. For several months thereafter he was "on the beach," living with and forcibly detained by the natives who, so he thought when he was low, might eventually eat him. Escaping from the Typees, he signed for a cruise in a second whaler, an Australian boat and an abominable one, to judge from all accounts. Half the men were sick and the crew were in open mutiny by the time the ship reached Tahiti. Melville, with the other mutineers, lingered on the island in mild confinement until he was picked up by a Nantucket sea captain in search of a crew. This voyage seems again to have stranded him in the Pacific for in 1843 he signed on as an ordinary seaman on an American man-of-war, from which he was honorably discharged a year later when the ship arrived home. Despite his uncle, that long "unseasonable exposure to the sun" was the very tonic Melville needed. For from these years came the source material and inspiration to publish *Typee* and *Omoo, Mardi, Moby Dick* (at thirty-two) and *Pierre*.

Melville's life as a whaler and beachcomber covered less than four years, but the experience was of a sort which would have left a smaller writer hard-bitten and vindictive. There is literal reality and plenty of vehemence in the books which he wrote immediately on coming ashore. Enough, at least, to offend his English publisher, John Murray, who

dropped Melville's name from his list after the publication of *Omoo* on the grounds that he wanted no such "obscenity" in his Colonial Library. But if *Moby Dick* and *White Jacket* vex us today it is not because of anything offensive in their realism but because some still find it difficult to follow the full course of the author's philosophy.

Nearly forty years later, when Melville came to write the story of Billy Budd, the Handsome Sailor, he was essentially more interested in exploring the psychology of seamen and in coping with the ageless conflict between good and evil than in harking back to a more direct narrative of life aboard ship. This distinction must be clearly understood by the reader before he begins. The author knows his ships through hard usage but in this story he deliberately subordinates action in order to concentrate upon the antagonism between the two sailors, Claggart, the master-at-arms, a kind of chief of police of the crew, and Billy Budd, the simple, handsome foretopman, a man of splendid physique whose essential goodness is betrayed by his lack of experience and his inarticulation. Claggart picks the fight because of envy; Billy falls into his trap because he is not on his guard; and since the conflict occurs only a few months after the mutiny at the Nore and therefore in an atmosphere of exaggerated discipline, it soon involves both the crew and the captain.

At first glance the story may seem to be oversimplified, Billy too good to be true, and Claggart the personification of all villainy. But this would be the superficial judgment of an audience not used to reading Melville. Not every novel is to be judged by its narrative alone, and this one, as Mr Freeman rightly says, is to be judged as you would judge Milton's *Paradise Regained*. The parallel is a good one, for both books are written in the calm after a stormy life and both reaffirm essential truths, which soak into you slowly and are not soon forgotten. Here are half-a-hundred side lights on human nature, as it is tested and irritated under the discipline of ship life. Here are vignettes on Nelson, on Napoleon, on old Dansker, an *Agamemnon* man who is the epitome of the cynical old salt. And here, strongly felt at the close, is the terrible decision of the captain and Billy's remarkable fortitude under stress. "In this, the simplest of stories," concludes John Freeman, "told with but little of the old digressive vexatiousness and based upon recorded incidents, Herman Melville uttered his everlasting yea, and died before a soul had been allowed to hear him."

Preface

THE year 1797, the year of this narrative, belongs to a period which, as every thinker now feels, involved a crisis for Christendom not exceeded in its undetermined momentousness at the time by any other era whereof there is record. The opening proposition made by the Spirit of that Age* involved rectification of the Old World's hereditary wrongs. In France, to some extent, this was bloodily effected. But what then? Straightway the Revolution itself became a wrongdoer, one more oppressive than the kings. Under Napoleon it enthroned upstart kings, and initiated that prolonged agony of continual war whose final throe was Waterloo. During those years not the wisest could have foreseen that the outcome of all would be what to some thinkers apparently it has since turned out to be—a political advance along nearly the whole line for Europeans.

Now, as elsewhere hinted, it was something caught from the Revolutionary Spirit that at Spithead emboldened the man-of-war's men to rise against real abuses, long-standing ones, and afterwards at the Nore to make inordinate and aggressive demands—successful resistance to which was confirmed only when the ringleaders were hung for an admonitory spectacle to the anchored fleet. Yet in a way analogous to the operation of the Revolution at large—the Great Mutiny, though by Englishmen naturally deemed monstrous at the time, doubtless gave the first latent prompting to most important reforms in the British navy.

*Crossed out; was one hailed by the noblest men of it. Even the dry tinder of a Wordsworth took fire.

BILLY BUDD, FORETOPMAN

WHAT BEFELL HIM IN THE YEAR OF THE GREAT MUTINY, ETC.

§ 1

(An inside Narrative)

In the time before steamships, or then more frequently than now, a stroller along the docks of any considerable seaport would occasionally have his attention arrested by a group of bronzed marines, man-of-war's men or merchant-sailors in holiday attire ashore on liberty. In certain instances they would flank, or, like a bodyguard, quite surround some superior figure of their own class, moving along with them like Aldebaran among the lesser lights of his constellation. That signal object was the "Handsome Sailor" of the less prosaic time, alike of the military and merchant navies. With no perceptible trace of the vainglorious about him, rather with the off-hand unaffectedness of natural regality, he seemed to accept the spontaneous homage of his shipmates. A somewhat remarkable instance recurs to me. In Liverpool, now half a century ago I saw under the shadow of the great dingy street-wall of Prince's Dock (an obstruction long since removed) a common sailor, so intensely black that he must needs have been a native African of the unadulterated blood of Ham. A symmetric figure, much above the average in height. The two ends of a gay silk handkerchief thrown loose about the neck danced upon the displayed ebony of his chest; in his ears were big hoops of gold, and a Scotch Highland bonnet with a tartan band set off his shapely head.

It was a hot noon in July, and his face, lustrous with perspiration, beamed with barbaric good-humour. In jovial sallies right and left, his white teeth flashing into view, he rollicked along, the centre of a company of his shipmates. These were made up of such an assortment of tribes and complexions as would have well fitted them to be marched up by Anacharsis Cloots before the bar of the first French Assembly as Representatives of the Human Race. At each spontaneous tribute rendered by the wayfarers to this black pagod of a fellow— the tribute of a pause and stare, and less frequent an exclamation— the motley retinue showed that they took that sort of pride in the evoker of it which the Assyrian priests doubtless showed for their grand sculptured Bull when the faithful prostrated themselves. To return—

If in some cases a bit of a nautical Murat in setting forth his person ashore, the Handsome Sailor of the period in question evinced nothing of the dandified Billy-be-Damn—an amusing character all but extinct now, but occasionally to be encountered, and in a form yet more amusing than the original, at the tiller of the boats on the tempestuous Erie Canal or, more likely, vapouring in the groggeries along the tow-path. Invariably a proficient in his perilous calling, he was also more or less of a mighty boxer or wrestler. It was strength and beauty. Tales of his prowess were recited. Ashore he was the champion; afloat the spokesman; on every suitable occasion always foremost. Close-reefing topsails in a gale, there he was—astride the weather yard-arm-end, foot in "stirrup," both hands tugging at the "ear-ring" as at a bridle, in very much the attitude of the young Alexander curbing the fiery Bucephalus. A superb figure, tossed up as by the horns of Taurus against the thunderous sky, cheerily ballooning to the strenuous file along the spar.

The moral nature was seldom out of keeping with the physical make. Indeed, except as toned by the former, the comeliness and power, always attractive in masculine perfection, hardly could have drawn the sort of homage the Handsome Sailor, in some examples, received from his less gifted associates.

Such a cynosure, as least in aspect, and something such too in nature, though with important variations made apparent as the story proceeds, was welkin-eyed Billy Budd, or Baby Budd—as more familiarly, under circumstances hereafter to be given, he at last came to be called—aged twenty-one, a foretopman of the fleet towards the close of the last decade of the eighteenth century. It was not very long prior to the time of the narration that follows, that he had entered the King's Service, having been impressed on the Narrow Seas from a homeward-bound English merchantman into a seventy-four outward-bound, H.M.S. *Indomitable;* which ship, as was not unusual in those hurried days, had been obliged to put to sea short of her proper complement of men. Plump upon Billy at first sight in the gangway the boarding officer, Lieutenant Ratcliffe, pounced, even before the merchantman's crew formally was mustered on the quarter-deck for his deliberate inspection. And him only he elected. For whether it was because the other men when ranged before him showed to ill advantage after Billy, or whether he had some scruples in view of the merchantman being rather short-handed; however it might be, the officer contented himself with his first spontaneous choice. To the surprise of the ship's company, though much to the Lieutenant's satisfaction, Billy made no demur. But indeed any demur would have been as idle as the protest of a goldfinch popped into a cage.

Noting this uncomplaining acquiescence, all but cheerful one might say, the shipmates turned a surprised glance of silent reproach at the sailor. The shipmaster was one of those worthy mortals found in every vocation,—even the humbler ones,—the sort of person whom everybody agrees in calling "a respectable man." And—nor so strange to report as it may appear to be—though a ploughman of the troubled waters, life-long contending with the intractable elements, there was nothing this honest soul at heart loved better than simple peace and quiet. For the rest, he was fifty or thereabouts, a little inclined to corpulence, a prepossessing face, unwhiskered, and of an agreeable colour—a rather full face, humanely intelligent in expression. On a fair day with a fair wind and all going well, a certain musical chime in his voice seemed to be the veritable unobstructed outcome of the innermost man. He had much prudence, much conscientiousness, and there were occasions when these virtues were the cause of overmuch disquietude in him. On a passage, so long as his craft was in any proximity to land, there was no sleep for Captain Graveling. He took to heart those serious responsibilities not so heavily borne by some shipmasters.

Now, while Billy Budd was down in the forecastle, getting his kit together, the *Indomitable's* Lieutenant—burly and bluff, nowise disconcerted by Captain Graveling's omitting to proffer the customary hospitalities on an occasion so unwelcome to him; an omission simply caused by preoccupation of thought—unceremoniously invited himself into the cabin, and also to a flask from the spirit locker, a receptacle which his experienced eye instantly discovered. In fact, he was one of those sea-dogs in whom all the hardship and peril of naval life in the great prolonged wars of his time never impaired the natural instinct for sensuous enjoyment. His duty he always faithfully did; but duty is sometimes a dry obligation, and he was for irrigating its aridity whensoever possible with a fertilizing decoction of strong waters. For the cabin's proprietor there was nothing left but to play the part of the enforced host with whatever grace and alacrity were practicable. As necessary adjuncts to the flask he silently placed tumbler and water-jug before the irrepressible guest. But excusing himself from partaking just then, he dismally watched the unembarrassed officer deliberately diluting his grog a little, then tossing it off in three swallows, pushing the empty tumbler away, yet not so far as to be beyond easy reach, at the same time settling himself in his seat and smacking his lips with high satisfaction, looking straight at the host.

These proceedings over the Master broke the silence; and there lurked a rueful reproach in the tone of his voice: "Lieutenant, you are going to take my best man from me, the jewel of 'em."

"Yes, I know," rejoined the other, immediately drawing back the tumbler preliminary to a replenishing; "Yes, I know. Sorry."

"Beg pardon, but you don't understand, Lieutenant. See here now. Before I shipped that young fellow, my forecastle was a rat-pit of quarrels. It was black times, I tell you, aboard the *'Rights'* here. I was worried to that degree my pipe had no comfort for me. But Billy came; and it was like a Catholic priest striking peace in an Irish shindy. Not that he preached to them or said or did anything in particular; but a virtue went out of him, sugaring the sour ones. They took to him like hornets to treacle; all but the bluffer of the gang, the big shaggy chap with the fire-red whiskers. He, indeed, out of envy perhaps of the newcomer, and thinking such a 'sweet and pleasant fellow,' as he mockingly designated him to the others, could hardly have the spirit of a game-cock, must needs bestir himself in trying to get up an ugly row with him. Billy forebore with him and reasoned with him in a pleasant way—he is something like myself, Lieutenant, to whom aught like a quarrel is hateful—but nothing served. So, in the second dog-watch one day the Red-Whiskers, in the presence of the others, under pretense of showing Billy just whence a sirloin steak was cut—for the fellow had once been a butcher—insultingly gave him a dig under the ribs. Quick as lightning Billy let fly his arm. I dare say he never meant to do quite as much as he did, but anyhow he gave the burly fool a terrible drubbing. It took about half a minute, I should think. And, Lord bless you, the lubber was astonished at the celerity. And will you believe it, Lieutenant, the Red-Whiskers now really loves Billy—loves him, or is the biggest hypocrite that ever I heard of. But they all love him. Some of 'em do his washing, darn old trousers for him; the carpenter is at odd times making a pretty little chest of drawers for him. Anybody will do anything for Billy Budd; and it's the happy family here. Now, Lieutenant, if that young fellow goes—I know how it will be aboard the *'Rights.'* Not again very soon shall I, coming up from dinner, lean over the capstan smoking a quiet pipe—no, not very soon again, I think. Ay, Lieutenant, you are going to take away the jewel of 'em; you are going to take away my peacemaker." And with that the good soul had really some ado in checking a rising sob.

"Well," answered the Lieutenant, who had listened with amused interest to all this, and now waxing merry with his tipple, "Well, blessed are the peacemakers, especially the fighting peacemakers! And such are the seventy-four beauties, some of which you see poking their noses out of the portholes of yonder warship lying-to there for me," pointing through the cabin window at the *Indomitable.* "But courage! don't look so down-hearted, man. Why, I pledge you in advance the royal approbation. Rest assured that His Majesty will be delighted to

know that in a time when his hard-tack is not sought for by sailors with such avidity as should be; a time also when some shipmasters privily resent the borrowing from them of a tar or two for the service; His Majesty, I say, will be delighted to learn that *one* shipmaster, at least, cheerfully surrenders to the King the flower of his flock: a sailor who with equal loyalty makes no dissent.—But where's my beauty? Ah," looking through the cabin's open door. "Here he comes; and, by Jove—lugging along his chest—Apollo with his portmanteau! My man," stepping out to him, "you can't take that big box on board a warship. The boxes there are mostly shot-boxes. Put up your duds in a bag, lad. Boot and saddle for the cavalryman, bag and hammock for the man-of-war's man."

The transfer from chest to bag was made. And, after seeing his man into the cutter, and then following him down, the Lieutenant pushed off from the *Rights-of-Man*. That was the merchant ship's name; though by her master and crew abbreviated in sailor fashion into the *"Rights."* The hard-headed Dundee owner was a staunch admirer of Thomas Paine, whose book in rejoinder to Burke's arraignment of the French Revolution had then been published for some time and had gone everywhere. In christening his vessel after the title of Paine's volume, the man of Dundee was something like his contemporary shipowner, Stephen Girard of Philadelphia, whose sympathies alike with his native land and its liberal philosophies he evinced by naming his ships after Voltaire, Diderot, and so forth.

But now, when the boat swept under the merchantman's stern, and officer and oarsmen were noting,—some bitterly and others with a grin, —the name emblazoned there; just then it was that the new recruit jumped up from the bow where the coxswain had directed him to sit, waving his hat to his silent shipmates sorrowfully looking over at him from the taffrail, and bade the lads a genial good-bye. Then making a salutation as to the ship herself, "And good-bye to you too, old *Rights-of-Man!*"

"Down, Sir," roared the Lieutenant, instantly assuming all the rigour of his rank, though with difficulty repressing a smile.

To be sure, Billy's action was a terrible breach of naval decorum. But in that decorum he had never been instructed; in consideration of which the Lieutenant would hardly have been so energetic in reproof but for the concluding farewell to the ship. This he rather took as meant to convey a covert sally on the new recruit's part—a sly slur at impressment in general, and that of himself in especial. And yet, more likely, if satire it was in effect, it was hardly so by intention, for Billy (though happily endowed with the gaiety of high health, youth and a free heart) was yet by no means of a satirical turn. The will to it and

the sinister dexterity were alike wanting. To deal in double meaning
and insinuations of any sort was quite foreign to his nature.

As to his enforced enlistment—that he seemed to take pretty much
as he was wont to take any vicissitude of weather. Like the animals,
though no philosopher, he was, without knowing it, practically a
fatalist. And, it may be, that he rather liked this adventurous turn in
his affairs which promised an opening into novel scenes and martial
excitements.

Aboard the *Indomitable* our merchant-sailor was forthwith rated as
an able seaman, and assigned to the starboard watch of the foretop.
He was soon at home in the service, not at all disliked for his unpre-
tentious good looks and his rather genial happy-go-lucky air. No mer-
rier man in his mess; in marked contrast to certain other individuals
included like himself among the impressed portions of the ship's com-
pany; for these when not actively employed were sometimes—and
more particularly in the last dog-watch, when the drawing near of
twilight induced revery—apt to fall into a saddish mood which in
some partook of sullenness. But they were not so young as our foretop-
man, and no few of them must have known a hearth of some sort,
others may have had wives and children left, too probably, in uncer-
tain circumstances, and hardly any but must have acknowledged kith
and kin; while for Billy, as will shortly be seen, his entire family was
practically invested in himself.

§ 2

Though our new-made foretopman was well received in the top and
on the gun-decks, hardly here was he that cynosure he had previously
been among those minor ship's companies of the merchant marine,
with which companies only had he hitherto consorted.

He was young; and despite his all but fully developed frame, in
aspect looked even younger than he really was. This was owing to a
lingering adolescent expression in the as yet smooth face, all but
feminine in purity of natural complexion, but where, thanks to his
seagoing, the lily was quite suppressed and the rose had some ado
visibly to flush through the tan.

To one essentially such a novice in the complexities of factitious life,
the abrupt transition from his former and simpler sphere to the ampler
and more knowing world of a great war-ship—this might well have
abashed him had there been any conceit or vanity in his composition.
Among her miscellaneous multitude, the *Indomitable* mustered sev-
eral individuals who, however inferior in grade, were of no common

natural stamp: sailors more signally susceptive of that air which continuous martial discipline and repeated presence in battle can in some degree impart even to the average man. As the "Handsome Sailor" Billy Budd's position aboard the seventy-four was something analogous to that of a rustic beauty transplanted from the provinces and brought into competition with the high-born dames of the court. But this change of circumstances he scarce noted. As little did he observe that something about him provoked an ambiguous smile in one or two harder faces among the blue-jackets. Nor less unaware was he of the peculiar favourable effect his person and demeanour had upon the more intelligent gentlemen of the quarter-deck. Nor could this well have been otherwise. Cast in a mould peculiar to the finest physical examples of those Englishmen in whom the Saxon strain would seem not at all to partake of any Norman or other admixture, he showed in face that humane look of reposeful good nature which the Greek sculptor in some instances gave to his heroic strong man, Hercules. But this again was subtly modified by another and pervasive quality. The ear, small and shapely, the arch of the foot, the curve in mouth and nostril, even the indurated hand dyed to the orange-tawny of the toucan's bill, a hand telling of the halyards and tar-buckets. But, above all, something in the mobile expression, and every chance attitude and movement, something suggestive of a mother eminently favoured by Love and the Graces; all this strangely indicated a lineage in direct contradiction to his lot. The mysteriousness here became less mysterious through a matter of fact elicited when Billy at the capstan was being formally mustered into the service. Asked by the officer, a small, brisk little gentleman as it chanced, among other questions, his place of birth, he replied, "Please, Sir, I don't know."

"Don't you know where you were born? Who was your father?"

"God knows, Sir."

Struck by the straightforward simplicity of these replies, the officer next asked, "Do you know anything about your beginning?"

"No, Sir. But I have heard that I was found in a pretty silk-lined basket hanging one morning from the knocker of a good man's door in Bristol."

" 'Found,' say you? Well," throwing back his head and looking up and down the new recruit; "well it turns out to have been a pretty good find. Hope they'll find some more like you, my man; the fleet sadly needs them."

Yes, Billy Budd was a foundling, a presumable by-blow, and, evidently, no ignoble one. Noble descent was as evident in him as in a blood horse.

For the rest, with little or no sharpness of faculty or any trace of the

wisdom of the serpent, nor yet quite a dove, he possessed that kind and degree of intelligence which goes along with the unconventional rectitude of a sound human creature—one to whom not as yet had been proffered the questionable apple of knowledge. He was illiterate. He could not read, but he could sing, and like the illiterate nightingale was sometimes the composer of his own song.

Of self-consciousness he seemed to have little or none, or about as much as we may reasonably impute to a dog of St. Bernard's breed.

Habitually being with the elements, and knowing little more of the land than as a beach, or, rather, that portion of the terraqueous globe, providentially set apart for dance-houses, doxies and tapsters, in short what sailors call a "fiddlers' green," his simple nature remained unsophisticated by those moral obliquities which are not in every case incomparable with that manufacturable thing known as respectability. But are sailors, frequenters of fiddlers' greens without vices? No; but less often than with landsmen do their vices, so called, partake of crookedness of heart, seeming less to proceed from viciousness than from exuberance of vitality after long restraint, frank manifestations in accordance with natural law. By his original constitution aided by the coöperating influences of his lot, Billy in many respects was little more than a sort of upright barbarian, much such perhaps as Adam presumably might have been ere the urbane Serpent wriggled himself into his company.

And here be it submitted that, apparently going to corroborate the doctrine of man's fall—a doctrine now popularly ignored—it is observable that where certain virtues pristine and unadulterate peculiarly characterize anybody in the external uniform of civilization, they will upon scrutiny seem not to be derived from custom or convention but rather to be out of keeping with these, as if indeed exceptionally transmitted from a period prior to Cain's City and citified man. The character marked by such qualities has to an unvitiated taste an untampered-with flavour like that of berries, while the man thoroughly civilized, even in a fair specimen of the breed, has to the same moral palate a questionable smack as of a compounded wine. To any stray inheritor of these primitive qualities found, like Caspar Hauser, wandering dazed in any Christian capital of our time, the poet's famous invocation, near two thousand years ago, of the good rustic out of his latitude in the Rome of the Cæsars, still appropriately holds:—

> *"Faithful in word and thought,*
> *What has Thee, Fabian, to the city brought."*

Though our Handsome Sailor had as much of masculine beauty as one can expect anywhere to see; nevertheless, like the beautiful woman

in one of Hawthorne's minor tales, there was just one thing amiss in him. No visible blemish, indeed, as with the lady; no, but an occasional liability to a vocal defect. Though in the hour of elemental uproar or peril, he was everything that a sailor should be, yet under sudden provocation of strong heart-feeling his voice, otherwise singularly musical, as if expressive of the harmony within, was apt to develop an organic hesitancy,—in fact more or less of a stutter or even worse. In this particular Billy was a striking instance that the arch interpreter, the envious marplot of Eden, still has more or less to do with every human consignment to this planet of earth. In every case, one way or another, he is sure to slip in his little card, as much as to remind us—I too have a hand here.

The avowal of such an imperfection in the Handsome Sailor should be evidence not alone that he is not presented as a conventional hero, but also that the story in which he is the main figure is no romance.

§ 3

At the time of Billy Budd's arbitrary enlistment into the *Indomitable* that ship was on her way to join the Mediterranean fleet. No long time elapsed before the junction was effected. As one of that fleet the seventy-four participated in its movements: though at times on account of her superior sailing qualities, in the absence of frigates, despatched on separate duty as a scout—and at times on less temporary service. But with all this the story has little concernment, restricted as it is to the inner life of one particular ship and the career of an individual sailor.

It was the summer of 1797. In April of that year had occurred the commotion at Spithead followed in May by a second and yet more serious outbreak in the fleet at the Nore. The latter is known, and without exaggeration in the epithet, as the Great Mutiny. It was indeed a demonstration more menacing to England than the contemporary manifestoes and conquering and proselyting armies of the French Directory.

To the Empire, the Nore Mutiny was what a strike in the fire-brigade would be to London threatened by general arson. In a crisis when the Kingdom might well have anticipated the famous signal that some years later published along the naval line of battle what it was that upon occasion England expected of Englishmen; *that* was the time when at the mast-heads of the three-deckers and seventy-fours moored in our own roadstead—a fleet, the right arm of a Power then all but the sole free conservative one of the Old World, the blue-jackets, to

be numbered by thousands, ran up with hurras the British colours with the union and cross wiped out; by that cancellation transmuting the flag of founded law and freedom defined, into the enemy's red meteor of unbridled and unbounded revolt. Reasonable discontent growing out of practical grievances in the fleet had been ignited into irrational combustion as by live cinders blown across the Channel from France in flames.

The event converted into irony for a time those spirited strains of Dibdin—as a song-writer no mean auxiliary to the English Government—at the European conjecture, strains celebrating, among other things, the patriotic devotion of the British tar:

> *"And as for my life, 'tis the King's!"*

Such an episode in the Island's grand naval story her naval historians naturally abridge; one of them (G. P. R. James) candidly acknowledging that fain would he pass it over did not "impartiality forbid fastidiousness." And yet his mention is less a narration than a reference, having to do hardly at all with details. Nor are these readily to be found in the libraries. Like some other events in every age befalling states everywhere, including America, the Great Mutiny was of such character that national pride along with views of policy would fain shade it off into the historical background. Such events cannot be ignored, but there is a considerate way of historically treating them. If a well-constituted individual refrains from blazoning aught amiss or calamitous in his family, a nation in the like circumstance may without reproach be equally discreet.

Though after parleyings between Government and the ring-leaders, and concessions by the former as to some glaring abuses, the first uprising—that at Spithead—with difficulty was put down, or matters for a time pacified; yet at the Nore the unforeseen renewal of insurrection on a yet larger scale, and emphasized in the conferences that ensued by demands deemed by the authorities not only inadmissible but aggressively insolent, indicated, if the red flag did not sufficiently do so, what was the spirit animating the men. Final suppression, however, there was, but only made possible perhaps by the unswerving loyalty of the marine corps, and a voluntary resumption of loyalty among influential sections of the crews. To some extent the Nore Mutiny may be regarded as analogous to the distempering *irruption* of contagious fever in a frame constitutionally sound, and which anon throws it off.

At all events, of these thousands of mutineers were some of the tars who not so very long afterwards—whether wholly prompted thereto by patriotism, or pugnacious instinct, or by both,—helped to win a coro-

net for Nelson at the Nile, and the naval crown of crowns for him at Trafalgar. To the mutineers those battles, and especially Trafalgar, were a plenary absolution; and a grand one; for all that goes to make up scenic naval display is heroic magnificence in arms. Those battles, especially Trafalgar, stand unmatched in human annals.

§ 4

Concerning *"The greatest sailor since the world began"*—TENNYSON.

In this matter of writing, resolve as one may to keep to the main road, some bypaths have an enticement not readily to be withstood. Beckoned by the genius of Nelson, I am going to err into such a by-path. If the reader will keep me company I shall be glad. At the least we can promise ourselves that pleasure which is wickedly said to be in sinning, for a literary sin the divergence will be.

Very likely it is no new remark that the inventions of our time have at last brought about a change in sea warfare in degree corresponding to the revolution in all warfare effected by the original introduction from China into Europe of gunpowder. The first European firearm, a clumsy contrivance, was, as is well known, scouted by no few of the knights as a base implement, good enough peradventure for weavers too craven to stand up crossing steel with steel in frank fight. But as ashore knightly valour, though shorn of its blazonry, did not cease with the knights, neither on the seas, though nowadays in encounters there a certain kind of displayed gallantry be fallen out of date as hardly applicable under changed circumstances, did the nobler qualities of such naval magnates as Don John of Austria, Doria, Van Tromp, Jean Bart, the long line of British admirals and the American Decaturs of 1812 become obsolete with their wooden walls.

Nevertheless, to anybody who can hold the Present at its worth without being inappreciative of the Past, it may be forgiven, if to such an one the solitary old hulk at Portsmouth, Nelson's *Victory,* seems to float there, not alone as the decaying monument of a fame incorruptible, but also as a poetic reproach, softened by its picturesqueness, to the *Monitors* and yet mightier hulls of the European ironsides. And this not altogether because such craft are unsightly, unavoidably lacking the symmetry and grand lines of the old battleships, but equally for other reasons.

There are some, perhaps, who while not altogether inaccessible to that poetic reproach just alluded to, may yet on behalf of the new order be disposed to parry it; and this to the extent of iconoclasm, if

need be. For example, prompted by the sight of the star inserted in the *Victory's* deck designing the spot where the Great Sailor fell, these martial utilitarians may suggest considerations implying that Nelson's ornate publication of his person in battle was not only unnecessary, but not military, nay, savoured of foolhardiness and vanity. They may add, too, that at Trafalgar it was in effect nothing less than a challenge to death: and death came; and that but for his bravado the victorious admiral might possibly have survived the battle, and so, instead of having his sagacious dying injunction overruled by his immediate successor in command, he himself when the contest was decided might have brought his shattered fleet to anchor, a proceeding which might have averted the deplorable loss of life by shipwreck in the elemental tempest that followed the martial one.

Well, should we set aside the more disputable point whether for various reasons it was possible to anchor the fleet, then plausibly enough the Benthamites of war may urge the above.

But it *might have been* is but boggy ground to build on. And certainly in foresight as to the larger issue of an encounter, and anxious preparation for it—buoying the deadly way and mapping it out, as at Copenhagen—few commanders have been so painstakingly circumspect as this reckless declarer of his person in fight.

Personal prudence, even when dictated by quite other than selfish considerations, is surely no special virtue in a military man; while an excessive love of glory, exercising to the uttermost heartfelt sense of duty, is the first. If the name of *Wellington* is not so much a trumpet to the blood as the simpler name of *Nelson,* the reason for this may be inferred from the above. Alfred in his funeral ode on the victor of Waterloo ventures not to call him the greatest soldier of all time, though in the same ode he invokes Nelson as "the greatest sailor since the world began."

At Trafalgar, Nelson, on the brink of opening the fight, sat down and wrote his last brief will and testament. If under the presentiment of the most magnificent of all victories, to be crowned by his own glorious death, a sort of priestly motive led him to dress his person in the jewelled vouchers of his own shining deeds; if thus to have adorned himself for the altar and the sacrifice were indeed vainglory, then affectation and fustian is each truly heroic line in the great epics and dramas, since in such lines the poet but embodies in verse those exaltations of sentiment that a nature like Nelson, the opportunity being given, vitalizes into acts.

§ 5

The outbreak at the Nore was put down. But not every grievance was redressed. If the contractors, for example, were no longer permitted to ply some practices peculiar to their tribe everywhere, such as providing shoddy cloth, rations not sound, or false in the measure; not the less impressment, for one thing, went on. By custom sanctioned for centuries, and judicially maintained by a Lord Chancellor as late as Mansfield, that mode of manning the fleet, a mode now fallen into a sort of abeyance but never formally renounced, it was not practicable to give up in those years. Its abrogation would have crippled the indispensable fleet, one wholly under canvas, no steam-power, its innumerable sails and thousands of cannon, everything, in short, worked by muscle alone; a fleet the more insatiate in demand for men, because then multiplying its ships of all grades against contingencies present and to come of the convulsed Continent.

Discontent foreran the Two Mutinies, and more or less it lurkingly survived them. Hence it was not unreasonable to apprehend some return of trouble, sporadic or general. One instance of such apprehensions: In the same year with this story, Nelson, then Vice-Admiral Sir Horatio, being with the fleet off the Spanish coast, was directed by the Admiral in command to shift his pennant from the *Captain* to the *Theseus;* and for this reason: that the latter ship having newly arrived in the station from home where it had taken part in the Great Mutiny, danger was apprehended from the temper of the men; and it was thought that an officer like Nelson was the one, not indeed to terrorize the crew into base subjection, but to win them by force of his mere presence back to an allegiance, if not as enthusiastic as his own, yet as true. So it was that for a time on more than one quarter-deck anxiety did exist. At sea precautionary vigilance was strained against relapse. At short notice an engagement might come on. When it did, the lieutenants assigned to batteries felt it incumbent on them in some instances to stand with drawn swords behind the men working the guns.

But on board the seventy-four in which Billy now swung his hammock, very little in the manner of the men and nothing obvious in the demeanour of the officers would have suggested to an ordinary observer that the Great Mutiny was a recent event. In their general bearing and conduct the commissioned officers of a war-ship naturally take their tone from the commander, that is if he has that ascendency of character that ought to be his.

Captain the Honourable Edward Fairfax Vere, to give his full title, was a bachelor of forty or thereabouts, a sailor of distinction, even in a time prolific of renowned seamen. Though allied to the higher nobility, his advancement had not been altogether owing to influences connected with that circumstance. He had seen much service, been in various engagements, always acquitting himself as an officer mindful of the welfare of his men, but never tolerating an infraction of discipline; thoroughly versed in the science of his profession, and intrepid to the verge of temerity, though never injudiciously so. For his gallantry in the West Indian waters as flag-lieutenant under Rodney in that Admiral's crowning victory, over De Grasse, he was made a post-captain.

Ashore in the garb of a civilian, scarce any one would have taken him for a sailor, more especially that he never garnished unprofessional talk with nautical terms, and grave in his bearing, evinced little appreciation of mere humour. It was not out of keeping with these traits that on a passage when nothing demanded his paramount action, he was the most undemonstrative of men. Any landsman observing this gentleman not conspicuous by his stature and wearing no pronounced insignia, emerging from his retreat to the open deck, and noting the silent deference of the officers retiring to leeward, might have taken him for the King's guest, a civilian aboard the King's ship, some highly honourable discreet envoy on his way to an important post. But, in fact, this unobtrusiveness of demeanour may have proceeded from a certain unaffected modesty of manhood sometimes accompanying a resolute nature, a modesty evinced at all times not calling for pronounced action, and which shown in any rank of life suggests a virtue aristocratic in kind.

As with some others engaged in various departments of the world's more heroic activities, Captain Vere, though practical enough upon occasion, would at times betray a certain dreaminess of mood. Standing alone on the weather-side of the greater deck, one hand holding by the rigging, he would absently gaze off at the black sea. At the presentation to him then of some minor matter interrupting the current of his thoughts, he would show more or less irascibility; but instantly he would control it.

In the navy he was popularly known by the appellation—Starry Vere. How such a designation happened to fall upon one who, whatever his sturdy qualities, was without any brilliant ones, was in this wise: a favourite kinsman, Lord Denton, a free-handed fellow, had been the first to meet and congratulate him upon his return to England from the West Indian cruise; and but the day previous turning over a copy of Andrew Marvell's poems had lighted, not for the first time,

however, upon the lines entitled "Appleton House," the name of one of the seats of their common ancestor, a hero in the German wars of the seventeenth century, in which poem occur the lines,

> "*This 'tis to have been from the first*
> *In a domestic heaven nursed,*
> *Under the discipline severe*
> *Of Fairfax and the starry Vere.*"

And so, upon embracing his cousin fresh from Rodney's victory, wherein he had played so gallant a part, brimming over with just family pride in the sailor of their house, he exuberantly exclaimed, "Give ye joy, Ed; give ye joy, my starry Vere!" This got currency, and the novel prefix serving in familiar parlance readily to distinguish the *Indomitable's* Captain from another Vere, his senior, a distant relative, an officer of like rank in the navy, it remained permanently attached to the surname.

§ 6

In view of the part that the commander of the *Indomitable* plays in scenes shortly to follow, it may be well to fill out that sketch of him outlined in the previous chapter. Aside from his qualities as a sea-officer Captain Vere was an exceptional character. Unlike no few of England's renowned sailors, long and arduous service with signal devotion to it, had not resulted in absorbing and *salting* the entire man. He had a marked leaning towards everything intellectual. He loved books, never going to sea without a newly replenished library, compact but of the best. The isolated leisure, in some cases so wearisome, falling at intervals to commanders even during a war-cruise, never was tedious to Captain Vere. With nothing of that literary taste which less heeds the thing conveyed than the vehicle, his bias was towards those books to which every serious mind of superior order occupying any active post of authority in the world, naturally inclines; books treating of actual men and events, no matter of what era— history, biography and unconventional writers, who, free from cant and convention, like Montaigne, honestly, and in the spirit of common sense, philosophize upon realities.

In this love of reading he found confirmation of his own more reserved thoughts—confirmation which he had vainly sought in social converse, so that as touching most fundamental topics, there had got to be established in him some positive convictions which he forefelt would abide in him essentially unmodified so long as his intelligent part re-

mained unimpaired. In view of the humbled position in which his lot was cast, this was well for him. His settled convictions were as a dyke against those invading waters of novel opinion social, political, and otherwise, which carried away as in a torrent no few minds in those days, minds by nature not inferior to his own. While other members of that aristocracy to which by birth he belonged were incensed at the innovators mainly because their theories were inimical to the privileged classes, Captain Vere disinterestedly opposed them because they semed to him incapable of embodiment in lasting institutions, but at war with the peace of the world and the good of mankind.

With minds less stored than his and less earnest, some officers of his rank, with whom at times he would necessarily consort, found him lacking in the companionable quality, a dry and bookish gentleman as they deemed. Upon any chance withdrawal from their company one would be apt to say to another something like this: "Vere is a noble fellow, Starry Vere. 'Spite the gazettes, Sir Horatio is at bottom scarce a better seaman or fighter. But between you and me now, don't you think there is a queer streak of the pedantic running through him? Yes, like the King's yarn in a coil of navy-rope?"

Some apparent ground there was for this sort of confidential criticism; since not only did the Captain's discourse never fall into the jocosely familiar, but in illustrating any point touching the stirring personages and events of the time, he would cite some historic character or incident of antiquity with the same easy air that he would cite from the moderns. He seemed unmindful of the circumstance that to his bluff company such remote allusions, however pertinent they might really be, were altogether alien to men whose reading was mainly confined to the journals. But considerateness in such matters is not easy to natures constituted like Captain Vere's. Their honesty prescribes to them directness, sometimes far-reaching, like that of a migratory fowl that in its flight never heeds when it crosses a frontier.

§ 7

The lieutenants and other commissioned gentlemen forming Captain Vere's staff it is not necessary here to particularize nor needs it to make mention of any of the warrant-officers. But among the petty officers was one who, having much to do with the story, may as well be forthwith introduced. This portrait I essay, but shall never hit it.

This was John Claggart, the master-at-arms. But that sea-title may to landsmen seem somewhat equivocal. Originally, doubtless, that petty-officer's function was the instruction of the men in the use of

arms, sword, or cutlass. But very long ago, owing to the advance in gunnery making hand-to-hand encounters less frequent—and giving to nitre and sulphur the pre-eminence over steel—that function ceased; the master-at-arms of a great war-ship becoming a sort of Chief of Police charged, among other matters, with the duty of preserving order on the populous lower gun-decks.

Claggart was a man of about five-and-thirty, somewhat spare and tall yet of no ill figure upon the whole. His hand was too small and shapely to have been accustomed to hard toil. The face was a notable one; the features, all except the chin, cleanly cut as those on a Greek medallion; yet the chin, beardless as Tecumseh's, had something of the strange protuberant heaviness in its make that recalled the prints of the Rev. Dr. Titus Oates, the historical deponent with the clerical drawl in the time of Charles II, and the fraud of the alleged Popish Plot. It served Claggart in his office that his eye could cast a tutoring glance. His brow was of the sort phrenologically associated with more than average intellect; silken jet curls partly clustering over it, making a foil to the pallor below, a pallor tinged with a faint shade of amber akin to the hue of time-tinted marbles of old.

This complexion singularly contrasting with the red or deeply bronzed visages of the sailors, and in part the result of his official seclusion from the sunlight, though it was not exactly displeasing, nevertheless seemed to hint of something defective or abnormal in the constitution and blood. But his general aspect and manner were so suggestive of an education and career incongruous with his naval function, that when not actively engaged in it he looked like a man of high quality, social and moral, who for reasons of his own was keeping incog. Nothing was known of his former life. It might be that he was an Englishman; and yet there lurked a bit of accent in his speech suggesting that possibly he was not such by birth, but through naturalization in early childhood. Among certain grizzled sea-gossips of the gun-decks and forecastle went a rumour perdue that the master-at-arms was a chevalier who had volunteered into the King's navy by way of compounding for some mysterious swindle whereof he had been arraigned at the King's bench. The fact that nobody could substantiate this report was, of course, nothing against its secret currency. Such a rumour once started on the gun-decks in reference to almost any one below the rank of a commissioned officer would, during the period assigned to this narrative, have seemed not altogether wanting in credibility to the tarry old wiseacres of a man-of-war crew. And indeed a man of Claggart's accomplishments, without prior nautical experience entering the navy at mature life, as he did, and necessarily allotted at the start to the lowest grade in it; a man, too, who never

made allusion to his previous life ashore; these were circumstances which in the dearth of exact knowledge as to his true antecedents opened to the invidious a vague field for unfavourable surmise.

But the sailors' dog-watch gossip concerning him derived a vague plausibility from the fact that now, for some period, the British Navy could so little afford to be squeamish in the matter of keeping up the muster-rolls, that not only were press-gangs notoriously abroad both afloat and ashore, but there was little or no secret about another matter, namely, that the London police were at liberty to capture any able-bodied suspect, and any questionable fellow at large, and summarily ship him to the dock-yard or fleet. Furthermore, even among voluntary enlistments, there were instances where the motive thereto partook neither of patriotic impulse nor yet of a random desire to experience a bit of sea-life and martial adventure. Insolvent debtors of minor grade, together with the promiscuous lame ducks of morality, found in the navy a convenient and secure refuge. Secure, because once enlisted aboard a King's-Ship, they were as much in sanctuary, as the transgressor of the middle ages harbouring himself under the shadow of the altar. Such sanctioned irregularities, which for obvious reasons the Government would hardly think to parade at the time— and which consequently, and as affecting the least influential class of mankind, have all but dropped into oblivion—lends colour to something for the truth whereof I do not vouch, and hence have some scruple in stating; something I remember having seen in print, though the book I cannot recall; but the same thing was personally communicated to me now more than forty years ago by an old pensioner in a cocked hat, with whom I had a most interesting talk on the terrace at Greenwich, a Baltimore negro, a Trafalgar man. It was to this effect: In the case of a war-ship short of hands, whose speedy sailing was imperative, the deficient quota, in lack of any other way of making it good, would be eked out by drafts called direct from the jails. For reasons previously suggested it would not perhaps be very easy at the present day directly to prove or disprove the allegation. But allowed as a verity, how significant would it be of England's straits at the time, confronted by those wars which, like a flight of harpies, rose shrieking from the din and dust of the fallen Bastille. That era appears measurably clear to us who look back at it, and but read of it. But to the grandfathers of us greybeards, the thoughtful of them, the genius of it presented an aspect like that of Camoen's "Spirit of the Cape," an eclipsing menace, mysterious and prodigious. Not America even was exempt from apprehension. At the height of Napoleon's unexampled conquests, there were Americans who had fought at Bunker Hill, who looked forward to the possibility that the Atlantic might prove no

barrier against the ultimate schemes of this portentous upstart from the revolutionary chaos, who seemed in act of fulfilling the judgment prefigured in the Apocalypse.

But the less credence was to be given to the gun-deck talk touching Claggart, seeing that no man holding his office in a man-of-war can ever hope to be popular with the crew. Besides, in derogatory comments upon any one against whom they have a grudge, or for any reason or no reason mislike, sailors are much like landsmen: they are apt to exaggerate or romance it.

About as much was really known to the *Indomitable's* tars of the Master-at-arms' career before entering the service as an astronomer knows about a comet's travels prior to its first observable appearance in the sky. The verdict of the sea *guid nunc's* has been cited only by way of showing what sort of moral impression the man made upon rude uncultivated natures whose conceptions of human wickedness were necessarily of the narrowest, limited to ideas of vulgar rascality, —a thief among the swinging hammocks during a night-watch, or the man-brokers and land-sharks of the seaports.

It was no gossip, however, but fact, that though, as before hinted, Claggart upon his entrance into the navy was, as a novice, assigned to the least honourable section of a man-of-war's crew, embracing the drudges, he did not long remain there.

The superior capacity he immediately evinced, his constitutional sobriety, his ingratiating deference to superiors, together with a peculiar ferreting genius manifested on a singular occasion, all this capped by a certain austere patriotism, abruptly advanced him to the position of Master-at-arms.

Of this maritime Chief of Police the ship's-corporals, so called, were the immediate subordinates, and compliant ones; and this—as is to be noted in some business departments ashore—almost to a degree inconsistent with entire moral volition. His place put various converging wires of underground influence under the Chief's control, capable when astutely worked through his understrappers of operating to the mysterious discomfort, if nothing worse, of any of the sea-commonalty.

§ 8

Life in the foretop well agreed with Billy Budd. There, when not actually engaged on the yards yet higher aloft, the topmen, who as such had been picked out for youth and activity, constituted an aerial club, lounging at ease against the smaller stun'sails rolled up into cushions, spinning yarns like the lazy gods, and frequently amused

with what was going on in the busy world of the decks below. No
wonder then that a young fellow of Billy's disposition was well content
in such society. Giving no cause of offence to anybody, he was always
alert at a call. So in the merchant service it had been with him. But
now such punctiliousness in duty was shown that his topmates would
sometimes good-naturedly laugh at him for it. This heightened alacrity
had its cause, namely, the impression made upon him by the first
formal gangway-punishment he had ever witnessed, which befell the
day following his impressment. It had been incurred by a little fellow,
young, a novice, an after-guardsman absent from his assigned post
when the ship was being put about, a dereliction resulting in a rather
serious hitch to that manœuvre, one demanding instantaneous prompt-
itude in letting go and making fast. When Billy saw the culprit's naked
back under the scourge gridironed with red welts, and worse; when he
marked the dire expression in the liberated man's face, as with his
woolen shirt flung over him by the executioner, he rushed forward
from the spot to bury himself in the crowd, Billy was horrified. He re-
solved that never through remissness would he make himself liable to
such a visitation, or do or omit aught that might merit even verbal
reproof. What then was his surprise and concern when ultimately he
found himself getting into petty trouble occasionally about such matters
as the stowage of his bag, or something amiss in his hammock, matters
under the police oversight of the ship's-corporals of the lower decks,
and which brought down on him a vague threat from one of them.

So heedful in all things as he was, how could this be? He could not
understand it, and it more than vexed him. When he spoke to his
young topmates about it, they were either lightly incredulous, or found
something comical in his unconcealed anxiety. "Is it your bag, Billy?"
said one; "well, sew yourself up in it, Billy boy, and then you'll be
sure to know if anybody meddles with it."

Now there was a veteran aboard who, because his years began to
disqualify him for more active work, had been recently assigned duty as
mainmast-man in his watch, looking to the gear belayed at the rail
round about that great spar near the deck. At off-times the foretopman
had picked up some acquaintance with him, and now in his trouble it
occurred to him that he might be the sort of person to go to for wise
council. He was an old Dansker long anglicized in the service, of few
words, many wrinkles and some honourable scars. His wizened face,
time-tinted and weather-stormed to the complexion of an antique
parchment, was here and there peppered blue by the chance explosion
of a gun-cartridge in action. He was an *Agamemnon*-man; some two
years prior to the time of this story having served under Nelson, when
but Sir Horatio, in that ship immortal in naval memory, and which,

dismantled and in part broken up to her bare ribs, is seen a grand skeleton in Hayden's etching. As one of a boarding-party from the *Agamemnon* he had received a cut slantwise along one temple and cheek, leaving a long pale scar like a streak of dawn's light falling athwart the dark visage. It was on account of that scar and the affair in which it was known that he had received it, as well as from his blue-peppered complexion, that the Dansker went among the *Indomitable's* crew by the name of "Board-her-in-the-smoke."

Now the first time that his small weazel-eyes happened to light on Billy Budd, a certain grim internal merriment set all his ancient wrinkles into antic play. Was it that his eccentric unsentimental old sapience, primitive in its kind, saw, or thought it saw, something which in contrast with the war-ship's environment looked oddly incongruous in the Handsome Sailor? But after slyly studying him at intervals, the old Merlin's equivocal merriment was modified. For now when the twain would meet, it would start in his face a quizzing sort of look, but it would be but momentary, and sometimes replaced by an expression of speculative query as to what might eventually befall a nature like that, dropped into a world not without some man-traps and against whose subtleties simple courage lacking experience and address and without any touch of defensive ugliness, is of little avail; and where such innocence as man is capable of does yet, in a moral emergency, not always sharpen the faculties or enlighten the will.

However it was, the Dansker in his ascetic way rather took to Billy. Nor was this only because of a certain philosophic interest in such a character. There was another cause. While the old man's eccentricities, sometimes bordering on the ursine, repelled the juniors, Billy, un-deterred thereby, would make advances, never passing the old *Aga-memnon*-man without a salutation marked by that respect which is seldom lost on the aged, however crabbed at times, or whatever their station in life. There was a vein of dry humour, or what not, in the mast-man; and whether in freak of patriarchal irony touching Billy's youth and athletic frame, or for some other and more recondite reason, from the first in addressing him he always substituted Baby for Billy. The Dansker, in fact, being the originator of the name by which the foretopman eventually became known aboard ship.

Well then, in his mysterious little difficulty going in quest of the wrinkled one, Billy found him off duty in a dog-watch ruminating by himself, seated on a shot-box of the upper gun-deck, now and then surveying with a somewhat cynical regard certain of the more swag-gering promenaders there. Billy recounted his trouble, again wonder-ing how it all happened. The salt seer attentively listened, accom-panying the foretopman's recitals with queer twitchings of his wrinkles

and problematical little sparkles of his small ferret eyes. Making an end of his story, the foretopman asked, "And now, Dansker, do tell me what you think of it."

The old man, shoving up the front of his tarpaulin and deliberately rubbing the long slant scar at the point where it entered the thin hair, laconically said, "Baby Budd, *Jimmy Legs*" (meaning the master-at-arms) "is down on you."

"*Jimmy Legs!*" ejaculated Billy his welkin eyes expanding; "what for? Why he calls me *the sweet and pleasant young fellow*, they tell me."

"Does he so?" grinned the grizzled one; then said, "Ay, Baby Lad, a sweet voice has *Jimmy Legs*."

"No, not always. But to me he has. I seldom pass him but there comes a pleasant word."

"And that's because he's down upon you, Baby Budd."

Such reiteration, along with the manner of it (incomprehensible to a novice), disturbed Billy almost as much as the mystery for which he had sought explanation. Something less unpleasingly oracular he tried to extract. But the old sea-chiron, thinking perhaps that for the nonce he had sufficiently instructed his young Achilles, pursed his lips, gathered all his wrinkles together, and would commit himself to nothing further.

Years, and those experiences which befall certain shrewder men subordinated life-long to the will of superiors, all this had developed in the Dansker the pithy guarded cynicism that was his leading characteristic.

§ 9

The next day an incident served to confirm Billy Budd in his incredulity as to the Dansker's strange summing up of the case submitted.

The ship at noon going large before the wind was rolling on her course, and he, below at dinner and engaged in some sportful talk with the members of his mess, chanced in a sudden lurch to spill the entire contents of his soup-pan upon the new scrubbed deck. Claggart, the master-at-arms, official rattan in hand, happened to be passing along the battery, in a bay of which the mess was lodged, and the greasy liquid streamed just across his path. Stepping over it, he was proceeding on his way without comment, since the matter was nothing to take notice of under the circumstances, when he happened to observe who it was that had done the spilling. His countenance changed. Pausing, he was about to ejaculate something hasty at the

sailor, but checked himself, and pointing down to the streaming soup, playfully tapped him from behind with his rattan, saying, in a low musical voice, peculiar to him at times, "Handsomely done, my lad! And handsome is as handsome did it, too!" and with that passed on. Not noted by Billy as not coming within his view was the involuntary smile, or rather grimace, that accompanied Claggart's equivocal words. Aridly it drew down the thin corners of his shapely mouth. But everybody taking his remark as meant for humorous, and at which therefore as coming from a superior they were bound to laugh, "with counterfeited glee" acted accordingly; and Billy tickled, it may be, by the allusion to his being the handsome sailor, merrily joined in; then addressing his messmates exclaimed, "There now, who says that Jimmy Legs is down on me!"

"And who said he was, Beauty?" demanded one Donald with some surprise. Whereat the foretopman looked a little foolish, recalling that it was only one person, Board-her-in-the-smoke, who had suggested what to him was the smoky idea that this master-at-arms was in any peculiar way hostile to him. Meantime that functionary resuming his path must have momentarily worn some expression less guarded than that of the bitter smile and, usurping the face from the heart, some distorting expression perhaps—for a drummer-boy, heedlessly frolicking along from the opposite direction, and chancing to come into light collision with his person was strangely disconcerted by his aspect. Nor was the impression lessened when the official, impulsively giving him a sharp cut with the rattan, vehemently exclaimed, "Look where you go!"

§ 10

What was the matter with the Master-at-arms? And, be the matter what it might, how could it have direct relation to Billy Budd, with whom prior to the affair of the spilled soup he had never come into any special contact, official or otherwise? What indeed could the trouble have to do with one so little inclined to give offence as the merchant-ship's *peacemaker,* even him who in Claggart's own phrase was "The sweet and pleasant young fellow"? Yes, why should *Jimmy Legs,* to borrow the Dansker's expression, be *down* on the Handsome Sailor?

But at heart and not for nothing, as the late chance encounter may indicate to the discerning, down on him, secretly down on him, he assuredly was.

Now to invent something touching the more private career of Claggart—something involving Billy Budd, of which something the

latter should be wholly ignorant, some romantic incident implying that Claggart's knowledge of the young blue-jacket began at some period anterior to catching sight of him on board the seventy-four—all this, not so difficult to do, might avail in a more or less interesting way to account for whatever enigma may appear to lurk in the case. But, in fact, there was nothing of the sort. And yet the cause, necessarily to be assumed as the sole one assignable, is in its very realism as much charged with that prime element of Radcliffian romance, *the mysterious,* as any that the ingenuity of the author of the "Mysteries of Udolpho" could devise. For what can more partake of the mysterious than an antipathy spontaneous and profound such as is evoked in certain exceptional mortals by the mere aspect of some other mortal, however harmless he may be?—if not called forth by that very harmlessness itself.

Now there can exist no irritating juxtaposition of dissimilar personalities comparable to that which is possible aboard a great warship fully manned and at sea. There, every day, among all ranks, almost every man comes into more or less of contact with almost every other man. Wholly there to avoid even the sight of an aggravating object one must needs give it Jonah's toss, or jump overboard himself. Imagine how all this might eventually operate on some peculiar human creature the direct reverse of a saint?

But for the adequate comprehending of Claggart by a normal nature, these hints are insufficient. To pass from a normal nature to him one must cross "The deadly space between," and this is best done by indirection.

Long ago an honest scholar, my senior, said to me in reference to one who like himself is now no more, a man so unimpeachably respectable that against him nothing was ever openly said, though among the few something was whispered, "Yes, X—— is a nut not to be cracked by the tap of a lady's fan. You are aware that I am the adherent of no organized religion, much less of any philosophy built into a system. Well, for all that, I think that to try and get into X——, enter his labyrinth and get out again, without a clue derived from some source other than what is known as *knowledge of the world*—that were hardly possible, at least for me."

"Why," said I, "X——, however singular a study to some, is yet human, and knowledge of the world assuredly implies the knowledge of human nature, and in most of its varieties."

"Yes, but a superficial knowledge of it, serving ordinary purposes. But for anything deeper, I am not certain whether to know the world and to know human nature be not two distinct branches of knowledge, which while they may co-exist in the same heart, yet either may exist

with little or nothing of the other. Nay, in an average man of the world, his constant rubbing with it blunts that fine spiritual insight indispensable to the understanding of the essential in certain exceptional characters, whether evil ones or good. In a matter of some importance I have seen a girl wind an old lawyer about her little finger. Nor was it the dotage of senile love. Nothing·of the sort. But he knew law better than he knew the girl's heart. Coke and Blackstone hardly shed so much light into obscure spiritual places as the Hebrew prophets. And who were they? Mostly recluses."

At the time my inexperience was such that I did not quite see the drift of all this. It may be that I see it now. And, indeed, if that lexicon which is based on Holy Writ were any longer popular, one might with less difficulty define and denominate certain phenomenal men. . . . As it is, one must turn to some authority not liable to the charge of being tinctured with the Biblical element.

In a list of definitions included in the authentic translation of Plato, a list attributed to him, occurs this: "Natural Depravity: a depravity according to nature." A definition which though savouring of Calvinism by no means involves Calvin's dogma as to total mankind. Evidently its intent makes it applicable but to individuals. Not many are the examples of this depravity which the gallows and jail supply. At any rate, for notable instances,—since these have no vulgar alloy of the brute in them, but invariably are dominated by intellectuality,— one must go elsewhere. Civilization, especially if of the austerer sort, is auspicious to it. It folds itself in the mantle of respectability. It has its certain negative virtues serving as silent auxiliaries. It never allows wine to get within its guard. It is not going too far to say that it is without vices or small sins. There is a phenomenal pride in it that excludes them from anything. Never mercenary or avaricious. In short, the depravity here meant partakes nothing of the sordid or sensual. It is serious, but free from acerbity. Though no flatterer of mankind it never speaks ill of it.

But the thing which in eminent instances signalizes so exceptional a nature is this: though the man's even temper and discreet bearing would seem to intimate a mind peculiarly subject to the law of reason, not the less in his soul's recesses he would seem to riot in complete exemption from that law, having apparently little to do with reason further than to employ it as an ambidexter implement for effecting the irrational. That is to say: towards the accomplishment of an aim which in wantonness of malignity would seem to partake of the insane, he will direct a cool judgment sagacious and sound.

These men are true madmen, and of the most dangerous sort, for their lunacy is not continuous, but occasional; evoked by some special

object; it is secretive and self-contained: so that when most active it is, to the average mind, not distinguished from sanity, and for the reason above suggested that whatever its aims may be (and the aim is never disclosed) the method and the outward proceeding is always perfectly rational.

Now something such was Claggart, in whom was the mania of an evil nature, not engendered by vicious training or corrupting books or licentious living, but born with him and innate, in short, "a depravity according to nature."

Can it be this phenomenon, disowned or not acknowledged, that in some criminal cases puzzles the courts? For this cause have our juries at times not only to endure the prolonged contentions of lawyers with their fees, but also the yet more perplexing strife of the medical experts with theirs? And why leave it to them? Why not subpoena as well the clerical proficients? Their vocation bringing them into peculiar contact with so many human beings, and sometimes in their least guarded hour, in interviews very much more confidential than those of physician and patient; this would seem to qualify them to know something about those intricacies involved in the question of moral responsibility; whether in a given case, say, the crime proceeded from manis in the brain or rabies of the heart. As to any differences among themselves which clerical proficients might develop on the stand, these could hardly be greater than the direct contradictions exchanged between the remunerated medical experts.

Dark sayings are these, some will say. But why? It is because they somewhat savour of Holy Writ in its phrase "mysteries of iniquity."

The point of the story turning on the hidden nature of the Master-at-arms has necessitated this chapter. With an added hint or two in connection with the incident at the mess, the resumed narrative must be left to vindicate as it may, its own credibility.

§ 11

(Pale ire, envy and despair)

That Claggart's figure was not amiss, and his face, save the chin, well moulded, has already been said. Of these favourable points he seemed not insensible, for he was not only neat but careful in his dress. But the form of Billy Budd was heroic; and if his face was without the intellectual look of the pallid Claggart's, not the less was it lit, like his, from within, though from a different source. The bonfire in his heart made luminous the rose-tan in his cheek.

In view of the marked contrast between the persons of the twain, it is more than probable that when the Master-at-arms in the scene last given applied to the sailor the proverb *Handsome is as handsome does* he there let escape an ironic inkling, not caught by the young sailors who heard it, as to what it was that had first moved him against Billy, namely, his significant personal beauty.

Now envy and antipathy, passions irreconcilable in reason, nevertheless in fact may spring conjoined like Chang and Eng in one birth. Is Envy then such a monster? Well, though many an arraigned mortal has in hopes of mitigated penalty pleaded guilty to horrible actions, did ever anybody seriously confess to envy? Something there is in it universally felt to be more shameful than even felonious crime. And not only does everybody disown it, but the better sort are inclined to incredulity when it is in earnest imputed to an intelligent man. But since its lodgment is in the heart, not the brain, no degree of intellect supplies a guarantee against it. But Claggart's was no vulgar form of the passion. Nor, as directed toward Billy Budd, did it partake of that streak of apprehensive jealousy which marred Saul's visage perturbedly brooding on the comely young David. Claggart's envy struck deeper. If askance he eyed the good looks, cheery health and frank enjoyment of young life in Billy Budd, it was because these happened to go along with a nature that, as Claggart magnetically felt, had in its simplicity never willed malice or experienced the reactionary bite of that serpent. To him, the spirit lodged within Billy, and looking out from his welkin eyes as from windows—that ineffability it was which made the dimple in his dyed cheeks, suppled his joints, and dancing in his yellow curls made him pre-eminently the Handsome Sailor. One person excepted, the Master-at-arms was perhaps the only man in the ship intellectually capable of adequately appreciating the moral phenomenon presented in Billy Budd, and the insight but intensified his passion, which, assuming various secret forms within him, at times assumed that of cynic disdain—disdain of innocence. To be nothing more than innocent! Yet in an æsthetic way he saw the charm of it, the courageous free-and-easy temper of it, and fain would have shared it, but he despaired of it.

With no power to annul the elemental evil in himself, though readily enough he could hide it; apprehending the good, but powerless to be it; a nature like Claggart's, surcharged with energy as such natures almost invariably are, what recourse is left to it but to recoil upon itself and like the scorpion for which the Creator alone is responsible, act out to the end the part allotted it.

Passion, and passion in its profoundest, is not a thing demanding a palatial stage whereon to play its part. Down among the groundlings,

among the beggars and rakers of the garbage, profound passion is enacted. And the circumstances that provoke it, however trivial or mean, are no measure of its power. In the present instance the stage is a scrubbed gun-deck, and one of the external provocations a man-of-war's man's spilled soup.

Now when the Master-at-arms noticed whence came that greasy fluid streaming before his feet, he must have taken it—to some extent wilfully perhaps—not for the mere accident it assuredly was, but for the sly escape of a spontaneous feeling on Billy's part more or less answering to the antipathy on his own. In effect a foolish demonstration he must have thought, and very harmless, like the futile kick of a heifer, which yet were the heifer a shod stallion would not be so harmless. Even so was it that into the gall of envy Claggart infused the vitriol of his contempt. But the incident confirmed to him certain tell-tale reports purveyed to his ear by *Squeak,* one of his more cunning corporals, a grizzled little man, so nicknamed by the sailors on account of his squeaky voice and sharp visage ferreting about the dark corners of the lower decks after interlopers, satirically suggesting to them the idea of a rat in a cellar.

Now his chief's employing him as an implicit tool in laying little traps for the worriment of the foretopman—for it was from the Master-at-arms that the petty persecutions heretofore adverted to had proceeded—the corporal, having naturally enough concluded that his master could have no love for the sailor, made it his business, faithful understrapper that he was, to ferment the ill blood by perverting to his chief certain innocent frolics of the good-natured foretopman, besides inventing for his master sundry contumelious epithets he claimed to have overheard him let fall. The Master-at-arms never suspected the veracity of these reports, more especially as to the epithets, for he well knew how secretly unpopular may become a Master-at-arms—at least a Master-at-arms of those days, zealous in his function—how the blue-jackets shot at him in private their raillery and wit; the nickname by which he goes among them (*Jimmy Legs*) implying under the form of merriment their cherished disrespect and dislike.

But in view of the greediness of hate for provocation, it hardly needed a purveyor to feed Claggart's passion. An uncommon prudence is habitual with the subtler depravity, for it has everything to hide. And in case of any merely suspected injury its secretiveness voluntarily cuts it off from enlightenment or disillusion; and not unreluctantly, action is taken upon surmise as upon certainty. And the retaliation is apt to be in monstrous disproportion to the supposed offence; for when in anybody was revenge in its exactions aught else but an inordinate usurer? But how with Claggart's conscience? For

though consciences are unlike as foreheads, every intelligence, not including the Scriptural devils who "believe and tremble," has one. But Claggart's conscience being but the lawyer to his will, made ogres of trifles, probably arguing that the motive imputed to Billy in spilling the soup just when he did, together with the epithets alleged—these, if nothing more, made a strong case against him; nay, justified animosity into a sort of retributive righteousness. The Pharisee is the Guy Fawkes prowling in the hid chambers underlying some natures like Claggart's. And they can really form no conception of an unreciprocated malice. Probably, the Master-at-arms' clandestine persecutions of Billy were started to try the temper of the man; but they had not developed any quality in him that enmity could make official use of, or ever pervert into even plausible self-justification; so that the occurrence at the mess, petty if it were, was a welcome one to that peculiar conscience assigned to be the private mentor of Claggart; and for the rest, not improbably it put him upon new experiments.

§ 12

Not many days after the last incident narrated, something befell Billy Budd that more gravelled him than aught that had previously occurred.

It was a warm night for the latitude; and the foretopman, whose watch at the time was properly below, was dozing on the uppermost deck whither he had ascended from his hot hammock—one of hundreds suspended so closely wedged together over a lower gun-deck that there was little or no swing to them. He lay as in the shadow of a hill-side stretched under the lee of the *booms,* a piled ridge of spare spars, and among which the ship's largest boat, the launch, was stowed. Alongside of three other slumberers from below, he lay near one end of the booms which approached from the foremast; his station aloft on duty as a foretopman being just over the deck station of the forecastlemen entitling him according to usage to make himself more or less at home in that neighbourhood.

Presently he was stirred into semi-consciousness by somebody, who must have previously sounded the sleep of the others, touching his shoulder, and then as the foretopman raised his head, breathing into his ear in a quick whisper, "Slip into the lee fore-chains, Billy; there is something in the wind—don't speak. Quick. I will meet you there;" and disappeared.

Now Billy—like sundry other essentially good-natured ones—had some of the weakness inseparable from essential good nature; and

among these was a reluctance, almost an incapacity of plumply saying *no* to an abrupt proposition not obviously absurd, on the face of it, nor obviously unfriendly, nor iniquitous. And being of warm blood he had not the phlegm to negative any proposition by unresponsive inaction. Like his sense of fear, his apprehension as to aught outside of the honest and natural was seldom very quick. Besides, upon the present occasion, the drowse from his sleep still hung upon him.

However it was, he mechanically rose and, sleepily wondering what could be *in the wind,* betook himself to the designated place, a narrow platform, one of six, outside of the high bulwarks and screened by the great dead-eyes and multiple columned lanyards of the shrouds and back-stays; and, in a great war-ship of that time, of dimensions commensurate to the ample hull's magnitude; a tarry balcony, in short, overhanging the sea, and so secluded that one mariner of the *Indomitable,* a non-conformist old tar of serious turn, made it even in daytime his private oratory.

In this retired nook the stranger soon joined Billy Budd. There was no moon as yet; a haze obscured the star-light. He could not distinctly see the stranger's face. Yet from something in the outline and carriage, Billy took him to be, and correctly, for one of the afterguard.

"Hist Billy!" said the man; in the same quick cautionary whisper as before; "You were impressed, weren't you? Well, so was I;" and he paused as to mark the effect. But Billy, not knowing exactly what to make of this, said nothing. Then the other: "We are not the only impressed ones, Billy. There's a gang of us. Couldn't you—help—at a pinch?"

"What do you mean?" demanded Billy here shaking off his drowse.

"Hist, hist!" the hurried whisper now growing husky, "see here;" and the man held up two small objects faintly twinkling in the night light; "See, they are yours, Bill, if you'll only—"

But Billy here broke in, and in his resentful eagerness to deliver himself his vocal infirmity somewhat intruded; "D-D-Damme, I don't know what you are d-driving at, or what you mean, but you had better g-g-go where you belong!" For the moment the fellow, as confounded, did not stir; and Billy, springing to his feet, said, "If you d-don't start, I'll t-t-toss you back over the r-rail!" There was no mistaking this, and the mysterious emissary decamped, disappearing in the direction of the mainmast in the shadow of the booms.

"Hallo, what's the matter?" here came growling from a forecastle-man awakened from his deck-doze by Billy's raised voice. And as the foretopman reappeared and was recognized by him; "Ah, *Beauty,* is it you? Well, something must have been the matter for you st-st-stuttered."

"Oh," rejoined Billy, now mastering the impediment; "I found an afterguardsman in our part of the ship here and I bid him be off where he belongs."

"And is that all you did about it, foretopman?" gruffly demanded another, an irascible old fellow of brick-coloured visage and hair, and who was known to his associate forecastlemen as *Red Pepper.*

"Such sneaks I should like to marry to the gunner's daughter!" by that expression meaning that he would like to subject them to disciplinary castigation over a gun.

However, Billy's rendering of the matter satisfactorily accounted to these inquirers for the brief commotion, since of all the sections of a ship's company the forcastlemen, veterans for the most part, and bigoted in their sea-prejudices, are the most jealous in resenting territorial encroachments, especially on the part of any of the after guard, of whom they have but a sorry opinion, chiefly landsmen, never going aloft except to reef or furl the mainsail, and in no wise competent to handle a marlingspike or turn in a *dead-eye,* say.

§ 13

This incident sorely puzzled Billy Budd. It was an entirely new experience—the first time in his life that he had ever been personally approached in underhanded intriguing fashion. Prior to this encounter he had known nothing of the afterguardsman, the two men being stationed wide apart, one forward and aloft during his watch, the other on deck and aft.

What could it mean? And could they really be guineas, those two glittering objects the interloper had held up to his (Billy's) eyes? Where could the fellow get guineas? Why, even buttons, spare buttons, are not so plentiful at sea. The more he turned the matter over, the more he was nonplussed, and made uneasy and discomfited. In his disgustful recoil from an overture which, though he but ill comprehended, he instinctively knew must involve evil of some sort—Billy Budd was like a young horse fresh from the pasture suddenly inhaling a vile whiff from some chemical factory and by repeated snortings trying to get it out of his nostrils and lungs. This frame of mind barred all desire of holding further parley with the fellow, even were it but for the purpose of gaining some enlightenment as to his design in approaching him. And yet he was not without natural curiosity to see how such a visitor in the dark would look in broad day.

He espied him the following afternoon in his first dog-watch below, one of the smokers on that forward part of the upper gun-deck allotted

to the pipe. He recognized him by his general cut and build, more than by his round freckled face and glassy eyes of pale blue, veiled with lashes all but white. And yet Billy was a bit uncertain whether indeed it were he—yonder chap about his own age, chatting and laughing in a free-hearted way, leaning against a gun,—a genial young fellow enough to look at, and something of a rattle-brain, to all appearance. Rather chubby, too, for a sailor, even an afterguardsman. In short the last man in the world—one would think—to be overburthened with thoughts, especially those perilous thoughts that must needs belong to a conspirator in any serious project, or even to the underling of such a conspirator.

Although Billy was not aware of it, the fellow, with one sidelong watchful glance had perceived Billy first, and then noting that Billy was looking at him, thereupon nodded a familiar sort of friendly recognition as to an old acquaintance, without interrupting the talk he was engaged in with the group of smokers. A day or two afterwards, chancing in the evening promenade on a gun-deck, to pass Billy, he offered a flying word of good-fellowship, as it were, which by its unexpectedness, and equivocalness under the circumstances, so embarrassed Billy that he knew not how to respond to it, and let it go unnoticed.

Billy was now left more at a loss than before. The ineffectual speculations into which he was led were so disturbingly alien to him that he did his best to smother them. It never entered his mind that here was a matter, which, from its extreme questionableness, it was his duty as a loyal blue-jacket to report in the proper quarter. And, probably, had such a step been suggested to him, he would have been deterred from taking it by the thought—one of novice-magnanimity—that it would savour overmuch of the dirty work of a tell-tale. He kept the thing to himself. Yet upon one occasion he could not forbear a little disburthening himself to the old Dansker, tempted thereto perhaps by the influence of a balmy night when the ship lay becalmed; the twain, silent for the most part, sitting together on deck, their heads propped against the bulwarks. But it was only a partial and anonymous account that Billy gave—the unfounded scruples above referred to preventing full disclosure to anybody. Upon hearing Billy's version, the sage Dansker seemed to divine more than he was told; and after a little meditation, during which his wrinkles were pursed as into a point— quite effacing for the time that quizzing expression his face sometimes wore—answered: "Didn't I say so, Baby Budd?"

"Say what?" demanded Billy.

"Why, *Jimmy Legs* is *down* on you."

"And what," rejoined Billy in amazement, "has *Jimmy Legs* to do with that cracked afterguardsman?"

"Ho, it was an afterguardsman, then: a cat's-paw, only a cat's-paw!" And with that exclamation, which, whether it had reference to a light puff of air just then coming over the calm sea, or subtler relation to the afterguardsman, there is no telling. The old Merlin gave a twisting wrench with his black teeth at his plug of tobacco—vouchsafing no reply to Billy's impetuous question, though now repeated, for it was his wont to relapse into grim silence when interrogated in sceptical sort as to any of his sententious oracles, not always very clear ones, but rather partaking of that obscurity which invests most Delphic deliverances from any quarter.

§ 14

Long experience had very likely brought this old man to that bitter prudence which never interferes in aught, and never gives advice.

Yes, despite the Dansker's pithy insistence as to the Master-at-arms being at the bottom of these strange experiences of Billy on board the *Indomitable,* the young sailor was ready to ascribe them to almost anybody but the man who, to use Billy's own expression, "always had a pleasant word for him." This is to be wondered at. Yet not so much to be wondered at. In certain matters, some sailors even in mature life, remain unsophisticated enough. But a young seafarer of the disposition of our athletic foretopman is yet very much of a child-man. And yet a child's utter innocence is but its blank ignorance, and the innocence more or less wanes as intelligence waxes. But in Billy Budd intelligence, such as it was, had advanced, while yet his simple-mindedness remained for the most part unaffected. Experience is a teacher indeed; yet did Billy's years make his experience small. Besides, he had none of that intuitive knowledge of the bad which in natures not good or incompletely so, foreruns experience, and therefore may pertain, as in some instances it too clearly does pertain, even to youth.

And what could Billy know of man except of man as a mere sailor? And the old-fashioned sailor, the veritable man-before-the-mast—the sailor from boyhood up—he, though indeed of the same species as a landsman, is in some respects singularly distinct from him. The sailor is frankness, the landsman is finesse. Life is not a game with the sailor, demanding the long head; no intricate game of chess where few moves are made in straightforwardness, and ends are attained by indirection; an oblique, tedious, barren game hardly worth that poor candle burnt out in playing it.

Yes, as a class, sailors are in character a juvenile race. Even their deviations are marked by juvenility. And this more especially holding true with the sailors of Billy's time. Then, too, certain things which apply to all sailors, do more pointedly operate here and there upon the junior one. Every sailor, too, is accustomed to obey orders without debating them; his life afloat is externally ruled for him; he is not brought into that promiscuous commerce with mankind where unobstructed free agency on equal terms—equal superficially, at least—soon teaches one that unless upon occasion he exercises a distrust keen in proportion to the fairness of the appearance, some foul turn may be served him. A ruled, undemonstrative distrustfulness is so habitual, not with business-men so much, as with men who know their kind in less shallow relations than business, namely certain men-of-the-world, that they come at last to employ it all but unconsciously; and some of them would very likely feel real surprise at being charged with it as one of their general characteristics.

§ 15

But after the little matter at the mess Billy Budd no more found himself in strange trouble at times about his hammock or his clothes-bag, or what not. While, as to that smile that occasionally sunned him, and the pleasant passing word: these were, if not more frequent, yet if anything more pronounced than before.

But for all that, there were certain other demonstrations now. When Claggart's unobserved glance happened to light on belted Billy rolling along the upper gun-deck in the leisure of the second dog-watch, exchanging passing broadsides of fun with other young promenaders in the crowd; that glance would follow the cheerful Sea Hyperion with a settled meditative and melancholy expression—his eyes strangely suffused with incipient feverish tears. Then would Claggart look like the man of sorrows. Yes, and sometimes the melancholy expression would have in it a touch of soft yearning, as if Claggart could even have loved Billy but for fate and ban. But this was an evanescence, and quickly repented of, as it were, by an immitigable look, pinching and shrivelling the visage into the momentary semblance of a wrinkled walnut. But sometimes, catching sight in advance of the foretopman coming in his direction, he would, upon their nearing, step aside a little to let him pass, dwelling upon Billy for the moment with the glittering dental satire of a Guise. Yet, upon an abrupt unforeseen encounter, a red light would flash forth from his eye, like a spark from an anvil in a dusky smithy. That quick fierce light was a strange one,

darted from orbs which in repose were of a colour nearest approaching
a deeper violet, the softest of shades.

Though some of these caprices of the pit could not but be observed
by their object, yet were they beyond the construing of such a nature.
And the thews of Billy were hardly comparable with that sort of sen-
sitive spiritual organization which in some cases instinctively conveys to
ignorant innocence an admonition of the proximity of the malign. He
thought the Master-at-arms acted in a manner rather queer at times.
That was all. But the occasional frank air and pleasant word went for
what they purported to be—the young sailor never having heard as
yet of the "too fair-spoken man."

Had the foretopman been conscious of having done or said anything
to provoke the ill will of the official, it would have been different with
him, and his sight might have been purged if not sharpened.

So was it with him in yet another matter. Two minor officers, the
Armourer, and Captain of the Hold, with whom he had never ex-
changed a word, his position on the ship not bringing him into contact
with them; these men now for the first began to cast upon Billy—
when they chanced to encounter him—that peculiar glance which
evidences that the man from whom it comes has been some way tam-
pered with, and to the prejudice of him upon whom the glance lights.
Never did it occur to Billy as a thing to be noted, or a thing suspicious
—though he well knew the fact that the Armourer and Captain of the
Hold, with the ship's yeoman, apothecary, and others of that grade,
were by naval usage, mess-mates of the Master-at-arms; men with
ears convenient to his confidential tongue.

But the general popularity that our Handsome Sailor's manly for-
wardness upon occasion, and irresistible good nature, indicating no
mental superiority tending to excite an invidious feeling; this good
will on the part of most of his ship-mates made him the less to concern
himself about such mute aspects toward him as those whereto allusion
has just been made.

As to the afterguardsman, though Billy for reasons already given,
necessarily saw little of him, yet when the two did happen to meet,
invariably came the fellow's off-hand cheerful recognition, sometimes
accompanied by a passing pleasant word or two. Whatever that
equivocal young person's original design may really have been, or the
design of which he might have been the deputy, certain it was from
his manner upon these occasions, that he had wholly dropped it.

It was as if his precocity of crookedness (and every vulgar villain is
precocious) had for once deceived him, and the man he had sought to
entrap as a simpleton had, through his very simplicity, baffled him.

But shrewd ones may opine that it was hardly possible for Billy to

refrain from going up to the afterguardsman and bluntly demanding to know his purpose in the initial interview, so abruptly closed in the fore-chains. Shrewd ones may also think it but natural in Billy to set about sounding some of the other impressed men of the ship in order to discover what basis, if any, there was for the emissary's obscure suggestions as to plotting disaffection aboard. The shrewd may so think. But something more, or rather, something else than mere shrewdness is perhaps needful for the due understanding of such a character as Billy Budd's.

As to Claggart, the monomania in the man—if that indeed it were —as involuntarily disclosed by stars in the manifestations detailed, yet in general covered over by his self-contained and rational demeanour; this, like a subterranean fire was eating its way deeper and deeper in him. Something decisive must come of it.

§ 16

After the mysterious interview in the fore-chains—the one so abruptly ended there by Billy—nothing especially germane to the story occurred until the events now about to be narrated.

Elsewhere it has been said that owing to the lack of frigates (of course better sailors than line-of-battle ships) in the English squadron up the Straits at that period, the *Indomitable* was occasionally employed not only as an available substitute for a scout, but at times on detached service of more important kind. This was not alone because of her sailing qualities, not common in a ship of her rate, but quite as much, probably, that the character of her commander—it was thought—specially adapted him for any duty where, under unforeseen difficulties, a prompt initiative might have to be taken in some matter demanding knowledge and ability in addition to those qualities employed in good seamanship. It was on an expedition of the latter sort, a somewhat distant one, and when the *Indomitable* was almost at her furthest remove from the fleet, that in the latter part of an afternoon-watch she unexpectedly came in sight of a ship of the enemy. It proved to be a frigate. The latter—perceiving through the glass that the weight of men and metal would be heavily against her—invoking her light heels, crowded on sail to get away. After a chase urged almost against hope—and lasting until about the middle of the first dog-watch she signally succeeded in effecting her escape.

Not long after the pursuit had been given up, and ere the excitement incident thereto had altogether waned away, the Master-at-arms, ascending from his cavernous sphere, made his appearance (cap in

hand) by the mainmast: respectfully awaiting the notice of Captain Vere—then solitary walking the weather-side of the quarter-deck— doubtless somewhat chafed at the failure of the pursuit. The spot where Claggart stood was the place allotted to the men of lesser grades when seeking some more particular interview either with the officer-of-the-deck or the Captain himself. But from the latter it was not often that a sailor or petty-officer of those days would seek a hearing; only some exceptional cause, would, according to established custom, have warranted that.

Presently, just as the Commander, absorbed in his reflections, was on the point of turning aft in his promenade, he became sensible of Claggart's presence, and saw the doffed cap held in deferential expectancy. Here be it said the Captain Vere's personal knowledge of this petty-officer had only begun at the time of the ship's last sailing from home, Claggart then for the first, in transfer from a ship detained for repairs, supplying on board the *Indomitable* the place of a previous Master-at-arms disabled and ashore.

No sooner did the Commander observe who it was that now so deferentially stood awaiting his notice, than a peculiar expression came over him. It was not unlike that which uncontrollably will flit across the countenance of one at unawares encountering a person, who, though known to him, indeed, has hardly been long enough known for thorough knowledge, but something in whose aspect nevertheless now, for the first time, provokes a vaguely repellent distaste. Coming to a stand and resuming much of his wonted official manner, save that a sort of impatience lurked in the intonation of the opening word, he said, "Well? what is it, Master-at-arms?"

With the air of a subordinate grieved at the necessity of being a messenger of ill tidings, and while conscientiously determined to be frank, yet equally resolved upon shunning overstatement, Claggart at this invitation, or rather summons to disburthen, spoke up. What he said, conveyed in the language of no uneducated man, was to the effect following if not altogether in these words, namely, that during the chase and preparations for the possible encounter he had seen enough to convince him that at least one sailor aboard was a dangerous character in a ship mustering some who not only had taken a guilty part in the late serious trouble, but others also who, like the man in question, had entered His Majesty's service under another form than enlistment.

At this point Captain Vere, with some impatience, interrupted him: "Be direct, man; say impressed men."

Claggart made a gesture of subservience and proceeded. Quite lately he (Claggart) had begun to suspect that some sort of movement

prompted by the sailor in question was covertly going on, but he had not thought himself warranted in reporting the suspicion so long as it remained indistinct. But from what he had that afternoon observed in the man referred to, the suspicion of something clandestine going on had advanced to a point less removed from certainty. He deeply felt— he added—the serious responsibility assumed in making a report involving such possible consequences to the individual mainly concerned, besides tending to augment those natural anxieties which every naval commander must feel in view of the extraordinary outbreak so recent as those which, he sorrowfully said it, it needed not to name.

Now at the first broaching of the matter Captain Vere, taken by surprise, could not wholly dissemble his disquietude, but as Claggart went on, the former's aspect changed into restiveness under something in the testifier's manner in giving his testimony. However, he refrained from interrupting him. And Claggart, continuing, concluded with this:

"God forbid, your honour, that the *Indomitable's* should be the experience of the—"

"Never mind that!" here peremptorily broke in the superior, his face altering with anger instantly, divining the ship that the other was about to name, one in which the Nore Mutiny assumed a singularly tragical character that for a time jeopardized the life of its Commander. Under the circumstances he was indignant at the purposed allusion. When the commissioned officers themselves were on all occasions very heedful how they referred to the recent events,—for a petty-officer unnecessarily to allude to them in the presence of his Captain, this struck him as a most immodest presumption. Besides, to his quick sense of self-respect, it even looked under the circumstances something like an attempt to alarm him. Nor at that was he without some surprise that one who, so far as he had hitherto come under his notice, had shown considerable tact in his function, should in this particular evince such lack of it.

But these thoughts and kindred dubious ones flitting across his mind were suddenly replaced by an intuitional surmise, which though as yet obscure in form, served practically to affect his reception of the ill tidings. Certain it is that, long versed in everything pertaining to the complicated gun-deck life (which like every other form of life has its secret mines and dubious side; the side popularly disclaimed), Captain Vere did not permit himself to be unduly disturbed by the general tenor of his subordinate's report. Furthermore, if in view of recent events prompt action should be taken at the first palpable sign of recurring insubordination—for all that, not judicious would it be, he thought, to keep the idea of lingering disaffection alive by undue

forwardness in crediting an informer, even if his own subordinate, and charged with police surveillance of the crew. This feeling would not perhaps have so prevailed with him were it not that upon a prior occasion the patriotic zeal officially evinced by Claggart had somewhat irritated him as appearing rather super-sensible and strained. Furthermore, something even in the official's self-possessed and somewhat ostentatious manner in making his specifications strangely reminded him of a bandsman, a perjured witness in a capital case before a court-martial ashore of which when a lieutenant he, Captain Vere, had been a member.

Now the peremptory check given to Claggart in the matter of the arrested allusion was quickly followed up by this: "You say that there is at least one dangerous man aboard. Name him."

"William Budd, a foretopman, your honour—"

"William Budd," repeated Captain Vere with unfeigned astonishment, "and mean you the man our Lieutenant Ratcliffe took from the merchantman not very long ago—the young fellow who seems to be so popular with the men—Billy, the Handsome Sailor, as they call him?"

"The same, your honour; but for all his youth and good looks, a deep one. Not for nothing does he insinuate himself into the good will of his shipmates, since at the least they will at a pinch say a good word for him at all hazards. Did Lieutenant Ratcliffe happen to tell your honour of that adroit fling of Budd's jumping up in the Cutter's bow under the merchantman's stern when he was being taken off? It is even masqued by that sort of good-humoured air· that at heart he resents his impressment. You have but noted his fair cheek. A man-trap may be under his fine ruddy-tipped daisies."

Now the *Handsome Sailor,* as a signal figure among the crew, had naturally enough attracted the Captain's attention from the first. Though in general not very demonstrative to his officers, he had congratulated Lieutenant Ratcliffe upon his good fortune in lighting on such a fine specimen of the *genus homo* who, in the nude, might have posed for a statue of young Adam before the fall.

As to Billy's adieu to the ship *Rights-of-Man,* which the boarding lieutenant had indeed reported to him, Captain Vere,—but in a deferential way—more as a good story than aught else,—though mistakenly understanding it as a satiric sally, had but thought so much the better of the impressed man for it; as a military sailor, admiring the spirit that could take an arbitrary enlistment so merrily and sensibly. The foretopman's conduct, too, so far as it had fallen under the Captain's notice had confirmed the first happy augury, while the new recruit's qualities as a *sailor-man* seemed to be such that he had thought of recommending him to the executive officer for promo-

tion to a place that would more frequently bring him under his own observation, namely, the captaincy of the mizzen-top, replacing there in the star-board watch a man not so young whom partly for that reason he deemed less fitted for the post. Be it parenthesized here that since the mizzen-top-men have not to handle such breadths of heavy canvas as the lower sailors on the main-mast and fore-mast, a young man if of the right stuff not only seems best adapted to duty there, but, in fact, is generally selected for the captaincy of that top, and the company under him are light hands, and often but striplings. In sum, Captain Vere had from the beginning deemed Billy Budd to be what in the naval parlance of the times was called a *"King's bargain,"* that is to say, for His Britannic Majesty's navy a capital investment at small outlay or none at all.

After a brief pause—during which the reminiscences above mentioned passed vividly through his mind—he weighed the import of Claggart's last suggestion, conveyed in the phrase, "pitfall under the clover," and the more he weighed it the less reliance he felt in the informer's good faith. Suddenly he turned upon him: "Do you come to me, Master-at-arms, with so foggy a tale? As to Budd, cite me an act or spoken word of his confirmatory of what you here in general charge against him. Stay," drawing nearer to him, "heed what you speak. Just now and in a case like this, there is a yard-arm-end for the false-witness."

"Ah, your honour!" sighed Claggart mildly shaking his shapely head as in sad deprecation of such unmerited severity of tone. Then bridling —erecting himself as in virtuous self-assertion, he circumstantially alleged certain words and acts, which collectively if credited, led to presumptions mortally inculpating Budd, and for some of these averments, he added, substantiating proof was not far.

With grey eyes now impatient and distrustful, essaying to fathom to the bottom Claggart's calm violet ones, Captain Vere again heard him out; then for the moment stood ruminating. The mood he evinced, Claggart—himself for the time liberated from the other's scrutiny— steadily regarded with a look difficult to render:—a look curious of the operation of his tactics, a look such as might have been that of the spokesman of the envious children of Jacob deceptively imposing upon the troubled patriarch the blood-dyed coat of young Joseph.

Though something exceptional in the moral quality of Captain Vere made him, in earnest encounter with a fellow-man, a veritable touchstone of that man's essential nature, yet now as to Claggart and what was really going on in him his feeling partook less of intuitional conviction than of strong suspicion clogged by strange dubieties. The perplexity he evinced proceeded less from aught touching the man

informed against—as Claggart doubtless opined—than from considera-
tions how best to act in regard to the informer. At first, indeed, he was
naturally for summoning that substantiation of his allegations which
Claggart said was at hand. But such a proceeding would result in the
matter at once getting abroad—which—in the present stage of it, he
thought, might undesirably affect the ship's company. If Claggart was
a false witness,—that closed the affair. And therefore, before trying
the accusation, he would first practically test the accuser; and he
thought this could be done in a quiet undemonstrative way.

The measure he determined upon involved a shifting of the scene—
a transfer to a place less exposed to observation than the broad quarter-
deck. For although the few gun-room officers there at the time had, in
due observance of naval etiquette, withdrawn to leeward the moment
Captain Vere had begun his promenade on the deck's weather side;
and though during the colloquy with Claggart they of course ventured
not to diminish the distance; and though throughout the interview
Captain Vere's voice was far from high, and Claggart's silvery and
low; and the wind in the cordage and the wash of the sea helped the
more to put them beyond ear-shot; nevertheless, the interview's con-
tinuance already had attracted observation from some topmen aloft,
and other sailors in the waist or further forward.

Having now determined upon his measures, Captain Vere forthwith
took action. Abruptly turning to Claggart he asked, "Master-at-arms,
is it now Budd's watch aloft?"

"No, your honour." Whereupon—"Mr. Wilkes," summoning the
nearest midshipman, "tell Albert to come to me." Albert was the
Captain's hammock-boy, a sort of sea-valet in whose discretion and
fidelity his master had much confidence. The lad appeared. "You
know Budd the foretopman?"

"I do, Sir."

"Go find him. It is his watch off. Manage to tell him out of ear-shot
that he is wanted aft. Contrive it that he speaks to nobody. Keep him
in talk yourself. And not till you get well aft here, not till then, let
him know that the place where he is wanted is my cabin. You under-
stand. Go.—Master-at-arms, show yourself on the decks below, and
when you think it time for Albert to be coming with his man, stand by
quietly to follow the sailor in."

§ 17

Now when the foretopman found himself closeted, as it were, in
the cabin with the Captain and Claggart, he was surprised enough. But

it was a surprise unaccompanied by apprehension or distrust. To an immature nature, essentially honest and humane, forewarning intimations of subtler danger from one's kind come tardily, if at all. The only thing that took shape in the young sailor's mind was this: "Yes, the Captain, I have always thought, looks kindly upon me. I wonder if he's going to make me his coxswain. I should like that. And maybe now he is going to ask the Master-at-arms about me."

"Shut the door there, sentry," said the commander. "Stand without and let nobody come in.—Now, Master-at-arms, tell this man to his face what you told of him to me;" and stood prepared to scrutinize the mutually confronting visages.

With the measured step and calm collected air of an asylum physician approaching in the public hall some patient beginning to show indications of a coming paroxysm, Claggart deliberately advanced within short range of Billy, and mesmerically looking him in the eye, briefly recapitulated the accusation.

Not at first did Billy take it in. When he did the rose-tan of his cheek looked struck as by white leprosy. He stood like one impaled and gagged. Meanwhile the accuser's eyes, removing not as yet from the blue, dilated ones, underwent a phenomenal change, their wonted rich violet colour blurring into a muddy purple. Those lights of human intelligence losing human expression, gelidly protruding like the alien eyes of certain uncatalogued creatures of the deep.

The first mesmeric glance was one of surprised fascination; the last was the hungry lurch of the torpedo-fish.

"Speak, man!" said Captain Vere to the transfixed one, struck by his aspect even more than by Claggart's, "Speak! defend yourself." Which appeal caused but a strange, dumb gesturing and gurgling in Billy; amazement at such an accusation so suddenly sprung on inexperienced nonage; this, and it may be horror at the accuser, serving to bring out his lurking defect, and in this instance for the time intensifying it into a convulsed tongue-tie; while the intent head and entire form straining forward in an agony of ineffectual eagerness to obey the injunction to speak and defend himself, gave an expression to the face like that of a condemned vestal priestess in the moment of her being buried alive, and in the first struggle against suffocation.

Though at the time Captain Vere was quite ignorant of Billy's liability to vocal impediment, he now immediately divined it, since vividly Billy's aspect recalled to him that of a bright young schoolmate of his whom he had seen struck by much the same startling impotence in the act of eagerly rising in the class to be foremost in response to a testing question put to it by the master. Going close up to the young sailor, and laying a soothing hand on his shoulder, he said, "There is

no hurry, my boy. Take your time, take your time." Contrary to the effect intended, these words, so fatherly in tone, doubtless touching Billy's heart to the quick, prompted yet more violent efforts at utterance—efforts soon ending for the time in confirming the paralysis, and bringing to the face an expression which was as a crucifixion to behold. The next instant, quick as the flame from a discharged cannon at night—his right arm shot out and Claggart dropped to the deck. Whether intentionally, or but owing to the young athlete's superior height, the blow had taken effect full upon the forehead, so shapely and intellectual-looking a feature in the Master-at-arms; so that the body fell over lengthwise, like a heavy plank tilted from erectness. A gasp or two and he lay motionless.

"Fated boy," breathed Captain Vere in a tone so low as to be almost a whisper, "what have you done! But here, help me."

The twain raised the felled one from the loins up into a sitting position. The spare form flexibly acquiesced, but inertly. It was like handling a dead snake. They lowered it back. Regaining erectness, Captain Vere with one hand covering his face stood to all appearance as impassive as to the object at his feet. Was he absorbed in taking in all the bearings of the event, and what was best not only now at once to be done, but also in the sequel? Slowly he uncovered his face; forthwith the effect was if the moon, emerging from eclipse, should reappear with quite another aspect than that which had gone into hiding. The father in him, manifested towards Billy thus far in the scene, was replaced by the military disciplinarian. In his official tone he bade the foretopman retire to a state-room aft, (pointing it out), and there remain till thence summoned. This order Billy in silence mechanically obeyed. Then, going to the cabin door where it opened on the quarterdeck, Captain Vere said to the sentry without, "Tell somebody to send Albert here." When the lad appeared his master so contrived it that he should not catch sight of the prone one. "Albert," he said to him, "tell the surgeon I wish to see him. You need not come back till called."

When the surgeon entered—a self-poised character of that grave sense and experience that hardly anything could take him aback—Captain Vere advanced to meet him, thus unconsciously interrupting his view of Claggart and interrupting the other's wonted ceremonious salutation, said, "Nay, tell me how it is with yonder man," directing his attention to the prostrate one.

The surgeon looked, and for all his self-command, somewhat started at the abrupt revelation. On Claggart's always pallid complexion, thick black blood was now oozing from mouth and ear. To the gazer's professional eyes it was unmistakably no living man that he saw.

"Is it so, then?" said Captain Vere intently watching him. "I

thought it. But verify it." Whereupon the customary tests confirmed the surgeon's first glance, who now looking up in unfeigned concern, cast a look of intense inquisitiveness upon his superior. But Captain Vere, with one hand to his brow, was standing motionless. Suddenly, catching the surgeon's arm convulsively, he exclaimed pointing down to the body,—"It is the divine judgment of Ananias! Look!"

Disturbed by the excited manner he had never before observed in the *Indomitable's* Captain, and as yet wholly ignorant of the affair, the prudent surgeon nevertheless held his peace, only again looking an earnest interrogation as to what it was that had resulted in such a tragedy.

But Captain Vere was now again motionless, standing absorbed in thought. Once again starting, he vehemently exclaimed—"Struck dead by an angel of God. Yet the angel must hang!"

At these interjections, incoherences to the listener as yet unapprised of the antecedent events, the surgeon was profoundly discomfited. But now, as recollecting himself, Captain Vere in less harsh tone briefly related the circumstances leading up to the event.

"But come; we must despatch," he added, "help me to remove him (meaning the body) to yonder compartment"—designating one opposite where the foretopman remained immured. Anew disturbed by a request that, as implying a desire for secrecy, seemed unaccountably strange to him, there was nothing for the subordinate to do but comply.

"Go now," said Captain Vere, with something of his wonted manner, "Go now. I shall presently call a drum-head court. Tell the lieutenants what has happened, and tell Mr. Morton"—meaning the captain of marines. "And charge them to keep the matter to themselves."

Full of disquietude and misgivings, the surgeon left the cabin. Was Captain Vere suddenly affected in his mind, or was it but a transient excitement brought about by so strange and extraordinary a happening? As to the drum-head court, it struck the surgeon as impolitic, if nothing more. The thing to do, he thought, was to place Billy Budd in confinement, and in a way dictated by usage, and postpone further action in so extraordinary a case to such time as they should again join the squadron, and then transfer it to the Admiral. He recalled the unwonted agitation of Captain Vere and his exciting exclamations so at variance with his normal manner. Was he unhinged? But assuming that he was, it were not so susceptible of proof. What then could he do? No worse trying situation is conceivable than that of an officer subordinated under a Captain whom he suspects to be, not mad indeed, but yet not quite unaffected in his intellect. To argue his order to him would be insolence. To resist him would be mutiny. In obedi-

ence to Captain Vere he communicated to the lieutenants and captain of marines what had happened; saying nothing as to the Captain's state. They stared at him in surprise and concern. Like him they seemed to think that such a matter should be reported to the Admiral.

Who in the rainbow can draw the line where the violet tint ends and the orange tint begins? Distinctly we see the difference of the colour, but where exactly does the first one visibly enter into the other? So with sanity and insanity. In pronounced cases there is no question about them. But in some cases, in various degrees supposedly less pronounced, to draw the line of demarkation few will undertake, though for a fee some professional experts will. There is nothing namable but that some men will undertake to do for pay. In other words, there are instances where it is next to impossible to determine whether a man is sane or beginning to be otherwise.

Whether Captain Vere, as the surgeon professionally surmised, was really the sudden victim of any degree of aberration, one must determine for himself by such light as this narrative may afford.

§ 18

The unhappy event which has been narrated could not have happened at a worse juncture. For it was close on the heel of the suppressed insurrections, an after-time very critical to naval authority, demanding from every English sea-commander two qualities not readily interfusable—prudence and rigour. Moreover, there was something crucial in the case.

In the jugglery of circumstances preceding and attending the event on board the *Indomitable* and in the light of that martial code whereby it was formally to be judged, innocence and guilt, personified in Claggart and Budd, in effect changed places.

In the legal view the apparent victim of the tragedy was he who had sought to victimize a man blameless; and the indisputable deed of the latter, navally regarded, constituted the most heinous of military crimes. Yet more. The essential right and wrong involved in the matter, the clearer that might be, so much the worse for the responsibility of a loyal sea-commander, inasmuch as he was authorized to determine the matter on that primitive legal basis.

Small wonder then that the *Indomitable's* Captain, though in general a man of rigid decision, felt that circumspectness not less than promptitude was necessary. Until he could decide upon his course, and in each detail; and not only so, but until the concluding measure was upon the point of being enacted he deemed it advisable, in view of

all the circumstances, to guard as much as possible against publicity. Here he may or may not have erred. Certain it is, however, that subsequently in the confidential talk of more than one or two gun-rooms and cabins he was not a little criticized by some officers, a fact imputed by his friends, and vehemently by his cousin Jack Denton, to professional jealousy of Starry Vere. Some imaginative ground for invidious comment there was. The maintenance of secrecy in the matter, the confining all knowledge of it for a time to the place where the homicide occurred—the quarter-deck cabin; in these particulars lurked some resemblance to the policy adopted in those tragedies of the palace which have occurred more than once in the capital founded by Peter the Barbarian, great chiefly by his crimes.

The case was such that fain would the *Indomitable's* Captain have deferred taking any action whatever respecting it further than to keep the foretopman a close prisoner till the ship rejoined the squadron, and then submitting the matter to the judgment of his Admiral.

But a true military officer is, in one particular, like a true monk. Not with more of self-abnegation will the latter keep his vows of monastic obedience than the former his vows of allegiance to martial duty.

Feeling that unless quick action were taken on it, the deed of the foretopman, as soon as it should be known on the gun-decks, would tend to awaken any slumbering embers of the Nore among the crews —a sense of the urgency of the case overruled in Captain Vere all other considerations. But though a conscientious disciplinarian, he was no lover of authority for mere authority's sake. Very far was he from embracing opportunities for monopolizing to himself the perils of moral responsibility, none at least that could properly be referred to an official superior, or shared with him by his official equals or even subordinates. So thinking, he was glad it would not be at variance with usage to turn the matter over to a summary court of his own officers, reserving to himself, as the one on whom the ultimate accountability would rest, the right of maintaining a supervision of it, or formally or informally interposing at need. Accordingly a drum-head court was summarily convened, he electing the individuals composing it, the First Lieutenant, the Captain of Marines, and the Sailing Master.

In associating an officer of marines with the sea-lieutenants in a case having to do with a sailor, the Commander perhaps deviated from general custom. He was prompted thereto by the circumstances that he took that soldier to be a judicious person, thoughtful and not altogether incapable of gripping with a difficult case unprecedented in his prior experience. Yet even as to him he was not without some latent misgiving, for withal he was an extremely good-natured man, an en-

joyer of his dinner, a sound sleeper, and inclined to obesity. The sort of man who, though he would always maintain his manhood in battle, might not prove altogether reliable in a moral dilemma involving aught of the tragic. As to the First Lieutenant and the Sailing Master, Captain Vere could not but be aware that though honest natures, of approved gallantry upon occasion, their intelligence was mostly confined to the matter of active seamanship, and the fighting demands of their profession. The court was held in the same cabin where the unfortunate affair had taken place. This cabin, the Commander's embraced the entire area under the poop-deck. Aft, and on either side, was a small state-room—the one room temporarily a jail, and the other a deadhouse—and a yet smaller compartment leaving a space between, expanding forward into a goodly oblong of length coinciding with the ship's beam. A sky-light of moderate dimension was overhead, and at each end of the oblong space were two sashed port-hole windows, easily convertible back into embrasures for short cannonades.

All being quickly in readiness, Billy Budd was arraigned, Captain Vere necessarily appearing as the sole witness in the case, and as such temporarily sinking his rank, though singularly maintaining it in a matter apparently trivial, namely, that he testified from the ship's weather-side, with that object having caused the court to sit on the lee-side. Concisely he narrated all that had led up to the catastrophe, omitting nothing in Claggart's accusation and deposing as to the manner in which the prisoner had received it. At this testimony the three officers glanced with no little surprise at Billy Budd, the last man they would have suspected, either of mutinous design alleged by Claggart, or of the undeniable deed he himself had done. The First Lieutenant, taking judicial primacy and turning towards the prisoner, said, "Captain Vere has spoken. It is or is it not as Captain Vere says?" In response came syllables not so much impeded in the utterances as might have been anticipated. They were these:

"Captain Vere tells the truth. It is just as Captain Vere says, but it is not as the Master-at-arms said. I have eaten the King's bread and I am true to the King."

"I believe you, my man," said the witness, his voice indicating a suppressed emotion not otherwise betrayed.

"God will bless you for that, your honour!" not without stammering said Billy, and all but broke down. But immediately was recalled to self-control by another question, with which the same emotional difficulty of utterance came: "No, there was no malice between us. I never bore malice against the Master-at-arms. I am sorry that he is dead. I did not mean to kill him. Could I have used my tongue I would not have struck him. But he foully lied to my face, and in the presence

of my Captain, and I had to say something, and I could only say it with a blow. God help me!"

In the impulsive above-board manner of the frank one the court saw confirmed all that was implied in words which just previously had perplexed them, coming as they did from the testifier to the tragedy, and promptly following Billy's impassioned disclaimer of mutinous intent—Captain Vere's words, "I believe you, my man."

Next it was asked of him whether he knew of or suspected aught savouring of incipient trouble (meaning a mutiny, though the explicit term was avoided) going on in any section of the ship's company.

The reply lingered. This was naturally imputed by the court to the same vocal embarrassment which had retarded or obstructed previous answers. But in main it was otherwise here; the question immediately recalling to Billy's mind the interview with the afterguardsman in the fore-chains. But an innate repugnance to playing a part at all approaching that of an informer against one's own shipmates—the same erring sense of uninstructed honour which had stood in the way of his reporting the matter at the time; though as a loyal man-of-war man it was incumbent on him and failure so to do charged against him and, proven, would have subjected him to the heaviest of penalties. This, was the blind feeling now his, that nothing really was being hatched, prevailing with him. When the answer came it was a negative.

"One question more," said the officer of marines now first speaking and with a troubled earnestness. "You tell us that what the Master-at-arms said against you was a lie. Now why should he have so lied, so maliciously lied, since you declare there was no malice between you?"

At that question unintentionally touching on a spiritual sphere wholly obscure to Billy's thoughts, he was nonplussed, evincing a confusion indeed that some observers, such as can be imagined, would have construed into involuntary evidence of hidden guilt. Nevertheless he strove some way to answer, but all at once relinquished the vain endeavour, at the same time turning an appealing glance towards Captain Vere as deeming him his best helper and friend. Captain Vere, who had been seated for a time, rose to his feet, addressing the interrogator. "The question you put to him comes naturally enough. But can he rightly answer it?—or anybody else? unless indeed it be he who lies within there," designating the compartment where lay the corpse. "But the prone one there will not rise to our summons. In effect though, as it seems to me, the point you make is hardly material. Quite aside from any conceivable motive actuating the Master-at-arms, and irrespective of the provocation of the blow, a martial court must needs in the present case confine its attention to

the blow's consequence, which consequence is to be deemed not otherwise than as the striker's deed!"

This utterance, the full significance of which it was not at all likely that Billy took in, nevertheless caused him to turn a wistful, interrogative look towards the speaker, a look in its dumb expressiveness not unlike that which a dog of generous breed might turn upon his master, seeking in his face some elucidation of a previous gesture ambiguous to the canine intelligence. Nor was the same utterance without marked effect upon the three officers, more especially the soldier. Couched in it seemed to them a meaning unanticipated, involving a prejudgment on the speaker's part. It served to augment a mental disturbance previously evident enough.

The soldier once more spoke, in a tone of suggestive dubiety addressing at once his associates and Captain Vere: "Nobody is present —none of the ship's company, I mean, who might shed lateral light, if any is to be had, upon what remains mysterious in this matter."

"That is thoughtfully put," said Captain Vere; "I see your drift. Ay, there is a mystery; but to use a Scriptural phrase, it is 'a mystery of iniquity,' a matter for only psychologic theologians to discuss. But what has a military court to do with it? Not to add that for us any possible investigation of it is cut off by the lasting tongue-tie of him in yonder," again designating the mortuary state-room. "The prisoner's deed. With that alone we have to do."

To this, and particularly the closing reiteration, the marine soldier, knowing not how aptly to reply, sadly abstained from saying aught. The First Lieutenant, who at the outset had not unnaturally assumed primacy in the court, now overrulingly instructive by a glance from Captain Vere (a glance more effective than words), resumed that primacy. Turning to the prisoner: "Budd," he said, and scarce in equable tones, "Budd, if you have aught further to say for yourself, say it now."

Upon this the young sailor turned another quick glance towards Captain Vere; then, as taking a hint from that aspect, a hint confirming his own instinct that silence was now best, replied to the Lieutenant, "I have said all, Sir."

The marine—the same who had been the sentinel without the cabin-door at the time that the foretopman, followed by the Master-at-arms, entered it—he, standing by the sailor throughout their judicial proceedings, was now directed to take him back to the after compartment originally assigned to the prisoner and his custodian. As the twain disappeared from view, the three officers, as partially liberated from some inward constraint associated with Billy's mere presence—

simultaneously stirred in their seats. They exchanged looks of troubled indecision, yet feeling that decide they must, and without long delay; for Captain Vere was for the time sitting unconsciously with his back towards them, apparently in one of his absent fits, gazing out from a sashed port-hole to windward upon the monotonous blank of the twilight sea. But the court's silence continuing, broken only at moments by brief consultations in low earnest tones, this seemed to assure him and encourage him. Turning, he to-and-fro paced the cabin athwart; in the returning ascent to windward, climbing the slant deck in the ship's lee roll; without knowing it symbolizing thus in his action a mind resolute to surmount difficulties even if against primitive instincts strong as the wind and the sea. Presently he came to a stand before the three. After scanning their faces he stood less as mustering his thoughts for expression, than as one in deliberating how best to put them to well-meaning men not intellectually mature—men with whom it was necessary to demonstrate certain principles that were axioms to himself. Similar impatience as to talking is perhaps one reason that deters some minds from addressing any popular assemblies; under which head is to be classed most legislatures in a Democracy.

When speak he did, something both in the substance of what he said and his manner of saying it, showed the influence of unshared studies, modifying and tempering the practical training of an active career. This, along with his phraseology now and then, was suggestive of the grounds whereon rested that imputation of a certain pedantry socially alleged against him by certain naval men of wholly practical cast, captains who nevertheless would frankly concede that His Majesty's Navy mustered no more efficient officers of their grade than "Starry Vere."

What he said was to this effect: "Hitherto I have been but the witness, little more; and I should hardly think now to take another tone, that of your coadjutor, for the time, did I not perceive in you—at the crisis too—a troubled hesitancy, proceeding, I doubt not, from the clashing of military duty with moral scruple—scruple vitalized by compassion. For the compassion, how can I otherwise but share it. But, mindful of paramount obligation, I strive against scruples that may tend to enervate decision. Not, gentlemen, that I hide from myself that the case is an exceptional one. Speculatively regarded, it well might be referred to a jury of casuists. But for us here, acting not as casuists or moralists, it is a case practical and under martial law practically to be dealt with.

"But your scruples! Do they move as in a dusk? Challenge them. Make them advance and declare themselves. Come now—do they import something like this: If, mindless of palliating circumstances, we

are bound to regard the death of the Master-at-arms as the prisoner's
deed, then does that deed constitute a capital crime whereof the
penalty is a mortal one? But in natural justice is nothing but the
prisoner's overt act to be considered? Now can we adjudge to sum-
mary and shameful death a fellow-creature innocent before God, and
whom we feel to be so?—Does that state it aright? You sign sad assent.
Well, I, too, feel that, the full force of that. It is Nature. But do these
buttons that we wear attest that our allegiance is to Nature? No, to the
King. Though the ocean, which is inviolate Nature primeval, though
this be the element where we move and have our being as sailors, yet
as the King's officers lies our duty in a sphere correspondingly natural?
So little is that true, that in receiving our commissions we in the most
important regards ceased to be natural free-agents. When war is de-
clared, are we the commissioned fighters previously consulted? We
fight at command. If our judgments approve the war, that is but co-
incidence. So, in other particulars. So now, would it be so much we
ourselves that would condemn as it would be martial law operating
through us? For that law and the rigour of it, we are not responsible.
Our vowed responsibility is in this: That however pitilessly that law
may operate, we nevertheless adhere to it and administer it.

"But the exceptional in the matter moves the heart within you.
Even so, too, is mine moved. But let not warm hearts betray heads that
should be cool. Ashore in a criminal case will an unright judge allow
himself when off the bench to be waylaid by some tender kinswoman
of the accused seeking to touch him with her tearful plea? Well, the
heart here is as that piteous woman. The heart is the feminine in man,
and hard though it be, she must here be ruled out."

He paused, earnestly studying them for a moment; then resumed.

"But something in your aspect seems to urge that it is not solely that
heart that moves in you, but also the conscience, the private conscience.
Then, tell me whether or not, occupying the position we do, private
conscience should not yield to that imperial one formulated in the code
under which alone we officially proceed?"

Here the three men moved in their seats, less convinced than agitated
by the course of an argument troubling but the more the spontaneous
conflict within. Perceiving which, the speaker paused for a moment;
then abruptly changing his tone, went on:

"To steady us a bit, let us recur to the facts.—In war-time at sea a
man-of-war's man strikes his superior in grade, and the blow kills.
Apart from its effect, the blow itself is, according to the Articles of
War, a capital crime. Furthermore—"

"Ay, Sir," emotionally broke in the officer of marines, "in one sense
it was. But surely Budd purposed neither mutiny nor homicide."

"Surely not, my good man. And before a court less arbitrary and more merciful than a martial one that plea would largely extenuate. At the Last Assizes it shall acquit. But how here? We proceed under the law of the Mutiny Act. In feature no child can resemble his father more than that Act resembles in spirit the thing from which it derives —War. In His Majesty's service—in this ship indeed—there are Englishmen forced to fight for the King against their will. Against their conscience, for aught we know. Though as their fellow-creatures some of us may appreciate their position, yet as Navy officers, what reck we of it? Still less recks the enemy. Our impressed men he would fain cut down in the same swath with our volunteers. As regards the enemy's naval conscripts, some of whom may even share our own abhorrence of the regicidal French Directory, it is the same on our side. War looks but to the frontage, the appearance. And the Mutiny Act, War's child, takes after the father. Budd's intent or non-intent is nothing to the purpose.

"But while, put to it by those anxieties in you which I cannot but respect, I only repeat myself—while thus strangely we prolong proceedings that should be summary, the enemy may be sighted and an engagement result. We must do; and one of two things must we do— condemn or let go."

"Can we not convict and yet mitigate the penalty?" asked the junior Lieutenant here speaking, and falteringly, for the first time.

"Lieutenant, were that clearly lawful for us under the circumstances, consider the consequences of such clemency. The people" (meaning the ship's company) "have native sense; most of them are familiar with our naval usage and tradition; and how would they take it? Even could you explain to them—which our official position forbids—they, long moulded by arbitrary discipline, have not that kind of intelligent responsiveness that might qualify them to comprehend and discriminate. No, to the people the foretopman's deed, however it be worded in the announcement, will be plain homicide committed in a flagrant act of mutiny. What penalty for that should follow, they know. But it does not follow. *Why?* they will ruminate. You know what sailors are. Will they not revert to the recent outbreak at the Nore? Ay, they know the well-founded alarm—the panic it struck throughout England. Your clement sentence they would account pusillanimous. They would think that we flinch, that we are afraid of them—afraid of practising a lawful rigour singularly demanded at this juncture lest it should provoke new troubles. What shame to us such a conjecture on their part, and how deadly to discipline. You see then whither, prompted by duty and the law, I steadfastly drive. But I beseech you, my friends, do not take me amiss. I feel as you do for this unfortunate

boy. But did he know our hearts, I take him to be of that generous nature that he would feel even for us on whom in this military necessity so heavy a compulsion is laid."

With that, crossing the deck, he resumed his place by the sashed port-hole, tacitly leaving the three to come to a decision. On the cabin's opposite side the troubled court sat silent. Loyal lieges, plain and practical, though at bottom they dissented from some points Captain Vere had put to them, they were without the faculty, hardly had the inclination to gainsay one whom they felt to be an earnest man—one, too, not less their superior in mind than in naval rank. But it is not improbable that even such of his words as were not without influence over them, less came home to them than his closing appeal to their instinct as sea-officers, in the forethought he threw out as to the practical consequences to discipline (considering the unconfirmed tone of the fleet at the time)—should a man-of-war's man's violent killing at sea of a superior in grade be allowed to pass for aught else than a capital crime, demanding prompt infliction of the penalty?

Not unlikely they were brought to something more or less akin to that harassed frame of mind which in the year 1842 actuated the commander of the U.S. brig-of-war *Somers* to resolve (under the so-called Articles of War—Articles modelled upon the English Mutiny Act) to resolve upon the execution at sea of a midshipman and two petty-officers as mutineers designing the seizure of the brig. Which resolution was carried out, though in a time of peace and within not many days' sail of home. An act vindicated by a naval court of inquiry subsequently convened ashore—history, and here cited without comment. True, the circumstances on board the *Somers* were different from those on board the *Indomitable*. But the urgency felt, well-warranted or otherwise, was much the same.

Says a writer whom few know, "Forty years after a battle it is easy for a non-combatant to reason about how it ought to have been fought. It is another thing personally and under fire to direct the fighting while involved in the obscuring smoke of it. Much so with respect to other emergencies involving considerations both practical and moral, and when it is imperative promptly to act. The greater the fog, the more it imperils the steamer, and speed is put on though at the hazard of running somebody down. Little ween the snug card-players in the cabin of the responsibilities of the sleepless man on the bridge."

In brief, Billy Budd was formally convicted and sentenced to be hung at the yard-arm in the early morning-watch, it being now night. Otherwise, as is customary in such cases, the sentence would forthwith have been carried out. In war-time on the field or in the fleet, a mortal punishment decreed by a drum-head court—on the field sometimes de-

creed by but a nod from the General—follows without a delay on the heel of conviction without appeal.

§ 19

It was Captain Vere himself who, of his own motion, communicated the finding of the court to the prisoner; for that purpose going to the compartment where he was in custody, and bidding the marine there to withdraw for the time.

Beyond the communication of the sentence, what took place at this interview was never known. But, in view of the character of the twain briefly closeted in that state-room, each radically sharing in the rarer qualities of one nature—so rare, indeed, as to be all but incredible to average minds however much cultivated—some conjectures may be ventured.

It would have been in consonance with the spirit of our Captain Vere should he on this occasion have concealed nothing from the condemned one—should he indeed have frankly disclosed to him the part he himself had played in bringing about the decision, at the same time revealing his actuating motives. On Billy's side it is not improbable that such a confession would have been received in much the same spirit that prompted it. Not without a sort of joy indeed he might have appreciated the brave opinion of him implied in his Captain making such a confidant of him. Nor as to the sentence itself could he have been insensible that it was imparted to him as to one not afraid to die. Even more may have been. Captain Vere in the end may have developed the passion sometimes latent under an exterior stoical or indifferent. He was old enough to have been Billy's father. The austere devotee of military duty, letting himself melt back into what remains primeval in our formalized humanity, may in the end have caught Billy to heart, even as Abraham may have caught young Isaac on the brink of resolutely offering him up in obedience to the exacting behest. But there is no telling the sacrament—seldom if in any case revealed to the gadding world wherever under circumstances at all akin to those here attempted to be set forth—two of great Nature's nobler order embrace. There is privacy at the time, inviolable to the survivor, and holy oblivion (the sequel to each diviner magnanimity) providentially covers all at last.

The first to encounter Captain Vere in the act of leaving the compartment was the senior Lieutenant. The face he beheld, for the moment one expressive of the agony of the strong, was to that officer, though a man of fifty, a startling revelation. That the condemned one

suffered less than he who mainly had effected the condemnation, was apparently indicated by the former's exclamation in the scene soon perforce to be touched upon.

Of a series of incidents within a brief term rapidly following each other, the adequate narration may take up a term less brief, especially if explanation or comment here and there seem requisite to the better understanding of such incidents. Between the entrance into the cabin of him who never left it alive, and him who when he did leave it left it as one condemned to die; between this and the closeted interview just given, less than an hour and a half had elapsed. It was an interval long enough, however, to awaken speculations among no few of the ship's company as to what it was that could be detaining in the cabin the Master-at-arms and the sailor, for it was rumoured that both of them had been seen to enter it and neither of them had been seen to emerge. This rumour had got abroad upon the gun-decks and in the tops; the people of a great war-ship being in one respect like villagers, taking microscopic note of every untoward movement or non-movement going on. When therefore in weather not at all tempestuous all hands were called in the second dog-watch, a summons under such circumstances not usual in those hours, the crew were not wholly unprepared for some announcement extraordinary, one having connection, too, with the continued absence of the two men from their wonted haunts.

There was a moderate sea at the time; and the moon, newly risen and near to being at its full, silvered the white spar-deck wherever not blotted by the clear-cut shadows horizontally thrown of fixtures and moving men. On either side of the quarter-deck the marine guard under arms was drawn up; and Captain Vere, standing up in his place surrounded by all the ward-room officers, addressed his men. In so doing his manner showed neither more nor less than that properly pertaining to his supreme position aboard his own ship. In clear terms and concise he told them what had taken place in the cabin; that the Master-at-arms was dead; that he who had killed him had been already tried by a summary court and condemned to death; and that the execution would take place in the early morning watch. The word *mutiny* was not named in what he said. He refrained, too, from making the occasion an opportunity for any preachment as to the maintenance of discipline, thinking, perhaps, that under existing circumstances in the navy the consequence of violating discipline should be made to speak for itself.

Their Captain's announcement was listened to by the throng of standing sailors in a dumbness like that of a seated congregation of believers in Hell listening to the clergyman's announcement of his Calvinistic text.

At the close, however, a confused murmur went up. It began to wax all but instantly, then, at a sign, was pierced and suppressed by shrill whistles of the Boatswain and his mates piping "Down one watch."

To be prepared for burial Claggart's body was delivered to certain petty-officers of his mess. And here, not to clog the sequel with lateral matters, it may be added that at a suitable hour, the Master-at-arms was committed to the sea with every funeral honour properly belonging to his naval grade.

In this proceeding, as in every public one growing out of the tragedy, strict adherence to usage was observed. Nor in any point could it have been at all deviated from, either with respect to Claggart or Billy Budd, without begetting undesirable speculations in the ship's company, the sailors, and more particularly the men-of-war's men, being of all men the greatest sticklers for usage.

For similar cause all communication between Captain Vere and the condemned one ended with the closeted interview already given, the latter being now surrendered to the ordinary routine preliminary to the end. This transfer under guard from the Captain's quarters was effected without unusual precautions—at least no visible ones.

If possible, not to let the men so much as surmise that their officers anticipate aught amiss from them, is the tacit rule in a military ship. And the more that some sort of trouble should really be apprehended, the more do the officers keep that apprehension to themselves; though not the less unostentatious vigilance may be augmented.

In the present instance the sentry placed over the prisoner had strict orders to let no one have communication with him but the Chaplain. And certain unobtrusive measures were taken absolutely to insure this point.

§ 20

In a seventy-four of the old order the deck known as the upper gundeck was the one covered over by the spar-deck, which last, though not without its armament, was for the most part exposed to the weather. In general it was at all hours free from hammocks; those of the crew swinging on the lower gun-deck, and berth-deck, the latter being not only a dormitory but also the place for the stowing of the sailors' bags, and on both sides lined with the large chests or movable pantries of the many messes of the men.

On the starboard side of the *Indomitable's* upper gun-deck, behold Billy Budd under sentry lying prone in irons in one of the bays formed by the regular spacing of the guns comprising the batteries on either

side. All these pieces were of the heavier calibre of that period.
Mounted on lumbering wooden carriages, they were hampered with
cumbersome harness of breeching and strong side-tackles for running
them out. Guns and carriages, together with the long rammers and
shorter lintstocks lodged in loops overhead—all these, as customary,
were painted black; and the heavy hempen breechings, tarred to the
same tint, wore the like livery of the undertakers. In contrast with the
funereal tone of these surroundings, the prone sailor's exterior apparel,
white *jumper* and white duck trousers, each more or less soiled, dimly
glimmered in the obscure light of the bay like a patch of discoloured
snow in early April lingering at some upland cave's black mouth. In
effect he is already in his shroud or the garments that shall serve him
in lieu of one. Over him, but scarce illuminating him, two battle-
lanterns swing from two massive beams of the deck above. Fed with
the oil supplied by war-contractors (whose gains, honest or otherwise,
are in every land an anticipated portion of the harvest of death), with
flickering splashes of dirty yellow light they pollute the pale moonshine
all but ineffectually struggling in obstructed flecks through the open
ports from which the tompined cannon protrude. Other lanterns at
intervals serve but to bring out somewhat the obscurer bays which, like
small confessionals or side-chapels in a cathedral, branch from the long,
dim-vasted, broad aisle between the two batteries of that covered tire.

Such was the deck where now lay the Handsome Sailor. Through
the rose-tan of his complexion, no pallor could have shown. It would
have taken days of sequestration from the winds and the sun to have
brought about the effacement of that young sea-bloom. But the skele-
ton in the cheek-bone at the point of its angle was just beginning deli-
cately to be defined under the warm-tinted skin. In fervid hearts self-
contained some brief experiences devour our human tissue as secret
fire in a ship's hold consumes cotton in the bale.

But now, lying between the two guns, as nipped in the vice of fate,
Billy's agony, mainly proceeding from a generous young heart's virgin
experience of the diabolical incarnate and effective in some men—the
tension of that agony was over now. It survived not the something
healing in the closeted interview with Captain Vere. Without move-
ment, he lay as in a trance, that adolescent expression previously noted
as his, taking on something akin to the look of a slumbering child in
the cradle when the warm hearth-glow of the still chamber of night
plays on the dimples that at whiles mysteriously form in the cheek,
silently coming and going there. For now and then in the gyved one's
trance, a serene happy light born of some wandering reminiscence or
dream would diffuse itself over his face, and then wane away only
anew to return.

The Chaplain coming to see him and finding him thus, and perceiving no sign that he was conscious of his presence, attentively regarded him for a space, then slipping aside, withdrew for the time, peradventure feeling that even he, the minister of Christ, though receiving his stipend from wars, had no consolation to proffer which could result in a peace transcending that which he beheld. But in the small hours he came again. And the prisoner, now awake to his surroundings, noticed his approach, and civilly, all but cheerfully, welcomed him. But it was to little purpose that in the interview following the good man sought to bring Billy Budd to some Godly understanding that he must die, and at dawn. True, Billy himself freely referred to his death as a thing close at hand; but it was something in the way that children will refer to death in general, who yet among their other sports will play a funeral with hearse and mourners. Not that like children Billy was incapable of conceiving what death really is. No, but he was wholly without irrational fear of it, a fear more prevalent in highly civilized communities than those so-called barbarous ones which in all respects stand nearer to unadulterate Nature. And, as elsewhere said, a barbarian Billy radically was; as much so, for all the costume, as his countrymen the British captives, living trophies made to march in the Roman triumph of Germanicus. Quite as much so as those later barbarians, young men probably, and picked specimens among the earlier British converts to Christianity, at least nominally such, and taken to Rome (as to-day converts from lesser isles of the sea may be taken to London), of whom the Pope of that time, admiring the strangeness of their personal beauty—so unlike the Italian stamp, their clear, ruddy complexions and curled flaxen locks, explained, "Angels" (meaning in English the modern derivative)—"Angels do you call them? And is it because they look so like *angels?*" Had it been later in time one would think that the Pope had in mind Fra Angelico's seraphs, some of whom, plucking apples in gardens of Hesperides, have the faint rose-bud complexion of the more beautiful English girls.

§ 21

If in vain the kind Chaplain sought to impress the young barbarian with ideas of death akin to those conveyed in the skull, dial and cross-bones on old tombstones; equally futile to all appearances were his efforts to bring home to him the thought of salvation and a Saviour. Billy listened, but less out of awe or reverence, perhaps, than from a certain natural politeness; doubtless at bottom regarding all that in much the same way which most mariners of his class take any discourse

abstract or out of the common tone of the workaday world. And this sailor way of taking clerical discourse is not wholly unlike the way in which the pioneer of Christianity—full of transcendent miracles—was received long ago on tropic isles by any superior *savage* so called: a Tahitian say of Captain Cook's time or shortly after that time. Out of natural courtesy he received but did not appreciate. It was like a gift placed in the palm of an out-stretched hand upon which the fingers do not close.

But the *Indomitable's* Chaplain was a discreet man possessing the good sense of a good heart. So he insisted not in his vocation here. At the instance of Captain Vere, a lieutenant had apprised him of pretty much of everything as to Billy; and since he felt that innocence was even a better thing than religion wherewith to go to judgment, he reluctantly withdrew; but in his emotion not without performing an act strange enough in an Englishman, and under the circumstances yet more so in any regular priest. Stooping over, he kissed on the fair cheek his fellow man, a felon in martial law, one who, though in the confines of death, he felt he could never convert to a dogma; nor for all that he did fear for his future.

Marvel not that, having been made acquainted with the young sailor's essential innocence, the worthy man lifted not a finger to avert the doom of such a martyr to martial discipline. So to do would not only have been as idle as invoking the desert, but would also have been an audacious transgression of the bounds of his function—one as exactly prescribed to him by military law as that of any other naval officer. Bluntly put, a chaplain is the minister of the Prince of Peace serving in the host of the God of War—Mars. As such, he is as incongruous as a musket would be on the altar at Christmas. Why then is he there? Because he indirectly subserves the purpose attested by the cannon; because, too, he lends the sanction of the religion of the meek to that which practically is the abrogation of everything but force.*

§ 22

The night so luminous on the spar-deck, but otherwise on the cavernous ones below—levels so very like the tiered galleries in a coalmine—the luminous night passed away. Like the prophet in the chariot disappearing in heaven and dropping his mantle to Elisha, the withdrawing night transferred its pale robe to the peeping day. A meek shy light appeared in the East, where stretched a diaphanous fleece of

*Melville notes on this passage: "An irruption of heretic thought hard to suppress."

white furrowed vapour. That light slowly waxed. Suddenly *one bell* was struck aft, responded to by one louder metallic stroke from forward. It was four o'clock in the morning. Instantly the silver whistles were heard summoning all hands to witness punishment. Up through the great hatchway rimmed with racks of heavy shot, the watch below came pouring, overspreading with the watch already on deck the space between the mainmast and foremast, including that occupied by the capacious *launch* and the black booms tiered on either side of it—boat and booms making a summit of observation for the powder boys and younger tars. A different group comprising one watch of topmen leaned over the side of the rail of that sea-balcony, no small one in a seventy-four, looking down on the crowd below. Man or boy, none spake but in whisper, and few spake at all. Captain Vere—as before, the central figure among the assembled commissioned officers—stood nigh the break of the poop-deck, facing forward. Just below him on the quarter-deck the marines in full equipment were drawn up much as at the scene of the promulgated sentence.

At sea in the old time, the execution by halter of a military sailor was generally from the fore-yard. In the present instance—for special reasons—the main-yard was assigned. Under an arm of that yard the prisoner was presently brought up, the Chaplain attending him. It was noted at the time, and remarked upon afterwards, that in this final scene the good man evinced little or nothing of the perfunctory. Brief speech indeed he had with the condemned one, but the genuine gospel was less on his tongue than in his aspect and manner towards him. The final preparations personal to the latter being speedily brought to an end by two boatswain's-mates, the consummation impended. Billy stood facing aft. At the penultimate moment, his words, his only ones, words wholly unobstructed in the utterance, were these—"God bless Captain Vere!" Syllables so unanticipated coming from one with the ignominious hemp about his neck—a conventional felon's benediction directed aft towards the quarters of honour; syllables, too, delivered in the clear melody of a singing-bird on the point of launching from the twig, had a phenomenal effect, not unenhanced by the rare personal beauty of the young sailor, spiritualized now through late experiences so poignantly profound.

Without volition, as it were, as if indeed the ship's populace were the vehicles of some vocal electric current, with one voice, from alow and aloft, came a resonant echo—"God bless Captain Vere!" And yet, at that instant, Billy alone must have been in their hearts, even as he was in their eyes.

At the pronounced words and the spontaneous echo that voluminously rebounded them, Captain Vere, either through stoic self-control

or a sort of momentary paralysis induced by emotional shock, stood erectly rigid as a musket in the ship-armour's rack.

The hull, deliberately recovering from the periodic roll to leeward, was just regaining an even keel—when the last signal, the preconcerted dumb one, was given. At the same moment it chanced that the vapoury fleece hanging low in the East, was shot through with a soft glory as of the fleece of the Lamb of God seen in mystical vision; and simultaneously therewith, watched by the wedged mass of upturned faces, Billy ascended; and ascending, took the full rose of the dawn.

In the pinioned figure, arrived at the yard-end, to the wonder of all no motion was apparent save that created by the slow roll of the hull, in moderate weather so majestic in a great ship heavy-cannoned.

A DIGRESSION

When, some days afterwards, in reference to the singularity just mentioned, the Purser (a rather ruddy, rotund person, more accurate as an accountant than profound as a philosopher) said at mess to the Surgeon, "What testimony to the force lodged in will-power," the latter, spare and tall, one in whom a discreet causticity went along with a manner less genial than polite, replied, "Your pardon, Mr. Purser. In a hanging so scientifically conducted—and, under special orders, I myself directed how Budd's was to be effected—any movement following the completed suspension and originating in the body suspended, such movement indicates mechanical spasm in the muscular system. Hence the absence of that is no more attributable to will-power, as you call it, than to horse-power—begging your pardon."

"But this muscular spasm you speak of—is not that, in a degree, more or less invariable in these cases?"

"Assuredly so, Mr. Purser."

"How then, my good sir, do you account for its absence in this instance?"

"Mr. Purser, it is clear that your sense of the singularity in this matter equals not mine. You account for it by what you call will-power, a term not yet included in the lexicon of science. As for me, I do not with my present knowledge pretend to account for it at all. Even should one assume the hypothesis that, at the first touch of the halyards, the action of Budd's heart, intensified by extraordinary emotion at its climax, abruptly stopped—much like a watch when in carelessly winding it up you strain at the finish, thus snapping the spring—even under that hypothesis, how account for the phenomenon that followed?"

"You admit, then, that the absence of spasmodic movement was phenomenal?"

"It was phenomenal, Mr. Purser, in the sense that it was an appearance, the cause of which is not immediately to be assigned."

"But tell me, my dear Sir," pertinaciously continued the other, "was the man's death effected by the halter, or was it a species of euthanasia?"

"*Euthanasia,* Mr. Purser, is something like your will-power; I doubt its authenticity as a scientific term—begging your pardon again. It is at once imaginative and metaphysical; in short, Greek. But," abruptly changing his tone, "there is a case in the sick-bay which I do not care to leave to my assistants. Begging your pardon, but excuse me." And rising from the mess he formally withdrew.

§ 23

The silence at the moment of execution, and for a moment or two continuing thereafter (but emphasized by the regular wash of the sea against the hull, or the flutter of a sail caused by the helmsman's eyes being tempted astray), this emphasized silence was gradually disturbed by a sound not easily to be here verbally rendered. Whoever has heard the freshet-wave of a torrent suddenly swelled by pouring showers in tropical mountains, showers not shared by the plain; whoever has heard the first muffled murmur of its sloping advance through precipitous woods, may form some conception of the sound now heard. The seeming remoteness of its source was because of its murmurous indistinctness, since it came from close by, even from the men massed on the ship's open deck. Being inarticulate, it was dubious in significance further in that it seemed to indicate some capricious revulsion of thought or feeling such as mobs ashore are liable to—in the present instance possibly implying a sullen revocation on the men's part of their involuntary echoing of Billy's benediction. But ere the murmur had time to wax into clamour it was met by a strategic command, the more telling that it came with abrupt unexpectedness.

"Pipe down the starboard watch, Boatswain, and see that they go."

Shrill as the shriek of the sea-hawk the whistles of the Boatswain and his Mates pierced that ominous low sound, dissipating it; and yielding to the mechanism of discipline the throng was thinned by one half. For the remainder most of them were set to temporary employments connected with trimming the yards and so forth, business readily to be found upon occasion by any officer-of-the-deck.

Now each proceeding that follows a mortal sentence pronounced at

sea by a drum-head court is characterized by a promptitude not perceptibly merging into hurry, though bordering that. The hammock—the one which had been Billy's bed when alive, having already been ballasted with shot and otherwise prepared to serve for his canvas coffin—the last offices of the sea-undertakers, the Sail-maker's Mates, were now speedily completed. When everything was in readiness, a second call for all hands, made necessary by the strategic movement before mentioned, was sounded: and now to witness burial.

The details of this closing formality it needs not to give. But when the tilted plank let slide its freight into the sea, a second strange human murmur was heard—blended now with another so inarticulate sound proceeding from certain larger sea-fowl, whose attention having been attracted by the peculiar commotion in the water resulting from the heavy sloped dive of the shotted hammock into the sea, flew screaming to the spot. So near the hull did they come, that the stridor or bony creak of their gaunt double-jointed pinions was audible. As the ship under light airs passed on, leaving the burial spot astern, they still kept circling it low down with the moving shadow of their outstretched wings and the cracked requiem of their cries.

Upon sailors as superstitious as those of the age preceding ours—all men-of-war's men, too, who had just beheld the prodigy of repose in the form suspended in air and now foundering in the deeps; to such mariners the action of the sea-fowl, though dictated by a mere animal greed for prey, was big with no prosaic significance. An uncertain movement began among them, in which some encroachment was made. It was tolerated but for a moment. For suddenly the drum beat to quarters—which familiar sound, happening at least twice every day, had upon the present occasion some signal peremptoriness in it. True martial discipline long continued superinduces in an average man a sort of impulse of docility, whose operation at the official tone of command much resembles in its promptitude the effect of an instinct.

The drum-beat dissolved the multitude, distributing most of them along the batteries of the two covered gun-decks. There, as wont, the gun crews stood by their respective cannon erect and silent. In due course the First officer, sword under arm and standing in his place on the quarter-deck, formally received the successive reports of the sworded Lieutenants commanding the sections of batteries below; the last of which reports being made, the summed report he delivered with the customary salute to the Commander. All of this occupied time, which, in the present case, was the object of beating to quarters at an hour prior to the customary one. That such variance from usage was authorized by an officer like Captain Vere (a martinet as some deemed him), was evidence of the necessity for unusual action implied

in what he deemed to be temporarily the mood of his men. "With mankind," he would say, "forms, measured forms, are everything; and that is the import couched in the story of Orpheus, with his lyre, spellbinding the wild denizens of the woods." And this he once applied to the disruption of forms going an across the Channel and the consequence thereof.

At this unwonted muster at quarters, all proceeded as at the regular hour. The band on the quarter-deck played a sacred air. After which the Chaplain went through with the customary morning service. That done, the drum beat the retreat, and toned by music and religious rites subserving the discipline and purpose of war, the men in their wonted, orderly manner dispersed to the places allotted them when not at the guns.

And now it was full day. The fleece of low-hanging vapour had vanished, licked up by the sun that late had so glorified it. And the circumambient air in the clearness of its serenity was like smooth white marble in the polished block not yet removed from the marble-dealer's yard.

§ 24

The symmetry of form attainable in pure fiction cannot so readily be achieved in a narration essentially having less to do with fable than with fact. Truth uncompromisingly told will always have its ragged edges; hence the conclusion of such a narration is apt to be less finished than an architectural finial.

How it fared with the Handsome Sailor during the year of the great mutiny has been faithfully given. But though properly the story ends with his life, something in way of a sequel will not be amiss. Three brief chapters will suffice.

In the general re-christening under the Directory of the craft originally forming the navy of the French Monarchy, the *St. Louis* line-of-battle ship was named the *Athéiste*. Such a name, like some other substituted ones in the Revolutionary fleet, while proclaiming the infidel audacity of the ruling power, was yet (though not so intended to be) the aptest name, if one consider it, ever given to a war-ship; far more so, indeed, than the *Devastation* or the *Eritus* (the Hell) and similar names bestowed upon fighting ships.

On the return passage to the full English fleet from the detached cruise during which occurred the events already recorded, the *Indomitable* fell in with the *Athéiste*. An engagement ensued; during which Captain Vere, in the act of putting his ship alongside the enemy with a view of throwing his boarders across the bulwarks, was hit by a

musket-ball from a port-hole of the enemy's main cabin. More than disabled, he dropped to the deck and was carried below to the same cock-pit where some of his men already lay. The senior Lieutenant took command. Under him the enemy was finally captured, and though much crippled, was by rare good fortune successfully taken into Gibraltar, an English fort not very distant from the scene of the fight. There Captain Vere with the rest of the wounded was put ashore. He lingered for some days, but the end came. Unhappily he was cut off too early for the Nile and Trafalgar. The spirit that, in spite of its philosophic austerity, may yet have indulged in the most secret of all passions—ambition—never attained to the fulness of fame.

Not long before death, while lying under the influence of that magical drug which, in soothing the physical frame, mysteriously operates on the subtler element in man, he was heard to murmur words inexplicable to his attendant—"Billy Budd, Billy Budd." That these were not the accents of remorse, would seem clear from what the attendant said to the *Indomitable's* potent senior officer of marines, who, as the most reluctant to condemn of the members of the drum-head court, too well knew (though here he kept the knowledge to himself) who Billy Budd was.

§ 25

Some few weeks after the execution, among other matters under the main head of *News from the Mediterranean,* there appeared in one naval chronicle of the time, an authorized weekly publication, an account of the affair. It was doubtless for the most part written in good faith, though the medium, partly rumour, through which the facts must have reached the writer, served to deflect and in part to falsify them. The account was as follows:—

"On the tenth of the last month a deplorable occurrence took place on board *H.M.S. Indomitable.* John Claggart, the ship's Master-at-arms, discovering that some sort of plot was incipient among an inferior section of the ship's company, and that the ringleader was one William Budd, he, Claggart, in the act of arraigning the man before the Captain was vindictively stabbed to the heart by the suddenly drawn sheath-knife of Budd.

"The deed and the implement employed sufficiently suggest that, though mustered into the service under an English name, the assassin was no Englishman but one of those aliens adopting English cognomen whom the present extraordinary necessities of the Service have caused to be admitted into it in considerable numbers.

"The enormity of the crime and the extreme depravity of the criminal, appear the greater in view of the character of the victim—a middle-aged man, respectable and discreet, belonging to that minor official grade, the petty-officers, upon whom, as none know better than the commissioned gentlemen, the efficiency of His Majesty's navy so largely depends. His function was a responsible one—at once onerous and thankless—and his fidelity in it the greater because of his strong patriotic impulse. In this instance, as in so many other instances in these days, the character of the unfortunate man signally refutes, if refutation were needed, that peevish saying attributed to the late Dr. Johnson, that patriotism is the last refuge of a scoundrel.

"The criminal paid the penalty of his crime. The promptitude of the punishment has proved salutary. Nothing amiss is now apprehended aboard the *H.M.S. Indomitable.*"

The above item appearing in a publication, now long ago super-annuated and forgotten in all that hitherto has stood in human record, to attest what manner of men respectively were John Claggart and Billy Budd.*

§ 26

Everything is for a season remarkable in navies. Any tangible object associated with some striking incident of the service is converted into a monument. The spar from which the foretopman was suspended was for some few years kept trace of by the bluejackets. Then knowledge followed it from ship to deck-yard, and again from deck-yard to ship, still pursuing it even when at last reduced to a mere deck-yard boom. To them a chip of it was as a piece of the Cross. Ignorant though they were of the real facts of the happening, and not thinking but that the penalty was unavoidably inflicted from the naval point of view, for all that they instinctively felt that Billy was a sort of man as incapable of mutiny as of wilful murder. They recalled the fresh young image of the Handsome Sailor, that face never deformed by a sneer of subtler vile freak of the heart within! This impression of him was doubtless deep-ened by the fact that he was gone, and in a measure mysteriously gone. On the gun-decks of the *Indomitable* the general estimate of his nature and its unconscious simplicity eventually found rude utterance from another foretopman, one of his own watch, gifted as some sailors are with an artless poetic temperament. Those tarry hands made some lines

*An author's note, crossed out, here appears in the original MS. It reads: Here ends a story not unwarranted in this incongruous world of ours—inno-cence and infirmity, spiritual depravity and fair respite.·

which, after circulating among the ship-board crew for a while, finally were rudely printed at Portsmouth as a ballad. The title given to it was the sailor's own:

BILLY IN THE DARBIES

Good of the Chaplain to enter Lone Bay
And down on his marrow-bones here and pray
For the likes just o' me, Billy Budd,—But look:
Through the port comes the moon-shine astray!
It tips the guard's cutlass and silvers this nook;
But 'twill die in the dawning of Billy's last day.
A jewel-block they'll make of me to-morrow,
Pendant pearl from the yard-arm-end
Like the ear-drop I gave to Bristol Molly—
O, 'tis me, not the sentence, they'll suspend.
Ay, Ay, all is up; and I must up too
Early in the morning, aloft from alow.
On an empty stomach, now, never it would do.
They'll give me a nibble—bit o' biscuit ere I go.
Sure, a messmate will reach me the last parting cup;
But, turning heads away from the hoist and the belay,
Heaven knows who will have the running of me up!
No pipe to those halyards—but aren't it all sham?
A blur's in my eyes, it is dreaming that I am.
A hatchet to my panzer? all adrift to go?
The drum roll to grog, and Billy never know?
But Donald he has promised to stand by the plank;
So I'll shake a friendly hand ere I sink.
But—no! It is dead then I'll be, come to think.—
I remember Taff the Welshman when he sank.
And his cheek it was like the budding pink.
But me, they'll lash me in hammock, drop me deep
Fathoms down, fathoms down, how I'll dream fast asleep.
I feel it stealing now. Sentry, are you there?
Just ease these darbies at the wrist.
And roll me over fair.
I am sleepy, and the oozy weeds about me twist.

END OF BOOK

April 19, 1891.

Jacob's Room

VIRGINIA WOOLF

VIRGINIA WOOLF *was born in London in 1882. The daughter of Sir Leslie Stephen, the noted biographer and critic, she was from her earliest years at home in a literary society. The Stephen girls, for Virginia and her sister Vanessa were inseparable, attracted to their home in Bloomsbury a brilliant group, most of them from Cambridge, including Clive Bell, E. M. Forster, Lytton Strachey and Leonard Woolf, whom Virginia married in 1912. Mr and Mrs Woolf presently set up a small hand press, producing limited editions and eventually the novels under her signature. Jacob's Room, which appeared in 1922, measures 54,000 words.*

INTRODUCTION

In this novel Rebecca West tells the story of Jacob Flanders, a young Englishman, unspoiled and undecided. Jacob's room is wherever he hangs his hat—or, to be more practical, his trousers, for Jacob never wears a hat; now it is in Neville's Court, Trinity College, where he is absorbed in the bachelordom of Cambridge; now it is in Great Ormond Street, where he reads for law and divides his time between Bohemia and Mayfair; now it is in the British Museum or a Paris *atelier* or a hotel room in Athens. Jacob's room is, if you like, the whole panorama of Edwardian England, with the many attractions and the small misgivings which it held out to a fastidious man in his early twenties whose romantic streak and Greek-cut distinction made him so instantly appealing to women and to men.

Virginia Woolf is one of the most elaborate stylists of our time and until you have accustomed yourself to it her style may be a source of some inconvenience. You first see Jacob as a little boy, playing with his brothers on the beach at Scarborough. In these early pages the author has two duties which she wants to get done with as swiftly as possible. She wants to give you a clear understanding of Jacob's middle-class background and she wants to show you that cheerful, energetic and somewhat sentimental widow, his mother. Clearly it is Mrs Woolf's design to set Jacob free of his mother and to accomplish her purpose she uses, of all people, red-haired Mr Floyd, the village rector. It appears that Mr Floyd has been teaching the boys Latin in his spare time, and, propinquity having done its work, he has fallen in love with Betty Flanders and now proposes to her by letter. That night when the boys are in bed Mrs Flanders, her mind still distracted by those domestic details which keep scurrying like mice, bends over her note paper, trying to tell Mr Floyd why she can't marry him. The

passage which follows is so characteristic of Mrs Woolf that I must quote it in full to show you how relative is time in the hands of a skillful novelist.

". . . it was such a motherly, respectful, inconsequential, regretful letter that he kept it for many years—long after his marriage with Miss Wimbush of Andover, long after he had left the village. For he asked for a parish in Sheffield, which was given him, and, sending for Archer, Jacob and John to say good-by, he told them to choose whatever they liked in his study to remember him by. Archer chose a paper knife, because he did not like to choose anything too good; Jacob chose the works of Byron in one volume; John, who was still too young to make a proper choice, chose Mr Floyd's kitten, which his brothers thought an absurd choice, but Mr Floyd upheld him when he said, 'It has fur like you.' Then Mr Floyd spoke about the king's navy (to which Archer was going) and about Rugby (to which Jacob was going) and next day he received a silver salver and went, first to Sheffield where he met Miss Wimbush, who was on a visit to her uncle, then to Hackney—then to Maresfield House, of which he became the principal, and finally, becoming editor of a well-known series of ecclesiastical biographies, he retired to Hampstead with his wife and daughter and is often to be seen feeding the ducks on Leg of Mutton Pond. As for Mrs Flanders' letter, when he looked for it the other day he could not find it and did not like to ask his wife whether she had put it away. Meeting Jacob in Piccadilly lately, he recognized him after three seconds. But Jacob had grown such a fine young man that Mr Floyd did not like to stop him in the street."

In those seemingly random details which occupy less than a page but which actually traverse twenty years Virginia Woolf has given you a delicious thumbnail sketch of Mr Floyd; she has indicated Jacob's taste for books, has put him through Rugby, freed him from his mother's apron strings and brought him to the ripeness where the story can begin in earnest. By such swift transitions, by suggesting so much in so little Mrs Woolf gives to her novel the sweep and development of many years.

Virginia Woolf was more dependent upon details than any other novelist of our time. Like Katherine Mansfield and Rebecca West, her sense of observation is acute. Always she is reaching for those few telling details which will unlock an entire scene in three swift sentences. Any style as exacting as this imposes an obligation upon the reader. It means that he must be sensitive to and, as it were, in the same key with the story.

It may help to put you in a receptive mood if I tell you of the three aspects of Mrs Woolf's narration which give me—as she intended they

should—a special kind of satisfaction. First there is her instinctive delight in the thumbnail sketch. *Jacob's Room* is crowded with human encounters that hit like a flash and are gone and with characters (to call them "minor" is to belittle the intensity of their being) whom we see for an instant but remember long after. Captain Barfoot, the punctilious and, I am sure, platonic lover of Jacob's mother, Miss Marchmont, the pathetic little drone in the British Museum, Sopwith, the talkative Don ("talking, talking, talking—as if everything could be talked—the soul itself slipped through the lips in thin silver discs which dissolve in young men's minds like silver, like moonlight"), Cruttendon, whose painting Jacob thought "a solid piece of work," Florinda, who talked more about virginity than women usually do, Fanny Elmer, the thin model . . . But there are fifty such excited, odd, talkative, friendly people crowding into *Jacob's Room.*

Notice also the curious tempo and the apparent jumble of sound with which Mrs Woolf conducts her dialogue. No sentence is ever completed, no conversation ever rounded off. Instead you pass from group to group, and the volley of talk as it rebounds against your mind tells you more than any one person could do. Beneath these sentences which seem to be so random are motives common to us all, little revelations of character which, for instance, make you so sure that you would like Mrs Durrant, so sure that Clara is falling in love with Jacob, so sure that Bonamy is the friend who understands him best. In short, once you have learned the code there is a telegraphic pleasure to be had in attending one of Virginia Woolf's parties.

In contrast to this there is the single-minded intentness with which she reveals to you Jacob's mind, the slowgoing, interpretative pages where the mind must pause while we see Jacob as he walks along the Cam "in the springy air of May," Jacob at St. Paul's, Jacob on a bus, taking in London, Jacob at the Parthenon—essays on loneliness, on beauty and on doubt, so rich in experience, so sensitive to the aspects of humanity that they take in, through Jacob's antennae, the sights and the sounds and the thoughts not only of an Englishman at the prime of life but of England in its hazy, golden prime, when the world was at peace and before the guns were heard across the Channel.

§ I

"So of course," wrote Betty Flanders, pressing her heels rather deeper in the sand, "there was nothing for it but to leave."

Slowly welling from the point of her gold nib, pale blue ink dissolved the full stop; for there her pen stuck; her eyes fixed, and tears slowly filled them. The entire bay quivered; the lighthouse wobbled; and she had the illusion that the mast of Mr. Connor's little yacht was bending like a wax candle in the sun. She winked quickly. Accidents were awful things. She winked again. The mast was straight; the waves were regular; the lighthouse was upright; but the blot had spread.

". . . nothing for it but to leave," she read.

"Well, if Jacob doesn't want to play" (the shadow of Archer, her eldest son, fell across the notepaper and looked blue on the sand, and she felt chilly—it was the third of September already), "If Jacob doesn't want to play"—what a horrid blot! It must be getting late.

"Where *is* that tiresome little boy?" she said. "I don't see him. Run and find him. Tell him to come at once." ". . . but mercifully," she scribbled, ignoring the full stop, "everything seems satisfactorily arranged, packed though we are like herrings in a barrel, and forced to stand the perambulator which the landlady quite naturally won't allow . . ."

Such were Betty Flanders's letters to Captain Barfoot—many-paged, tear-stained. Scarborough is seven hundred miles from Cornwall: Captain Barfoot is in Scarborough: Seabrook is dead. Tears made all the dahlias in her garden undulate in red waves and flashed the glass house in her eyes, and spangled the kitchen with bright knives, and made Mrs. Jarvis, the rector's wife, think at church, while the hymntune played and Mrs. Flanders bent low over her little boys' heads, that marriage is a fortress and widows stray solitary in the open fields, picking up stones, gleaning a few golden straws, lonely, unprotected, poor creatures. Mrs. Flanders had been a widow these two years.

"Ja—cob! Ja—cob!" Archer shouted.

"Scarborough," Mrs. Flanders wrote on the envelope, and dashed a bold line beneath; it was her native town; the hub of the universe. But a stamp? She ferreted in her bag; then held it up mouth downwards; then fumbled in her lap, all so vigorously that Charles Steele in the Panama hat suspended his paint-brush.

Like the antennae of some irritable insect it positively trembled. Here was that woman moving—actually going to get up—confound her! He struck the canvas a hasty violet-black dab. For the landscape needed it. It was too pale—greys flowing into lavenders, and one star or a white gull suspended just so—too pale as usual. The critics would say it was too pale, for he was an unknown man exhibiting obscurely, a favourite with his landladies' children, wearing a cross on his watch chain, and much gratified if his landladies liked his pictures—which they often did.

"Ja—cob! Ja—cob!" Archer shouted.

Exasperated by the noise, yet loving children, Steele picked nervously at the dark little coils on his palette.

"I saw your brother—I saw your brother," he said, nodding his head, as Archer lagged past him, trailing his spade, and scowling at the old gentleman in spectacles.

"Over there—by the rock," Steele muttered, with his brush between his teeth, squeezing out raw sienna, and keeping his eyes fixed on Betty Flanders's back.

"Ja—cob! Ja—cob!" shouted Archer, lagging on after a second.

The voice had an extraordinary sadness. Pure from all body, pure from all passion, going out into the world, solitary, unanswered, breaking against rocks—so it sounded.

Steele frowned; but was pleased by the effect of the black—it was just *that* note which brought the rest together. "Ah, one may learn to paint at fifty! There's Titian . . ." and so, having found the right tint, up he looked and saw to his horror a cloud over the bay.

Mrs. Flanders rose, slapped her coat this side and that to get the sand off, and picked up her black parasol.

The rock was one of those tremendously solid brown, or rather black, rocks which emerge from the sand like something primitive. Rough with crinkled limpet shells and sparsely strewn with locks of dry seaweed, a small boy has to stretch his legs far apart, and indeed to feel rather heroic, before he gets to the top.

But there, on the very top, is a hollow full of water, with a sandy bottom; with a blob of jelly stuck to the side, and some mussels. A fish darts across. The fringe of yellow-brown seaweed flutters, and out pushes an opal-shelled crab——

"Oh, a huge crab," Jacob murmured—and begins his journey on weakly legs on the sandy bottom. Now! Jacob plunged his hand. The crab was cool and very light. But the water was thick with sand, and so, scrambling down, Jacob was about to jump, holding his bucket in front of him, when he saw, stretched entirely rigid, side by side, their faces very red, an enormous man and woman.

An enormous man and woman (it was early-closing day) were stretched motionless, with their heads on pocket-handkerchiefs, side by side, within a few feet of the sea, while two or three gulls gracefully skirted the incoming waves, and settled near their boots.

The large red faces lying on the bandanna handkerchiefs stared up at Jacob. Jacob stared down at them. Holding his bucket very carefully, Jacob then jumped deliberately and trotted away very nonchalantly at first, but faster and faster as the waves came creaming up to him and he had to swerve to avoid them, and the gulls rose in front of him and floated out and settled again a little farther on. A large black woman was sitting on the sand. He ran towards her.

"Nanny! Nanny!" he cried, sobbing the words out on the crest of each gasping breath.

The waves came round her. She was a rock. She was covered with seaweed which pops when it is pressed. He was lost.

There he stood. His face composed itself. He was about to roar when, lying among the black sticks and straw under the cliff, he saw a whole skull—perhaps a cow's skull, a skull, perhaps, with the teeth in it. Sobbing, but absent-mindedly, he ran farther and farther away until he held the skull in his arms.

"There he is!" cried Mrs. Flanders, coming round the rock and covering the whole space of the beach in a few seconds. "What has he got hold of? Put it down, Jacob! Drop it this moment! Something horrid, I know. Why didn't you stay with us? Naughty little boy! Now put it down. Now come along both of you," and she swept round, holding Archer by one hand and fumbling for Jacob's arm with the other. But he ducked down and picked up the sheep's jaw, which was loose.

Swinging her bag, clutching her parasol, holding Archer's hand, and telling the story of the gunpowder explosion in which poor Mr. Curnow had lost his eye, Mrs. Flanders hurried up the steep lane, aware all the time in the depths of her mind of some buried discomfort.

There on the sand not far from the lovers lay the old sheep's skull without its jaw. Clean, white, wind-swept, sand-rubbed, a more unpolluted piece of bone existed nowhere on the coast of Cornwall. The sea holly would grow through the eye-sockets; it would turn to powder, or some golfer, hitting his ball one fine day, would disperse a little dust. —No, but not in lodgings, thought Mrs. Flanders. It's a great experiment coming so far with young children. There's no man to help with the perambulator. And Jacob is such a handful; so obstinate already.

"Throw it away, dear, do," she said, as they got into the road; but Jacob squirmed away from her; and the wind rising, she took out her bonnet-pin, looked at the sea, and stuck it in afresh. The wind was rising. The waves showed that uneasiness, like something alive, restive, expecting the whip, of waves before a storm. The fishing-boats were leaning to the water's brim. A pale yellow light shot across the purple sea; and shut. The lighthouse was lit. "Come along," said Betty Flanders. The sun blazed in their faces and gilded the great blackberries trembling out from the hedge which Archer tried to strip as they passed.

"Don't lag, boys. You've got nothing to change into," said Betty, pulling them along, and looking with uneasy emotion at the earth displayed so luridly, with sudden sparks of light from greenhouses in gardens, with a sort of yellow and black mutability, against this blazing sunset, this astonishing agitation and vitality of nature, which stirred Betty Flanders and made her think of responsibility and danger. She gripped Archer's hand. On she plodded up the hill.

"What did I ask you to remember?" she said.

"I don't know," said Archer.

"Well, I don't know either," said Betty, humorously and simply, and who shall deny that this blankness of mind, when combined with profusion, mother wit, old wives' tales, haphazard ways, moments of astonishing daring, humour, and sentimentality—who shall deny that in these respects every woman is nicer than any man?

Well, Betty Flanders, to begin with.

She had her hand upon the garden gate.

"The meat!" she exclaimed, striking the latch down.

She had forgotten the meat.

There was Rebecca at the window.

The bareness of Mrs. Pearce's front room was fully displayed at ten o'clock at night when a powerful oil lamp stood on the middle of the table. The harsh light fell on the garden; cut straight across the lawn; lit up a child's bucket and a purple aster and reached the hedge. Mrs.

Flanders had left her sewing on the table. There were her large reels of white cotton and her steel spectacles; her needle-case; her brown wool wound round an old postcard. There were the bulrushes and the *Strand* magazines; and the linoleum sandy from the boys' boots. A daddy-long-legs shot from corner to corner and hit the lamp globe. The wind blew straight dashes of rain across the window, which flashed silver as they passed through the light. A single leaf tapped hurriedly, persistently, upon the glass. There was a hurricane out at sea.

Archer could not sleep.

Mrs. Flanders stooped over him. "Think of the fairies," said Betty Flanders. "Think of the lovely, lovely birds settling down on their nests. Now shut your eyes and see the old mother bird with a worm in her beak. Now turn and shut your eyes," she murmured, "and shut your eyes."

The lodging-house seemed full of gurgling and rushing; the cistern overflowing; water bubbling and squeaking and running along the pipes and streaming down the windows.

"What's all that water rushing in?" murmured Archer.

"It's only the bath water running away," said Mrs. Flanders.

Something snapped out of doors.

"I say, won't that steamer sink?" said Archer, opening his eyes.

"Of course it won't," said Mrs. Flanders. "The Captain's in bed long ago. Shut your eyes, and think of the fairies, fast asleep, under the flowers."

"I thought he'd never get off—such a hurricane," she whispered to Rebecca, who was bending over a spirit-lamp in the small room next door. The wind rushed outside, but the small flame of the spirit-lamp burnt quietly, shaded from the cot by a book stood on edge.

"Did he take his bottle well?" Mrs. Flanders whispered, and Rebecca nodded and went to the cot and turned down the quilt, and Mrs. Flanders bent over and looked anxiously at the baby, asleep, but frowning. The window shook, and Rebecca stole like a cat and wedged it. The two women murmured over the spirit-lamp, plotting the eternal conspiracy of hush and clean bottles while the wind raged and gave a sudden wrench at the cheap fastenings.

Both looked round at the cot. Their lips were pursed. Mrs. Flanders crossed over to the cot.

"Asleep?" whispered Rebecca, looking at the cot.

Mrs. Flanders nodded.

"Good night, Rebecca," Mrs. Flanders murmured, and Rebecca

called her ma'm, though they were conspirators plotting the eternal conspiracy of hush and clean bottles.

Mrs. Flanders had left the lamp burning in the front room. There were her spectacles, her sewing; and a letter with the Scarborough postmark. She had not drawn the curtains either.

The light blazed out across the patch of grass; fell on the child's green bucket with the gold line round it, and upon the aster which trembled violently beside it. For the wind was tearing across the coast, hurling itself at the hills, and leaping, in sudden gusts, on top of its own back. How it spread over the town in the hollow! How the lights seemed to wink and quiver in its fury, lights in the harbour, lights in bedroom windows high up! And rolling dark waves before it, it raced over the Atlantic, jerking the stars above the ships this way and that.

There was a click in the front sitting-room. Mr. Pearce had extinguished the lamp. The garden went out. It was but a dark patch. Every inch was rained upon. Every blade of grass was bent by rain. Eyelids would have been fastened down by the rain. Lying on one's back one would have seen nothing but muddle and confusion—clouds turning and turning, and something yellow-tinted and sulphurous in the darkness.

The little boys in the front bedroom had thrown off their blankets and lay under the sheets. It was hot; rather sticky and steamy. Archer lay spread out, with one arm striking across the pillow. He was flushed; and when the heavy curtain blew out a little he turned and half-opened his eyes. The wind actually stirred the cloth on the chest of drawers, and let in a little light, so that the sharp edge of the chest of drawers was visible, running straight up, until a white shape bulged out; and a silver streak showed in the looking-glass.

In the other bed by the door Jacob lay asleep, fast asleep, profoundly unconscious. The sheep's jaw with the big yellow teeth in it lay at his feet. He had kicked it against the iron bed-rail.

Outside the rain poured down more directly and powerfully as the wind fell in the early hours of the morning. The aster was beaten to the earth. The child's bucket was half-full of rain-water; and the opal-shelled crab slowly circled round the bottom, trying with its weakly legs to climb the steep side; trying again and falling back, and trying again and again.

§ 2

"Mrs. Flanders"—"Poor Betty Flanders"—"Dear Betty"—"She's very attractive still"—"Odd she don't marry again!" "There's Captain

Barfoot to be sure—calls every Wednesday as regular as clockwork, and never brings his wife."

"But that's Ellen Barfoot's fault," the ladies of Scarborough said. "She don't put herself out for no one."

"A man likes to have a son—that we know."

"Some tumours have to be cut; but the sort my mother had you bear with you for years and years, and never even have a cup of tea brought up to you in bed."

(Mrs. Barfoot was an invalid.)

Elizabeth Flanders, of whom this and much more than this had been said and would be said, was, of course, a widow in her prime. She was half-way between forty and fifty. Years and sorrow between them; the death of Seabrook, her husband; three boys; poverty; a house on the outskirts of Scarborough; her brother, poor Morty's downfall and possible demise—for where was he? what was he? Shading her eyes, she looked along the road for Captain Barfoot—yes, there he was, punctual as ever; the attentions of the Captain—all ripened Betty Flanders, enlarged her figure, tinged her face with jollity, and flooded her eyes for no reason that any one could see perhaps three times a day.

True, there's no harm in crying for one's husband, and the tombstone, though plain, was a solid piece of work, and on summer's days when the widow brought her boys to stand there one felt kindly towards her. Hats were raised higher than usual; wives tugged their husbands' arms. Seabrook lay six foot beneath, dead these many years; enclosed in three shells; the crevices sealed with lead, so that, had earth and wood been glass, doubtless his very face lay visible beneath, the face of a young man whiskered, shapely, who had gone out duck-shooting and refused to change his boots.

"Merchant of this city," the tombstone said; though why Betty Flanders had chosen so to call him when, as many still remembered, he had only sat behind an office window for three months, and before that had broken horses, ridden to hounds, farmed a few fields, and run a little wild—well, she had to call him something. An example for the boys.

Had he, then, been nothing? An unanswerable question, since even if it weren't the habit of the undertaker to close the eyes, the light so soon goes out of them. At first, part of herself; now one of a company, he had merged in the grass, the sloping hillside, the thousand white stones, some slanting, others upright, the decayed wreaths, the crosses of green tin, the narrow yellow paths, and the lilacs that drooped in April, with a scent like that of an invalid's bedroom, over the church-

yard wall. Seabrook was now all that; and when, with her skirt hitched up, feeding the chickens, she heard the bell for service or funeral, that was Seabrook's voice—the voice of the dead.

The rooster had been known to fly on her shoulder and peck her neck, so that now she carried a stick or took one of the children with her when she went to feed the fowls.

"Wouldn't you like my knife, mother?" said Archer.

Sounding at the same moment as the bell, her son's voice mixed life and death inextricably, exhilaratingly.

"What a big knife for a small boy!" she said. She took it to please him. Then the rooster flew out of the hen-house, and, shouting to Archer to shut the door into the kitchen garden, Mrs. Flanders set her meal down, clucked for the hens, went bustling about the orchard, and was seen from over the way by Mrs. Cranch, who, beating her mat against the wall, held it for a moment suspended while she observed to Mrs. Page next door that Mrs. Flanders was in the orchard with the chickens.

Mrs. Page, Mrs. Cranch, and Mrs. Garfit could see Mrs. Flanders in the orchard because the orchard was a piece of Dods Hill enclosed; and Dods Hill dominated the village. No words can exaggerate the importance of Dods Hill. It was the earth; the world against the sky; the horizon of how many glances can best be computed by those who have lived all their lives in the same village, only leaving it once to fight in the Crimea, like old George Garfit, leaning over his garden gate smoking his pipe. The progress of the sun was measured by it; the tint of the day laid against it to be judged.

"Now she's going up the hill with little John," said Mrs. Cranch to Mrs. Garfit, shaking her mat for the last time, and bustling indoors.

Opening the orchard gate, Mrs. Flanders walked to the top of Dods Hill, holding John by the hand. Archer and Jacob ran in front or lagged behind; but they were in the Roman fortress when she came there, and shouting out what ships were to be seen in the bay. For there was a magnificent view—moors behind, sea in front, and the whole of Scarborough from one end to the other laid out flat like a puzzle. Mrs. Flanders, who was growing stout, sat down in the fortress and looked about her.

The entire gamut of the view's changes should have been known to her; its winter aspect, spring, summer, and autumn; how storms came up from the sea; how the moors shuddered and brightened as the clouds went over; she should have noted the red spot where the villas were building; and the crisscross of lines where the allotments were cut; and the diamond flash of little glass houses in the sun. Or, if details like these escaped her, she might have let her fancy play upon

the gold tint of the sea at sunset, and thought how it lapped in coins of gold upon the shingle. Little pleasure boats shoved out into it; the black arm of the pier hoarded it up. The whole city was pink and gold; domed; mist-wreathed; resonant; strident. Banjoes strummed; the parade smelt of tar which stuck to the heels; goats suddenly cantered their carriages through crowds. It was observed how well the Corporation had laid out the flower-beds. Sometimes a straw hat was blown away. Tulips burnt in the sun. Numbers of sponge-bog trousers were stretched in rows. Purple bonnets fringed soft, pink, querulous faces on pillows in bath chairs. Triangular hoardings were wheeled along by men in white coats. Captain George Boase had caught a monster shark. One side of the triangular hoarding said so in red, blue, and yellow letters; and each line ended with three differently coloured notes of exclamation.

So that was a reason for going down into the Aquarium, where the sallow blinds, the stale smell of spirits of salt, the bamboo chairs, the tables with ash-trays, the revolving fish, the attendant knitting behind six or seven chocolate boxes (often she was quite alone with the fish for hours at a time) remained in the mind as part of the monster shark, he himself being only a flabby yellow receptacle, like an empty Gladstone bag in a tank. No one had ever been cheered by the Aquarium; but the faces of those emerging quickly lost their dim, chilled expression when they perceived that it was only by standing in a queue that one could be admitted to the pier. Once through the turnstiles, every one walked for a yard or two very briskly; some flagged at this stall; others at that. But it was the band that drew them all to it finally; even the fishermen on the lower pier taking up their pitch within its range.

The band played in the Moorish kiosk. Number nine went up on the board. It was a waltz tune. The pale girls, the old widow lady, the three Jews lodging in the same boarding-house, the dandy, the major, the horse-dealer, and the gentleman of independent means, all wore the same blurred, drugged expression, and through the chinks in the planks at their feet they could see the green summer waves, peacefully, amiably, swaying round the iron pillars of the pier.

But there was a time when none of this had any existence (thought the young man leaning against the railings). Fix your eyes upon the lady's skirt; the grey one will do—above the pink silk stockings. It changes; drapes her ankles—the nineties; then it amplifies—the seventies; now it's burnished red and stretched above a crinoline—the sixties; a tiny black foot wearing a white cotton stocking peeps out. Still sitting there? Yes—she's still on the pier. The silk now is sprigged with roses, but somehow one no longer sees so clearly. There's no pier

beneath us. The heavy chariot may swing along the turnpike road, but
there's no pier for it to stop at, and how grey and turbulent the sea is
in the seventeenth century! Let's to the museum. Cannon-balls; arrow-
heads; Roman glass and a forceps green with verdigris. The Rev.
Jaspar Floyd dug them up at his own expense early in the forties in the
Roman camp on Dods Hill—see the little ticket with the faded writing
on it.

And now, what's the next thing to see in Scarborough?

Mrs. Flanders sat on the raised circle of the Roman camp, patch-
ing Jacob's breeches; only looking up as she sucked the end of her
cotton, or when some insect dashed at her, boomed in her ear, and was
gone.

John kept trotting up and slapping down in her lap grass or dead
leaves which he called "tea," and she arranged them methodically but
absent-mindedly, laying the flowery heads of the grasses together,
thinking how Archer had been awake again last night; the church
clock was ten or thirteen minutes fast; she wished she could buy
Garfit's acre.

"That's an orchid leaf, Johnny. Look at the little brown spots. Come,
my dear. We must go home. Ar—cher! Ja—cob!"

"Ar—cher—Ja—cob!" Johnny piped after her, pivoting round on
his heel, and strewing the grass and leaves in his hands as if he were
sowing seed. Archer and Jacob jumped up from behind the mound
where they had been crouching with the intention of springing upon
their mother unexpectedly, and they all began to walk slowly home.

"Who is that?" said Mrs. Flanders, shading her eyes.

"That old man in the road?" said Archer, looking below.

"He's not an old man," said Mrs. Flanders. "He's—no, he's not—I
thought it was the Captain, but it's Mr. Floyd. Come along, boys."

"Oh, bother Mr. Floyd!" said Jacob, switching off a thistle's head,
for he knew already that Mr. Floyd was going to teach them Latin,
as indeed he did for three years in his spare time, out of kindness, for
there was no other gentleman in the neighbourhood whom Mrs.
Flanders could have asked to do such a thing, and the elder boys were
getting beyond her, and must be got ready for school, and it was more
than most clergymen would have done, coming round after tea, or
having them in his own room—as he could fit it in—for the parish
was a very large one, and Mr. Floyd, like his father before him, visited
cottages miles away on the moors, and, like old Mr. Floyd, was a great
scholar, which made it so unlikely—she had never dreamt of such a
thing. Ought she to have guessed? But let alone being a scholar he was
eight years younger than she was. She knew his mother—old Mrs.
Floyd. She had tea there. And it was that very evening when she came

back from having tea with old Mrs. Floyd that she found the note in
the hall and took it into the kitchen with her when she went to give
Rebecca the fish, thinking it must be something about the boys.

"Mr. Floyd brought it himself, did he?—I think the cheese must
be in the parcel in the hall—oh, in the hall——" for she was reading.
No, it was not about the boys.

"Yes, enough for fish-cakes to-morrow certainly— Perhaps Captain
Barfoot——" she had come to the word "love." She went into the
garden and read, leaning against the walnut tree to steady herself. Up
and down went her breast. Seabrook came so vividly before her. She
shook her head and was looking through her tears at the little shifting
leaves against the yellow sky when three geese, half-running, half-
flying, scuttled across the lawn with Johnny behind them, brandishing
a stick.

Mrs. Flanders flushed with anger.

"How many times have I told you?" she cried, and seized him and
snatched his stick away from him.

"But they'd escaped!" he cried, struggling to get free.

"You're a very naughty boy. If I've told you once, I've told you a
thousand times. I won't *have* you chasing the geese!" she said, and
crumpling Mr. Floyd's letter in her hand, she held Johnny fast and
herded the geese back into the orchard.

"How could I think of marriage!" she said to herself bitterly, as she
fastened the gate with a piece of wire. She had always disliked red hair
in men, she thought, thinking of Mr. Floyd's appearance, that night
when the boys had gone to bed. And pushing her work-box away, she
drew the blotting-paper towards her, and read Mr. Floyd's letter again,
and her breast went up and down when she came to the word "love,"
but not so fast this time, for she saw Johnny chasing the geese, and
knew that it was impossible for her to marry any one—let alone Mr.
Floyd, who was so much younger than she was, but what a nice man—
and such a scholar too.

"Dear Mr. Floyd," she wrote.—"Did I forget about the cheese?"
she wondered, laying down her pen. No, she had told Rebecca that the
cheese was in the hall. "I am much surprised . . ." she wrote.

But the letter which Mr. Floyd found on the table when he got up
early next morning did not begin "I am much surprised," and it was
such a motherly, respectful, inconsequent, regretful letter that he kept
it for many years; long after his marriage with Miss Wimbush, of
Andover; long after he had left the village. For he asked for a parish in
Sheffield, which was given him; and, sending for Archer, Jacob, and
John to say good-bye, he told them to choose whatever they liked in
his study to remember him by. Archer chose a paper-knife, because

he did not like to choose anything too good; Jacob chose the works of Byron in one volume; John, who was still too young to make a proper choice, chose Mr. Floyd's kitten, which his brothers thought an absurd choice, but Mr. Floyd upheld him when he said: "It has fur like you." Then Mr. Floyd spoke about the King's Navy (to which Archer was going); and about Rugby (to which Jacob was going); and next day he received a silver salver and went—first to Sheffield, where he met Miss Wimbush, who was on a visit to her uncle, then to Hackney— then to Maresfield House, of which he became the principal, and finally, becoming editor of a well-known series of Ecclesiastical Biographies, he retired to Hampstead with his wife and daughter, and is often to be seen feeding the ducks on Leg of Mutton Pond. As for Mrs. Flanders's letter—when he looked for it the other day he could not find it, and did not like to ask his wife whether she had put it away. Meeting Jacob in Piccadilly lately, he recognized him after three seconds. But Jacob had grown such a fine young man that Mr. Floyd did not like to stop him in the street.

"Dear me," said Mrs. Flanders, when she read in the *Scarborough and Harrogate Courier* that the Rev. Andrew Floyd, etc., etc., had been made Principal of the Maresfield House, "that must be our Mr. Floyd."

A slight gloom fell upon the table. Jacob was helping himself to jam; the postman was talking to Rebecca in the kitchen; there was a bee humming at the yellow flower which nodded at the open window. They were all alive, that is to say, while poor Mr. Floyd was becoming Principal of Maresfield House.

Mrs. Flanders got up and went over to the fender and stroked Topaz on the neck behind the ears.

"Poor Topaz," she said (for Mr. Floyd's kitten was now a very old cat, a little mangy behind the ears, and one of these days would have to be killed).

"Poor old Topaz," said Mrs. Flanders, as he stretched himself out in the sun, and she smiled, thinking how she had had him gelded, and how she did not like red hair in men. Smiling, she went into the kitchen.

Jacob drew rather a dirty pocket-handkerchief across his face. He went upstairs to his room.

The stag-beetle dies slowly (it was John who collected the beetles). Even on the second day its legs were supple. But the butterflies were dead. A whiff of rotten eggs had vanquished the pale clouded yellows which came pelting across the orchard and up Dods Hill and away on

to the moor, now lost behind a furze bush, then off again helter-skelter in a broiling sun. A fritillary basked on a white stone in the Roman camp. From the valley came the sound of church bells. They were all eating roast beef in Scarborough; for it was Sunday when Jacob caught the pale clouded yellows in the clover field, eight miles from home.

Rebecca had caught the death's-head moth in the kitchen.

A strong smell of camphor came from the butterfly boxes.

Mixed with the smell of camphor was the unmistakable smell of seaweed. Tawny ribbons hung on the door. The sun beat straight upon them.

The upper wings of the moth which Jacob held were undoubtedly marked with kidney-shaped spots of a fulvous hue. But there was no crescent upon the underwing. The tree had fallen the night he caught it. There had been a volley of pistol-shots suddenly in the depths of the wood. And his mother had taken him for a burglar when he came home late. The only one of her sons who never obeyed her, she said.

Morris called it "an extremely local insect found in damp or marshy places." But Morris is sometimes wrong. Sometimes Jacob, choosing a very fine pen, made a correction in the margin.

The tree had fallen, though it was a windless night, and the lantern, stood upon the ground, had lit up the still green leaves and the dead beech leaves. It was a dry place. A toad was there. And the red underwing had circled round the light and flashed and gone. The red underwing had never come back, though Jacob had waited. It was after twelve when he crossed the lawn and saw his mother in the bright room, playing patience, sitting up.

"How you frightened me!" she had cried. She thought something dreadful had happened. And he woke Rebecca, who had to be up so early.

There he stood pale, come out of the depths of darkness, in the hot room, blinking at the light.

No, it could not be a straw-bordered underwing.

The mowing-machine always wanted oiling. Barnet turned it under Jacob's window, and it creaked—creaked, and rattled across the lawn and creaked again.

Now it was clouding over.

Back came the sun, dazzlingly.

It fell like an eye upon the stirrups, and then suddenly and yet very gently rested upon the bed, upon the alarum clock, and upon the butterfly box stood open. The pale clouded yellows had pelted over the moor; they had zigzagged across the purple clover. The fritillaries flaunted along the hedgerows. The blues settled on little bones lying on

the turf with the sun beating on them, and the painted ladies and the peacocks feasted upon bloody entrails dropped by a hawk. Miles away from home, in a hollow among teasles beneath a ruin, he had found the commas. He had seen a white admiral circling higher and higher round an oak tree, but he had never caught it. An old cottage woman living alone, high up, had told him of a purple butterfly which came every summer to her garden. The fox cubs played in the gorse in the early morning, she told him. And if you looked out at dawn you could always see two badgers. Sometimes they knocked each other over like two boys fighting, she said.

"You won't go far this afternoon, Jacob," said his mother, popping her head in at the door, "for the Captain's coming to say good-bye." It was the last day of the Easter holidays.

Wednesday was Captain Barfoot's day. He dressed himself very neatly in blue serge, took his rubber-shod stick—for he was lame and wanted two fingers on the left hand, having served his country—and set out from the house with the flagstaff precisely at four o'clock in the afternoon.

At three Mr. Dickens, the bath-chair man, had called for Mrs. Barfoot.

"Move me," she would say to Mr. Dickens, after sitting on the esplanade for fifteen minutes. And again, "That'll do, thank you, Mr. Dickens." At the first command he would seek the sun; at the second he would stay the chair there in the bright strip.

An old inhabitant himself, he had much in common with Mrs. Barfoot—James Coppard's daughter. The drinking-fountain, where West Street joins Broad Street, is the gift of James Coppard, who was mayor at the time of Queen Victoria's jubilee, and Coppard is painted upon municipal watering-carts and over shop windows, and upon the zinc blinds of solicitors' consulting-room windows. But Ellen Barfoot never visited the Aquarium (though she had known Captain Boase, who had caught the shark, quite well), and when the men came by with the posters she eyed them superciliously, for she knew that she would never see the Pierrots, or the brothers Zeno, or Daisy Budd and her troupe of performing seals. For Ellen Barfoot in her bath-chair on the esplanade was a prisoner—civilization's prisoner—all the bars of her cage falling across the esplanade on sunny days when the town hall, the drapery stores, the swimming-bath, and the memorial hall striped the ground with shadow.

An old inhabitant himself, Mr. Dickens would stand a little behind her, smoking his pipe. She would ask him questions—who people were —who now kept Mr. Jones's shop—then about the season—and had

Mrs. Dickens tried, whatever it might be—the words issuing from her lips like crumbs of dry biscuit.

She closed her eyes. Mr. Dickens took a turn. The feelings of a man had not altogether deserted him, though as you saw him cóming towards you, you noticed how one knobbed black boot swung tremulously in front of the other; how there was a shadow between his waistcoat and his trousers; how he leant forward unsteadily, like an old horse who finds himself suddenly out of the shafts drawing no cart. But as Mr. Dickens sucked in the smoke and puffed it out again, the feelings of a man were perceptible in his eyes. He was thinking how Captain Barfoot was now on his way to Mount Pleasant; Captain Barfoot, his master. For at home in the little sitting-room above the mews, with the canary in the window, and the girls at the sewing-machine, and Mrs. Dickens huddled up with the rheumatics—at home where he was made little of, the thought of being in the employ of Captain Barfoot supported him. He liked to think that while he chatted with Mrs. Barfoot on the front, he helped the Captain on his way to Mrs. Flanders. He, a man, was in charge of Mrs. Barfoot, a woman.

Turning, he saw that she was chatting with Mrs. Rogers. Turning again, he saw that Mrs. Rogers had moved on. So he came back to the bath-chair, and Mrs. Barfoot asked him the time, and he took out his great silver watch and told her the time very obligingly, as if he knew a great deal more about the time and everything than she did. But Mrs. Barfoot knew that Captain Barfoot was on his way to Mrs. Flanders.

Indeed he was well on his way there, having left the tram, and seeing Dods Hill to the southeast, green against a blue sky that was suffused with dust colour on the horizon. He was marching up the hill. In spite of his lameness there was something military in his approach. Mrs. Jarvis, as she came out of the Rectory gate, saw him coming, and her Newfoundland dog, Nero, slowly swept his tail from side to side.

"Oh, Captain Barfoot!" Mrs. Jarvis exclaimed.

"Good-day, Mrs. Jarvis," said the Captain.

They walked on together, and when they reached Mrs. Flanders's gate Captain Barfoot took off his tweed cap, and said, bowing very courteously:

"Good-day to you, Mrs. Jarvis."

And Mrs. Jarvis walked on alone.

She was going to walk on the moor. Had she again been pacing her lawn late at night? Had she again tapped on the study window and cried: "Look at the moon, look at the moon, Herbert!"

And Herbert looked at the moon.

Mrs. Jarvis walked on the moor when she was unhappy, going as far as a certain saucer-shaped hollow, though she always meant to go to a more distant ridge; and there she sat down, and took out the little book hidden beneath her cloak and read a few lines of poetry, and looked about her. She was not very unhappy, and, seeing that she was forty-five, never perhaps would be very unhappy, desperately unhappy that is, and leave her husband, and ruin a good man's career, as she sometimes threatened.

Still there is no need to say what risks a clergyman's wife runs when she walks on the moor. Short, dark, with kindling eyes, a pheasant's feather in her hat, Mrs. Jarvis was just the sort of woman to loose her faith upon the moors—to confound her God with the universal that is—but she did not lose her faith, did not leave her husband, never read her poem through, and went on walking the moors, looking at the moon behind the elm trees, and feeling as she sat on the grass high above Scarborough . . . Yes, yes, when the lark soars; when the sheep, moving a step or two onwards, crop the turf, and at the same time set their bells tinkling; when the breeze first blows, then dies down, leaving the cheek kissed; when the ships on the sea below seem to cross each other and pass on as if drawn by an invisible hand; when there are distant concussions in the air and phantom horsemen galloping, ceasing; when the horizon swims blue, green, emotional—then Mrs. Jarvis, heaving a sigh, thinks to herself, "If only some one could give me . . . if I could give some one . . ." But she does not know what she wants to give, nor who could give it her.

"Mrs. Flanders stepped out only five minutes ago, Captain," said Rebecca. Captain Barfoot sat him down in the arm-chair to wait. Resting his elbows on the arms, putting one hand over the other, sticking his lame leg straight out, and placing the stick with the rubber ferrule beside it, he sat perfectly still. There was something rigid about him. Did he think? Probably the same thoughts again and again. But were they "nice" thoughts, interesting thoughts? He was a man with a temper; tenacious; faithful. Women would have felt, "Here is law. Here is order. Therefore we must cherish this man. He is on the Bridge at night," and, handing him his cup, or whatever it might be, would run on to visions of shipwreck and disaster, in which all the passengers come tumbling from their cabins, and there is the captain, buttoned in his peajacket, matched with the storm, vanquished by it but by none other. "Yet I have a soul," Mrs. Jarvis would bethink her, as Captain Barfoot suddenly blew his nose in a great red bandanna handkerchief, "and it's the man's stupidity that's the cause of this, and the storm's my storm as well as his" . . . so Mrs. Jarvis would

bethink her when the Captain dropped in to see them and found Herbert out, and spent two or three hours, almost silent, sitting in the arm-chair. But Betty Flanders thought nothing of the kind.

"Oh, Captain," said Mrs. Flanders, bursting into the drawing-room, "I had to run after Barker's man . . . I hope Rebecca . . . I hope Jacob . . ."

She was very much out of breath, yet not at all upset, and as she put down the hearth-brush which she had bought of the oil-man, she said it was hot, flung the window further open, straightened a cover, picked up a book, as if she were very confident, very fond of the Captain, and a great many years younger than he was. Indeed, in her blue apron she did not look more than thirty-five. He was well over fifty.

She moved her hands about the table; the Captain moved his head from side to side, and made little sounds, as Betty went on chattering, completely at his ease—after twenty years.

"Well," he said at length, "I've heard from Mr. Polegate."

He had heard from Mr. Polegate that he could advise nothing better than to send a boy to one of the universities.

"Mr. Floyd was at Cambridge . . . no, at Oxford . . . well, at one or the other," said Mrs. Flanders.

She looked out of the window. Little windows, and the lilac and green of the garden were reflected in her eyes.

"Archer is doing very well," she said. "I have a very nice report from Captain Maxwell."

"I will leave you the letter to show Jacob," said the Captain, putting it clumsily back in its envelope.

"Jacob is after his butterflies as usual," said Mrs. Flanders irritably, but was surprised by a sudden afterthought, "Cricket begins this week, of course."

"Edward Jenkinson has handed in his resignation," said Captain Barfoot.

"Then you will stand for the Council?" Mrs. Flanders exclaimed, looking the Captain full in the face.

"Well, about that," Captain Barfoot began, settling himself rather deeper in his chair.

Jacob Flanders, therefore, went up to Cambridge in October, 1906.

§ 3

"This is not a smoking-carriage," Mrs. Norman protested, nervously

but very feebly, as the door swung open and a powerfully built young man jumped in. He seemed not to hear her. The train did not stop before it reached Cambridge, and here she was shut up alone, in railway carriage, with a young man.

She touched the spring of her dressing-case, and ascertained that the scent-bottle and a novel from Mudie's were both handy (the young man was standing up with his back to her, putting his bag in the rack). She would throw the scent-bottle with her right hand, she decided, and tug the communication cord with her left. She was fifty years of age, and had a son at college. Nevertheless, it is a fact that men are dangerous. She read half a column of her newspaper; then stealthily looked over the edge to decide the question of safety by the infallible test of appearance. . . . She would like to offer him her paper. But do young men read the *Morning Post?* She looked to see what he was reading—the *Daily Telegraph.*

Taking note of socks (loose), of tie (shabby), she once more reached his face. She dwelt upon his mouth. The lips were shut. The eyes bent down, since he was reading. All was firm, yet youthful, indifferent, unconscious—as for knocking one down! No, no, no! She looked out of the window, smiling slightly now, and then came back again, for he didn't notice her. Grave, unconscious . . . now he looked up, past her . . . he seemed so out of place, somehow, alone with an elderly lady . . . then he fixed his eyes—which were blue—on the landscape. He had not realized her presence, she thought. Yet it was none of *her* fault that this was not a smoking-carriage—if that was what he meant.

Nobody sees any one as he is, let alone an elderly lady sitting opposite a strange young man in a railway carriage. They see a whole—they see all sorts of things—they see themselves. . . . Mrs. Norman now read three pages of one of Mr. Norris's novels. Should she say to the young man (and after all he was just the same age as her own boy): "If you want to smoke, don't mind me"? No: he seemed absolutely indifferent to her presence . . . she did not wish to interrupt.

But since, even at her age, she noted his indifference, presumably he was in some way or other—to her at least—nice, handsome, interesting, distinguished, well built, like her own boy? One must do the best one can with her report. Anyhow, this was Jacob Flanders, aged nineteen. It is no use trying to sum people up. One must follow hints, not exactly what is said, nor yet entirely what is done—for instance, when the train drew into the station, Mr. Flanders burst open the door, and put the lady's dressing-case out for her, saying, or rather mumbling: "Let me" very shyly; indeed he was rather clumsy about it.

"Who . . ." said the lady, meeting her son; but as there was a great crowd on the platform and Jacob had already gone, she did not finish

her sentence. As this was Cambridge, as she was staying there for the week-end, as she saw nothing but young men all day long, in streets and round tables, this sight of her fellow-traveller was completely lost in her mind, as the crooked pin dropped by a child into the wishing-well twirls in the water and disappears for ever.

They say the sky is the same everywhere. Travellers, the ship-wrecked, exiles, and the dying draw comfort from the thought, and no doubt if you are of a mystical tendency, consolation, and even explanation, shower down from the unbroken surface. But above Cam-bridge—anyhow about the roof of King's College Chapel—there is a difference. Out at sea a great city will cast a brightness into the night. It is fanciful to suppose the sky, washed into the crevices of King's College Chapel, lighter, thinner, more sparkling than the sky else-where? Does Cambridge burn not only into the night, but into the day?

Look, as they pass into service, how airily the gowns blow out, as though nothing dense and corporeal were within. What sculptured faces, what certainty, authority controlled by piety, although great boots march under the gowns. In what orderly procession they ad-vance. Thick wax candles stand upright; young men rise in white gowns; while the subservient eagle bears up for inspection the great white book.

An inclined plane of light comes accurately through each window, purple and yellow even in its most diffused dust, while, where it breaks upon stone, that stone is softly chalked red, yellow, and purple. Neither snow nor greenery, winter nor summer, has power over the old stained glass. As the sides of a lantern protect the flame so that it burns steady even in the wildest night—burns steady and gravely illumines the tree-trunks—so inside the Chapel all was orderly. Gravely sounded the voices; wisely the organ replied, as if buttressing human faith with the assent of the elements. The white-robed figures crossed from side to side; now mounted steps, now descended, all very orderly.

. . . If you stand a lantern under a tree every insect in the forest creeps up to it—a curious assembly, since though they scramble and swing and knock their heads against the glass, they seem to have no purpose—something senseless inspires them. One gets tired of watching them, as they amble round the lantern and blindly tap as if for admittance, one large toad being the most besotted of any and shouldering his way through the rest. Ah, but what's that? A terrifying volley of pistol-shots rings out—cracks sharply; ripples spread—silence laps smooth over sound. A tree—a tree has fallen, a sort of death in the forest. After that, the wind in the trees sounds melancholy.

But this service in King's College Chapel—why allow women to take part in it? Surely, if the mind wanders (and Jacob looked extraor-

dinarily vacant, his head thrown back, his hymn-book open at the
wrong place), if the mind wanders it is because several hat shops and
cupboards upon cupboards of coloured dresses are displayed upon
rush-bottomed chairs. Though heads and bodies may be devout enough,
one has a sense of individuals—some like blue, others brown; some
feathers, others pansies and forget-me-nots. No one would think of
bringing a dog into church. For though a dog is all very well on a
gravel path, and shows no disrespect to flowers, the way he wanders
down an aisle, looking, lifting a paw, and approaching a pillar with a
purpose that makes the blood run cold with horror (should you be one
of a congregation—alone, shyness is out of the question), a dog de-
stroys the service completely. So do these women—though separately
devout, distinguished, and vouched for by the theology, mathematics,
Latin, and Greek of their husbands. Heaven knows why it is. For
one thing, thought Jacob, they're as ugly as sin.

Now there was a scraping and murmuring. He caught Timmy Dur-
rant's eye; looked very sternly at him; and then, very solemnly, winked.

"Waverley," the villa on the road to Girton was called, not that
Mr. Plumer admired Scott or would have chosen any name at all, but
names are useful when you have to entertain undergraduates, and as
they sat waiting for the fourth undergraduate, on Sunday at lunch-
time, there was talk of names upon gates.

"How tiresome," Mrs. Plumer interrupted impulsively. "Does any-
body know Mr. Flanders?"

Mr. Durrant knew him; and therefore blushed slightly, and said,
awkwardly, something about being sure—looking at Mr. Plumer and
hitching the right leg of his trouser as he spoke. Mr. Plumer got up
and stood in front of the fireplace. Mrs. Plumer laughed like a straight-
forward friendly fellow. In short, anything more horrible than the
scene, the setting, the prospect, even the May garden being afflicted
with chill sterility and a cloud choosing that moment to cross the
sun, cannot be imagined. There was the garden, of course. Every one
at the same moment looked at it. Owing to the cloud, the leaves
ruffled grey, and the sparrows—there were two sparrows.

"I think," said Mrs. Plumer, taking advantage of the momentary
respite, while the young men stared at the garden, to look at her
husband, and he, not accepting full responsibility for the act, never-
theless touched the bell.

There can be no excuse for this outrage upon one hour of human
life, save the reflection which occurred to Mr. Plumer as he carved
the mutton, that if no don ever gave a luncheon party, if Sunday after
Sunday passed, if men went down, became lawyers, doctors, members

of Parliament, business men—if no don ever gave a luncheon party—

"Now, does lamb make the mint sauce, or mint sauce make the lamb?" he asked the young man next him, to break a silence which had already lasted five minutes and a half.

"I don't know, sir," said the young man, blushing very vividly.

At this moment in came Mr. Flanders. He had mistaken the time.

Now, though they had finished their meat, Mrs. Plumer took a second helping of cabbage. Jacob determined, of course, that he would eat his meat in the time it took her to finish her cabbage, looking once or twice to measure his speed—only he was infernally hungry. Seeing this, Mrs. Plumer said that she was sure Mr. Flanders would not mind—and the tart was brought in. Nodding in a peculiar way, she directed the maid to give Mr. Flanders a second helping of mutton. She glanced at the mutton. Not much of the leg would be left for luncheon.

It was none of her fault—since how could she control her father begetting her forty years ago in the suburbs of Manchester? and once begotten, how could she do other than grow up cheese-paring, ambitious, with an instinctively accurate notion of the rungs of the ladder and an ant-like assiduity in pushing George Plumer ahead of her to the top of the ladder? What was at the top of the ladder? A sense that all the rungs were beneath one apparently; since by the time that George Plumer became Professor of Physics, or whatever it might be, Mrs. Plumer could only be in a condition to cling tight to her eminence, peer down at the ground, and goad her two plain daughters to climb the rungs of the ladder.

"I was down at the races yesterday," she said, "with my two little girls."

It was none of *their* fault either. In they came to the drawing-room, in white frocks and blue sashes. They handed the cigarettes. Rhoda had inherited her father's cold grey eyes. Cold grey eyes George Plumer had, but in them was an abstract light. He could talk about Persia and the Trade winds, the Reform Bill and the cycle of the harvests. Books were on his shelves by Wells and Shaw; on the table serious sixpenny weeklies written by pale men in muddy boots—the weekly creak and screech of brains rinsed in cold water and wrung dry—melancholy papers.

"I don't feel that I know the truth about anything till I've read them both!" said Mrs. Plumer brightly, tapping the table of contents with her bare red hand, upon which the ring looked so incongruous.

"O God, O God, O God!" exclaimed Jacob, as the four undergraduates left the house. "Oh, my God!"

"Bloody beastly!" he said, scanning the street for lilac or bicycle—anything to restore his sense of freedom.

"Bloody beastly," he said to Timmy Durrant, summing up his discomfort at the world shown him at lunch-time, a world capable of existing—there was no doubt about that—but so unnecessary, such a thing to believe in—Shaw and Wells and the serious sixpenny weeklies! What were they after, scrubbing and demolishing, these elderly people? Had they never read Homer, Shakespeare, the Elizabethans? He saw it clearly outlined against the feelings he drew from youth and natural inclination. The poor devils had rigged up this meagre object. Yet something to pity was in him. Those wretched little girls——

The extent to which he was disturbed proves that he was already agog. Insolent he was and inexperienced, but sure enough the cities which the elderly of the race have built upon the skyline showed like brick suburbs, barracks, and places of discipline against a red and yellow flame. He was impressionable; but the word is contradicted by the composure with which he hollowed his hand to screen a match. He was a young man of substance.

Anyhow, whether undergraduate or shop boy, man or woman, it must come as a shock about the age of twenty—the world of the elderly—thrown up in such black outline upon what we are; upon the reality; the moors and Byron; the sea and the lighthouse; the sheep's jaw with the yellow teeth in it; upon the obstinate irrepressible conviction which makes youth so intolerably disagreeable—"I am what I am, and intend to be it," for which there will be no form in the world unless Jacob makes one for himself. The Plumers will try to prevent him from making it. Wells and Shaw and the serious sixpenny weeklies will sit on its head. Everytime he lunches out on Sunday—at dinner parties and tea parties—there will be this same shock—horror—discomfort—then pleasure, for he draws into him at every step as he walks by the river such steady certainty, such reassurance from all sides, the trees bowing, the grey spires soft in the blue, voices blowing and seeming suspended in the air, the springy air of May, the elastic air with its particles—chestnut bloom, pollen, whatever it is that gives the May air its potency, blurring the trees, gumming the buds, daubing the green. And the river too runs past, not at flood, nor swiftly, but cloying the oar that dips in it and drops white drops from the blade, swimming green and deep over the bowed rushes, as if lavishly caressing them.

Where they moored their boat the trees showered down, so that their topmost leaves trailed in the ripples and the green wedge that lay in the water being made of leaves shifted in leaf-breadths as the real leaves shifted. Now there was a shiver of wind—instantly an edge of sky—and as Durrant ate cherries he dropped the stunted yellow cherries through the green wedge of leaves, their stalks twinkling

as they wriggled in and out, and sometimes one half-bitten cherry would go down red into the green. The meadow was on a level with Jacob's eyes as he lay back; gilt with buttercups, but the grass did not run like the thin green water of the graveyard grass about to overflow the tombstones, but stood juicy and thick. Looking up, backwards, he saw the legs of children deep in the grass, and the legs of cows. Munch, munch, he heard; then a short step through the grass; then again munch, munch, munch, as they tore the grass short at the roots. In front of him two white butterflies circled higher and higher round the elm tree.

"Jacob's off," thought Durrant, looking up from his novel. He kept reading a few pages and then looking up in a curiously methodical manner, and each time he looked up he took a few cherries out of the bag and ate them abstractedly. Other boats passed them, crossing the backwater from side to side to avoid each other, for many were now moored, and there were now white dresses and a flaw in the column of air between two trees, round which curled a thread of blue—Lady Miller's picnic party. Still more boats kept coming, and Durrant, without getting up, shoved their boat closer to the bank.

"Oh-h-h-h," groaned Jacob, as the boat rocked, and the trees rocked, and the white dresses and the white flannel trousers drew out long and wavering up the bank.

"Oh-h-h-h!" He sat up, and felt as if a piece of elastic had snapped in his face.

"They're friends of my mother's," said Durrant. "So-old Bow took no end of trouble about the boat."

And this boat had gone from Falmouth to St. Ives Bay, all round the coast. A larger boat, a ten-ton yacht, about the twentieth of June, properly fitted out, Durrant said . . .

"There's the cash difficulty," said Jacob.

"My people'll see to that," said Durrant (the son of a banker, deceased).

"I intend to preserve my economic independence," said Jacob stiffly. (He was getting excited.)

"My mother said something about going to Harrogate," he said with a little annoyance, feeling the pocket where he kept his letters.

"Was that true about your uncle becoming a Mohammedan?" asked Timmy Durrant.

Jacob had told the story of his Uncle Morty in Durrant's room the night before.

"I expect he's feeding the sharks, if the truth were known," said Jacob. "I say, Durrant, there's none left!" he exclaimed, crumpling the bag which had held the cherries, and throwing it into the river.

He saw Lady Miller's picnic party on the island as he threw the bag into the river.

A sort of awkwardness, grumpiness, gloom came into his eyes.

"Shall we move on . . . this beastly crowd . . ." he said.

So up they went, past the island.

The feathery white moon never let the sky grow dark; all night the chestnut blossoms were white in the green; dim was the cow-parsley in the meadows.

The waiters at Trinity must have been shuffling china plates like cards, from the clatter that could be heard in the Great Court. Jacob's rooms, however, were in Neville's Court; at the top; so that reaching his door one went in a little out of breath; but he wasn't there. Dining in Hall, presumably. It will be quite dark in Neville's Court long before midnight, only the pillars opposite will always be white, and the fountains. A curious effect the gate has, like lace upon pale green. Even in the window you hear the plates; a hum of talk, too, from the diners; the Hall lit up, and the swing-doors opening and shutting with a soft thud. Some are late.

Jacob's room had a round table and two low chairs. There were yellow flags in a jar on the mantelpiece; a photograph of his mother; cards from societies with little raised crescents, coats of arms, and initials; notes and pipes; on the table lay paper ruled with a red margin —an essay, no doubt—"Does History consist of the Biographies of Great Men?" There were books enough; very few French books; but then any one who's worth anything reads just what he likes, as the mood takes him, with extravagant enthusiasm. Lives of the Duke of Wellington, for example; Spinoza; the works of Dickens; the *Faërie Queene;* a Greek dictionary with the petals of poppies pressed to silk between the pages; all the Elizabethans. His slippers were incredibly shabby, like boats burnt to the water's rim. Then there were photographs from the Greeks, and a mezzotint from Sir Joshua—all very English. The works of Jane Austen, too, in deference, perhaps, to some one else's standard. Carlyle was a prize. There were books upon the Italian painters of the Renaissance, a *Manual of the Diseases of the Horse,* and all the usual text-books. Listless is the air in an empty room, just swelling the curtain; the flowers in the jar shift. One fibre in the wicker arm-chair creaks, though no one sits there.

Coming down the steps a little sideways (Jacob sat on the window-seat talking to Durrant; he smoked, and Durrant looked at the map), the old man, with his hands locked behind him, his gown floating black, lurched, unsteadily, near the wall; then, upstairs he went into

his room. Then another, who raised his hand and praised the columns, the gate, the sky; another, tripping and smug. Each went up a staircase; three lights were lit in the dark windows.

If any light burns above Cambridge, it must be from three such rooms; Greek burns here; science there; philosophy on the ground floor. Poor old Huxtable can't walk straight;—Sopwith, too, has praised the sky any night these twenty years; and Cowan still chuckles at the same stories. It is not simple, or pure, or wholly splendid, the lamp of learning, since if you see them there under its light (whether Rossetti's on the wall, or Van Gogh reproduced, whether there are lilacs in the bowl or rusty pipes), how priestly they look! How like a suburb where you go to see a view and eat a special cake! "We are the sole purveyors of this cake." Back you go to London; for the treat is over.

Old Professor Huxtable, performing with the method of a clock his change of dress, let himself down into his chair; filled his pipe; chose his paper; crossed his feet; and extracted his glasses. The whole flesh of his face then fell into folds as if props were removed. Yet strip a whole seat of an underground railway carriage of its heads and old Huxtable's head will hold them all. Now, as his eye goes down the print, what a procession tramps through the corridors of his brain, orderly, quick-stepping, and reinforced, as the march goes on, by fresh runnels, till the whole hall, dome, whatever one calls it, is populous with ideas. Such a muster takes place in no other brain. Yet sometimes there he'll sit for hours together, gripping the arm of the chair, like a man holding fast because stranded, and then, just because his corn twinges, or it may be the gout, what execrations, and, dear me, to hear him talk of money, taking out his leather purse and grudging even the smallest silver coin, secretive and suspicious as an old peasant woman with all her lies. Strange paralysis and constriction —marvellous illumination. Serene over it all rides the great full brow, and sometimes asleep or in the quiet spaces of the night you might fancy that on a pillow of stone he lay triumphant.

Sopwith, meanwhile, advancing with a curious trip from the fireplace, cut the chocolate cake into segments. Until midnight or later there would be undergraduates in his room, sometimes as many as twelve, sometimes three or four; but nobody got up when they went or when they came; Sopwith went on talking. Talking, talking, talking— as if everything could be talked—the soul itself slipped through the lips in thin silver disks which dissolve in young men's minds like silver, like moonlight. Oh, far away they'd remember it; and deep in dullness gaze back on it, and come to refresh themselves again.

"Well, I never. That's old Chucky. My dear boy, how's the world treating you?" And in came poor little Chucky, the unsuccessful provincial, Stenhouse his real name, but of course Sopwith brought back by using the other everything, everything, "all I could never be"—yes, though next day, buying his newspaper and catching the early train, it all seemed to him childish, absurd; the chocolate cake, the young men; Sopwith summing things up; no, not all; he would send his son there. He would save every penny to send his son there. Sopwith went on talking; twining stiff fibres of awkward speech—things young men blurted out—plaiting them round his own smooth garland, making the bright side show, the vivid greens, the sharp thorns, manliness. He loved it. Indeed to Sopwith a man could say anything, until perhaps he'd grown old, or gone under, gone deep, when the silver disks would tinkle hollow, and the inscription read a little too simple, and the old stamp look too pure, and the impress always the same—a Greek boy's head. But he would respect still. A woman, divining the priest, would, involuntarily, despise.

Cowan, Erasmus Cowan, sipped his port alone, or with one rosy little man, whose memory held precisely the same span of time; sipped his port, and told his stories, and without book before him intoned Latin, Virgil, and Catullus, as if language were wine upon his lips. Only —sometimes it will come over one—what if the poet strode in? *"This* my image?" he might ask, pointing to the chubby man, whose brain is, after all, Virgil's representative among us, though the body gluttonize, and as for arms, bees, or even the plough, Cowan takes his trips abroad with a French novel in his pocket, a rug about his knees, and is thankful to be home again in his place, in his line, holding up in his snug little mirror the image of Virgil, all rayed round with good stories of the dons of Trinity and red beams of port. But language is wine upon his lips. Nowhere else would Virgil hear the like. And though, as she goes sauntering along the Backs, old Miss Umphelby sings him melodiously enough, accurately too, she is always brought up by this question as she reaches Clare Bridge: "But if I met him, what should I wear?"—and then, taking her way up the avenue towards Newnham, she lets her fancy play upon other details of men's meeting with women which have never got into print. Her lectures, therefore, are not half so well attended as those of Cowan, and the thing she might have said in elucidation of the text for ever left out. In short, face a teacher with the image of the taught and the mirror breaks. But Cowan sipped his port, his exalation over, no longer the representative of Virgil. No, the builder, assessor, surveyor, rather; ruling lines between names, hanging lists above doors. Such is the fabric through

which the light must shine, if shine it can—the light of all these languages, Chinese and Russian, Persian and Arabic, of symbols and figures, of history, of things that are known and things that are about to be known. So that if at night, far out at sea over the tumbling waves, one saw a haze on the waters, a city illuminated, a whiteness even in the sky, such as that now over the Hall of Trinity where they're still dining, or washing up plates, that would be the light burning there—the light of Cambridge.

"Let's go round to Simeon's room," said Jacob, and they rolled up the map, having got the whole thing settled.

All the lights were coming out round the court, and falling on the cobbles, picking out dark patches of grass and single daisies. The young men were now back in their rooms. Heaven knows what they were doing. What was it that could *drop* like that? And leaning down over a foaming window-box one stopped another hurrying past, and upstairs they went and down they went, until a sort of fulness settled on the court, the hive full of bees, the bees home thick with gold, drowsy, humming, suddenly vocal; the Moonlight Sonata answered by a waltz.

The Moonlight Sonata tinkled away; the waltz crashed. Although young men still went in and out, they walked as if keeping engagements. Now and then there was a thud, as if some heavy piece of furniture had fallen, unexpectedly, of its own accord, not in the general stir of life after dinner. One supposed that young men raised their eyes from their books as the furniture fell. Were they reading? Certainly there was a sense of concentration in the air. Behind the grey walls sat so many young men, some undoubtedly reading, magazines, shilling shockers, no doubt; legs, perhaps, over the arms of chairs; smoking; sprawling over tables, and writing while their heads went round in a circle as the pen moved—simple young men, these, who would—but there is no need to think of them grown old; others eating sweets; here they boxed; and, well, Mr. Hawkins must have been mad suddenly to throw up his window and bawl: "Jo—seph! Jo—seph!" and then he ran as hard as ever he could across the court, while an elderly man, in a green apron, carrying an immense pile of tin covers, hesitated, balanced, and then went on. But this was a diversion. There were young men who read, lying in shallow armchairs, holding their books as if they had hold in their hands of something that would see them through; they being all in a torment, coming from midland towns, clergymen's sons. Others read Keats. And those long histories in many volumes—surely some one was now beginning at the begin-

ning in order to understand the Holy Roman Empire, as one must. That was part of the concentration, though it would be dangerous on a hot spring night—dangerous, perhaps, to concentrate too much upon single books, actual chapters, when at any moment the door opened and Jacob appeared; or Richard Bonamy, reading Keats no longer, began making long pink spills from an old newspaper, bending forward, and looking eager and contented no more, but almost fierce. Why? Only perhaps that Keats died young—one wants to write poetry too and to love—oh, the brutes! It's damnably difficult. But, after all, not so difficult if on the next staircase, in the large room, there are two, three, five young men all convinced of this—of brutality, that is, and the clear division between right and wrong. There was a sofa, chairs, a square table, and the window being open, one could see how they sat—legs issuing here, one there crumpled in a corner of the sofa; and, presumably, for you could not see him, somebody stood by the fender, talking. Anyhow, Jacob, who sat astride a chair and ate dates from a long box, burst out laughing. The answer came from the sofa corner; for his pipe was held in the air, then replaced. Jacob wheeled round. He had something to say to *that,* though the sturdy red-haired boy at the table seemed to deny it,wagging his head slowly from side to side; and then, taking out his pen-knife, he dug the point of it again and again into a knot in the table, as if affirming that the voice from the fender spoke the truth—which Jacob could not deny. Possibly, when he had done arranging the date-stones, he might find something to say to it—indeed his lips opened—only then there broke out a roar of laughter.

The laughter died in the air. The sound of it could scarcely have reached any one standing by the Chapel which stretched along the opposite side of the court. The laughter died out, and only gestures of arms, movements of bodies, could be seen shaping something in the room. Was it an argument? A bet on the boat races? Was it nothing of the sort? What was shaped by the arms and bodies moving in the twilight room?

A step or two beyond the window there was nothing at all, except the enclosing buildings—chimneys upright, roofs horizontal; too much brick and building for a May night, perhaps. And then before one's eyes would come the bare hills of Turkey—sharp lines, dry earth, coloured flowers, and colour on the shoulders of the women, standing naked-legged in the stream to beat linen on the stones. The stream made loops of water round their ankles. But none of that could show clearly through the swaddlings and blanketings of the Cambridge night. The stroke of the clock even was muffled; as if intoned by somebody reverent from a pulpit; as if generations of learned men

heard the last hour go rolling through their ranks and issued it, already smooth and time-worn, with their blessing, for the use of the living.

Was it to receive this gift from the past that the young man came to the window and stood there, looking out across the court? It was Jacob. He stood smoking his pipe while the last stroke of the clock purred softly round him. Perhaps there had been an argument. He looked satisfied; indeed masterly; which expression changed slightly as he stood there, the sound of the clock conveying to him (it may be) a sense of old buildings and time; and himself the inheritor; and then to-morrow; and friends; at the thought of whom, in sheer confidence and pleasure, it seemed, he yawned and stretched himself.

Meanwhile behind him the shape they had made, whether by argument or not, the spiritual shape, hard yet ephemeral, as of glass compared with the dark stone of the Chapel, was dashed to splinters, young men rising from chairs and sofa corners, buzzing and barging about the room, one driving another against the bedroom door, which giving way, in they fell. Then Jacob was left there, in the shallow arm-chair, alone with Masham? Anderson? Simeon? Oh, it was Simeon. The others had all gone.

". . . Julian the Apostate. . . ." Which of them said that and the other words murmured round it? But about midnight there sometimes rises, like a veiled figure suddenly woken, a heavy wind; and this now flapping through Trinity lifted unseen leaves and blurred everything. "Julian the Apostate"—and then the wind. Up go the elm branches, out blow the sails, the old schooners rear and plunge, the grey waves in the hot Indian Ocean tumble sultrily, and then all falls flat again.

So, if the veiled lady stepped through the Courts of Trinity, she now drowsed once more, all her draperies about her, her head against a pillar.

"Somehow it seems to matter."

The low voice was Simeon's.

The voice was even lower that answered him. The sharp tap of a pipe on the mantelpiece cancelled the words. And perhaps Jacob only said "hum," or said nothing at all. True, the words were inaudible. It was the intimacy, a sort of spiritual suppleness, when mind prints upon mind indelibly.

"Well, you seem to have studied the subject," said Jacob, rising and standing over Simeon's chair. He balanced himself; he swayed a little. He appeared extraordinarily happy, as if his pleasure would brim and spill down the sides if Simeon spoke.

Simeon said nothing. Jacob remained standing. But intimacy—

the room was full of it, still, deep, like a pool. Without need of move-
ment or speech it rose softly and washed over everything, mollifying,
kindling, and coating the mind with the lustre of pearl, so that if you
talk of a light, of Cambridge burning, it's not languages only. It's
Julian the Apostate.

But Jacob moved. He murmured good-night. He went out into
the court. He buttoned his jacket across his chest. He went back to his
rooms, and being the only man who walked at that moment back to
his rooms, his footsteps rang out, his figure loomed large. Back from
the Chapel, back from the Hall, back from the Library, came the
sound of his footsteps, as if the old stone echoed with magisterial au-
thority: "The young man—the young man—the young man—back to
his rooms."

§ 4

What's the use of trying to read Shakespeare, especially in one of
those little thin paper editions whose pages get ruffled, or stuck to-
gether with sea-water? Although the plays of Shakespeare had fre-
quently been praised, even quoted, and placed higher than the Greek,
never since they started had Jacob managed to read one through. Yet
what an opportunity!

For the Scilly Isles had been sighted by Timmy Durrant lying like
mountain-tops almost a-wash in precisely the right place. His calcula-
tions had worked perfectly, and really the sight of him sitting there,
with his hand on the tiller, rosy gilled, with a sprout of beard, looking
sternly at the stars, then at a compass, spelling out quite correctly his
page of the eternal lesson-book, would have moved a woman. Jacob,
of course, was not a woman. The sight of Timmy Durrant was no
sight for him, nothing to set against the sky and worship; far from
it. They had quarrelled. Why the right way to open a tin of beef, with
Shakespeare on board, under conditions of such splendour, should have
turned them to sulky schoolboys, none can tell. Tinned beef is cold
eating, though; and salt water spoils biscuits; and the waves tumble
and lollop much the same hour after hour—tumble and lollop all
across the horizon. Now a spray of seaweed floats past—now a log
of wood. Ships have been wrecked here. One or two go past, keeping
their own side of the road. Timmy knew where they were bound, what
their cargoes were, and, by looking through his glass, could tell the
name of the line, and even guess what dividends it paid its share-
holders. Yet that was no reason for Jacob to turn sulky.

The Scilly Isles had the look of mountain-tops almost a-wash. . . .
Unfortunately, Jacob broke the pin of the Primus stove.

The Scilly Isles might well be obliterated by a roller sweeping straight across.

But one must give young men the credit of admitting that, though breakfast eaten under these circumstances is grim, it is sincere enough. No need to make conversation. They got out their pipes.

Timmy wrote up some scientific observations; and—what was the question that broke the silence—the exact time or the day of the month? anyhow, it was spoken without the least awkwardness; in the most matter-of-fact way in the world; and then Jacob began to unbutton his clothes and sat naked, save for his shirt, intending, apparently, to bathe.

The Scilly Isles were turning bluish; and suddenly blue, purple, and green flushed the sea; left it grey; struck a stripe which vanished; but when Jacob had got his shirt over his head the whole floor of the waves was blue and white, rippling and crisp, though now and again a broad purple mark appeared, like a bruise; or there floated an entire emerald tinged with yellow. He plunged. He gulped in water, spat it out, struck with his right arm, struck with his left, was towed by a rope, gasped, splashed, and was hauled on board.

The seat in the boat was positively hot, and the sun warmed his back as he sat naked with a towel in his hand, looking at the Scilly Isles which—confound it! the sail flapped. Shakespeare was knocked overboard. There you could see him floating merrily away, with all his pages ruffling innumerably; and then he went under.

Strangely enough, you could smell violets, or if violets were impossible in July, they must grow something very pungent on the mainland then. The mainland, not so very far off—you could see clefts in the cliffs, white cottages, smoke going up—wore an extraordinary look of calm, of sunny peace, as if wisdom and piety had descended upon the dwellers there. Now a cry sounded, as of a man calling pilchards in a main street. It wore an extraordinary look of piety and peace, as if old men smoked by the door, and girls stood, hands on hips, at the well, and horses stood; as if the end of the world had come, and cabbage fields and stone walls, and coast-guard stations, and, above all, the white sand bays with the waves breaking unseen by any one, rose to heaven in a kind of ecstasy.

But imperceptibly the cottage smoke droops, has the look of a mourning emblem, a flag floating its caress over a grave. The gulls, making their broad flight and then riding at peace, seem to mark the grave.

No doubt if this were Italy, Greece, or even the shores of Spain, sadness would be routed by strangeness and excitement and the nudge of a classical education. But the Cornish hills have stark chimneys

standing on them; and, somehow or other, loveliness is infernally sad. Yes, the chimneys and the coast-guard stations and the little bays with the waves breaking unseen by any one make one remember the overpowering sorrow. And what can this sorrow be?

It is brewed by the earth itself. It comes from the houses on the coast. We start transparent, and then the cloud thickens. All history backs our pane of glass. To escape is vain.

But whether this is the right interpretation of Jacob's gloom as he sat naked, in the sun, looking at the Land's End, it is impossible to say; for he never spoke a word. Timmy sometimes wondered (only for a second) whether his people bothered him. . . . No matter. There are things that can't be said. Let's shake it off. Let's dry ourselves, and take up the first thing that comes handy. . . . Timmy Durrant's notebook of scientific observations.

"Now . . ." said Jacob.

It is a tremendous argument.

Some people can follow every step of the way, and even take a little one, six inches long, by themselves at the end; others remain observant of the external signs.

The eyes fix themselves upon the poker; the right hand takes the poker and lifts it; turns it slowly round, and then, very accurately, replaces it. The left hand, which lies on the knee, plays some stately but intermittent piece of march music. A deep breath is taken; but allowed to evaporate unused. The cat marches across the hearth-rug. No one observes her.

"That's about as near as I can get to it," Durrant wound up.

The next minute is quiet as the grave.

"It follows . . ." said Jacob.

Only half a sentence followed; but these half-sentences are like flags set on tops of buildings to the observer of external sights down below. What was the coast of Cornwall, with its violet scents, and mourning emblems, and tranquil piety, but a screen happening to hang straight behind as his mind marched up?

"It follows . . ." said Jacob.

"Yes," said Timmy, after reflection. "That is so."

Now Jacob began plunging about, half to stretch himself, half in a kind of jollity, no doubt, for the strangest sound issued from his lips as he furled the sail, rubbed the plates—gruff, tuneless—a sort of pæan, for having grasped the argument, for being master of the situation, sunburnt, unshaven, capable into the bargain of sailing round the world in a ten-ton yacht, which, very likely, he would do one of these days instead of settling down in a lawyer's office, and wearing spats.

"Our friend Masham," said Timmy Durrant, "would rather not be seen in our company as we are now." His buttons had come off.

"D'you know Masham's aunt?" said Jacob.

"Never knew he had one," said Timmy.

"Masham has millions of aunts," said Jacob.

"Masham is mentioned in Domesday Book," said Timmy.

"So are his aunts," said Jacob.

"His sister," said Timmy, "is a very pretty girl."

"That's what'll happen to you, Timmy," said Jacob.

"It'll happen to you first," said Timmy.

"But this woman I was telling you about—Masham's aunt——"

"Oh, do get on," said Timmy, for Jacob was laughing so much that he could not speak.

"Masham's aunt. . . ."

Timmy laughed so much that he could not speak.

"Masham's aunt . . ."

"What is there about Masham that makes one laugh?" said Timmy.

"Hang it all—a man who swallows his tie-pin," said Jacob.

"Lord Chancellor before he's fifty," said Timmy.

"He's a gentleman," said Jacob.

"The Duke of Wellington was a gentleman," said Timmy.

"Keats wasn't."

"Lord Salisbury was."

"And what about God?" said Jacob.

The Scilly Isles now appeared as if directly pointed at by a golden finger issuing from a cloud; and everybody knows how portentous that sight is, and how these broad rays, whether they light upon the Scilly Isles or upon the tombs of crusaders in cathedrals, always shake the very foundations of scepticism and lead to jokes about God.

> *"Abide with me:*
> *Fast falls the eventide;*
> *The shadows deepen;*
> *Lord, with me abide,"*

sang Timmy Durrant.

"At my place we used to have a hymn which began

> *Great God, what do I see and hear?"*

said Jacob.

Gulls rode gently swaying in little companies of two or three quite near the boat; the cormorant, as if following his long strained neck in

eternal pursuit, skimmed an inch above the water to the next rock; and the drone of the tide in the caves came across the water, low, monotonous, like the voice of some one talking to himself.

> "*Rock of Ages, cleft for me,*
> *Let me hide myself in thee,*"

sang Jacob.

Like the blunt tooth of some monster, a rock broke the surface; brown; overflown with perpetual waterfalls.

> "*Rock of Ages,*"

Jacob sang, lying on his back, looking up into the sky at mid-day, from which every shred of cloud had been withdrawn, so that it was like something permanently displayed with the cover off.

By six o'clock a breeze blew in off an icefield; and by seven the water was more purple than blue; and by half-past seven there was a patch of rough gold-beater's skin round the Scilly Isles, and Durrant's face, as he sat steering, was of the colour of a red lacquer box polished for generations. By nine all the fire and confusion had gone out of the sky, leaving wedges of apple-green and plates of pale yellow; and by ten the lanterns on the boat were making twisted colours upon the waves, elongated or squab, as the waves stretched or humped themselves. The beam from the lighthouse strode rapidly across the water. Infinite millions of miles away powdered stars twinkled; but the waves slapped the boat, and crashed, with regular and appalling solemnity, against the rocks.

Although it would be possible to knock at the cottage door and ask for a glass of milk, it is only thirst that would compel the intrusion. Yet perhaps Mrs. Pascoe would welcome it. The summer's day may be wearing heavy. Washing in her little scullery, she may hear the cheap clock on the mantelpiece tick, tick, tick, . . . tick, tick, tick. She is alone in the house. Her husband is out helping Farmer Hosken; her daughter married and gone to America. Her elder son is married too, but she does not agree with his wife. The Wesleyan minister came along and took the younger boy. She is alone in the house. A steamer, probably bound for Cardiff, now crosses the horizon, while near at hand one bell of a foxglove swings to and fro with a bumble-bee for clapper.

These white Cornish cottages are built on the edge of the cliff; the garden grows gorse more readily than cabbages; and for hedge, some

primeval man has piled granite boulders. In one of these, to hold, an historian conjectures, the victim's blood, a basin has been hollowed, but in our time it serves more tamely to seat those tourists who wish for an uninterrupted view of the Gurnard's Head. Not that any one objects to a blue print dress and a white apron in a cottage garden.

"Look—she has to draw her water from a well in the garden."

"Very lonely it must be in winter, with the wind sweeping over those hills, and the waves dashing on the rocks."

Even on a summer's day you hear them murmuring.

Having drawn her water, Mrs. Pascoe went in. The tourists regretted that they had brought no glasses, so that they might have read the name of the tramp steamer. Indeed, it was such a fine day that there was no saying what a pair of field-glasses might not have fetched into view. Two fishing luggers, presumably from St. Ives Bay, were now sailing in an opposite direction from the steamer, and the floor of the sea became alternately clear and opaque. As for the bee, having sucked its fill of honey, it visited the teasle and thence made a straight line to Mrs. Pascoe's patch, once more directing the tourists' gaze to the old woman's print dress and white apron, for she had come to the door of the cottage and was standing there.

There she stood, shading her eyes and looking out to sea.

For the millionth time, perhaps, she looked at the sea. A peacock butterfly now spread himself upon the teasle, fresh and newly emerged, as the blue and chocolate down on his wings testified. Mrs. Pascoe went indoors, fetched a cream pan, came out, and stood scouring it. Her face was assuredly not soft, sensual, or lecherous, but hard, wise, wholesome rather, signifying in a room full of sophisticated people the flesh and blood of life. She would tell a lie; though, as soon as the truth. Behind her on the wall hung a large dried skate. Shut up in the parlour she prized mats, china mugs, and photographs, though the mouldy little room was saved from the salt breeze only by the depth of a brick, and between lace curtains you saw the gannet drop like a stone, and on stormy days the gulls came shuddering through the air, and the steamers' lights were now high, now deep. Melancholy were the sounds on a winter's night.

The picture papers were delivered punctually on Sunday, and she pored long over Lady Cynthia's wedding at the Abbey. She, too, would have liked to ride in a carriage with springs. The soft, swift syllables of educated speech often shamed her few rude ones. And then all night to hear the grinding of the Atlantic upon the rocks instead of hansome cabs and footmen whistling for motor cars. . . . So she may have dreamed, scouring her cream pan. But the talkative nimble-witted people have taken themselves to towns. Like a miser, she has

hoarded her feelings within her own breast. Not a penny piece has she changed all these years, and, watching her enviously, it seems as if all within must be pure gold.

The wise old woman, having fixed her eyes upon the sea, once more withdrew. The tourists decided that it was time to move on to the Gurnard's Head.

Three seconds later Mrs. Durrant rapped upon the door.

"Mrs. Pascoe?" she said.

Rather haughtily, she watched the tourists cross the field path. She came of a Highland race, famous for its chieftains.

Mrs. Pascoe appeared.

"I envy you that bush, Mrs. Pascoe," said Mrs. Durrant, pointing the parasol with which she had rapped on the door at the fine clump of St. John's wort that grew beside it. Mrs. Pascoe looked at the bush deprecatingly.

"I expect my son in a day or two," said Mrs. Durrant. "Sailing from Falmouth with a friend in a little boat. . . . Any news of Lizzie yet, Mrs. Pascoe?"

Her long-tailed ponies stood twitching their ears on the road twenty yards away. The boy, Curnow, flicked flies off them occasionally. He saw his mistress go into the cottage; come out again; and pass, talking energetically to judge by the movements of her hands, round the vegetable plot in front of the cottage. Mrs. Pascoe was his aunt. Both women surveyed a bush. Mrs. Durrant stooped and picked a sprig from it. Next she pointed (her movements were peremptory; she held herself very upright) at the potatoes. They had the blight. All potatoes that year had the blight. Mrs. Durrant showed Mrs. Pascoe how bad the blight was on her potatoes. Mrs. Durrant talked energetically; Mrs. Pascoe listened submissively. The boy Curnow knew that Mrs. Durrant was saying that it is perfectly simple; you mix the powder in a gallon of water; "I have done it with my own hands in my own garden," Mrs. Durrant was saying.

"You won't have a potato left—you won't have a potato left," Mrs. Durrant was saying in her emphatic voice as they reached the gate. The boy Curnow became as immobile as stone.

Mrs. Durrant took the reins in her hands and settled herself on the driver's seat.

"Take care of that leg, or I shall send the doctor to you," she called back over her shoulder; touched the ponies; and the carriage started forward. The boy Curnow had only just time to swing himself up by the toe of his boot. The boy Curnow, sitting in the middle of the back seat, looked at his aunt.

Mrs. Pascoe stood at the gate looking after them; stood at the gate till the trap was round the corner; stood at the gate, looking now to the right, now to the left; then went back to her cottage.

Soon the ponies attacked the swelling moor road with striving fore-legs. Mrs. Durrant let the reins fall slackly, and leant backwards. Her vivacity had left her. Her hawk nose was thin as a bleached bone through which you almost see the light. Her hands, lying on the reins in her lap, were firm even in repose. The upper lip was cut so short that it raised itself almost in a sneer from the front teeth. Her mind skimmed leagues where Mrs. Pascoe's mind adhered to its solitary patch. Her mind skimmed leagues as the ponies climbed the hill road. Forwards and backwards she cast her mind, as if the roofless cottages, mounds of slag, and cottage gardens overgrown with foxglove and bramble cast shade upon her mind. Arrived at the summit, she stopped the carriage. The pale hills were round her, each scattered with an-cient stones; beneath was the sea, variable as a southern sea; she her-self sat there looking from hill to sea, upright, aquiline, equally poised between gloom and laughter. Suddenly she flicked the ponies so that the boy Curnow had to swing himself up by the toe of his boot.

The rooks settled; the rooks rose. The trees which they touched so capriciously seemed insufficient to lodge their numbers. The tree-tops sang with the breeze in them; the branches creaked audibly and dropped now and then, though the season was midsummer, husks or twigs. Up went the rooks and down again, rising in lesser numbers each time as the sager birds made ready to settle, for the evening was already spent enough to make the air inside the wood almost dark. The moss was soft; the tree-trunks spectral. Beyond them lay a silvery meadow. The pampas grass raised its feathery spears from mounds of green at the end of the meadow. A breadth of water gleamed. Already the convolvulus moth was spinning over the flowers. Orange and purple, nasturtium and cherry pie, were washed into the twilight, but the tobacco plant and the passion flower, over which the great moth spun, were white as china. The rooks creaked their wings together on the tree-tops, and were settling down for sleep when, far off, a familiar sound shook and trembled—increased—fairly dinned in their ears— scared sleepy wings into the air again—the dinner bell at the house.

After six days of salt wind, rain, and sun, Jacob Flanders had put on a dinner jacket. The discreet black object had made its appearance now and then in the boat among tins, pickles, preserved meats, and as the voyage went on had become more and more irrelevant, hardly to be believed in. And now, the world being stable, lit by candle-light, the dinner jacket alone preserved him. He could not be sufficiently thank-ful. Even so his neck, wrists, and face were exposed without cover, and

his whole person, whether exposed or not, tingled and glowed so as to make even black cloth an imperfect screen. He drew back the great red hand that lay on the table-cloth. Surreptitiously it closed upon slim glasses and curved silver forks. The bones of the cutlets were decorated with pink frills—and yesterday he had gnawn ham from the bone! Opposite him were hazy, semi-transparent shapes of yellow and blue. Behind them, again, was the grey-green garden, and among the pear-shaped leaves of the escallonia fishing-boats seemed caught and suspended. A sailing ship slowly drew past the women's backs. Two or three figures crossed the terrace hastily in the dusk. The door opened and shut. Nothing settled or stayed unbroken. Like oars rowing now this side, now that, were the sentences that came now here, now there, from either side of the table.

"Oh, Clara, Clara!" exclaimed Mrs. Durrant, and Timothy Durrant adding, "Clara, Clara," Jacob named the shape in yellow gauze Timothy's sister, Clara. The girl sat smiling and flushed. With her brother's dark eyes, she was vaguer and softer than he was. When the laugh died down she said: "But, mother, it was true. He said so, didn't he? Miss Eliot agreed with us. . . ."

But Miss Eliot, tall, grey-headed, was making room beside her for the old man who had come in from the terrace. The dinner would never end, Jacob thought, and he did not wish it to end, though the ship had sailed from one corner of the window-frame to the other, and a light marked the end of the pier. He saw Mrs. Durrant gaze at the light. She turned to him.

"Did you take command, or Timothy?" she said. "Forgive me if I call you Jacob. I've heard so much of you." Then her eyes went back to the sea. Her eyes glazed as she looked at the view.

"A little village once," she said, "and now grown. . . ." She rose, taking her napkin with her, and stood by the window.

"Did you quarrel with Timothy?" Clara asked shyly. "I should have."

Mrs. Durrant came back from the window.

"It gets later and later," she said, sitting upright, and looking down the table. "You ought to be ashamed—all of you. Mr. Clutterbuck, you ought to be ashamed." She raised her voice, for Mr. Clutterbuck was deaf.

"We *are* ashamed," said a girl. But the old man with the beard went on eating plum tart. Mrs. Durrant laughed and leant back in her chair, as if indulging him.

"We put it to you, Mrs. Durrant," said a young man with thick spectacles and a fiery moustache. "I say the conditions were fulfilled. She owes me a sovereign."

"Not *before* the fish—*with* it, Mrs. Durrant," said Charlotte Wilding.

"That was the bet; with the fish," said Clara seriously. "Begonias, mother. To eat them with his fish."

"Oh, dear," said Mrs. Durrant.

"Charlotte won't pay you," said Timothy.

"How dare you . . ." said Charlotte.

"That privilege will be mine," said the courtly Mr. Wortley, producing a silver case primed with sovereigns and slipping one coin on to the table. Then Mrs. Durrant got up and passed down the room, holding herself very straight, and the girls in yellow and blue and silver gauze followed her, and elderly Miss Eliot in her velvet; and a little rosy woman, hesitating at the door, clean, scrupulous, probably a governess. All passed out at the open door.

"When you are as old as I am, Charlotte," said Mrs. Durrant, drawing the girl's arm within hers as they paced up and down the terrace.

"Why are you so sad?" Charlotte asked impulsively.

"Do I seem to you sad? I hope not," said Mrs. Durrant.

"Well, just now. You're *not* old."

"Old enough to be Timothy's mother." They stopped.

Miss Eliot was looking through Mr. Clutterbuck's telescope at the edge of the terrace. The deaf old man stood beside her, fondling his beard, and reciting the names of the constellations: "Andromeda, Bootes, Sidonia, Cassiopeia. . . ."

"Andromeda," murmured Miss Eliot, shifting the telescope slightly.

Mrs. Durrant and Charlotte looked along the barrel of the instrument pointed at the skies.

"There are *millions* of stars," said Charlotte with conviction. Miss Eliot turned away from the telescope. The young men laughed suddenly in the dining-room.

"Let *me* look," said Charlotte eagerly.

"The stars bore me," said Mrs. Durrant, walking down the terrace with Julia Eliot. "I read a book once about the stars. . . . What are they saying?" She stopped in front of the dining-room window. "Timothy," she noted.

"The silent young man," said Miss Eliot.

"Yes, Jacob Flanders," said Mrs. Durrant.

"Oh, mother! I didn't recognize you!" exclaimed Clara Durrant, coming from the opposite direction with Elsbeth. "How delicious," she breathed, crushing a verbena leaf.

Mrs. Durrant turned and walked away by herself.

"Clara!" she called. Clara went to her.

"How unlike they are!" said Miss Eliot.

Mr. Wortley passed them, smoking a cigar.

"Every day I live I find myself agreeing . . ." he said as he passed them.

"It's so interesting to guess . . ." murmured Julia Eliot.

"When first we came out we could see the flowers in that bed," said Elsbeth.

"We see very little now," said Miss Eliot.

"She must have been so beautiful, and everybody loved her, of course," said Charlotte. "I suppose Mr. Wortley . . ." she paused.

"Edward's death was a tragedy," said Miss Eliot decidedly.

Here Mr. Erskine joined them.

"There's no such thing as silence," he said positively. "I can hear twenty different sounds on a night like this without counting your voices."

"Make a bet of it?" said Charlotte.

"Done," said Mr. Erskine. "One, the sea; two, the wind; three, a dog; four . . ."

The others passed on.

"Poor Timothy," said Elsbeth.

"A very fine night," shouted Miss Eliot into Mr. Clutterbuck's ear.

"Like to look at the stars?" said the old man, turning the telescope towards Elsbeth.

"Doesn't it make you melancholy—looking at the stars?" shouted Miss Eliot.

"Dear me no, dear me no," Mr. Clutterbuck chuckled when he understood her. "Why should it make me melancholy? Not for a moment —dear me no."

"Thank you, Timothy, but I'm coming in," said Miss Eliot. "Elsbeth, here's a shawl."

"I'm coming in," Elsbeth murmured with her eye to the telescope. "Cassiopeia," she murmured. "Where are you all?" she asked, taking her eye away from the telescope. "How dark it is!"

Mrs. Durrant sat in the drawing-room by a lamp winding a ball of wool. Mr. Clutterbuck read the *Times*. In the distance stood a second lamp, and round it sat the young ladies, flashing scissors over silver-spangled stuff for private theatricals. Mr. Wortley read a book.

"Yes; he is perfectly right," said Mrs. Durrant, drawing herself up and ceasing to wind her wool. And while Mr. Clutterbuck read the rest of Lord Lansdowne's speech she sat upright, without touching her ball.

"Ah, Mr. Flanders," she said, speaking proudly, as if to Lord Lansdowne himself. Then she sighed and began to wind her wool again.

"Sit *there*," she said.

Jacob came out from the dark place by the window where he had hovered. The light poured over him, illuminating every cranny of his skin; but not a muscle of his face moved as he sat looking out into the garden.

"I want to hear about your voyage," said Mrs. Durrant.

"Yes," he said.

"Twenty years ago we did the same thing."

"Yes," he said. She looked at him sharply.

"He is extraordinarily awkward," she thought, noticing how he fingered his socks. "Yet so distinguished-looking."

"In those days . . ." she resumed, and told him how they had sailed . . . "my husband, who knew a good deal about sailing, for he kept a yacht before we married" . . . and then how rashly they had defied the fishermen, "almost paid for it with our lives, but so proud of ourselves!" She flung the hand out that held the ball of wool.

"Shall I hold your wool?" Jacob asked stiffly.

"You do that for your mother," said Mrs. Durrant, looking at him again keenly, as she transferred the skein. "Yes, it goes much better."

He smiled; but said nothing.

Elsbeth Siddons hovered behind them with something silver on her arm.

"We want," she said. . . . "I've come . . ." she paused.

"Poor Jacob," said Mrs. Durrant, quietly as if she had known him all his life. "They're going to make you act in their play."

"How I love you!" said Elsbeth, kneeling beside Mrs. Durrant's chair.

"Give me the wool," said Mrs. Durrant.

"He's come—he's come!" cried Charlotte Wilding. "I've won my bet!"

"There's another bunch higher up," murmured Clara Durrant mounting another step of the ladder. Jacob held the ladder as she stretched out to reach the grapes high up on the vine.

"There!" she said, cutting through the stalk. She looked semi-transparent, pale, wonderfully beautiful up there among the vine leaves and the yellow and purple bunches, the lights swimming over her in coloured islands. Geraniums and begonias stood in pots along planks; tomatoes climbed the walls.

"The leaves really want thinning," she considered, and one green one, spread like the palm of a hand, circled down past Jacob's head.

"I have more than I can eat already," he said, looking up.

"It does seem absurd . . ." Clara began, "going back to London. . . ."

"Ridiculous," said Jacob, firmly.

"Then . . ." said Clara, "you must come next year, properly," she said, snipping another vine leaf, rather at random.

"If . . . if . . ."

A child ran past the greenhouse shouting. Clara slowly descended the ladder with her basket of grapes.

"One bunch of white, and two of purple," she said, and she placed two great leaves over them where they lay curled warm in the basket.

"I have enjoyed myself," said Jacob, looking down the greenhouse.

"Yes, it's been delightful," she said vaguely.

"Oh, Miss Durrant," he said, taking the basket of grapes; but she walked past him towards the door of the greenhouse.

"You're too good—too good," she thought, thinking of Jacob, thinking that he must not say that he loved her. No, no, no.

The children were whirling past the door, throwing things high into the air.

"Little demons!" she cried. "What have they got?" she asked Jacob.

"Onions, I think," said Jacob. He looked at them without moving.

"Next August, remember, Jacob," said Mrs. Durrant, shaking hands with him on the terrace where the fuchsia hung, like a scarlet earring, behind her head. Mr. Wortley came out of the window in yellow slippers, trailing the *Times* and holding out his hand very cordially.

"Good-bye," said Jacob. "Good-bye," he repeated. "Good-bye," he said once more. Charlotte Wilding flung up her bedroom window and cried out: "Good-bye, Mr. Jacob!"

"Mr. Flanders!" cried Mr. Clutterbuck, trying to extricate himself from his beehive chair. "Jacob Flanders!"

"Too late, Joseph," said Mrs. Durrant.

"Not to sit for me," said Miss Eliot, planting her tripod upon the lawn.

§ 5

"I rather think," said Jacob, taking his pipe from his mouth, "it's in Virgil," and pushing back his chair, he went to the window.

The rashest drivers in the world are, certainly, the drivers of post-office vans. Swinging down Lamb's Conduit Street, the scarlet van rounded the corner by the pillar box in such a way as to graze the kerb and make the little girl who was standing on tiptoe to post a letter look up, half frightened, half curious. She paused with her hand in the mouth of the box; then dropped her letter and ran away. It is seldom only that we see a child on tiptoe with pity—more often a dim discomfort, a grain of sand in the shoe which it's scarcely worth while to remove—that's our feeling, and so—Jacob turned to the bookcase. Long ago great people lived here, and coming back from Court past midnight stood, huddling their satin skirts, under the carved door-posts while the footman roused himself from his mattress on the floor, hurriedly fastened the lower buttons of his waistcoat, and let them in. The bitter eighteenth-century rain rushed down the kennel. Southampton Row, however, is chiefly remarkable nowadays for the fact that you will always find a man there trying to sell a tortoise to a tailor. "Showing off the tweed, sir; what the gentry wants is something singular to catch the eye, sir—and clean in their habits, sir!" So they display their tortoises.

At Mudie's corner in Oxford Street all the red and blue beads had run together on the string. The motor omnibuses were locked. Mr. Spalding going to the city looked at Mr. Charles Budgeon bound for Shepherd's Bush. The proximity of the omnibuses gave the outside passengers an opportunity to stare into each other's faces. Yet few took advantage of it. Each had his own business to think of. Each had his past shut in him like the leaves of a book known to him by heart; and his friends could only read the title, James Spalding, or Charles Budgeon, and the passengers going the opposite way could read nothing at all—save "a man with a red moustache," "a young man in grey smoking a pipe." The October sunlight rested upon all these men and women sitting immobile; and little Johnnie Sturgeon took the chance to swing down the staircase, carrying his large mysterious parcel, and so dodging a zigzag course between the wheels he reached the pavement, started to whistle a tune and was soon out of sight—for ever. The omnibuses jerked on, and every single person felt relief at being a little nearer to his journey's end, though some cajoled themselves past the immediate engagement by promise of indulgence beyond—steak and kidney pudding, drink, or a game of dominoes in the smoky corner of a city restaurant. Oh yes, human life is very tolerable on the top of an omnibus in Holburn, when the policeman holds up his arm and the sun beats on your back, and if there is such a thing as a shell secreted by man to fit man himself here we find it, on the banks of the Thames, where the great

streets join and St. Paul's Cathedral, like the volute on the top of the snail shell, finishes it off. Jacob, getting off his omnibus, loitered up the steps, consulted his watch, and finally made up his mind to go in. . . . Does it need an effort? Yes. These changes of mood wear us out.

Dim it is, haunted by ghosts of white marble, to whom the organ for ever chaunts. If a boot creaks, it's awful; then the order; the discipline. The verger with his rod has life ironed out beneath him. Sweet and holy are the angelic choristers. And for ever round the marble shoulders, in and out of the folded fingers, go the thin high sounds of voice and organ. For ever requiem—repose. Tired with scrubbing the steps of the Prudential Society's office, which she did year in year out, Mrs. Lidgett took her seat beneath the great Duke's tomb, folded her hands, and half closed her eyes. A magnificent place for an old woman to rest in, by the very side of the great Duke's bones, whose victories mean nothing to her, whose name she knows not, though she never fails to greet the little angels opposite, as she passes out, wishing the like on her own tomb, for the leathern curtain of the heart has flapped wide, and out steal on tiptoe thoughts of rest, sweet melodies. . . . Old Spicer, jute merchant, thought nothing of the kind though. Strangely enough he'd never been in St. Paul's these fifty years, though his office windows looked on the churchyard. "So that's all? Well, a gloomy old place. . . . Where's Nelson's tomb? No time now—come again—a coin to leave in the box. . . . Rain or fine is it? Well, if it would only make up its mind!" Idly the children stray in—the verger dissuades them—and another and another . . . man, woman, man, woman, boy . . . casting their eyes up, pursing their lips, the same shadow brushing· the same faces; the leathern curtain of the heart flaps wide.

Nothing could appear more certain from the steps of St. Paul's than that each person is miraculously provided with coat, skirt, and boots; an income; an object. Only Jacob, carrying in his hand Finlay's *Byzantine Empire*, which he had bought in Ludgate Hill, looked a little different; for in his hand he carried a book, which book he would at nine-thirty precisely, by his own fireside, open and study, as no one else of all these multitudes would do. They have no houses. The streets belong to them; the shops; the churches; theirs the innumerable desks; the stretched office lights; the vans are theirs, and the railway slung high above the street. If you look closer you will see that three elderly men at a little distance from each other run spiders along the pavement as if the street were their parlour, and here, against the wall, a woman stares at nothing, boot-laces extended, which she does not ask you to buy. The posters are theirs too; and the news

on them. A town destroyed; a race won. A homeless people, circling beneath the sky whose blue or white is held off by a ceiling cloth of steel filings and horse dung shredded to dust.

There, under the green shade, with his head bent over white paper, Mr. Sibley transferred figures to folios, and upon each desk you observe, like provender, a bunch of papers, the day's nutriment, slowly consumed by the industrious pen. Innumerable overcoats of the quality prescribed hung empty all day in the corridors, but as the clock struck six each was exactly filled, and the little figures, split apart into trousers or moulded into a single thickness, jerked rapidly with angular forward motion along the pavement; then dropped into darkness. Beneath the pavement, sunk in the earth, hollow drains lined with yellow light for ever conveyed them this way and that, and large letters upon enamel plates represented in the underworld the parks, squares, and circuses of the upper. "Marbel Arch—Shepherd's Bush"—to the majority the Arch and the Bush are eternally white letters upon a blue ground. Only at one point—it may be Acton, Holloway, Kensal Rise, Caledonian Road—does the name mean shops where you buy things, and houses, in one of which, down to the right, where the pollard trees grow out of the paving stones, there is a square curtained window, and a bedroom.

Long past sunset an old blind woman sat on a camp-stool, with her back to the stone wall of the Union of London and Smith's Bank, clasping a brown mongrel tight in her arms and singing out loud, not for coppers, no, from the depths of her gay wild heart—her sinful, tanned heart—for the child who fetches her is the fruit of sin, and should have been in bed, curtained, asleep, instead of hearing in the lamplight her mother's wild song, where she sits against the Bank, singing not for coppers, with her dog against her breast.

Home they went. The grey church spires received them; the hoary city, old, sinful, and majestic. One behind another, round or pointed, piercing the sky or massing themselves, like sailing ships, like granite cliffs, spires and offices, wharves and factories crowd the bank; eternally the pilgrims trudge; barges rest in mid stream heavy laden; as some believe, the city loves her prostitutes.

But few, it seems, are admitted to that degree. Of all the carriages that leave the arch of the Opera House, not one turns eastward, and when the little thief is caught in the empty market-place no one in black-and-white or rose-coloured evening dress blocks the way by pausing with a hand upon the carriage door to help or condemn— though Lady Charles, to do her justice, sighs sadly as she ascends her staircase, takes down Thomas à Kempis, and does not sleep till her mind has lost itself tunnelling into the complexity of things.

"Why? Why? Why?" she sighs. On the whole it's best to walk back from the Opera House. Fatigue is the safest sleeping draught.

The autumn season was in full swing. Tristan was twitching his rug up under his armpits twice a week; Isolde waved her scarf in miraculous sympathy with the conductor's baton. In all parts of the house were to be found pink faces and glittering breasts. When a Royal hand attached to an invisible body slipped out and withdrew the red and white bouquet reposing on the scarlet ledge, the Queen of England seemed a name worth dying for. Beauty, in its hothouse variety (which is none of the worst), flowered in box after box; and though nothing was said of profound importance, and though it is generally agreed that wit deserted beautiful lips about the time that Walpole died—at any rate when Victoria in her nightgown descended to meet her ministers, the lips (through an opera glass) remained red, adorable. Bald distinguished men with gold-headed canes strolled down the crimson avenues between the stalls, and only broke from intercourse with the boxes when the lights went down, and the conductor, first bowing to the Queen, next to the bald-headed men, swept round on his feet and raised his wand.

Then two thousand hearts in the semi-darkness remembered, anticipated, travelled dark labyrinths; and Clara Durrant said farewell to Jacob Flanders, and tasted the sweetness of death in effigy; and Mrs. Durrant, sitting behind her in the dark of the box, sighed her sharp sigh; and Mr. Wortley, shifting his position behind the Italian Ambassador's wife, thought that Brangaena was a trifle hoarse; and suspended in the gallery many feet above their heads, Edward Whittaker surreptitiously held a torch to his miniature score; and . . . and . . .

In short, the observer is choked with observations. Only to prevent us from being submerged by chaos, nature and society between them have arranged a system of classification which is simplicity itself; stalls, boxes, amphitheatre, gallery. The moulds are filled nightly. There is no need to distinguish details. But the difficulty remains— one has to choose. For though I have no wish to be Queen of England —or only for a moment—I would willingly sit beside her; I would hear the Prime Minister's gossip; the countess whisper, and share her memories of halls and gardens; the massive fronts of the respectable conceal after all their secret code; or why so impermeable? And then, doffing one's own head-piece, how strange to assume for a moment some one's—any one's—to be a man of valour who has ruled the Empire; to refer while Brangaena sings to the fragments of Sophocles, or see in a flash, as the shepherd pipes his tune, bridges and aqueducts. But no—we must choose. Never was there a harsher necessity! or one

which entails greater pain, more certain disaster; for wherever I seat myself, I die in exile: Whittaker in his lodging-house; a Lady Charles at the Manor.

A young man with a Wellington nose, who had occupied a seven-and-sixpenny seat, made his way down the stone stairs when the opera ended, as if he were still set a little apart from his fellows by the influence of the music.

At midnight Jacob Flanders heard a rap on his door.

"By Jove!" he exclaimed. "You're the very man I want!" and without more ado they discovered the lines which he had been seeking all day; only they come not in Virgil, but in Lucretius.

"Yes; that should make him sit up," said Bonamy, as Jacob stopped reading. Jacob was excited. It was first time he had read his essay aloud.

"Damned swine!" he said, rather too extravagantly; but the praise had gone to his head. Professor Bulteel, of Leeds, had issued an edition of Wycherley without stating that he had left out, disembowelled, or indicated only by asterisks, several indecent words and some indecent phrases. An outrage, Jacob said; a breach of faith; sheer prudery; token of a lewd mind and a disgusting nature. Aristophanes and Shakespeare were cited. Modern life was repudiated. Great play was made with the professorial title, and Leeds as a seat of learning was laughed to scorn. And the extraordinary thing was that these young men were perfectly right—extraordinary, because, even as Jacob copied his pages, he knew that no one would ever print them; and sure enough back they came from the *Fortnightly,* the *Contemporary,* the *Nineteenth Century*—when Jacob threw them into the black wooden box where he kept his mother's letters, his old flannel trousers, and a note or two with the Cornish postmark. The lid shut upon the truth.

This black wooden box, upon which his name was still legible in white paint, stood between the long windows of the sitting-room. The street ran beneath. No doubt the bedroom was behind. The furniture—three wicker chairs and a gate-legged table—came from Cambridge. These houses (Mrs. Garfit's daughter, Mrs. Whitehorn, was the landlady of this one) were built, say, a hundred and fifty years ago. The rooms are shapely, the ceilings high; over the doorway a rose, or a ram's skull, is carved in the wood. The eighteenth century has its distinction. Even the panels, painted in raspberry-coloured paint, have their distinction. . . .

"Distinction"—Mrs. Durrant said that Jacob Flanders was "distinguished-looking." "Extremely awkward," she said, "but so dis-

tinguished-looking." Seeing him for the first time that no doubt is the word for him. Lying back in his chair, taking his pipe from his lips, and saying to Bonamy: "About this opera now" (for they had done with indecency). "This fellow Wagner" . . . distinction was one of the words to use naturally, though, from looking at him, one would have found it difficult to say which seat in the opera house was his, stalls, gallery, or dress circle. A writer? He lacked self-consciousness. A painter? There was something in the shape of his hands (he was descended on his mother's side from a family of the greatest antiquity and deepest obscurity) which indicated taste. Then his mouth—but surely, of all futile occupations this of cataloguing features is the worst. One word is sufficient. But if one cannot find it?

"I like Jacob Flanders," wrote Clara Durrant in her diary. "He is so unworldly. He gives himself no airs, and one can say what one likes to him, though he's frightening because . . ." But Mr. Letts allows little space in his shilling diaries. Clara was not the one to encroach upon Wednesday. Humblest, most candid of women! "No, no, no," she sighed, standing at the greenhouse door, "don't break—don't spoil"—what? Something infinitely wonderful.

But then, this is only a young woman's language, one, too, who loves, or refrains from loving. She wished the moment to continue for ever precisely as it was that July morning. And moments don't. Now, for instance, Jacob was telling a story about some walking tour he'd taken, and the inn was called "The Foaming Pot," which, considering the landlady's name . . . They shouted with laughter. The joke was indecent.

Then Julia Eliot said "the silent young man," and as she dined with Prime Ministers, no doubt she meant: "If he is going to get on in the world, he will have to find his tongue."

Timothy Durrant never made any comment at all.

The housemaid found herself very liberally rewarded.

Mr. Sopwith's opinion was as sentimental as Clara's, though far more skilfully expressed.

Betty Flanders was romantic about Archer and tender about John; she was unreasonably irritated by Jacob's clumsiness in the house.

Captain Barfoot liked him best of the boys; but as for saying why. . . .

It seems then that men and women are equally at fault. It seems that a profound, impartial, and absolutely just opinion of our fellow-creatures is utterly unknown. Either we are men, or we are women. Either we are cold, or we are sentimental. Either we are young, or growing old. In any case life is but a procession of shadows, and God knows why it is that we embrace them so eagerly, and see them

depart with such anguish, being shadows. And why, if this and much more than this is true, why are we yet surprised in the window corner by a sudden vision that the young man in the chair is of all things in the world the most real, the most solid, the best known to us—why indeed? For the moment after we know nothing about him.

Such is the manner of our seeing. Such the conditions of our love.

("I'm twenty-two. It's nearly the end of October. Life is thoroughly pleasant, although unfortunately there are a great number of fools about. One must apply oneself to something or other—God knows what. Everything is really very jolly—except getting up in the morning and wearing a tail coat.")

"I say, Bonamy, what about Beethoven?"

("Bonamy is an amazing fellow. He knows practically everything —not more about English literature than I do—but then he's read all those Frenchmen.")

"I rather suspect you're talking rot, Bonamy. In spite of what you say, poor old Tennyson. . . ."

("The truth is one ought to have been taught French. Now, I suppose, old Barfoot is talking to my mother. That's an odd affair to be sure. But I can't see Bonamy down there. Damn London!") for the market carts were lumbering down the street.

"What about a walk on Saturday?"

("What's happening on Saturday?")

Then, taking out his pocket-book, he assured himself that the night of the Durrants' party came next week.

But though all this may very well be true—so Jacob thought and spoke—so he crossed his legs—filled his pipe—sipped his whisky, and once looked at his pocket-book, rumpling his hair as he did so, there remains over something which can never be conveyed to a second person save by Jacob himself. Moreover, part of this is not Jacob but Richard Bonamy—the room; the market carts; the hour; the very moment of history. Then consider the effect of sex—how between man and woman it hangs wavy, tremulous, so that here's a valley, there's a peak, when in truth, perhaps, all's as flat as my hand. Even the exact words get the wrong accent on them. But something is always impelling one to hum vibrating, like the hawk moth, at the mouth of the cavern of mystery, endowing Jacob Flanders with all sorts of qualities he had not at all—for though, certainly, he sat talking to Bonamy, half of what he said was too dull to repeat; much unintelligible (about unknown people and Parliament); what remains is mostly a matter of guess work. Yet over him we hang vibrating.

"Yes," said Captain Barfoot, knocking out his pipe on Betty Flanders's hob, and buttoning his coat. "It doubles the work, but I don't mind that."

He was now town councillor. They looked at the night, which was the same as the London night, only a good deal more transparent. Church bells down in the town were striking eleven o'clock. The wind was off the sea. And all the bedroom windows were dark—the Pages were asleep; the Garfits were asleep; the Cranches were asleep—whereas in London at this hour they were burning Guy Fawkes on Parliament Hill.

§ 6

The flames had fairly caught.

"There's St. Paul's!" some one cried.

As the wood caught the city of London was lit up for a second; on other sides of the fire there were trees. Of the faces which came out fresh and vivid as though painted in yellow and red, the most prominent was a girl's face. By a trick of the firelight she seemed to have no body. The oval of the face and hair hung beside the fire with a dark vacuum for background. As if dazed by the glare, her green-blue eyes stared at the flames. Every muscle of her face was taut. There was something tragic in her thus staring—her age between twenty and twenty-five.

A hand descending from the chequered darkness thrust on her head the conical white hat of a pierrot. Shaking her head, she still stared. A whiskered face appeared above her. They dropped two legs of a table upon the fire and a scattering of twigs and leaves. All this blazed up and showed faces far back, round, pale, smooth, bearded, some with billy-cock hats on; all intent; showed too St. Paul's floating on the uneven white mist, and two or three narrow, paper-white, extinguisher-shaped spires.

The flames were struggling through the wood and roaring up when, goodness knows where from, pails flung water in beautiful hollow shapes, as of polished tortoiseshell; flung again and again; until the hiss was like a swarm of bees; and all the faces went out.

"Oh, Jacob," said the girl, as they pounded up the hill in the dark, "I'm so frightfully unhappy!"

Shouts of laughter came from the others—high, low; some before, others after.

The hotel dining-room was brightly lit. A stag's head in plaster was at one end of the table; at the other some Roman bust blackened

and reddened to represent Guy Fawkes, whose night it was. The diners were linked together by lengths of paper roses, so that when it came to singing "Auld Lang Syne" with their hands crossed a pink and yellow line rose and fell the entire length of the table. There was an enormous tapping of green wine-glasses. A young man stood up, and Florinda, taking one of the purplish globes that lay on the table, flung it straight at his head. It crushed to powder.

"I'm so frightfully unhappy!" she said, turning to Jacob, who sat beside her.

The table ran, as if on invisible legs, to the side of the room, and a barrel organ decorated with a red cloth and two pots of paper flowers reeled out waltz music.

Jacob could not dance. He stood against the wall smoking a pipe.

"We think," said two of the dancers, breaking off from the rest, and bowing profoundly before him, "that you are the most beautiful man we have ever seen."

So they wreathed his head with paper flowers. Then somebody brought out a white and gilt chair and made him sit on it. As they passed, people hung glass grapes on his shoulders, until he looked like the figure-head of a wrecked ship. Then Florinda got upon his knee and hid her face in his waistcoat. With one hand he held her; with the other, his pipe.

"Now let us talk," said Jacob, as he walked down Haverstock Hill between four and five o'clock in the morning of November the sixth arm-in-arm with Timmy Durrant, "about something sensible."

The Greeks—yes, that was what they talked about—how when all's said and done, when one's rinsed one's mouth with every litera-ture in the world, including Chinese and Russian (but these Slavs aren't civilized), it's the flavour of Greek that remains. Durrant quoted Aeschylus—Jacob Sophocles. It is true that no Greek could have understood or professor refrained from pointing out—Never mind; what is Greek for if not to be shouted on Haverstock Hill in the dawn? Moreover, Durrant never listened to Sophocles, nor Jacob to Aeschylus. They were boastful, triumphant; it seemed to both that they had read every book in the world; known every sin, passion, and joy. Civilizations stood round them like flowers ready for picking. Ages lapped at their feet like waves fit for sailing. And surveying all this, looming through the fog, the lamplight, the shades of London, the two young men decided in favour of Greece.

"Probably," said Jacob, "we are the only people in the world who know what the Greeks meant."

They drank coffee at a stall where the urns were burnished and little lamps burnt along the counter.

Taking Jacob for a military gentleman, the stallkeeper told him about his boy at Gibraltar, and Jacob cursed the British army and praised the Duke of Wellington. So on again they went down the hill talking about the Greeks.

A strange thing—when you come to think of it—this love of Greek, flourishing in such obscurity, distorted, discouraged, yet leaping out, all of a sudden, especially on leaving crowded rooms, or after a surfeit of print, or when the moon floats among the waves of the hills, or in hollow, sallow, fruitless London days, like a specific; a clean blade; always a miracle. Jacob knew no more Greek than served him to stumble through a play. Of ancient history he knew nothing. However, as he tramped into London it seemed to him that they were making the flagstones ring on the road to the Acropolis, and that if Socrates saw them coming he would bestir himself and say "my fine fellows," for the whole sentiment of Athens was entirely after his heart; free, venturesome, high-spirited. . . . She had called him Jacob without asking his leave. She had sat upon his knee. Thus did all good women in the days of the Greeks.

At this moment there shook out into the air a wavering, quavering, doleful lamentation which seemed to lack strength to unfold itself, and yet flagged on; at the sound of which doors in back streets burst sullenly open; workmen stumped forth.

Florinda was sick.

Mrs. Durrant, sleepless as usual, scored a mark by the side of certain lines in the *Inferno*.

Clara slept buried in her pillows; on her dressing-table dishevelled roses and a pair of long white gloves.

Still wearing the conical white hat of a pierrot, Florinda was sick. The bedroom seemed fit for these catastrophes—cheap, mustard-coloured, half attic, half studio, curiously ornamented with silver paper stars, Welsh-women's hats, and rosaries pendent from the gas brackets. As for Florinda's story, her name had been bestowed upon her by a painter who had wished it to signify that the flower of her maidenhood was still unplucked. Be that as it may, she was without a surname, and for parents, had only the photograph of a tombstone beneath which, she said, her father lay buried. Sometimes she would

dwell upon the size of it, and rumour had it that Florinda's father had died from the growth of his bones which nothing could stop; just as her mother enjoyed the confidence of a royal master, and now and again Florinda herself was a princess, but chiefly when drunk. Thus deserted, pretty into the bargain, with tragic eyes and the lips of a child, she talked more about virginity than women mostly do; and had lost it only the night before, or cherished it beyond the heart in her breast, according to the man she talked to. But did she always talk to men? No, she had her confidante: Mother Stuart. Stuart, as the lady would point out, is the name of a royal house; but what that signified, and what her business was, no one knew; only that Mrs. Stuart got postal orders every Monday morning, kept a parrot, believed in the transmigration of souls, and could read the future in tea leaves. Dirty lodging-house wallpaper she was behind the chastity of Florinda.

Now Florinda wept, and spent the day wandering the streets; stood at Chelsea watching the river swim past; trailed along the shopping streets; opened her bag and powdered her cheeks in omnibuses; read love letters, propping them against the milk pot in the A.B.C. shop; detected glass in the sugar bowl; accused the waitress of wishing to poison her; declared that young men stared at her; and found herself towards evening slowly sauntering· down Jacob's street, when it struck her that she liked that man Jacob better than dirty Jews, and sitting at his table (he was copying his essay upon the Ethics of Indecency), drew off her gloves and told him how Mother Stuart had banged her on the head with the tea-cosy.

Jacob took her word for it that she was chaste. She prattled, sitting by the fireside, of famous painters. The tomb of her father was mentioned. Wild and frail and beautiful she looked, and thus the women of the Greeks were, Jacob thought; and this was life; and himself a man and Florinda chaste.

She left with one of Shelley's poems beneath her arm. Mrs. Stuart, she said, often talked of him.

Marvellous are the innocent. To believe that the girl herself transcends all lies (for Jacob was not such a fool as to believe implicitly), to wonder enviously at the unanchored life—his own seemed petted and even cloistered in comparison—to have at hand as sovereign specifics for all disorders of the soul Adonais and the plays of Shakespeare; to figure out a comradeship all spirited on her side, protective on his, yet equal on both, for women, thought Jacob, are just thé same as men—innocence such as this is marvellous enough, and perhaps not so foolish after all.

For when Florinda got home that night she first washed her head;

then ate chocolate creams; then opened Shelley. True, she was horribly bored. What on earth was it *about?* She had to wager with herself that she would turn the page before she ate another. In fact she slept. But then her day had been a long one, Mother Stuart had thrown the tea-cosy;—there are formidable sights in the streets, and though Florinda ignorant as an owl, and would never learn to read even her love letters correctly, still she had her feelings, liked some men better than others, and was entirely at the beck and call of life. Whether or not she was a virgin seems a matter of no importance whatever. Unless, indeed, it is the only thing of any importance at all.

Jacob was restless when she left him.

All night men and women seethed up and down the well-known beats. Late home-comers could see shadows against the blinds even in the most respectable suburbs. Not a square in snow or fog lacked its amorous couple. All plays turned on the same subject. Bullets went through heads in hotel bedrooms almost nightly on that account. When the body escaped mutilation, seldom did the heart go to the grave unscarred. Little else was talked of in theatres and popular novels. Yet we say it is a matter of no importance at all.

What with Shakespeare and Adonais, Mozart and Bishop Berkeley —choose whom you like—the fact is concealed and the evenings for most of us pass reputably, or with only the sort of tremor that a snake makes sliding through the grass. But then concealment by itself distracts the mind from the print and the sound. If Florinda had had a mind, she might have read with clearer eyes than we can. She and her sort have solved the question by turning it to a trifle of washing the hands nightly before going to bed, the only difficulty being whether you prefer your water hot or cold, which being settled, the mind can go about its business unassailed.

But it did occur to Jacob, half-way through dinner, to wonder whether she had a mind.

They sat at a little table in the restaurant.

Florinda leant the points of her elbows on the table and held her chin in the cup of her hands. Her cloak had slipped behind her. Gold and white with bright beads on her she emerged, her face flowering from her body, innocent, scarcely tinted, the eyes gazing frankly about her, or slowly settling on Jacob and resting there. She talked:

"You know that big black box the Australian left in my room ever so long ago? . . . I do think furs make a woman look old. . . . That's Bechstein come in now. . . . I was wondering what you

looked like when you were a little boy, Jacob." She nibbled her roll and looked at him.

"Jacob. You're like one of those statues. . . . I think there are lovely things in the British Museum, don't you? Lots of lovely things . . ." she spoke dreamily. The room was filling; the heat increasing. Talk in a restaurant is dazed sleepwalkers' talk, so many things to look at—so much noise—other people talking. Can one overhear? Oh, but they mustn't overhear *us*.

"That's like Ellen Nagle—that girl . . ." and so on.

"I'm awfully happy since I've known you, Jacob. You're such a *good* man."

The room got fuller and fuller; talk louder; knives more clattering.

"Well, you see what makes her say things like that is . . ."

She stopped. So did every one.

"To-morrow . . . Sunday . . . a beastly . . . you tell me . . . go then!" Crash! And out she swept.

It was at the table next them that the voice spun higher and higher. Suddenly the woman dashed the plates to the floor. The man was left there. Everybody stared. Then—"Well, poor chap, we mustn't sit staring. What a go! Did you hear what she said? By God, he looks a fool! Didn't come up to the scratch, I suppose. All the mustard on the table-cloth. The waiters laughing."

Jacob observed Florinda. In her face there seemed to him something horribly brainless—as she sat staring.

Out she swept, the black woman with the dancing feather in her hat.

Yet she had to go somewhere. The night is not a tumultuous black ocean in which you sink or sail as a star. As a matter of fact it was a wet November night. The lamps of Soho made large greasy spots of light upon the pavement. The by-streets were dark enough to shelter man or woman leaning against the doorways. One detached herself as Jacob and Florinda approached.

"She's dropped her glove," said Florinda.

Jacob, pressing forward, gave it her.

Effusively she thanked him; retraced her steps; dropped her glove again. But why? For whom?

Meanwhile, where had the other woman got to? And the man?

The street lamps do not carry far enough to tell us. The voices, angry, lustful, despairing, passionate, were scarcely more than the voices of caged beasts at night. Only they are not caged, nor beasts. Stop a man; ask him the way; he'll tell it you; but one's afraid to ask him the way. What does one fear?—the human eye. At once the pavement narrows, the chasm deepens. There! They've melted

into it—both man and woman. Further on, blatantly advertising its meritorious solidity, a boarding-house exhibits behind uncurtained windows its testimony to the soundness of London. There they sit, plainly illuminated, dressed like ladies and gentlemen, in bamboo chairs. The widows of business men prove laboriously that they are related to judges. The wives of coal merchants instantly retort that their fathers kept coachmen. A servant brings coffee, and the crochet basket has to be moved. And so on again into the dark, passing a girl here for sale, or there an old woman with only matches to offer, passing the crowd from the Tube station, the women with veiled hair, passing at length no one but shut doors, carved door-posts, and a solitary policeman, Jacob, with Florinda on his arm, reached his room and, lighting the lamp, said nothing at all.

"I don't like you when you look like that," said Florinda.

The problem is insoluble. The body is harnessed to a brain. Beauty goes hand in hand with stupidity. There she sat staring at the fire as she had stared at the broken mustard-pot. In spite of defending indecency, Jacob doubted whether he liked it in the raw. He had a violent reversion towards male society, cloistered rooms, and the works of the classics; and was ready to turn with wrath upon whoever it was who had fashioned life thus.

Then Florinda laid her hand upon his knee.

After all, it was none of her fault. But the thought saddened him. It's not catastrophes, murders, deaths, diseases, that age and kill us; it's the way people look and laugh, and run up the steps of omnibuses.

Any excuse, though, serves a stupid woman. He told her his head ached.

But when she looked at him, dumbly, half-guessing, half-understanding, apologizing perhaps, anyhow saying as he had said, "It's none of my fault," straight and beautiful in body, her face like a shell within its cap, then he knew that cloisters and classics are no use whatever. The problem is insoluble.

§ 7

About this time a firm of merchants having dealings with the East put on the market little paper flowers which opened on touching water. As it was the custom also to use finger-bowls at the end of dinner, the new discovery was found of excellent service. In these sheltered lakes the little coloured flowers swam and slid; surmounted smooth slippery waves, and sometimes foundered and lay like pebbles

on the glass floor. Their fortunes were watched by eyes intent and lovely. It is surely a great discovery that leads to the union of hearts and foundation of homes. The paper flowers did no less.

It must not be thought, though, that they ousted the flowers of nature. Roses, lilies, carnations in particular, looked over the rims of vases and surveyed the bright lives and swift dooms of their artificial relations. Mr. Stuart Ormond made this very observation; and charming it was thought; and Kitty Craster married him on the strength of it six months later. But real flowers can never be dispensed with. If they could, human life would be a different affair altogether. For flowers fade; chrysanthemums are the worst; perfect over night; yellow and jaded next morning—not fit to be seen. On the whole, though the price is sinful, carnations pay best;—it's a question, however, whether it's wise to have them wired. Some shops advise it. Certainly it's the only way to keep them at a dance; but whether it is necessary at dinner parties, unless the rooms are very hot, remains in dispute. Old Mrs. Temple used to recommend an ivy leaf—just one—dropped into the bowl. She said it kept the water pure for days and days. But there is some reason to think that old Mrs. Temple was mistaken.

The little cards, however, with names engraved on them, are a more serious problem than the flowers. More horses' legs have been worn out, more coachmen's lives consumed, more hours of sound afternoon time vainly lavished than served to win us the battle of Waterloo, and pay for it into the bargain. The little demons are the source of as many reprieves, calamities, and anxieties as the battle itself. Sometimes Mrs. Bonham has just gone out; at others she is at home. But, even if the cards should be superseded, which seems unlikely, there are unruly powers blowing life into storms, disordering sedulous mornings, and uprooting the stability of the afternoon—dressmakers, that is to say, and confectioners' shops. Six yards of silk will cover one body; but if you have to devise six hundred shapes for it, and twice as many colours?—in the middle of which there is the urgent question of the pudding with tufts of green cream and battlements of almond paste. It has not arrived.

The flamingo hours fluttered softly through the sky. But regularly they dipped their wings in pitch black; Notting Hill, for instance, or the purlieus of Clerkenwell. No wonder that Italian remained a hidden art, and the piano always played the same sonata. In order to buy one pair of elastic stockings for Mrs. Page, widow, aged sixty-three, in receipt of five shillings out-door relief, and help from her only son employed in Messrs. Mackie's dye-works, suffering in winter

with his chest, letters must be written, columns filled up in the same round, simple hand that wrote in Mr. Letts's diary how the weather was fine, the children demons, and Jacob Flanders unworldly. Clara Durrant procured the stockings, played the sonata, filled the vases, fetched the pudding, left the cards, and when the great invention of paper flowers to swim in finger-bowls was discovered, was one of those who most marvelled at their brief lives.

Nor were there wanting poets to celebrate the theme. Edwin Mallett, for example, wrote his verses ending:

And read their doom in Chloe's eyes,

which caused Clara to blush at the first reading, and to laugh at the second, saying that it was just like him to call her Chloe when her name was Clara. Ridiculous young man! But when, between ten and eleven on a rainy morning, Edwin Mallett laid his life at her feet she ran out of the room and hid herself in her bedroom, and Timothy below could not get on with his work all that morning on account of her sobs.

"Which is the result of enjoying yourself," said Mrs. Durrant severely, surveying the dance programme all scored with the same initials, or rather they were different ones this time—R. B. instead of E. M.; Richard Bonamy it was now, the young man with the Wellington nose.

"But I could never marry a man with a nose like that," said Clara.

"Nonsense," said Mrs. Durrant.

"But I am too severe," she thought to herself. For Clara, losing all vivacity, tore up her dance programme and threw it in the fender.

Such were the very serious consequences of the invention of paper flowers to swim in bowls.

"Please," said Julia Eliot, taking up her position by the curtain almost opposite the door, "don't introduce me. I like to look on. The amusing thing," she went on, addressing Mr. Salvin, who, owing to his lameness, was accommodated with a chair, "the amusing thing about a party is to watch the people—coming and going, coming and going."

"Last time we met," said Mr. Salvin, "was at the Farquhars. Poor lady! She had much to put up with."

"Doesn't she look charming?" exclaimed Miss Eliot, as Clara Durrant passed them.

"And which of them . . .?" asked Mr. Salvin, dropping his voice and speaking in quizzical tones.

"There are so many . . ." Miss Eliot replied. Three young men stood at the doorway looking about for their hostess.

"You don't remember Elizabeth as I do," said Mr. Salvin, "dancing Highland reels at Banchorie. Clara lacks her mother's spirit. Clara is a little pale."

"What different people one sees here!" said Miss Eliot.

"Happily we are not governed by the evening papers," said Mr. Salvin.

"I never read them," said Miss Eliot. "I know nothing about politics," she added.

"The piano is in tune," said Clara, passing them, "but we may have to ask some one to move it for us."

"Are they going to dance?" asked Mr. Salvin.

"Nobody shall disturb you," said Mrs. Durrant peremptorily as she passed.

"Julia Eliot. It *is* Julia Eliot!" said old Lady Hibbert, holding out both her hands. "And Mr. Salvin. What is going to happen to us, Mr. Salvin? With all my experience of English politics—My dear, I was thinking of your father last night—one of my oldest friends, Mr. Salvin. Never tell me that girls of ten are incapable of love! I had all Shakespeare by heart before I was in my teens, Mr. Salvin!"

"You don't say so," said Mr. Salvin.

"But I do," said Lady Hibbert.

"Oh, Mr. Salvin, I'm so sorry. . . ."

"I will remove myself if you'll kindly lend me a hand," said Mr. Salvin.

"You shall sit by my mother," said Clara. "Everybody seems to come in here. . . . Mr. Calthorp, let me introduce you to Miss Edwards."

"Are you going away for Christmas?" said Mr. Calthorp.

"If my brother gets his leave," said Miss Edwards.

"What regiment is he in?" said Mr. Calthorp.

"The Twentieth Hussars," said Miss Edwards.

"Perhaps he knows my brother?" said Mr. Calthorp.

"I am afraid I did not catch your name," said Miss Edwards.

"Calthorp," said Mr. Calthorp.

"But what proof was there that the marriage service was actually performed?" said Mr. Crosby.

"There is no reason to doubt that Charles James Fox . . ." Mr. Burley began; but here Mrs. Stretton told him that she knew his sister well; had stayed with her not six weeks ago; and thought the house charming, but bleak in winter.

"Going about as girls do nowadays——" said Mrs. Forster.

Mr. Bowley looked round him, and catching sight of Rose Shaw moved towards her, threw out his hands, and exclaimed: "Well!"

"Nothing!" she replied. "Nothing at all—though I left them alone the entire afternoon on purpose."

"Dear me, dear me," said Mr. Bowley. "I will ask Jimmy to breakfast."

"But who could resist her?" cried Rose Shaw. "Dearest Clara— I know we mustn't try to stop you . . ."

"You and Mr. Bowley are talking dreadful gossip, I know," said Clara.

"Life is wicked—life is detestable!" cried Rose Shaw.

"There's not much to be said for this sort of thing, is there?" said Timothy Durrant to Jacob.

"Women like it."

"Like what?" said Charlotte Wilding, coming up to them.

"Where have you come from?" said Timothy. "Dining somewhere, I suppose."

"I don't see why not," said Charlotte.

"People must go downstairs," said Clara, passing. "Take Charlotte, Timothy. How d'you do, Mr. Flanders."

"How d'you do, Mr. Flanders," said Julia Eliot, holding out her hand. "What's been happening to you?"

> *"Who is Silvia? what is she?*
> *That all our swains commend her?"*

sang Elsbeth Siddons.

Every one stood where they were, or sat down if a chair was empty.

"Ah," sighed Clara, who stood beside Jacob, half-way through.

> *"Then to Silvia let us sing,*
> *That Silvia is excelling;*
> *She excels each mortal thing*
> *Upon the dull earth dwelling.*
> *To her let us garlands bring,"*

sang Elsbeth Siddons.

"Ah!" Clara exclaimed out loud, and clapped her gloved hands; and Jacob clapped his bare ones; and then she moved forward and directed people to come in from the doorway.

"You are living in London?" asked Miss Julia Eliot.

"Yes," said Jacob.

"In rooms?"

"Yes."

"There is Mr. Clutterbuck. You always see Mr. Clutterbuck here. He is not very happy at home, I am afraid. They say that Mrs. Clutterbuck . . ." she dropped her voice. "That's why he stays with the Durrants. Were you there when they acted Mr. Wortley's play? Oh, no, of course not—at the last moment, did you hear—you had to go to join your mother, I remember, at Harrogate—At the last moment, as I was saying, just as everything was ready, the clothes finished and everything—Now Elsbeth is going to sing again. Clara is playing her accompaniment or turning over for Mr. Carter, I think. No, Mr. Carter is playing by himself—This is *Bach*," she whispered, as Mr. Carter played the first bars.

"Are you fond of music?" said Mrs. Durrant.

"Yes. I like hearing it," said Jacob. "I know nothing about it."

"Very few people do that," said Mrs. Durrant. "I dare say you were never taught. Why is that, Sir Jasper?—Sir Jasper Bigham—Mr. Flanders. Why is nobody taught anything that they ought to know, Sir Jasper?" She left them standing against the wall.

Neither of the gentlemen said anything for three minutes, though Jacob shifted perhaps five inches to the left, and then as many to the right. Then Jacob grunted, and suddenly crossed the room.

"Will you come and have something to eat?" he said to Clara Durrant.

"Yes, an ice. Quickly. Now," she said.

Downstairs they went.

But half-way down they met Mr. and Mrs. Gresham, Herbert Turner, Sylvia Rashleigh, and a friend, whom they had dared to bring, from America, "knowing that Mrs. Durrant—wishing to show Mr. Pilcher.—Mr. Pilcher from New York—This is Miss Durrant."

"Whom I have heard so much of," said Mr. Pilcher, bowing low.

So Clara left him.

§ 8

About half-past nine Jacob left the house, his door slamming, other doors slamming, buying his paper, mounting his omnibus, or, weather permitting, walking his road as other people do. Head bent down, a desk, a telephone, books bound in green leather, electric light. . . . "Fresh coals, sir?" . . . "Your tea, sir." . . . Talk about

football, the Hotspurs, the Harlequins; six-thirty *Star* brought in by the office boy; the rooks of Gray's Inn passing overhead; branches in the fog thin and brittle; and through the roar of traffic now and again a voice shouting: "Verdict—verdict—winner—winner," while letters accumulate in a basket, Jacob signs them, and each evening finds him, as he takes his coat down, with some muscle of the brain new stretched.

Then, sometimes a game of chess; or pictures in Bond Street, or a long way home to take the air with Bonamy on his arm, meditatively marching, head thrown back, the world a spectacle, the early moon above the steeples coming in for praise, the sea-gulls flying high, Nelson on his column surveying the horizon, and the world our ship.

Meanwhile, poor Betty Flanders's letter, having caught the second post, lay on the hall table—poor Betty Flanders writing her son's name, Jacob Alan Flanders, Esq., as mothers do, and the ink pale, profuse, suggesting how mothers down at Scarborough scribble over the fire with their feet on the fender, when tea's cleared away, and can never, never say, whatever it may be—probably this—Don't go with bad women, do be a good boy; wear your thick shirts; and come back, come back, come back to me.

But she said nothing of the kind. "Do you remember old Miss Wargrave, who used to be so kind when you had the whooping-cough?" she wrote; "she's dead at last, poor thing. They would like it if you wrote. Ellen came over and we spent a nice day shopping. Old Mouse gets very stiff, and we have to walk him up the smallest hill. Rebecca, at last, after I don't know how long, went into Mr. Adamson's. Three teeth, he says, must come out. Such mild weather for the time of year, the little buds actually on the pear trees. And Mrs. Jarvis tells me——" Mrs. Flanders liked Mrs. Jarvis, always said of her that she was too good for such a quiet place, and, though she never listened to her discontent and told her at the end of it (looking up, sucking her thread, or taking off her spectacles) that a little peat wrapped round the iris roots keeps them from the frost, and Parrot's great white sale is Tuesday next, "do remember,"—Mrs. Flanders knew precisely how Mrs. Jarvis felt; and how interesting her letters were, about Mrs. Jarvis, could one read them year in, year out—the unpublished works of women, written by the fireside in pale profusion, dried by the flame, for the blotting-paper's worn to holes and the nib cleft and clotted. Then Captain Barfoot. Him she called "the Captain," spoke of frankly, yet never without reserve. The Captain was enquiring for her about Garfit's acre; advised chickens; could promise profit; or had the sciatica; or Mrs. Barfoot had been indoors for weeks; or the Captain says things look bad,

politics that is, for as Jacob knew, the Captain would sometimes talk, as the evening waned, about Ireland or India; and then Mrs. Flanders would fall musing about Morty, her brother, lost all these years—had the natives got him, was his ship sunk—would the Admiralty tell her?—the Captain knocking his pipe out, as Jacob knew, rising to go, stiffly stretching to pick up Mrs. Flanders's wool which had rolled beneath the chair. Talk of the chicken farm came back and back, the woman, even at fifty, impulsive at heart, sketching on the cloudy future flocks of Leghorns, Cochin Chinas, Orpingtons; like Jacob in the blur of her outline; but powerful as he was; fresh and vigorous, running about the house, scolding Rebecca.

The letter lay upon the hall table; Florinda coming in that night took it up with her, put it on the table as she kissed Jacob, and Jacob seeing the hand, left it there under the lamp, between the biscuit-tin and the tobacco-box. They shut the bedroom door behind them.

The sitting-room neither knew nor cared. The door was shut; and to suppose that wood, when it creaks, transmits anything save that rats are busy and wood dry is childish. These old houses are only brick and wood, soaked in human sweat, grained with human dirt. But if the pale blue envelope lying by the biscuit-box had the feelings of a mother, the heart was torn by the little creak, the sudden stir. Behind the door was the obscene thing, the alarming presence, and terror would come over her as at death, or the birth of a child. Better, perhaps, burst in and face it than sit in the antechamber listening to the little creak, the sudden stir, for her heart was swollen, and pain threaded it. My son, my son—such would be her cry, uttered to hide her vision of him stretched with Florinda, inexcusable, ir-rational, in a woman with three children living at Scarborough. And the fault lay with Florinda. Indeed, when the door opened and the couple came out, Mrs. Flanders would have flounced upon her—only it was Jacob who came first, in his dressing-gown, amiable, authoritative, beautifully healthy, like a baby after an airing, with an eye clear as running water. Florinda followed, lazily stretching; yawn-ing a little; arranging her hair at the looking-glass—while Jacob read his mother's letter.

Let us consider letters—how they come at breakfast, and at night, with their yellow stamps and their green stamps, immortalized by the postmark—for to see one's own envelope on another's table is to realize how soon deeds sever and become alien. Then at last the power of the mind to quit the body is manifest, and perhaps we fear or hate or wish annihilated this phantom of ourselves, lying on the table. Still, there are letters that merely say how dinner's at seven;

others ordering coal; making appointments. The hand in them is scarcely perceptible, let alone the voice or the scowl. Ah, but when the post knocks and the letter comes always the miracle seems repeated—speech attempted. Venerable are letters, infinitely brave, forlorn, and lost.

Life would split asunder without them. "Come to tea, come to dinner, what's the truth of the story? have you heard the news? life in the capital is gay; the Russian dancers. . . ." These are our stays and props. These lace our days together and make of life a perfect globe. And yet, and yet . . . when we go to dinner, when pressing finger-tips we hope to meet somewhere soon, a doubt insinuates itself; is this the way to spend our days? the rare, the limited, so soon dealt out to us—drinking tea? dining out? And the notes accumulate. And the telephones ring. And everywhere we go wires and tubes surround us to carry the voices that try to penetrate before the last card is dealt and the days are over. "Try to penetrate," for as we lift the cup, shake the hand, express the hope, something whispers, Is this all? Can I never know, share, be certain? Am I doomed all my days to write letters, send voices, which fall upon the tea-table, fade upon the passage, making appointments, while life dwindles, to come and dine? Yet letters are venerable; and the telephone valiant, for the journey is a lonely one, and if bound together by notes and telephones we went in company, perhaps—who knows?—we might talk by the way.

Well, people have tried. Byron wrote letters. So did Cowper. For centuries the writing-desk has contained sheets fit precisely for the communications of friends. Masters of language, poets of long ages, have turned from the sheet that endures to the sheet that perishes, pushing aside the tea-tray, drawing close to the fire (for letters are written when the dark presses round a bright red cave), and addressed themselves to the task of reaching, touching, penetrating the individual heart. Were it possible! But words have been used too often; touched and turned, and left exposed to the dust of the street. The words we seek hang close to the tree. We come at dawn and find them sweet beneath the leaf.

Mrs. Flanders wrote letters; Mrs. Jarvis wrote them; Mrs. Durrant too; Mother Stuart actually scented her pages, thereby adding a flavour which the English language fails to provide; Jacob had written in his day long letters about art, morality, and politics to young men at college. Clara Durrant's letters were those of a child. Florinda—the impediment between Florinda and her pen was something impassable. Fancy a butterfly, gnat, or other winged insect, attached to a twig which, clogged with mud, it rolls across a page.

Her spelling was abominable. Her sentiments infantile. And for some reason when she wrote she declared her belief in God. Then there were crosses—tear stains; and the hand itself rambling and redeemed only by the fact—which always did redeem Florinda—by the fact that she cared. Yes, whether it was for chocolate creams, hot baths, the shape of her face in the looking-glass, Florinda could no more pretend a feeling than swallow whisky. Incontinent was her rejection. Great men are truthful, and these little prostitutes, staring in the fire, taking out a powder-puff, decorating lips at an inch of looking-glass, have (so Jacob thought) an inviolable fidelity.

Then he saw her turning up Greek Street upon another man's arm.

The light from the arc lamp drenched him from head to toe. He stood for a minute motionless beneath it. Shadows chequered the street. Other figures, single and together, poured out, wavered across, and obliterated Florinda and the man.

The light drenched Jacob from head to toe. You could see the pattern on his trousers; the old thorns on his stick; his shoe laces; bare hands; and face.

It was as if a stone were ground to dust; as if white sparks flew from a livid whetstone, which was his spine; as if the switchback railway, having swooped to the depths, fell, fell, fell. This was in his face.

Whether we know what was in his mind is another question. Granted ten years' seniority and a difference of sex, fear of him comes first; this is swallowed up by a desire to help—overwhelming sense, reason, and the time of night; anger would follow close on that—with Florinda, with destiny; and then up would bubble an irresponsible optimism. "Surely there's enough light in the street at this moment to drown all our cares in gold!" Ah, what's the use of saying it? Even while you speak and look over your shoulder towards Shaftesbury Avenue, destiny is chipping a dent in him. He has turned to go. As for following him back to his rooms, no—that we won't do.

Yet that, of course, is precisely what one does. He let himself in and shut the door, though it was only striking ten on one of the city clocks. No one can go to bed at ten. Nobody was thinking of going to bed. It was January and dismal, but Mrs. Wagg stood on her doorstep, as if expecting something to happen. A barrel-organ played like an obscene nightingale beneath wet leaves. Children ran across the road. Here and there one could see brown panelling inside the hall door. . . . The march that the mind keeps beneath the windows of others is queer enough. Now distracted by brown panelling; now by a fern in a pot; here improvising a few phrases to dance with the

barrel-organ; again snatching a detached gaiety from a drunken man; then altogether absorbed by words the poor shout across the street at each other (so outright, so lusty)—yet all the while having for centre, for magnet, a young man alone in his room.

"Life is wicked—life is detestable," cried Rose Shaw.

The strange thing about life is that though the nature of it must have been apparent to every one for hundreds of years, no one has left any adequate account of it. The streets of London have their map; but our passions are uncharted. What are you going to meet if you turn this corner?

"Holborn straight ahead of you," says the policeman. Ah, but where are you going if instead of brushing past the old man with the white beard, the silver medal, and the cheap violin, you let him go on with his story, which ends in an invitation to step somewhere, to his room, presumably, off Queen's Square, and there he shows you a collection of birds' eggs and a letter from the Prince of Wales's secretary, and this (skipping the intermediate stages) brings you one winter's day to the Essex coast, where the little boat makes off to the ship, and the ship sails and you behold on the skyline the Azores; and the flamingoes rise; and there you sit on the verge of the marsh drinking rum-punch, an outcast from civilization, for you have committed a crime, are infected with yellow fever as likely as not, and—fill in the sketch as you like.

As frequent as street corners in Holborn are these chasms in the continuity of our ways. Yet we keep straight on.

Rose Shaw, talking in rather an emotional manner to Mr. Bowley at Mrs. Durrant's evening party a few nights back, said that life was wicked because a man called Jimmy refused to marry a woman called (if memory serves) Helen Aitken.

Both were beautiful. Both were inanimate. The oval tea-table invariably separated them, and the plate of biscuits was all he ever gave her. He bowed; she inclined her head. They danced. He danced divinely. They sat in the alcove; never a word was said. Her pillow was wet with tears. Kind Mr. Bowley and dear Rose Shaw marvelled and deplored. Bowley had rooms in the Albany. Rose was re-born every evening precisely as the clock struck eight. All four were civilization's triumphs, and if you persist that a command of the English language is part of our inheritance, one can only reply that beauty is almost always dumb. Male beauty in association with female beauty breeds in the onlooker a sense of fear. Often have I seen them—Helen and Jimmy—and likened them to ships adrift, and feared for my own little craft. Or again, have you ever watched

fine collie dogs couchant at twenty yards' distance? As she passed him his cup there was that quiver in her flanks. Bowley saw what was up—asked Jimmy to breakfast. Helen must have confided in Rose. For my own part, I find it exceedingly difficult to interpret songs without words. And now Jimmy feeds crows in Flanders and Helen visits hospitals. Oh, life is damnable, life is wicked, as Rose Shaw said.

The lamps of London uphold the dark as upon the points of burning bayonets. The yellow canopy sinks and swells over the great fourposter. Passengers in the mail-coaches running into London in the eighteenth century looked through leafless branches and saw it flaring beneath them. The light burns behind yellow blinds and pink blinds, and above fanlights, and down in basement windows. The street market in Soho is fierce with light. Raw meat, china mugs, and silk stockings blaze in it. Raw voices wrap themselves round the flaring gas-jets. Arms akimbo, they stand on the pavement bawling—Messrs. Kettle and Wilkinson; their wives sit in the shop, furs wrapped round their necks, arms folded, eyes contemptuous. Such faces as one sees. The little man fingering the meat must have squatted before the fire in innumerable lodging-houses, and heard and seen and known so much that it seems to utter itself even volubly from dark eyes, loose lips, as he fingers the meat silently, his face sad as a poet's, and never a song sung. Shawled women carry babies with purple eyelids; boys stand at street corners; girls look across the road—rude illustrations, pictures in a book whose pages we turn over and over as if we should at last find what we look for. Every face, every shop, bedroom window, public-house, and dark square is a picture feverishly turned—in search of what? It is the same with books. What do we seek through millions of pages? Still hopefully turning the pages— oh, here is Jacob's room.

He sat at the table reading the *Globe*. The pinkish sheet was spread flat before him. He propped his face in his hand, so that the skin of his cheek was wrinkled in deep folds. Terribly severe he looked, set, and defiant. (What people go through in half an hour! But nothing could save him. These events are features of our landscape. A foreigner coming to London could scarcely miss seeing St. Paul's.) He judged life. These pinkish and greenish newspapers are thin sheets of gelatine pressed nightly over the brain and heart of the world. They take the impression of the whole. Jacob cast his eye over it. A strike, a murder, football, bodies found; vociferation from all parts of England simultaneously. How miserable it is that the *Globe* newspaper offers

nothing better to Jacob Flanders! When a child begins to read history one marvels, sorrowfully, to hear him spell out in his new voice the ancient words.

The Prime Minister's speech was reported in something over five columns. Feeling in his pocket, Jacob took out a pipe and proceeded to fill it. Five minutes, ten minutes, fifteen minutes passed. Jacob took the paper over to the fire. The Prime Minister proposed a measure for giving Home Rule to Ireland. Jacob knocked out his pipe. He was certainly thinking about Home Rule in Ireland—a very difficult matter. A very cold night.

The snow, which had been falling all night, lay at three o'clock in the afternoon over the fields and the hill. Clumps of withered grass stood out upon the hill-top; the furze bushes were black, and now and then a black shiver crossed the snow as the wind drove flurries of frozen particles before it. The sound was that of a broom sweeping —sweeping.

The stream crept along by the road unseen by any one. Sticks and leaves caught in the frozen grass. The sky was sullen grey and the trees of black iron. Uncompromising was the severity of the country. At four o'clock the snow was again falling. The day had gone out.

A window tinged yellow about two feet across alone combated the white fields and the black trees. . . . At six o'clock a man's figure carrying a lantern crossed the field. . . . A raft of twigs stayed upon a stone, suddenly detached itself, and floated towards the culvert. . . . A load of snow slipped and fell from a fir branch. . . . Later there was a mournful cry. . . . A motor car came along the road shoving the dark before it. . . . The dark shut down behind it. . . .

Spaces of complete immobility separated each of these movements. The land seemed to lie dead. . . . Then the old shepherd returned stiffly across the field. Stiffly and painfully the frozen earth was trodden under and gave beneath pressure like a treadmill. The worn voices of clocks repeated the fact of the hour all night long.

Jacob, too, heard them, and raked out the fire. He rose. He stretched himself. He went to bed.

§ 9

The Countess of Rocksbier sat at the head of the table alone with Jacob. Fed upon champagne and spices for at least two centuries (four, if you count the female line), the Countess Lucy looked well

fed. A discriminating nose she had for scents, prolonged, as if in quest of them; her underlip protruded a narrow red shelf; her eyes were small, with sandy tufts for eyebrows, and her jowl was heavy. Behind her (the window looked on Grosvenor Square) stood Moll Pratt on the pavement, offering violets for sale; and Mrs. Hilda Thomas, lifting her skirts, preparing to cross the road. One was from Walworth; the other from Putney. Both wore black stockings, but Mrs. Thomas was coiled in furs. The comparison was much in Lady Rocksbier's favour. Moll had more humour, but was violent; stupid too. Hilda Thomas was mealy-mouthed, all her silver frames aslant; egg-cups in the drawing-room; and the windows shrouded. Lady Rocksbier, whatever the deficiencies of her profile, had been a great rider to hounds. She used her knife with authority, tore her chicken bones, asking Jacob's pardon, with her own hands.

"Who is that driving by?" she asked Boxall, the butler.

"Lady Fittlemere's carriage, my lady," which reminded her to send a card to ask after his lordship's health. A rude old lady, Jacob thought. The wine was excellent. She called herself "an old woman" —"so kind to lunch with an old woman"—which flattered him. She talked of Joseph Chamberlain, whom she had known. She said that Jacob must come and meet—one of our celebrities. And the Lady Alice came in with three dogs on a leash, and Jackie, who ran to kiss his grandmother, while Boxall brought in a telegram, and Jacob was given a good cigar.

A few moments before a horse jumps it slows, sidles, gathers itself together, goes up like a monster wave, and pitches down on the further side. Hedges and sky swoop in a semicircle. Then as if your own body ran into the horse's body and it was your own forelegs grown with his that sprang, rushing through the air you go, the ground resilient, bodies a mass of muscles, yet you have command too, upright stillness, eyes accurately judging. Then the curves cease, changing to downright hammer strokes, which jar; and you draw up with a jolt; sitting back a little, sparkling, tingling, glazed with ice over pounding arteries, gasping: "Ah! ho! Hah!" the steam going up from the horses as they jostle together at the cross-roads, where the signpost is, and the woman in the apron stands and stares at the doorway. The man raises himself from the cabbages to stare too.

So Jacob galloped over the fields of Essex, flopped in the mud, lost the hunt, and rode by himself eating sandwiches, looking over the hedges, noticing the colours as if new scraped, cursing his luck.

He had tea at the Inn; and there they all were, slapping, stamping, saying, "After you," clipped, curt, jocose, red as the wattles of

turkeys, using free speech until Mrs. Horsefield and her friend Miss Dudding appeared at the doorway with their skirts hitched up, and hair looping down. Then Tom Dudding rapped at the window with his whip. A motor car throbbed in the courtyard. Gentlemen, feeling for matches, moved out, and Jacob went into the bar with Brandy Jones to smoke with the rustics. There was old Jevons with one eye gone, and his clothes the colour of mud, his bag over his back, and his brains laid feet down in earth among the violet roots and the nettle roots; Mary Sanders with her box of wood; and Tom sent for beer, the half-witted son of the sexton—all this within thirty miles of London.

Mrs. Papworth, of Endell Street, Covent Garden, did for Mr. Bonamy in New Square, Lincoln's Inn, and as she washed up the dinner things in the scullery she heard the young gentlemen talking in the room next door. Mr. Sanders was there again; Flanders she meant; and where an inquisitive old woman gets a name wrong, what chance is there that she will faithfully report an argument? As she held the plates under water and then dealt them on the pile beneath the hissing gas, she listened: heard Sanders speaking in a loud rather overbearing tone of voice: "good" he said, and "absolute" and "justice" and "punishment," and "the will of the majority." Then her gentleman piped up; she backed him for argument against Sanders. Yet Sanders was a fine young fellow (here all the scraps went swirling round the sink, scoured after by her purple, almost nailless hands). "Women"—she thought, and wondered what Sanders and her gentleman did in *that* line, one eyelid sinking perceptibly as she mused, for she was the mother of nine—three stillborn and one deaf and dumb from birth. Putting the plates in the rack she heard once more Sanders at it again ("He don't give Bonamy a chance," she thought). "Objective something," said Bonamy; and "common ground" and something else—all very long words, she noted. "Book learning does it," she thought to herself, and, as she thrust her arms into her jacket, heard something —might be the little table by the fire—fall; and then stamp, stamp, stamp—as if they were having at each other—round the room, making the plates dance.

"To-morrow's breakfast, sir," she said, opening the door; and there were Sanders and Bonamy like two bulls of Bashan driving each other up and down, making such a racket, and all them chairs in the way. They never noticed her. She felt motherly towards them. "Your breakfast, sir," she said, as they came near. And Bonamy, all his hair touzled and his tie flying, broke off, and pushed Sanders into the arm-

chair, and said Mr. Sanders had smashed the coffee-pot and he was teaching Mr. Sanders—
Sure enough, the coffee-pot lay broken on the hearthrug.

"Any day this week except Thursday," wrote Miss Perry, and this was not the first invitation by any means. Were all Miss Perry's weeks blank with the exception of Thursday, and was her only desire to see her old friend's son? Time is issued to spinster ladies of wealth in long white ribbons. These they wind round and round, round and round, assisted by five female servants, a butler, a fine Mexican parrot, regular meals, Mudie's library, and friends dropping in. A little hurt she was already that Jacob had not called.

"Your mother," she said, "is one of my oldest friends."

Miss Rosseter, who was sitting by the fire, holding the *Spectator* between her cheek and the blaze, refused to have a fire screen, but finally accepted one. The weather was then discussed, for in deference to Parkes, who was opening little tables, graver matters were postponed. Miss Rosseter drew Jacob's attention to the beauty of the cabinet.

"So wonderfully clever in picking things up," she said. Miss Perry had found it in Yorkshire. The North of England was discussed. When Jacob spoke they both listened. Miss Perry was bethinking her of something suitable and manly to say when the door opened and Mr. Benson was announced. Now there were four people sitting in that room. Miss Perry aged 66; Miss Rosseter 42; Mr. Benson 38; and Jacob 25.

"My old friend looks as well as ever," said Mr. Benson, tapping the bars of the parrot's cage; Miss Rosseter simultaneously praised the tea; Jacob handed the wrong plates; and Miss Perry signified her desire to approach more closely. "Your brothers," she began vaguely.

"Archer and John," Jacob supplied her. Then to her pleasure she recovered Rebecca's name; and how one day "when you were all little boys, playing in the drawing-room——"

"But Miss Perry has the kettle-holder," said Miss Rosseter, and indeed Miss Perry was clasping it to her breast. (Had she, then, loved Jacob's father?)

"So clever"—"not so good as usual"—"I thought it most unfair," said Mr. Benson and Miss Rosseter, discussing the Saturday *Westminster*. Did they not compete regularly for prizes? Had not Mr. Benson three times won a guinea, and Miss Rosseter once ten and sixpence? Of course Everard Benson had a weak heart, but still, to win prizes, remember parrots, toady Miss Perry, despise Miss Rosseter, give tea-parties in his rooms (which were in the style of Whistler, with

pretty books on tables), all this, so Jacob felt without knowing him, made him a contemptible ass. As for Miss Rosseter, she had nursed cancer, and now painted water-colours.

"Running away so soon?" said Miss Perry vaguely. "At home every afternoon, if you've nothing better to do—except Thursdays."

"I've never known you desert your old ladies once," Miss Rosseter was saying, and Mr. Benson was stooping over the parrot's cage, and Miss Perry was moving towards the bell. . . .

The fire burnt clear between two pillars of greenish marble, and on the mantelpiece there was a green clock guarded by Britannia leaning on her spear. As for pictures—a maiden in a large hat offered roses over the garden gate to a gentleman in eighteenth-century costume. A mastiff lay extended against a battered door. The lower panes of the windows were of ground glass, and the curtains, accurately looped, were of plush and green too.

Laurette and Jacob sat with their toes in the fender side by side, two large chairs covered in green plush. Laurette's skirts were short, her legs long, thin, and transparently covered. Her fingers stroked her ankles.

"It's not exactly that I don't understand them," she was saying thoughtfully. "I must go and try again."

"What time will you be there?" said Jacob.

She shrugged her shoulders.

"To-morrow?"

No, not to-morrow.

"This weather makes me long for the country," she said, looking over her shoulder at the back view of tall houses through the window.

"I wish you'd been with me on Saturday," said Jacob.

"I used to ride," she said. She got up gracefully, calmly. Jacob got up. She smiled at him. As she shut the door he put so many shillings on the mantelpiece.

Altogether a most reasonable conversation; a most respectable room; an intelligent girl. Only Madame herself seeing Jacob out had about her that leer, that lewdness, that quake of the surface (visible in the eyes chiefly), which threatens to spill the whole bag of ordure, with difficulty held together, over the pavement. In short, something was wrong.

Not so very long ago the workmen had gilt the final "y" in Lord Macaulay's name, and the names stretched in unbroken file round the dome of the British Museum. At a considerable depth beneath, many hundreds of the living sat at the spokes of a cart-wheel copying from

printed books into manuscript books; now and then rising to consult the catalogue; regaining their places stealthily, while from time to time a silent man replenished their compartments.

There was a little catastrophe. Miss Marchmont's pile overbalanced and fell into Jacob's compartment. Such things happened to Miss Marchmont. What was she seeking through millions of pages, in her old plush dress, and her wig of claret-coloured hair, with her gems and her chilblains? Sometimes one thing, sometimes another, to confirm her philosophy that colour is sound—or, perhaps, it has something to do with music. She could never quite say, though it was not for lack of trying. And she could not ask you back to her room, for it was "not very clean, I'm afraid," so she must catch you in the passage, or take a chair in Hyde Park to explain her philosophy. The rhythm of the soul depends on it—("how rude the little boys are!" she would say) and Mr. Asquith's Irish policy, and Shakespeare comes in, "and Queen Alexandra most graciously once acknowledged a copy of my pamphlet," she would say, waving the little boys magnificently away. But she needs funds to publish her book, for "publishers are capitalists—publishers are cowards." And so, digging her elbow into her pile of books it fell over.

Jacob remained quite unmoved.

But Fraser, the atheist, on the other side, detesting plush, more than once accosted her leaflets, shifted irritably. He abhorred vagueness—the Christian religion, for example, and old Dean Parker's pronouncements. Dean Parker wrote books and Frazer utterly destroyed them by force of logic and left his children unbaptized—his wife did it secretly in the washing basin—but Frazer ignored her, and went on supporting blasphemers, distributing leaflets, getting up his facts in the British Museum, always in the same check suit and fiery tie, but pale, spotted, irritable. Indeed, what a work—to destroy religion!

Jacob transcribed a whole passage from Marlowe.

Miss Julia Hedge, the feminist, waited for her books. They did not come. She wetted her pen. She looked about her. Her eye was caught by the final letters in Lord Macaulay's name. And she read them all round the dome—the names of great men which remind us—— "Oh damn," said Julia Hedge, "why didn't they leave room for an Eliot or a Brontë?"

Unfortunate Julia! wetting her pen in bitterness, and leaving her shoe laces untied. When her books came she applied herself to her gigantic labours, but perceived through one of the nerves of her exasperated sensibility how composedly, unconcernedly, and with every consideration the male readers applied themselves to theirs. That young man for example. What had he got to do except copy out

poetry? And she must study statistics. There are more women than men. Yes; but if you let women work as men work, they'll die off much quicker. They'll become extinct. That was her argument. Death and gall and bitter dust were on her pen-tip; and as the afternoon wore on, red had worked into her cheek-bones and a light was in her eyes.

But what brought Jacob Flanders to read Marlowe in the British Museum?

Youth, youth—something savage—something pedantic. For example there is Mr. Masefield, there is Mr. Bennett. Stuff them into the flame of Marlowe and burn them to cinders. Let not a shred remain. Don't palter with the second rate. Detest your own age. Build a better one. And to set that on foot read incredibly dull essays upon Marlowe to your friends. For which purpose one must collate editions in the British Museum. One must do the thing oneself. Useless to trust to the Victorians, who disembowel, or to the living, who are mere publicists. The flesh and blood of the future depends entirely upon six young men. And as Jacob was one of them, no doubt he looked a little regal and pompous as he turned his page, and Julia Hedge disliked him naturally enough.

But then a pudding-faced man pushed a note towards Jacob, and Jacob, leaning back in his chair, began an uneasy murmured conversation, and they went off together (Julia Hedge watched them), and laughed aloud (she thought) directly they were in the hall.

Nobody laughed in the reading-room. There were shiftings, murmurings, apologetic sneezes, and sudden unashamed devastating coughs. The lesson hour was almost over. Ushers were collecting exercises. Lazy children wanted to stretch. Good ones scribbled assiduously —ah, another day over and so little done! And now and then was to be heard from the whole collection of human beings a heavy sigh, after which the humiliating old man would cough shamelessly, and Miss Marchmont hinnied like a horse.

Jacob came back only in time to return his books.

The books were now replaced. A few letters of the alphabet were sprinkled round the dome. Closely stood together in a ring round the dome were Plato, Aristotle, Sophocles, and Shakespeare; the literatures of Rome, Greece, China, India, Persia. One leaf of poetry was pressed flat against another leaf, one burnished letter laid smooth against another in a density of meaning, a conglomeration of loveliness.

"One does want one's tea," said Miss Marchmont, reclaiming her shabby umbrella.

Miss Marchmont wanted her tea, but could never resist a last look at the Elgin Marbles. She looked at them sideways. waving her hand

and muttering a word or two of salutation which made Jacob and the other man turn round. She smiled at them amiably. It all came into her philosophy—that colour is sound, or perhaps it has something to do with music. And having done her service, she hobbled off to tea. It was closing time. The public collected in the hall to receive their umbrellas.

For the most part the students wait their turn very patiently. To stand and wait while some one examines white discs is soothing. The umbrella will certainly be found. But the fact leads you on all day through Macaulay, Hobbes, Gibbon; through octavos, quartos, folios; sinks deeper and deeper through ivory pages and morocco bindings into this density of thought, this conglomeration of knowledge.

Jacob's walking-stick was like all the others; they had muddled the pigeon-holes perhaps.

There is in the British Museum an enormous mind. Consider that Plato is there cheek by jowl with Aristotle; and Shakespeare with Marlowe. This great mind is hoarded beyond the power of any single mind to possess it. Nevertheless (as they take so long finding one's walking-stick) one can't help thinking how one might come with a notebook, sit at a desk, and read it all through. A learned man is the most venerable of all—a man like Huxtable of Trinity, who writes all his letters in Greek, they say, and could have kept his end up with Bentley. And then there is science, pictures, architecture,—an enormous mind.

They pushed the walking-stick across the counter. Jacob stood beneath the porch of the British Museum. It was raining. Great Russell Street was glazed and shining—here yellow, here, outside the chemist's, red and pale blue. People scuttled quickly close to the wall; carriages rattled rather helter-skelter down the streets. Well, but a little rain hurts nobody. Jacob walked off much as if he had been in the country; and late that night there he was sitting at his table with his pipe and his book.

The rain poured down. The British Museum stood in one solid immense mound, very pale, very sleek in the rain, not a quarter of a mile from him. The vast mind was sheeted with stone; and each compartment in the depths of it was safe and dry. The night-watchmen, flashing their lanterns over the backs of Plato and Shakespeare, saw that on the twenty-second of February neither flame, rat, nor burglar was going to violate these treasures—poor, highly respectable men, with wives and families at Kentish Town, do their best for twenty years to protect Plato and Shakespeare, and then are buried at Highgate.

Stone lies solid over the British Museum, as bone lies cool over the visions and heat of the brain. Only here the brain is Plato's brain

and Shakespeare's; the brain has made pots and statues, great bulls and little jewels, and crossed the river of death this way and that incessantly, seeking some landing, now wrapping the body well for its long sleep; now laying a penny piece on the eyes; now turning the toes scrupulously to the East. Meanwhile, Plato continues his dialogue; in spite of the rain; in spite of the cab whistles; in spite of the woman in the mews behind Great Ormond Street who has come home drunk and cries all night long, "Let me in! Let me in!"

In the street below Jacob's room voices were raised.

But he read on. For after all Plato continues imperturbably. And Hamlet utters his soliloquy. And there the Elgin Marbles lie, all night long old Jones's lantern sometimes recalling Ulysses, or a horse's head; or sometimes a flash of gold, or a mummy's sunk yellow cheek. Plato and Shakespeare continue; and Jacob, who was reading the *Phaedrus*, heard people vociferating round the lamp-post, and the woman battering at the door and crying, "Let me in!" as if a coal had dropped from the fire, or a fly, falling from the ceiling, had lain on its back, too weak to turn over.

The *Phaedrus* is very difficult. And so, when at length one reads straight ahead, falling into step, marching on, becoming (so it seems) momentarily part of this rolling, imperturbable energy, which has driven darkness before it since Plato walked the Acropolis, it is impossible to see to the fire.

The dialogue draws to its close. Plato's argument is done. Plato's argument is stowed away in Jacob's mind, and for five minutes Jacob's mind continues alone, onwards, into the darkness. Then, getting up, he parted the curtains, and saw, with astonishing clearness, how the Springetts opposite had gone to bed; how it rained; how the Jews and the foreign woman, at the end of the street, stood by the pillar-box, arguing.

Every time the door opened and fresh people came in, those already in the room shifted slightly; those who were standing looked over their shoulders; those who were sitting stopped in the middle of sentences. What with the light, the wine, the strumming of a guitar, something exciting happened each time the door opened. Who was coming in?

"That's Gibson."

"The painter?"

"But go on with what you were saying."

They were saying something that was far, far too intimate to be said outright. But the noise of the voices served like a clapper in little Mrs. Withers's mind, scaring into the air flocks of small birds, and then they'd settle, and then she'd feel afraid, put one hand to her hair,

bind both round her knees, and look up at Oliver Skelton nervously, and say:

"Promise, *promise,* you'll tell no one." . . . so considerate he was, so tender. It was her husband's character that she discussed. He was cold, she said.

Down upon them came the splendid Magdalen, brown, warm, voluminous, scarcely brushing the grass with her sandalled feet. Her hair flew; pins seemed scarcely to attach the flying silks. An actress of course, a line of light perpetually beneath her. It was only "My dear" that she said, but her voice went jodelling between Alpine passes. And down she tumbled on the floor, and sang, since there was nothing to be said, round ah's and oh's. Mangin, the poet, coming up to her, stood looking down at her, drawing at his pipe. The dancing began.

Grey-haired Mrs. Keymer asked Dick Graves to tell her who Mangin was, and said that she had seen too much of this sort of thing in Paris (Magdalen had got upon his knees; now his pipe was in her mouth) to be shocked. "Who is that?" she said, staying her glasses when they came to Jacob, for indeed he looked quiet, not indifferent, but like some one on a beach, watching.

"Oh, my dear, let me lean on you," gasped Helen Askew, hopping on one foot, for the silver cord round her ankle had worked loose. Mrs. Keymer turned and looked at the picture on the wall.

"Look at Jacob," said Helen (they were binding his eyes for some game).

And Dick Graves, being a little drunk, very faithful, and very simple-minded, told her that he thought Jacob the greatest man he had ever known. And down they sat cross-legged upon cushions and talked about Jacob, and Helen's voice trembled, for they both seemed heroes to her, and the friendship between them so much more beautiful than women's friendships. Anthony Pollett now asked her to dance, and as she danced she looked at them, over her shoulder, standing at the table, drinking together.

The magnificent world—the live, sane, vigorous world. . . . These words refer to the stretch of wood pavement between Hammersmith and Holborn in January between two and three in the morning. That was the ground beneath Jacob's feet. It was healthy and magnificent because one room, above a mews, somewhere near the river, contained fifty excited, talkative, friendly people. And then to stride over the pavement (there was scarcely a cab or policeman in sight) is of itself exhilarating. The long loop of Piccadilly, diamond-stitched, shows to best advantage when it is empty. A young man has nothing to fear. On the contrary, though he may not have said anything brilliant, he

feels pretty confident he can hold his own. He was pleased to have met Mangin; he admired the young woman on the floor; he liked them all; he liked that sort of thing. In short, all the drums and trumpets were sounding. The street scavengers were the only people about at the moment. It is scarcely necessary to say how well-disposed Jacob felt towards them; how it pleased him to let himself in with his latchkey at his own door; how he seemed to bring back with him into the empty room ten or eleven people whom he had not known when he set out; how he looked about for something to read, and found it, and never read it, and fell asleep.

Indeed, drums and trumpets is no phrase. Indeed, Piccadilly and Holborn, and the empty sitting-room and the sitting-room with fifty people in it are liable at any moment to blow music into the air. Women perhaps are more excitable than men. It is seldom that any one says anything about it, and to see the hordes crossing Waterloo Bridge to catch the non-stop to Surbiton one might think that reason impelled them. No, no. It is the drums and trumpets. Only, should you turn aside into one of those little bays on Waterloo Bridge to think the matter over, it will probably seem to you all a muddle—all a mystery.

They cross the bridge incessantly. Sometimes in the midst of carts and omnibuses a lorry will appear with great forest trees chained to it. Then, perhaps, a mason's van with newly lettered tombstones recording how some one loved some one who is buried at Putney. Then the motor car in front jerks forward, and the tombstones pass too quick for you to read more. All the time the stream of people never ceases passing from the Surrey side to the Strand; from the Strand to the Surrey side. It seems as if the poor had gone raiding the town and now trapesed back to their own quarters, like beetles scurrying to their holes, for that old woman fairly hobbles towards Waterloo, grasping a shiny bag, as if she had been out into the light and now made off with some scraped chicken bones to her hovel underground. On the other hand, though the wind is rough and blowing in their faces, those girls there, striding hand in hand, shouting out a song, seem to feel neither cold nor shame. They are hatless. They triumph.

The wind has blown up the waves. The river races beneath us, and the men standing on the barges have to lean all their weight on the tiller. A black tarpaulin is tied down over a swelling load of gold. Avalanches of coal glitter blackly. As usual, painters are slung on planks across the great riverside hotels, and the hotel windows have already points of light in them. On the other side the city is white as if with age; St. Paul's swells white above the fretted, pointed, or

oblong buildings beside it. The cross alone shines rosy-gilt. But what century have we reached? Has this procession from the Surrey side to the Strand gone on for ever? That old man has been crossing the Bridge these six hundred years, with the rabble of little boys at his heels, for he is drunk, or blind with misery, and tied round with old clouts of clothing such as pilgrims might have worn. He shuffles on. No one stands still. It seems as if we marched to the sound of music; perhaps the wind and the river; perhaps these same drums and trumpets—the ecstasy and hubbub of the soul. Why, even the unhappy laugh, and the policeman, far from judging the drunk man, surveys him humorously, and the little boys scamper back again, and the clerk from Somerset House has nothing but tolerance for him, and the man who is reading half a page of *Lothair* at the bookstall muses charitably, with his eyes off the print, and the girl hesitates at the crossing and turns on him the bright yet vague glance of the young.

Bright yet vague. She is perhaps twenty-two. She is shabby. She crosses the road and looks at the daffodils and the red tulips in the florist's window. She hesitates, and makes off in the direction of Temple Bar. She walks fast, and yet anything distracts her. Now she seems to see, and now to notice nothing.

§ 10

Through the disused graveyard in the parish of St. Pancras, Fanny Elmer strayed between the white tombs which lean against the wall, crossing the grass to read a name, hurrying on when the grave-keeper approached, hurrying into the street, pausing now by a window with blue china, now quickly making up for lost time, abruptly entering a baker's shop, buying rolls, adding cakes, going on again so that any one wishing to follow must fairly trot. She was not drably shabby, though. She wore silk stockings, and silver-buckled shoes, only the red feather in her hat drooped, and the clasp of her bag was weak, for out fell a copy of Madame Tussaud's programme as she walked. She had the ankles of a stag. Her face was hidden. Of course, in this dusk, rapid movements, quick glances, and soaring hopes come naturally enough. She passed right beneath Jacob's window.

The house was flat, dark, and silent. Jacob was at home engaged upon a chess problem, the board being on a stool between his knees. One hand was fingering the hair at the back of his head. He slowly brought it forward and raised the white queen from her square; then put her down again on the same spot. He filled his pipe; ruminated;

moved two pawns; advanced the white knight; then ruminated with
one finger upon the bishop. Now Fanny Elmer passed beneath the
window.

She was on her way to sit to Nick Bramham the painter.

She sat in a flowered Spanish shawl, holding in her hand a yellow
novel.

"A little lower, a little looser, so—better, that's right," Bramham
mumbled, who was drawing her, and smoking at the same time, and
was naturally speechless. His head might have been the work of a
sculptor, who had squared the forehead, stretched the mouth, and left
marks of his thumbs and streaks from his fingers in the clay. But the
eyes had never been shut. They were rather prominent, and rather
bloodshot, as if from staring and staring, and when he spoke they
looked for a second disturbed, but went on staring. An unshaded elec-
tric light hung above her head.

As for the beauty of women, it is like the light on the sea, never con-
stant to a single wave. They all have it; they all lose it. Now she is
dull and thick as bacon; now transparent as a hanging glass. The
fixed faces are the dull ones. Here comes Lady Venice displayed like a
monument for admiration, but carved in alabaster, to be set on the
mantelpiece and never dusted. A dapper brunette complete from head
to foot serves only as an illustration to lie upon the drawing-room table.
The women in the streets have the faces of playing cards; the outlines
accurately filled in with pink or yellow, and the line drawn tightly
round them. Then, at a top-floor window, leaning out, looking down,
you see beauty itself; or in the corner of an omnibus; or squatted in a
ditch—beauty glowing, suddenly expressive, withdrawn the moment
after. No one can count on it or seize it or have it wrapped in paper.
Nothing is to be won from the shops, and Heaven knows it would be
better to sit at home than haunt the plate-glass windows in the hope of
lifting the shining green, the glowing ruby, out of them alive. Sea glass
in a saucer loses its lustre no sooner than silks do. Thus if you talk of a
beautiful woman you mean only something flying fast which for a
second uses the eyes, lips, or cheeks of Fanny Elmer, for example, to
glow through.

She was not beautiful, as she sat stiffly; her underlip too prominent;
her nose too large; her eyes too near together. She was a thin girl, with
brilliant cheeks and dark hair, sulky just now, or stiff with sitting.
When Bramham snapped his stick of charcoal she started. Bramham
was out of temper. He squatted before the gas fire warming his hands.
Meanwhile she looked at his drawing. He grunted. Fanny threw on a
dressing-gown and boiled a kettle.

"By God, it's bad," said Bramham.

Fanny dropped on to the floor, clasped her hands round her knees, and looked at him, her beautiful eyes—yes, beauty, flying through the room, shone there for a second. Fanny's eyes seemed to question, to commiserate, to be, for a second, love itself. But she exaggerated. Bramham noticed nothing. And when the kettle boiled, up she scrambled, more like a colt or a puppy than a loving woman.

Now Jacob walked over to the window and stood with his hands in his pockets. Mr. Springett opposite came out, looked at his shop window, and went in again. The children drifted past, eyeing the pink sticks of sweetstuff. Pickford's van swung down the street. A small boy twirled from a rope. Jacob turned away. Two minutes later he opened the front door, and walked off in the direction of Holborn.

Fanny Elmer took down her cloak from the hook. Nick Bramham unpinned his drawing and rolled it under his arm. They turned out the lights and set off down the street, holding on their way through all the people, motor cars, omnibuses, carts, until they reached Leicester Square, five minutes before Jacob reached it, for his way was slightly longer, and he had been stopped by a block in Holborn waiting to see the King drive by, so that Nick and Fanny were already leaning over the barrier in the promenade at the Empire when Jacob pushed through the swing doors and took his place beside them.

"Hullo, never noticed you," said Nick five minutes later.

"Bloody rot," said Jacob.

"Miss Elmer," said Nick.

Jacob took his pipe out of his mouth very awkwardly.

Very awkward he was. And when they sat upon a plush sofa and let the smoke go up between them and the stage, and heard far off the high-pitched voices and the jolly orchestra breaking in opportunely he was still awkward, only Fanny thought: "What a beautiful voice!" She thought how little he said yet how firm it was. She thought how young men are dignified and aloof, and how unconscious they are, and how quietly one might sit beside Jacob and look at him. And how childlike he would be, come in tired of an evening, she thought, and how majestic; a little overbearing perhaps; "But I wouldn't give way," she thought. He got up and leant over the barrier. The smoke hung about him.

And for ever the beauty of young men seems to be set in smoke, however lustily they chase footballs, or drive cricket balls, dance, run, or stride along roads. Possibly they are soon to lose it. Possibly they look into the eyes of far-away heroes, and take their station among us

half contemptuously, she thought (vibrating like a fiddle-string, to be played on and snapped). Anyhow, they love silence, and speak beautifully, each word falling like a disc new cut, not a hubble-bubble of small smooth coins such as girls use; and they move decidedly, as if they knew how long to stay and when to go—oh, but Mr. Flanders was only gone to get a programme.

"The dancers come right at the end," he said, coming back to them.

And isn't it pleasant, Fanny went on thinking, how young men bring out lots of silver coins from their trouser pockets, and look at them, instead of having just so many in a purse?

Then there she was herself, whirling across the stage in white flounces, and the music was the dance and fling of her own soul, and the whole machinery, rock and gear of the world was spun smoothly into those swift eddies and falls, she felt, as she stood rigid leaning over the barrier two feet from Jacob Flanders.

Her screwed-up black glove dropped to the floor. When Jacob gave it her, she started angrily. For never was there a more irrational passion. And Jacob was afraid of her for a moment—so violent, so dangerous is it when young women stand rigid; grasp the barrier; fall in love.

It was the middle of February. The roofs of Hampstead Garden Suburb lay in a tremulous haze. It was too hot to walk. A dog barked, barked, barked down in the hollow. The liquid shadows went over the plain.

The body after long illness is languid, passive, receptive of sweetness, but too weak to contain it. The tears well and fall as the dog barks in the hollow, the children skim after hoops, the country darkens and brightens. Beyond a veil it seems. Ah, but draw the veil thicker lest I faint with sweetness, Fanny Elmer sighed, as she sat on a bench in Judges Walk looking at Hampstead Garden Suburb. But the dog went on barking. The motor cars hooted on the road. She heard a faraway rush and humming. Agitation was at her heart. Up she got and walked. The grass was freshly green; the sun hot. All round the pond children were stooping to launch little boats; or were drawn back screaming by their nurses.

At mid-day young women walk out into the air. All the men are busy in the town. They stand by the edge of the blue pond. The fresh wind scatters the children's voices all about. *My* children, thought Fanny Elmer. The women stand round the pond, beating off great prancing shaggy dogs. Gently the baby is rocked in the perambulator. The eyes of all the nurses, mothers, and wandering women are a little glazed, absorbed. They gently nod instead of answering when the little boys tug at their skirts, begging them to move on.

And Fanny moved, hearing some cry—a workman's whistle perhaps —high in mid air. Now, among the trees, it was the thrush trilling out into the warm air a flutter of jubilation, but fear seemed to spur him, Fanny thought; as if he too were anxious with such joy at his heart— as if he were watched as he sang, and pressed by tumult to sing. There! Restless, he flew to the next tree. She heard his song more faintly. Beyond it was the humming of the wheels and the wind rushing.

She spent tenpence on lunch.

"Dear, miss, she's left her umbrella," grumbled the mottled woman in the glass box near the door at the Express Dairy Company's shop.

"Perhaps I'll catch her," answered Milly Edwards, the waitress with the pale plaits of hair; and she dashed through the door.

"No good," she said, coming back a moment later with Fanny's cheap umbrella. She put her hand to her plaits.

"Oh, that door!" grumbled the cashier.

Her hands were cased in black mittens, and the finger-tips that drew in the paper slips were swollen as sausages.

"Pie and greens for one. Large coffee and crumpets. Eggs on toast. Two fruit cakes."

Thus the sharp voices of the waitresses snapped. The lunchers heard their orders repeated with approval; saw the next table served with anticipation. Their own eggs on toast were at last delivered. Their eyes strayed no more.

Damp cubes of pastry fell into mouths opened like triangular bags.

Nelly Jenkinson, the typist, crumbled her cake indifferently enough. Every time the door opened she looked up. What did she expect to see?

The coal merchant read the *Telegraph* without stopping, missed the saucer, and, feeling abstractedly, put the cup down on the table-cloth.

"Did you ever hear the like of that for impertinence?" Mrs. Parsons wound up, brushing the crumbs from her furs.

"Hot milk and scone for one. Pot of tea. Roll and butter," cried the waitresses.

The door opened and shut.

Such is the life of the elderly.

It is curious, lying in a boat, to watch the waves. Here are three coming regularly one after another, all much of a size. Then, hurrying after them comes a fourth, very large and menacing; it lifts the boat; on it goes; somehow merges without accomplishing anything; flattens itself out with the rest.

What can be more violent than the fling of boughs in a gale, the tree

yielding itself all up the trunk, to the very tip of the branch, streaming and shuddering the way the wind blows, yet never flying in dishevelment away?

The corn squirms and abases itself as if preparing to tug itself free from the roots, and yet is tied down.

Why, from the very windows, even in the dusk, you see a swelling run through the street, an aspiration, as with arms outstretched, eyes desiring, mouths agape. And then we peaceably subside. For if the exaltation lasted we should be blown like foam into the air. The stars would shine through us. We should go down the gale in salt drops—as sometimes happens. For the impetuous spirits will have none of this cradling. Never any swaying or aimlessly lolling for them. Never any making believe, or lying cosily, or genially supposing that one is much like another, fire warm, wine pleasant, extravagance a sin.

"People are so nice, once you know them."

"I couldn't think ill of her. One must remember——" But Nick perhaps, or Fanny Elmer, believing implicitly in the truth of the moment, fling off, sting the cheek, are gone like sharp hail.

"Oh," said Fanny, bursting into the studio three-quarters of an hour late because she had been hanging about the neighbourhood of the Foundling Hospital merely for the chance of seeing Jacob walk down the street, take out his latch-key, and open the door, "I'm afraid I'm late"; upon which Nick said nothing and Fanny grew defiant.

"I'll never come again!" she cried at length.

"Don't, then," Nick replied, and off she ran without so much as good-night.

How exquisite it was—that dress in Evelina's shop off Shaftesbury Avenue! It was four o'clock on a fine day early in April, and was Fanny the one to spend four o'clock on a fine day indoors? Other girls in that very street sat over ledgers, or drew long threads wearily between silk and gauze; or, festooned with ribbons in Swan and Edgars, rapidly added up pence and farthings on the back of the bill and twisted the yard and three-quarters in tissue paper and asked "Your pleasure?" of the next comer.

In Evelina's shop off Shaftesbury Avenue the parts of a woman were shown separate. In the left hand was her skirt. Twining round a pole in the middle was a feather boa. Ranged like the heads of malefactors on Temple Bar were hats—emerald and white, lightly wreathed or drooping beneath deep-dyed feathers. And on the carpet were her feet —pointed gold, or patent leather slashed with scarlet.

Feasted upon by the eyes of women, the clothes by four o'clock were flyblown like sugar cakes in a baker's window. Fanny eyed them too.

But coming along Gerrard Street was a tall man in a shabby coat. A shadow fell across Evelina's window—Jacob's shadow, though it was not Jacob. And Fanny turned and walked along Gerrard Street and wished that she had read books. Nick never read books, never talked of Ireland, or the House of Lords; and as for his finger-nails! She would learn Latin and read Virgil. She had been a great reader. She had read Scott; she had read Dumas. At the Slade no one read. But no one knew Fanny at the Slade, or guessed how empty it seemed to her; the passion for ear-rings, for dances, for Tonks and Steer—when it was only the French who could paint, Jacob said. For the moderns were futile; painting the least respectable of the arts; and why read anything but Marlowe and Shakespeare, Jacob said, and Fielding if you must read novels?

"Fielding," said Fanny, when the man in Charing Cross Road asked her what book she wanted.

She bought *Tom Jones*.

At ten o'clock in the morning, in a room which she shared with a school teacher, Fanny Elmer read *Tom Jones*—that mystic book. For this dull stuff (Fanny thought) about people with odd names is what Jacob likes. Good people like it. Dowdy women who don't mind how they cross their legs read *Tom Jones*—a mystic book; for there is something, Fanny thought, about books which if I had been educated I could have liked—much better than ear-rings and flowers, she sighed, thinking of the corridors at the Slade and the fancy-dress dance next week. She had nothing to wear.

They are real, thought Fanny Elmer, setting her feet on the mantelpiece. Some people are. Nick perhaps, only he was so stupid. And women never—except Miss Sargent, but she went off at lunch-time and gave herself airs. There they sat quietly of a night, reading, she thought. Not going to music-halls; not looking in at shop windows; not wearing each other's clothes, like Robertson who had worn her shawl, and she had worn his waistcoat, which Jacob could only do very awkwardly; for he liked *Tom Jones*.

There it lay on her lap, in double columns, price three and sixpence; the mystic book in which Henry Fielding ever so many years ago rebuked Fanny Elmer for feasting on scarlet, in perfect prose, Jacob said. For he never read modern novels. He liked *Tom Jones*.

"I do like *Tom Jones*," said Fanny at five-thirty that same day early in April when Jacob took out his pipe in the arm-chair opposite.

Alas, women lie! But not Clara Durrant. A flawless mind; a candid

nature; a virgin chained to a rock (somewhere off Lowndes Square) eternally pouring out tea for old men in white waistcoats, blue-eyed, looking you straight in the face, playing Bach. Of all women, Jacob honoured her most. But to sit at a table with bread and butter, with dowagers in velvet, and never say more to Clara Durrant than Benson said to the parrot when old Miss Perry poured out tea, was an insufferable outrage upon the liberties and decencies of human nature—or words to that effect. For Jacob said nothing. Only he glared at the fire. Fanny laid down *Tom Jones.*

She stitched or knitted.

"What's that?" asked Jacob.

"For the dance at the Slade."

And she fetched her head-dress; her trousers; her shoes with red tassels. What should she wear?

"I shall be in Paris," said Jacob.

And what is the point of fancy-dress dances? thought Fanny. You meet the same people; you wear the same clothes; Mangin gets drunk; Florinda sits on his knee. She flirts outrageously—with Nick Bramham just now.

"In Paris?" said Fanny.

"On my way to Greece," he replied.

For, he said, there is nothing so detestable as London in May.

He would forget her.

A sparrow flew past the window trailing a straw—a straw from a stack stood by a barn in a farmyard. The old brown spaniel snuffs at the base for a rat. Already the upper branches of the elm trees are blotted with nests. The chestnuts have flirted their fans. And the butterflies are flaunting across the rides in the Forest. Perhaps the Purple Emperor is feasting, as Morris says, upon a mass of putrid carrion at the base of an oak tree.

Fanny thought it all came from *Tom Jones.* He could go alone with a book in his pocket and watch the badgers. He would take a train at eight-thirty and walk all night. He saw fireflies, and brought back glow-worms in pill-boxes. He would hunt with the New Forest Staghounds. It all came from *Tom Jones;* and he would go to Greece with a book in his pocket and forget her.

She fetched her hand-glass. There was her face. And suppose one wreathed Jacob in a turban? There was his face. She lit the lamp. But as the daylight came through the window only half was lit up by the lamp. And though he looked terrible and magnificent and would chuck the Forest, he said, and come to the Slade, and be a Turkish knight or a Roman emperor (and he let her blacken his lips and clenched his teeth and scowled in the glass), still—there lay *Tom Jones.*

§ 11

"Archer," said Mrs. Flanders with that tenderness which mothers so often display towards their eldest sons, "will be at Gibraltar to-morrow."

The post for which she was waiting (strolling up Dods Hill while the random church bells swung a hymn tune about her head, the clock striking four straight through the circling notes; the grass purpling under a storm-cloud; and the two dozen houses of the village cowering, infinitely humble, in company under a leaf of shadow), the post, with all its variety of messages, envelopes addressed in bold hands, in slanting hands, stamped now with English stamps, again with Colonial stamps, or sometimes hastily dabbed with a yellow bar, the post was about to scatter a myriad messages over the world. Whether we gain or not by this habit of profuse communication it is not for us to say. But that letter-writing is practiced mendaciously nowadays, particularly by young men travelling in foreign parts, seems likely enough.

For example, take this scene.

Here was Jacob Flanders gone abroad and staying to break his journey in Paris. (Old Miss Birkbeck, his mother's cousin, had died last June and left him a hundred pounds.)

"You needn't repeat the whole damned thing over again, Crutten-don," said Mallinson, the little bald painter who was sitting at a marble table, splashed with coffee and ringed with wine, talking very fast, and undoubtedly more than a little drunk.

"Well, Flanders, finished writing to your lady?" said Cruttendon, as Jacob came and took his seat beside them, holding in his hand an envelope addressed to Mrs. Flanders, near Scarborough, England.

"Do you uphold Velasquez?" said Cruttendon.

"By God, he does," said Mallinson.

"He always gets like this," said Cruttendon irritably.

Jacob looked at Mallinson with excessive composure.

"I'll tell you the three greatest things that were ever written in the whole of literature," Cruttendon burst out. " 'Hang there like fruit my soul,' " he began. . . .

"Don't listen to a man who don't like Valesquez," said Mallinson.

"Adolphe, don't give Mr. Mallinson any more wine," said Crut-tendon.

"Fair play, fair play," said Jacob judicially. "Let a man get drunk

if he likes. That's Shakespeare, Cruttendon. I'm with you there. Shakespeare had more guts than all these damned frogs put together. 'Hang there like fruit my soul,'" he began quoting, in a musical rhetorical voice, flourishing his wine-glass. "The devil damn you black, you cream-faced loon!" he exclaimed, as the wine washed over the rim.

"'Hang there like fruit my soul,'" Cruttendon and Jacob both began again at the same moment, and both burst out laughing.

"Curse these flies," said Mallinson, flicking at his bald head. "What do they take me for?"

"Something sweet-smelling," said Cruttendon.

"Shut up, Cruttendon," said Jacob. "The fellow has no manners," he explained to Mallinson very politely. "Wants to cut people off their drink. Look here. I want grilled bone. What's the French for grilled bone? Grilled bone, Adolphe. Now you juggins, don't you understand?"

"And I'll tell you, Flanders, the second most beautiful thing in the whole of literature," said Cruttendon, bringing his feet down on to the floor, and leaning right across the table, so that his face almost touched Jacob's face.

"'Hey diddle diddle, the cat and the fiddle,'" Mallinson interrupted, strumming his fingers on the table. "The most ex-qui-sitely beautiful thing in the whole of literature. . . . Cruttendon is a very good fellow," he remarked confidentially. "But he's a bit of a fool." And he jerked his head forward.

Well, not a word of this was ever told to Mrs. Flanders; nor what happened when they paid the bill and left the restaurant, and walked along the Boulevard Raspaille.

Then here is another scrap of conversation; the time about eleven in the morning; the scene a studio; and the day Sunday.

"I tell you, Flanders," said Cruttendon, "I'd as soon have one of Mallinson's little pictures as a Chardin. And when I say that . . ." he squeezed the tail of an emaciated tube . . . "Chardin was a great swell. . . . He sells 'em to pay his dinner now. But wait till the dealers get hold of him. A great swell—oh, a very great swell."

"It's an awfully pleasant life," said Jacob, "messing away up here. Still, it's a stupid art, Cruttendon." He wandered off across the room. "There's this man, Pierre Louÿs now." He took up a book.

"Now my good sir, are you going to settle down?" said Cruttendon.

"That's a solid piece of work," said Jacob, standing a canvas on a chair.

"Oh, that I did ages ago," said Cruttendon, looking over his shoulder.

"You're a pretty competent painter in my opinion," said Jacob after a time.

"Now if you'd like to see what I'm after at the present moment," said Cruttendon, putting a canvas before Jacob. "There. That's it. That's more like it. That's . . ." he squirmed his thumb in a circle round a lamp globe painted white.

"A pretty solid piece of work," said Jacob, straddling his legs in front of it. "But what I wish you'd explain . . ."

Miss Jinny Carslake, pale, freckled, morbid, came into the room.

"Oh, Jinny, here's a friend. Flanders. An Englishman. Wealthy. Highly connected. Go on, Flanders. . . ."

Jacob said nothing.

"It's *that*—that's not right," said Jinny Carslake.

"No," said Cruttendon decidedly. "Can't be done."

He took the canvas off the chair and stood it on the floor with its back to them.

"Sit down, ladies and gentlemen. Miss Carslake comes from your part of the world, Flanders. From Devonshire. Oh, I thought you said Devonshire. Very well. She's a daughter of the church too. The black sheep of the family. Her mother writes her such letters. I say—have you one about you? It's generally Sundays they come. Sort of church-bell effect, you know."

"Have you met all the painter men?" said Jinny. "Was Mallinson drunk? If you go to his studio he'll give you one of his pictures. I say, Teddy . . ."

"Half a jiff," said Cruttendon. "What's the season of the year?" He looked out of the window.

"We take a day off on Sundays, Flanders."

"Will he . . ." said Jinny, looking at Jacob. "You . . ."

"Yes, he'll come with us," said Cruttendon.

And then, here is Versailles.

Jinny stood on the stone rim and leant over the pond, clasped by Cruttendon's arms or she would have fallen in. "There! There!" she cried. "Right up to the top!" Some sluggish, sloping-shouldered fish had floated up from the depths to nip her crumbs. "You look," she said, jumping down. And then the dazzling white water, rough and throttled, shot up into the air. The fountain spread itself. Through it came the sound of military music far away. All the water was puckered with drops. A blue air-ball gently bumped the surface. How all the nurses and children and old men and young crowded to the edge, leant over and waved their sticks! The little girl ran stretching her arms towards her air-ball, but it sank beneath the fountain.

Edward Cruttendon, Jinny Carslake, and Jacob Flanders walked in
a row along the yellow gravel path; got on to the grass; so passed
under the trees; and came out at the summer-house where Marie
Antoinette used to drink chocolate. In went Edward and Jinny, but
Jacob waited outside, sitting on the handle of his walking-stick. Out
they came again.

"Well?" said Cruttendon, smiling at Jacob.

Jinny waited; Edward waited; and both looked at Jacob.

"Well?" said Jacob, smiling and pressing both hands on his stick.

"Come along," he decided; and started off. The others followed him,
smiling.

And then they went to the little café in the by-street where people
sit drinking coffee, watching the soldiers, meditatively knocking ashes
into trays.

"But he's quite different," said Jinny, folding her hands over the top
of her glass. "I don't suppose you know what Ted means when he says
a thing like that," she said, looking at Jacob. "But I do. Sometimes I
could kill myself. Sometimes he lies in bed all day long—just lies
there. . . . I don't want you right on the table"; she waved her hands.
Swollen iridescent pigeons were waddling round their feet.

"Look at that woman's hat," said Cruttendon. "How do they come
to think of it? . . . No, Flanders, I don't think I could live like you.
When one walks down that street opposite the British Museum—what's
it called?—that's what I mean. It's all like that. Those fat women—
and the man standing in the middle of the road as if he were going to
have a fit . . ."

"Everybody feeds them," said Jinny, waving the pigeons away.
"They're stupid old things."

"Well, I don't know," said Jacob, smoking his cigarette. "There's
St. Paul's."

"I mean going to an office," said Cruttendon.

"Hang it all," Jacob expostulated.

"But you don't count," said Jinny, looking at Cruttendon. "You're
mad. I mean, you just think of painting."

"Yes, I know. I can't help it. I say, will King George give way about
the peers?"

"He'll jolly well have to," said Jacob.

"There!" said Jinny. "He really knows."

"You see, would if I could," said Cruttendon, "but I simply can't."

"I *think* I could," said Jinny. "Only, it's all the people one dislikes
who do it. At home, I mean. They talk of nothing else. Even people
like my mother."

"Now if I came and lived here——" said Jacob. "What's my share, Cruttendon? Oh, very well. Have it your own way. Those silly birds, directly one wants them—they've flown away."

And finally under the arc lamps in the Gare des Invalides, with one of those queer movements which are so slight yet so definite, which may wound or pass unnoticed but generally inflict a good deal of discomfort, Jinny and Cruttendon drew together; Jacob stood apart. They had to separate. Something must be said. Nothing was said. A man wheeled a trolley past Jacob's legs so near that he almost grazed them. When Jacob recovered his balance the other two were turning away, though Jinny looked over her shoulder, and Cruttendon, waving his hand, disappeared like the very great genius that he was.

No—Mrs. Flanders was told none of this, though Jacob felt, it is safe to say, that nothing in the world was of greater importance; and as for Cruttendon and Jinny, he thought them the most remarkable people he had ever met—being of course unable to foresee how it fell out in the course of time that Cruttendon took to painting orchards; had therefore to live in Kent; and must, one would think, see through apple blossom by this time, since his wife, for whose sake he did it, eloped with a novelist; but no; Cruttendon still paints orchards, savagely, in solitude. Then Jinny Carslake, after her affair with Lefanu, the American painter, frequented Indian philosophers, and now you find her in pensions in Italy cherishing a little jeweller's box containing ordinary pebbles picked off the road. But if you look at them steadily, she says, multiplicity becomes unity, which is somehow the secret of life, though it does not prevent her from following the macaroni as it goes round the table, and sometimes, on spring nights, she makes the strangest confidences to shy young Englishmen.

Jacob had nothing to hide from his mother. It was only that he could make no sense himself of his extraordinary excitement, and as for writing it down——

"Jacob's letters are so like him," said Mrs. Jarvis, folding the sheet.

"Indeed he seems to be having . . ." said Mrs. Flanders, and paused, for she was cutting out a dress and had to straighten the pattern, ". . . a very gay time."

Mrs. Jarvis thought of Paris. At her back the window was open, for it was a mild night; a calm night; when the moon seemed muffled and the apple trees stood perfectly still.

"I never pity the dead," said Mrs. Jarvis, shifting the cushion at her

back, and clasping her hands behind her head. Betty Flanders did not hear, for her scissors made so much noise on the table.

"They are at rest," said Mrs. Jarvis. "And we spend our days doing foolish unnecessary things without knowing why."

Mrs. Jarvis was not liked in the village.

"You never walk at this time of night?" she asked Mrs. Flanders.

"It is certainly wonderfully mild," said Mrs. Flanders.

Yet it was years since she had opened the orchard gate and gone out on Dods Hill after dinner.

"It is perfectly dry," said Mrs. Jarvis, as they shut the orchard door and stepped on to the turf.

"I shan't go far," said Betty Flanders. "Yes, Jacob will leave Paris on Wednesday."

"Jacob was always my friend of the three," said Mrs. Jarvis.

"Now, my dear, I am going no further," said Mrs. Flanders. They had climbed the dark hill and reached the Roman camp.

The rampart rose at their feet—the smooth circle surrounding the camp or the grave. How many needles Betty Flanders had lost there! and her garnet brooch.

"It is much clearer than this sometimes," said Mrs. Jarvis, standing upon the ridge. There were no clouds, and yet there was a haze over the sea, and over the moors. The lights of Scarborough flashed, as if a woman wearing a diamond necklace turned her head this way and that.

"How quiet it is!" said Mrs. Jarvis.

Mrs. Flanders rubbed the turf with her toe, thinking of her garnet brooch.

Mrs. Jarvis found it difficult to think of herself to-night. It was so calm. There was no wind; nothing racing, flying, escaping. Black shadows stood still over the silver moors. The furze bushes stood perfectly still. Neither did Mrs. Jarvis think of God. There was a church behind them, of course. The church clock struck ten. Did the strokes reach the furze bush, or did the thorn tree hear them?

Mrs. Flanders was stooping down to pick up a pebble. Sometimes people do find things, Mrs. Jarvis thought, and yet in this hazy moonlight it was impossible to see anything, except bones, and little pieces of chalk.

"Jacob bought it with his own money, and then I brought Mr. Parker up to see the view, and it must have dropped——" Mrs. Flanders murmured.

Did the bones stir, or the rusty swords? Was Mrs. Flanders' two-penny-halfpenny brooch for ever part of the rich accumulation? and if all the ghosts flocked thick and rubbed shoulders with Mrs. Flanders

in the circle, would she not have seemed perfectly in her place, a live English matron, growing stout?

The clock struck the quarter.

The frail waves of sound broke among the stiff gorse and the hawthorn twigs as the church clock divided time into quarters.

Motionless and broad-backed the moors received the statement "It is fifteen minutes past the hour," but made no answer, unless a bramble stirred.

Yet even in this light the legends on the tombstones could be read, brief voices saying, "I am Bertha Ruck," "I am Tom Gage." And they say which day of the year they died, and the New Testament says something for them, very proud, very emphatic, or consoling.

The moors accept all that too.

The moonlight falls like a pale page upon the church wall, and illumines the kneeling family in the niche, and the tablet set up in 1780 to the Squire of the parish who relieved the poor, and believed in God—so the measured voice goes on down the marble scroll, as though it could impose itself upon time and the open air.

Now a fox steals out from behind the gorse bushes.

Often, even at night, the church seems full of people. The pews are worn and greasy, and the cassocks in place, and the hymn-books on the ledges. It is a ship with all its crew aboard. The timbers strain to hold the dead and the living, the ploughmen, the carpenters, and fox-hunting gentlemen and the farmers smelling of mud and brandy. Their tongues join together in syllabling the sharp-cut words, which for ever slice asunder time and the broad-backed moors. Plaint and belief and elegy, despair and triumph, but for the most part good sense and jolly indifference, go trampling out of the windows any time these five hundred years.

Still, as Mrs. Jarvis said, stepping out on to the moors, "How quiet it is!" Quiet at midday, except when the hunt scatters across it; quiet in the afternoon, save for the drifting sheep; at night the moor is perfectly quiet.

A garnet brooch has dropped into its grass. A fox pads stealthily. A leaf turns on its edge. Mrs. Jarvis, who is fifty years of age, reposes in the camp in the hazy moonlight.

". . . and," said Mrs. Flanders, straightening her back, "I never cared for Mr. Parker."

"Neither did I," said Mrs. Jarvis. They began to walk home.

But their voices floated for a little above the camp. The moonlight destroyed nothing. The moor accepted everything. Tom Gage cries aloud so long as his tombstone endures. The Roman skeletons are in safe keeping. Betty Flanders' darning needles are safe too and her gar-

net brooch. And sometimes at midday, in the sunshine, the moor seems to hoard these little treasures, like a nurse. But at midnight when no one speaks or gallops, and the thorn tree is perfectly still, it would be foolish to vex the moor with questions—what? and why?

The church clock, however, strikes twelve.

§ 12

The water fell off a ledge like lead—like a chain with thick white links. The train ran out into a steep green meadow, and Jacob saw striped tulips growing and heard a bird singing, in Italy.

A motor car full of Italian officers ran along the flat road and kept up with the train, raising dust behind it. There were trees laced together with vines—as Virgil said. Here was a station; and a tremendous leave-taking going on, with women in high yellow boots and odd pale boys in ringed socks. Virgil's bees had gone about the plains of Lombardy. It was the custom of the ancients to train vines between elms. Then at Milan there were sharp-winged hawks, of a bright brown, cutting figures over the roofs.

These Italian carriages get damnably hot with the afternoon sun on them, and the chances are that before the engine has pulled to the top of the gorge the clanking chain will have broken. Up, up, up, it goes, like a train on a scenic railway. Every peak is covered with sharp trees, and amazing white villages are crowded on ledges. There is always a white tower on the very summit, flat red-frilled roofs, and a sheer drop beneath. It is not a country in which one walks after tea. For one thing there is no grass. A whole hillside will be ruled with olive trees. Already in April the earth is clotted into dry dust between them. And there are neither stiles nor footpaths, nor lanes chequered with the shadows of leaves nor eighteenth-century inns with bow-windows, where one eats ham and eggs. Oh, no, Italy is all fierceness, bareness, exposure, and black priests shuffling along the roads. It is strange, too, how you never get away from villas.

Still, to be travelling on one's own with a hundred pounds to spend is a fine affair. And if his money gave out, as it probably would, he would go on foot. He could live on bread and wine—the wine in straw bottles—for after doing Greece he was going to knock off Rome. The Roman civilization was a very inferior affair, no doubt. But Bonamy talked a lot of rot, all the same. "You ought to have been in Athens," he would say to Bonamy when he got back. "Standing on the Parthenon," he would say, or "The ruins of the Coliseum suggest some fairly

sublime reflections," which he would write out at length in letters. It might turn to an essay upon civilization. A comparison between the ancients and moderns, with some pretty sharp hits at Mr. Asquith—something in the style of Gibbon.

A stout gentleman laboriously hauled himself in, dusty, baggy, slung with gold chains, and Jacob, regretting that he did not come of the Latin race, looked out of the window.

It is a strange reflection that by travelling two days and nights you are in the heart of Italy. Accidental villas among olive trees appear; and menservants watering the cactuses. Black victorias drive in between pompous pillars with plaster shields stuck to them. It is at once momentary and astonishingly intimate—to be displayed before the eyes of a foreigner. And there is a lonely hill-top where no one ever comes, and yet it is seen by me who was lately driving down Piccadilly on an omnibus. And what I should like would be to get out among the fields, sit down and hear the grasshoppers, and take up a handful of earth—Italian earth, as this is Italian dust upon my shoes.

Jacob heard them crying strange names at railway stations through the night. The train stopped and he heard frogs croaking close by, and he wrinkled back the blind cautiously and saw a vast strange marsh all white in the moonlight. The carriage was thick with cigar smoke, which floated round the globe with the green shade on it. The Italian gentleman lay snoring with his boots off and his waistcoat unbuttoned. . . . And all this business of going to Greece seemed to Jacob an intolerable weariness—sitting in hotels by oneself and looking at monuments—he'd have done better to go to Cornwall with Timmy Durrant. . . . "O—h," Jacob protested, as the darkness began breaking in front of him and the light showed through, but the man was reaching across him to get something—the fat Italian man in his dicky, unshaven, crumpled, obese, was opening the door and going off to have a wash.

So Jacob sat up, and saw a lean Italian sportsman with a gun walking down the road in the early morning light, and the whole idea of the Parthenon came upon him in a clap.

"By Jove!" he thought, "we must be nearly there!" and he stuck his head out of the window and got the air full in his face.

It is highly exasperating that twenty-five people of your acquaintance should be able to say straight off something very much to the point about being in Greece, while for yourself there is a stopper upon all emotions whatsoever. For after washing at the hotel at Patras, Jacob had followed the tram lines a mile or so out; and then followed them a mile or so back; he had met several droves of turkeys; several strings of donkeys; and had got lost in back streets; had read advertisements of

corsets and of Maggi's consommé; children had trodden on his toes; the place smelt of bad cheese; and he was glad to find himself suddenly come out opposite his hotel. There was an old copy of the *Daily Mail* lying among coffee-cups; which he read. But what could he do after dinner?

No doubt we should be, on the whole, much worse off than we are without our astonishing gift for illusion. At the age of twelve or so, having given up dolls and broken our steam engines, France, but much more probably Italy, and India almost for a certainty, draw the superfluous imagination. One's aunts have been to Rome; and every one has an uncle who was last heard of—poor man—in Rangoon. He will never come back any more. But it is the governesses who start the Greek myth. Look at that for a head (they say)—nose, you see, straight as a dart, curls, eyebrows—everything appropriate to manly beauty; while his legs and arms have lines on them which indicate a perfect degree of development—the Greeks caring for the body as much as for the face. And the Greeks could paint fruit so that birds pecked at it. First you read Xenophon; then Euripides. One day—that was an occasion, by God—what people have said appears to have sense in it; "the Greek spirit"; the Greek this, that, and the other; though it is absurd, by the way, to say that any Greek comes near Shakespeare. The point is, however, that we have been brought up in an illusion.

Jacob, no doubt, thought something in this fashion, the *Daily Mail* crumpled in his hand; his legs extended; the very picture of boredom. "But it's the way we're brought up," he went on.

And it all seemed to him very distasteful. Something ought to be done about it. And from being moderately depressed he became like a man about to be executed. Clara Durrant had left him at a party to talk to an American called Pilchard. And he had come all the way to Greece and left her. They wore evening-dresses, and talked nonsense—what damned nonsense—and he put out his hand for the *Globe Trotter,* an international magazine which is supplied free of charge to the proprietors of hotels.

In spite of its ramshackle condition modern Greece is highly advanced in the electric tramway system, so that while Jacob sat in the hotel sitting-room the trams clanked, chimed, rang, rang, rang imperiously to get the donkeys out of the way, and one old woman who refused to budge, beneath the windows. The whole of civilization was being condemned.

The waiter was quite indifferent to that too. Aristotle, a dirty man, carnivorously interested in the body of the only guest now occupying the only arm-chair, came into the room ostentatiously, put something down, put something straight, and saw that Jacob was still there.

"I shall want to be called early to-morrow," said Jacob, over his shoulder. "I am going to Olympia."

This gloom, this surrender to the dark waters which lap us about, is a modern invention. Perhaps, as Cruttendon said, we do not believe enough. Our fathers at any rate had something to demolish. So have we for the matter of that, thought Jacob, crumpling the *Daily Mail* in his hand. He would go into Parliament and make fine speeches—but what use are fine speeches and Parliament, once you surrender an inch to the black waters? Indeed there has never been any explanation of the ebb and flow in our veins—of happiness and unhappiness. That respectability and evening parties where one has to dress, and wretched slums at the back of Gray's Inn—something solid, immovable, and grotesque—is at the back of it, Jacob thought probable. But then there was the British Empire which was beginning to puzzle him; nor was he altogether in favour of giving Home Rule to Ireland. What did the *Daily Mail* say about that?

For he had grown to be a man, and was about to be immersed in things—as indeed the chambermaid, emptying his basin upstairs, fingering keys, studs, pencils, and bottles of tabloids strewn on the dressing-table, was aware.

That he had grown to be a man was a fact that Florinda knew, as she knew everything, by instinct.

And Betty Flanders even now suspected it, as she read his letter, posted at Milan, "Telling me," she complained to Mrs. Jarvis, "really nothing that I want to know"; but she brooded over it.

Fanny Elmer felt it to desperation. For he would take his stick and his hat and would walk to the window, and look perfectly absent-minded and very stern too, she thought.

"I am going," he would say, "to cadge a meal off Bonamy."

"Anyhow, I can drown myself in the Thames," Fanny cried, as she hurried past the Foundling Hospital.

"But the *Daily Mail* isn't to be trusted," Jacob said to himself, looking about for something else to read. And he sighed again, being indeed so profoundly gloomy that gloom must have been lodged in him to cloud him at any moment, which was odd in a man who enjoyed things so, was not much given to analysis, but was horribly romantic, of course, Bonamy thought, in his rooms in Lincoln's Inn.

"He will fall in love," thought Bonamy. "Some Greek woman with a straight nose."

It was to Bonamy that Jacob wrote from Patras—to Bonamy who couldn't love a woman and never read a foolish book.

There are very few good books after all, for we can't count profuse histories, travels in mule carts to discover the sources of the Nile, or the volubility of fiction.

I like books whose virtue is all drawn together in a page or two. I like sentences that don't budge though armies cross them. I like words to be hard—such were Bonamy's views, and they won him the hostility of those whose taste is all for the fresh growths of the morning, who throw up the window, and find the poppies spread in the sun, and can't forbear a shout of jubilation at the astonishing fertility of English literature. That was not Bonamy's way at all. That his haste in literature affected his friendships, and made him silent, secretive, fastidious, and only quite at his ease with one or two young men of his own way of thinking, was the charge against him.

But then Jacob Flanders was not at all of his own way of thinking— far from it, Bonamy sighed, laying the thin sheets of notepaper on the table and falling into thought about Jacob's character, not for the first time.

The trouble was this romantic vein in him. "But mixed with the stupidity which leads him into these absurd predicaments," thought Bonamy, "there is something—something"—he sighed, for he was fonder of Jacob than of any one in the world.

Jacob went to the window and stood with his hands in his pockets. There he saw three Greeks in kilts; the masts of ships; idle or busy people of the lower classes strolling or stepping out briskly, or falling into groups and gesticulating with their hands. Their lack of concern for him was not the cause of his gloom; but some more profound conviction—it was not that he himself happened to be lonely, but that all people are.

Yet next day, as the train slowly rounded a hill on the way to Olympia, the Greek peasant women were out among the vines; the old Greek men were sitting at the stations, sipping sweet wine. And though Jacob remained gloomy he had never suspected how tremendously pleasant it is to be alone; out of England; on one's own; cut off from the whole thing. There are very sharp bare hills on the way to Olympia; and between them blue sea in triangular spaces. A little like the Cornish coast. Well now, to go walking by oneself all day—to get on to that track and follow it up between the bushes—or are they small trees?—to the top of that mountain from which one can see half the nations of antiquity——

"Yes," said Jacob, for his carriage was empty, "let's look at the map."

Blame it or praise it, there is no denying the wild horse in us. To

gallop intemperately; fall on the sand tired out; to feel the earth spin; to have—positively—a rush of friendship for stones and grasses, as if humanity were over, and as for men and women, let them go hang—there is no getting over the fact that this desire seizes us pretty often.

The evening air slightly moved the dirty curtains in the hotel window at Olympia.

"I am full of love for every one," thought Mrs. Wentworth Williams, "—for the poor most of all—for the peasants coming back in the evening with their burdens. And everything is soft and vague and very sad. It is sad, it is sad. But everything has meaning," thought Sandra Wentworth Williams, raising her head a little and looking very beautiful, tragic, and exalted. "One must love everything."

She held in her hand a little book convenient for travelling—stories by Tchekhoff—as she stood, veiled, in white, in the window of the hotel at Olympia. How beautiful the evening was! and her beauty was its beauty. The tragedy of Greece was the tragedy of all high souls. The inevitable compromise. She seemed to have grasped something. She would write it down. And moving to the table where her husband sat reading she leant her chin in her hands and thought of the peasants, of suffering, of her own beauty, of the inevitable compromise, and of how she would write it down. Nor did Evan Williams say anything brutal, banal, or foolish when he shut his book and put it away to make room for the plates of soup which were now being placed before them. Only his drooping bloodhound eyes and his heavy sallow cheeks expressed his melancholy tolerance, his conviction that though forced to live with circumspection and deliberation he could never possibly achieve any of those objects which, as he knew, are the only ones worth pursuing. His consideration was flawless; his silence unbroken.

"Everything seems to mean so much," said Sandra. But with the sound of her own voice the spell was broken. She forgot the peasants. Only there remained with her a sense of her own beauty, and in front, luckily, there was a looking-glass.

"I am very beautiful," she thought.

She shifted her hat slightly. Her husband saw her looking in the glass; and agreed that beauty is important; it is an inheritance; one cannot ignore it. But it is a barrier; it is in fact rather a bore. So he drank his soup; and kept his eyes fixed upon the window.

"Quails," said Mrs. Wentworth Williams languidly. "And then goat, I suppose; and then . . ."

"Caramel custard presumably," said her husband in the same cadence, with his toothpick out already.

She laid her spoon upon her plate, and her soup was taken away half finished. Never did she do anything without dignity; for hers was

the English type which is so Greek, save that villagers have touched
their hats to it, the vicarage reveres it; and upper-gardeners and
under-gardeners respectfully straighten their backs as she comes down
the broad terrace on Sunday morning, dallying at the stone urns with
the Prime Minister to pick a rose—which, perhaps, she was trying to
forget, as her eye wandered round the dining-room of the inn at
Olympia, seeking the window where her book lay, where a few min-
utes ago she had discovered something—something very profound it
had been, about love and sadness and the peasants.

But it was Evan who sighed; not in despair nor indeed in rebellion.
But, being the most ambitious of men and temperamentally the most
sluggish, he had accomplished nothing; had the political history of
England at his finger-ends, and living much in company with Chatham,
Pitt, Burke, and Charles James Fox could not help contrasting himself
and his age with them and theirs. "Yet there never was a time when
great men are more needed," he was in the habit of saying to himself,
with a sigh. Here he was picking his teeth in an inn at Olympia. He
had done. But Sandra's eyes wandered.

"Those pink melons are sure to be dangerous," he said gloomily.
And as he spoke the door opened and in came a young man in a grey
check suit.

"Beautiful but dangerous," said Sandra, immediately talking to her
husband in the presence of a third person. ("Ah, an English boy on
tour," she thought to herself.)

And Evan knew all that too.

Yes, he knew all that; and he admired her. Very pleasant, he
thought, to have affairs. But for himself, what with his height (Na-
poleon was five feet four, he remembered), his bulk, his inability to
impose his own personality (and yet great men are needed more than
ever now, he sighed), it was useless. He threw away his cigar, went up
to Jacob and asked him, with a simple sort of sincerity which Jacob
liked, whether he had come straight out from England.

"How very English!" Sandra laughed when the waiter told them
next morning that the young gentleman had left at five to climb the
mountain. "I am sure he asked you for a bath?" at which the waiter
shook his head, and said that he would ask the manager.

"You do not understand," laughed Sandra. "Never mind."

Stretched on the top of the mountain, quite alone, Jacob enjoyed
himself immensely. Probably he had never been so happy in the whole
of his life.

But at dinner that night Mr. Williams asked him whether he
would like to see the paper; then Mrs. Williams asked him (as they

strolled on the terrace smoking—and how could he refuse that man's cigar?) whether he'd seen the theatre by moonlight; whether he knew Everard Sherborn; whether he read Greek and whether (Evan rose silently and went in) if he had to sacrifice one it would be the French literature or the Russian?

"And now," wrote Jacob in his letter to Bonamy, "I shall have to read her cursed book"—her Tchekhoff, he meant, for she had lent it him.

Though the opinion is unpopular it seems likely enough that bare places, fields too thick with stones to be ploughed, tossing sea-meadows half-way between England and America, suit us better than cities.

There is something absolute in us which despises qualification. It is this which is teased and twisted in society. People come together in a room. "So delighted," says somebody, "to meet you," and that is a lie. And then: "I enjoy the spring more than the autumn now. One does, I think, as one gets older." For women are always, always, always talking about what one feels, and if they say "as one gets older," they mean you to reply with something quite off the point.

Jacob sat himself down in the quarry where the Greeks had cut marble for the theatre. It is hot work walking up Greek hills at mid-day. The wild red cyclamen was out; he had seen the little tortoises hobbling from clump to clump; the air smelt strong and suddenly sweet, and the sun, striking on jagged splinters of marble, was very dazzling to the eyes. Composed, commanding, contemptuous, a little melancholy, and bored with an august kind of boredom, there he sat smoking his pipe.

Bonamy would have said that this was the sort of thing that made him uneasy—when Jacob got into the doldrums, looked like a Margate fisherman out of a job, or a British Admiral. You couldn't make him understand a thing when he was in a mood like that. One had better leave him alone. He was dull. He was apt to be grumpy.

He was up very early, looking at the statues with his Baedeker.

Sandra Wentworth Williams, ranging the world before breakfast in quest of adventure or a point of view, all in white, not so very tall perhaps, but uncommonly upright—Sandra Williams got Jacob's head exactly on a level with the head of the Hermes of Praxiteles. The comparison was all in his favour. But before she could say a single word he had gone out of the Museum and left her.

Still, a lady of fashion travels with more than one dress, and if white suits the morning hour, perhaps sandy yellow with purple spots on it, a black hat, and a volume of Balzac, suit the evening. Thus she was arranged on the terrace when Jacob came in. Very beautiful she looked. With her hands folded she mused, seemed to listen to her

husband, seemed to watch the peasants coming down with brush-wood on their backs, seemed to notice how the hill changed from blue to black, seemed to discriminate between truth and falsehood, Jacob thought, and crossed his legs suddenly, observing the extreme shabbiness of his trousers.

"But he is very distinguished looking," Sandra decided.

And Evan Williams, lying back in his chair with the paper on his knees, envied them. The best thing he could do would be to publish, with Macmillans, his monograph upon the foreign policy of Chatham. But confound this tumid, queasy feeling—this restlessness, swelling, and heat—it was jealousy! jealousy! jealousy! which he had sworn never to feel again.

"Come with us to Corinth, Flanders," he said with more than his usual energy, stopping by Jacob's chair. He was relieved by Jacob's reply, or rather by the solid, direct, if shy manner in which he said that he would like very much to come with them to Corinth.

"Here is a fellow," thought Evan Williams, "who might do very well in politics."

"I intend to come to Greece every year so long as I live," Jacob wrote to Bonamy. "It is the only chance I can see of protecting oneself from civilization."

"Goodness knows what he means by that," Bonamy sighed. For as he never said a clumsy thing himself, these dark sayings of Jacob's made him feel apprehensive, yet somehow impressed, his own turn being all for the definite, the concrete, and the rational.

Nothing could be much simpler than what Sandra said as she descended the Acro-Corinth, keeping to the little path, while Jacob strode over rougher ground by her side. She had been left motherless at the age of four; and the Park was vast.

"One never seemed able to get out of it," she laughed. Of course there was the library, and dear Mr. Jones, and notions about things. "I used to stray into the kitchen and sit upon the butler's knees," she laughed, sadly though.

Jacob thought that if he had been there he would have saved her; for she had been exposed to great dangers, he felt, and, he thought to himself, "People wouldn't understand a woman talking as she talks."

She made little of the roughness of the hill; and wore breeches, he saw, under her short skirts.

"Women like Fanny Elmer don't," he thought. "What's-her-name Carslake didn't; yet they pretend . . ."

Mrs. Williams said things straight out. He was surprised by his own knowledge of the rules of behaviour; how much more can be said

than one thought; how open one can be with a woman; and how little he had known himself before.

Evan joined them on the road; and as they drove along up hill and down hill (for Greece is in a state of effervescence, yet astonishingly clean-cut, a treeless land, where you see the ground between the blades, each hill cut and shaped and outlined as often as not against sparkling deep blue waters, islands white as sand floating on the horizon, occasional groves of palm trees standing in the valleys, which are scattered with black goats, spotted with little olive trees and sometimes have white hollows, rayed and criss-crossed, in their flanks), as they drove up hill and down he scowled in the corner of the carriage, with his paw so tightly closed that the skin was stretched between the knuckles and the little hairs stood upright. Sandra rode opposite, dominant, like a Victory prepared to fling into the air.

"Heartless!" thought Evan (which was untrue).

"Brainless!" he suspected (and that was not true, either). "Still . . . !" He envied her.

When bedtime came the difficulty was to write to Bonamy, Jacob found. Yet he had seen Salamis, and Marathon in the distance. Poor old Bonamy! No; there was something queer about it. He could not write to Bonamy.

"I shall go to Athens all the same," he resolved, looking very set, with his hook dragging in his side.

The Williamses had already been to Athens.

Athens is still quite capable of striking a young man as the oddest combination, the most incongruous assortment. Now it is suburban; now immortal. Now cheap continental jewellery is laid upon plush trays. Now the stately woman stands naked, save for a wave of drapery above the knee. No form can he set on his sensations as he strolls, one blazing afternoon, along the Parisian boulevard and skips out of the way of the royal landau which, looking indescribably ramshackle, rattles along the pitted roadway, saluted by citizens of both sexes cheaply dressed in bowler hats and continental costumes; though a shepherd in kilt, cap, and gaiters very nearly drives his herd of goats between the royal wheels, and all the time the Acropolis surges into the air, raises itself above the town, like a large immobile wave with the yellow columns of the Parthenon firmly planted upon it.

The yellow columns of the Parthenon are to be seen at all hours of the day firmly planted upon the Acropolis; though at sunset, when the ships in the Piraeus fire their guns, a bell rings, a man in uniform (the waistcoat unbuttoned) appears; and the women roll up the black

stockings which they are knitting in the shadow of the columns, call to the children, and troop off down the hill back to their houses.

There they are again, the pillars, the pediment, the Temple of Victory and the Erechtheum, set on a tawny rock cleft with shadows, directly you unlatch your shutters in the morning and, leaning out, hear the clatter, the clamour, the whip cracking in the street below. There they are.

The extreme definiteness with which they stand, now a brilliant white, again yellow, and in some lights red, imposes ideas of durability, of the emergence through the earth of some spiritual energy elsewhere dissipated in elegant trifles. But this durability exists quite independently of our admiration. Although the beauty is sufficiently humane to weaken us, to stir the deep deposit of mud—memories, abandonments, regrets, sentimental devotions—the Parthenon is separate from all that; and if you consider how it has stood out all night, for centuries, you begin to connect the blaze (at midday the glare is dazzling and the frieze almost invisible) with the idea that perhaps it is beauty alone that is immortal.

Added to this, compared with the blistered stucco, the new love songs rasped out to the strum of guitar and gramophone, and the mobile yet insignificant faces of the street, the Parthenon is really astonishing in its silent composure; which is so vigorous that, far from being decayed, the Parthenon appears, on the contrary, likely to outlast the entire world.

"And the Greeks, like sensible men, never bothered to finish the backs of their statues," said Jacob, shading his eyes and observing that the side of the figure which is turned away from view is left in the rough.

He noted the slight irregularity in the line of the steps which "the artistic sense of the Greeks preferred to mathematical accuracy," he read in his guide-book.

He stood on the exact spot where the great statue of Athena used to stand, and identified the more famous landmarks of the scene beneath.

In short he was accurate and diligent; but profoundly morose. Moreover he was pestered by guides. This was on Monday.

But on Wednesday he wrote a telegram to Bonamy, telling him to come at once. And then he crumpled it in his hand and threw it in the gutter.

"For one thing he wouldn't come," he thought. "And then I daresay this sort of thing wears off." "This sort of thing" being that uneasy, painful feeling, something like selfishness—one wishes almost that the thing would stop—it is getting more and more beyond what is possible

—"If it goes on much longer I shan't be able to cope with it—but if some one else were seeing it at the same time—Bonamy is stuffed in his room in Lincoln's Inn—oh, I say, damn it all, I say."—the sight of Hymettus, Pentelicus, Lycabettus on one side, and the sea on the other, as one stands in the Parthenon at sunset, the sky pink feathered, the plain all colours, the marble tawny in one's eyes, is thus oppressive. Luckily Jacob had little sense of personal association; he seldom thought of Plato or Socrates in the flesh; on the other hand his feeling for architecture was very strong; he preferred statues to pictures; and he was beginning to think a great deal about the problems of civilization, which were solved, of course, so very remarkably by the ancient Greeks, though their solution is no help to us. Then the hook gave a great tug in his side as he lay in bed on Wednesday night; and he turned over with a desperate sort of tumble, remembering Sandra Wentworth Williams with whom he was in love.

Next day he climbed Pentelicus.

The day after he went up to the Acropolis. The hour was early; the place almost deserted; and possibly there was thunder in the air. But the sun struck full upon the Acropolis.

Jacob's intention was to sit down and read, and, finding a drum of marble conveniently placed, from which Marathon could be seen, and yet it was in the shade, while the Erechtheum blazed white in front of him, there he sat. And after reading a page he put his thumb in his book. Why not rule countries in the way they should be ruled? And he read again.

No doubt his position there overlooking Marathon somehow raised his spirits. Or it may have been that a slow capacious brain has these moments of flowering. Or he had, insensibly, while he was abroad, got into the way of thinking about politics.

And then looking up and seeing the sharp outline, his meditations were given an extraordinary edge; Greece was over; the Parthenon in ruins; yet there he was.

(Ladies with green and white umbrellas passed through the courtyard—French ladies on their way to join their husbands in Constantinople.)

Jacob read on again. And laying the book on the ground he began, as if inspired by what he had read, to write a note upon the importance of history—upon democracy—one of those scribbles upon which the work of a lifetime may be based; or again, it falls out of a book twenty years later, and one can't remember a word of it. It is a little painful. It had better be burnt.

Jacob wrote; began to draw a straight nose; when all the French ladies opening and shutting their umbrellas just beneath him ex-

claimed, looking at the sky, that one did not know what to expect—rain or fine weather?

Jacob got up and strolled across to the Erechtheum. There are still several women standing there holding the roof on their heads. Jacob straightened himself slightly; for stability and balance affect the body first. These statues annulled things so! He stared at them, then turned, and there was Madame Lucien Gravé perched on a block of marble with her kodak pointed at his head. Of course she jumped down, in spite of her age, her figure, and her tight boots—having, now that her daughter was married, lapsed with a luxurious abandonment, grand enough in its way, into the fleshy grotesque; she jumped down, but not before Jacob had seen her.

"Damn these women—damn these women!" he thought. And he went to fetch his book which he had left lying on the ground in the Parthenon.

"How they spoil things," he murmured, leaning against one of the pillars, pressing his book tight between his arm and his side. (As for the weather, no doubt the storm would break soon; Athens was under cloud.)

"It is those damned women," said Jacob, without any trace of bitterness, but rather with sadness and disappointment that what might have been should never be.

(This violent disillusionment is generally to be expected in young men in the prime of life, sound of wind and limb, who will soon become fathers of families and directors of banks.)

Then, making sure that the Frenchwomen had gone, and looking cautiously round him, Jacob strolled over to the Erechtheum and looked rather furtively at the goddess on the left-hand side holding the roof on her head. She reminded him of Sandra Wentworth Williams. He looked at her, then looked away. He looked at her, then looked away. He was extraordinarily moved, and with the battered Greek nose in his head, with Sandra in his head, with all sorts of things in his head, off he started to walk right up to the top of Mount Hymettus, alone, in the heat.

That very afternoon Bonamy went expressly to talk about Jacob to tea with Clara Durrant in the square behind Sloane Street where, on hot spring days, there are striped blinds over the front windows, single horses pawing the macadam outside the doors, and elderly gentlemen in yellow waistcoats ringing bells and stepping in very politely when the maid demurely replies that Mrs. Durrant is at home.

Bonamy sat with Clara in the sunny front room with the barrel organ piping sweetly outside; the water-cart going slowly along spray-

ing the pavement; the carriages jingling, and all the silver and chintz, brown and blue rugs and vases filled with green boughs, striped with trembling yellow bars.

The insipidity of what was said needs no illustration—Bonamy kept on gently returning quiet answers and accumulating amazement at an existence squeezed and emasculated within a white satin shoe (Mrs. Durrant meanwhile enunciating strident politics with Sir Somebody in the back room) until the virginity of Clara's soul appeared to him candid; the depths unknown; and he would have brought out Jacob's name had he not begun to feel positively certain that Clara loved him —and could do nothing whatever.

"Nothing whatever!" he exclaimed, as the door shut, and, for a man of his temperament, got a very queer feeling, as he walked through the park, of carriages irresistibly driven; of flower-beds uncompromisingly geometrical; of force rushing round geometrical patterns in the most senseless way in the world. "Was Clara," he thought, pausing to watch the boys bathing in the Serpentine, "the silent woman?—would Jacob marry her?"

But in Athens in the sunshine, in Athens, where it is almost impossible to get afternoon tea, and elderly gentlemen who talk politics talk them all the other way round, in Athens sat Sandra Wentworth Williams, veiled, in white, her legs stretched in front of her, one elbow on the arm of the bamboo chair, blue clouds wavering and drifting from her cigarette.

The orange trees which flourish in the Square of the Constitution, the band, the dragging of feet, the sky, the houses, lemon and rose coloured—all this became so significant to Mrs. Wentworth Williams after her second cup of coffee that she began dramatizing the story of the noble and impulsive Englishwoman who had offered a seat in her carriage to the old American lady at Mycenae (Mrs. Duggan)— not altogether a false story, though it said nothing of Evan, standing first on one foot, then on the other, waiting for the women to stop chattering.

"I am putting the life of Father Damien into verse," Mrs. Duggan had said, for she had lost everything—everything in the world, husband and child and everything, but faith remained.

Sandra, floating from the particular to the universal, lay back in a trance.

The flight of time which hurries us so tragically along; the eternal drudge and drone, now bursting into fiery flame like those brief balls of yellow among green leaves (she was looking at orange trees); kisses on lips that are to die; the world turning, turning in mazes of heat

and sound—though to be sure there is the quiet evening with its lovely pallor, "For I am sensitive to every side of it," Sandra thought, "and Mrs. Duggan will write to me for ever, and I shall answer her letters." Now the royal band marching by with the national flag stirred wider rings of emotion, and life became something that the courageous mount and ride out to sea on—the hair blown back (so she envisaged it, and the breeze stirred slightly among the orange trees) and she herself was emerging from silver spray—when she saw Jacob. He was standing in the Square with a book under his arm looking vacantly about him. That he was heavily built and might become stout in time was a fact.

But she suspected him of being a mere bumpkin.

"There is that young man," she said, peevishly, throwing away her cigarette, "that Mr. Flanders."

"Where?" said Evan. "I don't see him."

"Oh, walking away—behind the trees now. No, you can't see him. But we are sure to run into him," which, of course, they did.

But how far was he a mere bumpkin? How far was Jacob Flanders at the age of twenty-six a stupid fellow? It is no use trying to sum people up. One must follow hints, not exactly what is said, nor yet entirely what is done. Some, it is true, take ineffaceable impressions of character at once. Others dally, loiter, and get blown this way and that. Kind old ladies assure us that cats are often the best judges of character. A cat will always go to a good man, they say; but then, Mrs. Whitehorn, Jacob's landlady, loathed cats.

There is also the highly respectable opinion that character-mongering is much overdone nowadays. After all, what does it matter—that Fanny Elmer was all sentiment and sensation, and Mrs. Durrant hard as iron? that Clara, owing (so the character-mongers said) largely to her mother's influence, never yet had the chance to do anything off her own bat, and only to very observant eyes displayed deeps of feeling which were positively alarming; and would certainly throw herself away upon some one unworthy of her one of these days unless, so the character-mongers said, she had a spark of her mother's spirit in her— was somehow heroic. But what a term to apply to Clara Durrant! Simple to a degree, others thought her. And that is the very reason, so they said, why she attracts Dick Bonamy—the young man with the Wellington nose. Now *he's* a dark horse if you like. And there these gossips would suddenly pause. Obviously they meant to hint at his peculiar disposition—long rumoured among them.

"But sometimes it is precisely a woman like Clara that men of that temperament need . . ." Miss Julia Eliot would hint.

"Well," Mr. Bowley would reply, "it may be so."

For however long these gossips sit, and however they stuff out their victims' characters till they are swollen and tender as the livers of geese exposed to a hot fire, they never come to a decision.

"That young man, Jacob Flanders," they would say, "so distinguished looking—and yet so awkward." Then they would apply themselves to Jacob and vacillate eternally between the two extremes. He rode to hounds—after a fashion, for he hadn't a penny.

"Did you ever hear who his father was?" asked Julia Eliot.

"His mother, they say, is somehow connected with the Rocksbiers," replied Mr. Bowley.

"He doesn't overwork himself anyhow."

"His friends are very fond of him."

"Dick Bonamy, you mean?"

"No, I didn't mean that. It's evidently the other way with Jacob. He is precisely the young man to fall headlong in love and repent it for the rest of his life."

"Oh, Mr. Bowley," said Mrs. Durrant, sweeping down upon them in her imperious manner, "you remember Mrs. Adams? Well, that is her niece." And Mr. Bowley, getting up, bowed politely and fetched strawberries.

So we are driven back to see what the other side means—the men in clubs and Cabinets—when they say that character-drawing is a frivolous fireside art, a matter of pins and needles, exquisite outlines enclosing vacancy, flourishes, and mere scrawls.

The battleships ray out over the North Sea, keeping their stations accurately apart. At a given signal all the guns are trained on a target which (the master gunner counts the seconds, watch in hand—at the sixth he looks up) flames into splinters. With equal nonchalance a dozen young men in the prime of life descend with composed faces into the depths of the sea; and there impassively (though with perfect mastery of machinery) suffocate uncomplainingly together. Like blocks of tin soldiers the army covers the cornfield, moves up the hillside, stops, reels slightly this way and that, and falls flat, save that, through field-glasses, it can be seen that one or two pieces still agitate up and down like fragments of broken match-stick.

These actions, together with the incessant commerce of banks, laboratories, chancellories, and houses of business, are the strokes which oar the world forward, they say. And they are dealt by men as smoothly sculptured as the impassive policeman at Ludgate Circus. But you will observe that far from being padded to rotundity his face is stiff from force of will, and lean from the effort of keeping it so. When his right arm rises, all the force in his veins flows straight from

shoulder to finger-tips; not an ounce is diverted into sudden impulses, sentimental regrets, wire-drawn distinctions. The busses punctually stop.

It is thus that we live, they say, driven by an unseizable force. They say that the novelists never catch it; that it goes hurtling through their nets and leaves them torn to ribbons. This, they say, is what we live by —this unseizable force.

"Where are the men?" said old General Gibbons, looking round the drawing-room, full as usual on Sunday afternoons of well-dressed people. "Where are the guns?"

Mrs. Durrant looked too.

Clara, thinking that her mother wanted her, came in; then went out again.

They were talking about Germany at the Durrants, and Jacob (driven by this unseizable force) walked rapidly down Hermes Street and ran straight into the Williamses.

"Oh!" cried Sandra, with a cordiality which she suddenly felt. And Evan added, "What luck!"

The dinner which they gave him in the hotel which looks on to the Square of the Constitution was excellent. Plated baskets contained fresh rolls. There was real butter. And the meat scarcely needed the disguise of innumerable little red and green vegetables glazed in sauce.

It was strange, though. There were the little tables set out at intervals on the scarlet floor with the Greek King's monogram wrought in yellow. Sandra dined in her hat, veiled as usual. Evan looked this way and that over his shoulder; imperturbable yet supple; and sometimes sighed. It was strange. For they were English people come together in Athens on a May evening. Jacob, helping himself to this and that, answered intelligently, yet with a ring in his voice.

The Williamses were going to Constantinople early next morning, they said.

"Before you are up," said Sandra.

They would leave Jacob alone, then. Turning very slightly, Evan ordered something—a bottle of wine—from which he helped Jacob, with a kind of solicitude, with a kind of paternal solicitude, if that were possible. To be left alone—that was good for a young fellow. Never was there a time when the country had more need of men. He sighed.

"And you have been to the Acropolis?" asked Sandra.

"Yes," said Jacob. And they moved off to the window together, while Evan spoke to the head waiter about calling them early.

"It is astonishing," said Jacob, in a gruff voice.

Sandra opened her eyes very slightly. Possibly her nostrils expanded a little too.

"At half-past six then," said Evan, coming towards them, looking as if he faced something in facing his wife and Jacob standing with their backs to the window.

Sandra smiled at him.

And, as he went to the window and had nothing to say she added, in broken half-sentences:

"Well, but how lovely—wouldn't it be? The Acropolis, Evan—or are you too tired?"

At that Evan looked at them, or, since Jacob was staring ahead of him, at his wife, surlily, sullenly, yet with a kind of distress—not that she would pity him. Nor would the implacable spirit of love, for anything he could do, cease its tortures.

They left him and he sat in the smoking-room, which looks out on to the Square of the Constitution.

"Evan is happier alone," said Sandra. "We have been separated from the newspapers. Well, it is better that people should have what they want. . . . You have seen all these wonderful things since we met. . . . What impression . . . I think that you are changed."

"You want to go to the Acropolis," said Jacob. "Up here then."

"One will remember it all one's life," said Sandra.

"Yes," said Jacob. "I wish you could have come in the day-time."

"This is more wonderful," said Sandra, waving her hand.

Jacob looked vaguely.

"But you should see the Parthenon in the day-time," he said. "You couldn't come to-morrow—it would be too early?"

"You have sat there for hours and hours by yourself?"

"There were some awful women this morning," said Jacob.

"Awful women?" Sandra echoed.

"Frenchwomen."

"But something very wonderful has happened," said Sandra. Ten minutes, fifteen minutes, half an hour—that was all the time before her.

"Yes," he said.

"When one is your age—when one is young. What will you do? You will fall in love—oh, yes! But don't be in too great a hurry. I am so much older."

She was brushed off the pavement by parading men.

"Shall we go on?" Jacob asked.

"Let us go on," she insisted.

For she could not stop until she had told him—or heard him say—or was it some action on his part that she required? Far away on the horizon she discerned it and could not rest.

"You'd never get English people to sit out like this," he said.

"Never—no. When you get back to England you won't forget this—or come with us to Constantinople!" she cried suddenly.

"But then . . ."

Sandra sighed.

"You must go to Delphi, of course," she said. "But," she asked herself, "what do I want from him? Perhaps it is something that I have missed. . . ."

"You will get there about six in the evening," she said. "You will see the eagles."

Jacob looked set and even desperate by the light at the street corner; and yet composed. He was suffering perhaps. He was credulous. Yet there was something caustic about him. He had in him the seeds of extreme disillusionment, which would come to him from women in middle life. Perhaps if one strove hard enough to reach the top of the hill it need not come to him—this disillusionment from women in middle life.

"The hotel is awful," she said. "The last visitors had left their basins full of dirty water. There is always that," she laughed.

"The people one meets *are* beastly," Jacob said.

His excitement was clear enough.

"Write and tell me about it," she said. "And tell me what you feel and what you think. Tell me everything."

The night was dark. The Acropolis was a jagged mound.

"I should like to, awfully," he said.

"When we get back to London, we shall meet . . ."

"Yes."

"I suppose they leave the gates open?" he asked.

"We could climb them!" she answered wildly.

Obscuring the moon and altogether darkening the Acropolis the clouds passed from east to west. The clouds solidified; the vapours thickened; the trailing veils stayed and accumulated.

It was dark now over Athens, except for gauzy red streaks where the streets ran; and the front of the Palace was cadaverous from electric light. At sea the piers stood out, marked by separate dots; the waves being invisible, and promontories and islands were dark humps with a few lights.

"I'd love to bring my brother, if I may," Jacob murmured.

"And then when your mother comes to London——," said Sandra.

The mainland of Greece was dark; and somewhere off Euboea a

cloud must have touched the waves and spattered them—the dolphins circling deeper and deeper into the sea. Violent was the wind now rushing down the Sea of Marmara between Greece and the plains of Troy.

In Greece and the uplands of Albania and Turkey, the wind scours the sand and the dust, and sows itself thick with dry particles. And then it pelts the smooth domes of the mosques, and makes the cypresses, standing stiff by the turbaned tombstones of Mohammedans, creak and bristle.

Sandra's veils were swirled about her.

"I will give you my copy," said Jacob. "Here. Will you keep it?"

(The book was the poems of Donne.)

Now the agitation of the air uncovered a racing star. Now it was dark. Now one after another lights were extinguished. Now great towns—Paris—Constantinople—London—were black as strewn rocks. Waterways might be distinguished. In England the trees were heavy in leaf. Here perhaps in some southern wood an old man lit dry ferns and the birds were startled. The sheep coughed; one flower bent slightly towards another. The English sky is softer, milkier than the Eastern. Something gentle has passed into it from the grass-rounded hills, something damp. The salt gale blew in at Betty Flanders' bedroom window, and the widow lady, raising herself slightly on her elbow, sighed like one who realizes, but would fain ward off a little longer—oh, a little longer!—the oppression of eternity.

But to return to Jacob and Sandra.

They had vanished. There was the Acropolis; but had they reached it? The columns and the Temple remain; the emotion of the living breaks fresh on them year after year; and of that what remains?

As for reaching the Acropolis who shall say that we ever do it, or that when Jacob woke next morning he found anything hard and durable to keep for ever? (Still, he went with them to Constantinople.)

Sandra Wentworth Williams certainly woke to find a copy of Donne's poems upon her dressing-table. And the book would be stood on the shelf in the English country house where Sally Duggan's *Life of Father Damien* in verse would join it one of these days. There were ten or twelve little volumes already. Strolling in at dusk, Sandra would open the books and her eyes would brighten (but not at the print), and subsiding into the arm-chair she would suck back again the soul of the moment; or, for sometimes she was restless, would pull out book after book and swing across the whole space of her life like an acrobat from bar to bar. She had had her moments. Meanwhile, the great clock on the landing ticked and Sandra would hear time accumulating, and ask herself, "What for? What for?"

"What for? What for?" Sandra would say, putting the book back, and strolling to the looking-glass and pressing her hair. And Miss Edwards would be startled at dinner, as she opened her mouth to admit roast mutton, by Sandra's sudden solicitude: "Are you happy, Miss Edwards?"—a thing Cissy Edwards hadn't thought of for years.

"What for? What for?" Jacob never asked himself any such question, to judge by the way he laced his boots; shaved himself; to judge by the depth of his sleep that night, with the wind fidgeting at the shutters, and half-a-dozen mosquitoes singing in his ears. He was young—a man. And then Sandra was right when she judged him to be credulous as yet. At forty it might be a different matter. Already he had marked the things he liked in Donne, and they were savage enough. However, you might place beside them passages of the purest poetry in Shakespeare.

But the wind was rolling the darkness through the streets of Athens, rolling it, one might suppose, with a sort of trampling energy of mood which forbids too close an analysis of the feelings of any single person, or inspection of features. All faces—Greek, Levantine, Turkish, English—would have looked much the same in that darkness. At length the columns and the Temples whiten, yellow, turn rose; and the Pyramids and St. Peter's arise, and at last sluggish St. Paul's looms up.

The Christians have the right to rouse most cities with their interpretation of the day's meaning. Then, less melodiously, dissenters of different sects issue a cantankerous emendation. The steamers, resounding like gigantic tuning-forks, state the old old fact—how there is a sea coldly, greenly, swaying outside. But nowadays it is the thin voice of duty, piping in a white thread from the top of a funnel, that collects the largest multitudes, and night is nothing but a long-drawn sigh between hammer-strokes, a deep breath—you can hear it from an open window even in the heart of London.

But who, save the nerve-worn and sleepless, or thinkers standing with hands to the eyes on some crag above the multitude, see things thus in skeleton outline, bare of flesh? In Surbiton the skeleton is wrapped in flesh.

"The kettle never boils so well on a sunny morning," says Mrs. Grandage, glancing at the clock on the mantelpiece. Then the grey Persian cat stretches itself on the window-seat, and buffets a moth with soft round paws. And before breakfast is half over (they were late to-day) a baby is deposited in her lap, and she must guard the sugar basin while Tom Grandage reads the golfing article in the *Times*, sips his coffee, wipes his moustaches, and is off to the office, where he is the greatest authority upon the foreign exchanges and marked for promotion.

The skeleton is well wrapped in flesh. Even this dark night when the wind rolls the darkness through Lombard Street and Fetter Lane and Bedford Square it stirs (since it is summer-time and the height of the season) plane trees spangled with electric light, and curtains still preserving the room from the dawn. People still murmur over the last word said on the staircase, or strain, all through their dreams, for the voice of the alarum clock. So when the wind roams through a forest innumerable twigs stir; hives are brushed; insects sway on grass blades; the spider runs rapidly up a crease in the bark; and the whole air is tremulous with breathing; elastic with filaments.

Only here—in Lombard Street and Fetter Lane and Bedford Square —each insect carries a globe of the world in his head, and the webs of the forest are schemes evolved for the smooth conduct of business; and honey is treasure of one sort and another; and the stir in the air is the indescribable agitation of life.

But colour returns; runs up the stalks of the grass; blows out into tulips and crocuses; solidly stripes the tree trunks; and fills the gauze of the air and the grasses and pools.

The Bank of England emerges; and the Monument with its bristling head of golden hair; the dray horses crossing London Bridge show grey and strawberry and iron-coloured. There is a whir of wings as the suburban trains rush into the terminus. And the light mounts over the faces of all the tall blind houses, slides through a chink and paints the lustrous bellying crimson curtains; the green wine-glasses; the coffee-cups; and the chairs standing askew.

Sunlight strikes in upon shaving-glasses; and gleaming brass cans; upon all the jolly trappings of the day; the bright, inquisitive, armoured, resplendent, summer's day, which has long since vanquished chaos; which has dried the melancholy mediæval mists; drained the swamp and stood glass and stone upon it; and equipped our brains and bodies with such an armoury of weapons that merely to see the flash and thrust of limbs engaged in the conduct of daily life is better than the old pageant of armies drawn out in battle array upon the plain.

§ 13

"The height of the season," said Bonamy.

The sun had already blistered the paint on the backs of the green chairs in Hyde Park; peeled the bark off the plane trees; and turned the earth to powder and to smooth yellow pebbles. Hyde Park was circled, incessantly, by turning wheels.

"The height of the season," said Bonamy sarcastically.

He was sarcastic because of Clara Durrant; because Jacob had come back from Greece very brown and lean, with his pockets full of Greek notes, which he pulled out when the chair man came for pence; because Jacob was silent.

"He has not said a word to show that he is glad to see me," thought Bonamy bitterly.

The motor-cars passed incessantly over the bridge of the Serpentine; the upper classes walked upright, or bent themselves gracefully over the palings; the lower classes lay with their knees cocked up, flat on their backs; the sheep grazed on pointed wooden legs; small children ran down the sloping grass, stretched their arms, and fell.

"Very urbane," Jacob brought out.

"Urbane," on the lips of Jacob had mysteriously all the shapeliness of a character which Bonamy thought daily more sublime, devastating, terrific than ever, though he was still, and perhaps would be for ever, barbaric, obscure.

What superlatives! What adjectives! How acquit Bonamy of sentimentality of the grossest sort; of being tossed like a cork on the waves; of having no steady insight into character; of being unsupported by reason, and of drawing no comfort whatever from the works of the classics?

"The height of civilization," said Jacob.

He was fond of using Latin words.

Magnanimity, virtue—such words when Jacob used them in talk with Bonamy meant that he took control of the situation; that Bonamy would play round him like an affectionate spaniel; and that (as likely as not) they would end by rolling on the floor.

"And Greece?" said Bonamy. "The Parthenon and all that?"

"There's none of this European mysticism," said Jacob.

"It's the atmosphere, I suppose," said Bonamy. "And you went to Constantinople?"

"Yes," said Jacob.

Bonamy paused, moved a pebble; then darted in with the rapidity and certainty of a lizard's tongue.

"You are in love!" he exclaimed.

Jacob blushed.

The sharpest of knives never cut so deep.

As for responding, or taking the least account of it, Jacob stared straight ahead of him, fixed, monolithic—oh, very beautiful!—like a British Admiral, exclaimed Bonamy in a rage, rising from his seat and walking off; waiting for some sound; none came; too proud to look back; walking quicker and quicker until he found himself gazing into motor cars and cursing women. Where was the pretty woman's

face? Clara's—Fanny's—Florinda's? Who was the pretty little
creature?

Not Clara Durrant.

The Aberdeen terrier must be exercised, and as Mr. Bowley was
going that very moment—would like nothing better than a walk—they
went together, Clara and kind little Bowley—Bowley who had rooms
in the Albany, Bowley who wrote letters to the *Times* in a jocular vein
about foreign hotels and the Aurora Borealis—Bowley who liked young
people and walked down Piccadilly with his right arm resting on the
boss of his back.

"Little demon!" cried Clara, and attached Troy to his chain.

Bowley anticipated—hoped for—a confidence. Devoted to her
mother, Clara sometimes felt her a little, well, her mother was so sure
of herself that she could not understand other people being—being
—"as ludicrous as I am," Clara jerked out (the dog tugging her for-
wards). And Bowley thought she looked like a huntress and turned
over in his mind which it should be—some pale virgin with a slip of
the moon in her hair, which was a flight for Bowley.

The colour was in her cheeks. To have spoken outright about her
mother—still, it was only to Mr. Bowley, who loved her, as everybody
must; but to speak was unnatural to her, yet it was awful to feel, as
she had done all day, that she *must* tell some one.

"Wait till we cross the road," she said to the dog, bending down.

Happily she had recovered by that time.

"She thinks so much about England," she said. "She is so anx-
ious——"

Bowley was defrauded as usual. Clara never confided to any one.

"Why don't the young people settle it, eh?" he wanted to ask.
"What's all this about England?"—a question poor Clara could not
have answered, since, as Mrs. Durrant discussed with Sir Edgar the
policy of Sir Edward Grey, Clara only wondered why the cabinet
looked dusty, and Jacob had never come. Oh, here was Mrs. Cowley
Johnson . . .

And Clara would hand the pretty china teacups, and smile at the
compliment—that no one in London made tea so well as she did.

"We get it at Brocklebank's," she said, "in Cursitor Street."

Ought she not to be grateful? Ought she not to be happy? Espe-
cially since her mother looked so well and enjoyed so much talking to
Sir Edgar about Morocco, Venezuela, or some such place.

"Jacob! Jacob!" thought Clara; and kind Mr. Bowley, who was
ever so good with old ladies, looked; stopped; wondered whether
Elizabeth wasn't too harsh with her daughter; wondered about

Bonamy, Jacob—which young fellow was it?—and jumped up directly Clara said she must exercise Troy.

They had reached the site of the old Exhibition. They looked at the tulips. Stiff and curled, the little rods of waxy smoothness rose from the earth, nourished yet contained, suffused with scarlet and coral pink. Each had its shadow; each grew trimly in the diamond-shaped wedge as the gardener had planned it.

"Barnes never gets them to grow like that," Clara mused; she sighed.

"You are neglecting your friends," said Bowley, as some one, going the other way, lifted his hat. She started; acknowledged Mr. Lionel Parry's bow; wasted on him what had sprung for Jacob.

("Jacob! Jacob!" she thought.)

"But you'll get run over if I let you go," she said to the dog.

"England seems all right," said Mr. Bowley.

The loop of the railing beneath the statue of Achilles was full of parasols and waistcoats; chains and bangles; of ladies and gentlemen, lounging elegantly, lightly observant.

" 'This statue was erected by the women of England . . .' " Clara read out with a foolish little laugh. "Oh, Mr. Bowley! Oh!" Gallop—gallop—gallop—a horse galloped past without a rider. The stirrups swung; the pebbles spurted.

"Oh, stop! Stop it, Mr. Bowley!" she cried, white, trembling, gripping his arm, utterly unconscious, the tears coming.

"Tut-tut!" said Mr. Bowley in his dressing-room an hour later. "Tut-tut!"—a comment that was profound enough, though inarticulately expressed, since his valet was handing his shirt studs.

Julia Eliot, too, had seen the horse run away, and had risen from her seat to watch the end of the incident, which, since she came of a sporting family, seemed to her slightly ridiculous. Sure enough the little man came pouncing behind with his breeches dusty; looked thoroughly annoyed; and was being helped to mount by a policeman when Julia Eliot, with a sardonic smile, turned towards the Marble Arch on her errand of mercy. It was only to visit a sick old lady who had known her mother and perhaps the Duke of Wellington; for Julia shared the love of her sex for the distressed; liked to visit death-beds; threw slippers at weddings; received confidences by the dozen; knew more pedigrees than a scholar knows dates, and was one of the kindliest, most generous, least continent of women.

Yet five minutes after she had passed the statue of Achilles she had the rapt look of one brushing through crowds on a summer's afternoon,

when the trees are rustling, the wheels churning yellow, and the tumult of the present seems like an elegy for past youth and past summers, and there rose in her mind a curious sadness, as if time and eternity showed through skirts and waistcoats, and she saw people passing tragically to destruction. Yet, Heaven knows, Julia was no fool. A sharper woman at a bargain did not exist. She was always punctual. The watch on her wrist gave her twelve minutes and a half in which to reach Bruton Street. Lady Congreve expected her at five.

The gilt clock at Verrey's was striking five.

Florinda looked at it with a dull expression, like an animal. She looked at the clock; looked at the door; looked at the long glass opposite; disposed her cloak; drew closer to the table, for she was pregnant—no doubt about it, Mother Stuart said, recommending remedies, consulting friends; sunk, caught by the heel, as she tripped so lightly over the surface.

Her tumbler of pinkish sweet stuff was set down by the waiter; and she sucked, through a straw, her eyes on the looking-glass, on the door, now soothed by the sweet taste. When Nick Bramham came in it was plain, even to the young Swiss waiter, that there was a bargain between them. Nick hitched his clothes together clumsily; ran his fingers through his hair; sat down, to an ordeal, nervously. She looked at him; and set off laughing; laughed—laughed—laughed. The young Swiss waiter, standing with crossed legs by the pillar, laughed too.

The door opened; in came the roar of Regent Street, the roar of traffic, impersonal, unpitying; and sunshine grained with dirt. The Swiss waiter must see to the newcomers. Bramham lifted his glass.

"He's like Jacob," said Florinda, looking at the newcomer.

"The way he stares." She stopped laughing.

Jacob, leaning forward, drew a plan of the Parthenon in the dust in Hyde Park, a network of strokes at least, which may have been the Parthenon, or again a mathematical diagram. And why was the pebble so emphatically ground in at the corner? It was not to count his notes that he took out a wad of papers and read a long flowing letter which Sandra had written two days ago at Milton Dower House with his book before her and in her mind the memory of something said or attempted, some moment in the dark on the road to the Acropolis which (such was her creed) mattered for ever.

"He is," she mused, "like that man in Molière."

She meant Alceste. She meant that he was severe. She meant that she could deceive him.

"Or could I not?" she thought, putting the poems of Donne back in the bookcase. "Jacob," she went on, going to the window and look-

ing over the spotted flower-beds across the grass where the piebald cows grazed under beech trees, "Jacob would be shocked."

The perambulator was going through the little gate in the railing. She kissed her hand; directed by the nurse, Jimmy waved his.

"*He's* a small boy," she said, thinking of Jacob.

And yet—Alceste?

"What a nuisance you are!" Jacob grumbled, stretching out first one leg and then the other and feeling in each trouser-pocket for his chair ticket.

"I expect the sheep have eaten it," he said. "Why do you keep sheep?"

"Sorry to disturb you, sir," said the ticket-collector, his hand deep in the enormous pouch of pence.

"Well, I hope they pay you for it," said Jacob. "There you are. No. You can stick to it. Go and get drunk."

He had parted with half-a-crown, tolerantly, compassionately, with considerable contempt for his species.

Even now poor Fanny Elmer was dealing, as she walked along the Strand, in her incompetent way with this very careless, indifferent, sublime manner he had of talking to railway guards or porters; or Mrs. Whitehorn, when she consulted him about her little boy who was beaten by the schoolmaster.

Sustained entirely upon picture post cards for the past two months, Fanny's idea of Jacob was more statuesque, noble, and eyeless than ever. To reinforce her vision she had taken to visiting the British Museum, where, keeping her eyes downcast until she was alongside of the battered Ulysses, she opened them and got a fresh shock of Jacob's presence, enough to last her half a day. But this was wearing thin. And she wrote now—poems, letters that were never posted, saw his face in advertisements on hoardings, and would cross the road to let the barrel-organ turn her musings to rhapsody. But at breakfast (she shared rooms with a teacher), when the butter was smeared about the plate, and the prongs of the forks were clotted with old egg yolk, she revised these visions violently; was, in truth, very cross; was losing her complexion, as Margery Jackson told her, bringing the whole thing down (as she laced her stout boots) to a level of mother-wit, vulgarity, and sentiment, for she had loved too; and been a fool.

"One's godmothers ought to have told one," said Fanny, looking in at the window of Bacon, the mapseller, in the Strand—told one that it is no use making a fuss; this is life, they should have said, as Fanny said it now, looking at the large yellow globe marked with steamship lines.

"This is life. This is life," said Fanny.

"A very hard face," thought Miss Barrett, on the other side of the glass, buying maps of the Syrian desert and waiting impatiently to be served. "Girls look old so soon nowadays."

The equator swam behind tears.

"Piccadilly?" Fanny asked the conductor of the omnibus, and climbed to the top. After all, he would, he must, come back to her.

But Jacob might have been thinking of Rome; of architecture; of jurisprudence; as he sat under the plane tree in Hyde Park.

The omnibus stopped outside Charing Cross; and behind it were clogged omnibuses, vans, motor-cars, for a procession with banners was passing down Whitehall, and elderly people were stiffly descending from between the paws of the slippery lions, where they had been testifying to their faith, singing lustily, raising their eyes from their music to look into the sky, and still their eyes were on the sky as they marched behind the gold letters of their creed.

The traffic stopped, and the sun, no longer sprayed out by the breeze, became almost too hot. But the procession passed; the banners glittered far away down Whitehall; the traffic was released; lurched on; spun to a smooth continuous uproar; swerving round the curve of Cockspur Street; and sweeping past Government offices and esquetrian statues down Whitehall to the prickly spires, the tethered grey fleet of masonry, and the large white clock of Westminster.

Five strokes Big Ben intoned; Nelson received the salute. The wires of the Admiralty shivered with some far-away communication. A voice kept remarking that Prime Ministers and Viceroys spoke in the Reichstag; entered Lahore; said that the Emperor travelled; in Milan they rioted; said there were rumours in Vienna; said that the Ambassador at Constantinople had audience with the Sultan; the fleet was at Gibraltar. The voice continued, imprinting on the faces of the clerks in Whitehall (Timothy Durrant was one of them) something of its own inexorable gravity, as they listened, deciphered, wrote down. Papers accumulated, inscribed with the utterances of Kaisers, the statistics of rice-fields, the growling of hundreds of work-people, plotting sedition in back streets, or gathering in the Calcutta bazaars, or mustering their forces in the uplands of Albania, where the hills are sand-coloured, and bones lie unburied.

The voice spoke plainly in the square quiet room with heavy tables, where one elderly man made notes on the margin of type-written sheets, his silver-topped umbrella leaning against the bookcase.

His head—bald, red-veined, hollow-looking—represented all the heads in the building. His head, with the amiable pale eyes, carried the burden of knowledge across the street; laid it before his colleagues, who

came equally burdened; and then the sixteen gentlemen, lifting their pens or turning perhaps rather wearily in their chairs, decreed that the course of history should shape itself this way or that way, being manfully determined, as their faces showed, to impose some coherency upon Rajahs and Kaisers and the muttering in bazaars, the secret gatherings, plainly visible in Whitehall, of kilted peasants in Albanian uplands; to control the course of events.

Pitt and Chatham, Burke and Gladstone looked from side to side with fixed marble eyes and an air of immortal quiescence which perhaps the living may have envied, the air being full of whistling and concussions, as the procession with its banners passed down Whitehall. Moreover, some were troubled with dyspepsia; one had at that very moment cracked the glass of his spectacles; another spoke in Glasgow to-morrow; altogether they looked too red, fat, pale or lean, to be dealing, as the marble heads had dealt, with the course of history.

Timmy Durrant in his little room in the Admiralty, going to consult a Blue book, stopped for a moment by the window, and observed the placard tied round the lamp-post.

Miss Thomas, one of the typists, said to her friend that if the Cabinet was going to sit much longer she should miss her boy outside the Gaiety.

Timmy Durrant, returning with his Blue book under his arm, noticed a little knot of people at the street corner; conglomerated as though one of them knew something; and the others, pressing round him, looked up, looked down, looked along the street. What was it that he knew?

Timothy, placing the Blue book before him, studied a paper sent round by the Treasury for information. Mr. Crawley, his fellow-clerk, impaled a letter on a skewer.

Jacob rose from his chair in Hyde Park, tore his ticket to pieces, and walked away.

"Such a sunset," wrote Mrs. Flanders in her letter to Archer at Singapore. "One couldn't make up one's mind to come indoors," she wrote. "It seemed wicked to waste even a moment."

The long windows of Kensington Palace flushed fiery rose as Jacob walked away; a flock of wild duck flew over the Serpentine; and the trees were stood against the sky, blackly, magnificently.

"Jacob," wrote Mrs. Flanders, with the red light on her page, "is hard at work after his delightful journey . . ."

"The Kaiser," the far-away voice remarked in Whitehall, "received me in audience."

"Now I know that face——" said the Reverend Andrew Floyd, coming out of Carter's shop in Piccadilly, "but who the dickens——?" and he watched Jacob, turned round to look at him, but could not be sure——

"Oh, Jacob Flanders!" he remembered in a flash.

But he was so tall; so unconscious; such a fine young fellow.

"I gave him Byron's works," Andrew Floyd mused, and started forward, as Jacob crossed the road; but hesitated, and let the moment pass, and lost the opportunity.

Another procession, without banners, was blocking Long Acre. Carriages, with dowagers in amethyst and gentlemen spotted with carnations, intercepted cabs and motor-cars turned in the opposite direction, in which jaded men in white waistcoats lolled, on their way home to shrubberies and billiard-rooms in Putney and Wimbledon.

Two barrel-organs played by the kerb, and horses coming out of Aldridge's with white labels on their buttocks straddled across the road and were smartly jerked back.

Mrs. Durrant, sitting with Mr. Wortley in a motor-car, was impatient lest they should miss the overture.

But Mr. Wortley, always urbane, always in time for the overture, buttoned his gloves, and admired Miss Clara.

"A shame to spend such a night in the theatre!" said Mrs. Durrant, seeing all the windows of the coach-makers in Long Acre ablaze.

"Think of your moors!" said Mr. Wortley to Clara.

"Ah! but Clara likes this better," Mrs. Durrant laughed.

"I don't know—really," said Clara, looking at the blazing windows. She started.

She saw Jacob.

"Who?" asked Mrs. Durrant sharply, leaning forward.

But she saw no one.

Under the arch of the Opera House large faces and lean ones, the powdered and the hairy, all alike were red in the sunset; and, quickened by the great hanging lamps with their repressed primrose lights, by the tramp, and the scarlet, and the pompous ceremony, some ladies looked for a moment into steaming bedrooms near by, where women with loose hair leaned out of windows, where girls—where children —(the long mirrors held the ladies suspended) but one must follow; one must not block the way.

Clara's moors were fine enough. The Phoenicians slept under their piled grey rocks; the chimneys of the old mines pointed starkly; early moths blurred the heather-bells; cart-wheels could be heard grinding

on the road far beneath; and the suck and sighing of the waves sounded gently, persistently, for ever.

Shading her eyes with her hand Mrs. Pascoe stood in her cabbage-garden looking out to sea. Two steamers and a sailing-ship crossed each other; passed each other; and in the bay the gulls kept alighting on a log, rising high, returning again to the log, while some rode in upon the waves and stood on the rim of the water until the moon blanched all to whiteness.

Mrs. Pascoe had gone indoors long ago.

But the red light was on the columns of the Parthenon, and the Greek women who were knitting their stockings and sometimes crying to a child to come and have the insects picked from its head were as jolly as sand-martins in the heat, quarrelling, scolding, suckling their babies, until the ships in the Piraeus fired their guns.

The sound spread itself flat, and then went tunnelling its way with fitful explosions among the channels of the islands.

Darkness drops like a knife over Greece.

"The guns?" said Betty Flanders, half asleep, getting out of bed and going to the window, which was decorated with a fringe of dark leaves.

"Not at this distance," she thought. "It is the sea."

Again, far away, she heard the dull sound, as if nocturnal women were beating great carpets. There was Morty lost, and Seabrook dead; her sons fighting for their country. But were the chickens safe? Was that some one moving downstairs? Rebecca with the toothache? No. The nocturnal women were beating great carpets. Her hens shifted slightly on their perches.

§ 14

"He left everything just as it was," Bonamy marvelled. "Nothing arranged. All his letters strewn about for any one to read. What did he expect? Did he think he would come back?" he mused, standing in the middle of Jacob's room.

The eighteenth century has its distinction. These houses were built, say, a hundred and fifty years ago. The rooms are shapely, the ceilings high; over the doorways a rose or a ram's skull is carved in the wood. Even the panels, painted in raspberry-coloured paint, have their distinction.

Bonamy took up a bill for a hunting-crop.

"That seems to be paid," he said.

There were Sandra's letters.

Mrs. Durrant was taking a party to Greenwich.

Lady Rocksbier hoped for the pleasure . . .

Listless is the air in an empty room, just swelling the curtain; the flowers in the jar shift. One fibre in the wicker arm-chair creaks, though no one sits there.

Bonamy crossed to the window. Pickford's van swung down the street. The omnibuses were locked together at Mudie's corner. Engines throbbed, and carters, jamming the brakes down, pulled their horses sharp up. A harsh and unhappy voice cried something unintelligible. And then suddenly all the leaves seemed to raise themselves.

"Jacob! Jacob!" cried Bonamy, standing by the window. The leaves sank down again.

"Such confusion everywhere!" exclaimed Betty Flanders, bursting open the bedroom door.

Bonamy turned away from the window.

"What am I to do with these, Mr. Bonamy?"

She held out a pair of Jacob's old shoes.

The Aspern Papers

HENRY JAMES

HENRY JAMES *was born in New York City on April 15,*
1843. He was educated for the most part abroad, studying
under tutors; then at the University at Bonn. He returned
to this country in 1862, and since a physical infirmity pre-
vented his enlisting, he went on to Cambridge where he
studied at the Harvard Law School and came both socially
and intellectually under the influence of Charles Eliot Nor-
ton and William Dean Howells. His first story appeared
in the Atlantic Monthly *in 1865. Thereafter, as literature*
claimed him, he made his headquarters in London, where
in the 1880s the best of his fifty volumes were written. The
Aspern Papers, *which appeared in 1888, measures 42,000*
words.

INTRODUCTION

With Henry James, as with Joseph Conrad, I was faced with an embarrassment of riches. Each man had done much of his best work in the short novel, and with so many to choose from I simply had to play my favorites.

There were two good reasons for selecting *The Aspern Papers*. In the first place, it is unquestionably the best literary detective story that has yet been written by an American. Secondly, the narrative, which was written in 1887, marked the peak of James's early power. In that year he was working on three short novels; he was in his early forties, refreshed from seven delightful months in Florence and Venice where he had lived for a time in Browning's old apartment and then later in the splendid old Palazzo Barbaro. Finally, material circumstances have their bearing upon any book and at the time he wrote *The Aspern Papers,* Henry James was trying hard to secure a wider public for his work. As he wrote to William Dean Howells, "I am still staggering a good deal under the mysterious and (to me) inexplicable injury wrought—apparently—upon my situation by my two last novels, the *Bostonians* and the *Princess,* from which I expected so much and derived so little. They have reduced the desire, and the demand, for my productions to zero—as I judge from the fact that though I have for a good while past been writing a number of good short things, I remain irremediably unpublished. However, I don't despair, for I think I am now really in better form than I have ever been in my life, and I propose yet to do many things." James was short of funds and more than ever determined to advance his reputation. In this predicament he was compelled to give as much—perhaps even more—attention to his narrative than he did to the refinement of his style. James always indulged in qualifying phrases; he wrote without

the lyrical ear and with a kind of searching hesitation for the idea or picture he had in mind. But at this stage in his career there was not that condescension in his voice which is heard later, when he had acquired the habit of modifying and explaining endlessly, with a subtlety infuriating to the more direct reader.

On one of his earlier visits to Italy, James had discovered that Jane Clairmont (half-sister of Mary Godwin), for a time the mistress of Byron and the mother of his daughter Allegra, was still living as an ancient recluse in Florence. Henry James never saw her. But the fact that Jane Clairmont had lived on, into his own day, preserving her rich associations with Byron and Shelley and, so far as one could tell, preserving her letters, perhaps a journal, became for him a romantic cocoon from which this short novel was to emerge. It is easy to see how his mind flirted with the situation. Suppose Jane Clairmont had been in love not with an English but with an American poet— call him Jeffrey Aspern—and suppose that Henry James, an American man of letters, had appointed himself the biographer of Aspern, the poet. You can see at once how important it would be for him to break through the old lady's reticence and, invading her hermitage by one means or another, secure before she died those literary papers which might throw such light upon the past. Here was an assignment which would challenge any detective, and with these thoughts, Henry James set himself to work.

As I have said, the novelist substituted an American poet, Jeffrey Aspern, for Lord Byron. Aspern pays his first visit to Europe in 1820, which identifies him at once with the romantic poets. He has been long dead by the time the novel opens. But he is an American, and that point was important to James, who was not at that stage trying to live it down. "Jeffrey Aspern isn't even feebly localized," he wrote, "but I *thought* New York as I wrote him." To complicate the chase, the novelist allows for the possibility that Jane's daughter Allegra might have lived. In short, Jane Clairmont, now in her nineties and very feeble, becomes that "wasted antiquity" the elder Miss Bordereau, who is now defended and now betrayed by her niece Miss Tina. The biographer from America comes to Venice, hot on the scent and sure that literary remains of inestimable value have been secreted somewhere in the old palazzo occupied by the Misses Bordereau. With no little skill he forces himself upon their hospitality, being careful to use an assumed name. In his first meeting with the old lady, baffled somewhat by the fact that her features are concealed by a green eye-shade and by the momentary suspicion that she sees through his stratagem, he arranges to live with them as a paying guest—and the reader chuckles at the price he has to pay. In the nearness of success he boasts to a

friend in Venice that if necessary he will make love to the niece in order to gain the Aspern Papers. Thus, he is competing against three adversaries, suspicious old Juliana, who has all the tyranny of age; timid Miss Tina; and Death, which may intervene at any moment.

It is a tribute to the fine craftsmanship of Henry James that before you have gone many pages you yourself have a feverish interest in the pursuit. You *know* that the relics are there, you feel that the young American deserves them—at least he won't abuse them—and you apprehend that the old lady is going to keep them out of his clutches if she can possibly do so. A lesser novelist would have destroyed this tension by too-frequent encounters between the opposing forces. But James, who is a master of subtlety, keeps your interest on the rise. The young biographer in his apartment is as far apart from the ladies as if they lived in separate towns. Between them stretch the vast, silent corridors of the palazzo, and an air of musty mystery which the novelist reproduces with incredible skill. So well are you held in suspense, so rare are the encounters, that you must check the impulse to page ahead in order to see what happens. As you read, you feel how slow-going is the life in Venice. "There could be no Venetian business without patience," writes the novelist, "and since I adored the place I was much more in the spirit of it for having laid in a large provision. That spirit kept me perpetual company and seemed to look out at me from the revived immortal face—in which all his genius shone—of the great poet who was my prompter. I had invoked him and he had come; he hovered before me half the time. It was as if he had said: 'Poor dear, be easy with her; she has some natural prejudices; only give her time. Strange as it may appear to you, she was very attractive in 1820. Meanwhile aren't we in Venice together . . . See how it glows with the advancing summer; how the sky and the sea and the rosy air and the marble of the palaces all shimmer and melt together.' "

In no one of his stories has James ever been more successful in invoking that spirit of the place for which he was famous. Here is the dilapidated palazzo overlooking its "clean, melancholy, rather lonely canal"; here are the golden days in the arbor, as the American "worked and waited and mused and hoped, while the golden hours elapsed and the plants drank in the light and the inscrutable old palace turned pale and then, as the day waned, began to recover and flush and my papers rustled in the wandering breeze of the Adriatic"; and here is the imperishable beauty of Venice, "without streets and vehicles, the uproar of wheels, the brutality of horses, and with its little winding ways where people crowd together, where voices sound as in the corridors of a house, where the human step circulates as if it skirted the angles of furniture and shoes never wear out . . ."

§ I

I HAD TAKEN Mrs. Prest into my confidence; without her in truth I should have made but little advance, for the fruitful idea in the whole business dropped from her friendly lips. It was she who found the short cut and loosed the Gordian knot. It is not supposed easy for women to rise to the large free view of anything, anything to be done; but they sometimes throw off a bold conception—such as a man would n't have risen to—with singular serenity. "Simply make them take you in on the footing of a lodger"—I don't think that unaided I should have risen to that. I was beating about the bush, trying to be ingenious, wondering by what combination of arts I might become an acquaintance, when she offered this happy suggestion that the way to become an acquaintance was first to become an intimate. Her actual knowledge of the Misses Bordereau was scarcely larger than mine, and indeed I had brought with me from England some definite facts that were new to her. Their name had been mixed up ages before with one of the greatest names of the century, and they now lived obscurely in Venice, lived on very small means, unvisited, unapproachable, in a sequestered and dilapidated old palace: this was the substance of my friend's impression of them. She herself had been established in Venice some fifteen years and had done a great deal of good there; but the circle of her benevolence had never embraced the two shy, mysterious and, as was somehow supposed, scarcely respectable Americans—they were believed to have lost in their long exile all national quality, besides being as their name implied of some remoter French affiliation—who asked no favours and desired no attention. In the early years of her residence she had made an attempt to see them, but this had been successful only as regards the little one, as Mrs. Prest called the niece; though in fact I afterwards found her the bigger of the two in inches. She had heard Miss Bordereau was ill and had a suspicion she was in want, and had gone to the house to offer aid, so that if there were suffering, American suffering in particular, she should n't have it on

her conscience. The "little one" had received her in the great cold tarnished Venetian *sala,* the central hall of the house, paved with marble and roofed with dim cross-beams, and had n't even asked her to sit down. This was not encouraging for me, who wished to sit so fast, and I remarked as much to Mrs. Prest. She replied, however, with profundity "Ah, but there 's all the difference: I went to confer a favour and you 'll go to ask one. If they 're proud you 'll be on the right side." And she offered to show me their house to begin with— to row me thither in her gondola. I let her know I had already been to look at it half a dozen times; but I accepted her invitation, for it charmed me to hover about the place. I had made my way to it the day after my arrival in Venice—it had been described to me in advance by the friend in England to whom I owed definite information as to their possession of the papers—laying siege to it with my eyes while I considered my plan of campaign. Jeffrey Aspern had never been in it that I knew of, but some note of his voice seemed to abide there by a roundabout implication and in a "dying fall."

Mrs. Prest knew nothing about the papers, but was interested in my curiosity, as always in the joys and sorrows of her friends. As we went, however, in her gondola, gliding there under the sociable hood with the bright Venetian picture framed on either side by the moveable window, I saw how my eagerness amused her and that she found my interest in my possible spoil a fine case of monomania. "One would think you expected from it the answer to the riddle of the universe," she said; and I denied the impeachment only by replying that if I had to choose between that precious solution and a bundle of Jeffrey Aspern's letters I knew indeed which would appear to me the greater boon. She pretended to make light of his genius and I took no pains to defend him. One does n't defend one's god: one's god is in himself a defence. Besides, to-day, after his long comparative obscuration, he hangs high in the heaven of our literature for all the world to see; he's a part of the light by which we walk. The most I said was that he was no doubt not a woman's poet: to which she rejoined aptly enough that he had been at least Miss Bordereau's. The strange thing had been for me to discover in England that she was still alive: it was as if I had been told Mrs. Siddons was, or Queen Caroline, or the famous Lady Hamilton, for it seemed to me that she belonged to a generation as extinct. "Why she must be tremendously old—at least a hundred," I had said; but on coming to consider dates I saw it not strictly involved that she should have far exceeded the common span. None the less she was of venerable age and her relations with Jeffrey Aspern had occurred in her early womanhood. "That's her excuse," said Mrs. Prest half sententiously and yet also somewhat as if she were ashamed

of making a speech so little in the real tone of Venice. As if a woman needed an excuse for having loved the divine poet! He had been not only one of the most brilliant minds of his day—and in those years, when the century was young, there were, as every one knows, many— but one of the most genial men and one of the handsomest.

The niece, according to Mrs. Prest, was of minor antiquity, and the conjecture was risked that she was only a grand-niece. This was possible; I had nothing but my share in the very limited knowledge of my English fellow-worshipper John Cumnor, who had never seen the couple. The world, as I say, had recognised Jeffrey Aspern, but Cumnor and I had recognised him most. The multitude to-day flocked to his temple, but of that temple he and I regarded ourselves as the appointed ministers. We held, justly, as I think, that we had done more for his memory than any one else, and had done it simply by opening lights into his life. He had nothing to fear from us because he had nothing to fear from the truth, which alone at such a distance of time we could be interested in establishing. His early death had been the only dark spot, as it were, on his fame, unless the papers in Miss Bordereau's hands should perversely bring out others. There had been an impression about 1825 that he had "treated her badly," just as there had been an impression that he had "served," as the London populace says, several other ladies in the same masterful way. Each of these cases Cumnor and I had been able to investigate, and we had never failed to acquit him conscientiously of any grossness. I judged him perhaps more indulgently than my friend; certainly, at any rate, it appeared to me that no man could have walked straighter in the given circumstances. These had been almost always difficult and dangerous. Half the women of his time, to speak liberally, had flung themselves at his head, and while the fury raged—the more that it was very catching—accidents, some of them grave, had not failed to occur. He was not a woman's poet, as I had said to Mrs. Prest, in the modern phase of his reputation; but the situation had been different when the man's own voice was mingled with his song. That voice, by every testimony, was one of the most charming ever heard. "Orpheus and the Mænads!" had been of course my foreseen judgement when first I turned over his correspondence. Almost all the Mænads were unreasonable and many of them unbearable; it struck me that he had been kinder and more considerate than in his place—if I could imagine myself in any such box—I should have found the trick of.

It was certainly strange beyond all strangeness, and I shall not take up space with attempting to explain it, that whereas among all these other relations and in these other directions of research we had to deal with phantoms and dust, the mere echoes of echoes, the one living

source of information that had lingered on into our time had been unheeded by us. Every one of Aspern's contemporaries had, according to our belief, passed away; we had not been able to look into a single pair of eyes into which his had looked or to feel a transmitted contact in any aged hand that his had touched. Most dead of all did poor Miss Bordereau appear, and yet she alone had survived. We exhausted in the course of months our wonder that we had not found her out sooner, and the substance of our explanation was that she had kept so quiet. The poor lady on the whole had had reason for doing so. But it was a revelation to us that self-effacement on such a scale had been possible in the latter half of the nineteenth century—the age of newspapers and telegrams and photographs and interviewers. She had taken no great trouble for it either—hadn't hidden herself away in an undiscoverable hole, had boldly settled down in a city of exhibition.

The one apparent secret of her safety had been that Venice contained so many much greater curiosities. And then accident had somehow favoured her, as was shown for example in the fact that Mrs. Prest had never happened to name her to me, though I had spent three weeks in Venice—under her nose, as it were—five years before. My friend indeed had not named her much to any one; she appeared almost to have forgotten the fact of her continuance. Of course Mrs. Prest had n't the nerves of an editor. It was meanwhile no explanation of the old woman's having eluded us to say that she lived abroad, for our researches had again and again taken us—not only by correspondence but by personal enquiry—to France, to Germany, to Italy, in which countries, not counting his important stay in England, so many of the too few years of Aspern's career had been spent. We were glad to think at least that in all our promulgations—some people now consider I believe that we have overdone them—we had only touched in passing and in the most discreet manner on Miss Bordereau's connexion. Oddly enough, even if we had had the material—and we had often wondered what could have become of it—this would have been the most difficult episode to handle.

The gondola stopped, the old palace was there; it was a house of the class which in Venice carries even in extreme dilapidation the dignified name. "How charming! It's gray and pink!" my companion exclaimed; and that is the most comprehensive description of it. It was not particularly old, only two or three centuries; and it had an air not so much of decay as of quiet discouragement, as if it had rather missed its career. But its wide front, with a stone balcony from end to end of the *piano nobile* or most important floor, was architectural enough, with the aid of various pilasters and arches; and the stucco with which in the intervals it had long ago been endued was rosy in the April

afternoon. It overlooked a clean melancholy rather lonely canal, which had a narrow *riva* or convenient footway on either side. "I don't know why—there are no brick gables," said Mrs. Prest, "but this corner has seemed to me before more Dutch than Italian, more like Amsterdam than like Venice. It's eccentrically neat for reasons of its own; and though you may pass on foot scarcely any one ever thinks of doing so. It's as negative—considering *where* it is—as a Protestant Sunday. Perhaps the people are afraid of the Misses Bordereau. I dare say they have the reputation of witches."

I forget what answer I made to this—I was given up to two other reflexions. The first of these was that if the old lady lived in such a big and imposing house she couldn't be in any sort of misery and therefore wouldn't be tempted by a chance to let a couple of rooms. I expressed this fear to Mrs. Prest, who gave me a very straight answer. "If she didn't live in a big house how could it be a question of her having rooms to spare? If she were not amply lodged you'd lack ground to approach her. Besides, a big house here, and especially in this *quartier perdu,* proves nothing at all: it's perfectly consistent with a state of penury. Dilapidated old palazzi, if you'll go out of the way for them, are to be had for five shillings a year. And as for the people who live in them—no, until you've explored Venice socially as much as I have, you can form no idea of their domestic desolation. They live on nothing, for they've nothing to live on." The other idea that had come into my head was connected with a high blank wall which appeared to confine an expanse of ground on one side of the house. Blank I call it, but it was figured over with the patches that please a painter, repaired breaches, crumblings of plaster, extrusions of brick that had turned pink with time; while a few thin trees, with the poles of certain rickety trellises, were visible over the top. The place was a garden and apparently attached to the house. I suddenly felt that so attached it gave me my pretext.

I sat looking out on all this with Mrs. Prest (it was covered with the golden glow of Venice) from the shade of our *felze,* and she asked me if I would go in then, while she waited for me, or come back another time. At first I couldn't decide—it was doubtless very weak of me. I wanted still to think I *might* get a footing, and was afraid to meet failure, for it would leave me, as I remarked to my companion, without another arrow for my bow. "Why not another?" she enquired as I sat there hesitating and thinking it over; and she wished to know why even now and before taking the trouble of becoming an inmate—which might be wretchedly uncomfortable after all, even if it succeeded—I hadn't the resource of simply offering them a sum of money down. In that way I might get what I wanted without bad nights.

"Dearest lady," I exclaimed, "excuse the impatience of my tone when I suggest that you must have forgotten the very fact—surely I communicated it to you—which threw me on your ingenuity. The old woman won't have her relics and tokens so much as spoken of; they 're personal, delicate, intimate, and she has n't the feelings of the day, God bless her! If I should sound that note first I should certainly spoil the game. I can arrive at my spoils only by putting her off her guard, and I can put her off her guard only by ingratiating diplomatic arts. Hypocrisy, duplicity are my only chance. I 'm sorry for it, but there 's no baseness I would n't commit for Jeffrey Aspern's sake. First I must take tea with her—then tackle the main job." And I told over what had happened to John Cumnor on his respectfully writing to her. No notice whatever had been taken of his first letter, and the second had been answered very sharply, in six lines, by the niece. "Miss Bordereau requested her to say that she could n't imagine what he meant by troubling them. They had none of Mr. Aspern's 'literary remains,' and if they *had* had would n't have dreamed of showing them to any one on any account whatever. She could n't imagine what he was talking about and begged he would let her alone." I certainly did n't want to be met that way.

"Well," said Mrs. Prest after a moment and all provokingly, "perhaps they really have n't anything. If they deny it flat how are you sure?"

"John Cumnor's sure, and it would take me long to tell you how his conviction, or his very strong presumption—strong enough to stand against the old lady's not unnatural fib—has built itself up. Besides, he makes much of the internal evidence of the niece's letter."

"The internal evidence?"

"Her calling him 'Mr. Aspern.' "

"I don't see what that proves."

"It proves familiarity, and familiarity implies the possession of mementoes, of tangible objects I can't tell you how that 'Mr.' affects me—how it bridges over the gulf of time and brings our hero near to me—nor what an edge it gives to my desire to see Juliana. You don't say 'Mr.' Shakespeare."

"Would I, any more, if I had a box full of his letters?"

"Yes, if he had been your lover and some one wanted them!" And I added that John Cumnor was so convinced, and so all the more convinced by Miss Bordereau's tone, that he would have come himself to Venice on the undertaking were it not for the obstacle of his having, for any confidence, to disprove his identity with the person who had written to them, which the old ladies would be sure to suspect in spite of dissimulation and a change of name. If they were to ask him point-

blank if he were not their snubbed correspondent it would be too awk-
ward for him to lie; whereas I was fortunately not tied in that way. I
was a fresh hand—I could protest without lying.

"But you 'll have to take a false name," said Mrs. Prest. "Juliana
lives out of the world as much as it is possible to live, but she has none
the less probably heard of Mr. Aspern's editors. She perhaps possesses
what you 've published."

"I 've thought of that," I returned; and I drew out of my pocket-
book a visiting card neatly engraved with a well-chosen *nom de guerre*.

"You 're very extravagant—it adds to your immorality. You might
have done it in pencil or ink," said my companion.

"This looks more genuine."

"Certainly you 've the courage of your curiosity. But it will be
awkward about your letters; they won't come to you in that mask."

"My banker will take them in and I shall go every day to get them.
It will give me a little walk."

"Shall you depend all on that?" asked Mrs. Prest. "Are n't you
coming to see me?"

"Oh you 'll have left Venice for the hot months long before there
are any results. I 'm prepared to roast all summer—as well as through
the long hereafter perhaps you 'll say! Meanwhile John Cumnor will
bombard me with letters addressed, in my feigned name, to the care of
the padrona."

"She 'll recognise his hand," my companion suggested.

"On the envelope he can disguise it."

"Well, you 're a precious pair! Does n't it occur to you that even if
you 're able to say you 're not Mr. Cumnor in person they may still
suspect you of being his emissary?"

"Certainly, and I see only one way to parry that."

"And what may that be?"

I hesitated a moment. "To make love to the niece."

"Ah," cried my friend, "wait till you see her!"

§ 2

"I must work the garden—I must work the garden," I said to my-
self five minutes later and while I waited, upstairs, in the long, dusty
sala, where the bare scagliola floor gleamed vaguely in a chink of the
closed shutters. The place was impressive, yet looked somehow cold
and cautious. Mrs. Prest had floated away, giving me a rendezvous
at the end of half an hour by some neighbouring water-steps; and I
had been let into the house, after pulling the rusty bell-wire, by a small

red-headed and white-faced maid-servant, who was very young and not ugly and wore clicking pattens and a shawl in the fashion of a hood. She had not contented herself with opening the door from above by the usual arrangement of a creaking pulley, though she had looked down at me first from an upper window, dropping the cautious challenge which in Italy precedes the act of admission. I was irritated as a general thing by this survival of mediæval manners, though as so fond, if yet so special, an antiquarian I suppose I ought to have liked it; but, with my resolve to be genial from the threshold at any price, I took my false card out of my pocket and held it up to her, smiling as if it were a magic token. It had the effect of one indeed, for it brought her, as I say, all the way down. I begged her to hand it to her mistress, having first written on it in Italian the words: "Could you very kindly see a gentleman, a travelling American, for a moment?" The little maid was n't hostile—even that was perhaps something gained. She coloured, she smiled and looked both frightened and pleased. I could see that my arrival was a great affair, that visits in such a house were rare and that she was a person who would have liked a bustling place. When she pushed forward the heavy door behind me I felt my foot in the citadel and promised myself ever so firmly to keep it there. She pattered across the damp stony lower hall and I followed her up the high staircase—stonier still, as it seemed—without an invitation. I think she had meant I should wait for her below, but such was not my idea, and I took up my station in the sala. She flitted, at the far end of it, into impenetrable regions, and I looked at the place with my heart beating as I had known it to do in dentists' parlours. It had a gloomy grandeur, but owed its character almost all to its noble shape and to the fine architectural doors, as high as those of grand frontages, which, leading into the various rooms, repeated themselves on either side at intervals. They were surmounted with old faded painted escutcheons, and here and there in the spaces between them hung brown pictures, which I noted as speciously bad, in battered and tarnished frames that were yet more desirable than the canvases themselves. With the exception of several straw-bottomed chairs that kept their backs to the wall the grand obscure vista contained little else to minister to effect. It was evidently never used save as a passage, and scantly even as that. I may add that by the time the door through which the maid-servant had escaped opened again my eyes had grown used to the want of light.

I had n't meanwhile meant by my private ejaculation that I must myself cultivate the soil of the tangled enclosure which lay beneath the windows, but the lady who came toward me from the distance over the hard shining floor might have supposed as much from the way in

which, as I went rapidly to meet her, I exclaimed, taking care to speak Italian: "The garden, the garden—do me the pleasure to tell me if it's yours!"

She stopped short, looking at me with wonder; and then, "Nothing here is mine," she answered in English, coldly and sadly.

"Oh you're English; how delightful!" I ingenuously cried. "But surely the garden belongs to the house?"

"Yes, but the house does n't belong to me." She was a long lean pale person, habited apparently in a dull-coloured dressing-gown, and she spoke very simply and mildly. She did n't ask me to sit down, any more than years before—if she were the niece—she had asked Mrs. Prest, and we stood face to face in the empty pompous hall.

"Well then, would you kindly tell me to whom I must address myself? I'm afraid you will think me horribly intrusive, but you know I *must* have a garden—upon my honour I must!"

Her face was not young, but it was candid; it was not fresh, but it was clear. She had large eyes which were not bright, and a great deal of hair which was not "dressed," and long fine hands which were—possibly—not clean. She clasped these members almost convulsively as, with a confused alarmed look, she broke out: "Oh, don't take it away from us; we like it ourselves!"

"You have the use of it then?"

"Oh yes. If it was n't for that—!" And she gave a wan vague smile.

"Is n't it a luxury, precisely? That's why intending to be in Venice some weeks, possibly all summer, and having some literary work, some reading and writing to do, so that I must be quiet and yet if possible a great deal in the open air—that's why I've felt a garden to be really indispensable. I appeal to your own experience," I went on with as sociable a smile as I could risk. "Now can't I look at yours?"

"I don't know, I don't understand," the poor woman murmured, planted there and letting her weak wonder deal—helplessly enough, as I felt—with my strangeness.

"I mean only from one of those windows—such grand ones as you have here—if you'll let me open the shutters." And I walked toward the back of the house. When I had advanced halfway I stopped and waited as in the belief she would accompany me. I had been of necessity quite abrupt, but I strove at the same time to give her the impression of extreme courtesy. "I've looked at furnished rooms all over the place, and it seems impossible to find any with a garden attached. Naturally in a place like Venice gardens are rare. It's absurd if you like, for a man, but I can't live without flowers."

"There are none to speak of down there." She came nearer, as if, though she mistrusted me, I had drawn her by an invisible thread. I

went on again, and she continued as she followed me: "We've a few, but they're very common. It costs too much to cultivate them; one has to have a man."

"Why shouldn't I be the man?" I asked. "I'll work without wages; or rather I'll put in a gardener. You shall have the sweetest flowers in Venice."

She protested against this with a small quaver of sound that might have been at the same time a gush of rapture for my free sketch. Then she gasped: "We don't know you—we don't know you."

"You know me as much as I know you; or rather much more, because you know my name. And if you're English I'm almost a countryman."

"We're not English," said my companion, watching me in practical submission while I threw open the shutters of one of the divisions of the wide high window.

"You speak the language so beautifully: might I ask what you are?" Seen from above the garden was in truth shabby, yet I felt at a glance that it had great capabilities. She made no rejoinder, she was so lost in her blankness and gentleness, and I exclaimed, "You don't mean to say you're also by chance American?"

"I don't know. We used to be."

"Used to be? Surely you haven't changed?"

"It's so many years ago. We don't seem to be anything now."

"So many years that you've been living here? Well, I don't wonder at that; it's a grand old house. I suppose you all use the garden," I went on, "but I assure you I shouldn't be in your way. I'd be very quiet and stay quite in one corner."

"We all use it?" she repeated after me vaguely, not coming close to the window but looking at my shoes. She appeared to think me capable of throwing her out.

"I mean all your family—as many as you are."

"There's only one other than me. She's very old. She never goes down."

I feel again my thrill at this close identification of Juliana; in spite of which, however, I kept my head. "Only one other in all this great house!" I feigned to be not only amazed but almost scandalized. "Dear lady, you must have space then to spare!"

"To spare?" she repeated—almost as for the rich unwonted joy to her of spoken words.

"Why you surely don't live (two quiet women—I see *you* are quiet, at any rate) in fifty rooms!" Then with a burst of hope and cheer I put the question straight: "Couldn't you for a good rent *let* me two or three? That would set me up!" I had now struck the note that

translated my purpose, and I need n't reproduce the whole of the
tune I played. I ended by making my entertainer believe me an un-
designing person, though of course I did n't even attempt to persuade
her I was not an eccentric one. I repeated that I had studies to pursue;
that I wanted quiet; that I delighted in a garden and had vainly
sought one up and down the city; that I would undertake that before
another month was over the dear old house should be smothered in
flowers. I think it was the flowers that won my suit, for I afterwards
found that Miss Tina—for such the name of this high tremulous spin-
ster proved somewhat incongruously to be—had an insatiable appetite
for them. When I speak of my suit as won I mean that before I left
her she had promised me she would refer the question to her aunt.
I invited information as to who her aunt might be and she answered
"Why Miss Bordereau!" with an air of surprise, as if I might have
been expected to know. There were contradictions like this in Miss
Tina which, as I observed later, contributed to make her rather
pleasingly incalculable and interesting. It was the study of the two
ladies to live so that the world should n't talk of them or touch them,
and yet they had never altogether accepted the idea that it did n't hear
of them. In Miss Tina at any rate a grateful susceptibility to human
contact had not died out, and contact of a limited order there would
be if I should come to live in the house.

"We 've never done anything of the sort; we 've never had a lodger
or any kind of inmate." So much as this she made a point of saying to
me. "We 're very poor, we live very badly—almost on nothing. The
rooms are very bare—those you might take; they 've nothing at all
in them. I don't know how you 'd sleep, how you 'd eat."

"With your permission I could easily put in a bed and a few tables
and chairs. *C'est la moindre des choses* and the affair of an hour or
two. I know a little man from whom I can hire for a trifle what I
should so briefly want, what I should use; my gondolier can bring the
things round in his boat. Of course in this great house you must have a
second kitchen, and my servant who 's a wonderfully handy fellow"—
this personage was an evocation of the moment—"can easily cook me
a chop there. My tastes and habits are of the simplest; I live on
flowers!" And then I ventured to add that if they were very poor it
was all the more reason they should let their rooms. They were bad
economists—I had never heard of such a waste of material.

I saw in a moment my good lady had never before been spoken to in
any such fashion—with a humorous firmness that did n't exclude sym-
pathy, that was quite founded on it. She might easily have told me
that my sympathy was impertinent, but this by good fortune did n't
occur to her. I left her with the understanding that she would submit

the question to her aunt and that I might come back the next day for their decision.

"The aunt will refuse; she'll think the whole proceeding very *louche!*" Mrs. Prest declared shortly after this, when I had resumed my place in her gondola. She had put the idea into my head and now—so little are women to be counted on—she appeared to take a despondent view of it. Her pessimism provoked me and I pretended to have the best hopes; I went so far as to boast of a distinct prevision of success. Upon this Mrs. Prest broke out, "Oh I see what's in your head! You fancy you've made such an impression in five minutes that she's dying for you to come and can be depended on to bring the old one round. If you do get in you'll count it as a triumph."

I did count it as a triumph, but only for the commentator—in the last analysis—not for the man, who had not the tradition of personal conquest. When I went back on the morrow the little maid-servant conducted me straight through the long sala—it opened there as before in large perspective and was lighter now, which I thought a good omen—into the apartment from which the recipient of my former visit had emerged on that occasion. It was a spacious shabby parlour with a fine old painted ceiling under which a strange figure sat alone at one of the windows. They come back to me now almost with the palpitation they caused, the successive states marking my consciousness that as the door of the room closed behind me I was really face to face with the Juliana of some of Aspern's most exquisite and most renowned lyrics. I grew used to her afterwards, though never completely; but as she sat there before me my heart beat as fast as if the miracle of resurrection had taken place for my benefit. Her presence seemed somehow to contain and express his own, and I felt nearer to him at that first moment of seeing her than I ever had been before or ever have been since. Yes, I remember my emotions in their order, even including a curious little tremor that took me when I saw the niece not to be there. With her, the day before, I had become sufficiently familiar, but it almost exceeded my courage—much as I had longed for the event—to be left alone with so terrible a relic as the aunt. She was too strange, too literally resurgent. Then came a check from the perception that we weren't really face to face, inasmuch as she had over her eyes a horrible green shade which served for her almost as a mask. I believed for the instant that she had put it on expressly, so that from underneath it she might take me all in without my getting at herself. At the same time it created a presumption of some ghastly death's-head lurking behind it. The divine Juliana as a grinning skull—the vision hung there until it passed. Then it came to me that she *was* tremendously old—so old that death might take her

at any moment, before I should have time to compass my end. The next thought was a correction to that; it lighted up the situation. She would die next week, she would die to-morrow—then I could pounce on her possessions and ransack her drawers. Meanwhile she sat there neither moving nor speaking. She was very small and shrunken, bent forward with her hands in her lap. She was dressed in black and her head was wrapped in a piece of old black lace which showed no hair.

My emotion keeping me silent she spoke first, and the remark she made was exactly the most unexpected.

§ 3

"Our house is very far from the centre, but the little canal is very *comme il faut*."

"It 's the sweetest corner of Venice and I can imagine nothing more charming," I hastened to reply. The old lady's voice was very thin and weak, but it had an agreeable, cultivated murmur and there was wonder in the thought that that individual note had been in Jeffrey Aspern's ear.

"Please to sit down there. I hear very well," she said quietly, as if perhaps I had been shouting; and the chair she pointed to was at a certain distance. I took possession of it, assuring her I was perfectly aware of my intrusion and of my not having been properly introduced, and that I could but throw myself on her indulgence. Perhaps the other lady, the one I had had the honour of seeing the day before, would have explained to her about the garden. That was literally what had given me courage to take a step so unconventional. I had fallen in love at sight with the whole place—she herself was probably so used to it that she did n't know the impression it was capable of making on a stranger—and I had felt it really a case to risk something. Was her own kindness in receiving me a sign that I was not wholly out in my calculation? It would make me extremely happy to think so. I could give her my word of honour that I was a most respectable inoffensive person and that as a co-tenant of the palace, so to speak, they would be barely conscious of my existence. I would conform to any regulations, any restrictions, if they would only let me enjoy the garden. Moreover I should be delighted to give her references, guarantees; they would be of the very best, both in Venice and in England, as well as in America.

She listened to me in perfect stillness and I felt her look at me with great penetration, though I could see only the lower part of her bleached and shrivelled face. Independently of the refining process of

old age it had a delicacy which once must have been great. She had been very fair, she had had a wonderful complexion. She was silent a little after I had ceased speaking; then she began: "If you're so fond of a garden why don't you go to *terra firma,* where there are so many far better than this?"

"Oh it's the combination!" I answered, smiling; and then with rather a flight of fancy; "It's the idea of a garden in the middle of the sea."

"This isn't the middle of the sea; you can't so much as see the water."

I stared a moment, wondering if she wished to convict me of fraud. "Can't see the water? Why, dear madam, I can come up to the very gate in my boat."

She appeared inconsequent, for she said vaguely in reply to this: "Yes, if you've got a boat. I haven't any; it's many years since I have been in one of the *gondole.*" She uttered these words as if they designed a curious far-away craft known to her only by hearsay.

"Let me assure you of the pleasure with which I would put mine at your service!" I returned. I had scarcely said this however before I became aware that the speech was in questionable taste and might also do me the injury of making me appear too eager, too possessed of a hidden motive. But the old woman remained impenetrable and her attitude worried me by suggesting that she had a fuller vision of me than I had of her. She gave me no thanks for my somewhat extravagant offer, but remarked that the lady I had seen the day before was her niece; she would presently come in. She had asked her to stay away a little on purpose—had had her reasons for seeing me first alone. She relapsed into silence and I turned over the fact of these unmentioned reasons and the question of what might come yet; also that of whether I might venture on some judicious remark in praise of her companion. I went so far as to say I should be delighted to see our absent friend again: she had been so very patient with me, considering how odd she must have thought me—a declaration which drew from Miss Bordereau another of her whimsical speeches.

"She has very good manners; I bred her up myself!" I was on the point of saying that that accounted for the easy grace of the niece, but I arrested myself in time, and the next moment the old woman went on: "I don't care who you may be—I don't want to know; it signifies very little to-day." This had all the air of being a formula of dismissal, as if her next words would be that I might take myself off now that she had had the amusement of looking on the face of such a monster of indiscretion. Therefore I was all the more surprised when she added in her soft venerable quaver: "You may have as

many rooms as you like—if you 'll pay me a good deal of money."

I hesitated but an instant, long enough to measure what she meant in particular by this condition. First it struck me that she must have really a large sum in her mind; then I reasoned quickly that her idea of a large sum would probably not correspond to my own. My deliberation, I think, was not so visible as to diminish the promptitude with which I replied: "I will pay with pleasure and of course in advance whatever you may think it proper to ask me."

"Well then, a thousand francs a month," she said instantly, while her baffling green shade continued to cover her attitude.

The figure, as they say, was startling and my logic had been at fault. The sum she had mentioned was, by the Venetian measure of such matters, exceedingly large; there was many an old palace in an out-of-the-way corner that I might on such terms have enjoyed the whole of by the year. But so far as my resources allowed I was prepared to spend money, and my decision was quickly taken. I would pay her with a smiling face what she asked, but in that case I would make it up by getting hold of my "spoils" for nothing. Moreover if she had asked five times as much I should have risen to the occasion, so odious would it have seemed to me to stand chaffering with Aspern's Juliana. It was queer enough to have a question of money with her at all. I assured her that her views perfectly met my own and that on the morrow I should have the pleasure of putting three months' rent into her hand. She received this announcement with apparent complacency and with no discoverable sense that after all it would become her to say that I ought to see the rooms first. This did n't occur to her, and indeed her serenity was mainly what I wanted. Our little agreement was just concluded when the door opened and the younger lady appeared on the threshold. As soon as Miss Bordereau saw her niece she cried out almost gaily: "He 'll give three thousand—three thousand to-morrow!"

Miss Tina stood still, her patient eyes turning from one of us to the other; then she brought out, scarcely above her breath: "Do you mean francs?"

"Did you mean francs or dollars?" the old woman asked of me at this.

"I think francs were what you said," I sturdily smiled.

"That 's very good," said Miss Tina, as if she had felt how over-reaching her own question might have looked.

"What do *you* know? You 're ignorant," Miss Bordereau remarked; not with acerbity but with a strange soft coldness.

"Yes, of money—certainly of money!" Miss Tina hastened to concede.

"I'm sure you've your own fine branches of knowledge," I took the liberty of saying genially. There was something painful to me, somehow, in the turn the conversation had taken, in the discussion of dollars and francs.

"She had a very good education when she was young. I looked into that myself," said Miss Bordereau. Then she added: "But she has learned nothing since."

"I have always been with *you*," Miss Tina rejoined very mildly, and of a certainty with no intention of an epigram.

"Yes, but for that—!" her aunt declared with more satirical force. She evidently meant that but for this her niece would never have got on at all; the point of the observation however being lost on Miss Tina, though she blushed at hearing her history revealed to a stranger. Miss Bordereau went on, addressing herself to me: "And what time will you come to-morrow with the money?"

"The sooner the better. If it suits you I'll come at noon."

"I am always here, but I have my hours," said the old woman as if her convenience were not to be taken for granted.

"You mean the times when you receive?"

"I never receive. But I'll see you at noon when you come with the money."

"Very good, I shall be punctual." To which I added: "May I shake hands with you on our contract?" I thought there ought to be some little form; it would make me really feel easier, for I was sure there would be no other. Besides, though Miss Bordereau could n't to-day be called personally attractive and there was something even in her wasted antiquity that bade one stand at one's distance, I felt an irresistible desire to hold in my own for a moment the hand Jeffery Aspern had pressed.

For a minute she made no answer, and I saw that my proposal failed to meet with her approbation. She indulged in no movement of withdrawal, which I half expected; she only said coldly: "I belong to a time when that was not the custom."

I felt rather snubbed but I exclaimed good-humouredly to Miss Tina "Oh you'll do as well!" I shook hands with her while she assented with a small flutter. "Yes, yes, to show it's all arranged!"

"Shall you bring the money in gold?" Miss Bordereau demanded as I was turning to the door.

I looked at her a moment. "Are n't you a little afraid, after all, of keeping such a sum as that in the house?" It was not that I was annoyed at her avidity, but was truly struck with the disparity between such a treasure and such scanty means of guarding it.

"Whom should I be afraid of if I'm not afraid of you?" she asked with her shrunken grimness.

"Ah well," I laughed, "I shall be in point of fact a protector and I'll bring gold if you prefer."

"Thank you," the old woman returned with dignity and with an inclination of her head which evidently signified my dismissal. I passed out of the room, thinking how hard it would be to circumvent her. As I stood in the sala again I saw that Miss Tina had followed me, and I supposed that as her aunt had neglected to suggest I should take a look at my quarters it was her purpose to repair the omission. But she made no such overture; she only stood there with a dim, though not a languid smile, and with an effect of irresponsible incompetent youth almost comically at variance with the faded facts of her person. She was not infirm, like her aunt, but she struck me as more deeply futile, because her inefficiency was inward, which was not the case with Miss Bordereau's. I waited to see if she would offer to show me the rest of the house but I did n't precipitate the question, inasmuch as my plan was from this moment to spend as much of my time as possible in her society. A minute indeed elapsed before I committed myself.

"I've had better fortune than I hoped. It was very kind of her to see me. Perhaps you said a good word for me."

"It was the idea of the money," said Miss Tina.

"And did you suggest that?"

"I told her you'd perhaps pay largely."

"What made you think that?"

"I told her I thought you were rich."

"And what put that into your head?"

"I don't know; the way you talked."

"Dear me, I must talk differently now," I returned. "I'm sorry to say it's not the case."

"Well," said Miss Tina, "I think that in Venice the *forestieri* in general often give a great deal for something that after all is n't much." She appeared to make this remark with a comforting intention, to wish to remind me that if I had been extravagant I was n't foolishly singular. We walked together along the sala, and as I took its magnificent measure I said that I was afraid it would n't form a part of my *quartiere*. Were my rooms by chance to be among those that opened into it? "Not if you go above—to the second floor," she answered as if she had rather taken for granted I would know my proper place.

"And I infer that that's where your aunt would like me to be."

"She said your apartments ought to be very distinct."

"That certainly would be best." And I listened with respect while she told me that above I should be free to take whatever I might like; that there was another staircase, but only from the floor on which we stood, and that to pass from it to the garden-level or to come up to my lodging I should have in effect to cross the great hall. This was an immense point gained; I foresaw that it would constitute my whole leverage in my relations with the two ladies. When I asked Miss Tina how I was to manage at present to find my way up she replied with an access of that sociable shyness which constantly marked her manner:

"Perhaps you can't. I don't see—unless I should go with you." She evidently had n't thought of this before.

We ascended to the upper floor and visited a long succession of empty rooms. The best of them looked over the garden; some of the others had above the opposite rough-tiled house-tops a view of the blue lagoon. They were all dusty and even a little disfigured with long neglect, but I saw that by spending a few hundred francs I should be able to make three or four of them habitable enough. My experiment was turning out costly, yet now that I had all but taken possession I ceased to allow this to trouble me. I mentioned to my companion a few of the things I should put in, but she replied rather more precipitately than usual that I might do exactly what I liked: she seemed to wish to notify me that the Misses Bordereau would take none but the most veiled interest in my proceedings. I guessed that her aunt had instructed her to adopt this tone, and I may as well say now that I came afterwards to distinguish perfectly (as I believed) between the speeches she made on her own responsibility and those the old woman imposed upon her. She took no notice of the unswept condition of the rooms and indulged neither in explanations nor in apologies. I said to myself that this was a sign Juliana and her niece—disenchanting idea!—were untidy persons with a low Italian standard; but I afterwards recognised that a lodger who had forced an entrance had no *locus standi* as a critic. We looked out of a good many windows, for there was nothing within the rooms to look at, and still I wanted to linger. I asked her what several different objects in the prospect might be, but in no case did she appear to know. She was evidently not familiar with the view—it was as if she had not looked at it for years —and I presently saw that she was too preoccupied with something else to pretend to care for it. Suddenly she said—the remark was not suggested:

"I don't know whether it will make any difference to you, but the money is for me."

"The money—?"

"The money you're going to bring."

"Why you 'll make me wish to stay here two or three years!" I spoke as benevolently as possible, though it had begun to act on my nerves that these women so associated with Aspern should so constantly bring the pecuniary question back.

"That would be very good for me," she answered almost gaily.

"You put me on my honour!"

She looked as if she failed to understand this, but went on: "She wants me to have more. She thinks she 's going to die."

"Ah not soon I hope!" I cried with genuine feeling. I had perfectly considered the possibility of her destroying her documents on the day she should feel her end at hand. I believed that she would cling to them till then, and I was as convinced of her reading Aspern's letters over every night or at least pressing them to her withered lips. I would have given a good deal some view of those solemnities. I asked Miss Tina if her venerable relative were seriously ill, and she replied that she was only very tired—she had lived so extraordinarily long. That was what she said herself—she wanted to die for a change. Besides, all her friends had been dead for ages; either they ought to have remained or she ought to have gone. That was another thing her aunt often said: she was not at all resigned—resigned, that is, to life.

"But people don't die when they like, do they?" Miss Tina inquired. I took the liberty of asking why, if there was actually enough money to maintain both of them, there would not be more than enough in case of her being left alone. She considered this difficult problem a moment and then said: "Oh well, you know, she takes care of me. She thinks that when I'm alone I shall be a great fool and shan't know how to manage."

"I should have supposed rather that you took care of *her*. I'm afraid she 's very proud."

"Why, have you discovered that already?" Miss Tina cried with a dimness of glad surprise.

"I was shut up with her there for a considerable time and she struck me, she interested me extremely. It did n't take me long to make my discovery. She won't have much to say to me while I'm here."

"No, I don't think she will," my companion averred.

"Do you suppose she has some suspicion of me?"

Miss Tina's honest eyes gave me no sign I had touched a mark. "I should n't think so—letting you in after all so easily."

"You call it easily? She has covered her risk," I said. "But where is it one could take an advantage of her?"

"I ought n't to tell you if I knew, ought I?" And Miss Tina added, before I had time to reply to this, smiling dolefully: "Do you think we 've any weak points?"

"That's exactly what I'm asking. You'd only have to mention them for me to respect them religiously."

She looked at me hereupon with that air of timid but candid and even gratified curiosity with which she had confronted me from the first; after which she said: "There's nothing to tell. We're terribly quiet. I don't know how the days pass. We've no life."

"I wish I might think I should bring you a little."

"Oh we know what we want," she went on. "It's all right."

There were twenty things I desired to ask her: how in the world they did live; whether they had any friends or visitors, any relations in America or in other countries. But I judged such probings premature; I must leave it to a later chance. "Well, don't *you* be proud," I contented myself with saying. "Don't hide from me altogether."

"Oh I must stay with my aunt," she returned without looking at me. And at the same moment, abruptly, without any ceremony of parting, she quitted me and disappeared, leaving me to make my own way downstairs. I stayed a while longer, wandering about the bright desert—the sun was pouring in—of the old house, thinking the situation over on the spot. Not even the pattering little *serva* came to look after me, and I reflected that after all this treatment showed confidence.

§ 4

Perhaps it did, but all the same, six weeks later, towards the middle of June, the moment when Mrs. Prest undertook her annual migration, I had made no measurable advance. I was obliged to confess to her that I had no results to speak of. My first step had been unexpectedly rapid, but there was no appearance it would be followed by a second. I was a thousand miles from taking tea with my hostesses—that privilege of which, as I reminded my good friend, we both had had a vision. She reproached me with lacking boldness and I answered that even to be bold you must have an opportunity: you may push on through a breach, but you can't batter down a dead wall. She returned that the breach I had already made was big enough to admit an army and accused me of wasting precious hours in whimpering in her salon when I ought to have been carrying on the struggle in the field. It is true that I went to see her very often—all on the theory that it would console me (I freely expressed my discouragement) for my want of success on my own premises. But I began to feel that it didn't console me to be perpetually chaffed for my scruples, especially since I was really so vigilant; and I was rather glad when my ironic friend closed her house for the summer. She had expected to gather

amusement from the drama of my intercourse with the Misses Bordereau, and was disappointed that the intercourse, and consequently the drama, had not come off. "They'll lead you on to your ruin," she said before she left Venice. "They'll get all your money without showing you a scrap." I think I settled down to my business with more concentration after her departure.

It was a fact that up to that time I had not, save on a single brief occasion, had even a moment's contact with my queer hostesses. The exception had occurred when I carried them according to my promise the terrible three thousand francs. Then I found Miss Tina awaiting me in the hall, and she took the money from my hand with a promptitude that prevented my seeing her aunt. The old lady had promised to receive me, yet apparently thought nothing of breaking that vow. The money was contained in a bag of chamois leather, of respectable dimensions, which my banker had given me, and Miss Tina had to make a big fist to receive it. This she did with extreme solemnity though I tried to treat the affair a little as a joke. It was in no jocular strain, yet it was with a clearness akin to a brightness that she enquired, weighing the money in her two palms: "Don't you think it's too much?" To which I replied that this would depend on the amount of pleasure I should get for it. Hereupon she turned away from me quickly, as she had done the day before, murmuring in a tone different from any she had used hitherto: "Oh pleasure, pleasure—there's no pleasure in this house!"

After that, for a long time, I never saw her, and I wondered the common chances of the day should n't have helped us to meet. It could only be evident that she was immensely on her guard against them; and in addition to this the house was so big that for each other we were lost in it. I used to look out for her hopefully as I crossed the sala in my comings and goings, but I was not rewarded with a glimpse of the tail of her dress. It was as if she never peeped out of her aunt's apartment. I used to wonder what she did there week after week and year after year. I had never met so stiff a policy of seclusion; it was more than keeping quiet—it was like hunted creatures feigning death. The two ladies appeared to have no visitors whatever and no sort of contact with the world. I judged at least that people could n't have come to the house and that Miss Tina could n't have gone out without my catching some view of it. I did what I disliked myself for doing— considering it but as once in a way: I questioned my servant about their habits and let him infer that I should be interested in any information he might glean. But he gleaned amazingly little for a knowing Venetian: it must be added that where there is a perpetual fast there are very few crumbs on the floor. His ability in other ways was suf-

ficient, if not quite all I had attributed to him on the occasion of my first interview with Miss Tina. He had helped my gondolier to bring me round a boat-load of furniture; and when these articles had been carried to the top of the palace and distributed according to our associated wisdom he organized my household with such dignity as answered to its being composed exclusively of himself. He made me in short as comfortable as I could be with my indifferent prospects. I should have been glad if he had fallen in love with Miss Bordereau's maid or, failing this, had taken her in aversion; either event might have brought about some catastrophe, and a catastrophe might have led to some parley. It was my idea that she would have been sociable, and I myself on various occasions saw her flit to and fro on domestic errands, so that I was sure she was accessible. But I tasted of no gossip from that fountain, and I afterwards learned that Pasquale's affections were fixed upon an object that made him heedless of other women. This was a young lady with a powdered face, a yellow cotton gown and much leisure, who used often to come to see him. She practised, at her convenience, the art of a stringer of beads—these ornaments are made in Venice to profusion; she had her pocket full of them and I used to find them on the floor of my apartment—and kept an eye on the possible rival in the house. It was not for me of course to make the domestics tattle, and I never said a word to Miss Bordereau's cook.

It struck me as a proof of the old woman's resolve to have nothing to do with me that she should never have sent me a receipt for my three months' rent. For some days I looked out for it and then, when I had given it up, wasted a good deal of time in wondering what her reason had been for neglecting so indispensable and familiar a form. At first I was tempted to send her a reminder; after which I put by the idea—against my judgement as to what was right in the particular case—on the general ground of wishing to keep quiet. If Miss Bordereau suspected me of ulterior aims she would suspect me less if I should be businesslike, and yet I consented not to be. It was possible she intended her omission as an impertinence, a visible irony, to show how she could overreach people who attempted to overreach her. On that hypothesis it was well to let her see that one did n't notice her little tricks. The real reading of the matter, I afterwards gathered, was simply the poor lady's desire to emphasise the fact that I was in the enjoyment of a favour as rigidly limited as it had been liberally bestowed. She had given me part of her house, but she would n't add to that so much as a morsel of paper with her name on it. Let me say that even at first this did n't make me too miserable, for the whole situation had the charm of its oddity. I foresaw that I should have a summer after my own literary heart, and the sense of playing with my

opportunity was much greater after all than any sense of being played with. There could be no Venetian business without patience, and since I adored the place I was much more in the spirit of it for having laid in a large provision. That spirit kept me perpetual company and seemed to look out at me from the revived immortal face—in which all his genius shone—of the great poet who was my prompter. I had invoked him and he had come; he hovered before me half the time; it was as if his bright ghost had returned to earth to assure me he re-garded the affair as his own no less than as mine and that we should see it fraternally and fondly to a conclusion. It was as if he had said: "Poor dear, be easy with her; she has some natural prejudices; only give her time. Strange as it may appear to you she was very attractive in 1820. Meanwhile are n't we in Venice together, and what better place is there for the meeting of dear friends? See how it glows with the advancing summer; how the sky and the sea and the rosy air and the marble of the palaces all shimmer and melt together." My eccen-tric private errand became a part of the general romance and the general glory—I felt even a mystic companionship, a moral fraternity with all those who in the past had been in the service of art. They had worked for beauty, for a devotion; and what else was I doing? That element was in everything that Jeffrey Aspern had written, and I was only bringing it to light.

I lingered in the sala when I went to and fro; I used to watch—as long as I thought decent—the door that led to Miss Bordereau's part of the house. A person observing me might have supposed that I was trying to cast a spell on it or attempting some odd experiment in hypnotism. But I was only praying it might open or thinking what treasure probably lurked behind it. I hold it singular, as I look back, that I should never have doubted for a moment that the sacred relics were there; never have failed to know the joy of being beneath the same roof with them. After all they were under my hand—they had not escaped me yet; and they made my life continuous, in a fashion, with the illustrious life they had touched at the other end. I lost my-self in this satisfaction to the point of assuming—in my quiet extrava-gance—that poor Miss Tina also went back, and still went back, as I used to phrase it. She did indeed, the gentle spinster, but not quite so far as Jeffrey Aspern, who was simple hearsay to her quite as he was to me. Only she had lived for years with Juliana, she had seen and handled all mementoes and—even though she was stupid—some esoteric knowledge had rubbed off on her. That was what the old woman represented—esoteric knowledge; and this was the idea with which my critical heart used to thrill. It literally beat faster often, of an evening when I had been out, as I stopped with my candle in the re-

echoing hall on my way up to bed. It was as if at such a moment as that, in the stillness and after the long contradiction of the day, Miss Bordereau's secrets were in the air, the wonder of her survival more vivid. These were the acute impressions. I had them in another form, with more of a certain shade of reciprocity, during the hours I sat in the garden looking up over the top of my book at the closed windows of my hostess. In these windows no sign of life ever appeared; it was as if, for fear of my catching a glimpse of them, the two ladies passed their days in the dark. But this only emphasised their having matters to conceal; which was what I had wished to prove. Their motionless shutters became as expressive as eyes consciously closed, and I took comfort in the probability that, though invisible themselves, they kept me in view between the lashes.

I made a point of spending as much time as possible in the garden, to justify the picture I had originally given of my horticultural passion. And I not only spent time, but (hang it! as I said) spent precious money. As soon as I had got my rooms arranged and could give the question proper thought I surveyed the place with a clever expert and made terms for having it put in order. I was sorry to do this, for personally I liked it better as it was, with its weeds and its wild rich tangle, its sweet characteristic Venetian shabbiness. I had to be consistent, to keep my promise that I would smother the house in flowers. Moreover I clung to the fond fancy that by flowers I should make my way— I should succeed by big nosegays. I would batter the old women with lilies—I would bombard their citadel with roses. Their door would have to yield to the pressure when a mound of fragrance should be heaped against it. The place in truth had been brutally neglected. The Venetian capacity for dawdling is of the largest, and for a good many days unlimited litter was all my gardener had to show for his ministrations. There was a great digging of holes and carting about of earth, and after a while I grew so impatient that I had thoughts of sending for my "results" to the nearest stand. But I felt sure my friends would see through the chinks of their shutters where such tribute *could n't* have been gathered, and might so make up their minds against my veracity. I possessed my soul and finally, though the delay was long, perceived some appearances of bloom. This encouraged me and I waited serenely enough till they multiplied. Meanwhile the real summer days arrived and began to pass, and as I look back upon them they seem to me almost the happiest of my life. I took more and more care to be in the garden whenever it was not too hot. I had an arbour arranged and a low table and an armchair put into it; and I carried out books and portfolios—I had always some business of writing in hand—and worked and waited and mused and hoped, while

the golden hours elapsed and the plants drank in the light and the inscrutable old palace turned pale and then, as the day waned, began to recover and flush and my papers rustled in the wandering breeze of the Adriatic.

Considering how little satisfaction I got from it at first it is wonderful I should n't have grown more tired of trying to guess what mystic rites of ennui the Misses Bordereau celebrated in their darkened rooms; whether this had always been the tenor of their life and how in previous years they had escaped elbowing their neighbours. It was supposable they had then had other habits, forms and resources; that they must once have been young or at least middle-aged. There was no end to the questions it was possible to ask about them and no end to the answers it was not possible to frame. I had known many of my country-people in Europe and was familiar with the strange ways they were liable to take up there; but the Misses Bordereau formed altogether a new type of the American absentee. Indeed it was clear the American name had ceased to have any application to them—I had seen this in the ten minutes I spent in the old woman's room. You could never have said whence they came from the appearance of either of them; wherever it was they had long ago shed and unlearned all native marks and notes. There was nothing in them one recognised or fitted, and, putting the question of speech aside, they might have been Norwegians or Spaniards. Miss Bordereau, after all, had been in Europe nearly three-quarters of a century; it appeared by some verses addressed to her by Aspern on the occasion of his own second absence from America—verses of which Cumnor and I had after infinite conjecture established solidly enough the date—that she was even then, as a girl of twenty, on the foreign side of the sea. There was a profession in the poem—I hope not just for the phrase—that he had come back for her sake. We had no real light on her circumstances at that moment, any more than we had upon her origin, which we believed to be of the sort usually spoken of as modest. Cumnor had a theory that she had been a governess in some family in which the poet visited and that, in consequence of her position, there was from the first something unavowed, or rather something quite clandestine, in their relations. I on the other hand had hatched a little romance according to which she was the daughter of an artist, a painter or a sculptor, who had left the Western world, when the century was fresh, to study in the ancient schools. It was essential to my hypothesis that this amiable man should have lost his wife, should have been poor and unsuccessful and should have had a second daughter of a disposition quite different from Juliana's. It was also indispensable that he should have been accompanied to Europe by these young ladies and should have

established himself there for the remainder of a struggling saddened life. There was a further implication that Miss Bordereau had had in her youth a preverse and reckless, albeit a generous and fascinating character, and that she had braved some wondrous chances. By what passions had she been ravaged, by what adventures and sufferings had she been blanched, what store of memories had she laid away for the monotonous future?

I asked myself these things as I sat spinning theories about her in my arbour and the bees droned in the flowers. It was incontestable that, whether for right or for wrong, most readers of certain of Aspern's poems (poems not as ambiguous as the sonnets—scarcely more divine, I think—of Shakespeare) had taken for granted that Juliana had not always adhered to the steep footway of renunciation. There hovered about her name a perfume of impenitent passion, an intimation that she had not been exactly as the respectable young person in general. Was this a sign that her singer had betrayed her, had given her away, as we say nowadays, to posterity? Certain it is that it would have been difficult to put one's finger on the passage in which her fair fame suffered injury. Moreover was not any fame fair enough that was so sure of duration and was associated with works immortal through their beauty? It was a part of my idea that the young lady had had a foreign lover—and say an unedifying tragical rupture—before her meeting with Jeffrey Aspern. She had lived with her father and sister in a queer old-fashioned expatriated artistic Bohemia of the days when the æsthetic was only the academic and the painters who knew the best models for *contadina* and *pifferaro* wore peaked hats and long hair. It was a society less awake than the coteries of to-day—in its ignorance of the wonderful chances, the opportunities of the early bird, with which its path was strewn—to tatters of old stuff and fragments of old crockery; so that Miss Bordereau appeared not to have picked up or have inherited many objects of importance. There was no enviable *bric-à-brac,* with its provoking legend of cheapness, in the room in which I had seen her. Such a fact as that suggested bareness, but none the less it worked happily into the sentimental interest I had always taken in the early movements of my countrymen as visitors to Europe. When Americans went abroad in 1820 there was something romantic, almost heroic in it, as compared with the perpetual ferryings of the present hour, the hour at which photography and other conveniences have annihilated surprise. Miss Bordereau had sailed with her family on a tossing brig in the days of long voyages and sharp differences; she had had her emotions on the top of yellow diligences, passed the night at inns where she dreamed of travellers' tales, and was most struck, on reaching the Eternal City, with the elegance of

Roman pearls and scarfs and mosaic brooches. There was something
touching to me in all that, and my imagination frequently went back
to the period. If Miss Bordereau carried it there of course Jeffrey As-
pern had at other times done so with greater force. It was a much more
important fact, if one was looking at his genius critically, that he had
lived in the days before the general transfusion. It had happened to
me to regret that he had known Europe at all; I should have liked to
see what he would have written without that experience, by which he
had incontestably been enriched. But as his fate had ruled otherwise
I went with him—I tried to judge how the general old order would
have struck him. It was not only there, however, I watched him; the
relations he had entertained with the special new had even a livelier
interest. His own country after all had had most of his life, and his
muse, as they said at that time, was essentially American. That was
originally what I had prized him for: that at a period when our native
land was nude and crude and provincial, when the famous "atmos-
phere" it is supposed to lack was not even missed, when literature was
lonely there and art and form almost impossible, he had found means
to live and write like one of the first; to be free and general and not at
all afraid; to feel, understand and express everything.

§ 5

I was seldom at home in the evening, for when I attempted to
occupy myself in my apartments the lamplight brought in a swarm of
noxious insects, and it was too hot for closed windows. Accordingly
I spent the late hours either on the water—the moonlights of Venice
are famous—or in the splendid square which serves as a vast forecourt
to the strange old church of Saint Mark. I sat in front of Florian's
café eating ices, listening to music, talking with acquaintances: the
traveller will remember how the immense cluster of tables and little
chairs stretches like a promontory into the smooth lake of the Piazza.
The whole place, of a summer's evening, under the stars and with all
the lamps, all the voices and light footsteps on marble—the only
sounds of the immense arcade that encloses it—is an open-air saloon
dedicated to cooling drinks and to a still finer degustation, that of the
splendid impressions received during the day. When I did n't prefer to
keep mine to myself there was always a stray tourist, disencumbered
of his Bädeker, to discuss them with, or some domesticated painter re-
joicing in the return of the season of strong effects. The great basilica,
with its low domes and bristling embroideries, the mystery of its
mosaic and sculpture, looked ghostly in the tempered gloom, and the

sea-breeze passed between the twin columns of the Piazzetta, the lintels of a door no longer guarded, as gently as if a rich curtain swayed there. I used sometimes on these occasions to think of the Misses Bordereau and of the pity of their being shut up in apartments which in the Venetian July even Venetian vastness could n't relieve of some stuffiness. Their life seemed miles away from the life of the Piazza, and no doubt it was really too late to make the austere Juliana change her habits. But poor Miss Tina would have enjoyed one of Florian's ices, I was sure; sometimes I even had thoughts of carrying one home to her. Fortunately my patience bore fruit and I was not obliged to do anything so ridiculous.

One evening about the middle of July I came in earlier than usual —I forget what chance had led to this—and instead of going up to my quarters made my way into the garden. The temperature was very high; it was such a night as one would gladly have spent in the open air, and I was in no hurry to go to bed. I had floated home in my gondola, listening to the slow splash of the oar in the dark narrow canals, and now the only thought that occupied me was that it would be good to recline at one's length in the fragrant darkness on a garden bench. The odour of the canal was doubtless at the bottom of that aspiration, and the breath of the garden, as I entered it, gave consistency to my purpose. It was delicious—just such an air as must have trembled with Romeo's vows when he stood among the thick flowers and raised his arms to his mistress's balcony. I looked at the windows of the palace to see if by chance the example of Verona—Verona being not far off—had been followed; but everything was dim, as usual, and everything was still. Juliana might on the summer nights of her youth have murmured down from the open windows at Jeffrey Aspern, but Miss Tina was not a poet's mistress any more than I was a poet. This however did n't prevent my gratification from being great as I became aware on reaching the end of the garden that my younger padrona was seated in one of the bowers. At first I made out but an indistinct figure, not in the least counting on such an overture from one of my hostesses; it even occurred to me that some enamoured maidservant had stolen in to keep a tryst with her sweetheart. I was going to turn away, not to frighten her, when the figure rose to its height and I recognised Miss Bordereau's niece. I must do myself the justice that I did n't wish to frighten her either, and much as I had longed for some such accident I should have been capable of retreating. It was as if I had laid a trap for her by coming home earlier than usual and by adding to that oddity my invasion of the garden. As she rose she spoke to me, and then I guessed that perhaps, secure in my almost inveterate absence, it was her nightly practice to take a lonely

airing. There was no trap in truth, because I had had no suspicion. At first I took the words she uttered for an impatience of my arrival; but as she repeated them—I had n't caught them clearly—I had the surprise of hearing her say: "Oh dear, I'm so glad you 've come!" She and her aunt had in common the property of unexpected speeches. She came out of the arbour almost as if to throw herself in my arms.

I hasten to add that I escaped this ordeal and that she did n't even then shake hands with me. It was an ease to her to see me and presently she told me why—because she was nervous when out-of-doors at night alone. The plants and shrubs looked so strange in the dark, and there were all sorts of queer sounds—she could n't tell what they were —like the noises of animals. She stood close to me, looking about her with an air of greater security but without any demonstration of interest in me as an individual. Then I felt how little nocturnal prowlings could have been her habit, and I was also reminded—I had been afflicted by the same in talking with her before I took possession—that it was impossible to allow too much for her simplicity.

"You speak as if you were lost in the backwoods," I cheeringly laughed. "How you manage to keep out of this charming place when you 've only three steps to take to get into it is more than I 've yet been able to discover. You hide away amazingly so long as I 'm on the premises, I know; but I had a hope you peeped out a little at other times. You and your poor aunt are worse off than Carmelite nuns in their cells. Should you mind telling me how you exist without air, without exercise, without any sort of human contact? I don't see how you carry on the common business of life."

She looked at me as if I had spoken a strange tongue, and her answer was so little of one that I felt it make for irritation. "We go to bed very early—earlier than you 'd believe." I was on the point of saying that this only deepened the mystery, but she gave me some relief by adding: "Before you came we were n't so private. But I 've never been out at night."

"Never in these fragrant alleys, blooming here under your nose?"

"Ah," said Miss Tina, "they were never nice till now!" There was a finer sense in this and a flattering comparison, so that it seemed to me I had gained some advantage. As I might follow that further by establishing a good grievance I asked her why, since she thought my garden nice, she had never thanked me in any way for the flowers I had been sending up in such quantities for the previous three weeks. I had not been discouraged—there had been, as she would have observed, a daily armful; but I had been brought up in the common forms and a word of recognition now and then would have touched me in the right place.

"Why I did n't know they were for me!"

"They were for both of you. Why should I make a difference?"

Miss Tina reflected as if she might be thinking of a reason for that, but she failed to produce one. Instead of this she asked abruptly: "Why in the world do you want so much to know us?"

"I ought after all to make a difference," I replied. "That question 's your aunt's; it is n't yours. You would n't ask it if you had n't been put up to it."

"She did n't tell me to ask you," Miss Tina replied without confusion. She was indeed the oddest mixture of shyness and straightness.

"Well, she has often wondered about it herself and expressed her wonder to you. She has insisted on it, so that she has put the idea into your head that I 'm insufferably pushing. Upon my word I think I 've been very discreet. And how completely your aunt must have lost every tradition of sociability, to see anything out of the way in the idea that respectable intelligent people, living as we do under the same roof, should occasionally exchange a remark! What could be more natural? We are of the same country and have at least some of the same tastes, since, like you, I 'm intensely fond of Venice."

My friend seemed incapable of grasping more than one clause in any proposition, and she now spoke quickly, eagerly, as if she were answering my whole speech: "I 'm not in the least fond of Venice. I should like to go far away!"

"Has she always kept you back so?" I went on, to show her I could be as irrelevant as herself.

"She told me to come out to-night; she has told me very often," said Miss Tina. "It is I who would n't come. I don't like to leave her."

"Is she too weak, is she really failing?" I demanded, with more emotion, I think, than I meant to betray. I measured this by the way her eyes rested on me in the darkness. It embarrassed me a little, and to turn the matter off I continued genially: "Do let us sit down together comfortably somewhere—while you tell me all about her."

Miss Tina made no resistance to this. We found a bench less secluded, less confidential, as it were, than the one in the arbour; and we were still sitting there when I heard midnight ring out from those clear bells of Venice which vibrate with a solemnity of their own over the lagoon and hold the air so much more than the chimes of other places. We were together more than an hour and our interview gave, as it struck me, a great lift to my undertaking. Miss Tina accepted the situation without a protest; she had avoided me for three months, yet now she treated me almost as if these three months had made me an old friend. If I had chosen I might have gathered from this that though she had avoided me she had given me a good deal of considera-

tion to doing so. She paid no attention to the flight of time—never worried at my keeping her so long away from her aunt. She talked freely, answering questions and asking them and not even taking advantage of certain longish pauses by which they were naturally broken to say she thought she had better go in. It was almost as if she were waiting for something—something I might say to her—and intended to give me my opportunity. I was the more struck by this as she told me how much less well her aunt had been for a good many days, and in a way that was rather new. She was markedly weaker; at moments she showed no strength at all; yet more than ever before she wished to be left alone. That was why she had told her to come out—not even to remain in her own room, which was alongside; she pronounced poor Miss Tina "a worry, a bore and a source of aggrava- tion." She sat still for hours together, as if for long sleep; she had always done that, musing and dozing; but at such times formerly she gave, in breaks, some small sign of life, of interest, liking her com- panion to be near her with her work. This sad personage confided to me that at present her aunt was so motionless as to create the fear she was dead; moreover she scarce ate or drank—one could n't see what she lived on. The great thing was that she still on most days got up; the serious job was to dress her, to wheel her out of her bedroom. She clung to as many of her old habits as possible and had always, little company as they had received for years, made a point of sitting in the great parlour.

I scarce knew what to think of all this—of Miss Tina's sudden con- version to sociability and of the strange fact that the more the old woman appeared to decline to her end the less she should desire to be looked after. The story hung indifferently together, and I even asked myself if it might n't be a trap laid for me, the result of a design to make me show my hand. I could n't have told why my companions (as they could only by courtesy be called) should have this purpose—why they should try to trip up so lucrative a lodger. But at any hazard I kept on my guard, so that Miss Tina should n't have occasion again to ask me what I might really be "up to." Poor woman, before we parted for the night my mind was at rest as to what *she* might be. She was up to nothing at all.

She told me more about their affairs than I had hoped; there was no need to be prying, for it evidently drew her out simply to feel me listen and care. She ceased wondering why I *should*, and at last, while describing the brilliant life they had led years before, she almost chat- tered. It was Miss Tina who judged it brilliant; she said that when they first came to live in Venice, years and years back—I found her essentially vague about dates and the order in which events had

occurred—there was never a week they had n't some visitor or did n't make some pleasant *passeggio* in the town. They had seen all the curiosities; they had even been to the Lido in a boat—she spoke as if I might think there was a way on foot; they had had a collation there, brought in three baskets and spread out on the grass. I asked her what people they had known and she said Oh very nice ones—the Cavaliere Bombicci and the Contessa Altemura, with whom they had had a great friendship! Also English people—the Churtons and the Goldies and Mrs. Stock-Stock, whom they had loved dearly; she was dead and gone, poor dear. That was the case with most of their kind circle—this expression was Miss Tina's own; though a few were left, which was a wonder considering how they had neglected them. She mentioned the names of two or three Venetian old women; of a certain doctor, very clever, who was so attentive—he came as a friend, he had really given up practice; of the *avvocato* Pochintesta, who wrote beautiful poems and had addressed one to her aunt. These people came to see them without fail every year, usually at the *capo d'anno,* and of old her aunt used to make them some little present—her aunt and she together: small things that she, Miss Tina, turned out with her own hand, paper lamp-shades, or mats for the decanters of wine at dinner, or those woollen things that in cold weather are worn on the wrists. The last few years there had n't been many presents; she could n't think what to make and her aunt had lost interest and never suggested. But the people came all the same; if the good Venetians liked you once they liked you for ever.

There was affecting matter enough in the good faith of this sketch of former social glories; the picnic at the Lido had remained vivid through the ages and poor Miss Tina evidently was of the impression that she had had a dashing youth. She had in fact had a glimpse of the Venetian world in its gossiping home-keeping parsimonious professional walks; for I noted for the first time how nearly she had acquired by contact the trick of the familiar soft-sounding almost infantile prattle of the place. I judged her to have imbibed this invertebrate dialect from the natural way the names of things and people—mostly purely local—rose to her lips. If she knew little of what they represented she knew still less of anything else. Her aunt had drawn in— the failure of interest in the table-mats and lamp-shades was a sign of that—and she had n't been able to mingle in society or to entertain it alone; so that her range of reminiscence struck one as an old world altogether. Her tone, had n't it been so decent, would have seemed to carry one back to the queer rococo Venice of Goldoni and Casanova. I found myself mistakenly think of her too as one of Jeffrey Aspern's contemporaries; this came from her having

so little in common with my own. It was possible, I indeed reasoned, that she had n't even heard of him; it might very well be that Juliana had forborne to lift for innocent eyes the veil that covered the temple of her glory. In this case she perhaps would n't know of the existence of the papers, and I welcomed that presumption—it made me feel more safe with her—till I remembered we had believed the letter of disavowal received by Cumnor to be in the handwriting of the niece. If it had been dictated to her she had of course to know what it was about; though the effect of it withal was to repudiate the idea of any connexion with the poet. I held it probable at all events that Miss Tina had n't read a word of his poetry. Moreover if, with her companion, she had always escaped invasion and research, there was little occasion for her having got it into her head that people were "after" the letters. People had not been after them, for people had n't heard of them. Cumnor's fruitless feeler would have been a solitary accident.

When midnight sounded Miss Tina got up; but she stopped at the door of the house only after she had wandered two or three times with me round the garden. "When shall I see you again?" I asked before she went in; to which she replied with promptness that she should like to come out the next night. She added, however, that she should n't come—she was so far from doing everything she liked.

"You might do a few things *I* like," I quite sincerely sighed.

"Oh you—I don 't believe you!" she murmured at this, facing me with her simple solemnity.

"Why don't you believe me?"

"Because I don't understand you."

"That's just the sort of occasion to have faith." I could n't say more, though I should have liked to, as I saw I only mystified her; for I had no wish to have it on my conscience that I might pass for having made love to her. Nothing less should I have seemed to do had I continued to beg a lady to "believe in me" in an Italian garden on a midsummer night. There was some merit in my scruples, for Miss Tina lingered and lingered: I made out in her the conviction that she should n't really soon come down again and the wish therefore to protract the present. She insisted too on making the talk between us personal to ourselves; and altogether her behaviour was such as would have been possible only to a perfectly artless and a considerably witless woman.

"I shall like the flowers better now that I know them also meant for me."

"How could you have doubted it? If you 'll tell me the kind you like best I 'll send a double lot."

"Oh I like them all best!" Then she went on familiarly: "Shall you study—shall you read and write—when you go up to your rooms?"

"I don't do that at night—at this season. The lamplight brings in the animals."

"You might have known that when you came."

"I did know it!"

"And in winter do you work at night?"

"I read a good deal, but I don't often write." She listened as if these details had a rare interest, and suddenly a temptation quite at odds with all the prudence I had been teaching myself glimmered at me in her plain mild face. Ah yes, she was safe and I could make her safer! It seemed to me from one moment to another that I could n't wait longer—that I really must take a sounding. So I went on: "In general before I go to sleep (very often in bed; it 's a bad habit, but I confess to it) I read some great poet. In nine cases out of ten it 's a volume of Jeffrey Aspern."

I watched her well as I pronounced that name, but I saw nothing wonderful. Why should I indeed? Was n't Jeffrey Aspern the property of the human race?

"Oh *we* read him—we *have* read him," she quietly replied.

"He's my poet of poets—I know him almost by heart."

For an instant Miss Tina hesitated; then her sociability was too much for her. "Oh by heart—that's nothing;" and, though dimly, she quite lighted. "My aunt used to know him—to know him"—she paused an instant and I wondered what she was going to say—"to know him as a visitor."

"As a visitor?" I guarded my tone.

"He used to call on her and take her out."

I continued to stare.. "My dear lady, he died a hundred years ago!"

"Well," she said amusingly, "my aunt 's a hundred and fifty."

"Mercy on us!" I cried; "why did n't you tell me before? I should like so to ask her about him."

"She would n't care for that—she would n't tell you," Miss Tina returned.

"I don't care what she cares for! She *must* tell me—it 's not a chance to be lost."

"Oh you should have come twenty years ago. Then she still talked about him."

"And what did she say?" I eagerly asked.

"I don't know—that he liked her immensely."

"And she—did n't she like *him?*"

"She said he was a god." Miss Tina gave me this information flatly, without expression; her tone might have made it a piece of trivial

gossip. But it stirred me deeply as she dropped the words into the summer night; their sound might have been the light rustle of an old unfolded love-letter.

"Fancy, fancy!" I murmured. And then, "Tell me this, please—has she got a portrait of him? They're distressingly rare."

"A portrait? I don't know," said Miss Tina; and now there was discomfiture in her face. "Well, good-night!" she added; and she turned into the house.

I accompanied her into the wide dusky stone-paved passage that corresponded on the ground floor with our grand sala. It opened at one end into the garden, at the other upon the canal, and was lighted now only by the small lamp always left for me to take up as I went to bed. An extinguished candle which Miss Tina apparently had brought down with her stood on the same table with it. "Good-night, good-night!" I replied, keeping beside her as she went to get her light. "Surely you'd know, should n't you, if she had one?"

"If she had what?" the poor lady asked, looking at me queerly over the flame of her candle.

"A portrait of the god. I don't know what I would n't give to see it."

"I don't know what she has got. She keeps her things locked up." And Miss Tina went away toward the staircase with the sense evidently of having said too much.

I let her go—I wished not to frighten her—and I contented myself with remarking that Miss Bordereau would n't have locked up such a glorious possession as that: a thing a person would be proud of and hang up in a prominent place on the parlour-wall. Therefore of course she had n't any portrait. Miss Tina made no direct answer to this and, candle in hand, with her back to me, mounted two or three degrees. Then she stopped short and turned round, looking at me across the dusky space.

"Do you write—do you write?" There was a shake in her voice—she could scarcely bring it out.

"Do I write? Oh don't speak of my writing on the same day with Aspern's!"

"Do you write about *him*—do you pry into his life?"

"Ah that's your aunt's question; it can't be yours!" I said in a tone of slightly wounded sensibility.

"All the more reason then that you should answer it. Do you, please?"

I thought I had allowed for the falsehoods I should have to tell, but I found that in fact when it came to the point I had n't. Besides, now that I had an opening there was a kind of relief in being frank. Lastly—it was perhaps fanciful, even fatuous—I guessed that Miss

Tina personally would n't in the last resort be less my friend. So after a moment's hesitation I answered: "Yes, I 've written about him and I 'm looking for more material. In heaven's name have you got any?"

"*Santo Dio!*" she exclaimed without heeding my question; and she hurried upstairs and out of sight. I might count upon her in the last resort, but for the present she was visibly alarmed. The proof of it was that she began to hide again, so that for a fortnight I kept missing her. I found my patience ebbing and after four or five days of this I told the gardener to stop the "floral tributes."

§ 6

One afternoon, at last, however, as I came down from my quarters to go out, I found her in the sala: it was our first encounter on that ground since I had come to the house. She put on no air of being there by accident; there was an ignorance of such arts in her honest angular diffidence. That I might be quite sure she was waiting for me she mentioned it at once, but telling me with it that Miss Bordereau wished to see me: she would take me into the room at that moment if I had time. If I had been late for a love-tryst I would have stayed for this, and I quickly signified that I should be delighted to wait on my benefactress. "She wants to talk with you—to know you," Miss Tina said, smiling as if she herself appreciated that idea; and she led me to the door of her aunt's apartment. I stopped her a moment before she had opened it, looking at her with some curiosity. I told her that this was a great satisfaction to me and a great honour; but all the same I should like to ask what had made Miss Bordereau so markedly and suddenly change. It had been only the other day that she would n't suffer me near her. Miss Tina was not embarrassed by my question; she had as many little unexpected serenities, plausibilities almost, as if she told fibs, but the odd part of them was that they had on the contrary their source in her truthfulness. "Oh my aunt varies," she answered; "it 's so terribly dull—I suppose she 's tired."

"But you told me she wanted more and more to be alone."

Poor Miss Tina coloured as if she found me too pushing. "Well, if you don't believe she wants to see you, I have n't invented it! I think people often are capricious when they 're very old."

"That's perfectly true. I only wanted to be clear as to whether you 've repeated to her what I told you the other night."

"What you told me?"

"About Jeffrey Aspern—that I'm looking for materials."

"If I had told her do you think she 'd have sent for you?"

"That's exactly what I want to know. If she wants to keep him to herself she might have sent for me to tell me so."

"She won't speak of him," said Miss Tina. Then as she opened the door she added in a lower tone: "I told her nothing."

The old woman was sitting in the same place in which I had seen her last, in the same position, with the same mystifying bandage over her eyes. Her welcome was to turn her almost invisible face to me and show me that while she sat silent she saw me clearly. I made no motion to shake hands with her; I now felt too well that this was out of place for ever. It had been sufficiently enjoined on me that she was too sacred for trivial modernisms—too venerable to touch. There was something so grim in her aspect—it was partly the accident of her green shade—as I stood there to be measured, that I ceased on the spot to doubt her suspecting me, though I did n't in the least myself suspect that Miss Tina had n't just spoken the truth. She had n't betrayed me, but the old woman's brooding instinct had served her; she had turned me over and over in the long still hours and had guessed. The worst of it was that she looked terribly like an old woman who at a pinch would, even like Sardanapalus, burn her treasure. Miss Tina pushed a chair forward, saying to me: "This will be a good place for you to sit." As I took possession of it I asked after Miss Bordereau's health; expressed the hope that in spite of the very hot weather it was satisfactory. She answered that it was good enough—good enough; that it was a great thing to be alive.

"Oh as to that, it depends upon what you compare it with!" I returned with a laugh.

"I don't compare—I don't compare. If I did that I should have given everything up long ago."

I liked to take this for a subtle allusion to the rapture she had known in the society of Jeffrey Aspern—though it was true that such an allusion would have accorded ill with the wish I imputed to her to keep him buried in her soul. What it accorded with was my constant conviction that no human being had ever had a happier social gift than his, and what it seemed to convey was that nothing in the world was worth speaking of if one pretended to speak of that. But one did n't pretend! Miss Tina sat down beside her aunt, looking as if she had reason to believe some wonderful talk would come off between us.

"It's about the beautiful flowers," said the old lady; "you sent us so many—I ought to have thanked you for them before. But I don't write letters and I receive company but at long intervals."

She had n't thanked me while the flowers continued to come, but she departed from her custom so far as to send for me as soon as she began to fear they would n't come any more. I noted this; I remembered

what an acquisitive propensity she had shown when it was a question of extracting gold from me, and I privately rejoiced at the happy thought I had had in suspending my tribute. She had missed it and was willing to make a concession to bring it back. At the first sign of this concession I could only go to meet her. "I 'm afraid you have n't had many, of late, but they shall begin again immediately—to-morrow, to-night."

"Oh do send us some to-night!" Miss Tina cried as if it were a great affair.

"What else should you do with them? It is n't a manly taste to make a bower of your room," the old woman remarked.

"I don't make a bower of my room, but I 'm exceedingly fond of growing flowers, of watching their ways. There 's nothing unmanly in that: it has been the amusement of philosophers, of statesmen in retirement; even I think of great captains."

"I suppose you know you can sell them—those you don't use," Miss Bordereau went on. "I dare say they would n't give you much for them; still, you could make a bargain."

"Oh I 've never in my life made a bargain, as you ought pretty well to have gathered. My gardener disposes of them and I ask no questions."

"I 'd ask a few, I can promise you!" said Miss Bordereau; and it was so I first heard the strange sound of her laugh, which was as if the faint "walking" ghost of her old-time tone had suddenly cut a caper. I could n't get used to the idea that this vision of pecuniary profit was most what drew out the divine Juliana.

"Come into the garden yourself and pick them; come as often as you like; come every day. The flowers are all for you," I pursued, addressing Miss Tina and carrying off this veracious statement by treating it as an innocent joke. "I can 't imagine why she does n't come down," I added for Miss Bordereau's benefit.

"You must make her come; you must come up and fetch her," the old woman said to my stupefaction. "That odd thing you 've made in the corner will do very well for her to sit in."

The allusion to the most elaborate of my shady coverts, a sketchy "summer-house," was irreverent; it confirmed the impression I had already received that there was a flicker of impertinence in Miss Bordereau's talk, a vague echo of the boldness or the archness of her adventurous youth and which had somehow automatically outlived passions and faculties. None the less I asked: "Would n't it be possible for you to come down there yourself? Would n't it do you good to sit there in the shade and the sweet air?"

"Oh sir, when I move out of this it won't be to sit in the air, and

I'm afraid that any that may be stirring around me won't be particularly sweet! It will be a very dark shade indeed. But that won't be just yet," Miss Bordereau continued cannily, as if to correct any hopes this free glance at the last receptacle of her mortality might lead me to entertain. "I 've sat here many a day and have had enough of arbours in my time. But I'm not afraid to wait till I 'm called."

Miss Tina had expected, as I felt, rare conversation, but perhaps she found it less gracious on her aunt's side—considering I had been sent for with a civil intention—than she had hoped. As to give the position a turn that would put our companion in a light more favourable she said to me: "Did n't I tell you the other night that she had sent me out? You see I can do what I like!"

"Do you pity her—do you teach her to pity herself?" Miss Bordereau demanded, before I had time to answer this appeal. "She has a much easier life than I had at her age."

"You must remember it has been quite open to me," I said, "to think you rather inhuman."

"Inhuman? That's what the poets used to call the women a hundred years ago. Don't try that; you won't do as well as they!" Juliana went on. "There 's no more poetry in the world—that *I* know of at least. But I won't bandy words with you," she said, and I well remember the old-fashioned artificial sound she gave the speech. "You make me talk, talk, talk! It is n't good for me at all." I got up at this and told her I would take no more of her time; but she detained me to put a question, "Do you remember, the day I saw you about the rooms, that you offered us the use of your gondola?" And when I assented promptly, struck again with her disposition to make a "good thing" of my being there and wondering what she now had in her eye, she produced: "Why don't you take that girl out in it and show her the place?"

"Oh dear aunt, what do you want to do with me?" cried the "girl" with a piteous quaver. "I know all about the place!"

"Well then go with him and explain!" said Miss Bordereau, who gave an effect of cruelty to her implacable power of retort. This showed her as a sarcastic profane cynical old woman. "Have n't we heard that there have been all sorts of changes in all these years? You ought to see them, and at your age—I don't mean because you 're so young— you ought to take the chances that come. You 're old enough, my dear, and this gentleman won't hurt you. He 'll show you the famous sunsets if they still go on—*do* they go on? The sun set for me so long ago. But that 's not a reason. Besides, I shall never miss you; you think you 're too important. Take her to the Piazza; it used to be very pretty," Miss Bordereau continued, addressing herself to me. "What have they done

with the funny old church? I hope it has n't tumbled down. Let her look at the shops; she may take some money, she may buy what she likes."

Poor Miss Tina had got up, discountenanced and helpless, and as we stood there before her aunt it would certainly have struck a spectator of the scene that our venerable friend was making rare sport of us. Miss Tina protested in a confusion of exclamations and murmurs; but I lost no time in saying that if she would do me the honour to accept the hospitality of my boat I would engage she really should n't be bored. Or if she did n't want so much of my company, the boat itself, with the gondolier, was at her service; he was a capital oar and she might have every confidence. Miss Tina, without definitely answering this speech, looked away from me and out of the window, quite as if about to weep, and I remarked that once we had Miss Bordereau's approval we could easily come to an understanding. We would take an hour, whichever she liked, one of the very next days. As I made my obeisance to the old lady I asked her if she would kindly permit me to see her again.

For a moment she kept me; then she said: "Is it very necessary to your happiness?"

"It diverts me more than I can say."

"You 're wonderfully civil. Don't you know it almost kills *me?*"

"How can I believe that when I see you more animated, more brilliant than when I came in?"

"That 's very true, aunt," said Miss Tina. "I think it does you good."

"Is n't it touching, the solicitude we each have that the other shall enjoy herself?" sneered Miss Bordereau. "If you think me brilliant to-day you don't know what you are talking about; you 've never seen an agreeable woman. What do you people know about good society?" she cried; but before I could tell her, "Don't try to pay me a compliment; I 've been spoiled," she went on. "My door 's shut, but you may sometimes knock."

With this she dismissed me and I left the room. The latch closed behind me, but Miss Tina, contrary to my hope, had remained within. I passed slowly across the hall and before taking my way downstairs waited a little. My hope was answered; after a minute my conductress followed me. "That 's a delightful idea about the Piazza," I said. "When will you go—to-night, to-morrow?"

She had been disconcerted, as I have mentioned, but I had already perceived, and I was to observe again, that when Miss Tina was embarrassed she did n't—as most women would have in like case— turn away, floundering and hedging, but came closer, as it were, with a deprecating, a clinging appeal to be spared, to be protected. Her

attitude was a constant prayer for aid and explanation, and yet no woman in the world could have been less of a comedian. From the moment you were kind to her she depended on you absolutely; her self-consciousness dropped and she took the greatest intimacy, the innocent intimacy that was all she could conceive, for granted. She didn't know, she now declared, what possessed her aunt, who had changed so quickly, who had got some idea. I replied that she must catch the idea and let me have it: we would go and take an ice together at Florian's and she should report while we listened to the band.

"Oh, it will take me a long time to be able to 'report'!" she said rather ruefully; and she could promise me this satisfaction neither for that night nor for the next. I was patient now, however, for I felt I had only to wait; and in fact at the end of the week, one lovely evening after dinner, she stepped into my gondola, to which in honour of the occasion I had attached a second oar.

We swept in the course of five minutes into the Grand Canal; whereupon she uttered a murmur of ecstasy as fresh as if she had been a tourist just arrived. She had forgotten the splendour of the great water-way on a clear summer evening, and how the sense of floating between marble palaces and reflected lights disposed the mind to freedom and ease. We floated long and far, and though my friend gave no high-pitched voice to her glee I was sure of her full surrender. She was more than pleased, she was transported; the whole thing was an immense liberation. The gondola moved with slow strokes, to give her time to enjoy it, and she listened to the plash of the oars, which grew louder and more musically liquid as we passed into narrow canals, as if it were a revelation of Venice. When I asked her how long it was since she had thus floated, she answered: "Oh I don't know; a long time—not since my aunt began to be ill." This was not the only show of her extreme vagueness about the previous years and the line marking off the period of Miss Bordereau's eminence. I was not at liberty to keep her out long, but we took a considerable *giro* before going to the Piazza. I asked her no questions, holding off my design from her life at home and the things I wanted to know; I poured, rather, treasures of information about the objects before and around us into her ears, describing also Florence and Rome, discoursing on the charms and advantages of travel. She reclined, receptive, on the deep leather cushions, turned her eyes conscientiously to everything I noted and never mentioned to me till some time afterwards that she might be supposed to know Florence better than I, as she had lived there for years with her kinswoman. At last she said with the shy impatience of a child: "Are we not really going to the Piazza? That's what I want to see!" I immediately gave the order that we should go straight, after

which we sat silent with the expectation of arrival. As some time still passed, however, she broke out of her own movement: "I've found out what's the matter with my aunt: she's afraid you'll go!"

I quite gasped. "What has put that into her head?"

"She has an idea you've not been happy. That's why she is different now."

"You mean she wants to make me happier?"

"Well, she wants you not to go. She wants you to stay."

"I suppose you mean on account of the rent," I remarked candidly.

Miss Tina's candour but profited. "Yes, you know; so that I shall have more."

"How much does she want you to have?" I asked with all the gaiety I now felt. "She ought to fix the sum, so that I may stay till it's made up."

"Oh that wouldn't please me," said Miss Tina. "It would be unheard of, your taking that trouble."

"But suppose I should have my own reasons for staying in Venice?"

"Then it would be better for you to stay in some other house."

"And what would your aunt say to that?"

"She wouldn't like it at all. But I should think you'd do well to give up your reasons and go away altogether."

"Dear Miss Tina," I said, "it's not so easy to give up my reasons!"

She made no immediate answer to this, but after a moment broke out afresh: "I think I know what your reasons are!"

"I dare say, because the other night I almost told you how I wished you'd help me to make them good."

"I can't do that without being false to my aunt."

"What do you mean by being false to her?"

"Why she would never consent to what you want. She has been asked, she has been written to. It makes her fearfully angry."

"Then she *has* papers of value?" I precipitately cried.

"Oh she has everything!" sighed Miss Tina, with a curious weariness, a sudden lapse into gloom.

These words caused all my pulses to throb, for I regarded them as precious evidence. I felt them too deeply to speak, and in the interval the gondola approached the Piazzetta. After we had disembarked I asked my companion if she would rather walk round the square or go and sit before the great café; to which she replied that she would do whichever I liked best—I must only remember again how little time she had. I assured her there was plenty to do both, and we made the circuit of the long arcades. Her spirits revived at the sight of the bright shop-windows, and she lingered and stopped, admiring or disapproving of their contents, asking me what I thought of things,

theorizing about prices. My attention wandered from her; her words of a while before "Oh she has everything!" echoed so in my consciousness. We sat down at last in the crowded circle at Florian's, finding an unoccupied table among those that were ranged in the square. It was a splendid night and all the world out-of-doors; Miss Tina could n't have wished the elements more auspicious for her return to society. I saw she felt it all even more than she told, but her impressions were well-nigh too many for her. She had forgotten the attraction of the world and was learning that she had for the best years of her life been rather mercilessly cheated of it. This did n't make her angry; but as she took in the charming scene her face had, in spite of its smile of appreciation, the flush of a wounded surprise. She did n't speak, sunk in the sense of opportunities, for ever lost, that ought to have been easy; and this gave me a chance to say to her: "Did you mean a while ago that your aunt has a plan of keeping me on by admitting me occasionally to her presence?"

"She thinks it will make a difference with you if you sometimes see her. She wants you so much to stay that she's willing to make that concession."

"And what good does she consider I think it will do me to see her?"

"I don't know; it must be interesting," said Miss Tina simply. "You told her you found it so."

"So I did; but every one does n't think that."

"No, of course not, or more people would try."

"Well, if she's capable of making that reflexion she's capable also of making this further one," I went on: "that I must have a particular reason for not doing as others do, in spite of the interest she offers—for not leaving her alone." Miss Tina looked as if she failed to grasp this rather complicated proposition; so I continued: "If you've not told her what I said to you the other night may she not at least have guessed it?"

"I don't know—she's very suspicious."

"But she has n't been made so by indiscreet curiosity, by persecution?"

"No, no; it is n't that," said Miss Tina, turning on me a troubled face. "I don't know how to say it; it's on account of something—ages ago, before I was born—in her life."

"Something? What sort of thing?"—and I asked it as if I could have no idea.

"Oh she has never told me." And I was sure my friend spoke the truth.

Her extreme limpidity was almost provoking, and I felt for the moment that she would have been more satisfactory if she had been less

ingenuous. "Do you suppose it's something to which Jeffrey Aspern's letters and papers—I mean the things in her possession—have reference?"

"I dare say it is!" my companion exclaimed as if this were a very happy suggestion. "I've never looked at any of those things."

"None of them? Then how do you know what they are?"

"I don't," said Miss Tina placidly. "I've never had them in my hands. But I've seen them when she has had them out."

"Does she have them out often?"

"Not now, but she used to. She's very fond of them."

"In spite of their being compromising?"

"Compromising?" Miss Tina repeated as if vague as to what that meant. I felt almost as one who corrupts the innocence of youth.

"I allude to their containing painful memories."

"Oh I don't think anything's painful."

"You mean there's nothing to affect her reputation?"

An odder look even than usual came at this into the face of Miss Bordereau's niece—a confession, it seemed, of helplessness, an appeal to me to deal fairly, generously with her. I had brought her to the Piazza, placed her among charming influences, paid her an attention she appreciated, and now I appeared to show it all as a bribe—a bribe to make her turn in some way against her aunt. She was of a yielding nature and capable of doing almost anything to please a person markedly kind to her; but the greatest kindness of all would be not to presume too much on this. It was strange enough, as I afterwards thought, that she had not the least air of resenting my want of consideration for her aunt's character, which would have been in the worst possible taste if anything less vital—from my point of view— had been at stake. I don't think she really measured it. "Do you mean she ever did something bad?" she asked in a moment.

"Heaven forbid I should say so, and it's none of my business. Besides, if she did," I agreeably put it, "that was in other ages, in another world. But why shouldn't she destroy her papers?"

"Oh she loves them too much."

"Even now, when she may be near her end?"

"Perhaps when she's sure of that she will."

"Well, Miss Tina," I said, "that's just what I should like you to prevent."

"How can I prevent it?"

"Couldn't you get them away from her?"

"And give them to you?"

This put the case, superficially, with sharp irony, but I was sure of her not intending that. "Oh I mean that you might let me see them

and look them over. It is n't for myself, or that I should want them at any cost to any one else. It 's simply that they would be of such immense interest to the public, such immeasurable importance as a contribution to Jeffrey Aspern's history."

She listened to me in her usual way, as if I abounded in matters she had never heard of, and I felt almost as base as the reporter of a newspaper who forces his way into a house of mourning. This was marked when she presently said: "There was a gentleman who some time ago wrote to her in very much those words. He also wanted her papers."

"And did she answer him?" I asked, rather ashamed of not having my friend's rectitude.

"Only when he had written two or three times. He made her very angry."

"And what did she say?"

"She said he was a devil," Miss Tina replied categorically.

"She used that expression in her letter?"

"Oh no; she said it to me. She made me write to him."

"And what did you say?"

"I told him there were no papers at all."

"Ah poor gentleman!" I groaned.

"I knew there were, but I wrote what she bade me."

"Of course you had to do that. But I hope I shan't pass for a devil."

"It will depend upon what you ask me to do for you," my companion smiled.

"Oh if there 's a chance of *your* thinking so my affair 's in a bad way! I shan't ask you to steal for me, nor even to fib—for you *can't* fib, unless on paper. But the principal thing is this—to prevent her destroying the papers."

"Why I 've no control of her," said Miss Tina. "It 's she who controls me."

"But she does n't control her arms and legs, does she? The way she would naturally destroy her letters would be to burn them. Now she can't burn them without fire, and she can't get fire unless you give it to her."

"I've always done everything she has asked," my poor friend pleaded. "Besides, there's Olimpia."

I was on the point of saying that Olimpia was probably corruptible, but I thought it best not to sound that note. So I simply put it that this frail creature might perhaps be managed.

"Every one can be managed by my aunt," said Miss Tina. And then she remembered that her holiday was over; she must go home.

I laid my hand on her arm, across the table, to stay her a moment. "What I want of you is a general promise to help me."

"Oh how *can* I, how *can* I?" she asked, wondering and troubled. She was half-surprised, half-frightened at my attaching that importance to her, at my calling on her for action.

"This is the main thing: to watch our friend carefully and warn me in time, before she commits that dreadful sacrilege."

"I can't watch her when she makes me go out."

"That's very true."

"And when you do too."

"Mercy on us—do you think she'll have done anything to-night?"

"I don't know. She's very cunning."

"Are you trying to frighten me?" I asked.

I felt this question sufficiently answered when my companion murmured in a musing, almost envious way: "Oh but she loves them— she loves them!"

This reflexion, repeated with such emphasis, gave me great comfort; but to obtain more of that balm I said: "If she should n't intend to destroy the objects we speak of before her death she'll probably have made some disposition by will."

"By will?"

"Has n't she made a will for your benefit?"

"Ah she has so little to leave. That's why she likes money," said Miss Tina.

"Might I ask, since we're really talking things over, what you and she live on?"

"On some money that comes from America, from a gentleman—I think a lawyer—in New York. He sends it every quarter. It is n't much!"

"And won't she have disposed of that?"

My companion hesitated—I saw she was blushing. "I believe it's mine," she said; and the look and tone which accompanied these words betrayed so the absence of the habit of thinking of herself that I almost thought her charming. The next instant she added: "But she had in an *avvocato* here once, ever so long ago. And some people came and signed something."

"They were probably witnesses. And you were n't asked to sign? Well then," I argued, rapidly and hopefully, "it's because you're the legatee. She must have left all her documents to you!"

"If she has it's with very strict conditions," Miss Tina responded, rising quickly, while the movement gave the words a small character of decision. They seemed to imply that the bequest would be accompanied with a proviso that the articles bequeathed should remain

concealed from every inquisitive eye, and that I was very much mistaken if I thought her the person to depart from an injunction so absolute.

"Oh of course you 'll have to abide by the terms," I said; and she uttered nothing to mitigate the rigour of this conclusion. None the less, later on, just before we disembarked at her own door after a return which had taken place almost in silence, she said to me abruptly: "I 'll do what I can to help you." I was grateful for this— it was very well so far as it went; but it did n't keep me from remembering that night in a worried waking hour that I now had her word for it to re-enforce my own impression that the old woman was full of craft.

§ 7

The fear of what this side of her character might have led her to do made me nervous for days afterwards. I waited for an intimation from Miss Tina; I almost read it as her duty to keep me informed, to let me know definitely whether or no Miss Bordereau had sacrificed her treasures. But as she gave no sign I lost patience and determined to put the case to the very touch of my own senses. I sent late one afternoon to ask if I might pay the ladies a visit, and my servant came back with surprising news. Miss Bordereau could be approached without the least difficulty; she had been moved out into the sala and was sitting by the window that overlooked the garden. I descended and found this picture correct; the old lady had been wheeled forth into the world and had a certain air, which came mainly perhaps from some brighter element in her dress, of being prepared again to have converse with it. It had not yet, however, begun to flock about her; she was perfectly alone and, though the door leading to her own quarters stood open, I had at first no glimpse of Miss Tina. The window at which she sat had the afternoon shade and, one of the shutters having been pushed back, she could see the pleasant garden, where the summer sun had by this time dried up too many of the plants—she could see the yellow light and the long shadows.

"Have you come to tell me you 'll take the rooms for six months more?" she asked as I approached her, startling me by something coarse in her cupidity almost as much as if she had n't already given me a specimen of it. Juliana's desire to make our acquaintance lucrative had been, as I have sufficiently indicated, a false note in my image of the woman who had inspired a great poet with immortal lines; but I may say here definitely that I after all recognised large

allowance to be made for her. It was I who had kindled the unholy flame; it was I who had put into her head that she had the means of making money. She appeared never to have thought of that; she had been living wastefully for years, in a house five times too big for her, on a footing that I could explain only by the presumption that, excessive as it was, the space she enjoyed cost her next to nothing and that, small as were her revenues, they left her, for Venice, an appreciable margin. I had descended on her one day and taught her to calculate, and my almost extravagant comedy on the subject of the garden had presented me irresistibly in the light of a victim. Like all persons who achieve the miracle of changing their point of view late in life, she had been intensely converted; she had seized my hint with a desperate tremulous clutch.

I invited myself to go and get one of the chairs that stood, at a distance, against the wall—she had given herself no concern as to whether I should sit or stand; and while I placed it near her I began gaily: "Oh dear madam, what an imagination you have, what an intellectual sweep! I'm a poor devil of a man of letters who lives from day to day. How can I take palaces by the year? My existence is precarious. I don't know whether six months hence I shall have bread to put in my mouth. I've treated myself for once; it has been an immense luxury. But when it comes to going on——!"

"Are your rooms too dear? If they are you can have more for the same money," Juliana responded. "We can arrange, we can *combinare*, as they say here."

"Well yes, since you ask me, they're too dear, much too dear," I said. "Evidently you suppose me richer than I am."

She looked at me as from the mouth of her cave. "If you write books don't you sell them?"

"Do you mean don't people buy them? A little, a very little—not so much as I could wish. Writing books, unless one be a great genius—and even then!—is the last road to fortune. I think there's no more money to be made by good letters."

"Perhaps you don't choose nice subjects. What do you write about?" Miss Bordereau implacably pursued.

"About the books of other people. I'm a critic, a commentator, an historian, in a small way." I wondered what she was coming to.

"And what other people now?"

"Oh better ones than myself: the great writers mainly—the great philosophers and poets of the past; those who are dead and gone and can't, poor darlings, speak for themselves."

"And what do you say about them?"

"I say they sometimes attached themselves to very clever women!"

I replied as for pleasantness. I had measured, as I thought, my risk, but as my words fell upon the air they were to strike me as imprudent. However, I had launched them and I was n't sorry, for perhaps after all the old woman would be willing to treat. It seemed tolerably obvious that she knew my secret; why therefore drag the process out? But she did n't take what I had said as a confession; she only asked:

"Do you think it 's right to rake up the past?"

"I don't feel that I know what you mean by raking it up. How can we get at it unless we dig a little? The present has such a rough way of treading it down."

"Oh I like the past, but I don't like critics," my hostess declared with her hard complacency.

"Neither do I, but I like their discoveries."

"Are n't they mostly lies?"

"The lies are what they sometimes discover," I said, smiling at the quiet impertinence of this. "They often lay bare the truth."

"The truth is God's, it is n't man's; we had better leave it alone. Who can judge of it?—who can say?"

"We 're terribly in the dark, I know," I admitted; "but if we give up trying what becomes of all the fine things? What becomes of the work I just mentioned, that of the great philosophers and poets? It 's all vain words if there 's nothing to measure it by."

"You talk as if you were a tailor," said Miss Bordereau whimsically; and then she added quickly and in a different manner: "This house is very fine; the proportions are magnificent. To-day I wanted to look at this part again. I made them bring me out here. When your man came just now to learn if I would see you I was on the point of sending for you to ask if you did n't mean to go on. I wanted to judge what I 'm letting you have. This sala is very grand," she pursued like an auctioneer, moving a little, as I guessed, her invisible eyes. "I don't believe you often have lived in such a house, eh?"

"I can't often afford to!" I said.

"Well then how much will you give me for six months?"

I was on the point of exclaiming—and the air of excruciation in my face would have denoted a moral fact—"Don't, Juliana; for *his* sake, don't!" But I controlled myself and asked less passionately: "Why should I remain so long as that?"

"I thought you liked it," said Miss Bordereau with her shriveled dignity.

"So I thought I should."

For a moment she said nothing more, and I left my own words to suggest to her what they might. I half-expected her to say, coldly enough, that if I had been disappointed we need n't continue the

discussion, and this in spite of the fact that I believed her now to have in her mind—however it had come there—what would have told her that my disappointment was natural. But to my extreme surprise she ended by observing: "If you don't think we've treated you well enough perhaps we can discover some way of treating you better." This speech was somehow so incongruous that it made me laugh again, and I excused myself by saying that she talked as if I were a sulky boy pouting in the corner and having to be "brought round." I had n't a grain of complaint to make; and could anything have exceeded Miss Tina's graciousness in accompanying me a few nights before to the Piazza? At this the old woman went on: "Well, you brought it on yourself!" And then in a different tone: "She's a very fine girl." I assented cordially to this proposition, and she expressed the hope that I did so not merely to be obliging, but that I really liked her. Meanwhile I wondered still more what Miss Bordereau was coming to. "Except for me, to-day," she said, "she has n't a relation in the world." Did she by describing her niece as amiable and unencumbered wish to represent her as a *parti?*

It was perfectly true that I could n't afford to go on with my rooms at a fancy price and that I had already devoted to my undertaking almost all the hard cash I had set apart for it. My patience and my time were by no means exhausted, but I should be able to draw upon them only on a more usual Venetian basis. I was willing to pay the precious personage with whom my pecuniary dealings were such a discord twice as much as any other *padrona di casa* would have asked, but I was n't willing to pay her twenty times as much. I told her so plainly, and my plainness appeared to have some success, for she exclaimed: "Very good; you've done what I asked—you've made an offer!"

"Yes, but not for half a year. Only by the month."

"Oh I must think of that then." She seemed disappointed that I would n't tie myself to a period, and I guessed that she wished both to secure me and to discourage me; to say severely: "Do you dream that you can get off with less than six months? Do you dream that even by the end of that time you'll be appreciably nearer your victory?" What was most in my mind was that she had a fancy to play me the trick of making me engage myself when in fact she had sacrificed her treasure. There was a moment when my suspense on this point was so acute that I all but broke out with the question, and what kept it back was but an instinctive recoil—lest it should be a mistake—from the last violence of self-exposure. She was such a subtle old witch that one could never tell where one stood with her. You may imagine whether it cleared up the puzzle when, just after she had said she would think of my proposal

and without any formal transition, she drew out of her pocket with an embarrassed hand a small object wrapped in crumpled white paper. She held it there a moment and then resumed: "Do you know much about curiosities?"

"About curiosities?"

"About antiquities, the old gimcracks that people pay so much for to-day. Do you know the kind of price they bring?"

I thought I saw what was coming, but I said ingenuously: "Do you want to buy something?"

"No, I want to sell. What would an amateur give me for that?" She unfolded the white paper and made a motion for me to take from her a small oval portrait. I possessed myself of it with fingers of which I could only hope that they did n't betray the intensity of their clutch, and she added: "I would part with it only for a good price."

At the first glance I recognized Jeffrey Aspern, and was well aware that I flushed with the act. As she was watching me however I had the consistency to exclaim: "What a striking face! Do tell me who it is."

"He's an old friend of mine, a very distinguished man in his day. He gave it me himself, but I 'm afraid to mention his name, lest you never should have heard of him, critic and historian as you are. I know the world goes fast and one generation forgets another. He was all the fashion when I was young."

She was perhaps amazed at my assurance, but I was surprised at hers; at her having the energy, in her state of health and at her time of life, to wish to sport with me to that tune simply for her private entertainment—the humour to test me and practise on me and befool me. This at least was the interpretation that I put upon her production of the relic, for I could n't believe she really desired to sell it or cared for any information I might give her. What she wished was to dangle it before my eyes and put a prohibitive price on it. "The face comes back to me, it torments me," I said, turning the object this way and that and looking at it very critically. It was a careful but not a supreme work of art, larger than the ordinary miniature and representing a young man with a remarkably handsome face, in a high-collared green coat and a buff waistcoat. I felt in the little work a virtue of likeness and judged it to have been painted when the model was about twenty-five. There are, as all the world knows, three other portraits of the poet in existence, but none of so early a date as this elegant image. "I 've never seen the original, clearly a man of a past age, but I 've seen other reproductions of this face," I went on. "You expressed doubt of this generation's having heard of the gentleman, but he strikes me for all the world as a celebrity. Now who is he? I can't put my finger on him—I can't give him a label. Was n't he a

writer? Surely he's a poet." I was determined that it should be she, not I, who should first pronounce Jeffrey Aspern's name.

My resolution was taken in ignorance of Miss Bordereau's extremely resolute character, and her lips never formed in my hearing the syllables that meant so much for her. She neglected to answer my question, but raised her hand to take back the picture, using a gesture which though impotent was in a high degree peremptory. "It's only a person who should know for himself that would give me my price," she said with a certain dryness.

"Oh then you have a price?" I didn't restore the charming thing; not from any vindictive purpose, but because I instinctively clung to it. We looked at each other hard while I retained it.

"I know the least I would take. What it occurred to me to ask you about is the most I shall be able to get."

She made a movement, drawing herself together as if, in a spasm of dread at having lost her prize, she had been impelled to the immense effort of rising to snatch it from me. I instantly placed it in her hand again, saying as I did so: "I should like to have it myself, but with your ideas it would be quite beyond my mark."

She turned the small oval plate over in her lap, with its face down, and I heard her catch her breath as after a strain or an escape. This however did not prevent her saying in a moment: "You'd buy a likeness of a person you don't know by an artist who has no reputation?"

"The artist may have no reputation, but that thing's wonderfully well painted," I replied, to give myself a reason.

"It's lucky you thought of saying that, because the painter was my father."

"That makes the picture indeed precious!" I returned with gaiety; and I may add that a part of my cheer came from this proof I had been right in my theory of Miss Bordereau's origin. Aspern had of course met the young lady on his going to her father's studio as a sitter. I observed to Miss Bordereau that if she would entrust me with her property for twenty-four hours I should be happy to take advice on it; but she made no other reply than to slip it in silence into her pocket. This convinced me still more that she had no sincere intention of selling it during her lifetime, though she may had desired to satisfy herself as to the sum her niece, should she leave it to her, might expect eventually to obtain for it. "Well, at any rate, I hope you won't offer it without giving me notice," I said as she remained irresponsive. "Remember me as a possible purchaser."

"I should want your money first!" she returned with unexpected rudeness; and then, as if she bethought herself that I might well complain of such a tone and wished to turn the matter off, asked abruptly

what I talked about with her niece when I went out with her that way of an evening.

"You speak as if we had set up the habit," I replied. "Certainly I should be very glad if it were to become our pleasant custom. But in that case I should feel a still greater scruple at betraying a lady's confidence."

"Her confidence? Has my niece confidence?"

"Here she is—she can tell you herself," I said; for Miss Tina now appeared on the threshold of the old woman's parlour. "Have you confidence, Miss Tina? Your aunt wants very much to know."

"Not in her, not in her!" the younger lady declared, shaking her head with a dolefulness that was neither jocular nor affected. "I don't know what to do with her; she has fits of horrid imprudence. She's so easily tired—and yet she has begun to roam, to drag herself about the house." And she looked down at her yoke-fellow of long years with a vacancy of wonder, as if all their contact and custom had n't made her perversities, on occasion, any more easy to follow.

"I know what I 'm about. I 'm not losing my mind. I dare say you 'd like to think so," said Miss Bordereau with a crudity of cynicism.

"I don't suppose you came out here yourself. Miss Tina must have had to lend you a hand," I interposed for conciliation.

"Oh she insisted we should push her; and when she insists!" said Miss Tina, in the same tone of apprehension; as if there were no knowing what service she disapproved of her aunt might force her next to render.

"I 've always got most things done I wanted, thank God! The people I 've lived with have humoured me," the old woman continued, speaking out of the white ashes of her vanity.

I took it pleasantly up. "I suppose you mean they 've obeyed you."

"Well, whatever it is—when they like one."

"It 's just because I like you that I want to resist," said Miss Tina with a nervous laugh.

"Oh I suspect you 'll bring Miss Bordereau upstairs next to pay me a visit," I went on; to which the old lady replied:

"Oh no; I can keep an eye on you from here!"

"You 're very tired; you 'll certainly be ill to-night!" cried Miss Tina.

"Nonsense, dear; I feel better at this moment than I 've done for a month. To-morrow I shall come out again. I want to be where I can see this clever gentleman."

"Should n't you perhaps see me better in your sitting-room?" I asked.

"Don't you mean should n't you have a better chance at *me?*" She returned, fixing me a moment with her green shade.

"Ah I have n't that anywhere! I look at you but don't see you."

"You agitate her dreadfully—and that's not good," said Miss Tina, giving me a reproachful deterrent headshake.

"I want to watch you—I want to watch you!" Miss Bordereau went on.

"Well then let us spend as much of our time together as possible— I don't care where. That will give you every facility."

"Oh I've seen you enough for to-day. I'm satisfied. Now I'll go home," Juliana said. Miss Tina laid her hands on the back of the wheeled chair and began to push, but I begged her to let me take her place. "Oh yes, you may move me this way—you shan't in any other!" the old woman cried as she felt herself propelled firmly and easily over the smooth hard floor. Before we reached the door of her own apartment she bade me stop, and she took a long last look up and down the noble sala. "Oh it's a prodigious house!" she murmured; after which I pushed her forward. When we had entered the parlour Miss Tina let me know she should now be able to manage, and at the same moment the little red-haired *donna* came to meet her mistress. Miss Tina's idea was evidently to get her aunt immediately back to bed. I confess that in spite of this urgency I was guilty of the indiscretion of lingering; it held me there to feel myself so close to the objects I coveted—which would be probably put away somewhere in the faded unsociable room. The place had indeed a bareness that suggested no hidden values; there were neither dusky nooks nor curtained corners, neither massive cabinets nor chests with iron bands. Moreover it was possible, it was perhaps even likely, that the old lady had consigned her relics to her bedroom, to some battered box that was shoved under the bed, to the drawer of some lame dressing-table, where they would be in the range of vision by the dim night-lamp. None the less I turned an eye on every article of furniture, on every conceivable cover for a hoard, and noticed that there were half a dozen things with drawers, and in particular a tall old secretary with brass ornaments of the style of the Empire—a receptacle somewhat infirm but still capable of keeping rare secrets. I don't know why this article so engaged me, small purpose as I had of breaking into it; but I stared at it so hard that Miss Tina noticed me and changed colour. Her doing this made me think I was right and that, wherever they might have been before, the Aspern papers at that moment languished behind the peevish little lock of the secretary. It was hard to turn my attention from the dull mahogany front when I reflected that a plain panel divided me from the goal of my hopes; but I gathered up my slightly

scattered prudence and with an effort took leave of my hostess. To make the effort graceful I said to her that I should certainly bring her an opinion about the little picture.

"The little picture?" Miss Tina asked in surprise.

"What do *you* know about it, my dear?" the old woman demanded. "You need n't mind. I've fixed my price."

"And what may that be?"

"A thousand pounds."

"Oh Lord!" cried poor Miss Tina irrepressibly.

"Is that what she talks to you about?" said Miss Bordereau.

"Imagine your aunt's wanting to know!" I had to separate from my younger friend with only those words, though I should have liked immensely to add: "For heaven's sake meet me to-night in the garden!"

§ 8

As it turned out the precaution had not been needed, for three hours later, just as I had finished my dinner, Miss Tina appeared, unannounced, in the open doorway to the room in which my simple repasts were served. I remember well that I felt no surprise at seeing her; which is not a proof of my not believing in her timidity. It was immense, but in a case in which there was a particular reason for boldness it never would have prevented her from running up to my floor. I saw that she was now quite full of a particular reason; it threw her forward— made her seize me, as I rose to meet her, by the arm.

"My aunt's very ill; I think she's dying!"

"Never in the world," I answered bitterly. "Don't you be afraid!"

"Do go for a doctor—do, do! Olimpia's gone for the one we always have, but she does n't come back; I don't know what has happened to her. I told her that if he was n't at home she was to follow him where he had gone; but apparently she's following him all over Venice. I don't know what to do—she looks so as if she were sinking."

"May I see her, may I judge?" I asked. "Of course I shall be delighted to bring some one; but had n't we better send my man instead, so that I may stay with you?"

Miss Tina assented to this and I dispatched my servant for the best doctor in the neighbourhood. I hurried downstairs with her, and on the way she told me that an hour after I quitted them in the afternoon Miss Bordereau had had an attack of "oppression," a terrible difficulty in breathing. This had subsided, but had left her so exhausted that she did n't come up: she seemed all spent and gone. I repeated that she was n't gone, that she would n't go yet; whereupon Miss Tina gave

me a sharper sidelong glance than she had ever favoured me withal
and said: "Really, what do you mean? I suppose you don't accuse her
of making-believe!" I forget what reply I made to this, but I fear that
in my heart I thought the old woman capable of any weird manœuvre.
Miss Tina wanted to know what I had done to her; her aunt had told
her I had made her so angry. I declared I had done nothing whatever
—I had been exceedingly careful; to which my companion rejoined
that our friend had assured her she had had a scene with me—a scene
that had upset her. I answered with some resentment that the scene
had been of *her* making—that I could n't think what she was angry
with me for unless for not seeing my way to give a thousand pounds
for the portrait of Jeffrey Aspern. "And did she show you that? Oh
gracious—oh deary me!" groaned Miss Tina, who seemed to feel the
situation pass out of her control and the elements of her fate thicken
round her. I answered her I'd give anything to possess it, yet that I
had no thousand pounds; but I stopped when we came to the door of
Miss Bordereau's room. I had an immense curiosity to pass it, but I
thought it my duty to represent to Miss Tina that if I made the
invalid angry she ought perhaps to be spared the sight of me. "The
sight of you? Do you think she can *see?*" my companion demanded,
almost with indignation. I did think so but forbore to say it, and I
softly followed my conductress.

I remember that what I said to her as I stood for a moment beside
the old woman's bed was: "Does she never show you her eyes then?
Have you never seen them?" Miss Bordereau had been divested of
her green shade, but—it was not my fortune to behold Juliana in
her nightcap—the upper half of her face was covered by the fall of a
piece of dingy lacelike muslin, a sort of extemporised hood which,
wound round her head, descended to the end of her nose, leaving
nothing visible but her white withered cheeks and puckered mouth,
closed tightly and, as it were, consciously. Miss Tina gave me a glance
of surprise, evidently not seeing a reason for my impatience. "You
mean she always wears something? She does it to preserve them."

"Because they 're so fine?"

"Oh to-day, to-day!" And Miss Tina shook her head speaking very
low. "But they used to be magnificent!"

"Yes indeed—we 've Aspern's word for that." And as I looked again
at the old woman's wrappings I could imagine her not having wished
to allow any supposition that the great poet had overdone it. But I
did n't waste my time in considering Juliana, in whom the appearance
of respiration was so slight as to suggest that no human attention could
ever help her more. I turned my eyes once more all over the room,
rummaging with them the closets, the chests of drawers, the tables.

Miss Tina at once noted their direction, and read, I think, what was in them; but she did n't answer it, turning away restlessly, anxiously, so that I felt rebuked, with reason, for an appetite well-nigh indecent in the presence of our dying companion. All the same I took another view, endeavouring to pick out mentally the receptacle to try first, for a person who should wish to put his hand on Miss Bordereau's papers directly after her death. The place was a dire confusion; it looked like the dressing-room of an old actress. There were clothes hanging over chairs, odd-looking shabby bundles here and there, and various pasteboard boxes piled together, battered, bulging and discoloured, which might have been fifty years old. Miss Tina after a moment noticed the direction of my eyes again, and, as if she guessed how I judged such appearances—forgetting I had no business to judge them at all—said, perhaps to defend herself from the imputation of complicity in the disorder:

"She likes it this way; we can't move things. There are old bandboxes she has had most of her life." Then she added, half-taking pity on my real thought: "Those things were *there*." And she pointed to a small low trunk which stood under a sofa that just allowed room for it. It struck me as a queer superannuated coffer, of painted wood, with elaborate handles and shrivelled straps and with the colour—it had last been endued with a coat of light green—much rubbed off. It evidently had travelled with Juliana in the olden time—in the days of her adventures, which it had shared. It would have made a strange figure arriving at a modern hotel.

"*Were* there—they are n't now?" I asked, startled by Miss Tina's implication.

She was going to answer, but at that moment the doctor came in—the doctor whom the little maid had been sent to fetch and whom she had at last overtaken. My servant, going on his own errand, had met her with her companion in tow, and in the sociable Venetian spirit, retracing his steps with them, had also come up to the threshold of the padrona's room, where I saw him peep over the doctor's shoulder. I motioned him away the more instantly that the sight of his prying face reminded me how little I myself had to do there—an admonition confirmed by the sharp way the little doctor eyed me, his air of taking me for a rival who had the field before him. He was a short fat brisk gentleman who wore the tall hat of his profession and seemed to look at everything but his patient. He kept me still in range, as if it struck him I too should be better for a dose, so that I bowed to him and left him with the women, going down to smoke a cigar in the garden. I was nervous; I could n't go further; I could n't leave the place. I don't know exactly what I thought might happen, but I felt it im-

portant to be there. I wandered about the alleys—the warm night had come on—smoking cigar after cigar and studying the light in Miss Bordereau's windows. They were open now, I could see; the situation was different. Sometimes the light moved, but not quickly; it did n't suggest the hurry of a crisis. Was the old woman dying or was she already dead? Had the doctor said that there was nothing to be done at her tremendous age but to let her quietly pass away? or had he simply announced with a look a little more conventional that the end of the end had come? Were the other two women just going and coming over the offices that follow in such a case? It made me uneasy not to be nearer, as if I thought the doctor himself might carry away the papers with him. I bit my cigar hard while it assailed me again that perhaps there were now no papers to carry!

I wandered about an hour and more. I looked out for Miss Tina at one of the windows, having a vague idea that she might come there to give me some sign. Would n't she see the red tip of my cigar in the dark and feel sure I was hanging on to know what the doctor had said? I 'm afraid it 's a proof of the grossness of my anxieties that I should have taken in some degree for granted at such an hour, in the midst of the greatest change that could fall on her, poor Miss Tina's having also a free mind for them. My servant came down and spoke to me; he knew nothing save that the doctor had gone after a visit of half an hour. If he had stayed half an hour then Miss Bordereau was still alive: it could n't have taken so long to attest her decease. I sent the man out of the house; there were moments when the sense of his curiosity annoyed me, and this was one of them. *He* had been watching my cigar-tip from an upper window, if Miss Tina had n't; he could n't know what I was after and I could n't tell him, though I suspected in him fantastic private theories about me which he thought fine and which, had I more exactly known them, I should have thought offensive.

I went upstairs at last, but I mounted no higher than the sala. The door of Miss Bordereau's apartment was open, showing from the parlour the dimness of a poor candle. I went toward it with a light tread, and at the same moment Miss Tina appeared and stood looking at me as I approached. "She 's better, she 's better," she said even before I had asked. "The doctor has given her something; she woke up, came back to life while he was there. He says there 's no immediate danger."

"No immediate danger? Surely he thinks her condition serious!"

"Yes, because she had been excited. That affects her dreadfully."

"It will do so again then, because she works herself up. She did so this afternoon."

"Yes, she must n't come out any more," said Miss Tina with one of her lapses into a deeper detachment.

"What 's the use of making such a remark as that," I permitted myself to ask, "if you begin to rattle her about again the first time she bids you?"

"I won't—I won't do it any more."

"You must learn to resist her," I went on.

"Oh yes, I shall; I shall do so better if you tell me it 's right."

"You must n't do it for me—you must do it for yourself. It all comes back to you, if you 're scared and upset."

"Well, I 'm not upset now," said Miss Tina placidly enough. "She 's very quiet."

"Is she conscious again—does she speak?"

"No, she does n't speak, but she takes my hand. She holds it fast."

"Yes," I returned, "I can see what force she still has by the way she grabbed that picture this afternoon. But if she holds you fast how comes it that you 're here?"

Miss Tina waited a little; though her face was in deep shadow—she had her back to the light in the parlour and I had put down my own candle far off, near the door of the sala—I thought I saw her smile ingenuously. "I came on purpose—I had heard your step."

"Why I came on tiptoe, as soundlessly as possible."

"Well, I had heard you," said Miss Tina.

"And is your aunt alone now?"

"Oh no—Olimpia sits there."

On my side I debated. "Shall we then pass in there?" And I nodded at the parlour; I wanted more and more to be on the spot.

"We can 't talk there—she 'll hear us."

I was on the point of replying that in that case we 'd sit silent, but I felt too much this would n't do, there was something I desired so immensely to ask her. Thus I hinted we might walk a little in the sala, keeping more at the other end, where we should n't disturb our friend. Miss Tina assented unconditionally; the doctor was coming again, she said, and she would be there to meet him at the door. We strolled through the fine superfluous hall, where on the marble floor—particularly as at first we said nothing—our footsteps were more audible than I had expected. When we reached the other end—the wide window, inveterately closed, connecting with the balcony that overhung the canal—I submitted that we had best remain there, as she would see the doctor arrive the sooner. I opened the window and we passed out on the balcony. The air of the canal seemed even heavier, hotter than that of the sala. The place was hushed and void; the quiet neighbourhood had gone to sleep. A lamp, here and there, over the

narrow black water, glimmered in double; the voice of a man going homeward singing, his jacket on his shoulder and his hat on his ear, came to us from a distance. This did n't prevent the scene from being very *comme il faut,* as Miss Bordereau had called it the first time I saw her. Presently a gondola passed along the canal with its slow rhythmical plash, and as we listened we watched it in silence. It did n't stop, it did'n't carry the doctor; and after it had gone on I said to Miss Tina:

"And where are they now—the things that were in the trunk?"

"In the trunk?"

"That green box you pointed out to me in her room. You said her papers had been there; you seemed to mean she had transferred them."

"Oh yes; they 're not in the trunk," said Miss Tina.

"May I ask if you 've looked?"

"Yes, I 've looked—for you."

"How for me, dear Miss Tina? Do you mean you 'd have given them to me if you had found them?"—and I fairly trembled with the question.

She delayed to reply and I waited. Suddenly she broke out: "I don't know what I 'd do—what I would n't!"

"Would you look again—somewhere else?"

She had spoken with a strange unexpected emotion, and she went on in the same tone: "I can't—I can't—while she lies there. It is n't decent."

"No, it is n't decent," I replied gravely. "Let the poor lady rest in peace." And the words, on my lips, were not hypocritical, for I felt reprimanded and shamed.

Miss Tina added in a moment, as if she had guessed this and were sorry for me, but at the same time wished to explain that I did push her, or a least harp on the chord, too much: "I can't deceive her that way. I can't deceive her—perhaps on her deathbed."

"Heaven forbid I should ask you, though I 've been guilty myself!"

"You 've been guilty?"

"I 've sailed under false colours." I felt now I must make a clean breast of it, must tell her I had given her an invented name on account of my fear her aunt would have heard of me and so refuse to take me in. I explained this as well as that I had really been a party to the letter addressed them by John Cumnor months before.

She listened with great attention, almost in fact gaping for wonder, and when I had made my confession she said: "Then your real name —what is it?" She repeated it over twice when I had told her, accompanying it with the exclamation "Gracious, gracious!" Then she added: "I like your own best."

"So do I,"—and I felt my laugh rueful. "Ouf! it's a relief to get rid of the other."

"So it was a regular plot—a kind of conspiracy?"

"Oh a conspiracy—we were only two," I replied, leaving out of course Mrs. Prest.

She considered; I thought she was perhaps going to pronounce us very base. But this was not her way, and she remarked after a moment, as in candid impartial contemplation: "How much you must want them!"

"Oh I do, passionately!" I grinned, I fear to admit. And this chance made me go on, forgetting my compunction of a moment before. "How can she possibly have changed their place herself? How can she walk? How can she arrive at that sort of muscular exertion? How can she lift and carry things?"

"Oh when one wants and when one has so much will!" said Miss Tina as if she had thought over my question already herself and had simply had no choice but that answer—the idea that in the dead of night, or at some moment when the coast was clear, the old woman had been capable of a miraculous effort.

"Have you questioned Olimpia? Hasn't she helped her—hasn't she done it for her?" I asked; to which my friend replied promptly and positively that their servant had had nothing to do with the matter, though without admitting definitely that she had spoken to her. It was as if she were a little shy, a little ashamed now, of letting me see how much she had entered into my uneasiness and had me on her mind. Suddenly she said to me without any immediate relevance: "I rather feel you a new person, you know, now that you've a new name."

"It isn't a new one; it's a very good old one, thank fortune!"

She looked at me a moment. "Well, I do like it better."

"Oh if you didn't I would almost go on with the other!"

"Would you really?"

I laughed again, but I returned for all answer: "Of course if she can rummage about that way she can perfectly have burnt them."

"You must wait—you must wait," Miss Tina mournfully moralised; and her tone ministered little to my patience, for it seemed after all to accept that wretched possibility. I would teach myself to wait, I declared nevertheless; because in the first place I couldn't do otherwise and in the second I had her promise, given me the other night, that she would help me.

"Of course if the papers are gone that's no use," she said; not as if she wished to recede, but only to be conscientious.

"Naturally. But if you could only find out!" I groaned, quivering again.

"I thought you promised you'd wait."

"Oh you mean wait even for that?"

"For what then?"

"Ah, nothing," I answered rather foolishly, being ashamed to tell her what had been implied in my acceptance of delay—the idea that she would perhaps do more for me than merely find out.

I know not if she guessed this; at all events she seemed to bethink herself of some propriety of showing me more rigour. "I did n't promise to deceive, did I? I don't think I did."

"It does n't much matter whether you did or not, for you could n't!"

Nothing is more possible than that she would n't have contested this even had n't she been diverted by our seeing the doctor's gondola shoot into the little canal and approach the house. I noted that he came as fast as if he believed our proprietress still in danger. We looked down at him while he disembarked and then went back into the sala to meet him. When he came up, however, I naturally left Miss Tina to go off with him alone, only asking her leave to come back later for news.

I went out of the house and walked far, as far as the Piazza, where my restlessness declined to quit me. I was unable to sit down; it was very late now though there were people still at the little tables in front of the cafés: I could but uneasily revolve, and I did so half a dozen times. The only comfort, none the less, was my having told Miss Tina who I really was. At last I took my way home again, getting gradually and all but inextricably lost, as I did whenever I went out in Venice: so that it was considerably past midnight when I reached my door. The sala, upstairs, was as dark as usual and my lamp as I crossed it found nothing satisfactory to show me. I was disappointed, for I had notified Miss Tina that I would come back for a report, and I thought she might have left a light there as a sign. The door of the ladies' apartment was closed; which seemed a hint that my faltering friend had gone to bed in impatience of waiting for me. I stood in the middle of the place, considering, hoping she would hear me and perhaps peep out, saying to myself too that she would never go to bed with her aunt in a state so critical; she would sit up and watch—she would be in a chair, in her dressing-gown. I went nearer the door; I stopped there and listened. I heard nothing at all and at last I tapped gently. No answer came and after another minute I turned the handle. There was no light in the room; this ought to have prevented my entrance, but it had no such effect. If I have frankly stated the importunities, the indelicacies, of which my desire to possess myself of Jeffrey Aspern's papers had made me capable I need n't shrink, it seems to me, from

confessing this last indiscretion. I regard it as the worst thing I did, yet there were extenuating circumstances. I was deeply though doubtless not disinterestedly anxious for more news of Juliana, and Miss Tina had accepted from me, as it were, a rendezvous which it might have been a point of honour with me to keep. It may be objected that her leaving the place dark was a positive sign that she released me, and to this I can only reply that I wished not to be released.

The door of Miss Bordereau's room was open and I could see beyond it the faintness of a taper. There was no sound—my footstep caused no one to stir. I came further into the room; I lingered there lamp in hand. I wanted to give Miss Tina a chance to come to me if, as I could n't doubt, she were still with her aunt. I made no noise to call her; I only waited to see if she would n't notice my light. She did n't, and I explained this—I found afterwards I was right—by the idea that she had fallen asleep. If she had fallen asleep her aunt was not on her mind, and my explanation ought to have led me to go out as I had come. I must repeat again that it did n't, for I found myself at the same moment given up to something else. I had no definite purpose, no bad intention, but felt myself held to the spot by an acute, though absurd, sense of opportunity. Opportunity for what I could n't have said, inasmuch as it was n't in my mind that I might proceed to thievery. Even had this tempted me I was confronted with the evident fact that Miss Bordereau did n't leave her secretary, her cupboard and the drawers of her tables gaping. I had no keys, no tools and no ambition to smash her furniture. None the less it came to me that I was now, perhaps alone, unmolested, at the hour of freedom and safety, nearer to the source of my hopes than I had ever been. I held up my lamp, let the light play on the different objects as if it could tell me something. Still there came no movement from the other room. If Miss Tina was sleeping she was sleeping sound. Was she doing so—generous creature—on purpose to leave me the field? Did she know I was there and was she just keeping quiet to see what I would do—what I *could* do? Yet might I, when it came to that? She herself knew even better than I how little.

I stopped in front of the secretary, gaping at it vainly and no doubt grotesquely; for what had it to say to me after all? In the first place it was locked, and in the second it almost surely contained nothing in which I was interested. Ten to one the papers had been destroyed, and even if they had n't the keen old woman would n't have put them in such a place as that after removing them from the green trunk—would n't have transferred them, with the idea of their safety on her brain, from the better hiding-place to the worse. The secretary was more conspicuous, more exposed in a room in which she could

no longer mount guard. It opened with a key, but there was a small brass handle, like a button as well; I saw this as I played my lamp over it. I did something more, for the climax of my crisis; I caught a glimpse of the possibility that Miss Tina wished me really to understand. If she did n't so wish me, if she wished me to keep away, why hadn't she locked the door of communication between the sitting-room and the sala? That would have been a definite sign that I was to leave them alone. If I did n't leave them alone she meant me to come for a purpose—a purpose now represented by the super-subtle inference that to oblige me she had unlocked the secretary. She had n't left the key, but the lid would probably move if I touched the button. This possibility pressed me hard and I bent very close to judge. I did n't propose to do anything, not even—not in the least—to let down the lid; I only wanted to test my theory, to see if the cover *would* move. I touched the button with my hand—a mere touch would tell me; and as I did so—it is embarrassing for me to relate it—I looked over my shoulder. It was a chance, an instinct, for I had really heard nothing. I almost let my luminary drop and certainly I stepped back, straightening myself up at what I saw. Juliana stood there in her nightdress, by the doorway of her room, watching me; her hands were raised, she had lifted the everlasting curtain that covered half her face, and for the first, the last, the only time I beheld her extraordinary eyes. They glared at me; they were like the sudden drench, for a caught burglar, of a flood of gaslight; they made me horribly ashamed. I never shall forget her strange little bent white tottering figure, with its lifted head, her attitude, her expression; neither shall I forget the tone in which as I turned, looking at her, she hissed out passionately, furiously:

"Ah you publishing scoundrel!"

I can't now say what I stammered to excuse myself, to explain; but I went toward her to tell her I meant no harm. She waved me off with her old hands, retreating before me in horror; and the next thing I knew she had fallen back with a quick spasm, as if death had descended on her, into Miss Tina's arms.

§ 9

I left Venice the next morning, directly on learning that my hostess had not succumbed, as I feared at the moment, to the shock I had given her—the shock I may also say she had given me. How in the world could I have supposed her capable of getting out of bed by herself? I failed to see Miss Tina before going; I only saw the *donna*, whom I entrusted with a note for her younger mistress. In this note I men-

tioned that I should be absent but a few days. I went to Treviso, to Bassano, to Castelfranco; I took walks and drives and looked at musty old churches with ill-lighted pictures; I spent hours seated smoking at the doors of cafés, where there were flies and yellow curtains, on the shady side of sleepy little squares. In spite of these pastimes, which were mechanical and perfunctory, I scantly enjoyed my travels: I had had to gulp down a bitter draught and could n't get rid of the taste. It had been devilish awkward, as the young men say, to be found by Juliana in the dead of night examining the attachment of her bureau; and it had not been less so to have to believe for a good many hours after that it was highly probable I had killed her. My humiliation galled me, but I had to make the best of it, had, in writing to Miss Tina to minimise it, as well as account for the posture in which I had been discovered. As she gave me no word of answer I could n't know what impression I made on her. It rankled for me that I had been called a publishing scoundrel, since certainly I did publish and no less certainly had n't been very delicate. There was a moment when I stood convinced that the only way to purge my dishonour was to take myself straight away on the instant; to sacrifice my hopes and relieve the two poor women for ever of the oppression of my intercourse. Then I reflected that I had better try a short absence first, for I must already have had a sense (unexpressed and dim) that in disappearing completely it would n't be merely my own hopes I should condemn to extinction. It would perhaps answer if I kept dark long enough to give the elder lady time to believe herself rid of me. That she would wish to be rid of me after this—if I was n't rid of her—was now not to be doubted: that midnight monstrosity would have cured her of the disposition to put up with my company for the sake of my dollars. I said to myself that after all I could n't abandon Miss Tina, and I continued to say this even while I noted that she quite ignored my earnest request—I had given her two or three addresses, at little towns, *poste restante*—for some sign of her actual state. I would have made my servant write me news but that he was unable to manage a pen. Could n't I measure the scorn of Miss Tina's silence—little disdainful as she had ever been? Really the soreness pressed; yet if I had scruples about going back I had others about not doing so, and I wanted to put myself on a better footing. The end of it was that I did return to Venice on the twelfth day; and as my gondola gently bumped against our palace steps a fine palpitation of suspense showed me the violence my absence had done me.

I had faced about so abruptly that I had n't even telegraphed to my servant. He was therefore not at the station to meet me, but he poked out his head from an upper window when I reached the house.

"They have put her into earth, *quella vecchia*," he said to me in the lower hall while he shouldered my valise; and he grinned and almost winked as if he knew I should be pleased with his news.

"She 's dead!" I cried, giving him a very different look.

"So it appears, since they 've buried her."

"It 's all over then? When was the funeral?"

"The other yesterday. But a funeral you could scarcely call it, signore: *roba da niente—un piccolo passeggio brutto* of two gondolas. Poveretta!" the man continued, referring apparently to Miss Tina. His conception of funerals was that they were mainly to amuse the living.

I wanted to know about Miss Tina, how she might be and generally where; but I asked him no more questions till we had got upstairs. Now that the fact had met me I took a bad view of it, especially of the idea that poor Miss Tina had had to manage by herself after the end. What did she know about arrangements, about the steps to take in such a case? Poveretta indeed! I could only hope the doctor had given her support and that she had n't been neglected by the old friends of whom she had told me, the little band of the faithful whose fidelity consisted in coming to the house once a year. I elicited from my servant that two old ladies and an old gentleman had in fact rallied around Miss Tina and had supported her—they had come for her in a gondola of their own—during the journey to the cemetery, the little red-walled island of tombs which lies to the north of the town and on the way to Murano. It appeared from these signs that the Misses Bordereau were Catholics, a discovery I had never made, as the old woman could n't go to church and her niece, so far as I perceived, either did n't, or went only to early mass in the parish before I was stirring. Certainly even the priests respected their seclusion; I had never caught the whisk of the curato's skirt. That evening, an hour later, I sent my servant down with five words on a card to ask if Miss Tina would see me for a few moments. She was not in the house, where he had sought her, he told me when he came back, but in the garden walking about to refresh herself and picking the flowers quite as if they belonged to her. He had found her there and she would be happy to see me.

I went down and passed half an hour with poor Miss Tina. She had always had a look of musty mourning, as if she were wearing out old robes of sorrow that would n't come to an end; and in this particular she made no different show. But she clearly had been crying, crying a great deal—simply, satisfyingly, refreshingly, with a primitive retarded sense of solitude and violence. But she had none of the airs or graces of grief, and I was almost surprised to see her stand there in the first dusk with her hands full of admirable roses and smile at me

with reddened eyes. Her white face, in the frame of her mantilla, looked longer, leaner than usual. I had n't doubted her being irreconcilably disgusted with me, her considering I ought to have been on the spot to advise her, to help her; and, though I believed there was no rancour in her composition and no great conviction of the importance of her affairs, I had prepared myself for a change in her manner, for some air of injury and estrangement, which should say to my conscience: "Well, you 're a nice person to have professed things!" But historic truth compels me to declare that this poor lady's dull face ceased to be dull, almost ceased to be plain, as she turned it gladly to her late aunt's lodger. That touched him extremely and he thought it simplified his situation until he found it did n't. I was as kind to her that evening as I knew how to be, and I walked about the garden with her as long as seemed good. There was no explanation of any sort between us; I did n't ask her why she had n't answered my letter. Still less did I repeat what I had said to her in that communication; if she chose to let me suppose she had forgotten the position in which Miss Bordereau had surprised me and the effect of the discovery on the old woman, I was quite willing to take it that way: I was grateful to her for not treating me as if I had killed her aunt.

We strolled and strolled, though really not much passed between us save the recognition of her bereavement, conveyed in my manner and in the expression she had of depending on me now, since I let her see I still took an interest in her. Miss Tina's was no breast for the pride or the pretense of independence; she did n't in the least suggest that she knew at present what would become of her. I forbore to press on that question, however, for I certainly was not prepared to say that I would take charge of her. I was cautious; not ignobly, I think, for I felt her knowledge of life to be so small that in her unsophisticated vision there would be no reason why—since I seemed to pity her—I should n't somehow look after her. She told me how her aunt had died, very peacefully at the last, and how everything had been done afterwards by the care of her good friends—fortunately, thanks to me, she said, smiling, there was money in the house. She repeated that when once the "nice" Italians like you they are your friends for life, and when we had gone into this she asked me about my *giro*, my impressions, my adventures, the places I had seen. I told her what I could, making it up partly, I 'm afraid, as in my disconcerted state I had taken little in; and after she had heard me she exclaimed, quite as if she had forgotten her aunt and her sorrow, "Dear, dear, how much I should like to do such things—to take an amusing little journey!" It came over me for the moment that I ought to propose some enterprise, say I would accompany her anywhere she liked; and I remarked at any

rate that a pleasant excursion—to give her a change—might be managed; we would think of it, talk it over. I spoke never a word of the Aspern documents, asked no question as to what she had ascertained or what had otherwise happened with regard to them before Juliana's death. It was n't that I was n't on pins and needles to know, but that I thought it more decent not to show greed again so soon after the catastrophe. I hoped she herself would say something, but she never glanced that way, and I thought this natural at the time. Later on, however, that night, it occurred to me that her silence was matter for suspicion; since if she had talked of my movements, of anything so detached as the Giorgione at Castelfranco, she might have alluded to what she could easily remember was in my mind. It was not to be supposed that the emotion produced by her aunt's death had blotted out the recollection that I was interested in that lady's relics, and I fidgeted afterwards as it came to me that her reticence might very possibly just mean that no relics survived. We separated in the garden —it was she who said she must go in; now that she was alone on the *piano nobile* I felt that (judged at any rate by Venetian ideas) I was on rather a different footing in regard to the invasion of it. As I shook hands with her for good-night I asked her if she had some general plan, had thought over what she had best do. "Oh yes, oh yes, but I have n't settled anything yet," she replied quite cheerfully. Was her cheerfulness explained by the impression that I would settle for her?

I was glad the next morning that we had neglected practical questions, as this gave me a pretext for seeing her again immediately. There was a practical enough question now to be touched on. I owed it to her to let her know formally that of course I did n't expect her to keep me on as a lodger, as also to show some interest in her own tenure, what she might have on her hands in the way of a lease. But I was not destined, as befell, to converse with her for more than an instant on either of these points. I sent her no message; I simply went down to the sala and walked to and fro there. I knew she would come out; she would promptly see me accessible. Somehow I preferred not to be shut up with her; gardens and big halls seemed better places to talk. It was a splendid morning, with something in the air that told of the waning of the long Venetian summer; a freshness from the sea that stirred the flowers in the garden and made a pleasant draught in the house, less shuttered and darkened now than when the old woman was alive. It was the beginning of autumn, of the end of the golden months. With this it was the end of my experiment—or would be in the course of half an hour, when I should really have learned that my dream had been reduced to ashes. After that there would be nothing left for me but to go to the station; for seriously—and as it struck me

in the morning light—I could n't linger there to act as guardian to a piece of middle-aged female helplessness. If she had n't saved the papers wherein should I be indebted to her? I think I winced a little as I asked myself how much, if she *had* saved them, I should have to recognise and, as it were, reward such a courtesy. Might n't that service after all saddle me with a guardianship? If this idea did n't make me more uncomfortable as I walked up and down it was because I was convinced I had nothing to look to. If the old woman had n't destroyed everything before she pounced on me in the parlour she had done so the next day.

It took Miss Tina rather longer than I had expected to act on my calculation; but when at last she came out she looked at me without surprise. I mentioned I had been waiting for her and she asked why I had n't let her know. I was glad a few hours later on that I had checked myself before remarking that a friendly intuition might have told her: it turned to comfort for me that I had n't played even to that mild extent on her sensibility. What I did say was virtually the truth—that I was too nervous, since I expected her now to settle my fate.

"Your fate?" said Miss Tina, giving me a queer look; and as she spoke I noticed a rare change in her. Yes, she was other than she had been the evening before—less natural and less easy. She had been crying the day before and was not crying now, yet she struck me as less confident. It was as if something had happened to her during the night, or at least as if she had thought of something that troubled her —something in particular that affected her relations with me, made them more embarrassing and more complicated. Had she simply begun to feel that her aunt's not being there now altered my position?

"I mean about our papers. *Are* there any? You must know now."

"Yes, there are a great many; more than I supposed." I was struck with the way her voice trembled as she told me this.

"Do you mean you 've got them in there—and that I may see them?"

"I don't think you can see them," said Miss Tina, with an extraordinary expression of entreaty in her eyes, as if the dearest hope she had in the world now was that I would n't take them from her. But how could she expect me to make such a sacrifice as that after all that had passed between us? What had I come back to Venice for but to see them, to take them? My joy at learning they were still in existence was such that if the poor woman had gone down on her knees to beseech me never to mention them again I would have treated the proceeding as a bad joke. "I 've got them but I can 't show them," she lamentably added.

"Not even to me? Ah Miss Tina!" I broke into a tone of infinite remonstrance and reproach.

She coloured and the tears came back to her eyes; I measured the anguish it cost her to take such a stand which a dreadful sense of duty had imposed on her. It made me quite sick to find myself confronted with that particular obstacle; all the more that it seemed to me I had been distinctly encouraged to leave it out of account. I quite held Miss Tina to have assured me that if she had no greater hindrance than that——! "You don't mean to say you made her a death-bed promise? It was precisely against your doing anything of that sort that I thought I was safe. Oh I would rather she had burnt the papers outright than have to reckon with such a treachery as that."

"No, it is n't a promise," said Miss Tina.

"Pray what is it then?"

She hung fire, but finally said: "She tried to burn them, but I prevented it. She had hid them in her bed."

"In her bed—?"

"Between the mattresses. That's where she put them when she took them out of the trunk. I can't understand how she did it, because Olimpia did n't help her. She tells me so and I believe her. My aunt only told her afterwards, so that she should n't undo the bed—anything but the sheets. So it was very badly made," added Miss Tina simply.

"I should think so! And how did she try to burn them?"

"She did n't try much; she was too weak those last days. But she told me—she charged me. Oh it was terrible! She could n't speak after that night. She could only make signs."

"And what did you do?"

"I took them away. I locked them up."

"In the secretary?"

"Yes, in the secretary," said Miss Tina, reddening again.

"Did you tell her you 'd burn them?"

"No, I did n't—on purpose."

"On purpose to gratify me?"

"Yes, only for that."

"And what good will you have done me if after all you won't show them?"

"Oh none. I know that—I know that," she dismally sounded.

"And did she believe you had destroyed them?"

"I don't know what she believed at the last. I could n't tell—she was too far gone."

"Then if there was no promise and no assurance I can't see what ties you."

"Oh she hated it so—she hated it so! She was so jealous. But here's the portrait—you may have that," the poor woman announced, taking the little picture, wrapped up in the same manner in which her aunt had wrapped it, out of her pocket.

"I may have it—do you mean you give it to me?" I gasped as it passed into my hand.

"Oh yes."

"But it's worth money—a large sum."

"Well!" said Miss Tina, still with her strange look.

I did n't know what to make of it, for it could scarcely mean that she wanted to bargain like her aunt. She spoke as for making me a present. "I can't take it from you as a gift," I said, "and yet I can't afford to pay you for it according to the idea Miss Bordereau had of its value. She rated it a thousand pounds."

"Could n't we sell it?" my friend threw off.

"God forbid! I prefer the picture to the money."

"Well then keep it."

"You 're very generous."

"So are you."

"I don't know why you should think so," I returned; and this was true enough, for the good creature appeared to have in her mind some rich reference that I did n't in the least seize.

"Well, you 've made a great difference for me," she said.

I looked at Jeffrey Aspern's face in the little picture, partly in order not to look at that of my companion, which had begun to trouble me, even to frighten me a little—it had taken so very odd, so strained and unnatural a cast. I made no answer to this last declaration; I but privately consulted Jeffrey Aspern's delightful eyes with my own—they were so young and brilliant and yet so wise and so deep; I asked him what on earth was the matter with Miss Tina. He seemed to smile at me with mild mockery; he might have been amused at my case. I had got into a pickle for him—as if he needed it! He was unsatisfactory for the only moment since I had known him. Nevertheless, now that I held the little picture in my hand I felt it would be a precious possession. "Is this a bribe to make me give up the papers?" I presently and all perversely asked. "Much as I value this, you know, if I were to be obliged to choose the papers are what I should prefer. Ah but ever so much!"

"How can you choose—how can you choose?" Miss Tina returned slowly and woefully.

"I see! Of course there's nothing to be said if you regard the interdiction that rests on you as quite insurmountable. In this case it must

seem to you that to part with them would be an impiety of the worst kind, a simple sacrilege!"

She shook her head, only lost in the queerness of her case. "You'd understand if you had known her. I'm afraid," she quavered suddenly—"I'm afraid! She was terrible when she was angry."

"Yes, I saw something of that, that night. She was terrible. Then I saw her eyes. Lord, they were fine!"

"I see them—they stare at me in the dark!" said Miss Tina.

"You've grown nervous with all you've been through."

"Oh yes, very—very!"

"You mustn't mind; that will pass away," I said kindly. Then I added resignedly, for it really seemed to me that I must accept the situation: "Well, so it is, and it can't be helped. I must renounce." My friend, at this, with her eyes on me, gave a low soft moan, and I went on: "I only wish to goodness she had destroyed them; then there would be nothing more to say. And I can't understand why, with her ideas, she didn't."

"Oh she lived on them!" said Miss Tina.

"You can imagine whether that makes me want less to see them," I returned not quite so desperately. "But don't let me stand here as if I had it in my soul to tempt you to anything base. Naturally, you understand, I give up my rooms. I leave Venice immediately." And I took up my hat, which I had placed on a chair. We were still rather awkwardly on our feet in the middle of the sala. She had left the door of the apartments open behind her, but had not led me that way.

A strange spasm came into her face as she saw me take my hat. "Immediately—do you mean to-day?" The tone of the words was tragic—they were a cry of desolation.

"Oh no; not so long as I can be of the least service to you."

"Well, just a day or two more—just two or three days," she panted. Then controlling herself she added in another manner: "She wanted to say something to me—the last day—something very particular. But she couldn't."

"Something very particular?"

"Something more about the papers."

"And did you guess—have you any idea?"

"No, I've tried to think—but I don't know. I've thought all kinds of things."

"As for instance?"

"Well, that if you were a relation it would be different."

I wondered. "If I were a relation—?"

"If you weren't a stranger. Then it would be the same for you as for me. Anything that's mine would be yours, and you could do what

you like. I should n't be able to prevent you—and you'd have no responsibility."

She brought out this droll explanation with a nervous rush and as if speaking words got by heart. They gave me an impression of a subtlety which at first I failed to follow. But after a moment her face helped me to see further, and then the queerest of lights came to me. It was embarrassing, and I bent my head over Jeffrey Aspern's portrait. What an odd expression was in his face! "Get out of it as you can, my dear fellow!" I put the picture into the pocket of my coat and said to Miss Tina: "Yes, I'll sell it for you. I shan't get a thousand pounds by any means, but I shall get something good."

She looked at me through pitiful tears, but seemed to try to smile as she returned: "We can divide the money."

"No, no, it shall be all yours." Then I went on: "I think I know what your poor aunt wanted to say. She wanted to give directions that her papers should be buried with her."

Miss Tina appeared to weigh this suggestion; after which she answered with striking decision, "Oh no, she would n't have thought that safe!"

"It seems to me nothing could be safer."

"She had an idea that when people want to publish they 're capable ——!" And she paused, very red.

"Of violating a tomb? Mercy on us, what must she have thought of me!"

"She was n't just, she was n't generous!" my companion cried with sudden passion.

The light that had come into my mind a moment before spread further. "Ah don't say that, for we *are* a dreadful race." Then I pursued: "If she left a will that may give you some idea."

"I 've found nothing of the sort—she destroyed it. She was very fond of me," Miss Tina added with an effect of extreme inconsequence. "She wanted me to be happy. And if any person should be kind to me—she wanted to speak of that."

I was almost awestricken by the astuteness with which the good lady found herself inspired, transparent astuteness as it was and stitching, as the phrase is, with white thread. "Depend upon it she did n't want to make any provision that would be agreeable to *me.*"

"No, not to you, but quite to me. She knew I should like it if you could carry out your idea. Not because she cared for you, but because she did think of me," Miss Tina went on with her unexpected persuasive volubility. "You could see the things—you could use them." She stopped, seeing I grasped the sense of her conditional—stopped long enough for me to give some sign that I did n't give. She must

have been conscious, however, that though my face showed the greatest embarrassment ever painted on a human countenance it was not set as a stone, it was also full of compassion. It was a comfort to me a long time afterwards to consider that she could n't have seen in me the smallest symptom of disrespect. "I don't know what to do; I 'm too tormented, I 'm too ashamed!" she continued with vehemence. Then turning away from me and burying her face in her hands she burst into a flood of tears. If she did n't know what to do it may be imagined whether I knew better. I stood there dumb, watching her while her sobs resounded in the great empty hall. In a moment she was up at me again with her streaming eyes. "I 'd give you everything, and she 'd understand, where she is—she 'd forgive me!"

"Ah Miss Tina—ah Miss Tina," I stammered for all reply. I did n't know what to do, as I say, but at a venture I made a wild vague movement in consequence of which I found myself at the door. I remember standing there and saying "It would n't do, it would n't do!" —saying it pensively, awkwardly, grotesquely, while I looked away to the opposite end of the sala as at something very interesting. The next thing I remember is that I was downstairs and out of the house. My gondola was there and my gondolier, reclining on the cushions, sprang up as soon as he saw me. I jumped in and to his usual *"Dove commanda?"* replied, in a tone that made him stare: "Anywhere, anywhere; out into the lagoon!"

He rowed me away and I sat there prostrate, groaning softly to myself, my hat pulled over my brow. What in the name of the preposterous did she mean if she did n't mean to offer me her hand? That was the price—that was the price! And did she think I wanted it, poor deluded infatuated extravagant lady? My gondolier, behind me, must have seen my ears red as I wondered, motionless there under the fluttering *tenda* with my hidden face, noticing nothing as we passed— wondered whether her delusion, her infatuation had been my own reckless work. Did she think I had made love to her even to get the papers? I had n't, I had n't; I repeated that over to myself for an hour, for two hours, till I was wearied if not convinced. I don't know where, on the lagoon, my gondolier took me; we floated aimlessly and with slow rare strokes. At last I became conscious that we were near the Lido, far up, on the right hand, as you turn your back to Venice, and I made him put me ashore. I wanted to walk, to move, to shed some of my bewilderment. I crossed the narrow strip and got to the sea-beach—I took my way toward Malamocco. But presently I flung myself down again on the warm sand, in the breeze, on the coarse dry grass. It took it out of me to think I had been so much at fault, that I had unwittingly but none the less deplorably trifled. But I had n't

given her cause—distinctly I had n't. I had said to Mrs. Prest that I
would make love to her; but it had been a joke without consequences
and I had never said it to my victim. I had been as kind as possible
because I really liked her; but since when had that become a crime
where a woman of such an age and such an appearance was con-
cerned? I am far from remembering clearly the succession of events
and feelings during this long day of confusion, which I spent entirely
in wandering about, without going home, until late at night; it only
comes back to me that there were moments when I pacified my con-
science and others when I lashed it into pain. I did n't laugh all day—
that I do recollect; the case, however it might have struck others,
seemed to me so little amusing. I should have been better employed
perhaps in taking in the comic side of it. At any rate, whether I had
given cause or not, there was no doubt whatever that I could n't pay
the price. I could n't accept the proposal. I could n't, for a bundle of
tattered papers, marry a ridiculous pathetic provincial old woman. It
was a proof of how little she supposed the idea would come to me that
she should have decided to suggest it herself in that practical argu-
mentative heroic way—with the timidity, however, so much more
striking than the boldness, that her reasons appeared to come first and
her feelings afterward.

As the day went on I grew to wish I had never heard of Aspern's
relics, and I cursed the extravagant curiosity that had put John
Cumnor on the scent of them. We had more than enough material
without them, and my predicament was the just punishment of that
most fatal of human follies, our not having known when to stop. It
was very well to say it was no predicament, that the way out was
simple, that I had only to leave Venice by the first train in the morn-
ing, after addressing Miss Tina a note which should be placed in her
hand as soon as I got clear of the house; for it was strong proof of
my quandary that when I tried to make up the note to my taste in
advance—I would put it on paper as soon as I got home, before going
to bed—I could n't think of anything but "How can I thank you for
the rare confidence you 've placed in me?" That would never do; it
sounded exactly as if an acceptance were to follow. Of course I might
get off without writing at all, but that would be brutal, and my idea
was still to exclude brutal solutions. As my confusion cooled I lost
myself in wonder at the importance I had attached to Juliana's
crumpled scraps; the thought of them became odious to me and I
was as vexed with the old witch for the superstition that had pre-
vented her from destroying them as I was with myself for having al-
ready spent more money than I could afford in attempting to control
their fate. I forget what I did, where I went after leaving the Lido,

and at what hour or with what recovery of composure I made my way back to my boat. I only know that in the afternoon, when the air was aglow with the sunset, I was standing before the church of Saints John and Paul and looking up at the small square-jawed face of Bartolommeo Colleoni, the terrible *condottiere* who sits so sturdily astride of his huge bronze horse on the high pedestal on which Venetian gratitude maintains him. The statue is incomparable, the finest of all mounted figures, unless that of Marcus Aurelius, who rides benignant before the Roman Capitol, be finer: but I was not thinking of that; I only found myself staring at the triumphant captain as if he had had an oracle on his lips. The western light shines into all his grimness at that hour and makes it wonderfully personal. But he continued to look far over my head, at the red immersion of another day—he had seen so many go down into the lagoon through the centuries—and if he were thinking of battles and stratagems they were of a different quality from any I had to tell him of. He could n't direct me what to do, gaze up at him as I might. Was it before this or after that I wandered about for an hour in the small canals, to the continued stupefaction of my gondolier, who had never seen me so restless and yet so void of a purpose and could extract from me no order but "Go anywhere—everywhere—all over the place?" He reminded me that I had not lunched and expressed therefore respectfully the hope that I would dine earlier. He had had long periods of leisure during the day, when I had left the boat and rambled, so that I was not obliged to consider him, and I told him that till the morrow, for reasons, I should touch no meat. It was an effect of poor Miss Tina's proposal, not altogether auspicious, that I had quite lost my appetite. I don't know why it happened that on this occasion I was more than ever struck with that queer air of sociability, of cousinship and family life, which makes up half the expression of Venice. Without streets and vehicles, the uproar of wheels, the brutality of horses, and with its little winding ways where people crowd together, where voices sound as in the corridors of a house, where the human step circulates as if it skirted the angles of furniture and shoes never wear out, the place has the character of an immense collective apartment, in which Piazza San Marco is the most ornamented corner and palaces and churches, for the rest, play the part of great divans of repose, tables of entertainment, expanses of decoration. And somehow the splendid common domicile, familiar domestic and resonant, also resembles a theatre with its actors clicking over bridges and, in straggling processions, tripping along fondamentas. As you sit in your gondola the footways that in certain parts edge the canals assume to the eye the importance of a stage, meeting it at the same angle, and the Venetian figures, moving to and fro

against the battered scenery of their little houses of comedy, strike you as members of an endless dramatic troupe.

I went to bed that night very tired and without being able to compose an address to Miss Tina. Was this failure the reason why I became conscious the next morning as soon as I awoke of a determination to see the poor lady again the first moment she would receive me? That had something to do with it, but what had still more was the fact that during my sleep the oddest revulsion had taken place in my spirit. I found myself aware of this almost as soon as I opened my eyes: it made me jump out of my bed with the movement of a man who remembers that he has left the house-door ajar or a candle burning under a shelf. Was I still in time to save my goods? That question was in my heart; for what had now come to pass was that in the unconscious cerebration of sleep I had swung back to a passionate appreciation of Juliana's treasure. The pieces composing it were now more precious than ever and a positive ferocity had come into my need to acquire them. The condition Miss Tina had attached to that act no longer appeared an obstacle worth thinking of, and for an hour this morning my repentant imagination brushed it aside. It was absurd I should be able to invent nothing; absurd to renounce so easily and turn away helpless from the idea that the only way to become possessed was to unite myself to her for life. I might n't unite myself, yet I might still have what she had. I must add that by the time I sent down to ask if she would see me I had invented no alternative, though in fact I drew out my dressing in the interest of my wit. This failure was humiliating, yet what could the alternative be? Miss Tina sent back word I might come; and as I descended the stairs and crossed the sala to her door—this time she received me in her aunt's forlorn parlour—I hoped she would n't think my announcement was to be "favourable." She certainly would have understood my recoil of the day before.

As soon as I came into the room I saw that she had done so, but I also saw something which had not been in my forecast. Poor Miss Tina's sense of her failure had produced a rare alteration in her, but I had been too full of stratagems and spoils to think of that. Now I took it in; I can scarcely tell how it startled me. She stood in the middle of the room with a face of mildness bent upon me, and her look of forgiveness, of absolution, made her angelic. It beautified her; she was younger; she was not a ridiculous old woman. This trick of her expression, this magic of her spirit, transfigured her, and while I still noted it I heard a whisper somewhere in the depths of my conscience: "Why not, after all—why not?" It seemed to me I *could* pay the price. Still more distinctly however than the whisper I heard

Miss Tina's own voice. I was so struck with the different effect she made on me that at first I was n't clearly aware of what she was saying; then I recognised she had bade me good-bye—she said something about hoping I should be very happy.

"Good-bye—good-bye?" I repeated with an inflection interrogative and probably foolish.

I saw she did n't feel the interrogation, she only heard the words; she had strung herself up to accepting our separation and they fell upon her ear as a proof. "Are you going to-day?" she asked. "But it does n't matter, for whenever you go I shall not see you again. I don't want to." And she smiled strangely, with an infinite gentleness. She had never doubted my having left her the day before in horror. How *could* she, since I had n't come back before night to contradict, even as a simple form, even as an act of common humanity, such an idea? And now she had the force of soul—Miss Tina with force of soul was a new conception—to smile at me in her abjection.

"What shall you do—where shall you go?" I asked.

"Oh I don't know. I 've done the great thing. I 've destroyed the papers."

"Destroyed them?" I waited.

"Yes; what was I to keep them for? I burnt them last night, one by one, in the kitchen."

"One by one?" I coldly echoed it.

"It took a long time—there were so many." The room seemed to go round me as she said this and a real darkness for a moment descended on my eyes. When it passed, Miss Tina was there still, but the transfiguration was over and she had changed back to a plain dingy elderly person. It was in this character she spoke as she said "I can't stay with you longer, I can't;" and it was in this character she turned her back upon me, as I had turned mine upon her twenty-four hours before, and moved to the door of her room. Here she did what I had n't done when I quitted her—she paused long enough to give me one look. I have never forgotten it and I sometimes still suffer from it, though it was not resentful. No, there was no resentment, nothing hard or vindictive in poor Miss Tina; for when, later, I sent her, as the price of the portrait of Jeffrey Aspern, a larger sum of money than I had hoped to be able to gather for her, writing to her that I had sold the picture, she kept it with thanks; she never sent it back. I wrote her that I had sold the picture, but I admitted to Mrs. Prest at the time—I met this other friend in London that autumn—that it hangs above my writing-table. When I look at it I can scarcely bear my loss—I mean of the precious papers.

The Bridge of
San Luis Rey

THORNTON WILDER

THORNTON NIVEN WILDER *was born in Madison, Wisconsin, April 17, 1897. When he was nine years old his family took him to China, where his father was to be the American consul general at Hong Kong, and where he may have acquired that love of far horizons which has been with him ever since. He studied for two years at Oberlin, took his A.B. at Yale in 1920, and then spent two years in the American Academy in Rome. Traveling, teaching and writing are his pastimes.* The Cabala, *his first novel, was written while he was a master of French at Lawrenceville School.* The Bridge of San Luis Rey, *which appeared in 1927, established him as a free lance and one of the ablest novelists of our day. It measures 34,500 words.*

INTRODUCTION

In the spring of 1926 I was serving my apprenticeship as an editor. On one of my visits to New York I stopped in at the Sunwise Turn, a bookstore then famous for its discovery of the new, and there for the first time heard the name of Thornton Wilder. The clerk recommended him as a young Yale graduate of about my age whose first novel, *The Cabala,* I ought to read. I took it home that night and found myself as covetous as one contemporary can be of another. For here was the kind of book I should like to have written—a delightful story—or, rather, a succession of stories—about Rome. The author had either lived in Italy or read everything about it he could get his hands on—I couldn't tell which. I was fascinated by his blending of the past and present; for instance, Wilder would take the story of Keats's last visit, when he was dying and had only Severn to hold his head up, and this he would retell in modern circumstances, with fresh emphasis. I know I envied him his knowledge, and with it his colorful style, a kind of tapestry English, so beautifully neat but not gaudy.

At the time I speak of, I was the third assistant editor of the *Atlantic* and I was naturally doing my utmost to people the magazine with my contemporaries. I wrote to Thornton Wilder at Yale Station, told him of my admiration for *The Cabala,* and of my hope that he would let me see, as a possible serial for the *Atlantic,* the next book on which he was working. In due time he sent me the first two thirds of a new novel about Peru, a story in which, I am sorry to say, I could interest my seniors very little. So I was under the necessity of dissimulating my private enthusiasm in a letter of rejection. But to keep the record clear, let me say that I think now, and thought then, that *The Bridge of San Luis Rey* is one of the well-tempered and classic novels of our time.

When he came to write *The Bridge,* Wilder applied to perfection

the very same methods which he had been experimenting with in *The Cabala*. It mattered little that he had never been in Peru. He knew it by map. He knew its history. Best of all, he had been cruising widely in Spanish and French literature—so widely that he already possessed an intimate, confiding knowledge of the Latin temperament. The novel opens with a coincidence. The Bridge of San Luis Rey was, so Wilder tells us—the finest bridge in all Peru, up until Friday noon, July 20, 1714, when the osier of which it had been woven by the Incas snapped with a twanging noise and the five pedestrians on it were flung to their deaths in the valley below. On this coincidence the novel turns.

Who were these five that perished? And how much did they matter in the little city of Lima? To answer that curiosity, the novelist re-creates the whole enchanting society of Peru as it was—or ought to have been—in the years leading up to the accident. Graciously and with great urbanity he introduces the reader to those in high place and those in low—individuals all: the Viceroy, Don Andrés de Ribera, the remnant of a delightful man; the Abbess with her plain red face, her great heart and her angry impudence with God; Uncle Pio so worn by disease and bad company that he was like a soiled pack of cards; Esteban and Manuel, the twins, with their deathless love and their secret language; Pepita the orphan; the hideous old Marquesa, so lonely and yet so captivating in those longing letters to her daughter in Spain; the adventurer, Captain Alvarado, "blackened and cured by all weather"; and most lustrous of them all, Señora Micaela Villégas, called the Perichole, half Castilian, and no better actress in the world! Some of these, one suspects, will put foot on that fateful bridge. But it is part of the novelist's suspense that he gives you no warning.

Mr Wilder writes with the air of knowing much more than he tells. This, I believe, is partly the effect of his enormous reading and of the relish with which he stores up every aspect of experience, and partly it is the effect of a craftsmanship which can make a sentence so sensitive to humor, or pathos, or irony. I stress this point because Wilder's prose is so smooth flowing, so outwardly restrained that one is tempted to take for granted the beauty it reveals. Let me illustrate. Speaking of the twins, the novelist says that they had grown up in the convent "until they were a little past the age when their presence began to be a slight distraction to the dedicated sisters." Of the old Marquesa in a re-pentant mood he says, "Perhaps she would learn in time to permit both her daughter and her gods to govern their own affairs"; of Uncle Pio, "he wanted to be always near beautiful women, of whom he was always in the best and worst sense the worshipper"; and of Esteban, "now he discovered that secret from which one never quite recovers, that even in the most perfect love one person loves less profoundly than another."

This poignancy is the keynote of Wilder's style, the poignancy arising from the struggle of people so variously marked by experience, trying so desperately to get through to those they love.

The novel begins on the bridge, and it ends on the bridge. But a world of meaning has passed in between. For the victims and the survivors of the Bridge of San Luis Rey are threaded together by the tenuous strands of love, and these threads give the story its unity and its philosophy. As the story is unfolded, we first perceive and then sympathize with the possessive love of the Marquesa for her daughter, the adoration of Pepita for the Abbess, the deep filial affection of Esteban for Manuel, the Pygmalion love of Uncle Pio for the Perichole, and the love of the oppressed felt by the Abbess, Madre María del Pilar, whom no man ever loved. This theme runs through the story from beginning to end, never intrusive, always sustaining, and because of it we feel no resentment at the death of the five, but rather a kind of satisfaction with as much as they have. No words of mine can express it as well as the closing sentences of the author's: "We ourselves shall be loved for a while, and forgotten, but the love will have been enough. . . . Even memory is not necessary for love. There is a land of the living and a land of the dead and the bridge is love, the only survival, and the only meaning."

THE BRIDGE OF SAN LUIS REY

PART I

Perhaps An Accident

On FRIDAY NOON, July the twentieth, 1714, the finest bridge in all Peru broke and precipitated five travellers into the gulf below. This bridge was on the highroad between Lima and Cuzco and hundreds of persons passed over it every day. It had been woven of osier by the Incas more than a century before and visitors to the city were always led out to see it. It was a mere ladder of thin slats swung out over the gorge, with handrails of dried vine. Horses and coaches and chairs had to go down hundreds of feet below and pass over the narrow torrent on rafts, but no one, not even the Viceroy, not even the Archbishop of Lima, had descended with the baggage rather than cross by the famous bridge of San Luis Rey. St. Louis of France himself protected it, by his name and by the little mud church on the further side. The bridge seemed to be among the things that last forever; it was unthinkable that it should break. The moment a Peruvian heard of the accident he signed himself and made a mental calculation as to how recently he had crossed by it and how soon he had intended crossing by it again. People wandered about in a trance-like state, muttering; they had the hallucination of seeing themselves falling into a gulf.

There was a great service in the Cathedral. The bodies of the victims were approximately collected and approximately separated from one another, and there was great searching of hearts in the beautiful city of Lima. Servant girls returned bracelets which they had stolen from their mistresses, and usurers harangued their wives angrily, in defense of usury. Yet it was rather strange that this event should have so impressed the Limeans, for in that country those catastrophes which lawyers shockingly call the "acts of God" were more than usually frequent. Tidal waves were continually washing away cities; earthquakes arrived every week and towers fell upon good men and women all the time. Diseases were forever flitting in and out of the provinces and old age carried away some of the most admirable citizens. That

is why it was so surprising that the Peruvians should have been especially touched by the rent in the bridge of San Luis Rey.

Everyone was very deeply impressed, but only one person did anything about it, and that was Brother Juniper. By a series of coincidences so extraordinary that one almost suspects the presence of some Intention, this little red-haired Franciscan from Northern Italy happened to be in Peru converting the Indians and happened to witness the accident.

It was a very hot noon, that fatal noon, and coming around the shoulder of a hill Brother Juniper stopped to wipe his forehead and to gaze upon the screen of snowy peaks in the distance, then into the gorge below him filled with the dark plumage of green trees and green birds and traversed by its ladder of osier. Joy was in him; things were not going badly. He had opened several little abandoned churches and the Indians were crawling in to early Mass and groaning at the moment of miracle as though their hearts would break. Perhaps it was the pure air from the snows before him; perhaps it was the memory that brushed him for a moment of the poem that bade him raise his eyes to the helpful hills. At all events he felt at peace. Then his glance fell upon the bridge, and at that moment a twanging noise filled the air, as when the string of some musical instrument snaps in a disused room, and he saw the bridge divide and fling five gesticulating ants into the valley below.

Anyone else would have said to himself with secret joy: "Within ten minutes myself. . . !" But it was another thought that visited Brother Juniper: "Why did this happen to *those* five?" If there were any plan in the universe at all, if there were any pattern in a human life, surely it could be discovered mysteriously latent in those lives so suddenly cut off. Either we live by accident and die by accident, or we live by plan and die by plan. And on that instant Brother Juniper made the resolve to inquire into the secret lives of those five persons, that moment falling through the air, and to surprise the reason of their taking off.

.

It seemed to Brother Juniper that it was high time for theology to take its place among the exact sciences and he had long intended putting it there. What he had lacked hitherto was a laboratory. Oh, there had never been any lack of specimens; any number of his charges had met calamity,—spiders had stung them; their lungs had been touched; their houses had burned down and things had happened to their children from which one averts the mind. But these occasions of human woe had never been quite fit for scientific exam-

ination. They had lacked what our good savants were later to call *proper control*. The accident had been dependent upon human error, for example, or had contained elements of probability. But this collapse of the bridge of San Luis Rey was a sheer Act of God. It afforded a perfect laboratory. Here at last one could surprise His intentions in a pure state.

You and I can see that coming from anyone but Brother Juniper this plan would be the flower of a perfect skepticism. It resembled the effort of those presumptuous souls who wanted to walk on the pavements of Heaven and built the Tower of Babel to get there. But to our Franciscan there was no element of doubt in the experiment. He knew the answer. He merely wanted to prove it, historically, mathematically, to his converts,—poor obstinate converts, so slow to believe that their pains were inserted into their lives for their own good. People were always asking for good sound proofs; doubt springs eternal in the human breast, even in countries where the Inquisition can read your very thoughts in your eyes.

This was not the first time that Brother Juniper had tried to resort to such methods. Often on the long trips he had to make (scurrying from parish to parish, his robe tucked up about his knees, for haste) he would fall to dreaming of experiments that justify the ways of God to man. For instance, a complete record of the Prayers for Rain and their results. Often he had stood on the steps of one of his little churches, his flock kneeling before him on the baked street. Often he had stretched his arms to the sky and declaimed the splendid ritual. Not often, but several times, he had felt the virtue enter him and seen the little cloud forming on the horizon. But there were many times when weeks went by . . . but why think of them? It was not himself he was trying to convince that rain and drought were wisely apportioned.

Thus it was that the determination rose within him at the moment of the accident. It prompted him to busy himself for six years, knocking at all the doors in Lima, asking thousands of questions, filling scores of notebooks, in his effort at establishing the fact that each of the five lost lives was a perfect whole. Everyone knew that he was working on some sort of memorial of the accident and everyone was very helpful and misleading. A few even knew the principal aim of his activity and there were patrons in high places.

The result of all this diligence was an enormous book, which as we shall see later, was publicly burned on a beautiful Spring morning in the great square. But there was a secret copy and after a great many years and without much notice it found its way to the library of the University of San Marco. There it lies between two great wooden

covers collecting dust in a cupboard. It deals with one after another of the victims of the accident, cataloguing thousands of little facts and anecdotes and testimonies, and concluding with a dignified passage describing why God had settled upon that person and upon that day for His demonstration of wisdom. Yet for all his diligence Brother Juniper never knew the central passion of Doña María's life; nor of Uncle Pio's, not even of Esteban's. And I, who claim to know so much more, isn't it possible that even I have missed the very spring within the spring?

Some say that we shall never know and that to the gods we are like the flies that the boys kill on a summer day, and some say, on the contrary, that the very sparrows do not lose a feather that has not been brushed away by the finger of God.

PART II

The Marquesa De Montemayor

Any Spanish schoolboy is required to know today more about Doña María, Marquesa de Montemayor, than Brother Juniper was to discover in years of research. Within a century of her death her letters had become one of the monuments of Spanish literature and her life and times have ever since been the object of long studies. But her biographers have erred in one direction as greatly as the Franciscan did in another; they have tried to invest her with a host of graces, to read back into her life and person some of the beauties that abound in her letters, whereas all real knowledge of this wonderful woman must proceed from the act of humiliating her and of divesting her of all beauties save one.

She was the daughter of a cloth-merchant who had acquired the money and the hatred of the Limeans within a stone's-throw of the Plaza. Her childhood was unhappy: she was ugly; she stuttered; her mother persecuted her with sarcasms in an effort to arouse some social charms and forced her to go about the town in a veritable harness of jewels. She lived alone and she thought alone. Many suitors presented themselves, but as long as she could she fought against the convention of her time and was determined to remain single. There were hysterical scenes with her mother, recriminations, screams and slamming of doors. At last at twenty-six she found herself penned into marriage with a supercilious and ruined nobleman and the Cathedral of Lima

fairly buzzed with the sneers of her guests. Still she lived alone and thought alone, and when an exquisite daughter was born to her she fastened upon her an idolatrous love. But little Clara took after her father; she was cold and intellectual. At the age of eight she was calmly correcting her mother's speech and presently regarding her with astonishment and repulsion. The frightened mother became meek and obsequious but she could not prevent herself from persecuting Doña Clara with nervous attention and a fatiguing love. Again there were hysterical recriminations, screams and slamming of doors. From the offers of marriage that fell to her, Doña Clara deliberately chose the one that required her removal to Spain. So to Spain she went, to that land from which it takes six months to receive an answer to one's letter. The leave-taking before so long a voyage became in Peru one of the formal services of the Church. The ship was blessed and as the space widened between the vessel and the beach both companies knelt and sang a hymn that never failed to sound weak and timid in all that open air. Doña Clara sailed with most admirable composure, leaving her mother to gaze after the bright ship, her hand pressing now her heart and now her mouth. Blurred and streaked became her view of the serene Pacific and the enormous clouds of pearl that hang forever motionless above it.

Left alone in Lima the Marquesa's life grew more and more inward. She became increasingly negligent in her dress and like all lonely people she talked to herself audibly. All her existence lay in the burning center of her mind. On that stage were performed endless dialogues with her daughter, impossible reconciliations, scenes eternally recommenced of remorse and forgiveness. On the street you beheld an old woman her red wig fallen a little over one ear, her left cheek angry with a leprous affection, her right with a complementary adjustment of rouge. Her chin was never dry; her lips were never still. Lima was a city of eccentrics, but even there she became its jest as she drove through the streets or shuffled up the steps of its churches. She was thought to be continuously drunk. Worse things were said of her and petitions were afloat that she be locked up. She had been denounced three times before the Inquisition. It is not impossible that she might have been burned had her son-in-law been less influential in Spain and had she not somehow collected a few friends about the viceregal court who suffered her for her oddity and her wide reading.

The distressing character of the relations between mother and daughter were further embittered by misunderstandings over money. The Condesa received a handsome allowance from her mother and frequent gifts. Doña Clara soon became the outstanding woman of intelligence at the Spanish court. All the wealth of Peru would have

been insufficient to maintain her in the grandiose style she fancied for herself. Strangely enough her extravagance proceeded from one of the best traits in her nature: she regarded her friends, her servants and all the interesting people in the capital, as her children. In fact there seemed only one person in the world towards whom she did not expend herself in kind offices. Among her *protégés* was the cartographer De Blasiis (whose *Maps of the New World* was dedicated to the Marquesa de Montemayor amid the roars of the courtiers at Lima who read that she was the *"admiration of her city and a rising sun in the West"*); another was the scientist Azuarius whose treatise on the laws of hydraulics was suppressed by the Inquisition as being too exciting. For a decade the Condesa literally sustained all the arts and sciences of Spain; it was not her fault that nothing memorable was produced in that time.

About four years after Doña Clara's departure Doña María received her permission to visit Europe. On both sides the visit was anticipated with resolutions well nourished on self-reproach: the one to be patient, the other to be undemonstrative. Both failed. Each tortured the other and was on the point of losing her mind under the alternations of self-rebuke and the outbursts of passion. At length one day Doña María rose before dawn, daring no more than to kiss the door behind which her daughter was sleeping, took ship and returned to America. Henceforth letter-writing had to take the place of all the affection that could not be lived.

Hers were the letters that in an astonishing world have become the text-book of schoolboys and the ant-hill of the grammarians. Doña María would have invented her genius had she not been born with it, so necessary was it to her love that she attract the attention, perhaps the admiration, of her distant child. She forced herself to go out into society in order to cull its ridicules; she taught her eye to observe; she read the masterpieces of her language to discover its effects; she insinuated herself into the company of those who were celebrated for their conversation. Night after night in her baroque palace she wrote and rewrote the incredible pages, forcing from her despairing mind those miracles of wit and grace, those distilled chronicles of the viceregal court. We know now that her daughter barely glanced at the letters and that it is to the son-in-law that we owe their preservation.

The Marquesa would have been astonished to learn that her letters were immortal. Yet many critics have accused her of keeping one eye on posterity and point to a number of letters that have all the air of being bravura pieces. To them it seems impossible that Doña María should have put herself to the same pains to dazzle her daughter that most artists expend on dazzling the public. Like her son-in-law they

misunderstood her; the Conde delighted in her letters, but he thought that when he had enjoyed the style he had extracted all their richness and intention, missing (as most readers do) the whole purport of literature, which is the notation of the heart. Style is but the faintly contemptible vessel in which the bitter liquid is recommended to the world. The Marquesa would even have been astonished to learn that her letters were very good, for such authors live always in the noble weather of their own minds and those productions which seem remarkable to us are little better than a day's routine to them.

This was the old woman who hour by hour would sit upon her balcony, her odd straw hat casting a purple shadow across her lined and yellow face. How often as she turned her pages with her gemmed hands, she would ask herself, almost with amusement, whether the constant pain at her heart had an organic seat. She wondered whether a subtle doctor cutting through to that battered throne could at last discover a sign and lifting his face to the amphitheatre cry out to his students: "This woman has suffered, and her suffering has left its mark upon the structure of her heart." This idea had so often visited her that one day she wrote it into a letter and her daughter scolded her for an introspective and for making a cult of sorrow.

The knowledge that she would never be loved in return acted upon her ideas as a tide acts upon cliffs. Her religious beliefs went first, for all she could ask of a god, or of immortality, was the gift of a place where daughters love their mothers; the other attributes of Heaven you could have for a song. Next she lost her belief in the sincerity of those about her. She secretly refused to believe that anyone (herself excepted) loved anyone. All families lived in a wasteful atmosphere of custom and kissed one another with secret indifference. She saw that the people of this world moved about in an armour of egotism, drunk with self-gazing, athirst for compliments, hearing little of what was said to them, unmoved by the accidents that befell their closest friends, in dread of all appeals that might interrupt their long communion with their own desires. These were the sons and daughters of Adam from Cathay to Peru. And when on the balcony her thoughts reached this turn, her mouth would contract with shame for she knew that she too sinned and that though her love for her daughter was vast enough to include all the colours of love, it was not without a shade of tyranny: she loved her daughter not for her daughter's sake, but for her own. She longed to free herself from this ignoble bond; but the passion was too fierce to cope with. And then on that green balcony a strange warfare would shake the hideous old lady, a singularly futile struggle against a temptation to which she would never have the opportunity of succumbing. How could she rule her

daughter when her daughter saw to it that four thousand miles lay between them? Nevertheless Doña María wrestled with the ghost of her temptation and was worsted on every occasion. She wanted her daughter for herself; she wanted to hear her say: "You are the best of all possible mothers"; she longed to hear her whisper: "Forgive me."

About two years after her return from Spain there took place a series of inconspicuous events that had a great deal to tell about the inner life of the Marquesa. Only the faintest allusion to them occurs in the Correspondence, but as that is found in Letter XXII which contains other signs I shall do my best to give a translation and commentary of the first part of the letter:

"Are there no doctors in Spain? Where are those good men from Flanders that used to help you so? Oh, my treasure, how can we punish you enough for letting your cold endure so many weeks? Don Vicente, I implore you to make my child see reason. Angels of Heaven, I implore you to make my child see reason. Now that you are better, I beg of you, resolve that when the first warning of a cold comes you will steam yourself well and go to bed. Here in Peru I am helpless; I can do nothing. Do not be self-willed, my beloved. God bless you. I am enclosing in today's packet the gum of some tree which the sisters of San Tomás peddle from door to door. Whether it be of much use I know not. It can do no harm. I am told that in the convent the silly sisters inhale it so diligently that one cannot smell the incense at Mass. Whether it be worth anything I know not; try it.

"Rest easy, my love, I am sending His Most Catholic Majesty the perfect gold chain." (Her daughter had written her: *"The chain arrived in good condition and I wore it at the christening of the Infante. His Most Catholic Majesty was gracious enough to admire it and when I told Him that you had given it me He sent you His compliments upon your taste. Do not fail to send Him one as like it as possible; send it at once, by way of the Chamberlain."*) *"He need never know that in order to obtain it I had to walk into a picture. Do you remember that in the sacristy of San Martín there is a portrait by Velasquez of the Viceroy who founded the monastery and of his wife and brat? and that his wife is wearing a gold chain? I resolved that only that chain would do. So one midnight I slipped into the sacristy, climbed upon the robing-table like a girl of twelve and walked in. The canvas resisted for a moment, but the painter himself came forward to lift me through the pigment. I told him that the most beautiful girl in Spain wished to present the finest gold chain that could be found to the most gracious king in the world. It was as simple as that, and there we stood talking, we four, in the gray and silvery air that makes a Velasquez. Now I keep thinking about a more golden*

light; I keep looking at the Palace: I must pass the evening in a Titian. Would the Viceroy let me?

"But His Excellency has the gout again. I say 'again' because the *flattery of the court insists that there are times when he is free of it. This being Saint Mark's day His Excellency started out to visit the University where twenty-two new doctors were being brought into the world. He had hardly been carried from his divan to his coach when he screamed and refused to go any farther. He was carried back to his bed where he broke a most delicious cigar and sent for the Perichole. And while we listened to long doctrinal addresses, more or less in Latin, he heard all about us, more or less in Spanish, from the reddest and cruellest lips in town.*" (Doña María permitted herself this passage, although she had just read in her daughter's last letter: "*How many times must I tell you to be more cautious in the things you say in your letters? They often show signs of having been opened on the journey. Nothing could be more ill-judged than your remarks on the you-know-what-I-mean at Cuzco. Such remarks are not funny, even though Vicente did compliment you upon them in his postscript, and they might get us into a great deal of trouble with Certain Persons here in Spain. I continue to be astonished that your indiscretions have not long since led to your being ordered to retire to your farm.*")

"There was a great press at the Exercises and two women fell from the balcony, but God in His goodness saw that they fell on Doña Merced. All three are badly hurt, but will be thinking of other things within a year. The President was speaking at the moment of the accident and being short-sighted could not imagine what the disturbance of cries and talk and falling bodies could be about. It was very pleasant to see him bowing, under the impression that he was being applauded.*

"Speaking of the Perichole, and of applause, you should know that Pepita and I decided to go to the Comedia this evening. The public still idolizes its Perichole; it even forgives her her years. We are told that she saves what she can, every morning, by passing alternate pencils of ice and fire across her cheeks.*" (Translation falls especially short of this conceit which carries the whole flamboyance of the Spanish language. It was intended as an obsequious flattery of the Condesa, and was untrue. The great actress was twenty-eight at this time; her cheeks had the smoothness and polish of dark yellow marble and would certainly have retained that quality for many years. Apart from the cosmetics required by her performances the only treatment Camila Perichole afforded her face was to throw cold water at it twice a day, like a peasant woman at a horse trough.) "*That curious man they call Uncle Pio is by her all the time. Don Rubio says that he cannot make out whether Uncle Pio is her father, her lover, or her*

son. The Perichole gave a wonderful performance. Scold me all you like for a provincial ninny, you have no such actresses in Spain." And so on.

It is on this visit to the theatre that further matter hangs. She decided to go to the Comedia where the Perichole was playing Doña Leonor in Moreto's *Trampa Adelante;* perhaps some material could be derived from the visit for her daughter's next letter. She took with her Pepita, a little girl about whom later we shall learn much. Doña María had borrowed her from the orphanage connected with the Convent of Santa María Rosa de las Rosas to be her companion. The Marquesa sat in her box gazing with flagging attention at the brilliant stage. Between the acts it was the Perichole's custom to lay aside the courtly rôle and appear before the curtain to sing a few topical songs. The malicious actress had seen the Marquesa arrive and presently began improvising couplets alluding to her appearance, her avarice, her drunkenness, and even to her daughter's flight from her. The attention of the house was subtly directed to the old woman and a rising murmur of contempt accompanied the laughter of the audience. But the Marquesa, deeply moved by the first two acts of the comedy, scarcely saw the singer and sat staring before her, thinking about Spain. Camila Perichole became bolder and the air was electric with the hatred and glee of the crowd. At last Pepita plucked the Marquesa's sleeve and whispered to her that they should go. As they left the box the house arose and burst into a roar of triumph; the Perichole flung herself into a frenzied dance, for she saw the manager at the back of the hall and knew that her salary had been increased. But the Marquesa remained unaware of what had taken place; in fact she was quite pleased, for during the visit she had contrived a few felicitous phrases, phrases (who knows) that might bring a smile to her daughter's face and might make her murmur: "Really, my mother is charming."

In due time the report reached the Viceroy's ears that one of his aristocrats had been openly baited in the theatre. He summoned the Perichole to the Palace and ordered her to call upon the Marquesa and to apologize. The trip was to be made barefoot and in a black dress. Camila argued and fought, but all she gained was a pair of shoes.

The Viceroy had three reasons for insisting. In the first place the singer had taken liberties with his court. Don Andrés had contrived to make exile endurable by building up a ceremonial so complicated that it could be remembered only by a society that had nothing else to think about. He nursed his little aristocracy and its minute distinctions and any insult paid to a Marquesa was an insult to His Person. In the second place, Doña María's son-in-law was an increasingly important

personage in Spain, laden with possibilities of injury to the Viceroy, nay with the possibility of supplanting him. The Conde Vicente d'Abuirre must not be vexed, even through his half-wit mother-in-law. Finally, the Viceroy was delighted to humble the actress. He suspected that she was deceiving him with a matador, perhaps with an actor,— between the flattery of the court and the inertia of gout he could not quite make out who it was; at all events, it was clear that the singer was beginning to forget that he was one of the first men in the world.

The Marquesa, beside not having heard the scurrilous songs, was in other ways unprepared for the actress's visit. You should know that after the departure of her daughter, Doña María had lighted upon a certain consolation: she had taken to drinking. Everyone drank *chicha* in Peru and there was no particular disgrace in being found unconscious on a feast day. Doña María had begun to discover that her feverish monologues had a way of keeping her awake all night. Once she took a delicate fluted glassful of *chicha* on retiring. Oblivion was so sweet that presently she stole larger amounts and tried dissimulating their effects from Pepita; she hinted that she was not well, and represented herself as going into a decline. At last she resigned all pretense. The boats that carried her letter to Spain did not leave oftener than once a month. During the week that preceded the making of the packet she observed a strict regimen and cultivated the city assiduously for material. At last on the eve of the post she wrote the letter, making up the bundle towards dawn and leaving it for Pepita to deliver to the agent. Then as the sun rose she would shut herself up in her room with some flagons and drift through the next few weeks without the burden of consciousness. Finally she would emerge from her happiness and prepare to go into a state of "training" in preparation for the writing of another letter.

Thus on the night following the scandal in the theatre she wrote Letter XXII and retired to bed with a carafe. All next day Pepita moved about the room, glancing anxiously at the figure on the bed. The next afternoon Pepita brought her needlework into the room. The Marquesa lay staring at the ceiling with wide-open eyes, talking to herself. Towards dusk Pepita was called to the door and informed that the Perichole had come to see the mistress. Pepita remembered the theatre very well and sent back word angrily that the mistress refused to see her. The man carried the message to the street door, but returned awe-struck with the news that the Señora Perichole was armed with a letter from the Viceroy presenting her to the lady. Pepita tiptoed to the bed and started talking to the Marquesa. The glazed eyes moved to the girl's face. Pepita shook her gently. With great effort Doña María tried to fix her mind on what was being said

to her. Twice she lay back, refusing to seize the meaning, but at last, like a general calling together in a rain and by night the dispersed division of his army she assembled memory and attention and a few other faculties and painfully pressing her hand to her forehead she asked for a bowl of snow. When it was brought her, she long and drowsily pressed handfuls of it against her temples and cheeks; then rising she stood for a long time leaning against the bed and looking at her shoes. At last she raised her head with decision, she called for her fur-trimmed cloak and a veil. She put them on and tottered into her handsomest reception room where the actress stood waiting for her.

Camila had intended to be perfunctory and if possible impudent, but now she was struck for the first time with the dignity of the old woman. The mercer's daughter could carry herself at times with all the distinction of the Montemayors and when she was drunk she wore the grandeur of Hecuba. For Camila the half-closed eyes had the air of weary authority and she began almost timidly:

"I come, señora, to make sure that you could not have misunderstood anything I said on the evening that Your Grace did me the honour to visit my theatre."

"Misunderstood? Misunderstood?" said the Marquesa.

"Your Grace might have misunderstood and thought that my words were intended to be disrespectful to Your Grace."

"To me?"

"Your Grace is not offended at her humble servant? Your Grace is aware that a poor actress in my position may be carried beyond her intentions . . . that it is very difficult . . . that everything. . . ."

"How can I be offended, señora? All that I can remember is that you gave a beautiful performance. You are a great artist. You should be happy, happy. My handkerchief, Pepita. . . ."

The Marquesa brought out these words very rapidly and vaguely, but the Perichole was confounded. A piercing sense of shame filled her. She turned crimson. At last she was able to murmur:

"It was in the songs between the acts of the comedy. I was afraid Your Grace . . ."

"Yes, yes. I remember now. I left early. Pepita, we left early, did we not? But, señora, you are good enough to forgive my leaving early, yes, even in the middle of your admirable performance. I forget why we left. Pepita . . . oh, some indisposition. . . ."

It was impossible that anyone in the theatre could have missed the intention of the songs. Camila could only assume that the Marquesa, out of a sort of fantastic magnanimity, was playing the farce of not having noticed it. She was almost in tears: "But you are so good to overlook my childishness, señora,—I mean Your Grace. I did not know.

I did not know your goodness. Señora, permit me to kiss your hand."

Doña María held out her hand astonished. She had not for a long time been addressed with such consideration. Her neighbors, her tradespeople, her servants—for even Pepita lived in awe of her,—her very daughter had never approached her thus. It induced a new mood in her; one that must very likely be called maudlin. She became loquacious:

"Offended, offended at you, my beautiful, . . . my gifted child? Who am I, a . . . an unwise and unloved old woman, to be offended at you? I felt, my daughter, as though I were—what says the poet?— *surprising through a cloud the conversation of the angels.* Your voice kept finding new wonders in our Moreto. When you said:

> '*Don Juan, si mi amor estimas,*
> *Y la fe segura es necia,*
> *Enojarte mis temores*
> *Es no quererme discreta.*
> *¿Tan seguros. . . .*'

and so on,—that was true! And what a gesture you made at the close of the First Day. There, with your hand *so.* Such a gesture as the Virgin made, saying to Gabriel: *How is it possible that I shall have a child?* No, no, you will begin to have resentment at me, for I am going to tell you about a gesture that you may remember to use some day. Yes, it would fit well into that scene where you forgive your Don Juan de Lara. Perhaps I should tell you that I saw it made one day by my daughter. My daughter is a very beautiful woman . . . everyone thinks. Did . . . did you know my Doña Clara, Señora?"

"Her Grace often did me the honour of visiting my theatre. I knew the Condesa well by sight."

"Do not remain so, on one knee, my child.—Pepita, tell Jenarito to bring this lady some sweetcakes at once. Think, one day we fell out, I forget over what. Oh, there is nothing strange in that; all we mothers from time to time. . . . Look, can you come a little closer? You must not believe the town that says she was unkind to me. You are a great woman with a beautiful nature and you can see further than the crowd sees in these matters.—It is a pleasure to talk to you. What beautiful hair you have! What beautiful hair!—She had not a warm impulsive nature, I know that. But, oh, my child, she has such a store of intelligence and graciousness. Any misunderstandings between us are so plainly my fault; is it not wonderful that she is so quick to forgive me? This day there fell one of those little moments. We both said hasty things and went off to our rooms. Then each turned back to be forgiven. Finally only a door separated us and there

we were pulling it in contrary ways. But at last she . . . took my . . . face . . . thus, in her two white hands. So! Look!"

The Marquesa almost fell out of her chair as she leaned forward, her face streaming with happy tears, and made the beatific gesture. I should say the mythical gesture, for the incident was but a recurring dream.

"I am glad you are here," she continued, "for now you have heard from my own lips that she is not unkind to me, as some people say. Listen, señora, the fault was mine. Look at me. Look at me. There was some mistake that made me the mother of so beautiful a girl. I am difficult. I am trying. You and she are great women. No, do not stop me: you are rare women, and I am only a nervous . . . a foolish . . . a stupid woman. Let me kiss your feet. I am impossible. I am impossible. I am impossible."

Here indeed the old woman did fall out of her chair and was gathered up by Pepita and led back to her bed. The Perichole walked home in consternation and sat for a long time gazing into her eyes in the mirror, her palms pressed against her cheeks.

But the person who saw most of the difficult hours of the Marquesa was her little companion, Pepita. Pepita was an orphan and had been brought up by that strange genius of Lima, the Abbess Madre María del Pilar. The only occasion upon which the two great women of Peru (as the perspective of history was to reveal them) met face to face was on the day when Doña María called upon the directress of the Convent of Santa María Rosa de las Rosas and asked if she might borrow some bright girl from the orphanage to be her companion. The Abbess gazed hard at the grotesque old woman. Even the wisest people in the world are not perfectly wise and Madre María del Pilar who was able to divine the poor human heart behind all the masks of folly and defiance, had always refused to concede one to the Marquesa de Montemayor. She asked her a great many questions and then paused to think. She wanted to give Pepita the worldly experience of living in the palace. She also wanted to bend the old woman to her own interests. And she was filled with a sombre indignation, for she knew she was gazing at one of the richest women in Peru, and the blindest.

She was one of those persons who have allowed their lives to be gnawed away because they have fallen in love with an idea several centuries before its appointed appearance in the history of civilization. She hurled herself against the obstinacy of her time in her desire to attach a little dignity to women. At midnight when she had finished adding up the accounts of the House she would fall into insane vision of an age when women could be organized to protect women, women

travelling, women as servants, women when they are old or ill, the women she had discovered in the mines of Potosi, or in the workrooms of the cloth-merchants, the girls she had collected out of doorways on rainy nights. But always the next morning she had to face the fact that the women in Peru, even her nuns, went through life with two notions: one, that all the misfortunes that might befall them were merely due to the fact that they were not sufficiently attractive to bind some man to their maintenance and, two, that all the misery in the world was worth his caress. She had never known any country but the environs of Lima and she assumed that all its corruption was the normal state of mankind. Looking back from our century we can see the whole folly of her hope. Twenty such women would have failed to make any impression on that age. Yet she continued diligently in her task. She resembled the swallow in the fable who once every thousand years transferred a grain of wheat, in the hope of rearing a mountain to reach the moon. Such persons are raised up in every age; they obstinately insist on transporting their grains of wheat and they derive a certain exhilaration from the sneers of the bystanders. "How queerly they dress!" we cry. "How queerly they dress!"

Her plain red face had great kindliness, and more idealism than kindliness, and more generalship than idealism. All her work, her hospitals, her orphanage, her convent, her sudden journeys of rescue, depended upon money. No one harbored a fairer admiration for mere goodness, but she had been obliged to watch herself sacrificing her kindliness, almost her idealism, to generalship, so dreadful were the struggles to obtain her subsidies from her superiors in the church. The Archbishop of Lima, whom we shall know later in a more graceful connection, hated her with what he called a Vatinian hate and counted the cessation of her visits among the compensations for dying.

Lately she had felt not only the breath of old age against her cheek, but a graver warning. A chill of terror went through her, not for herself, but for her work. Who was there in Peru to value the things she had valued? And rising one day at dawn she had made a rapid journey through her hospital and convent and orphanage, looking for a soul she might train to be her successor. She hurried from empty face to empty face, occasionally pausing more from hope than conviction. In the courtyard she came upon a company of girls at work over the linen and her eyes fell at once upon a girl of twelve who was directing the others at the trough and at the same time recounting to them with great dramatic fire the less probable miracles in the life of Saint Rose of Lima. So it was that the search ended with Pepita. The education for greatness is difficult enough at any time, but amid the sensibilities and jealousies of a convent it must be conducted with fantastic indirec-

tion. Pepita was assigned to the most disliked tasks in the House, but she came to understand all the aspects of its administration. She accompanied the Abbess on her journeys, even though it was in the capacity of custodian of the eggs and vegetables. And everywhere, by surprise, hours would open up in which the Directress suddenly appeared and talked to her at great length, not only on religious experience, but on how to manage women and how to plan contagious wards and how to beg for money. It was a step in this education for greatness that led to Pepita's arriving one day and entering upon the crazy duties of being Doña María's companion. For the first two years she merely came for occasional afternoons, but finally she came to the palace to live. She never had been taught to expect happiness, and the inconveniences, not to say terrors, of her new position did not seem to her excessive for a girl of fourteen. She did not suspect that the Abbess, even there, was hovering above the house, herself estimating the stresses and watching for the moment when a burden harms and not strengthens.

A few of Pepita's trials were physical: for example, the servants in the house took advantage of Doña María's indisposition; they opened up the bedrooms of the palace to their relatives; they stole freely. Alone Pepita stood out against them and suffered a persecution of small discomforts and practical jokes. Her mind, similarly, had its distresses: when she accompanied Doña María on her errands in the city, the older woman would be seized with the desire to dash into a church, for what she had lost of religion as faith she had replaced with religion as magic. "Stay here in the sunlight, my dear child; I shall not be long," she would say. Doña María would then forget herself in a reverie before the altar and leave the church by another door. Pepita had been brought up by Madre María del Pilar to an almost morbid obedience and when after many hours she ventured into the church and made sure that her mistress was no longer there, still she returned to the street-corner and waited while the shadows fell gradually across the square. Thus waiting in public she suffered all the torture of a little girl's self-consciousness. She still wore the uniform of the orphanage (which a minute's thoughtfulness on the part of Doña María could have altered) and she suffered hallucinations wherein men seemed to be staring at her and whispering—nor were these always hallucinations. No less her heart suffered, for on some days Doña María would suddenly become aware of her and would talk to her cordially and humorously, would let appear for a few hours all the exquisite sensibility of the Letters; then, on the morrow she would withdraw into herself again and, while never harsh, would become impersonal and unseeing. The beginnings of hope and affection that Pepita had such need to expend would be wounded. She tiptoed about the palace, silent, bewildered, clinging

only to her sense of duty and her loyalty to her "mother in the Lord," Madre María del Pilar, who had sent her there.

Finally a new fact appeared that was to have considerable effect on the lives of both the Marquesa and her companion: *"My dear mother,"* wrote the Condesa, *"the weather has been most exhausting and the fact that the orchards and gardens are in bloom only makes it the more trying. I could endure flowers if only they had no perfume. I shall therefore ask your permission to write you at less length than usual. If Vicente returns before the post leaves he will be delighted to finish out the leaf and supply you with those tiresome details about myself which you seem to enjoy so. I shall not go to Grignan in Provence as I expected this Fall, as my child will be born in early October."*
What child? The Marquesa leaned against the wall. Doña Clara had foreseen the exhausting importunities that this news would waken in her mother and had sought to mitigate them by the casualness of her announcement. The ruse did not succeed. The famous Letter XLII was the answer.
Now at length the Marquesa had something to be anxious about: her daughter was to become a mother. This event, which merely bored Doña Clara, discovered a whole new scale of emotions in the Marquesa. She became a mine of medical knowledge and suggestion. She combed the city for wise old women and poured into her letters the whole folk-wisdom of the New World. She fell into the most abominable superstition. She practiced a degrading system of taboos for her child's protection. She refused to allow a knot in the house. The maids were forbidden to tie up their hair and she concealed upon her person ridiculous symbols of a happy delivery. On the stairs the even steps were marked with red chalk and a maid who accidentally stepped upon an even step was driven from the house with tears and screams. Doña Clara was in the hands of malignant Nature who reserves the right to inflict upon her children the most terrifying jests. There was an etiquette of propitiation which generations of peasant women had found comforting. So vast an army of witnesses surely implied that there was some truth in it. At least it could do no harm, and Perhaps it did good. But the Marquesa did not only satisfy the rites of paganism; she studied the prescriptions of Christianity as well. She arose in the dark and stumbled through the streets to the earliest Masses. She hysterically hugged the altar-rails trying to rend from the gaudy statuettes a sign, only a sign, the ghost of a smile, the furtive nod of a waxen head. Would all be well? Sweet, sweet Mother, would all be well?

At times, after a day's frantic resort to such invocations, a revulsion would sweep over her. Nature is deaf. God is indifferent. Nothing in man's power can alter the course of law. Then on some street-corner she would stop, dizzy with despair, and leaning against a wall would long to be taken from a world that had no plan in it. But soon a belief in the great Perhaps would surge up from the depths of her nature and she would fairly run home to renew the candles above her daughter's bed.

At last the time came to satisfy the supreme rite of Peruvian households looking forward to this event: she made the pilgrimage to the shrine of Santa María de Cluxambuqua. If there resided an efficacy in devotion at all, surely it lay in a visit to this great shrine. The ground had been holy through three religions; even before the Incan civilization distraught human beings had hugged the rocks and lashed themselves with whips to wring their will from the skies. Thither the Marquesa was carried in her chair, crossing the bridge of San Luis Rey and ascending up into the hills toward that city of large-girdled women, a tranquil town, slow-moving and slow-smiling; a city of crystal air, cold as the springs that fed its many fountains; a city of bells, soft and musical, and tuned to carry on with one another the happiest quarrels. If anything turned out for disappointment in the town of Cluxambuqua the grief was somehow assimilated by the overwhelming immanence of the Andes and by the weather of quiet joy that flowed in and about the side-streets. No sooner did the Marquesa see from a distance the white walls of this town perched on the knees of the highest peaks than her fingers ceased turning the beads and the busy prayers of her fright were cut short on her lips.

She did not even alight at the inn, but leaving Pepita to arrange for their stay she went on to the church and knelt for a long time patting her hands softly together. She was listening to the new tide of resignation that was rising within her. Perhaps she would learn in time to permit both her daughter and her gods to govern their own affairs. She was not annoyed by the whispering of the old women in padded garments who sold candles and medals and talked about money from dawn to dark. She was not even distracted by an officious sacristan who tried to collect a fee for something or other and who, from spite, made her change her place under the pretext of repairing a tile on the floor. Presently she went out into the sunshine and sat on the steps of the fountain. She watched the little processions of invalids slowly revolving about the gardens. She watched three hawks plunging about the sky. The children who had been playing by the fountain stared at her for a moment, and went away alarmed, but a llama (a lady with a long neck and sweet shallow eyes, burdened down by a fur cape too

heavy for her and picking her way delicately down an interminable staircase) came over and offered her a velvet cleft nose to stroke. The llama is deeply interested in the men about her, is even fond of pretending that she too is one of them and of inserting her head into their conversations as though in a moment she would lift her voice and contribute a wan and helpful comment. Soon Doña María was surrounded by a number of these sisters who seemed on the point of asking her why she clapped her hands so and how much her veiling cost a yard.

Doña María had arranged that any letters arriving from Spain should be brought to her at once by a special messenger. She had travelled slowly from Lima and even now as she sat in the square a boy from her farm ran up and put into her hand a large packet wrapped in parchment and dangling some nuggets of sealing-wax. Slowly she undid the wrappings. With measured stoic gestures she read first an affectionate and jocose note from her son-in-law; then her daughter's letter. It was full of wounding remarks rather brilliantly said, perhaps said for the sheer virtuosity of giving pain neatly. Each of its phrases found its way through the eyes of the Marquesa, then, carefully wrapped in understanding and forgiveness it sank into her heart. At last she arose, gently dispersed the sympathetic llamas, and with a grave face returned to the shrine.

While Doña María was passing the late afternoon in the Church and in the Square, Pepita was left to prepare their lodging. She showed the porters where to lay down the great wicker hampers and set about unpacking the altar, the brazier, the tapestries and the portraits of Doña Clara. She descended into the kitchen and gave the cook exact instructions as to the preparations of a certain porridge upon which the Marquesa principally subsisted. Then she returned to the rooms and waited. She resolved to write a letter to the Abbess. She hung for a long time over the quill, staring into the distance with trembling lip. She saw the face of Madre María del Pilar, so red and scrubbed, and the wonderful black eyes. She heard her voice as at the close of supper (the orphans sitting with lowered eyes and folded hands) she commented on the events of the day, or as, by candelight, she stood among the beds of the hospital and announced the theme for meditation during the night. But most clearly of all Pepita remembered the sudden interviews when the Abbess (not daring to wait until the girl was older) had discussed with her the duties of her office. She had talked to Pepita as to an equal. Such speech is troubling and wonderful to an intelligent child and Madre María del Pilar had abused it. She had expanded Pepita's vision of how she should feel and act beyond the measure of her years. And she had unthinkingly turned

upon Pepita the full blaze of her personality, as Jupiter had turned his upon Semele. Pepita was frightened by her sense of insufficiency; she hid it and wept. And then the Abbess had cast the child into the discipline of this long solitude, where Pepita struggled, refusing to let herself believe that she had been abandoned. And now from this strange inn in these strange mountains, where the altitude was making her lightheaded, Pepita longed for the dear presence, the only real thing in her life.

She wrote a letter, all inkstains and incoherence. Then she went downstairs to see about fresh charcoal and to taste the porridge.

The Marquesa came in and sat down at the table. "I can do no more. What will be, will be," she whispered. She unbound from her neck the amulets of her superstition and dropped them into the glowing brazier. She had a strange sense of having antagonized God by too much prayer and so addressed Him now obliquely. "After all it is in the hands of another. I no longer claim the least influence. What will be, will be." She sat for a long time, her palms against her cheeks, making a blank of her mind. Her eyes fell on Pepita's letter. She opened it mechanically and started to read. She had read a full half of it before her attention was aware of the meaning of the words: ". . . *but all this is nothing if you like me and wish me to stay with her. I oughtn't to tell you but every now and then the bad chambermaids lock me up in rooms and steal things and perhaps My Lady will think that I steal them. I hope not. I hope you are well and not having any trouble in the hospital or anywhere. Though I never see you I think of you all the time and remember what you told me, my dear mother in God. I want to do only what you want, but if you could let me come back for a few days to the convent, but not if you do not wish it. But I am so much alone and not talking to anyone, and everything. Sometimes I do not know whether you have forgotten me and if you could find a minute to write me a little letter or something, I could keep it, but I know how busy you are. . . .*"

Doña María read no further. She folded the letter and put it aside. For a moment she was filled with envy: she longed to command another's soul as completely as this nun was able to do. Most of all she longed to be back in this simplicity of love, to throw off the burden of pride and vanity that hers had always carried. To quiet the tumult in her mind she picked up a book of devotion and tried to fix her attention upon the words. But after a moment she suddenly felt the need to reread the whole letter, to surprise, if possible, the secret of so much felicity.

Pepita returned bringing the supper in her hands followed by a maid. Doña María watched her over the top of her book as she would

have watched a visitor from Heaven. Pepita tiptoed about the room laying the table and whispering directions to her assistant.

"Your supper is ready, My Lady," she said at last.

"But, my child, you are going to eat with me?" In Lima Pepita generally sat down at the table with her mistress.

"I thought you would be tired, My Lady. I had my supper downstairs."

"She does not wish to eat with me," thought the Marquesa. "She knows me and has rejected me."

"Would you like me to read aloud to you while you are eating, My Lady?" asked Pepita, who felt that she had made a mistake.

"No. You may go to bed, if you choose."

"Thank you, My Lady."

Doña María had risen and approached the table. With one hand on the back of the chair she said haltingly: "My dear child, I am sending off a letter to Lima in the morning. If you have one you can enclose it with mine."

"No, I have none," said Pepita. She added hastily: "I must go downstairs and get you the new charcoal."

"But, my dear, you have one for . . . Madre María del Pilar. Wouldn't you . . . ?"

Pepita pretended to be busy over the brazier. "No, I'm not going to send it," she said. She was aware during the long pause that followed that the Marquesa was staring at her in stupefaction. "I've changed my mind."

"I know she would like a letter from you, Pepita. It would make her very happy. I know."

Pepita was reddening. She said loudly: "The innkeeper said that there would be some new charcoal ready for you at dark. I'll tell them to bring it up now." She glanced hastily at the old woman and saw that she had not ceased from staring at her with great sad inquiring eyes. Pepita felt that these were not things one talked about, but the strange woman seemed to be feeling the matter so strongly that Pepita was willing to concede one more answer: "No, it was a bad letter. It wasn't a good letter."

Doña María fairly gasped. "Why, my dear Pepita, I think it was very beautiful. Believe me, I know. No, no; what could have made it a bad letter?"

Pepita frowned, hunting for a word that would close the matter.

"It wasn't . . . it wasn't . . . brave," she said. And then she would say no more. She carried the letter off into her own room and could be heard tearing it up. Then she got into bed and lay staring

into the darkness, still uncomfortable at having talked in such a fashion. And Doña María sat down to her dish amazed.

She had never brought courage to either life or love. Her eyes ransacked her heart. She thought of the amulets and of her beads, her drunkenness . . . she thought of her daughter. She remembered the long relationship, crowded with the wreckage of exhumed conversations, of fancied slights, of inopportune confidences, of charges of neglect and exclusion (but she must have been mad that day; she remembered beating upon the table). "But it's not my fault," she cried. "It's not my fault that I was so. It was circumstance. It was the way I was brought up. Tomorrow I begin a new life. Wait and see, oh my child." At last she cleared away the table and sitting down wrote what she called her first letter, her first stumbling misspelled letter in courage. She remembered with shame that in the previous one she had piteously asked her daughter how much she loved her, and had greedily quoted the few and hesitant endearments that Doña Clara had lately ventured to her. Doña María could not recall those pages, but she could write some new ones, free and generous. No one else has regarded them as stumbling. It is the famous Letter LVI, known to the Encyclopedists as her Second Corinthians because of its immortal paragraph about love: "Of the thousands of persons we meet in a lifetime, my child . . ." and so on. It was almost dawn when she finished the letter. She opened the door upon her balcony and looked at the great tiers of stars that glittered above the Andes. Throughout the hours of the night, though there had been few to hear it, the whole sky had been loud with the singing of these constellations. Then she took a candle into the next room and looked at Pepita as she slept, and pushed back the damp hair from the girl's face. "Let me live now," she whispered. "Let me begin again."

Two days later they started back to Lima, and while crossing the bridge of San Luis Rey the accident which we know befell them.

Part III

Esteban

One morning twin boys were discovered in the foundlings' basket before the door of the Convent of Santa María Rosa de las Rosas. Names were found for them almost before the arrival of the wetnurse, but the names were not as useful to them as our names are to most of us, for no one ever succeeded in telling the boys apart. There

was no way of knowing who their parents were, but Limean gossips, noticing as the boys grew older how straight they held themselves and how silent and sombre they were, declared them to be Castilian and laid them in turn at all sorts of crested doorways. The person in the world who came nearest to being their guardian was the Abbess of the Convent. Madre María del Pilar had come to hate all men, but she grew fond of Manuel and Esteban. In the late afternoon she would call them into her office, send for some cakes from the kitchen, and tell them stories about the Cid and Judas Maccabeus and the thirty-six misfortunes of Harlequin. She grew to love them so, that she would catch herself gazing deep into their black and frowning eyes, looking for those traits that would appear when they grew to be men, all that ugliness, all that soullessness that made hideous the world she worked in. They grew up about the convent until they were a little past the age when their presence began to be a slight distraction to the dedicated sisters. From thence they became vaguely attached to all the sacristies in town: they trimmed all the cloister hedges; they polished every possible crucifix; they passed a damp cloth once a year over most of the ecclesiastical ceilings. All Lima knew them well. When the priest rushed through the streets carrying his precious burden into a sickroom either Esteban or Manuel was to be seen striding behind him, swinging a censer. As they grew older, however, they showed no desire for the clerical life. They gradually assumed the profession of the scribe. There were few printing presses in the New World and the boys soon made a fair living transcribing comedies for the theatre, ballads for the crowds, and advertisements for the merchants. Above all they were the coypists of the choirmasters and made endless parts of the motets of Morales and Vittoria.

Because they had no family, because they were twins, and because they were brought up by women, they were silent. There was in them a curious shame in regard to their resemblance. They had to live in a world where it was the subject of continual comment and joking. It was never funny to them and they suffered the eternal pleasantries with stolid patience. From the years when they first learned to speak they invented a secret language for themselves, one that was scarcely dependent on the Spanish for its vocabulary, or even for its syntax. They resorted to it only when they were alone, or at great intervals in moments of stress whispered it in the presence of others. The Archbishop of Lima was something of a philologist; he dabbled in dialects; he had even evolved quite a brilliant table for the vowel and consonant changes from Latin into Spanish and from Spanish into Indian-Spanish. He was storing up notebooks of quaint lore against an amusing old age he planned to offer himself back on his estates out-

side Segovia. So when he heard one day about the secret language of the twin brothers, he trimmed some quills and sent for them. The boys stood humiliated upon the rich carpets of his study while he tried to extract from them their *bread* and *tree* and their *I see* and *I saw*. They did not know why the experience was so horrible to them. They bled. Long shocked silences followed each of the Archbishop's questions, until finally one of the other mumbled an answer. The priest thought for a while that they were merely in awe before his rank and before the luxury of his apartment, but at last, much perplexed, he divined the presence of some deeper reluctance and sadly let them go.

This language was the symbol of their profound identity with one another, for just as resignation was a word insufficient to describe the spiritual change that came over the Marquesa de Montemayor on that night in the inn at Cluxambuqua, so *love* is inadequate to describe the tacit almost ashamed oneness of these brothers. What relationship is it in which few words are exchanged, and those only about the details of food, clothing and occupation; in which the two persons have a curious reluctance even to glance at one another; and in which there is a tacit arrangement not to appear together in the city and to go on the same errand by different streets? And yet side by side with this there existed a need of one another so terrible that it produced miracles as naturally as the charged air of a sultry day produces lightning. The brothers were scarcely aware of it themselves, but telepathy was a common occurrence in their lives, and when one returned home the other was always aware of it when his brother was still several streets away.

Suddenly they discovered that they were tired of writing. They went down to the sea and found an occupation in loading and unloading vessels, not ashamed of working side by side with Indians. They drove teams across the provinces. They picked fruit. They were ferrymen. And always they were silent. Their sombre faces took on from these labors a male and gypsy cast. Their hair was seldom cut and under the dark mat their eyes looked up suddenly surprised and a little sullen. All the world was remote and strange and hostile except one's brother.

But at last the first shadow fell across this unity and the shadow was cast by the love of women. They had returned to the city and resumed the copying of parts for the theatre. One night the manager, foreseeing a thinning house, gave them a free admission. The boys did not like what they found there. Even speech was for them a debased form of silence; how much more futile is poetry which is a debased form of speech. All those allusions to honour, reputation, and the flame of

love, all the metaphors about birds, Achilles and the jewels of Ceylon were fatiguing. In the presence of literature they had the same darkling intelligence that stirs for a time behind the eyes of a dog, but they sat on patiently, gazing at the bright candles and the rich clothes. Between the acts of the comedy the Perichole stepped out of her rôle, put on twelve petticoats and danced before the curtain. Esteban had some copying still to do, or pretended so, and went home early; but Manuel stayed on. The red stocking and shoes of the Perichole had made their impression.

Both brothers had fetched and carried their manuscripts up and down the dusty stairs behind the stage. There they had seen an irritable girl in a soiled bodice mending her stockings before a mirror while her stage director read aloud her lines for memorization. She had let fall upon the boys for a moment the detonation of her amazing eyes, immediately dissipated in her amused recognition that they were twins. Forthwith she had dragged them into the room and placed them side by side: Carefully, amusedly and remorselessly she had peered into every square inch of their faces, until finally laying one hand on Esteban's shoulder she had cried out: "This one is the younger!" That had been several years before and neither brother had thought of the episode again.

Henceforth all Manuel's errands seemed to lead him past the theatre. Late at night he would drift about among the trees beneath her dressing-room window. It was not the first time that Manuel had been fascinated by a woman (both brothers had possessed women, and often, especially during their years at the waterfront; but simply, latinly), but it was the first time that his will and imagination had been thus overwhelmed. He had lost that privilege of simple nature, the disassociation of love and pleasure. Pleasure was no longer as simple as eating; it was being complicated by love. Now was beginning that crazy loss of one's self, that neglect of everything but one's dramatic thoughts about the beloved, that feverish inner life all turning upon the Perichole and which would so have astonished and disgusted her had she been permitted to divine it. This Manuel had not fallen in love through any imitation of literature. It was not of him, at all events, that the bitterest tongue in France had remarked only fifty years before: that many people would never have fallen in love if they had not heard about it. Manuel read little; he had only been once to the theatre (where above all there reigns the legend that love is a devotion) and the Peruvian tavern-songs that he might have heard, unlike those of Spain, reflected very little of the romantic cult of an idealized woman. When he said over to himself that she was beautiful and rich and fatiguingly witty and the Viceroy's mistress, none of these

attributes that made her less obtainable had the power to quench his curious and tender excitement. So he leaned against the trees in the dark, his knuckles between his teeth, and listened to his loud heart-beats.

But the life that Esteban was leading had been full enough for him. There was no room in his imagination for a new loyalty, not because his heart was less large than Manuel's, but because it was of a simpler texture. Now he discovered that secret from which one never quite recovers, that even in the most perfect love one person loves less profoundly than the other. There may be two equally good, equally gifted, equally beautiful, but there may never be two that love one another equally well. So Esteban sat up in their room by a guttering candle, his knuckles between his teeth, and wondered why Manuel was so changed and why the whole meaning had gone out of their life.

One evening Manuel was stopped on the street by a small boy who announced to him that the Perichole wished him to call upon her at once. Manuel turned in his path and went to the theatre. Straight, sombre and impersonal, he entered the actress's room and stood waiting. Camila had a service to ask of Manuel and she thought a few preliminary blandishments were necessary, but she scarcely paused in combing a blond wig that was dressed upon the table before her.

"You write letters for people, don't you? I want you to write a letter for me, please. Please come in."

He came forward two steps.

"You never pay me the least visit either of you. That's not Spanish of you."—meaning 'courteous.'—"Which are you, Manuel or Esteban?"

"Manuel."

"It doesn't matter. You are both unfriendly. Neither of you ever comes to see me. Here I sit learning stupid lines all day and no one ever comes to see me but a lot of peddlers. It is because I am an actress, no?"

This was not very artful, but for Manuel it was unspeakably complicated. He merely stared at her from the shadows of his long hair and left her to improvise.

"I am going to engage you to write a letter for me, a very secret letter. But now I can see that you don't like me and that to ask you to write a letter would be as good as reading it aloud in all the wine-shops. What does that look mean, Manuel? Are you my friend?"

"Yes, señora."

"Go away. Send me Esteban. You do not even say *Yes, señora* as a friend would say it."

Long pause. Presently she raised her head: "Are you still there, Unfriendly?"

"Yes, señora . . . you can trust me to do anything for you . . . you can trust . . ."

"If I ask you to write one letter for me, or two letters, you promise never to mention to a human being what is in them, or even that you wrote them?"

"Yes, señora."

"What do you promise by?—by the Virgin Mary?"

"Yes, señora."

"And by the heart of Saint Rose of Lima?"

"Yes, señora."

"Name of the Name, Manuel, anyone would think you were as stupid as an ox. Manuel, I am very angry with you. You are not stupid. You don't look stupid. Please don't say just *Yes, señora* again. Don't be stupid or I'll send for Esteban. Is anything the matter with you?"

Here Manuel cast himself upon the Spanish language and exclaimed with unnecessary vigor: "I swear by the Virgin Mary and the heart of St. Rose of Lima that all that has to do with the letter will be secret."

"Even from Esteban," prompted the Perichole.

"Even from Esteban."

"Well, that's better." She motioned him to sit down at a table where writing materials were already laid out. As she dictated she strode about the room, frowning, swinging her hips. With her arms akimbo, she hugged her shawl about her shoulders defiantly.

"*Camila Perichole kisses the hands of Your Excellency and says—*No, take another piece of paper and begin again. *The señora Micaela Villegas, artist, kisses the hands of Your Excellency and says that, being the victim of the envious and lying friends that Y. E.'s goodness permits about Him, she can no longer endure Y. E.'s suspicions and jealousy. Y. E.'s servant has always valued Y. E.'s friendship and has never committed, nor even thought, an offense against it, but she can no longer fight against the calumnies that Y. E. believes so readily. Señora Villegas, artist, called the Perichole, therefore returns herewith such of Y. E.'s gifts as have not been placed beyond recall, since without Y. E.'s confidence, Y. E.'s servant can take no pleasure in them.*"

Camila continued walking about the room for several minutes, consumed by her thoughts. Presently without so much as glancing at her secretary, she commanded: "Take another leaf. *Have you gone mad? Do not ever think of dedicating another bull to me again. It has caused a frightful war. Heaven protect you, my colt. Friday night, the same place, the same time. I may be a little late, for the fox is wide-awake.* That will be all."

Manuel rose.

"You swear that you have made no errors?"

"Yes, I swear."

"There is your money."

Manuel took the money.

"I shall want you to write me more letters from time to time. My uncle Pio generally writes my letters; these I do not wish him to know about. Good night. Go with God."

"Go with God."

Manuel descended the stairs and stood for a long time among the trees, not thinking, not moving.

Esteban knew that his brother was continually brooding over the Perichole, but he never suspected that he saw her. From time to time during the next two months a small boy would approach him in great haste and ask whether he were Manuel or Esteban, and being informed that he was only Esteban, the boy would add that Manuel was wanted at the theatre. Esteban assumed that the call was for copyist's work and was therefore utterly unprepared for a visit that they received one night in their room.

It was almost midnight. Esteban had gone to bed, and lay gazing out from under the blanket at the candle beside which his brother was working. There was a light tap at the door and Manuel opened to admit a lady heavily veiled, out of breath and nervous. She threw back the scarf from her face and said hurriedly:

"Quick, ink and paper. You are Manuel, yes? You must do a letter for me at once."

For a moment her glance fell on the two bright eyes that glared at her from the edge of the cot. She murmured: "Eu . . . you must excuse me. I know it is late. It was necessary . . . I must come." Then turning to Manuel, she whispered into his ear: "Write this: *I, the Perichole, am not accustomed to wait at a rendez-vous.* Have you finished that? *You are only a cholo, and there are better matadors than you, even in Lima. I am half Castilian and there are no better actresses in the world. You shall not have the opportunity*—Have you got that?—*to keep me waiting again, cholo, and I shall laugh the last, for even an actress does not grow old as fast as a bullfighter.*"

To Esteban in the shadows the picture of Camila leaning over his brother's hand and whispering into his ear was complete evidence that a new congeniality had formed such as he would never know. He seemed to shrink away into space, infinitely tiny, infinitely unwanted. He took one more glance at the tableau of love, all the paradise from which he was shut out, and turned his face to the wall.

Camila seized the note the moment it was done, pushed a coin along the table and in a last flurry of black lace, scarlet beads and excited

whispers left the room. Manuel turned from the door with his candle. He sat down, put his hand over his ears, his elbows on his knees. He worshipped her. He murmured to himself over and over again that he worshipped her, making of the sound a sort of incantation and an obstacle to thought.

He emptied his mind of everything but a sing-song, and it was this vacancy that permitted him to become aware of Esteban's mood. He seemed to hear a voice that proceeded from the shadows saying: "Go and follow her, Manuel. Don't stay here. You'll be happy. There's room for us all in the world." Then the realization became even more intense and he received a mental image of Esteban going a long way off and saying good-bye many times as he went. He was filled with terror; by the light of it he saw that all the other attachments in the world were shadows, or the illusions of fever, even Madre María del Pilar, even the Perichole. He could not understand why Esteban's misery should present itself as demanding a choice between him and the Perichole, but he could understand Esteban's misery, as misery. And at once he sacrificed everything to it, if it can be said we ever sacrifice anything save what we know we can never attain, or what some secret wisdom tells us it would be uncomfortable or saddening to possess. To be sure there was nothing on which Esteban could base a complaint. It was not jealousy, for in their earlier affairs it had never occurred to either of them that their loyalty to one another had been diminished. It was merely that in the heart of one of them there was left room for an elaborate imaginative attachment and in the heart of the other there was not. Manuel could not quite understand this and, as we shall see, he nourished a dim sense of being accused unjustly. But he did understand that Esteban was suffering. In his excitement he groped for a means of holding this brother who seemed to be receding into the distance. And at once, in one unhesitating stroke of the will, he removed the Perichole from his heart.

He blew out the candle and lay down on his bed. He was trembling. He said aloud with exaggerated casualness: "Well, that's the last letter I write for that woman. She can go and find a pander somewhere else. If ever she calls here or sends for me when I'm out, tell her so. Make it plain. That's the last I have to do with her," and with that he began reciting his evening psalm aloud. But he had hardly reached *A sagitta volante in die* when he became aware that Esteban had risen and was lighting the candle.

"What's the matter?" he asked.

"I'm going out for a walk," replied Esteban sombrely, fastening his belt. After a moment, he broke out with an assumption of anger: "You don't have to say . . . what you just said, for me. I don't care whether

you write her letters or not. You don't have to change for me. I haven't anything to do with that."

"Go to bed, you fool. God, you're a fool, Esteban. What made you think I said that, for you? Don't you believe I mean it when I say I'm through with her? Do you think I want to write any more of her dirty letters and get paid for them like that?"

"It's all right. You love her. You don't have to change because of me."

" '*Love* her?' *Love* her? You're crazy, Esteban. How could I love her? What chance would there be for me? Do you suppose she'd give me those letters to write if there were any chance? Do you suppose she'd push a piece of money across the table every time. . . . You're crazy, Esteban, that's all."

There was a long pause. Esteban would not go to bed. He sat by the candle in the middle of the room, tapping with his hand on the edge of the table.

"Go to bed, you fool," shouted Manuel, rising on one elbow under the blanket. He was talking in their secret language and the new pain at his heart, gave a greater ring of reality to his assumption of rage. "I'm all right."

"I won't. I'm going out for a walk," replied Esteban picking up his coat.

"You can't go out for a walk. It's two o'clock. It's raining. You can't go and walk about for hours like that. Look, Esteban, I swear to you there's nothing left to all that. I don't love her. I only did for a time."

By now Esteban stood in the dark of the open door. In the unnatural voice with which we make the greatest declarations of our lives, he muttered: "I'm in your way," and turned to go.

Manuel leapt out of his bed. His head seemed to be full of a great din, a voice crying out that Esteban was going away forever, was leaving him alone forever. "In the name of God, in the name of God, Esteban, come back here."

Esteban came back and went to bed and the matter was not mentioned again for many weeks. The very next evening Manuel had an opportunity of declaring his position. A messenger arrived from the Perichole and was told harshly to inform the actress that Manuel would write no more letters for her.

One evening Manuel tore open the flesh on his knee against a piece of metal.

Neither brother had ever been ill for as much as a day in his life, and now Manuel, utterly bewildered, watched his leg swell and felt the

waves of pain rise and fall in his body. Esteban sat by and stared at his face trying to imagine what great pain was. At last one midnight Manuel remembered that the signboard of a certain hairdresser in the city described the proprietor as an experienced barber and surgeon. Esteban ran through the streets to fetch him. He pounded on the door. Presently a woman leaned out of a window and announced that her husband would be back in the morning. During the fearful hours that followed, they told one another that when the doctor had seen the leg all would be well. He would do something about it, and Manuel would be out around the town in a day or two, even in a day perhaps, even less than a day.

The barber arrived and prescribed various draughts and ointments. Esteban was instructed to lay cold cloths on his brother's leg every hour. The barber withdrew and the brothers sat down to wait for the pain to subside. But while they continued staring into one another's face waiting for the miracle of science the pain grew worse. Hour after hour Esteban approached with his dripping towel and they discovered that the moment of its application was the worst of all. With all the fortitude in the world Manuel could not prevent himself from shouting and from flinging himself about upon the bed. Night came on and still Esteban stolidly waited and watched and worked. Nine, ten, eleven. Now when the time drew near to apply the cloths (the hour struck so musically from all those towers) Manuel would plead with Esteban not to do his work. He would resort to guile and declare that he scarcely felt it. But Esteban, his heart bursting with pain and his lips a line of iron, would roll back the blanket and bind the towel fiercely in its place. Manuel gradually became delirious and under this application all the thoughts he did not permit himself in his right mind would burst magnified from his mouth.

Finally at two o'clock, out of his mind with rage and pain, and flinging himself half out of the bed until his head struck the floor, Manuel cried: "God condemn your soul to the hottest hell there is. A thousand devils torture you forever, Esteban. God condemn your soul, do you hear?" At first, the air gone out of his body, Esteban went out into the hall and leaned against the door, his mouth and eyes wide open. Still he heard from within: "Yes, Esteban, may God damn your beastly soul forever, do you hear that? For coming between me and what was mine by right. She was mine, do you hear, and what right had you. . . ." and he would go off into an elaborate description of the Perichole.

These outbursts recurred hourly. It was some time before Esteban was able to realize that his brother's mind was not then clear. After some moments of horror, in which his being a devout believer had its

part, he would return to the room and go about his duties with bent head.

Towards dawn his brother became serener. (For what human ill does not dawn seem to be an alleviation?) It was in one of these intervals that Manuel said quite calmly:

"God's son! I feel better, Esteban. Those cloths must be good after all. You'll see. I'll be up and around tomorrow. You haven't slept for days. You'll see I won't cause you any more trouble, Esteban."

"It's no trouble, you fool."

"You mustn't take me seriously when I try and stop you putting on the cold cloths, Esteban."

A long pause. At last Esteban brought out, barely audible:

"I think . . . don't you think it would be fine if I sent for the Perichole? She could just come and see you for a few minutes, I mean. . . ."

"Her? You still thinking about her? I wouldn't have her here for anything. No."

But Esteban was not content yet. He dragged up a few more phrases from the very centre of his being:

"Manuel, you still feel, don't you, that I came between you and the Perichole and you don't remember that I told you it was all right with me. I swear to you I'd have been glad if you'd gone away with her, or anything."

"What are you bringing that up for, Esteban? I tell you, in God's own name, I never think of that. She's nothing to me. When are you going to forget that, Esteban? I tell you I'm glad things are as they are. Look, I got to get angry when you keep going back to that."

"Manuel, I wouldn't speak of it again, only when you get angry at me about the cloths . . . you, you get angry at me about that, too. And you talk about it and you . . ."

"Look, I'm not responsible what I say. My old leg hurts then, see."

"Then you don't damn me to hell because . . . it looks like I came between you and the Perichole?"

"Damn you to . . . ? What makes you say that? You're going crazy, Esteban; you're imagining things. You haven't had any sleep, Esteban. I've been a curse to you and you're losing your health because of me. But you'll see, I won't trouble you much more. How could I damn you to hell, Esteban, when you're all I've got? Understand, see, that when the cold cloths go on, I just lose myself, see. You know. Don't think about it twice. It's time to put them on now. I won't say a word."

"No, Manuel, I'll skip this time. It won't do you any harm, I'll just skip this time."

"I've got to get well, Esteban. I've got to get up soon, you know.

Put them on. But one minute—give me the crucifix. I swear by the blood and body of Christ that if I say anything against Esteban, I don't mean it and it's just the foolish words when I'm dreaming because of the pain in my leg. God make me well again soon, amen. Put it back. There. Now I'm ready."

"Look, Manuel, it won't hurt if I skip just this once, see. It'll be good for you, sure, to not get it all stirred up just this once."

"No, I've got to get well. The doctor said it had to be done. I won't say a word, Esteban."

And it would begin all over again.

During the second night a prostitute in the next room started beating on the wall, outraged at such language. A priest in the room on the other side would come out into the hall and beat on the door. The whole floor would gather before the room in exasperation. The innkeeper came up the stairs, loudly promising his guests that the brothers would be dumped into the street the very next morning. Esteban, holding his candle, would go into the hall and permit them to rage at him for as long as they pleased; but after that he took to pressing his hand firmly over his brother's mouth during the moments of greatest stress. This increased Manuel's personal rage at him and he would babble all through the night.

On the third night, Esteban sent for the priest and amidst the enormous shadows Manuel received the sacrament, and died.

Thereafter Esteban refused to come near the building. He would start off upon long walks, but presently drifting back, would hang about, staring at passers-by, within two streets of where his brother lay. The innkeeper failing to make any impression upon him and remembering that the boys were brought up at the Convent of Santa Maria Rosa de las Rosas, sent for the Abbess. Simply and soundly she directed all that was to be done. At last she went down to the street corner and spoke to Esteban. He watched her approach him, a glance mixed of longing and distrust. But when she stood near him he turned sideways and looked away.

"I want you to help me. Won't you come in and see your brother? Won't you come in and help me?"

"No."

"You won't help me!" A long pause. Suddenly she stood there full of her helplessness there flashed through her mind an incident of many years before: the twin brothers about fifteen years old were sitting at her knee and she was telling them the story of the crucifixion. Their large grave eyes were fixed upon her lips. Suddenly Manuel had cried out loudly: "If Esteban and I had been there we would have prevented it."

"Well, then, if you won't help me, will you tell me which you are?"

"Manuel," said Esteban.

"Manuel, won't you come and sit with me up there for just a short time?"

After a long pause: "No."

"But Manuel, dear Manuel, can't you remember as children how you did so many things for me? You were willing to go across the town on some little errand. When I was ill you made the cook let you bring me my soup?" Another woman would have said: "Do you remember how much I did for you?"

"Yes."

"I, too, Manuel have lost. I too . . . once. We know that God has taken them into His hands. . . ." But this did not do at all. Esteban turned vaguely and walked away from her. When he had gone about twenty paces he stopped and stared down a side-street, like a dog who wants to go away, but is reluctant to offend the master who calls him back.

That was all they could get out of him. When the fearful procession passed through the city, with its black hoods and masks, its candles in broad daylight, its display of heaped-up skulls, its terrifying psalms, Esteban followed it in the parallel streets, catching glimpses of it from a distance, like a savage.

All Lima was interested in this separation of the brothers. Housewives whispered together sympathetically about it as they unfurled their carpets from the balconies. The men in the wineshops, alluding to it, shook their heads and smoked in silence for a while. Travellers from the interior told of seeing Esteban as he strayed with eyes like coals along the dried-up beds of rivers or through the great ruins of the old race. A herder of llamas had come upon him standing upon a hilltop, asleep or dazed, wet with dew under the stars. Some fishermen surprised him swimming far out from shore. From time to time he would find work to do, he would become a shepherd or a carter, but after a few months he would disappear and stride from province to province. But he always returned to Lima. One day he appeared at the door of the Perichole's dressing-room; he made as though to speak, gazed earnestly at her and vanished. One day a sister came running into the office of Madre María del Pilar with the news that Esteban (whom the world called Manuel) was lingering about the door of the convent. The Abbess hurried out into the street. For months she had been asking herself what strategy could reconcile this half-demented boy to living among them again. She assembled as grave and calm a manner as she was able and appearing at the street door murmured "My friend" and looked at him. He gazed back at her with the same

glance of longing and distrust that he had shown her before, and stood
trembling. Again she whispered "My friend" and moved a step for-
ward. Suddenly Esteban turned and breaking into a run disappeared.
Madre María del Pilar rushed stumbling back to her desk and fell
upon her knees, exclaiming angrily: "I have prayed for wisdom and
You have given me none. You have not chosen to give me the least
grace. I am a mere scrubber of floors. . . ." But during the penance
she set herself for this impudence the thought came to her to send for
Captain Alvarado. Three weeks later she had a ten-minute conversa-
tion with him. And the next day he started for Cuzco where, it was
said, Esteban was doing some copying for the University.

There was this strange and noble figure in Peru during these years,
the Captain Alvarado, the traveller. He was blackened and cured by
all weathers. He stood in the Square with feet apart as though they
were planted on a shifting deck. His eyes were strange, unaccustomed
to the shorter range, too used to seizing the appearances of a constella-
ation between a cloud and a cloud, and the outline of a cape in rain.
His reticence was sufficiently explained for most of us by his voyages,
but the Marquesa de Montemayor had other light on the matter.
"Captain Alvarado is bringing you this letter in person," she wrote to
her daughter. *"Introduce him to some of your geographers, my
treasure, though it may make them a little uncomfortable, for he is the
diamond of sincerity. They will never see anyone who has travelled so
far. Last night he described to me some of his voyages. Imagine him
pushing his prow through a sea of weeds, stirring up a cloud of fish like
grasshoppers in June; or sailing between islands of ice. Oh, he has been
to China and up the rivers of Africa. But he is not merely an ad-
venturer; and he seems to take no pride in discovering new places; nor
is he a mere merchant. One day I asked him narrowly why he lived
so, and he avoided my question. I found out from my laundress what
I think is the reason of his wandering: My child, he had a child; my
daughter, he had a daughter. She was just old enough to cook a
holiday meal, and do a little sewing for him. In those days he merely
sailed between Mexico and Peru and hundreds of times she waved him
farewell or welcome. We have no way of knowing whether she was
more beautiful or intelligent than the thousands of other girls that
lived about him, but she was his. I suppose it seems ignoble to you that
a great oak of a man should go about the world like a blind man about
an empty house merely because a chit of a girl has been withdrawn
from it. No, no, you cannot understand this, my adored one, but I
understand and grow pale. Last night he sat with me and talked of
her. He laid his cheek against his hand and looking into the fire, he
said: 'It sometimes seems to me that she is away upon a voyage and*

that I shall see her again. It seems to me that she is in England.' You will laugh at me, but I think he goes about the hemispheres to pass the time between now and his old age."

The brothers had always entertained a great respect for Captain Alvarado. They had worked for him a short time and the silence of the three of them had made a little kernel of sense in a world of boasting, self-excuse and rhetoric. So now when the great traveller came into the dark kitchen where Esteban was eating the boy drew his chair farther into the shadow, but at a distance, he was glad. The Captain gave no sign of recognizing or even of seeing him until he had finished his meal. Esteban had finished long before, but not wishing to be spoken to, waited until the Captain should have left the cave. At last the Captain walked over to him and said:

"You are Esteban or Manuel. You helped me once with some unloading. I am Captain Alvarado."

"Yes," said Esteban.

"How are you?"

Esteban muttered something.

"I am looking for some strong fellows to go on my next trip with me." Pause. "Would you like to come?" Longer pause. "England. And Russia. . . . Hard work. Good wages. . . . A long way from Peru. —Well?"

Apparently Esteban had not been listening. He sat with his eyes on the table. At last the Captain raised his voice, as to a deaf person:

"I said: Do you want to go on my next trip with me. . . ."

"Yes, I'll go," answered Esteban suddenly.

"Fine. That's fine. I want your brother, too, of course."

"No."

"What's the matter? Wouldn't he want to come?"

Esteban mumbled something, looking away. Then half rising, he said: "I got to go now. I've got to see somebody about something."

"Let me see your brother myself. Where is he?"

". . . 'dead," said Esteban.

"Oh, I didn't know. I didn't know. I'm sorry."

"Yes," said Esteban. "I got to go."

"Hmm.—Which are you? What's your name?"

"Esteban."

"When did Manuel die?"

"Oh, just a . . . just a few weeks. He hit his knee against something and . . . just a few weeks ago."

They both kept their eyes on the floor.

"How old are you, Esteban?"

"Twenty-two."

"Well, that's settled then, you're coming with me?"

"Yes."

"You may not be used to the cold."

"Yes, I'm used to it.—I've got to go now. I got to go in the city and see somebody about something."

"Well, Esteban. Come back here for supper and we'll talk about the trip. Come back and have some wine with me, see. Will you?"

"Yes, I will."

"Go with God."

"Go with God."

They had supper together and it was arranged that they were to start for Lima in the next morning. The Captain got him very drunk. At first they poured and drank and poured and drank in silence. Then the Captain began to talk about ships and their courses. He asked Esteban questions about tackle and about the guide-stars. Then Esteban began to talk about other things, and to talk very loudly:

"On the ship you must give me something to do all the time. I'll do anything, anything. I'll climb up high and fix ropes; and I'll watch all night,—because, you know, I don't sleep well anyway. And, Captain Alvarado, on the ship you must pretend that you don't know me. Pretend that you hate me the most. So that you'll always give me things to do. I can't sit still and write at a table any more.—And don't tell the other men about me . . . that is, about . . ."

"I hear you went into a burning house, Esteban, and pulled someone out."

"Yes. I didn't get burned or anything. You know," cried Esteban, leaning across the table, "you're not allowed to kill yourself; you know you're not allowed. Everybody knows that. But if you jump into a burning house to save somebody, that wouldn't be killing yourself. And if you became a matador and the bull caught you that wouldn't be killing yourself. Only you mustn't put yourself in the bull's way on purpose. Did you ever notice that animals never kill themselves, even when they're sure to lose? They never jump into a river or anything, even when they're sure to lose. Some people say that horses run into bonfires. Is that true?"

"No, I don't think that's true."

"I don't think it's true. We had a dog once. Well, I mustn't think of that.—Captain Alvarado, do you know Madre María del Pilar?"

"Yes."

"I want to give her a present before I go away. Captain Alvarado, I want you to give me all my wages before I start—I won't need any money anywhere—and I want to buy her a present now. The present isn't from me only. She was . . . was . . . " Here Esteban wished to

say his brother's name, but was unable to. Instead he continued in a lower voice: "She had a kind of . . . she had a serious loss, once. She said so. I don't know who it was, and I want to give her a present. Women can't bear that kind of a thing like we can."

The Captain promised him that they would choose something in the morning. Esteban talked about it at great length. At last the Captain saw him slip under the table, and himself, rising up, went out into the square before the inn. He looked at the line of the Andes and at the streams of stars crowding forever across the sky. And there was that wraith hanging in mid-air and smiling at him, the wraith with the silvery voice that said for the thousandth time: "Don't be gone long. But I'll be a big girl when you get back." Then he went within and carried Esteban to his room and sat looking at him for a long while.

The next morning he was waiting at the bottom of the stairs when Esteban appeared:

"We're starting when you're ready," said the Captain.

The strange glitter had returned to the boy's eyes. He blurted out: "No, I'm not coming. I'm not coming after all."

"Aïe! Esteban! But you have promised me that you would come."

"It's impossible. I can't come with you," and he turned back up the stairs.

"Come here a moment, Esteban, just a moment."

"I can't come with you. I can't leave Peru."

"I want to tell you something."

Esteban came down to the foot of the stairs.

"How about that present for Madre María del Pilar?" asked the Captain in a low voice. Esteban was silent, looking over the mountains. "You aren't going to take that present away from her? It might mean a lot to her . . . you know."

"All right," murmured Esteban, as though much impressed.

"Yes. Besides the ocean's better than Peru. You know Lima and Cuzco and the road. You have nothing more to know about them. You see it's the ocean you want. Besides on the boat you'll have something to do every minute. I'll see to that. Go and get your things and we'll start."

Esteban was trying to make a decision. It had always been Manuel who had made the decisions and even Manuel had never been forced to make as great a one as this. Esteban went slowly upstairs. The Captain waited for him and waited so long that presently he ventured half the way up the stairs and listened. At first there was silence; then a series of noises that his imagination was able to identify at once. Esteban had scraped away the plaster about a beam and was adjusting a rope about it. The Captain stood on the stairs trembling: "Perhaps it's best," he

said to himself. "Perhaps I should leave him alone. Perhaps it's the only thing possible for him." Then on hearing another sound he flung himself against the door, fell into the room and caught the boy. "Go away," cried Esteban. "Let me be. Don't come in now."

Esteban fell face downward upon the floor. "I am alone, alone, alone" he cried. The Captain stood above him, his great plain face ridged and gray with pain; it was his own old hours he was reliving. He was the awkwardest speaker in the world apart from the lore of the sea, but there are times when it requires a high courage to speak the banal. He could not be sure the figure on the floor was listening, but he said "We do what we can. We push on, Esteban, as best we can. It isn't for long, you know. Time keeps going by. You'll be surprised at the way time passes."

They started for Lima. When they reached the bridge of San Luis Rey, the Captain descended to the stream below in order to supervise the passage of some merchandise, but Esteban crossed by the bridge and fell with it.

PART IV

Uncle Pio

In one of her letters (the XXIXth) the Marquesa de Montemayor tries to describe the impression that Uncle Pio *"our aged Harlequin"* made upon her: *"I have been sitting all morning on the green balcony making you a pair of slippers, my soul,"* she tells her daughter. *"As the golden wire did not take up my whole attention I was able to follow the activity of a coterie of ants in the wall beside me. Somewhere behind the partition they were patiently destroying my house. Every three minutes a little workman would appear between two boards and drop a grain of wood upon the floor below. Then he would wave his antennae at me and back busily into his mysterious corridor. In the meantime various brothers and sisters of his were trotting back and forth on a certain highway, stopping to massage one another's heads, or if the messages they bore were of first importance, refusing angrily to massage or to be massaged. And at once I thought of Uncle Pio. Why? Where else but with him had I seen that very gesture with which he arrests a passing abbé or a courtier's valet, and whispers, his lips laid against his victim's ear? And surely enough, before noon I saw him hurry by on one of those mysterious errands of his. As I am the idlest and silliest of women I sent Pepita to get me a piece of*

nougat which I placed on the ant's highway. Similarly I sent word to the Café Pizarro asking them to send Uncle Pio to see me if he dropped in before sunset. I shall give him that old bent salad fork with the turquoise in it, and he will bring me a copy of the new ballad that everyone is singing about the d—q—a of Ol—v—s. My child, you shall have the best of everything, and you shall have it first."

And in the next letter: *"My dear, Uncle Pio is the most delightful man in the world, your husband excepted. He is the second most delightful man in the world. His conversation is enchanting. If he weren't so disreputable I should make him my secretary. He could write all my letters for me and generations would rise up and call me witty. Alas, however, he is so moth-eaten by disease and bad company, that I shall have to leave him to his underworld. He is not only like an ant, he is like a soiled pack of cards. And I doubt whether the whole Pacific could wash him sweet and fragrant again. But what divine Spanish he speaks and what exquisite things he says in it! That's what one gets by hanging around a theatre and hearing nothing but the conversation of Calderón. Alas, what is the matter with this world, my soul, that it should treat such a being so ill! His eyes are as sad as those of a cow that has been separated from its tenth calf."*

You should know first that this Uncle Pio was Camila Perichole's maid. He was also her singing-master, her coiffer, her masseur, her reader, her errand-boy, her banker; rumor added: her father. For example, he taught her her parts. There was a whisper around town that Camila could read and write. The compliment was unfounded; Uncle Pio did her reading and writing for her. At the height of the season the company put on two or three new plays a week, and as each one contained a long and flowery part for the Perichole the mere task of memorization was not a trifle.

Peru had passed within fifty years from a frontier state to a state in renaissance. Its interest in music and the theatre was intense. Lima celebrated its feast days by hearing a Mass of Tomás Luis da Victoria in the morning and the glittering poetry of Calderón in the evening. It is true that the Limeans were given to interpolating trivial songs into the most exquisite comedies and some lachrymose effects into the austerest music; but at least they never submitted to the boredom of a misplaced veneration. If they had disliked heroic comedy the Limeans would not have hesitated to remain at home; and if they had been deaf to polyphony nothing would have prevented their going to an earlier service. When the Archbishop returned from a short trip to Spain, all

Lima kept asking: "What has he brought?" The news finally spread abroad that he had returned with tomes of masses and motets by Palestrina, Morales and Vittoria, as well as thirty-five plays by Tirso de Molina and Ruiz de Alarçon and Moreto. There was a civic fête in his honor. The choirboys' school and the green room of the Comedia were swamped with the gifts of vegetables and wheat. All the world was eager to nourish the interpreters of so much beauty.

This was the theatre in which Camila Perichole gradually made her reputation. So rich was the repertory and so dependable the prompter's box that few plays were given more than four times a season. The manager had the whole flowering of the 17th Century Spanish drama to draw upon, including many that are now lost to us. The Perichole had appeared in a hundred plays of Lope de Vega alone. There were many admirable actresses in Lima during these years, but none better. The citizens were too far away from the theatres of Spain to realize that she was the best in the Spanish world. They kept sighing for a glimpse of the stars of Madrid whom they had never seen and to whom they assigned vague new excellences. Only one person knew for certain that the Perichole was a great performer and that was her tutor Uncle Pio.

Uncle Pio came of a good Castilian house, illegitimately. At the age of ten he ran away to Madrid from his father's hacienda and was pursued without diligence. He lived ever after by his wits. He possessed the six attributes of the adventurer—a memory for names and faces, with the aptitude for altering his own; the gift of tongues; inexhaustible invention; secrecy; the talent for falling into conversation with strangers; and that freedom from conscience that springs from a contempt for the dozing rich he preyed upon. From ten to fifteen he distributed handbills for merchants, held horses, and ran confidential errands. From fifteen to twenty he trained bears and snakes for travelling circuses; he cooked, and mixed punches; he hung about the entries of the more expensive taverns and whispered informations into the travellers' ears—sometimes nothing more dubious than that a certain noble house was reduced to selling its plate and could thus dispense with the commission of a silversmith. He was attached to all the theatres in town and could applaud like ten. He spread slanders at so much a slander. He sold rumors about crops and about the value of land. From twenty to thirty his services came to be recognized in very high circles—he was sent out by the government to inspirit some half-hearted rebellions in the mountains, so that the government could presently arrive and whole-heartedly crush them. His discretion was so profound that the French party used him even when they knew that the Austrian party used him also. He had long interviews with the Princesse des Ursins, but he came and went by the back stairs. During

this phase he was no longer obliged to arrange gentlemen's pleasures, nor to plant little harvests of calumny.

He never did one thing for more than two weeks at a time even when enormous gains seemed likely to follow upon it. He could have become a circus manager, a theatrical director, a dealer in antiquities, an importer of Italian silks, a secretary in the Palace or the Cathedral, a dealer in provisions for the army, a speculator in houses and farms, a merchant in dissipations and pleasures. But there seemed to have been written into his personality, through some accident or early admiration of his childhood, a reluctance to own anything, to be tied down, to be held to a long engagement. It was this that prevented his thieving, for example. He had stolen several times, but the gains had not been sufficient to offset his dread of being locked up; he had sufficient ingenuity to escape on the field itself all the police in the world, but nothing could protect him against the talebearing of his enemies. Similarly he had been reduced for a time to making investigations for the Inquisition, but when he had seen several of his victims led off in hoods he felt that he might be involving himself in an institution whose movements were not evenly predictable.

As he approached twenty, Uncle Pio came to see quite clearly that his life had three aims. There was first this need of independence, cast into a curious pattern, namely: the desire to be varied, secret and omniscient. He was willing to renounce the dignities of public life, if in secret he might feel that he looked down upon men from a great distance, knowing more about them than they knew themselves; and with a knowledge which occasionally passed into action and rendered him an agent in the affairs of states and persons. In the second place he wanted to be always near beautiful women, of whom he was always in the best and worst sense the worshipper. To be near them was as necessary to him as breathing. His reverence for beauty and charm was there for anyone to see and to laugh at, and the ladies of the theatre and the court and the houses of pleasure loved his connoisseurship. They tormented him and insulted him and asked his advice and were singularly comforted by his absurd devotion. He suffered greatly their rages and their meanness and their confiding tears; all he asked was to be accepted casually, to be trusted, to be allowed like a friendly and slightly foolish dog to come and go in their rooms and to write their letters for them. He was insatiably curious about their minds and their hearts. He never expected to be loved by them (borrowing for a moment another sense of that word); for that, he carried his money to the obscurer parts of the city; he was always desperately unprepossessing, with his whisp of a moustache and his whisp of a beard and his big ridiculous sad eyes. They constituted his parish; it

was from them that he acquired the name of Uncle Pio and it was when they were in trouble that he most revealed himself; when they fell from favour he lent them money, when they were ill he outlasted the flagging devotion of their lovers and the exasperation of their maids; when time or disease robbed them of their beauty, he served them still for their beauty's memory; and when they died his was the honest grief that saw them as far as possible on their journey.

In the third place he wanted to be near those that loved Spanish literature and its masterpieces, especially in the theatre. He had discovered all that treasure for himself, borrowing or stealing from the libraries of his patrons, feeding himself upon it in secrecy,—behind the scenes, as it were, of his mad life. He was contemptuous of the great persons who for all their education and usage, exhibited no care nor astonishment before the miracles of word order in Calderón and Cervantes. He longed himself to make verses. He never realized that many of the satirical songs he had written for the vaudevilles passed into folk-music and have been borne everywhere along the highroads.

As the result of one of those quarrels that arise so naturally in brothels his life became too complicated and he removed to Peru. Uncle Pio in Peru was even more versatile than Uncle Pio in Europe. Here too he touched upon real-estate, circuses, pleasures, insurrections and antiques. A Chinese junk had been blown from Canton to America; he dragged up the beach the bales of deep-red porcelain and sold the bowls to the collectors of virtú. He traced down the sovereign remedies of the Incas and started a smart trade in pills. Within four months he knew practically everyone in Lima. He presently added to this acquaintance the inhabitants of scores of seacoast towns, mining camps and settlements in the interior. His pretensions to omniscience became more and more plausible. The Viceroy discovered Uncle Pio and all this richness of reference; he engaged his services in many affairs. In the decay of his judgment Don Andrés had retained one talent, he was a master of the technique of handling confidential servants. He treated Uncle Pio with great tact and some deference; he understood which errands the other should not be asked to undertake and he understood his need for variety and intermission. Uncle Pio in turn was perpetually astonished that a prince should make so little use of his position, for power, or for fantasy, or for sheer delight in the manipulation of other men's destinies; but the servant loved the master because he could quote from any of Cervantes' prefaces and because his tongue had a little Castilian salt about it still. Many a morning Uncle Pio entered the Palace through corridors where there was no one to cross but a confessor or a confidential bully and sat with the Viceroy over his morning chocolate.

But for all his activity nothing made Uncle Pio rich. One would have said that he abandoned a venture when it threatened to prosper. Although no one knew it, he owned a house. It was full of dogs that could add and multiply and the top floor was reserved for birds. But even in this kingdom he was lonely, and proud in his loneliness, as though there resided a certain superiority in such a solitude. Finally he stumbled upon an adventure that came like some strange gift from the skies and that combined the three great aims of his life: his passion for overseeing the lives of others, his worship of beautiful women, and his admiration for the treasures of Spanish literature. He discovered Camila Perichole. Her real name was Micaela Villegas. She was singing in cafés at the age of twelve and Uncle Pio had always been the very soul of cafés. Now as he sat among the guitarists and watched this awkward girl singing ballads, imitating every inflection of the more experienced singers who had preceded her, the determination entered his mind to play Pygmalion. He bought her. Instead of sleeping locked up in the wine bin, she inherited a cot in his house. He wrote songs for her, he taught her how to listen to the quality of her tone, and bought her a new dress. At first all she noticed was that it was wonderful not to be whipped, to be offered hot soups, and to be taught something. But it was Uncle Pio who was really dazzled. His rash experiment flourished beyond all prophecy. The little twelve-year-old, silent and always a little sullen, devoured work. He set her endless exercises in acting and mimicry; he set her problems in conveying the atmosphere of a song; he took her to the theatres and made her notice all the details of a performance. But it was from Camila as a woman that he was to receive his greatest shock. The long arms and legs were finally harmonized into a body of perfect grace. The almost grotesque and hungry face became beautiful. Her whole nature became gentle and mysterious and oddly wise; and it all turned to him. She could find no fault in him and she was sturdily loyal. They loved one another deeply but without passion. He respected the slight nervous shadow that crossed her face when he came too near her. But there arose out of this denial itself the perfume of a tenderness, that ghost of passion which, in the most unexpected relationship, can make even a whole lifetime devoted to irksome duty pass like a gracious dream.

They travelled a great deal, seeking new taverns, for the highest attribute of a café singer will always be her novelty. They went to Mexico, their odd clothes wrapped up in the self-same shawl. They slept on beaches, they were whipped at Panama and shipwrecked on some tiny Pacific islands plastered with the droppings of birds. They tramped through jungles delicately picking their way among snakes

and beetles. They sold themselves out as harvesters in a hard season. Nothing in the world was very surprising to them.

Then began an even harder course of training for the girl, a regimen that resembled more the preparation for an acrobat. The instruction was a little complicated by the fact that her rise to favor was very rapid; and there was some danger that the applause she received would make her content with her work too soon. Uncle Pio never exactly beat her, but he resorted to a sarcasm that had terrors of its own.

At the close of a performance Camila would return to her dressing room to find Uncle Pio whistling nonchalantly in one corner. She would divine his attitude at once and cry angrily:

"Now what is it? Mother of God, Mother of God, what is it now?"

"Nothing, little pearl. My little Camila of Camilas, nothing."

"There was something you didn't like. Ugly fault-finding thing that you are. Come on now, what was it? Look, I'm ready."

"No, little fish. Adorable morning star, I suppose you did as well as you could."

The suggestion that she was a limited artist and that certain felicities would be forever closed to her never failed to make Camila frantic. She would burst into tears: "I wish I had never known you. You poison my whole life. You just think I did badly. It pleases you to pretend that I was bad. All right then, be quiet."

Uncle Pio went on whistling.

"The fact is I know I was weak to-night, and don't need you to tell me so. So there. Now go away. I don't want to see you around. It's hard enough to play that part without coming back and finding you this way."

Suddenly Uncle Pio would lean forward and ask with angry intensity: "Why did you take that speech to the prisoner so fast?"

More tears from the Perichole: "Oh God, let me die in peace! One day you tell me to go faster and another to go slower. Anyway I shall be crazy in a year or two and then it won't matter."

More whistling.

"Besides the audience applauded as never before. Do you hear me? *As never before.* There! Too fast or too slow is nothing to them. They wept. I was divine. That's all I care for. Now be silent. Be silent."

He was absolutely silent.

"You may comb my hair, but if you say another word I shall never play again. You can find some other girl, that's all."

Thereupon he would comb her hair soothingly for ten minutes, pretending not to notice the sobs that were shaking her exhausted body. At last she would turn quickly and catching one of his hands would

kiss it frantically: "Uncle Pio, was I so bad? Was I a disgrace to you? Was it so awful *that you left the theatre?*"

After a long pause Uncle Pio would admit judiciously: "You were good in the scene on the ship."

"But I've been better, Uncle Pio. You remember the night you came back from Cuzco———?"

"You were pretty good at the close."

"Was I?"

"But my flower, my pearl, *what was the matter in the speech to the prisoner?*"

Here the Perichole would fling her face and arms upon the table amid the pomades, caught up into a tremendous fit of weeping. Only perfection would do, only perfection. And that had never come.

Then beginning in a low voice Uncle Pio would talk for an hour, analyzing the play, entering into a world of finesse in matters of voice and gesture and tempo, and often until dawn they would remain there declaiming to one another the lordly conversation of Calderón.

Whom were these two seeking to please? Not the audiences of Lima. They had long since been satisfied. We come from a world where we have known incredible standards of excellence, and we dimly remember beauties which we have not seized again; and we go back to that world. Uncle Pio and Camila Perichole were tormenting themselves in an effort to establish in Peru the standards of the theatres in some Heaven whither Calderón had preceded them. The public for which masterpieces are intended is not on this earth.

With the passing of time Camila lost some of this absorption in her art. A certain intermittent contempt for acting made her negligent. It was due to the poverty of interest in women's rôles throughout Spanish classical drama. At a time when the playwrights grouped about the courts of England and France (a little later, of Venice) were enriching the parts of women with studies in wit, charm, passion and hysteria, the dramatists of Spain kept their eyes on their heroes, on gentlemen torn between the conflicting claims of honour, or, as sinners, returning at the last moment to the cross. For a number of years Uncle Pio spent himself in discovering ways to interest the Perichole in the rôles that fell to her. Upon one occasion he was able to announce to Camila that a granddaughter of Vico de Barrera had arrived in Peru. Uncle Pio had long since communicated to Camila his veneration for great poets and Camila never questioned the view that they were a little above the kings and not below the saints. So it was in great excitement that the two of them chose one of the master's plays to perform before his granddaughter. They rehearsed the poem

a hundred times, now in the great joy of invention, now in dejection. On the night of the performance Camila peering out between the folds of the curtain had Uncle Pio point out to her the little middle-aged woman worn with the cares of penury and a large family; but it seemed to Camila that she was looking at all the beauty and dignity in the world. As she waited for the lines that preceded her entrance she clung to Uncle Pio in reverent silence, her heart beating loudly. Between the acts she retired to the dusty corner of the warehouse where no one would find her and sat staring into the corners. At the close of the performance Uncle Pio brought the granddaughter of Vico de Barrera into Camila's room. Camila stood among the clothes that hung upon the wall, weeping with happiness and shame. Finally she flung herself on her knees and kissed the older woman's hands, and the older woman kissed hers, and while the audience went home and went to bed the visitor remained telling Camila the little stories that had remained in the family, of Vico's work and of his habits.

Uncle Pio was at his happiest when a new actress entered the company, for the discovery of a new talent at her side never failed to bestir the Perichole. To Uncle Pio (standing at the back of the auditorium, bent double with joy and malice) it seemed that the body of the Perichole had become an alabaster lamp in which a strong light had been placed. Without any resort to tricks or to false emphasis, she set herself to efface the newcomer. If the play were a comedy she became the very abstraction of wit, and (as was more likely) it was a drama of wronged ladies and implacable hates, the stage fairly smouldered with her emotion. Her personality became so electric that if she so much as laid her hand upon that of a fellow actor a sympathetic shudder ran through the audience. But such occasions of excellence became less and less frequent. As her technique became sounder, Camila's sincerity became less necessary. Even when she was absent-minded the audience did not notice the difference and only Uncle Pio grieved.

Camila had a very beautiful face, or rather a face beautiful save in repose. In repose one was startled to discover that the nose was long and thin, the mouth tired and a little childish, the eyes unsatisfied—a rather pinched peasant girl, dragged from the cafés-chantants and quite incapable of establishing any harmony between the claims of her art, of her appetites, of her dreams, and of her crowded daily routine. Each of these was a world in itself, and the warfare between them would soon have reduced to idiocy (or triviality) a less tenacious physique. We have seen that in spite of her discontent with her parts, the Perichole knew very well the joy that might reside in acting and

warmed herself from time to time at that flame. But that of love attracted her more often, though with no greater assurance of happiness, until Jupiter himself sent her some pearls.

Don Andrés de Ribera, the Viceroy of Peru, was the remnant of a delightful man, broken by the table, the alcove, a grandeeship and ten years of exile. As a youth he had accompanied embassies to Versailles and Rome; he had fought in the wars in Austria; he had been in Jerusalem. He was a widower and childless of an enormous and wealthy woman; he had collected coins a little, wines, actresses, orders and maps. From the table he had received the gout; from the alcove a tendency to convulsions; from the grandeeship a pride so vast and puerile that he seldom heard anything that was said to him and talked to the ceiling in a perpetual monologue; from the exile, oceans of boredom, a boredom so persuasive that it was like pain,—he woke up with it and spent the day with it, and it sat by his bed all night watching his sleep. Camila was passing the years in the hard-working routine of the theatre, savoured by a few untidy love-affairs, when this Olympian personage (for he had a face and port fit to play gods and heroes on the scene) suddenly transported her to the most delicious midnight suppers at the Palace. Contrary to all the traditions of the stage and state she adored her elderly admirer; she thought she was going to be happy forever. Don Andrés taught the Perichole a great many things and to her bright eager mind that was one of the sweetest ingredients of love. He taught her a little French; to be neat and clean; the modes of address. Uncle Pio had taught her how great ladies carry themselves on great occasions; he taught her how they relax. Uncle Pio and Calderón had trained her in beautiful Spanish; Don Andrés furnished her with the smart slang of *El Buen Retiro*.

Uncle Pio was made anxious by Camila's invitation from the Palace. He would have much preferred that she continue with her little vulgarian love-affairs in the theatrical ware-house. But when he saw that her art was gaining a new finish he was well content. He would sit in the back of the theatre, rolling about in his seat for sheer joy and amusement, watching the Perichole intimate to the audience that she frequented the great world about whom the dramatists wrote. She had a new way of fingering a wine-glass, of exchanging an adieu, a new way of entering a door that told everything. To Uncle Pio nothing else mattered. What was there in the world more lovely than a beautiful woman doing justice to a Spanish masterpiece?—a performance (he asks you), packed with observation, in which the very spacing of the words revealed a comment on life and on the text—delivered by a beautiful voice—illustrated by a faultless carriage, considerable personal beauty and irresistible charm. "We are almost ready

to take this marvel to Spain," he would murmur to himself. After the performance he would go around to her dressing-room and say "Very good!" But before taking his leave he would manage to ask her where, in the name of the eleven thousand virgins of Cologne, she had acquired that affected way of saying *Excelencia*.

After a time the Viceroy asked the Perichole whether it would amuse her to invite a few discreet guests to their midnight suppers, and he asked her whether she would like to meet the Archbishop. Camila was delighted. The Archbishop was delighted. On the eve of their first meeting he sent the actress an emerald pendant as big as a playing-card.

There was something in Lima that was wrapped up in yards of violet satin from which protruded a great dropsical head and two fat pearly hands; and that was its archbishop. Between the rolls of flesh that surrounded them looked out two black eyes speaking discomfort, kindliness and wit. A curious and eager soul was imprisoned in all this lard, but by dint of never refusing himself a pheasant or a goose or his daily procession of Roman wines, he was his own bitter jailer. He loved his cathedral; he loved his duties; he was very devout. Some days he regarded his bulk ruefully; but the distress of remorse was less poignant than the distress of fasting and he was presently found deliberating over the secret messages that a certain roast sends to the certain salad that will follow it. And to punish himself he led an exemplary life in every other respect.

He had read all the literature of antiquity and forgotten all about it except a general aroma of charm and disillusion. He had been learned in the Fathers and the Councils and forgotten all about them save a floating impression of dissensions that had no application to Peru. He had read all the libertine masterpieces of Italy and France and reread them annually; even in the torments of the stone (happily dissolved by drinking the water from the springs of Santa María de Cluxambuqua), he could find nothing more nourishing than the anecdotes of Brantôme and the divine Aretino.

The Archbishop knew that most of the priests of Peru were scoundrels. It required all his delicate Epicurean education to prevent his doing something about it; he had to repeat over to himself his favourite notions: that the injustice and unhappiness in the world is a constant; that the theory of progress is a delusion; that the poor, never having known happiness, are insensible to misfortune. Like all the rich he could not bring himself to believe that the poor (look at their houses, look at their clothes) could really suffer. Like all the cultivated he believed that only the widely-read could be said to *know* that they were unhappy. On one occasion, the iniquities in his see having been

called to his notice, he almost did something about it. He had just heard that it was becoming a rule in Peru for priests to exact two measures of meal for a fairly good absolution, and five measures, for a really effective one. He trembled with indignation; he roared to his secretary and bidding him bring up his writing materials, announced that he was going to dictate an overwhelming message to his shepherds. But there was no ink left in the inkwell; there was no ink left in the next room; there was no ink to be found in the whole palace. This state of things in his household so upset the good man that he fell ill of the combined rages and learned to guard himself against indignations.

The addition of the Archbishop to the suppers was so successful that Don Andrés began to think of new names. He had grown increasingly dependent upon Uncle Pio, but waited until Camila should propose his inclusion of her own accord. And in due time Uncle Pio brought with him that courser of the seas, the Captain Alvarado. Generally the reunion had been several hours under way before Camila was able to join them after her performance at the theatre. She would arrive towards one o'clock, radiant and bejewelled and very tired. The four men received her as they would a great queen. For an hour or so she would carry the conversation, but gradually reclining more and more against Don Andrés' shoulder she would follow the talk as it flitted from one humorous lined face to the other. All night they talked, secretly comforting their hearts that longed always for Spain and telling themselves that such a symposium was after the manner of the high Spanish soul. They talked about ghosts and second-sight, and about the earth before man appeared upon it and about the possibility of the planets striking against one another; about whether the soul can be seen, like a dove, fluttering away at the moment of death; they wondered whether at the second coming of Christ to Jerusalem, Peru would be long in receiving the news. They talked until the sun rose, about wars and kings, about poets and scholars, and about strange countries. Each one poured into the conversation his store of wise sad anecdotes and his dry regret about the race of men. The flood of golden light struck across the Andes and entering the great window fell upon the piles of fruit, the stained brocade upon the table, and the sweet thoughtful forehead of the Perichole as she lay sleeping against the sleeve of her protector. There would ensue a long pause, no one wishing to make the first move to go, and the glances of them all would rest upon this strange beautiful bird who lived among them. But Uncle Pio's glance had been upon her all night, a quick glance from his black eyes, full of tenderness and anxiety, resting on the great secret and reason of his life.

But Uncle Pio never ceased watching Camila. He divided the inhabitants of this world into two groups, into those who had loved and those who had not. It was a horrible aristocracy, apparently, for those who had no capacity for love (or rather for suffering in love) could not be said to be alive and certainly would not live again after their death. They were a kind of straw population, filling the world with their meaningless laughter and tears and chatter and disappearing still lovable and vain into thin air. For this distinction he cultivated his own definition of love that was like no other and that had gathered all its bitterness and pride from his odd life. He regarded love as a sort of cruel malady through which the elect are required to pass in their late youth and from which they emerge, pale and wrung, but ready for the business of living. There was (he believed) a great repertory of errors mercifully impossible to human beings who had recovered from this illness. Unfortunately there remained to them a host of failings, but at least (from among many illustrations) they never mistook a protracted amiability for the whole conduct of life, they never again regarded any human being, from a prince to a servant, as a mechanical object. Uncle Pio never ceased watching Camila because it seemed to him that she had never undergone this initiation. In the months that followed her introduction to the Viceroy he held his breath and waited. He held his breath for years. Camila bore the Viceroy three children, yet remained the same. He knew that the first sign of her entrance into the true possession of the world would be the mastery of certain effects in her acting. There were certain passages in the plays that she would compass some day, simply, easily, and with secret joy, because they alluded to the new rich wisdom of her heart; but her treatment of such passages became more and more cursory, not to say embarrassed. He presently saw that she had tired of Don Andrés and had returned to a series of furtive love-affairs with the actors and matadors and merchants of the town.

She became more and more impatient of acting and another parasite found its way into her mind. She wanted to be a lady. She slowly contracted a greed for respectability and began to refer to her acting as a pastime. She acquired a duenna and some footmen and went to church at the fashionable hours. She attended the prize days at the University and appeared among the donors of the great charities. She even learned to read and write a little. Any faint discrimination against her as a bohemian she challenged with fury. She led the Viceroy a horrible life with her passion for concessions and her gradual usurpation of privileges. The new vice displaced the old and she became noisily virtuous. She invented some parents and produced some cousins. She obtained an undocumented legitimization of her children.

In society she cultivated a delicate and languid magdelinism, as a great lady might, and she carried a candle in the penitential parades, side by side with ladies who had nothing to regret but an outburst of temper and a furtive glance into Descartes. Her sin had been acting and everyone knows that there were even saints who had been actors, —there was Saint Gelasius and Saint Genesius and Saint Margaret of Antioch and Saint Pelagia.

There was a fashionable watering place in the hills not far from Santa María de Cluxambuqua. Don Andrés had travelled in France and had thought to build himself a little mock Vichy; there was a pagoda, some drawing-rooms, a theatre, a little arena for bull-fights and some French gardens. Camila's health had never known a shadow, but she built herself a villa in the vicinity and sipped the hateful waters at eleven o'clock. The Marquesa de Montemayor has left a brilliant picture of this *opéra bouffe* paradise with the reigning divinity parading her fierce sensitiveness along the avenues of powdered shell and receiving the homage of all those who could not afford to offend the Viceroy. Doña María draws a portrait of this ruler, stately and weary, gambling all through the night in sums that would have raised another Escurial. And beside him she sets the portrait of his son, Camila's little Don Jaime. Don Jaime, at seven years, was a rachitic little body who seemed to have inherited not only his mother's forehead and eyes, but his father's liability to convulsions. He bore his pain with the silent bewilderment of an animal, and like an animal he was mortally ashamed when any evidences of it occurred in public. He was so beautiful that the more trivial forms of pity were hushed in his presence and his long thoughts about his difficulties had given his face a patient and startling dignity. His mother dressed him in garnet velvet, and when he was able he followed her about at a distance of several yards, extricating himself gravely from the ladies who tried to detain him in conversation. Camila was never cross to Don Jaime and she was never demonstrative. When the sun was shining the two could be seen walking along those artificial terraces in silence, Camila wondering when the felicity would begin that she had always associated with social position, Don Jaime rejoicing merely in the sunlight and anxiously estimating the approach of a cloud. They looked like figures that had strayed there from some remote country, or out of an old ballad, that had not yet learned the new language and had not yet found any friends.

Camila was about thirty when she left the stage and it required five years for her to achieve her place in society. She gradually became almost stout, though her head seemed to grow more beautiful every year. She took to overdressing and the floors of the drawing-rooms

reflected a veritable tower of jewels and scarves and plumes. Her face and hands were covered with a bluish powder against which she drew an irritable mouth in scarlet and orange. The almost distraught fury of her temper was varied by the unnatural sweetness of her address in the company of the dowagers. In the earliest stages of her progress upward she had intimated to Uncle Pio that he was not to be seen with her in public, but finally she became impatient even of his discreeter visits. She conducted the interviews with formality and evasion. Her eyes never crossed his and she angled for pretexts to quarrel with him. Still he ventured out once a month to try her patience and when the call had become impossible he would climb the stairs and finish the hour among her children.

One day he arrived at her villa in the hills and, through her maid, begged for an opportunity to talk with her. He was told that she would see him in the French gardens a little before sunset. He had come up from Lima on a strange sentimental impulse. Like all solitary persons he had invested friendship with a divine glamour: he imagined that the people he passed on the street, laughing together and embracing when they parted, the people who dined together with so many smiles,—you will scarcely believe me, but he imagined that they were extracting from all that congeniality great store of satisfaction. So that suddenly he was filled with the excitement of seeing her again, of being called "Uncle Pio," and of reviving for a moment the trust and humour of their long vagabondage.

The French Gardens were at the southern end of the town. Behind them rose the higher Andes and before them there was a parapet overlooking a deep valley and overlooking wave after wave of hills that stretched toward the Pacific. It was the hour when bats fly low and the smaller animals play recklessly underfoot. A few solitaries lingered about the gardens, gazing dreamily into the sky that was being gradually emptied of its colour, or leaned upon the balustrade and looked down into the valley, noting in which village a dog was barking. It was the hour when the father returns home from the fields and plays for a moment in the yard with the dog that jumps upon him, holding his muzzle closed or throwing him upon his back. The young girls look about for the first star to fix a wish upon it, and the boys grow restless for supper. Even the busiest mother stands for a moment idlehanded, smiling at her dear and exasperating family.

Uncle Pio stood against one of the chipped marble benches and watched Camila coming towards him:

"I am late," she said. "I am sorry. What is it you wish to say to me?"

"Camila,—" he began.

"My name is Doña Micaela."

"I do not wish to offend you, Doña Micaela, but when you let me call you Camila for twenty years, I should think——"

"Oh, do as you like. Do as you like."

"Camila, promise me that you will listen to me. Promise me that you will not run away at my first sentence."

At once she burst out with unexpected passion: "Uncle Pio, listen to me. You are mad if you think you can make me return to the theatre. I look back at the theatre with horror. Understand that. The theatre! The theatre, indeed! The daily payment of insults in that filthy place. Understand that you are wasting your time."

He answered gently: "I would not have you come back if you are happy with these new friends."

"You don't like my new friends, then?" she answered quickly. "Whom do you offer me in their stead?"

"Camila, I only remember . . ."

"I will not be criticized. I don't want any advice. It will be cold in a moment, I must go back to my house. Just give me up, that's all. Just put me out of your mind."

"Dear Camila, don't be angry. Let me talk to you. Just suffer me for ten minutes."

He did not understand why she was weeping. He did not know what to say. He talked at random: "You never even come to see the theatre, and they all notice it. The audiences are falling away now, too. They only put on the Old Comedy twice a week; all the other nights are these new farces in prose. All is dull and childish and indecent. No one can speak Spanish any more. No one can even walk correctly any more. On Corpus Christi Day they gave *Belshazzar's Feast* where you were so wonderful. Now it was shameful."

There was a pause. A beautiful procession of clouds, like a flock of sheep, was straying up from the sea, slipping up the valleys between the hills. Camila suddenly touched his knee, and her face was like her face twenty years before: "Forgive me, Uncle Pio, for being so bad. Jaime was ill this afternoon. There's nothing one can do. He lies there, so white and . . . so surprised. One must just think of other things. Uncle Pio, it would be no good if I went back to the theatre. The audiences come for the prose farces. We were foolish to try and keep alive the Old Comedy. Let people read the old plays in books if they choose to. It is not worth while fighting with the crowd."

"Wonderful Camila, I was not just to you when you were on the stage. It was some foolish pride in me. I grudged you the praise that you deserved. Forgive me. You have always been a very great artist. If you come to see that you are not happy among these people you might think about going to Madrid. You would have a great triumph

there. You are still young and beautiful. There will be time later to be called Doña Micaela. We shall be old soon. We shall be dead soon."

"No, I shall never see Spain. All the world is alike, Madrid or Lima."

"Oh, if we could go away to some island where the people would know you for yourself. And love you."

"You are fifty years old and you are still dreaming of such islands, Uncle Pio."

He bent his head and mumbled: "Of course I love you, Camila, as I always must and more than I can say. To have known you is enough for my whole life. You are a great lady now. And you are rich. There is no longer any way that I can help you. But I am always ready."

"How absurd you are," she said smiling. "You said that as boys say it. You don't seem to learn as you grow older, Uncle Pio. There is no such thing as that kind of love and that kind of island. It's in the theatre you find such things."

He looked shamefaced, but unconvinced.

At last she rose and said sadly: "What are we talking about! It is growing cold. I must be going in. You must be resigned. I have no heart for the theatre." There was a pause. "And for the rest? . . . Oh, I do not understand. It is just circumstance. I must be what I must. Do not try to understand either. Don't think about me, Uncle Pio. Just forgive, that's all. Just try to forgive."

She stood still a moment, searching for something deeply felt to say to him. The first cloud reached the terrace; it was dark; the last stragglers were leaving the gardens. She was thinking of Don Jaime, and of Don Andrés and of himself. She could not find the words. Suddenly she bent down and kissed his fingers and went quickly away. But he sat for a long time in the gathering clouds trembling with happiness and trying to penetrate into the meaning of these things.

Suddenly the news was all over Lima. Doña Micaela Villegas, the lady that used to be Camila the Perichole, had the small-pox. Several hundred other persons had the small-pox also, but popular interest and malignity were concentrated upon the actress. A wild hope ran about the town that the beauty would be impaired that had enabled her to despise the class from which she sprang. The news escaped from the sick-room that Camila had become ludicrous in homeliness and the cup of the envious overflowed. As soon as she was able she had herself carried from the city to her villa in the hills; she ordered the sale of her elegant little palace. She returned her jewels to their givers and she sold her fine clothes. The Viceroy, the Archbishop, and the few men at court who had been her sincerest admirers besieged her door still with messages and gifts; the messages were ignored and the

gifts were returned without comment. No one but her nurse and maids had been permitted to see her since the commencement of her illness. As an answer to his repeated attempts Don Andrés received a large sum of money from her with a letter compounded of all that is possible in bitterness and pride.

Like all beautiful women who have been brought up amid continual tributes to her beauty she assumed without cynicism that it must necessarily be the basis of anyone's attachment to herself; henceforth any attention paid to her must spring from a pity full of condescension and faintly perfumed with satisfaction at so complete a reversal. This assumption that she need look for no more devotion now that her beauty had passed proceeded from the fact that she had never realized any love save love as passion. Such love, though it expends itself in generosity and thoughtfulness, though it give birth to visions and to great poetry, remains among the sharpest expressions of self-interest. Not until it has passed through a long servitude, through its own self-hatred, through mockery, through great doubts, can it take its place among the loyalties. Many who have spent a lifetime in it can tell us less of love than the child that lost a dog yesterday. As her friends continued in their efforts to draw her again into society she grew more and more angry and dispatched insulting messages to the city. It was said for a time that she was retiring into religion. But new rumours that all was fury and despair on the little farm, contradicted the old. For those near to her the despair was fearful to behold. She was convinced that her life was over, her life and children's. In her hysterical pride she had given back more than she owed and the approach of poverty was added to the loneliness and the gloom of her future. There was nothing left for her to do but to draw out her days in jealous solitude in the center of the little farm that was falling into decay. She brooded for hours upon the joy of her enemies and could be heard striding about her room with strange cries.

Uncle Pio did not allow himself to be discouraged. By dint of making himself useful to the children, by taking a hand in the management of the farm and by discreetly lending her some money he obtained his entrance into the house and even into the presence of its veiled mistress. But even then Camila, convinced in her pride that he *pitied* her, lashed him with the blade of her tongue and derived some strange comfort from heaping him with sneers. He loved her the more, understanding better than she did herself all the stages in the convalescence of her humiliated spirit. But one day an accident befell that lost him his share in her progress. He pushed open a door.

She thought she had locked it. For just one hour a foolish secret hope had come to her; she wondered whether she could make a paste

of chalk and cream to spread upon her face. She who had sneered so often at the befloured grandmothers of the court wondered for a few moments whether she had learned anything on the stage that would aid her now. She thought she had locked the door and with hurried hands and beating heart she laid on the coat, the grotesque pallor, and as she gazed into the mirror and recognized the futility of her attempt she caught the image of Uncle Pio standing in the door amazed. She rose from the chair with a cry and covered her face with her hands.

"Go away. Go away out of my house forever," she screamed. "I never want to see you again." In her shame she drove him out with blasphemy and hatred, she pursued him down the corridor and hurled objects down the stairs. She gave her farmer orders that Uncle Pio was forbidden to come into the grounds. But he continued for a week trying to see her again. At last he went back to Lima; he filled in the time as best he could, but he longed to be by her as a boy of eighteen would long. At last he devised a stratagem and returned up into the hills to put it into effect.

One morning before dawn he arose and lay on the ground below her window. He imitated in the darkness the sound of weeping, and, as nearly as he could, of a young girl's weeping. He continued in this for the whole quarter of an hour. He did not let his voice rise above that degree of loudness which Italian musicians would represent by the direction *piano,* but he frequently intermitted the sound trusting that if she were asleep it would insinuate itself into her mind as well by duration as by degree. The air was cool and agreeable. The first faint streak of sapphire was appearing behind the peaks and in the east the star of morning was pulsating every moment with a more tender intention. A profound silence wrapped all the farm buildings, only an occasional breeze set all the grasses sighing. Suddenly a lamp was lit in her room and a moment later the shutter was thrown back and a head wrapped in veils leaned far out.

"Who is there?" asked the beautiful voice.

Uncle Pio remained silent.

Camila said again in a tone edged with impatience:

"Who is there? Who is there weeping?"

"Doña Micaela, my lady, I beg of you to come here to me."

"Who are you and what do you want?"

"I am a poor girl. I am Estrella. I beg of you to come and help me. Do not call your maid. I pray you, Doña Micaela, to come yourself."

Camila was silent a moment, then said abruptly: "Very well," and closed the shutter. Presently she appeared around the corner of the

house. She wore a thick cloak that dragged in the dew. She stood at a distance and said: "Come over here to where I am standing,—Who are you?"

Uncle Pio rose up. "Camila, it is I,—Uncle Pio. Forgive me, but I must speak to you."

"Mother of God, when shall I be free of this dreadful person! Understand: I want to see no one. I don't want to speak to a soul. My life is over. That is all."

"Camila, by our long life together, I beg of you to grant me one thing. I shall go away and never trouble you again."

"I grant you nothing, nothing. Stay away from me."

"I promise you I shall never trouble you again if you listen to me this once." She was hurrying around to the door on the other side of the house and Uncle Pio was obliged to run beside her to make sure that she heard what he was saying. She stopped:

"What is it then? Hurry. It is cold. I am not well. I must go back to my room."

"Camila, let me take Don Jaime for a year to live with me in Lima. Let me be his teacher. Let me teach him the Castilian. Here he is left among the servants. He is learning nothing."

"No."

"Camila, what will become of him? He has a good mind and he wants to learn."

"He is sick. He is delicate. Your house is a sty. Only the country is good for him."

"But he has been much better these last few months. I promise you I shall clean out my house. I shall apply to Madre María del Pilar for a housekeeper. Here he is in your stables all day. I shall teach him all that a gentleman should know,—fencing and Latin and music. We shall read all. . . ."

"A mother cannot be separated from her child like that. It is impossible. You are crazy to have thought of it. Give up thinking of me and of everything about me. I no longer exist. I and my children will get on as best we can. Do not try to disturb me again. I do not want to see any human being."

Now it was that Uncle Pio felt obliged to use a hard measure. "Then pay me the money that you owe me," he said.

Camila stood still, confounded. To herself she said: "Life is too fearful to bear. When may I die?" After a moment she answered him, in a hoarse voice: "I have very little money. I will pay you what I can. I will pay you now. I have a few jewels here. Then we need never see one another again." She was ashamed of her poverty. She took a few

steps, then turned and said: "Now I see that you are a very hard man. But it is right that I pay you what I owe you."

"No, Camila, I only said that to enforce my request. I shall take no money from you. But lend me Don Jaime for one year. I shall love him and take every care of him. Did I harm you? Was I a bad teacher to you in those other years?"

"It is cruel of you to keep urging gratitude, gratitude, gratitude. I was grateful,—good, good! but now that I am no longer the same woman there remains nothing to be grateful for." There was a silence. Her eyes were resting on the star that seemed to be leading forth the whole sky in its wonder. A great pain lay at her heart, the pain of a world that was meaningless. Then she said: "If Jaime wishes to go with you, very well. I shall talk to him in the morning. If he wishes to go with you, you will find him at the Inn about noon. Good night. Go with God."

"Go with God."

She returned to the house. The next day the grave little boy appeared at the Inn. His fine clothes were torn and stained now and he carried a small bundle for change. His mother had given him a gold piece for spending-money and a little stone that shone in the dark to look at in his sleepless nights. They set off together in a cart, but soon Uncle Pio became aware that the jolting was not good for the boy. He carried him on his shoulder. As they drew near to the bridge of San Luis Rey, Jaime tried to conceal his shame for he knew that one of those moments was coming that separated him from other people. He was especially ashamed because Uncle Pio had just overtaken a friend of his, a sea-captain. And just as they got to the bridge he spoke to an old lady who was travelling with a little girl. Uncle Pio said that when they had crossed the bridge they would sit down and rest, but it turned out not to be necessary.

PART V

Perhaps An Intention

A new bridge of stone has been built in the place of the old, but the event has not been forgotten. It has passed into proverbial expressions. "I may see you Tuesday," says a Limean, "unless the bridge falls." "My cousin lives by the bridge of San Luis Rey," says another, and a smile goes around the company, for that also means: under the

sword of Damocles. There are some poems about the accident, classics to be found in every Peruvian anthology, but the real literary monument is Brother Juniper's book.

There are a hundred ways of wondering at circumstance. Brother Juniper would never have arrived at his method had it not been for his friendship with a certain master in the University of San Martín. This student's wife had stolen away one morning on a boat for Spain, following a soldier, and had left him the care of two daughters in their cradle. He was possessed of all the bitterness that Brother Juniper lacked and derived a sort of joy from the conviction that all was wrong in the world. He whispered into the Franciscan's ear such thoughts and anecdotes as belied the notion of a guided world. For a moment a look of distress, almost of defeat, would come into the Brother's eyes; then he would begin patiently explaining why such stories held no difficulty for a believer. "There was a queen of Naples and Sicily," the student would say, "who discovered that she was carrying an angry tumor in her side. In great dismay she commanded her subjects to fall to their prayers and ordered that all the garments in Sicily and Naples be sewn with votive crosses. She was well loved by her people and all their prayers and embroideries were sincere, but ineffectual. Now she lies in the splendor of Monreale, and a few inches above her heart may be read the words: *I shall fear no evil.*"

It was by dint of hearing a great many such sneers at faith that Brother Juniper became convinced that the world's time had come for proof, tabulated proof, of the conviction that was so bright and exciting within him. When the pestilence visited his dear village of Puerto and carried off a large number of peasants, he secretly drew up a diagram of the characteristics of fifteen victims and fifteen survivors, the statistics of their value *sub specie aeternitatis*. Each soul was rated upon a basis of ten as regards its goodness, its diligence in religious observance, and its importance to its family group. Here is a fragment of this ambitious chart:

	Goodness	Piety	Usefulness
Alfonso G.	4	4	10
Nina	2	5	10
Manuel B.	10	10	0
Alfonso V.	—8	—10	10
Vera N.	0	10	10

The thing was more difficult than he had foreseen. Almost every soul in a difficult frontier community turned out to be indispensable economically, and the third column was all but useless. The examiner was driven to the use of minus terms when he confronted the personal

character of Alfonso V., who was not, like Vera N., merely bad: he was a propagandist for badness and not merely avoided church but led others to avoid it. Vera N. was indeed bad, but she was a model worshipper and the mainstay of a full hut. From all this saddening data Brother Juniper contrived an index for each peasant. He added up the total for victims and compared it with the total for survivors, to discover that the dead were five times more worth saving. It almost looked as though the pestilence had been directed against the really valuable people in the village of Puerto. And on that afternoon Brother Juniper took a walk along the edge of the Pacific. He tore up his findings and cast them into the waves; he gazed for an hour upon the great clouds of pearl that hang forever upon the horizon of that sea, and extracted from their beauty a resignation that he did not permit his reason to examine. The discrepancy between faith and the facts is greater than is generally assumed.

But there was another story of the master of San Martín (not so subversive, this one) that probably gave to Brother Juniper the hint for his procedure after the fall of the bridge of San Luis Rey.

This master was one day walking through the Cathedral of Lima and stopped to read the epitaph of a lady. He read with an increasingly prominent lower lip that she had been for twenty years the centre and joy of her home, that she had been the delight of her friends, that all who met her went away in astonishment at her goodness and beauty, and that there she lay awaiting the return of her Lord. Now on the day that he read these words, the master of San Martín had had much to fret him, and raising his eyes from the tablet he spoke aloud in his rage: "The shame of it, the persecution of it! Everyone knows that in the world we do nothing but feed our wills. Why perpetuate this legend of selflessness? Why keep this thing alive, this rumour of disinterestedness?"

And so saying he resolved to expose this conspiracy of the stone-cutters. The lady had been dead only twelve years. He sought out her servants, her children and her friends. And everywhere he went, like a perfume, her dear traits had survived her and wherever she was mentioned these arose a suffering smile and the protest that words could not describe the gracious ways of her. Even the eager youth of her grandchildren, who had never seen her, was made more difficult by the news that it was possible to be as good as that. And the man stood amazed; only at last he muttered: "Nevertheless, what I said was true. This woman was an exception, perhaps an exception."

In compiling his book about these people Brother Juniper seemed to be pursued by the fear that in omitting the slightest detail he might lose some guiding hint. The longer he worked the more he felt that

he was stumbling about among great dim intimations. He was forever being cheated by details that looked as though they were significant if only he could find their setting. So he put everything down on the notion perhaps that if he (or a keener head) reread the book twenty times, the countless facts would suddenly start to move, to assemble, and to betray their secret. The Marquesa de Montemayor's cook told him that she lived almost entirely on rice, fish and a little fruit and Brother Juniper put it down on the chance that it would some day reveal a spiritual trait. Don Rubío said of her that she used to appear at his receptions without invitation in order to steal the spoons. A midwife on the edge of the own declared that Doña María called upon her with morbid questions until she had been obliged to order her away from the door like a beggar. The bookseller of the town reported that she was one of the three most cultivated persons in Lima. Her farmer's wife declared that she was absent-minded, but compact of goodness. The art of biography is more difficult than is generally supposed.

Brother Juniper found that there was least to be learned from those who had been most closely associated with the subjects of his inquiry. Madre María del Pilar talked to him at length about Pepita, but she did not tell him of her own ambitions for her. The Perichole was at first difficult of approach, but presently even liked the Franciscan. Her characterization of Uncle Pio flatly contradicted the stores of unsavory testimonies that he had acquired elsewhere. Her allusions to her son were few and conceded with pain. They closed the interview abruptly. The Captain Alvarado told what he could of Esteban and of Uncle Pio. Those who know most in this realm, venture least.

I shall spare you Brother Juniper's generalizations. They are always with us. He thought he saw in the same accident, the wicked visited by destruction and the good called early to Heaven. He thought he saw pride and wealth confounded as an object lesson to the world, and he thought he saw humility crowned and rewarded for the edification of the city. But Brother Juniper was not satisfied with his reasons. It was just possible that the Marquesa de Montemayor was not a monster of avarice, and Uncle Pio of self-indulgence.

The book being done fell under the eyes of some judges and was suddenly pronounced heretical. It was ordered to be burned in the Square with its author. Brother Juniper submitted to the decision that the devil had made use of him to effect a brilliant campaign in Peru. He sat in his cell that last night trying to seek in his own life the pattern that had escaped him in five others. He was not rebellious. He was willing to lay down his life for the purity of the church, but he longed for one voice somewhere to testify for him that his intention,

at least, had been for faith; he thought there was no one in the world who believed him. But the next morning in all that crowd and sunlight there were many who believed, for he was much loved.

There was a little delegation from the village of Puerto, and Nina (Goodness 2, Piety 5, Usefulness 10) and others stood with drawn puzzled faces while their little friar was given to the congenial flames. Even then, even then, there remained in his heart an obstinate nerve insisting that at least St. Francis would not utterly have condemned him, and (not daring to call upon a greater name, since he seemed so open to error in these matters) he called twice upon St. Francis and leaning upon a flame he smiled and died.

.

The day of the service was clear and warm. The Limeans, their black eyes wide with awe, poured through the streets into their Cathedral and stood gazing at the mound of black velvet and silver. The Archbishop enclosed in his wonderful and almost wooden vestments perspired upon his throne, lending from time to time a connoisseur's ear to the felicities of Vittoria's counterpoint. The choir had restudied the pages that, as his farewell to music, Tomás Luis had composed for his friend and patron, the Empress of Austria, and all that grief and sweetness, all that Spanish realism filtering through an Italian mode, rose and fell above the sea of mantillas. Don Andrés, under the colours and feathered hangings of his office, knelt, ill and troubled. He knew that the crowd was furtively glancing at him, expecting him to play the father who has lost his only son. He wondered whether the Perichole was present. He had never been obliged to go so long without smoking. The Captain Alvarado pushed in from the sunny square for a moment. He looked across the fields of black hair and lace at the trooping of the candles and the ropes of incense. "How false, how unreal," he said and pushed his way out. He descended to the sea and sat on the edge of his boat, gazing down into the clear water. "Happy are the drowned, Esteban," he said.

Behind the screen the Abbess sat among her girls. The night before she had torn an idol from her heart and the experience had left her pale but firm. She had accepted the fact that it was of no importance whether her work went on or not; it was enough to work. She was the nurse who tends the sick who never recover; she was the priest who perpetually renews the office before an altar to which no worshippers come. There would be no Pepita to enlarge her work; it would relapse into the indolence and the indifference of her colleagues. It seemed to be sufficient for Heaven that for a while in Peru a disinterested love had flowered and faded. She leaned her forehead upon her hand,

following the long tender curve that the soprano lifts in the Kyrie. "My affection should have had more of that colour, Pepita. My whole life should have had more of that quality. I have been too busy," she added ruefully and her mind drifted into prayer.

Camilla had started from the farm to attend the service. Her heart was filled with consternation and amazement. Here was another comment from the skies; that was the third time she had been spoken to. Her small-pox, Jaime's illness, and now the fall of the bridge,—oh, these were not accidents. She was as ashamed as though letters had appeared on her forehead. An order from the Palace announced that the Viceroy was sending her two daughters to a convent-school in Spain. That was right. She was alone. She gathered a few things together mechanically and started to the city for the Service. But she fell to thinking of the crowds gaping over her Uncle Pio and over her son; she thought of the vast ritual of the church, like a chasm into which the beloved falls, and of the storm of the *dies irae* where the individual is lost among the millions of the dead, features grow dim and traits fade. At a little more than half the journey, at the mud church of San Luis Rey she slipped in and knelt against a pillar to rest. She wandered through her memory, searching for the faces of her two. She waited for some emotion to appear. "But I feel nothing," she whispered to herself. "I have no heart. I am a poor meaningless woman, that's all. I am shut out. I have no heart. Look, I won't try and think of anything; let me just rest here." And scarcely had she paused when again that terrible incommunicable pain swept through her, the pain that could not speak once to Uncle Pio and tell him of her love and just once offer her courage to Jaime in his sufferings. She started up wildly: "I fail everybody," she cried. "They love me and I fail them." She returned to the farm and carried for a year the mood of her self-despair. One day she heard by accident that the wonderful Abbess had lost two persons whom she loved in the same accident. Her sewing fell from her hand: then *she* would know, she would explain. "But no, what would she say to me! She would not even believe that such a person as I could love or could lose." Camila decided to go to Lima and look at the Abbess from a distance. "If her face tells me that she would not despise me, I will speak to her," she said.

Camila lurked about the convent church and fell humbly in love with the homely old face, though it frightened her a little. At last she called upon her.

"Mother," she said, "I . . . I . . ."

"Do I know you, my daughter?"

"I was the actress, I was the Perichole."

"Oh, yes. Oh, I have wished to know you for a long while, but they told me you did not wish to be seen. You too, I know, lost in the fall of the bridge of San. . . ."

Camila rose and swayed. There! again that access of pain, the hands of the dead she could not reach. Her lips were white. Her head brushed the Abbess's knee: "Mother, what shall I do? I am all alone. I have nothing in the world. I love them. What shall I do?"

The Abbess looked at her closely. "My daughter, it is warm here. Let us go into the garden. You can rest there." She made a sign to a girl in the cloister to bring some water. She continued talking mechanically to Camila. "I have wished to know you for a long while, señora. Even before the accident I had wished much to know you. They told me that in the *autos sacramentales* you were a very great and beautiful actress, in *Belshazzar's Feast.*"

"Oh, Mother, you must not say that. I am a sinner. You must not say that."

"Here, drink this, my child. We have a beautiful garden, do you not think so? You will come and see us often and some day you will meet Sister Juana who is our gardener-in-chief. Before she entered religion she had almost never seen a garden, for she worked in the mines high up in the mountains. Now everything grows under her hand.—A year has gone by, señora, since our accident. I lost two who had been children in my orphanage, but you lost a real child of your own?"

"Yes, Mother."

"And a great friend?"

"Yes, Mother."

"Tell me. . . ."

And then the whole tide of Camila's long despair, her lonely obstinate despair since her girlhood, found its rest on that dusty friendly lap among Sister Juana's fountains and roses.

.

But where are sufficient books to contain the events that would not have been the same without the fall of the bridge? From such a number I choose one more.

"The Condesa d'Abuirre wishes to see you," said a lay-sister at the door of the Abbess's office.

"Well," said the Abbess, laying down her pen, "who is she?"

"She has just come from Spain. I don't know."

"Oh, it is some money, Inez, some money for my house for the blind. Quick, bid her come in."

The tall, rather languorous beauty entered the room. Doña Clara,

who was generally so adequate, seemed constrained for once. "Are you busy, dear Mother, may I talk to you for a while?"

"I am quite free, my daughter. You will excuse an old woman's memory; have I known you before?"

"My mother was the Marquesa de Montemayor. . . ." Doña Clara suspected that the Abbess had not admired her mother and would not let the older woman speak until she herself had made a long passionate defense of Doña María. The languor fell away in her self-reproach. At last the Abbess told her of Pepita and Esteban, and of Camila's visit. "All, all of us have failed. One wishes to be punished. One is willing to assume all kinds of penance, but do you know, my daughter, that in love—I scarcely dare say it—but in love our very mistakes don't seem to be able to last long?"

The Condesa showed the Abbess Doña María's last letter. Madre María dared not say aloud how great her astonishment was that such words (words that since then the whole world has murmured over with joy) could spring in the heart of Pepita's mistress. "Now learn," she commanded herself, "learn at last that anywhere you may expect grace." And she was filled with happiness like a girl at this new proof that the traits she lived for were everywhere, that the world was ready. "Will you do me a kindness, my daughter? Will you let me show you my work?"

The sun had gone down, but the Abbess led the way with a lantern down corridor after corridor. Doña Clara saw the old and the young, the sick and the blind, but most of all she saw the tired, bright old woman who was leading her. The Abbess would stop in a passageway and say suddenly: "I can't help thinking that something could be done for the deaf-and-dumb. It seems to me that some patient person could, . . . could study out a language for them. You know there are hundreds and hundreds in Peru. Do you remember whether anyone in Spain has found a way for them? Well, some day they will." Or a little later: "Do you know, I keep thinking that something can be done for the insane. I am old, you know, and I cannot go where these things are talked about, but I watch them sometimes and it seems to me . . . In Spain, now, they are gentle with them? It seems to me that there is a secret about it, just hidden from us, just around the corner. Some day back in Spain, if you hear of anything that would help us, you will write me a letter . . . if you are not too busy?"

At last after Doña Clara had seen even the kitchens, the Abbess said: "Now will you excuse me, for I must go into the room of the very sick and say a few words for them to think about when they cannot sleep. I will not ask you to come with me there, for you are not accustomed to such . . . such sounds and things. And besides I only

talk to them as one talks to children." She looked up at her with her modest rueful smile. Suddenly she disappeared a moment to return with one of her helpers, one who had likewise been involved in the affair of the bridge and who had formerly been an actress. "She is leaving me," said the Abbess, "for some work across the city and when I have spoken here I must leave you both, for the flour-broker will not wait for me any longer, and our argument will take a long time."

But Doña Clara stood in the door as the Abbess talked to them, the lamp placed on the floor beside her. Madre María stood with her back against a post; the sick lay in rows gazing at the ceiling and trying to hold their breaths. She talked that night of all those out in the dark (she was thinking of Esteban alone, she was thinking of Pepita alone) who had no one to turn to, for whom the world perhaps was more difficult, without meaning. And those who lay in their beds there felt that they were within a wall that the Abbess had built for them; within all was light and warmth, and without was the darkness they would not exchange even for a relief from pain and from dying. But even while she was talking, other thoughts were passing in the back of her mind. "Even now," she thought, "almost no one remembers Esteban and Pepita, but myself. Camila alone remembers her Uncle Pio and her son; this woman, her mother. But soon we shall die and all memory of those five will have left the earth, and we ourselves shall be loved for a while and forgotten. But the love will have been enough; all those impulses of love return to the love that made them. Even memory is not necessary for love. There is a land of the living and a land of the dead and the bridge is love, the only survival, the only meaning."